Deadly Propensity

A Novel

by

Tim McDermott

TELEMACHUS PRESS

DEADLY PROPENSITY

Cover Designed by Telemachus Press, LLC

Cover Art:
Copyright © 12922371/iStock
Copyright © 5803157/iStock
Copyright © 16858984/iStock

Cover Photo of Christian Dodd Copyright © Tim McDermott

Published by Telemachus Press, LLC
http://www.telemachuspress.com

Visit the author's art website:
http://www.tmacgallery.com

ISBN: 978-1-939337-54-2 (eBook)
ISBN: 978-1-939337-55-9 (Paperback)

Version 2013.03.20

For my wife, Mary, who has always been my loving anchor to wind, and to my daughters, Megan and Kelly, who always make me proud and who, in active conspiracy with their mother and our great son-in-law, Derek, always make me laugh.

Deadly Propensity

A Novel

CHAPTER 1

JENNY HAWKINS SMILED to herself as she dabbed the thin film of sweat from her forehead with the rolled-up sleeve of her blue work shirt. She couldn't believe she had allowed Sarah, her eight-year-old daughter, to talk her into serving as the troop mom responsible for this year's Girl Scout cookie drive. When she had relented and agreed to do it, she had no idea the troop would be selling so many cookies. *Never underestimate the determination of a group of eight-year old girls,* she mused.

As she struggled to push her side of the large carton of boxed cookies into the rear of her forest green SUV, she was grateful that Ellen, one of the other troop mothers, was there to help. Both of the young women were short and slight in build, making the job of lifting and loading the large, heavy cartons an awkward task.

She brushed a damp strand of long auburn hair away from her face as the oppressive heat and humidity bore down upon her. It was surprisingly uncomfortable weather for a February afternoon in South Florida. Both women instinctively looked up at the same time as the loud rumble of thunder sounded above them. What had been a bright sunny afternoon when they started loading had quickly deteriorated as the gathering storm clouds announced an imminent rain storm. If they hurried, Jenny calculated, they could beat the rain that looked to be only minutes away.

The two women bent, lifted the last large box into the SUV's cargo area and shoved it next to the others. Hopefully, the tailgate will close, Jenny thought. She was irritated that her husband had forgotten to unload the eight cartons of house paint lining the left side of the Mesa's cargo area. Hadn't she reminded him twice that morning to unload the heavy paint cartons before he left for work? Well, she reflected, at least I finally talked him into repainting the house.

"How many billion fat grams do you think we're about to unleash on our troop's unsuspecting customers?" Jenny asked as she slammed the tailgate closed.

"I hate to admit it," Ellen laughed, "but I don't care. S'mores and Thin Mints are going to be my downfall. I'm a closet snacker when it comes to Girl Scout cookies. Thank God they're only available once a year," she said, patting her waist. "Otherwise, I'd weigh as much as your Mesa," nodding her head towards the loaded SUV.

"Rest easy," Jenny chuckled, "your binging secret is safe with me."

"Don't forget the paperwork that you'll need for sorting the cookie orders," Ellen reminded her as they left the SUV and walked across the brick drive towards Ellen's front door.

"Got it. It's inside the house with Ryan's diaper pack," Jenny replied. "I really do appreciate your sister watching him while we loaded up. I'm sure he's up from his nap by now and wondering where I'm at."

"No problem, she's happy to help. I'm just glad I was able to give you a hand. Those boxes are a lot heavier than you would think," she added, referring to the eight large boxes they had loaded in the Mesa. Each large box contained dozens of individual boxes of cookies. "Do you have help to unload them when you get home?"

"Sure," Jenny said, "that's what husbands are for, isn't it?" They both looked at each other and laughed heartily as they entered the front door of the two-story peach-colored house just as a light rain started to fall.

Dressed in khaki shorts, brown Docksiders and a blue work shirt with rolled-up sleeves, Jenny emerged from the house ten minutes later. She walked briskly in the light rain as she headed for the right rear passenger door of her SUV. With a white envelope clenched between her teeth, her one-year-old son grasped firmly against her chest with her left arm, and a Mickey Mouse diaper pack slung over her right shoulder, she was still able to open the right rear door in one fluid motion, showing the skill of a mother with a practiced hand.

Working quickly in the falling rain, she leaned into the SUV and belted her young son into his infant car seat. It was tethered to the short split section of rear seat closest to the door that had not been folded down for cargo. Immediately to the left of the car seat, and lying on top of the folded-down remaining rear seat area, were boxes of the recently-loaded Girl Scout cookies. Finally getting the seatbelt latched, she slammed the back door and bolted around the front of the vehicle to the driver's door. Opening it quickly, she entered and got out of the light rain. She shook the rain off her hair and opened the diaper pack to remove her keys and a small brown fuzzy teddy bear. Turning and putting her knee on the driver's seat to be able to make the reach and leaning towards the passenger side to avoid the loaded boxes, she snaked her upper body between the two front seats and tossed the teddy bear onto Ryan's lap. A perfect delivery onto his lap, the young boy's face instantly lit up in a big smile as he grabbed it, immediately jammed it into his toothless mouth and started gumming away. *Life's small pleasures*, she thought. Turning back around and seating herself in the driver's seat, she pulled her own seatbelt across her body and buckled it next to her right hip.

Backing into the palm-lined street of the Weston suburb, she put the Mesa in gear, and headed towards the interstate for the twenty-mile trip back to Ft. Lauderdale. Ryan was concentrating all of his attention on busily gumming the soft fuzzy ear of his teddy bear.

About a mile from Ellen's house, Jenny guided the Mesa onto the entrance ramp and entered the interstate heading east. Traffic was sparse, and she quickly accelerated to the posted speed limit of fifty-five. As she moved her vehicle into the middle of the three eastbound lanes, the light rain that had been falling ended abruptly and the soft rays of the late afternoon sun slowly re-emerged. Traffic on the interstate coming in the opposite direction was still light, she noted. The Friday afternoon rush hour of homeward-bound suburban commuters was not yet underway.

Directly ahead of her vehicle, also in the center lane was an old dilapidated pickup truck. Its body, which had probably been a light green color twenty years ago when new, was now sun-bleached, dented and spotted with rusted blotches of gray primer paint. An aluminum step ladder was precariously tied by thin strands of twine to the top of a makeshift rusty steel frame which had been welded to the truck's bed at some pre-Cambrian time long ago. A hodgepodge mound of miscellaneous tools, sawhorses and extension cords filled the bed of the rickety truck where they had been haphazardly piled like seven weeks of dirty clothes in a teenager's bedroom. Protruding from the truck's open driver's door window, and resting on its window sill, was the weathered leathery left arm of the pickup truck's driver. Its appearance matched that of the truck. The entire surface area of the visible arm, including the backside of its hand, sported an inky-black and orange-colored tattooed pattern of spider webbing, which culminated in a cigarette dangling casually from its tattooed fingers that rested on the sill. Gracing the truck's rear bumper was a red, white and blue bumper sticker proudly proclaiming "*Shit Happens: re-elect Obama*," which had not been removed post-election.

As she followed the pickup, Jenny's mind wandered to the list of items she needed to pick up at the grocery store on her way home.

Without warning, the step ladder on the old pickup suddenly broke free from the rusty metal frame to which it had been tied. It whipped off the truck, forced loose by the wind pushing against it. Jenny's reverie was broken instantly as she saw it slam down violently on the roadway immediately in front of her, where it bounced off the roadway and directly towards the front of her vehicle. She sat momentarily frozen as she tried to grasp the sudden event.

"Oh my God!" she exclaimed out loud. Instinctively, she clenched the steering wheel with both hands and, in a quick but controlled movement, turned it sharply to the right to avoid the imminent collision with the ladder. In response, the front of her vehicle swerved immediately towards the lane to her right. She felt an odd rocking sensation in the body of the Mesa as it quickly and sharply sliced into and across the right eastbound lane. Her panic spiraled when she immediately saw the continuous, four-foot tall concrete barrier aligning the right shoulder coming at her. Her reflexes went into automatic. She quickly hit, then released, the brakes and counter-steered to the left in an attempt to avoid colliding with the oncoming wall.

The Mesa's responsive swerve to the left was immediate but overwhelming and seemingly out of proportion to her corrective steering input. The entire vehicle leaned violently to her right, almost as if its two left-side wheels were somehow lifting off the roadway. It also started spinning, in a counter-clockwise direction. Her mind, flooded with panic and adrenaline, paid no notice to Ryan's teddy bear flying across the inside of the passenger compartment as a terrible, coppery dread suddenly washed over her. The spinning and tilting Mesa crossed the three eastbound lanes of traffic towards the wide grassy median which separated her eastbound lanes from the three westbound interstate lanes.

Despite the fact that everything was happening at lightning speed, she felt the loss of control unfolding in terrifyingly slow motion. She let out an involuntary cry as she sought to regain control of the SUV. Her frantic efforts were in vain. The tilting Mesa continued both skidding sideways and rotating counter-clockwise as it headed for the grassy median, with its passenger side leading the way. As it approached the edge of the asphalt roadway, but while still on the roadway, she felt the driver's side suddenly lift upwards as the SUV began a violent rollover towards its passenger side.

Inside the vehicle, terror and an immediate loss of all orientation were the only sensations she felt. The full force of her body strained against her seatbelt as the roll developed. Her hands were ripped from the steering wheel, while her head and neck felt like they were being centrifugally pulled from her body as the Mesa underwent its violent rolling action to its right.

As it rolled onto and over its roof, the entire vehicle suddenly sprung three feet off the ground, the result of its stiff passenger side roof rail coming into violent contact with the ground beneath. Continuing in its rotation as it did so, the Mesa landed violently, and with full force, on its driver's side with a sickening loud crunch of metal and exploding glass. Its kinetic energy was not dissipated by the violent crush of the landing but continued in its completion of a full three hundred sixty degree roll of the vehicle, with the SUV finally coming to rest sitting upright on its wheels in the middle of the grassy median. A settling cloud of dirt, broken debris and glass shards surrounded the now quiet Mesa.

It was then that the fire started.

It appeared to originate from underneath the rear door on the driver's side. Its small orange tongues quickly increased in size and hungrily moved upwards into the rear cargo and passenger compartment through the now open windows on the driver's side which had exploded into tiny particles of glass during the rollover landing.

Manny Abadin and Alex Fuentes, two house painters on their way home from a Miami jobsite, jumped from Manny's van which had abruptly stopped in the median 100 feet rear of the Mesa. They had been following at a distance behind the Mesa when the accident happened.

"Llame a 911 ahora mismo en mi cellular!" *Call 911 on my cell!* Manny screamed to Alex as he sprang from the van and started running towards the flaming vehicle. Cursing himself for his panic, Manny suddenly remembered the fire extinguisher in the back of his painting van. He stopped in his tracks, slipping on the grass as he did so, and doubled back to his van where he frantically opened its rear cargo door. He reached inside, tossing paint cans and piles of drop cloths out of the way until he emerged with a small red fire extinguisher in hand.

"Mira, ver si otra persona tiene más de éstos!" *See if any of these other people have any more of these!* he ordered Alex as he sprinted past him towards the Mesa. Alex was already on his portable phone excitedly calling 911 as he ran towards other cars which had come to a stop on both sides of the interstate.

"Save my baby! Save my baby!" Manny heard a female voice inside the vehicle scream hysterically as he approached. He ran to the passenger side of the SUV which had not yet caught fire, pulling the safety pin on the extinguisher as he did so. Dark gray and black smoke rolled from the broken windows of the Mesa. With some difficulty, he yanked the badly dented rear passenger door open to find a young infant belted in a rear-facing car seat amidst the black smoke and flames which overwhelmed the inside of the vehicle. To his horror, he saw through the thick, black smoke pouring out of the door that the child's clothing and hair were on fire. A quick glance beyond the child confirmed that the brilliant, orange flames had advanced forward from the adjacent cargo area, both behind the child's seat, and from the child's left, from what looked like cardboard boxes that were engulfed in fire. Frantically, his eyes immediately darted forward, to the driver's seat, where he observed a woman belted into the seat writhing and flailing her arms at the flames which were also engulfing and burning her hair and shirt. Her face was covered with deep crimson-colored blood which stood in sharp contrast to the adjacent orange flames. Both the woman and the child were shrieking in pain and agony.

Equally compelled by horror and self-preservation, he instinctively took a step back before he caught himself, leaned forward again, pulled the ring from the extinguisher's handle, and started wildly spraying the foamy contents. He first sprayed the infant, then forward towards the driver, and, finally, the flaming cargo area directly next to the infant and immediately behind him. In his adrenaline rush, he quickly emptied the foamy contents of his small red extinguisher.

While able to momentarily subdue the flames inside the vehicle, he could see that the fire continued unabated on the outside the driver's side of the vehicle. Despite her obvious pain and shock, the woman looked back at him and croaked in a desperate voice that sounded hardly human, "Please! ... Please! ... Get my baby out of here!" She was then suddenly wracked with heavy coughing and gasping for breath. Despite the layer of white chemical foam now covering her, he saw that her entire upper body was burned and charred black, rendering the reddened whites of her eyes stark in their utter panic and terror.

Now coughing badly himself from the acrid smoke he was ingesting, Manny steeled himself to remain calm.

"Ma'am! ... Lady!" he yelled excitedly in his heavy Cuban accent, "I get both of you out of here, but you must hurry! Can you unbuckle?" he screamed to her as he reached over the infant seat in front of him in a desperate attempt to find the seat belt latch that held the infant seat in place. Feeling a painful burning sensation in his extended arm and hand from the intensely hot and still-smoldering burned cargo as he groped for the release buckle, he finally found it and depressed it. The seat belt popped free immediately. He instantaneously wrenched the child seat from the vehicle, with the small shrieking child still belted within it, just as Alex was running up with two more small extinguishers. Manny couldn't tell if the fire-blackened child was a boy or girl. Alex threw the two extinguishers down at Manny's feet, and, without comment, quickly took the child seat, along with its charred, whimpering infant, from his friend's arms.

The flames on the driver's side of the SUV suddenly erupted upwards and forward again, through the broken-out driver's door window. As if by a hidden, pyrrhic signal, the blackened and heavily smoking cardboard boxes in the rear cargo area re-ignited and their flames also shot forward again.

"Help me! ... I don't want to die!" Jenny again screamed to him.

Manny reacted immediately.Ignoring the pain from his burned arm and hand, he reached down and grabbed one of the two small extinguishers at his feet and yanked open the front passenger door of the SUV ...

"Quick, lean 'dis way, ma'am!" he yelled. Wild-eyed and whimpering, she did what she was told. Leaning into the front seat through the now-open right front door, he sprayed the contents of the second extinguisher towards her and the driver's door area. In response to the dousing effects of the chemical foam, the orange and smoky flames again angrily retreated in response, but he could see that his victory was only temporary. The heavy smell of gasoline suddenly caught his attention for the first time. He realized with a sudden jolt of panic that time was working against him.

He threw the extinguisher down and, ignoring the rapidly rebuilding smoke and heat, jumped into the right front seat with his entire body to get her out. The woman was sobbing and whimpering in fear and agony as she strained her body towards him and away from the ever-advancing flames coming from the driver's door and the backside of the front seats, from the burning cargo boxes. The unmistakable smell of burned flesh and hair, mixed in with the heavy black smoke in the vehicle's interior he was gulping, threatened to over-whelm him. Coughing heavily, he groped along the center console next to her right hip until his fingers found her seatbelt buckle release button. Working on reflexes, he pushed it down. The metal latch released just as the relentless flames simultaneously re-entered the open window of the driver's door and again started to lap over the top of the seatback behind them.

Willing himself to fight off his renewed panic, he immediately reached over, grabbed her upper torso with both hands and fiercely jerked her body towards him in an effort to pull her from the vehicle. He could feel a burning pain on the left side of his face from the oncoming flames as he yanked. In response, her body started moving towards him but then suddenly stopped at the same time as the woman let out a blood curdling scream.

"I'm caught!" she screamed, "I'm caught!"

The advancing flames again electrified him into action.

Peering through the increasingly heavy smoke, Manny could make out the inward deformation of the driver's door which had occurred during the violent rollover. It was somehow pinning the lower part of her left leg against the left side of the driver's seat. Again resisting the ever-increasing panic that was about to overwhelm him from the advancing heat and flames, he knew he had to act decisively. Without saying a word, he quickly bent towards her, sliding both his hands around the middle of her left thigh. Flames were now advancing towards him, between the gap separating the two front seats from one another. Bending down and grabbing her left thigh in both of his hands, he yanked the leg with all his strength, hoping to forcibly free it.

"Aaaaaaaaaaaahhhhhhhhhhhh!" she screamed in animal agony. He could feel her fractured thigh bone move in his hands, directly beneath where he had grabbed her. She shrieked and grabbed at his hand reflexively as she continued to cry out in pain and sobs. It was then that he saw through the smoke that her lower leg, in addition to being pinned, was broken. Splintered ends of a white fractured bone protruded from its surrounding fleshy tissue directly below her knee joint.

He quickly backed out from the front seat area of the Mesa through the passenger door he had entered. Frantically bending down and picking up the half-spent extinguisher he had thrown down to the ground only seconds before, as well as the one remaining full one, he sprinted around the front of the vehicle to the driver's side. Positioning himself ten feet away from the driver's door, he tossed the full extinguisher down and fired the remaining contents of the second one directly at the driver's door and the area immediately beneath it from which the flames seemed to be emanating. Once again, the foam was able to momentarily drive the flames back to the rear door when that tank also went dry.

"Coño!" *Shit!* He screamed in angry frustration as he slammed the empty tank to the ground. The woman's animal-like screams and wails continued from within the vehicle. He gave a frenzied look to Alex as he picked up the last extinguisher from the ground. Alex, now bare-chested, had taken his T-shirt off and had wrapped the child within it. Next to him stood an older couple who looked like tourists. The man, in his 70s, was futilely yelling to other onlookers in stopped cars across the road for more fire extinguishers. There were no responses. The older woman, his wife, was sobbing uncontrollably. Both of her hands were held to her mouth in shock at what she was seeing.

"Busque más de estas piezas de mierda, coño!" *Look for more of these pieces of shit, damnit!* Manny bellowed in mixed English and Spanish as he pulled the pin on the last extinguisher.

"No hay más!" *There aren't any more*, Alex shouted back. "Esa la única que queda!" *That's the only one left!*

Manny swallowed hard and pointed the last tank directly at the brilliant orange and yellow flames and unrelenting heavy black smoke, which continued to billow without mercy from beneath the vehicle. He guessed the accident had caused some type of tear or hole in the gas tank which was allowing escaping raw gasoline to feed the fire. The flames were fierce and growing in intensity.

"Alex," he screamed again at his friend in Spanish, "dé el niño a alguien y ayúdeme con esta mujer!" *Give the baby to someone else and help me with this woman!* "Su pierna es atrapada—hágalo ahora!" *Her leg is caught—do it now!* "No tengo mucha espuma dejada!" *I don't have much foam left!*

The older man, standing next to Alex, carefully but quickly took the burned child which Alex handed to him. Shirtless, Alex raced to the front passenger door of the Mesa and jumped into the front seat. He was shocked and momentarily paralyzed by the sight of the badly burned woman he managed to see through the black smoke. The intense heat, advancing flames and acrid smoke in the vehicle slammed at his senses.

"Please ... please, help me," Jenny begged. Her voice, though hoarse, was now a frantic but quiet whimper. She was now unable to clearly pronounce her words. "I'm so afraid. I don't want to die. Please ..." she struggled.

"Uh ... I try," is all that Alex could think to utter, his words also strong with his heavy Cuban accent. He bent over the top of her body which was still stretched out, over the console area, desperately seeking her pinned lower left leg. He kept low to avoid the flames which were again charging over the seats and between the two front seats. The ceiling liner above him was now on fire, with burning portions falling down onto his skin. He felt the intense pain against his bare skin, but he focused all of his attention on getting her out. Grasping her pinned left leg with both hands around her upper thigh, he yanked with all the strength he could muster. She screamed in agony once again. "Lo siento!" he said, again momentarily lapsing into his native Spanish in his panic. *I'm sorry.* Catching himself, he quickly added in English, "I sorry, but I must do this, señora."

Now ignoring her curdling screams of pain, he repeatedly and violently yanked her broken leg in an attempt to free it, all without success. He then saw that the lower portion of her leg was tightly pinned by the inwardly crushed and bent metal door panel. It was not coming free.

"Donde están los condenados bomberos!" *Where the hell are the damn fire fighters!* Manny roared out of frustration outside the driver's door. "Ya no me queda nada!" *I don't have anything left!* he said in reference to his now empty fire extinguishers. He stepped forward to the driver's door in front of him. Oblivious to the scorching heat of the metal now against his bare palms and to the ever-advancing flames to his immediate right, he grabbed the window sill with his left hand and strained to pull it open while his right hand worked the door handle. The deformed door didn't move, even when he frantically lifted his right leg up and braced it against the charred and paint-blistered side of the truck for leverage. The metal buckling the door had suffered in the rollover, preventing its opening. Caustic black smoke continued pouring forward at an increasing rate from the burning cargo area of the Mesa.

Without more foam to retard its path, the angry fire on the left side of the Mesa's exterior now roared back unabatedly, forcing Manny away from the driver's door altogether. Jenny screamed again in agony and primal fear from inside the Mesa as she sensed approaching death. Manny frantically charged back around the front of the vehicle to the open front passenger door where Alex, seeing him coming, quickly got out of his way by backing out of the vehicle. Manny entered the front seat again, desperately looking for a solution to get her out. There was none. He saw that the woman was now racked in heavy coughing and gasping for breath as she was enveloped in the deathly grasp of the increasingly superheated air and black smoke. Through his own burning and watering eyes, Manny could make out that she was openly sobbing and desperately trying to move her body off her driver's seat and down towards the floor-mounted gear shift console, away from the rapidly advancing heat and flames. Her efforts were in vain. Her leg remained pinned as the fire now engulfed the back, top and sides of both front seats as it charged into the front seat area.

With an instant and crushing awareness, Manny realized it was useless. The lady was going to die, and he was impotent to stop it from happening. Pressing his upper body lower inside the front seat area in order to avoid the advancing flames above, he moved a few inches closer towards her and gently touched her blackened shoulder with his left hand. With emotions overflowing, he looked at the now whimpering woman through the heavy screen of hot black smoke.

"Lo siento ... lo siento ..." *I'm sorry ... I'm sorry ...* he cried softly, his voice breaking. "Perdóname!" *Forgive me!* With that, he quickly withdrew from the Mesa just as the hot and hungry flames above and around him proceeded to engulf the entire interior. He withdrew just as the first sounds of distant rescue vehicles were heard by the onlookers.

Once out, he numbly walked a short distance outside the fire's range, where he slowly crumpled to the ground. With his soot-covered and burned hands, he covered his blackened face and cried uncontrollably as the animal screams came, and then stopped, from inside the Mesa.

CHAPTER 2

I WAS PLAYING with the red swizzle stick in my Jack and water as I listened to Avery Wilcox. He was my law firm's chairman, and he was busily addressing my firm's partners. Standing militarily erect, dressed in his usual sincere dark blue suit and crimson tie, and wearing his no-nonsense gold wire rim glasses, Avery certainly fit the part. As I gazed around the room, I could see that he had the undivided attention of all forty-one of my partners. We were assembled in one of the large meeting rooms at the Lauderdale Athletic Club, seated around white linen-covered circular tables crowded into the room.

Surveying his subjects from his podium, Avery's head suddenly stopped as his eyes zeroed in on my drink. His glare shifted up from my drink to my face, clearly not pleased with my breach of his rules of order. Avery was all business, and he loved to issue rules. Six months ago he had made it known, by another of his frequent memo edicts: He didn't want any partner of Hunt & Baxter drinking at these quarterly partners' meetings until all formal firm business matters were concluded. "The law is serious business," his memo intoned. He wanted our "full and undivided attention," as he put it, on all matters dealing with firm business.

I looked directly back at him, smiled slightly and nodded cordially. It didn't work. He maintained his stern expression as he finally looked away.

Ever since being elected firm chairman eighteen months ago, Avery had been constantly preaching that while a law firm is a profession, it is, first and foremost, a business. He made no apologies about his philosophy. The legal highways here in South Florida, as well as around the country, he relentlessly warned, were littered with the bleached and sun-dried bones of law firms that didn't understand that fact. And with two consecutive years of flat overall profits at Hunt & Baxter resulting from the real estate bust preceding his election as chairman, his philosophy found a ready and accepting audience in most of my partners. Avery recognized that support and quickly and decisively moved the firm in the direction of his monopsychotic focus on the firm's financial 'bottom line.'

I suppose I could have waited to have a drink. But, what the hell, I lamented to myself, I needed a drink after the difficult phone conversation I had just finished with Willis Cole shortly before leaving the office for this meeting.

Cole was chief product liability litigation counsel at Global Motors Corporation. With annual firm billings at around one-point-eight million, Global, my client, was one of the firm's most important and prestigious clients. After my conversation with Cole, I wasn't in the mood, quite frankly, to really care about what King Avery felt about my breach of his little anal-retentive rules of order. Besides, one needed a drink—and a stiff one at that—to get through all of the nonsense the management committee was presently going over.

Scanning the room, I spotted Jack Franklin, one of my partners, trying to camouflage a yawn. He was obviously enjoying Avery's droning on as much as I was. He saw me catch him in the act and smiled when I discreetly frowned and shook my head in feigned disgust at his lack of interest.

Jack had joined the firm fifteen years ago, two years after I did. He had a lot more hair then. With his penchant for bow ties, it was only natural that his practice area was wills, probate and estate planning, or, as the rest of us called them, "the Mod Squad"—the 'merchants of death.' He was one of the few lawyers I liked who wore bow ties. Jack was an excellent lawyer with a great wit, and we had grown to be good friends over the years. I trusted his intelligence and good judgment. I made a mental note to get his thoughts about my conversation with Cole when we broke for dinner.

Avery finally turned to the last item on the agenda. It was the big one, and the only one that guaranteed one hundred percent attendance by the partners at one of these meetings—partner compensation.

Avery cleared his throat and waited for complete silence. "Your management committee and your compensation sub-committee have spent a great deal of time this year on the compensation guide point recommendations we are about to distribute," he pronounced with importance. "I can assure all of you that it was not an easy task to accomplish. We collectively reviewed a considerable amount of information in order to arrive at these guide point recommendations, including a very thorough review of your respective client billings, billable hours, work revenues, and administrative responsibilities. And, as we know you can well appreciate, we sometimes were required to make tough decisions. The recommendations you're about to receive are the product of that hard work. While we don't pretend they're perfect, we believe they are fair and reasonable to all of us in this room."

His use of the 'Royal We' was my first inkling of trouble. He only used it, I observed over the last year-and-a-half, when he was running for cover.

With that pronouncement, Avery nodded to Robert Harrington, one of my litigation partners, to hand out the written recommendation sheets. Harrington sat at the committee table, immediately to Avery's right—to the right hand of god, at least in Harrington's view.

The 'guide point recommendation' was the method by which the firm split up its profits at the end of every year. The recommendation listed every partner's name with a specific percentage number typed next to it. The percentage was that partner's individual share of the net profits, which would be determined at the end of the firm's fiscal year, which fell on June thirtieth, some four months from now. The next column listed what that partner's projected dollar bonus would be based upon the percentage, and the last column showed each partner's total projected compensation for both base salary and expected bonus. This had been the way profits had been split up since Richard Hunt and Jonathon Baxter started the firm in 1955 and built it to the one hundred twenty lawyers it was today. Since our monthly salaries were intentionally set at a very low number, with the balance of our compensation made up by what traditionally had been a healthy year-end bonus, this bonus recommendation approval meeting was, bar none, the most important partner meeting of the year.

Its importance was amplified by the fact that many of my partners in the room had predicated their spending habits over the past eight months of the current fiscal year on assumptions they had made last June thirtieth as to what their own share of the bonus pie would be. However, as all of us in the room knew, the numbers being handed out were hardly "recommendations" at all. Barring some exception, which I had never seen occur, the deal was done. It only needed what had become a ceremonial 'rubber stamp' of approval from the partners at large to the management committee's recommendation.

Under the firm's partnership agreement, there were only a few 'fundamental' issues which the partners had to approve. These included annual compensation decisions, the hiring or termination of partners, and mergers with other firms.

Traditionally, the management committee's recommended compensation had been received and accepted by the group with an amazing sense of collective good will, with only a few bruised egos in the process. If my instincts were correct, however, that tradition was about to be sorely tested.

At King Avery's nod, his lap dog, Harrington, opened his soft, belted leather briefcase, lifted out a stack of the recommendation sheets and started distributing them to the various tables. Harrington was wearing his usual powder blue shirt with his *RJH* initials monogrammed on the cuff, along with a pair of expensive suspenders which matched his club tie. Ever the 'blue blood,' Harrington preferred to call them 'straps,' not suspenders. It figured. While always quick to inform clients and other lawyers that he graduated from Yale Law School, he never mentioned that he was born in Beaver Dam, Wisconsin.

Harrington was taking great pleasure in this job. He and Jacob Forman, a real estate partner, were selected by the management committee to serve on this year's compensation sub-committee. In Avery's zest to thank the subcommittee a few moments ago for its hard work, he omitted to mention that the sub-committee was comprised of his own very same management committee as supplemented only by two partners at large. And, I should add, the management committee also chose the two partners at large. This managerial incest was lost on no one in the room. I started thinking about a second Jack and water, *sans* the water.

Before the reign of King Avery, the seven-member compensation subcommittee was comprised of only two members of the management committee. The other five were intentionally chosen from the partners at large to better ensure a more complete and democratic view of each partner's individual economic worth to the firm. But that was before Avery's bottom line re-organization of all things firm. Don't get me wrong. This wasn't sour grapes on my part. When the guide point recommendations were issued in the past, I had always done well. However, with the management committee's relentless focus on 're-tooling the foundation of the firm,' as Avery recently called it, I had bad vibes as to how that 're-tooling' would translate in our guidepoints.

Actually, the bad vibes began a month ago. That was when I heard that Harrington and Forman had been appointed to the compensation subcommittee. Both of them, ass kissers of the first order, shared the same, somewhat limited three-item agenda: me, myself and mine.

Forman handed me a copy of the recommendations. Like everyone else in the room, I immediately scanned the page until I found my own percentage first. My percentage had increased dramatically over my last year's number, meaning that my earnings would be significantly more this year based on our projected year-end revenues. I was enjoying a very good year with Global and my other client billings, but even I had to question the degree of the recommended substantial increase, especially since it obviously would be coming at the expense of someone else.

Scanning down the list, I quickly saw that my hunch had been right. The Royal We on the management committee had collectively given themselves robust compensation increases, along with six other partners who were not on the committee, me included. These eleven partners controlled perhaps forty percent of the firm's total client revenue. The message being sent was clear: If you owned the big clients, you were protected. If you didn't, and were only a 'worker bee,' your days of sharing in the honey were over. In years past, Hunt partners with the big clients were generous in taking care of those worker bee partners who toiled away on their clients. Not anymore. If you didn't have your own clients, you were now viewed as expendable. The Royal We knew that without a book of their own clientele, the worker bee partners weren't going anywhere. And the worker bees knew it, too.

Studying the guide point recommendation more carefully, I could see that the Mod Squad partners took a major cut—some by as much as thirty-five percent. The real estate attorneys, whose practice suffered greatly from the continuing real estate bust, also got a big-time haircut. In fact, some of them would actually end up with no bonus at all, causing them to have to repay money from the draw they had previously been paid during the year. The rest of the partners were left with no increase in income over their last year's level, and many with slight decreases—decreases which were funding the extra percentage points needed in order to provide the Royal We and their cronies, including myself, with their major compensation increases.

Overall, the collective good will of the group had just been dealt a ruthless body slam by the management committee and its Harrington-led compensation sub-committee.

It suddenly dawned on me that the committee would not have adopted this proposal without first passing it quietly by the other power partners in the firm for their 'heads up' approval. Interestingly, I thought, no one had talked to me about it first.

I threw down the remains of my drink and surveyed the group's reaction around the room, awaiting the fireworks to start from my partners. George Benson, an estate planning partner of twenty years, was one of those who had just had his proposed compensation cut by thirty-five percent. Benson, an excellent lawyer, knew the tax and estate planning area backwards and forwards, but he didn't have much of his own client base. He serviced the clients of the other partners, including those of the Royal We.

Benson's face was beet red. He had his pen out and was doing some fast calculations on the backside of the handout, undoubtedly doing the math to determine just how much money he was going to have to pay back. I knew that he certainly wasn't preparing a list of other law firms that he would be joining.

At his age and salary, even after this major pay whack, he wasn't going any-where. A law firm, even this one, could replace him tomorrow with a six-year lawyer at a fraction of his overall cost. Benson knew that as well, and his pre-sent angry, but accepting, reaction was undoubtedly just what the committee was gambling on. I could see a lot of Bensons in the room.

A few more partners were quietly shaking their heads, but the vast major-ity was simply looking at the head table. All wore long faces. One of the older real estate partners seated in the back of the room, whose income had just been slashed by twenty percent, got up from his table, disgustedly threw his crum-pled copy of the schedule down onto the table in front of him and exited the room. He headed for the bar, staring angrily at the head table on his way out. Avery ignored him.

"This is ridiculous!" the young female partner next to me whispered defi-antly. "I had a great year." She had. Looking down at the list, her projected annual compensation had been cut by thirty thousand dollars. She had few cli-ents of her own, and like Benson and many of the others serviced the clients of the Royal We.

I looked at her and nodded. "I agree. This is bullshit."

Hank Ollin finally broke the silence from the middle of the room. "Avery, I find these recommendations ... well ... uh ... er ... unacceptable," he finally stammered. "Just exactly what message is the management committee trying to send us here?"

Ted Gunther, one the other members of the management committee, and who had quickly surfaced as King Avery's hatchet man, quickly responded instead.

"Hank, there's no new message here," he said calmly, with the same tone a father would have when addressing an impetuous teenager being denied the keys to the family car. "It's the same message that this committee has been em-phasizing to all of you since you elected us eighteen months ago to turn around this firm's finances and its future. Competition for legal business is brutal."

"Frankly," he continued, "that shouldn't be a secret to any of us. This firm can no longer be run as a gentleman's club if it's to grow and prosper. Those partners and those practice areas that are bringing in the clients will do well. Those that don't, won't. It's as simple as that. The recommendations we're making here tonight," he stated, as he calmly lifted both palms up, "do nothing more than reward those attorneys who are producing significant client revenues from their efforts. That's the lifeblood of this firm."

With his reprimand delivered, undoubtedly just as he had practiced, Gunther leaned contentedly back into his chair. I studied him as he did so. There were a few people in the firm that I didn't particularly like or trust.

Gunther was one of them. The fact is, I had never liked him or trusted him. He was in his early 50s and of medium build. His massive ego refused to admit the reality of fast-approaching baldness. The long, thin black hairs now lying across the top of his head were not indigenous to that area. Trump-like, they had been swept up and over the top of his scalp, in a valiant, but losing, effort to feign hair on the top of his head. I'd wager even money that hair plug transplants were in his near future.

Ollin, a paunchy corporate attorney in his late fifties with only a modest clientele of his own was now hot. Gunther's lecture and condescending attitude caused him to overcome his usual timidity. He rose from his chair.

"Well, if that's the committee's criteria," he countered, looking directly at Gunther, "why did *your* percentage and Harrington's percentage both increase by twenty-five percent? You're both having great client billing years, but let's face it," he added sarcastically, "you both got your major clients the old-fashioned way—you inherited them. You didn't find them and drag them into this firm. You didn't get them referred to you by another attorney in the community who was impressed with the quality of your hard work. You didn't get them through hard work at all. No," he challenged with undisguised contempt in his voice, "since you're into 'speaking frankly' tonight, Ted, let's tell it like it really is. You and Robert were both *given* your major clients from Jonathon Baxter when he became ill and had to retire. *But for* that inheritance," he angrily added, removing and pointing his glasses with his right hand at Gunther to punctuate his comments, "both of you would be in the same damn client situation that most of us are in presently. Where the hell is *that* fortuitous inheritance reflected on your recommendation list here?!" He threw his glasses onto the linen tablecloth in front of him and sat down angrily.

As soon as he finished, Harrington rocketed upwards from his chair. He stood to his full imposing height of six-feet-four-inches and entered the fray. There was no doubt as to what side of the battle he was on. Wilcox, Gunther and the rest of the Royal We were buttering his bread. Having inherited his clients, he was not about to tolerate any insurrection in the ranks of the worker bees.

"Hank, that was a damn cheap shot!" he angrily charged. "There's no question that Ted and I were given continued responsibility for those clients by Jonathan, but we've proceeded to invest a great deal of valuable time and resources in handling those clients. Like Ted, I've expanded the legal areas of practice, which we now perform for those 'inherited' clients, as you call them. We did that ourselves, and I didn't see you knocking on my door to offer to help out in those expansion efforts." Harrington glanced over at Gunther on that point. Gunther was nodding his assent. They made a great tag team, I thought.

"I also might add that we have both increased our billings to those clients by over fifty percent since we accepted responsibility. Your comments are way out of line!"

Harrington truly looked hurt. I could see why he was considered one of the best trial attorneys in South Florida. He was quick on his feet, believed his own rhetoric, and had a superb appreciation for the dramatic. Last fall he had handled a piece of environmental litigation for Global Motors which I had given him. I felt Harrington was the best partner to handle it. I hadn't spent any time on environmental matters over the years; instead, I'd concentrated on products liability defense cases. As it turned out, Harrington and Willis Cole of Global had hit it off quite well. Cole, who had taken an interest in the case due to the potential environmental liability exposure to Global, had been very pleased with Harrington's work. Harrington had both bullied and finessed his way to a successful jury trial verdict through a minefield of complex environmental issues and unfavorable evidence. Cole called me the day after the jury had come back with glowing accolades for Harrington.

"Goddamn Rambo is what that man is! Goddamn Rambo!" Cole kept repeating admiringly. I passed the compliment on to Harrington. He ate it up.

"Hank," Harrington continued, "if you bring in, or expand existing client billings, like Ted and I have done, you're going to be treated the same as we are. Until that time, however," he added sharply, "I would appreciate it if you would knock off the unfounded comments." With that he sat down, glanced confidently over at the head table, looking for a regal blessing from King Avery as he did so.

That did it. The prudent voice inside told me to shut up, but I couldn't. Maybe it was the Jack Daniels.

"I hadn't intended to speak on this," I quietly announced as I rose next to my chair, "but I must." I saw all eyes turn to me. I also caught the puzzled look on Avery's face as well. I turned to squarely face the management committee sitting at the head table in the front of the room.

"I have to agree with Hank; this guide point proposal is unacceptable. All of us here certainly appreciate the time and effort which you and the subcommittee have put into this, Avery," I said holding up my copy of the recommendation. "However, this is inconsistent with the firm's long-term best interests and its historical values." I tossed it on the middle of the table in front of me.

"As a law firm, we have to make a realistic and equitable distinction between partners who inherit their major clients and those who get theirs by beating the bushes and working their asses off to bring in new ones. As everyone here knows, it's a hell of a lot harder to get new clients than it is to inherit or expand existing ones. And I think I can safely get away with saying that since, as all of you know, I inherited Global Motors from Peter Herman when he took early retirement eight years ago. Yes, like many of you have done with your inherited firm clients," I said, nodding at members at the head table, "I too have grown and expanded the firm's services and billings to Global since then. But the simple fact is, had it not been for that fortuitous twist of great timing, I would never have been able to bring that client into the firm on my own, at least not at that stage of my career. And there are a couple of other litigators here," I added, as I scanned the room, "who undoubtedly could have done just as well with Global as I have done if they'd been lucky enough to have been in the right place at the right time, as I was."

I paused for effect. I could see that I had everyone's attention, including Avery's cold, angry glare from the head table. He was furious. *Well, I thought, 'in for a penny, in for a pound.'* I continued.

"There's no question we need to encourage the retention and expansion of inherited clients by increasing the compensation of those partners who assume responsibility for them and do so successfully. But these guide point numbers, including my own for that matter, aren't fair and aren't smart for the firm. They introduce two elements that have never played a role in this firm: greed and divisiveness. It's been the historical, intangible sense of camaraderie that's made this firm different from our competitors over the years. It's been the feeling that we all work hard and we share the spoils; that's the glue that has gotten us through thick and thin in the past, and it's the same glue that will get us through this current economic slump. Your guide point recommendations destroy that glue."

Gunther quickly sat forward in his seat. His calm, placating demeanor of five minutes ago had disappeared. "Mike," he angrily interrupted, "I think—"

"Excuse me, Ted," I politely but forcefully cut him off, raising my hand to ward off his interruption. "I've got the floor right now, and I'm not quite finished yet." I maintained steady eye contact with him, and he angrily relented and sat back in his seat. From the grimaces on their faces, the other members of the management committee were equally incensed at my comments. They apparently had assumed that a beneficiary of their *largesse* would keep quiet. However, I had had enough of Avery's hectoring, and his new philosophy, and I needed to get it off my chest.

"The partners joined this firm because we wanted to practice law with each other in a group practice. We figured that we wouldn't starve, and that we would treat each other fairly. However, over the last year," I said looking directly at the Royal We and their head table, "this firm has been moving in an unhealthy direction. This compensation proposal is but one more step—and a damn poor one—in that direction. We are developing an absolute fixation on making money, whatever the costs might be. Well, that fixation, in my humble opinion, is causing some people in this room to put their own selfish interests ahead of what I believe—and I think a majority of partners in this room believe—are the best long-term interests of the group as a whole. If we don't reverse this trend, this firm will cease to exist, at least with the values that have historically defined us. Now, if this is the direction that everyone here wants to go, then that's fine, but I don't think it is, and it certainly isn't the direction in which I want to be headed."

The room was very quiet.

"Avery," I concluded, now addressing him directly, "I'm respectfully asking that your committee withdraw these recommendations and re-issue them in an amended fashion, consistent with some of the historical values of the firm. If the management committee wishes to use compensation as a means of persuading many of the partners in this room to encourage them to bring in new clients, then I suggest that we establish a sub-committee—with full representation of the partnership at large—to immediately develop a plan for adoption by June thirtieth year end. We can phase in economic carrots and clubs over a two year period, rather than the draconian plan that your committee has presented here. That's my motion," I said, finally taking my seat.

I saw most of the other partners in the room nod their heads in silent agreement. It was a sentiment not shared by the management committee members who were giving me icy glares. Harrington was furious. The adoption of my motion would be reducing the size of his feedbag at Hunt.

"No!" exploded Derek Rodgers, an older tax attorney, and a member of the Royal We. "I don't agree one damn bit with your assessment of the firm's direction, Mike, and I certainly don't agree with your motion to amend these recommendations. We're not going to do it! This firm gave this committee the duty, and the responsibility I might add, to make tough decisions to protect and guide the firm in this dog-eat-dog legal market we're all caught in. Well, they've done just that. They're sending important messages to this group that, quite frankly, need to be sent if we are to remain in business." He paused as he scanned the partners in the room with a challenging glower. "Rejecting these guide point recommendations would be a grave mistake. In fact, I feel so strongly about this, that I hereby move that the committee's guide point recommendations be approved without amendment and without further discussion! Otherwise, I'll have to seriously consider my own options."

With that threat, he forcefully nodded at Avery, urging him to re-take charge of the discussions.

Rodgers, I knew, had been a close friend of Avery's for many years. He sponsored Avery's membership application at the Lauderdale Yacht Club a number of years ago. He controlled a profitable group of clients in the leisure travel industry, along with the trade association to which they belonged. Not coincidentally, Avery had been servicing many of those clients with Rodgers and lusted to be heir to them and to their billings if and when Rodgers retired as he recently hinted would likely occur in the next few years. Rodgers apparently wanted to play golf full time instead of the half time that he now played.

"I agree with Derek," another powerful Royal We partner chimed in. "I second his motion." Not a surprise there, either. His daughter also happened to marry Rodgers' son ten years ago.

The room was silent. The cold political reality of what was happening was not lost on the less powerful partners sitting around the room. While those partners might have enjoyed a numerical voting majority, they lacked the political majority. They didn't control the source of the real power in the law firm—clients. If Avery and his cronies pulled out of the firm and took their client base with them, the remaining partners would be left with a terminal problem—few clients and even less income.

Avery didn't miss the reality either. Rodger's motion had its desired effect of nudging him back into action.

"All right, we have a motion and a second," he declared decisively as he walked over to the podium again, taking charge. "Any further discussion?" His demeanor and tone announced that the question was purely rhetorical. He wanted and expected no further discussion as he looked challengingly around the room. The intimidation worked—no one squeaked.

With rising anger, I couldn't believe what I was witnessing. The other partners were remaining the frightened and mute little mice they had become. If they were to collectively object, and do so with a strong united front, I was convinced that a number of the Royal We would probably back down and support the motion I had suggested. If the other partners were going to speak, it was now or never.

Not a hand went in the air to discuss or oppose Rodger's motion. Jesus Christ, I thought to myself. *Pass the cheese. The mice are ready to vote.*

"Let's call for a vote then," Avery said. "All in favor of the motion to adopt the guide point recommendations as presently proposed signify by raising your hand," he ordered.

Immediately, all hands at the committee's table ascended. Slowly, the other hands around the room followed suit. Many waited to see how others were voting, including their department practice heads. Over the course of a slow ten seconds, all of the partners finally raised their hands in approval. All except for me and three others.

Unbelievable, I thought to myself. This is exactly why drinking should be *mandatory* at a partners' meeting—alcohol sometimes gives you a set of balls when you need them the most.

"Well, the motion clearly carries," Avery declared. "No sense calling for a negative vote count, unless, of course, someone wants to." He was looking directly at me. I shrugged and shook my head in disgust. "The board hereby adopts the recommendations of the committee based upon your collective approval," he proclaimed. He smiled at the group.

The dirty little deed was done and the mayhem completed.

"Since that is the last item on the agenda," he confidently stated, "this meeting is hereby adjourned. Dinner is being served in the dining room," he said as he stared frostily over at me. "At least for those of you who would like to join the rest of us."

CHAPTER 3

DRIVING HOME AFTER the meeting, I tried to calculate just how much damage I had inflicted upon myself. What was that old saying: 'If you decide to shoot the king, don't miss?' I figured I not only shot at the king tonight, but also at his entire royal court. And I missed them all. Well, I reassured myself, it needed to be said.

I turned off Las Olas Boulevard onto Coral Reef Drive, one of the old waterfront isles near downtown Ft. Lauderdale. My house was third from the point at the end of the street. The isles abutting Las Olas were thin man-made peninsulas built during the land boom of the 1920s when developers dredged the swampy areas and used the sandy muck to create long finger-like peninsulas extending outward from Las Olas Boulevard at their base. Each of the peninsulas was only about two hundred-fifty feet wide and a quarter mile long. The narrow width allowed for only one street down the middle of each isle, with approximately thirty waterside homes lining each side. Their yards were covered with lush and exotic tropical plants and trees. Typically, the closer a home was to the point, that is, the far end of the peninsula, the more expensive it was.

Most residents had a boat or yacht tied to their dock. I hated to fish. My 'yacht' was a small, open Boston Whaler.

Coming home to my place each night was like escaping to a tropical paradise. Buying it was one of the smarter things that Liz and I did eight years earlier. We certainly couldn't afford to buy the place in this location at today's prices I reminded myself as I pulled into the drive and parked my car. Even with the crash of the real estate market, homes in the Las Olas area held their expensive price and value. As I got out and strolled up the bougainvillea-lined walk to the front door, I could feel the heavy, oppressive layer of humidity, unusual for February, still in the February air. There was absolutely no breeze.

"The mighty warrior returns," my wife announced as I walked into the family room carrying my briefcase. The room was located in the back of the house overlooking the rear yard and canal beyond. Liz was curled up on the couch in her bathrobe, reading a novel on her Kindle.

I put down my briefcase and threw my suit coat over the back of a chair at the little eating area just off the kitchen. "Hi," I laughed in response as she got up and came over. We quick-kissed hello.

"Sorry I'm so late, but I had a couple of drinks at the bar after the partners' dinner. There were a few things I needed to discuss. How are the ladies?" I asked, referring to our two daughters in high school.

"They're fine. They're both in bed. I treated them to pizza out tonight to celebrate their quarterly report cards. Erin got her perfect 4.0 GPA again, while Ann pulled a 3.7."

"That's great. I can't believe how well they're doing in school. Where do you suppose they got their brains?"

"Well, I think it's becoming painfully obvious, don't you?" She smiled ever so sweetly. "They've inherited my genes, Michael, not yours."

I laughed again.

"How did the partners' meeting go?" she asked. "Are you hungry?"

"Yeah, actually, I'm starved. The dinner at the Club was some odd combination of spinach and chicken. Awful. I just picked at it." I slipped off my tie. "I'll get something out of the fridge. As far as the meeting went," I said, returning to her original question, "I'd prefer to forget it. In fact," I added, "I'd prefer to forget the whole damn day."

"Why, what happened?"

"Well, for starters, I had a major blow up on the phone this afternoon with one of the big-dog, in-house lawyers at Global. Then I capped that off by completely pissing off Avery and the management committee over their compensation recommendations."

"Was tonight the big vote on everyone's compensation?" she asked. After years of experience, Liz also knew what the annual compensation meeting meant.

"Yeah, tonight was the big vote, alright." I reached into my pocket and, without comment, handed her the folded sheet with the bonus recommendations on it. She took it over to the kitchen table, sat down and started to read. Meanwhile, I headed over to the refrigerator, opened the door and started scrounging for a snack. I was one of those lucky guys that were born with a super-active metabolism. I could munch all day and only rarely put on an extra pound. It killed Liz who claimed she gained weight brushing her teeth. Her figure defied that claim. God help me if my metabolism ever turned on me.

After a minute, Liz looked up from the document with a puzzled look. "I don't understand. If I read this right, your points actually went up from last year, didn't they?"

"That's right," I answered without further elaboration.

"Well, doesn't that mean that you're going to be making more money this year?"

"That's right," I again responded as I reached into the fridge.

"Then what's the problem?" she asked. "Why would this cause you a problem at the meeting?"

I walked over and joined her at the kitchen table, sitting across from her with a cold slice of pizza on a small plate. The pointed end of the slice was gone, the half-moon outline of someone's teeth marks evident. It was obvious that Liz had been at work. Bites like this out of leftovers in the fridge had been her signature since early in our marriage. While I no longer said anything, it still drove me crazy.

I proceeded to explain the events of the partners' meeting to her, including a description of the details of the various partner comments. Liz loved details. If I didn't volunteer them when relating a story to her, she would invariably question me to great lengths until she got them. I learned more of the finer points of effective cross-examination tactics from her over the years of our marriage than I ever did in court. Compared to Liz, F. Lee Bailey, even in his prime, was a piker.

"You know what I think of those people on your management committee," she said after I finished. "They're not half the quality of the men that originally started your firm, Michael. You can't even begin to compare Wilcox or Gunther with Hunt in his prime or even Baxter for that matter," she continued. "I still remember how impressive both of those two guys were when they were alive and active in the firm."

She reached over, picked up the bottle of Corona in front of me which I had pulled from the fridge and took a drink. "Avery can pontificate until the cows come home, but he'll never be their match, and you know it," she added as she put my bottle of beer back down. She was right, and, unfortunately, I knew it.

I shrugged. "Well, all the same, I probably should have kept my mouth shut, or at least toned down my comments. I'm sure I made some enemies tonight."

"Nonsense, Michael. That firm is as much your firm as it is anyone else's there. You've got to speak out on issues like that, and I'm sure even Avery respects you for that. Besides, you probably only said what most of the rest of them were thinking anyway. The real problem with your firm," she offered, "is that Avery, Harrington, Gunther and the rest of that 'new power group,'" she added sarcastically, "are only out for themselves."

I shrugged. "Maybe we're both being too critical of them."

She looked at me, frowning. "I don't think so. They may be your partners, but they're selfish little shits. And you know it, too. Thank goodness you've got the protection of having Global Motors as a client. With the firm changing the way it is, Michael, Global is like a welcome clove of garlic against some of your vampire partners."

I laughed and shook my head back and forth, thinking about her comments. I took another plug from the Corona.

"Speaking of Global," she added, suddenly recalling my earlier comment, "what was that problem you had with Global today?"

"You know the *Bertson* case that I'm working on for Global?" I asked. I knew that asking her to remember the specific name of one of my cases wasn't going to happen. Liz could never remember case names. Unlike her other great talents, this was a condition that had never improved over the twenty-one years of our married life. Once again it was the details of my cases that she was interested in, not the names. Give her a case detail, however, and she would recall the case immediately. As I took a bite out of the cold pizza, I could see that all-too-familiar vacant look in her eyes. She had absolutely no idea what the *Bertson* case was about.

"You know," I prompted, "the one where the airbag in the van supposedly didn't go off properly in the head-on collision, and the chiropractor was killed?" Bingo. Armed with those little details, she remembered. I could read it in her eyes.

"Sure," she replied as if she knew exactly which case I was referring to from the outset. "I recall it. What about it?"

"I had a very ugly conversation today about that case with Willis Cole, the senior in-house attorney at Global who oversees all their product liability cases around the country. He supervises Don Kean. Kean is the Global in-house staff attorney covering the State of Florida who I usually deal with. Anyway, do you remember me saying that the in-house engineer at Global assigned to the *Bertson* case was very concerned about the case and wanted it settled in a big way?"

"Was that the guy who inspected the wrecked van and concluded that some kind of air bag part was possibly not installed correctly or was broken when it was originally installed at the factory?" Liz had locked on.

"Very good," I nodded and smiled. "I'm impressed. Yeah, the sensor was either broken when it was originally installed at the factory, in which case Global is at fault, or the sensor was broken as a result of the crash itself, in which case there is no liability for Global. The problem is that there was so much damage from the crash itself that it's really very difficult to determine what the actual situation was. In view of the fact that the deceased chiropractor was making a lot of money and due to some not-so-helpful information we discovered at Global, the Global engineer didn't feel comfortable putting it in front of a jury. He wanted the case settled for reasonable dollars if at all possible. So last week," I continued, "when I was in Detroit, I met with Don Kean and the engineer. The three of us recognized that it was a good case to settle, and we also agreed on a settlement dollar value within which they wanted the case settled. Kean told me to try to settle the case for no more than one hundred thousand dollars. The plaintiff's lawyer isn't the sharpest knife in the drawer and his expert hasn't really focused on the important issues yet. I told Kean that I thought I could get it settled for under that amount."

Liz, nodding and listening intently, smoothly reached over and took the piece of pizza off my plate. Leaning forward over the table towards me, she took a bite out of it and replaced it back on my plate. I stopped my explanation mid-sentence, staring at her and then down at my piece of pizza.

"I only want a bite," she innocently protested. "You know," she added on obvious second thought, "when you think about it, the girls and I didn't have to even bring the rest of the unfinished pizza home from the restaurant. We could have left it there, and then where would you be right now? Sitting here with nothing to eat is where. So, you should be *thanking me* instead of glaring at me," she offered, raising both eyebrows and smiling at the same time.

Territorially, I moved the plate closer to me and picked up what remained of the communal piece of pizza.

I sighed in resignation and continued. "Anyway, all three of us agreed on that course of action. I was to settle the case as soon as possible, and I did. I called the plaintiff's attorney when I got back to Lauderdale, and over the course of this past week, I was able to get him to settle for seventy thousand dollars. In fact, he and I had our concluding telephone conversation first thing this morning in which we agreed on all the settlement terms."

"So, what's the issue? I don't understand," she said.

"Hear me out. Anyway, I called Kean in Michigan after I concluded it with the plaintiff's lawyer and reported the settlement to him. He was ecstatic. 'Good job,' he told me. Well, at around five o'clock today, just as I'm getting ready to head over to the club for the partners' meeting, I got a call out of the blue from Cole at Global."

"Who's Cole?"

"Willis Cole. He's Kean's boss," I reminded her. "Anyway, Cole told me that Kean had reported the settlement to him. Cole said he was not happy with the settlement. He said that he felt the *Bertson* case was a good one to try, and that he disagreed with Don Kean's settlement views on the case. He told me that since he had taken over management of all product liability cases at Global last fall, he was in the process of revamping the company's settlement philosophy around the country. He said that, in his opinion, a lot of the attorneys around the country representing Global had 'lost their nerve,' as he put it, to try the tough cases. In fact, he volunteered his opinion that my percentage of settlements was too high for his own personal satisfaction. He felt I should be trying a lot more cases than I am. It's total baloney, and he knows it."

"What's his problem?" Liz asked, defending me.

"Well, the worst is yet to come. Cole repeated that he was convinced that the *Bertson* case was a good one to try. He instructed me to call up the plaintiff's attorney in that case and tell him that I was 'withdrawing the settlement offer,' as he put it."

Her forehead frowned. "I thought you said that you had already settled the case earlier this morning with the other lawyer."

"Very good. I did. And that's both the point and the problem. I told Cole that there was no longer any 'settlement offer' on the table. I pointed out that based upon the express settlement authority and instructions that Kean and engineering had given me, I made the call to the plaintiff's lawyer that morning. We had orally agreed to a settlement at seventy thousand dollars in return for a dismissal of the case, with a full release. I pointed out that I had promised the opposing attorney that I'd be faxing him a letter of settlement confirmation on Monday." I took another swig from the Corona.

"What did Cole say to that?"

I shook my head in disgust. "The weasel. He told me that he wanted me to call the plaintiff's attorney back and tell him that I had 'misunderstood' my client's settlement authority guidelines and that I had not been authorized to settle the case."

Liz leaned forward and rested both arms on the kitchen table. "That's not even legal is it?" she asked. It was more of a statement than a question.

I responded sharply. "It's an outright lie is what it is, and that son of a bitch Cole knows it. I told him that I had a problem with what he was asking me to do and that I couldn't make that call. Liz, when I told him that, you could just feel his fury over the phone."

"Did he back off when you told him that?"

"No. And here is what's bothering me about the call. When I told him that I had a problem with his request, he didn't say anything for a good five seconds. I mean, not a word. And neither did I. I figured that he finally realized that he had stepped over the line and would drop it. But he didn't. He then asked me in a very cold tone: 'Are you going to do what I have instructed'?"

Liz was staring intently at me. Anger and concern both registered in her blue eyes. "And ...?" she asked.

"I was very direct with him. I told him that what he was asking me to do was to lie and, quite frankly, to practice law in a manner that I don't. I told him that I had represented Global for over eight years now, and that I had never been put in the position he was putting me in. I told him that while I could appreciate the fact that he and Don Kean may have had a miscommunication between themselves, or even a difference of opinion about the wisdom of settling the case, Don had *unequivocally* told me that he had one hundred thousand dollars in authority to settle the case, that he and engineering wanted the case settled, and that I was to get it settled at or under that number as soon as I could. I also stressed to him that Don followed the established Global settlement procedure which his predecessor at Global, Jeff Gordon, put in place requiring a legal-engineering conference with local counsel on any case where the settlement authority exceeds fifty thousand dollars. We did that, I told him, and all three of us agreed to settlement authority of up to one hundred thousand dollars. While I tried to put it as diplomatically as possible, I had to tell him that he shouldn't be asking me to do what he was asking."

Liz tilted her head to one side, concern now clearly etched on her face. "And what did he say to that?"

"He said that he wasn't really *asking* me to make the call. He said that as a vice-president and the in-house counsel in charge of Global's national product liability defense program, he was *directing* me to make that call, that I must have made a mistake in what I understood Kean to have told me."

"You've got to be kidding me!"

"Liz, at that point, I flat out told him that I wasn't going to make that call, and that my good name and self respect outweighed his feelings on the matter. Global made a deal with the plaintiff's lawyer, and I was duty bound to send out the confirmation letter to the *Bertson* lawyer on Monday morning. Since I was at it, and since I was a little pissed off as well, I also told him that his new defense philosophy was fine, but that I did not agree with his opinion regarding my Global representation. I suggested that if it was a philosophical problem that the two us were having, that I would not be adverse at all to discussing it with Rex Folger, who is Cole's boss in the Legal Department. I've known Rex for four or five years, and I think that he would be shocked at the discussion."

"Was he agreeable with that suggestion?" she asked.

"Are you kidding me? He immediately fired back and told me that he was in charge of this area of Global's business, and that I was *not* to discuss the matter with Folger. Period."

Liz just listened. She let me talk.

"I reminded him that I had received years of nothing but high praise from both Folger and Gordon, and that I only recommended settlement in cases where the exposure to Global warranted it. I pointed out that of the dozen Global cases that I have tried over the last eight years, I lost only two, and, frankly, that those two deserved losing. They were tough defense cases, and I told them that. The two Global engineers assigned to the cases, however, wanted to take the chance in those two cases, and we did. At that point, Cole interrupted me and said something to the effect that he didn't think that he and I really had anything more to talk about. With that, he hung up."

Liz leaned back in her chair. She folded her arms across her chest. "Michael, what exactly does all of this mean?" she asked. Concern was evident in her voice.

"It means that Cole is a power-hungry little prick that can't be trusted, for starters. From what I hear from the staff attorneys who work for him, he has his eyes glued on Rex Folger's position of general counsel and will absolutely stop at nothing to get it. He co-chairs the product safety committee at Global which reports directly to the Global executive committee. I'm sure he thinks that if he can show a tougher stance on these defense cases, he'll cement his position as a rising star to the powers that be at Global. I had a little flap with him a few months ago over a document production that had been served on Global in one of my cases. For some reason, Cole decided to get personally involved in the case. He called me one afternoon and claimed that, using his words, I was 'too pro-plaintiff' in my interpretation of the document request. He told me that from what he could see, I was in favor of turning over more documents than he felt the document request actually required."

"What happened?" she asked, again leaning forward in her chair.

"I politely told him that he apparently was not given all of the facts from his staff. I explained that I had gone over the document request very carefully and had already made the very objections to the court that he was now suggesting. The trial judge, I explained, had disagreed and had ruled against Global. He found the documents were relevant and ordered them produced. Consequently, I pointed out that Global was now required to produce them. However, I could tell that he was still miffed about it. I hate to say this, but I remember having the distinct feeling then that Cole would have ignored the court order and would not have produced them at all except for the fact that I had previously seen the documents myself and knew of their existence. Bottom line, I made a mental note then about the guy. Now," I said, shaking my head, "this only confirms my instincts. He's trouble. And an asshole to boot."

"What do you think will happen now?"

"I don't really know, but I think Cole took my refusal as a personal slap at either his judgment or his authority. Either way, it's not good."

What I didn't tell Liz was that Cole was in a position to hurt the firm if he really wanted to. Cole was the Global attorney who hired and fired outside law firms.

Liz got up from the table without a word, picked up my dirty plate and walked over to the dishwasher where she put it inside. I remained sitting at the table.

Closing the dishwasher door, she turned and looked over at me. "Suppose that he does take it personally. What can he do to the firm?" she asked. Her sixth sense was scary.

Recognizing her concern, I realized that I had probably overreacted.

"Hey, I don't mean to get you alarmed. I'm sure I'm reading way too much into the conversation," I assured her. "I'll wager that when Cole thinks the matter over, he'll quickly realize that he was way off base. I'm going to be in Detroit at the end of next week on another Global case. I'll drop in on him and smooth everything over." I gave her a confident smile.

It worked. She smiled.

I looked over at the time displayed on the digital clock on the microwave. "Gosh, I can't believe that it's already eleven-thirty. Let's get to bed, I'm beat."

With that, Liz came out from the kitchen area and stood directly in front of me as I was still seated at the table. She bent towards me and casually started unfastening and removing my tie. *"Oh, my poor little Michael,"* she teased, *"is he all tuckered out?"* With a mischievous look in her eyes and a seductive voice, she added, "shall I put you to bed and make it all better?"

A broad smile came instantly to my face. "It seems that your warrior has a sudden sense of renewed energy after all, my queen," I responded, laughing. "I accept your kind offer, my lady, to put it to me in bed," I said, as I reached over and untied the sash tying her robe. She offered no resistance. The robe opened, and I was rewarded immediately; she had nothing on beneath.

"Now those are world-class tits," I announced quietly, as I drew her body to me, "world class. Even the Russian judge would have to give them a ten."

"They are called *breasts*," she corrected, giggling.

"Call them anything you want, my dear," I said softly, as my lips moved forward to kiss my favorite breast. "They're still 'world class,'" I mumbled.

She took in a shallow breath and let out a moan. Without saying more, she reached down, lifted my head in both of her warm hands and kissed me gently on the lips. She then hooked her forefinger under the top button of my shirt, pulled me out of my chair and walked me towards our bedroom at the other end of the house. Her robe was fully off before we made it out of the family room.

CHAPTER 4

THE RINGING OF the phone jarred me awake. Groggily, I eyed the green digital numbers illuminated on the clock radio next to my bed and struggled to make out the time. Two-thirty-nine a.m. Liz and I had only been asleep a few hours I mentally noted as I groped in the darkness for the phone on the nightstand.

"Hello," I managed.

"Mike, this is Todd Hawkins. Eric's brother," he said. "I'm sorry to call and wake you at this hour, but Eric asked me to call. There's been a terrible car accident," he quietly stated.

I was instantly awake. "What happened?" Part of me didn't want to know. The Hawkins' were close family friends; Liz and I were godparents to Jenny and Eric's young son, Ryan. The call and tone of my voice apparently alerted Liz to a problem. She was awake and sat up in bed beside me.

"Who is it? What is it?" she asked with immediate concern.

I held my hand up to her as I listened to the voice on the other end of the phone explain.

"It's Jenny and Ryan. They had a terrible car accident on the interstate this afternoon on their way home from Weston. Jenny's ..." his voice broke. He recovered. "... Jenny's dead and Ryan is burned real bad." His voice was breaking again.

"Oh my God," was the only response I could utter.

"What is it?" Liz now asked worriedly. She turned on the lamp on the night table next to her side of the bed.

"Just a moment, Todd," I said as I turned to Liz, putting the phone down in my lap, with one hand over the speaker.

"It's the Hawkins—there was a car accident," I said quietly. "Jenny was killed and Ryan badly burned."

"Oh my god," she cried, covering her mouth with the palm of her right hand.

I brought the phone back to my mouth. "Todd ..." I managed to say, trying to comprehend what I had just heard, "I just can't believe this. We had dinner with them only last weekend. Were Eric and Sarah in the car?"

"No, thank god, it was just the two of them. Jenny was coming home late this afternoon with Ryan on I-595 after picking up some Girl Scout cookies out in Weston. I haven't heard any of the details except that there was a rollover and a fire." He paused, "none of us can believe it either. We're all in shock."

"How badly is Ryan burned?"

"Bad," he said with a quivering voice. "The doctors told Eric that he has third degree burns over something like thirty percent of his body. His left ear and most of his nose have been burned off according to what I could get out of Eric." He started to choke up again. I knew that Todd was close to his niece and nephew.

Despite knowing that I was trying to listen and obtain information, Liz couldn't contain her concern. "Is Ryan badly burned?" she whispered between quiet sobs.

I nodded affirmatively as I listened to Todd.

"Eric is still over at the hospital with Ryan," Todd continued. "He's in the burn center. I ..." he struggled, "I was over at the mortuary taking care of some of those details earlier this evening, after the authorities released Jenny's body. Debbie and I just got home from the hospital. Eric wanted me to be sure to give you a call to let you and Liz know. He apologizes for not being able to call you himself tonight."

"How are Eric and Sarah holding up?" I asked. Sarah was their daughter.

"Not well, not well at all. Eric called us as soon as he heard. He had us pick Sarah up from one of her friend's homes where she had been working on a school project. We brought her over to the hospital for her dad to tell her the news. It was awful."

That did it for Todd. He started sobbing. "Eric wanted to be with her when she was told. Sarah was so upset when she was told," he related between stifled sobs. "She's staying with us tonight. Our family doctor went ahead and put her on a mild tranquilizer just so she could get some sleep tonight. She's utterly devastated."

"I can't imagine. Are you okay?" I asked. His grief was tangible.

"Just a minute," he said. I could hear him rest the phone on a desk or counter, followed by the sound of him blowing his nose in the background.

Another few seconds passed until he got back on the phone. "I'm sorry about that," he apologized in a more controlled voice. "I'm really concerned about Eric though. He's devastated. If it weren't for his having to deal right now with Sarah's needs and Ryan's medical problems, I don't know what he'd do. I've never seen him like this."

"Todd, I'm going to throw some clothes on and head over right now to the hospital to be with him."

"No, I think he needs to be by himself right now. He told me that he doesn't want to see anybody tonight, Mike. Thank you for your offer though. I'm going to catch a few hours of sleep and go over to the hospital tomorrow morning to be with him."

"What hospital are he and Ryan at?"

"Jackson Memorial, in Miami. Ryan's in the burn center on the third floor."

"If it's okay with you Todd, Liz would like to come over to your place tomorrow morning to see Sarah. The two of them are pretty close, and it might help." I looked over at Liz who was nodding her agreement as she blew her own nose in a Kleenex.

"I know they're close. That would be nice, Mike."

"I'm going to head over to Jackson Memorial first thing in the morning to be with them if you think that would be alright," I offered.

"That would be much appreciated, Mike. I know that Eric would like to see you. He just needs to be alone tonight with himself and with Ryan."

"I understand. Todd, thank you for letting us know. All of you will be in our thoughts and prayers."

We both hung up.

I slid over on the bed and put my arms around Liz who was sitting with her back against the headboard. Her knees were pulled against her chest with her long nightie T-shirt pulled over her knees and legs. Her head was down, resting on her arms which were crossed on her knees. Quiet crying was the only sound from her as her shoulders rocked up and down in response to her quiet sobs. We didn't say a word. I just held her tightly.

CHAPTER 5

LIZ AND I talked until just after four a.m. when we finally turned out the lights. Despite the short night, we both got up early the next morning, a Saturday. Neither one of us got much sleep after the call.

We broke the news to Erin and Anne when they came down for breakfast. No one in our house was a late sleeper. They both took the news very badly with a lot of tears. Jenny had been more like a favorite aunt to them over the years than a close friend of the family. My daughters babysat for Ryan on a few occasions over the last few months. We didn't tell them the details of his burn injuries, only that they were quite severe.

Erin, however, had inherited her mother's affinity for details. "Dad, where was Ryan burned?"

"His uncle gave me some general information, but I haven't seen Ryan myself," I related, dodging the specifics.

"Did it get his face?" she persisted. "I saw something on the Discovery Channel about burn injuries. It said there isn't much that can be done if a person's face is badly burned. I remember some doctor said that even after all the skin grafting and stuff that a person will still end up with terrible scars that never go away."

I finally answered her directly. "Yes, I was told that one of his ears may have been burned off, along with a good portion of his nose. Ryan's going to need a lot of medical care and even more love and support, I'm afraid."

That information started a new round of quiet discussion and more wet eyes.

"I'm going to the hospital," I announced. I said goodbye and headed out the door, kissing Liz and the girls on the way out.

I stopped by a donut shop on the way, picking up donuts and some fresh orange juice for Eric. I figured that he'd had his fill of black coffee by now. I grabbed an extra large cup of strong, black Cuban coffee for myself.

After inquiring at the nurses' station on the hospital's third floor, I rounded the corner of the burn center unit and spotted Eric in the hall. He was talking to a doctor. Since I had come up behind him, he still didn't see me, so I stood back while they finished their conversation.

"We've been able to stabilize your son, Mr. Hawkins," a middle-aged doctor calmly told Eric. A burn specialist from the sounds of his comments, I guessed; he was calm, completely confident and matter-of-fact in his tone and presentation. Eric was hanging on his every word and occasionally posed a question which the doctor took time to thoughtfully consider before answering.

"It's much too early for me to give you any reliable opinions regarding his overall survival chances," the doctor cautioned. "He is severely burned. But I can tell you, Mr. Hawkins," he added in an upbeat tone, "Ryan is showing us an excellent fighting and survival attitude. The traditional medical texts say that young children of Ryan's tender years all react in the same way to burn injuries, but we've found just the opposite. Some children will fight to survive while others just give up. Your son is a real fighter. That's a very important factor in his favor. The biggest risks we face at this stage are infection and pneumonia. The initial debridement of his burned skin went very well." He was very clinical, but upbeat in his presentation. He and Eric continued for another five minutes.

I saw the doctor reach over and grasp Eric on his shoulder as he ended his discussion. "Mr. Hawkins," he soothed, "I know that you're going to worry about your son, and nothing I'm going to say will likely change that fact. But I want you to know that this burn unit team is one of the best there is in the country. We're going to do everything we can to help him, okay?" He gave Eric a warm, reassuring smile.

"Thank you Doctor," Eric responded. "I can't tell you how much I appreciate your help." With that, the doctor gave him a final pat on the shoulder and proceeded down the hall.

"Eric," I finally announced, causing him to turn. His expression was one of fatigue and pain. His eyes were red and his face drawn, with his unshaven black stubble noticeable. He looked like he had aged five years since I had seen him recently.

"Mike," is all that he uttered as we walked to each other and warmly hugged. Liz and I had known Eric and Jenny for probably eleven years. They had been our next door neighbors at our previous home before we bought our house on Coral Reef Drive. What had started out as a neighborly relationship had broadened over the years to one of close friendship. While Liz and I were somewhat older than the two of them, we had hit it off immediately. They asked us to serve as godparents for Ryan after his birth.

"Eric, I can't tell you how sorry we are," I offered weakly as we stepped back to face each other. "We still can't believe it."

At that, he broke down. He lowered his head and put his right hand to his face and forehead. "Why? Why did this happen?" he managed. "I kissed her goodbye when I went to work yesterday morning ... and ... and ... then all of a sudden she's gone. Why her? ... Why her? ... I ... I ... loved her so much ..." he managed, his voice breaking. "She was my best friend," he whispered, trying to regain his emotional control. Speaking almost to himself, he quietly mumbled. "We were going to grow old together ... And Ryan, he's so little. He has his whole life ..." He stopped and now sobbed uncontrollably. "I don't think I can go on ..."

Two nurses at the nearby nurses' station didn't even bother to look up at the sight of this grown man weeping and sobbing like a child. It apparently was a common scene in the burn unit. Unfortunately, on this burn unit floor, they had obviously seen it hundreds of times before. A young male hospital clerk dressed in high top Nike sneakers was pushing a cart by at the time. He gaped wide-eyed as he passed by, and continued to glance back over his shoulder as he moved the cart down the hall. He apparently had not yet become immune to this type of scene.

I put my arm around Eric's shoulders and tried to console his grief. This was a new experience for me, one that I wasn't comfortable with. I couldn't imagine myself in that situation and what someone else could possibly say to make me feel any better.

"I'm going to miss her, too. Jenny was truly a special person," I lamely offered. "You know, Eric, one of the things that made her so unique," I continued, "was the fact that she was such a spirited fighter." At that point, I started choking up myself, but I willed myself to continue. "Do you remember how fierce a tennis player she was?" I asked, stepping back to face him. I almost used the verb 'is.'

When he heard the questioning tone in my voice, his swollen red eyes looked up at me.

I continued. "Do you remember that time the four of us were playing doubles and Jenny was paired against you at the net? I remember that you started getting overly aggressive, and she warned you that she was going to send the next return right at your groin. You made the mistake of laughing her off, remember? And her next return was right on the mark, wasn't it?"

A sad beginning of a smile came to his red eyes as he remembered.

"Yeah ... yeah," he repeated, almost to himself. "She was a tough competitor." He looked distantly past me, apparently recollecting other images of his wife. "That's one of the things that I really loved about her."

"Eric, the reason I'm reminded of that story is because that's one of the things that she also loved about you so much. You both share that same fighting spirit. I think the most important gift that you can give to Jenny right now is to draw upon that spirit and work your way through this. I know it's hell for you, but Sarah, and especially Ryan, are both going to need you more than anything else to get through this terrible time. It's going to be very painful and very difficult, Eric, but Jenny knows that you can do it for her and for the kids. And she also knows that you've got your family and friends to help you out," I quietly added. I hoped that I didn't sound like I was preaching.

He didn't say a word but just looked at me and nodded his head.

Not mentioning that I had overheard his conversation with the doctor, I asked him about Ryan's condition. I was hoping to get him talking and functioning. It was clear that he wanted to talk about Ryan and did so.

From what the doctor had related, Ryan would likely be in the hospital for months. Further debridement, skin grafting, reconstruction and months of rehabilitation were planned. I knew from some of the injury cases that I had handled over the years involving burn victims that Ryan would be forced to undergo excruciating pain in the process. Eric could not yet know the full extent of the painful road that awaited his son.

At the nurses' station, one of the nurses started to object to my going in to see Ryan since I was not immediate family. Eric intervened and explained that I was a close family friend as well as Ryan's godfather. That did the trick. After donning a sterile gown and surgical mask along with Eric, I was permitted to accompany him to see his son. The hospital wasn't taking any chances about spreading any potential infection.

While I had been told about Ryan's burn injuries, I was nonetheless unprepared for the damage I saw. The young child in front of me was absolutely unrecognizable from the little infant I saw just last week when Liz and I dropped by their house to pick up Jenny and Eric for a movie. Those parts of his face not covered by the heavy dressings were swollen, discolored and badly burned. His nose and ear areas were heavily covered in dressings. His breathing was labored and he was asleep, obviously the result of drugs for the pain his ravaged body was experiencing.

Eric gently rubbed Ryan's unburned right foot with his gloved hand and spoke to him in a soft, comforting voice. The helpless appearing man I had been speaking with barely ten minutes ago was now nowhere to be seen. He had been replaced by a loving father whose sole focus was now on his badly injured son.

Late that afternoon, Trooper Martelli of the Florida Highway Patrol came by the hospital to speak with Eric about the accident. Martelli was the trooper assigned to investigate the accident and prepare the final accident report. A nurse took them to a conference room near the burn unit to talk. Eric asked me if I wouldn't mind sitting in on their discussion.

Martelli related the events that an eyewitness, a Manny Abadin, had reported, including the fact that a step ladder falling from a pickup truck started the whole terrible event.

"I know that this is very difficult for you Mr. ... uh ... Hawkins," he said, glancing down at his notes for Eric's last name, "but I'm very familiar with that part of I-595 where the accident happened. Traffic can get going at a pretty good clip in that area, especially on Friday afternoons. I see it all the time. You get a little too much speed on that roadway and you can get into a lot of trouble real fast." His suggestion of 'driver error' on the part of Jenny was not particularly subtle. I disliked him and his heavy New Jersey accent immediately.

"Did the witness see anything that tells us why the Mesa rolled?" I was interested in fact, not his self-professed 'experience.' Rollovers are unusual events I knew from the accident cases I had handled over the years.

Martelli looked at me and shrugged. "Oh, he made some offhand comment about the Mesa moving kind of 'weird' on the road as it headed for the grassy median," he said, dismissively, "but I don't put much stock in it. He was too vague for me. Quite frankly, I think he was a bit excited about the whole event. He's Hispanic. While I'm certainly going to be looking at everything, my initial inspection of the sport utility vehicle—the SUV—rules out anything mechanically wrong with it. It looks good mechanically. Unfortunately, I'm leaning towards the obvious cause of the rollover and fire."

"And what's that?" Eric asked.

"A combination of excessive speed and probable driver error by the deceased."

That comment ignited Eric.

"What the hell do you mean 'excessive speed.' My wife is ... was ... not a speeder!" he angrily snapped. "*I'm* the speeder in the family. Jenny was a plodder. Her last speeding ticket was probably twenty years ago for god's sake. So, I don't know how you come off telling me that she was speeding! I thought you just told me that you hadn't even finished your investigation yet, so how can you say that, god dammit!" His face was red and angry.

Martelli, a muscle-bound patrolman in his late 20's, did not have a great bedside manner. "Look mister," he defensively fired back, "I realize that this is not a good time for you, but my preliminary investigation leads me to conclude that your wife was likely speeding when she reacted to avoid a ladder in the road. I think she oversteered in her panic and drove into the grassy median, causing the rollover to occur. That in turn caused the fire. My job is to make these types of determinations when a fatality is involved. I'm sorry to have to tell you all this now, but that's the way I see it at this stage," he said adamantly. "If I discover any facts which cause me to change that preliminary conclusion, I'll reconsider it," he ended, snapping his notepad closed. It was clear that this conversation was over. He obviously resented being challenged.

I could see that Eric was about to erupt. I jumped in. "Trooper Martelli," I calmly asked, "did this Abadin witness you spoke of actually report seeing Jenny speeding? Also, what did the driver of the truck with the stepladder have to say about it?"

Martelli turned his head and gave me a cold stare. He did not like uninvited interlopers questioning him or trying to turn this discussion into a tag team wrestling event involving Eric and me. With his muscle-bound arms and his machismo wrestler attitude, that was the first image that popped into my head.

"And just who are you, by the way?" he challenged.

"I'm a close family friend who also happens to be a lawyer, if that's important to you."

"Doesn't make any difference to me," he indifferently shrugged. "The vehicle with the ladder didn't bother to stop, and the witness said that he was coming home from a jobsite in Miami. He was traveling pretty fast himself, so he couldn't say what her speed was. The fact is I don't think the guy got much of a good view."

"Well, if that's the case," I asked, "what exactly is it that you base your preliminary opinion on that she was speeding?"

Martelli leaned forward towards me in the orange plastic hospital chair in which he was sitting. "The fact is that if she was driving at or below the speed limit, sir, she should have been able, under the circumstances, to have maintained control of her vehicle and still have avoided the ladder. Couple that with the erratic behavior of her vehicle on the roadway, as reported by that witness, and you've got speeding," he icily replied. "She obviously overreacted, oversteered and simply lost control. It happens every day of the week out there."

Trooper Martelli didn't like having his opinion challenged, especially by a lawyer who was not even family.

"Trooper Martelli," I responded as politely as I could, "surely you would agree, with your obvious experience in these matters, that you don't have a very solid basis at this stage of your investigation upon which to conclude that Jenny was speeding. I mean, do you have any physical evidence such as skid marks from which you calculated speeds, which would have more of an objective basis to it?"

Martelli was not about to let some lawyer in a hospital waiting room cross-examine him on some of the finer points of his accident investigation. He ignored my question. Instead, he reached into his pocket, took out a business card, wrote a number on it, and handed it directly to Eric, intentionally by-passing me in the process. Looking at Eric, he told him, "That's the accident report number that has been assigned to the accident," he said, pointing to the number he had written on the card. "I'll provide you with a copy of the accident report as soon as I finalize it."

At that point, I reached into my wallet, pulled out a business card of my own and handed it to Martelli. "I would appreciate it if you could fax me a copy of the report as well when it's done."

"I'm sorry ... Mr ... Culhane," he said, stopping to read my name off my card, "but the department only provides a copy to the family. Feel free to either get your copy from the family or drop by the office to pick one up. I'm sure you understand." He gave me a cop's smile that politely said, "*Fuck you.*"

"Sure, I understand completely," I smiled back.

Picking up his notebook from the Formica coffee table, along with his pair of blue-block Oakley sunglasses, he rose and headed for the door. "Because this case involves a fatality," he announced, "it will take a little longer for me to finalize the accident report. Good day." With that, he exited the room.

It seemed, I thought to myself, that death has a way of complicating a lot of people's lives.

"That son of a bitch," Eric angrily uttered to no one in particular after Martelli was gone.

Late that afternoon, Liz, Todd and Debbie brought Sarah by the hospital to see her dad. I ushered Eric and Sarah into the same conference room that we had used earlier that day for our discussion with Trooper Martelli. We left the two of them alone for privacy. After an hour, they emerged. It was obvious there had been a lot of talking and crying on the other side of the door. Sarah didn't want to leave but relented when her father quietly took her aside and softly emphasized that her mother was watching from heaven above and needed her help.

As I drove home from the hospital that evening, I was thoroughly de-pressed. All I knew was that the Hawkins family would never be the same. As a result of one quick and brutal accident, Jenny Hawkins, the nucleus of that family, was gone, and her surviving family was devastated. And my blond-haired, handsome and thoroughly typical godson had been hideously damaged. His future would be anything but typical, I thought.

CHAPTER 6

I ARRIVED AT my office around ten o'clock on Monday morning, having stopped first at the hospital to check in on Ryan and Eric. It was status quo, both medically and emotionally, although Eric was talking more. He had finally shaved.

"Morning Evelyn," I announced to my secretary as I got to my office door. She sat directly outside of my office at her secretarial workstation.

As I greeted her, she was tacking up yet another photo of one of her many cats to the wall of her work area. The two walls around her workstation were filled with photos of her beloved cats. There must have been ten photos. I couldn't tell if they were ten photos of the same cat or ones of ten different cats. While I hated cats, I'd never dare tell Evelyn that. She was the Will Rogers of cats—she'd never met one that she didn't like.

Evelyn had been my secretary for eight years. She was thirty-eight, matronly, and still lived with her mother somewhere in Lauderhill Lakes, one of the zillion small little politically-fractured suburban communities that comprise the greater Ft. Lauderdale area. She was one of those people who never quite fit in socially, at least comfortably. As a result, she largely kept to herself while in the office and to her cats while outside the office.

For me, she was a great secretary, a nine on a ten-scale. If she had a good sense of humor, she would have been the perfect ten. But a good sense of humor Evelyn didn't have, and never would. She was all work, good with clients, extremely competent and loyal to me. What more could I ask for? I figured that when I was starved for a good dose of humor around the office, I could always go to a partners' meeting.

"Good morning Mike," she replied.

"So, how was your weekend?" I asked, setting my briefcase down by her desk.

"Really nice. The Florida Professional Cat Groomers held their annual show this weekend at the convention center, and I spent the entire weekend there," she beamed. "How was yours?"

I shook my head. "Not good." I told her of the accident and the details.

"That's terrible," she offered, "I'm really sorry to hear that."

At that point, I heard my phone ringing in my office. I was back in the rat race once again.

My first order of business today, I reminded myself, would be a letter to my opposing attorney in the *Bertson* case confirming the settlement agreement reached on Friday morning. Dealing with Eric's problems over the weekend caused me to completely forget about the Global Motors matter until driving into work this morning when I mentally went over my "to do" list for the day.

While I was on the phone talking to a client, I went over my accumulated email. There was one from the opposing attorney in the *Bertson* case confirming the deal and asking for my prompt confirmation by reply email. If that guy only knew how close he had come, I thought to myself.

After getting off the phone, I prepared the confirmatory return email and hit the send button on my computer. I copied Don Kean at Global in Detroit on the email. I figured that Kean would persuade Cole that he overstepped the line last Friday and needed to back off.

In any event, I decided that I wasn't going to worry about it right now. This was Monday morning, my schedule for the week looked like hell, and I had other fish to fry. Cole would just have to get over it.

I DIDN'T ARRIVE home until after eight-thirty that evening since I stopped at the hospital on the way to check on Ryan and Eric. Dark bags had formed under Eric's eyes. It was obvious that he had not been sleeping and was still in a state of shock.

Liz and the girls had eaten dinner already, but they all sat around the butcher block table as I ate the re-warmed lasagna Liz had made for dinner. Erin and Anne had a lot of questions about Ryan, and I related the medical information that I had learned about his condition.

Later in the evening, after the girls had done their homework and gone to bed, I sat on the couch in the family room going over some motion papers for a motion I had the next morning. The file materials were spread out over the rest of the couch and on top of the old wooden, antique carpenter's trunk we used as a coffee table. I had the Heat game on the television as background noise.

"Anymore on the details yet as to how Jenny's accident happened?" Liz asked, taking a sip of her white wine. She was sitting in a stuffed chair with two of her patient case files for tomorrow neatly placed on her lap. She worked as office manager three days a week for two plastic surgeons who did in-office cosmetic surgery. It was a great job for her. It got her out of the house working at a job she really liked, allowed us to put aside her salary for the girls' college fund, and kept her in the work force at the top of her skills—well oiled and ready to work full time when I had my inevitable lawyer thrombo at age fifty and dropped over dead. She had her bare feet up propped on the foot stool in front of her, with her glass of wine resting on the side table to her left.

My bare feet were resting on the old carpenter's trunk.

"Only a few so far," I answered. "The Highway Patrol hasn't finished its accident report yet, but the patrolman in charge of the investigation dropped by the hospital Saturday afternoon and talked a little about it. He said that it was his preliminary opinion that Jenny was speeding." I watched her reaction.

"That doesn't sound right. I've driven with her a lot of times, and she was not a fast driver."

"Eric had the same reaction. He damned near went after the guy when he essentially accused Jenny of causing her own death."

"Did that cop seem to know what he was talking about?"

"He was pretty young. I only spoke with him for a few minutes, but if first impressions mean anything, I was not impressed. He sure seemed opinionated and quick to jump to an easy conclusion. He also struck me as lazy. Interestingly, there was an eyewitness who told the cop that he felt that her Mesa behaved kind of strangely when she responded to the ladder in the road. It probably needs to be checked out. I'm hoping that Eric and I motivated him to do a more complete investigation."

Liz looked puzzled. "What did the witness mean when he said that the Mesa acted strangely?"

"I don't know. That's all that the patrolman said, but that's an odd description by an eyewitness."

"What do you mean?"

"Well, from what I've seen in the cases I've handled, witnesses usually say things like: 'the car went out of control,' or 'it just went off the road,' or 'the driver was driving crazy,' and comments like that. Apparently, this guy referred to the Mesa she was driving as acting 'weird.' That's a strange comment."

She frowned and took another sip of wine. "What do you think it means?"

"In all likelihood, it probably doesn't mean a damn thing," I responded. "Car accidents are short and intensely-startling events to eyewitnesses who are not expecting them to happen. Things happen very fast. As a result, their observations are often dead wrong, good-intentioned as they may be. In fact, there are a number of studies that have been done by psychologists under controlled circumstances where they have tested the accuracy of that kind of eye-witness testimony. The reports all conclude that eyewitness testimony is actually very unreliable. The eyewitness thinks that he sees something that, in reality, just didn't happen."

"Interesting. I'm sure that the guy whose stepladder fell on the roadway felt pretty badly about what happened. Who was he, anyway?"

"They don't know. He didn't even bother stopping, and no one got his tag number."

She put her file down on her lap. "He didn't stop! What a low life. You know that he had to see what happened."

I got up, casually walked over to her chair, leaned over and took a big sip from her wine glass. "Oh, I'm sure that he saw it all. It's a little hard to miss a large utility vehicle right behind you going off the roadway and rolling over as it tries to avoid hitting a stepladder that fell off your truck. He just didn't want his own ass sued."

Liz stopped and looked up at me. "Do you want your own glass of wine?"

I smiled. "No, really ... I'll just have a sip of yours." *Payback time for the pizza bite of the other night.*

"Isn't the Mesa made by Global Motors?" Liz asked. She was aware of the Mesa only because we started looking at buying a third car a few months ago now that Erin had started driving. She was driving herself and Anne to high school this year. The Mesa was one of the cars we had looked at.

"Yeah, it's a brand new model that Global came out with last year." Other than looking at it on a showroom floor, I really didn't know much about it. I knew generally that it was intended to represent Global's attempt to compete with the Japanese imports in the profitable but competitive SUV category. With Toyota's recent problems with brakes, stuck accelerators and recalls, Global saw a golden opportunity to steal market share.

"Eric and Jenny didn't really own it all that long before the accident, did they?" I asked.

"No, Eric just got it after Christmas at one of those year-end sales promotions."

Liz started opening the second of her office administration files. "Oh, before I forget," she added, "I think that we had better start finalizing our plans if we hope to take any kind of vacation this summer. I downloaded some information from a couple of really neat places in Colorado that I Googled. Can you get away during July? I need to know so that I can start making reservations." She looked over expectantly at me for my response.

I focused my attention on the motion papers in front of me. "I can't do it in June or July. I'm on trial dockets during those two months on two different cases I have for Global and two others for other clients. I'm pretty sure that all of those cases won't settle either," I added. "To be safe, let's make reservations for the middle two weeks in August instead." I knew exactly where this conversation was going. South.

"Michael, that's really too close to when the girls have to be heading back to school." Liz was about to ignite. "Can't you get somebody else in the firm to cover these trials?" she asked, with growing frustration. She absolutely hated being held hostage, once again, to my trial schedule since most of the trial judges didn't much care about 'family vacations' of the lawyers practicing before them. Despite all of our many discussions on this point over the years, Liz simply couldn't fathom the tyranny typically displayed by many of the judges.

The problem, you see, was that Liz, like most non-lawyers, had this notion that trial court judges were like Andy Hardy's father in the old 1940s movies—easy going, fair-minded and judicious individuals with whom attorneys could reason in a civilized fashion, including working out reasonable scheduling accommodations to allow overworked, pasty-complexioned lawyers a break in the summer to go on a family vacation. Forget it. The cold reality was that many of them either took a perverse pleasure in being difficult with lawyers' schedules or were so mired in trying to deal with the incredible volume of civil cases on their docket, that they used the attorneys' personal scheduling problems as an effective tool to force settlements of cases just to get them off their docket. In fairness to the judges, the lawyers historically had played a major role in causing the problem. Every time trial dockets were called in the summer months, those lawyers who were unprepared to try the case—usually because they had been too damn lazy to get it properly worked up for trial, or had erroneously gambled that it would settle—suddenly claimed that they had a 'pre-existing family vacation' planned which necessitated their excusal from the trial docket. After an epidemic of these excuses, many judges had no alternative but to assume that *none* of the lawyers could be trusted to tell the truth about their schedules. As a result, no scheduling breaks were given to anyone for claimed summer vacations.

Liz and I had this same 'vacation discussion' every year. Without fail, here in South Florida, you weren't given a specific date for a trial before a particular judge. Rather, your case, along with three dozen others, was put on a two to four-week trial docket, meaning that you were required to be ready to appear for trial anytime during that docket time period, often with as little as twenty-four hours advance notice. It was a ridiculous system, and one which played hell with a lawyer's business and personal schedule.

Liz's frustration and short fuse stemmed from the fact that we often had to reschedule family vacations in the past due to my suddenly being called to trial, sometimes the very morning of the day that we had planned to leave. To avoid the uncertainty and capriciousness of the trial judges, I now tried to schedule a vacation only when I could reasonably be assured of not being on a trial docket.

I knew that her resentment was justified, but there wasn't a hell of a lot that could be done about it. "Honey, we've had this conversation before," I said with irritation. "You know and I know that I can't do a damn thing about it. If I could, I would. I can't, so let's drop it, okay?"

"You can have one of the other litigators down there handle some of those trials," she countered, dismissively. She was again looking for a 'silver bullet' to eliminate the problem.

"God dammit," I responded, testily, "you know that Global expects me, and only me, to try its more serious cases. They don't mind a different face on the 'small potatoes' cases, but it's me on the others. We'll just have to work around it, and that's all there is to it. The two Global cases I'm talking about are serious ones. I'm the one who's going to try them."

"Great! What about giving one of those cases to Harrington? He's supposed to be a big-shot litigator down there. In fact," her forehead wrinkled as she suddenly remembered, "didn't he actually try a big case for Global last year for you?"

Amazing how she can remember this stuff when she wants to, I thought to myself.

I'd never concede this to her, but she usually won most of our arguments. Her logic was excellent; her tongue could either be razor sharp or soft as silk; and she always intuitively knew just where the soft underbelly of my argument was located.

"Nope," I quickly defended, "that was a commercial case for Global, not a products liability case. I'm the products liability partner for Global at the firm. That's the only reason that I asked him to handle that case instead of handling it myself; Global would never accept Harrington to handle a products case for them."

"Well—"

"And," I quickly added, "as you can appreciate from our conversation the other night about the importance of Global to me at the firm, I'd just as soon not do anything right now. Quite frankly, that would irritate Global. They'd see it as me trying to pawn off one of their important cases on someone less experienced at the firm for trial. That would not go over well, at all."

"Fine!" she finally relented. "I'll schedule the vacation for August then, but I don't like it."

It appeared that I was up off the canvass. With great irritation, she delved into her patient file and said no more.

I was smart enough to drop it while I was ahead. I put my head down and dove into my papers, relieved to have survived, for one more year, what had become a very unpleasant annual discussion for both of us.

CHAPTER 7

I GOT UP the next morning, jogged down Las Olas to the beach before breakfast, and arrived in my office at my usual eight-thirty. I had just enough time to grab the balance of my file for my eight forty-five motion hearing. I walked the two blocks over to the Broward County Courthouse from the Hunt & Baxter offices.

You wouldn't consider the Broward courthouse one of the great architectural wonders of the world, unless, of course, you wonder how an architect could design a building with so little imagination. It was built in the 1950s as a ten-story box. Its exterior was comprised of vertical aluminum metal strips, thirty feet apart, between which were inlaid aqua-colored mosaic tile for what its architect undoubtedly thought was dramatic aesthetic effect. It was dramatic all right. With the exception of limited remodeling over the years, the courthouse had remained the dark, utilitarian box it was. The civil court judges were housed on the higher floors of the building, accessible, at least theoretically, by a bank of four elevators. I say theoretically since they are sometimes broken, usually jammed with an eclectic cross section of humanity, and always impossibly slow to arrive.

I passed through the metal detector in the lobby and walked over to the elevator banks where I waited my obligatory five minutes for an elevator. I rode it to the ninth floor, with fifteen other sardines, for my hearing with Judge Paulette Morgenthal. In her early fifties, Morgenthal had been on the bench for close to twenty-five years. In the opinion of most defense lawyers practicing in front of her, that had been about twenty-six years too long. Her late husband, Simon, much older than her, and also a lawyer, had been a big-shot Democratic Party fund-raiser for a couple of Florida governors. His support and, more importantly, his financial contributions had been repaid by appointing his wife as a circuit court judge. His money—most of it having been inherited from a family business in New York—guaranteed her re-elections thereafter. Now his money was hers, and she didn't need to work. Most of us hoped that she would get bored with the job and retire, but, unfortunately, she hadn't shown any signs of fulfilling our wishes anytime soon. She loved the power and being in control.

It was widely assumed that Simon, a rather demanding guy with quite a reputation in his day as a lady's man around town, had not been attracted to her originally by her intellectual depth, which was somewhat like the Platte River in Nebraska—a mile wide, but only an inch deep, as William Jennings Bryan once said. No, the bar members were in agreement that her original allure to the late Mr. Morgenthal had undoubtedly been her once-gorgeous face, and I've been told, an equally gorgeous body. You couldn't have guessed that now since she had let herself go over the ensuing years. She was now a fleshy, corpulent woman who usually came to work dressed in an expensive suit sporting a bad disposition and an over-inflated opinion of both her brains and importance.

The courthouse scuttlebutt was that a few years after she snagged and married Simon, she arrived late one evening and walked into his office. Supposedly working late, Simon was caught giving one of his female divorce clients something more than learned advice on top of his desk. Paulette had apparently shown up unexpectedly to exchange car keys with him. Instead of switching keys, she threw the client out of the office and started switching roles with Simon. She started making demands on him over threat of a divorce and a punitive property settlement. One of her first demands was a judicial appointment which repentant Simon was only too happy to provide with a few phone calls.

She had been a mediocre sole practitioner while in private practice. Once on the bench, not only did her mediocrity blossom, but she also quickly displayed a merciless pro-plaintiff and pro-little-guy philosophy in her rulings and opinions. If there was a close call on an evidentiary issue in a personal injury trial, she'd invariably rule for the injured plaintiff instead of the defendant or its insurance company. Even on not-so-close evidentiary issues during trial, she would bend over backwards to help out the plaintiff. Defense lawyers quickly realized that she had absolutely no grasp of the rules of evidence and likely couldn't even tell when the evidence issue presented to her was close or not. It mattered not that she was one of the more frequently overturned trial court judges on appeal. Morgenthal proudly wore her independence and her pro-plaintiff bent almost as a badge. If there was a massive and largely irrelevant request for production of documents served by a plaintiff upon a defendant manufacturer in a products liability case, 'Judge Neanderthal,' as the defense bar fondly dubbed her, would invariably deny the manufacturer's objections and require it to produce the documents, even if it meant producing boxes and boxes of tens of thousands of irrelevant documents gathered at great cost to the manufacturer. Such rulings had caused many manufacturers to settle cases in her court rather than run the risk of her draconian discovery rulings and her hostile attitude at trial.

I had represented Global and other manufacturers in front of her on a number of personal injury cases over the years. Put simply, she was a colossal pain in the ass to deal with. Every favorable jury verdict I had won in her courtroom over the years came with the same ease and pleasure as passing a large, irregularly shaped kidney stone.

Most trial judges who were not respected by the local lawyers stood the risk of being voted out of office when one of the trial lawyers finally had enough and ran against them. With Judge Morgenthal, however, that wasn't going to happen. She always had the loyal support of her fans—the plaintiffs' bar—and she had her own substantial financial reserves to draw upon for campaign costs to ward off any serious challenge.

Like most judges in Broward County, Neanderthal was holding her motion calendar hearings in her chambers, rather than open court. She had her desk perpendicular to, and flush against, another very long table that had four sets of old wooden chairs pulled up to it on each side. Pushed together as they were, the two tables resembled a long "T," with Neanderthal seated at the top of the T. The opposing lawyers appearing before her sat on opposing sides of the long table. The two attorneys seated in the chairs closest to her would argue their motion, she would rule, and they would exit. The two attorneys seated immediately next to them would quickly pop up, move over to occupy the chairs that the departing lawyers had just left, and start their arguments. The game of musical chairs would continue until motion calendar was over, usually at nine-thirty, or until Neanderthal threw a temper tantrum as she was often prone to do, and declare motion calendar over. Ever the consistent one, the good judge had no good working knowledge of the rules of evidence, no appreciation at all for the rules of civil procedure, and an utter lack of judicial temperament. She was moody and harbored a tinderbox temper. When you appeared in front of her, you never knew exactly which mood *du jour* you were in for.

When my opponent and I entered her chambers and sat down at the opposite end of the lawyers' table, we were fourth in line to be heard. Neanderthal was listening to a discovery dispute. An insurance company's lawyer was arguing for permission to take the deposition of a urologist who had treated the male plaintiff for impotence five years before the intersection accident, which was now the subject of their lawsuit. From what I could discern from the arguments, the plaintiff, a guy named Carbo, was claiming in the present lawsuit that he had been rendered impotent as a result of the severe concussion that his lawyer said he received in the car accident. The insurance company's attorney, a young, aggressive guy that I had seen on other cases in the courthouse, was exasperated.

"Your honor," he argued, "this is a clear cut case. My client has an absolute right to take the deposition of that prior treating doctor. Mr. Carbo is claiming that his sexual impotence was caused by the car accident. I want to take this deposition to show that this gentleman was complaining of sexual impotence problems *five years before* the accident due to psychological problems. My client has a right to discover the nature and extent of those earlier problems since they go right to the issue of causation. I'd like to cite the court to the case of *Rudolph v—*."

"Mr. Shapiro," Neanderthal curtly cut him off, turning to the opposing attorney, "let's hear your side of this."

I had not run into Shapiro before. He was much older than the defense lawyer, had the deep Florida tan of one who spent a lot of time on a boat or a tennis court, and was wearing an expensive Brioni double-breasted olive suit with an expensive Versace tie.

"Thank you, Your Honor," he said smoothly. "My client suffered a very severe closed-head injury in this accident. It has affected every aspect of his being, from the obvious medical injuries to severe psychological trauma. Mr. Collings is correct that my client did see a urologist a number of years ago for what I would classify, Your Honor, as strictly a situational problem with situational sexual dysfunction. It had nothing to do with this accident. You see, Mr. Carbo had ... well ... he engaged in an extra-marital indiscretion, shall we say," Shapiro finally managed, stroking his salt and pepper goatee. "He realized immediately that it had been a mistake, and the guilt from that one transgression in his otherwise impeccable marriage, caused him a transient sexual performance problem. I should add," Shapiro continued in his syrupy smooth fashion, "that Mrs. Carbo is presently not aware of her husband having seen this urologist, nor is she aware of his prior marital transgression."

Shapiro stopped for a moment and removed his glasses before addressing Neanderthal for his summation. "Your Honor, I consider a marital relationship to be sacrosanct. Permitting Mr. Collings access to that doctor's file, and allowing him to depose that doctor, will cause an unwarranted judicial intrusion into that sacrosanct relationship. It could cause a break-up of that marriage. I beg this court to prohibit the deposition and to issue an order forbidding Mr. Collings and his witnesses from making any reference whatsoever throughout this case to this prior indiscretion. It has nothing to do with the issues involved in this case, and will only cause the breakup of a wonderful fifteen year marriage."

"Mr. Collings," Neanderthal commented, looking over her half glasses at the defense attorney, "while I don't countenance the plaintiff's apparent philanderings, I fail to see the relevance of this line of evidence. We're apparently talking about a fifteen year marriage, and an impotence problem that occurred five years ago. I don't see the relevance of that deposition you want to take," she said, shaking her head as she spoke. "I'm not going to allow you or your witnesses to get into it."

"But Your Honor," Collings pleaded, "this is only the discovery phase of the case. It may prove to be that his previous impotence problem was an aberration, but I have a right to view his doctor's records and depose the doctor to elicit the information to determine if that is, in fact, the case. Mr. Shapiro's assessment here," Collings added sarcastically, "saying that it was 'merely a transient problem' doesn't make it so. Let's see if the *treating doctor* says that is the case under oath. As for the fact that Mr. Carbo's wife is unaware of his prior affairs, that should not be a bar to my client's ability to discover this information as it may pertain to Mr. Carbo's present damage claim for his present impotence problem. Judge, I should probably remind the Court that Mrs. Carbo is also a named plaintiff in this case. She is also claiming loss of consortium damages against my client. A jury should have all of—"

"Mr. Collings, I've made my ruling. You're engaged in nothing more than a defense fishing expedition. You are not permitted to delve into that area at all, either during discovery or during trial. Is that clear?" she demanded.

Collings, to his credit, kept his composure, although was obviously furious at her ruling. Every attorney in the room could see that Neanderthal was wrong on the law. This was only the discovery stage, and the deposition should have been permitted, subject to a confidentiality order if she felt it necessary.

"Perfectly, Your Honor," he answered evenly.

"Thank you, Your Honor," Shapiro purred as he rose out of his chair. "I'll prepare the order."

Score another one for the plaintiffs, I thought, as the rest of us moved forward in our chairs towards the good judge.

I sat through the other two motions in front of mine and finally argued my own. I had no better luck this morning in front of Neanderthal, losing my motion to require the plaintiff in my case to undergo a second independent medical inspection by a second doctor having a different medical area of expertise.

I got back to my office around ten-thirty. I answered a couple of calls and was in the process of going through my mail when Evelyn popped her head into my office.

"Mr. Wilcox wants to see you down in his office. His secretary said that it was important."

"Why did he call you instead of me?" I asked, somewhat puzzled as I came out of my office and passed her desk.

"I don't know," she shrugged. "It actually was his secretary that called for him."

"Well, it shouldn't take too long, whatever it is." I walked by her and headed for Avery's corner office at the opposite end of the floor.

"Also," Evelyn called after me, "Eric Hawkins called you while you were on the phone with Mr. Bailey. He said that he would really like to speak with you regarding the accident when you get a chance."

"Okay," I called back to her, "remind me to call him back."

Avery's secretary was busy pounding away on her keyboard with her head down when I got to his office. His door was closed.

"Hey Judy, what's up?" I asked, hoping to get a heads up on what client matter Avery wanted to see me about.

Judy looked up at me with a somewhat flustered look on her face. "Uh ..." she hesitated, "Mr. Wilcox said for you to go right in," looking quickly back down at her screen without further comment.

"Okay," I shrugged as I knocked on his door. I didn't wait but immediately entered his office. Avery was sitting at his enormous antique partners' desk, facing the door through which I had entered. Gunther and Harrington, to my surprise, were both in the room, sitting in two of the antique lacquered leather chairs in front of Avery's desk, facing Avery. Neither one turned his head towards me as I entered the room. A third empty chair was located between theirs.

"Good Morning," I offered to all of them. Since I had been at the courthouse and squirreled away in my office, I hadn't yet seen any of them that morning.

I didn't get a response as I took a seat in the middle chair. From the serious faces on all three men, I speculated that we must have had some kind of malpractice incident involving someone on the litigation team. As with all firms, one of our attorneys will periodically screw up on a client's legal matter. When it occurs, representatives of the management committee try to meet promptly with the partners in charge of the practice area in order to engage in damage control. Odd, I thought to myself, I hadn't heard of any screw up, and I usually heard about these things right off the bat.

Avery cleared his throat and addressed me immediately.

"We have a very serious problem," Avery said directly, without any preamble. "We received a telephone call Saturday afternoon from Willis Cole at Global regarding a case that you are apparently handling for him. I believe he referred to it as the *Bertson* case." He looked pointedly at me through his wire rim glasses.

Oh shit, I thought to myself as my stomach tightened. I looked evenly and directly back at him. "Yes, that's one of my Global cases. What's the issue?"

"Mr. Cole was extremely upset to put it mildly when he called Robert Saturday to discuss the matter."

I look over at Harrington. I was puzzled as to why he hadn't called me immediately to discuss Cole's call to him. He was staring straight ahead at Avery. He didn't even try to look at me.

Avery continued, "Mr. Cole said that you went and settled that case without Global's consent or authorization. He said that it was a very defensible case that Global wanted very much to try, and that Global felt that it was a winner." His tone was irritating and very accusatorial.

"That's not correct," I quickly answered, trying to keep my cool. "I spoke—"

I was immediately cut short by Avery who leaned forward at his desk, raised his voice and imperiously shot back, "You'll get your say, but I'm going to outline the problem and its ramifications first."

I angrily sat back in my chair. "Fine, you've got the floor, Avery. Let's hear it."

"As I was saying, Mr. Cole is very concerned for a number of reasons. That settlement was contrary to Global's consent, and by settling that case, you've put Global at risk of being sued in countless other accidents by other Global drivers who were involved in frontal collisions like *Bertson's*. Cole told us that once word of your settlement is disseminated throughout the American Trial Lawyers' Association, every plaintiff's lawyer and his brother will raise that same baseless allegation which was raised in the *Bertson* case in cases involving that same vehicle. And all of those plaintiff sharks will be trying to squeeze settlement money out of Global just like you allowed *Bertson* to do here."

Avery paused momentarily and quickly glanced at Gunther and Harrington. I willed myself to shut up and let him finish, but I was about to explode in anger.

"I must tell you," Avery said gravely, "this problem is much greater than I think you apparently realized when you did what you did in settling that case. Mr. Cole has threatened both to pull all of the Global work from the firm immediately and to sue us all for malpractice and punitive damages for breach of our duty of trust and confidence as a result of your actions. The—"

"Wait one goddamn minute!" I finally exploded. "I'll be damned if I'm going to sit here one more nanosecond and listen to you 'outline' the problem,

Avery, when your 'outline' is full of bullshit and is flat ass wrong." I had their attention. "You aren't outlining, you're indicting, and you've not even heard me talk. You may have forgotten," I sarcastically added as I looked around at the three of them, "but the last time I checked I was a partner of yours and have been for a number of years."

I got up from my chair and walked over and stood next to the large expanse of window located to the left and rear of Wilcox. I didn't like being squeezed in what I viewed as a hot seat between Gunther and Harrington, the little pompous bookends they were.

"I can tell you that—"

Gunther interrupted me. "I think that you would do well to let Avery finish," he said as he smoothed the field of relocated hair on the top of his head. "You might want to hear what we have to say first."

"No, I don't think so. Ted," I said sarcastically, "I realize that you've never stepped foot inside a courtroom, but I'm going to let you in on a little secret. Even juries are required to hear both sides of a case before arriving at a verdict. Now, that's probably a somewhat radical idea for you, but let's give it a shot anyway, okay?"

He shot me an angry glare, but he said nothing.

"I was *instructed* by Global to settle the *Bertson* case," I continued. "I met with Don Kean, the in-house Global attorney, and the Global engineer assigned to the case, at a legal-engineering conference to discuss the case. *We*— not me—*we* collectively came to the conclusion that the case should be settled for a number of reasons, including the potential damage exposure and the difficulty we believed we would face in winning in front of a jury. *We*," I paused and slowly looked at each of them for emphasis, "collectively agreed that if the case could be settled for one hundred thousand dollars or less that I should get it settled as soon as possible. And those were my marching instructions. And that's exactly what I did—with full client authority and direction."

I walked behind Avery, over to the window to his right. He was irritated at having to swing around in his chair the other way in order to face me as I kept talking. *Good.*

"I followed the Global settlement procedures to the letter, and Cole knows damn well that I did. In fact, I called Kean right after I settled the case for seventy thousand dollars last Friday morning just to let him know, and he congratulated me. He told me that Global had reserved the case on its books at four hundred fifty thousand dollars of exposure. Later that same day—that's last Friday—I received a call out of the blue from Cole. He told me that he had heard about the settlement from Kean. He told me that he personally thought that the case should not have been settled. Now," I said with sarcasm, "what he apparently didn't tell you, and what you didn't care to find out from me before indicting my ass, is that he then instructed me to call up the plaintiff's lawyer in the *Bertson* case and to lie and tell him that I originally didn't have the authority to settle the case after all. As you can imagine, I was surprised, to say the least, about his instruction to me. I told him flat out that I wouldn't do that, and, in fact, I told him that I would be sending out a letter to the plaintiff's lawyer confirming our oral agreement. At that point, we ended out discussion, and I thought that he then realized his gross indiscretion—and I'm being kind in calling it that—and would drop it."

"And now you tell me that he called with his cock-and-bull story, threatened us, and now all of you are running for cover?" I continued, "Well, I've got to tell you, I'm dumbfounded that Cole would lie like this, but I'm even more dumbfounded that my own partners didn't give me the basic courtesy and respect of informing me immediately of his call and didn't provide me with the opportunity to put the correct facts on the table before the accusations started." I fired a final volley in my anger.

The three of them just stared blankly at me.

"I suggest that you take the time to call Don Kean, Cole's staff attorney at Global, directly. He'll confirm everything that I have just told you."

"We have," Avery quickly responded, with finality in its tone. His comment caught my attention. "After Robert got all the facts from Mr. Cole and discussed them immediately with the management committee by phone, he called Cole back and requested the opportunity to discuss the matter over directly with Mr. Kean in view of the seriousness of the allegation. Cole kindly agreed." I glanced over to see Harrington nodding his head up and down, confirming the story. "What Mr. Kean told Robert," Avery somberly continued, "is one hundred eighty degrees from the story you just told us."

"What! That's bullshit!" I exploded. I walked over and sat down on Avery's dark brown leather tufted couch that aligned the far wall of his office.

At that point, Harrington looked at me directly for the first time since I had been in the room. His voice was an equal mix of contempt and arrogance.

"Mike, Kean told me flat out that you did *not* have his authority, consent or instructions to settle that case at all," he challenged. "All that was agreed upon at the legal-engineering conference you referred to was that you were merely to call the plaintiff's attorney and see if he had *an interest* in settling. If he did," Harrington said, "you were only supposed to find out what kind of money he was looking for and to report back to Kean. In fact, he told me that you were pointedly informed that any positive response from the plaintiff's lawyer to your settlement overture had to be specifically first run by and approved by Mr. Cole before any specific settlement discussions were to be commenced. Kean stated that only a nuisance settlement value would even be considered since it was a clear-cut winner of a case from Global's standpoint."

"That lying son of a bitch," I slowly uttered.

"Stow it for a second," Gunther said to me, harshly.

It was suddenly obvious to me as I sat there and listened to him that Harrington was actually enjoying this. He continued.

"Kean told me that he told you at that conference that Cole was implementing a radically different settlement philosophy at Global that required Cole's approval on any settlement—"

"That's bullshit," I interrupted Harrington's continued lecture.

"—on any settlement over fifty thousand dollars. You apparently decided to settle it right away, before Cole got more fully involved. He told me that both he and Cole have been reviewing the performance of Global's local counsel around the country. They said they've noticed that you seem to prefer to settle cases rather than try them. They figured that with *Bertson*, you must have thought that if you waited until Cole got more closely involved with the case, that you would reluctantly have to try the case. So," he concluded, "they told me that you took this immediate settlement action on your own to avoid going to trial."

No one in the room spoke after Harrington finished. I was both shell-shocked and furious at this utter pack of lies, including the fact that I had tried more cases over the last eight years than virtually any other lawyer in the firm, and many for Global. Only Harrington's trial experience at Hunt was close to mine. I could smell Cole's ruthless machinations all over this.

Before I could respond, however, Gunther spoke first, addressing me from his chair across the room.

"We looked at your *Bertson* file late yesterday evening," he announced. "There's no letter in there from you to Kean or from Kean to you confirming your supposed authority to settle the case. There's no email on your computer to that effect either, or even a single memo to file confirming your *claimed* settlement authority from Global." He shook his head in disapproval.

"I don't believe this! Are you telling me that you went through my computer and my file on this case without first telling me?"

"In view of the allegations," Avery intoned, "we thought it best to do just that."

His officious use of the Royal We set me off, royally.

"You won't find any 'confirming' letter or email to that effect in that file. I've been representing Global for damn near eight years now. As a result, our working relationship has become very informal about that sort of thing. A lot of what I do with Global is not formally documented like I do with most of my other clients with whom I don't have such a long or close relationship. Let's face it," I said suddenly feeling defensive, "all of us in this room get a little loose with our paperwork when dealing with long-time clients that we've developed a relationship of trust with." I could feel the tightness which had suddenly developed in the back of my neck. "If I'm guilty of anything, it's that I trusted my client. But that's the *only* mistake I made on that case! Everything I told you is absolutely true. Jesus, I just can't believe this is happening."

"Well it is happening," Avery lectured sharply. "And it's put this entire firm at risk of a major suit for damages and the loss of one of our most important clients."

With that, Avery looked at Harrington and then over at Gunther. He cleared his throat again and then looked at me. "In view of these very serious facts and consequences, we need to inform you that the management committee called a special emergency meeting of the partners last night at the club."

"You what," I bellowed, "and I wasn't notified?"

"Your attendance would not have been appropriate under the circumstances," Avery replied bluntly. "It's your actions which have gotten all of us in this mess! Your actions have placed this firm's employees and families in jeopardy. As a result of your actions, Robert had a number of lengthy conversations with Mr. Cole well into the early evening last night. He was able to calm Cole down and to settle Global's claims against the firm and yourself, and to allow us to continue our representation of Global."

Harrington was fidgeting in his chair. I didn't like the smell of this.

"What kind of settlement?" I asked.

"Cole demanded that Robert take over the Global account from you. Robert has kindly agreed to undertake that responsibility," Avery said. "However, as a condition to this settlement, Global demanded two other things: first, that the firm repay Global seventy thousand dollars as reimbursement for the settlement money which you obligated Global to pay in the *Bertson* case, and, two, that you have absolutely nothing to do ever again with the Global account here at the firm."

"You can't be serious," I managed.

"Dead serious," Avery replied "and the partnership has agreed to Global's demands. We had no choice. Moreover," he cleared his throat again, "in view of your misconduct, and the jeopardy to which you subjected this firm, it is my unfortunate duty to inform you that your partners voted you out of the firm last night, effective immediately. The fact is, we've lost all confidence in you and, quite frankly, we don't believe a word of what you've told us here today. The scars that you have caused to the trust of your partners cannot be cured."

With the announcement of that bombshell, Avery became silent. He and the two bookends waited for my response. The silence in the room was broken only by the soft 'tick tock' being made by the swinging pendulum on the expensive wall clock to Avery's right.

"You've got to be kidding me?" I quietly managed to say, with great effort. The air had been knocked out of me. "None of my partners even heard the facts that I've just told you about. How could they have voted on such a fundamental issue as my continued partnership with this firm without first giving me a chance to tell them the facts?"

"They *were* given all the facts," Gunther responded, harshly. "The sad fact is that you blew it, plain and simple. Your partners chose to believe the assistant general counsel of Global Motors and his staff counsel who worked on the case with you. Those two people have no motive to make this stuff up, and they certainly can't be said to have any type of grudge against you." He then added, almost as an afterthought: "Frankly, after you cool down, I think you'll realize that we've probably done you a big favor. From the tone of your comments at the partners' meeting Friday night, it's pretty clear to us that you aren't in step anyway with where this firm and its management committee are going. It was probably time for you and the firm to go our separate ways anyway." With that comment, he sat back confidently in his chair and crossed his legs. He removed a piece of lint from his pants as he did so.

I laughed, mockingly, "So, *that's* what this is *really* all about, isn't it? What an idiot I am for not spotting it earlier myself. You bastards! You've used a client's absolutely baseless—I repeat, baseless—allegations as a means to throw me under the bus to bolster your little power base, isn't that right?" As I spoke, the angrier I was getting. "Isn't this all nice and convenient for you! You should be ashamed of yourselves. All three of you know me. You've practiced with me for many years. You know that I'm telling the truth and that Cole and Kean are lying, don't you?" I stopped talking for a moment and looked directly at each of them to let my words sink in. All three just stared silently at me in return. Their faces weren't showing any emotion.

"And you intentionally called a quick meeting of the partners without me there so that you could blackmail, bludgeon or bullshit the rest of them into voting me out," I said, shaking my head in contempt. "And," I added, with insult, "we certainly know the three of you aren't above those tactics, don't we?" They still said nothing. I looked at Harrington with a full dose of contempt. "Robert, I always knew that you were a selfish, greedy son of a bitch, but I never suspected that even you would stoop this low. You must have really *lusted* for the Global billings. Well," I said, now looking from one to the other of the three, "if you all think that I intend to simply let you get away with this and let this purge die quietly, then you really don't know me very well."

At that point, I rose from the couch and headed for the door.

"We're not finished," Avery acidly announced, causing me to stop in my tracks and look back at the group. "As of this moment, you are no longer an employee of this firm. As we speak, your personal effects in your office are being placed in boxes and will be made available to you to take with you when you leave these premises. If you agree to sign a general release in favor of Global, this firm and all of your partners, we are prepared to continue to pay you your base salary through our fiscal year-end, June thirtieth, and to issue you a severance payment of twenty-five thousand dollars in addition to returning your partnership contribution." He glared at me with venom through his gold wire-rimmed glasses.

My expected bonus of one hundred thousand dollars was obviously being stripped from me in their little offer.

"If you refuse this proposal," Avery warned, "you will be paid through this pay period, you will be re-paid your partnership capital contribution at five thousand dollars per month, per the terms of the partnership agreement, until your capital account has been paid out, and that will be the *last* money that you will ever see from this firm. You have until five o'clock tomorrow afternoon to let me personally know if you are agreeable to those terms. They aren't negotiable. Do you understand?" he asked as he calmly laced his two hands together as they rested on the desk in front of him.

I looked directly back at him, then at Gunther and finally at Harrington. I mentally summoned all the control I could muster and started laughing, shaking my head back and forth at the same time. My reaction surprised them. It surprised me too.

"You know, boys, my only regret is that I didn't stand up to the three of you earlier. I represent the good things that this law firm has stood for over all the years that it has been around. You, however, don't. Your little regime doesn't view issues in terms of what's right or wrong, or what's honorable or dishonorable; rather, since you've been elected as the new management of this place, your little team sees everything in terms of power, money and having your own way, doesn't it? No more and no less." I scanned their impassive faces.

"I guess I've really known all of that since I've seen your new management committee's actions in play, but I chose to persuade myself that I should give you the benefit of the doubt and not be so critical. Stupid me," I said.

I turned to face Gunther. "Ted, you may by absolutely right. Forcing me out of this firm may well be the best thing for me, after all. You see, I couldn't practice law with any of you anymore after what you've done, and I've lost all respect for my gutless partners who've signed on to your bullshit little coup."

They again didn't say a word but only looked coldly at me. I turned and took four or five strides to the door, opened it and stopped. I turned one final time towards the three of them, with my hand on the doorknob. "And by the way," I said in a very loud voice that I hoped would be heard by everyone down the hall, "I don't need until five o'clock tomorrow afternoon to respond to your little offer, King Avery. You and your merry little gang of thieves here can take my base salary, my hard-earned bonus, and your proposed severance payment and go royally fuck yourselves! Send my personal items and my capital funds to my home tomorrow!" I commanded.

Having said that, I looked at them one final moment, turned and exited the room. I took impotent but immense joy in seeing the fury on their collective faces as they got dressed down in front of their subjects.

Not even bothering to walk back to my office, I walked out of the Hunt offices trying to keep my head high. But I was dying inside.

CHAPTER 8

WHAT THE HELL have I done, I repeatedly asked myself. After leaving the firm's offices, I got into my car, drove down to the beach off of A1A, the road that parallels the ocean. I parked on the beach side of AIA, across from the Elbow Room, a mainstay on the beach since the 60s for students on winter break. I needed to sort this all out. I couldn't get up the nerve to drive home, and the beach was as good a place as any to get a grip.

A chesty young brunette in a neon orange halter top and a thong roller-bladed by as I sat there and looked at her vacantly. She gave me a quick suspicious look as I sat there in eighty-five degree weather with my tie on and the windows rolled down. Probably thought I was some kind of pervert.

What was I going to tell Liz and my daughters? I knew that I hadn't done anything wrong, but I still felt sick with a sense of guilt and shame, all the same. I should have documented the settlement authority and instructions I received from Global, I painfully reminded myself. One of the first rules that I drilled, and re-drilled, into every one of the lawyers and paralegals working on my products' liability team was to document a client's authority and instructions. My anger at what happened suddenly returned, but I blamed myself for having let my guard down. And now, I would be paying the price.

While I was trying to think it through in a forward-moving fashion, I just couldn't stop going over the discussion in Avery's office. The more I thought about it, the more I was sure that it was Harrington, the Boy Wonder, who'd come up with the plan to use the Cole telephone call as the perfect way to get rid of me and steal the client. I could spot his conniving handiwork. I was equally sure that Gunther was quick to seize onto the plan after Harrington hatched it. It had his odor about it, as well. I also started questioning whether I should have beaten up the management committee so publicly at the recent partners' meeting. Well, the boys got their licks in today.

And then there was Avery. He might have been a worthless leader of the firm, I acidly contemplated, but he certainly understood the first rule of power—subjugate or annihilate your enemies. My little speech Friday night, I figured, apparently had the effect of painting a big red bull's eye on my ass, which the three of them certainly zeroed in on today. The price for shooting at the king ... and missing.

On a sudden impulse, I reached down and picked up my cell phone. I needed to talk with my partner, or, more accurately I quickly reminded myself, my ex-partner, Jack Franklin. I wanted to find out why he didn't call me and tell me what was going on? I started getting worked up all over again just thinking about it.

"Hunt & Baxter," Jean Beckman, the firm's receptionist answered.

A question suddenly grabbed me; how was the firm responding to calls for me? "Mr. Culhane, please," I asked. I hoped that Jean wouldn't recognize my voice as I acted out what I suddenly felt was a stupid charade. Jean knew me too well. A classy lady in her late fifties with a great sense of humor and a bubbling view of life, she and I constantly traded jokes and humorous passing remarks with each other as I passed her reception desk during the work day.

There was a distinct pause before she responded. "I'm sorry, but Mr. Culhane is no longer with the firm. May I direct your call to Mr. Harrington? He's taking Mr. Culhane's calls."

"No, thanks, I'll take Mr. Franklin, instead," I said.

"Michael ..." she tentatively asked, "is that you?"

It was my turn to momentarily pause. "Yes," I admitted sheepishly, "it's me." I should have known better than to think that I could ever fool the 'junk-yard dog' as I referred to her over the years. She exhibited tenacious skills at protecting the firm's attorneys from the ever-persistent stockbrokers, insurance agents, and crazies who would constantly try to get through to make a sale or talk to a lawyer.

"Michael, what in the world happened?" she asked quietly, keeping her voice low. The concern in her voice was real. "We were all called into a big emergency staff meeting right after you stormed out of here. Mr. Wilcox told us that you and the firm had decided to part ways over what he called 'fundamental philosophical differences.'"

As she was talking, I could hear the other phone lines ringing in the background. Contrary to her standard practice of quickly fielding all incoming calls and transferring the caller on, she let them ring. She was waiting for a response from me instead.

"Jean, I don't want to get you involved in this mess. I have a feeling that anyone there who is seen or heard 'fraternizing with me' may quickly become *persona non grata*, if you know what I mean."

"Michael, I don't really care," she defiantly stated. She was the only person other than my wife and my mother who routinely called me 'Michael.' "I don't know what happened, but I know there is more to this story than what we've been told. I just want you to know that you're one of the few people in this firm that I truly respect and enjoy; something bad happened to you with this, and I'm sick—just sick—over your leaving." Her voice started to choke up. Meanwhile, the other phone lines were continuing to ring madly. She remained oblivious to them.

"Jean," I quietly responded, "thank you. I share the same feelings for you. I'm going to miss you and a lot of other people there." I was moved by her compliment and heartfelt emotions. "You'd probably better grab those other lines. I don't want the Gestapo to come and haul you off," I said, trying to inject some humor into the moment.

"Bastards," she said quietly, but fiercely, as she transferred me to Franklin's extension. I was momentarily stunned; I had never heard her utter one swear word during the many years that I have known her. Her rare expletive in my defense was probably the highest compliment that she probably could have given me.

Two rings passed, and then I heard the pickup. "Jack Franklin," he answered.

"Jack, it's Mike."

There was an uncomfortable pause before he responded. "Mike, where are you calling from? I've been hoping to talk to you."

"Really?" My tone was intentionally cool to my good friend.

"I wanted to call you yesterday afternoon as soon as I got word from the management committee of the special partnership meeting," he quickly offered, "but Avery's email to all of us told us that under absolutely no circumstances were we to inform you of the meeting or even talk to you about it." I noticed that Jack, who was normally a slow talker, was racing with his apologies. "His email made it clear that 'adverse consequences' would occur to any of us who did."

"And you certainly didn't want to put yourself at risk in talking to me about those odd developments, did you? And I guess you also didn't want to chance calling me at home after the expulsion vote last night, did you?" I wasn't used to directing sarcasm towards him, but I couldn't stop myself. I felt betrayed. "Since when have you ever been afraid of talking to me one-on-one and worrying about any breach of confidence between the two of us? Since when did you lose your nerve and your fucking guts, Jack?" I wanted the words to hurt.

Franklin didn't say anything for five or six seconds. "I'm sorry. I should have called you," he quietly said. "I'm truly sorry, Mike."

"Christ, Jack, I can't believe that not one of my 'partners' bothered to call me about the special meeting or demand at the meeting that it be adjourned until I was given an opportunity to come and defend myself against those bullshit allegations."

"I know it won't change things," he said, "but I want you to know that two other partners and I did make that motion. However, Avery and Gunther intimidated everyone else there into voting against it. They said that they had fully investigated the Global charges themselves. They made a big point that they had looked at your file and your emails, had spoken with Mr. Cole, and had even gone so far as to verify Cole's story with the other Global attorney involved. They said that there was, as Gunther told us, 'not even a scintilla of doubt' that you were guilty of the bad acts. Avery told us that to have you there, after the proof was irrefutable, would only add an unnecessary and divisive rancor to the discussions and decisions that they felt had to be made, and made immediately."

"And all those supposedly seasoned lawyers in that room bought that sewage?"

"Let's put it this way," he answered. "I don't think that a majority of the partners bought it, but those with the clients and the power in the firm—most of whom are close to Avery—did. The rest were intimidated into going along with the management committee's expulsion motion. If it makes any difference, Mike, there were ten of us who voted against it." He proceeded to tell me who the other nine were when I asked him.

"I assume you know, Jack, that not a damn thing they said is true. I had clear—"

"Please, you don't have to tell me that," he said with embarrassment. "I know it already. I know it and I'm sure everybody else in that room knew it, too. But I also think that there were some who saw it as a way of freeing up your percentage share of the bonus pool in order to fatten a lot of everybody else's."

"I'm perversely curious. Who made the original motion to expel me from the partnership?"

"It was Harrington, seconded by Gunther."

"Figures. Fucking weasels," I said, evenly.

"Mike, I've been sitting here this morning giving some thought to trying to get enough partner support to call a second emergency meeting of the partnership to rescind the vote and allow you to come back to address the group. I've read over the partnership agreement, and it provides that a special meeting can be called by fifteen partners."

"Don't bother. It's over. You know that old saying, 'you can't go home again?' Well, that's where it's at. Loyalties and friendships which I foolishly thought existed obviously didn't. And I'm not very good at begging."

There was another momentary and uncomfortable silence. Jack finally broke it. "What are you going to do, Mike?"

"That's a good question. I only wish that I had an answer for it. I always thought I was a hot stuff litigator. Now I'll get a chance to see if my stock with other firms around here is as high as I always thought it was."

I didn't feel much like talking any further. "I've got to be going," I said abruptly. "I'll keep in touch." We both knew that I wouldn't.

"Mike, good luck. If there is anything I can do …" his voice trailed off.

"Sure, take care." With that, I hit the off button on my cell.

I started the car and headed home. Liz would be home around three-thirty and my daughters about six-thirty.

What the hell have I done, I asked myself again.

CHAPTER 9

WHEN I GOT home, I threw on a T-shirt and some old khaki shorts, grabbed a legal pad and a beer, and headed for my back yard, next to the water. I decided not to call Liz at work. I sat at a circular black wrought iron table in the shade next to a thick cluster of traveler's palms and started making notes on my pad. I needed to pencil out a course of action.

I started putting together a 'to do' list. After an hour of jotting, the preliminary list I had was extensive. It ranged from getting my mail from the firm forwarded to figuring out my financial situation.

With regard to finances, I started second guessing myself, my judgment and my ego in rejecting the firm's offer to pay me the modest severance and my base salary through the end of June. It would have bought me a few more months of security, that's for sure. While it felt satisfying to tell Avery to go to hell on that issue, as I started thinking about the monthly expenses I'd be facing—that I previously never had to give a whole lot of thought to—I felt the beginning of panic. I realized that I had to find another job, and find one quickly. The substantial expenses of maintaining my family's lifestyle, I soberly recognized, had never been a major concern to me in the past. There was always the comfort and security of knowing that next month's paycheck, and the year-end bonus, would always be there to draw on. Not anymore.

All the news I'd seen on Fox TV about layoffs and unemployment statistics over the past two years, with only the slightest of a passing interest on my part, suddenly came to mind, front and center. With a feeling of some guilt, I realized that I really hadn't given much thought to the employees that were being affected in those articles. They were just numbers and statistics, and they certainly didn't affect my protected little life. Well, the worm certainly had turned.

I also realized that I needed to talk with my secretary and Sandy Stevens, my paralegal. I owed them a call about all of this. They undoubtedly were trying to figure out just what the hell had happened. I picked up my cell phone and gave my secretary a call on her direct dial number.

"Mike!" Evelyn said, answering on the second ring. She'd read the caller ID on her phone and had seen it was me. "What is going on?" she excitedly asked into the phone. Her whispered voice told me that Avery had probably issued another one of his edicts banning any employee from talking to me during office hours.

"It's a long story, believe me," I said. "In twenty words or less, some of my former partners made some serious accusations about me which I wasn't given the chance to rebut. So I got fired." It served no purpose to get Evelyn involved in any of the details. The last thing I wanted her to do was to start defending me in the coffee room, which is exactly what she would do.

"You're not going to let them get away with this, are you?" she asked, indignantly.

"What's done is done," I responded. "Frankly, I wouldn't want to come back after what's happened anyway. I just wanted you to know that it's bullshit and to tell you that the nasty little rumors about me that I'm sure will begin circulating shortly are not true. I'm not ashamed of one thing that I ever did at the firm, and it's important to me that you know that."

"Are you kidding? You know that I could never believe anything bad about you. I know you too well. I'm just sitting here, still in a state of shock that you're gone," she sighed. "This won't be the same firm without you here. I really don't want to work for anybody else here. Mike," she offered quietly, "I always felt that you treated me like a professional. I'm going to miss that."

"Evelyn, I can't believe this is happening either, but it is, and both of us will land on our feet. I treated you like a professional because that's exactly what you are. You're an incredibly good secretary, and I don't know how I could have done it without you there. I know that I didn't compliment you enough on that score, but believe me, I'll miss you. I'm just sorry that it ended like this, and we have to end up saying our goodbyes over the phone."

She started to cry. "I don't want to work for anyone else here, not after this."

"It's okay, really it is," I calmly tried to reassure her. "If you want to know the truth, in a way, it was probably time for me to move on anyway," I said, trying to believe it myself. "I just didn't figure that I would be getting the bum's rush out of there, that's all," I laughed. I was trying to lighten the mood of this wake.

She managed a chuckle in response.

"I'll be sending Wilcox an email tomorrow, with a copy to you, giving the firm instructions as to the forwarding of my mail and other administrative details. If you can birddog those details for me I would appreciate it."

"Don't worry. I'll be sure to take care of it. Is there anything else that I can do for you? I'd really like to help."

"Actually, there is one thing that you can get for me, but only if you are absolutely sure that you can do it without getting caught." I felt like a thief and a conspirator in my own firm, but what I was asking her to provide was mine.

"Just say the word," she said, enthusiastically.

"Can you download onto a thumb drive my computer-stored directory of my existing clients, and reference sources, with their contact addresses and telephone numbers? I kept them on the firm's C: drive, under the name MAC-CLIENTS.'"

She paused for a second and then told me. "They've been wiped out."

"What do you mean? That directory was there this morning. I used it to call Mark Mahan at Overland Bank."

"About ten minutes after you left this morning, Harrington and his snotty secretary, Wendy, came over here. They told me to access your client list and give them a hard copy printout of it. Also," she sarcastically added, "I was *ordered* to copy it onto a CD, which that little snot brought with her."

Evelyn despised Harrington's secretary. Perky Wendy was blonde, conniving and snotty. Perky Wendy absolutely fawned over "Mr. Harrington," as she always formally referred to him. She dutifully had 'Mr. Harrington's' *Wall Street Journal* and a cup of perfectly-mixed coffee waiting for him every morning when he arrived in the office. She knew that he was an up and coming political power in the firm, and she was riding his rising star. Actually, it was well known among a few of the partners that Mr. Harrington's star was not his only rising attribute that perky little Wendy was riding. Howard Levy, a real estate partner happened, by chance, to observe both of them coming out of one of Ft. Lauderdale's lesser known motels over by the airport during lunchtime last month. Howard had been inspecting the motel for a possible purchase by one of his clients at the time. Although they didn't see Howard, he told a few of us in confidence that there certainly was no mistaking perky little Wendy and her 'Mr. Harrington' as they exited one of the motel rooms over the lunch hour. I kind of doubted that Mr. Harrington had told Mrs. Harrington about young Wendy.

Wendy used her vicarious stature in the firm to lord it over other secretaries and staff employees every chance she got. Evelyn tried to avoid her as much as possible. I could understand and appreciate her ire at Perky Wendy standing with Harrington at her side barking out directives to her.

"I did what they ordered me to do, and I gave them the printout and the duplicate disc. Once that was done, she ordered me to delete the information from the network. They must not have trusted me to do it because they physically stood right there next to me while I deleted it. Then they left."

"Goddammit, that was my property!" I angrily said.

"I think they ordered me to delete it so that you would have no easy or quick way to contact your clients to try and persuade them to come with you to whatever new firm you go to," she said with amazing insight. "I'm sure they'll be on the phone to your clients this afternoon, trying to persuade them to keep their legal work with Hunt & Baxter."

I cooled my jets. I decided I wasn't going to get worked up any further over this, at least not in front of Evelyn. "I'm calling Harrington directly about this," I said as calmly as I could.

"Why would you want to do that?" Evelyn said with an unusually mischievous quality to her voice. "I thought you wanted me to get that information over to you."

I was confused. "I do, but I thought that you just told me that you erased all of that information from the network, with the little snot breathing down your neck. What are you saying?"

"No," she giggled, "what I said was that the snot ordered me to pull it up on my computer screen and to delete it, which I did. Well, that little ditz apparently doesn't know or understand the automatic backup information system that we have in place at the firm."

"What are you talking about?" My lack of knowledge about the details of the firm's computer system was appalling.

"I'm talking about the fact that the firm installed a system about eight years ago where all the information put on our computer system is automatically backed up on remote hard drives every three minutes. Mike," she patiently explained, "it's done to protect us in the event of a power shutdown in the system, or in the event of a fire or hurricane to the office here. Each Friday, that week's data on the hard drives is downloaded onto data storage devices that are taken down to the fireproof vault on the eighteenth floor for safekeeping. The remote hard drives are then erased in order to receive new data. If you know the date that the information was put on the system, or you have the document number, you can access that storage device and retrieve it easily," she explained. "Before I deleted that data with that little snot looking over my shoulder this morning, I noted the document number of your client and resource list. I waited until Wendy left, then I went down to the eighteenth floor, located the backup information I had deleted from my PC and downloaded it onto a thumb drive. I have it in my purse. I figured that if they wanted to destroy that information, you would probably want to have it."

I could almost hear her big smile over the phone. *Evelyn: 1, Perky Wendy: 0.*

"Evelyn," I laughed heartily for the first time all day, "I think I'm in love with you! Remind me never to double cross you in my lifetime!"

"And why is that?"

"Because you're ruthless, unpredictable and you never forget, that's why!" We both laughed over our little victory.

"Thanks a million. Can you transfer me to Sandy?"

"Yeah, Sandy told me that she hoped that you would call in. Bye." With that I was transferred over to my paralegal. I fastened my seatbelt. I could only imagine what reaction I was going to get from her.

"Mike! I'm coming with you! I don't care where you go, but I'm coming with you!" she firmly announced as she came onto the line. No hellos, no explanations and no breaths.

"Whoa, wait a minute," I laughed. "What do you mean you're coming with me?"

"I'm not working here without you is what I mean. Nobody will tell us exactly what happened, but I overheard bits and pieces from two of the partners outside the coffee room talking about it. You wouldn't believe the bullshit they are saying about you, Mike."

"Well I'm glad that you recognize it as that, because that's exactly what it is. But—"

"Mike," she interrupted, "I've learned more about products liability working with you over the last six years than I could ever have imagined. You're the best lawyer and teacher I know, and, besides, I don't want to work with these creepos around here. You've got to take me with you to your next firm, okay?"

I hired Sandy six years ago to work with me on the Global cases. Before she came to me, she had been working in Miami as a secretary, paralegal and over-all 'girl Friday' for a sole practitioner specializing in plaintiff's personal injury. She spent four years with him until, as she told me, she had her fill.

When he started spending most of his time out fishing on his forty-five foot Hatteras, she ended up doing most of the substantive work-up on his cases, including meeting with insurance adjusters and negotiating with defense lawyers. She demanded that he hire another person half time to help her out. He refused, saying that he couldn't afford it. That did it. She gave him a month's notice of her resignation so that he could find a replacement for her. When she handed him the resignation, he started screaming obscenities at her and called her ungrateful. At that point, she told him that she was sorry, saying that she had exercised bad judgment in giving him a month's notice of her leaving—it should have been immediate. She picked up her purse, grabbed the personal photos on her desk and calmly walked out.

Thank goodness for the bad business judgment of lawyers. His loss had been my gain. She proved to be an exceptional assistant to me, worth five times her weight of one hundred twenty pounds in lawyers. Sandy was thirty-five, single and lived an active lifestyle in a rented guest house on an old estate off Ft. Lauderdale Beach. With a great sense of humor, she was as irreverent as she was bright and independent. And when she got fired up, as she was now, watch out.

"Sandy, I don't have any idea where I'm going. The smoke from the firing squad still hasn't cleared yet."

"All I'm asking is that when you do figure out where you're going, that you ask the new firm if they have room for me."

"All right," I promised, "I'll make the inquiry. But I think you know you don't owe me a thing. You have a great future there at Hunt, and I'd hate to see you throw away six years of seniority just because you're pissed off over what they did to me." Inside, I was touched and delighted that she wanted to come with me. She was smooth with clients, helpful with witnesses, and tough, but professional, with opposing lawyers. She was not one to be intimidated.

"Don't kid yourself, Mike. As I see it, my future here is not particularly rosy now that you're gone. At the emergency staff meeting that Avery called this morning to explain your departure, he informed us that Harrington would be taking over the Global account."

"Yeah, I heard," I commented without more.

"I don't think I am part of the long-term plan around here now that you're gone."

"What do you mean?"

"First of all, everyone here knows that you and I have been working very closely as a team on the Global cases for many years now. From what I overheard the two partners say outside the coffee room this morning, your name is bad news now at Global. I'm guessing that Harrington will remove me from the Global cases, as well." She then surprised me by laughing.

"What's so funny?"

"Because I also don't think that Gunther is going to do much to save me from Harrington's vindictiveness after what I did to him at the Christmas party last year."

That was the first that I had heard about that. "What happened?"

"I never told you about it, but I stepped outside the club after dinner for a breath of fresh air during the Christmas party. Gunther came out alone right after I did. He had too much to drink, but that's no excuse. He started coming on to me and making crude remarks about what neat little things he could do for my sex life. I told him that I wasn't the least bit interested, particularly with married men. When I walked past him to return inside, the pervert grabbed me and started groping me and trying to kiss me."

"Jesus, you should have told me."

"It doesn't matter. I can handle myself. Well, anyway," she continued, "I shoved him away and slapped him as hard as I could right across his little face. He hasn't said a word to me since, and that's just fine with me. I think the man is repulsive. With you there, he kept his distance. With you now gone, I know that it's just a matter of time before he'd cause me enough grief to want to leave, as well."

"Knowing that, you're probably right," I conceded. "I'm really sorry that my issues are putting your job in peril."

"That's ridiculous. I'm a big girl, and I'm quite capable of taking care of myself. They own the problem, Mike, not you or me. Do you have any idea what you are going to be doing?" she asked, changing the focus of the conversation.

"No, I've got some ideas, but I haven't really focused yet."

"Well, please keep my situation in mind, okay? Also, if you call, use my cell, will you."

"I will, believe me." Then I added, "Sandy ... I just want you to know that whatever happens, I can't tell you how much I appreciate all the great help you've given me. You're superb. I thought we made a hell of a team."

"Thanks Mike. I feel the same." We hung up. I felt better that I had made those two calls. I did have a great team.

I LOOKED UP as I heard the French door on the back of the house open. Liz came outside.

"Hi," she said with a hint of suspicion in her voice. "Don't tell me that you're finally acting reckless and taking an afternoon off." She leaned over and gave me her usual 'hello kiss.' She had been on me for months to take an afternoon off work. I always begged off. I was too busy.

"I guess, in a way, you could say that I took the afternoon off."

"What's that supposed to mean?" she chuckled as she pulled a chair out at the table to join me. As she did so, she laid a small pile of mail on the table which she had picked up from the mailbox to sort through.

I looked at her evenly, not reacting to her tease. "Liz, I'm not quite sure how to put this, but I'm out of the firm. I've been fired." I decided that the direct way was probably the best course to take.

Her brow wrinkled. "What are you talking about?"

"Do you recall the telephone conversation I had on Friday with the in-house attorney for Global, Willis Cole?"

"Yes," she said, slowly registering concern.

"Well, that son of a bitch called up Harrington over the weekend and told him that I had settled the *Bertson* case without Global's approval."

"But I thought—"

"He supposedly told Harrington that he was going to sue the firm and all its partners, and pull all of Global's business. So, without telling me about it, or giving me any chance to respond with the correct facts, Wilcox, Gunther and Harrington called a special meeting of the partners last night. They voted to oust me from the firm. Avery summoned me to his office to break the news." I paused for a moment to let it sink in. "It's over—just like that, and after this next paycheck, so are any further paychecks except a limited monthly capital repayment amount." I was surprisingly calm.

"What! This is a joke, right? You aren't serious about this, are you?"

"Honey, this isn't a joke." My face told her more than my words did that it wasn't.

"What in the hell is going on down there! Are you telling me that those people at your firm believed a client's story over you?" she asked. Her voice was laced with anger and disbelief. "Were they told of your side of it?"

I wiped the rivulets of condensation off the outside of the beer can in front of me with my thumb. "What my partners were told was that Harrington had thoroughly investigated the allegations and had found them true. Avery told them that my presence at the partnership meeting would only be divisive in view of the allegations and the proof they had assembled, as he related it to me."

"Michael, they can't do this, can they? You've been there for years now. They just can't vote you out." Her words were angry statements.

"I re-read the partnership agreement this afternoon when I got home. That son of a bitch Wilcox read it right. A two-thirds vote of the partners can terminate any partner, with or without cause. You know," I added, "I don't think I have read that document since I was made partner years ago. I certainly never thought that I would be reading it for anything like this."

"If that's the case, you're telling me that not even one-third of those people stuck up for you, after all those years and everything that you have done for the firm? They didn't support you? I can't believe this!" she bitterly said as she got up out of the chair. Liz was a pacer when she got angry or nervous. She was pacing now.

"The sad thing is I'm really not all that surprised that I didn't get more support from the rest of them. When I stop and think how cowardly the great masses acted the other night at the partners' meeting in refusing to stand up and challenge the board's bullshit on the compensation issue, it only stands to reason that they certainly weren't about to grow a set and save my ass," I said, sarcastically. "I'm sure many of them are worrying about whether they will be next to go under the committee's claim of 'operating efficiencies.'"

"Well you're not going to let them get away with this, are you?"

"What do you mean?" I asked.

"Can't you sue them or that Global lawyer for lying about you?" Liz was not one to sit back and lick her wounds.

"Sure, I could sue them for defamation and probably a bunch of other theories I could come up with, but I'm not suing anyone. It—"

"And why not? You just can't allow them to steal your job and your good name, goddammit. Remember," she added, angrily, "this is not just about you. This family also has an interest in this just as much as you do."

"I know goddamn well who has a stake in this, and I sure as hell don't need you to give me a lecture on it!" I suddenly exploded in return. "That comment *really* pisses me off."

"All I'm—"

"If you'd have let me finish," I said sharply, "I would have told you that the reason I'm not going to sue anybody is that a suit would just boil down to Global's word against mine. It's a goddamn swearing contest, and it would be Cole's and his pissant subordinate's word against mine. Think about it. People will ask 'why would they lie about this'? Cole and his assistant will say that they settle individual cases every day of the week for millions of dollars, and that a seventy thousand dollar settlement like this one—if they had authorized it— has as little effect on Global Motors as does pissing in the ocean. It wouldn't make one damn bit of difference to them. So, if the amount of the settlement isn't the reason they're complaining, that only leaves one issue in dispute— whether I had been given authority to settle it. You'd better believe that both Cole and Kean will put on their black suits, their sincere shoes, and their solemn lying little faces, and will swear on a stack of dog-eared bibles that I settled this case without one scintilla of permission from them. They'll claim that I settled it because I am 'too afraid to try the tough cases' in the words of Willis Cole."

"That's crazy, nobody would believe that story. You've tried a lot of cases for them over the years. How could they say it in view of that? No one would believe that," she repeated as she paced around the table.

I lifted the beer and took the final sip left in the can. "They would say it because I haven't tried a serious Global case for about two years now."

"Why is that?"

"It's a combination of the luck of the draw, and, quite frankly, the fact that I have discovered and prepared those cases for trial so well that the opposing attorneys have buckled prior to trial in the last two years. After I beat them up in discovery, they agreed to take a cheap nuisance settlement amount to dismiss their suits. In one case, Kean and I determined that there were, in fact, legitimate questions about the existence of a problem with the Global vehicle that was involved and settled it. The *Bertson* case is a great example. During my pre-trial preparation and investigation, we found that there were some production lots of the same air bag sensor component that were at issue in our case that came broken from Global's component supplier."

"How could they come already broken?" she asked sitting back down.

"Don't ask me. Maybe a worker dropped the box on the dock. Maybe a fork truck ran into the box. Who the hell knows? The fact is Global had rejection slips during vehicle assembly which confirmed the existence of a problem, which would be extremely helpful to the plaintiff in that case at trial. While the assembly people *think* that they caught *most of them* before they were actually installed on cars that went out the door, they as much as admitted to me that they can't rule out the possibility that they missed some, including the one on the *Bertson* van. That van was built during the same time period that this problem was discovered. That's the very reason that Kean, the Global engineer and I wanted that case settled."

I knew I was sounding defensive. But I needed Liz, of all people, to know the truth. I continued, "We all agreed that the *Bertson* attorney, even as inexperienced as he was, sooner or later probably would discover the bad lots and the rejection slips at some point prior to trial. If and when that happened, you can kiss a reasonable settlement goodbye. Had that happened, as we all anticipated it would, it would have cost Global at least a half million in view of the plaintiff's earning's history." I crumpled my now empty beer can in frustration. "Those two Global cases I mentioned the other night, which are scheduled for trial this summer, which I was trying to work our family vacation around, they're likely not going to be settled and will be going to trial then. I was looking forward to trying them."

"Well couldn't you show all of this stuff in a trial against Global and the firm?" she persisted. She was standing next to me, her arms crossed on her chest.

"Liz, get real," I snapped, "look at the bigger picture. Where is a lawsuit going to get me? Do I ask a judge to force my partners to take me back? Hell no. I don't want to go back to them, not after this. Do I sue my partners, gut-less cowards as they are, for money damages? No," I said, shaking my head, "I have no desire or stomach for that. And what are my damages against Global if I win? I'm simply out of a job. I'm supposed to be a big shot defense lawyer in this town," I said with sarcasm. "I have no real damages. I can get another job." I took a deep breath and looked squarely at her. "The only sure thing re-sulting from a suit is that I will end up looking overly defensive about my set-tlement performance for Global, and every lawyer in this town would love to witness that sideshow of a trial. I'd end up looking like an idiot in the process, and I'm not going to do that. Period. So, don't bring that up again—okay?" I ended testily.

Without saying another word, she turned her back to me and walked over to our wooden dock on the canal. She sat down with her back to me, facing the water. Her lower legs were dangling over the edge of the dock. I was still smarting from our exchange and was angry that my decisions were being chal-lenged. However, when I looked over a few moments later, I could see the tell-tale signs that tears were starting to fall; her shoulders were quietly moving up and down.

Oh shit.

I walked over and quietly sat down next to her on the dock, with my lower legs also now hanging over the edge of the wooden dock. "I'm sorry I yelled and snapped at you," I apologized quietly. "I guess I'm more upset and angry about all this than I want to admit. It's a big a shock to me, too, Liz. I'm sorry for taking it out on you."

I reached over and put my left hand over her right hand which was braced against the dock's edge. We both looked out over the water.

"I would never in a million years have believed that my partners would have betrayed me like this, or that a client that I've been so utterly loyal to for all these years would do this to me … I'm sorry, my anger has absolutely nothing to do with you."

"No, I'm the one who's sorry," she offered, "I just reacted. I didn't think it through myself. I know it's your firm, but I can't help but feel like it's part of me as well, and part of this family. What they did to you, I feel they also did to me and to the girls. We know all of them, their wives and kids, and they know all of us." She reflected for a moment, "I guess the world is changing. Those kinds of relationships don't seem to matter much to people anymore, do they?" She continued looking out, towards the water, wiping the tears from her cheeks.

"No, I guess they don't. I always thought that Hunt & Baxter was differ-ent, that it was family, but I was obviously wrong. Liz," I said, turning to look at her, "I want you to know that I love you very much. I hope you know just how much. We'll come out of this just fine."

"Michael, I love you too," she smiled in return as she turned her head to look at me. "I know we'll be fine."

"Look, I don't want to be melodramatic about all of this; we absolutely will be fine. You and I have always landed on our feet, and we're certainly going to this time as well. Call it the luck of the Irish," I smiled. "I'll have no trouble at all finding another job with another good firm, and life will go on, okay. Maybe a little bruised in the process, but we'll be just fine." I put my left arm around her shoulder and pulled her close to my side. She put her head on my shoulder.

My confidence had its intended immediate effect on her.

"Well, I guess I should be happy this happened," she said, finally managing a small smile. Her tears had stopped. "Maybe this new challenge in your life will keep you from going through a mid-life crisis and going after twenty-year-old nymphomaniac secretaries like everybody else's husband seems to be doing these days." She turned her head towards mine and managed a soft smile.

I leaned over and kissed her gently on the lips. However, what started out as a gentle, soft kiss quickly escalated to something more as her tongue slipped gently against my lips and slid smoothly between them. I quickly returned the unexpected invitation, with Liz slowly leaning backwards onto her back on the dock with me, by instinct, now rolling partially on top of her. By that same hungry instinct, my right hand was at her neck, then down the top of her loose blouse and under her bra, gently sliding where I enveloped her breast and her rapidly swelling nipple. Her left hand reached over where she massaged my suddenly-rising little friend who was quickly making his appearance beneath my slacks.

I groaned. I was quickly losing control.

"I think we had better do something about this," she quietly whispered as she nibbled the lobe of my left ear. "The girls aren't home until six-thirty, but I'm not sure that this dock in broad daylight is the right place," she laughed as she pulled her head back and looked up at me.

I removed my hand from her top, took a handful of her dark hair into my hand, raised it to my nose and breathed in its aroma. "I don't think that you have to worry about any twenty-year old nymphomaniac secretaries. I've got my hands full trying to handle my forty-year old nymphomaniac wife," I whispered in return. I leaned down and started kissing the nape of her neck. "And yes, let's get the hell inside. You're about to get a house call from 'The Little Leprechaun.'"

We laughed, disentangled and headed for the house, her leading me, hand-in-hand. While walking to the house, I was thinking that this had been one hell of a day. Once inside, on the living room throw rug, she stopped and turned towards me. Letting go of my hand and smiling suggestively, she stepped back, slowly unbuttoned and removed her blouse and black lace bra, revealing her still-slim and incredibly sexy body, with her gravity-defying breasts, (*not tits, I reminded myself*). She knew the captivating effect they had on me. Like the sirens of Greek mythology beckoning the passing sailors to their rocks, her breasts had always irresistibly drawn and beckoned me to her arms. Once again, her charms were irresistible, and I happily succumbed. I took her and pulled her down to the rug on the floor. Then, I wasn't thinking at all anymore. I was simply and only deliciously feeling. And so was Liz.

I EXPLAINED THE day's events, at least most of them, to Erin and Anne when they got home for dinner after their daily school swimming practice. They were on the St. Cecilia's High School swim team during the school year and on a private club team during the off-season to keep in shape. While I tried to keep it upbeat and matter of fact, they weren't buying it.

Erin, the junior, eventually asked me a question which I didn't expect.

"Dad, does this mean that we'll have to leave St. Cecilia's and go to public school if you can't find another job like the one you had?" She was helping Liz clean up the kitchen after dinner when she posed the question. Her sister sat over at the kitchen table looking at me intently, awaiting my response.

It dawned on me what was on their minds. Their high school swimming team came in second place at the state championship meet in Orlando last year. They lost the last event of the meet to the team from Satellite Beach who took first place with that event. Since their team only lost two seniors, they had been planning on making a run again for the championship this fall. They had a lot of great friends on the team, both male and female, and they were obviously concerned that they were at risk as well. I hadn't even thought about that scenario.

I decided to duck a straight answer. "Erin, I don't want you or your sister to lose one night's sleep over this. These days, lawyers change jobs and law firms as frequently as teenage girls change moods. It's no big deal." I smiled innocently. My daughters were normal teenage girls, which meant that the hormones were coursing through their veins at twice the speed of light. Their moods changed constantly, often by the millisecond. Liz and I periodically had heated words with both of them over their mercurial mood changes. I assumed they saw the humor in my analogy. As a dad, part of my job around here was to bring comic relief to the place.

Ignoring my assurance, her reaction was quick. "Dad, do you know how pathetic the swim team is over at Ft. Lauderdale East?" East was the public high school, which both of them would attend if they changed schools. "They barely have a swim team. They had to forfeit some of their meets last year because a bunch of the swimmers on their team didn't feel like swimming those days! I'm not leaving St. Cecilia's! My friends are there, and I don't want to spend my senior year trying to make a bunch of new friends! I'll get a job part-time if I have to in order to pay the tuition next year."

With that, she stormed out of the room, with her sister following, before I could even respond.

Liz walked after them to talk it over, looking very upset once again. I decided to stay out of their discussions for the time being. I didn't have the answers myself.

CHAPTER 10

I GOT UP the next morning out of habit, even though I had no place to go. I decided to fix my breakfast specialty for everyone, cinnamon French toast. Everyone ate on the run, and the three of them were gone for school and work by seven-fifteen, leaving me feeling a little strange. Home alone.

Evelyn dropped by on her way to work with the thumb drive containing my client information and reference sources. I made it a point to have showered, shaved and dressed in jeans and a polo shirt before she arrived. I wasn't going to start looking like a street person.

I inserted the thumb drive into the computer in my den and scrolled through my client list. I was glad I had kept this current. I printed out a hard copy to make notes on, complete with phone numbers and email addresses. A number of them I knew by memory anyway. Around ten-thirty, I started making some client calls to let them know of my departure from the firm and of my desire to continue my representation on their pending cases.

I decided to let clients know that while I hadn't yet linked up with a new firm, I intended to do so shortly. I knew how important it was for an attorney looking to associate with another law firm in today's market to have his own sizable clientele. Despite the public's perception to the contrary, while good attorneys were easy to find, good attorneys *with* a sizable stable of established clients were not. And as with most other things in life, timing is everything. I knew from my own experience in interviewing potential laterals at Hunt & Baxter that there were three key questions we always asked before we would consider making an offer: Did we have a need for the potential lateral right then; would he/she be able to bring with them a sizable annual level of client billings and lawyer work revenue; and was the lateral honest, competent and easy to get along with? If any one of those questions was answered in the negative, we wouldn't consider making an offer.

My first priority was to secure my client base and then I'd start talking with the other law firms. My projected total client billings at Hunt for this year, had I been there when the firm closed its books on June thirtieth, would have been around two million, of which Global would have accounted for about one-point-five million. The rest was comprised of clients, mostly corporate ones, whom I acquired over the years on the basis of referrals from other satisfied corporate clients, or from other attorneys with whom and against whom I had litigated. They ranged from national insurance companies and manufacturers to smaller local businesses. With the Global billings up in smoke, I knew that I needed to focus on this other half-million of clientele.

I decided to start first with Lincoln Assurance, a large insurance company out of Chicago. I had represented Lincoln for almost four years in connection with life and disability insurance policy litigation. It accounted for an average of one hundred thousand to one hundred twenty-five thousand dollars of billings per year and was an excellent client to deal with.

"Good morning, Tom," I said as Tom Edwards answered my call. He was Lincoln's in-house attorney who handled Florida litigation. "Mike Culhane here. How are you?"

"Uh ... Mike," he was somewhat hesitant in his answer, "I'm fine. Thanks. I guess the more important question, is how are you doing?"

"What do you mean?" I asked with some confusion.

"Hunt & Baxter. I spoke with Ted Gunther yesterday afternoon. He called to let me know that ... uh ... you and the firm had some kind of parting of the ways, and that you had left. I'm really sorry to hear that, but I realize that it happens to everyone it seems like anymore. Who are you going with now?" he asked, speaking more rapidly than usual. He was clearly uncomfortable talking with me. I didn't expect that he or any of my clients would know about all of this, at least this quickly. His awareness of my departure, however, put me immediately on the defensive. That was exactly what I wanted to avoid in dealing with my clients in my first call to them.

"Actually, I'm speaking with some firms right now," I white-lied, "but I haven't decided which one I want to hook up with. At this stage of my career, I want to be fairly selective about who I choose. They each have some interesting aspects, but I'm going to take my time on this one." *Jesus Christ, I can't believe I'm saying this!* I quickly tried to collect myself and to take control of the conversation and its direction.

"One of the reasons for my call, Tom, is that I wanted you to be one of the first to know of my decision to leave Hunt. I want you and my other clients to know that I will be linking up with one of the other excellent firms shortly. In the meantime, I'm calling to reassure you that I am completely committed to continuing our relationship, including my continued work on the pending liti-gation files I have of yours. That is, of course, that you have the same desire." I tried to keep my voice upbeat, calm and entirely confident.

"Well, ... uh ..." he fumbled. "We probably need to talk about that, Mike." I immediately sensed that I was in trouble. "I ... uh ... spoke with our general counsel about our representation in South Florida after Gunther called yesterday. I'm sure that you can appreciate that I have certain responsibilities to the company here when something like this happens, Mike." I'm not sure what he meant by 'this.' No doubt my good friend Gunther has adroitly let him know that I was fired by the firm without actually using the magic words. I'm sure that he made damn sure that the waters were well-poisoned by the time their conversation was over. Edwards probably thought I was caught in a bath-house with a five-year-old boy, or something worse.

"Tom," I quickly injected, "whenever a law firm and one of its partners decide to sever their relationship, like I did with Hunt & Baxter, I know that it can tend to put the partner's clients feeling like they're caught somewhat in the middle. I apologize for that, believe me. I know that I can probably speak for Hunt when I emphasize that we both have, as our top priority, the best inter-ests of our clients. That's why I am making this call to you. I would welcome the opportunity to continue to represent Lincoln on the present cases I'm on, as well as future ones. It's a relationship which started with me at Hunt, and it's one which I would like to continue, particularly in view of the success, which I believe I've provided in the cases, which I have personally handled for you over the years." I decided to make my pitch immediate and direct, drawing upon the fact that the Lincoln cases came to me in the beginning—not to Hunt.

"Mike, you're absolutely correct in pointing out that the cases which we sent to Hunt over the years were sent to you. And you've done a great job in representing our interests in Florida. However," he cleared his throat, "I am charged with the responsibility of making sure that the company's immediate and long-term interests are best served by the decisions which I make, even if they may be difficult ones for me to make personally."

I didn't like the sounds of where this conversation was going, but I quietly listened.

"Our general counsel feels that, for the time being anyway, we probably should keep the cases right where they are now, Mike, and that's at Hunt. I want you to know that our decision is based on a couple of factors, and that you shouldn't take this as any reflection on you personally, whatsoever. We just know from our experience in the past that it's always a difficult problem transi-tioning a group of pending cases from a firm that has been handling them for some time, to a completely different firm that would have to get up to speed on them." He nervously cleared his throat. "Mike, I'm sure that you can appreciate the fact that on some of the smaller cases, the associates at Hunt who were handling them are still at Hunt. We don't think that it would be financially prudent for us to move those to either you or to some new attorney at a completely new firm at this late date. Also," he hesitated somewhat, "Ted emphasized that as an indication of the firm's commitment to the company's business, Hunt is reducing its billing rates for all of our work by twenty per cent, effective immediately. My general counsel has emphasized to me that he believes that our stockholders have an interest in cost savings, and that we can't ignore the economic savings from the firm's proposal to keep our work."

I didn't immediately respond to what he said. I was stunned both at Gunther's speed and craftiness in getting to, and stealing, my clients so quickly—and at Tom's reluctance to stick with me on the representation. He and I had gotten along very well over the years. I knew that he had expressed complete confidence in my handling of his cases. Until talking to Gunther, that is. Despite my anger, however, I also realized, in fairness to Tom, that he had to protect his institutional rear end. Big companies don't like to take risks if they can avoid it, and staff lawyers for big companies don't want to have their boss challenging their judgment in taking unnecessary risks in the choice of counsel. I couldn't fault Tom. I'd probably do the same thing if I were in his shoes.

"Tom ... I understand," I said with resignation. "I'm very disappointed with your decision. I'm not going to try and hide it. I've thoroughly enjoyed representing Lincoln and working with you. While I'm convinced you would continue to be professionally and personally very pleased with my representation, I also understand your decision."

He responded, with relief in his voice. "I want you to know, Mike, that I'm only talking about the cases which are pending right now. With future cases, we may have an entirely different situation after you get re-established." He and I both knew that was unlikely. Lincoln's decision was for both the present and the future. Gunther would ensure that with billing rate bait.

"I appreciate that Tom. Listen, I'll let you go. I know that you're busy. I do want to thank you for your support in the past. I mean it when I tell you that I have enjoyed our professional and personal relationship very much. Best of luck with Hunt & Baxter, it's a good firm, and I know that you'll be well served by them. Take care."

"Mike, I appreciate the work you've performed for us in the past, and I hope our paths cross again in the future. Good-bye." We both hung up.

I just sat and stared out the window into the side yard. I now understood exactly why Harrington wanted my copy of my client list copied and destroyed

yesterday. He knew full well that Gunther and the others were planning to immediately contact my clients and seek to persuade them to stay with Hunt
rather than go with me. He wanted me handicapped. Little did he have to
worry, I thought. I was so damn naïve that I didn't even think about racing to
solicit my clients at the firm. I've got a hell of a lot to learn. I'll bet those guys
were on the phones with my clients yesterday morning at the same time as the
firm's etched glass reception door was hitting me in the ass on my way out.

I quickly realized that my hoped-for 'book' of business might well be a
hell of a lot thinner than I had projected. Anorexic was probably a better
description.

I scanned the list of clients before me and decided that I had better get in
gear and start making calls, if it wasn't already too late.

I SPENT THE rest of the morning and early afternoon on the phone. I had
to hand it to the boys over at Hunt. They had beaten me to every last one, and
they offered the same twenty percent discount as bait for keeping the work.
After the second call, I reluctantly realized I had to do what lawyers hate to
do—cut fees. I started offering a twenty-five percent discount on my rate at
Hunt to each of the clients, with a corresponding twenty-five percent discount
for any paralegal that I would use on their cases during the next year. At least
there was some benefit in going last in the solicitation effort.

After completing the calls, I had assurances from clients with annual billings of between only one hundred thousand and one hundred fifty thousand
dollars, less, of course, the twenty-five percent discount, which I promised for
the first year. It was a very disappointing result, but it was at least something to
offer up to a new firm.

When discussing my departure with the clients, a few openly expressed
concern about the nature of my rather quick departure from Hunt & Baxter,
and two actually asked for the details. While I refused to name names or give
details due to the attorney-client privilege, I told them that I had a major and
very unpleasant ethical disagreement with one of the firm's large clients, and
that I refused to take certain actions on behalf of that client which I felt were
unethical. Hence, I told them, my departure was less than amicable. One of the
inquiring clients accepted my explanation and elected to come with me after all,
while the other stated that her company would be staying with Hunt.

My last client conversation of the day, with Eli Chernov, boosted my
spirits. Eli, in his 60s, originally moved from Brooklyn to Ft. Lauderdale, in the
early 70s and opened a small auto parts store. His business grew over the years
to the point where he now owned fifteen stores over South Florida. He still

had a tough Brooklyn accent, and a tough demeanor which hid a heart the size of his ever-expanding waistline. I had been handling his litigation and some of his contract work for about ten years. We had developed a good relationship.

I hadn't gotten ten words out of my mouth to Eli when he interrupted me.

"What the fuck happened to you, Counselor? I figured you'd be calling pretty soon," he chuckled.

"I got fired Eli, that's what." I never tap danced with Eli.

"Yeah," he continued, "some guy named Gunter or Gunther called me this morning and pussyfooted around it, but he wasn't none too subtle. He wanted me to know that you got tossed out, and not the other way around. I couldn't believe that the little prick asked me to stop using you on that exploding battery case you're working on for me. He wanted me to start using some other attorney there. He even started pandering by offering some type of discount. Jesus, I thought I was talking to a hooker back in Redhook, the way he was trying to make the sale."

"What did you tell him?" I laughed.

"Whad'ya think I told him? Told him to keep his filthy hands off my files. Told him I already had a lawyer, and he's an altar boy by the name of Culhane. Told him to take his 'discount' and shove it cuz I wasn't changing attorneys."

I was laughing heartily at that point. What I would have given to have been a fly on Gunther's wall during that conversation. "How did Gunther take your reaction?"

"I'd guess badly. The little prick! I ended up hanging up on him. Does that answer your question?"

"Eli, you may not know it," I said, laughing out loud, "but you just made my day. I really want to tell you how much I appreciate your comments and your loyalty. It means a lot." I then explained that I was going to pass along the same twenty-five percent discount that I was giving to other clients.

"Bullshit," he immediately replied.

"What?" I asked.

"I said bullshit. I ain't taking no damn discount from you, Mike. I—"

"Eli," I protested, "I must—"

"I've been around the block a few times myself. That was no discount that your old firm offered to me for your business. That was thirty pieces of silver. I don't sell out my friends," he stubbornly said. "And besides, with the shit you know about me and my business, I can't risk having you out there with me not knowing where the hell you are or what the hell you're doing." He chuckled.

"I don't know what to say Eli, other than thanks. I appreciate your comments more than you'll ever know."

"Now, if that dumb son of a bitch from your old firm had offered me a thirty per cent discount," he added, "I'd a gone with him in a heartbeat."

"You bastard," I laughed, "your billing rate just went *up* twenty percent."

He laughed heartily. "Listen," he offered on a more serious note, "take my advice, Mike. Open your own shop; be your own boss. You're a good lawyer. Work hard, treat people fair, and the work will come. That's what I did, and I wasn't a hell of a lot younger than you are now when I started my business here in Ft. Lauderdale, over on Davie Road." He hesitated, "Maybe I'm putting my nose in your business, and I shouldn't. Anyway, you got my legal work, for what that's worth, whatever you decide to do."

"Thanks a million. I'll keep your advice in mind."

After completing my client calls, I telephoned the three Ft. Lauderdale law firms on my list that I was interested in talking with about joining as a partner: Druck and Shores; Michaels, Fields and Gray; and Hammond and Lewis. Speaking with friends of mine who were partners at the three firms, I arranged for a meeting with two of the firms the next afternoon, with the third the following afternoon. All three of my friends at the firms were surprised at my call. They had not yet heard of my departure.

As one commented, "Mike, I was sure they would have carried you out of Hunt & Baxter in a box when you retired."

I dodged giving any specifics on the "why" of my leaving Hunt, stating only that the firm and I had reached a 'fundamental difference of opinion' on a certain client matter. While they didn't press it further, I fully expected that they would inquire more specifically when I met with them. I would if I were in their shoes.

The balance of the afternoon was spent at the computer in my den, preparing a standardized engagement letter for each of my all-too-few clients to sign to confirm they were sticking with me. The letter, addressed to Avery, informed him that the client was aware of my departure from the firm and was electing to transfer its pending legal cases and work files to me for my continued representation. The letter, to be signed by each client, ended by requesting Hunt's full cooperation in the transition and directed that all such files be assembled for their immediate pick-up by me.

I proofed them, prepared a cover letter to each client, and emailed them all by four-thirty. I requested in my cover letter that they email their letter to Hunt as soon as possible in order to enable me to start the transition immediately, with no loss of attention to their files. An equally important motive was to get those files in my hands before Gunther and Company could figure out yet another, new and equally devious way of persuading my clients to reconsider and stay with Hunt after all. I could hope that the clients coming with me remained resolute.

My momentary reverie was broken by a call from Eric. Damn, I suddenly realized, I hadn't returned his call to me the morning before.

"Mike, what's the deal with your job? I just called down there and spoke with your old secretary. She told me that you had left your firm. What happened?"

"It's a long story. When you have more time, I'll share the details with you. How's Ryan?"

"Status quo, I'm afraid. It's going to be a very, very slow process."

"Sorry I didn't return your call. What is it?"

"Would it be possible to see you for a few minutes tonight?"

"Sure, what's on your mind?"

"I received the final police report yesterday. I need to talk about it with you." He sounded very upset.

"I'll plan on seeing you right after dinner over at the hospital."

"I appreciate it. I'll see you then."

LIZ AND I drove south on I-95 and arrived at Jackson Memorial around seven-thirty. We left Anne and Erin biking around the Las Olas islands when we left, with promises to hit their homework upon their return.

When we arrived, Eric was in a conference room, spending some private time with Sarah. Eric had informed the nursing staff that Liz and I were god-parents and were to be considered family. This meant that we could gown, mask and glove to go in and see Ryan anytime we were there, so long as there was no medical order to the contrary.

Ryan, while under some pain medication, was still in a lot of pain. It was heart wrenching to watch the young boy in such misery and not be able to do anything about it.

We left the isolation room to visit with Sarah and Eric. Sarah was obviously planning on staying with her dad and brother for some time tonight. She had her fourth grade homework and school books with her in the room adjoining the burn unit. After spending only a few moments with her, it was quite apparent that she wasn't the same Sarah we were used to. While polite, her usual vivacious and spunky personality was absent. She acted more serious and withdrawn. Liz decided to try and spend a few quiet moments alone with her and persuaded Sarah to accompany her down to the hospital cafeteria for some ice cream and talk.

I waited alone in the meeting room while Eric spent a few moments checking in on his son. Ten minutes later, he emerged from the critical care isolation room and sat down beside me on one of the bright orange molded plastic chairs. The room was ours tonight since no one else was around except for the periodic nurse or clerk who walked by in the outer hall.

"Thanks for coming by tonight, Mike." He still looked very tired and emotionally worn out.

"No, not at all." I decided to get to the point. "What's troubling you, Eric?"

"It's the final police report. I read it over," he said as he opened the manila folder he was carrying and handed it to me. "Take a look at it, will you?"

I read it over fairly quickly. When I came to page four, I saw the narrative section in which Trooper Martelli outlined his conclusion regarding the 'probable cause' of the accident:

> Decedent driver's loss of control of her vehicle, and its rollover, were due to a combination of a step ladder not being adequately secured to unknown leading vehicle, coupled with decedent's speeding and exercising a lack of due care in the control of her vehicle in trying to avoid hitting it. The fire resulted from a tear in the filler pipe connection with the gas tank occurring during the violent rollover phase of the accident, allowing gasoline to escape from the vehicle.

In short, 'driver error.' After reading the report, I looked up at Eric. He was visibly angry, and the scene last week with Martelli quickly came to mind.

"Mike, that conclusion is bullshit! While the ladder flying onto the road is right, that's the only finding he got right. There's no way that Jenny was speeding or caused any 'loss of control' or rollover," he said angrily. "She was not a speeder, and I don't give a damn what that cop says to the contrary. Jesus, she was always hounding me to slow down when I drove with her on the highway." His eyes were intense as he spoke. "I've been giving this a lot of thought. There's something about the Mesa that caused that accident, I just know it." He got up out of the chair and started to pace around the room as he continued.

I made no attempt to comment yet, or to interrupt him.

"Look at the description that the witness gave in the report. That house painter, Abadin, says that the Mesa looked like it was acting weird on the roadway. I'm convinced that something strange did happen out there with the Mesa and that is what caused that rollover. It wasn't Jenny's driving, I can tell you that!" Eric finally took a deep breath and looked at me directly. A stubborn, fierce determination was in his eyes.

"I want you to represent me and my family in a lawsuit against Global Motors, Mike. I have to find out what the problem was. I can't let this rest, no matter how much I've tried to tell myself to do just that. It's all I can think about." He paused and looked at the floor for a moment, and, again, I didn't interrupt him. I let him talk.

"I've got to do this, or I'm going to go crazy," he continued after a moment. "I need your help, Mike. Will you help me out and take the case? I want to sue Global and find out what happened. There's got to be a problem in that Mesa. I know there is. And I obviously expect to pay you for it; I don't expect anything like this for free. I just need to know why ... why all of this happened," he said nodding towards Ryan's room down the hall. "Will you represent me and my family in a suit against Global?"

He stopped talking and looked at me, waiting for my response.

I took a deep breath. "Eric, I've got to make two very important points in answer to your question. First, maybe I tend to think too much like a defense lawyer, but I'm not sure that you have any grounds to legitimately believe that a problem of some type exists with the Mesa. Please, don't misunderstand me," I quickly added, putting both of my hands up defensively when I saw the puzzled frown develop on his face. "I'm not saying that there was anything wrong with the way that Jenny was driving. I don't mean that at all. All I'm saying is that you have almost nothing to go on to prove some type of defect in the Mesa based on what I have heard. The—"

"You read the accident description of the eyewitness! He said that he thought that something was wrong with the way the Mesa was operating and handling. He didn't say that she was speeding or driving recklessly like that lazy goddamn cop says. What more do we need?"

"Eric, let's be precise about what that Abadin witness told the cops," I cautioned. "He said that he *thought* that the Mesa acted 'weird' on the road, at least as he saw it. And remember, the guy was obviously witnessing a startling event. You can't put too much stock in the accuracy of what he *thinks* he saw. The guy didn't say that it looked like some type of 'defect' existed in the Mesa. I agree with you—and I felt this way from the first time that Martelli spoke to us—that Abadin's use of the word 'weird' is encouraging and does raise some legitimate questions, but to jump from that observation to the conclusion that there must be something wrong with the Mesa and that a lawsuit should be started, is a jump that I'm not comfortable making as a lawyer. I know you're very upset about all this, but as a friend and a lawyer, you don't really have much to go on, that's all I'm telling you. I'm giving you my unvarnished advice."

Eric looked at me with anger and frustration. "Jesus, Mike! Tell me, what else do you need to justify a lawsuit? I don't want this happening to any other family out there. I don't want anybody else to suffer what my family did," he managed before his voice started breaking.

"Eric," I countered, "I realize that Jenny's death and Ryan's injuries have been extremely difficult for you to deal with. I'm not sure how a person can cope with that kind of tragedy. I think it's only normal that you would have feelings that make you want to strike out and find some kind of reason for all of this to have happened. But it may not be there. Bad things happen to nice people every second of every day, and most of the time there's no rhyme or reason for it either. I see it happen every day." I shook my head. "Look around here," I said, gesturing at the rooms filling the hospital hall next to us. "Why is this hospital crammed with nice people who are filled with cancer? Why are there kids upstairs laying there with brain tumors?" I stopped for a moment and took a breath as he just stared at me. I was already feeling guilty, but I didn't want to give him false hopes or expectations.

"The hard fact," Eric, "is that it's extremely unlikely there was anything wrong with Jenny's Mesa. I think that you need to accept that, otherwise you're going to end up fighting an expensive battle that you're not going to win, and you're likely to prolong the emotional damage flowing from your family's tragedy. You've got to put this part of the tragedy behind you, for your own good and that of the kids."

Eric stubbornly persisted, "What would it take to convince you to take this case and sue Global? I know that I'm right on this. It's not guilt or vengeance speaking either. I know Jenny. She would not have been speeding."

"It would take something, Eric … something that takes the cause of her loss of control out of the realm of pure speculation and into the realm of real possibilities."

"Give me an example, a 'for instance'?"

I sighed with some frustration at his stubbornness. "Okay, give me a witness who says that he saw Jenny driving at the time of the accident and can verify first-hand that she wasn't speeding. Give me evidence that Jenny's accident, and the odd behavior of her Mesa on the roadway, as observed by that Abadin witness, is not the only such accident that the Mesa model has had around this country where odd vehicle instability was reported by the drivers involved in other rollover accidents. That's the kind of hard evidence that you need for starters, Eric. That's something that has a basis in fact, not fiction. As it stands now, you and I are only aware of *her* accident, and for all we know it's an isolated incident. Look," I continued, "I've represented Global for years. I haven't heard of any other incidents with the Mesa, although I'll admit that it's a newly-produced model for Global, and I wouldn't expect them to have a lot of any such problems reported yet. But I've not heard of any, and I'd expect that I would have heard through the Global grapevine if Global is having any stability problems with the Mesa."

I could see that Eric wasn't buying any of this. He stood facing me with his arms folded across his chest.

I realized that I needed to tell him why I couldn't take any potential suit against Global, in any event.

"Eric, I mentioned that I have two points to make to you about your desire to have me represent you in a case against Global. The fact is, even if there were grounds to believe that a defect in the Mesa exists and that Global should be sued, I personally couldn't represent you in that suit."

"What do you mean you couldn't represent me? You're my lawyer! You were Jenny's lawyer as well!"

"I know that, but I've also been Global's lawyer on product liability cases for almost eight years now. I would have what the lawyers call an 'ethical conflict of interest' in representing you in a suit against Global. I was privy to a lot of inside information about their overall defense procedures and strategies, as well as some of their manufacturing information. While I don't have any information about the Mesa model, specifically, the rules of ethics would still prohibit me from taking the case. You're an accountant. You have the same type of ethical constraints, though probably not as rigorous or pervasive as the ones lawyers have."

"Jesus, Mike," he said with exasperation, "you're the only lawyer that I'd even consider having as my attorney on a case against Global. I know you. You're Ryan's godfather. You know Sarah. I don't want some sleazebag lawyer on the back of the telephone book or the side of a bus representing me. I want you."

"Thanks for the confidence," I said, "but even if you felt you had good grounds to start a suit, I couldn't do it myself. The decision is not mine to make. It's Global's. I have a conflict. I couldn't take the case. Eric, I hope that you can understand that. Believe me, if you had grounds, and I didn't have this conflict, I'd relish the opportunity to go after Global for you. But I can't."

"It would be you or nothing, Mike," he stubbornly persisted. "I wouldn't be doing it for the money. Any other lawyer would be in it only for the money, and they would end up making me feel dirty about it."

"I can't do it, Eric … I can't tell you how bad I feel about this, but I just can't do it ethically," I said, holding up both of my hands, palms up, as I pleaded my ethical problem. "Believe me, I have no love for Global after the shit they pulled on me, but it's out of my control." An uncomfortable silence fell between us. It was a feeling that I wasn't used to experiencing with him. I didn't respond to his comments any further, hoping that he would move on to another topic.

After a few somewhat strained moments of silence, Liz returned with Sarah, and we said our goodbyes for the night.

When we left the hospital, I had a hollow feeling in my stomach. While I knew that my prior representation ethically prevented my representing Eric, it still didn't feel right. I knew Eric well enough to know that he wouldn't let any other lawyer represent his family in a suit against Global. He was stubborn, and he disliked lawyers.

CHAPTER 11

THE NEXT DAY, I spent the morning again in my study drafting a current résumé. It was a weird experience preparing one after all these years out of the job market. After attempting a number of different formats, I decide on the simplest layout that I could think of. I recognized that my paper credentials, at this stage in my career, didn't mean a hell of a lot anyway.

I arrived at Druck and Shores a few minutes early for my one-thirty appointment with Keith Cahill, a friend of mine who was also a litigator at the firm. Keith was about the same age as I was, having been a partner with Druck for about ten years. As I sat in the waiting room, I took notice of the furnishings. There was the obligatory oriental rug, the dark walnut furniture and the framed prints of the English landed gentry, with horses, about to embark on the fox hunt. I was wondering if the fox ever won when out came Keith with an open smile and his right arm extended for a strong handshake.

"Mike, it's great to see you," he beamed as we shook hands and exchanged greetings. "Come on back to my office." He led the way through the dark walnut and beveled glass door separating the reception area from the offices.

We spent the first few minutes talking about our families and just generally catching up on personal matters. I finally got to the point.

"Keith, I certainly appreciate your seeing me on short notice. As I mentioned briefly in our telephone conversation, I've left Hunt & Baxter and am looking at different options available for me and my practice at this point. I'm hoping to join a solid firm here in Ft. Lauderdale, one that I'm familiar with, and one which I would want to practice law with for the rest of my career. I naturally thought of Druck and Shores when I started compiling my list of possible candidates, and that's why I'm here."

"I appreciate the complement, Mike. As you know, lateral moves into a large firm can pose some real problems for the firm. We have to worry about the wrong type of reaction from our existing attorneys, and then there is the economic factor." Keith looked very nervous and not at ease. "I've got to tell you that, presently, the most recent lateral moves that we have made here at the firm have created some serious problems on both fronts for us. Two years ago, we brought in a young partner with a beginning healthcare practice. The firm represents two growing hospitals, and we decided that we needed to make the big commitment to having a legitimate healthcare practice which would not only satisfy those two clients, but also allow us to go after some of the big national healthcare companies who seem to be monopolizing the industry. Well, we brought the guy in, paid him a healthy salary, and invested a lot of money in helping him develop a practice. Last fall he left us and took one of the hospitals with him," Cahill said, shaking his head. "As you can imagine, there were not a lot of happy partners around here. We felt that we were betrayed, frankly. Lateral partners are not currently in vogue here."

"I can imagine," I replied. "Are you telling me that the firm is simply not interested in laterals?"

"No, but we are being very selective."

"As far as my situation is concerned, I think that you and a number of your partners know my legal skills. I'm in a position to bring a modest, but very loyal, book of clients with me, and I would be a very positive addition to your existing firm practice."

"Mike, can you give me some idea of what range of annual billings you think that you'll be able to bring with you?"

"Yeah, I'd put it in the range of two hundred thousand dollars. I'm intentionally being conservative since I don't want to promise what I don't reasonably believe I could deliver. I know that I will be able to increase that significantly within the next few years. At Hunt, I spent the vast majority of my time representing Global Motors, as you may know, and that did not leave me a great deal of time to devote to the development of new, non-Global clients. Since I won't be representing Global any longer, I intend to concentrate on client development, and I'm optimistic that I'll be able to double those numbers within a year, and expand well beyond those numbers in years to follow."

Cahill frowned. "I've got to be honest with you, Mike. Two hundred thousand dollars a year for an attorney with the years of experience that you have is not significant. The disastrous healthcare attorney who we brought in, and that I mentioned to you, brought in billings of one hundred fifty thousand dollars a year, but we decided to take a chance on him. There were an awful lot of partners here who were negative on bringing on any lateral who could not at least pay his own salary, plus overhead share. Two hundred thousand dollars won't do that for you," he said.

Cahill picked up the phone and called out to his secretary for a cup of coffee. I declined his offer for a cup.

"I also should tell you, Mike," he continued, "that there will be some serious questions raised in your case about the nature of your departure from Hunt. I'm not sure that there will be sufficient support here at this firm to warrant serious discussions about a position with us."

"What do you mean the nature of my departure?" I asked, with a sudden sinking feeling. *How could he know about the Global mess?*

"Well, the whole deal involving Global," he answered. He apparently read the questioning on my face. "You know," he added, "the stuff that was in *The Daily Business Gazette* article this morning."

It was my turn to look confused. "I'm sorry, but what newspaper article are you talking about?"

He got up out of his maroon leather chair and walked over to his black leather briefcase which was on the floor over by the window. Opening it up, he took out a copy of what appeared to be this morning's edition of the *Gazette*. The *Gazette* is the local scandal sheet which focuses on business and legal developments. It's one step up from *The Enquirer*, but just barely. The *Gazette* had a habit of snooping high and low for juicy news stories, finding them, and then sensationalizing them for its readers' voyeuristic pleasure. Hidden among the trash, however, were fast-breaking legitimate stories which were often of interest to law firms and businesses in South Florida. Needless to say, everyone subscribed to the *Gazette*, and most attorneys read it over every morning with their coffee before getting started on the day's pillage. It was delivered daily to office doors. I read it at Hunt.

"This is the story I was referring to," Keith said as he handed me the paper.

I quickly scanned the front page. The headline caused an unpleasant warm rush to pass through my body: 'HUNT LAWYER SHOWN THE DOOR,' the headline proclaimed.

"I'm sorry, Mike. I thought that you had seen the story."

I didn't respond to him. I was busy reading. The story reported that I had been 'booted out' of Hunt & Baxter by a nearly unanimous vote of my partners. The reporter of the story related that while Ted Gunther, spokesperson for the firm, would only say that the firm and I had experienced 'sudden irreconcilable differences,' she went on to state that 'certain unidentified sources within the firm' had nonetheless disclosed that my termination was pegged to 'major dissatisfaction' that Global Motors, a long-time client of the firm, had expressed about my handling of a serious case for them.

The story ended by quoting Avery Wilcox to the effect that my departure was considered 'inconsequential' to the firm's operations. He emphasized that the firm had spoken with its clients, and that 'only a very few' would be following me. The rest had chosen to stay with Hunt. Cahill's secretary knocked on the door and brought in his cup of coffee and left as I finished the story. It carried over to page three.

"Goddammit," is all that I could undiplomatically muster. "Those sons of bitches. Keith, I am terribly disappointed at the insinuations Hunt is making in this piece of trash. While I'll concede I was voted out of the firm by a majority of my partners, the facts are not at all as they appear in this paper," I said defensively. I realized how this must look from Cahill's vantage point. What else was the indicted criminal going to say—'I didn't do it; I was framed.'

"Look," he calmly suggested, "why don't I go ahead and speak informally with the firm's management committee and see if there is an interest in opening discussions on the issue of your possibly joining us. I'll take it up with them promptly, and I'll get back to you as soon as I can, okay?" As he said this, he was rising up from his chair. It was obvious that he was uncomfortable and wanted me out of his office. It was equally clear that I wouldn't be getting any positive call back from him.

I got up out of my chair as well, putting the newspaper on the top of his desk. "Uh ... sure," I responded, "that would be great."

He walked me to the reception area where we said goodbye.

I left the Druck offices, both furious and embarrassed at the bilge in the newspaper article. There was no doubt in my mind that the 'unidentified sources within the firm' were members of the management committee. Gunther had been currying favor with the press from the moment he was elected to the committee for positive press for Hunt. He obviously decided that he needed to both put the right spin on my departure and to use it as a way of ensuring that some of my clients would have serious questions about taking their business with me after all. *The little shit.*

I pulled my cell phone out of my pocket and called my home to retrieve any messages on my answering machine. There were three, two of which were for me. Both the Michaels firm and the Hammond firm had called to cancel their interviews. The Michaels lawyer's message said that he had informally canvassed the partners, and they had decided that they were not interested at the present time in taking on a lateral in the litigation area. They were probably overstaffed the way it was, he explained. He apologized for any inconvenience and wished me good luck in my employment efforts.

The Hammond lawyer was equally apologetic. He stated that they had just brought on some other lateral hires last year and had decided to 'put off' hiring any more until perhaps next year. The attorney stated that he was sorry, but that he had not correctly gauged the willingness of his firm's partners at the present time to hire more laterals. He wished me luck.

I noted that both calls had come in just after lunch. It wasn't hard to determine that it was just long enough for their various partners to read this morning's *Gazette*, huddle, and determine that they didn't want to have anything to do with 'damaged goods.'

I headed home. As I turned onto Coral Reef, I saw old Mrs. Montcrief, one of my elderly neighbors, out in her yard gardening. She stopped and stared at me as I drove past. I was beginning to wonder if she had read the *Gazette* article, too. Cool it, I told myself, she's been strange since the day we moved in.

Liz's car was in the drive when I got there. I didn't look forward to my discussions with her about my interviews.

"Hi!" she said when I entered the family room. I immediately loosened and removed my tie and threw my suit jacket over the chair next to the eating area off the kitchen. "Well, how did they go?" she asked.

"I have a problem," I responded. "It seems like my buddies down at Hunt leaked the fact of my departure to the *Gazette*, and they managed to arrange for a little interview with the reporter in the process. The story was front page of today's *Gazette*."

"Oh, no, what did it say?"

"What didn't it say?" I related to her the substance of the story, including the fact that I had been 'shown the door.'

"Who reads that paper?"

"No one except most of the lawyers in town, and that's the problem. Both of my other interviews canceled, and I'm sure it was because of the story." I sat down at the table.

"How did your interview with Druck go?" You could read the anxiety in her eyes.

"It was pleasant enough, but there's no doubt in my mind that I'm not going to be getting any offer from them either. Believe me, they would have canceled as well if they had been given enough lead time between having read the article this morning and my appointment with Cahill right after lunch. So, to answer your question, don't hold your breath on Druck. It's not going to produce anything."

"Who else is there in Ft. Lauderdale that you have an interest in joining? There have to be others."

"I don't think I could get a job cleaning the wastebaskets at any other halfway decent law firm in this town after that *Gazette* article. My name is shit. Period."

"Then you have no alternative now. You have to sue Hunt and Global to get your name back, Michael."

"We've had this conversation already," I responded angrily. "I'm not going to be suing Hunt or Global or anybody else, okay. So, please do both of us a favor and don't bring that up again. They've screwed me royally, but there's no way that I'm going to ever be able to fully disprove everything that they will say about me. I'll end up slathered in mud." I was again suddenly overwhelmed with a raw burning hate and frustration over what had happened to me at the hands of Global and my former partners. My inability to strike back was a knife in my gut.

Liz kept her cool and came over to the table and sat down opposite me. "If you're not going to even consider a suit, what do you suggest for a job? Are you going to interview with some of the Miami law firms?"

I shook my head. "No, I'm not going to do the commute bit into Miami. I'm not going to spend two hours or more every day in my car driving to and from Miami to work, and we're not going to move to Miami, either. We're not going to raise our kids in Miami. And let's face it, the *Gazette* also publishes its daily newspaper in Dade and Palm Beach counties as well. They're all going to know about the nasty little questions surrounding my departure from Hunt, as well, so I don't realistically think that I'm going to be exactly swamped with offers from Miami firms either." I pulled my tie off and threw it onto the table.

"Then what are you going to do? You had better figure out a game plan for this." She was clearly nervous about where this was going.

"I've been thinking about that since after the Druck interview today. I'm going out on my own."

She cocked her head at that response. "Michael, didn't you always tell me that the last thing that you would ever do would be to go out on your own because of the hours, the administrative hassles and the paperwork? Am I missing something? Also, I hate to ask this question, but can you support us on your own? I mean, I don't want to put added pressure on you right now, but isn't it really risky to try and set up your own firm when you don't really have much in the way of clients?"

"Yes, it is risky, but what's my alternative? My name is mud right now and with the limited book of clientele I have, I'm not going to be a hot commodity with any decent firm. So, if we're going to stay here in Ft. Lauderdale, it looks like I'm going to have to bite the bullet and go out on my own. I figure I can rent an office in one of those executive office suites where I don't have to have a full time secretary. I can share one who will handle my calls and my typing." Liz was listening, but I could see she was very skeptical.

"Let's look on the bright side; if I do as well as I think I can, I stand to make a lot more money than I could ever have made at Hunt. I know a number of attorneys who have broken away from large law firms on their own who have done great. In fact," I continued, "I recently spoke with John Westbrook who used to be with a big firm in Miami. He went out on his own and ended up hiring two associates to help him handle all his newfound work within the first year after he left. It can be done Liz."

While I expected some nervous tears from her at this point, I didn't get any. Instead, she nodded her head slowly. "Alright, if that's what you think is the best way to handle it, let's do it. We're in this together though. If it means that we have to cut our expenses, or to move from this house to a cheaper one, we'll do it, Michael. I want you to know that," she said with a stubborn resilience in her eyes. "We've always said that the most important thing in this life is us and the girls. Well, it looks like we're about to put that to the test," she smiled with some effort.

Her smile was contagious.

"Thanks."

"I'm serious about my willingness to work full time and to cut expenses."

"I know you are, and I appreciate that. There will probably have to be cuts made, but let me do some review of our expenses for the time being, okay? We still have a decent balance in the savings account, and I will start getting the monthly reimbursements shortly from Hunt for my partnership contribution. It's not going to be much, but it will be something."

As we talked, I considered the fact that the house carried an annual property tax bill of fourteen thousand dollars alone. I was going to have to do some serious reviewing of our expenses. Scratch any new car. And you can cancel any reservations for a vacation in Colorado this summer, I also thought. I wasn't about to point that out now. It was ironic, I thought. Now that I had the time for a hassle-free summer vacation, I didn't have the money. *Figures.*

I left the kitchen and headed for the den. The decision just made spurred me into action. I needed to get my ass in gear if I was going to keep those clients who indicated that they would follow me with their work. I started making another list of everything that I needed to do, from leasing an office to designing my own new letterhead. While common sense told me that I should be worried about the risks that I was taking on, I was surprisingly filled with a sense of energy and purpose. *The Law Offices of Michael A. Culhane?* I liked the ring of it.

CHAPTER 12

I SPENT THE next week looking for office space. While I was intent on going cheap, I was also determined to avoid the appearance of financial desperation. Clients can sense desperation in a lawyer much like sharks can smell a thimble of blood in the vast ocean of water. It's amazing. Clients may raise a suspicious eye at a well-appointed law office and grumble 'I hope I'm not paying for all this,' but down deep, they want to feel absolutely secure in the prominence and success of their lawyer and his abilities. And, somehow, a lot of dark wood, shining brass, oriental rugs and china coffee cups always give clients that requisite warm, fuzzy feeling in their little fee-paying hearts.

Large law firms know it, and that's why they decorate their offices accordingly. I'm convinced that they'd use walnut-encased phones and all brass toilets if they made them. The fact of the matter, however, is there are a lot of very mediocre lawyers charging five hundred dollars an hour hiding behind horned-rimmed glasses and dark walnut desks the size of aircraft carriers. While their clients probably don't have a clue as to their legal skills, they figured that they must be worth the price or else they wouldn't be able to afford the expensive digs. Put those same clients in front of an excellent sole practitioner working out of a shoestring budget office, and I guarantee that they'll question not only the attorney's hourly rate of two hundred fifty dollars, but almost every bit of his legal advice as well.

All of this was running through my mind as I searched for office space. After checking out six different office possibilities, I ended up paying a little more per month than I had planned on. I would be sharing office space with three other attorneys on the fifteenth floor of a new twenty-five story office building in downtown Ft. Lauderdale. I would be only five minutes by foot from the courthouse and ten minutes driving from home. I worked out an arrangement to be able to use half of the receptionist, Tina, who also functioned as the secretary for one of the other attorneys. The office manager assured me that Tina was hell on wheels on the computer and was great with clients.

Walking through that office, I didn't see any photos around her desk of cats or dogs. She did have a picture of herself with a stocky, bearded guy dressed in a tank top and Miami Marlins baseball hat. And, yes, the offices did have a client reception area with a red oriental rug and dark walnut upholstered chairs.

Once I locked down the space, I called Hunt & Baxter regarding the immediate transfer of the client files, which my clients had directed them to make. It was clear I was considered an irritating annoyance by the old gang. When I asked to speak to Avery, Jean, the receptionist-operator at the firm, told me that she had been directed to route any call from me to Harrington's secretary, Perky Wendy.

Jean routed me to Wendy who got on the phone and officiously informed me that I was to deal with her in connection with the transfer of any client transition matters. I asked her to deliver the files to my new offices by Friday so that I could immediately attend to pending matters which needed to be handled.

"I'm sorry, but you're going to have to wait a few days. I'm busy on other matters for Mr. Harrington. I couldn't possibly even begin to attend to those files until after I finish his matters." I could picture her working her emery board.

You little Bitch. "I see. In that case, tell me Wendy, what is Harrington's Florida Bar number and his middle name. Also, exactly how do you spell your last name?"

A moment's hesitation preceded her crisp little reply. "What does that information have to do with the transfer of those files, may I ask?"

"Well, I know that Harrington is a real stickler for detail. I'm sure he'd want me to get it right when I file my ethics grievance with the Florida Bar tomorrow morning for his refusal to turn over client files in accordance with explicit client instructions. That's the only reason I want it," I answered nonchalantly. "I'm sure that when he receives the bar complaint he'll want to know who at Hunt was helpful in causing that complaint to be issued against him. That's why I want to make damn sure that I spell your name right. So, how do you spell it?"

There was uncharacteristic sudden silence on the other end of the phone. *Did she drop the emery board?* She finally responded. "Well, if you're going to be so difficult about all this, I'll re-arrange my schedule just to deal with your difficult demands," she huffed.

"Gee, that would be great, Wendy. That's awfully nice of you. I'll tell you what, since you've freed up your busy little schedule, what do you say that I just go ahead and hold off filing this old grievance unless, of course, I don't get those files delivered to my office by noon sharp tomorrow? Does that sound fair to you?"

"Fine," she snapped. "You'll get your files."

"By noon?" I persisted.

"You'll get them by noon!" she said nastily.

"Great," I said nicely. "That really works out well for both of us. Give my regards to *Mr. Harrington*, will you?"

She slammed down the phone.

Just like clockwork, the boxes of client files arrived via courier at my new offices precisely at noon the next day. I spent the afternoon sorting through them to review case status on all the matters. I ended up taking three boxes home with me on Friday afternoon to complete the review.

On the way home from my office on Friday, I called Tina on my cell to have her email and fax a letter to all of my clients first thing Monday morning to let them know that I had custody of their files now, and that their matters were well under control. Frankly, I wanted them to see my new letterhead and my new office address. I wanted them to know that my office was for real. Let the warm fuzzies begin.

I had just gotten home from work when Liz told me that Eric had just called. He wanted me to call him right back.

"He seemed pretty excited about something," she said. "He was about to leave work and suggested that you try to catch him at home before he and Sarah headed out to grab a bite and go over to the hospital to see Ryan."

I called him back using the phone in my study. He answered on the second ring.

After exchanging pleasantries and discussing how Ryan and Sarah were doing, he got right to the point.

"I got a call at home last night on my answering machine. It came in while Sarah and I were over at the hospital. It was from a Carole Merton who lives in Naples. She left her telephone number, but I was too tired to call her back last night. I wrote her number down and took it to work with me today." He was talking quickly and excitedly, with a noticeable lift to his voice. "I've been jammed at work, and I only was able to return her call a few hours ago. Mike, she says that she was on I-595 that same day as Jenny's accident and had passed Jenny's Mesa just a few minutes before the accident. She was driving to Ft. Lauderdale to spend the weekend with a friend. She told me that while she didn't see the accident happen, she remembers that when she passed Jenny, the Mesa wasn't speeding at all!"

"What exactly did she say?"

"She said that she passed Jenny's Mesa about a mile after the Weston entrance ramp onto I-595. She said that Jenny wasn't speeding at all!" he repeated, excitedly. "I knew that cop was wrong ... the lazy bastard!"

"Take it easy," I said calmly. "How did she get your name, and why did she call you now?"

The excitement in his voice not ten seconds before suddenly vanished. There was a brief pause before Eric answered. "She said that she saw the film footage on the evening news of the Mesa burning. Some cameraman from Channel 7 ran a ten second shot on their local eleven o'clock news. She said that when she saw the green Mesa on fire and the news reporter said where and when the accident occurred, she realized that it was the same lady that she had seen on I-595 with her son in the baby seat as she had passed them. Merton said that she happened to pay pretty close attention to the Mesa as she passed it since she was thinking about getting one, and she liked the color of the one that she saw in front of her. She eyed it over as she passed it and saw a lady driving it. She didn't pay any more attention to it than that. She felt terrible about it and called the highway patrol earlier this week and persuaded them to give her the name of the family involved. She called information for my telephone number since the police wouldn't give that out."

"What was her reason for calling?"

"She says that she lost her mother in a terrible car accident last year, and for some reason, she just wanted to call the family of the Mesa driver and say that she was sorry that it happened. I asked her about Jenny's speed when she passed her, and she told me that she was going the speed limit. She is sure of that."

"That's amazing. That kind of concern and follow-up doesn't happen very often in South Florida," I commented.

"Mike," he said with a firm conviction in his voice, "I told you that Jenny was not a speeder and that she didn't cause that accident. I'm more convinced than ever that there's something wrong with that Mesa. That's what killed her and destroyed my son."

"Did she—"

"I can't let this just drop, Mike," he said insistently. "I'm suing Global, and that's that. I've got to find out what happened. I'm not going to just sit by and do nothing when I know that they sold my family an SUV that caused this accident. It's that simple to me." He was measuring his words, and he was speaking very slowly and with conviction.

"What I want to know from you, Mike, is whether you'll represent the kids and me in a suit against Global. Jenny should not have died, and Ryan should not be laying over in that intensive care hospital bed right now as a burned up baby boy! He should be a normal, healthy little boy at home with us cutting more teeth instead of fighting for his every breath to keep a hold on a life that sure as hell won't be like the one that you or I have enjoyed."

"Eric—"

"Please ... please don't say no, Mike. I need your help now more than ever. My family needs your help," he quietly pleaded.

His anger and pleas for help hit me like a fist. All I could see was Willis Cole trying to do everything in his ugly little power to squash any suit that Eric and his family brought against Global. And I now had no doubt whatsoever that Global would stoop to any means possible to do just that. Perhaps it was also the anger and frustration that I was selfishly feeling right now at having been taken advantage of by Global that was the final straw. I thought quietly to myself about the representation, and the huge ethical conflict I faced, not saying a word.

I needed to remind him of my representation issue. "Eric, the problem is that I can't *ethically* take your case. As much as I want to, it would be a breach of my ethical duties and I'd lose my license to practice law if I took your case against Global."

"I don't understand," he replied.

"Under the ethical rules to which I'm bound, a lawyer can't sue a former client—here, that would be Global—on behalf of a new client—that would be you and your family—if the proposed lawsuit against the former client involves *the same or substantially related matter* for which the lawyer represented the former client in the past. That's what the ethical rule clearly states. The only exception is where the former client *consents*. And I can tell you, former clients *never* give consent."

"So, how does that apply to my wanting to hire you to sue Global for the Mesa? From what you've told me, you've never handled any other Mesa suits for Global, did you? It's a brand new model Global just put on the market. So, what's the problem," he asked, with mounting exasperation in his voice.

"It's not that simple. A suit against Global alleging the Mesa was defective would, unfortunately, involve the same matter for which I had represented Global. I did this for over eight years, namely, products liability claims against its motor vehicles. The definition under the ethical rules of *same or substantially related* matter is very broad. It covers *any* vehicle asserting a claim for *any* type of defect, so the fact that I didn't work for Global on the defense of any Mesa vehicle, in particular, won't remove the conflict. I'm stuck," I said, with the same growing level of frustration that Eric had expressed. "Those weasels at Global would never consent to allowing me to represent you in a Mesa lawsuit."

"But from what you've told me the last week, Global caused you to be fired from your law firm," Eric persisted, his voice now angry. "Since Global was part of your firing, it can't possibly now be able to object and claim any ethical violation if you sue them, can it?" he asked, in frustrated disbelief.

I sighed. "Crazy as it sounds, Global can still raise the objection, and believe me, the nasty in-house lawyer at Global who got me fired would love to stick it to me once again. There is no way he would allow me to sue them on your behalf on a Mesa suit, especially since its their new flagship SUV product. It's unfair under these circumstances, but the ethical rules are really stacked in favor of the former client."

Crushed with the bad news, Eric was dejected. "So, I guess that's it, isn't it? You can't represent me?" It was more of a final plea for my help than a statement of acceptance.

I sat there quietly thinking the ethical problem over one final time in my head. I was absently pondering the definition of *same or substantially related* matter I had just explained to Eric. *There has to be a way to solve this problem,* I considered.

"Mike, are you there?" Eric said after a moment.

"I'm thinking," I replied. Finally, after a full minute passed, I had the kernel of an idea. I smiled for the first time in our difficult conversation. "Eric, do you trust me?"

"You know I do," he said. "Why do you even need to ask?"

"You asked me if I would represent you and your family in a suit against Global. I'm not going to answer you right now. I'm—"

"But Mike—"

"Hear me out. Let me finish," I said calmly. "I'm going to ask that you trust me, and suggest that you not discuss any possible lawsuit against Global with anyone else for a couple of weeks, okay? I'll tell you then whether I'll represent you."

"But Mike, I don't understand what—"

"Eric, I have my reasons for telling you this. You're just going to have to trust me implicitly, okay?"

"Mike, I'll do whatever you ask me to do, but I don't understand any of this."

"Thanks. There is one thing that I want to emphasize to you right now, though, and that is that as I am talking to you right now, I still have not agreed to represent you. If you want to go out and hire some other lawyer to represent you and your family in the meantime in a suit against Global, you should go ahead and do that. Do you understand that?"

"I don't understand what you're doing exactly, but, yes, I understand what you've just told me. I'm not hiring any other lawyer except you, Mike. You're the only lawyer that I could trust. Promise that you'll tell me what this is all about in a couple of weeks?"

"I think it'll all become very clear to you on its own," I answered. The seeds of my plan to free me from my conflict in representing Eric were beginning to take solid root.

"Do you still have the remains of the Mesa in the locked storage bin since the accident?" I asked, now suddenly re-engaged in the idea of a suit against Global by me.

"Yeah, it's still there. No one has touched it or even viewed it since I had it towed there from the police impound lot after the highway patrol finished their accident report and released it."

"Good. You'll want to make sure that it stays that way if you're going to bring a lawsuit," I reminded him. "Don't let anyone in to see it or to change anything about it. Eric, I appreciate your asking me to represent all of you. Actually, I'm humbled. You'll get an answer from me within a few weeks, I promise."

"Thank you, Mike. I'll be waiting for your answer. I only hope that it's the response that I'm asking you for."

After I hung up, I sat at my desk mentally fleshing out my plan in greater detail. I was still sitting there thirty minutes later when Liz came in to get me for dinner. "What are you smiling about?" she asked.

"Do you think that Brutus had just cause to slay Caesar?" I asked.

"What are you talking about?"

"I'm beginning to think that when Caesar said those historical words, *et tu Brute*, that maybe Caesar actually had it coming to him, that's all."

Liz looked at me with puzzlement on her face. "Do you want to tell me what's going on in that head of yours?"

I got up from the desk and put my hand on the back of her neck as we headed out the door for the dinner table. "Liz, for the first time since I left Hunt, I finally feel like I'm back in the game. And, yes, I'll tell you exactly what I'm smiling about over dinner. I'm starved."

CHAPTER 13

I CALLED SANDY Stevens, my former paralegal, the next morning. It was a Saturday, and my call caught her as she was walking out the door for a day of windsurfing off Key Biscayne.

"How are things going for you at Hunt now that I'm not there to cover all your mistakes?"

"You've got that backwards!" she laughed. "Suffice it to say, the Global team at Hunt is a whole different creature with you gone and that pompous ass Harrington in charge. He is something else, and he brought his sweet little darling of a secretary with him. She just loves to bark out orders 'per Mr. Harrington.' Don't let me get started, okay?" she laughed. "Mike, tell me that you're calling to take me away from all of this," she joked.

"Actually, I am," I retorted.

"Seriously?" she asked.

"As my first heart attack. Are you still interested? You need to know," I quickly added, "that I'm running a shoestring budget. I can't pay Hunt's salaries. If I could, I would. What I'd like to do is pay you at about seventy-five percent of your present salary, with a potential bonus based on how well I do, and you do. My intention is to hopefully allow you to make a hell of a lot more money in the long run with me than you would ever make at Hunt. But it would be a big risk for you, and I certainly will understand if you'd prefer to stay there."

"Mike, are you kidding? Yes, I'm interested!" she said excitedly, "and don't worry about the money; that will work itself out. You're a better investment than this place will ever be, at least for me. I don't have a husband or kids, and I don't need a lot. In fact," she added dryly, "I should be paying you to get me out of here. Harrington told me this past week that he has decided to transfer me off the Global team. His story was that he is so used to using his own paralegal, Robin, that it would be *more productive*, as he put it, for me to transfer over to the trusts and estates team. Can you believe that?"

"Trusts and estates?" I asked. "You've got to be kidding me. Is he an idiot?"

"It's banishment, I'm sure, for having been so closely identified with you. And no one there is going to challenge him in assigning me to that dead-end estate-planning team. I know he's probably hoping that I'll just resign instead of suffering a transfer to that team. Can you imagine me working on drafting wills?"

"Not exactly."

"The fact is, as much as I'm sure he'd love to, I don't think Harrington has the guts to fire me."

Her comment caught me off guard. I paused for a moment, reflecting on a new thought.

"Do you think that you could goad Harrington into firing you for refusing to be re-assigned off the Global team?" I asked.

"What? Why would I want to do that?"

"Because," I answered, "I am considering a potential client's request that I take a very serious products liability case against Global, and I think that it may prove important to me—if you are going to join my office—that you were *fired* from Hunt & Baxter, and not merely that you resigned and elected to join me. That's why."

"*You* are going to take a case *against* Global?" she asked incredulously. "I don't mean to be rude, Mike, but how can you ethically do that after you've represented them for all these years? Isn't there some type of ethics rule on that?"

"I didn't agree yet to take the case. I'm only considering it at this point," I carefully pointed out. "As far as the ethical issues are concerned, I have something in mind to hopefully deal with that."

"Okay, but why would the circumstances of my departure from Hunt have any bearing on the ethics of your taking a possible case against Global?"

"Sandy, I know that I'm asking a lot from you, but if my hunch is correct, I'm going to get into a hell of a dogfight with Global over the fact of my prior representation of Global on products liability defense cases. In view of what you've just told me—that Harrington is going to probably re-assign you off the Global team anyway—I think that the details of your departure may have a bearing on that conflict of interest issue. I would prefer to not get into the details with you for your own protection at this point, but my instincts tell me that a *firing* as opposed to a *resignation* may very well prove important. However,

I also recognize that it's your employment record we're talking about, Sandy, and it's strictly your call."

Sandy laughed again on the other end of the phone. "I stopped worrying about my employment record when I walked out on my last boss. I've always assumed that I wouldn't be receiving what you'd call a sterling reference from him, and even a 'pleasant resignation' from Hunt & Baxter isn't going to guarantee me a great reference in the future anyway. Mike, I knew that I missed your scheming, but I had forgotten just how much! Count me in."

"Done."

"Under the circumstances," she continued, "I think that I would love to orchestrate Harrington into firing me. Just tell me that eventually I'll have the pleasure of knowing that he will realize that I set him up."

"I think that the best that we can hope for is that he will always wonder whether that was the case. Can your black heart be content with only that?" I asked, chuckling as I posed the question.

"Actually, that's probably even better. When do we want my termination to occur?" she asked, conspiratorially.

"How does a week from this coming Monday sound?" I chuckled.

"That'll work. I'm going to use up some of my vacation days this week and have my discussion with him on that Monday morning. Is there anything that I can do for you in the interim?"

"Nope, not a thing."

"Mike, I'm really excited about this. I appreciate your asking me first."

"Sandy," I deadpanned, letting a few seconds pass, "you weren't first on my list. I had six rejections before I made this call."

"You're rotten!"

I SPENT MONDAY morning over at the courthouse on motion hearings on the cases I was handling and the rest of the day writing a brief I had to get out. Late in the day, I called over to the Broward County Bar Association offices to determine if they had a pending *pro bono* automobile case against Global Motors in their current inventory of cases being handled by private attorneys in Broward County. About fifteen years ago, the Florida Supreme Court adopted a rule encouraging all practicing attorneys in Florida to provide a certain number of hours of legal services per year, free of charge, to persons who would not otherwise be able to afford to hire attorneys to represent them. The Broward County *pro bono* program was a Bar-funded program, which identified needy recipients of legal representation and attempted to hook them up with attorneys in private practice who volunteered to provide it, free of charge. I kept my fingers crossed that *pro bono* would have just the case I was looking for.

It didn't. So, I called down to the *pro bono* section of the Dade County Bar Association in Miami. I told the section representative that I wanted to fulfill my pro bono obligations but wanted to do it in my field of experience, products liability. If I could represent a person in a products liability claim against an automobile company like Global, I explained, I could be putting my talents to their best use. She cheerfully thanked me for volunteering and asked me to hold while she looked at her existing inventory of new cases to be assigned.

She was back on the phone after only a brief moment and informed me that she actually had one such case. However, it had "some problems," she said.

"What kind of problems?"

"Well, it appears from the file jacket that the client, a Mr. Rocky Watson, had an accident in a small car made by Global, and that he wanted to bring a suit against Global for the damages he incurred. The damages only amount to a little over two thousand dollars. The problem," she said, "is that this case had been assigned to an attorney about three weeks ago, but Mr. Watson fired him and has asked for a different lawyer."

"So, I guess you're telling me that Mr. Watson 'is difficult'?" I asked, diplomatically.

She hesitated. "Uh ... yes, that appears to be the case."

She elaborated. The Watson case had been sitting in their offices for the last two weeks while her assistant shopped for someone else who might be interested in taking his case against Global. She related that while the Supreme Court had encouraged *pro bono* services by every attorney, it was still difficult to persuade a busy attorney to find room for a non-paying case, particularly one that *was difficult*. Finding a home, as she called it, for a small case like Mr. Watson's, especially where he had already fired the first attorney assigned to him, was particularly challenging.

I could tell by the spring in her voice, however, that she felt she had a live one on the line for this problematic case.

"Does the file indicate why the prior attorney was fired?" I asked.

"All it says on the file jacket is that he and Mr. Watson experienced 'irreconcilable differences.' I have no idea what the specific problem was, but I'm sure that you'll be able to resolve it," she said soothingly.

She offered that Mr. Watson qualified for *pro bono* services since he only had irregular work as a kitchen worker. He had apparently suffered some serious physical and emotional injuries from the first Gulf War, according to the intake summary. He had very little in the way of steady money, other than a small monthly disability payment he received from the army.

I asked for Watson's telephone number and told her to tentatively put my name on the case. In the meantime, I informed her that I first needed to speak with Watson to verify the nature of the case and to clear a potential conflict with a former client. With the prospect of unloading a problem file, she was only too happy to oblige.

I called Watson on the cell phone number he had given the *pro bono* offices. After five rings, an answering machine came on to take a message. Watson had a voice like a chainsaw cutting through wet oak. It didn't sound any too friendly, either. "Leave a message," his taped voice commanded, "you know the drill." It did not end with any 'have a good day' comment.

I left a message, telling him who I was and why I was calling. I left him callback numbers for my cell, office and home. I asked him to give me a call at his first chance regarding my possible representation.

He returned my call that evening at my home number just after dinner.

"This is Rocky Watson. Are you the lawyer who called me?" he challenged more than asked. He had the same loud, harsh voice as his voice message.

"Yes, thank you for calling back. Is this a good time for you to spend a few moments talking about your case?"

"Good as any, I suppose. What do you want to know?"

"Well, tell me what happened and why you want to sue Global?" I asked. No reason not to start at the beginning.

"I should have bought a fuckin' Ford," he growled. "I bought that piece of shit of a car new from Global about five years ago with a lump sum disability payment I got. It's one of those little two-door, four-cylinder models that Global makes. They call it their Carriage model. You're probably not familiar with that car if you're a lawyer," he added. "I don't see too many lawyers driving little cheap cars like that around. They all drive the big Cadillacs or the expensive Jap cars."

His tone caught me off guard. He was hostile and irritatingly baiting. I could see that I was getting a fast introduction to the 'irreconcilable differences' that undoubtedly arose between Watson and his prior *pro bono* lawyer.

"As a matter of fact, Mr. Watson, I know that model very well. Did you get it with the aluminum block, or was it one of the earlier model years when they still had the cast iron block?" I calmly asked. "I can't exactly remember when Global went to the aluminum one on that model."

What I didn't mention was that I had represented Global on a case involving the Carriage model a few years ago where the claimed defect was that the motor mounts in the car had broken, causing the drunk teenage driver to lose control one Saturday night as he rounded a sharp curve up by Lake Okeechobee. He was killed, and his parents sued Global. I tried the case to verdict, and the jury found no liability. In the course of defending the case, I picked up a lot of information about the Carriage model, including the worthless piece of trivia about its aluminum engine block. I used it now to give me credibility with Watson, if that was possible.

"No shit," he grunted. The trivia I offered apparently had the desired inoculative effect. "My car was the first year that they went with the aluminum block," he answered. "I think they made a big mistake with putting an aluminum engine in. The piece of shit burns oil like crazy."

"So, what exactly happened in your accident? Why do you want to sue Global?" I asked, hoping to get him re-focused.

"I'm a big boy, around six-foot-four and two hundred eighty pounds. I was driving that car down a steep exit ramp in one of those indoor parking garages in downtown Miami a couple of months ago. There was an expensive Jap car in front of me as I came towards the bottom. I put on my brakes to stop. Hell, I was only going maybe like five miles an hour. Anyway, as I hit my brakes, my fuckin seat all of a sudden slid forward on its track. I wasn't expecting that to happen. I lost control of my car as my goddamn seat slid forward, and I ended up slamming into the car in front of me in the confusion. I got threatened by the driver of the car I hit for all the damage to his car. He was a goddamn lawyer who worked in the building. My fuckin luck. The son of a bitch said that he didn't care if my story about the seat slipping on its track was true or not. Said I hit his car and he wanted to get paid, and it didn't cost him no money to sue me for it. Asshole," he grumbled.

"Did you end up paying?"

"Hell, I had no choice. I don't have no insurance, and my record stinks the way it is. He wanted three thousand six hundred dollars for the damage, but I didn't have that kind of money," he said, with great irritation. "I ended up paying him one thousand six hundred dollars which was all of the money I had left over from my lump sum disability payment. It goddamn wiped me out! I also had another five hundred dollars of damage to my car that I can't get fixed because I don't have any money. That's why I want to sue those fuckers!"

He didn't seem to have any problem expressing himself, I thought. "Did you receive any physical injuries from the accident?" I asked, hoping for the right answer.

"I got a bloody nose when my face hit the steering wheel, and my knees got bruised when they hit the bottom of the dash, that's all. No big deal. Course, I wasn't wearing a seatbelt. Seatbelts are bullshit," he said, with emphasis. "I've read stories where drivers go into a canal and get trapped in their cars by their seatbelts and drown. No way am I gonna wear any damn belts."

The beauty of a telephone interview is that the person on the other end can't see my reaction. As I listened to Watson, I closed my eyes and slowly shook my head back and forth. I realized, however, that I couldn't afford to be picky under the circumstances.

"Well, if you want me to take the case, Mr. Watson, I would be willing to represent you."

"Yeah," he said after a moment, "I guess you sound like you'd be okay. Do you know anything about taking on a big company like Global? They treated me like shit when I wrote them about the accident and demanded that they pay for the damages. The letter they sent me was a 'kiss my ass' letter if I ever read one."

"Yes, I—"

"You know," he bulldozed on, "I might not be the most important guy around, but I earned my rights to get treated with a little respect. I didn't go over to Iraq and get my ass shot for the hell of it. The way I figure it," he continued, "I went over at the goddamn invitation of Mr. George Fuckin' Bush Junior and his goddamn war machine. And that war machine included Global and all of the other big companies in this country who made a mother fuckin' fortune off the war in the process," he added bitterly.

"Uh-huh," is all I bothered to offer. I could see that he was on a roll.

"You'd think that they would have the courtesy to call me and at least ask me about the accident or to send someone out to look at the seat track before they told me to get lost. Well, they haven't heard the last from me!" he ended angrily.

"Let me ask you something," I said. "Why don't you just bring this in regular small claims court on your own without an attorney? You do know that you can do that, don't you?"

"I've been in small claims court before when I was sued for not paying a repair bill on my car about two years ago. The repair guy that sued me took me to small claims court. I got to see the way that drill went. It's set up to favor the big companies. I sat there waiting for my case to get called, and the judge never did believe the little guy far's I could see. The collection companies would all come in with copies of bills and tell the judge all this bullshit in a smooth talking way, and the judge would try to get a settlement from the little guy. If the little guy didn't cave in, the judge would always go with the company. He did the same with me, and I had to pay the company, even though they overcharged me. No thanks! I don't want nothing to do with that little baby court bullshit. That's why I want a real lawyer for my case in front of a real jury."

I could see that his motive for wanting to bring his case probably had as much—or more—to do with Global's trampling on his feelings of self-respect as it had to do with any seat-track problem in his car. I wasn't going to try and question his motives. He needed a lawyer, and I was only too happy to be his. I had to admit to myself that I felt a little bit guilty not letting him know that his case was going to hopefully help me out on my conflicts problem, but where was the harm? He was going to get free representation from me, and the fact that I might also be helped out by his case in the process, I figured, was only a coincidental plus. However, I did need to discuss one final matter with him before I formally took his case.

"I need to tell you, Mr. Watson, that I've represented Global in auto defect cases on many occasions in the past. I'm going to be contacting Global and letting them know that you've asked me to take this case, but I need to inform you of my previous representation of Global and ask you, point blank, whether you have any objection to my representing you on this case in view of that."

"Doesn't mean monkey shit to me if it doesn't to you. I just don't want you pulling any fuckin punches against them in this case because you used to do work for them. Is that something I gotta worry about?"

"Rocky—may I call you Rocky?"

"Yeah, go ahead." he barreled.

"You don't have to worry about me 'pulling any punches' against Global in your case. The fact is, I don't represent them anymore, and, frankly, I don't have any love for Global or its lawyers. So, that's not a worry, okay?"

"Fair enough. When are you gonna start my lawsuit against them?" he asked impatiently.

"I plan on calling the Global attorney tomorrow or Wednesday and ask them for their consent to be able to represent you in this case. I need their consent because of my prior representation of them. I'm hoping that there won't be a problem. If there is, I'll have to pass on this case, but I'll find another lawyer to take the case. I promise you that." I clearly owed him that much.

"Well, just let me know when ya start it. Do you have my file with all the bills and the letters that went between me and Global?"

"The *pro bono* people told me that they have the complete file. I'll pick it up tomorrow morning. I'll call you back after I speak with Global. In the meantime, is the bad seat track still around?"

"Hell no, I replaced the fuckin' thing. I went to a bone yard and bought me a used one off a wrecked Carriage. I pitched the old one. Why would I want to keep it?"

Oh shit. "That could be a problem. It's important in a case like yours, where you allege that the original seat track was bad," I explained, "to have the original still around for the manufacturer to be able to inspect it."

"Are you saying I'm dead in the water?"

"Well, it's definitely going to be a problem, but we'll just have to try and work around it. We can try and establish the existence of a defect by your testimony regarding the details of its failure in your accident. Hopefully, the problem in the seat track is one that Global has had with others as well. Anyway, let's take it one step at a time," I urged him. "Thanks for your time, Rocky. I'll be in touch."

After I hung up, I sat at the desk in my study for another hour thinking over the best way to approach Willis Cole in order to induce him into giving me his consent to represent Mr. Watson. Knowing Cole, I concluded that the best approach was a full-blown grovel, coupled, if necessary, with a contrite ass kissing. *If only I could swallow my pride to do it.*

CHAPTER 14

THE NEXT MORNING, I called Dade *pro bono* and informed them that I was taking the case, subject to my clearing a conflict I had with Global Motors. They were kind enough to let me send a courier down to their offices to pick up their file on Watson's case, which I received after lunch. I spent a few moments going over the file, which was thin. I was impressed. Initially representing himself, Watson had sent his own complaint letter to Global after the accident. While crudely worded, it got the point across that Watson felt that his seat track assembly had failed and had caused his minor rear-ending of another car. His letter mentioned his bloody nose as well. *Perfect.*

Global's response was from its Customer Relations department. It was a predictable corporate response that I had seen Global use dozens of times over the years on cases I had represented them on. It thanked him for his letter, stated that the company was sorry to hear of his accident, but regretted to inform him that Global was not aware of any problem with the seat track assembly in its Carriage model. It ended by wishing him well, but stated that Global was closing its file on the matter.

I pulled Watson's demand letter and Global's response letter from the file. I emailed both of them to Cole along with a cover letter in which I told Cole that I had been asked to represent Mr. Watson in his "minor County Court suit," which was outlined in Watson's enclosed demand letter. I tried to be as self-effacing as possible, pointing out that I had been unsuccessful thus far in associating with another law firm since I had parted ways with Hunt & Baxter. I was opening my doors as a sole practitioner and was taking what I could get. I ended by saying that I "would be most appreciative if you would permit me to represent Mr. Watson on a *pro bono* basis in his modest claim against Global." I pointed out that it involved a claim for a few thousand dollars for minor property damage to Mr. Watson's car and a few bumps and bruises to his face. I emphasized that I was fulfilling my *pro bono* representation requirements under Florida Bar requirements and would be calling him regarding the matter later in the afternoon.

Around three-thirty I called Cole. He was in his office and had read my email and attachments. He was his predictable self and was not the least bit uncomfortable or apologetic about talking to me. That fact alone made me angry, although I willed myself to act this one out according to the script.

"Willis, as you can appreciate, I'm on my own right now and trying to build a modest practice. It's tough enough without having to fulfill my *pro bono* requirements and not even get paid for it," I added, attempting to sound 'sheepish.'

"It must be tough," he responded sarcastically. "I'm not sure I'd even call this a real case. But, then again, maybe this is more in line with your talents. In fact, maybe you can try and settle it so you don't have to try it," he added in cheap-shot fashion.

It was all I could do to keep from ripping into him.

"Look," I answered, trying to sound embarrassed, "it was stupid of me to even ask. Forget it. I don't want trouble with you or Global. If it's—"

"No, I want you to take it, Culhane. I want you to consider it as a crumb from the Global table," he said, his voice again laden with sarcasm and disdain. "But I've got to tell you, you're not going to make it on your own. You thought that you were so high and mighty, but I guess you're finding out now that you aren't. Well, welcome to the real world. Don't bother me again, okay?" he ended. "I'm not fond of taking calls from second-class lawyers, especially from ones I've fired."

I squeezed the phone in my right hand with all my might to help me keep my focus and contain my temper.

"I'll send you a confirmatory letter," is all that I quietly said. Without another word, Cole hung up.

I slammed the phone down. Grabbing a brass-plated paper weight in the shape of an arrow from the top of my desk, I hurled it across the room, embedding its pointed end with a loud boom in the opposite wall. "Goddammit!" I yelled.

Tina immediately appeared through my open office door.

"What was that?" she asked animatedly. Her eyes then caught the paper weight protruding from the opposite wall at about eye level.

"What happened?"

"It's not worth explaining," I said, still angry. I looked over at the damage done to the wall. "I'm sorry about that. I'll get it fixed."

Tina looked back at me, busily chewing her gum. "You know, I think there's a side to you that we haven't seen yet," she said smiling as she left the room. She poked her head back around the door. "Hang a picture or something over it," she said, nodding at the hole in the wall. "It's about the right height." She popped her gum and was gone.

After cooling down, I dictated and emailed a letter to Cole confirming our conversation and the fact that Global had consented to my representation of Mr. Watson in his suit against Global. I asked him to email me back a copy of my letter with his signature on the signature line I provided at the bottom of the letter to document his consent.

Cole's email reply came about an hour later. He had signed and attached the consent letter I had sent him without any qualifications or reservations expressed.

"Well, you dumb son of a bitch," I said out loud after I read over his consent. "Let's just see who gets the last word on this."

I called Watson the next morning and informed him that I was on the case for sure. I promised to have his suit papers filed within the week. Since his case involved limited monetary damages, it had to be filed in County Court, as opposed to Circuit Court, which handles the more significant cases from a money damages standpoint. The balance of the week was spent on putting out fires on a couple of my cases, as well as taking depositions in two cases which the Hunt associate assigned to those files had been neglecting somewhat, even before my departure from the firm. I certainly couldn't afford to alienate any of my paying clients at the present time, so I vowed to get back into the thick of things in those two cases as quickly as possible.

On Friday morning, I called Eric at work. I told him that I was taking his case against Global.

"Mike, you don't know what this means to me," he said with obvious relief. "Thank you. I knew that you'd come through."

"I'm gratified to take it, but I want to warn you that I expect Global to try to get me kicked off your case since I previously represented them. We aren't out of the woods yet on that issue, but I'm prepared now to deal with it."

"What do we do from here?" he asked.

"I'll sit down with you and go over the general game plan, at least as it exists at this preliminary stage. Eric, I hate to bring this up, but I need to. It's about the money terms of my representation. If it's okay with you, I would propose a flat twenty-five percent contingency fee arrangement, rather than the thirty-three and one-third percent, and forty percent on appeal, that plaintiff's attorneys typically charge here in Florida." I felt embarrassed to talk money with my good friend, but bar rules demanded that I do so.

"Mike, I don't expect you to give me any special deals. I realize that this case will probably end up taking a lot of your time and energy, and I'd feel badly if you shorted yourself on the monetary end of things. I've told you before; this case is not about money from my standpoint, so I don't care how much you take. I'm in this case to keep this same thing from happening to other people, and to prove that Jenny didn't cause her own death or the injuries to Ryan."

"I understand that, but you're family to me just the same. It's a flat twenty-five percent. Enough said."

I drafted an engagement letter to Eric confirming that I was taking his case. In view of the anticipated objections from Global after the proverbial hit the fan, I wanted a neat paper trail showing that I didn't accept Eric's case until after Global had expressly consented to my representation against them in Watson's case.

Around five-thirty, Tina routed a call to me from Sandy.

"Hello Boss," she opened with.

I had forgotten that today was 'the day' she was getting fired. "Good! Tell me, how did it go?"

"Perfectly, if one can use that term describing your own firing," she laughed. "I called Harrington this morning and scheduled an appointment with him in his office at four o'clock this afternoon. At the meeting, I told him that I was not happy with the direction that my career was taking with the firm, and that I needed to address some basic issues. He must have known that it was an important meeting because he had Gunther in his office when I got there."

"Any surprises?"

"Thankfully, no. I was direct. I informed Harrington that I disagreed with his decision to re-assign me to the estate planning team. I had worked for many years developing a products liability expertise, and, quite frankly, I viewed my transfer as a punitive measure. I told them that I was refusing to be re-assigned from the Global team, and I wanted to know how they planned to deal with that fact."

"And?"

"It was a short meeting," she quipped. "Harrington was undoubtedly ecstatic at my reaction, I'm sure. I had barely gotten my refusal out of my mouth when he looked at me and told me that I was 'impertinent' and 'insubordinate.' He told me that I could consider myself fired as of that moment, and that I was to gather all of my personal effects from the offices and to be gone by the end of the day."

"And how did you take this firing?"

"I expressed my shock and outrage and stormed out of his office," she said over her laughter. "It took me about half an hour to collect my personal things, and I was out of there. And get this—Harrington had the nerve to stand right outside my office as I was packing up. As if I would be taking any of their precious property!" she said indignantly. "The jerk!"

"Well, the guy is consistent, that's for sure. I'm sure that he fully expected you to go into your computer and destroy data bases out of spite. That's the way he thinks," I said, shaking my head. "I'm sure that he also wanted to prevent you from downloading any of the litigation forms you've been using and from taking them with you to your next place of employment."

"Too late. I already downloaded a copy of all those forms first thing this morning onto a couple of thumb drives. They're in my purse as we speak," she laughed. "I spent a ton of time creating many of those myself on my own time after work over the course of the last few years, and I'll be damned if I'm not taking a copy of them with me now!"

"Great, that'll save us a big investment in time to develop our own. Are you ready to dig in on Monday? My cases, limited as they are, are starting to heat up. And I suspect that things are going to get a lot worse when I start the products case against Global on the Mesa rollover."

"So, you took on that case for sure?" she asked.

"Yeah, and I think that it's going to get very ugly and very nasty before it's all over. I'll tell you all about it next week when you start. Sandy, it's going to be fun working with you again."

"I've got to tell you, I want to start enjoying going to work again. It hasn't been that way at Hunt since you left and they started treating me like I was a leper or something. It will be fun. I'll see you bright and early Monday, Mike."

CHAPTER 15

I HAD WATSON come by my office early the next week to talk over his case facts and to approve the county court civil complaint I had drafted in his case against Global.

His appearance matched his telephone voice and demeanor. Under his very fleshy exterior were the remnants of a guy who had once been a ruggedly handsome man. He was every bit of the two hundred eighty pounds he alluded to on the phone, yet he managed to carry it surprisingly well on his big, bony frame. His brown hair, now heavily streaked with gray, was long and pulled back into a pony tail. His hair didn't look like it had seen shampoo for a while, and it was obvious that Rocky Watson didn't really give a damn if people cared either. I assumed that his war injuries must have caused the slight limp he carried in his left leg as he entered my office. He was wearing dirty jeans and a Harley-Davidson T-shirt that was more of a well worn gray than its original white color. He had two or three days' growth of beard stubble.

Tina brought him back to my office where I offered him a chair. A heavy wave of body odor accompanied him into my office, and I had to suppress a grin when I saw Tina's raised eyebrows as she closed the door to my office, leaving the two of us alone.

Despite his 'let-go-of-himself' exterior, he had extremely piercing and intelligent-looking green eyes. I noticed that the green in his eyes matched the shade of green in the tattoo of the large dragon that had been stenciled onto his huge forearm.

I like to obtain a little personal information about my clients. It makes it a lot easier to communicate with them about case issues and helps me develop a personality for the case that fits the client's. Despite my efforts, Watson wasn't exactly what I'd call 'forthcoming' in talking about himself or his past. From the little that I was able to drag out of him, he got into some minor trouble with the law right after he graduated from high school in a small town somewhere in the middle of Nebraska. Rather than face jail time, the judge, who knew the local recruiter, gave him the option to join the Marines. He opted for the Marines and was inducted. He did one tour in Iraq, only to get caught in an intense fire fight while on a patrol two days before he was scheduled to return to the states. He ended up coming home, but with a bullet-shattered left hip, a Purple Heart and an inner anger that had not yet subsided. When he admitted to the Purple Heart, he reached into his pocket with a sardonic smile, pulled a key chain out and held it up for me to see. I took it and examined it. There was his Purple Heart medal. He had drilled a hole in the medal itself through which he had threaded a leather string which now held his keys. He was one of only two survivors on his squad from that firefight, and he spent a great deal of time in a couple of veterans' hospitals recovering. I suspected that his injuries were as profoundly mental as they were physical. He made a passing comment that after he got his hip repaired, he had to spend a little time in 'another place to get my head screwed on again.' I didn't pursue that comment.

He was struggling to keep his life in control, working at different laborer day jobs in Miami, ranging from working as a dishwasher, to driving tow trucks, to helping as a loader for a couple of moving companies. From the job history he gave me, he apparently had a problem sticking with any job for more than a few weeks. He was fiercely independent and displayed a feisty disposition, as I had already witnessed, first-hand.

When Tina came in after ten minutes to offer him some coffee, he just looked at her and growled: "No, did I ask for any?" She quickly apologized, looked at me with a confused look on her face and swiftly escaped my office.

Rocky Watson wasn't going to win any personality contests.

He lived by himself in a room off North Biscayne Boulevard. I recognized his address as being in a tough area, inhabited by a lot of people who were either down-and-out or headed in that direction. He would be just another non-descript person in that area of the city.

I obtained all of the case facts I needed for the time being from him in order to get the suit started. As drafted, his suit papers asked for Global to pay him for the damage to his car, to reimburse him for the repair damages he had to pay the other driver and to pay him an unspecified sum for his personal injuries, i.e., the non-serious injuries to his face and leg. He said that if Global paid him a total of three thousand dollars, he'd be a happy camper. He wasn't worried that the replacement driver's seat he put in the car would fail like the original one. A buddy, he explained, welded the seat track to the seat position that fit him when he drove the car. I guess he didn't expect, or care, if other people who drove his car might need, or prefer to have, a different seat position. With his prickly personality, however, I didn't think friends, of any size, driving his car were going to pose a real problem.

Sandy had done some quick checking with the National Highway Transportation Safety Administration and found that there had been no federal safety recalls issued by Global for the driver's seat in any of the Carriage model cars. However, NHTSA documents indicated that there had been problems with front seats on some of the other Global models that year suddenly slipping in their seat track under certain conditions. The problem in those other models, it appeared from the information obtained from NHTSA, was not of design, but of manufacture. Some springs used in the holding mechanism that kept the spring-loaded pawl in place, so that the seat wouldn't slip, were metallurgically bad. Over time, the coils in the steel spring lost their 'spring,' causing the seat to fail if it was subjected to a substantial load, such as a heavy driver in the seat during heavy braking. I suspected that this was the problem that Watson had experienced. Unfortunately, his having thrown out the seat track assembly, which included the original coiled spring that came with the Carriage, eliminated the direct evidence of any defect itself.

After providing the balance of the information I needed, Watson approved the complaint I had drafted and was on his way. Not a guy at a loss of words to express his feelings, his parting directions to me were pretty clear: "Kick their fuckin' asses!" he barked as he walked out of my office.

The timing of his departure actually couldn't have come sooner. After an hour with him, I was about to pass out from the over-powering presence of his body odor. Tina popped in my office two minutes after he had gone spraying air freshener out of an aerosol can all over the place.

"I'm not saying a word," she said as she shook her head and sprayed.

I filed Watson's suit the following Monday and had Global's registered agent in Florida served with the suit papers. Global didn't use Hunt & Baxter for small suits when the dollar amount, like Watson's case, was under fifteen thousand dollars. Instead, it used a sole practitioner out of Miami by the name of Jessie Mears. Mears also handled Global's 'lemon law' suits and arbitrations since Hunt charged too much for these types of cases. Jessie was a nice guy who I had always gotten along with very well. He was a former assistant U. S. attorney who left the government ten years ago to go out onto his own in the civil arena.

He called me two days later after getting a copy of the suit papers faxed to him by the registered agent.

"Mike, I didn't think I would ever see the day when I saw your name representing a plaintiff against Global. Think you might have a possible conflict?" It was classic Jessie understatement.

"I would have if Global hadn't expressly consented to my representation in this case," I explained. "I spoke with Willis Cole who gave me the green light to go ahead and represent this *pro bono* plaintiff. I'll send you over a copy of my letter to Cole, as well as a copy of his response to me approving it." Cole had merely taken the confirmation letter I had emailed to him, scribbled the words "OK" on it, signed it and emailed it back to me.

"I'd appreciate that, Mike. I figured that it must have been something like that. What's the scoop with this monster of a case?" he asked with a good deal of humor in his voice.

"Watson says that he had a defect on the seat track mechanism of his Carriage. He was coming down a steep structure in a parking garage when it suddenly slipped. It caused him to lose control and his focus as his seat shot forward. He ended up plowing into some lawyer in his new Lexus who was immediately ahead of him."

He laughed when he heard that. "Anybody I know?"

"A criminal defense lawyer by the name of Pryor. Know him?"

"Pryor? Barry Pryor?"

"That's the guy," I answered.

"That's perfect!" he chortled. "Yeah, I knew him from my days at the U.S. Attorney's Office. If your client was going to rear-end someone, it couldn't have happened to a nicer target. Pryor is a real piece of work. I'm sure that he hasn't changed his spots over the years. Is the seat track assembly still in the car and available for inspection and photographing by my investigator?"

"No. My client was so angry over it that he took it out of the car after Global wrote him and told him to get lost. He welded a used replacement seat he bought out of a bone yard in the car so that it wouldn't move again."

"You're kidding me, aren't you?"

"No," I laughed. "Mr. Watson is a 'can do' kind of guy. As far as I can see, he gave Global the opportunity to inspect it when he wrote them about it. It appears that your client chose to decline an inspection when they claimed that it wasn't their problem. So, Watson engaged in a little self help to fix the defect when Global wouldn't fix it themselves and pay for the damages."

"Good luck trying to get anywhere on this case, Mike," he chuckled. "You and I both know that you're pissing in the wind if you think that you're going to win a products liability case after having disposed of the product before trial. You know probably better than I do that Global doesn't settle cases where the product has been destroyed like this one has."

"Well, I guess that I'm going to just have to prove the existence of a defect by circumstantial evidence. It's difficult to do, but I don't have any choice, do I?"

"Sounds to me that the best choice you had was to punt on taking this loser of a case to begin with. Well, I'll be sending out an answer and some discovery demands early next week. I may need an extension of time to answer the first round of discovery demands you served with the suit papers. Give me an additional two weeks, okay?"

"No problem. Just drop me an email to confirm the extension."

"Mike, I realize that this is *pro bono* for you, so I won't make you jump over too many expensive hoops."

"Thanks Jessie. I appreciate that. I'll be talking to you."

I CALLED SANDY into my office to chart out a list of 'to do' tasks that needed to be done on the Hawkins case. The other lawyers from whom I leased the office space agreed to let me use the only other remaining space in the office as Sandy's office. It was an area next to Tina's desk just big enough for a desk and a file cabinet. The trade-off was that they were free to use Sandy from time to time on isolated projects of theirs, at no charge. Sandy was fine with the arrangement, although she looked a little surprised at how small and open her work area was. Her office back at Hunt was lavish by our spartan standards.

"I want you to get a complete copy of all the photos taken by the police and any news photographers who were at the Hawkins accident scene, including the Channel Seven film footage. They might have some 'witness marks' in them, like tire smears, that we might be able to use in the case."

"They're already ordered," she said. "Channel Seven was the only station that sent a crew out, and they suggested that I come by the news station to look at their archived videotape footage to see if I want to order a copy. I've set that up for next week."

"Perfect. Also, get your hands on a copy of the final motor vehicle homicide report and any photos that the medical examiner may have taken of Jenny for evidence purposes. I don't expect to find anything helpful from those photos, but I know that Global will get them, and I want to be on the same page as they are."

"Do you have any special information sources you want me to be looking into regarding the liability issues surrounding the design of the Mesa?"

I had my shirt sleeves rolled up at my desk and my tie loosened at the neck. I was jotting the assignments down on my own pad as well.

"First thing," I replied, "check with NHTSA to see if they have anything that might be of help to us on the Mesa model. Who knows? Maybe we'll get lucky and find that there have been product recall investigations underway for rollover complaints or fuel system fires. Also, call the Institute of Consumer

Products Safety. They have a database of problems which consumers are experiencing with various car models. I'm not sure exactly where they get their data, but I know from a couple of the Global cases that I was in at Hunt, that some of the plaintiff lawyers had gotten nuggets of good stuff from that institute from time to time. It's worth a shot."

"You have to be a paying member to receive information from that institute. Don't you remember? We had to pay something like three hundred dollars to have them do a data search in the *Coffey* case that you and I worked on? Do you want me to go ahead and pay that?"

"Oh damn, that's right. I forgot." The subject of costs reminded me of what was becoming an unpleasant and uncomfortable subject. I had received my first check from Hunt for my partnership contribution return, but it was being used up quickly. I had to buy malpractice insurance out of my own pocket for the first time in my life. At Hunt, it had always been paid for by the firm, and nobody really cared what it cost since it was inconsequential in the overall scheme of things. There was plenty of money coming in to cover those costs, just like the electricity costs, rent, etc. The economics of being on my own were starting to hurt. The malpractice insurance alone cost me nine thousand five hundred for the year, and that was only for seven hundred fifty thousand dollars of coverage per year. Between that cost, the rent, the secretarial sharing, my paralegal, and everything else, I could see that I would be rapidly draining the savings that I had put away if I didn't start bringing some revenue in pretty damn fast.

"Yeah," I sighed, "go ahead and pay it. We're going to need to use that membership in other cases anyway. Also, call over to Mark Pangburn and ask him if he would do me the favor of running an inquiry in The National Trial Lawyers' Association newsletter to see if any other plaintiff lawyers are handling any cases against Global involving a Mesa rollover or fire. I'm sure he won't object. I've done him a few favors." NTLA, as that organization was known, also charged for membership, and only members were entitled to use their national newsletter for inquiries like that. Defense attorneys were not allowed to join. I didn't want to spend more money at this stage joining another organization. Besides, I still didn't view myself as a plaintiff's lawyer. Old habits truly do die hard.

"Do you think that there's a problem with the fuel system on the Mesa?" Sandy asked.

"I don't know. From the highway patrol photos, it looks like it landed pretty hard on its side during the rollover. I suspect that one of the fuel lines or fasteners was damaged during the violence, but I need to check out all of the possibilities."

"Are you ordering up an engineering survey of the accident scene? I'll need to know so that I can make arrangements to coordinate the scene visit with the surveyor."

"Yes, we're going to have to get one. The accident reconstructionist will need one for sure," I said. "I hesitate to ask, but do you remember what the surveyor charged us for that scene survey he did for us in the *Nelson* case?" The irony here is the fact that I had probably hired and paid for twenty accident scene surveys over the course of the last year-and-a-half in the various cases I had handled for Global back at Hunt. But I couldn't even tell you what each had cost. Global's defense philosophy was to give its defense attorneys *carte blanche* authority when it came to defense costs. The focus was on beating the plaintiff—not on scrimping on costs. As a result, at Hunt, I didn't care about the costs, only that the expert was good, prepared and effective in front of a jury. Now, costs were a big priority for me. I knew that Eric was required to pay for all of the experts, including their expert witness fees, their time spent in working the case up, as well as their travel and lodging costs for depositions and trial time. However, I also knew that he wasn't Fort Knox. He and Jenny had always lived very modestly and frugally, especially since Jenny had stopped working in order to stay home and raise the kids. Eric was not going to be able to pay for all of these costs without my helping him out by advancing a good share of them.

"If I remember correctly, we paid that firm over six thousand dollars for the scaled drawing, the elevations and the various skid marks on the intersection made by the tires of the vehicles. Do you want me to use the same firm?"

"You're kidding me! That's grand theft! We didn't pay it, did we?"

Sandy looked at me like I was nuts. "Sure we paid it. That's the going rate, Mike, look, if money is going to be tight on this case, should we try to get by without one and maybe use a scaled aerial photograph that we can blow up? We did that in the *Heifitz* case, if you remember, and it really worked out pretty well I thought."

"Yeah, you're right, it did work out well. What did that run?"

"It was a lot cheaper. A scaled aerial, including the costs of the airplane and the enlargement should only run about eighteen hundred dollars. There's nothing unusual about the interstate in the area of the crash site. Everything is flat and pretty basic. I drove past it yesterday to get an idea of the area."

"That sounds a lot better. Let's do it. The accident scene is flat, and there's nothing at this scene that a scaled aerial photo wouldn't be able to capture for use by the accident reconstructionist. See," I added, smiling, "I knew there was a reason that I hired you back."

"Do I get a commission on the cost savings?" She smiled sweetly.

"Nice try," I laughed. "We're going to need a good accident reconstructionist on this case, particularly in view of the highway patrol's accident report saying that Jenny was speeding and not paying attention."

"Who do you have in mind?"

"I'm thinking about talking to Townsend. He doesn't have any cases that I was using him on for Global when I left Hunt. He's good."

"Do you really think that he'll take on a case testifying against Global? He's probably done a dozen cases for Global that you had him on."

"I'll use my charm. The fact is, there aren't a hell of a lot of plaintiff's accident reconstruction experts that I've seen over the years that I thought were very good. I'll give him a call directly and let you know. Until I get a handle on some of this preliminary information, I'm not prepared to figure out what kind of design expert we're going to need."

"That leaves us with damages. What are your thoughts now as to who you want to use there?"

I started absently drumming the pencil against the desktop as I thought. "Clearly, we'll want to use the burn team at Jackson Memorial that is working with Ryan. I got a chance to observe the burn specialist physician who heads up the team speaking with Eric over at the hospital. He'll make an excellent witness. Let's figure out who the primary nurses are, as well as the plastic surgeons assigned to him. We'll probably need a vocational rehab expert, a psychologist and an economist to pin down the numbers on his loss of earning capacity." The specter of costs again nagged at me. None of these experts would be cheap. *Shit!*

"How is the little boy doing, anyway?" She lowered her legal pad when she asked the question.

"Not well. I spoke with Eric last night. He was very down. The head doctor, this guy I was telling you about, Dr. Stuart Olive, told him that Ryan has pneumonia now. The smoke which he ingested during the fire damaged his lungs, and he's taken a turn for the worse. He's optimistic, but the little guy is really hurting."

"Oh my god, it just won't stop, will it?"

"No, it doesn't, and Sarah is having some serious psychological adjustment problems on top of all this. It's not good for Eric or his family right now. He's burning the candle at both ends trying to deal with the kids' problems as well as his own adjustment problems. I don't know how he does it and still tries to keep on top of his job. He has me worried."

"It sounds like we may need to consider psychologist testimony for Eric and Sarah as well, Mike. Shall I start looking at that?"

"I don't think that we have any alternative. At this point, let's just get some names of potential experts who have expertise in this area. I don't want to address the subject yet with Eric, at least about his own personal situation. He's pretty old-fashioned about things like that, you know, the old 'I don't need any help from anybody else to get me through this' attitude."

"Well, I'll get on this right away," Sandy said as she rose from one of my client chairs. Since coming to work for me, she also started wearing more casual attire to work. She had asked if I cared. I didn't. She had on blue jeans and a pressed powder-blue work shirt. Her blonde hair was pulled back in a pony tail.

"Do you mind if I take off a little early today? I'm going down to Key West for the weekend, and I wanted to get a jump on the Friday traffic headed down there."

"What's going on there this weekend?"

"There is a triathlon tomorrow morning in Key West. It sounds like fun. I'll be back Sunday afternoon."

"Sounds great. Be careful with the traffic going down," I added. The two-lane road down to the Keys was an extremely dangerous one. It was infested with tourists who were holding up traffic looking at the sights, boats on trailers being pulled behind pickups and others who had too much to drink who were hell bent on passing the above two groups. The combination made for a lot of traffic problems.

"Okay, Dad," she laughed as she walked out of my office. "You ought to get out of here early yourself."

That was actually the best advice I had received all day.

CHAPTER 16

THE PROBLEM I faced in choosing experts for Eric's case was that the best experts in the area of automobile liability were usually those who routinely worked for the insurance companies and the auto manufacturers. They had the money to spend. They identified the best reconstructionists around the country, hired them, and fed them a steady and lucrative diet of defense cases to feed on. These experts, oftentimes low paid professors of engineering at local colleges or universities, were only too happy to supplement their modest salaries with consulting jobs at two hundred to two hundred fifty dollars an hour for work done on defense files. Moreover, after building a profitable consulting business on the side for these clients, many of the professors abandoned their university jobs and set up consulting practices on a full time basis, specializing in representing—you guessed it—insurance companies and manufacturers.

In return for the financial feedbag they provided, the auto manufacturers in particular, demanded absolute loyalty and service from their outside experts. The expert was expected to stay "on the defense" side of the fence. If an expert was foolish enough to take a case against the auto industry, word of that fact would spread quickly among the defense lawyers and their counterparts of in-house attorneys at the auto companies. The punishment for "going over to the dark side," as it was often called, was usually swift and always severe: that expert would never again receive any work for the auto companies. The feedbag was pulled and the expert left to starve.

There was a hell of an irony to all this, I thought, as I sat at my desk and sketched out my potential experts. A month ago, I had been a part of that system. *Live by the sword, die by the sword.*

Most of the accident reconstruction experts who testified on behalf of plaintiffs against auto manufacturers that I had run up against in South Florida when I represented Global were not appealing. They were either not very experienced, were 'hired guns' who would give any 'expert' opinion they were paid to give by a plaintiff's lawyer, or simply weren't very competent.

In Eric's case, I knew I was going to need a good reconstructionist. With a fatality, a badly burned infant, and two other grieving family members, Global would be investing a lot of money in defending the case. The reconstruction expert would set the stage for the design expert since it was his job to put the pieces of the accident puzzle together and explain what the Mesa's movements were both immediately before and during the accident event.

I called Seth Cohen, an extremely capable plaintiff's lawyer that I had litigated against in the past. Seth and I had become decent friends over the years. I figured he would be a good resource for the name of an expert that could help me out.

Cohen was becoming a hard guy to find in the office ever since he had hit on a "bad baby" medical malpractice case a year ago. He walked away with something over three million in attorney's fees from the huge jury verdict his client was awarded. I got lucky when I called his office hoping to talk to him. He was in, having just returned from a fishing trip to Belize.

"Any suggestions?" I asked after outlining the basic facts.

"How serious a case do you think you have?"

"Serious. I've got a fatality and a seriously burned infant that survived. They're friends of mine."

"I guess what I'm really asking is whether you have the money to pump into this case? If you've got the cash and the willingness and ability to gamble it on winning the case or forcing a successful settlement, then I could direct you to some very competent reconstructionists that I have used in other cases. But they're expensive as hell."

"What kind of money are you talking about for them? I have no idea what plaintiff's experts are charging these days. I've been hanging around with the defense boys too long." The subject of further outlays of money again caused me to twinge inside.

"Something in the neighborhood of fifty thousand to sixty thousand dollars per expert after all the smoke clears in a case like the one you're talking about. That's what the very good ones are going for."

"Holy shit. You've got to be kidding. That's a problem," I lamented. "The client isn't flush with cash, and I'm … uh, kind of just getting my own practice set up. As it is, I'm sure that I'm going to have to front the costs of the case expenses for my clients, so I don't have a lot to spend."

Cohen was quiet for a moment, thinking. "I'll tell you what," he finally offered. "While I haven't used him myself, and I can't therefore vouch for his abilities, I heard there is a guy over in Ft. Myers that moved down to Florida a year ago that is doing some reconstruction work. I was told by one of the plaintiff's attorneys I know from that side of the state that he's good and pretty inexpensive. He's a retired highway patrolman from Pennsylvania who did a lot of accident reconstruction for the Pennsylvania highway patrol over the years. He doesn't have much in the way of formal degrees though, so he's vulnerable in that regard."

"Do you have a name?"

I could hear Cohen type away at his computer, searching for the contact information. After a minute, he gave it to me. "The name is Ralph Cargill. All I've got is a telephone number and an address." He gave me the details, and I thanked him for the help.

No sooner had I hung up the phone when Tina yelled into my office from her desk. "Mike, I have Liz on the phone. She's been holding and says that she needs to talk to you. I'll transfer."

"Hi. What's up?" I asked.

"It's Ryan. It's his lungs. One of them has collapsed from the pneumonia, and they've put him on a respirator to deal with it. I'm over at the hospital with Eric right now," she said, crying softly.

"How bad is it? Is he going to make it?"

"They don't know. He's in such bad condition from the burn injuries and the grafting that it's a terrible assault for his system to deal with right now. Eric is a wreck," she managed.

"I'll be right over."

I hung up, told Tina to cancel a late afternoon deposition I had scheduled, and jumped into the car for the hospital.

When is it going to stop? I asked myself on the way over.

CHAPTER 17

LIZ CALLED ME at work the next afternoon to report that Ryan was responding favorably to the treatment. Eric had called her from the hospital, stating that the damaged lung had been re-inflated and was functioning well. The infection seemed to be under control, and the medical team was encouraged. According to Liz, Dr. Olive and his team were amazed at the young boy's stubborn resilience. She thought that Ryan's resilience had as much to do with Eric's devotion to his son. Eric had stayed by Ryan's bed all night long. When his son had shown the improvement, he went home, showered, shaved and headed off to work to catch up. He was concerned that he wasn't pulling his share of the load at the office.

"He's an incredible father," Liz commented over the phone.

"I know he is. I just hope he isn't burning himself out."

IT WAS AFTER ten-thirty when I finally got home from the office that night. I had stayed late trying to catch up on matters that I was behind on. The girls were in bed and already asleep, so I quietly went into their bedrooms and planted a goodnight kiss on their cheeks.

Liz was sitting at the eating table off the kitchen working on some type of list when I came into the room. I grabbed a bottle of Corona out of the fridge, opened it and joined her.

"What are you working on?" I asked as I grabbed the day's pile of mail sitting on the table and started to rummage through it.

"I made the mistake of volunteering to help Father Murphy organize and computerize an updated list of the school's alumni," she said rather absently. "It's way out of date."

"Oh no, does this mean what I think it means? Another pinch by 'The Artful Dodger' for more money?" I asked in my best Irish brogue. 'The Artful Dodger' was my reference to Father Patrick Rooney Murphy, the principal of St. Cecilia's. Murphy, born in Ireland, still spoke with a heavy Gaelic accent. He could charm even the most difficult parents and alumni into supporting the school with their financial donations. He usually marshaled a group of mothers into all types of volunteer projects around the school, including fundraising events. From what I could see, the man probably belonged in prison for all the pockets of alumni and parents he had 'picked' with his fund raisers. He had almost single-handedly kept the school financially sound and committed to academic excellence.

She looked across at me and laughed. "You've got that right. Father Murphy wants to send a letter out next month seeking money to build a new high-tech computer center for the students at the school. We're not state of the art as far as he's concerned."

Being a Catholic school, which received limited financial support from the diocese, St. Cecilia's was forever looking for funds to stay in business and provide an excellent education for its students.

"I'm sure we'll be on the list as well," she added as she lowered her head and again focused her attention to the list she was working on.

"I'm sure we will, too," I mumbled. Well, I thought, this may be one year where we're going to have to give a little less. The well is dry.

Liz went back to her project and I started rummaging through the day's mail. "Jesus Christ" I said out loud as I started going over a new bill that had come in. I put my bottle of beer down sharply on the table. "I don't believe it."

"What is it?" Liz asked. My eruption had taken her by surprise, and she put down the document that she had been working on.

"It's this damn house, that's what. Did you look over this escrow summary we got from the mortgage company?" I handed her the piece of paper. It showed that we had to come up with another four thousand dollars to cover the fact that the escrow amount we had been paying with our monthly mortgage payment had been insufficient to cover the major increase that we had experienced in our property taxes and homeowner's insurance. Ever since Hurricane Andrew blew through South Florida in 1992, the insurance companies had pumped up the homeowners' insurance rates dramatically. In addition, the property taxes on the island homes off Las Olas had also been going nuts over the last few years, especially since the Las Olas shopping and restaurant area had become the hottest commercial area in Ft. Lauderdale. I knew that my mortgage escrow was going to be short, but I hadn't figured on a shortfall of this amount.

"Calm down, will you? We have a shortfall, Michael. We've had them before and we'll have them again. What's with you, anyway? We've had escrow shortfalls every year we have been in this house, haven't we?"

"And don't we also have the next big installment payment due this month on the girl's tuition at St. Cecilia's? That's another five thousand dollars. And what other damn bills are out there that are waiting in line to bite us in the ass!" My frustration was evident.

Liz sat back in her chair and studied me for a moment. "What's this all about Michael," she calmly asked. "I know you well enough to know that something else is eating at you. Talk to me."

She had a calming effect on me. "It's the money, Liz," I finally said, lowering my voice. "It's the damn money. I don't know how we're going to make it happen. We're living the lifestyle we have been living for the last ten years, but I don't see how I can keep it going. I don't make the money I used to make. I don't think that we can afford to keep it up."

"How bad is it?" Liz didn't get involved in the details of the family's finances.

"It's getting bad. I used up the partnership capital return I received from Hunt on a ton of stuff that I needed to pay for in my new practice—malpractice insurance, rent, a computer, the computerized legal research system, stationery, and salary payments for Tina and Sandy. I've had to dig into our savings to cover the remainder of those expenses. And the problem is that I don't see any big light at the end of the tunnel—at least not in the immediate future. I've started getting some revenue coming in from some of the files that I took with me from Hunt, but there just isn't enough to cover all of the expenses in the short run. And on top of all of those expenses, I'm staring at a big outlay of costs to pay for some of the experts and costs on Eric's case against Global that are going to start up shortly."

Liz was quietly taking all of this in, allowing me to vent.

"Do you want to know something scary?" I asked after a moment. "For the first time in my life, I feel that we could have a serious financial problem as a family. It's a feeling that I'm having a tough time dealing with. We always used to have the year-end bonus at Hunt to bail us out of any cash flow squeezes. That's not there now."

"What are our options?"

"I've been mulling that over for the last couple of nights in bed."

"Is that why you were thrashing around? Why didn't you say something, Michael?"

"No sense getting both of us worked up over it. The way I see it, we have three basic options: increase family revenue, shave family expenses, or some combination of the two."

"Well, I can try to get on full time at the clinic. I ..."

"Liz, I don't want you to go full time. I've always been able to support you, and I'm not going to stop now, damn it."

"Oh spare me from that mentality. We need the money, Michael, and that's all there is to it. I told you when you made the decision to go it on your own that we were in this together, and I meant that. Besides, with Ann and Erin in high school, I can only do so much volunteer work. I was getting bored with that stuff anyway."

"Liz, I don't want to panic about this. If we can focus on some cost cutting, I'd like to try that first."

"I understand, but I've made up my mind. Save your breath."

She had that look of determination, which she displayed periodically in some of our discussions. In our early years of marriage, I had been foolish enough to try to change her mind after she had expressed that look. I no longer wasted the energy. We had been married too long.

"Hey, I really appreciate this. I want you to know that. I'm hoping to get my practice to take off one of these days, and then you can—"

She put up her hand to end the discussion on that issue. "The only reason I stopped working full time years ago was to raise the kids. I think it's time for me to get back into it full time anyway, so I think that it's fortuitous that this is happening right now to get me redirected. Besides," she added smiling, "it'll probably be better for me to be working full time when you have your major thrombo from working so hard anyway."

"You're a vicious woman. You know that, don't you?"

She laughed. "Now, do you have any suggestions for cost savings around here?"

"Yeah, I do. I'm going to drop our club membership over at the Yacht Club. It's too expensive, and we really don't use it that much. Besides, if I want to take a client out, there's no reason why I can't simply take them to a regular restaurant like the rest of humanity." I took a swig of my beer. Liz reached over as I was putting it down and took a draw on it as well.

"There's really no reason to keep using the cleaning lady either," Liz injected. "We're paying her one hundred dollars a week, and the girls and I can just as easily clean the house on Saturday mornings. I did the house clean-up before we could afford to have someone else do it for me, and there's no reason that our daughters can't learn how to do it as well."

"Good, that will help. I'm also thinking that we need to cut back on vacations and keep any that we do take short and simple, like we used to do when we were younger, you know? I'm not going to have a lot of time for vacations the way it is, but I'm thinking that instead of going out to Colorado like we were talking about, that we should maybe rent a cheap beach cottage over by Sanibel Island or down in the Keys. I figure that alone would save us three to four thousand."

"That's fine with me, but I'm not doing any camping. Can we reach agreement on that fine point?" she laughed. She hated camping, and so did I.

"I was also thinking that we should probably pass on the girls going to camp this summer. That alone would save us four thousand dollars in their airfare and camp tuition. I really hate to do that, but the reality is that we need to save the money."

Liz nodded her head. "If it has to be, it has to be."

"I know, but I know how much they look forward to camp and seeing their old friends."

"Michael, I hope you're not giving any thought to pulling the girls out of St. Cecilia's. I consider that school to be an investment rather than an expense. They can't get the same education at a public school. Do you agree?"

"Yeah, I do. Their tuition is a hell of a hit, but we'll just have to find a way to make it work, that's all there is to it." *How, I didn't really know at the moment.*

We went over some other miscellaneous cost-cutting moves, with emphasis on household items like dropping HBO, reducing the number of visits by the company that sprayed fertilizer and chemicals on the yard and plants, and other smaller items.

"How are we doing?" Liz finally asked after we had exhausted the list of potential cost-saving moves. "Are we out of the woods?"

"These will definitely help, but it's still going to depend on my practice. The cases and the money both have to increase. If not, we still have a problem."

"How are you doing on getting new cases?"

"I've received a few new ones from the clients I took from Hunt, but I'm not getting the types of referrals that I had hoped. That little newspaper article in the *Gazette* on my departure from Hunt probably has a lot to do with that fact. I think everybody has the impression that I've got a big problem of some type, and that Hunt had to ask me to leave."

"What can you do to dispel that?"

"I've just got to try some cases and win them. Other attorneys have to see that I 'haven't lost it.' I think that the referrals will start up again. In the meantime, I'm working on some of the business clients I have to send me some of their non-litigation work, like drafting business contracts, leases and that type of stuff. I've gotten some of that type of new work from three of them so far."

"Do you know how to do that kind of work? You haven't drafted any serious business agreements have you?"

"Hey, I'm learning how to fake it," I laughed. "Seriously, the key is to get the work in the door. I'll figure out how to get it done right after that. I'm not in a position to be too picky right now. The funny thing is that I'm kind of enjoying the challenge of doing entirely different things than just pure old litigation. That's all I've done since I got out of law school."

"I just don't want you dropping over dead, Michael. You're working too hard right now the way it is. We don't see you much during the week, and you're either working in your study on the weekends or your mind is on your work. It's not good, and I think that you need to ease off a little. I don't want to end up a widow. You and I have a lot of living and traveling to do, and the girls need you around to harass them when they start dating, okay?"

"All right," I solemnly answered, "I'll work on it." It was my standard response. She just looked at me and said nothing. We had this conversation frequently.

I started to reach for my beer to finish the last swig left in it.

"Michael!" she said suddenly, looking with fear in her eyes over my shoulder towards the doors leading out to the backyard, "there's someone out there! Look, right there!" she said thrusting her pointed hand towards the doors.

I turned sharply in the chair, looking immediately towards the doors to which she had pointed. Jumping quickly out of my chair, I took a few steps towards the doors. "What did you see?" I asked excitedly.

"Honey ...?" Liz said evenly, an odd inflection in her voice.

I turned quickly around to her. She was calmly sitting in her chair at the table just finishing the last dregs in my bottle of beer. She put it down and grinned. "Thanks for saving me the last sip."

"You bitch!" I quietly said. She just laughed, got up and tossed the empty bottle in the recycling bin under the sink.

"Gee, I could have sworn I saw someone there. Hmmm. It must have been a reflection on the glass."

Goddamn it. She had done it again.

CHAPTER 18

THE FOLLOWING DAY, I spoke by phone with Ralph Cargill, the accident reconstructionist recommended to me by Seth Cohen. Cargill was very pleasant and direct when I interviewed him by phone from his home in Ft. Myers on the West coast of Florida.

Cargill, speaking in almost a surprising, easygoing drawl, confirmed that he had retired to Florida the previous year from Pennsylvania. He had taken early retirement from the Pennsylvania highway patrol after having served with them for approximately forty years. I couldn't believe that anybody still worked for the same employer for forty years anymore.

I quizzed him on his background. He had joined the patrol after having spent four years in the Navy after graduating from high school in Oklahoma. A friend in the Navy gave him a line on a job with the Pennsylvania state patrol where he applied and was accepted. His first ten years on the force, he related, were spent as a road trooper until he unwittingly pulled over a speeder who had just robbed a bank. The bank robber was in no mood to talk about speed limits. He pulled a pistol and put two bullets into Cargill's chest, leaving him for dead. Cargill eventually recovered, but not without receiving permanent injuries. One of his lungs was badly scarred by the bullets and surgery. He had to give up his road patrol duties to take a desk job which would keep him out of the cold winter weather which played havoc with his scarred lung.

He opted for a position with one of the patrol's motor vehicle homicide teams where he could couple 'riding a desk,' as he put it, with getting out in the field periodically to work the investigation and reconstruction of motor vehicle accidents, which resulted in a fatality to passengers or third parties. He talked the patrol into sending him to night school at a local junior college where he obtained an associate's degree in criminology and traffic investigation. From the animated tone of his voice as he related this history to me, I could see that he was a person who had truly enjoyed his work with the patrol.

However, I was concerned as we spoke that he didn't possess a bachelor's degree, or other traditional college degree. Nor had he authored any articles on the subject of accident reconstruction in any of the professional journals in that field. My concern was due to the fact that I knew full well that Harrington would undoubtedly be hiring pedigreed experts who possessed a host of degrees and publications to their names. Harrington would be adeptly making the jury painfully aware of the comparison. Hell, I could just about hear his paternalistic closing arguments to the jury already about the 'well-intentioned, though unfortunately undertrained and incorrect opinions of Mr. Cargill.'

Mr. Cargill apparently detected my concern when I 'tested' him on some of the technical concepts of accident reconstruction I had managed to absorb over the years from my handling of cases for Global. Cargill handled my questions directly and very accurately. He finally addressed the issue openly, much to his credit.

"Mr. Culhane," he said at last, "I understand your apparent concern about my lack of a traditional college degree. Working for the patrol, I never needed one. After getting my associate's degree, I had planned on going back and getting a bachelor's degree, but a couple kids came along and I didn't have the time. I also soon realized that I was receiving a lot more 'on the job' training in accident reconstruction by performing them every day than I felt I would ever get in a college atmosphere. I was performing as many as one hundred plus reconstructions a year. And," he chuckled, "the fact is I found that when I walked into those courtrooms over the years dressed in my trooper's uniform, and I opened my briefcase on the witness stand with all my calculations of closing speeds, conservation of momentum and the like, I had instant credibility. I was the reconstruction expert representing the State of Pennsylvania. I don't care what the legal textbooks say about formal credentials, people love a uniform, especially if the guy wearing it seems fair, intelligent and professional. I think I held my own against a lot of PhDs over the years."

"Mr. Cargill," I responded, "I don't mean any disrespect, but you won't be wearing a patrolman's uniform when you walk into courtrooms these days. I have a duty to my clients to make sure that I'm hiring very competent experts. I hope you understand."

"No offence taken. I understand completely."

"In twenty words or less, what do you consider to be the trade-off for your lack of a formal college degree?"

"It's experience, plain and simple. I reckon that over the last thirty years, I've conducted well over two thousand accident reconstructions, many of which were complex. I've dealt with almost every type of vehicle and accident scenario you can imagine, and then some. I've learned a lot in the process." He paused for a moment and then added: "Mr. Culhane, let me put it this way. If you're looking for a reconstructionist with a sheepskin degree on the wall, I'm not your man. But if you're interested in hiring someone who knows what he's talking about in this area, who isn't going to sugarcoat his findings and opinions, and who can explain what all this technical stuff means to a jury in pretty simple terms, then I think I'm your man. That's kind of how I see it."

He won me over. I liked the guy and his straight-forward approach. I hired him, subject to some reference checks from other attorneys he had worked with over the last year. He was quick to give me three or four names. I also liked his price. At one hundred dollars an hour, he was a bargain by South Florida billing standards. I promised to express him a comprehensive packet of preliminary information that I had compiled on the accident, and we agreed to meet at the accident scene the following Saturday.

Cargill was already at the accident scene Saturday morning when I drove up. I parked my car immediately behind his, well onto the grass, well off the asphalt shoulder of the interstate roadway. I noted that he drove an older Ford station wagon that had some rust in the fender areas. Undoubtedly, he had driven it down from Pennsylvania.

Ralph Cargill was in his early sixties. At five-foot-eight, he stood six inches shorter than me. He was built like a beer keg, barrel-chested and robust. There was only a modest paunch to his stomach, which was in keeping with his military-like appearance. His brown hair, flecked with a good measure of white, sported a flattop haircut with the sides of his head buzz-cut to about a half-inch in length. Although we were meeting at ten o'clock in the morning and he had clean-shaven earlier that morning, his cheeks showed the dark outline of his thick underlying beard. When he extended his hand and shook mine, my first impression of him was that of a panda bear due to the heavy, dark bags prominent under his dark brown eyes. He flashed a broad, warm smile as we shook hands. He had the grip of an ex-cop, strong and forceful. He was wearing khaki pants and a yellow polo shirt and was carrying a digital camera and notepad.

He had read over the materials Sandy had sent to him and was well prepared to discuss the reconstruction issues in the case. To that end, I was impressed with the fact that he had prepared a list of preliminary questions regarding some information that was not evident in the materials sent to him, such as other eyewitnesses, vehicle maintenance and the like. I gave him what I had and ended up making a list of follow-up tasks that I needed to perform for him.

After walking and discussing the accident scene for an hour and a half, he followed my car over to the storage bin where the remains of the Mesa were being stored. He got another positive assessment from me when he pulled a one-piece, zippered nylon body suit from his car and put it on over his slacks and shirt prior to inspecting the Mesa. It was a good sign to me that he intended to get dirty if necessary in order to fully inspect the Mesa.

As it turned out, Cargill got plenty dirty in performing his inspection. He was all over every square inch of the Mesa. I had it stored on a roller plate so that it could be pushed out of the garage. Its two driver-side tires had been burned badly, leaving its two wheel rims essentially resting on the remains of the tires and on the concrete floor. Its acrid burnt odor was heavy. We used a forklift to help pull the vehicle on the roller plate out of the garage and to lift its back end and its front end, alternately, off the ground high enough for Cargill to crawl under for his inspection and photography.

He was careful not to remove or change the condition of any of the Mesa's components or remains. I didn't want Global to claim that we had somehow "spoiled" the evidence by altering the condition of the Mesa before Global's attorneys and experts had an opportunity to inspect it as well. As a precaution, I videotaped every minute of Cargill's inspection in order to document that he had not made any changes to the vehicle. The only change I allowed him to make to the Mesa was the removal of the soggy, charred remains of the boxes of Girl Scout cookies and cartons from the back of the Mesa. Most had been burned up in the fire, but those remaining were already starting to mold badly when the vehicle was released by the police from their impound lot after their investigation was completed. Sandy was kind enough to 'volunteer' for the job.

"I don't see any obvious mechanical failure like a broken suspension system or strut that would explain any of the handling problems some of the witnesses referred to, Mike." Cargill had completed his examination of the vehicle after two hours. He was cleaning the soot and grime from his hands using some liquid soap and some Handi-Wipes he pulled from a bottle dispenser out of the cargo area of his station wagon. The clipboard containing a soot-smudged yellow pad with his field inspection notes was lying on the garage's cement floor. He had compiled about ten pages of detailed notes. He had precise and neat handwriting. Another good sign, I thought to myself.

After cleaning his hands, he went to work removing the last roll of exposed film from his Nikon 35mm automatic and replaced the camera neatly into the foam-filled carrying interior of an aluminum traveling case. The five rolls of exposed film he took of both the accident scene and the Mesa were secured in the travel case, which he closed. He had apparently not made the transition to the digital camera age.

"I'm curious," I finally asked, "did you see any evidence of any non-standard modifications to the Mesa made by either the factory or dealer?"

"No, from the measurements I took, she's all standard for this model, including her trim height." Trim height was a term used to refer to the height or elevation that the body of a vehicle has from the ground beneath it.

During his examination, Cargill told me that he had taken the liberty of stopping in at a Global dealership in Ft. Myers to look at a standard Mesa of the same type that Eric had owned. He had taken certain measurements of its trim height, wheel base, and other elements that might prove helpful to his reconstruction. He also had obtained a number of glossy, colored sales brochures for the Mesa which gave some vehicle specifications, including wheel-base, weight, suspension information and the like. I was impressed with his initiative. Many of the big-shot experts that I had worked with over the years, particularly those that did work all around the country for Global on the more serious liability cases, had become spoiled. They expected the attorney to spoon feed them all of the documents and background information for their analysis, like sales brochures.

"Damn," I said, "I was hoping we'd get lucky and find an assembly screw-up at the factory level. You know, some guy on the assembly line forgetting to put all of the bolts in the suspension components, or putting on the wrong part. I should have known that would be too easy," I lamented, wiping the sweat from my forehead with the rolled up sleeve of my blue work shirt. It had to be ninety degrees out with ninety-five percent humidity, I thought. Summer was upon us. Surprisingly, Cargill only showed a minimal sweat, despite the nylon body suit he had on.

"I'm going to be taking the scene and vehicle information I have and start playing around with some basic dynamics next week. All of that will only be preliminary, you understand, to be updated with additional case information. I'm going to be looking at the Mesa's vehicle speed at the time she faced the falling ladder. That should be a bit difficult to pin down in a single vehicle accident without skid marks from braking on the roadway and with the rollover dynamics we had here. The investigating trooper didn't take any photos of the highway, so we don't have any witness marks to use from any tire marks that might have been on the highway leading up to, or during, the accident scenario."

"Why didn't Trooper Martelli take those shots? Isn't that pretty standard?"

"It should be. All of his photos are of the burning Mesa, but that doesn't tell us much at all of the events leading up to the roll at all. I suspect that he just overlooked them in all the activity. They sure would have been helpful to a reconstruction if they were taken and showed tire rubs and the like."

"Can you work around the lack of road photos?"

"I'll work around it. For one thing, I'm going to take a peek at some studies I used a couple of years ago dealing with speed estimates based on the number of rolls which various rolling vehicles at various pre-determined speeds actually underwent. There's some published data on that."

"What do you mean?"

"In this accident, the Mesa rolled and eventually ended up landing back on its four tires. As you know, that's considered a full or three hundred sixty degree rollover. If it had rolled another half roll and ended up resting upside down, that's considered a roll and a half. The authors of the particular study I'm referring to, a couple of engineers working for Volkswagen in Germany, as I recall, did a workup with a number of different types of vehicles to try to determine the relationship between vehicle speed and the number of rolls that a vehicle undergoes. In short, they were trying to determine the speed at the point of roll by figuring the number of rolls it underwent in the accident."

"Did they come up with anything?"

"Yes. They actually found definite relationships, depending on the different types of geometry of the vehicles involved in the roll. Their paper presented a matrix of calculations that reflected what speed a vehicle would be traveling at in order to result in the number of rolls experienced in the given accident. It was an interesting study. I might be able to find some helpful data in it to apply here."

"Good. Say, Ralph, let me ask you something." I had quickly and comfortably moved to a first-name basis with him. "I realize that you aren't an expert in fuel containment systems, but I'm curious to know if you were able to determine what the cause of the fire was. I'm going to have to look at not only the stability issue, but also whether there was any potential defect in the Mesa's fuel system that resulted in the fire. I mean, I've seen a number of rollover accidents over the years when I worked on Global cases, but this is the only fire that ever occurred in any of those cases. I'm curious why there was a fire with this accident."

"I did take a look at the fuel system," he answered, "more out of professional curiosity than anything else. While I don't pretend to be a fuel systems design expert, it looked to me like the Mesa's fuel system was fine. I found a broken clamp that was supposed to secure the gasoline filler pipe to the side of the gas tank. I don't know whether you noticed it or not, but out at the accident site on the interstate, there was a concrete pad about twelve inches square in the grassy median that was elevated up from the ground about a foot."

"Yeah, I saw that."

"It looks like it is the base for a large road sign pole that is to be bolted to it."

"Yeah, what role did it play?"

"Well, there is a forest green paint transfer from the sheet metal of the Mesa on it. Based on what I've seen so far, including my review of what some of the witnesses told the investigating officers, the Mesa did one complete three hundred sixty degree roll during the rollover. As you know, the Mesa was headed eastbound towards Ft. Lauderdale when the accident occurred. It appears that Mrs. Hawkins took some evasive action in response to the step ladder that fell off the truck in front of her, and that somehow she started losing control of the vehicle. It went back and forth across the road lanes as she was trying to regain control, and a roll started. During the scenario, the Mesa ended up going into the grassy median that separated eastbound traffic from westbound interstate traffic. When it entered that median, the front of the Mesa was pointing towards that median, but the vehicle's overall directional movement was still largely in an easterly direction," he explained, demonstrating with his hands.

"You mean that when the roll started, the Mesa was essentially moving sideways and moving in the original easterly direction where Jenny was originally headed?"

"Exactly. It rolled onto the passenger door, and when it started to roll onto the roof, it became airborne from what I can see, probably a couple of feet off the ground. It continued to roll while it was airborne. When it came crashing down to earth it landed on the driver's side of the Mesa. From the damage pattern I can see, it came down right on that raised concrete pad. The pad smashed into the area of the gas cap door on the driver's side of the Mesa. It landed with a lot of force, and the concrete pad crushed in the Mesa's sheet metal around that gas cap door. Here," he said, walking over to the Mesa and pointing to an area of sheet metal on the driver's side immediately to the rear of the passenger's door that was crushed severely inward, "is the area of deformation I'm referring to." He pointed to a caved-in and smashed-in area of burnt sheet metal located about two feet to the rear of the passenger's door on the driver's side of the Mesa.

I bent down to inspect it more closely.

"Behind that crushed gas cap door is the gas cap that, in turn, is connected to a filler tube that, in turn, is connected to the gas tank itself. The crushing caused a leak to develop at the attachment fitting."

"So, how does the broken clamp you talk about play into all this?" I asked.

"If you look under here," he said, kneeling down, lying on his back and sliding under the side of the left side of the Mesa, "you can see that when the inward crushing occurred, it went far enough inward to actually reach the attachment clamp that secured the filler tube to the gas tank and tear it loose." I lay down next to him and slid my head under the side of the Mesa to eyeball the area he was talking about. "Once that clamp broke," he continued, "and the Mesa made another ninety degree roll to finally end up back on its wheels, the laws of gravity simply took over. The gas in that tank started leaking out through that opening towards the ground. And when gas fumes and vapor came into contact with the hot exhaust pipes or the muffler, that's when ignition occurred and the fire started."

"I see what you're referring to."

We both looked at it for a moment and then slid back out and stood up, looking at the charred remains of the vehicle. The fiery, horrendous death of Jenny Hawkins was on our minds. It was eerie for me. I had been at a lot of vehicle inspections over the years where the drivers or occupants had been killed or terribly injured. Those were just statistics and 'evidence' to me. This one was different. I knew the victims here.

"So, bottom line," I finally said, "your off-the-cuff opinion is that there isn't any real fuel system defect?"

"Yes, that's the way I see it. That concrete platform did a lot of damage, and the Mesa's fuel system took a nasty blow. It was freakish, I'll grant you that, landing right on that pad and all, but I just don't see that there was a fuel design defect."

"I see."

"I want you to talk with an honest-to-god expert who knows something about fuel system design though. I don't pretend to be one, but I have seen my share of collision fires, and this doesn't strike me as a problem. That's all I'm trying to say."

"Understood," I responded.

CHAPTER 19

IT WAS THURSDAY when Cargill got back to me by phone with his initial reconstruction opinions.

"This is a strange one," he opened with.

"In what respect?"

"Well, based on my review of the vehicle, the scene and doing the math, I'm getting a big inconsistency between what I believe the vehicle should have done during that accident and what the witness says he saw it do. Specifically, the witness, Abadin, says that he saw the Mesa's wheels lift off the road after Mrs. Hawkins attempted to swerve to avoid the stepladder, right?"

"Yes, he told the police he saw the wheels on one side lift from the roadway as it started to rotate and head towards the median."

"According to my calculations, the Mesa shouldn't have done that, not at the speed she was traveling. I have her at an estimated speed of between fifty-two and fifty-five miles per hour. Even if she cranked the steering wheel pretty aggressively to avoid hitting the ladder, she should have been able to both avoid the ladder and yet still maintain full control of the vehicle. There's no way that you would expect to see any wild, out-of-control movement, with wheels pulling off the roadway that eyewitness Abadin refers to."

"So, what explanation do you have for the inconsistency?"

"As I see it, there are only three realistic alternatives. First," he explained, "this Abadin witness could just be wrong in what he thinks he saw. After all, it happened very fast, and maybe the big adrenaline rush he got when he saw it all happen confused him. I've seen it happen a lot over the years."

"And the other two explanations?" I queried.

"The second is that Mrs. Hawkins was actually going faster—a lot faster—than the speed of fifty-two to fifty-five I have her at when the ladder fell off the truck in front of her."

"Well, how fast would she have to have been going for her wheels to have lifted off the roadway under a swerve like that?"

He paused for a moment. I could hear him on the other end of the phone, shuffling what must have been his work papers and calculations, apparently looking through some of his numbers.

"Here it is," he finally said out loud. "She would have to have been going around eighty miles an hour in a vehicle like that in order to see the potential for a loss of control and wheel lift like Mr. Abadin referred to. And even then," he offered, "in order to get major instability like that, she would have to have turned the steering wheel very dramatically and very quickly in order to cause it to show the kind of movement, and wheel lift, that Abadin says he saw. At speeds of eighty or better, a person could induce some pretty serious instability in that type of sport utility vehicle."

"Eighty!" I exclaimed. "That doesn't square with the speed at which the other witness, Carole Merton, told Eric she saw Jenny driving only a few miles before the accident. It also doesn't comport with the type of driver that she was," I added. "She wasn't a speeder, by all accounts. I don't see that as a realistic scenario, although that's exactly what Martelli, the investigating police officer, is saying."

"The third explanation," Cargill continued, "is that there's something wrong with the stability design of the Mesa that caused it to behave much differently—much more out of control, if you will—than it should have under the circumstances. I'm only an accident reconstructionist, but a well-designed SUV should not go out of control and roll over at fifty-five miles per hour if the driver turns the steering wheel, even sharply, to avoid hitting an object on the roadway. And I've considered the load she was carrying at the time, as well."

His comment reminded me of the load of Girl Scout cookies, as well as the paint and heavy paint compressor Jenny was hauling at the time of her accident.

"Was she overloaded in any respect?" I asked.

"Not at all. When I was at the Global dealership getting information for this case, I looked at the load capacity of a similar Mesa SUV they had on their dealership floor. When you add up the weight of the paint cartons, the compressor and the boxes of cookies, she wasn't even close to the maximum rated load-carrying capacity for the vehicle."

I mulled over his comments for a moment.

"The problem I'm going to face with trying to prove a stability defect is that I'm going to have to start the lawsuit and then hope to find the evidence of the problem during discovery prior to trial. This is a new vehicle for Global

Motors," I said to him, "which means that there isn't going to be much design information that I'm going to be able to get from lawyers in other lawsuits representing other plaintiffs around the country about this model's stability profile and experience. I don't even know if there are any other rollover cases involving the Mesa."

"Well, along those lines," Cargill added, "I think I should caution you that this is a difficult case to accurately pin a speed number from an accident reconstruction standpoint."

Like all good experts, he was warning against unfulfilled expectations. He didn't want me to foolishly invest a ton of time and money into starting an expensive products liability case against Global without having all the facts.

"Are you telling me that you aren't comfortable with the speed estimate of fifty-two to fifty-five miles per hour that you just spoke of?"

"No. I'm comfortable with it just fine. Those are the speeds that I've come up with and that I am quite convinced existed. However, I would be stretching it if I led you to believe that this is an easy case to reconstruct. The fact is, there aren't a lot of good traditional indicators for a reconstructionist to go on, like skid marks or vehicle crush damage, to use in order to come up with a solid speed estimate. I will be a bit exposed on cross-examination," he cautioned.

"Okay," I said. "This information is helpful. I'll get back to you. Thanks for jumping on this case so quickly with your preliminary work."

"My pleasure," he said. "Incidentally," he added, "there's one other item that I noted that I still don't know if it's significant. I'm passing it along for your design expert to consider."

"What's that?"

"The Mesa's tires. When I was in the Global dealership looking at the similar model to get vehicle data, I happened to observe the SUV's decal on its door jamb, you know," he continued, "the one that has all vehicles weights, load carrying capacities, and that type of thing."

"Yes, I'm familiar with that specifications decal. NHTSA requires it to be on all new vehicles. But, what about its tires?"

"Well, the Mesa comes equipped with Powergrip AP brand tires as standard equipment. When I inspected the tires on that showroom Mesa, they carried an imprint reading on their sidewall recommending thirty psi. Yet," he added, "the door jamb decal on the Mesa instructs the owner to maintain a maximum tire pressure of only twenty-six psi. I don't understand that inconsistency, or the reason for the difference in pressure recommendations. Anyway, I'm passing this information on to you. The Hawkins' Mesa had the same Powergrip AP tires on it."

"What tire pressure did the Hawkins' Mesa have?"

"I can't tell you as far as the tires on the driver's side. They burned in the fire. The two on the passenger side had twenty-nine and thirty psi of air in them when I checked them. The fire department was able to put out the fire before the fire got to them."

"Thanks for the information. I'll pass it along to the design engineer I will be using."

Before we signed off, I had Cargill list for me some of the additional information he needed from Global in order to be more precise and thorough in his accident reconstruction if the client decided to proceed and start a suit against Global. I jotted down the information he needed, such as the build documents for Jenny's Mesa, which established its precise unloaded weight, wheel base, steering system details, suspension system, operator's manual, and the like.

IN VIEW OF the catastrophic fire which the Mesa had undergone in the accident, I needed to hire an expert to determine if there was any defect that caused the fire itself, whether by design or manufacture. Based on Cargill's preliminary information, I suspected that if the Mesa had a defect, it was in its stability, not in its fuel system. From a legal standpoint, if there was a problem with the Mesa's stability that caused Jenny to lose control and roll over, then it would be deemed to be the cause of the fire, as well, since if the Mesa hadn't lost control and rolled over, there wouldn't have been a fire. Cargill's preliminary assessment of no defect in the Mesa's fuel system made a lot of sense, even if he wasn't qualified as a fuel system expert. Even I could see that the concrete platform in the median, which Cargill had pointed out to me, had put a big-time impact on the Mesa's filler pipe assembly, causing the leak to occur.

The problem was that while Cargill's off-the-cuff observation of the fuel system made sense, it would be legal malpractice for me to rely on those observations as a basis for not pursuing a fuel system defect. Long gone were the days when a lawyer could intuitively size up a serious case and decide which defect issues to pursue and which to abandon. The advent of legal malpractice lawsuits against attorneys had changed all that now. Even attorneys were subject to being second guessed in the way they identified defect issues in a case, how they prepared for trial, and how they tried a case to a jury.

The painful result of all this was that I was going to have to spend more money on Eric's case. I needed an engineer with some expertise in fuel systems to evaluate the potential for any defect that could have played a role in causing the fire. While Eric wasn't about to sue me for malpractice if I decided to make the call myself and abandon a fuel system defect, I wanted to be sure on this case.

I was sitting with my paralegal discussing case ideas with her. "Sandy," I said matter-of-factly, "I'm going to have Bobbie Rudolph take a look at the fuel system on the Hawkins' Mesa. Could you get a copy of the police report and a set of the photos which Cargill took of the damaged Mesa and send them over to him for his review?"

She was on the carpeted floor, sitting cross-legged in her jeans, going through a box of documents I had to produce in a very boring breach of contract case I was handling. With the cramped quarters we had, I had started simply storing boxes of client documents in my office along one of the walls. At the mention of Rudolph's name, she looked up immediately.

"Are you kidding, we're that desperate?" she asked.

Her comments were focused on Rudolph. I had no love for the guy myself. He had appeared as an expert witness in probably a dozen products cases against my clients over the years. Formerly a professor of mechanical engineering at the University of Miami, he had been in the lawsuit consulting business, testifying only for plaintiffs, for about five years. The man had excellent academic credentials but absolutely no shame, it seemed, when it came to conjuring up a possible theory of defect against any given manufacturer in a case. He was so pro-plaintiff in his philosophy and approach that the facts of a case didn't much bother Rudolph when it came to coming up with an opinion of 'defect.' He could dream up theories of defect like no one else I had run across.

The depth of his imagination was matched only by the breadth of his claimed areas of expertise. So rich and varied was his self-proclaimed knowledge, that he had testified as a design expert in products ranging from sewing machines, to autos and to pistols. In fact, the local defense bar had nicknamed him 'Du Jour'—if this was Monday, Du Jour was an expert in motorcycle design, if Tuesday, he might be an expert in guarding devices on table saws, etc.

Sandy's question made me laugh. "No, it's really not that bad," I explained. "I recall from Du Jour's résumé that he's actually had some honest-to-god experience with fuel system design."

"How, by filling up his car at gas stations?" she asked, sarcastically.

The sad reality was that the legal system is set up such that any guy with a degree in mechanical engineering was usually permitted by the courts to give an 'expert' opinion in virtually any aspect of design to a jury.

"Actually," I answered, ignoring her sarcasm, "I remember from my prior depositions of him that his master's thesis dealt with the analysis of fuel tanks on Army helicopters involved in crash landings. The professor that he was studying under at the time had some type of government contract grant after the Vietnam War. Rudolph helped him work on improving the system to prevent leaks in the event of a crash landing."

"Well that's a first!" she said. "Seriously, Mike, you can't really be considering using *Du Jour* in the Hawkins' case, are you? He's a slime ball with no integrity. You've said that a million times yourself," she reminded me.

God, I hated it when she was right. "Yeah, I'm going to use him," I said, holding up my hands apologetically. "Understand, I don't think that there's any fuel system defect, at all. But I think I need an engineer to tell me that just to be sure."

"Well, you know that he's going to come up with some type of wacked out theory of defect."

"Oh, I'm sure that he's going *to try*," I said, quickly, "but I intend to make it clear that I want a flat-out, no bullshit, honest opinion. The point is that I am really looking to have him go over the Mesa's fuel system and tell me if he spots any obvious and realistic fuel system flaws, either in design or in assembly that played a role in causing the fire. I'm not interested in any of his wacked-out, bullshit theories. Don't worry, I haven't lost all my common sense. I do think he's competent to find an obvious fuel system defect, if there is one, that Cargill didn't see, that's all."

"Well, what happens if he actually finds a real defect in the Mesa's fuel system? You know that Global will rip his heart out on cross examination."

"If he finds a real defect," I replied, "we'll hire a legitimate expert in fuel systems to pursue that theory. On the other hand, if he's only able to come up with one of his lame-brained theories, I'm going to ignore him. So, when you talk with him to set this up, just make sure that you diplomatically inform him that—"

"When I talk to him? I thought you were going to talk to him," she interrupted.

"Just set it up," I said, a bit testier than I had intended. "I'll take care of talking to him about what we need in his assessment." She really did despise the guy.

IN BETWEEN THE telephone calls, the motion hearings and depositions I had going on in my other cases, I needed to address the big defect issue that I saw in the Hawkins' case—that of stability. While Cargill would be able to tell the jury *what* the Mesa did during the accident scenario that afternoon, including a detailed description of its unfolding loss of control, he couldn't tell them *why* it went out of control or why Jenny was unable to regain control of the Mesa before it left the roadway. I needed another expert for that.

Specifically, I needed an engineer who knew something about motor vehicle stability.

Finding such an expert, I realized, was going to be measurably more difficult than finding an accident reconstructionist. Stability was a very narrow area of engineering expertise. There weren't a lot of engineers who really knew what the hell they were talking about in this area. Those engineers who did were either employed by, or retired from, the auto manufacturers. And let's face it, most of them weren't interested in helping out people who wanted to sue the manufacturer and throw mud at some of their old pals in the industry. Nor did they want to help plaintiffs win lawsuits that put their pensions further at risk, especially after surviving one auto industry bailout initiated by Bush and carried out by Obama. Most of the plaintiff's experts that I had run across when I defended Global weren't acceptable. Most were cut from the tattered cloth, as was *Du Jour*.

Being an optimist, I made a call to two retired design engineers who had formerly worked for General Motors and who I had used as defense experts in cases for Global. Not surprisingly, I hit a stone wall with both. Things were very cordial in my conversations with each until I informed them that I was calling on behalf of a plaintiff in a case against Global.

"I'm just too busy right now to take on any more cases," one had responded immediately, almost before I got the word "plaintiff" out of my mouth.

"Sorry," the other said. "I don't do plaintiff work. Never have. Never will," he said curtly. "And," he added, "I think I've got a conflict." He didn't elaborate, and I didn't push it.

The next engineer I tried was an engineer in Columbus, Ohio. He had incredible credentials, having been an up-and-coming design engineer with Ford in the mid-1970s. When passed over for a chief engineer's position, which he felt should have been his, he got angry and then he decided to get even. He left the manufacturer shortly thereafter and started testifying for plaintiffs in product liability actions. His defendant of choice was Ford, and he was very effective at his new-found occupation. An article I read indicated that last year the cases in which he was involved for plaintiffs' lawyers resulted in over eighteen million dollars in verdicts. This did not even count the settlements he had assisted in securing for plaintiffs.

The problem was that he had become almost prohibitively expensive. When I spoke with him, he was quick to start talking about his success. In fact, I didn't think that the guy was going to shut up. He caught his breath, however, long enough to inform me that he was now charging a flat, non-refundable retainer of ten thousand dollars to become involved in a case. He demanded the money before he would even look over the first file. He added his hourly rate to that fee at three hundred fifty dollars per hour. We had a short conversation. He might be great, but he was obnoxious. More importantly, however, I couldn't afford him. I didn't have that kind of money to gamble on this case, and Eric didn't either.

After racking my brain for other potential stability experts, I finally recalled an individual I had run up against a few years earlier. I gave him a call.

"Mechanical engineering department," the young male voice announced at the other end of the phone. I was calling the Massachusetts Polytechnic Institute of Technology in Worcester, Massachusetts.

"Do you still have a professor there by the name of Braxton? I think it was Dr. Hubert Braxton," I added.

"Are you kidding? Old Braxton will be here forever. Need me to transfer you to his office?"

"That'd be great," I said. "Thanks."

While the call was in the process of being transferred, I wondered whether Braxton would remember me. He had appeared about three years ago as the plaintiff's expert in a case against a Japanese motorcycle manufacturer that I had represented. The motorcycle had gone out of control at a high speed on a sharp curve outside of Homestead, Florida. The bike had gone down and slid across the road, slamming into a twelve-year-old girl who happened to be riding her bicycle in the opposite direction. She was bringing a sack of McDonald's hamburgers to her grandfather at the time. Bad timing. The six hundred fifty pounds of cycle slammed into her and her bicycle at a speed of sixty-five miles per hour. She was rendered a quadriplegic who now spent her days as a vegetable, drooling.

Her parents had sued the operator of the cycle for negligence. He, of course, had survived the accident with only a bad case of road rash. However, he brought my motorcycle manufacturing client into the suit, alleging that the motorcycle had gone out of control because a high-speed 'weave' had suddenly occurred as his cycle was entering the curve, all as a result of a "design defect" in the cycle.

The unique pattern of rubber tire marks left on the roadway by the cycle as reflected in the police photos substantiated that a weave had indeed occurred. My client's in-house design engineers admitted that a high-speed "weave" had likely occurred, but they denied it was due to any "design error." Rather, they vigorously testified in deposition that the weave was caused by a steering bearing on the cycle which had been maladjusted by the cycle's operator, or the dealership that had previously serviced the cycle.

Dr. Braxton had been the expert for the plaintiff's lawyer representing the girl and her family in the suit. He testified at his deposition that, in his opinion, the weave was caused by a design defect in the cycle itself. Namely, there was an insufficient rigidity in the cycle's metal frame, which caused it to dynamically twist under unique circumstances, thereby inducing a 'weave' phenomenon.

The case eventually settled before trial, but not before I had taken Braxton's deposition. I had been very impressed with his education—a master's in physics and a doctorate in mechanical engineering—as well as with his intelligent and detailed analysis of the motorcycle's design from a stability standpoint. He taught courses, I recalled, on fundamental concepts of vehicle design. It was the kind of stuff that made a student's head hurt. The motorcycle case had been only the fourth or fifth litigation case upon which he had consulted. Another positive attribute of Braxton, I remembered, is that his billing rate was only something like one hundred dollars an hour at that time—an absolute bargain for that type of expertise at twice the price. I was into bargains right now.

"Professor Braxton," a pleasant voice finally answered. "I'm sorry if you had to wait. They had to pull me out of one of my graduate labs." I had forgotten how thick his Massachusetts accent was.

"No problem at all," I answered. "Thanks for taking the call. Dr. Braxton, my name is Michael Culhane. I don't know if you remember me, but I was the attorney who represented the motorcycle manufacturer in the *Fabio* case, which you were involved in about three years ago."

"*Fabio* ... *Fabio* ..." he thought out loud. "Oh yes, I recall you rather well. You're the gentleman who took my deposition over the course of two full days, aren't you? That's still the record for me in terms of length," he laughed good-naturedly. He was referring to the fact that I had painstakingly gone through every opinion and sub-opinion he held.

"If you hadn't been so thorough and so well prepared for that deposition," I countered in the same light tone, "I wouldn't have been such a pest."

We both chuckled at the exchange.

"Dr. Braxton," I said, breaking the pause, "Are you still consulting on litigation cases?"

"Well, yes and no, actually."

"Oh?"

"I'm trying to be very selective in the cases in which I become involved. I've found that the time demands required on the litigation work interfere terribly with my teaching responsibilities and the time that I feel I should be devoting to my doctoral candidates. As a consequence," he continued, "I'm limiting myself to only two cases at any one time. I presently have two open files, and so, I'm afraid I won't be in a position to help you out," he ended, almost apologetically.

"I appreciate your candor, and I can also appreciate what you are saying about the time demands. However," I offered quickly, hoping to bait the hook, "I have a case which I think you would find extremely interesting from a professional point of view. It presents a challenging issue on SUV vehicle stability, particularly as it relates to the relationship between physics and design. My case involves an SUV which lost control on the interstate, left the road and rolled over. The young mother was killed and her infant son was badly burned and disfigured. It's still an open question as to whether he's going to make it," I added. I sensed that I needed to pull out all the stops and play both to his heart as well as his professional curiosity.

"Mr. Cochran—"

"Culhane," I politely corrected.

"Pardon me. Mr. Culhane, it does sound rather interesting, but as I mentioned, I really am awfully jammed this semester. I did promise my wife that I would hold to the line at only handling two litigation consultation cases, if at all possible. I'm afraid—"

"Dr. Braxton," I persisted, "I'm wondering if I could impose on you to at least eyeball some of the brief case materials I would like to Fed Ex to you before you make up your mind not to take this case. Look, I know that probably just about every attorney that calls you tells you that their case is a 'special case,' but this one truly is. I'd also be less than honest with you if I didn't tell you that I'm also very selective in the cases I take." I had his ear, so I plowed on.

"I've been a defense lawyer for too many years now," I continued. "I think I could count on one hand the plaintiff's design engineers that I have deposed over the years in products liability cases who both had the credentials and who had done their homework to support their opinions of defect in their case. I'm not trying to soft soap you with false praise. But, the fact is, Professor, I was very impressed with you on both counts when I deposed you in the *Fabio* case. I'd very much like to work with you." I paused for a moment. "And, there's also another factor at play here that I haven't discussed, and that's the fact that the injured infant is my godson. His family is very close to mine, and I don't want to entrust their case to just anyone. I need someone who is good. The case is special to me, both personally and professionally. Could you at least take a peek at the case materials I'd be willing to send before saying 'no'?"

Braxton was quiet for a moment. "I'll take a look at your materials. I don't see any harm in that, but I can't make any promises, okay?"

"That would be terrific. That's all I can ask," I said.

"You mentioned a fire, Mr. Culhane. Are you asking me to look at that design aspect in addition to the stability issue?"

"No. At this stage, I'm only interested in your preliminary review of the stability issue, that's all." I figured that if *Du Jour* surprised me and came up with a plausible fuel system defect, I could always cross that bridge with Dr. Braxton at that time.

Part of me found his self-imposed scheduling constraints a bit on the anal-retentive side. Yet, I found I had a begrudging respect for his ability and willingness to forego the substantial extra income he was turning away from added litigation consulting in order to safeguard and protect his private and academic time demands. It was an attitude rarely apparent in the experts I had been dealing with for so many years.

"When did you say you thought you might have those materials to me?" he asked.

"Today is Wednesday. I'll have them emailed to you by Friday morning. I mentioned that I've had an accident reconstructionist take a preliminary look at the dynamics of the accident," I added. "His preliminary observation is that there is a defect of some origin in the vehicle itself that gave rise to the loss of control and, ultimately, the rollover that caused the fire that killed and injured my clients. That's why I'm seeking to involve your expertise."

"Very good," he ended. "I'll look for your packet and call you after I've reviewed it. I would think that I could get back to you by the end of next week."

"That would be great. Again, I really appreciate your time."

We both hung up. I immediately went out to Sandy's desk. As I was walking past Tina's desk, I almost stopped dead in my tracks. Tina was taping a Polaroid photo of a kitten next to her phone.

"What's that?" I asked, nodding towards the photo.

"Isn't she cute?" she replied. "She's a little stray kitten that I took in. You know, all these years I thought that I didn't like cats. Well, I'm really enjoying the dickens out of little Cleo here. I'm almost tempted to get her a playmate."

"Uh huh," is all I could muster. *It's started, I thought to myself. First Evelyn, now Tina.* I shook my head. It's contagious. I moved on to Sandy's desk.

I filled her in on the conversation I had with Braxton, gave her his contact information and told her that I needed a comprehensive set of materials emailed to him for his review. I mentioned his reluctance to get involved due to his time demands.

She considered for a moment. "I'm going to throw in a family photo of the Hawkins' family taken before the accident, along with her autopsy photos and one or two of Ryan in his burned condition. I realize they don't bear on his opinions, but, believe me," she smiled wryly, "after looking at those, I guarantee you he'll take the case."

"You're really a manipulator, aren't you?" I laughed.

"Wait until raise-time if you think I'm manipulating now. I'll get the information to him by Friday morning. Let's keep our fingers crossed."

I started to walk away. "Incidentally," Sandy called after me, "if he does agree to get involved, what kind of retainer is he going to require?" Since coming with me, she had agreed to also take responsibility for paying the day-to-day bills of the firms and depositing the fees received. There had been a steady stream of the former so far and, unfortunately, a paucity of the latter.

"I didn't get into any discussion with him about the economics, but I'd guess that he's not going to break the bank. Let's hope so anyway."

Sandy motioned me with her head to come closer to her. I did. She then whispered to me in a very low voice so as not to be heard by Tina. "You do realize that you only have about four thousand dollars left in your checking account balance right now, don't you?"

"Yeah, I know that. We should be getting some of the payments in from the first batch of invoices we sent out recently, don't you think?"

"Mike, at most, we're due to receive only about ten thousand dollars from that first group. You lost a lot of time, as you know, on the transition. Do you have any kind of line of credit set up? We're going to need one at the rate we're going." She looked concerned.

"Thanks for reminding me," I said. "I'll take care of it."

I headed back into my office and started assembling a file for a deposition that I was heading to cover. I made a mental note to double check on the loan limit of my line of credit with my bank. I had a 'credit line' of up to one hundred thousand dollars with the bank, secured by a second mortgage on my home. Presently, the debt balance was only forty-five hundred dollars on that credit line. I had used it to purchase a state-of-the-art sound and TV system for my entire home for Christmas last year. Well, I figured, if I needed more capital to get the practice started, I could draw on that line of credit.

My thoughts were interrupted by the ringing of my desk phone.

"Mike," Tina said, "I've got a Mr. Windsor on your other line. He was referred to you by one of your other clients, Mr. Chernov. He says he just moved down from New York and needs a lawyer. He's buying a business in Boca and needs a contract proposal drafted. I know you don't do that type of law, but I thought you'd want to talk to him and refer him to someone else that does."

"Tina, there's nothing more exciting than drafting a contract. Didn't I ever tell you that before?"

"Uh … no, I don't think I heard you say that before."
"Put Mr. Windsor through to me."

CHAPTER 20

ONE OF THE great pleasures of practicing at Hunt & Baxter was that I was largely insulated from having to deal with one of the more frustrating aspects of running a law firm: collecting money from bills sent out to clients. In large law firms like Hunt, the job of collections is largely left to a bookkeeping department staff and one or two partners who oversee the firm's administrative tasks. They're the ones who have to write the friendly reminder letters to clients on older unpaid bills, make phone calls to the clients and cajole them into payment, or get mired down in answering the clients' requests for more information. The rest of the attorneys are left to practice law.

I received my first hard dose of 'billing reality,' or more aptly, 'collection reality,' when I looked for my clients' checks in response to the first group of invoices I had sent out for my legal services. Only half of them paid by the end of thirty days after the bills had been sent out.

"How can they do that?" Liz asked with exasperation. The two of us were sitting outside on the backyard patio overlooking the water. It was late in the evening, and I was nursing a beer. I had brought up the subject of our finances and my dismal collections.

"Don't they know that you're relying on their payments to pay our bills, too?"

In retrospect, I realized, it probably wasn't one of my brighter ideas to even discuss the money situation with Liz tonight. I had been in the doghouse since arriving home late once again. I didn't get home until nine-thirty p.m., having missed dinner with the family for the third straight night in a row. Liz wasn't a happy camper, but I thought she had since cooled down. I guessed wrong.

My late arrival was due to my working on Windsor's project. When he had dropped off the contract offer materials yesterday, he assured me that there was no particular rush to have me prepare the contract proposal since the seller was out of town for a few days. Perhaps predictably, he showed up at my office at three this afternoon in a panic, stating that the seller had unexpectedly popped back into town. He needed to have the finished contract proposal in his hands tonight. Wheezing and appearing like a hyperactive walrus, he both sounded and looked like a man flirting with a major stroke. A second bidder had suddenly and unexpectedly appeared in the wings, and Windsor was convinced that the success of the deal hinged on his getting his contract offer into the seller's hands first thing in the morning.

I pushed aside the other matter I was working on when he showed up and put his project on the front burner. It wasn't completed until eight-thirty, at which time I emailed him a copy and sent the original over by an after-hours commercial courier. He was back and forth on the phone with non-stop changes to earlier contract provisions I had been emailing him as I drafted.

Despite her claims to the contrary, Liz didn't either fully understand or appreciate emergencies at the office. Emergencies are when kids get sick, the dishwasher starts leaking, or the car won't start. A demanding client doesn't fit into that same category, no matter the circumstances. In fairness to her, I realized that ever since I had started practicing on my own, my work schedule had changed drastically from what it had been at Hunt. At Hunt, if I wasn't in trial, I would generally be home by six-fifteen and would only work maybe one night a week at home. The weekends were free, other than a periodic Saturday morning. Now, I rarely got home before seven-thirty p.m., if I was lucky. Even after dinner, I gravitated towards the den where I worked on client files almost every night during the week. I also head into the office every Saturday, although I try not to work on Sundays. The hard reality, as I have tried to explain to Liz, is that I don't have the luxury of an associate or a law clerk to perform my legal research or take care of a lot of the more elementary aspects of my cases. Sandy is able to handle a great deal, but I have to take care of the rest. The scheduling issues created by my clients' needs are not easy for Liz to deal with. And the fact that a bunch of my clients aren't timely in paying my bills only aggravates the situation.

"They're clients, Liz. What can I tell you?" I finally said, with some exasperation. "Some are great about paying their bills immediately, and some aren't. I'm going to give the non-payers another fifteen days to pay before making any calls to them. I can't afford to be too aggressive in my collection efforts right now. Christ, it's not like I can exactly afford to lose any clients right now."

"Well, if they don't pay you, what good is it to have them?" she said, crossing her arms over her chest.

"They'll pay. Don't worry about it," I assured her. "The problem is that it may take me sixty to ninety days to collect from some of them, that's all."

"Sixty to ninety! And just what are we going to do in the meantime for money to pay the bills?"

I took a swig from my bottle of beer before answering. I didn't have any shoes on, and my feet were resting up on the seat of another of the patio chairs.

"I'm going to be borrowing money from the bank under our line of credit. We've got about ninety-five thousand available to us from that. I'll be paying that off as soon as my practice gets in gear. Don't worry," I calmly reassured her, "it's only a temporary cash flow problem, Liz."

"A temporary cash flow problem!" she said, in immediate response. She uncrossed her arms and put her hands on the arms of the patio chair in which she was sitting. "You can't be serious, Michael. We can't just start borrowing on our home. We're putting our home in jeopardy if we can't make the payments."

I looked at her and did not say anything for a moment, hoping to calm her down. I put my beer down on the wrought iron table around which we were seated.

"First of all, unless you have a better idea, that's the only source of money I have available to my practice right now. Even if I went to a bank and asked for a traditional line of credit, they're going to demand a second mortgage on the house as security anyway. There's just no getting around it. And, yes, there is a risk, but I'm confident that things will pick up with my practice. Besides, I don't expect to be borrowing more than twenty or thirty thousand anyway. After that, I'm sure that the cash flow at work will start rolling."

Liz grew quiet and looked out over the ink dark water of the canal in front of us. "It doesn't look like we have much of a choice, does it?"

"No, it doesn't."

"I'm not comfortable with all this new debt, Michael. When we started out, we didn't have two nickels to rub together. Remember those days? We weren't afraid of any risks and really didn't even think twice about it. Now," she said, looking over her shoulder at the home behind us, "we have something. And, it … it … just seems like we're in increasing financial jeopardy, all of a sudden. This is our home. We've raised the girls here … It just … just makes me nervous and angry at the same time."

I knew her anxiety was also fueled by the fact that the doctors she worked for could not use her on a full time basis. The best she could get was four days a week. It was better than the two days she was previously averaging, but the growing financial squeeze was on both of our minds.

"Liz, it's going to be fine. I know it," I assured her, trying to sound convincing.

She nodded. She wasn't buying it. "I'm going to bed."

"What do you say we take the Whaler out for a few minutes with a few beers?" I asked, trying to change the subject. "This is a perfect night for being on the water."

"No," she said, "I'm tired, Michael. I'm going to bed."

With that, she walked off and into the house.

I stayed up and drank three more beers, finally getting into bed at one a.m. I knew that Liz was still awake, but she didn't say anything as I slid into bed. Nor did I. This was not going according to script, I thought to myself.

CHAPTER 21

TRUE TO HIS word, Braxton called me at my office the following Wednesday.

"How sure are you that Mrs. Hawkins wasn't speeding when she attempted to avoid the ladder in the road?" he asked after we discussed some of his preliminary observations.

"Very," I answered. "Her husband tells me that she was never a fast driver and hadn't had a speeding ticket in years. Also, we have a witness who will testify that she passed Mrs. Hawkins only five minutes or so before the accident and is sure that she wasn't speeding. Furthermore, the accident reconstructionist I hired puts her speed at about the speed limit at the time. I assume from your question that the speed of her Mesa is important?"

"Yes, it's a critical factor in my analysis of your facts," he said. His Massachusetts' accent was thick as maple syrup. "At speeds over seventy-five miles per hour, even well-designed SUVs will be difficult to control and may see wheel lift if the driver starts introducing sharp turning maneuvers with the steering wheel. That's just the nature of the beast from the standpoints of the physics involved."

"Well, I'm very comfortable that I've got the evidence to prove that she wasn't speeding," I said. "But, in any event," I continued, "at speeds of only fifty-five to sixty miles per hour, with a well-designed SUV, even with sharp steering inputs by the driver, would you expect to see the wheels of the utility vehicle lift off the roadway?" I was thinking of the general observations of the witness, Abadin, who had made a comment to that effect to Trooper Martelli.

"No, you shouldn't, not if the vehicle is designed correctly. If you start getting that phenomenon, you've got a fundamental design flaw, in my opinion, from the standpoint of vehicle stability and vehicle control. Now," he added, "don't get me wrong. Global's engineers will probably disagree with me on that point, but I believe that good engineering will support me. You're going to face an uphill battle from Global on this case. You know that, don't you?"

"Without a doubt, I'm sure, but I'm prepared for a hard-fought contest." I cleared my throat. "Dr. Braxton, I'm not going to beat around the bush. What I need to know is whether I can count on you to help my clients out in that fight? I need the benefit of your expertise as my expert design witness, and your commitment to defend your opinions aggressively."

I tried not to sound like I was begging, which was just about what I was doing. I had no alternative. I needed to get the ball into the end zone.

He didn't answer immediately, obviously weighing his vow to his wife to limit his case consultations to two at a time.

"Yes," he finally said. "I'll just have to somehow fit it in my schedule, I guess. From the data you sent me, I believe that you have a case. How strong that case is will depend on further discovery information from Global, and your ability to rule out driver error, you know, excessive speed on her part."

"I understand that," I responded, relieved.

"What a shame," he added on a personal note, "it looks like she was a nice lady from the family photo you sent. My wife was sure upset about that little boy getting burned so badly and losing his mother in the process. She happened to see the photos you sent along."

I made a mental note to thank Sandy for thinking to attach a photo of Eric's family to her email to Braxton.

"Dr. Braxton, thanks for taking on the case. I know it violates your two-case rule. I appreciate it. It sure means a great deal to the Hawkins family as well."

"Don't worry. I'll get it all done. Besides," he added, "the case does present some very interesting issues."

"I'm glad to hear that," I said.

"I'll need a ten thousand dollar retainer," he said. "Also, I've increased my hourly rate somewhat since you deposed me a few years ago. I'm currently charging one hundred seventy-five dollars an hour if that's okay."

He almost sounded apologetic

"That's fair," I responded. The up-front retainer would be depleting the existing balance in my firm checking account. I'd be drawing on my line of credit on my home earlier than I had hoped, I realized.

Before hanging up, Braxton outlined for me the kinds of additional engineering and design documents and information he would need from Global in order for him to arrive at definite defensible opinions. I noted which of these in his list he considered to be the more important since I anticipated a major dogfight with Global and Harrington over turning over my discovery demands that were to be served on Global with the complaint. If I had to offer up any 'compromises' to the judge, I needed to know which were less important than the others.

With Cole and Harrington in charge, I anticipated a Rambo-like struggle over discovery. Global was sure to utilize its own version of 'give and take.' It gave nothing of value voluntarily and took every scintilla of information that the plaintiff might possibly possess. By interposing its constant objections to discovery, Global would attempt to delay the case, demoralize my client and drain my money and resources.

BY FRIDAY, I had finished drafting the complaint and the broad-ranging discovery demands against Global. Sandy had prepared a first draft of both sets of documents. I had given her my handwritten notes of the various discovery documents and information which Braxton and Cargill needed from Global, as well as my outline of additional types of Global internal documents which I knew existed from my years of Global representation in the areas of fuel containment and vehicle stability.

Du Jour had called me the day before, confirming what Cargill had suggested regarding the Mesa's fuel containment system. It looked okay, *Du Jour* had reluctantly reported, although he suggested that 'we could argue,' as he phrased it, that the Mesa's filler pipe, which had been forcibly ripped loose from its attachment to the fuel tank 'should have been designed' with some new space-age, flexible and forgiving attachment technology that NASA had developed for the space shuttle.

It was typical and predictable *Du Jour*. While I was certainly all for an aggressively innovative approach against Global, I had this old-fashioned notion that a defect theory ought to be tied, however gossamer-thin, to reality. Nor did I have the money to try oddball theories.

"Don't you think that theory kind of sounds like we're asking Global to design a 'perfect' vehicle and not just a 'reasonably designed' one?" I challenged. I knew that I shouldn't spar with my own experts, but the man just got under my skin.

"Absolutely not," he responded indignantly. "If engineers can invent and use it on the space shuttle, then Global's engineers have an engineering obligation to use it on the fuel system attachments on its cars and trucks as well. It's always dollars over safety with the auto companies, you know," he pontificated.

I quietly shook my head on the other end of the phone as I listened to his comments.

"Well," I said, "I'm going to think the fuel system issue over for awhile. I can't get excited about your attachment theory."

In the final version of the complaint I drafted against Global, I limited the defect allegation to that of the Mesa's stability design. The case was going to be expensive enough to litigate just on the stability issue. No sense in dragging in fuel tank issues based on what I had seen.

THE LAWSUIT AGAINST global, entitled '*Eric Hawkins, as the Personal Representative of The Estate of Jennifer Hawkins, et al. versus Global Motors Company,* was filed the following Tuesday in Broward County Circuit Court in Ft. Lauderdale. Eric had reviewed and approved the complaint before I filed it.

I called Eric at his office after my process server had telephoned to inform me that he had filed the complaint against Global and had served the papers on Global's agent in Ft. Lauderdale.

"The good news," I told Eric, "is that we drew Judge Morgenthal as our judge."

"Is he good for us?"

"He's a 'she.' Let me put it to you this way," I chuckled. "She hates big companies, especially if she thinks that there's insurance around."

"Great! Is she smart?" he asked.

"No, not exactly," I again chuckled. "Her nickname around the courthouse is 'Neanderthal' if that tells you anything." He laughed.

I gave Eric a short course on the history of Neanderthal and her rise to the bench. In doing so, I felt as if I was stripping him of all the sugar-coated views he had acquired of the American judicial system in his seventh grade civics class.

"When do they have to answer the suit papers?" he finally asked.

"Twenty days," I responded. "I expect them to file a pretty aggressive response."

"Meaning what?"

"Meaning the war has started."

I wasn't wrong. On the twentieth day, Sandy came into my office carrying a five-inch stack of papers which had just been hand-delivered by courier from Hunt & Baxter.

"What's that, the new phone book?" I asked.

"It's Global's court filing," she said. "It's really serious, Mike. You need to read it over, I think." It wasn't like Sandy to be so solemn.

She brought it over and laid it on my desk in front of me. I read over the various documents.

As predicted, Harrington had signed all the filings as lead counsel for Global. I was surprised, however, to see an attorney by the name of Aubrey Trenton III and his law firm, appearing as co-counsel for Global out of Atlanta. I wasn't familiar with Trenton or his firm.

Global had filed two motions. The first, the more extensive of the two, was a motion to disqualify me from representing the Hawkins family. The grounds, predictably, were that since I had represented Global for many years in defending it against products liability suits, I was ethically barred from representing the Hawkins' family—personal injury plaintiffs themselves—in their products suit against Global. An 'ethical conflict of interest' is what I was suffering from, according to Global.

The second motion was to dismiss the Hawkins lawsuit. Global's argument was that since I had a conflict of interest and since I had 'undoubtedly divulged confidential information' to my clients that I had supposedly acquired about Global's operations, the Hawkins family should be barred from proceeding with their action.

As I read, Sandy sat quietly in one of my two client chairs. She had obviously read over the documents before she had brought them into my office.

I looked at the other documents that were included in the Global filing. They included a cover letter to Judge Morgenthal from Harrington, as well as an affidavit from Avery Wilcox, on behalf of the Hunt & Baxter firm. His affidavit had five inches of my old time sheets attached to it, reflecting all of the work which I had performed on Global defense cases over the many years that I had been an attorney at Hunt.

Avery's affidavit stated that the firm was both ethically and professionally embarrassed by the 'grossly unethical conduct displayed' by me, a former attorney and partner in that firm, now seeking to represent a plaintiff in a products case against my principal former client. He really laid it on. My actions, he said, were 'legally impermissible, morally reprehensible and professionally offensive.' To permit my continued representation, he continued, would be to encourage other attorneys in the legal community to likewise violate their ethical obligations. Wilcox ended by emphasizing to the court that Sandy, my current paralegal on the Hawkins case, was also a former Hunt employee. He characterized her as an 'aider and abettor' of the ethical breach, and copies of her time sheets were also attached to illustrate to the court the breadth of Global work she had personally performed while at Hunt.

The last filing was an affidavit signed by my old pal, Willis Cole of Global. It reeked of self-righteous indignation in my having 'betrayed,' as he put it, the complete trust, confidence and inside information which Global had entrusted to me over the many years of my defense representation. He referred to my current representation of the Hawkins family, as well as that by Sandy, as 'legal treachery.' He implored Neanderthal to disqualify Sandy and me from the case altogether and concluded by informing the court that Global had found my conduct so unethical that it had filed a formal written grievance against me with The Florida Bar.

"Well," I finally said to Sandy after I had completed reading the documents, "can you imagine the poor grunt at Hunt that had to go over all our time sheets for all those years and extract our Global entries," I chuckled.

She didn't laugh. "I told you it was serious. I can't believe they filed a formal grievance against you with the bar."

"I expected the disqualification motion. As far as the ethics complaint, well, I didn't think the little ferrets would stoop to that kind of bullshit."

"Mike, what do we do now?"

"Take a deep breath. Unless I have really screwed up, I think we're okay."

"But how are you going to get around everything they're saying in those affidavits about all your previous representation for Global?"

I held up both palms, in a calming fashion. "Put aside the legal defenses to their motion for a moment. You seem to have completely overlooked our single most potent weapon in response to their motion."

"What's that?" she asked.

"Neanderthal. Remember, she's the judge assigned to this case. Harrington hasn't been in front of her much. He's about to get a cram course in 'Neanderthal 101.'"

She finally laughed. "I sure hope you're right," she said as she rose out her chair and left my office.

So do I, I thought. So do I.

IT WAS MORE than a coincidence, I thought, that on the day after I received the hand-delivered disqualification motion papers from Harrington I got a call from Jessie Mears, Global's attorney on the *Watson* case. Tina told me he was on the line and put him through to my office.

"Man, what the fuck did you do wrong?" he opened with. No 'hellos' or 'hey, how you doing?'

"Geez, that question covers a lot of territory, Jessie. Want to try and narrow it down a little so I can maybe identify which of my many fuck ups you're referring to?"

He laughed, although somewhat nervously. "I'm talking about your starting that other lawsuit against Global. I got a call yesterday afternoon from Willis Cole of Global. You know him pretty well, don't you?"

"Oh, sure, best of pals. And what did Little Willie have to say?"

"Between you and me, okay?" he asked, lowering his voice.

"Jessie," I replied, "we didn't have this conversation. You're getting me interested."

"Well, he was rip-shit mad at you when he called. Said that Global was pulling the *Watson* case from me and wanted the entire file delivered by messenger immediately to Robert Harrington over at Hunt & Baxter. He made the comment that you were going to wish you had never met Global Motors before all this was over. Apparently you sued Global in some other case, too? That's the drift I got from Cole. He didn't seem interested in sharing a lot of information with me."

"Yeah, that's true. It's a bit more serious than Mr. Watson's case is, I'll admit." I didn't elaborate.

"Well, I sure hope you know what you're doing Mike because Cole is out to fuck you over. I mean fuck you over," he repeated for emphasis. "Look, you and I've always gotten along well. I don't know any of the shit that is going on in that other case you've got going against Global, or what your conflict of interest problems are—and I don't want to know," he quickly added, "but you better be careful in dealing with him. I'm talking to you as a friend. Besides," he added, almost as a secondary justification for the call to me, "I wanted to let you know that I don't think that Global is going to honor the informal commitment I made to you in the *Watson* case—that I wouldn't put you through the ringer since it was a *pro bono* case for you. I think it's safe to say that all bets are off in that regard."

"Yeah, I'm sure that it's a scorched earth policy in *Watson's* case from this point out."

"Count on it," he added.

"Hey, Jessie," I ended, "I do appreciate this heads up call. You're a classy guy. Thanks."

"I figured you'd do the same for me, that's all."

"You know I would."

THE NEXT MORNING I had a one inch stack of discovery demands hand delivered to my office in the *Watson* case, along with a Notice of Substitution informing me and the court that Harrington of Hunt & Baxter was substituting as counsel of record for Jessie Mears. The discovery demands contained voluminous interrogatories, i.e. questions, for Mr. Watson to answer under oath, along with an extensive request for Watson to produce his car, the allegedly defective seat track assembly, and any documents he had pertaining to his case. A Notice of Deposition was included, which scheduled Mr. Watson's deposition. I noted that Harrington had not extended the courtesy of calling my office first to attempt to schedule the deposition on a mutually-agreeable date, which was the typical practice among the lawyers in town. He set the date unilaterally.

Harrington had also sent along a copy of the bar grievance complaint letter which Global had filed against me with The Florida Bar.

"What do you make of all this discovery over a piddly little small claims suit?" Sandy asked, pointing to the *Watson* discovery package on my desk. She was carrying a cup of coffee into me.

"This is not about the merits of this small claims suit. This is retribution. They're telling us that it's war. Cole wants us to know that they're going to make us work our asses off on this case, knowing that I'm not going to get paid a dime since it's a *pro bono* case. If you noticed, Harrington also served us with an Offer of Judgment there," I said, nodding my head in the direction of the packet delivered by him. "Global is offering to settle Watson's case in return for a payment to him of one hundred dollars."

"That's ridiculous. They know that Watson isn't going to accept one hundred dollars to settle his case. Who are they kidding?"

"Absolutely they know that. But that's the point. They're setting him up to force him into bankruptcy. That's what they're really up to. Remember that under Florida's Offer of Judgment statute, if Watson refuses to accept Global's one hundred dollar offer and he later loses his case, Global will be entitled to obtain a money judgment against Watson for its attorney's fees and costs spent defending against his suit."

Sandy took a sip from the can of Coke she was drinking and shook her head. "At the kind of hourly rates that Hunt is charging for its time, you know it's going to end up with a bill of maybe twenty thousand dollars, don't you think?"

"Try again," I suggested. "If I gauge the venom of Global & Hunt on this whole deal, I'd wager that the final bill will be closer to fifty thousand dollars after they get through with all their discovery bullshit. That," I said, nodding at the discovery demands we had received from Harrington on the Watson case, "is only an *hors d'oeuvre.*"

"Am I missing something here?" she asked. "What good does it do for Global to put him into bankruptcy if he has no money to pay them if he does lose?"

I got up and walked over to the windows in my office and looked down to the small public park below. Two street persons were sitting on a park bench next to a shopping cart that looked to contain their worldly possessions. Even from the height of my office I could see their coppery, sun-weathered faces. They were passing a bottle wrapped in a paper bag back and forth between them and talking. I wondered if that was where Rocky Watson was eventually headed.

"I'm not quite sure I really understand Global's actions myself," I finally answered, looking over at Sandy. "But I think they're telling me that they hate my guts. I think their message is that if I drop Eric's case, Global will back off and not go after Watson. If I stay on it, they'll go after him and put him into bankruptcy, whatever the costs." I turned to face her. "The problem is that Global is creating a practical conflict of interest between me and Rocky Watson's best interests. The best thing I can do for Watson's personal interests is to get out of his case or drop Eric's case."

"Is that true? Does all this cause you to have to withdraw from Watson's case?"

"I'll find out. I've got to talk to him about all of this and give him the option of getting another attorney. Do me a favor, Sandy, and leave a message on Watson's cell phone for him to call me. Leave my office and home numbers."

Rocky Watson did call me back at home that night—at one a.m. The ringing of the phone jarred me out of a dead sleep. I grabbed the phone off the night table next to my bed.

"Hello," I grunted, trying to clear my head.

"You wanted to talk to me?" is all the unidentified voice on the other end asked.

"Who is this?" I asked testily, coming awake.

"It's Rocky Watson, that's who!" the voice shot back, indignantly. "I just got back to my room and got your girl's message from my cell. So, do ya wanna talk or not?" he challenged.

He was exhibiting his usual characteristic charisma. The slight slur in his voice told me that he had obviously had more than a few beers.

Jesus Christ, I thought to myself. "Let me get on another phone," is what came out of my mouth. Liz had been awakened by the call and was looking at me with her eyes half closed.

"It's a crazy client," I whispered as I covered the mouthpiece of the phone and placed it on the nightstand. "I'll take it in the other room and get rid of him," I offered in marital supplication.

"I hope you're getting paid a lot for this," she mumbled as she turned her head on the pillow and went back to sleep.

I made my way through the darkened house to the kitchen where I picked up the phone in that room and turned on a light under one of the cupboards.

"Thanks for calling back," I managed. Putting it as simply as I could, I explained to him the recent developments in his case, including the one hundred dollar settlement offer and the potential bankruptcy consequences if he didn't accept the offer. I made a point of fully disclosing Global's personal vendetta against me for starting the other case against them and the probability that a new attorney in my place would probably be better for him in his lawsuit.

"Culhane, you're my combat point man against those assholes," was his slurred response. "If those cocksucking ragheads think I'm not supporting my point man, they're fuckin crazy in the head. Tell them to come on down here and kiss my rosy red ass. We're in this baby together. Unless," he asked suddenly, "you're fuckin' chickening out on me!" It was an accusation rather than a question.

Oh, just great, I thought to myself. It's the middle of the night, and I'm trying to get a halfway intelligent decision out of a client who is loaded and whose mind, or what's left of it, is stuck in a Gulf War I time warp.

"Well, let me put it to you this way, Rocky. The ragheads here, Global, have us kind of pinned down. I may be your point man, but you're still the sergeant of this squad. If you sacrifice me, you can probably get yourself and the rest of the squad out of this ambush and back to camp to fight and win another day. But if you try to save me, or keep me as your lawyer, you could be putting the whole squad, and yourself, at risk of getting killed. I say you cut your losses and get the rest of the guys out while you can." It was the best I could come up with.

"You weren't in the Marines, were you?" His voice was condescending.

"Uh ... no." I felt like a real wimp all of a sudden.

"Figured. *Semper fi*, man. That's what it's all about," he slurred. "I ain't about to fuckin' sneak away from a firefight with those assholes. We stay together. If one of us is under fire, all of us stay and fight. So tell those fuckheads over at Global to take their little white settlement flag and wipe their asses with it!" he barked. "That's all it's good for."

"Well," I laughed heartily, "is that a 'no' to their settlement offer?"

"Fucking A John," he declared. It was the first time that I heard him actually pronounce the 'g' in "fucking" since meeting him weeks ago.

"I'll let the ragheads know your views on the matter. I'll keep you posted."

He might be a crazy son of a bitch, I smiled to myself as I hung up, but I was growing to like the guy.

"Who was that?" Liz sleepily asked when I slid back into bed. Her head was on her pillow facing me. She didn't bother to open her eyes.

"John Wayne," I answered.

"Who?" she mumbled.

"I'll tell you about it in the morning."

CHAPTER 22

ERIC, SANDY AND I rolled into Judge Morgenthal's courtroom about ten minutes prior to the hearing on Global's motions for disqualification. Her courtroom, located on the seventh floor, was old and tired. Just like the rest of the Broward County Courthouse.

The three of us entered through the two heavy swinging walnut doors, which connected her courtroom to the narrow tiled hallway; beyond that the building was yellowed with age. The courtroom, with its very low ceiling and poor lighting, only added to the drab and depressive 'ambiance' of the place.

Avery Wilcox and Ted Gunther were seated in the bench seats on the right side, three rows from the front. My glance over to them was met with an icy glare from both.

"Something tells me they aren't happy about being subpoenaed by you for these hearings," Sandy leaned over and quietly whispered next to me as we approached the rail.

"Avery, Ted," I greeted them with a big smile as I got to the rail, which separated the bench seats for the public from the area in front of the rail where the judge, his staff, the parties and the attorneys in the case sat. "Glad you both were able to take the time from your busy schedules to join us today." I couldn't resist the taunt. At their billing rates of five hundred twenty five dollars an hour, they were losing a lot of money sitting in the courtroom in response to my subpoena. *Tough shit.*

Harrington was seated at counsel table. Willis Cole was seated next to him. A third lawyer, who I could only assume was Aubrey Trenton, Harrington's co-counsel, was seated off to the side.

Harrington had already placed an easel in place facing the judge's bench for his argument. There were probably twenty various enlarged and colored documents stacked upright and leaning against the base of the easel. They were all mounted on light foam board and were obviously exhibits for his presentation. Consistent with her pre-Cambrian mentality, Neanderthal didn't believe in technology in her courtroom. PowerPoint presentations were not welcome. She liked a simple trial with simple presentations. To his credit, Harrington had learned of her preference and had modified his presentation accordingly.

As a professional courtesy, I normally always introduced my client to opposing counsel. That was not going to happen in this case. This was the first time I had seen Harrington since our meeting in Avery's office on the day I left Hunt, and I was itching for a fight.

"Bob, how ya doing?" I asked of Harrington as I moved Eric to his chair to my left and loudly plunked my briefcase down on the plaintiff's table in front of me. Sandy sat in a chair off to my side. "Looks like you're loaded for bear today," I said, nodding my head towards his stack of enlarged exhibits. A stranger would have thought I was gushing with cordiality. I said nothing to Cole who pointedly ignored me altogether.

Harrington hated to be called 'Bob.' It was 'Robert,' if you please. He was forever correcting people who addressed him otherwise. The thought came to mind as to whether Perky Wendy, during their passionate trysts, was required to scream: "Oh ... oh ... oh ... Robert!! ... yes ... yes ... oh yes, Robert!" in the climatic throes of passion, or did she dare sneak in a simple "Oh fuck me, Bobbie!" every now and then, without any recrimination back at the office? My money was on the former.

"I would have expected a juvenile comment like that from you," Harrington said. "It certainly fits your lack of style. It's Robert to you, and I'd appreciate it if you would remember that," he admonished me.

"Oh geez, I forgot. I guess I've been gone from the Hunt too long. I'll try to remember. I'm not very good with names. Now, faces, I'm good at, especially if a person has two of them. For example," I quipped with a chuckle, "your two faces, I have no problem remembering, Bob."

Harrington shook his head in disgust and said nothing. Sandy looked at me with disapproval in her eyes.

Our table was to the left of the Global table as we faced the judge's bench. The empty jury box was to my left. While Harrington had his easel, his stack of exhibits and his pile of voluminous documents on the table in front of him, I pulled only a single, thin manila folder from my briefcase. I laid it on the table in front of me and put my briefcase on the floor beside me. The folder's light color stood in stark contrast to the brown desktop beneath it.

Both sides sat quietly for a few minutes until Ruth Taskey, the judge's judicial assistant, popped her head out from behind the door at the rear of the elevated judge's bench.

"Are all parties here and ready?" she inquired.

"Yes," Harrington replied, "the defense team is here."

"The plaintiff is ready as well," I added. I looked at Eric next to me and nodded, giving him confidence. He looked uncomfortable.

Twenty seconds later, Judge Morgenthal popped through the door behind her bench like a champagne cork out of its bottle. The attorneys rose in unison from their chairs.

"Please be seated, everyone," she ordered over her half glasses as she sat down in her high-backed leather chair. She had on her black robe and was carrying a stack of Global's motion papers. Her glasses were connected to a silver-beaded retention chain, which hung loosely from each side of her face. We took our seats.

"Are all the parties represented here today?" she asked.

"Michael Culhane, Your Honor," I stood and replied. "I'm here for the Hawkins family, along with the plaintiff, Eric Hawkins, who is the personal representative." I sat back down.

"Robert J. Harrington of the Hunt & Baxter law firm, your Honor," he announced smoothly as he rose from his chair. He was sporting his usual power ensemble: light powder blue, athletic-cut shirt, gold cufflinks, straps, dark navy Brooks Brothers suit and red foulard tie. "I am here with my associate, Tucker Craige, and Mr. Willis Cole, in-house counsel for Global Motors Company. I also have with me, as my co-counsel today, Mr. Aubrey Trenton III who practices in Atlanta and serves as regional counsel for Global. We are representing Global."

"Quite a full house," Neanderthal commented, with amusement. She liked an audience.

"Yes, Your Honor," Harrington continued, "with the court's permission, I would like to move to have Mr. Trenton's admission to practice here in Florida for this case on a *pro hac vice* basis. I can attest that he is a member in good standing of the Georgia Bar."

Neanderthal rotated her head slightly to look at me. "Any objection?"

I smiled graciously and shook my head, rising out of my chair. "If Mr. Harrington has a need to call in additional legal reinforcements from our sister state of Georgia, Judge, I'm certainly not going to object."

"Judge Morgenthal," Harrington started to explain, "Mr. Trenton routinely serves as regional counsel for Global on cases—"

"Mr. Harrington," she quickly cut him off, "let's not waste this court's time giving me a playbill on the job description of all the Global attorneys here today. The man said he has no objection," she said, nodding in my direction. "I'll grant your motion. Now, let's get on with this hearing. I have two more motions to hear after yours, so let's get started." Neanderthal was in classic form.

"Thank you," Harrington offered, sneaking a glance over at Cole to his right. It was one of those 'Can you believe this fucking idiot' type of glances. Cole remained stoned-faced.

"Let's see here," Neanderthal continued, looking at the papers in front of her, "we're here today on the defendant's motions to disqualify Mr. Culhane and to dismiss his client's suit on related grounds. I've read over your rather hefty submittal of supporting papers, Mr. Harrington. I think I'd like to hear some testimony on the issues. What's your pleasure?" she inquired of him.

"Very well, Your Honor. The defendants call as their first witness, Mr. Avery Wilcox, the chairman of the Hunt & Baxter law firm," Harrington announced as he started walking towards the wooden podium, which stood a few feet forward of the attorneys' desks. Lawyers were expected to conduct their examination of witnesses while standing at the podium.

Neanderthal suddenly leaned forward in her high-backed leather chair and placed her arms on the top of the top of the bench in front of her. "Did you say that Mr. Wilcox is a lawyer in your own firm?" She removed the glasses from her nose as she posed the question.

"Why ... yes," Harrington stammered, caught off guard by the judge's unexpected question.

"You can't do that, can you? Isn't there a rule of professional conduct out there that prohibits a lawyer in one law firm from calling as a witness in a case another lawyer from his same firm? Isn't that unethical?" she queried of Harrington.

Harrington quickly regained his composure and turned to his associate, Tucker Craige, sitting in the chair immediately behind him. Craige, who was a perfect clone of Harrington, complete with "straps," apparently had anticipated the issue. With little hesitation, he dipped into his briefcase, quickly extracted a legal research memo of some sort, and slammed it into Harrington's hand as if it were a surgeon's scalpel. Harrington nodded.

"There is such a rule, Judge Morgenthal," he responded, suddenly confident once again. "However, case law provides that where a party is involved in obtaining the trial court's ruling on a preliminary legal matter, outside the presence of the jury, the ethical constraint to which Your Honor correctly alludes is not applicable. The pending motions at bar today are precisely that: requested rulings on purely legal matters."

"Judge Morgenthal," I offered magnanimously, again rising from my chair, "if it will assist, and to expedite this hearing, my client waives any objection to Mr. Harrington and Mr. Wilcox both being involved in this hearing as interrogator and witness. We prefer to get to the merits." I sat back down.

"Thank you, Mr. Culhane. Your concession is accepted by the court." She turned back to Harrington. "Go ahead and have Mr. Wilcox take the witness stand."

Wilcox did, walking poker-spined to the witness stand where the clerk swore him in. He sat down and gave a sober, deferential nod to the judge. He sat stiffly in the witness chair facing the lawyers. As a corporate lawyer, he did not 'mix' with trial court judges or their courtrooms. He preferred the board rooms of his clients, instead.

Harrington quickly took him through the many years that Hunt had represented Global Motors in defense of its product liability suits and claims in Florida. He followed the general context of his prior affidavit, placing great emphasis on the fact that I had been *entrusted*, Avery's word, to personally supervise the Global defense work, with Sandy as my chief Global paralegal. He gilded the lily by stating that Global's relationship with the firm had been 'rocked to its core' when Global learned that I had taken what appeared to be a serious plaintiff's products liability suit against Global. As the firm's chairman, he pontificated self-righteously, he was duty-bound to bring this matter to the Court's attention and ask for the disqualification order since the client was naturally angry about the breach of ethical obligations. He informed her that Global had also demanded it.

I sat through his testimony, watching him impassively. Eric followed the request I had made of him, namely remaining calm and not reacting to the dynamics of the discussion or testimony.

Throughout Wilcox's testimony, Harrington used his easel and a number of enlarged exhibits very effectively. He was good, I had to admit. He had apparently learned that Neanderthal liked pictures, preferably big colorful ones. So he gave her big cartoons. Representative copies of my old time sheets, which contained my handwritten entries of a multitude of work entries I had performed over the years for Global, were splashed effectively before her. To apparently drive the point home—they were taking no chances with Neanderthal—Wilcox presented an enlarged summary of every Global file I had ever worked on during my entire tenure at Hunt. It was presented on a dark blue background with brilliant yellow letters. The double-spaced list went on for three-and-a-half enlarged pages. He also emphasized that Global had paid Hunt over eight million dollars in legal fees for handling the cases I had worked on over the years I was on their account. He pointed out that I had also recently hired Sandy Stevens, a former Hunt paralegal, who was also now working on the *Hawkins'* suit.

Avery gave his wind-up pitch. "Global is very disturbed at this new development since Ms. Stevens was also privy to extremely sensitive and confidential Global product liability information when she was at Hunt. We believe that is an ethical violation as well," he proclaimed, evincing vast professional disappointment.

While he tried his best to mask it on the stand, Wilcox was unable to completely conceal his contempt for my 'turncoat' conduct.

At one point, I caught Neanderthal herself, with knitted brow, looking down at me from her perch up on the bench. She was listening to Global's arguments. I remained poker-faced.

Eric leaned over. "Is this a problem for us?" he quietly whispered to me.

I reached over with my left hand and patted his forearm. "We're okay," I whispered back.

After fifteen minutes of testimony, Harrington finished his direct of Wilcox. "Thank you, Mr. Wilcox. You've been very helpful. Your witness," he nodded to me as he confidently left the podium and headed back to his seat at counsel's table. I looked over, catching the not-so-well concealed smirk on Cole's face as Harrington sat down.

I strode to the podium without pad, paper or documents. "Good afternoon, Mr. Wilcox," I opened with. He didn't return the salutation. I shrugged.

"As chairman of Hunt & Baxter, you are aware of the ethical responsibilities that your firm and its attorneys are required to carry out under the Rules of Professional Conduct, are you not?"

"I am, and, unfortunately," he gratuitously added, "it's your failure to abide by those rules that obligated me to come here and testify today." The King had been waiting to zip me. I ignored his jab.

"I see. Since you're fully versed in your firm's ethical duties and responsibilities, I assume you're equally aware of the requirements imposed on every lawyer here in Florida by the bar to perform *pro-bono* legal representation to the less than fortunate members of our society, right?"

"Yes, I am, but I don't quite see the relevance of—"

"Mr. Wilcox," I said, cutting him off sharply. "I'm making every effort to pose simple little questions to you that properly call only for a simple, uncomplicated 'yes' or 'no' response from you. Please answer my questions and not the ones you apparently want to pose to yourself, okay?"

"I object!" Harrington shouted as he shot up from his chair. "Mr. Culhane is cutting off the response of the witness before he has had a chance to give his full answer. He's bullying the witness and arguing with him, Your Honor. That's improper."

"Tut, tut, Mr. Harrington," Judge Morgenthal admonished, jumping into the fray. "This is cross-examination. Mr. Culhane is entitled to be controlling with an adverse witness under the rules, especially if the witness, like Mr. Wilcox here," she said looking down at him over her glasses, "tries to add unsolicited information to his answer. Now, it seems to me that Mr. Culhane's question to your partner, Mr. Harrington, called for a simple 'yes' or 'no' response, without the extra little spin that the witness wants to add. Your objection," she added anticlimactically, "is overruled."

She then turned to Wilcox and directed him to answer the questions and save the 'add-ons' as she called them.

Avery stated that he understood her rules. He was working to contain his anger at her chastising comments. The King wasn't used to being reprimanded, let alone in public, and certainly never in front of his clients. He was pissed.

"Very good," she said. "Continue Mr. Culhane."

"Thank you. Now, Mr. Wilcox, when your firm's attorneys represent a person on a *pro-bono* case, do they get paid for it?"

"No, it's just what you said, *pro bono*. It's free."

"Do you agree that the case of a *pro bono* client is entitled to receive the same level of seriousness and respect that a paying client's case gets?"

"Yes," he answered tersely. King Avery didn't give a shit about *pro bono* cases, but he wasn't about to admit that in open court. He'd save it for partners' meetings.

"So, in other words, if a lawyer takes on a *pro bono* client's case, is that lawyer required to ethically treat that case as important as, say, the case of a long-time firm client like Global Motors Corporation, which has paid your firm, say, over eight million dollars over the years?"

"Well ... uh ..." he stammered, trying to figure out where I was headed.

"Yes or no, sir?" I tapped my finger on the edge of the podium to indicate my impatience with his equivocation.

"Yes," he answered.

"Thank you, sir. You have been most helpful. No more questions."

Avery looked surprised for a second, then got up and walked back to his bench in the audience section of the courtroom, on the other side of the rail.

For his next witness, Harrington called Willis Cole. Cole looked like he just stepped out of an ad from *Gentleman's Quarterly* as he confidently walked to the witness stand. He took his oath and sat down. He wore a very expensive looking dark navy suit, white shirt and vibrant yellow Hermes tie over his powerfully built but lean body. Despite being in his mid 40s, his hair was still jet black, except for only the most modest beginnings of gray at his temples. His general 'corporate' image was accentuated by his 'John Edwards' razor-cut hair. You had the impression that not a hair on his head had the guts to get out of place. However, his eyes were his most prominent feature. They had the color and warmth of mica. He was a man who liked power and being in control of the situation.

After taking Cole through his position at Global as the chief attorney in charge of its products liability defense group, Harrington finally got to the important questions that Neanderthal wanted to hear.

"Did there come a time when you learned that this *Hawkins* action had been filed?"

"Yes. I receive a daily summary of all new actions involving significant products liability claims against the company, including the name of the plaintiff's attorney. That is how I came to discover that Mr. Culhane had filed the suit on behalf of the Hawkins family."

"Does Global take objection to Mr. Culhane's representation?" Harrington asked.

"Absolutely, as his former client, we strenuously object."

"Would you tell the court why you object, sir?" Harrington asked, feeding him the question they had carefully rehearsed.

He turned, facing the judge. "Yes. He is prejudicing my company's rights, Your Honor. He is using confidential information about Global's operations that he learned as our attorney. I can't put it any more direct than that. When we entrusted him and the Hunt law firm with our products liability defense work, we expected to receive utmost loyalty and confidence in return. In the course of the last eight years that he has been representing Global, he has been our primary outside defense counsel in South Florida. We have literally communicated a great deal of sensitive and confidential inside information to him." His face was a portrait of serious concern.

"Can you provide the court with some specifics," Harrington asked. He was leading Cole along very smoothly. Their dog and pony show was going smoothly.

"Sure," Cole offered firmly. "In reviewing our case records, he has worked on potential recall issues, the production and review of confidential product information, internal settlement standards and procedures, and he has been provided with some very intense technical training regarding our products. For example," Cole rolled on, "I estimate that over the last five years alone, Mr. Culhane has spent thirty to forty days at our engineering evaluation facility in Flint, Michigan where Global engineers taught him about the technical aspects of our products."

"Was this training broad or narrow?" Harrington led him on.

"Extremely broad and extremely varied. In the *Mondello* case, for example," he said, reading from some notes he pulled from his coat pocket, "our Global engineers taught him about airbags. In *Toomey*, we educated Mr. Culhane on the subject of ABS brakes. In the *Swiatoviak* case, it was cruise control. Judge," Cole finally said, turning and facing her squarely from his witness chair, "I could spend all afternoon recounting a litany of different types of cases and information that Global provided to Mr. Culhane on a confidential basis, if you would like. The fact of the matter, however, is that Global retained him and trusted him not to turn on us and use that inside information against us. But that's just what he's done in taking the Hawkins' case against us."

"I object," I finally said, "I can see that Mr. Cole here is just itching to give you his closing arguments on this motion, but I think it would be more orderly if he were to act like a real witness and limit his responses to the questions that are being posed to him." The little weasel was finally starting to get under my skin.

"Oh, don't get your underwear all in a bundle Mr. Culhane," Neanderthal calmly ruled. "I can safely tell the difference between testimony and lawyer talk. Continue Mr. Harrington."

Eric shifted in his seat, growing uncomfortable with the direction the hearing was going. I looked over at Sandy. She remained poker-faced, but I could read the mounting concern in her eyes.

Cole proceeded over the next fifteen minutes to embellish upon his fundamental claim of prejudice. And he laid it on thick. He also seized upon the opportunity to claim that my conflict of interest was all the more flagrant given the fact that I had employed Sandy, the former paralegal at Hunt who was assigned to the Global defense team, and who had supervisory responsibility over Hunt's team of paralegals.

Cole was an effective witness. After he was finally through, a casual observer would have thought that I had been the most important and informed outside defense attorney that Global had retained in the lower forty-eight states. I should have charged the son of a bitch a higher billing rate, I thought to myself.

"Your witness, Mr. Culhane," Harrington finally offered as he turned away from the podium and calmly returned to his chair at his counsel table. A cocky arrogance was evident in the look he gave me as he passed.

I walked up to the podium where I leaned against it, resting on my left elbow.

"Mr. Cole, you're the big cheese in the Global product liability defense group, aren't you?"

"Big cheese? I'm not sure what you're asking me, Mr. Culhane," he said, as he removed and discarded a piece of lint from his neatly-pressed slacks.

"Well, you're the top decision-maker at Global who decides which attorneys will be hired on the outside by Global for products cases, and which will be fired, right?"

"That's correct."

"And you're the person who decides which cases to try and which to settle, correct?"

"Correct again, Mr. Culhane," he answered, "and you of all people should know that since you were Global's lawyer for many years. That's why we are here," he added, enjoying the chance to add the gratuitous jab.

"And are you the person who approves or disapproves the billing rates that outside attorneys charge Global?"

He gave a big sigh. I was obviously starting to bore him. "Yes, although I don't know what any of this has to do with the conflict issue that we're supposed to be dealing with," he lectured.

"Well," I responded, "having been given this broad range of authority by Global, you're certainly authorized to waive a conflict of interest that an outside Global attorney might bring to your attention, isn't that true, sir?"

"That really depends, Mr. Culhane," he answered, now suddenly wary for the first time. His eyes flickered momentarily to glance at Harrington, before he glanced back at me. He suddenly knew where I was headed. "What exactly do you mean by a 'conflict of interest'?" he parried.

"Well, now, let's not quibble over semantics, Mr. Cole," I responded with sarcasm in my voice as I walked over to my desk to my left. I leaned over and picked up the manila folder laying on it.

"A few months ago, you and I had a little telephone conversation, did we not?" My tone was not cordial. I wasn't smiling anymore. Neither was Cole.

"I don't keep track of all my telephone conversations with outside attorneys, Mr. Culhane," he snapped, irritation now evident in his voice.

"You mean that when you and Mr. Harrington and Mr. Wilcox and your Atlanta co-counsel assembled that six-inch stack of records and time sheets and summaries of all my life's work for Global that's sitting there in front of Mr. Harrington's nose," I said pointing, "you didn't bother to gather your records of that telephone conversation we had in the case of *Rocky Watson versus Global Motors Corporation?*"

"The records we gathered for this motion deal with when you were a lawyer at the Hunt law firm, Mr. Culhane. When you and I had the telephone conversation I believe you are referring to, you had been *fired* by that firm," he said with relish.

I ignored his baiting. "You remember that conversation we had in the *Watson* matter, don't you sir?"

"Vaguely," he replied.

"And when we spoke that day, you knew that I was no longer working on any of Global's legal matters. Isn't that true?"

"Yes, I—"

"In fact, you had personally demanded that the partners at Hunt strip me of all Global cases before they fired me, right?"

"For your unauthorized and damaging actions on the *Bertson* case, yes, I requested that action."

"So, when you and I had our telephone conversation earlier this year about my taking the Watson case, you knew full well that I wasn't representing Global at that time, right? Yes or no?" I commanded.

"Yes," he replied crisply.

"And you knew that I wouldn't be representing Global on any other legal cases in the future. Isn't that also true?" I stepped to the left side of the podium as I finished the question for emphasis.

"I no longer wanted you working on my company's matters, if that's what you are driving at, Mr. Culhane." The calm demeanor we had seen moments ago from the corporate warrior was beginning to crack with growing irritation.

"So, that's a 'yes' to my question?" I asked, subjecting him to my control.

"That's what I just said," he said, shortly.

"Now, with all of that said, sir, I want to spend a moment on the substance of what you and I talked about in that conversation." I paced slowly and thoughtfully to my left before I stopped, turned and posed the question.

"In that telephone conversation, I informed you that I was calling for your consent—for Global's consent rather—to represent a *pro bono* plaintiff in a lawsuit against Global. Isn't that right?"

"Yes, but that was a little *pro bono* case, as you explained to me. It was not a case like this Hawkins case, and you well knew it!" he fired back.

"Baby steps, Mr. Cole. Let's take this in baby steps," I retorted, raising my hand in a halting fashion to slow him down. "Did I tell you that I was asking for your consent to waive the conflict of interest issue presented by my representation of that *pro bono* plaintiff? Yes or no?"

"It seemed—"

"Yes or no, sir?" I cut in sharply.

"Yes," he replied, angrily, remembering Neanderthal's admonition to Wilcox.

"Thank you. And I specifically told you," I said, pointing my finger at him for emphasis, "that Mr. Watson—the *pro bono* plaintiff that I was being asked to represent—was asking me to start a lawsuit in county court here in Florida against Global on his behalf for property damages and minor personal injuries, right? Yes or no?" I wasn't about to give Willie any slack.

"Yes," he answered in a clipped fashion.

"And I also specifically told you, did I not, that his lawsuit involved a claim for damages that he alleged occurred from a product liability claim?" I kept slowly pacing next to the podium, with my arms crossed on my chest.

"You didn't use the term 'product liability' action, Mr. Culhane. In fact, looking back at that conversation, I recall you as being rather vague in describing the details of that *pro bono* case."

"Really? Does this letter help you refresh your recollection?" I asked, removing a copy of the letter from my manila folder which I had emailed to Cole after our telephone conversation confirming his consent to my representing Mr. Watson in his *pro bono* case against Global. It was the letter that he had signed and emailed back to me. I knew that he wouldn't have considered my letter worthy of keeping in his important corporate files.

I calmly walked over to the witness stand and handed him the copy. "Read it over to yourself, Mr. Cole," I instructed. As he did so, I walked over to Neanderthal and handed her a copy for her review, as well. I tossed a copy onto Harrington's table as I passed by his table, like a paper boy with a bad attitude. I didn't bother to look at him.

"I really don't remember much about this letter," he replied matter-of-factly. Again, I caught the quick, furtive glance at Harrington. His quick look, with his mica black eyes, were those of a rat trying to avoid the trap.

I chuckled, exhibiting disbelief in my tone. "That's your counter signature on that letter I sent to you, isn't it?"

"It appears to be."

"You're not suggesting that I forged your signature on that letter, are you?" I asked mockingly.

"No."

"And that's your email address that appears at the top of the letter, isn't that true, as well?"

"Yes." He was now a bit quieter and less combative.

"You do know how to read, don't you Mr. Cole?" It was a low blow, but it worked.

"Your Honor!" Harrington protested—.

"I'll rephrase," I offered. "Being the astute and careful lawyer that you are, sir, you certainly read this letter of mine over before you signed it, didn't you?"

"I signed it."

"Well, for the record, the letter says, and I quote: 'This will confirm that Global Motors has kindly consented to my representation of Mr. Rocky Watson in his *pro bono products liability action against the Company for his property damage and personal injuries*,'" I said, with emphasis on the key words. "That's what the document says, doesn't it?"

"I don't think I probably read it over, to be honest with you. You told me it was only a little pro *bono case*, that's all I relied on, what you told me orally."

I suddenly stopped pacing and just stared at Cole. "As the manager of the products liability group at Global Motors Company," I asked incredulously, "with all of that profound authority and responsibility, which you so carefully described to Mr. Harrington, is it your sworn testimony that you routinely sign documents that are placed in front of your nose *without reading them*?" My voice and sarcasm clearly betrayed my delight in seeing him squirm.

"I said that I don't remember this letter," he fumed. "You're forgetting, Mr. Culhane, that I testified that in our telephone conversation, you emphasized more of the *pro bono* aspect of the action than the details. In fact, I don't remember you even mentioning the products liability feature. In any event," he recovered, "I didn't feel that I was *carte blanche* consenting to your representation of plaintiffs in serious products liability suits against Global like this *Hawkins* suit."

"Mr. Cole, are you, on behalf of Global Motors, telling this court that if a poor person in this country buys a defective Global car and sues for personal injuries and property damages, that Global Motors doesn't treat that poor person's lawsuit as being *serious*, but that if a middle income or rich person sues you, that's a *serious* suit?"

His eyes smoldered. "Uh … no … What I really … uh, meant to say, and as you well know …" He angrily stammered as he groped to come up with an explanation to erase his prior comment.

I cut him off. "Mr. Cole, as the biggest cheese at Global in the product liability group, wouldn't you agree that Global treats even *pro bono* suits filed by poorer citizens of this country, like Mr. Watson, as *serious*?"

"Well … yes … of course," he begrudgingly conceded, knowing that Global's public relations consequences and "political correctness" prevented him from telling me and the court what he really believed: He didn't give a shit about small claims actions or the 'little people' that brought them.

"I certainly thought so, sir. So, to recap," I said, loudly and with exaggerated emphasis, "if I understand all of this correctly, *you* signed a letter just a few months ago, as *the most senior person* at Global's legal department in charge of its product liability group, *consenting* to my representing Mr. Rocky Watson, a Global customer, in a plaintiff's *serious* products liability action against the company seeking damages for *both* property damages and personal injury. Isn't that correct?"

"I strenuously object!" Harrington barked from his seat. "Counsel has misrepresented Mr. Cole's testimony and has improperly asked multiple questions."

"Overruled," Neanderthal ruled, playing with the beaded lanyard connected to her glasses. "I want to hear your answer." Her comment was more of a challenge than a ruling.

Cole stared at her for a full three seconds before responding. His anger and contempt for her had been unwrapped. "IF-YOU-WANT-TO-TWIST-IT-THAT-WAY,-COUNSEL," he said, articulating every word slowly and distinctly.

"Is that a *yes*, Mr. Cole?" I asked, raising my voice. Again, I knew the forced control that I had over him; using the structured power that the court rules provide to the interrogating lawyer on cross-examination had him apoplectic.

He glared at me. "Yes!" he finally spat out in response.

"Thank you, Mr. Cole. You, too, have been most helpful," I said, mimicking Harrington's comment to King Avery. I turned and headed back to my chair. "I'm through with him, Bob," I announced as I walked past Harrington. I looked over at Eric as I sat down. He smiled very discretely and nodded. I winked back at him.

Harrington proceeded to ask some generally ineffectual redirect questions in an attempt to rehabilitate Cole. It went over like a fart at a wedding reception. I didn't bother to re-cross him.

Harrington rested his case after Cole's testimony.

I only called two witnesses: Eric Hawkins and Sandy. Eric was shown the letter of representation that he and I had signed. It post-dated the Watson consent letter signed by Cole. He confirmed that I had not agreed to represent him at any time before my engagement letter with him had been signed by the both of us.

On cross, Harrington focused on establishing that Eric had generally discussed a potential case against Global with me before I had agreed to take it.

"Eric," I asked on re-direct examination, "did I suggest to you that you seek other counsel during that same time period that you were trying to persuade me to take your case?"

"Yes, constantly," he replied. "It wasn't until sometime later that you changed your mind and agreed to represent me and my family against Global. To be honest with you, I still don't understand all the technicalities of this conflict stuff, but my family is grateful that you finally agreed to take the case."

"And during that time period, did I provide you with any information about Global that even sounded remotely 'confidential'?"

"Not at all."

Sandy was asked only a handful of questions by me. She related that she was fired by Hunt when she had objected to being *removed* from the Global team and being re-assigned to the estate planning team.

"Those two men, right there," she said, pointing at Harrington and Gunther with great theatric embellishment, "are the two that fired me." She turned, looking directly at Neanderthal now, with great hurt and frustration. "I don't quite understand how they can now say what they are saying to you, Your Honor. If I really had possession of important or confidential Global information as they are saying today, why did they yank me from the Global team?"

It was all I could do to suppress a laugh. I had seen her practice that line six or seven times in my office before we left today for the hearing. Her frustration and anger looked absolutely sincere and spontaneous.

After I rested, Neanderthal permitted ten minutes of argument per side. Harrington used his entire allotment. Mine took maybe sixty seconds.

"Judge Morgenthal," I argued as I rose from my chair, not even bothering to go to the podium, "Global's motions should be denied. The conflict issue in this case is squarely governed by the decision of *Lucas v. Superior Metal Products, Inc.*, a 1979 Florida Supreme Court ruling." I walked up to the bench and handed her a copy of the case. "In that case, the Court ruled that once a client knowingly consents to allowing one of its former defense counsel to sue it on behalf of a plaintiff, the client is thereafter deemed to have forever waived its right to object to that same attorney representing other plaintiffs in suits against it." I tossed a copy of the case onto Harrington's table. "In short, Judge, it's the old horse out of the barn situation. When Global, per Mr. Cole, consented to my representation of Mr. Watson in his serious products liability action against Global, Global forever waived its right to object to my representation of *any* other products liability plaintiffs against them, including the Hawkins family, in this case. Global can't undo its consent. It cannot 'unring' the bell." I shrugged both of my shoulders, for emphasis. "I realize that Global's lawyers have made quite a fuss about this, but it's really a very open-and-shut issue, given the *Lucas* precedent." I tossed my pen onto the table in front of me and sat down.

Harrington rose again from his seat and started walking towards the podium, apparently intending to offer a few additional morsels of argument in rebuttal to my comments. The judge looked up, ignored him and made her ruling, catching him in mid-stride.

"I'm finding for Mr. Culhane and his client on these issues before me today. Mr. Cole," she said, as she peered down at him, over her half glasses, as he sat in his chair next to Harrington at counsel table, "the court finds that if you hadn't consented to Mr. Culhane's representation of Mr. Watson, I would have granted your company's motions. The fact is, however, you did. And you did it broadly, and with no limitation or exception. So, I'm going to apply the *Lucas* precedent and allow Mr. Culhane to represent the Hawkins family in their products case against your company. Also, the court finds that since the Hunt firm fired Ms. Stevens and had removed her from the Global account before her departure, there is no legal basis available for the court to bar her from working on the Hawkins matter either. Accordingly, Mr. Harrington, both of your motions are denied. Your client has ten days to file an answer to the complaint. Thank you, gentlemen," she announced, as she promptly rose from her upholstered chair to leave the bench and back into chambers.

At that point, Cole did what his genetic and hormonal makeup drove him to do. He tried to control the situation and have the last word with the judge. Big mistake.

"Your Honor, I take great personal issue with the comments that you directed towards me. I was tricked by Mr. Culhane's obviously sneaky tactics. Consent by deceit doesn't constitute legal consent."

Upon hearing his comments, Neanderthal stopped dead in her tracks, turned and faced him as he stood next to Harrington. Her eyes suddenly blazed with fury. "Mr. Harrington, you had better control your client in this case. If I hear any more legal backtalk from Mr. Cole, I'll throw him in jail for civil contempt, and you will regret the consequences as co-counsel of record. The fact is," she volunteered, with a certain degree of venom suddenly injected into her voice, "your client apparently got outfoxed on this consent issue. Either Mr. Cole didn't pay the close attention he should have, or he didn't care. Either way, the consequences are the same. He waived the conflict. But either way, I don't appreciate your client, or its in-house counsel, now coming into my courtroom and trying to have this court save your client from its own ineptitude! Do I make myself clear to you?" she barked.

"Perfectly, Your Honor. I apologize for my client's comments," Harrington groveled.

Neanderthal stared wordlessly for two or three full seconds at Cole before she stormed, without further comment, from the bench and out her chambers' door. Her judicial assistant quickly followed behind her.

No sooner had she exited the room when Cole stormed over to my table, putting his face within inches of mine, as I stood next to my table. He had pushed past Harrington who tried to restrain him from a confrontation with me.

"You and your clients will rue the fucking day you crossed me!" he hissed, with spittle flying. "The fucking day!" he repeated. He was inches from my face and millimeters from losing all control.

"Willis," I calmly said, without flinching, "you'd do well to spend less time threatening people and more time reading important documents before you sign them. It's kind of a helpful habit for a lawyer to get into. And, by the way, you've got bad breath," I added. "Now, get out of my fucking face!" I commanded.

Eric quickly reached over and grabbed my right arm. I'm right handed.

"Easy, Mike, easy," Eric calmly said, "let's get out of here."

Harrington came over and likewise tugged at Cole's arm, finally pulling him away. I casually turned and gathered up the now empty manila folder from the table in front of me. I reached down and picked up my briefcase.

"Good day, gentlemen," I said, as the three of us headed towards the door. On her way out, Sandy winked and smiled at Gunther sitting in the audience section of the courtroom as we passed them. He didn't smile back.

CHAPTER 23

TINA PUNCHED THE hold button on her phone and looked up at me as I walked through the front door of the office. I was returning from a deposition. "It's a Mr. Moskowitz on the phone. He says he wants to hire you for his wife's products liability case."

"Did he give you any information what it's about?" I asked as I headed for my office to grab the call.

"No, he said he wants to talk to you directly."

"I could use a new fat case. Put him through," I called back over my shoulder as I passed into my office. I dropped my briefcase onto the desk, picked up the ringing phone and dropped into my desk chair.

"Michael Culhane here."

"Ah, yes. Mr. Culhane, my name is Jacob Moskowitz," an elderly-sounding voice announced. It bore a heavy New York accent. "I would like you to represent my wife in a products liability lawsuit."

"I see. As a preliminary matter, may I ask you how you came to call me?" I am always curious when I get a call out of the blue.

"I picked your name out of the new phone directory that just came out."

Well, I thought, so much for my ego. "Well, why don't you go ahead and tell me some of the facts, including a little preliminary information about you and your wife for my records." I pulled my desk drawer open, pulled out a legal pad and grabbed a pen off the desk.

"Sure, my wife's name is Rachel. We live over here in Century Club Estates in Miramar. I took early retirement from my job for the New York Transit Authority last year." I knew the retirement village he was living in. It catered to moderate income retirees from the Northeast. "We don't really do much now. I play a little golf and Rachel likes to play the horses, you know."

"So, tell me, what's the problem that causes your wife to want to start a lawsuit?"

"It's really bad. Rachel opened a box of Post Toasties this morning for breakfast, and there were mice feces in it. Can you believe that—mice feces!" he announced with great emotion.

There was a momentary pause on my end of the line. "Uh ... mice feces?" is all I could offer. I laid my pen back down on the desk.

"Yeah, unbelievable! She saw the things floating right there in her cereal bowl, right in her milk. We want to sue the cereal company for damages."

Listening to him, you would have thought that his wife had been fatally impaled on a defective turnstile out at the horse track. He apparently was waiting for me to share in his outrage. I couldn't resist the next question.

"Mr. Moskowitz, did your wife eat any of the feces?"

"Oh my god, such a tragedy. Let me put her on so you can talk to her directly." Before I could tell him that wasn't necessary, the unfortunate victim herself got on the line.

"It was terrible!" she opened with, no hellos or other pleasantries.

I cut in before she repeated the same information her husband had already related to me. "Ma'am, can you tell me? Did you eat any of these ... uh ... foreign objects?" is what I asked. *Did you wolf down any of the mouse turds is what I thought.*

"Who's to know? It was a brand new box of cereal that I had opened this morning. Jacob and I had just sat down for breakfast, and I had fixed myself a bowl of cereal. I poured the milk on the cereal and had taken my first bite when I saw them floating right there in the white milk. Little specks of mice feces. Thought I should die!" she exclaimed.

"So you only had one bite of the cereal, is that right?"

"Such an offensive event!" she lamented. I had visions of a Saturday Night Live skit.

"Mrs. Moskowitz," I repeated. "Did you only have one bite of the cereal," I persisted.

"Yes."

"Do you know if you actually ate any of the feces in that one bite, Mrs. Moskowitz?" I was dying to ask her the next question that came to mind: *Did they taste like chicken?*

"I can't say, but I'm just sure I must have. They were floating all around the bowl," she victim-whined.

"Did you actually get sick or throw up?"

"Oh yeah, I did."

I cross examined, "You got sick? I mean, you actually threw up?"

"Well, no, I didn't actually vomit, if that's what you mean, but I wanted to. I just wanted to vomit," she repeated the new idea I just gave her with emphasis. "When I showed my bowl to Jacob, we decided to call a lawyer and sue the company for our damages."

I rolled my eyes and shook my head on my end of the phone. *So much for the great case and the easy slam-dunk money.* I was desperate for cases, but not that desperate.

"I'll tell you what, Mrs. Moskowitz, it's probably not a good case for you to waste your time pursuing, either from a proof or damages standpoint. Not only is it questionable whether you actually consumed any of the feces, but I don't really see much in the way of compensable damages under Florida law. Also, the cereal company will fight you all the way, on every issue, you can count on that. They'll make you prove that the mouse turds ... excuse me, the mice feces—were in your cereal box when it was manufactured as opposed to having been introduced into the box at the grocery store, or at your home after it was purchased, from dirty dishes, or weren't in the jug of milk you poured on the cereal. So," I urged the poor victim, "you actually might be better off just calling the cereal company and letting them know of the problem. They might just send you some coupons for some free replacement cereal," I suggested.

"No, I want to fight this! We aren't going to be treated like that, and we think they owe us some money for our pain and ... uh ..." she groped for the word that she had undoubtedly read in the newspapers.

"Pain and suffering, Mrs. Moskowitz?" I suggested.

"Yeah, for our pain and suffering," she echoed.

"I appreciate your perspective, Ma'am, but it's not the kind of case that I'm interested in pursuing for you. I'm a sole practitioner, and I simply don't have the resources for your case."

"Uh, huh."

"I'll tell you what," I suddenly brightened, "let me give you the name of another excellent attorney here in Ft. Lauderdale that you'll probably want to talk to about taking the case."

"That would be fine," she said.

"Robert Harrington. Heck of a good lawyer. He goes by 'Bob.' He practices with the Hunt & Baxter law firm." I gave her the firm's general telephone number and suggested that she give him a call. "Tell him I referred you to him. If he can't take it, try the Broward County Bar Association for a recommendation."

"Thank you," she said, reluctantly accepting my dissing of her case.

"My pleasure," I smiled as I hung up.

I was still chuckling from the call when Sandy walked into my office a moment later, holding the day's mail. "Bad news. Global has moved to disqualify Neanderthal from the Hawkins case," she said, without preamble. She handed the stack of mail to me. The motion was on top. "They also served us with an Offer of Judgment for twenty-five thousand dollars."

"Dog shit," I grimaced. "I knew it was too good to be true to have pulled Neanderthal as our trial judge. What are their grounds?"

"Her berating Cole and Harrington at the close of the disqualification motion," she said, sitting in one of my client chairs. "Cole signed an affidavit on behalf of Global saying that her comments last week reflect a prejudice against Global. Can't receive a fair trial in front of her is the long and short of it. Can we fight it?"

"Not successfully. Florida law gives a party to a lawsuit essentially an unqualified right to bump a sitting judge from the case if that party files a sworn affidavit attesting that he doesn't believe he can receive a fair trial before that judge and there's even a hint of evidence in the record to support it. Global has said all the magic words," I said, scanning the motion I lifted from the pile. "Nine times out of ten a disqualification motion is upheld on appeal, and we don't have the resources to go fighting an appeal as well. This is not a good development," I said.

"Well, if you're not happy about that development, you're sure not going to like who we drew as the replacement judge either."

"Oh, shit, don't do this to me. You're killing me! Who did we get?"

"Vaughn," she said, shaking her head.

"Shit squared!" I murmured, shaking my head.

"I thought you'd see it that way."

"Global is going to love the Honorable Baylor T. Vaughn," I lamented.

"What's he like on a case? I've only heard bits and pieces, but I know that you've tried a couple of cases before him before I joined Hunt, didn't you?"

"Only one, actually. It was a case for a table saw manufacturer I represented. It was obvious from the evidentiary rulings he gave me that he loves the business community. Half of his rulings for me were dead wrong on the law, but I wasn't about to complain. Looks like the worm has turned," I said with concern.

Vaughn was a staunch conservative. Now in his mid-60s, he had been on the trial court bench for ten years, having previously practiced as an average insurance defense trial lawyer with a below average three-man firm in Ft. Lauderdale. He liked to run his courtroom with a tight rein and a stern disposition. His evidentiary rulings were rarely even-tempered, often questionable and always unpredictable. He struck me as a lawyer who had practiced too long and burnt out in the process before ascending to the bench. His mood hadn't improved on the bench either.

"Is he a straight shooter, or is he an old fraternity brother or drinking buddy of any of the old farts at Hunt?" Sandy asked.

"He's honest enough, but I also know he's a friend of the Hunt firm. He and Derek Rodgers, one of the senior partners at Hunt, both served on the judicial nominating committee for this district for two terms before he took the bench. It was well known that Rodgers pulled a few strings with the committee to get him nominated for the bench. I'm sure the two of them have downed their share of martinis together, so I figure that Harrington will get the benefit of the close calls. Nothing dishonest, but he knows the firm a hell of a lot better than he knows me. And he also doesn't like to change his mind once he makes it up," I added, pointing out another of his sterling qualities. "More problematic than anything else, though, is his staunchly conservative philosophy. Having represented nothing but manufacturers and insurance companies when he practiced, he doesn't like plaintiffs."

"Great!" she said, shaking her head in frustration. Then, with a hint of a smile, she asked, "So, if Global bumped Neanderthal, can't we bump him, too? You know, file a motion to disqualify him just like they did?"

"You're pretty Machiavellian, you know that?"

"I do my best," she shrugged. "So, can we?"

"No. He hasn't made any prejudicial statement to us, like Neanderthal made to Cole and Harrington, which would give us the opportunity to file on him. And Vaughn's too smart to make that mistake. He's very careful about protecting his record."

"So, we're stuck?"

"Yes, we're stuck, dammit. He's going to be a problem, but we'll have to deal with it." I was trying to convince myself as much as Sandy. "I'll give Eric a call and let him know the bad news."

"Oh," she suddenly recalled as she rose from the chair, "what about the offer of judgment? Are you going to mention it to Eric and let him know of its consequences?" She was referring to the fact that if Eric rejected the offer and Global won at trial, Global would get a judgment against Eric for the full amount of fees and costs it paid to defend the lawsuit. That would be a staggering sum in this case. The offer of judgment was another sign that Cole was 'playing for keeps' in Eric's case.

"Yeah," I shrugged, "I'll discuss the O.J. with him when I tell him about the change in judges. He's in this fight to win. He'll reject it, of course, but I need to alert him about the severe economic consequences if we lose the case."

"Also, I don't know if you saw it yet in that stack of mail," Sandy pointed out as she walked towards my office door, "but Global also served us with its answer and its objections to about ninety percent of the discovery demands we served on them with the complaint in this case."

I read over Global's discovery objections after she left my office. Predictably, they were heavy on objections and thin on substantive information. I emailed a copy over to my experts for their review and analysis and then prepared my first, of what would undoubtedly be many, motions to compel Global to produce the discovery information I had asked for regarding the Mesa. I would need to file a motion and request a hearing before Judge Vaughn. Global's war of economic attrition had started. Harrington knew that, as a sole practitioner on a contingent fee, I would be burning up valuable time and limited resources attending hearings over ridiculous discovery objections he would be asserting in the case. He was getting paid by the hour, and he knew that time truly was money. Every hour I spent bringing motions fighting over his discovery demands in the Hawkins case was another hour that I would not be paid, nor spent on another of my clients who were paying me by the hour. It was a powerful club, and Global intended to use it.

AT THE MOTION to compel hearing, which was held before Judge Vaughn the following week, I focused my arguments on six distinct categories of documents and information concerning the fuel system and stability design of the Mesa that I wanted but Global had objected to. These included internal Mesa engineering design memoranda, documents and email; product specifications relating to the Mesa's stability system, including vehicle weight, height of various aspects such as its center of gravity (c.g.), length of wheelbase; design, layout and assembly drawings; marketing and sales information; all testing conducted on the Mesa's stability or fuel containment systems; and records reflecting complaints or lawsuits received by Global in which a problem or defect was alleged to exist in the Mesa's stability or fuel containment systems. It was exhaustive but straight-forward and elementary information in a products liability case like the Hawkins case. To provide it, Global would be required to spend a not insubstantial chunk of internal time to identify, gather and copy it for production. Most trial courts were prone to conclude that these documents, and the costs to gather them, were simply part of a manufacturer's overhead, i.e., just another cost of doing business in the United States. I was hoping that Vaughn had finally come around to this line of thinking. I hadn't been before him since the table saw case a few years ago. Discovery in that case had been modest and did not provide me with any clues as to his philosophy on discovery.

If you talk to the average guy on the street, he will tell you that a products liability suit against a manufacturer is won in the courtroom with flashy cross-examination and a stable full of smooth, silver-tongued experts. He's wrong. It isn't. A products liability case is usually won in the very tedious, boring and low-profile trenches of pre-trial discovery. It's in those trenches, which requires hundreds of hours of reading through literally thousands of pages of documents, drawings and emails, that defects are hopefully (from the plaintiff's perspective) identified and theories of liability crystallized. Hence, getting one's grubby hands on these internal documents is vital.

Harrington knew this as well, and he argued vigorously at the hearing to prevent Global from being required to produce the documents and information I had demanded.

"Your Honor, what's at issue in this case is the *final* design, the *as built* design that was actually sold to the public, not all the countless *preliminary* designs and testing information that Global considered before that final design. Mr. Culhane is demanding the production of the voluminous design history of the Mesa, including earlier design variations which might have been later changed. After all," he argued, "Mr. Culhane isn't criticizing the Mesa that *wasn't built*. He's trying this case on the final Mesa design that *was built*. If you allow him to obtain discovery of this irrelevant information, I can assure you that he'll be parading a great deal of it before the jury at trial. They'll be hopelessly lost and confused in this design case."

Harrington was very effectively playing to Vaughn's penchant for control over his courtroom. He was a judge who liked to keep trials as simple as possible for the benefit of the jury. And for him.

"Mr. Culhane?" Judge Vaughn succinctly asked as he drew a big puff on his cigar, "your response?" We were sitting in Vaughn's chambers for the motion hearing rather than in open court. This was his preference.

The courthouse was supposed to be a smoke-free building, but Vaughn utterly disregarded the rule, and none of the attorneys appearing before him was about to complain. His poison of choice was a cheap, fat black cigar whose odor was as pungent as it was overpowering. It matched Vaughn.

Baylor T. Vaughn was a big-boned, fleshy man. He sported a perfectly bald head, adorned with a medley of liver spots which floated on top from way too much sun. His triple chin was a matching combination to his heavily-hooded and dark, baggy eyes, which looked more like horizontal pill-box gun slits than eye openings. A set of thick, old-fashioned, black-framed Joe McCarthy glasses sat perched upon his undersized nose. Vaughn wasn't much into style. With his rather odd, triangular-shaped, flat ears, he gave me the overall impression of an old loggerhead turtle puffing on a big stogie.

I looked at him through the blue haze. "Your Honor, as you can appreciate, this case has only recently commenced, it's brand new. This is my first discovery demand. To avoid any legitimate objections from Global, I made my
document request very narrow and relevant to the specific issues in this case.
My experts and client are entitled to this elementary design-related information.
Without it, my client's rights will be irreparably prejudiced. The docu—"

"Jury confusion," Vaughn interrupted, shaking his head back and forth as
he blew a stream of blue smoke from his mouth. His chins undulated as he did
so. "I'm very concerned with jury confusion in this case," he continued. "In the
last couple of years, I've witnessed more and more lawyers in these product
liability cases ask for every type of document imaginable from the manufacturer. It's especially bad, I think, in the auto cases. I used to allow it, but I don't
anymore. I've seen what happens," he puffed. "The plaintiff starts the lawsuit
without the foggiest idea of any particular defect and then tries to get boxcars
of company records in hope of finding a relevant needle somewhere in that
haystack. Well, it leads to a colossal waste of everybody's time, including the
court's since I end up refereeing constant discovery disputes between the attorneys over design and discovery issues that are far removed from the real issues
in the case."

"I certainly can appreciate Your Honor's feelings on the discovery issues,"
I politely interrupted, taking advantage of his drag on his cigar, "but I respectfully remind the court that this is the first discovery request in the case. A certain degree of latitude, I believe, is required at this stage, particularly since I
have identified two very specific defect claims in my clients' complaint: the
Mesa's stability system and the attachment of the fuel filler pipe to the Mesa's
gas tank. This isn't a fishing expedition, Judge." I hoped to placate his
concerns.

"Well, I intend to keep it that way, gentlemen." The Turtle looked at me
and then over at Harrington. "There will be no fishing expeditions conducted
in my courtroom. I'm the game warden here, and I post the fishing rules. I'm
sorry Mr. Culhane, but I'm not going to allow you to obtain the scope of
documents you desire. I don't believe they're relevant. What's the name of the
vehicle that's involved in this case?" he asked, looking down with confusion at
the pleadings in front of him. Either he had not been paying attention or had
already forgotten.

"A Mesa, Your Honor. It's an SUV, a sport utility vehicle," I answered.

"Your clients allege that they were damaged by a defectively designed
Mesa that they purchased from Global through its dealer. It's the *final,
production* design of the Mesa that is at issue in these proceedings," he said with
emphasis, "not the *preliminary* designs for that vehicle, which were not

ultimately selected, nor sold, to your clients. That's the scope of your discovery that I'm going to permit," he ordered. "I'm ordering Global to produce for you only the final design documents, including the testing documents which Global conducted of that final production Mesa model. I'll permit some leeway to you, Mr. Culhane, in your depositions of the Global engineers regarding the design history, but not a lot. However, I will allow you to see complaints and suit papers against Global regarding allegations of fuel containment defects and stability defects in the Mesa. Also, I'm not permitting you access to the marketing or design team memos which aren't related to the final design chosen." He stubbed out the now-stubby remnants of his cigar in the base of a cut-off empty brass artillery shell casing that served as his ashtray. "Is my ruling clear enough, gentlemen?"

"Perfectly," Harrington bubbled. He was barely managing to contain his delight at his victory.

"Yes, Your Honor," I said evenly, not showing my anger at his screwed up ruling. I wasn't about to let Harrington witness my clear disappointment in the restrictive ruling.

"Also, while I have both of you here," Vaughn added, momentarily clearing phlegm from his throat, "I'm setting this case down for trial on December first. As both of you probably know, I keep a very current docket, and I move my cases along. That date will give both of you almost six months to complete your discovery and get this case ready for trial. My judicial assistant will be sending you out a scheduling order to that effect with all of the deadlines and disclosures I require of the attorneys in my court."

My surprise at the extremely quick trial date he just announced must have registered on my face.

"Is there a problem with that date, Mr. Culhane?" The Turtle asked.

"Judge," I protested, "this is a very serious products case. One of my clients died in the accident. Her one-year-old infant son was horribly burned and is just beginning treatment. There is going to be significant discovery of complex engineering issues in this case. Judge," I pleaded, "there's no way that we can be reasonably expected to be ready to try a case of this magnitude by December. I ask that you reconsider and set it for next year, your Honor. Even March or April would be tight, but we can get it ready by that time."

"No. I'm not going to do that," he said gruffly. "I used to do a lot of trial work myself, Mr. Culhane. Lawyers work under deadlines. I have found as a judge that if I don't push the lawyers, they certainly aren't going to push themselves. They'll delay and delay 'til the cows come home.' No," he said resolutely, "December first is plenty of time for you and your experts to do what you have to do to get this case ready. Besides, it's going to be the same deadline for the defendants here, too. Do you have any problem with that date Mr. Harrington?" he asked, turning his substantial corpulence towards him.

"Judge Vaughn," he responded, "you've hit it on the head. This case could be tried tomorrow. Mr. Culhane's over-reacting. December first is more than enough time for both sides to get this case ready. It's a simple case."

"December first it is," The Turtle pronounced with finality.

"Well, if you're setting deadlines in this case," I quickly recovered, "I'm requesting that you also set a common deadline by which all testing by the parties or their experts must be completed and disclosed to the other party. November first would be a logical date for both sides."

"While I agree that a deadline for testing and disclosures should be set," Harrington quickly countered, "I disagree with Mr. Culhane's proposal that the deadline be the same date for both sides. The plaintiff should disclose any testing that it does first, if it decides to do testing, with Global's testing and disclosure deadline 30 days thereafter. That way, if the plaintiff doesn't perform testing, my client may decide not to do it either."

As a defense lawyer for Global, I always made the same argument that Harrington was now making since a staggered disclosure deadline gave the defendant manufacturer a distinct strategic advantage. Testing for a manufacturer always created the risk that the test of the product would help the plaintiff prove the plaintiff's defect theory. The prevailing defense strategy was to avoid testing if the plaintiff opted not to perform any.

"Judge," I now whined, "Mr. Harrington is trying to play tactical games here with your scheduling order. If November first is sauce for the plaintiff's goose in this case, then it ought to likewise be sauce for the defendant's gander. Besides," I reminded him with sarcasm, "didn't we just hear Mr. Harrington tell this court that he could 'try this case tomorrow,' something about this being a 'simple case'?"

I detected the slightest trace of a smile on The Turtle's face. One of his chin folds moved.

He thought for a moment and then finally nodded in assent. "A common date it is," he ordered. "November first will be the common deadline for the completion and disclosure of all case testing by both parties. Results are to be hand delivered to the opposing attorney's office by five p.m. on that date. Is there anything else we need to address?"

"No," Harrington and I said in chorus. It was the only thing we had agreed to all day.

CHAPTER 24

HARRINGTON SCHEDULED ROCKY Watson's deposition for the next week. Global was putting on a full court press. I demanded that it be held in my offices since I wanted Watson to be as comfortable as possible. I was hoping that on our "battleground," Rocky would be easier to control. To say that he was unpredictable would be akin to saying that the Titanic took on a little water just before it went down. Given the small amount of money involved in his lawsuit, taking his deposition was intended to be nothing more than a punitive salvo from Global. Normally, Global wouldn't waste its time with a deposition in such a small case. The case would simply be set for trial and tried. Clearly, every hour that they forced me to spend on the Watson case was an hour less spent by me on the Hawkins case, and in neither one was I getting paid by the hour, as Harrington was.

"What a ridiculous waste of time," I grumbled to Liz as the two of us lay in bed the night before Watson's deposition. I was commenting on the Watson deposition in the morning. Liz was reading her Kindle in bed, her usual practice before going to sleep.

She put her Kindle down and took off her reading glasses, putting them on the night table next to her side of the bed. "Since you're determined to frustrate my reading, you must want to talk."

"Frustrate your reading? I'm trying to engage in meaningful discussion, that's all. I haven't seen my wife all day, and here she is with her nose buried in a dime store novel," I joked.

"Dime store novel?" she laughed. "This is serious literature I'm reading, if you don't mind—Mary Higgins Clark."

"Aren't you always telling me that I need to pay more attention to relationships? Well, that's what I'm trying to do here—have a 'relationship conversation.'"

"*A relationship* conversation? Is that what this is?" she asked, mockingly. "Men really are from Mars. Okay, so tell me, what are you fuming about?"

"It's this *pro bono* case I'm handling against Global for that burned-out vet down in Miami, a guy named Rocky Watson. I'm just venting over Global's bullshit tactics to get me to waste more of my time, without getting paid, as punishment for taking the Hawkins case. They know that Watson faces an impossible task in proving his case, even without considering his having destroyed the seat track that he had the problem with. They don't need to do this; it's just goddamn harassment."

"Why would Global want to waste its money paying Hunt & Baxter lawyers to hassle you? I know they're not happy that you beat them on the conflict of interest issue, but aren't they spending a lot more money on the Watson case than it really deserves?"

"Yes, it's pure retribution."

"Wait a minute," she said suddenly, her brow knitting, "is Watson the guy that called us in the middle of the night?"

"The one and only."

"Oh brother," she replied as she snuggled over and put her head on my chest, "I hope he shows better judgment at his deposition tomorrow than what he's shown to me. Didn't you say that he's a little on the strange side?"

I laughed. "Yeah, he's a bit of an artichoke, I think—all tough leaves and nasty thistles on the outside, but a nice guy with a decent heart on the inside. Life's been tough for him," I said, coming to his defense. "He told Sandy that he's been estranged from his parents for years, and has no other family. He's kind of all alone out there and likes to do his own thing. Apparently, he's become a little 'difficult' in the process."

"Well, good luck tomorrow. How do you think he will fare in a deposition setting?" Liz asked as she moved back onto her side of the bed and turned her reading light off.

"That's the twenty dollar question," I chuckled as I turned my light off, as well.

THE ANSWER TO that question came the next day.

Harrington sent over his associate in training, Tucker Craige, to take Watson's deposition. Craige was one of the few associates back at Hunt who had always rubbed me the wrong way from the day he was hired. Upon crossing the firm's threshold as a newbie associate, he had kept one unwavering eye on the partnership ladder and the other on what political steps he needed to take to climb to its top.

If the associates started griping about a particular Hunt policy that irritated them as a group—and what group of associates worth their salt didn't—you could always count on Craige to remain non-committal on the issue until he had comfortably gauged how the political winds were blowing on the issue at the partnership level. If the partners frowned on the associates' request, Craige would be distancing himself as quickly as possible from his fellow associates. If the partners liked the idea, he'd lead the associate charge.

He went unloved by his fellow associates. They recognized his conniving ways. At the last firm Christmas party before I left, Craige received an anonymous Christmas gift from a couple of the associates: a supersized tube of Chapstick with a card suggesting his need for the gift for all the ass kissing he did. Craige could care less. He figured out early that the associates didn't sign his paycheck nor did they control his advancement in the firm. The partners did. He was very capable and had managed to work his way into becoming Harrington's senior litigation associate of choice over the last three years. He emulated Harrington's approach in all respects. As a result, he was on the fast track towards partnership.

Concerned about Watson's independent and unpredictable streak, I spent two hours with him in my office in advance of the deposition trying to prepare him. We went over the facts again and again, and I stressed the rules I wanted him to follow during the deposition: tell the truth, answer the question, don't volunteer information, be firm but polite and don't get emotional. He promised he would follow them.

"What do ya take me for, a fuckin' stupid idiot?" he asked, irritably, after we had gone over the rules for the third time that morning. "It's just questions and answers, *and I'll be a good boy,*" he said, shortly.

"No, I'm not treating you as an idiot, Rocky," I both assured and tried to placate him. "I repeat all of these rules, over and over, with all of my clients before their first deposition." *Okay, maybe I spent a lot more time on them with you, I acknowledged to myself.* "Depositions are very important, and it's damn important that you know and abide by the rules, that's all."

He showed up at my office wearing dirty and worn jeans and a 'wife beater shirt'—a white tank top that could have used a spin or two in the washing machine with a gallon of Oxy-Clean. It also looked like it had remnants of last weeks' meals on it.

"Keep cool, Rocky," I urged him again as we ended our prep session. "I know the lawyer who will be asking you the questions this morning. He's a little shit with a big time ego. He may intentionally try to get under your skin to get you angry. Don't fall for it. Just keep focused on the information he is asking for, answer it and keep your cool. It shouldn't take more than a couple of hours. Okay?"

"I don't know why I gotta take time off work to give this deposition thing, anyway," he said, with continued irritation. "Didn't we already answer a whole fuckin' bushel basket of goddamn written questions about all this stuff?" He was referring to the extensive set of written questions that Global had served us with immediately after the suit was started. Those questions went on for ten pages and went into excruciating detail about his ownership of the Carriage model, its maintenance and the facts of his accident. Watson was right. He had already provided all the information that was important. I tried again. "I understand your frustration, Rocky, but Global's lawyers get the right to ask you oral questions as well, under oath. It's no big deal, really. It will be over before you know it, and you can get back to work. Just keep a poker face and take your time answering the questions. And," I quickly added—*how could I have forgotten this part*—"don't use swear words or profanity. Everything you say will be taken down by the court reporter, word for word. If you start swearing, Global's lawyers are just going to read it all back to the jury at trial and try to embarrass us. Juries don't like to hear profanity by witnesses in a lawsuit, okay?"

He just looked at me and frowned. Asking him to stop swearing was like asking him to quit breathing.

I scheduled the deposition to take place down the hall from my offices in the large conference room of a title insurance company. They allowed me to use the room when it wasn't being used for their real estate closings. Craige showed up right on time, all business, and was led into the conference room by Tina. Watson and I were already there along with the female court reporter Craige had hired to take down the testimony.

Predictably, Craige made no effort to shake hands with either me or my client when he came in and sat down at the table. All business, he set his expensive Tumi leather briefcase down, pulled out his legal pad that I could see was chock full of questions, and started arranging his materials on the conference room table in front of him. It was obvious that he was bent on making the point that he was now my 'equal' since we were on opposite sides of a case; no more 'partner-associate' deferential butt kissing for him.

"Care for something to drink, Tucker, a Coke, coffee or water?" I offered as he was prepared to start his questions. The reporter sat at the end of the long, dark, polished mahogany conference table, while Rocky sat at the end on my side, immediately to my right. Craige sat on the other side of the four foot wide table, directly across from Watson.

"Won't be necessary," he responded stiffly, not bothering to even look at me. "I brought my own bottle of water." He pulled a plastic bottle of water from his litigation bag, unscrewed its lid and put it on the table next to his pad. Craige looked, well, *resplendent* was the only adjective that came to mind, as he sat at the table. He was dressed every bit the corporate litigator. The pattern in his expensive-looking red print tie matched the fabric in his suspenders. He was even beginning to look like Harrington, I chuckled inwardly.

"Let's proceed, Madame Reporter," he curtly instructed the diminutive brunette court reporter. "Please swear in the witness." She did, and we were off.

After listening to Craige's questions for sixty minutes, it was painfully obvious that his marching orders from Harrington were to drag the deposition out for as long as possible. And he carried out those orders well. The same basic question would be repeatedly posed to Rocky in ten different thinly-disguised ways.

Rocky was getting pissed, and so was I.

"Tucker," I finally but politely said on the record after about an hour, "let's move this deposition along. I've been very tolerant so far, but you're wasting Mr. Watson's time and mine with the repetitious questions. You're plowing and re-plowing the same old ground."

"Are you instructing Mr. Watson not to answer my question, Mr. Culhane?" he icily challenged, his voice rising. He was looking for a fight and was trying to assert himself in the process. I refused to rise to the bait.

"Tucker, come on, let's get moving," I implored, good-naturedly. "You didn't hear me instruct him not to answer your questions. I'm just asking you to move the questions along and get to where the rubber meets the road in this case. That's all I'm suggesting, okay? Incidentally, loosen up a little," I suggested, "this is just a deposition, for god's sake, not trial. Incidentally," I added, "do me a favor and call me Mike. Our days at Hunt, and the formal pecking order we had there, are long gone," I offered, trying to be nice.

"Believe me, Mr. Culhane," he smirked, keeping his icy and formal distance, "I'm well aware that you're gone from Hunt. I'm taking this deposition the way I want to take it, and I'll ask any questions I want to ask. Is that clear?" He asked shortly and defensively. "And you're free to make any objections you desire, Mr. Culhane," he replied, stiffly. He had his agenda, and he was sticking to it.

"Mr. Watson," he said, finally turning back to the witness and continuing, "when was the first time after you bought the car that the seat problem, *as you claim*, first manifested itself?" His emphasis of the phrase, "as you claim," was intended to be an insult and a challenge to the veracity of the claim.

Rocky leaned his head to one side and looked at Craige, confused. "I don't understand. What do you mean, 'manifest'?" Rocky asked. He was not used to big words.

Craige closed his eyes, pinched the bridge of his nose and shook his head back and forth in apparent disbelief at Rocky's inability to comprehend the word. After an audible sigh, he opened his eyes and looked directly at Rocky. "'*Pop up,*' Mr. Watson," he said sarcastically, "is that better for you? When did the seat track problem you *claim* existed first '*pop up*'?" he repeated, his voice laden with sarcasm.

"Watch it, Tucker," I advised, "your tone and sarcasm are inappropriate and unprofessional. Don't persist."

Craige didn't even look at me. He ignored my admonition altogether. "Can you answer my question with that *easier* definition thrown in for you?" The insulting tone in his voice could not be mistaken.

I noticed the court reporter started looking uncomfortable at the deteriorating tone and tenor of Craige's questions.

Rocky, sitting directly across the table from Craige, folded his arms across his chest, defensively. His eyes narrowed at hearing Craige's insulting sarcasm. Without changing his facial expression, and while looking Craige straight in the eye, Rocky slowly leaned his upper body to his right in his chair, to about a forty-five degree angle, at which point he let a huge bullfrog of a fart audibly rumble out from down below. Its klaxon-like bellow lasted a good three seconds. It was truly of Oscar quality, and its malodorous aroma quickly engulfed our entire end of the table.

It was all I could do to keep from laughing. Craige looked aghast and disgusted. Harrington's instructions for the deposition apparently had not included this scenario.

Continuing to keep his eyes locked on Craige, Rocky finally slowly leaned back to being perfectly vertical in his chair. After waiting another three or four seconds, he finally answered Craige's question.

"It first *popped up* after the car had about fifty thousand miles on it." His voice barely masked his anger at being demeaned.

"Did you bring it into the Global dealership for remedial work when that happened? ... *Repair work*, Mr. Watson," Craige clarified, seeing that Rocky was also having trouble understanding the word 'remedial.'

Always count on a lawyer, I thought, to take a perfectly simple word and recast it into non-English, technical garbage.

"Yeah, I brought the car to a friend of mine who runs a repair shop." he answered. "Twice. But he could never find no problem with the fuckin' seat track when he looked. The problem was that it wouldn't slip around all the time, only every now and then. Damn thing never did it at the repair shop."

I winced. *So much for my 'deposition rules.'* Craige smiled. He was getting under Rocky's skin and getting profanity-laced testimony to eventually read back to the judge or jury at trial to paint Rocky in a bad light.

"Mr. Watson, you eventually, *and intentionally*, removed that *allegedly* defective driver's seat track from your car and threw it away, didn't you?" Craig continued, both challenging and attacking Rocky with his choice of words.

"Yep, and you can drop that 'alleged' word from our little chat here. I know what that word means, and there was nothing 'alleged' about that seat track problem. It was a piece of shit, pure and simple." Rocky was hot, getting hotter and starting to lose control. Craige's tactics and attitude of disrespect towards Rocky were finally getting to him. I had warned him this would occur and that he was to keep cool and not react. So much for that.

"And when you removed that seat track from your car, you certainly knew that you were *tampering* with potentially important evidence, didn't you?" Craige's tone continued its ugly and accusatorial tone.

The court reporter quickly looked up with a new frown on her face.

"I knew I was removing it. There was no fuckin' 'tampering' going on," he angrily shot back.

"You don't think that removing the seat track from the car and trashing it before you start a lawsuit over it isn't 'tampering' with it, Mr. Watson?"

"No, I don't." He kept his eyes locked on Craige, like a Patriot missile on an incoming scud.

Craige's only response was to shake his head softly back and forth and look up at the ceiling in obvious disbelief before asking his next question.

"And you never gave my client any fair opportunity to inspect the seat for any alleged defects before you started your lawsuit, did you?"

"Look, I didn't think shit about it," Rocky shot back. "I've already told you that about five times now. I just wanted a seat that wouldn't unexpectedly slide around under my ass when I was driving the street like that piece of shit did! Global had already wrote me and told me that it wasn't taking any responsibility for a damn thing, anyway. So, tell me why I should have to come back and beg you and Global a second time to come out and inspect it before I throw the worthless piece of shit away, will ya?" he said angrily.

"Sir," Craige quickly and imperiously shot back at him, "*I'm* the one asking the questions here. *Your* job is *to sit there* and answer them unless your lawyer there tells you not to. Now, those rules are *simple enough* for even you to understand, aren't they?" His insolence and disrespect was undisguised.

I didn't think that Rocky was capable of moving as fast as he did. Craige had no sooner finished mouthing his smart-ass question when Rocky sprang forward out of his chair, in one fluid motion, with his piston-like left arm and hand shooting across the table at Craige. He violently grabbed the now wide-eyed Craige by his sporty red tie, about six inches below its knot, and literally yanked him across the table towards himself. Craige's nattily dressed body immediately came following closely behind his stretched and reddening neck and tie, gagging uncontrollably as he did. His designer bottle of water went flying in the process, with the water flying towards our side of the table.

Reacting almost reflexively, I jumped out of my chair next to Rocky and threw my arms around his upper arms and torso just as his right arm was pulling back to punch Craige's lights out. It was like holding on for dear life on a raging bull. I heard the court reporter scream down at the end of the table and saw a blur of her as she ran for the door. Her machine was knocked over in her frantic attempt to get out of the way.

"You little fuckin' nightcrawler!" Watson bellowed in his rage. "Nobody treats me like fuckin' white trash, nobody!"

"Rocky! Rocky!" I yelled as I managed to pin both his arms and keep from sending Craige into his next week's docket call. "Let him go! Let him go! It's okay."

While my focus and energy was on trying to control Rocky, I managed to catch a glance at Craige. He was on his belly, completely lying on top of the conference table, having been pulled into that position by Rocky who still held the tie in a vise-like grip with his left fist. Craige looked like a tournament-winning tuna being pulled wide-eyed onto a fishing boat. Only a gaff was missing.

Finally responding to my grip and my loud pleas in his ear, Rocky regained some degree of control and let go of the tie, flinging it at Craige's beet-red face. Craige's upper body immediately dropped down to rest on the table-top below where he laid gasping and rasping for air. A fish out of water. He was clawing at his tie with both hands trying to unloosen its now-restrictive encirclement of his neck.

"You! ... you! ..." he blubbered and screamed at Rocky between gasps as he unceremoniously crawled off the table on the other side and slumped into his chair. "You ... are dead meat!! You're going to pay for this, you son of a bitch, so help me god!"

"Careful there Tucker," I calmly suggested as I tentatively released Rocky from my bear hug. Rocky was still breathing heavily, and I continued to watch him carefully as I spoke. "I don't think you really want to provoke my client anymore today. I have a feeling that you just tasted only the *hors d'oeuvre*. Trust me, stay away from the main course," I cautioned.

Rocky stared coldly at Craige for a final moment, looked over at me, and then calmly walked out of the room. His firefight was over.

"I'm suing him for assault!" Craige spat after Watson left the room. "Count on it!" He was massaging his red and swollen neck. "You have no idea of the trouble that guy is in!" All pretenses of his former 'calm control' and 'refined breeding' at Hunt were gone. "He's fucking dead!" he screamed, once again.

"Tucker," I said calmly, "after you cool down and get back to your office to change your underwear, I suggest that you might want to think long and hard before running off and doing that. The fact is you provoked the man. And you did it in a most unprofessional manner, with your arrogant, sarcastic questions and your demeaning attitude with him."

"I'm going to sue that son—"

"Not a good idea," I cut him off. "Should you do that, or try to use what happened here today for some type of sanctions in Mr. Watson's case against Global, well, I'd probably have to file for counter sanctions and follow that up with a bar grievance against you for unprofessional conduct. I can assure you our court reporter will be my first witness. Oh yeah," I casually added as I started walking out the door to find my client, "if I remember correctly, aren't you up for partnership over at Hunt next year? Well, I used to sit on partnership decisions there at Hunt. For what it's worth, I don't think the partners over there would like what happened here today one bit. It doesn't fit the image of a Hunt partner. Not at all. Egging on a semi-literate *pro bono* plaintiff and causing him to protect his pride by throttling your pin-striped little ass? No," I added, shaking my head, "this all raises vexatious little questions, Tucker. But, don't let me prevent you from doing what you think you have to do," I smiled politely as I momentarily stopped at the door before exiting.

Craige was sitting there, listening with narrowed eyes between wheezes. He was slowly getting ahold of himself. If Craige was anything, he was a survivor.

"You can drop it right here, and only you and I will know what happened here today, or you can try to use this to your advantage—if you really think it is going to give you some type of advantage. Choose your poison," I declared. "Incidentally, I assume that you're done with your deposition?"

He sat there and looked at me with rage and smoldering anger in his eyes. But I also saw fear. Fear that the partnership rung was getting away from his controlled grip. He apparently made up his mind. "You ... son ... of ... a ... bitch, Culhane." Then, after a moment, he added, "alright, this stays here. Understood?"

"Wise choice." I said. "Kind of glad you didn't take a video deposition, aren't you?" I added, with a chuckle as I left the room. The deposition was over.

I found Rocky down by my office door, pacing the hall. The court reporter, who was still wide-eyed and wary, was standing off to the side, well away from him. "Excuse me for a moment, Rocky." I walked over to the reporter. I knew her, though not well, from having been in a few depositions with her over the years.

"You okay?"

She laughed, somewhat nervously. She was a veteran and had undoubtedly seen other depositions go badly, like this one had. "Thank you, I'm fine. Are we going to continue?"

"No. The lawyers have agreed that the deposition is over. We've also agreed that your deposition transcript will merely conclude with the last question that was not responded to by my client being deleted from the transcript. Craige is in agreement. We both want this to look just like a regular old boring deposition to anybody who reads the thing. Feel free to verify what I'm telling you with Tucker, okay?"

"That's fine with me," she replied. "More than fine."

"Oh, one more thing. Tucker has asked that this whole little event stays in that room. You know, from a professional embarrassment standpoint," I smiled.

She held up both hands, palms facing me. "Whatever floats your boat. I just report on the written transcript, the rest is nobody's business." She smiled and walked back down to retrieve her machine.

"I'm sorry I lost it," Rocky growled in an apologetic tone as I got over to him. It was as close as I had seen him to actually being humble.

"What's done is done. I've got to take some of the blame myself. I should have stepped in and terminated the deposition when he started getting particularly sarcastic at the end."

"Have I blown the case for us?" he asked, concerned.

"If that other lawyer asks for sanctions against you, I think we've got problems. Strangling opposing counsel is generally frowned upon, even if they probably deserve it," I laughed, trying to lighten it up. "However, I don't think that Craige is inclined to report the episode. To be honest with you, however, I'm more concerned with the fact that Global has enough evidence to move for summary judgment against your case, and that would not be good."

"What's that mean?"

"It means that they would be asking the judge on your case to throw it out, even before you get to a jury, on the grounds that you can't prove that a 'defect' existed in your seat track. Your testimony today establishes that you not only threw out the seat track item, but the repair shop that inspected your track didn't find a problem."

"But, like I said," he countered, "the problem would only come and go."

"I understand what you're telling me, but I also know the way judges think. I'm just alerting you to a problem, that's all. Let's take it one step at a time."

The two of us finished our talk in the hall and he left.

CHAPTER 25

A FEW DAYS after Rocky's deposition, Harrington sent over the additional Global discovery documents and information which Judge Vaughn had ordered produced. To my surprise and relief, I hadn't heard a peep from anyone at Hunt about Rocky's actions. Craige was apparently keeping his mouth shut on the matter, even from Harrington. The allure of the Hunt partnership brass ring obviously had its benefits.

I had Sandy make an extra copy of the more important Mesa documents and information from Global and emailed them on to my experts. My cover letter asked Dr. Braxton to give me a call after he had reviewed the information.

He called back a few days later.

"Anything in the packet look significant from a stability standpoint?" I asked.

"Well, there are a couple of interesting things I see from the design documents that I will need you to follow up on in your depositions of the Global engineers. I can help you frame the questions in order to get the information I need to know."

"What items are you referring to?"

"For starter, the Mesa's center of gravity, or c.g. as it's referred to. Do you mind if I explain a little something about the importance of the c.g. factor in the stability of a motor vehicle? I realize you have a fairly extensive background in these auto design cases, but it's very important that you and I completely understand each other as we work this Hawkins case up. It doesn't help either of us if I'm using certain engineering terms one way, and I find out on the eve of trial that you actually have a totally different understanding of those terms."

I could see the professor coming out in Braxton. I liked his approach. "Fair enough, go ahead."

"As you know, gravity is the earth's force that pulls all things containing matter towards the center of the earth. Gravity acts on everything, including you, me and motor vehicles running down the road. The center of gravity of any physical object, in its simplest terms, is the location on the object where the 'center' of that object's overall, collective weight, or mass, is located. Every motor vehicle has its own c.g. The taller the motor vehicle is on the road, generally speaking, the higher its c.g. For example, a semi-tractor and trailer has a very high c.g. due to the fact that it is so high and tall on the road. A low-to-the-ground sports car, say a Corvette, on the other hand, has a very low c.g."

"I'm with you."

"As a vehicle is running down the road, the forces of the earth's gravity are acting on that vehicle's c.g., trying to pull it towards the earth. However, there are other forces acting on that moving vehicle that are effectively trying to upset and capsize that vehicle. Those other forces, which I'll generically call 'capsizing forces,' occur whenever the forward-moving mass of the motor vehicle is suddenly shifted in a different direction from the direction the vehicle was traveling in. To illustrate, let's take the Hawkins case. In that situation, it appears that Mrs. Hawkins was driving her Mesa eastbound on the interstate, heading for Ft. Lauderdale. The forward direction of her Mesa on the interstate was suddenly shifted when she was forced to turn her steering wheel quickly to avoid the step ladder that flew off the pickup truck in front of her. When she quickly turned the steering wheel, the nose of the Mesa started going in a different direction. In changing the direction of the Mesa, she introduced 'lateral forces' that wanted to push, or tip, the c.g. of her Mesa sideways. At that point, the pull of gravity on the vehicle's shifting c.g. would act to destabilize the Mesa and, unless properly controlled by correct design features, would cause it to begin to tip and roll over."

I interrupted in order to ensure my understanding.

"Isn't all of this supposed to be taken into account by the design engineers when the Mesa, or any other vehicle for that matter, is designed."

"Precisely. As a general proposition, when a company properly designs a motor vehicle, whether it's a car or an SUV, it needs to keep very focused on the location of the c.g. of that vehicle since its location will have a dramatic effect on its stability on the roadway when significant lateral forces are introduced. Those forces could come in a number of different ways: a sudden steering wheel input due to something in the road, sudden high winds, a shifting of cargo, a major tire blow-out, icy roads—a host of causes. The lower the c.g., the more stable you generally are—the more resistant to rollover, if you will—because a lower c.g. tends to help the vehicle fight off, or resist, the more significant capsizing forces it might be confronted with."

"Well, is there any 'magic' or 'safe' c.g. height on an SUV?" I asked.

"No, there isn't. Theoretically, you could have a number of alternative safe c.g. heights, provided—and this is the important qualifier—that the designers safely account for adequate stabilizing features in other aspects of the vehicle's design. But what it does mean is that the higher the c.g., the more challenging it will be for the design engineer to properly design the appropriate compensating stability features into the SUV. For example, if a higher c.g. is chosen, the engineer may have to design a much wider wheelbase into the vehicle in order to cause it to act 'more squat' on the road to resist destabilizing side-to-side forces. Or, the designer might have to install a stiffer suspension to better avoid unwanted side-to-side 'sway,' or tilt, from occurring in the heavy body of the SUV when its driver is forced to suddenly steer aggressively. By the same token, maybe the designer will find it necessary to add stabilizer bars to the SUV. He may have to incorporate a combination of compensating features to render the vehicle 'stable' and more resistant to rollover, under the range of expected driving environments. The location and height of a vehicle's c.g. is a very important starting point in the stability and handling analysis. And remember," he cautioned, "the behavior of an SUV's c.g., in response to lateral forces, changes the moment you start adding passengers or cargo into the SUV because they add weight to the vehicle."

"I get it," I said. "What is it about the c.g. of the Mesa that you found unusual?"

"Well, the Mesa has a relatively high c.g. According to the design documents you sent, it has a ground clearance of nine-point-two inches. As you know, the ground clearance is the distance between the ground and the underside of a vehicle. Ground clearance is a factor in a vehicle's c.g. height. The higher the ground clearance, the higher the vehicle's mass is, therefore, the higher its c.g."

"Is nine-point-two inches high for a sport utility vehicle?"

"Quite. If you look at the Vista model, which is the only other sport utility vehicle that Global designed and sold before coming out with the Mesa model last year, it had a ground clearance of only seven-point-six inches. A one-point-six inch increase in an unloaded vehicle is quite significant from a stability standpoint. It tells me right off the bat that the Global designers had a lot of work to do to ensure safe stability with the Mesa."

"Interesting. Why would a manufacturer want a high ground clearance, anyway?"

"The traditional reason is for off-road use. The higher the ground clearance on an SUV, the less rocks and tree stumps you have to worry about ripping off the bottom of your vehicle. Also, I've been doing some investigation of the new Japanese SUV model that came on the market about six months before the Mesa came out. Koyo Motor Company, its Japanese manufacturer, calls it the Klondike. Like the Mesa, it also has a nine-point-two ground clearance. I drove to a few dealerships around the city yesterday afternoon and picked up some literature on their competing utility vehicles. Interestingly, unless I'm missing something, the Klondike is the only other utility vehicle out there presently with the same height of ground clearance as the Mesa."

"How do the track widths compare between the Klondike and the Mesa?" I asked.

"That's another noteworthy item I observed in the Global documents you sent me. Let's first define our terms again here," he chuckled. "Track width is, for all practical purposes, the width of a vehicle. It is a measurement of the side-to-side distance between the centerline of the tires on one side of the vehicle to the centerline of the tires on the other side. The track width on the Mesa, according to the design drawings you sent me, is fifty eight-point-one inches. For comparison, I measured the wheelbase on a new Klondike that one of the grad students has here at the school. The Klondike has a full two inches more in track width than the Mesa has. And for added comparison, Global's Vista model had a wheelbase of fifty seven-point-nine inches according to one of the older brochures that one of the local Global dealers here still had. As you may know, Global discontinued the Vista model when the Mesa model came out."

"I was aware of that. I understand that the Mesa is being heralded by Global as the new family vehicle of the twenty-first century. They spent a hell of a lot of money to develop and market it."

"The last two things I noticed from the design documents you sent," he continued, "is that the Mesa was built with a front and rear stabilizer bar on it. The older Vista didn't have one. I want to look at the item as well and get an understanding as to why Global felt it necessary to add that stability aid. Also, the rear cargo capacity on the Mesa is huge as compared with competitive models and the older Vista model. With the rear seat folded down, as Mrs. Hawkins had her Mesa configured at the time of the accident, the Mesa has fifty-four cubic feet of capacity. Compare that to the Vista's capacity of forty-six cubic feet. The Klondike is at fifty-three, while the Jeep Verano is at forty-six."

"I take it that the more weight that the SUV is carrying in the rear cargo area, the more difficult it is to design for vehicle stability?"

"You got it. Adding cargo—in Mrs. Hawkins' case, she was carrying heavy paint and a heavy compressor, along with boxes of cookies—puts more mass at a higher level in the Mesa and effectively challenges the performance of its c.g."

"Dr. Braxton, isn't there a rough rule of thumb ratio that design engineers use as a measure of a vehicle's stability?" I asked. I was referencing one I had become aware of in prior stability cases I had handled over the years for other motor vehicle manufacturers.

"Yes, there is," he answered, pleased. "You're referring to the ratio between a vehicle's track width and its c.g. height. It's often referred to, on an abbreviated basis, as 'track width divided by two times the c.g. height,' or, short-handedly by the engineers, as *t over 2h*."

"That's the one I've heard referenced in the past."

"The mathematical figure generated by this short equation gives you a rough rollover threshold for any vehicle you're dealing with. Low sports cars, as an example, will generate a rollover threshold of anywhere from about one-point-two Gs to one-point-seven Gs, meaning that it takes one-point-two to one-point-seven Gs of lateral force to start a rollover of that vehicle on a flat roadway. Compare that number, for example, with tall semi or dump trucks that will have a very low rollover threshold of only about zero-point-four to zero-point-six Gs. The SUVs have an industry rollover threshold range of between zero-point-nine to one-point-one Gs."

"So," I said, "looking at it simplistically, the higher the G number, the better, from a stability standpoint?"

"Precisely."

"If you apply the *t over 2h* rollover formula to the Mesa, where does it put its rollover threshold in comparison to the industry range?"

"That's the fascinating part," he explained in his heavy Massachusetts accent making the word 'part' sounded like '*paaaart.*' "The formula, when applied to the Mesa, reflects a rollover threshold of only zero-point-eighty eight Gs. Now, that's just below the industry rollover threshold range. Incidentally," he added, "I don't know whether you caught it or not, but there doesn't appear to be any dynamic stability tests performed on the final, production-approved Mesa model. I find that to be most puzzling."

"What do you mean by dynamic' stability tests? The U.S. government and its federal motor vehicle safety standards don't require *any* stability tests, do they?" I had never heard of any.

"Dynamic stability testing refers to actual test driving of an SUV on a test track or test pad. And you are correct; the federal motor vehicle safety standards don't require any stability testing, if you can believe that. However, I know from my prior experience in the late 1980s acting as an automotive design consultant for *Consumers' Review* that, for a number of years, the industry has used a standard 'S' steering test-drive maneuver in order to check for obvious problems in a vehicle's handling and stability. In the S test, the vehicle is

being driven straight ahead at thirty-five miles per hour when the driver suddenly cranks the steering wheel sharply to the left to a pre-determined level of
rotation and then sharply back to the right to see how the vehicle responds
from a stability standpoint. The test is also repeated at fifty miles per hour. The
vehicle's steering wheel and other stability-related elements are heavily instrumented in order to accurately gather and record the results. I can't believe that
Global didn't perform an S stability test for the Mesa model before it was
cleared for production. I'd really like to know why they didn't do that test to
the final approved design of the Global."

"I'm starting to schedule the depositions of the in-house design engineers
at Global who signed off on the final design drawings for the Global. When we
discuss formulating the engineering questions for those depositions, should we
be thinking about having an S stability test done by you or some testing lab
ourselves to see how the Mesa fares?"

"It would be a great idea if you have the money to pay for it. With the
necessary instrumentation, the outriggers, the testing lab facilities' rent, the high
speed and regular video equipment, you're easily talking thirty-five thousand to
forty thousand dollars to perform one of these tests correctly."

"You've got to be kidding!" I gagged. "I can't believe it would be that
much."

"Believe me, that's an accurate estimate if you want to have the results in
a form that is not subject to challenge in a court of law. The engineers for
Global would rip apart any S testing that we did that didn't dot all the engineering Is and cross the Ts."

"Well, forget that," I sighed, "we don't have the money to do that."
Changing the focus for a moment, I pressed Braxton on the other information
I had sent him from Global.

"Incidentally, did you observe in the documents produced that there have
been four other lawsuits so far against Global in which the plaintiffs alleged
that the Mesa was unstable?"

"Yes, I did see that and made a note to follow up on that with you. If I
read the information correctly, Global settled all four of those suits before trial,
is that correct?"

"You read it right. I'm doing some checking up on the details of those
four suits right now. Also, I was astonished to see that Global had received
over forty complaints from Mesa owners around the United States claiming
problems with the Mesa's handling. I think that's an incredible number of
complaints when you realize that the Mesa is only one model-year old."

"That seems awfully high, but they've sold a lot of them, and it just may
be that there are a lot of them on the road," he cautioned. "The more drivers,

the more complaints you're going to get. I'm curious, though. Is this information about other suits or complaints about the Mesa's handling and stability going to be admissible for the jury to hear?"

"It depends. Under Florida's rules of evidence, in order for me to get these other accidents or instances of claimed poor handling into evidence, I've got to prove, to Judge Vaughn's satisfaction, that they involved situations which were 'the same or substantially similar to' the specific events of Jenny Hawkins' accident. If I can't show that, he's not going to allow them into evidence. I've got a very tough burden on that score."

"Hmmm. Well," he announced, signaling the end of our discussion, "I'm intrigued by what I'm seeing from these documents. However, I still have a great deal of work and analysis to perform before I will have definitive opinions as to whether there is any defect."

I ended our conversation by obtaining from him specific information he needed to acquire from the Global design engineers at their upcoming depositions. I was pleased with his quick analysis of the preliminary design documents and information on the Mesa. Judge Vaughn's pre-trial order limiting my discovery rights to the final design was handicapping Braxton from obtaining a greater appreciation of the actual design history of the Mesa from its original concept on paper to prototype and to final production vehicle. I would need to extract more of that information from the Global design engineers at the depositions.

I CALLED HARRINGTON the following day to arrange mutually-convenient dates for my taking the depositions of Global's chief design project engineers on the Mesa vehicle. I had identified their names from the internal engineering documents produced by Global. There were literally dozens of different engineers whose names appeared on the documents. While I informed Harrington that I wanted to depose four of them that I identified, the one I was particularly interested in was an Arthur Markov. His signature was on the final engineering approval for the design release of the Mesa. Stability would have been part of his design responsibility.

Predictably, Harrington stonewalled.

"These are busy people. You're not taking their depositions."

"Nice try. They were involved. I'm entitled to them, and I want them," I informed him.

"Take the depositions of some of the more junior design engineers who signed off on the documents. Their time and scheduling commitments are a lot more flexible."

"I'm sorry, but that won't do. Those four were project-level engineers. I don't want the worker bees. I want the bees in the corner offices, and I'm entitled to them."

"Well, you're not getting them," he answered nonchalantly. "File a motion if you want to. I don't care. Also, just so you're not confused on the procedures that Global is using in this case, I'm not agreeing to voluntarily produce any of my employees for your depositions. If you want them, and the court lets you depose them, you're going to have to get subpoenas issued out of a Michigan court and have each of them served personally."

He knew that Vaughn would order Global to produce the four engineers I had designated, but he also knew that I'd have to file a motion for a court hearing to obtain that order—all at my expense and with the limited discovery clock running. It took a week to get a hearing on the motion calendar before the judge on a discovery dispute. It was already June twenty-third, and the November first court-ordered deadline for the disclosure of each side's expert witnesses and testing results was quickly approaching. The requirement of a subpoena for the engineers was tactical icing on the obstructive cake. Getting these guys served in Michigan ate up time and, again, cost more money on my part.

"You're too predictable, Bob," I said, probably showing more irritation than I had wanted. "You'll get my motion papers this afternoon." I was madder than hell at the tactical roadblocks he was throwing at me, but I didn't want to give him the satisfaction of knowing it. I was probably not doing as good a job at that as I hoped.

CHAPTER 26

JUDGE VAUGHN WAS not happy to see us the next week when we appeared before him on my motion to compel the Global depositions.

"Weren't you just here on a prior motion to compel, Mr. Culhane?" he asked irritably. My hearing caught him on a Monday morning. I had the misfortune to be the first motion hearing of the week on his jammed calendar. First in his line of fire. Not recognizing, as usual, that hearing discovery disputes between lawyers before him was part of his job description, The Turtle viewed our presence as taking precious time from his calendar. His foul mood was evident to all dozen or so lawyers sitting in his chambers with me. "I thought we had all these discovery problems ironed out," he grumbled, looking at the large round wall clock to his right. *With his fixation on that damn clock, you'd think he was a third grader watching the classroom clock for recess time, I thought.*

"I thought so as well, Your Honor," I said, attempting a half grovel to placate him, "but Mr. Harrington here is refusing to let me depose four of the senior Global project design engineers on the Mesa product. They signed the final design approval papers at Global, Judge, and I need to depose them," I argued, holding one of the Global design approval sheets in the air as if it was a smoking gun. "Their personal importance and relevance to the issues in this case can hardly be questioned. Also," I added, with my own dose of irritation, "I'm now being told that Global won't agree to produce these four men voluntarily; I'm being required to waste everybody's time and my poor client's money chasing them down with personal subpoenas to require their personal attendance in Detroit at the depositions. Judge, I'm asking you to order Global to produce them voluntarily."

Harrington had come to the hearing with Tucker Craige in tow. Craige sat on the other side of the table, with flint in his eyes. I ignored him.

"Judge Vaughn," Harrington smoothly and calmly responded, waiving his horn-rimmed glasses for effect, "I've told Mr. Culhane here that we want to cooperate and give him a full opportunity to conduct his discovery of Global design engineers. The problem is that he is being unreasonable about it. As the court can appreciate, the four men he has asked to depose are extremely senior in their engineering positions. They have substantial engineering demands and should not be put to the task of giving a deposition in a products liability case. Global has no objection to the depositions of their immediate engineering subordinates who undoubtedly have as much information about the Mesa as their bosses do. Also, Global may be their employer, but it certainly can't order them to appear for a sworn deposition. They have rights, too. Let Mr. Culhane subpoena them just like any other lawsuit. He shouldn't be asking for favors."

"Gentlemen, you're wasting my time. Look at all these other lawyers I have sitting around these chambers right now," he scowled, referring to the ten other lawyers sitting around his chambers for their turn at justice. "The court can't be bothered with disputes, which the two of you can't seem to work out as professionals. I'm ruling that you get to depose two of the project managers of your choosing, Mr. Culhane, not four. The other two depositions, if you still want them, are going to be of their subordinates. And this court isn't going to order a corporation to order its employees who are not officers or directors to show up at a deposition. If you want to depose them Mr. Culhane, you'd better make arrangements to get commissions issued out of this court and subpoenas issued out of a Michigan state court and have them served personally on the witnesses you want to depose," he ordered, testily. Pulling what appeared to be his first fat black cigar of the day from the glossy black and gold trimmed humidor sitting on the corner of his desk, he stopped and looked directly at me. "And I don't want to see you in here again on any more motions to compel in this case. I expect you and Mr. Harrington there," he said, pointing the fat cigar at Harrington, "to act like professionals and work your issues out without this court's intervention. Is that clear Mr. Culhane?"

The Turtle's attitude, self-importance and impatience, which were unfairly and unilaterally directed at me, suddenly set me off. *You get paid for ruling on motions, for god's sake*, I exploded within. Instead, what I said was a bit more diplomatic and restrained. "Judge, I understand that your time is valuable. But so is mine. And while I have every intention to comply with your admonition—just as I have to date with all of the judges in this courthouse—cooperation, as you know, is a *two-sided* street. Mr. Harrington here has to meet me half way as well." I was venting, not only to keep the judge's unfounded impatience at me in check going forward in this case, but probably just as much for the sake of my reputation in front of the other lawyers in the room who had obviously heard of my ignominious 'departure' from Hunt. "I can assure you, Judge," I continued, "the *only* reason I'm here this morning is because Mr. Harrington refused to negotiate these matters in good faith with me. Had he done so, I wouldn't be here, ruining this fine morning for you. I can tell you," I added for good measure, nodding at Harrington, for emphasis, "that when I represented Global, it *routinely* agreed to produce its engineers for depositions without requiring the plaintiff's attorney to get subpoenas issued."

"I take great issue—"

The Turtle cut Harrington off mid-sentence as his sausage-like fingers jammed the newly-lit cigar down into the ashtray in front of him. "I'm not going to get into this gentleman! You heard my admonition, and you'd *both* better follow it. Understood?" he asked rhetorically. "Next case!" he said dismissively, slamming the file closed. He picked his cigar back up and grabbed the next case file from the six-inch pile in front of him.

"Thank you, Your Honor, and fully understood," Harrington quickly said as he rose. He had gotten more than half of what he wanted and had reason to gloat.

I gathered my papers and rose from the table. Craige looked at me with a cocky smile on his face. We both knew that Global was going to do all it could to force me to keep coming back to The Turtle on discovery disputes and to make it look, each time, like I was the unreasonable one who couldn't seem to negotiate my discovery problems with Harrington in good faith. With his disposition, if they were able to get The Turtle increasingly angry at me on simple discovery motion matters, he would stop basing his decisions on the law and start basing them on his emotional impatience. We both knew that he had a fuse whose length was as short as his judicial temperament.

As I exited chambers and walked into his judicial assistant's adjacent office to obtain a duplicate copy of the signed discovery order, Harrington apparently couldn't resist piling it on.

"Mike, you just don't get it, do you? You've got a dog shit case. While I'll give you kudos for going to bat for a family friend, you'd do well to show some objectivity and get out of this case. It's going nowhere, and you and I both know it. And if you think that you're going to get one inch of cooperation from Global, you're on cocaine. I'm telling you," he said, with confidence, as he grabbed the doorknob of the door leading to the outer hall, with Craige one step behind him. "You'd be well advised to start spending your time on cases that can put some money in your pocket. You're not getting any money in this case."

The judicial assistant, who was confirming the judge's order for me, ignored our discussion. She looked to be in her late 50s and had likely seen too many lawyers posturing with each other over her years to give our discussion any note.

"Thanks for the fatherly advice," I said evenly. I took my copy of the order from the clerk as she handed it to me. "If it's all the same to you, I'm going to see this one through to verdict." I moved towards the hall door as well.

"Suit yourself. We're getting paid by the hour," Harrington replied over his shoulder as he and Craige exited the door.

"Oh, by the way," Craige's voice suddenly added, "I'm working with Robert on the Global depositions in Detroit that you're planning to take. There's no way that the schedules of those four engineers are going to permit you to take them on consecutive days in Detroit. You're likely going to have to make at least three and possibly four different trips to Detroit for their depositions. Also, the engineers are busy until the middle of August." He gave me a wry smile.

I now knew the reason for his earlier shit grin; he knew that I couldn't risk Judge Vaughn's ire if I brought another motion to force the four depositions on consecutive days. I'd have to accede to their unreasonable demand which, of course, was aimed at requiring me to pay for four different airfares and incur the inefficiencies of lost travel time on four different trips to Detroit. A war of attrition it was.

I stopped and looked steadily at him for a moment. He knew he had me and was enjoying my reaction.

"Tucker," I said evenly, "there was a time when I had my doubts about you. I've changed my mind, however. I think you're going to make a great Hunt partner. You remind me a lot of your mentor here," I added, smiling and nodding towards Harrington who was walking two steps in front of both of us as we made it out into the hall. "The two of you share a lot of the same characteristics, but class isn't one of them. Incidentally," I asked, "on a fashion note, are you doing something different these days with the way you're wearing your necktie? You seem to be wearing it a lot looser around your neck than the last time I saw you wearing one."

His grin disappeared. He was without a quick comeback. Harrington looked at me like I was nuts.

"Hmmm ... just thought I'd ask." I turned and left the room.

"What was that comment all about?" I heard Harrington ask Craige.

"Who knows, for Christ's sake," he answered, "he's weird."

When I arrived back at the office, I filled Sandy in on Vaughn's order. She started the process of getting the paperwork out to obtain subpoenas for the Global engineers in Michigan. In the meantime, I finished putting together the drafts of Eric's answers to Global's massive discovery demands to him. I made arrangements to drop by his house tonight and have him review the accuracy of the responses before he signed the interrogatory answers. I also needed to pick up the stack of documents that Global had demanded: tax returns, maintenance records on the Mesa, school report cards for Sarah, etc.

Erin and Anne accompanied me that evening when I stopped by the Hawkins' home to meet with Eric. They had asked me if they could tag along and visit with Sarah and Ryan. We grabbed dinner at Taco Bell's on the way since Liz was out at a volunteer's meeting over at St. Cecilia's. The school had its annual foundation dinner coming up, and the foundation board, of which Liz was a member, was busy concocting new and innovative ways for The Artful Dodger, Father Patrick Rooney Murphy, to pick a few new pockets this year for the school's fund-raising drive.

While Erin and Anne had seen Sarah on a few occasions with Liz since the accident, this was going to be their first time visiting—and seeing—Ryan. During dinner, I tried my best to prepare them for what they were going to see. I emphasized the importance of letting Sarah and Ryan feel perfectly normal and avoiding creating the impression that Ryan was some type of odd-looking sideshow object.

"Dad," Erin protested, "give us credit for some brains, will you?" She gave me the ever-present, teenage daughter roll of the eyes.

When we arrived at the Hawkins' home, Eric greeted the three of us and took us into Ryan's room to say hello. He was home for a short stint between further grafting surgeries. Sarah was in with him. After saying hello to Sarah, they looked over at Ryan who was lying on his back. Despite our previous conversation and Eric's efforts to be upbeat in his conversation, the shock at Ryan's injuries was reflected immediately in their eyes. An elastic Jobst stocking covered his face, with cutouts for his eyes, ears, nose and mouth. The preliminary graft on his nose was visible, as was his obviously missing left ear. It was a grotesque picture, and one could only imagine the damage under the stocking which was not visible.

To her credit, Erin quickly caught herself, smiled ear-to-ear, went to the crib and leaned over the side rails. She playfully squeezed his little hands.

"Hi Ryan! You are really growing! I'm waiting for your dad to let me start helping Sarah babysit for you."

His eyes appeared to brighten somewhat at the attention. His legs moved in response to her presence and stimulation.

Anne was much more timid. "Hi Ryan!" she added, walking over to the crib as well.

Sarah, I noted, just stood off to the side of the room and watched quietly and passively. I saw none of the fun-loving, impish eight-year-old's behavior I had known before her mother's death.

"Dad," Erin said to me, "we'll be all right in here. We're just going to, like, talk and stuff. Go ahead and meet with Mr. Hawkins if you want."

"All right," Eric responded for both of us, "we'll be in the family room. Don't hesitate to call us, though, if you need anything." His protective concern for Ryan was evident.

Eric and I moved to the small family room where we went over the documents and discoveries we were putting in the mail the next day to Global's attorneys.

"How are the kids getting along," I asked after we had finished. The kids had come out of Ryan's room only once, to get popsicles. They were still in Ryan's room.

Eric grew quiet, pensive for a moment before answering. "I can see Ryan's injuries. The burns, the disfigurement, and the grafting are all there for the world to see." His voice had gone from the steady, factual voice of a moment ago—when the two of us had been reviewing discovery responses—to one laden with painful emotion. Eric was a tough guy, not a whiner used to breaking down. "But what I can't see, and what I can't know, is what's going on inside of his mind right now. Those internal scars and damages are the ones that probably terrify me the most, Mike. If his inner person is disfigured anything like his outside, I'm afraid I will have lost him as a normal person. I'm very concerned … very scared," he said. "What's going to happen to him as he starts getting older and is subjected to the ridicule of the other kids? You know how cruel kids can be." His eyes welled with tears, but they didn't flow.

I just sat and tried to be a good listener. It was obvious that he needed to talk with someone about concerns that he had been dwelling on for some weeks now.

"And I'm also really worried about Sarah," he continued. "She's become very withdrawn and angry, almost about everything. Her grades have gone from As and Bs at school to Ds. Her teacher has met with me twice to discuss the situation because she is very concerned, as well. Sarah has started fights with other girls in her class, according to the teacher, and she has stopped eating lunch with other kids at school. She sits by herself." He rubbed the back of his neck as he spoke. His tension and worry were obvious. "I've talked with her, but she won't talk to me about what is going on. I know it's all related to

Jenny's death. I think she blames herself for it in some way, as if her Girl Scout cookies caused all of this to happen. She just won't talk to me about it though." He let out an exhausted sigh.

"Do you have her seeing a child psychologist?" I asked. "It sounds like she might need a real specialist to talk with about some of the things that are obviously troubling her. Things that she will need a professional to help her with; things that a child isn't going to share with a parent."

"I'm at my wit's end," he admitted, rubbing his eyes. He was obviously very troubled about her situation and his inability to help. "My insurance doesn't cover psychological coverage. It was an option that Jenny and I discussed when the new insurance coverage plan was offered at work last year. We've always been stable as a rock. We decided," he shrugged, exuding the irony that he felt, "that it was coverage that our family didn't need. We decided to save the money and take the dental coverage instead. No," he finally answered, "she hasn't seen a specialist. She needs the help, but I've been having money problems, finding extra cash to pay for it. I'm just going to have to find the money somewhere."

I knew that Eric's accounting firm had recently hit some difficult times with the bottomed-out economy. One of their most important clients, a national jewelry distribution chain, had been acquired last year. Its accounting work was lost to a competitor who had the acquiring company's work. As a result, his company, like everyone else, it seemed, in this terrible economy, had been forced to further downsize, and Eric had worried about his position. He had survived last year's cuts, but his pay, like everyone else's, had been further reduced in response to the lost revenue. Even before Jenny's death, he had informed me of his concern that he was on thin ice at work if there were other cuts, because he was only experienced in the audit area of the business. He did not have the tax accounting experience to draw upon to better justify his own job in the face of potential additional cutbacks.

"Eric," I offered, "Liz and I want to help out if we could. I know——"

"No, Mike," he responded immediately, knowing automatically of the financial help I was ready to offer, even from our ever-decreasing savings account, "you've done way too much already for us. I caused you to get a bar complaint filed against you, and I know you're spending an immense amount of time and money on our lawsuit against Global. No, I can't let you do more. I won't have it," he said, with stubbornness.

I shook my head. "Eric, let's make this clear. The bar complaint against me is a bullshit harassment tactic that Global is pushing for leverage purposes. It's going nowhere anyway, but, in any event, it's one that I take full responsibility for. *I'm* the lawyer in this deal, not you." I waived it off with my hand for emphasis, as if shooing a vexatious mosquito. "If it helps, I'd be happy to help you pick out the psychologist since I think I'll need one for trial anyway. I want the jury hearing this case to fully understand Sarah's injuries and damages from the product defect. The accident didn't just injure Jenny and Ryan."

Eric nodded quietly to my suggestion.

"I think you should find the right expert for Sarah as quickly as possible, Eric. If you're that concerned about her, the sooner she gets help, the better off she'll be. I know that money is a little tight for you right now, so I'll fund the psychologist's treatment costs as part of the case costs. If we recover, you can repay me then, okay?"

"Mike, I told you that—"

"Good, we're agreed," I quickly said, nixing his objection in mid-sentence, "I'll get on it first thing tomorrow. I know a female child psychologist, Paula Price, who I deposed in a case last year. I made a mental note then that I'd use her if I ever needed one in any of my cases, or for Erin or Anne. She was excellent and would relate well to Sarah, I believe. As I recall, she has her master's and she specializes in children and young adults exclusively." I changed directions in our discussions. "So, tell me, how are *you* holding up?"

"I'm fine. A little tired, that's all." He wasn't fooling me. His eyes said it all. They were tired alright, but they also showed something else—a deep loneliness for Jenny.

"Are you talking to anybody professionally? You know, a counselor or some other type of professional to help you deal with some of this grief and hurt? You're carrying a lot of emotional stress, right now, Eric. I don't want to see you overlook your own needs in your attempts to hold the family together. You'll only end up paying a little later, it seems to me." Our relationship was a good one. I could speak to him this way without it sounding like preaching.

"That's the one thing I can't afford to think about," he said, sighing heavily. "If I start down that road," he looked sadly at me, "I'm afraid I'd have a hard time coming back." His eyes looked past me as he spoke, obviously focusing on memories. "Some nights, when I lay in bed, I can't get to sleep. Not all night. I just keep thinking of all the plans Jenny and I had for the four of us. Of all the good times that she and I had. Do you know," he recounted, quietly, "she was the only woman I ever made love to? Imagine that," he added, letting his guard down completely. "There are times when I hurt so bad for her, and for the way it was, that I can hardly go on. But I've got to," he said, suddenly breaking his momentary trance-like stare, and his memories, as he looked directly at me. And reality. "The kids need me, and I'm going to be here for them."

"Eric, won't you at least spend one or two conferences with a counselor to just talk generally about it? I think you'd benefit."

"Thanks for your thoughts, but I can't do it. I'll deal with it myself." His tone was one of finality. I let it drop just as Anne, Erin and Sarah came out of Ryan's room to join us. We all talked about small things for a few moments, and the three of us left for home.

I let Erin drive while I sat in the front seat. She was happy for the time behind the wheel under her learner's permit. All the way home, my attention to her driving was interrupted by the recurring thought I was having about the hell that Eric's nights must have become. A phrase from a poem I had remembered from a long-forgotten college English class came to mind as Erin drove north on A1A along the beach. It was the only part of the poem I remembered: *Black furies visit the soul during the dead hours of the night*, the remembered phrase went. I now realized that they were more than just words. The black furies were Eric's reality. Every night.

CHAPTER 27

FT. LAUDERDALE, LIKE the rest of Florida, is unbelievably hot and humid during the summer. Before air conditioning, it must have been atrocious, especially if you didn't live on the water. As we rolled into mid-August, I was actually looking forward to a trip up to Detroit for my depositions of the Global engineers. It had to be cooler in Michigan.

Throughout July and the first two weeks of August, I was mired in virtual non-stop discovery with Harrington and his defense team, as he kept referring to them, including 'The Confederate,' as I referred to Aubrey Trenton III. The Confederate showed up at every deposition that was taken, which was substantial. Harrington had taken the depositions of every person who was at the accident scene, including Manny Abadin, Alex Fuentes, the older retired couple—Mr. and Mrs. Jack Juel—who had held Ryan while Abadin fought the fire, and Carole Merton, the lady who had passed Jenny's Mesa shortly before the accident and remembered her speed as being at or below the speed limit. Harrington didn't stop with those witnesses either. He proceeded to notice and depose every cop, fireman, ambulance employee, and tow truck operator who was involved or at the scene. His goal was consistent, albeit irritating as hell: He was seeking to wear me and my wallet down. While I considered myself a reasonably thorough defense lawyer when at Hunt, even I wouldn't have taken all those depositions. It was overkill. Nonetheless, I had to attend every one of them. It was killing the rest of my practice, and my revenue stream showed it.

While I realized that Willis Cole personally also had the jaws for me, as did Harrington, I nonetheless had the nagging feeling that something just wasn't making sense here. Beating Eric and me up economically in this case was one thing, but this seemed different. Global was employing nothing short of a scorched earth approach in defending the Hawkins case. My instincts told me that Global's actions somehow signaled more than simple vindictiveness.

I also couldn't figure out just what The Confederate was doing in the case either. In the past, Global had used various law firms around the country as national counsel to oversee repetitive cases in which Global had heightened concerns about its potential exposure from the same component or the same model. The fuel tanks on two particular models of its cars were one instance that readily came to mind. A seatbelt recall problem on one of Global's luxury cars was another. I knew that Global's rationale for their national counsel approach in those repetitive cases involving the same model was to bring in one outside law firm as co-counsel in all of the lawsuits around the country in order to orchestrate a consistent defense strategy, organize the Global internal documents and witnesses, and identify the outside experts to use for these repetitive cases that were brought against the company. It was beginning to look like The Confederate was playing that role with the Mesa in this case. But why, I kept asking myself. Why would Global involve what looked like national counsel for a Mesa stability case where it was reported that there had only been four other lawsuits against the Mesa alleging a stability problem, or so the company reported, and all had been settled. It didn't make sense. Could it be that Global was thinking of taking all of the Global work away from Hunt and rolling it up into The Confederate's firm? My investigation revealed that his firm did all of Global's work in many of the southeastern states in the country, displacing the local law firms that had previously represented Global in those states. Very strange, but, at the end of the day, I didn't care. I had enough problems to deal with on my own side of the fence without fixating on the political machinations that might be underway on Global's side of the fence.

At the same time that Global was running me around the flagpole with depositions in Ft. Lauderdale, I wasn't getting any cooperation regarding the depositions the court had permitted me to take in Detroit. Harrington horsed me around for two weeks while he informed me that Global was obtaining their home addresses to give me for purposes of having to serve each of them with subpoenas for their depositions. Layered on top of that loss of time was the fact that the process server I had hired in Detroit, a deep-voiced man that went by the name of Maurice Smoke, 'Mo Smoke' to his friends as he quickly informed me, initially hit a brick wall in his efforts to serve the four engineers. Global had obviously warned them of their impending subpoena and undoubtedly 'suggested' that they be unavailable for easy service.

Mo finally got the job done after literally sleeping outside of their residences in the back of his van and catching them as they came out to go to work. His efforts, though necessary in view of The Turtle's ridiculous ruling, were expensive. It cost me close to sixteen hundred dollars out of my own pocket to hire a Michigan lawyer to get the subpoenas issued out of a Michigan court and to cover Mo's bill. It was money I couldn't afford, particularly since Harrington was doing a great job monopolizing my time on this contingency fee case.

Between Liz's modest extra work income, the reduction in our family spending, and the revenue I was pulling in from my struggling practice, the major financial hemorrhaging at the beginning of July, while not gone, had been partially stemmed. The upcoming discovery schedule, however, in the Hawkins' case had me again worried since I would have to pull myself off hourly-paying files and onto Eric's contingent fee case.

Ultimately, the depositions of the four Global engineers were scheduled in Detroit over the course of four fractured dates of August sixteen, twenty-third and twenty-fourth, the twenty-third and twenty-fourth and the twenty-ninth, all thanks to Global's truculence. I scheduled the deposition of the chief project engineer, Markov, to be taken last so that I would have the benefit of having learned some of the more important design information from the other three engineers. Armed with that preliminary information, I would be able to pose much more effective questions to Markov; at least, that was my goal. Since he was the top design engineer approving the Mesa's design, any admissions or concessions that I could manage to extract from him in his deposition testimony would be extremely valuable evidence I could offer at trial against Global.

Harrington realized that as well, for he faxed me a letter on the afternoon of August eleventh, a Wednesday, informing me that the schedules of Markov and one of the other engineers had changed. Markov, the fax related, had to be changed to the sixteenth, the first day.

"This is bullshit!" I exploded out loud when Harrington's fax came into my office. I called him immediately.

"This is totally unacceptable! I want Markov last. I don't care if you move the other three guys any which way you want, just put Markov last. I remind you, Robert," I said angrily, "I specifically cleared all of those dates, and the identity of the engineers on each date, with your office before I sent out the notices, and you didn't have any problems with any claimed scheduling problems then. So, do what you have to internally," I ended, "but I'm going with Markov last."

"Sorry to shoot down your little anal-retentive schedule," Harrington stated, mater-of-factly, "but you're just going to have to change your schedule. What can I say? Their schedules are important and fluid. Their schedules changed at work, for reasons beyond their control. So," he concluded, "you're just going to have to buck up and adjust our schedules accordingly."

"Beyond their control, my ass! This is pre-meditated, and you know it. If Global told those four engineers to piss in a shot glass and drink it down, believe me, they'd do it. And they'd make like they enjoyed it, too. You're forgetting that I set up depositions of Global engineers for eight years. I know their internal procedures. I know the engineers receive the deposition notices and are *told* to block out those dates and to arrange their other scheduling demands to work around the deposition schedules agreed to by Global's counsel. They may not like it, but they do it. This is total bullshit," I repeated again, unavoidably allowing my growing case frustration to boil over.

Knowing how to get under my skin, he chuckled in reply. "Well, I guess the internal protocol changed," he said evenly. "All I know is that I'm being told that they have scheduling problems that couldn't be avoided. The only good date for Markov is the first depo slot on the sixteenth. Now," he added, trying to pretend that he was having a spur of the moment constructive idea, "if you're telling me that you are demanding that Markov go last, and that you are not budging, I guess we have no alternative but to reschedule all of the depositions. The problem is, however, I can't reschedule them until the end of September. I've got a couple of trials in the way. So, what do you want to do?"

He knew damn well that putting off the depositions until the end of October was strategic suicide for me. With Vaughn's court-ordered deadline of November first for disclosing each side's expert witnesses, who were obligated to have their final opinions in hand at that time, rescheduling the depositions until mid-October wouldn't leave me with enough time to prepare my experts for their final opinions two weeks later. After taking the depositions of the Global engineers, I would need to have their deposition transcripts typed by the court reporter, provide the deposition transcripts to my experts for analysis, to analyze them myself, and to discuss the important aspects of the testimony with the experts.

"You don't leave me with any choice, Robert," I immediately replied. "I'm filing an emergency discovery motion this afternoon to see if Judge Vaughn will hear this dispute on his motion hearing calendar tomorrow morning at eight forty-five a.m. You'll get a copy of the motion faxed over to you in an hour," I said coolly.

"Suit yourself," he responded. "Let's see how pleased Vaughn is at having to deal with your latest hissy fit."

I hung up, hit the keys of my desktop and knocked out a quick motion to the court asking Judge Vaughn to order Global to produce Markov first. I didn't look forward in the least to going before The Turtle once again on another discovery dispute, but I had no choice. The order of the witnesses was important.

Vaughn did agree to hear my motion the next morning, if one could be so bold to call what he gave me a hearing.

"Are you in here *again* on these same engineering depositions?" he growled in his opening question. He posed it to me in chambers just as we sat down the next morning for the hearing on my motion. "Didn't I already rule on this issue?"

"I apologize for having to revisit the issue, Your Honor, but Mr. Harrington is trying to play games after we had reached a specific agreement regarding the sequence of the depositions, which you ordered I could take." Knowing the razor-thin thickness of both his patience and his attention span, I quickly outlined the problem, including the strategic importance in a products liability action of taking the most senior design engineer last.

The Turtle didn't bother to listen to Harrington's rebuttal argument before sending me packing.

"I'm denying your motion, Mr. Culhane," he ruled summarily. "Take those engineers in the order that Global Motors gives them to you. Now," he added gratuitously, with his comments directed at me, "I realize that when I tried insurance defense cases years ago, they probably weren't anything as sophisticated as the products liability cases that you're involved in. But, for the life of me, I can't see that it makes a tinker's difference who goes first. Global Motors is a major manufacturer in this country with a lot of busy engineers. I don't need to tell you that. If they say that their engineers have suddenly developed scheduling conflicts, then that's sufficient for me. And it's going to be sufficient for you too. I'm not about to question their integrity, their motives or their request for a scheduling change, and I'm certainly not about to order them to re-arrange the work schedules of their workers in this lawsuit. This economy is tough enough on companies and this court is not going to further hamstring them in their day-to-day operations." His pro-manufacturer, conservative philosophy was becoming painfully evident in his rulings, and, probably more importantly, in his attitude towards my case. "Your motion is denied."

"Thank you, Judge, I'll prepare the order," Harrington quickly offered as he rose from his chair and headed for the chambers' door.

I licked my wounds all the way back to the office. Getting hammered by Vaughn was becoming an uncomfortable habit.

CHAPTER 28

MARKOV SHOWED UP for his deposition the following week in Detroit. As his first witness. Harrington had demanded that the depos be held in Global's world headquarters' building. Markov entered the room accompanied by Harrington, Cole and The Confederate. I was surprised that Cole himself was there rather than Don Kean, the staff attorney who would have normally had day-to-day responsibility for handling the case with outside counsel.

Markov, a Brillo-haired, medium-framed man in his mid-50's, looked the part of an upper-level engineering executive at Global. His mannerism was smooth, he carried himself with a great deal of confidence, and he had the look of a guy who had probably stepped on a few bodies on his climb to the top of the engineering pile. To get to his level at Global, you had to be a good politician as well as a good engineer.

He was extremely well prepared, having spent all day Friday, he acknowledged, with the attorneys preparing for the deposition. A graduate engineer of Cornell University, he had spent his entire professional career of twenty-nine years employed at Global. He rose through the ranks to Chief Project Engineer for the Utility Vehicles Group. He was a company man through and through.

The deposition was filled with volleys of objections and arguments made by Harrington throughout. His goal wasn't hard to see: disrupt the rhythm and concentration of my deposition questions and coach his witness as much as possible. On some of the more critical areas, Markov started doing just what I figured he would—'not recalling.' Going first, he knew that I was not yet armed with more specific information that the other design engineers would have provided me with had they gone first, which would have armed me with factual information that would have allowed me to successfully refresh his memory or make him look very stupid if he persisted in his amnesia.

While the Global design documents provided during discovery allowed me to stop every so often and try to refresh his recollection with specifics, the majority of the time he was able to tap dance all around the questions. Either the documents, he claimed, didn't contain the necessary information to enable him to answer the question I posed, or he ducked a meaningful answer by saying that he would have to review the documents in great detail before responding. When that happened, he would often proceed to spend fifteen minutes reviewing a single document I had laid in front of him, only to finally say that a definitive opinion couldn't be provided without analyzing the matter further. It was obvious that he had been told that the court's standing rules limited every deposition to a maximum of one day, seven hours in length. He was running out the clock at every chance he got. And effectively.

It was largely a frustrating exercise that didn't conclude until six that night. On the plane trip back to Lauderdale, I outlined the limited important information he had provided.

The Mesa was a new model, having been conceived a little over two years prior to its market introduction, as a replacement for the older, successful Vista model, which was now viewed as too small and stylistically outdated by the public. When I attempted to extract information about the design history of the Mesa as it evolved from the drawing board to actual final design approval and production, Harrington strenuously objected. He instructed Markov not to answer the questions I posed regarding that area, citing Judge Vaughn's earlier discovery ruling, which prohibited me from litigating non-final designs. I noticed the normally unruffled Markov shoot a quick glance over to Cole when I pressed him with questions, which Harrington refused to let him answer anyway, regarding whether the final ground clearance measurement of nine-point-two inches reflected in the final Mesa production vehicle had ever been lower during the earlier design stages of the Mesa. After you've tried a lot of cases and examined a lot of witnesses, you begin to gain an appreciation for the truth of the old saying that 'the eyes are the windows to the soul.' Markov's windows piqued my curiosity when he seemed uncomfortable and on edge while I posed questions regarding the Mesa's design history. Unfortunately, The Turtle's earlier ruling, and lecture to me, about the limited scope of discovery he was allowing me in this case, prohibited me from pursing the issue further when Harrington repeatedly interposed an instruction for Markov not to answer.

When asked why Global had chosen such a relatively high ground clearance for the Mesa, Markov stated that it was to make it easier for drivers to take the four-wheel drive Mesa off road. The extra ground clearance, he explained, shaking his head with an attitude of 'I can't believe you'd ask such a stupid question,' made it easier for the vehicle to clear rocks, ruts and gullies

while off road. The customers, he emphasized, wanted a higher ground clearance, and the Mesa gave them just that. By contrast, he pointed out, the Vista
was much lower and not in step with what the consuming public wanted.

He acknowledged that the Mesa, while having one-point-six inches of additional ground clearance over the Vista model, only had less than a half inch
of increased track width over that of the Vista. However, he pooh-poohed the
suggestion that the relatively narrow track width dimension on the Mesa caused
it to have any potential stability, i.e., rollover problems.

"Counsel," he lectured, "you fail to understand that the Vista and the
Mesa are two radically different vehicles. I was very satisfied with the stability
characteristics of the Mesa, particularly with the added stability features that we
designed into the vehicle." Those added features, he related, were the stiffer,
semi-active suspension on the Mesa and the front and rear stabilizer bars. Both
were designed into the vehicle, he explained, to provide it with even more sta-
bilization than it probably really needed.

"Global typically *over designs* its products from a safety standpoint," he
added. I thought he was finished with that response when he suddenly looked
down and then quickly looked back up. He then added, "I would have thought
that as a former lawyer of ours, you would have already known that."

Harrington and Cole did educate him well. I suspected that Cole prepared
that last line, spoon fed it to him during their pre-deposition prep, and told him
to give it when Cole kicked him at the right time during the deposition. I realized that Markov's looking down a moment ago was in response to being
kicked by Cole, who sat next to him, to 'spit out the line now.'

Markov's last comment hit me like salt in an open wound. I had been representing Global for approximately three years when I happened to discover
that the Global designers had an internal, informal and unpublished design
credo to which their design teams had historically and proudly adhered in designing their products: 'If it can be reasonably over designed for safety, do it.'
The irony of his comment was that once I had learned of the Global credo, I
had successfully persuaded Willis Cole's boss, Rex Folger, to make sure this
design credo was emphasized strongly to the juries in all of its products liability
defense cases nationwide. And it had proven to be a very impressive defense
weapon in the cases Global tried around the country since that time. I certainly
had used it in every one of my Global trials. It was ironic that my own clever
defense tactic suggestion had now gone full circle to bite me in the ass in this
case.

When I asked about the lack of stability testing conducted on the Mesa, as
evidenced by the lack of any test reports produced during discovery, Markov
initially fidgeted and cast a quick glance over to Cole. I thought his glance

exhibited an uncomfortable expression. However, I didn't know him. Whatever the meaning, he recovered and again quickly took the opportunity to lecture me, in sarcastic fashion, about my ignorance of engineering design and proper testing.

"As you are undoubtedly aware, Counsel," he jabbed, "there are no motor vehicle safety standards, either here in the United States, or in the international arena, which require dynamic stability tests on a vehicle. And it's obvious why. There are simply too many variables that go into the stability issue to develop any meaningful, repeatable dynamic testing procedures. It's true that Global has, in some instances, subjected some of our cars and trucks to what the engineering world has informally called an S driving test, but that is only a very rough tool to evaluate a vehicle's overall stability personality. The results of that test are certainly subject to interpretation, and, more importantly, it's a test procedure which we often do not bother using at all in the design of a new vehicle if the lead engineer on the project believes that it isn't necessary to adequately assess the stability of a new design. Take this case," he continued. "Here I was in charge of approving this Mesa model. If you bothered to look at the written engineering and design data which you were supplied with in this case, you would have seen that my staff conducted *computer modeling* of the final design in which we subjected the Mesa to all different types of projected steering inputs, loads, and varying road undulations—all separately and in conjunction with one another. The results from those computer simulations were very instructive. They confirmed that the vehicle was eminently stable and that spending a lot of money to take some of the production prototype Mesas out to a test track and running expensive, instrumented S tests would have been a colossal waste of money and time."

Cole shook his head, in mock confirmation of my ignorance.

"Mr. Markov," I said, "I don't want to get bogged down in using the wrong type of engineering nomenclature, so please listen to this very simple question: Did Global run *any* type of *dynamic* tests on the proposed Mesa model in which its stability was addressed directly or indirectly?" Since I wanted to prevent him from any weaseling on this critical question, I broke it down even further. "Let me clarify, sir, so that there is no misunderstanding as to what I'm asking. What I'm talking about is whether Global, or any of its agents, ever ran any tests other than computer modeling, where a Mesa was taken on any type of test track and subjected to any type of testing while the Mesa was in motion, where any type of steering input was introduced to the Mesa's steering, and any type of response was observed or recorded or instrumented?" I asked the question in the interest of being complete. Global had not produced any such documents, and he had testified that there had been no such testing, but I wanted to make sure, for the record, with no weasel room left for the witness to hide behind.

"No. There were none. There wouldn't have been a need to, Mr. Culhane, as I have previously explained to you," he answered with irritation. Cole nodded in agreement.

I thought his irritation was out of proportion to my question, but I realized that I was probably starting to irritate him with my somewhat obsessive nitpicking and mining for the engineering details I was trying to pin down in definitive terms.

In addressing the number of handling and stability complaints, as well as the four Mesa stability suits, he scoffed at the idea that they were reflective of any problem. "For the vast number of Mesas out on the roadway," he argued, "the number of complaints by people who *think* they had a stability problem is completely expected. The sheer numbers tell you that you're going to get complaints about every component of our vehicle. Just saying that you have a problem doesn't mean that, in fact, you have a problem. And the Mesa doesn't have any stability or handling problem. The same holds true for those four lawsuits. If you look at the facts of all those complaints and those suits, Mr. Culhane, I'm sure you will see that what is alleged to be a Mesa stability problem is, in fact, a *human driver* problem. Whether it was too much alcohol, too much speed, inattentive driving or icy roads, it's the same old story. Blame the vehicle for a terrible death or injury caused solely by driver error. It's the same here. I'm sorry to tell you, but it's clear that Mrs. Hawkins was driving way too fast for those conditions and simply lost control."

One of the few interesting exchanges actually took place towards the end of the deposition when I asked Markov if he had been involved in any discussions with defense counsel as to whether Global would be performing any actual dynamic stability testing of the Mesa in the Hawkins case for disclosure on November first. I realized that the question invaded the attorney-client privilege, but, what the hell, I was curious. Harrington immediately jumped in with an objection on that basis and instructed him not to answer my question.

"So, are you going to do a test, Robert?" I challenged him in a bantering way. "If the Mesa is the stable vehicle that Mr. Markov here says it is it seems to me that a little dynamic S test would be just the thing for a jury to chew on, don't you think?"

"You've got the burden of proof, my friend. I don't," he replied. "I don't see the slightest reason for an expensive dynamic test based on what I'm hearing here today," he said nodding supportively to Markov. Cole sat stone faced, watching the exchange. "Besides," he countered, throwing his pen onto the yellow pad in front of him that was filled with his depo notes, "I think it would be more interesting if you were to try and run one. Don't you?" He crossed his arms over his chest and leaned back in his chair.

It was a strange question, I thought to myself. It was more than a challenge, and I had the distinct feeling that it was more of an inquisitive probe than an idle challenge from Harrington. Was Harrington trying to find out if we were going to be performing any stability tests? It showed the first inkling of Global's interest in my case. Knowing Harrington as I did, and the fact that he was obviously discussing Global's defense strategy in the case with Cole and The Confederate, it raised my suspicions as to whether Global might be concerned about a dynamic S test on a Mesa going the speed that Jenny was going and loaded as Jenny's was. I made a mental note to give the exchange more thought. However, remembering Braxton's admonition that it would cost around forty thousand dollars to run an admissible S test on the Mesa, I knew that we couldn't afford to do one. I sure didn't have the money, and Eric had already informed me that he didn't have any more money to advance for case costs. The five thousand dollars he had advanced at the beginning of the case was long spent.

I lamented as I polished off a Heineken on the trip back to Ft. Lauderdale, Markov's deposition was largely an expensive exercise in futility. I didn't get any plums, nor did I find any smoking guns. My hope was that the other engineers would provide some clear evidence of a defect in the designing stages, but I was a realist. I made a note to send the expedited deposition transcript of Markov on to my experts for their prompt analysis. Maybe they could find gems that I was overlooking.

I SPENT THE next morning on the phone with two of the four attorneys who had represented plaintiffs in lawsuits filed against Global in which it was alleged that the Mesa was unstable. I was fishing for information they may have gotten from Global during their case discovery which would be helpful to mine. While I had spoken with all four, two of the attorneys flat-out refused to talk at all, citing the confidentiality provisions of the settlement agreement which Global had insisted on. The other two were willing to talk, so long as they didn't discuss the specific terms of the settlement agreements their clients had entered into with Global since they were also "confidential."

The first attorney, a guy out of Denver, also was a sole practitioner. However, his practice was a general one, and he had no previous experience in products cases. From the summary he gave me regarding his discovery against Global in his Mesa case, he hadn't mounted much of a campaign. His discovery consisted of no more than sending out a set of interrogatories and taking one deposition of a lower-level staff designer on the Mesa project, which I was sure Global's local defense attorney had snookered him into accepting. Without having done a request for Global's design documents, he wasn't in any position to know which engineers played which design roles. I was disappointed to learn that he hadn't even bothered to go to Detroit to look at design documents of the Mesa. In fact, the guy was so laid back that he agreed to take the deposition of the low-level Global designer by telephone from his office in Denver! But then again, I reconsidered and reminded myself not to be so critical. Where had my hot-shot products' experience, intense document production and face-to-face deposition gotten me? Markov, the top Mesa design engineering dog, gave me precious little helpful information in the deposition I took of him. Maybe I should have saved the money after all and taken his by telephone as well.

His clients, Charlton and Robbie Perry, were a father and his six-year old son who rolled their Mesa just outside of Greeley, Colorado when the father swerved to avoid a deer, which the boy said suddenly jumped out into the roadway in front of them. The father was delivering a couple of heavy welding machines loaded in the Mesa's cargo area and had taken his son on the trip to keep him company. The unbelted Mr. Perry was killed from head injuries suffered during the rollover, while the son had miraculously survived with a broken right arm and other minor injuries.

According to the Denver attorney, Global had mounted a vigorous defense, alleging that the father was speeding excessively when the deer jumped out, causing the loss of control and rollover off the road when he made the sudden rotation of the steering wheel to avoid the impact. This was despite the investigating police officer's inquiry that concluded that the Mesa had actually started its roll while still on the roadway, not off the roadway as Global had argued. Due to his young age and the trauma he had suffered, the young boy was incapable of offering much evidence in the way of his observations regarding the accident details.

Interestingly, however, was the fact that on the eve of trial, Global had settled the case with the attorney and the Perry family. He wouldn't divulge the amount of money that Global had paid, again reminding me that Global had demanded a confidentiality clause in the settlement agreement, which prohibited him from disclosing that number. While not disclosing the settlement amount paid, the attorney couldn't resist telling me that he was 'very pleased' with the amount.

I found his settlement with Global intriguing since Global's *modus operandi* had always been *not* to settle with an attorney who both was inexperienced and who had a weak case on the merits. The Global defense policy in such cases— which the global defense attorneys cynically referred to as 'bankers,' meaning that you could take an expected victory to the bank—was to take them to trial, win the case, and then hold a major press conference to endlessly publicize the victory. The company's philosophy, which I agreed with, was that a victory, coupled with the media exposure of the victory, was the best inoculation in that local area of the country against further lawsuits. Contingent-fee plaintiffs' lawyers—who only get paid if they win—would think long and hard before taking on an expensive and risky legal battle with Global in a similar case. The certainty of having to invest substantial amounts of time and fork out big dollars in out-of-pocket costs to wage a battle that Global was aggressively touting that it would win—and had shown in other earlier trials *that it had won*—chilled them from taking such cases. Global knew, after all, that despite their lofty back-of-the-phonebook slogans to the contrary ('we've got your back' ... 'we're on your team,' 'we put you first,' etc.), most plaintiffs' lawyers were cold, calculating businessmen, ironically, not all that different from the businessmen and businesses they sued every day. They, too, were out to make a profit.

The Perry settlement ran contrary to that policy. Granted, I only had a limited conversation with the Perry's attorney, but it was long enough to realize that he was a weak sister when it came to taking on Global. And with his lack of an aggressive case workup, coupled with no helpful accident witness, the Perry case certainly smelled like a banker. Its settlement, especially at a confidential price, which was substantial enough to make the attorney 'very pleased,' didn't make any sense to me. Why would Global settle a case like that? I kept asking myself. It didn't make sense.

Nor did the second settled Mesa suit I was able to obtain information on.

That suit arose in Knoxville, Tennessee. The plaintiff's attorney in that suit, Curtis DuPuy, practiced with five other attorneys who specialized in medical malpractice and products liability litigation. Reese, a pleasant, smooth-talking guy with a pronounced Tennessee drawl, gave me the case summary. He represented the front-seat passenger of the Mesa, a Brant Stafford, who survived a rollover, but with severe injuries. Stafford and his younger brother, Ray, both in their mid-twenties, were headed home to a small town just outside Knoxville after having spent three days deer hunting. Their four-hundred-pound, sixteen-point buck was lashed to the top of the Mesa, and the cargo area was loaded with their camping supplies.

Ray, the driver, claimed that he was doing the speed limit when he hit a patch of ice on the two lane country roadway. When he attempted to quickly counter steer and regain control of the left-swerving front end of the Mesa, he told the police that the Mesa had reacted in a completely overly-responsive fashion. It had whipped suddenly the other way at the same time as the offside wheels lifted from the roadway, causing the Mesa to rollover one-and-a-half times. His younger brother was rendered a quadriplegic when his belted body apparently slammed head first into the downwardly crushed roof when the Mesa was upside down during the roll.

"It sure enough was a strange case for me," Reese related. "You know, I've litigated two other products cases against Global over the last four years. They weren't great cases, to tell you the truth, but I wanted to give them a try. Damages were pretty fair and all. I tried my damnedest to work them up and hope that Global would settle the darn things. Didn't happen that way though."

"They played hardball?" I asked.

"Most surely did. I served all kind a discovery demands and took all kind a depositions of Global people in both of those cases," he related in his heavy, folksy Tennessee drawl. "Thought World War III was going to break out the way I had to fight with their defense lawyer in those two cases over darn near every issue. Well, I ended up losing both of those cases at trial. The Stafford case," he chuckled to himself, "well, that was a horse of a different color. Hell, I had barely filed the darn thing when I got a call out of the blue from some lawyer in Atlanta who said he represented Global. Said that before we both started to spend a lot of money on the case, he wanted to know if I would be interested in talking settlement."

"That early in the case?"

"Yeah, damndest thing. Well, let me tell you," he went on, "twice burnt before, I jumped at the chance. See, the driver of the Mesa, as I mentioned to you already, was my client's kin. The police ran a blood test on him after the accident, and he was pert near twice the legal limit of intoxication here in this state. While those boys both swore up and down that they were going the speed limit and the Mesa just plumb acted up from a handling standpoint, I knew from my prior rassling matches with Global that they would have a field day with the alcohol at trial."

"Did you settle?"

"Quick as mercury. They paid us a real good chunk of change if you can believe that. They made us sign a confidentiality agreement; otherwise I'd be happy to tell you the amount."

"Let me ask you something," the thought jumping suddenly to mind, "do you remember the name of the lawyer out of Atlanta that you dealt with?"

"Are you kidding me?" he laughed heartily, "I can't forget his name. I sent the man a case of fine Jack Daniels whiskey after we settled that case. Trenton … Aubrey Trenton was the man's name."

"Well I'll be damned," I uttered out loud.

"You know him?"

"In a way, yes. Did you get your hands on any Global documents regarding the Mesa or take any depositions before you settled?"

"Nope, I had served a thick document request and a deposition notice with my initial discovery demand that was served on Global with the suit papers. I asked for all the good stuff, you know, design history information, testing, names and addresses of the engineers on the projects. The case settled before we all got into that."

I thanked Reese for his help and asked him to send me a copy of his complaint and the discovery demands he had served in his case. He was kind enough to agree to persuade the Stafford brothers to attend my trial as witnesses if I picked up their travel costs.

"It doesn't make sense," I again muttered to myself as I hung up and looked at my notes of the two telephone conversations. Both of those cases unquestionably were bankers, yet Global had apparently paid good money to resolve both of them before trial. Global didn't want them tried. That much was obvious. But why? I was coming up dry.

CHAPTER 29

I SPENT THREE days during the last two weeks of August deposing the other three Global design engineers in the Hawkins' case, as well as an additional engineer I noticed up for deposition in Rocky's case. The trial judge in Rocky's case, unlike Vaughn, ordered Global to produce the engineer I wanted for his deposition in Detroit without the necessity and costs of a subpoena served upon him personally. *So much for consistency in the law.* Taking the seat track engineers' depositions on the same trip as the Mesa depositions allowed me to obtain discovery information for Rocky's case at little incremental costs. I was in Detroit anyway.

The three Mesa design engineers didn't provide much more help to my case than Markov had. They deftly sidestepped many of my critical questions about why Global chose this or that design feature on the Mesa by deferring to Markov, claiming that he was the chief project design engineer on the Mesa Project who approved all final design decisions. As they well knew from Harrington's pre-deposition coaching, I wouldn't get another shot at Markov until trial. In short, Harrington's rescheduling tactic had worked. I was getting run around the block, and there wasn't a thing that The Turtle would do about it.

The only tangible accomplishment I could discern from the depositions of the Mesa engineers had been to increase my overwhelming investment of time and money in the Hawkins case. The time I spent on the case in July and August was much worse than I had counted on, all thanks to Harrington and his pals. My loss of incoming revenue at the office was again becoming severe.

To tourniquet the financial hemorrhaging, I sold my two favorite toys at the beginning of September: my Boston Whaler and my 1961 Jaguar XK-E, Series I coupe. I had purchased the British green racing Jag fifteen years ago and had lovingly restored it to mint condition. Its sleek fastback lines and exotic appeal caught my eye the first time I saw it, and the love affair hadn't waned over the years. Having been built in the first few months of production, it exhibited the exterior chrome hood releases, which were deleted in later production. Its biscuit interior still smelled of the new replacement leather I had put in the car the summer before. During the week, it sat in my garage under a tarp, awaiting Sundays when it was my preferred wheels for driving around Lauderdale. Liz called it *my British penis*, a comment on the love affair I had with the car.

It killed me to sell them, particularly the Jag, but I needed the money.

To my disappointment, I was receiving no case referrals from other attorneys in town. I had counted on referrals to help make my solo practice work, but they weren't there and I knew why. The rumors surrounding my departure from Hunt, still fueled undoubtedly by Gunther, Wilcox and Harrington were having their predictable effect. The word on the street obviously was that I was not to be trusted, and I had lost the ability to try a serious case. My concerns about my finances and the viability of my practice were mounting as the Hawkins case headed into mid-September.

I was mulling over my finances when Sandy came into my office carrying the day's mail. She was wearing a gray hoodie, with the words "White Cliffs" stenciled in navy blue across its front, and a pair of black jeans. Her blonde hair was pulled back in a ponytail. "I finally received a response back from the National Highway Traffic Safety Administration in Washington on any recall information they had on the Mesa," she announced.

Her practice was to calendar all of the scheduling dates and court-ordered deadlines in my cases before she turned the mail stack over to me.

"So, give me some good news for a change."

"Sorry, take a look," she said, handing me the NHTSA correspondence. "There are no recalls pending on the Mesa, and they have not opened any investigations of any sort either."

"Damn. We need a break if the case is going to get some momentum going."

"It looks like it's going to have to come from some other source," she responded. "Also, you may recall that you had me circulate an inquiry in the National Trial Lawyers' Association quarterly newsletter seeking information from any plaintiffs' attorneys around the country regarding stability or handling problems that any of their clients had experienced with the Mesa?"

"Yeah, did we get a response?"

"I have twelve attorneys around the country that replied and said that they are investigating a potential claim against Global for problems that their clients have had with the Mesa's stability. None has any pending lawsuit against Global for Mesa instability. Two of the complaints were rollovers with personal injuries, while the rest were loss of control situations with minor property damage. I've summarized the information from those twelve attorneys and put it in the memo paper-clipped to the NHTSA letter in front of you."

"Twelve! Are any of them included in the stability complaints that Global identified in its answers to interrogatories?"

"Only three, the others are entirely new and different."

"Jesus, that's a hell of a lot of stability complaints for a utility vehicle that's only been in production for a little over a year. Does your summary include any description of the different factors of each accident, you know, speed, alcohol, loading conditions, and all that like we talked about? If I'm going to have any chance of getting this stuff in evidence, I'm going to have to prove that the other accidents are substantially similar in accident circumstances."

"Way ahead of you," she announced. "It's all there, Mike. I ended up calling the responding attorneys directly and went over their accident facts in great detail so that my summary would be worthwhile for you. I also called all of the Mesa drivers who Global identified in its interrogatory answers who had complained to the company of a handling and stability complaint with the Mesa. The specific circumstances of their handling problems are also included in that memo in front of you."

"Thanks, Sandy, this is perfect."

"Let me know which, if any, you want to depose for use at trial, and I'll get the depositions set up. I took the liberty of highlighting the ones that appear to be arguably similar to Jenny's accident in terms of the same general speed, no alcohol, loading, and all that stuff. I saw five possible candidates," she offered, "but I'll defer to you."

I was busy scanning the chart she had compiled. "I'll look this over in more detail tonight and let you know tomorrow." I noticed that there was only one other complaint from a person in Florida, and that one didn't look similar at all. The five that she had identified as similar accidents were located in New Mexico, Pennsylvania, Ohio, Wisconsin and California. Since they were located outside of Florida, I would have to travel to them and take their depositions, probably by video-tape, if I wanted to use their stability problems in my case as evidence of a defect in the Mesa. I would be able to play back their sworn video-tape testimony for the Hawkins jury, assuming, of course, that his benevolence, The Turtle, found that their episodes of instability with the Mesa were 'substantially similar' to those presented in Jenny's accident, and, therefore, admissible in evidence.

Sandy was reading my mind.

"Not to dwell on the negative, but any out of state depositions are going to cost us a lot of money," Sandy commented. "Do you or Eric have the funds to pay for them?"

"I'm going to have to find the money," I said with a sigh. "It may be that I'll end up taking only three depositions of the best of these other stability complaints. If I can get them in evidence, that will make the point as effectively as five or six. In any event, it's going to have to do. I can't fund any more than that."

"Also," she said, looking over a checklist of 'to do' work-up tasks on a yellow legal pad she had with her that we had outlined a few weeks ago in the case, "I hate to be a nag, but I'm reminding you that we have a November first deadline for the completion and disclosure of all testing and all trial expert witnesses in this case. I know that money is a sore subject, Mike, but you need to remember those deadlines."

"Yes, Mother, I remember."

"I need to confirm. Is it final that we're not going to do any testing of the Mesa?" she asked, looking at the 'to do' tasks that we had charted out. "If we are, you probably need to start lining up a test facility." She was relentless in her case preparation.

I leaned back in my spring-loaded leather chair. My hands were clasped behind my head. "I'd love to do a dynamic S test on a Mesa in this case. I'd wager that the results would give us good data."

"Then let's do one," she suggested, energetically.

"I can't afford it," I said bluntly. "Braxton tells me that it would cost us somewhere around thirty-five to forty thousand dollars to do it in a proper, instrumented engineering manner to render it admissible at trial. I don't have that kind of money."

"Well, it's a shame that Global didn't do any S testing on the Mesa," Sandy commented. "It would be great to be able to use their own testing against them, all at no cost to us."

I thought about her comment for a moment. Then, it hit me.

"That's it!" I said, coming forward suddenly in my chair and slapping my palms against the top of my desk. "You just gave me the idea we needed!" I said excitedly.

"What are you talking about?"

"Testing! We want to see the Mesa put through the S test, right?"

"Of course ..."

"But we can't afford it, right?"

"That's what your bank statement says."

"Well, we're going to get our friends at Global to do the test for us!" I said, laughing.

She cocked her head, knitted her brows and looked at me like I was crazy. "And just how do you expect to persuade them to do our testing at their expense?"

"I don't know why I didn't consider this earlier," I said, thinking. "This is going to be goddamn great!"

"I'm still waiting," she said, continuing to look at me oddly.

"What's the one thing that we *know* we can count on with Harrington and Cole?"

"That they're assholes?" she replied.

"Yes," I chuckled, "but besides that?"

Sandy didn't reply this time but, instead, just sat and let me finish.

"They're sneaky, and they dearly want to win this case, that's what. We need to use those attributes to our advantage."

"Sure. I understand that, but how are you going to get them to go and run tests for us? I think you've been working too late, Mike."

"I don't think so," I said, smiling at the plan that had suddenly developed. "I know that they're peeing in their pants right now trying to figure out if we're going to do any testing ourselves. That's why Harrington posed that question to me at Markov's deposition. It wasn't a passing comment. Nothing Harrington says is casual. Like himself, all of his comments are calculating," I reminded her. "I think they're scared shitless that I'm going to scrape up the cash and run some tests that might show that the Mesa has a stability problem. They know as well as I do that juries get bored to tears listening to all the dry engineers talk about engineering defect theories. However, one thing that juries love is show and tell."

"Show and tell?" she asked.

"Testing," I replied. "Juries love to watch tests being performed on the vehicle that is the subject of the lawsuit. It reduces all of the engineering mumbo jumbo into a concrete demonstration of the principles at issue. If the plaintiff or the manufacturer can run an actual test and prove, or disprove, the other side's theory in the case, the case is over."

"Well, Cole and Harrington will know from your days representing Global that you love to do testing in your cases, won't they?"

"No question about it. If there was a chance to do a test, have it filmed and present it to the jury in my Global defense cases, Cole and Harrington both know that I always jumped at the chance. That was always my *m.o.* in defending Global. They know that I've been a firm believer that testing results displayed on a television monitor in the courtroom for the jury to see is overpowering evidence. That's why they're nervous about it now."

"So," she continued, still puzzled, "having said all that, how are you going to persuade them to run an S test for us? I still don't understand."

"Try this on for size. It's just crazy enough to work," I said. "I'm going to dictate a memo to you in this case. It's going to be stamped 'Confidential, Attorney-Client\Work Product Privileged' on the top. In that memo, I'm going to instruct you to finalize the S test procedures with our outside expert, giving you the precise speeds that he is going to test the Mesa at, along with the details, such as how many dummies are to be in the Mesa, how it's to be loaded with an identical paint compressor, cartons of paint, etc., just like Jenny's Mesa was loaded. I'll probably specify that the Mesa be equipped with outriggers on each side of it in the event that it actually starts to roll. It's also going to specify some of the camera setups I want our test facility to arrange. The memo will warn you to keep me posted on the test setup since I don't expect Global to run any S tests of its own." I thought for a moment, reflecting. "I think I'll even comment that our S tests will go uncontradicted by Global defense at trial because they haven't run any S tests of their own. Now," I said, "this is where you come in."

"I think I like this," she laughed, responding quickly to the idea.

"When is Craige supposed to be over here to review those additional documents we're required to produce in Hawkins?"

"October tenth is the date our production is required. He's already left me a couple of voice mails telling me that he wants to come over as soon as they are physically ready to be looked at. I can set the production up for the tenth."

"Perfect. Your job is to make damn sure that you *inadvertently* leave a copy of that memo in a spot where Craige will be sure to spot it. It can't be obvious that we're setting him up, or they'll smell a rat. I want him to read it."

"You know he'll read it if he gets the chance. Most lawyers would probably turn it over if they spotted an inadvertent production of a privileged document or call me in once they spotted what it is. Not Craige. He'll read it in a heartbeat."

"Absolutely, he will," I nodded in agreement, "and that's the key. Once he does, he'll be back reporting its contents to Harrington and Cole within the hour. Believe me," I laughed conspiratorially, "once he learns of the testing that we're supposedly doing, Harrington will want Global to run its own test, identical to ours, to rebut any test results that we might get that help prove our case. He'll have no option. He doesn't trust us. He's going to have to run his own tests to ensure that they are run correctly."

Sandy then raised the obvious question. "Okay, suppose they run their own S test. And suppose the testing shows that the Mesa is not stable. How are we going to ever get access to their test results? If their testing turns out badly won't they just claim 'work product,' not produce it and try the case without it? Also," she reflected further, "if their S testing actually proves the Mesa is stable, that's going to kill our case, won't it?"

"All of that's true, but you're forgetting one thing, Sandy. Who does Global use for *all* of its litigation testing? Who is the *only* company that you and I used when we recommended testing for Global cases?" I queried.

"Vehicle Testing Labs out of Tempe, Arizona," she answered. "They always use VTL," referencing its acronym.

"Bingo. If they take the bait and do S testing, there's no doubt in my mind that they'll use Vehicle Testing Labs for that testing and do it in Tempe. You know it! So," I said, "I'm going to place a guy on the side of that mountain that is located adjacent to VTL's desert test facility and have him film the whole damn thing with a telephoto lens. Did I ever take you to the VTL test facility in our prior cases?"

"No. You were always too cheap to spring for me to go on any of those testing trips when we were at Hunt," she chided.

"VTL's test facility is in the desert ten miles outside of Tempe. It sits at the base of a cactus-covered mountain on one side. Setting up a camera on that mountain will give a camera a perfect, unobstructed view of their test pad."

"But how are we going to know when they do their testing? You can't exactly position someone on that mountain for the next couple of months and have him film every day."

"We don't have to. Think about it," I said, as I got up and leaned against the door frame of my office. "The beauty of this is that since Global isn't going to *learn* of our testing until October tenth, when Craige comes over to look at our document production, and since Global has to produce its testing results—if it intends to use those results—by November first according to Judge Vaughn's order, we therefore know, by definition, that its testing has to be done sometime during that twenty-day window. We only need to cover that window." I smiled at her, very pleased with myself.

Sandy nodded her head. A smile appeared on her face. "It just might work at that."

"Well, nothing to lose if it doesn't," I replied. "Didn't you have an old guy that used to do camera work? Some old retired guy you knew?"

"Yes, George Krueger. He's retired and did some filming for us on that nighttime accident scene shoot we did in the *Hanna Family Enterprises* case. His wife recently died. I don't know if he's still around or doing shooting, but I'd guess that he would be cheap. If he's still doing it, I'm sure he'd work a deal for us."

"That's the guy I'm thinking of. He was pretty laid back, but he did a nice job in the *Hanna* case. I'd fly him out to Tempe and pay him a set price to do it if he's interested."

"Wait a minute," she suddenly said. "November first is the same day that we have to produce our testing under Vaughn's order as well. When they see on that day that we don't have any testing to produce, will Harrington decide to not produce his testing after all?"

"Not to worry. I'll take care of that at the time. If our video shows that their own test results are bad for them and good for us, I'll produce a copy of my video. Sponge Bob Harrington will shit in his little Square Pants!" I laughed heartily.

"This is going to be fun!" she added wryly, immediately warming to the crazy scheme. "There's nothing illegal or unethical about any of this, is there?"

"Hell no. If there's any unethical conduct, it would be on the part of Craige for the unauthorized reading of my confidential memo and not stopping or pointing the inadvertent disclosure out to you or me at the time. There's no law that says we can't hire a retired guy who happens to get his jollies sitting in the desert sun shooting video of a testing facility that happens, just coincidentally, to be testing a Mesa!"

We both laughed deeply. We both needed it. The Hawkins case had not been progressing well, and the financial problems of my practice were on both our minds.

"I'll get a hold of Krueger right away and see what we can work out," Sandy offered, as she got out of the chair and passed by me and out of my office.

"Just make sure that he fully understands that this is all confidential," I yelled after her.

"Understood," she shot back as she headed for her office.

CHAPTER 30

SANDY CONTACTED KRUEGER. As luck would have it, he had just sold his home in Pompano Beach and was about to move to San Diego where relatives of his lived. With the recent death of his wife of forty-five years, he had decided to be closer to family in Southern California. He had no children and no other ties to Florida. He was driving his RV to California, he explained to Sandy, with his furniture and belongings to follow by moving van. He and his wife had been avid RV travelers, usually staying at Good Sam RV Park stopovers around the country.

He was only too happy to plan his trip around the Tempe stop outside of Phoenix and shoot the video we wanted. Sandy had explained that the tests we wanted filmed were on a hunch, so he might end up doing a lot of waiting around watching for Mesa testing which might not even happen. That was okay with him, he reported. With no family, sixty-six years old and no pressing demands on his time, he was in no hurry and had no schedule, as he put it. He'd just leave a few days earlier than he had anticipated.

The other good news was his price tag. He was only going to charge us for half his gas to Arizona, his video film, his meals in Tempe, and a flat fee of one hundred dollars a day. It was a bargain. If his testimony proved necessary, he agreed to have us fly him back for trial.

I had him come by my office where I went over the type of testing that I expected him to look for, including providing him with photos of what the Mesa model looked like so that he would be able to identify the correct test. With the Mesa as Global's only present sport utility model in production and with its Mesa logo conspicuously imprinted on the right rear corner of the vehicle, identification shouldn't be a problem.

He agreed to start his trip so as to be in Tempe by the eleventh of October. I assured him that he wouldn't likely see any action until the week of the twentieth since it would undoubtedly take Global, even with all its engineers and organization, a good week to plan the test, determine the necessary instrumentation, and arrange for the correct loading to replicate the cartons of heavy paint, the compressor and the cartons of cookies, which Jenny had been transporting at the time. They would also need some time to obtain a Mesa and equip it with a set of outriggers—the instrumented, long steel devices which were affixed to, and extended outward from, each side of a vehicle being stability-tested. The outrigger arms were fitted with downward directed steel members at their outboard ends, which had wheels attached, to prevent the Mesa from rolling over in the event it tipped. The wheels on the ends of the steel outriggers were usually positioned to be about twelve inches above the road in order to allow for some body-lean during the tests.

Krueger promised to call us as soon as he actually witnessed the tests run. The driving portion of the S test itself shouldn't take more than a few minutes, I explained. The majority of the test time would be spent by Vehicle Testing Lab personnel instrumenting the vehicle and setting up the high speed cameras to record the actual test driving results.

Meanwhile, I was busy lining up my damage experts for trial in Eric's case. In addition to Paula Price, the child psychologist who was now treating Sarah, I retained Dr. Natalie Avalos, a psychologist who specialized in the emotional and psychological injuries resulting to victims with severe burn injuries. Dr. Avalos, a Cuban refugee who fled as a young child with her parents from Havana, practiced out of Shands Hospital, which is the large University of Florida Medical Center in Gainesville. Dr. Avalos agreed to review Ryan's medical injuries, including meeting with his main burn treatment doctor, Dr. Stuart Olive, and to meet with Eric in order to testify about the psychological damage resulting from the burn injuries which Ryan would likely carry with him to his grave. Avalos had written and lectured extensively on the subject, having acquired a strong personal interest in the subject matter after watching her younger brother's emotional struggle dealing with horrible facial burn injuries. His burn injuries were compliments of a Cuban gunboat which had riddled her family's escaping speed boat with machine gunfire. The bullets punctured a fuel tank, causing the tank to explode.

Although I had never met her before, she was very enjoyable to converse with over the phone. It was clear that she would make a very favorable impression on a jury. She was also surprisingly reasonable in her fees. She enjoyed the litigation consulting work, she said, and the intellectual challenges it offered. As a result, she charged the same rate as she charged her regular clients, one hundred fifty dollars an hour.

Dr. Olive, the physician I had overheard speaking with Eric in the hall of Broward General Hospital the day after the accident, rounded out the stable of medical experts I planned on using at trial. He also proved to be very helpful and genuinely kind, emphasizing that if his trial testimony was needed, there would be no charge. That was a much-appreciated offer, recognizing that some specialists in South Florida, even treating doctors, were charging lawyers and clients as much as seven hundred fifty dollars an hour for deposition and trial time. With his specialty, he would have easily commanded those boxcar rates.

For economic damages, I retained Peter Cianciolo. He held the rather unique distinction of having both a master's in vocational rehabilitation as well as a Ph.D. in economics. He agreed to formulate and quantify the economic damages which Ryan would likely incur during his lifetime based upon Dr. Avalos's opinions of Ryan's probable psychological problems as well as Cianciolo's own opinions of probable employment and financial prejudice, which Ryan would likely experience as a result of his grotesque facial burn injuries. Economic doors that would have otherwise been wide open, but for the burn injuries, would now be closed to him.

I had originally planned on having Cianciolo also quantify what the economic loss would be to the Hawkins family from the loss of Jenny's future employment. However, Eric would have nothing to do with that claim when I explained it to him. Blood money was the term he quietly, but emphatically, called it. He instructed me to abandon that aspect of the damage claim. I didn't argue the point with him.

Unlike the other expert witnesses I had been able to line up, Cianciolo lacked the warm bedside manner. While very qualified and very knowledgeable about his subject matter, he was in the business strictly for the money. He had a unique combination of talents which made him a necessary witness for my clients' case, but I still didn't care for the guy. He was smart, but arrogant in attitude and sloppy in demeanor. At two hundred ninety dollars an hour, he was one of the most expensive experts on board, but I desperately needed his expertise.

The various retainers I was getting billed for by the newly-hired medical and damage experts, along with the invoices I was now receiving monthly from Braxton and Cargill were mounting up. The case costs caused me to once again discuss the matter with Eric since I couldn't afford to fund them all myself. He had no savings to speak of and had not previously been in a position to help me fund the costs. I was getting desperate, and I decided to speak with him about the money problem to see if the two of us could come up with any bright ideas.

"I think I've got a partial solution," Eric announced over the phone after I started to relate the problem. "I just received insurance proceeds this morning from a twenty-five thousand dollar insurance policy that Jenny had on her life. Her dad had taken it out on her when she started high school. I wasn't even aware that it existed until I received the check today. Her dad filled out all the claim forms himself since he still was the owner of the policy. He had been making the payments on it over all these years. Take the money, Mike, and use it on costs of the case," he instructed. There was no hesitation in his voice. "I had passing thoughts about investing it for the kid's college education, but you need it for the case. The costs of the suit are my responsibility, and I can't ask you to front the whole cost bill."

"Eric ... uh ..." I stammered, embarrassed, "we're in desperate need for cost money, but I have some real reservations about using that money. I want you to be sure because ... well ... there's no guarantee that I'll win your case. As I've discussed with you, we haven't really turned up any clear evidence of any stability defects in the Mesa. Braxton certainly thinks that it has stability problems, but even he can't point to any smoking gun to show to the jury. The case isn't going to be decided on anything like that. That only happens in a Grisham novel. So, I want you to think long and hard before you commit that money to the case."

"Take the money, Mike. If Jenny was anything, she was stubborn about standing on principle," he commented quietly. "I know she'd support me on this. I'll figure out something for the kids' college. This case is important to me. I'm in it for her, for Ryan and Sarah. I'm convinced it's an unsafe vehicle. It took her from me, and I have to see this through, win or lose."

"Eric, I'd rather you thought it over, maybe slept on it. That money is important for—"

"My mind is made up, Mike. I'm going to be sending over a check this week for the immediate amount you need."

MY BAR GRIEVANCE hearing was held at the end of the week. The grievance committee had refused to summarily dismiss Global's complaint as I had requested. The committee wanted to hear live testimony from me and Global's representative before deciding to either dismiss it altogether or recommend that formal disciplinary charges be brought against me by The Florida Bar.

If Hunt hadn't been on the other side representing Global in the proceedings, the Committee would not have wasted their time with live testimony. The complaint would have been drop kicked out the window in view of the transcript of Cole's cross-examination at the disqualification hearing in front of Neanderthal. However, Hunt was on the other side, and its political clout could

not be ignored. Several of the senior Hunt partners had previously either
chaired or served on that grievance committee, and they still enjoyed influence
with the existing committee members. Hunt wanted formal disciplinary charges
pressed against me in no uncertain terms. I had little doubt that Avery, at Willis
Cole's bidding, was doing his best to spread the word around the local bar that
I was the subject of a bar investigation. I knew that the bar's rule that the proceeding was supposed to be confidential at this stage was one of those rules
honored more in its breach than its observance. Old gossipy women in local
neighborhood coffee klatches had nothing on lawyers in Ft. Lauderdale when it
came to gossip involving their fellow bar members. No doubt, this was one of
the reasons that I wasn't getting any local referrals on legal cases. The irony of
the proceedings, regardless of the outcome, was bitter in my mouth. Over the
many years of my practice, I had never received so much as a letter even questioning my ethics, much less a formal complaint filed against me.

Despite my frustration with the process, I wasn't concerned about the
outcome of the investigation; the facts supporting my position spoke loudly
and clearly.

The hearing took place in the offices of the chairman, a managing partner
with a small corporate law firm off Broward Boulevard in downtown Ft.
Lauderdale. He reserved his large conference room for the group which filled
the room. The room had a fabulous view of the New River whose sinuous path
wove its way through the downtown and the wealthy Rio Vista neighborhood
area on its way to the ocean.

Cole had sent Don Kean to the hearing in his place, as the client bringing
the ethic's charge, while Harrington appeared as Global's counsel. I didn't
bother to retain an attorney on my own behalf since the facts were clearly in
my favor, as buttressed by Neanderthal's ruling.

The seven-member committee, composed of five lawyers I knew, and two
I didn't, spent an hour posing questions to me and to Harrington. We were
each permitted to provide a fifteen minute argument at its close in support of
our respective positions. You would have thought I was attending a revival at a
tent jamboree of fundamentalist Baptists in the sugar cane fields of
Okeechobee. Harrington was preaching fire and brimstone, clothed in arguments of 'the long and honored ethical tradition of lawyers' I had violated. I
don't know which planet he had been practicing on. That long and honored
tradition he was talking about sure wasn't evident in the brawling legal environment of the South Florida I was familiar with.

I expected a quick committee vote finding no probable cause to proceed
with any formal bar disciplinary complaint.

After spending thirty minutes in an adjoining conference room discussing the evidence and arguments, the committee re-convened with the rest of us. Its chairman was Gordon Dillon, a small-statured man with the gaunt look of the long-distance jogger he was. "Mr. Culhane," he announced, "the committee has conferred. It is our duty, as the investigative body of The Florida Bar, to inform you that we find probable cause to believe that Rule 4-1.9 of the Florida Rules of Professional Conduct was violated by you in connection with your representation of the Hawkins family in its present action against Global Motors. That rule, as you should know, prohibits an attorney from representing a person in an action against a former client unless the former client 'consents after consultation regarding the matter,'" he announced, reading from some notes in front of him.

Interestingly, I observed, the notes he was reading from were located on the first page of his legal pad. Since I had seen him make notes on later pages during the 'hearing,' it was evident to me that he already made his mind up when he had entered the room, even before hearing any of the testimony. My Irish temper ignited anew.

"Excuse me for interrupting, Chairman Dillon, but I am well aware of that rule. Is the committee electing to ignore the specific telephone conversation I had with Mr. Cole *or* the consent letter I had him sign to confirm Global's consent? I was given *explicit* authority by Global to represent an adverse party, Rocky Watson, against Global in a products liability action. Judge Morgenthal correctly applied the law. I am both mystified and stunned," I said, looking around the room as I spoke, at the faces of the seven committee members, "that this is even an issue at all. It should be dead as a doornail."

The Chairman quickly responded. "The committee has serious questions regarding the issue, Mr. Culhane. Certain members of this committee believe that you were ethically required to have a broader discussion with Global's representative, Mr. Cole, when you obtained his consent regarding the Watson case. It is for that reason that we are recommending that formal disciplinary procedures be initiated against you."

I rose out of my chair in anger. "*Broader discussions* with Mr. Cole? You can't be serious! The rule doesn't require or envision the type of discussion you are suggesting. Mr. Cole is an extremely sophisticated lawyer who knew damn well what he was agreeing to. He isn't even here to substantiate your conclusion. He has a third person, his lawyer, make that claim. And the fact that he now claims that he didn't fully *think through* the legal ramifications of his knowing consent is irrelevant. He consented to my representation and that consent put me in one hundred ten percent compliance with the bar rule you just cited.

I respectfully demand that you reconsider your ruling and dismiss the complaint."

While a couple of the seven committee members shifted nervously in their chairs at the long table before me, Dillon was stoic and unmoved. "I strongly suggest that you retain an attorney, sir. Your license to practice law is at stake. Our recommendation will be submitted to Tallahassee."

Harrington nodded solicitously to Dillon. Kean looked straight ahead, unwilling to look at me.

"A point of procedure, Chairman Dillon," I persisted. "I am entitled to a roll call of the vote on the issue by each committee member, am I not?"

"You are, but it ... uh ... it is a procedural right rarely requested Mr. Culhane."

"Well, consider me rare, Mr. Chairman. I want each member to announce his or her vote on the record. Frankly, I am convinced that there are some things going on behind the scenes that I fully intend to investigate myself."

"What are you suggesting, sir?" Dillon haughtily shot back.

I ignored him. "I am waiting for the call of the votes, Mr. Dillon."

Dillon glared at me for a moment before nodding to the committee member at the far end of the table to state what her vote had been. After her, all of the remaining six announced their votes. The vote was four to three, with Dillon announcing his vote last. Not surprisingly, he voted against me.

"If we are going on the record with our individual votes," one of the committee members who had voted in my favor suddenly stated, "then I want the record to note that my vote against the committee's actions is a very strenuous one. There is absolutely no basis for any ethics violation based on the record we have heard." All heads in the room turned to her.

"Ms. Wellerby," Dillon immediately jumped in sharply, trying to maintain control, "while the record as to how each of the committee members voted is open to Mr. Culhane, I remind you that the *substance* of our committee discussions is not. They are to be treated as absolutely confidential. There will be no further discussion in this open forum on any aspect of our deliberations, including how strongly each of us feels about his or her vote."

Having been sharply rebuked, Wellerby folded her arms across her chest and looked straight up at the ceiling, apparently in silent protest. However, she said nothing more.

The four members voting to pursue a formal grievance charge were all close to the Hunt firm. Two of them, including Dillon, routinely received client and conflict referrals from various Hunt partners, including Avery Wilcox. One of the female attorneys on the committee was a tennis doubles partner with Gunther's wife. They knew where their business and social bread was buttered.

I walked out of the grievance hearing as furious at myself as I was at the committee's action. Hunt's influential political tentacles extended deeply into the Ft. Lauderdale legal and business establishment, and I had stupidly ignored that influence. My failure to retain an attorney with equal heavyweight influence to level the playing field politically before the committee had now put my most important meal ticket at risk—my law license.

Driving home after the evening grievance committee hearing, I felt equal measures of frustration, self-doubt, anger and depression. How could my professional life have turned so badly so quickly, I lamented to myself. What had been, professionally speaking, a virtual bowl of cherries for me only a short eight months ago was quickly turning into a shit sandwich. And I seemed to be taking increasingly bigger bites.

CHAPTER 31

IT CAME AS no real surprise when I received Global's motion for summary judgment against Rocky Watson's lawsuit in the mail. In its motion papers, Harrington was asking the trial judge sitting on Rocky's case to throw it out because Rocky had tossed the allegedly defective Global seat track before the lawsuit was started. Global claimed that Rocky's actions had prejudiced Global's ability to defend itself. The legal terminology was that Rocky had engaged in 'spoliation' of the evidence by preventing Global's engineers a post-litigation inspection of the seat track.

If Global's motion had been predictable, so also was Rocky's reaction when I called him and explained the nature and legal consequences of their motion if the judge granted it. He'd be out of court and would be facing the likelihood of having a judgment entered against him by Global for its litigation fees and costs.

Watson was not impressed with their motion, as he so eloquently expressed. "Those chicken-livered sons-a-bitches. They don't want to fight me fair and square in front of a jury, do they? They're trying to sneak out of this on a damn ... a damn ..." he groped, searching for the right word to finish his thought.

"Technicality," I finished for him.

"Yeah, a fuckin' technicality!" he echoed. "That's fuckin' bullshit."

"Well, it's a little more than a technicality, but, yes, they don't want to have to even address the merits of your lawsuit if they don't have to. I can't say that you'd probably do it any differently if you were in their shoes," I said, trying to keep him calm.

"So, what do we do now, hot shot? You're my lawyer. Any bright ideas?"

Thankfully, Rocky was one of those rare clients to whom I could comfortably respond in kind.

"Hey, you're the one who ripped the fucking seat track out of your car and tossed it in the trash, not me," I pushed back sharply, keeping him in check. "Remember, it's your seat track removal that's at issue here. Now," I said more calmly, "if you're asking me whether I can legally beat their motion in court, the answer is maybe. Your ace in the hole is the fact that in your complaint letter to Global *before* you removed the seat track, you did tell them to come and look at it. Your letter just might do the trick."

"Yeah?"

"Yeah. Can I ask you something? Don't take this the wrong way, but you don't exactly strike me as the kind of guy who is a letter writer. What caused you to write Global with your complaint in the first place?"

"My dad was a real pain in the ass when I was growing up. Always on my case. I guess he was good for something after all though. Big companies don't pay no attention to no complaints that 'ain't in writing, he once told me. I remembered that."

"Well, that was good advice. It may work. I'm going to argue that Global was given the *opportunity* to inspect the part before you tossed it. That's all the law should require. However, this spoliation stuff is still a pretty gray area in the law since it is a fairly recent defense that the manufacturers have come up with. I'll keep you posted on how we do. The court hearing isn't until December twenty-eighth. I'll want you there, Rocky." I didn't give him an option.

He grunted, which, from him, I took as a resounding 'yes, I'll be there.'

We hung up.

With the Hawkins' case set to begin trial on December first, and with my efforts to get caught up with the stack of other clients' work piling up on my desk as a result of the monopolization of my time that the Hawkins case was causing, I was going to back burner Rocky's case for a while.

THE MOST PRESSING front burner problem I had to deal with presently on Eric's case was the decision as to whether to take the depositions of other drivers around the country who had claimed to have experienced stability problems while driving the Mesa. If Vaughn permitted the testimony of their handling and stability problems with the Mesa to come before the jury, the impact could be very important. It's one thing for an expert like Braxton to take the stand and *talk* about his opinion that the Mesa has a stability problem. It's quite another, however, if the jury hears that these same theorized defect opinions actually occurred to other Mesa drivers around the country. That testimony would clothe Braxton's opinions in credibility.

Because of the highly persuasive effect, which evidence of other problems and other accidents inevitably has on a jury in a products case, I expected Vaughn to be especially vigilant in deciding whether these other accidents presented facts and circumstances which would be *substantially similar*—the criterion for their admissibility in our case—to those occurring in the Hawkins' accident.

Given the difficulty we would be facing at trial in persuading The Turtle to let these other accidents into evidence, the question was whether to spend the time and money to take the depositions. Through discovery, we had identified other Mesa drivers, in addition to the Perry and Stafford suits settled quickly by Global, who had experienced arguably similar stability episodes as Jenny had experienced. The problem was that we could not subpoena them to attend trial since they lived outside of Florida, and the taking of their sworn depositions, at which Harrington would appear and cross-examine them, would be damn expensive. One lived in California, and the others in New Mexico, Pennsylvania, Ohio and Wisconsin. Each would require my airfare, a court reporter, as well as a videographer to take the videotape of their testimony. That was an awful lot of money to spend on evidence which Vaughn, in any event, might not even allow at trial.

After discussing the situation with Eric, we elected to make the financial investment. Based upon what each of the other five had related to Sandy when she had interviewed them over the phone, they had important testimony. The same was true for Brant Stafford, the quadriplegic living in Knoxville with whom Global had settled. Sandy scheduled their depositions for the last two weeks in September.

As it turned out, I was very pleased with our decision. All five witnesses were only too happy to tell of their frightening experiences with the Mesa. All were angry about what they felt was an unsafe, unstable vehicle, and they wanted to help. They made excellent witnesses as they related their stories. While the specific details of their various accidents were somewhat different from Jenny's, they all presented a common problem—severe instability exhibited by the Mesa when sudden steering movements were required at normal highway speeds in response to an unexpected road hazard. Their specific road hazards included ice on the roadway, a deer running onto the road at night in one case, a dog on the roadway in another, and two cars running a stop sign in the remaining two.

Harrington's deposition cross-examination was aggressive and effective. He focused almost exclusively on accentuating the differences in the specific details of their individual accidents from those in Jenny's, including differences in speeds, road conditions, lighting, loading conditions of the Mesa, number of occupants, and any evidence of alcohol consumption by the five other drivers in the hours before their accidents.

At trial, my experts would be trying to get the jury to understand some rather dry, complex concepts of engineering and physics. Seeing these other Mesa drivers explain the similar terrifying experiences they had encountered in being unable to control their Mesa would be visually powerful evidence. If we could get them in evidence, that is.

Three of these other accidents involved rollovers of the Mesa, while the remaining two resulted in the Mesa running off the roadway. All three of the rollovers resulted in serious personal injuries—quadriplegia, paraplegia and a depressed skull fracture with severe neurological deficits. The other two were much more fortunate for the occupants of the Mesa—body damage to the Mesa itself or damage to property off road, including a utility pole in one of those cases.

Harrington scoffed at their testimony, commenting at one point during a break in one of their depositions, that they presented wide chasms of material differences from the Hawkins accident.

"You'll never get those depositions into evidence," he laughed after we had concluded the last one. "I hope you appreciate that you just spent a colossal waste of your time and money."

"WHAT TIME IS Craige scheduled to come by tomorrow to review our documents?" I asked Sandy and Tina late on the afternoon of October ninth. The three of us were sitting at an outdoor table at a bar on the New River having a drink. I told them to consider it a 'firm retreat.' They had both been working hard and welcomed sneaking out of the office at four p.m. for a drink. I had cleared it first with the other three lawyers in the shared office space for whom Tina worked.

We were trying to come up with a plausible scenario for tomorrow's planned, 'inadvertent' disclosure of our Mesa test plan memo to Craige.

"Ten o'clock is when he's coming by to look at the damage documents. He called me this morning to remind me," Sandy informed us over her frozen margarita. She, like Tina and me, was wearing her sunglasses to deflect the sun that was still high in the sky. The canopy of overhead fronds from the row of queen palms aligning the New River to our right shielded us from most of the direct sunlight. The river traffic was heavy, which was the norm for a Friday afternoon.

"Well, have the two of you figured out how we're going to pull this off?" I asked, sucking on a bottle of beer.

"Yeah," Sandy replied, putting down her drink. "I told Craige that you and I wouldn't be in when he came by due to other matters we were doing, but that Tina would show him into the conference room down the hall and bring him the files for his review. I explained that Tina works for us on a part-time basis; that I would tell her where in my office the specific files he was to review would be located. I implied that Tina was a bit of a ditz," she said, smiling proudly at Tina. "We have this all worked out. Right?" she asked, looking at Tina.

Tina was nursing her second frozen daiquiri. "Perfectly," she giggled. She was the only person I'd ever seen continue chewing gum while having a drink.

"The way we have it planned," Sandy continued, "is that Tina will put him in the conference room and come in five minutes later carrying the damage files for him to view. However, I've put two additional manila folders on the very bottom of that stack. One will be labeled 'Dr. Hubert Braxton,' which will actually have Braxton's résumé and the original of the retainer agreement that we entered into with him for this case."

I looked over as she was talking. Tina was smiling conspiratorially. She had met Craige when he showed up for Rocky's deposition and had taken an immediate dislike to him.

"The other file," Sandy said, "will be marked 'Mesa Stability Testing' and will have a memo from you to me outlining the details of the planned S stability test along the lines that you suggested. It makes reference to the fact that the stability design expert you retained wants to simulate the specific details of Jenny's accident as our expert believes existed, including a fifty-five mph speed. It specifies having the Mesa loaded with a fifty-percentile-sized female dummy belted into the driver's seat to simulate Jenny, an infant dummy belted in the second seat, passenger side, to simulate the location and weight of Ryan and his child's seat, and the rear cargo area of the test Mesa loaded with eight cartons containing the same heavy thirty-two gallons of paint that Jenny's Mesa had in it at the time of the rollover, a heavy spray paint compressor weighing a couple hundred pounds equating to the same weight as the one that was in Jenny's at the time of the accident, and eight large cardboard cartons each filled with the same weight as that of the large cartons of Girl Scout cookies that were also in her Mesa at the time of the accident," she recounted, in detail. "In fact," she suddenly remembered, "I brought the memo with me for you to look at to make sure you don't want to add or change anything." She reached down from her oversized purse and pulled a two page memo from the manila folder within it. She handed it over to me.

"I'm planning on using my best 'air head' impression for Mr. Craige," Tina added, again giggling. The alcohol was loosening her up. She was loose before she started. "In fact, I'm going to rat my hair up a little, for effect, of course. When Craige gets to those two files at the bottom, he's going to think I mistakenly grabbed those two files for his review."

I shook my head back and forth, chuckling at their duplicity. I eyeballed the memo. It looked legitimate, complete with a dried circular ring of stained coffee on it from the base of a coffee cup that had apparently been placed on it when it had sat on Sandy's desk after receiving it from me. "Nice touch," I said, pointing to the coffee ring.

"That was Tina's idea."

Tina beamed, obviously pleased that I noticed and appreciated her contribution to the scheming effort. "I saw that done on an old *Mission Impossible* re-run I watched on television last week. It does kind of make it look more real, doesn't it?"

"It does at that," I admitted. "Sandy, I'm assuming that you put that legitimate Braxton file in there to add believability?"

"Yes, Harrington and Craige know how carefully you guard the identity of your trial experts from all your years at Hunt. They know how you always fight to avoid having to disclose the name and identity of your trial experts until the court-ordered disclosure date in a case."

"That's true."

"Well, if Craige sees the Braxton file *now*, complete with the original of our retainer agreement, he's going to think that Tina really did screw up in delivering those extra two files to him since you wouldn't want him or Global to know who you are going to use until November first, which is the court-ordered deadline for disclosure. It will look legit," she finished.

I reviewed the balance of the memo's contents. Without raising any suspicions on his part, I had asked Braxton to outline the details of what the necessary instrumentation and test procedures would actually be if one were to conduct an S stability test on a Mesa. His procedures, including instrumentation details, were outlined in the memo, without attribution to him by name, in order to weave engineering credibility into the memo when Global's engineers read over Craige's verbatim handwritten notes of the memo's contents. I didn't expect Craige to filch the file or the memo itself.

"As you suggested," Sandy said as I finished reading, "I didn't identify in the memo where we were going to have the S test run. I merely had you inform me in there that you had been told by your design engineer that he had secured the test facility and that the S test would be conducted before the November first test disclosure deadline."

"Good job. Let's all hope that Global takes the bait, runs the test and that it shows that the Mesa has a stability problem like Braxton says it does. We

could use a break in this case. It's going to be a hard case to prove, especially
with all these complex engineering issues."

"Mike," Sandy added, "I was wondering. When November first rolls
around and we don't produce any test at all, will Harrington and Global be able
to cross-examine Braxton and some of our other witnesses at trial and ask them
about the results of our test? I'm a little concerned that if they do that, the jury
may think that we ran the S test, that the Mesa did just fine, and that we're
hiding the test results since they damage our case."

"Don't worry, that's the beauty of this ruse. I don't see any downside
from that standpoint. If Harrington asks Braxton at trial about whether he ran
any tests on an actual Mesa, Braxton will honestly be able to tell him that he
didn't. In fact, he'll probably wonder what the hell Harrington is even talking
about since I haven't told Braxton what we're doing. And," I added,
"Harrington can't even refer to our memo because, to do so, would be to admit
that he and Craige were engaged in unethical behavior. Under the ethical rules,
if a lawyer comes across the internal, confidential files or documents of the
other party or the other party's attorney, like this memo," I said, holding it up,
"he's ethically prohibited from reading it. His duty is to immediately bring the
inadvertent disclosure to the other attorney's attention."

"So they can't say a thing?"

"They can't say a damn thing." We both looked at each other and broke
out laughing.

"Sweet," Tina chimed in.

"Incidentally," I asked, "have you confirmed that Krueger will be in place
to videotape the Global testing?"

Sandy nodded. "He called in after lunch this afternoon, as a matter of
fact. He will be there in Tempe tomorrow morning and plans to check into a
motel and get in place with his tripod and tele-video equipment set up for
filming right after lunch. He said he brought a bunch of detective murder
mysteries to read to pass the time during the days as he waits. His only concern
expressed to me was whether you're sure that he can get within a hundred to a
hundred-fifty yards of the test pad at the Vehicle Testing Lab facility to get a
clear video shot."

"Believe me, that's not going to be a problem. VTL is only about ten
miles outside of Tempe, but it might just as well be one hundred miles. It's in
the middle of the desert. It has a ten foot tall chain link fence all around its
thirty to forty acres. There's nothing but cactus, sagebrush, rocks and low hills
surrounding its other three sides. Krueger should be able to park, set up his
equipment on the mountainside he'll be on and shoot without being noticed by
any Global engineers conducting the test. Even if they should see his RV

parked there, I'm sure they'll take him for a solitary desert camper and pay him no mind. Let me know if and when Krueger reports with any news of any Mesa testing, okay?"

"I will."

"Office meeting adjourned," I grinned as the three of us finished our drinks.

CHAPTER 32

I WAS OUT of the office at depositions the next day in another case I was handling. I called in to Sandy around five o'clock to see how the document inspection went with Craige.

"God, it went perfectly," Sandy gushed, "just perfectly. Tina makes a great bimbo."

"Did he say anything to Tina about having brought in the two wrong files?"

"Are you kidding me? Not a word. And I know that he saw them because I had placed the memo in the Mesa Testing file face up, but upside down. When I inspected the file after he left, he had replaced it right side up. He read it, all right. In fact, Tina told me that she went unannounced into his conference room after two hours to ask him if he wanted a soda or a cup of coffee, and she saw him looking at that file and writing a whole bunch of notes on his legal pad. She said he acted a little uncomfortable and put his legal pad over it when she came closer to the table he was working at, but she could still tell what it was. She didn't let on anything," Sandy assured me.

"Well, let's hope the fish takes the worm and runs with it."

AS IT TURNED out, the fish took it all—hook, worm, line and sinker. A week later, on October eighteenth, Sandy came rushing excitedly into my office. It was at close of the business day. "Mike, I have George Krueger on your second line! He says that they ran the Global tests today! I told him that you would want to speak with him directly. He's holding," she said, nodding triumphantly towards my phone.

"Thanks," I said, hitting the speaker button so that Sandy could listen to our conversation as well. She pulled a client chair closer to the phone, which was sitting on the corner of my desk.

"Mr. Krueger, it's Mike Culhane here. I've got you on the speaker phone with Sandy. So, what did you see?" I asked excitedly.

"I saw the tests done this morning. I usually get here about seven o'clock in the morning, but I got caught up in a little traffic jam in Tempe this morning and didn't get to my usual place on the mountainside outside the Vehicle Testing Labs facility until about seven-thirty. Sorry about that. Anyway, when I arrived, I noticed a bunch of activity out on the big open asphalt-paved lot on the South side of the main building. It's that lot that you figured that they'd do the Mesa testing on if they did it?"

"Yes," I responded, "it's what Vehicle Testing Labs calls its skid pad. It's where VTL normally conducts its braking and tire performance tests. Since the accident occurred on asphalt, I figured they would be using that asphalt skid pad for any testing they did."

"Well, when I got there, there was already a forest green-colored Mesa sitting there. When I got my equipment out and set it up, I was able to get a close look at it through my telephoto video lens."

"How was it loaded?" I asked.

"I didn't see them load it since they must have done that either before I got there late, or they loaded it back at the VTL shop area," he explained, quickly picking up its business acronym. "In any event, you could see through its windows that it had a big load in it. Through my close-up lens, I could see that it had large boxes that looked like they contained paint because all of them had the name of Sherwin Williams stenciled on them, you know, the paint company," he added, stating the obvious. "And there were also a lot of large cardboard boxes that were not marked with any markings on them, but they were big. The last thing that was already loaded in the cargo area looked like it was some kind of big, heavy piece of metal equipment. I couldn't make out exactly what it was, only that it was metal looking, like I said, and it looked heavy."

That would have been the heavy paint compressor and spray machine that Eric had planned on using to spray paint his house with, I mentally calculated. It fit the description. The four large unmarked boxes would have been weighted with sandbags, or the equivalent, to replicate the weight of the eight large cartons of cookies that were in Jenny's Mesa, and Global was using actual boxes of paint, each containing four gallons of paint. They had the load right.

"Did the Mesa have the test outriggers attached to it like we discussed?"

"It sure did, one on each side. Kinda weird looking things."

"How about dummies?" I questioned.

"They had a dummy in the driver's seat and it looked like a baby dummy strapped in a baby car seat in the rear seat, passenger side."

"Go ahead, I apologize for interrupting your description. Tell us what you saw."

"That's okay. Anyway, there were four engineer types around the Mesa. One was fiddling with all the high speed cameras they had set up, one looked like he was in charge of some pretty fancy instrumentation equipment that was there, and another one was the test driver. The last one looked like he was in charge. He was giving the orders, and everybody came to ask him questions from time to time. None of the four looked like they were VTL employees because their guys wear khaki-colored uniforms with the VTL logo over the shirt pocket. The four engineers involved in the test wore blue uniforms that had the words 'Global Motors Engineering' printed on the back."

"Did you see any VTL engineers around during the test?" I thought his description of the personnel odd. In all of the six or seven testing events I had done at its Tempe facility, VTL had its own engineers crawling all over the place. In all of the testing I had done over the years there, VTL had used its own cameras and its own camera techs to oversee those cameras and their set-ups. Also, in the prior testing I had done there, there were always two or three Vehicle Testing engineers who hung around the test site. They loved to watch the tests, even if they weren't directly involved. They would usually jump in a VTL pickup and head out to watch from the sidelines. Must have been busy with other tests for the day, I figured.

"No, just the four guys that I described. Well," he continued, "it took them until about noon to get all the cameras and equipment all set up. That's when the one driver got into the Mesa, started driving up to a pretty good speed and then looked like he started turning the steering wheel hard to the right, then again to the left, then again to the right and then, for the last time, back again to the left."

"What did the Mesa do when he did that?" I held my breath waiting for the answer. *This was the whole lawsuit.*

"It looked like a normal vehicle that was being steered back and forth quickly as best I could tell."

"Did you see it start to tip or anything like that? Did any of its wheels rise off the concrete or the ends of the outriggers touch the pavement?"

"No, nothing like that. When the driver turned the steering wheel each time pretty sharply in one direction, I mean, you could see the body of the

Mesa sway pretty good in the opposite direction, but there was no lifting of its wheels off the ground though. I'm sure of that."

Sandy looked over at me, and I at her. There was a depressing silence between us as our eyes met. Words didn't need to tell each other what our eyes communicated.

"Son of a bitch," I finally managed to say, dejectedly.

Sandy didn't say anything.

This was devastating news. The old saying about being careful what you ask for came quickly to mind. We had asked for Global to run 'our test' to prove our theory of defect, and they did just that. The results of that test were now going to bury us at trial.

"Are you still there?" Krueger asked, responding to the silence that he experienced from my end of the phone after my momentary swearing.

"Yes ... yes ... Go ahead. Sorry," I said, finally.

"Well, they re-ran the same test three more times, and it always looked the same to me. The four engineers running the tests all looked pretty pleased with the tests, too. They were all smiles and the like, far as I could see."

"I see," I said with a sigh. "Well, I appreciate everything you've done, George. Why don't you go ahead and send me a copy of the videotape when you get to California in a few days. I'm not going to need it Fed Exed to me as quickly as I thought I would," I said with disappointment.

"Is what I told you good or bad for your lawsuit?" he asked.

"It's not good at all," I acknowledged. "Thanks for taping it for us, though."

"I've already burned a copy for you onto a DVD, and I just put it in a Fed Ex pouch for delivery to you tomorrow," he said. "I stopped at a CVS on the way back into town since I thought that you would want to see it right away. They were nice enough to insert my video card into their copying system there and get it burned. Amazing what they can do nowadays, even at CVS," he added, "amazing. Anyway, I wanted to get this out of the way right now since I may just take a side trip to Sedona tomorrow while I'm this close. I'll be leaving my motel here in the morning."

"That would be fine," I said. My thoughts were still on the damage that the tape would have on our case in front of a jury.

"You know," Krueger added, chuckling, "I should tell you that the Global engineers weren't too happy with me being there."

"What do you mean?" I asked, "they saw you?" That scenario was not in my script.

"Yeah, they did. After the four tests were done, I was just letting the video camera run on the tripod to catch their clean-up operations in case you wanted it.

I went inside my RV to get something to eat, and when I came out ten minutes later, I saw a red Vehicle Testing pickup truck charging up the mountain road. One of the Global test guys from the Mesa tests was driving the truck. He came out, mad as a wet hen and slammed the door of the truck shut. I had grabbed the tripod that my video camera was on when I saw him coming and quickly shut it off and put it inside the side door of my RV just before he got there."

"Do you think he saw your video camera?" My professional pride didn't want this to get back to Harrington in some way for him to figure out that my little ruse had backfired right into my face. I'd never hear the last of it.

"I don't know. I suspect he may have gotten a glimpse of it as he approached and I was moving it into my RV. Anyway, he was all nasty when he walked towards my RV and asked me what the hell I was doing out there. I told him that I was a nature buff visiting Tempe on vacation," Krueger laughed, "and that I had been collecting desert flowers and photographing a unique variety of desert cactus that blossom this time of the year. I asked him why it was any business of his. He grumbled about the area being private property and that he was asking me to leave right then, which I did. The guy even took down my license plate and demanded to know where I was staying in Tempe."

"Did you tell him?"

"Sure, I figured that I had nothing to hide, and if it was private property, or something, that I didn't want to get into any trouble. Besides, I packed up my stuff and left then. He watched me go."

"I apologize if you were embarrassed over this, George. VTL doesn't own the property that you were on. I've seen other people camp out in those hills myself when I've been out there for other tests in other cases. VTL could care less about it, and I don't know what that guy's problem was."

"No apologies needed. I'm leaving the Fed Ex drop off bin now and heading back to my motel for the day. I'll keep the master of the video card in the event they lose yours en route. Let me know if you need the original or another copy. In the meantime, I'll call you when I get to my brother's place in California in a few days to give you my final bill if that's okay."

"That would be fine. Give Sandy a call directly. Thanks again for your help." We hung up.

The disappointment in the room was thick. "I can't believe this," Sandy lamented after I hung up. "This isn't good, is it?"

"Not at all. You know that Harrington is going to jam that test down our throats at trial, and he's going to emphasize that Global ran that test at only fifty-five mph—the very speed that we say that Jenny was traveling at—rather than at the much higher speed that Global's experts and Trooper Martelli will undoubtedly claim Jenny was going at. Shit," I added.

"I don't understand those test results," she continued. "How does that test square with what Braxton has been telling you in your conversations with him? He says that the Mesa is unstable from a design standpoint? And how do you account for the other people that you deposed around the country that all swear that they also had tipping of the Mesa on the roadway when they turned the steering wheel sharply like Krueger described they did on that Mesa? It doesn't make sense."

"It does if those other five drivers we deposed are simply mistaken about their speed or what the Mesa actually did in their accidents. It's hard to argue with a test, *our test* as a matter of fact," I said, with obvious irony in my voice. "I need to confer with Braxton. I can't say anything to him about their test until Harrington formally discloses it on November first, but as soon as he does, I want to go over it with Braxton. He has reviewed all the materials, the engineering documents, and the accident reconstruction opinions that Cargill will testify occurred in Jenny's accident. I just can't believe this," I repeated, again expressing my disappointment. "Braxton reconfirmed to me only yesterday in my telephone conference with him that he is absolutely convinced there is no way that a safely-designed utility vehicle traveling at only fifty-five miles per hour should have tipped up and started to roll over while it was still on the roadway like Jenny's did."

"Could he be wrong?" Sandy was asking the obvious question that was also on my mind.

"What can I say? Sure he could be wrong. But he seems to really know what he's talking about. And don't forget, Cargill is firm in his opinion that Jenny was only doing fifty-two to fifty-five miles per hour, which is also entirely consistent with Jenny's usual driving practices. She wasn't a speeder. She was a very safe and careful driver according to Eric. Also," I added, trying to rebuild my own confidence once again in our case, "you can't ignore that eyewitness, Abadin, who testified in his deposition that he saw the Mesa act weirdly before it left the roadway and got onto the grassy median. You put all those facts together, along with the complaints of those other five drivers we deposed who also experienced the same type of stability problem with the Mesa, and something just doesn't fit."

Sandy just nodded. My recitation sounded just as defensive to her as it did to me, I admitted. *Shit.*

I called Braxton the next day and told him that I was flying up to meet with him to go over his calculations and opinions. He agreed to meet with me over the weekend since he was busy with teaching commitments. I set up a similar meeting with Ralph Cargill over in Ft. Myers the next week. Before I disclosed both of them as my experts on November first, I needed to assure myself that neither they, nor I, had overlooked anything. I couldn't say anything to them about Global's S testing since I hadn't officially received it yet from Harrington. I'd be given a copy on November first, and I planned to provide them each with a copy at that time.

When Krueger's 'unofficial' DVD of the S testing was delivered by the Fed Ex deliveryman the next morning, I walked to the title insurance company offices down the hall to play it. They had a DVD player in one of their two closing rooms, with a high definition LED wall-mounted screen, which they had kindly allowed me to use. I popped it in and watched.

Unfortunately, Krueger had accurately described what he had seen. A Mesa, identical in color to the one Jenny was driving, was loaded exactly as hers had been at the time of the accident. The eight heavy boxes loaded with cans of paint and the heavy paint compressor were visible through the windows of the vehicle. While the top of the Mesa rocked dramatically back and forth during the severe steering movements, the vehicle managed to negotiate the sharp turning maneuvers without any lifting of the offside tires from the surface of the asphalt.

I had to complement Krueger on his close-up videotaping. He had picked an excellent spot which gave him sufficient elevation from the adjacent mountainside to see over the chain link fence for a clear, unobstructed view of the Mesa. As I was beginning to watch the four Global test personnel engage in their post-test cleanup operations of test cable disconnections and removal of camera film, I was mentally trying to calculate just how much damage the tests had done to my stability defect theory. I kept arriving at the same assessment. This testing would inflict a mortal wound to our case. In that one series of four S tests, Global had taken my theory of what had happened and had visually shot it out of the sky.

"Excuse me?" one of the title insurance employees interrupted my thoughts as she opened the door of the conference room, "is there any chance you might be done? I need this room for a closing this morning, and everybody is here. I wouldn't rush you, but the seller needs to close the sale of his house and catch a plane. I'm sorry."

"No problem. I'm really done anyway," I said as I hit the stop button and ejected the DVD from their player. I had seen all that I needed to see, and, unfortunately, more than I wanted to see. I recalled Krueger mentioning that the balance of the tape was just the housekeeping of the test crew finishing with the breakdown of the test site and cameras.

"Thanks for the use of your equipment," I said to her as I gathered my DVD, threw it back into the file and headed back to my office. The results of what I had seen weighed heavily on my mind.

NOVEMBER FIRST CAME, and I disclosed all of my experts, both liability and damage. Along with each, I produced a copy of their respective curriculum vitaes and an extensive summary of their respective opinions in the case. I received Global's disclosure via hand delivery at around four-thirty p.m. that same day. Harrington had sent it over by messenger. As expected, Harrington produced not only the names and CVs of Global's experts, but also a complete package of its Mesa S test results. The package included a single DVD of the four filmed tests along with a ten page report which set forth the data from the four tests as captured by the expensive instrumentation attached to the Mesa by cables which were connected to its underside. Global's footage was as impressive as it was depressing. While it depicted exactly what Krueger had filmed, albeit from a little different camera angle, Global had created a bold blue introductory video headboard in advance of each of the four tests, with vivid white lettering which identified each of the four tests in the same official format:

GLOBAL MOTORS CORPORATION
LITIGATION TESTS

HAWKINS vs. GLOBAL MOTORS CORPORATION
DATE: OCTOBER 18, 2012
SITE: VEHICLE TESTING LABS, INC. [VTL], TEMPE, AZ
VEHICLE TESTED: 2012 PRODUCTION MESA
LOAD: LOADED WITH SAME WEIGHTED PASSENGERS AND CARGO AS THE HAWKINS ACCIDENT MESA.
TEST SPEED: 55 mph
TEST CONDUCTED: STABILITY 'S' DRIVING TESTS

The next morning I received a call from Harrington. It wasn't unexpected.

"I want to set up depositions as soon as possible of all your experts," he announced. All business. "Why don't you give them a call and phone me tomorrow. I want to get this done."

"Do you really feel you need to depose all of them? If you noticed, I gave you a detailed report in my disclosure, which sets forth their respective opinions. If we can avoid the costs and expenses involved in their separate depositions, I think it would be in the best interests of both of our clients." It was worth a chance. Depositions by him would simply cost me more money and time into the case. Even though Global would have to pick up the fees and costs of my experts who were deposed by him, I still had to eat the substantial fees which each of them would likely generate in spending the four or five hours preparing for those depositions. Further, I would have to pick up the costs of the plane fare and hotels for the depositions of Braxton and Avalos.

"You've got to be kidding," he said mockingly. "I'm taking every one, and I figure that each one will likely take a complete day." His voice was filled with cutting delight.

"I can see a full day with Braxton, perhaps, but you don't need more than half a day with the rest."

"Wrong. You and your client are the ones who are alleging that this is a *big dollar case*," he said sarcastically. "Well, you've got to live by those claims. And, accordingly, I'm taking as much time as I damn well please to depose them. If you have a problem with that, let me know now so that I can schedule a motion to compel with Vaughn. I wouldn't exactly call your luck with his discovery rulings so far particularly good, would you?" he asked, mockingly.

"You know, Bob, I think I did a major disservice recently to your associate, Tucker Craige, when I told him that he reminded me a lot of you. I was wrong. You're in a class all by yourself."

"Oh, by the way," Harrington added, "I didn't see any test results in your disclosure materials. I hope you're not trying to sandbag me and try to produce any testing which you didn't disclose by yesterday's deadline. I'll yell like hell if you do, and you know Vaughn. He will prohibit the use of any late-disclosed tests. I'd probably even have to ask for sanctions if you're holding out on me," he challenged.

"Why would I even think of running tests in this case, Bob. I won't need any to prove my case, especially after Vaughn lets me use those five other Mesa drivers who had problems with their Mesas, too."

"You should live so long to see those get into evidence. They're not going to be allowed in evidence, and you know it. I'll grant you that Morgenthal undoubtedly would have let them in, but not Vaughn. We got lucky when we got him on this case, and you're stuck. The shoe is on the other foot, my friend," he chided, laughing to himself. "I'll look for your call tomorrow with some deposition dates."

"Well get me dates for all of your experts, too. I'm not interested in deposing your damage experts, only the liability ones."

"Suit yourself. I'm getting paid by the hour," he quipped before hanging up.

I was left sulking over the probable accuracy of his comments. Vaughn wasn't about to limit the number of hours that he allowed Harrington to depose my experts, so there was no sense going before him to get him angry at my case all over again. Harrington's predictions regarding Vaughn's evidentiary rulings also left me with a hollow feeling in my stomach. If The Turtle kept in character and philosophy, and I didn't see any evidence to the contrary so far in this case, the video depos of the other five Mesa drivers would probably never see the eyes of the jurors in our case. That meant that Eric's case would be won, if at all, on the strength of Braxton's analysis and opinions, as well as my ability to cross-examine Harrington's experts at trial and somehow neutralize the value or impact of Global's S tests. It was a daunting prospect.

CHAPTER 33

HARRINGTON AND I fought but finally agreed on the dates and sequence for our respective depositions of each other's expert witnesses. The
depositions would take us through November and right up to the start of the
trial on December first. We agreed to depose the accident reconstructionists
first, followed by the design experts, and, finally, the damage experts.

As expected, Harrington spent a full day examining Ralph Cargill on his
accident reconstruction opinions. His questioning was tough and thorough.
Cargill's lack of formal engineering degrees, as well as his lack of publications in
the reconstruction field, were prime areas of Harrington's focus.

To his credit, and undoubtedly due to his many years as a patrolman used
to testifying in court, Cargill maintained a calm composure despite subtle baiting by Harrington throughout the deposition. Cargill doggedly insisted that his
reconstruction confirmed that Jenny's speed at the time the stepladder fell onto
the roadway in front of her was in the range of only fifty-two to fifty-five mph.

As support for his speed opinions, he pointed out the rollover study published by engineers for Volkswagen that correlated a full vehicle roll for large
van-like vehicles with speeds of between forty-eight and fifty-seven mph.
Above fifty-seven mph, the VW engineers found that the vans would usually
roll one-and-one-half times or more. Since Jenny's Mesa had only rolled one
full revolution, Cargill pointed out, it was likely traveling within that forty-eight
to fifty-seven mph band at the time.

On an important foundational point for Braxton's stability defect opinions,
Cargill testified that the rollover of the vehicle started while the Mesa was still on
the roadway, and not, as Harrington kept suggesting, in the grassy median.

"Do you have any tire mark evidence on the roadway to support your
theory?" Harrington asked sarcastically.

"The highway patrolman, Martelli, did not record either the existence or the non-existence of tire marks on the roadway in his police report," Cargill answered. "If he had, I'm confident that you would have seen four tire side slip yaw marks, which transitioned into only two when the other two offside tires raised off the asphalt roadway as Mrs. Hawkins' struggled for control."

"Are you in the habit of basing your *expert* reconstruction opinions on evidence which is not recorded sir? That's rank speculation, isn't it?"

"No, my opinions stand on the strength of underlying facts. My comments about the lack of tire marks were in response to your question, sir."

"Are you also basing your opinions upon the supposed eyewitness testimony of Mr. Abadin and Ms. Merton?"

"I wouldn't say that I'm basing my opinions on their testimony. My opinions are based upon my own calculations, my wealth of experience, and the laws of physics, Mr. Harrington. However," he conceded, "I will say that I do reference their eyewitness testimony, as reported in their depositions in this case, as corroborative of my calculations."

In general, Cargill did a reasonably good job articulating his opinions and fending off Harrington's cross-examination.

Cargill's deposition demeanor, however, was in sharp contrast with that of Dr. Lee Quarles, the reconstructionist hired by Harrington, who I deposed a few days later. Quarles was a former chair of the Mechanical Engineering Department at Ohio State where he had taught for twenty-two years. While at that University, his department had received countless grants from the automotive industry for use in developing and improving accident reconstruction techniques, including computer animation. His CV, which looked more like a phone book than a professional résumé, listed numerous engineering awards received and professional articles published, including a textbook on accident reconstruction techniques. Since leaving the university three years ago, at age fifty-eight, he had consulted for the automotive companies on a full time basis. While I had not had occasion to use him on any of my previous Global defense cases, I had heard of him by reputation. At his deposition, Quarles came across as extremely bright, and he knew it. His confidence bordered on outright cockiness, which made for an interesting comparison with Cargill's quiet, yet firm, self-confidence. Their marked differences didn't stop with personality. Where Cargill appeared for his deposition as a flat-topped, panda-eyed, barrel-chested working man's expert, Quarles was the epitome of the good-looking, articulate, pedigreed expert who knew how to effectively communicate his message to his audience.

"I was asked by Mr. Harrington to do two thing," he said matter of factly, "reconstruct this accident and illustrate the accident scenario for the jury's assistance at trial by means of computer-generated animation. However, it was clear to me very quickly in my own reconstruction analysis that Trooper Martelli's reconstruction opinions, as set forth in his traffic accident report, were right on the mark in terms of accuracy. Accordingly, I simply adopted his opinions as reflecting the correct reconstruction variables and proceeded to generate the computer animation video that is in front of you there." He nodded at the DVD sitting on the stack of papers and notes on the table between us that comprised his work file in the case.

I turned to Harrington down at the end of the table. "I asked you if Dr. Quarles would be having any CDs or DVDs to look at during this deposition. You told me that he wouldn't. Now he produces this," I said, holding the reconstruction animation DVD. "You knew very well that I needed to know if he had any videos or DVDs so that I could arrange to have a video player at this deposition, or my laptop, in order to play it and ask the witness questions." I had forgotten to bring my laptop with me.

"Wait a minute," Harrington responded, "we did talk about that subject, but you must have misunderstood me. Why would I say that when I know that the witness was being hired to produce a computer-generated re-creation of the accident?" The court reporter was, of course, taking down every word the lawyers spoke.

I just shook my head. "There wasn't any misunderstanding, Bob. I'm being sandbagged." Without a laptop, I would have to wait until I was back in my office to view Quarles' digital accident simulation. As a result, I would be foreclosed from the opportunity to ask the witness any meaningful questions about the simulation until the trial itself. Score another one for Global, I thought.

Harrington shrugged. "That's not true. Don't blame me for your own ineptitude."

I looked at Quarles. He smirked, raised both his hands, palms up, and shrugged. "Does that mean that my deposition is over?"

I ignored him and plowed on, spending the next two hours of his deposition inquiring about the details of the information and assumptions he used in his computer animation. He told me that his reconstruction assumed that Jenny Hawkins was traveling at seventy-five miles per hour when the step ladder fell in front of her, that she had made severe, uncontrolled and panicked rotations of the steering wheel, and that the rollover didn't start until the Mesa was sliding sideways on the median grass.

"What, in your opinion, sir, caused it to tip and roll?"

"We're not talking about any instability defect, counselor," he responded, shaking his head as if he were teaching a beginning student who just wasn't getting it. "The rollover was caused by a basic trip lever. I'm sure you don't want to hear this, but when your client steered her Mesa off the roadway to her left and onto the grassy median, it was actually moving *sideways*. While the front of her Mesa was pointed towards the median, the body of the Mesa was, in effect, actually *traveling sideways*, to its right, in the same direction towards Ft. Lauderdale as it had been going in before she made the turn to her left. This is due to the Mesa's original direction and its original inertial direction. However, when the two right side wheels of the Mesa skidded sideways on the soft earth in the median, they built up an increasing mound of the soft dirt as they skidded. Once that happened," he shrugged, leaning back in his chair, "a rollover was no longer a mere possibility. It was a guarantee. The laws of physics took over."

"And why do you say that?"

"Because the mounds of dirt being created by the two sliding right side wheels were what accident reconstructionists call trip levers. Those mounds of dirt, small as they undoubtedly were, caused a drag on those two wheels, which in turn, caused the lower portion of the Mesa to slow down and dig into the earth. However, at the same time that the lower portion of the Mesa was slowing down and digging in, the top half of the Mesa continued moving to the right without any similar drag acting against it. As a result, the tip-over of the Mesa and its roll to the right was mandated, if you will, by the laws of physics. Put simply Mr. Culhane, there wasn't any defect-induced roll as your reconstruction expert, Mr. Cargill, suggests, unless, of course, he wants to quarrel with the laws of physics." With that, he looked over at Harrington and smiled like a Cheshire cat. He knew that his cocky and arrogant demeanor wouldn't show up on the typed transcript. At trial, of course, we both knew that his demeanor would show nothing but solemn concern and sincerely. Harrington chuckled himself.

I marked his entire file as a deposition exhibit and asked for copies, including a copy of his DVD animation.

I was at the Detroit airport after the Quarles deposition awaiting my return flight to Ft. Lauderdale when I called back to my office for messages. Tina transferred me immediately to Sandy.

"Can you believe it? George Krueger's dead!" Sandy announced. The shock was apparent in her voice.

"What?" I replied, shocked. "What happened?"

"He had an accident out in the desert. I was waiting for his final bill to come in. When it didn't, I called his brother in San Diego to make sure that

Krueger had our mailing address. His brother answered and told me that he died in a terrible accident back on October eighteenth, just outside of Tempe."

"October eighteenth ... isn't that the same day that Krueger shot the Mesa video footage for us?"

"Yes, that was the first thing I thought of, too, when I heard the date. His brother is beside himself with grief. He told me that Krueger's smashed RV was found at the bottom of an isolated gorge on the morning of the nineteenth about thirty miles southeast of Tempe. He had a major frontal skull fracture and internal injuries, apparently from the drop. Some mountain hiker found the RV with Krueger in it when he was on a hike that morning and called the police. Krueger's brother said that the police theorize that he lost his way out in the desert at night and mistakenly drove his vehicle off the side of the cliff in the dark. They figure he received his skull fracture from hitting the steering wheel when the RV landed at the base of the gorge, nose first."

"That's awful," I said. "What was he doing driving out in the middle of the desert at night? Didn't he tell us when we last spoke with him that afternoon that he was heading back to his hotel?"

"Yeah, he did, and what's strange, if you remember," Sandy added, "is that Krueger also told us that he was heading the next day for Sedona. Remember?"

"That's right. I do remember him saying that. But what's the issue there?" I asked. I was missing what she meant by this being strange.

"Well, Sedona is *north* of Tempe. His RV was found 30 miles *south* of Tempe. That's in the opposite direction for Sedona."

"He must have changed his mind at the last minute for some reason," I said, shaking my head on my end of the line. "What a shame, he was a nice old guy."

"He really was. What a shock though. Oh," Sandy interjected, "I almost forgot to mention it, but there's another thing that doesn't seem to make a lot of sense about his accident. When I asked Mr. Krueger's brother if he wouldn't mind sending us the video footage from the video card of the Global S tests that his brother had taken for us, he seemed surprised. He told me that the police had released all of the personal contents of the RV to him. While there was a video camera in the RV, it had no video card in it, nor were there any other video cards in the RV."

"Wait a minute," I said. "Didn't Krueger tell us that he had downloaded a copy of the original from his video card at a CVS and put that copy in a Federal Express pouch to us that afternoon just before he called us? I thought he specifically told us that he was keeping the original video card with him in the event the copy was lost in shipment."

"That's what he told us," Sandy replied. "I distinctly remember him telling us that was what he was doing. It's just odd that he would not have kept the video card in the video camera itself; that card should have been in the camera."

"I agree." *Who in the heck keeps a video card outside of the video camera itself?* "That doesn't make any sense at all. Where do you suppose his original video card could be?"

"That's why I called it strange, just like where his accident happened. That doesn't make any sense either. Well," she concluded, "I suppose that the cops either missed it in the debris inside the RV or just tossed it as junk after the accident. I'm sure the insides of that RV at the bottom of that ravine were a jumbled mess."

"I suppose," I responded, still thinking of a logical explanation for the missing video card. *It's still very odd.*

"Anyway," Sandy said, "now that Harrington has produced his official video of those S tests and we have the copy that Krueger Federal Expressed to us, do you want me to follow up further with the cops on the original video card?"

I hesitated for a moment. The absence of the video card from Krueger's video camera just didn't smell right. But, thinking of everything else that Sandy already had on her to do list for me on Eric's case, not to mention the other cases I had her working on, I realized that she didn't have the time. "No," I finally replied, "you're right, there's no need to do that. We have Global's official film of the test now, and Krueger's video footage is nothing more than a copy of Global's testing anyway. Forget it."

Sandy gave a sigh. "Okay. Have a safe trip back, Mike. I'll see you in the office when you get back."

"Are you okay?" I asked, sensing a sadness in her voice.

"Yeah, I just feel badly about the old guy, that's all."

"I know what you mean. He was a sweet guy. I'll see you tomorrow."

CHAPTER 34

HARRINGTON TOOK BRAXTON'S deposition in Massachusetts. I was puzzled, to say the least, when Harrington announced after only two hours of deposition time, that he was done. After all his previous whining, I expected that he'd be filibustering all day with Braxton just to wear us down.

"Why was it so short?" Braxton asked after Harrington and Craige packed their briefcases and left the court reporter's offices for the airport.

I frowned. "I don't really know. He didn't really ask you to go into your opinions in a big way, nor did he even ask for your critique of the Global S test video that Harrington produced. That's strange, all right."

"Could it be that he is so enamored with those S test results that he doesn't much care what my defect opinions are?"

"It may be as simple as that," I nodded, "but it's unlike Harrington to not burn an entire day with you, like he did with Ralph Cargill. It's a free kick at the cat. It doesn't make a lot of sense."

MY CORRESPONDING DEPOSITION of Dr. Murray Winchester, Global's design expert, on the other hand, went a full day in Detroit. It was held in the law offices of Global's Detroit counsel, which were located in the cold, cavernous and dismal Renaissance Center. The architect who designed that monstrosity deserved to serve five to ten.

A short, intense looking man in his late 40's, Winchester received his bachelor's degree in automotive engineering from Global Motors' own Institute of Automotive Technology located in Troy, Michigan. Working part time at Global and going to Wayne State University in Detroit, he received his master's and doctorate degrees at age twenty eight. Over the ensuing twelve years, he had been involved in vehicle handling design, spending eight years working on pickup design, and the next four years designing step vans, which were commonly known as bread trucks. For the last seven years, Winchester had moved over to product engineering analysis staff, or PEA staff as it was called at Global, where he focused on the evaluation of product performance. In truth, he and I both knew that while he and other PEA staff engineers would testify that their job was 'to analyze the company's products out in the field,' his actual job was more basic. He was effectively paid to be Global's own in-house expert witness at trials around the country. His unofficial job description was to testify for Global, plain and simple.

I had dealt with, and used, a good number of the PEA staff engineers over the years at Global. Many had been my witnesses in my defense cases for Global. Since they were each selected to focus on a narrow area of vehicle design, brakes, stability, seatbelts, steering, etc., the PEA staff engineers were extremely effective witnesses. Armed with their narrow specialization, they were difficult for plaintiff's attorneys to effectively cross-examine since they knew everything there was about their narrow area of expertise. On the other hand, plaintiffs' design experts were usually generalists whose design expertise was broader and thinner.

I knew that an appointment of a Global design engineer to a position on the PEA staff was considered to be a plum. They were worked hard, but they enjoyed special status and privileges not afforded to general engineers at Global, such as a company-paid car and their own shared secretarial pool. PEA engineers who testified effectively and successfully at trial were promoted up the food chain and were paid well. While no one ever admitted it as true, it was widely rumored that the managing directors of the PEA department kept a 'scorecard' of the successes of the staff engineers who testified at trial. An engineer advanced if he was a winner. While an infrequent loss of a defense case would be tolerated by PEA staff management, those engineers who lost at trial on more than a rare frequency were soon gone. They were banished back to general staff duty along with the rest of the design grunts who were slotted for comfortable, but not sterling, careers at Global Motors. And while the PEA staff position had its obvious occupational hazards, it was not without its longer term rewards. After testifying eight to ten years, PEA staffers would often leave the company, set up their own consulting business, and be fed thereafter a steady and lucrative diet of automotive defense cases, both by Global and by the other industry manufacturers. Global sanctioned their leaving at that point, since they now would appear as witnesses who were independent of Global since they were no longer employed there. Juries usually bought that argument, although the lawyers certainly knew the reality.

I had seen Winchester around the PEA staff offices over the years, but he had never been assigned to one of my cases in Florida. Obviously fed the company position on the case, Winchester gave me a steely cold reception.

As expected, he testified that the Mesa was solidly designed from a stability and handling standpoint. In addition to his technical assessment of its design, Winchester placed great emphasis on the S testing that had been performed in Tempe for the case.

"If the Mesa had a stability defect, as your Professor Braxton contends," he emphasized, "you would have seen it in living color in that S testing that Global performed and videotaped in this case. I hope you noted that our test used a speed of only fifty-five mph."

"Why fifty-five?" I asked. I knew he had used the speed since Craige had read it off the memo that we had 'inadvertently' disclosed to Craige.

"We put it at the speed limit for that stretch of I-595," he said. "We wanted to give your case every benefit of the doubt. We think Mrs. Hawkins was clearly speeding, but we assumed you would allege that she was traveling at the speed limit."

I couldn't challenge him on that point.

"I also point out," he related, "that we were careful in running those S tests to use an identically-equipped Mesa which was loaded in a fashion identical to the Hawkins' Mesa at the time of her accident. As you saw for yourself from the videotape, the Mesa performed wonderfully. Its wheels never even came close to lifting off the road."

The balance of the deposition was spent fleshing out the nature of his various opinions and the factual basis for them. I needed to know the edges of the envelope to avoid stepping on any land mines during cross-examination of Winchester during trial. It would not be an easy task. He was well armed, and he knew how and when to hurt me.

TOWARDS THE END of November, and what became his patter, Harrington spent complete days deposing my medical damage experts. Collectively and individually, I felt that they had held up fairly well under his aggressive cross-examination. They recounted the severe physical, emotional and financial price that the Hawkins family had paid as a result of the accident.

On the day before Thanksgiving, Harrington finally got around to taking the depositions of Eric and Sarah. To his credit, Harrington was gentle in his examination of Sarah, asking her only a handful of questions about her school, her hobbies and her friends. He was more interested in trying to gauge what kind of sentimental appeal she would make to a jury. From what I saw, she would have plenty.

Harrington's questions to Eric, on the other hand, were not gentle. He was caustic and invasive in his questioning; he was giving Eric fair notice of the type of vigorous and uncomfortable cross-examination he would be subjected to in front of a jury at trial.

"My god," Eric finally exploded in anger in response to Harrington's questioning about Eric's and Jenny's sex life over the course of their marriage before her death, "what business do you have asking about that information? I consider that to be personal and private."

"Mr. Hawkins," Harrington responded, with an insolent tone to his voice, "refusing to answer my question is not an option for you. You've alleged that my client damaged your relationship with your wife. My client is entitled to determine the nature and quality of that relationship from a damage standpoint. Now, answer the question."

"Excuse me," I interjected, "do you have to be so nasty in your tone to this witness? It's offensive and uncalled for. You're entitled to the information you've asked about, but I would have expected a little more sensitivity on the issue, for god's sake. You're not asking about mortgage payments."

"I intend to ask these questions any way I want and they are not being asked in a nasty fashion, as you suggest. They are entirely proper," he retorted. "If he doesn't like them, then I suggest that he withdraw his claims for loss of companionship and consortium and I will stay out of this area."

Eric rose from his chair on the other side of the large conference table and headed for the door in anger over Harrington's attitude. "We're taking a fifteen minute break," I announced as I rose to leave the conference room to cool Eric off before resuming.

I looked over at Harrington as I headed for the door.

"Off the record," I instructed the court reporter who took her hands off her machine. She complied. "Robert, you're a perfect shit, do you know that? You and I may have our differences, but you don't need to treat this man like you're doing. My god, win or lose, he's lost his wife and has a terribly damaged family. Every time that I think I've seen it all from you, you manage to surprise me one more time and outdo yourself."

"Look," he said in icy response, "if your client doesn't have the heart for this, he shouldn't have brought this bogus suit to begin with. Having brought it, and having sued my client for a lot of money, I'm damn well going to go into these areas, and I'll do it in any style I want. If the fire is too hot, stay out of the kitchen."

I looked over at him, shook my head in disgust, and left the room.

THE LAST WEEK before trial was spent with final trial preparation, including having witness subpoenas served on local witnesses, finalizing my trial notebook, figuring which documents I wanted enlarged for trial exhibits, and working on my opening statement. I was working at my office every night until midnight trying to get caught up on my other cases before the Hawkins trial started. My other cases had become neglected due to the pressing pretrial demands of the Hawkins case, and my other clients were grumbling. My inability to work on their cases, which were hourly fee cases, continued to interfere with my income. The contingent fee nature of the Hawkins case was killing me. However, I had committed my services to Eric for the case, and I was going to see it through.

I was in my office working through lunch on the Friday before trial started when Tina called into my office to inform me that Harrington was on the phone for me. I hadn't expected any calls from him. He apparently didn't like speaking with me anymore than I did with him. When he needed to communicate with me, he usually had his stable boy, Craige, call me for him, or he simply emailed me. He preferred the impersonal mode.

"Let me guess," I opened with, "you're wanting to take some more depositions three days before trial starts? Am I warm?"

He ignored my sarcasm. "I just got off the phone with Global. This is your lucky day. Since—"

"Lucky day?" I interrupted, "this may come as a shock to you, but I don't exactly equate Global with good luck."

Harrington continued, ignoring my comment. "Since trial starts Monday, Cole called me with Kean on the line to go over expected trial witness schedules and projected trial costs. As you know, this is going to be an expensive case for Global to try since it has to bring in so many out of state witnesses. Global will prevail, and I think you know that. The S tests we performed are going to kill your case. They say more about the incompetence of your experts than any of my cross examination ever could. I know—"

"Look, I'm a busy guy, Robert," I said, with rising anger and irritation. "What's on your mind other than trash-talking my case?"

"Look," Harrington shot back, "I'm making this call at Cole's specific direction, okay? It's not my idea in the least. Global doesn't think shit of your case, but it would just as soon avoid incurring the ridiculously expensive trial costs of bringing in its experts and paying my defense costs if your client would finally get ahold of himself and consider settling the case on a realistic basis."

The impact of his reference to settlement caught me completely off guard and caused a sudden silence over the phone. I wasn't sure that I had heard him correctly. With Global's scorched earth policy to date in this case, settlement was the last word that I expected to hear Harrington utter.

After a few seconds, I regained my balance. "Really ... now that's a refreshing change of heart for my old pal Cole. I thought that Mr. Testosterone wasn't settling cases these days? Why the sudden change of heart?"

"Listen," he said, his voice rising, "I'm making this call at my client's direction. But I'm not going to sit here and debate you over my client's orders, or the wisdom of those orders. Are you interested in settling the case, or not? That's all I'm interested in. If it were strictly up to me," he announced, viciously, "I wouldn't give you or your client the time of day. In fact, I'm hoping that you're as unreasonable as you usually are and that we end up trying this case. Nothing would give me greater pleasure than to kick your overrated ass all around that courtroom. You always held yourself as high and mighty when you were at Hunt, and I'm finally welcoming the chance to go at it one on one with you in this case. So, tell me that you aren't interested in hearing what I've been ordered to tell you about settlement so that I can report that to Cole."

"Bob," I couldn't resist, "get a grip. I have no intention of being drawn into a personal little 'fight' with you as to who is the better lawyer. I didn't give a shit when I was at Hunt, and I don't give a shit now. The only thing I'm interested in is my clients' interests. So, if you've been ordered by your master to carry the water of a settlement offer to me, I'm listening. What is it?"

"It's not my offer. It's my client's offer," he again repeated.

"Look, no offense, but spare me the window dressing, will you? If you have an offer to make, make it. If not, goodbye."

"The offer is five hundred thousand dollars."

I tried my best to avoid dropping the phone. Harrington surprised me with that number.

"A half-a-million, huh? That's at least a starting point," I responded nonchalantly.

"Listen, smart ass," he immediately snapped, "offering your client five hundred thousand on this bullshit case is a gift, and you and I both know it. If you're even half the lawyer you think you are, you'd know that you should grab that offer and run. The only reason Global is being so generous is the fact that you've got a burned baby and a dead crispy-critter mother. If we end up with a bunch of wet-eyed jurors in this case, we'll still win, but it will only make my job a little harder. It's cost of defense and sentimentality money, that's all. And I need an answer by noon tomorrow, otherwise it's withdrawn." It was an order not a request.

"You're all heart," I said sarcastically. "I'll speak with Mr. Hawkins about your offer and give you a call."

"Just so you're not operating under any illusions, don't try and negotiate a better offer. It's not open to negotiation. Take it or leave it. Understood? Remember, an answer by tomorrow noon."

"I heard you the first time. It's my judgment that's bad, not my hearing," I wise-cracked back. "I'll get back to you. Give me your home number," I said, remembering that tomorrow was a Saturday.

"Call me at the office tomorrow. I don't want to be bothered by you at home. I'll be in my office tomorrow morning until noon."

"Oh, Robert ...?"

"Yeah?"

"I hope you were smart enough to get that settlement authority from Cole in writing. He has a habit of double-crossing his local counsel. But I guess you would know all about that, wouldn't you?" I hung up without waiting for a reply.

I asked Sandy to come in to my office to discuss the offer. She had great instincts, and I wanted to get her reaction.

"They offered *five hundred thousand dollars*?" she exclaimed after I related the call. "I don't believe it, not after the threats that Cole made to you at the disqualification hearing that you'd 'regret that you ever took this case.' I never thought that we would see them offer a dime, especially after those S stability tests they ran."

"You're having the same reaction I'm having," I said, scratching the back of my head. "I realize that we have some huge sympathetic factors going for us in front of a jury, but still, that's a lot of money to offer on a case where discovery hasn't been going very great for us."

"You can say that again!" she said, stating the obvious. Then, reflecting for a moment, she stopped and looked questioningly at me. "Eric will take it, won't he? That's a great offer. Besides," she added, crossing her arms across her chest, "I hope I'm not stepping out of bounds with this, but we can use the cash infusion to finally get on our feet financially around here. I realize that it's the client's decision, but if you end up trying that case for a couple of weeks and we lose ... uh ... well ... I ... just don't know how you're going to be able to make it, Mike—how *we're* going to make it," she corrected. "Look, I apologize if I'm out of line, but I think it needs to be said, that's all."

I nodded at her. "Thanks for your candor. And you're not out of line," I assured her. "Believe me, I'm painfully aware of the fact that I'm at a tough spot in my practice. I know that winning this case is vital to making it on my own, but I've told myself that I'm not going to worry about it, Sandy. If I start doing that, I'll lose my focus altogether."

She nodded, saying nothing, for a change.

"You asked if Eric will take it," I said, getting back to the offer. "I don't know what his reaction will be. I'll put the pros and cons on the table, but I'm also going to tell him that there's something that just doesn't feel right about their offer."

"You don't *feel right* about their offer?" she asked incredulously. "I think you're crazy, Mike. Five-hundred thousand to the Hawkins family with the liability problems we have in this case is a hell of an offer. In fact, Harrington was right in labeling it a gift. You're over-analyzing it. The fact of the matter is that Global is nervous that the jury will simply disregard the strong evidence that it has and will decide the case on the basis of their emotions. If the jury does that, Global's screwed, and they know it. That's what is driving their offer. You're over-analyzing it," she repeated, with an uncharacteristic degree of frustration beginning to show in her voice.

I shrugged my shoulders at her comment. "I hear what you're saying, and your reasoning is hard to argue with. It's exactly what Harrington said about the motivation for the offer, but I don't know if I buy it. For starters, Cole wanted to pee in my porridge for humiliating him in front of Neanderthal. Four or five million in damages to Global if we were to win this case is small potatoes to Global, frankly. Cole is the type of guy who wouldn't give it a second thought to bet his company's money for the chance to rip my guts out at trial and send me packing with a defense verdict." I leaned back in my chair. "Why now? Why is Cole supposedly worried about defense costs? It smells, Sandy, but I just can't put my finger on why."

After years both making and receiving settlement offers in cases, most lawyers tend to develop a sixth sense, a gut feel, about both the amount and the timing of a settlement offer. Both the 'when' and the 'how much' of an offer needs to pass the smell test. *This one didn't pass mine.*

"Well," she said as she rose from the chair and headed out of my office, "I think you're paranoid, and I think you're foolish not to push Eric to grab it. It's an offer that I hope he takes. We have too much riding on this."

"Well, you're probably right," I said after a moment of further reflection, "I'm sure it's just me. I've undoubtedly lost some objective perspective in dealing with Global and Harrington, that's all. Anyway," I said, looking at my watch, "I'm calling Eric now to see if he can drop by this afternoon on his way home to discuss it. We've got to respond to it by noon tomorrow."

Sandy said nothing more as she left my office.

I CAUGHT ERIC at his office just as he was preparing to leave for home. He agreed to swing by my office when I told him that Global had made a settlement offer, which I needed to discuss with him.

He arrived thirty minutes later, putting his wet umbrella in the reception area. The skies had opened up with a downpour just before he arrived. Since it was six o'clock, Tina had already gone home for the night, while Sandy was out meeting a friend for a quick dinner. She and I were working late to finalize the exhibits for the opening day of trial on Monday.

Eric looked emotionally and physically tired as I led him into my office from the reception area. His face had aged five years in the nine short months since the accident. The gray business suit he wore hung loosely from his tall frame, a clear confirmation of the weight he had lost.

"What did Global have to say?" he asked after we exchanged hellos. He plunked down in one of the client chairs on the other side of my desk.

"They've offered you, Sarah and Ryan five hundred thousand dollars to settle," I stated directly, without preamble. "Harrington called me late this afternoon. He emphasized that the offer is not open to negotiation, and I'm sure it isn't."

The expression on his face didn't change at all upon hearing the figure. "What are they going to do about the Mesa?" he asked, looking at me intently.

"I'm not sure that I understand. What do you mean?"

"From my own personal standpoint, this case isn't about money, Mike. I didn't start it to collect money for Liz's death or the injuries to either Ryan or Sarah. Any money that's recovered is going to my kids, not me. I don't want it, and I don't need it. I started this lawsuit to get the Mesa model off the road. It's a death trap that took Liz from us."

"I understand what you're saying, Eric, and I respect your feelings. However, I'm going to take my hat off as your friend and talk with you strictly as your lawyer, okay?"

"Please, go ahead," he answered.

"In considering Global's offer, it's important that you understand that our court system is not really set up to deal very effectively with the removal of a defective product from the market."

"What do you mean exactly?"

"I mean that even if we win the case, the jury can only award money damages to try to compensate you, Sarah and Ryan for your injuries and loss. The jury can't order Global Motors to recall the Mesa from the market."

"Even if they find that it has a serious defect in its stability that causes it to kill and maim people?" he asked in disbelief.

"That's correct. Your remedy in a civil trial like this is limited to money damages. You—"

"Well, who sees to it that a defective car or utility vehicle gets pulled off the market so that it doesn't happen to other people?" he asked with rising anger in his voice.

"I'll give you both the legal answer and the reality answer. Legally speaking, the National Highway Traffic Safety Administration, NHTSA, has that duty. It's supposed to order investigations of any motor vehicle it suspects has a problem to determine if it has a safety defect. If it does, it has the jurisdiction and authority to order a manufacturer to stop the sales of that vehicle, or to recall any that have been sold and to require they be fixed."

"Okay," he said, "so what's the reality answer?"

"The hard truth is that NHTSA doesn't do squat. It talks a great game, but generally it doesn't have the budget or the political guts to take on the auto industry in a big recall fight. And the auto manufacturers know it. With the companies making huge political campaign contributions, and with so many jobs tied to the auto industry in this country, especially after Obama's bailout, the manufacturers carry a huge political and economic stick."

"But I've read about safety recalls over the years that the U.S. government has ordered. I remember Toyota and its problems with the stuck accelerator pedal. Didn't NHTSA end up fining them something like seventeen million dollars in fines for being late in reporting a defect in its vehicles?"

"Yeah, finally, but believe me, that's the exception that proves the rule," I answered. "I hate to be cynical, but the reason many vehicle defects are not uncovered is because it's cheaper for the auto manufacturer to pay money to settle the claims rather than to actually report the defect and fix the problem. Where the defect is not obvious or so frequent in causing accidents, NHTSA is more like a toothless pup, rather than a junkyard dog, when it comes to keeping unsafe vehicles off the road."

"And you think the Mesa's stability problem falls into that category?"

"Yes, I do. While we're now starting to hear about a few other Mesa stability-related accidents and rollovers around the country, the defect is not an obvious or easily provable one," I explained. "Global has the convenient defense in those other cases to do just what they're doing in this case—blame the loss of control or the rollover on the Mesa driver: speeding, driving recklessly, inattentive driving, over-reaction in steering, and things like that. And, if you'll notice," I added, "they're quickly settling them before they get any notoriety. That's a lesson they learned from Toyota's missteps."

I let my comments sink in for a moment before I continued. Eric sat quietly, absorbing my words.

"The reason I'm telling you this is because I want your evaluation of Global's settlement offer to be based on realistic case expectations, Eric, and removing the Mesa from the market is simply not a realistic result, in this case. I apologize if I sound insensitive or blunt, but that's the cold reality. It's more of an economic decision that you're faced with here, as much as I really hate putting it that way. Also," I continued, "I need to emphasize that there is by no means any guarantee that we're going to win this case. Not by any stretch. In fact, winning this case is going to be very difficult based on what I have seen and heard during discovery."

He looked up, with puzzlement on his face. "But what about the defect opinions of Dr. Braxton?" Eric countered. "I've read over his deposition. He says that the Mesa has a defect in its stability. A jury isn't going to just ignore what he has to say, will they?"

"Eric, Braxton has an *opinion* that the Mesa has a stability defect. The jury isn't going to just hear his opinion. They're also going to hear the contrary opinions of Markov, the design engineer on the Mesa project, as well as those of Dr. Winchester, and their opinions are backed up by the Global stability S test videotape footage. That footage is powerful evidence, as you had to admit when I showed it to you in my office a couple of weeks ago," I reminded him. "There's simply no getting around it. We've got an exceptionally difficult job ahead of us if we're going to win this case. It's an uphill battle to say the least. I just want you to be aware of all the risks when you make your settlement decision here. Also," I added cautiously, "remember that if you choose to reject their offer, and we lose, Global will be entitled to a judgment against you for all its defense costs and attorneys' fees. I would peg those fees and costs to come in at six hundred thousand to seven hundred thousand dollars, Eric. Hunt has a partner, two associates and a couple of paralegals working on this case pretty much full time. Their expert witness fees and their trial prep costs are huge. A judgment like that against you will bankrupt you." I took a sip from the cup of coffee in my hand, letting my words sink in. "Global has demanded an answer to the offer by noon tomorrow."

"What do you think I should do?" he asked, finally looking directly at me.

"I hesitate giving you my recommendation, Eric. I know your commitment to pursuing this case to the bitter end."

He nodded, looked down at the floor and then back up at me. "I still need to hear what you think I should do, as my lawyer."

I looked at him for a moment before answering. "As your lawyer, and looking strictly at risks and probabilities, I have to recommend that you accept their offer. The odds aren't with us winning. I want to emphasize that it's your call, and I'll support it one hundred ten percent, whatever it is, both as your friend and as your lawyer."

Eric got up out of his chair and walked over to stare out of the windows of my office towards the New River, which cut through downtown Ft. Lauderdale in the distance. The rain had stopped, but the dark of early evening was just settling in. I could see the River Queen, a double-decker paddle wheeler tourist boat that traveled up and down the New River loaded with tourists, making its last run, headed back to the harbor for the night.

I couldn't decipher what he was thinking. I didn't want to interrupt his thoughts. As he quietly stood there thinking, the rhythmic tick-tock of the Regulator clock on my office wall was the only sound that was heard.

"I don't want to belabor the issue, Mike, but if we were to win," he finally asked, still staring out the window, "and the jury found the Mesa to be defective in its stability design, would I then be in a position to ask NHTSA as a private citizen to investigate the Mesa and use that verdict as a credible basis for a recall investigation?"

"Yes, you could, but I don't want you to operate on any realistic hope that NHTSA would pay a great deal of attention to only one jury verdict against the Mesa. It likely would take a number of such verdicts to get their serious attention. One thing that you should bear in mind, though, is that even if NHTSA elects not to pursue a formal defect investigation on the Mesa, if Global gets tagged enough times by juries around the country, it might decide itself to recall the Mesa."

He finally turned and looked at me. His eyes were welled with tears. "Mike, I'm torn. I want to make sure that Ryan and Sarah are financially protected as much as possible for their own injuries from the accident. At some point, my insurance is going to run out on Ryan. He still needs a lot of skin grafting. I've got to try to protect him for those costs. After your fees and costs are taken out, there's not a lot left for that, but it's something. Sarah's also going to need some money for counseling. She's making progress with the lady you found for her, but she's got a ways to go," he said, reflecting and thinking as he spoke out loud. "Like I said, I don't want or need anything. And accepting the offer would also allow you to get paid for all the time and costs that you've invested in this case for us. You've done more than any other attorney or friend would do, and I appreciate it. I'll never be able to tell you how much, either."

"Don't even think about it."

Eric quietly raised his hands with his palms facing me, gesturing me to allow him to continue. I did.

"Those are all reasons, good reasons, for me to take the money. But ... but," his voice cracked with emotion, "I don't think I could live with myself if I did, Mike. God forgive me, but I think that my family has to take a stand on principle. We need to prove in court that the Mesa *is* defective; that it *did* kill my wife, burned my son and took my kids' mother away forever. If we don't take our stand, Global will just be buying off another family rather than being forced to deal with taking that vehicle off the market, and the same miserable thing will only happen to other families like mine." He lowered his head and put his left palm to his eyes, rubbing them in a futile effort to remove his mental anguish and despair.

I got out of my desk chair and walked over to him where I put my right arm around his shoulders and hugged him.

"You're a good man and a good father, Eric. I want you to know that whatever decision you make on this will be the right one. You know that your kids have a lot of Jenny in them. They're fighters just like she was, and they will both understand and respect whatever decision you make when they get older. And as far as I go, don't even give my fee or costs situation a second thought. I mean that," I said seriously, "this is a rare case for me. I've spent all these years trying cases for companies that were certainly appreciative, in a corporate sense, for my efforts, but it never got personal for me. They were always the client, and I knew I'd get paid. To be honest, there was plenty of professional satisfaction, but not a hell of a lot of personal satisfaction. Your case is the first case that makes me feel like I might be making a difference in somebody's life. And it's a good feeling, Eric. I haven't had this feeling for many years. The truth is, I think my soul needs this case just as much as yours does, in a strange sort of way. So," I said, squeezing his shoulders for emphasis, "when I tell you to ignore my financial interests in this case, I mean it. This is your case, your family and your decision. I'm perfectly content either way you go. If you reject the offer, we're going in that courtroom Monday morning and kick their ass," I said, trying my best to generate a positive and enthusiastic note. I gave him a final squeeze on the shoulder and released him from my arm.

He sighed and nodded. "Thanks. Can I think it over tonight and call you first thing in the morning?"

"I think you should. It's a lot to consider. I'll be back here in my office around nine-thirty tomorrow. If you need to talk about it some later tonight, or if you have any other questions, call me."

"Thanks Mike," he repeated, "I really appreciate everything you've done for us. I want you to know that."

I nodded and smiled.

He left, and I grabbed my sports coat and car keys and headed home for a quick meal with Liz and the girls before returning to work on trial exhibits with Sandy.

On the drive home, I tried to recall the number of clients I had represented over the years, either corporate or individual, who had held fast to principle over dollars. I had difficulty coming up with even a handful. The dollar had an almost irresistible alluring quality to it.

ERIC CALLED ME at my office the next morning, about ten o'clock. We talked over his decision for ten minutes, and I called Harrington to relay it.

"So, what's your decision?" he opened with after I called him on the direct dial number in his office. He obviously had caller ID. Spending a Saturday morning in the office was not what Harrington typically did. I figured he was in either doing exhibits or Perky Wendy.

"He's going to accept the money," I said.

"Why doesn't that surprise me? Your client is finally showing some common sense."

"I'm not through."

"What do you mean you're not through?"

"Mr. Hawkins will accept the money, *provided* that Global will acknowledge in open court that the Mesa has a stability defect and that it will voluntarily recall the model from the market."

"You're kidding, aren't you?"

"Serious as a procto exam, Bob."

There was quiet on the line for four or five seconds. I could almost feel the steam emanating from the phone. "Your client is one very foolish and greedy son of a bitch," he finally said. "I hope you have your malpractice ass covered with a letter to Hawkins telling him that he is going to lose this lawsuit, my friend, because I assure you that when he's sitting there after my defense verdict with no money in his pocket and facing bankruptcy to pay Global's judgment for its fees and costs, he's going to sue you. And I'll be his first witness as to your incompetence."

"Is that a 'no' to our counter-offer?" I asked sarcastically.

"I'll see you in court on Monday morning. Bring your nut cup. You're going to need it." He hung up.

CHAPTER 35

"ANNIE, LET'S JUMP in the car and grab a Baskin Robbins," I suggested to my daughter. It was Sunday night, and I started the Hawkins trial the next morning. After finishing some last minute pre-trial details at my office earlier in the day, I spent the afternoon on a long list of domestic 'honey do's' that Liz had been accumulating for the last month. I needed to get out of the house.

Anne was busy working on homework at the butcher block table in the eating area off the kitchen. Liz was across town at a St. Cecilia's Foundation meeting, undoubtedly conspiring on new ways to raise money for the school. Erin was out with some of her friends at the recently-released newest James Bond movie.

"Sure," Anne brightened, "Jamoca Almond Fudge for me!"

"Throw on some shoes and let's go," I said, grabbing the keys to my Acura.

We had no more than backed out of the garage onto Coral Reef Drive when Anne started surfing the radio stations for music fitting her tastes. She was a master surfer. She detested my country station.

The rain, which had started last Friday morning, had continued over the weekend. A light drizzle persisted as we drove up Coral Reef towards Las Olas Boulevard at the end of the street, making the dark night even darker. "Sooner or later," I joked as I pulled my car past a dark-colored van parked on the right shoulder close to the end of the street, "your musical ear will mature and you'll finally acquire a taste for country. So, you might as well not fight it and turn it to country now."

"I don't know how you can listen to that awful hick music, Dad," she said emphatically as she finally found a station she liked.

I stopped at the stop sign and turned left onto Las Olas Boulevard, taking the curb lane of the two westbound lanes. The waters of the Intracoastal canal lined both sides of Las Olas. With the drab rain falling, there was little boat traffic out in the canal tonight.

I looked over at Anne who was wearing her hair in her usual ponytail. She had her mother's freckles and her natural smile. "And which awful band is that?" I teased, nodding at her musical selection, 'Post Nasal Drip?'

She rolled her eyes. "Lady Gaga, Dad. Don't you know anything? Someday you're musical tastes are going to mature and you'll find that you like her," she teased back.

I laughed as I looked over to her sitting in the front seat. "Is that—"

"Dad! Watch out!" she suddenly screamed, looking past me to my left, out the driver's door window beside me.

At the same instant of her scream, I felt the violent jar of another vehicle as it slammed sharply and violently into the left front side of my car. The jolt of the collision jostled me roughly in my seat as my steering wheel turned involuntarily to my right in response to the violent collision against the left side of my car. Before I had any chance to react, my car was pushed up over the curb to my right, across the twenty foot strip of grass and towards the three-foot retaining wall and the watery canal immediately behind it.

My quick glance to my left caught a view of a dark-colored van. Despite the quickly happening events, I recognized it as the same van that had been parked at the end of my street, complete with smoky-black windows that did not permit one to see inside. The van did not disengage, but kept pushing my car off the road as it drove parallel to my car. What was happening in seconds seemed to me to be unfolding in slow motion.

"Jesus!" I yelled out loud as I reflexively grabbed the steering wheel and tried to both steer my car away from the retaining wall rushing towards me and slam on the brakes at the same time.

"Hang on Anne!" I bellowed to my screaming daughter. My efforts were too little and too late. With a final jarring push from the van as it careened away, my car plowed through the concrete wall and plunged nose first into the black waters of the canal behind it. Both of the airbags in my front seat exploded upon impact of the front end with the water below, enveloping each of us in airbag as my car came to a watery stop.

All was eerily quiet for a moment as I tried to regain my senses. I heard Anne screaming next to me, and, as dark as it was in the car, I could see that the passenger compartment was filled with the smoky talcum-like powder given off by our airbag explosions. The dim lighting created by the overhead streetlight fixtures instantly and eerily disappeared as the car was quickly engulfed by the ink-black waters of the canal. I could immediately sense that the front of the car was sinking faster than the lighter back end. Water was gushing into the passenger compartment through the doors, the bottom of the instrument panel, and the air conditioning vents.

"Dad! … Dad!" Anne continued shrieking in a terrified voice I had never heard before. It sent chills through me to hear it.

Fighting panic and terror myself, I willed myself to remain in control of my senses. "Annie!" I yelled loudly but evenly. "Annie, listen to me!" I reached over with my right hand and grabbed her left arm, just above her elbow. I suddenly realized that, incredibly, the car's headlights and instrument gauges were still illuminated, giving the inside of the car a ghostly cast with the murky water apparent outside all of the car's windows.

I could make out only the vaguest outlines of Anne. Her white face, arms and legs were the most obvious in the watery darkness. Thank god she had buckled her seatbelt as I had, I thought to myself. Her airbag, like mine, had deflated.

"Anne. Listen to me!" I again commanded as I shook her arm violently to get her attention. As I did so, I reached down to my right hip area with my left hand and popped the seatbelt release button which immediately released my body from the belt. I could feel the rapidly-rising water coming over the top of the front seat as I did so. The speed at which the Acura was filling with water was frightening.

"Dad, we're going to die! We're going to die!" she screamed out of control as I felt her desperately straining against the seatbelt strap to get out of her seat to avoid the rising water.

"We're not going to die! Now listen to me!" I barked with authority. "I'm going to release your seatbelt. We won't be able to open the doors until the water in here is just about up to the top of this compartment. The pressure has to equalize in order to get the door open. Do you understand that?"

She was just whimpering. I received no response.

"Do you understand me?" I again yelled at her, trying to get her to focus.

"She was sobbing, but she nodded her head."

"Good," I said. Still keeping a firm grasp on her left arm with my right hand, I leaned over and, as the water rose, I used my left hand to fish around by her left hip area trying to locate her seatbelt release button. Finding it, I depressed it. It didn't release. I depressed it again and wiggled it at the same time. Still no release of the metal tongue. A surge of panic rolled over me as the cold water rose now up to my chest and to the base of Anne's chin. Anne's screaming started anew as she fought to get her head above the rapidly rising water. At the same time, I felt the car suddenly even out and stop its descent. We had come to the murky black bottom of the twenty-foot deep canal.

Still struggling with her seatbelt release, it suddenly hit me. Her straining against the seatbelt webbing was putting the metal locking tongue under tension and pressure, preventing its release.

"Hold your breath," I yelled. She immediately did, and an instant later, I violently shoved her backwards and downwards against the seat, which momentarily removed the tension on the belt. Her head went under water as I did so, but her seatbelt immediately released when I pushed the button this time. She immediately rose, coughing and screaming again. She now kneeled on the seat, bending over to allow for the roof while, at the same time, trying to keep her head above the rising pitch black water.

I pulled her over to me as I also put my right knee on the driver's seat and fought to keep my head up. "Anne! You must stop screaming and pay attention. I need your help! Please, Anne!" I said forcefully.

She again stopped screaming but continued sobbing. Her water-logged hair was plastered against her head.

I spoke calmly but quickly. "Okay, keep as tall as you can get. Keep your head above the water and hang tightly onto the top of my T-shirt! Don't let go, whatever happens! I'm going to be opening my door. You and I are going to be pushing ourselves out of the car. It's going to all be underwater, so take a big breath of air when I say so."

I tried to keep my voice even, though I felt my own rising panic. "When we get out of the car, you and I are going to swim directly up to the surface. Hold your breath all the way! It's just like swimming. It'll be easy," I lied.

I could only make out the general outline of her facial features when the lights of the car suddenly went out. The inside of the car went black as death, and I could see her no longer. I could only hang on to her. I redoubled my grip on her arm.

"Okay, hold your breath! We're going!" I yelled to her in the darkness as I gulped a final lung full of air, put my upper body under water, grabbed the driver's door latch and pushed with all my might against the door. It slowly opened, but only after great effort on my part. I refused to release my grip on Anne's left arm. I could feel her death grip on my T-shirt as well. Bracing my left foot on the bottom of the now-open door sill, I pushed myself out at the same time as I pulled her with me. She was remarkably passive and light, I found myself thinking as I kicked and pushed free of the car. My lungs were burning already from the oxygen I had expended in my efforts against the door, but I kicked violently for the surface. My mental focus was entirely on the surface, and the life-sustaining air above it, only a few short feet away. I could feel Anne kicking alongside of me, although I couldn't see her at all in the ink of the water.

My lungs were at the bursting point when my head finally broke the surface of the water. I gasped savagely for air as I pulled at Anne at the same time. Her head and upper body burst from the water a second after mine had. She was also rasping and coughing, apparently having taken in water on the ascent.

She started screaming and grasping at my neck for security. I fended off her terrified clinging and quickly moved behind her in the water where I held her from behind. I attempted to keep her head above water as best I could as I gulped down fresh air myself.

"You're alive!" I heard a male voice yell, followed by a splash in the water. "I'm coming to help you. Hold on!" the voice said between strokes as it came closer.

I looked over as a face appeared in the water next to both of us. It was the red, excited face of a young man in his twenties. "I have her, Mister. Go ahead and let her go."

I refused, keeping my grip on my daughter.

"No ... no" ... I managed between gasps in the water. "Pull her and let's all swim for the canal wall together ... I'm not letting her go."

The three of us awkwardly swam, almost crab-like, over to the canal wall some thirty feet away. A big black Lab was waiting at the broken canal wall, a leash hanging round its neck. The young rescuer pulled himself out of the water first, laid flat on the concrete ledge above and reached down to grab Anne by her shoulders. He pulled her up, but she refused to let go of my collar, almost pulling the man back in.

"Let go of him!" he yelled, "you need to let go of him so I can pull you out!"

"Anne," I joined in, seeing the problem ... "it's ... it's ... okay now. Let go of me so he can pull you out! It's okay, you're safe now." I grabbed her hand and physically wrenched its death grip from my shirt. The man immediately pulled her up onto the ledge to safety.

"You ... you ... watch her," I told him, gasping for air, "I'll pull myself out." I grabbed the ledge above the water and pulled. I finally made it on the third try. My arms felt like rubber bands, weak and wobbly.

Out of the water, I immediately went over to Anne on the grass and cradled her in my arms. She was crying uncontrollably. The young man sat next to her, his shorts, T-shirt and tennis shoes soaked from the water. His face was laden with concern. He kept patting Anne's shoulder, saying, "It's going to be all right. It's going to be all right."

"Thank you," I whispered to him. "Thank you. I'll take her."

IT WAS WELL after midnight when Anne and I got home. The police came along with an ambulance. The ambulance crew insisted that we both be seen by the emergency room over at Broward General Hospital for any latent problems from the accident and near-drowning. Aside from the fright, we were both physically fine. Anne had swallowed a few mouthfuls of saltwater, but she was okay.

The EMT team called Liz's cell phone from the back of the ambulance en route to the hospital. She left her meeting and drove over immediately to the hospital's emergency room to be with us. While Liz comforted Anne as the trauma room staff physician checked her over, I spent a few moments with two City of Ft. Lauderdale police officers who were investigating the accident. Their squad car had followed the ambulance over to the hospital.

"What do you mean that it was intentional?" the cop questioned me after I had told him of the details of the collision.

"Just that, this was no accident! That fucking maniac intentionally slammed into my car and pushed us off the road and into the canal. He just kept pushing all the way, angling me and slamming me into the canal."

The older, burly cop glanced at his partner, a younger red-haired cop who looked young enough to have been my paper boy, and then looked back at me.

"Mr. Culhane, don't you think you're over-reacting a little bit? After all, the roads were wet. It looks to me like the other guy that hit you probably just lost control, banged into you and took off rather than get a ticket for reckless driving."

"This wasn't an accident," I said stubbornly. "I'm telling you that it was premeditated. The son of a bitch in the van went after us. You had to be there."

"All right, the burly one acknowledged, assume it was intentional. While this sounds like it's right out of the movies Mr. Culhane, is there anybody you know who would have any reason at all to kill you?" His voice betrayed his doubt that the accident was intentional.

"No, not that I know of, anyway. Look, I know that I probably sound crazy but I know it was no accident," I continued to insist.

"What do you do for a living, sir?" the redhead asked.

"I'm a lawyer."

The older cop's eyes quickly took on that knowing look as he glanced over at his partner. *Who doesn't want to kill a lawyer*, they read. "Are you involved in any criminal cases, or anything like that, which might give rise to somebody wanting to take you out?" He was obviously groping, trying to humor me.

"No, I don't do criminal. I only do civil cases, you know, lawsuits over breaches of contracts, bad products, that kind of stuff. Nobody would have any reason to want to hurt me for the cases I handle. It's all boring stuff. If I did divorces, I could understand it, but I don't." I was still sitting in my wet clothes. I had a dry towel around my neck and a blanket over my back.

"Well, we talked with the young guy that helped rescue you from the water. His name is ..." he looked down at his notepad as he searched for the name. "Franco ... Brent Franco. He says that he was out walking his black Lab and heard the collision and the splash. He didn't get a good view of the collision because he was down the street a ways. He came running down Las Olas after he saw your car plunge into the water. He says that the other vehicle that collided with you, which he identified as either a black or dark-blue van, didn't stop. He couldn't see who was driving it since its windows were dark-tinted. It sped westbound on Las Olas. He didn't get any license since he didn't realize then that it had been involved in the collision. Since you told us that it was a dark van, we put two and two together. It sounds like it was the van that crashed into you."

"You know," I said, slowly thinking out loud to myself, "there was a dark-colored van sitting on at the end of my street, Coral Reef, when I left my house tonight. It was sitting on the side of the street down by the Las Olas intersection. I only got a quick glance at it during the event, but I'm sure it was the same one that I saw parked there. I didn't pay any attention to it when we drove by since we get tourists driving down Coral Reef all the time looking at the homes on the islands."

"Well," the burly one said, closing his notebook, "I want to be honest with you. I wouldn't hold out much hope that we will find this guy. We've issued a BOLO to the police for that van." Seeing that we were not following him, he immediately explained himself. "I'm sorry, we've issued a BOLO, which is our code to other police officers on the street to 'be on the lookout' for, which in your case, is for any dark-colored van with a damaged right side with silver paint on it matching the color of your Acura. However, since there was no ... uh ... fatality involved," he said somewhat embarrassed, "it will only get a few days of attention."

"What about my car? Who will pull it up?"

"A barge will be sent over tomorrow to pull it up. It's a total loss, although I probably don't need to tell you that. Your insurance company will pick it up. Check with your agent."

Liz came inside the room. "They're through with Anne, Michael. Can we go?" She was very upset.

"Yes, we're done here," I said. "I'm coming now." I got up, asked the officers to let me know of any developments and went to be with Liz and Anne. We walked out together. Liz drove us home in her car, with Annie and me sitting together in the back seat. I had my arm wrapped protectively around Anne all the way home. En route, no one said a word. We were all emotionally shot.

Liz finally lost her stoic reserve after the girls got to sleep. Erin slept with Anne in Anne's double bed to comfort her. Liz broke down in our bedroom, crying uncontrollably. It was too close a call for all of us. She and I didn't fall asleep until three a.m.

CHAPTER 36

THE ALARM CLOCK jarred me awake at six-thirty the next morning. Liz looked equally tired herself as she pulled herself out of bed to check on Anne. We had resolved to push her into going to school and back into her old routine. We didn't want her dwelling on the terrible event she had been through by staying home from school. It was the old *get back on the horse* approach.

I dragged myself into the bathroom where I showered, shaved and climbed into a suit and tie. Trial opened at nine, but I had Eric meeting me at my office at eight o'clock. I was still a bit unfocused from the events of the preceding night. An hour, two shaving nicks, and two doses of Visine later, I was out the door and on my way to the office. I stopped in the kitchen only long enough to talk with Liz and the girls for a few moments, assure myself that they were okay, and grab a kiss from all three. Liz handed me a Styrofoam cup of black coffee as I shot out the door.

"Good luck, Michael," she offered. Her embrace was a long one this morning.

SANDY, ERIC AND I walked into the Broward County Courthouse lobby at eight-thirty. Sandy and I were each wheeling a dolly loaded down with cardboard boxes containing the voluminous case files, trial exhibits and general lawyer junk. Eric carried my briefcase to help us out, along with Sandy's laptop. Of course, we had to wait our obligatory ten minutes for an available elevator in the antiquated and not-so-venerable Broward County Courthouse to take us up to The Turtle's courtroom on the tenth floor. We were wet from the drizzle which had continued intermittently to come down through the night. It persisted even now, making for a thoroughly gray and depressing Monday morning.

As we opened the courtroom and rolled our boxes in, our esteemed opposition was already there, dry and dug in. Harrington, dressed in a navy blue suit, white shirt and brilliant red tie, was sitting at counsel's table speaking in low tones to the woman next to him. She was in her late 40s, professional appearing and attractive, although not overly so. Dressed in a sincere navy blue suit and conservative white blouse, she was obviously the Global corporate trial representative designated to sit at its defense table. I had to hand it to Harrington. He was doing what I would have done: pick a female employee who looked appropriately caring and responsible to sit next to him throughout the trial in order to soften the corporate persona of Global Motors Corporation.

Juries tend to expect the corporate defendant to be cold and uncaring. Putting a female representative in the saddle next to Harrington was a good strategic ploy to attempt to counterbalance the sentiment that would be naturally flowing towards the Hawkins family. Dollars to doughnuts, I mentally wagered to myself, she didn't know beans about any aspect of the Mesa design. Harrington wouldn't take that risk. As Global's corporate representative at trial, he knew that I could put her on the stand as an adverse witness at any time during the trial and try to obtain damaging admissions from her regarding issues in the case. If she knew anything, that is. That's why he wanted her to be a pretty, 'caring' potted plant. It was a smart move by him.

I laughed silently to myself when I saw Harrington wearing his trial glasses, as he called them. The man had perfect vision. However, he read somewhere that lawyers carried a higher degree of credibility with juries if they wore glasses. As a result, he purchased an expensive pair of tortoiseshell glasses and had simple clear, non-prescription lenses inserted in them. He never tried a case without them anymore.

The Boy Wonder, Craige, was over fiddling around next to the four black metal filing cabinets that Global had brought to trial to house its trial documents and its trial tricks. The Confederate, Aubrey Trenton III, was sitting in the first row of the spectator seats, next to the gutless Don Kean of Global Motors. I hadn't seen or spoken with him since my departure from Hunt. He looked away as I glanced over towards him.

A female paralegal flitted around putting pencils and pads next to Harrington and Craige's chairs. She was carrying what looked like some sort of master index to the file cabinets on a clipboard under her right arm. No doubt about it, the gang was loaded for bear. I was hoping to stay out of the crosshairs.

"Good morning," I said to the Global defense team. *Nothing like putting on your game face when you feel like shit.* While the paralegal replied with a quick 'good morning,' the rest of the Global team ignored me. Harrington didn't even bother to look over at us as we set up our boxes and unpacked our files. Sandy glanced at me as she rolled her dolly to a stop, shook her head and started unloading.

Okay, we might as well get this trial off on the right foot.

"Don, how's your back problem coming along?" I asked loudly to Kean as I started setting up my files. "I heard that it was serious."

"Huh?" he managed, somewhat uncomfortably, in response. "What are you talking about? What back problem?"

"Your spine," I deadpanned as I started removing the lids from the bankers' boxes, not bothering to look up at him as I spoke, "I heard that it was recently removed."

He said nothing. I could feel his embarrassment from the twenty feet that separated us.

At nine sharp, the bailiff, a stick-skinny old guy obviously on the verge of retirement from the Broward County Sheriff's Department, entered the courtroom dressed in his dark green county sheriff's uniform with a gold fabric department star stitched to the shirt pocket of his uniform. He was followed by the court clerk, an attractive Hispanic woman in her 40s. The female court reporter, a young redhead, was already seated at her desk to the side of the judge's bench in front of us. She was chewing gum, waiting for the proceedings to begin.

"All rise!" the skinny old bailiff ordered to the sparsely-filled courtroom. "This honorable court is now in session. The Honorable Baylor T. Vaughn is presiding. Silence is commanded!"

On cue, The Turtle, clothed in ample black robes to cover his more than ample body, marched—it was more like waddled—out of the door behind his bench, walked the three steps to his upholstered, high-backed leather chair and sat down.

"Good morning, ladies and gentlemen. Before I call for the jury panel to be brought in, are there any last minute matters which need addressing? I don't like to keep my jury panels waiting." He was all business this morning.

"Your honor," Harrington stated smoothly as he rose quickly from his chair, "There is one small matter. I anticipate that Mr. Culhane will attempt in opening statement or in jury *voir dire* to comment to the jury about other Mesa accidents and rollovers which have happened around the country to other drivers. I filed motions *in limine* this morning with your clerk asking that this court issue a pre-trial order preventing Mr. Culhane or his witnesses from referring to those other accidents in any respect since they are irrelevant to the issues in this case. They involve completely different factual situations, Your Honor. If he were permitted to refer to them now, and it later proves to be the case that the court grants my motion to exclude any evidence of those other accidents, I'll have to move for a mistrial. My client certainly doesn't want that to occur, and I'm sure the court is of the same persuasion."

"There will be no mistrial in my courtroom," Vaughn boomed, looking first at Harrington then over at me. "This court can't waste its resources retrying the same case over and over. I don't have hardly enough time to try cases the first time, for that matter. It's premature for me to issue an evidentiary ruling at this stage, Mr. Harrington, since I'll need to see the proffer of evidence by Mr. Culhane when it is made, together with the context of that evidence. In the meantime," he announced, "for purposes of the opening statement and jury selection, I'll consider a preliminary limit that won't prejudice either one of you. Mr. Harrington, any suggestions?"

Harrington went for the green light. "Yes, in fact I do, Judge. I ask that you forbid Mr. Culhane from even mentioning other accidents until after opening statements and the evidence itself is offered. By then, the court will have had an opportunity to consider both the nature of the evidence and the merits of my motion *in limine*."

"Your honor," I immediately countered, rising from my chair, "depriving me of my ability to refer to those other accidents in opening statements will unfairly prejudice my ability to outline the whole factual story to the jury of what we intend to prove. I fully expect that the court will allow all or part of those other accidents to be heard by the jury since that evidence will establish the dangerous propensity of the Mesa to roll over under normal, expected use on the open highways around this country. The jury needs to know that evidence and how it fits into my case. After all," I added, "you will be advising the jury that what the lawyers say during opening statement or jury selection is not evidence. I ask that Global's motion be denied and that you merely give the jury a cautionary instruction." This was an important initial ruling.

"I'm granting your request, Mr. Harrington," The Turtle ruled without further reflection. "I'm not issuing a ruling on the merits of that evidence when you offer it, you understand," as he looked at me, "but only for purposes of opening statements. So, consistent with my ruling, you are to say nothing about those other accidents in your comments to the jury, Mr. Culhane. If they come into evidence, I have no doubt that you'll make the jury painfully aware of the relevance and significance of that evidence."

I rose again and faced the judge. "I understand your ruling, your honor. However, if the court is inclined to prevent counsel from commenting in opening about evidence that is the subject of a motion *in limine*, I would respectfully request that the playing field be leveled. I have a motion pending,

which I filed this past Friday afternoon, in which I have asked the court to preclude the investigating police officer from testifying as to his opinion regarding
the speed the Mesa was allegedly traveling at the time of the accident. The
depositions reflect that Trooper Martelli has absolutely no competent, factual
basis for his speed opinions. Accordingly, I also ask you to forbid Mr.
Harrington in opening from mentioning Trooper Martelli's opinion that Jenny
Hawkins, the decedent, was speeding at the time of the accident."

"Wait a minute," The Turtle responded, not even waiting for Harrington
to carry his own water, "that's a different creature altogether, isn't it? You're
talking about the official conclusions of an investigating police officer, are you
not?"

"He is the investigating officer, but his opinions—"

The Turtle cut me off. He wasn't buying my argument. He loved police
officers.

"I'm not about to presumptively find, as your request essentially implies,
that a police officer in this state can't give an opinion as to the speeds of
vehicles involved in accidents that he investigates. That flies in the face of
just about every case that I tried when I was down there on your side of the
bench as a practicing attorney, as well as all the cases I have presided over as
a judge up here. I'm denying your request. If you have a legitimate objection
to his expert opinions when he takes the stand, I'll entertain them at that
time. In the meantime, Mr. Harrington is free to tell the jury what he expects
Trooper Martelli to testify to when he takes the stand. Is that all gentlemen?"
he asked with finality. "Frankly, these matters should have been addressed
last week by both of you on motion calendar," he added with irritation,
looking at the clock on the wall of his courtroom. "I have a jury panel
waiting. Let's go." The liver spots seemed to float on his lightly tanned scalp
this morning.

Neither attorney offered anything more, and he motioned to his scarecrow bailiff to bring in the jury panel from which we would select a jury to hear
the case. I looked over to catch Trenton winking and smiling at Harrington.
Score two for the home team, it said.

"Did we lose something important?" Eric whispered quietly to me as the
jury panel slowly filed into the courtroom.

"It's not a big deal. We're okay," I said, playing it nonchalantly. I didn't
want to rattle him at this early stage. Vaughn was showing his pro-
manufacturer philosophical bend in the two brief rulings he had just issued. It
was going to be an uphill march I could see.

THE JURY SELECTION went slowly. At three that afternoon, we finally had a jury of six, with three alternates. Since the case was expected to go for the better part of an entire week, the Turtle didn't want to run the risk of a mistrial in the event one or more of the required six jurors got sick or arrested. This was South Florida after all, not Ft. Wayne, Indiana. As a safety valve, he required us to select three alternates to serve as substitutes in the event the need arose.

The jury ultimately selected was composed of four men and two women, while the alternates were all men. My wish list had been for a much higher percentage of females who would likely be more apt to identify with Jenny. Unfortunately, I ended up using all three of my peremptory strikes on women.

One of my strikes was an anorexic-looking woman in her 60s with a pinched face who displayed, in her *voir dire* answers, that she either had a heart of dry ice, or a bad case of hemorrhoids, or both, since she never smiled. Either way, I didn't want her sitting on my case. The second woman I struck was a claims adjuster for a property insurance company, the proverbial kiss of death for a plaintiff in a personal injury case, or so the commonly-held wisdom foretold. I wasn't about to challenge traditional wisdom. My last strike was expended on a tough-looking woman sporting a butch haircut of bleach blond hair, tattoos running the length of each arm, and a t-shirt reading: *Nixon was right!* No thanks. Not only did she look too weird, even for South Florida, but Nixon was never right.

The diverse jury we were left with included a 50-ish quality control supervisor who worked at a computer software company; a mid-30's x-ray nurse technician, sporting a sleeve tattoo of a bird of paradise on his right arm ; a retired dry cleaning store owner in his 60's who was the only juror appearing in a suit and tie; a chubby, older female kindergarten teacher who, perhaps predictably, giggled her way through most of her *voir dire* responses to the lawyers. *Is it just my imagination or do all kindergarten teachers giggle?;* a 30-something fast-food employee at a Bubba Burger restaurant who was the only African-American member of the jury and the second female. *And didn't Harrington unsuccessfully try his damndest to get her removed for cause during his voir dire questioning?;* and a mid-40s owner of a small family-run hardware store who, rather unbelievably in today's world, actually wore a pencil protector in the front pocket of his white short-sleeve shirt. It was a motley group that comprised our jury, but, certainly by South Florida standards, I considered it a decent cross section. All three alternates were men, two of which had retired as public sector employees, and the last worked as a salesman at one of the two local country radio stations.

The Turtle instructed us to give our opening statements immediately following jury selection. Thirty minutes per side, he admonished us, was all the time he was going to permit.

As the plaintiff, I went first. I briefly outlined the facts of the case, our belief that the Mesa had a deadly defect—a propensity to go out of control and roll over on the roadway in reasonably foreseeable and normal use. "The evidence will show that the Mesa's deadly defect," I concluded, standing directly before the old wooden jury box, "killed Jenny Hawkins, horribly disfigured her young son, psychologically maimed her young daughter, and drove a stake of pain into the heart of her husband and her children. I urge you not to automatically accept as gospel what the automotive design engineers or experts from Global tell you on that witness stand," I said, pointing with emphasis at the empty wooden and raised witness box located in the courtroom between them and Judge Vaughn. "Critically analyze the testimony of each and every witness that takes that stand, including my own," I urged. "Make those witnesses satisfy you that what they are saying squares with what *you* see as the facts and with your own common sense. If it doesn't, reject it," I ended.

I intentionally kept my comments understated. I didn't want to give Harrington the opportunity in closing arguments at the end of the case to gut whatever credibility and favor I had won with the jury by pointing out my failure to prove overly-bold claims I had made at the beginning of the case.

Harrington was not so reserved in the tone or content of his opening.

"Does Global Motors feel terrible about the horrifying accident, which the Hawkins' family had on that Friday afternoon in February? Unquestionably," he said, his voice laden with concern, sincerity and compassion. "What human being or responsible manufacturer wouldn't? However, the evidence which Mr. Culhane here will offer," his tone changing to one of rebuke as he pointed over at me in my chair, "will utterly fail to show any *defect* or *problem* with the Mesa. Rather, as tragic and as unfortunate as that accident was, it was caused by two factors and two factors alone: the negligence of the driver of the pickup truck in failing to properly and safely secure the stepladder to his truck to prevent it from falling onto the roadway and the negligence of Mrs. Hawkins in the operation of her vehicle at the time. As difficult as it is for the Hawkins family and their lawyer to accept it, the *facts*, as you will see, unfortunately demonstrate that Mrs. Hawkins was speeding at the time of the accident. The speed limit in that area of the Interstate was only fifty-five mph, yet she was traveling *at over seventy-five mph*." He stopped for a moment to let the importance of his last comment soak in.

As he did so, he took his glasses off and, pulling out his handkerchief, proceeded to clean their lenses as he started up again. "The state trooper who officially investigated the accident will tell you that. Furthermore, you will also hear, from some of the finest and most competent experts in the country, which Global has brought into this case, that Mrs. Hawkins, in her panic at seeing the step ladder suddenly appear in front of her, simply overreacted in her steering response to that ladder. The rollover occurred not due to any defect, but simply due to the fact that the side-sliding wheels of the Mesa burrowed a deep rut in the soft, grassy shoulder of the interstate median. The engineering experts will tell you that when those ruts of gouged dirt were built up high enough, they acted as what engineers call a 'trip lever,' which caused the Mesa's sliding wheels to dig in so deep that they suddenly stopped sliding. This caused the Mesa, in turn, with its continuing momentum and kinetic energy, to simply trip, that is, to start rolling over. In effect, those two ruts of built-up dirt acted to trip the Mesa and cause its rollover, just like you would see a football player react by falling to the ground and rolling over if he were running fast along the sidelines and someone on the sidelines suddenly stuck out their leg and tripped the player's legs from beneath him. And that is exactly what those dirt ruts in the shoulder did in this accident to the sliding wheels of the Mesa. The engineers who will take that stand," he said, dramatically pointing towards the witness stand, "will also tell you that during its violent rollover, the driver's side of the Mesa slammed into a concrete stanchion that, unfortunately, happened to be located in the middle of that median that protruded above the ground. The immense crushing this stanchion did to the side of the Mesa fractured a bracket leading to its gas tank which, in turn, caused the gas to leak out of the gas tank. This, in turn, caused the very terrible fire when escaping gas and fumes came into contact with a hot muffler pipe or other hot engine components of the SUV."

Harrington stopped momentarily at that point, for dramatic effect, allowing the sober facts he had just summarized to sink into the jurors. They were captivated, I could see.

Gathering his rich, sincere voice, he continued. "Unfortunately, ladies and gentlemen, that's what this case is really about, and that's *all* it's about. The evidence in this case will demonstrate but one very crystal-clear conclusion: The Mesa is a superbly designed utility vehicle that proudly wears the Global mark. What Mr. Culhane did not mention in his opening statement, but I will, is that Global is so confident in the stability design characteristics of its Mesa, that it put Mr. Culhane's defect theory," he said with sarcasm, nodding over to me, "to the test under the very same conditions that Mr. Culhane's experts say existed in this accident. You will see film of a very important test that was conducted in this case. My client took a Mesa that was identical to the one that Mrs. Hawkins was operating at the time of her accident. We loaded it in the identical way that her Mesa was heavily loaded at that time of her accident. We then ran it through a very rigorous and challenging stability test, which the engineers call an S test. That is a test specifically designed to determine if a vehicle has a problem in its stability or control on the roadway under emergency driving circumstances. My client ran that test at fifty-five mph, which is the speed at which Mr. Culhane's so-called expert believes that her Mesa was traveling at the time of the accident. Global ran it at that speed, you will see, *just to be fair*," he emphasized. "Global took their speed when running that test so that the results couldn't be argued with, and the results were dramatic as all of you will be able to see for yourselves."

Harrington was firing on all eight cylinders in his delivery. He smiled warmly and sincerely to the jurors. "The S test results will show you that there was no rollover. There was no wheel lift of the wheels of that Mesa from the asphalt below, nor was there any loss of control. Rather, as you will see for yourself, the Mesa responded with supreme control and smooth stability.

"In short," he ended, "we've all heard the old saying that 'the proof is in the pudding.' Well, in this case, as all of us will witness, the proof is in the testing video pudding, ladies and gentlemen. Thank you for your attention." He smiled warmly to the jury, nodded and took his seat.

It was an effective opening, I had to begrudgingly admit. He personalized Global's enemy in this case as the Hawkins' attorney rather than the poor grief-stricken Hawkins family itself. He captured the full attention of the entire panel, despite the fact that it was near five o'clock when we had finished.

With that, Vaughn announced that he was concluding the proceedings for the day. "Mr. Culhane," he admonished in front of the jury, "be prepared to call your first witness at nine sharp tomorrow morning." With a much milder demeanor, he turned and addressed the jury. "Have a good evening, ladies and gentlemen, and I will look forward to seeing you here at nine a.m. tomorrow morning, as well." He smiled enthusiastically at the jury. "Remember what I told you earlier. Don't talk about the case, either among yourselves or with your family."

You would think that old Vaughn was their best friend. The Turtle, like all trial judges, loved to pander to jurors sitting on cases before them. They weren't just jurors. They were also votes in the next judicial election, and he wasn't about to waste the opportunity to ingratiate himself with them in the process. It was free campaign exposure.

INSTEAD OF CALLING Eric as my first witness the next morning, I chose to call Manny Abadin, the young house painter who had tried to put the fire out. After Harrington's painfully effective opening statement, I knew that I needed to reverse and maintain the momentum of the case. Abadin could supply it.

He took the witness stand wearing a pair of black slacks, a short-sleeved white shirt and a gray tie. I hadn't told him to dress up for trial. It was obviously something he did on his own out of apparent respect for the court and the serious nature of the proceedings.

I took the young, good looking Cuban-American in some detail through his eyewitness observations of the accident scenario. While he sometimes stumbled, he was generally articulate in English, his second language.

"Based upon your own observations, Mr. Abadin, of the Mesa on the roadway in front of you" I asked, "what speed would you estimate Jenny Hawkins to have been traveling at the time of the accident?"

"No more than fifty-five. She not going fast," he said. "I know fifty-five is the speed limit there, and she no faster than speed limit, I say."

"Did you actually see the rollover of her Mesa occur as you were driving in your painting van behind her?"

"Yes sir, I never forget it," he said soberly with his pronounced Cuban accent. "I still dream badly about it. I never forget it. It troubles me much."

"What did the Mesa do after the stepladder fell in front of it?"

He waited for a moment before answering, mentally remembering.

"It looked like the lady driver must have turned the steering wheel pretty good to right because the Mesa started going very quickly in that direction, you know, to her right. It ... it ... looked kind of weird as it did, though."

"Let me stop you a moment and ask a question about that last comment you made. Would you describe what the vehicle was doing that made you think that it was acting weird, as you said?"

His forehead wrinkled as he pondered the question. "I don't exactly know how to say it in English," he said. "It just seem, you know, to rock much on the road when she went to the right. Yes, that is best way to describe it—that it just rocked with a lot of ... how do you say ...?" He struggled to find the correct English word ... "with much action, that is the word. The Mesa rocked with much back-and-forth action at the same time that it started going to the right. It all happen very fast, but it seem to me that it kind of looked like it wanted to tip. Do you know what I mean?" he asked, searching for the right words.

"Yes," I assured him, "we do. Did you see the Mesa's wheels coming off the roadway at all at that stage?" I asked, hoping to jog his recollection of what he had told me during my discussions with him in the months since the accident.

"Objection! That's leading," Harrington argued, rising from his seat.

"Sustained. Don't lead the witness Mr. Culhane," The Turtle admonished. He was right.

"Let me ask you this way, sir. At that point in the accident, when she had first steered to her right to avoid hitting the ladder, were you able to make any observations about any of the tires on that vehicle?"

"Not really. Later I do," he added. "Like I say, it all happen very *rapido*—fast, and I very much surprised."

"Tell us what you saw next," I asked. I had a large thirty-six by thirty-six-inch overhead photo of the accident scene mounted on a foam board sitting on an easel in front of the jury so that they could follow along with his description of the movement of the Mesa during the unfolding accident.

"I saw her heading to hit the concrete wall to right, the one there in that photo," he said pointing at the exhibit, "but, all of sudden, she must have turn her steering wheel very *rapido*—fast," he again caught himself speaking in Spanish, "the other way, to left, to avoid hitting the wall because her car turn fast back the other way."

"You mean, to her left now?" I interrupted for clarification.

"Yes, to left. She start driving towards that grassy area to the left."

"This grassy median?" I again asked for clarification, pointing at the grassy area visible on the large photo that separated the westbound lanes from the eastbound lanes on the interstate.

"Si … yes," he quickly corrected himself. "When that happen, it look to me like her car was rocking side to side very much. I never see that kind of rocking before. It was weird. That's when I remember seeing the two wheels lift up into the air, and the Mesa just rolled over onto its right side."

"I apologize for interrupting you again, but when you saw the two wheels lift up in the air, *where* was the Mesa located when that happened—on the asphalt roadway, or on the grassy median?"

"It all happen very fast, very speedy, but I think it was still on the road when that happen. It was already rolling over onto its right side before it got to the grass," he said, nodding his head, almost as if he was trying to confirm his memory of the details.

I paused for a moment and glanced over at the jury to emphasize the significance of his last point of testimony. If the Mesa started rolling over while it was still on the roadway, then Global's engineers were all wrong. In their depositions prior to trial, they had testified that it was impossible for that vehicle to have started to roll on a flat road surface at only fifty-five mph. I caught the eye of the hardware store owner. He was paying attention.

"Thank you. Now, please continue with what you saw after that."

"The car ... it roll onto right side and off the road, into the grass, then it roll on to its top, and then," he said, demonstrating by jerking both of his hands upwards into the air, "it like jump up into the air and then came down with a much big hit on the driver's side. Then it made one more roll back onto its four wheels. That is when I pull over and stop to see if my friend and me could help. That is also when the fire start," he said more quietly. He took a drink from the Styrofoam glass of water I took up to him.

At the mention of the fire, I glanced briefly to my counsel table to my right where Eric was sitting. He was sitting there, stone-faced and staring intently ahead. This was not going to be easy on him, but I had no alternative.

"Mr. Abadin, I'm sorry to have to do this, but I need to have you tell us what happened next."

The young man dropped his head down, took a short breath, exhaled and looked up. "It was the most bad thing I ever see in my whole life."

For the next ten minutes, Abadin related, in graphic and poignant detail, the last moments of Jenny's life. He described her screams about her son's safety, as well as her desperate but futile efforts to free herself from the advancing flames and the certain death they brought. He related, with some embarrassment, his own futile attempts to keep the flames at bay with the various fire extinguishers. As he described his final words with her in the seat of the Mesa and her final blood curdling screams as the flames engulfed her, his voice finally cracked with emotion. Even his youthful machismo couldn't prevent the inevitable. The memories were too painful.

I thanked him for his testimony and ended my direct exam. As I headed back to my chair from the podium, I managed a glance at Eric. He had his head down, with his right hand covering his face and eyes in an attempt to deal with the grief. Though not a word or sound was coming from him, his shoulders were moving up and down from his grief. The courtroom was deathly silent.

Judge Vaughn leaned forward in his chair. "Counsel, I think this would be a good time for a ten minute break. Court is adjourned for ten minutes," he informed the jury.

As the jury filed out into the jury room, all faces were grim. The two women were watery-eyed from the testimony.

HARRINGTON'S CROSS-EXAMINATION was short and to the point.

"Mr. Abadin, we can all see that this was a very traumatic event for you, wasn't it?" he opened with.

"Yes."

"And it all happened very fast, isn't that right, as well?"

"Yes sir, very speedy."

"And would it be fair to say that it caused your adrenaline to pump very quickly when this terrible event started to unfold before your very eyes?" Harrington was setting the bait.

"I'm sorry. You use a word I that I ... uh ... no ... I don't understand," he said with some embarrassment.

"Adrenaline. I'm sorry, excuse me for that. What I'm asking is whether the excitement of the event caused your heart to race?"

"Oh, yes," he now nodded enthusiastically, understanding the question. "My heart very speedy too," he admitted politely.

"And you had just gotten off work after a long day, right?"

"Yes, we work on a job site in Pembroke Pines all day."

"I take it that having worked all day in the sun painting houses, you were probably pretty tired?"

"I was not like needing to go home and take a nap, but yes, I a little tired. I work since early in morning."

"Now, if I understand your testimony, your painting van was not very close to the Mesa when the stepladder fell off the pickup truck in front of her. Isn't that correct?"

"I not very good with distances, but I was not too far from her. Maybe a one hundred or so feet."

"Mr. Abadin," Harrington said, suddenly raising his voice and looking at the jury, then back at the witness, "isn't it true that you were a lot further than one hundred feet away from her Mesa?"

"No sir, I say it was around one hundred feet. I saw it good."

Harrington calmly reached over and picked up a deposition transcript that was lying on his counsel table. He held it up in the air with his right hand for emphasis. "I took your sworn deposition in this case a couple of months ago, didn't I?"

"Yes, I remember that."

"And in your deposition, Mr. Abadin, I asked you a lot of very specific questions about the details of this accident, didn't I?"

"Uh huh."

"Is that 'yes'?"

"Uh, yes, I'm sorry."

"And in your *sworn* testimony at that time, didn't you say that you were about *three hundred feet* behind her Mesa, not hundred feet, when the accident happened?"

He knitted his brows, confused. "I not remember exactly what I tell you then."

"Well, that's exactly what you said then, Mr. Abadin, just a few short months ago," Harrington said, now reading from the typed deposition transcript, "at page 87, line four, you said that the distance of your painting van from her SUV when all of this happened was, and I'm quoting your words now, 'about three hundred feet.' That's what you testified to under oath, didn't you?"

"I no remember what I say," he replied, "but I saw it," he said, holding stubbornly to his testimony on direct like a dog on a bloody bone.

"Judge, may I approach the witness?" Harrington asked?

"You may," Vaughn said.

Harrington approached Abadin, held the page of his deposition transcript open for him to read, and asked, "What you testified to then, 'about three hundred feet,' is that right?" he asked, pressing the witness.

"Yes," Abadin admitted. "That is what this page say I say."

"Three hundred feet," Harrington continued as he walked back to the podium, looking up at the ceiling, as if for inspiration. He then turned to face Abadin. "You've been to a Dolphins football game here in Miami, haven't you, sir?"

"Yes."

"So, based on what you told us under oath in your deposition, at the time of this accident, you were three hundred feet—*the length of an entire football field away from her* when you supposedly made all of these observations, right?" Harrington asked with staged disbelief at the immense distance he was trying to create in the minds of the jurors.

Abadin sat quietly for a moment, thinking. "I not think it was that far the more I remember about it," he responded.

"So, are you *admitting* that in your sworn testimony, which you gave only a few months after the accident, you were wrong in your recollection?" Harrington tilted his head for effect.

"Well ... uh ... I don't know. I just think I was more closer than a football field to her when all this happen," Abadin defended. There clearly was now more hesitation evident in his voice.

"Sir, wouldn't you agree that a driver who is traveling *the length of a football field* behind another car in front of him is not in a very good position to either make accurate estimates of the speed of the vehicle in front of him, or to take the stand in a courtroom and tell a jury that he could accurately see, in precise detail, the specific movements that supposedly took place in a fast-unfolding, speedy accident that happened in front of him?"

"I object, Your Honor. The question is argumentative and compound," I said.

"Overruled," Vaughn ruled, "I think it's fair cross. You may answer the question Mr. Abadin."

He squirmed uncomfortably in the witness chair. "I don't know. I can see what you mean, but I still think I saw it good."

Harrington skillfully took advantage of Abadin's momentary drop in self-confidence. "We all know that you are here trying to give us your honest recollection, sir. However, would you agree that there is a real possibility that in the moment of all the excitement that was happening, with your heart beating 'very speedy,' as you say, and with your van not being all that close to the Mesa, and with you being tired and just coming home from work, that your recollection about her vehicle speed, about this supposed *wheels lifting* and the location of exactly where her SUV was when it started its rollover that you talked about this morning, may, in fact, be incorrect?"

The courtroom was entirely quiet. Abadin's brow was knitted together as he thought over the question before answering. He was conscientious and was struggling to be absolutely accurate.

"Yes," he finally said, wilting like a water-deprived flower, "it happen *rapido.*"

"I'm sorry," Harrington quickly injected for the record and the jury, "*rapido* in English means rapidly ... fast, right?"

"Yes," Abadin politely answered, losing all fight and not wanting to argue in front of the jury.

Shit! I thought. Poker face is what I showed to the jury.

"That's what I thought," Harrington retorted with a confident smile. "Thank you for your honesty, sir. No further questions." He turned from the podium and returned with satisfaction to his table. The female representative from Global at the table was concealing the beginning of a smile at the crucial concession just given by Abadin.

In redirect, I did my best to rekindle the strength of the convictions Abadin had manifested in his earlier testimony during my direct examination about what he saw, including the fact that he had 20/20 vision, regardless of what the precise distance was between his painting truck and the Mesa when he saw what he saw. However, Harrington had successfully rattled his self-confidence. He refused to provide the same degree of firmness of recollection, which I knew the jury would be demanding of him.

When he was excused a few minutes later, we broke for lunch.

"Why did Abadin melt like that on the stand?" Sandy asked in frustration as the three of us walked down the street to a deli shop for a quick sandwich.

"He didn't have any doubt about his observations in his deposition, or in all the times we spoke with him about it, regardless of the distance."

"Like a snow cone on hot asphalt at noon," I said. "It hurt, too. I caught a glance from the computer company supervisor on the jury after Abadin said that he wasn't sure. I think he was expecting me to be able to rehabilitate his recollection."

"No luck there," Sandy said.

I PUT ERIC on as my next witness after we resumed trial. The jury needed to gain an appreciation for who Jenny Hawkins was.

Eric walked to the stand, was sworn in, and he sat down. He nervously cleared his throat, adjusted his tie, and then pulled the microphone closer.

My direct with him went for the better part of the afternoon. He did an excellent job providing the background facts regarding the family decision to purchase a Mesa sport utility vehicle rather than a station wagon.

"We thought it would be a much safer vehicle to drive," Eric related quietly. "Jenny was going to be driving it with the kids most of the time. I felt that its large size would provide more protection in the event that she ever got in an accident while driving it." The irony wasn't lost on the jury.

"Did Jenny have any habit over the years as to what kind of speed she would drive cars at?"

"Objection, your Honor!" Harrington bellowed from his chair. "May I be heard at sidebar?"

"Yes," The Turtle acquiesced with some hesitation. He hated sidebars. He thought they were a waste of time. We both walked to the side of Vaughn's bench opposite the jury box. The court reporter followed with her machine in hand to record the conference and the ruling.

"What's your objection to the question, Mr. Harrington?" Vaughn whispered so as not to be heard by the jurors.

"It's legally irrelevant under Section 90.402 of The Evidence Code," Harrington pressed in whisper. "Mr. Culhane hasn't laid the proper predicate to show that it was a 'habit' of the late Mrs. Hawkins to drive at any particular speeds. And as the court is aware, unless a practice rises to the level of a true 'habit,' meaning that the person *invariably* engages in the practice, *without exception*, then it isn't a 'habit.' And if it's not a habit, it's legally irrelevant."

"Judge," I countered, "this man will testify that his wife had a habit of driving at or below the speed limit every time she drove her vehicle. That is clearly relevant in this case to establish that on the date of her accident she was acting in conformance with that habit. Global claims that she was speeding. The evidence, as you can appreciate, is critical."

Harrington then pulled a piece of paper from a manila folder which he had carried with him from counsel's table. He handed it to the judge. He gave me a copy.

"Not true. Judge," he corrected, "Take a look at this."

"What is this?" The Turtle inquired?

"It's a certified copy of a public record—a speeding record, to be more precise. It reflects that the late Jenny Hawkins was previously ticketed for speeding in a school zone. The speed limit was fifteen miles per hour, yet she was caught going twenty-five. This," he said, pointing to the document in The Turtle's hand, "eviscerates Mr. Culhane's *habit* theory. She had about as much of a habit of not speeding as I do, Judge. And, unfortunately, like everybody else, I speed every now and then, too."

"Judge Vaughn," I quickly responded, "I'm aware of that ticket. It has nothing to do with any speeding propensities of Jenny Hawkins, as Mr. Harrington argues. Mr. Hawkins informed me that this happened on the first day of a new school year—over five years ago, I might add. A new school had just been opened in their neighborhood, but she was not aware of the school zone. She was traveling at the *regular* speed limit of twenty-five miles per hour, just as the ticket confirms. The slower fifteen mile per hour school zone speed limit was only in effect between seven-fifteen a.m. and eight a.m. This ticket only confirms what Mr. Hawkins has been saying. An awareness problem is not the same thing as a speeding problem. Besides, it's over *five years ago*," I pleaded.

"I understand your argument, Mr. Culhane," The Turtle said, massaging one of his chin rolls as he spoke quietly. "However, I'm afraid that Mr. Harrington has you on this one. A speed limit is a speed limit and she was caught for speeding in excess of a speed limit in the past. A 'habit' means just that, 'an invariable practice.' We don't seem to have that here. Given this," he said, waving the certified document in front of me, "the best that Mr. Hawkins can tell this jury would be that his late wife had a typical practice of driving at or under the posted speed limit, but a typical practice is far short of an habitual practice. So," he concluded, "I'm sustaining his objection, and the witness will not be permitted to give that testimony. And, as far as the age of the ticket goes, five years ago isn't that far removed from the present time as to render it immaterial. Let's proceed," he ordered.

"I request a curative instruction, Your Honor," Harrington interjected.

The Turtle nodded affirmatively, "You'll get one."

I returned to the podium while Harrington returned to his table.

"Ladies and gentlemen," The Turtle wheezed to the jury after we had resumed our seats. He was winded from having to move around to deal with the sidebar discussion we had. "You are to disregard any inference or suggestion that you may have gained from the question that was posed to Mr. Hawkins about any supposed habit that his late wife had, or did not have, about driving at, below or above posted speed limits. The court has found that the plaintiffs have failed to establish the existence of a habit within the meaning of the Florida Rules of Evidence. Continue, Mr. Culhane," he directed, adjusting his thick black glasses on the bridge of his nose.

I quickly tried to regroup from the blow inflicted on our case by his ruling.

"Well, was your wife under any particular schedule or deadline that afternoon of the accident, like having to be at a specific destination that would require her to hurry along?"

"No, I had picked up a movie at a Red Box over lunch hour. We were just planning to watch it that night after dinner."

I shifted gears. "Do you know what Jenny was carrying in the back of the Mesa at the time of her accident?"

"Yes. She had just picked up some large cartons of Girl Scout cookies from another scout mother in Weston just before the accident. She and another mother had volunteered to act as the troop leaders for the group of girls that included our daughter, Sarah. She had asked me that morning if I could take off from work a little early and pick them up myself before I came home. I told her that I couldn't," he added, his voice breaking. "I was ... I was too busy with a tax project I had to get out," he added slowly, looking down. He was stoically trying to control his emotions and the irrational guilt he still harbored.

"I understand," I said. "What else was in the vehicle?"

He looked at me somewhat vacantly a full three or four seconds before his thoughts focused on my question. "There were eight boxes of house paint still in the Mesa. I had purchased them the night before, but I hadn't gotten around to unloading them yet. Also, I had a rented spray paint machine with a heavy compressor. I had planned on painting the house that weekend. I had laid the rear bench seat down so that I could take full advantage of the cargo area."

"How many gallons of house paint were in each of those eight boxes?"

"Four per box, I had thirty-two gallons of paint. The stucco on our house eats a lot of paint."

"Your Honor, based upon the discovery done in the case, the parties were able to agree that the total weight of the equipment, the paint and the cookies in the Mesa at the time was six hundred twenty pounds and that Mrs. Hawkins and her son weighed a total of one hundred forty pounds. As a result, the Mesa was carrying a total load of seven hundred sixty pounds at the time of the accident."

Vaughn looked over at Harrington. "Is that correct?"

"Yes, those are agreed facts," he replied.

"Ladies and gentlemen, since the parties have agreed as to those facts, you are to take them as true. Proceed."

"Was Jenny athletic? I mean, did you consider her to be coordinated in her body movements?" I moved around the courtroom to keep the jury's attention.

"Objection," Harrington blurted, "irrelevant."

"Mr. Culhane?" Vaughn peered and awaited a brief response.

"It bears directly on the human reaction and accident reconstruction issues, Your Honor."

"Overruled. Go ahead and answer, sir," Vaughn instructed the witness.

"Yes, she was a jogger and a tennis player when she could break away from being a mom," he smiled for the first time since being on the stand. "She took great joy in beating me regularly on the tennis court."

"And how were her reflexes?"

"Better than mine, she was very quick and agile."

"Over the years of your marriage, did you observe whether she was one to panic in an emergency?"

"Jenny was one of the calmest people I knew. Some people get hysterical when an emergency occurs, but that wasn't her. She was always very good in a stressful situation."

"So, when the stepladder flew off the pickup truck in front of her that Friday afternoon, would she have been one to panic and start steering the Mesa wildly and out of control?"

"Objection," fired Harrington, "the question calls for speculation."

"Sustained," The Turtle intoned. "I think you're getting into speculation, Mr. Culhane."

The point of my question was not lost on the jury. That was what I was after.

I finished Eric's direct examination by focusing on the injuries and damages to Ryan and Sarah. After wading through the details of Ryan's burn injuries, his hospitalization, the surgeries and the medical expenses to date, I felt the jury needed to receive a jolt of reality. Thus far, I had intentionally kept both Sarah and Ryan out of the courtroom.

"Did I ask you to bring the photographs which the hospital took of your son's burned condition immediately after his admission to the hospital?"

"Yes ... I have them here," he said, tapping a large white envelope which he had brought up to the witness stand with him. He refused to look at them.

I walked up, took the envelope and pulled out the dozen eight by ten photos of Ryan. They were in vivid stomach-turning color.

"Judge Vaughn," Harrington announced as he stood at his table, "I must respectfully, but emphatically, object to those photographs being viewed by the jury. They are merely historical in nature and have no relevance to his present condition. Moreover, any tangential relevance is clearly outweighed by their prejudicial tendency to inflame this jury."

"Counselor," Vaughn said, holding his hand out towards me, "let me take a look at those."

I walked over to the bench and handed the photos to him.

His facial reaction was immediate and obvious to the jury. He winced as he paged through them. The burned-off ear and the charred and black-crusted face of the young child were dramatic. The missing portion of his nose was also evident. "Let me see both of you at sidebar."

"These are terribly graphic, Mr. Culhane. I'm inclined to sustain his objection, but I'm going to give you a shot at convincing me otherwise."

"Judge, they are graphic. I concede that fact. But that's the very nature of burn injuries. They are excruciatingly painful and catastrophically injurious to the person who suffers them. The only way that this jury can even begin to appreciate the shear torture that Ryan Hawkins went through in that fire is to view the cooked and charred remains of his body immediately afterwards. He was cooked for God's sakes! They are also going to be commented on from a treatment standpoint both by the treating burn specialist who will be testifying, Dr. Stuart Olive, and the burn psychologist, Dr. Natalie Avalos."

"You're representing to the court that both of those witnesses will be testifying and will be commenting on these photos?" Vaughn pondered.

"These photos and the injuries they reflect. Absolutely, your honor," I emphasized. "I'm entitled to have this jury know what the consequences were to my clients from the stability defect that the Mesa had. Mere words or descriptions are impotent substitutes for those pictures. They are most relevant as to issues of damages."

"But they don't—"

The Turtle held up his paw to silence Harrington. He had made up his mind, and he was not the kind of guy to change it.

"Because of the potential inflammatory nature of these, I'm not going to let you show them to the jury at this time. If I believe, after I hear the totality of your case in chief, that you have made a prima facie case for negligent design on the part of the manufacturer in connection with the design of the Mesa, I'll allow you to display them to the jury at the time that you call your damage witnesses to the stand. If you fail to prove a prima facie case, they won't be coming into evidence. In the meantime, they are simply too inflammatory for a jury to handle."

Being an optimist, I decided to push the envelope. "Your Honor," I said, reaching for my best non-whiny voice, "I've cited the *Hansen v. Ford Motors* case in my trial brief. In that case, as the court may recall, the Florida Supreme Court emphasized that even terribly inflammatory photos are permissible to be shown to the jury if words can't adequately describe the nature of a plaintiff's injuries or suffering. This is precisely—"

"I've read your brief, counsel," Vaughn responded, in a surprisingly decent tone, "and I'm well aware of the *Hansen* case. The Supreme Court ultimately leaves it to the discretion of the trial judge, and I'm exercising that discretion now. I've stated my ruling, and the reasons underlying it, so let's proceed." I chalked up his unexpected restraint to his own awareness that his ruling was iffy.

"Thank you, judge, I'll offer them later on the basis of your ruling," I acceded as I headed back to my podium. I was not happy with his ruling.

"Good luck trying," Harrington quietly whispered sarcastically as he walked past me to his table. To the jury, it undoubtedly looked like Harrington was commenting to me on some procedural matter.

I ignored him.

"Mr. Hawkins, I realize that this is very difficult for you, but it's important for the jury to have all of the facts. Did your son appear to be in any pain when you got to the hospital that night?"

He looked down for a moment, took a deep breath to compose himself, and finally looked up. "Two things occurred that night that will never leave my memory. Having to identify Jenny's burned and lifeless body ... and seeing my little boy all burned up and screaming in pain in the burn unit at the hospital. It ... it ... it was terrible," he finally managed with his voice shaking with emotion. "And there was nothing ... nothing that I could do to help him out. He was in agony, pure agony."

I waited for a moment to allow him to collect himself.

"Could you tell the jury whether Sarah, your daughter, has been affected by the accident?"

"Yes, she has. In some ways, I worry more about her than I do about Ryan. She's become withdrawn and very depressed. Before the accident, Sarah was the life of our household," he recounted. "She was forever laughing around the house and talking a mile a minute. Jenny and I always saw her as the most outgoing of the family."

"Has that changed?"

"She isn't the Sarah that was my daughter before the accident. She cries a lot. She doesn't want to talk to me or anybody else, and her grades at school have dropped from straight As to Ds in almost all of her classes." He sighed, "I'm trying to spend as much time as possible with her, and I have her seeing a child psychologist to help her deal with the grief, but the spark that made her Sarah is no longer there. I'd do anything to make it come back."

"And how are you doing?" I asked.

"I miss Jenny ... I ... miss her a lot, but I'm fine," he said woodenly, trying to convince himself. "It's the kids that have me worried. Their problems haven't even begun, I'm afraid."

"Thank you, Mr. Hawkins. I have no more questions."

Vaughn looked over at the jury and then at the Regulator clock hanging on the wall at the rear of the courtroom. "It's four forty-five. I'm not inclined to allow you to start your cross-examination of the witness at this hour since it will undoubtedly carry over into the morning. I'm going—"

"My apologies for interrupting, Your Honor," Harrington offered, rising from his chair, "but I actually only have but a few questions for Mr. Hawkins. I'll defer to the court's preferences, but I will finish my cross in a matter of minutes only."

Harrington wanted Eric off that witness stand and away from the eyes of the jury. There was nothing like starting a fresh day of testimony with a sympathetic and grieving husband back on the stand to rekindle the emotions of the jury in favor of the Hawkins family.

"That's fine with the court. If you believe you can finish your cross, let's begin." Vaughn was not about to waste fifteen minutes in his courtroom if he could avoid it.

Hawkins strode to the podium in front of the counsel tables where he laid his pad down.

"Mr. Hawkins, I know that this is very difficult for you. Please bear with me."

"That's fine," Eric replied.

"You and your wife had owned that Mesa for three months prior to the unfortunate accident, isn't that correct?"

"Yes, we bought it in December."

"And your wife drove it almost every day during that three-month stretch?"

"Yes, I drove it some, too."

"And neither one of you ever experienced *any* problems with the handling or stability of that Mesa during that entire three month stretch prior to the accident, did you?"

"That's true, but——"

"And you and your wife drove that vehicle over forty-five hundred miles in that three month stretch, isn't that correct?" Harrington machine-gunned.

"Yes, it was something like that. We drove it up to North Carolina for Christmas with my brother and his family."

"And on that trip, you drove it at all types of speeds, did you not? I mean, you drove it at twenty-five miles per hour all the way up to seventy miles per hour, did you not?" Harrington had covered all this in Eric's deposition, so he knew what the answers would be.

"That's right."

"And at no time at any of those speeds did you have *any* problem with the Mesa that my client designed and sold to you, did you?" Harrington had picked up his pad, signaling that his questioning was over. He had made his point.

"What you said is correct," Eric conceded.

"Oh, one final question," Harrington stated, stopping on his walk back to his table to feign that the next question was an almost forgotten afterthought. He turned and faced the witness. "Since you were not in the Mesa at the time of your wife's accident, would it be fair to say that you have no *personal knowledge* whatsoever as to what speed she was traveling at, or whether she simply panicked when she saw that stepladder coming right at her and her son?"

"I know my wife, Mr. Harrington," Eric shot back, "and I know the kind of driver she is."

"I think that the jury can certainly appreciate your feelings for your wife, sir, but my question is really one of simple fact. Since you weren't there, you don't have any *actual personal* knowledge at all about those things, do you?"

"Objection, Your Honor," I argued, "Mr. Harrington is being argumentative with the witness."

"Overruled. Answer the question Mr. Hawkins," the judge ordered evenly.

"No, I was not with her that afternoon riding in the Mesa that your client designed and sold to my family, Mr. Harrington, if that's what you want to know," Eric said slowly and with rising anger.

"Yes, that's all I wanted to confirm for the record. Thank you, sir." Harrington calmly and confidently walked back to his table, taking his seat.

Vaughn looked over at me. "Any redirect?"

"Yes, briefly," I replied.

Rising in my chair, I walked over and stood immediately next to Harrington as he was sitting in his chair. "Mr. Harrington asked you if your Mesa showed any stability problems during the three months and forty-five hundred miles that you and your wife drove it prior to the day of the accident. Do you remember those questions?"

"Yes."

"Tell us, were either of you put in the predicament of having to steer aggressively under *emergency circumstances* during that three month period of use?"

"No. It was only routine driving before Jenny's accident. We never had to avoid a stepladder or anything like that before the afternoon of Jenny's death. It was all just simple driving."

"Nothing further. Thank you."

The Turtle looked over at Harrington who technically had the right to recross the witness if he desired. He shook his head dismissively. He had what he wanted from Eric.

"All right, ladies and gentlemen," he said, swiveling his head to face the jury, "I will expect to see all of you here first thing tomorrow morning at nine a.m. when we resume. Do not discuss the case among yourselves in the meantime. Good evening."

CHAPTER 37

"YOU'RE NOT PUTTING the cop who investigated the accident on the witness stand?" Liz asked me, skeptically. "Isn't the jury going to expect to hear from him as part of your proof?"

We were lying next to one another in the rope hammock strung between two coconut palms in our back yard, adjacent to the canal having a beer about eleven p.m. The skies had finally cleared late in the day, leaving a brilliant moon in the indigo night sky. Its moon river reflection lazily undulated across the gently rocking top of the black canal water. My left leg was swung over the side of the hammock, with my foot gently pushing it back and forth in the cool night breeze. The crickets were going nuts all around us as I discussed the day's events in the case with my chief critic and sounding board, including my plans for the next day's witnesses.

I had been at the office since trial ended for the day, working on loose ends for tomorrow's witnesses and dictating letters and pleadings in response to the day's mail that was waiting on my desk. I sorely missed having an associate to keep up with the ongoing calls and pleadings coming into the office while my focus was on the trial. Before getting to what Liz called my boring case stuff, we had just finished catching up on Anne's day. She appeared to be fine, though still pretty shaken from the canal episode of last night. My car was totaled, and Liz had rented a replacement for the next two weeks.

"I can't afford to put him on," I said, referring to Trooper Martelli. "The guy is lazy. He did a half-assed investigation and had pre-conceived opinions that Jenny was at fault even before he started doing his workup. I'm convinced of that. The problem is he's trouble for my case. I know from his deposition that he'll testify that it is his conclusion that Jenny was speeding and that her rollover started only *after* the Mesa left the roadway and *after* its side-moving tires started digging into the median's soft grass as it slid sideways into and across the grassy median." I needed to think out loud, and Liz was a good ear. "I think he's flat-ass wrong, but the guy wears a uniform and was the investigating officer at the scene. Juries love police officers in traffic accident cases."

"So," she challenged me, "isn't that the point? Isn't it going to be worse for you if Harrington puts him on in his case and he clobbers you then? I mean, isn't there a risk that once they finally hear his opinions that the jury will think that you kind of hid him from them? Michael," she repeated her opinion, "I think that the jury will get angry at you for doing that."

"No question about it, but that's the risk I'm going to have to take." I reached down to the small wicker yard table next to the hammock, grabbed my bottle of beer and took a big swig. "If I put him on in my case, he's going to be so contradictory to the testimony of my experts that I'm afraid I'll be cooked. That's the power that an investigating police officer has in these kinds of cases. I'll take my lumps later on, after the jury has had a chance to hear my side of the story."

"Are you happy with the first day's testimony?" She took a sip from a can of diet Coke that she was resting on the flat of her stomach, surrounded by both of her hands.

"It would have been terrific if Abadin, the house painter, wouldn't have crumpled on cross-examination. I'll give Harrington his due. He did a nice job to get Abadin to start second-guessing his earlier recollection and testimony, which was very favorable to my case. The kid just wanted to be absolutely sure, and Harrington took advantage of that to unnerve him just enough." I finished off the beer in a final guzzle. "I'm just hoping that the jury understands that. I think the jury really liked Eric, though. He made a solid witness."

She finally patted my thigh. "You need to get to bed. You look really tired."

"Yeah, I'm wasted. I'm still dragging from last night." The mention of last night suddenly brought concern back to me. "Liz, I still can't figure out why that maniac was trying to drive us off the road. It's almost like he was trying to kill us. The son of a bitch."

Liz swung her legs over her side of the hammock and got out. I did the same as the rebound of the hammock pushed me out, as well.

"This is South Florida, remember?" she replied. "People don't need much of a reason anymore. That's the scary part of all this. That guy is probably out there trying to run someone else off the road tonight." She leaned over next to me and put her head on my shoulder as we started walking back inside. "I'm just thankful that you and Anne are okay."

"Yeah," I said, "we were lucky. I'm kind of glad to be here too," I smiled.

"Come on," she ended. "Let's go to bed. You need some sleep. We both do."

WE ENDED UP having to wait fifteen minutes to resume trial the next morning. One of the alternate jurors was late. After The Turtle politely, but forcefully, laid into him for 'holding up my entire courtroom,' the juror apologized.

"I got caught in a speed trap doing seventy on I-95," he admitted sheepishly. "I told the officer that I would be late for a trial where I was serving as a juror. He didn't believe me."

At the mention of the word *speeding*, I caught Harrington leaning over and whispering to Linda Mirek, the Global trial representative next to him. It wasn't lost on them that the rest of the panel also heard that the juror, like a lot of people in South Florida, drove at excessive rates of speed all the time. They were hoping that the jury would be thinking that Mrs. Hawkins was probably no different.

"Your apology is accepted, sir, but I don't want a repeat. This court's time and that of your fellow jurors is valuable," he huffed in a self-important way to the jury. Turning to me, he nodded and grumbled in his phlegmy voice, "Call your next witness, Mr. Culhane."

"Plaintiffs call Mr. Ralph Cargill to the stand," I announced. He had been sequestered out in the hall so that he could not hear the testimony of the other witnesses, per the order of Judge Vaughn. Sandy, standing back by the courtroom door when Vaughn had retaken the bench, exited the room and brought the reconstructionist into the courtroom. He walked forward, pushed aside the swinging section of the waist-high hinged railing that separated the audience seats from the lawyers' tables, the jury box and the judge's elevated bench, and approached the witness box. He walked directly in front of the jury box as he did so.

Cargill was sworn in by the court clerk then climbed the two steps up to the witness chair. He carried his old battered brown leather briefcase with him. It looked new maybe 20 years ago. His conservative dark gray suit, white shirt and navy blue tie were in keeping with his conservative bearing. In a humorous sort of way, his old-fashioned flat top and crew cut haircut had come full circle to match what kids were now sporting again.

The personable side of Cargill quickly came to the surface as I took him through his background and training over the thirty-eight years he had spent with the Pennsylvania Highway Patrol. I could see that the jury was warming up to him quickly. His self-deprecating personal manner, however, was in sharp contrast to the confidence and intelligence his strong voice and manner exuded as he provided the accident reconstruction information I requested.

"How many motor vehicle accidents have you investigated over the course of the thirty-eight years you worked for the Highway Patrol?"

"I never kept a count, per se," he answered, "but it would have been well over two thousand that I would have classified as being of the serious variety. I probably had three times that amount of the minor accident variety. Since the patrol had jurisdiction over state highways, and since their speeds were generally at fifty miles per hour or higher, the accidents often involved high speed events and graduated to what I would call the serious category."

"And over the years, did you teach accident investigation techniques to anyone?"

"Yes, every two years, the Patrol in Pennsylvania held a statewide school for traffic homicide investigative teams. I taught accident reconstruction principles and techniques at those schools for the last eight years of my career with the Patrol. I retired last year."

"Were you accorded any honors or awards for the accident reconstruction work you performed?"

"Well," he chuckled, I guess you could call it an award. When my retirement was announced, the governor of the State of Pennsylvania officially declared my last day of work as 'Patrolman Ralph C. Cargill Appreciation Day' in the state of Pennsylvania in honor of my contributions to the Patrol and to accident investigation." He smiled proudly. "Some of my good friends on the Patrol suggested that giving that award was the only way that they could finally get rid of me."

The jurors laughed at his comment. They like him. Enough of the background. The jury, I sensed, wanted to hear his professional opinions.

"Did I ask you to investigate the Hawkins accident?'"

"You did."

"Before getting into your specific opinions, Mr. Cargill, would you briefly outline for the jury the investigation, work and information you conducted and reviewed in order to arrive at your opinions in this case?'"

He opened his old battered briefcase and pulled out a thick three-ring binder, which contained his organized work papers. Paging through them as he spoke, he summarized the extensive work he had undertaken in the case. He related his scene investigation, his review of the police report and photographs, his review of the deposition testimony of the witnesses taken before trial, his physical examination of the charred remains of the Hawkins Mesa, and his analysis of various technical papers and engineering data.

"Did you arrive at an opinion as to the speed Jenny Hawkins was operating the Mesa when the step ladder flew onto the roadway in front of her?"

"I did. She was traveling in the range of only fifty-two to fifty-five miles an hour."

"How did you arrive at that speed, Mr. Cargill?" He and I had rehearsed my direct exam the evening before, one last time, over the phone when I was at my office.

"On the evidence, I based it on the evidence," he said, evenly. "I applied generally-accepted principles dealing with the conservation of momentum, together with the resting point of the vehicle, its degree of body damage, and the fact that it only underwent one three hundred sixty degree roll. I also considered the testimony of the eyewitnesses to the accident, including … Mr. Abadin and Carole Merton," he finally said, verifying their names in notes he read from his three-ring binder laid on the ledge in front of him.

I broke from my habit of yesterday, when I had conducted all of my questioning standing behind the podium the court had provided, which was located between the lawyers' tables, facing the judge. Today, I was walking slowly around in the area in front of the jury box as I asked him my questions. He and I were having more of a matter-of-fact conversation rather than a rigid examination. He was very engaging and easy for the jury to follow. He enjoyed talking to the jury, and I could see that they were paying close attention to his answers. I wanted to take advantage of that rapport in my approach.

"You mentioned that in arriving at your speed opinion, you considered the fact that the Mesa only made one complete three hundred sixty degree roll," I repeated his testimony. "Why was the degree of the Mesa's roll in this accident important to you?"

"That's correct, I did consider its degree of roll. My investigation in this case uncovered an accident reconstruction article published by engineers who work for Volkswagen. It was published by the Society of Automotive Engineers which," he explained, turning to face the jurors directly, "is the leading professional engineering organization in the world in the automotive design and accident-cause area." A couple of the older male jurors nodded, as if they had heard of the organization in some context over the years. "The VW engineers," he continued, "were interested in determining if one could derive the *pre-rollover* speed of a van or utility-type vehicle by looking at the number of rolls which the vehicle actually underwent. In other words, can the accident reconstructionist actually reasonably determine and bracket categories of *pre-rollover* accident speed based upon the known or determined number of times that the vehicle rolled over in the accident in question?"

"Were the VW engineers able to do so?"

"Yes, they were."

"And were you able to make a correlation of the VW data in this case?"

Eric leaned forward, resting on both elbows he had placed on the table in front of him. The witness had his full interest and attention.

"Yes," Cargill answered, "they went out and ran actual rollovers of vans and utility vehicles at various speeds. They kept track of the number of rolls that the vehicles made at the different speeds tested. While there are a number of very difficult variables that one needs to either factor in or factor out in any given accident, they did conclude that for a utility-type of vehicle, a three hundred sixty degree roll is *generally* associated with pre-rollover speeds in the fifty to sixty mile per hour range. At speeds of sixty to seventy-five, in comparison, the energy generated by those higher speeds usually results in a utility vehicle of the Mesa variety rolling a full one-and-a-half to two full revolutions. At speeds of over seventy-five miles per hour," he recounted, continuing to speak directly to the jurors with his answers, and not to me or to the judge, "utility vehicles tend to roll two-and-a-half or more revolutions before they come to rest."

"And in this case, you believe that the Mesa only rolled one full revolution of three hundred sixty degrees?"

"Yes, in fact," he said, nodding at both me and Harrington, "I believe you two lawyers have agreed that to be true in your pretrial submissions. As a result of that fact, and the VW study, it's entirely consistent with the speed that I otherwise found of only fifty-two to fifty-five that Mrs. Hawkins was traveling at the time the step ladder fell in front of her."

I walked back to the podium and let his information sink in for the jury.

"What was the legal speed limit on the stretch of interstate where Jenny Hawkins' accident occurred?" I asked, looking over at the jury myself.

"It was fifty-five in that area of I-595."

"Did you find any evidence that she was speeding at that time?"

"None at all," he said strongly. "What I found was that her vehicle was at or just below the legal speed limit when she was confronted with a stepladder that had blown off the pickup truck in front of her, causing her to take sudden and quick evasive action."

"Is the stepladder here?" I asked.

"Yes. The investigating officer found it at the scene. I understand that the police have since turned it over to your office."

I looked up at The Turtle. He was sitting back in his chair with his short arms folded across his more than ample chest, with his hooded eyes almost closed. For a fleeting second, the image of a sleeping reptile waiting quietly for unsuspecting prey to walk in front of a quickly-thrusted tongue came to mind.

He was paying close attention, too, but his horizontal slits for eyes wouldn't have readily disclosed that.

"Your Honor, with the court's permission, I would like to bring the ladder into the courtroom and have it marked." Harrington said nothing.

"That's fine, go ahead," he responded, only slightly opening his eyes.

I nodded to Sandy who rose from her chair, exited the courtroom and returned carrying the large seven-foot aluminum ladder which Tina had delivered to the courtroom hall after we started the day's proceedings. I wanted the jury to see Sandy struggle to lug the large ladder into the courtroom to emphasize Jenny's prudence in attempting to take immediate evasive action in the Mesa rather than simply electing to run it over.

She brought it forward, through the swinging wooden doors of the courtroom, towards the front of the room. While not particularly heavy, since it was made of aluminum, it was nonetheless difficult to carry due to its size and bulk. I stepped through the swinging wooden rail section and helped her carry it the last twenty feet. We spread its legs and stood it upright on the far side of the courtroom in plain view of the jury.

"That's it," Cargill said as I walked over and marked it with an exhibit sticker. It looked oddly ominous as it stood there in its damaged condition. Its bouncing on the roadway had bent its legs slightly to one side. The jury took an interest in the object that had started the deathly series of events, which brought all of us here today.

"Mr. Cargill, as part of your experience over the decades that you investigated accidents for the Highway Patrol, did you study the subject of human perception and human reaction to roadway perils?"

"Objection," Harrington said, "Mr. Cargill is not qualified to give opinions in the area of human factors, Your Honor."

"I disagree," Vaughn responded, not even waiting for my counter argument, "the witness served as an accident investigator for literally decades. Reviewing and assessing roadway perils and the driver's reaction to those accidents is something that strikes me as inherent in what he did. Would that be correct, sir?" Vaughn asked, as he spoon fed Cargill the question. Vaughn looked down to Cargill who was seated to Vaughn's right in the witness box. The jury, in turn, was to the right of the witness.

For once, I pleasantly realized, Vaughn's conservative philosophy was working in my favor. The man loved police, and Cargill had demonstrated that he had earned his police stripes. The optimism the judge's attitude had unexpectedly given me, however, was almost as suddenly dashed when I remembered that this same philosophy might backfire against me when Martelli took the stand.

"Yes, you would," Cargill answered, turning to more directly face The Turtle. "I also taught that whole subject area to new patrol investigators in the patrol and accident investigation courses I referred to earlier."

"Very well, objection overruled. Proceed," Vaughn said, as he swung his right arm permissively in a short arc.

"Based on that experience, do you have an opinion as to whether Jenny Hawkins took appropriate responsive reaction in attempting to swerve to avoid that ladder?" I said, pointing to the gray ladder across the room.

"Without question, her actions mirrored what the normal driver would have done when suddenly confronted with that large metal structure, and without warning, flying towards her from the back of the truck in front of her. And remember," he added, looking at the jury, "this all happened in the matter of a second or so. She would not have had the luxury that all of us have sitting here in this courtroom to dissect the wisdom of what action to take, or not take. She had to react and do so immediately. She did just that by swerving sharply to her right to avoid hitting it."

"Would you describe what occurred from that point on according to your review of the case?"

"The testimony had her in the middle of the three eastbound lanes on the interstate when the ladder first came at her. She immediately swerved to her right, that is, to the south, in order to get over. It appears that to do that, she turned the steering wheel sharply to her right in a controlled but very quick fashion."

"From your analysis, did she hit her brakes?"

"She may have started to, but I wouldn't have expected that. Slowing down her vehicle would have acted contrary to the first instinctive reaction she would have had, namely, to get away from the ladder. Also, remember that the Mesa didn't have ABS brakes. You can't steer a vehicle without ABS brakes if you slam on its brakes and lock the wheels."

"Are you critical of her not hitting her brakes, then, at the same time that she swerved sharply to her right?"

"No, not at all."

"Continue. I interrupted you."

"It was at that point that the eyewitness, Mr. Abadin, reported to the police officer, Officer Martelli, that he saw her Mesa start to act weirdly, in his words. I believe that what he was actually seeing was the Mesa's response to her sharp swerve to her right. I believe that it showed signs of significant instability and control at that point. It's likely that what Mr. Abadin was referring to was the first indication that the upper body of the Mesa actually started to sharply lean to its left. If the Mesa's right two wheels were not off the roadway

at that point, they were close to being so. Mrs. Hawkins was not able to control
the Mesa's unusual movements at that point, and she had to counter steer
sharply in the other direction, that is, to her left, which would be to the north,
in order to avoid hitting the concrete wall to her right."

I introduced enlarged blow-ups of photos of the four-foot concrete wall
that aligned the right shoulder of the interstate at the area of the accident. The
jury followed along with his explanation.

"What happened next?" I asked.

"The right front of her Mesa had made it to within three feet of the concrete wall to her right before she was able to quickly counter steer to her left to
avoid it. She had very quick reflexes, I might add, to do that. At that point ...
May I actually come down and demonstrate what I'm talking about in front of
the jury, Judge?" he suddenly asked up to Vaughn who was seated to his left. "I
think it would help them to better understand what happened there."

"If you believe that it would assist the jury, you're free to do so," he said. I
could see that Vaughn appreciated being asked for permission by the witness.

This is where Cargill's years of testifying in court hit pay dirt. He was eminently comfortable in the courtroom setting from his many years testifying for
the highway patrol, and he took full advantage of it. He reached into his briefcase and removed a small model of a utility vehicle which he had spray painted
primer gray. He stepped down and stood directly in front of the jury box, about
six feet away from them.

I walked over and pulled another large four-foot by four-foot foam board
exhibit from the stack I had leaning against the wooden railing behind my table.
It contained a scaled overhead colored photo of the accident scene which
Cargill had prepared for trial. It was taken from a helicopter at an elevation of
two hundred feet and showed the three eastbound lanes, the four-foot barrier
wall aligning the right shoulder, and the left shoulder and grassy median where
the Mesa eventually came to rest. Harrington had stipulated to its accuracy before trial.

"Would this scaled photo of the accident scene help out?" I asked.

"That would be very helpful," he answered as I placed it on an aluminum
easel directly in front of the jury.

He stood directly in front of the large photo. "As I indicated, her first reaction was to swerve sharply to her right," he repeated, moving the model vehicle to the right in the lanes on the photo in simulation of the actions of
Jenny's Mesa. "She was not able to control the Mesa and keep it on the roadway to her right when she did that. In order to avoid the hazard of hitting the
concrete wall we see here to the right, she was forced to steer sharply to her
left," he said, again demonstrating with the small model. "When she did that,

my reconstruction reflects that her Mesa's instability got worse, much worse. As the nose of the Mesa turned sharply to her left, towards the grassy median on her left, which separated the three lanes of eastbound interstate traffic from the westbound three lanes, the body of the Mesa didn't react in a controlled fashion. Rather, in response to her sharp counter-steer to the left, the body of the Mesa rocked and its two left-side wheels lifted completely off the roadway." He emphasized his point by lifting the left side of the model up from the surface of the photo to simulate the movement of the Mesa.

The jury continued to follow along closely. All eyes were focused on the model he was holding. Cargill had spent a total of maybe ten dollars for the simple model he was using. It would be a far cry from the fancy, expensive computer animation of the accident which PhD. Lee Quarles had put together for Global.

"When you say that the two left wheels of the Mesa lifted off the roadway, what exactly do you mean?" I asked to drive the point home.

"I mean the Mesa started its rollover."

"When does a rollover *start*, as you say?"

"Well, according to strict engineering principles, a rollover starts only when the roll angle of the vehicle becomes so large that the center of gravity of the vehicle passes outside of the line of contact of the outside wheels of the vehicle. That definition," he said, smiling at the jury as he saw the eyes of a couple of jurors in front of him start to glaze over, "kind of makes your head hurt." Three of the jurors chuckled. "In simple layman's terms, a rollover starts whenever the vehicle's inside wheels experience wheel lift from the roadway below since the vehicle becomes inherently unstable at that point. The speed at which the completion of the rollover occurs after wheel lift is very quick. Short of an expert driver behind the wheel, the average human driver simply cannot counter steer fast enough to bring the two wheels back down and avoid a roll."

I glanced over at Harrington. He was doodling on the legal pad in front of him, doing his best to act bored.

"Once the rollover started, what happened next?" I asked. He and I were acting like two guys having an interesting chat over a beer at the corner pub, and there wasn't a damn thing that Harrington could do at this point to disrupt our flow.

"Well, as I mentioned, the Mesa had turned to the left and was now coming back across the three eastbound lanes when this wheel lift started. Its front bumper was just about even with the left asphalt shoulder when its left wheels lifted and the rollover started." He again demonstrated using the photo in front of the jury. "At that point, while the nose of the Mesa was pointed towards the grassy median separating the eastbound lanes from the westbound lanes, it was also skidding and rolling to its right due to the Mesa's own inertial forces. Once the rollover started, there was nothing that Mrs. Hawkins could do to prevent it. It rolled quickly onto its right side and then onto its roof. However," he said, raising his pointer finger on his left hand to emphasize the point, "the Mesa has a well-defined roof line. When the roll got to the roof, its geometry actually caused it to be flung vertically into the air as it continued its rotation. It landed with a great deal of violence on the driver's side and then completed its roll by ending up rolling back onto its four wheels. That's when it came to a complete rest."

"How high off the ground did the Mesa get when it rolled onto its roof?"

"I believe it reached a good three feet. That was a function of the geometry of the roof line acting in response to the momentum of the vehicle."

Harrington got up and walked over to the water cooler which was located along the far wall of the room, directly across from the jury. He was attempting to subtly suggest to the jury that the witness was not worth listening to.

"And how did the fire happen?"

Cargill nodded his head, as if I had asked a good question that needed answering. "Do you see this concrete pad here in the middle of the grassy median?" he asked, pointing to the photo. "It was installed at that location only a few weeks before the accident. It was going to serve as the support base for a large road sign that is still on order by the state. If you look closely," he said, pointing the jury's attention to the detail on the large photo, "you can see the raised bolts that are embedded within its concrete to accept the bolting of the base of the sign, when installed. That support base is 18 inches square by twelve inches tall. When the Mesa came down during the roll and landed on the driver's side, its rear quarter panel happened to land squarely on that concrete base. The force of the landing on that base caused the sheet metal of the Mesa to crush inwards about fifteen inches. That crushing induced a metal attachment that held the neoprene filler tube to the side of the gas tank to pull loose, allowing gasoline and fumes to escape. Ignition occurred when they came into contact with the hot muffler pipe. From that point on," he said, somberly, "simple gravity took over. The slowly escaping gas continued to spill downward from the leak, feeding the flames."

"Were you able to determine why Jenny Hawkins was not able to free herself from the Mesa during the fire?"

"Yes. When the Mesa landed on the driver's side during the rollover, the driver's door was pushed inward from the crush. During the rollover, she had apparently moved her left leg back towards the door for support. She probably did it reflexively," he added. "Her left foot and ankle were located between the side of her driver's seat and the inner panel of the door when it landed on the driver's side. The inward crush of the door trapped her lower left leg against the seat, effectively … effectively imprisoning her in that vehicle when the fire erupted."

I let his last comment sink in for a moment before asking him my final question. The chubby older female juror had the flat palm of her right hand resting on her upper chest and neck, reflecting the horror of Jenny's predicament that Cargill was describing.

"Mr. Cargill, based upon your reconstruction, was there anything that Jenny Hawkins could have physically done to have avoided her accident, her rollover, or her incineration in that vehicle?"

"Absolutely nothing."

"Thank you, sir. Your witness," I announced to Harrington as I looked at the jury and took my seat.

"Mr. Harrington?" Judge Vaughn said.

"Thank you, Your Honor," Harrington replied as he strode confidently to the podium with his black four-inch-thick cross-examination binder.

"Accident reconstruction involves a great deal of engineering knowledge, does it not, Mr. Cargill?" he asked. His tone was even, with no sense of baiting.

"Yes. I would agree with that."

"From what university did you obtain your engineering degree?" he asked, equally evenly.

"I don't have an engineering degree, Mr. Harrington. Any knowledge and expertise that I have acquired has been through my on-the-job training and experience for over two decades doing this type of work, along with the dozens of specialized courses I've attended over the years." Cargill kept his response professional, with no hint of any defensiveness.

"So, you have no engineering degree, yet you are working in an area that requires an accurate understanding and application of engineering concepts and principles, is that right?"

"Yes."

"I see," was Harrington's only response. He was making no attempt to mask his incredulity.

"Would I also be correct that over the many years that you have engaged in your work, you never authored even one scholarly publication in any recognized engineering or accident reconstruction publication dealing with the subject of accident reconstruction?"

"That's correct. However, I did submit one article a few years ago."

"And that was to the S.A.E.—the Society of Automotive Engineers, correct?"

"Yes."

"That's a very prestigious organization that publishes extensive technical papers on motor vehicles, as well as accident reconstruction theory and principles, isn't it?" Harrington's tone was slowly ratcheting up in subtle sarcasm.

"That's true."

"Probably the foremost recognized professional association that publishes in that area in the world?"

"Yes."

"And, incidentally, the 'E' in S.A.E. stands for engineering, doesn't it?"

"You're correct."

"And you're not a degreed engineer, right?"

"Objection, Mr. Harrington has been over that ground once before, Your Honor."

"Sustained. Move along, counsel," The Turtle ordered. Harrington had made his point, however.

"The S.A.E. refused to publish the article that you submitted, didn't they?"

"I don't know if I would be quite as strong as you put it, but the S.A.E. chose not to publish it. I don't know if they felt that it was merely repetitious of previous articles, which had been published on the same topic as mine, or what."

"Let's talk about the *or what*. Isn't it true that the S.A.E. actually informed you that they provided a copy of your article to a peer review sub-committee for their professional critique and assessment."

"I do recall that, yes."

"And your *peers* who reviewed your submission, were engineers, weren't they?"

"I would imagine," he said, keeping his calm demeanor.

"And your *peers* who read your article didn't believe that it was worthy of publication, did they?" Harrington was obviously enjoying his screw tightening.

"I don't know what their thinking was. All I was told was that the S.A.E. chose not to publish my article. Only about twenty percent of the articles submitted every year are actually chosen by the S.A.E. for publication. They try to publish only new and innovative topics or treatment of existing topics. I wasn't shocked when they chose not to publish my submittal," he answered matter-of-factly.

"I see. Now, you also mentioned as part of your qualifications as an *expert*, did you not, that you taught the accident reconstruction course every few years for the Pennsylvania Highway Patrol?"

"Yes."

"Sir, I don't mean to split hairs, but in the interest of full and accurate disclosure, isn't it true that the actual title of that course was: 'Techniques in Traffic Accident *Investigation*'?" emphasizing the last word.

"I believe that you are correct, although I don't really understand your comment about 'full and accurate disclosure.'" Cargill was starting to show irritation in his responses.

"Sir, you know that there is a big difference between traffic investigation and accident reconstruction, don't you?" The very tone of his question suggested to the jury that Cargill had somehow been less that fully forthright in his earlier description of his experience and qualifications. "Isn't it a fact that traffic accident investigation, which you taught, is a much broader subject area than the more precise and disciplined area of accident reconstruction?"

"One is a subset of the other as far as I am concerned. I had to be knowledgeable with respect to both areas to teach the class." He was put off by the question.

"Well, the proclamation that you actually received from the Governor of Maryland stated that it was to acknowledge your contributions in the area of traffic accident *investigation*, isn't that true?"

"Yes, that's what the award actually said in the typed words, but it was understood by everyone involved to be an award for my accident *reconstruction* accomplishments."

"But it doesn't say that on its face, does it, Mr. Cargill?" As he asked the question, Harrington pulled a photocopy of the written proclamation from his binder. He had obviously had one of his investigators obtain a copy from the State of Maryland. He was leaving no stone unturned.

"Sir," Cargill responded with growing irritation, "I will concede that it uses the words 'traffic accident investigation' on the face of that award, just as you can see from the proclamation you are reading from in front of you there."

"And, yet, you are here this morning to testify to this jury that you have correct *reconstruction* opinions and conclusions regarding what happened in this accident, aren't you?"

"I am here to give this jury my opinions as to the accident reconstruction facts, Mr. Harrington, based upon the benefit of my experience. And I believe that my opinions are correct. The evidence is very clear," he said, starting to sound defensive. "Mrs. Hawkins was not speeding. She was going only fifty-two to fifty-five miles per hour at the time. My investigation establishes that she did everything humanly possible to try to maintain control of her Mesa, yet the Mesa's instability caused it to roll over despite her efforts." Cargill's rising irritation with the line of questioning was showing a steely edge, which had not existed on my direct exam.

"Well, let's see if we can dig into some of those opinions of yours, Mr. Cargill," Harrington said, leafing to a new page of carefully crafted questions in the black binder laying on the podium in front of him.

A couple of jurors were looking at each other, obviously interested in Harrington's cross.

"With respect to your speed estimate of fifty-two to fifty-five miles per hour, you relied, in part, upon the eyewitness testimony of Mr. Abadin. Isn't that right?"

"Yes."

"Are you aware, sir, that Mr. Abadin, upon whose observations your opinions are premised, sat in the very seat you are sitting in now and told this jury that it's possible that he may not have been only one hundred feet behind her when he made his supposed observations, but, instead, could have been *the length of a football field* away from her Mesa!" he asked, phrasing the question as a declarative statement, instead.

Because the court had ordered the attorneys and their clients not to tell upcoming witnesses what the testimony was of the earlier witnesses before them, Harrington knew that Cargill was clueless as to this important fact.

"No, I'm not," Cargill conceded, "but I'm aware of his deposition testimony in which he was quite emphatic about what he saw, sir. And, in any event," Cargill continued, seeking cover, "even at the farther distance of around three hundred feet, his line of sight would have been very good to have seen the gross vehicle movements, which he has testified to. I did confirm with him that he has 20\20 eyesight, and he appears to be a responsible young man."

Harrington looked down and slowly shook his head back and forth, like a parent listening to the feeble excuses of his child being caught not doing his homework. "As an *expert* in the area of accident reconstruction, you certainly know that the studies show that eyewitness testimony is probably the most unreliable evidence an accident reconstructionist should rely on. Isn't that true?" He looked at the jury as he finished the question.

"I've read those studies, and they do say that. However, I'm not resting my opinions entirely on his eyewitness observations. Rather, I used his eyewitness observations *to confirm* what my own analysis of the vehicle dynamics concluded. The studies you refer to Mr. Harrington, especially the study by Arseneau, which is recognized as the best of those studies, emphasizes that confirmatory usage is the preferred use of such testimony. That's what I used Mr. Abadin's for."

"And yet, Mr. Abadin is a young man who has given *different* information in his deposition and to this jury, isn't he?"

"I will agree that he apparently gave a different estimate in his deposition than he gave in this courtroom as to the distance that his van was behind the Hawkins Mesa at the time of the accident. I think that is the only inconsistency you are referring to, Mr. Harrington. Nowhere did I see a substantive difference in what he said he saw."

"And in arriving at your opinions," Harrington asked, ignoring the witness's qualification, "I assume that you obtained and read the traffic accident homicide report, did you not?"

Here it comes, I mentally cringed.

"Certainly, that was one of the first things I did."

"Did you read it cover to cover, so to speak?" Harrington was toying with him.

"Yes."

"Then you noticed, did you not, that the officer in charge of that investigation, Trooper Anthony Martelli, concluded that Mrs. Hawkins' speed was not driving at fifty-two to fifty-five miles per hour, as you believe, but," he said with new emphasis, "*she was speeding at an estimated seventy-five miles per hour—*right?"

Harrington gazed over at the jury as he finished the question, looking for the effect that the much higher speed had on them. It was the first time in the trial that they had heard evidence of this high rate of speed. The retired owner of the dry cleaning business, I noticed, raised his eyebrows at the mention of the high rate of speed. He shot a glance at the juror next to him who likewise looked surprised at hearing the high rate of speed that the investigating police officer had found. Sandy caught their look as well, I could see.

"That was his opinion, correct," Cargill conceded. "I happen to think it is incorrect."

"The speed limit on I-595 at that area is *only fifty-five miles per hour*, right?" Harrington said, drawing the words out for dramatic effect.

"Correct."

"And there is a world of difference, in terms of vehicle dynamics, between the behavior of an SUV traveling at fifty-two to fifty-five miles per hour and that same SUV traveling *at seventy-five miles per hour*, isn't there, sir?"

"Yes, I would agree with that."

Harrington nodded, relishing the concession Cargill had given him.

"Sir, wouldn't you agree that the investigating officer who was at the scene and who conducted on the spot interviews and observations is in a much better position to determine the speed of the vehicles than you are, who weren't even there?"

"As a general proposition, if the investigating officer knows what he's doing, and has conducted the investigation in a thorough fashion, and if there are witness marks on the roadway, like skid marks, for example, that are not available to later experts, then I would agree with you. However, I don't believe that was the situation in this case. Officer Martelli, in my humble opinion, did not do a thorough job. He didn't even keep his log sheets, which reflected his actual reconstruction calculations. That is standard protocol, especially where the reconstruction is a difficult one like this one was. Additionally, there were no witness marks or other similar critical scene-related evidence, which he had available to him at the time of the accident that were not available to me after the fact."

"So, you're telling this jury that you're smarter than Trooper Martelli. Isn't that what you're really saying?" His voice reflected his disdain for the witness.

"No. You're not listening to me," Cargill said, curtly. "I'm saying that he wasn't particularly thorough on this one, that's all. I think it's probably a function of the fact that, as I understand it, he has only been doing accident reconstruction for two years now. This was a fairly difficult one to reconstruct, even for an experienced person."

"Mr. Cargill," he asked, gripping the sides of the podium in each of his hands as he leaned forward, "can we at least agree that if Mrs. Hawkins was going *seventy-five* at the time that the ladder fell, as Trooper Martelli concluded, she would have been speeding under Florida traffic laws?"

"Yes."

"By twenty miles an hour?"

"Yes."

"And at seventy-five miles per hour, if she made severe, out of control steering inputs into her steering wheel, can we also agree that those steering inputs could cause her to lose control of her Mesa, *even if* it was designed *perfectly*, from a stability standpoint?" His tone was laced with sarcasm.

"I object, Your Honor, there is no foundation in the record at this stage for Mr. Harrington's factual assumptions in his hypothetical question."

"Overruled. This is cross, counsel. You've got the burden of proof, not the defendant. I'm also assuming," The Turtle said, looking back at Harrington, "that he will prove up the assumptions in his question later in his case."

"That's correct, Judge," Harrington replied.

"Please answer the question, sir," the judge ordered. His deferential attitude towards Cargill was waning.

Cargill looked at the jury. "If you have me *assume* that she was going seventy-five miles per hour, and *assume further* that she started turning her steering wheel in *severe, out of control* ways, as you suggest, then I would agree with the general proposition that such a combination of factors can cause a driver to lose control of a utility vehicle like this."

"And a loss of control under those conditions would be true for even a *safe and well designed vehicle*, correct?" He was repeating his point to drill it into the jury.

"That's true. However," Cargill retorted, "while I'm not a design engineer, I still don't see why you would expect to see the wheels of a utility vehicle like Mrs. Hawkins' lift off the roadway like this one did, even under your assumed facts, which I don't believe existed in this accident."

"So, we're back to your reliance on the ability of Mr. Abadin to make accurate observations under excited circumstances from his vantage position about the length of a football field away, is that it?"

"I'm relying on what the man said he saw in his deposition," Cargill stubbornly persisted.

"Sir, you don't have a clue as to what that man testified to yesterday morning in this courtroom, do you?" It was not intended to be a question but a partial closing argument to the jury.

"I don't know what he testified to in this chair, counselor, other than what you have suggested. However, I do know that in his deposition testimony, he very clearly and unqualifiedly stated that he saw the two left side wheels lift off the road as the Mesa was moving across the roadway, and that she was not speeding. The rollover, he said, started while the Mesa was still on the highway."

"Would you defer to what he told this jury yesterday under oath?"

Cargill was showing irritation. "His testimony is his testimony. I guess the jurors will have to make their own determinations about what he saw or didn't see. All I know is that his earlier testimony in his deposition squares exactly with my reconstruction opinions in this case. The rollover *started* while the Mesa was *still on the roadway*, not when it got to the grassy median as you apparently want to suggest, sir." He raised his voice in emphasizing his opinion. Harrington was getting to him.

"Mr. Cargill," Harrington said, taking off his trial glasses and pointing them at the witness, "you're very sure of your opinions in this case, aren't you?"

"Yes, I am. I believe they correctly recap what the Mesa actually did in this accident, including the speeds in question."

"So, I take it that you don't feel that you made any mistakes in coming to *your opinions* in this case. Is that about right?"

"I'm confident that my reconstruction opinions are correct, if that's what you mean."

Harrington paused for a moment, looked at Cargill and then calmly turned and walked back to pick up a small folder of documents from the top of his counsel table. He put his tortoiseshells back on, walked back to the podium and looked again at the witness and then over to the jury.

"You're familiar with the case of *State of Pennsylvania vs. Congelio*, aren't you Mr. Cargill?"

"Yes, I recall that case." The jury and I both noticed the distinct hesitation in his response.

Harrington casually strolled around the area in front of the podium. I did my best to keep a poker face. I had never heard of the *Congelio* case, or of its significance, but I didn't like where this was going.

"For the jury's edification, that was a case in Pennsylvania about five years ago, wasn't it?"

"Yes," Cargill answered. His voice had suddenly lost the air of assurance it had held only seconds ago.

"And Mr. Congelio was charged with motor vehicular homicide in connection with a fatality involving an accident in Pennsylvania in which he was a driver of one of the cars, correct?"

"I'm going to have to object, Your Honor. This is all very interesting, but it bears absolutely no relevance to this case. Mr. Congelio, whoever he is, isn't on trial here."

"Overruled. I'm assuming that Mr. Harrington is about to link up its relevance. Am I correct?"

"You certainly are, Judge Vaughn," he answered, polishing the judge's apple.

"Go ahead and answer the question, Mr. Cargill," The Turtle instructed.

"That is correct. He was charged with speeding and driving recklessly, resulting in the death of his passenger."

"And when the State of Pennsylvania prosecuted Mr. Congelio for that charge, you were the accident reconstructionist who testified on behalf of the state in that criminal trial. Isn't that true?"

'*Oh ... shit*', my alarm systems sounded silently. I saw Sandy's nervous glance over to me.

"Yes," he answered rather quietly.

"And in that trial, you told *that jury* that based on your accident reconstruction that Mr. Congelio was, in fact, traveling at a speed of seventy miles per hour in a forty-five mile per hour speed zone—right?"

"Yes, I—"

Harrington cut him off, not allowing any explanation. "And the jury convicted him of criminal speeding and reckless driving, didn't they?"

"They did, but—"

"And he was sentenced to prison for a term of eighteen months, wasn't he?" Harrington was about to pounce.

"Yes."

Harrington turned and walked slowly towards the jury box. Stopping three or four feet short, he finally turned towards the witness, drawing out the jury's curiosity. He folded his arms across his chest.

"Mr. Cargill, isn't it true that while Mr. Congelio's case was on appeal, you discovered that you were *dead wrong* in your accident reconstruction?"

Cargill blinked twice before answering. "Mr. Harrington, I discovered I was wrong about one very important aspect of my opinion, yes." Cargill turned to face the jury himself. "I discovered that I had used the wrong coefficient of friction for the type of roadway that was involved in that accident. As a result, my ultimate opinions were in error. My error, I discovered, had overstated Mr. Congelio's speed by twenty-five miles per hour. His actual speed was forty-five, not seventy. The moment I discovered my error, I called the government attorney who had tried the case and let him know. He informed the trial court, and Mr. Congelio's conviction was reversed. He was freed from prison. It was an unfortunate error that I had completely overlooked. It should not have occurred," he admitted with sincere conviction to the jury.

Eric turned his head and looked over to me. He looked like I felt, which was like I had been hit in the solar plexus. I tried my best to keep cool since I could see a couple of the jurors quickly swivel their heads to catch my expression. I leaned over and whispered quietly to him. "This is all news to me, too, but do *not* lose your cool in front of this jury," I cautioned, keeping the expression on my face calm. "Now, turn and keep a poker face for the jury to see. I'll try to clean up some of the damage in redirect."

As I pulled back from whispering to Eric, I snuck a peak over at the jury to catch their reaction. The retired owner of the dry cleaning store suddenly crossed his arms, shook his head side to side and leaned back in his chair. The body language of a number of the other jurors was equally negative and dismissive.

"*Unfortunate ... unfortunate?*" Harrington mocked. "Well, your *unfortunate* error, as you call it, caused that jury to come to the wrong verdict, didn't it?" Harrington slashed. He was thoroughly enjoying the pounding he was giving.

"I believe it did. That's why I felt it necessary to disclose it to the government."

"And from an accident reconstruction standpoint, that was a colossal error you made in that case, wasn't it, sir?"

"It was a major error, yes," he admitted quietly. The wind had been sucked out of his sails.

"And I'll bet that you're just as sure of the accuracy of your opinions in this case as you were when you were sitting in front of the Congelio jury giving them erroneous opinions, Mr. Cargill, is that a fair statement?"

"Objection, Your Honor! He's being argumentative and sarcastic with the witness," I said, rising from my chair.

"I'll withdraw the question," Harrington said. The effect of his question had obtained its desired effect anyway with the jury. "I have nothing more for this ... *expert witness.*"

Harrington picked up his black binder, cast one last look of only mildly camouflaged disgust at the witness and headed for his seat.

"Could I see counsel at sidebar?" Vaughn asked. While he addressed the order to both lawyers, he was looking at me and my client when he said it. Eric, sitting next to me, was clearly upset, and even Vaughn could see it. We approached the bench, on the side opposite the jury box. In what was his first surprising bone to my case, The Turtle said, "Gentlemen, I need a smoke. Why don't we take a fifteen minute break so I can do that? Mr. Culhane," he also offered, "you can probably use that time to do a bit of ... uh ... bandaging for your rehabilitation of this witness."

Bandaging, I thought to myself. *It's more like CPR.*

"Thank you, Judge," I said, grateful for the bone he had thrown me. "This is a perfect time for a break." Harrington knew better than to object at the judge's professional largesse.

"Ladies and gentlemen," The Turtle announced, removing his black glasses and putting them on the bench before him, "we're going to take a fifteen minute break at this point for our morning recess. Don't discuss the case and be back here in fifteen minutes."

"WHY THE HELL didn't you at least tell me about the *Congelio* disaster?" I asked Cargill in one of the lawyer's conference rooms adjacent to the courtroom as soon as the door closed. "I could have at least addressed it during your direct examination and neutralized the devastating effect of Harrington bringing it out on cross like he just did."

"I forgot about it," Cargill answered, rubbing his flattop head of hair with his right hand. He was clearly upset about it and the damage that it had brought to this case. "I testified in maybe fifty cases since the *Congelio* case and it has never been even referred to at all. The public at large isn't really aware of it since the state's attorney I was dealing with handled it immediately with Mr. Congelio and his criminal defense attorney. I'm just amazed that Harrington would have been aware of it at all."

"Well, he was aware of it, and now so is this jury," I said shortly. "Okay," I tried to regroup, "it's water over the dam. What's done is done," I said, mouthing nothing better than the old clichés. "Let's focus on damage control and rehabilitation for the moment." Eric stood to the side as I spoke with Cargill. He was as upset as I was about the *Congelio* issue, but he let me handle it. He stayed out of it. So did Sandy.

Cargill and I spent the balance of the short recess going over areas that needed to be covered in redirect. I didn't try to fool myself. Harrington's cross was ruthlessly effective, and he knew it as well as I did. An objective review of his cross would reflect that he hadn't done much to challenge the substance of Cargill's opinions in this case. Instead, he had done what all good trial lawyers are trained to do in cross-examination if the opportunity presents itself: Throw an incredibly prejudicial ham bone on the table for the jury to chew on, even if it has little to do with the specific facts or testimony of the witness, in hopes that the jury will be irreparably poisoned in their overall assessment of the witness. The *Congelio* screw-up by Cargill was a big ham bone, and its taste was bitter for my case.

AFTER THE RECESS, I put Cargill back on and attempted rehabilitation. My focus was on the fact that since the *Congelio* case, as I had quickly learned during our discussion in the hall, he had instituted a practice of double-checking all of his underlying data as well as his conclusions. The jury listened attentively, but I wasn't going to kid myself. Cargill had been badly bloodied on cross.

Harrington didn't even bother to re-cross, a fact meant to signal to the jury his utter scorn for the witness and his opinions.

I finished the morning and the rest of the day reading testimony from the depositions of the Global engineers I had taken in Detroit. Though boring to the jury, reading the depositions was necessary in order to put important underlying engineering information into the court record. True to form,

Harrington refused my offer, made to Judge Vaughn at a sidebar, that we enter into a written stipulation of the many boring engineering facts which the Global engineers had conceded during their lengthy depositions. Harrington wanted to force me to read the lengthy depositions into evidence, thereby both boring and irritating the jury's patience and attention span.

One of the Global concessions, which I felt was key, was the admission I obtained from my deposition of Markov, the lead Global design engineer on the Mesa project, that Global had not run any separate S tests, or any other type of dynamic tests, prior to production approval, in order to evaluate the stability of the new Mesa model. They relied on what Markov kept stressing was *independent engineering judgment*, as well as pre-production computer-simulations of S tests utilizing the Mesa's engineering measurements and the like. As far as I was concerned, Global could talk about 'independent engineering judgment' until the cows came home. Without concrete, confirmatory pre-production tests in their pocket, they had exposure. Or so I was convinced.

CHAPTER 38

"DID OUR CASE get hurt today as much as I think it did?" Eric asked as he, Sandy and I sat in my office after returning from the courthouse. We were all flat from Cargill's cross.

"Yes, it did," I admitted, as I undid my tie. "The Congelio issue hurt a lot."

Sandy was sipping on a can of diet Coke as she was scrolling through her I-phone, looking at the day's emails that had piled up while we were at trial. She stopped and looked up. "I agree. The jury didn't care for that fact, at all."

"But it doesn't have a damn thing to do with his opinions in this case!" Eric argued.

I popped the top on a can of Coke and took a big swig. "Unfortunately, it has everything to do with this case, Eric," I reluctantly acknowledged. "Forget what your logical mind tells you. Juries often decide cases not on what the objective evidence is, but on what their gut instincts and hearts tell them. Hell, take a look at the O.J. murder trial for a classic example. I'm afraid we may have jurors who are going to dismiss Cargill's opinions as those of a man who's careless. People don't like careless experts."

Eric shook his head back and forth in disgust and frustration. "So, what do we do to correct it?"

"We've done all that we can to rehabilitate Cargill's accident reconstruction opinions. Let's just hope that we have a forgiving jury that can set aside his screw-up in the Congelio case and evaluate the merits of his opinions in this case. On that aspect, he did a nice job. Harrington threw some nice body punches, but he didn't land any knockout blows to Cargill's opinions in this case, at least from what I saw."

"No, I think that he did okay fending himself off on the merits of the cross-examination," Sandy added. "The owner of the hardware store and the teacher, I noticed, were paying pretty close attention to his testimony on direct."

"Well, what's done is done," I finally shrugged. Putting the Coke down, I rolled up my sleeves. "We've got Carole Merton first thing tomorrow morning, followed by Dr. Braxton to give his opinions on the design issues. He's the most important witness we've got on the liability issue."

"He's in town," Sandy said. "Tina left me a note saying that his plane got in around four o'clock this afternoon. He's checked in at the Marriott off 17th Street, and he's going to be here tonight around seven o'clock to do some final preparation with you for tomorrow as you requested, Mike."

We sent Eric home for the night and ordered two pizzas to be delivered for us and Braxton. It was going to be another late one. Braxton arrived at my office a little after seven, and the three of us spent the next three hours going over his direct examination and anticipated areas of cross. He was as ready as he was going to be. I hoped it was enough. We had ground to make up.

CHAPTER 39

"GOOD MORNING LADIES and gentlemen." The Turtle greeted the assembled jurors the next morning. All of them were on time today. "Are you ready with your next witness, Mr. Culhane?" he asked, impatiently. He had barely waited for the jury to take their seats the next morning when he asked the question. Forced to handle an emergency motion in another case earlier that morning, he was in a foul mood. The motion hearing had rattled his anal-retentive fixation on keeping his trial schedule moving.

"Yes, your honor. The plaintiffs call Carole Merton."

The young woman rose from the front row of seats behind the rail and came forward to be sworn in. Dressed in black slacks, a yellow blouse and a wrist laden with a silver charm bracelets, Merton was in her early 30s, intelligent looking and articulate. Her direct exam was short. She related how she had been driving eastbound on I-595 on the afternoon of the accident. She remembered passing Jenny's Mesa about five miles before what proved to be the accident site. She explained how she remembered passing her because she had been interested in possibly buying a Mesa herself, and she liked the color of Jenny's. The fact that she happened to see the film footage on the television the evening of the accident was fortuitous and helped her remember passing Jenny's SUV, she testified. When I asked her the home-run question, that is, whether Jenny was speeding at that point in time, Harrington pounced.

"Objection, Your Honor, relevance. Her speed five miles earlier in the trip is not relevant to her speed at the time of the accident. People change speed on a trip all the time."

The Turtle quickly reprimanded Harrington. "I don't want any speaking objections in front of my jury, counsel," he said sternly, looking at Harrington. "Sidebar now," he ordered. We both immediately obeyed and met him on the side of his bench, opposite the jury box.

"Your Honor," I countered in a whispered tone, "we're only talking a distance of five miles and only a few minutes between her firsthand observation and the accident. I believe the relevance is clear." I needed this evidence to bolster the discredited testimony of Abadin and to substantiate the bruised speed opinion of Cargill.

The Turtle weighed the issue for a few seconds, then ruled. "I'm going to permit her to answer the question, but I'm going to give the jury a cautionary instruction."

Not wanting to anger the beast, I nonetheless disagreed with his ruling and had to document my objection for the record. "Your Honor," I responded, "if you give a cautionary instruction, that is tantamount to telling the jury that they might just as well ignore what the witness is saying. I must object to any such instruction."

"Judge, Global stands by its objection to any of this testimony being allowed into evidence, but if you allow it in, it would be an error if you failed to give an instruction. Your instincts in issuing a cautionary instruction were absolutely correct," Harrington brown-nosed.

"I've heard enough, gentlemen," he ruled, pinching his second chin with the stubby, sausage-like fingers of his right hand. "The instruction will be given. You've made your record, Mr. Culhane."

I returned to the podium, with Harrington returning back to his table.

"Ladies and gentlemen," The Turtle instructed, clearing his throat, "I'm going to permit Ms. Merton to answer the last question posed, which asked her to tell you what approximate speed Mrs. Hawkins' vehicle was travelling when Ms. Merton saw her five miles back up the road. However, while I'll allow her to answer, I must instruct you that you should weigh her testimony very carefully. The speed that the Mesa was travelling five miles before the accident, while relevant, is not necessarily indicative of the speed that it was traveling at the time of the accident. Remember, it is her speed at the time of the accident that is relevant here, and oftentimes people driving cars change their speed on the roadway." He swiveled and now looked back at me standing at the podium and then over at Merton.

"Go ahead, ma'am. Answer the question," he instructed her.

Merton didn't understand the procedural niceties that she had just observed. Neither did the jury, I thought. What they did know is that whatever Merton was about to tell them carried a negative footnote as to its worth, all compliments of The Turtle.

"I'd say she was travelling right at the speed limit of fifty-five," she answered. "I was going about sixty myself and I passed her vehicle without any problem."

"Thank you," I said, "nothing further."

Harrington's cross was short.

"Ms. Merton, isn't it true that you didn't specifically recall seeing Mrs. Hawkins and her child in a Mesa. In other words, from what I heard you say, I gather you are telling this jury that you saw a Mesa just like the accident Mesa about five miles before the accident site and you have *assumed* that it was the Hawkins Mesa?"

She fidgeted in her chair before answering. "As I told you at my deposition, I can't swear that it was Mrs. Hawkins in the Mesa that I saw. All I know is that I do remember seeing an identical Mesa and that there was a young woman and what looked like a bunch of boxes in the cargo area of that SUV. I didn't see any baby or baby seat. I've always assumed that it was her."

Harrington picked up a sheet that was on his desk.

"Would it surprise you to know that this is a print-out of all identical colored Mesa utility vehicles in the State of Florida, and that there are thirty-eight identically-colored Mesas registered in South Florida alone?"

"No, I wouldn't know anything like that," she answered.

"So, you would concede that *your assumption*, that it was Mrs. Hawkins in the Mesa you saw, could be wrong?"

She nodded slowly. "I suppose that could be true, yes."

"And if it was another Mesa that you saw, its speed has no relevance to the issues that this jury here is being asked to decide?" He pointed his tortoise-shelled specs towards the jury to make his point.

"Yes, that's true, too."

"Thank you, ma'am," he ended.

I offered no re-direct. She left the stand and nodded politely to me as she passed.

The Turtle wasted no time as ringmaster.

"Who is your next witness, Mr. Culhane?"

"The plaintiffs call Dr. Hubert Braxton to the stand," I said, turning towards the rear of the courtroom where Sandy had gone in the hall to bring him into the courtroom to take the stand.

The jurors' heads turned in unison to watch Braxton walk through the courtroom doors and make the walk up the aisle and through the double-swinging wooden rail doors. He stopped in front of The Turtle's bench long enough to be sworn in by the clerk, after which he stepped up the two short steps and sat down in the witness chair.

If there were a stereotype for a college professor, Braxton was it. He wore a black and gray tweed sports jacket over a barely pressed white shirt, which was complemented by a baby blue tie that didn't even pretend to match the colors in the tweed jacket. *Gentleman's Quarterly* he wasn't. His ruddy face was capped by a full head of thick, tousled salt and pepper hair. The effect of the absent-minded professor was made complete by the six inches of assorted, loose papers and notes he carried to the witness stand with him in his left hand. He had made no attempt whatsoever to organize them into any folders or binders. A few of the papers were wrinkled and crumpled, with a few bundled sideways in the mess. In his right hand, he carried a large, brown paper shopping bag with two large handles, with the words "GAP" on its exterior. Its contents were bulky and obviously heavy. It apparently was what he considered the equivalent of a briefcase.

Over the first half hour, I had him recount his background and experience to the jury. In his heavily-accented Massachusetts' voice, he informed the jury of his master's degree in engineering and his doctorate in physics. He pointed out that he chaired the engineering department at the college where he had taught upper level physics courses to undergraduate students, master's degree students and doctoral candidates for almost twenty years. His one hundred thirty scholarly publications were all in the field of dynamics and kinetics which he described as the study of the motion of objects and the forces that act upon them. His *pièce de résistance*, he noted with some pride, was authoring a chapter in a well-known, well used advanced physics textbook, which dealt with solving complex equations of motion.

"Have you designed any motor vehicles over the years, Doctor Braxton?" I asked, hoping to defuse some of Harrington's anticipated cross-examination regarding his credentials.

"Only indirectly," he replied. "My publications in dynamics and kinetics address the same principles and laws of physics that every motor vehicle designer would have to use. Also, I should note that in the mid-80s I served as a consultant to *Consumers' Review* on their evaluation of the handling of new motor vehicles that they would review periodically."

"How did that come about?"

"One of my former students left the automotive design field and took the position of lead editorial writer for that magazine's automotive section. He asked me to provide him with my evaluations, from a handling standpoint, of new cars that the magazine would assess." The female school teacher on the jury smiled warmly at him. He smiled back.

"Have you served as an expert witness in other courtrooms in the area of motor vehicle design?" I asked.

"Yes, I have been qualified as an expert on the design of vehicles as it pertains to handling and stability in three other cases that went to trial."

After walking through his other credentials, I moved directly to his opinions in this case. I wanted to hit the jury with his key opinions before they started dozing off.

"Have you evaluated the design of the Mesa utility vehicle from the standpoint of its handling and stability in this case?"

"Yes, I did so at your request," he said.

"And do you hold any opinions to a reasonable degree of certainty, Dr. Braxton, with respect to its stability and handling?"

"I do."

"What are those opinions, sir?"

"I object, your honor!" Harrington shouted, registering his first objection with this witness. He stood to make this objection. "This man doesn't have the competency to give expert opinions in the area of motor vehicle design. He's a college professor, not a design engineer."

The Turtle's hooded eyes appeared to shift over to Harrington. "Do you wish to *voir dire* the witness on the issue of competency and qualifications?" *Voir dire* of a witness was a tool that allows the opposing attorney, out of turn, to ask preliminary questions to an opposing witness that are aimed at some element of competence, or lack thereof. If those questions elicit admissions showing that the witness is not legally competent to give the opinions that he or she seeks to give, the judge can, and will, disqualify the witness and preclude the opinions from being given. Harrington was using the tool as a soapbox upon which he could tarnish the witness's opinions, even if he was technically found to be competent to give them. I had to begrudgingly acknowledge that it was a smart tactical move on his part.

"I sure do," he said with aggression in his voice. He stood up and walked to the podium. I took a few steps back and leaned against the edge of my table, arms crossed, allowing him to pose his *voir dire* questions.

"Isn't it true, sir, that you have never designed *any* component in *any* motor vehicle at *any* time?"

Braxton tugged at the lapels of his tweed jacket as he answered. "That's technically correct. However, I have taught mechanical engineering courses for the last twenty years, including the subject of mechanical design. The principles of design are universal, Mr. Harrington, and they apply whether one is designing an SUV or a skateboard."

"Well, even if this jury accepts that statement as true, the fact is that you haven't designed even one product of any type, have you sir? And that includes skateboards, doesn't it?" he countered.

"No, I haven't. I haven't experienced the need to do so."

"In fact, you can't point to even the simplest component of the simplest product that you've ever personally designed, can you?"

"As I just said, that's correct." Braxton was keeping his cool, although like most professors who are insulated in their academic towers, he didn't like having his credentials or his expertise challenged.

"Have you ever taught automotive design courses?" Harrington persisted.

"Again, as I mentioned, automotive design, though perhaps more complex than, say, designing sewing machines, must use the same basic principles of design. The designer must identify the function that the product is intended to serve, must determine the most efficient means of building a product which performs those functions in a cost effective manner, and must identify and address any dangers and risks that are reasonably expected to surface from the use of that product." He was completely comfortable, as if he were teaching Design 101 to a freshman class. "That means," he continued, "designing the product in such a way as to design out those dangers altogether, if reasonably possible, and if not, to design in guards or warnings to alert the person using the product to those dangers if it is determined that the product is safe enough with those dangers to still produce." He sat back in his chair, relaxed at his explanation.

"Thank you for that explanation, professor. However, that wasn't my question."

"I object. Mr. Harrington is arguing with the witness, your honor," I said.

"Overruled. This is *voir dire*. I allow free rein," Vaughn ruled. "Go ahead, Mr. Harrington."

"Please answer my question, sir. You haven't taught even one course on *automotive* design, have you?"

"No."

Harrington just shook his head back and forth, in feigned incredulity over the witness's credentials. He finally raised both hands, in a pleading gesture to the court. "Your honor, based on that *voir dire*, I must reiterate my previous objection to this witness being qualified as an expert to give expert testimony regarding *any* aspect of motor vehicle design, whether stability or otherwise."

"Gentlemen, let me see both of you at the sidebar," Vaughn ordered. His growing impatience at having to sidebar us on an ongoing basis was apparent.

"Mr. Culhane," Vaughn whispered after Harrington and I were assembled to his side, "I know that Florida law is increasingly liberal as to who can qualify as an expert witness in a case like this. However, I have serious doubts about this man's expertise in the area of actual design. My god, by his own admission, the man hasn't even designed so much as a pencil sharpener. How can I let him sit here and give opinions dealing with complex automotive design? Don't you think that I'm merely inviting error to allow that?"

I had anticipated Vaughn's concern. "Not at all, Judge." I lifted the pages of my legal pad and withdrew a copy of a case that I had inserted there that morning. I handed it to him. "This is a copy of the *Riley* case, Your Honor. As you can see, it's a decision that came down from the Florida Supreme Court last year. In that case, the court ruled that in order to qualify as an expert witness in design, the witness is not required to have actually designed products himself. Rather, all that is required is that the witness, due to either experience or training, has demonstrated some specialized knowledge and competence in the area of design and its underlying principles. In the *Riley* case," I quickly barged ahead, not wanting to yield the floor until I had made my point, "the court ruled that a foundry worker with over twenty-five years of experience repairing large industrial ovens had sufficient specialized knowledge to give opinions on the safe design of oven-guarding devices. Here," I argued, "Dr. Braxton has demonstrated over twenty years of teaching proper design theory, for goodness sake. He holds engineering degrees in the very field he will be giving opinions in, the principles of motion and stability." Having given him all the legal precedent I felt was needed, I implored The Turtle, "With all due respect, your Honor, it would be an error for you *not* to allow him to testify. And that's not just me arguing that point; it's what our Supreme Court says." I then stepped back, allowing my argument to hopefully soak in.

Looking through his black-rimmed Coke bottle glasses, Vaughn quietly but quickly reviewed the head notes in the case I had handed him, squinting over the text of the case as he digested the ruling. As he read, I recognized that if he ruled against me on this point, the case was over since I had no other admissible evidence of design defect, expert or otherwise. I had to prove the existence of a design defect as part of my prima facie case, and Harrington knew it. With his mono-psychotic penchant for clearing his case docket, I was concerned that The Turtle would use this ruling to dismiss my case and thus be able to use the rest of his now-freed-up-time this week to move on to other cases and matters on his busy docket.

"I guess you're legally correct," he finally said after he finished reading the case, with what appeared to be some degree of disappointment in his tone. "However, I must tell you that I personally don't agree with this trend of liberality in expert qualifications that our Supreme Court has been permitting. It allows individuals like Dr. Braxton here to give expert opinions on matters in which they really don't have any proven experience. I think it's a great mistake," he lectured, "and such testimony only serves to confuse juries, but I guess I'm bound to follow it." He handed me back the case.

Internally, I gave a sigh of immense relief. *I could give a rat's ass what you personally think*, I thought to myself. "Thank you, Judge," is what I said. Harrington and I both walked back. Harrington resumed his seat.

"Motion is denied," Vaughn ruled after I was back at the podium. Then, in what must have been a stubborn desire to let the jury know his own personal views, Vaughn added an additional comment to the jury. "Ladies and gentlemen, throughout this trial, you will likely hear from a number of witnesses who take this stand and profess to be experts in any given area of expertise. I caution you that you, and you alone, are the sole arbiters of the weight or credibility of any witnesses who take this stand and give you expert testimony. You are free to accept or utterly reject the testimony or credentials of any so-called expert witness that the court allows to take the stand and give expert testimony."

The Turtle's unsolicited and unexpected comments to the jury lit my fuse.

"Oh, Your Honor," I said politely and evenly, trying not to exhibit my inner anger to the jury, "there is an additional matter that I neglected to bring to the court's attention at the previous sidebar. I must respectfully ask the court's indulgence to approach the sidebar once again for a moment with the court and opposing counsel."

Vaughn showed his great irritation at my request. We were eating into his precious schedule.

"Mr. Culhane, I'd prefer that you save it for the next break. We can make a record of whatever it is at that time," he said, dismissively.

"I'm afraid it is a rather pressing matter, your honor," I persisted. "Respectfully, it needs to be done now."

Harrington looked over, puzzled.

"Well, let's make it quick!" he ordered, again looking up at the wall clock.

I signaled the court reporter to bring her machine over in order to record our sidebar discussion. As soon as the three of us were at sidebar with Vaughn, I turned my full anger at The Turtle.

"Your Honor, I take great issue with what you just stated to the jury about them being 'free to reject the testimony of an expert.'" I kept my voice low but forceful. "That comment, which was entirely uncalled for, clearly signaled to this jury that you *personally* don't believe that Dr. Braxton's opinions aren't worthy of any credibility. That is extremely prejudicial and damaging to my clients' case. You made a similar instruction to the jury in connection with another of my witnesses, and the overall effect that all of these comments are having on this jury is to thoroughly discredit my witnesses!" I was hot, and I did not hide my Irish temper.

"That is—"

Vaughn cut Harrington off. He didn't need any help in responding to my comments. His eyes suddenly blazed with equal fire. "I take great issue, counsel, with your comments. My instruction to the jury was neutral and appropriate. My cautionary remarks applied to everyone's experts, not just yours! As far as the earlier witness you reference, I've already ruled on that one and I fully and adequately explained my ruling on that score. I will not allow you to revisit it and re-argue it again!"

I dug in. "I disagree. Timing and context has *everything* to do with the way the jury is going to take your comments. *They* think that your comments about experts are addressed to Dr. Braxton and Dr. Braxton alone. I think that you've poisoned the well of credibility for this witness. You leave me with no alternative but to move for a mistrial, and I so move."

I knew that my motion would ignite him. If granted, a mistrial erases the trial and allows the parties to retry the case, from day one, with a new jury. Judges absolutely hate to grant mistrials. Not only does a mistrial cause a major problem in their own schedule, but also, the granting of a mistrial is often an implicit admission that the trial judge screwed up in some fashion. Trial judges, like the rest of us, don't like to admit failure. They have to report them to their boss, the chief judge, since a mistrial impacts the court's budget.

"You are way off base on this counsel, and as far as I'm concerned, your comments border on contemptuous conduct! Your motion for a mistrial is denied!" His already full, fleshy face was further bloated and red with anger. "Do you have anything else you want to add?" It was not exactly an invitation but more of a challenge.

"Not yet," I shot back, barely camouflaging my anger.

"Good. Now get back and resume your questioning before I think twice and hold you in contempt!"

I nodded at him, biting my tongue from re-igniting the fire. Harrington turned away as well. He looked amused at the sudden fireworks and was staying the hell out of firing range.

The three of us returned to our positions. Harrington sat down at his table and leaned over to explain the sudden events with the Global female representative next to him.

I walked over to my table to pick up some notes for Braxton's direct exam. The jury had sensed from the animated discussion at sidebar that trouble was brewing and that I was the focus. The Turtle's face, still blotchy crimson from his fit, was also a clue.

"What was that all about?" Eric leaned over and asked, cupping his hand next to his mouth to prevent the jury from hearing our discussion. From his vantage point, Eric had been able to witness The Turtle's facial ire during the sidebar exchange, a treat not directly perceived by the jury.

"I'll tell you about it later," I said evenly. I headed back to the podium.

"Dr. Braxton," I resumed, "Judge Vaughn has recognized your qualifications to testify as an expert witness in this case. I believe you were about to give us the benefit of your opinions regarding the design of the Mesa."

"Yes. In simplest terms, the Mesa was badly designed from the standpoint of its stability. It wasn't designed or built to be able to safely handle reasonably foreseeable sudden steering inputs at lower highway speeds without exhibiting a propensity to roll over. As a result, the Mesa is unreasonably dangerous and defective." His response was short and sweet, just as it should be.

"Would you tell us why?" I invited.

"Well, I think the best way for me to answer that question is to first discuss what a safely designed vehicle should provide to its occupants."

"Go ahead."

He turned in his chair to face the jury directly. I could see that his many years of teaching were coming in handy since he was extremely comfortable in the setting of trying to enlighten others about esoteric engineering points.

"When most of us think about driving a vehicle, we tend to naturally think about the typical uses that we put our vehicle to: driving to and from work, driving over to friends for dinner, transporting bags of yard mulch in the trunk on the weekend, that type of thing. All of that driving is pretty normal and routine and doesn't usually involve any driving experiences that are particularly unique or challenging. However, the designers who design cars, vans and SUVs know that all driving is not of this controlled, normal type as I just described. Rather, the designers know that in the real world a certain percentage of vehicle drivers will be confronted with sudden driving emergencies and sudden uncontrollable events, which will present the vehicle being designed with unique handling and stability demands." He took a moment to sip from the cup of water in front of him. "For example, the designer knows—or should know, I should add," he corrected, "that some of these utility vehicles will be driven in Wisconsin in the wintertime and that some of those roadways will have large, unexpected patches of ice on them. Some of the vehicles, on the other hand, will be driven over high bridges on the coast of Oregon where they will be subjected to sudden gusts of very high winds. And yet some of these vehicles will be driven in wooded areas around this country and will be called upon during the course of the vehicle's useful life to suddenly be asked to aggressively swerve on a highway to avoid hitting a deer or another car that unexpectedly entered their lane."

"Would that reasonably-foreseeable driving environment," I injected, seeking to tie his comments into the facts of this case, "also include driving on Florida interstates?"

"Of course," he replied. "The point to be made from all of this," he continued, "is that these types of reasonably foreseeable events subject the vehicle to substantial and potential capsizing forces, as I refer to them. These capsizing forces act to directly challenge the stability of the vehicle. The vehicle must be designed to safely control and overcome these forces in a stable manner. If it isn't, the vehicle can end up losing control and rolling over in response to the driver's normal responsive actions in trying to deal with those reasonably foreseeable capsizing forces."

Still smarting from our sidebar fight, The Turtle was sitting in his chair, looking at the ceiling while Braxton spoke, with the fingers of his two beefy hands interlaced behind his bald head. He was making his personal opinion of the witness's testimony and credentials known to the jury.

"It's the job of the designer," Braxton continued, "to anticipate these types of capsizing forces and to design the specific vehicle on the drawing board in front of him so that it will remain controllable and stable on the roadway, and not roll over, when faced with these events and the capsizing forces which they produce." His Massachusetts' accident was heavy and added to his professorial demeanor.

"How does the designer accomplish that design goal of avoiding a loss of control and preventing rollover?" I asked.

He nodded, anticipating the question. "By putting together a carefully considered design," he responded. "You see, in its simplest terms, the ability of a vehicle—any vehicle for that matter—to properly control capsizing forces to avoid a rollover on a flat highway is essentially dependent on the design of three basic elements: the vehicle's *geometry*, that is, its height, width and weight; its *suspension system*; and its *tires*," he said, emphasizing the words. "All three of these separate components must be viewed as parts of but one single stability design system. If designed correctly, the vehicle should be able to confront capsizing forces of a flat roadway and permit the operator to avoid rolling over."

"Having said that, can you relate your analysis to the Mesa's specific design?" I needed to take his theory out of the clouds and back to this case.

"Yes, I can. In the case of the Mesa, its geometry component is a major problem. The vehicle is too tall and not wide enough. As a result, it is top heavy and unstable. In the automotive design field, there is what is referred to as a mathematical stability ratio, which designers use to arrive at a *quick check* of a vehicle's *rollover propensity*."

"And what are the variables in that ratio?" I asked, tossing him the soft-balls that we had rehearsed the night before.

"The height of the vehicle's center of gravity, or c.g. for short, and the width of the vehicle's track width." Seeing the confusion registering on the faces of the jurors, Braxton stopped to define the terms he was using.

"C.g. is a term that sounds more complicated than it really is," he said smiling to the jury. "Every object has mass to it, whether it is a car, a book or a human being. Mass is what gives an object weight and material substance. This chair I'm sitting on has mass, for example, as does that glass of water sitting over there on the table in front of Mr. Harrington."

Harrington kept a poker face as the jury, in unison, swiveled their heads to look at the water glass.

"A utility vehicle is no different," he lectured. "It has a great deal of mass as reflected by its steel, fluids and other components. The c.g. of any object is the central horizontal and vertical location on the object where its overall mass is most concentrated. On an SUV, for example, the c.g. is located in the middle of the vehicle, between the two front doors, and, from a vertical standpoint, is located about at the height of the seat bottoms. That is where the overall mass of the vehicle is centrally located." He took another sip from the glass of water in front of him.

"The *higher* the c.g. of a vehicle is off the ground, the easier it is to roll it over if a capsizing force is set upon it. Let me illustrate the principle," he said. He reached down and pulled two objects from the rumpled brown shopping bag at his feet. "It's the same concept as comparing a short, wide mouth jar of peanut butter, like the one I brought with me here," he said, putting it on the wooden ledge in front of him, "with a tall glass vase that happens to weigh the same as the jar of peanut butter." He pulled the tall, heavy glass vase from the bag as well. It was approximately ten inches tall; he set it on the ledge alongside the jar of peanut butter, which stood perhaps only five inches tall. "As I men-tioned, both of these items weigh the same. However, as you can see, the vase has a lot of heavy glass located at the elevation of its top. The c.g. of this jar of peanut butter is located about two and a half inches from the desk top here that it's sitting on, while the c.g. of the vase is located about five-and-a-half inches from the table beneath it. Now watch when I take the flat of my hand and push it sideways against the jar of peanut butter at the top of its rim."

As he did so, the jar merely slid sideways, with no tendency to tip over.

"Now, let's apply the same lateral push against the taller vase, with my hand pushing against the top of the vase." As he did so, the vase immediately tipped over and fell in the direction of his pouch. He caught it with his other hand before it hit the rail top.

I noticed juror heads nodding. They were getting it.

Braxton was enjoying his 'class.' "What you are witnessing, in simplistic but accurate terms, is the significance of the stability role that the c.g. height of an object has on its ability to ward off a side-thrusting capsizing force. This very same phenomenon applies to the design of motor vehicles. The auto company designers should be designing the vehicle so that its c.g. is as low as possible, consistent, of course, with the intended function and purpose of the vehicle in order to make that vehicle, like our peanut butter jar here, if you will," he said smiling, "as resistant to tip-over, or rollover, as is reasonably possible. The stability ratio I referred to earlier is a fairly simple mathematical formula, which is aimed at arriving at a *quick check*, from a design standpoint, to assess a vehicle's overall rollover tendencies taking into account, in a mathematical way, this little c.g. experiment I just demonstrated for you. The formula itself is known as the 't over 2h' formula, meaning that you take the track width of the vehicle—that is, the distance between the centerline of the left-side tires and the centerline of the right side tires—and divide that number by two times the vertical height of the vehicle's c.g. The resulting quotient gives the engineer a very rough numerical indicator as to the vehicle's rollover propensity."

While technical in content, jurors were following him.

"Is there any resulting 't over 2h' numerical quotient that tells the designer if a particular vehicle under consideration is safe versus unsafe from a stability standpoint?"

He nodded. "Over the years, certain general ranges or guidelines have evolved in the industry. The higher the quotient number, the less prone the vehicle is to rollover. For low-slung sports cars, for example, which have a very low c.g., you will typically see rollover quotient in the range of one-point-two Gs, meaning that it requires lateral forces as high as one-point-two to one-point-seven Gs to cause that vehicle to begin to tip over. For heavy semi-trucks, on the other hand, which are built to pull very tall trailers to haul cargo having a very high c.g., the rollover threshold for them is as low as point-four to point-six Gs. In short, they will tip very easily due to their height and relatively narrow width."

"What is the industry range for an acceptable rollover threshold for utility vehicles of the type that the Mesa would fall within?"

"Objection" Harrington finally rose from his chair. He had enough and needed to disrupt the nice flow and rapport that Braxton was having with the jury. "There has been no testimony whatsoever by the professor here that these various numerical ranges, which he has been talking about, whatever their supposed worth, are viewed as acceptable or unacceptable in the industry. He's not even involved as a designer in the auto industry!"

"I'm sustaining that objection," Vaughn growled.

"Let me be more precise," I countered and clarified. "From the reported engineering literature in the industry, would you tell us what is the range of numbers utility vehicles, as a group, have demonstrated when this rollover threshold formula has been applied to them?"

"The t over 2h analysis for utility vehicles has resulted in a range of point-nine Gs to one-point-one Gs."

"Did you apply this threshold formula to the Mesa?" I asked, casually glancing over at the jury. To my relief, they were still paying attention.

"I did."

"And where did the Mesa end up?" I asked.

"At point-eighty-eight, which is below the very bottom of the industry range," he answered.

"*Below* the bottom of the range?" I asked, with some rehearsed surprise to drive the point home.

"That's correct."

"Have you made any attempt to determine the reason for that low reading?"

"I did. It appears that the designers of the Mesa did two things which caused it to have a fairly high c.g. height. First, they used a minimum ground clearance distance, that is, the distance between the underside of the Mesa and the ground—of nine-point-two inches. That is a significant vertical distance for utility vehicles. To give you some appreciation for the magnitude of that distance, I performed a survey of what the ground clearance distances are for other utility vehicles in the same class as the Mesa. The Range Rover Grenadier model, for example, is only eight-point-four inches, the Mitsubishi Montana is seven-point-four and the Ford Exponent is six-point-seven inches. In fact, my investigation reflects that the Mesa is at the very top of the pack when it comes to ground clearances. The Global utility model that the Mesa replaced, the Vista, only had a ground clearance distance of seven-point-six inches."

I walked to the side of my podium and leaned on it. "So what you are saying is that the Mesa is *higher* off the ground, so to speak, than every other utility vehicle you observed?" I elevated my voice at the word, as if I, like the jury, was hearing this fact for the first time.

"From the standpoint of c.g., that's true. There are one or two of those other SUVs you mentioned," Braxton explained, "which are technically an inch or two taller in overall height than the Mesa, but even their ground clearance is less than that of the Mesa, meaning that the extra one or two inches of their cab height was only sheet metal, and the Mesa's *overall c.g.*—that is, its overall central mass location—was still vertically higher than theirs. Only the Japanese Koyo Klondike model had the same ground clearance as the Mesa had."

"And what was the other design feature of the Mesa that causes it to be at the lower end of the stability range for utility vehicles?"

Braxton nodded as he reached over and pulled a wrinkled paper out of the stack in front of him. He put it on top of the mess of papers. "It deals with cargo-carrying capacity," he answered. "The Mesa has a much greater cargo-carrying capacity than the other utility vehicles in its class. With its rear seat folded down, like it was at the time of the Hawkins accident, the Mesa is capable of carrying a hundred-and-two cubic feet of cargo. That is really quite amazing when you consider that the Range Rover Grenadier model has only ninety-two cubic feet, the 8-Runner has eighty-three, and the Nissan Seeker VX has only eighty-five cubic feet. The prior Vista model sold by Global, I note, only had a capacity of eighty-three-point-five cubic feet. I suspect that the Mesa designers felt that it was necessary to have greater ground clearance to allow for the fact that the body of the vehicle would be descending downwards by a margin of a few inches when it was fully loaded with its maximum load of passengers and cargo."

"Of what significance from a rollover standpoint is the larger cargo capacity of the Mesa?" Braxton was on a professorial roll. The jury was awake and following his discourse, including the young x-ray tech with the sleeve tattoo. I noted that even the female Bubba Burger juror was jotting down notes on the pad that the bailiff made available to all jurors.

"Well, as I mentioned, it causes the Mesa to travel down the road at a higher elevation to begin with. As a result, it is more top heavy, if I could use that layman's term," he said, looking at the jury for acknowledgement. The hardware store owner nodded back, in understanding. "Moreover, when it's loaded up, the Mesa has more weight than other vehicles in its class located at a higher elevation off the ground. That's not a good thing to have from a stability standpoint," he added, frowning a bit as he related that fact to the jury. "More weight at a higher elevation means that any sudden lateral force, which a loaded Mesa is subjected to due to the lateral forces generated by a sudden swerve at highway speed, say for example, to avoid hitting something in the road, will have a much more magnified effect on its ability to control itself than would be the case if it were not loaded."

Now, two more jurors started jotting down notes on their pads.

"According to the manufacturer's specifications, what is the maximum load that the Mesa that Jenny Hawkins was driving can transport?" I wanted the jury to know that she was well within those guidelines.

"It is capable of carrying a *payload*, as Global calls it, of 1,400 pounds, including occupants and cargo."

"Have you calculated the maximum payload that Jenny Hawkins was carrying at the time of her accident?"

"Yes, I have." He again shuffled through his pile of dog-eared and unkempt papers for a moment before finding the document he was looking for. "Combining her weight, her son's weight, and the combined weight of the paint compressor, the paint and the Girl Scout cookies was a tad over half of that capacity. It's a heavy load, but its well within Global's design specifications."

"Are you critical of any other aspect of the Mesa's design from a stability standpoint?"

"I am," he said confidently. "If the Mesa designers were determined to make it taller, they should have correspondingly made its width, its tire track width, considerably wider. Track width is the distance between the right side tires, if you will, and the left side tires on a vehicle. The Mesa's width was inappropriately narrow for its height," he said critically. "That geometry only invited rollover problems to occur when the operator was required to make sudden, sharp steering inputs into the steering wheel while going at highway speed, particularly if they were carrying any significant load. In fact, that leads me to my final design criticism of the Mesa: its suspension system."

"And what are your observations and opinions in that regard, Dr. Braxton?"

"As I mentioned previously, stability of a vehicle is a function of an integrated design analysis of the vehicle's c.g., height, width, weight, its suspension and its tires."

"What role does a suspension system play in preventing rollover?" So far, the script which Braxton and I had rehearsed was going as planned.

"A very important one," he responded immediately. "Let me use an example to explain the role it plays," he suggested. "Let's assume that a utility vehicle is driving down the highway and a deer suddenly jumps onto the highway from a thicket of bushes on the side of the road," Braxton said. "If the driver suddenly swerves to his left to avoid hitting it, that swerve will cause a significant lateral force to be put onto the vehicle's center of gravity, just like in our peanut butter jar and vase illustration," he explained, pointing to the jar and vase in front of him. "That force will act to push laterally, or sideways, against the vehicle. When that happens, the body of the utility vehicle will want to immediately lean to one side in response. The purpose of a suspension system is to *capture and distribute* the sudden spike in lean energies and movements," he emphasized, "so that the vehicle's body will not cause a rollover. It controls these sudden forces by way of suspension leaf springs or stabilizing bars."

"Can a badly designed geometry be overcome by a well-designed suspension system?" I asked. Judge Vaughn was busy signing a stack of orders in other cases and not paying any attention to what the witness was saying. He was reiterating, in the way that only trial judges can, that he was getting the last word on the tiff with me. He didn't like Braxton or the fact that the Florida Supreme Court's ruling in the *Riley* case required him, at the trial court level, to allow Braxton's opinions into evidence.

"No, not really," he replied. "At best, if you have a basic geometry on a vehicle that is poorly designed, a good suspension will help you perhaps *sandpaper* some of the more extreme edges of the stability envelope, if you will, under certain circumstances. But, the inescapable fact of the matter is that if your basic vehicle geometry is bad, like the Mesa's is, even the best suspension can only act as a Band-Aid, not a panacea." He leaned back in his witness chair and comfortably rested his right hand over his left.

I caught a glimpse of Harrington. He was the epitome of boredom. He didn't bother to write down any of Braxton's testimony for purposes of cross. He wanted the jury to know that he thought even less of Braxton than he did of Cargill. Or than The Turtle, for that matter.

"Did you assess the Mesa's suspension components?"

"I did. The Mesa came equipped with front and rear stability bars. They are Band-Aids, that's all, for its overall poor design," he said, bluntly.

"Dr. Braxton. Based on all the information you have been supplied with, including Mr. Cargill's opinions regarding the accident reconstruction of Jenny Hawkins' accident, to a reasonable degree of certainty, how does your opinion of design defect apply to the facts of that accident?" It was the home run question which every member of the jury wanted to hear.

"In its simplest terms, this terrible catastrophe would not have happened had that Mesa been designed safely and appropriately. When she steered suddenly and sharply to her right to avoid the stepladder, which had fallen off the pickup truck in front of her, she should have experienced—if the Mesa had been designed correctly—a momentary sensation of her vehicle and her body both being pushed to her left. She would have felt that because the mass of her utility vehicle and her own human body would still want to travel in the same direction that they had been traveling in immediately prior to the steering wheel swerve to her right. That has to do with their original inertial forces. The upper cab of the Mesa would have felt as if it were lagging, or leaning, a bit to her left as it attempted to make the change in its direction of travel to follow where the steering wheel was then trying to send the Mesa. However, the Mesa should have responded quickly and moved to her right in response to the steering wheel rotation to her right." He was using his body in the witness chair to simulate and demonstrate his testimony, pretending that he was turning an imaginary steering wheel in front of him.

The giggly kindergarten teacher started leaning forward, in her chair. Eric glanced at me in recognition as he noticed it too. *Excellent.*

"All four of the Mesa's wheels should have remained planted firmly on the flat roadway, with no lift off whatsoever of any of those wheels. She should have been able to maneuver safely into the first lane of travel and bring her vehicle from that point to a stop if she had so desired, since she would have had full and complete control over its movement. After all, we are only talking about a speed which Mr. Cargill estimates at around fifty-five miles per hour. However, from what Mr. Cargill opines, and as I understand what witness Abadin testified to in his deposition, Mrs. Hawkins didn't get the response that I just described. Rather, what she experienced when she steered to her right was a pronounced lag in the body of the Mesa, followed by it whipping around to her left, with a pronounced lean of the top of the Mesa to her left, which likely resulted in the two wheels of the Mesa lifting somewhat off the flat roadway, preventing her from gaining control over the Mesa."

"Let me stop you right there for a moment," I said, hoping to tie down a point for the jury. "Wouldn't some lift off of the Mesa's tires from the roadway at that point have been consistent with a well-designed vehicle simply reacting to a severe steering input from Mrs. Hawkins? After all, if I can picture it, you have the Mesa driving in a straight line in an easterly direction towards Ft. Lauderdale, and all of a sudden, she cranks the steering wheel sharply to the right to avoid hitting the ladder that is suddenly in front of her. Wouldn't even a well-designed utility vehicle show some wheel lift?"

"No, not at all!" he said, shaking his head vigorously. "If that vehicle was properly designed, and she was driving at only fifty-five miles per hour on a flat surface like the highway she was on, the *most* that the Mesa should have done would be to experience some vehicle body lean to the left, coupled with the possibility of having its rear tires slide out somewhat in a clockwise fashion. There should have been absolutely no lift off of any of the wheels, and she should have been able to control the Mesa. Mr. Culhane," he lectured, "motor vehicles are not supposed to have tire lift off or rollover on a flat surface while traveling at only fifty-five miles per hour. I can't say it any plainer than that. A rollover of a soundly designed vehicle needs some type of trip lever to exist, like a curb or a flat tire or a dirt trench."

"I apologize for interrupting you. Please proceed with your application of the Mesa's stability defect to the facts of this accident," I encouraged, stepping back to give him full attention.

"When the Mesa moved to the right and started losing control, Mrs. Hawkins counter steered to her left in order to avoid hitting the concrete retaining wall to her right. When that happened, according to Mr. Cargill's reconstruction, the nose of the Mesa now swung to her left, pointing towards the grassy median that separated the eastbound traffic on I-595 from the westbound traffic. It appears from his reconstruction, along with the testimony of Mr. Abadin, the witness, that the body of the Mesa now rotated completely in the opposite direction, causing it to lean substantially to the right, with the two wheels on the Mesa's left side, lifting completely off the roadway. That was the beginning of the rollover and the ensuing fire. From the point that the wheels lifted off the roadway," he said soberly, looking at the jury, "there was *absolutely nothing* that she could do to stop it from happening. Her fate was cast, I'm afraid."

"Why is that? Couldn't she have steered her way out of it, even at that point?"

"No, you have to understand that from an engineering point of view," he said, continuing to lecture the jury in the friendly, straightforward manner of an old and experienced teacher, "when those two offside wheels left the ground, the vehicle became instantaneously unstable due to the shift of the vehicle's center of gravity. In order for the driver to halt the rollover action under those circumstances, he or she must *immediately*—within a fraction of a second— quickly steer out of the turn in order to reduce the lateral acceleration to a level that will return the vehicle to an upright position. Normal drivers are not quick enough or experienced enough to spot the problem, decide what must be done and act on that decision, all within the split second that we are talking about."

"Haven't you seen those car drivers at the circus that can drive a car on only two wheels as they drive along?"

"Sure, but that's why they're in the circus performing that trick for the audience. They are well trained professional drivers, and they *know* what's coming. And they've spent hours and hours practicing how to react. They're not normal housewives who are faced with this type of an emergency only once in a lifetime." His reference was a specific reference to Jenny Hawkins.

"Dr. Braxton, is there anything at all that Jenny Hawkins or her son did that contributed to this rollover?"

"Nothing at all. Their fault, if one can call it that, was simply being in the Mesa at the wrong time. From its overall design, it was a time bomb waiting to go off under the right circumstances," he ended with emphasis. "Unfortunately, the stepladder falling on the roadway was the fuse that lit that time bomb."

I caught three of the jurors lean over to start writing in their pads as he finished. *Write down 'time bomb,'* I mentally urged.

I looked solemnly at the witness, then at the jury. "Thank you, sir. Your witness, counsel." I grabbed my legal pad and headed back to my table.

CHAPTER 40

HARRINGTON WASTED NO time with pleasant preliminaries. He grabbed a new three-ring notebook, a red one no less, and headed for the examining podium.

"Dr. Braxton, do you consider a utility vehicle to be a fairly complex product to design from an engineering standpoint?"

"Yes, it has some very sophisticated systems."

"And not to beat a dead horse, but you haven't even designed so much as a screw or a nut on any motor vehicle, have you?"

"You're correct."

"You mentioned in your qualifications that you have taught design courses, isn't that correct?"

"Yes, at least one a year."

"So, if you've been teaching for about twenty years that means that you've taught about twenty of those design courses. Right?"

"Your math squares with mine," Braxton responded with a pleasant smile.

"So, tell us, in all twenty years of teaching design, how many times have you used *auto design* as the focal point of your design course, Professor?" He knew the answer from the deposition.

"I've never used auto design as a focal point in any of my courses."

"*Never?*" he asked, with renewed incredulity.

"That's correct."

"I see," Harrington said, knitting his brows for the jury to see. "Well, if you haven't *taught* auto design, then could you at least list for us all of the engineering publications that you've *authored* over the years dealing with *automotive* design, in particular. I recall that in direct exam to Mr. Culhane's questions, you mentioned that you had authored around one hundred and thirty engineering publications. dealing with motion"

Again, Harrington knew the answer in advance of Braxton's reply.

"My engineering articles have not dealt with automotive design, per se, Mr. Harrington. They have dealt with the concept of dynamics of bodies in motion, which obviously has application to the automotive design environment. Mr. Newton's laws and principles," he said calmly, "apply equally to cars as they do to bicycles." The witness took another sip of water from the glass in front of him.

"Do you own a utility vehicle, Professor?" Harrington persisted.

"No, never have."

"Have you ever driven a Mesa before giving your opinions in this case?" he asked with growing skepticism in his voice. His face wore a bemused look as well.

"As I told you in my deposition, Mr. Harrington, I have not. I don't believe that it's necessary for me to do so in order to arrive at my opinions. It's largely a function of the laws of physics and mathematics that I'm opining on, and my driving a particular vehicle won't change those laws of the universe." He was displaying irritation with Harrington's line of questioning.

"So, let me get this straight," Harrington said, removing his stage glasses and holding them for Hollywood effect, pointing them directly at the witness, "you've never designed one component on any motor vehicle. You've never taught a single class that focused on motor vehicle design. You've never owned a utility vehicle. And you've never even driven a Mesa, which is the subject of this lawsuit. Did I get that all right?"

"Yes."

"Yet, despite all of that," he asked, lifting both hands, palm up, in feigned disbelief, "you waltz into this courtroom and claim to be an expert in the design of the Mesa. Is that a fair statement?" The sarcasm was not lost on the jury.

"I think you've got it all right except the waltzing part."

"Interesting." Harrington said out loud to no one in particular.

"Your Honor, I must object to Mr. Harrington's commentaries."

The Turtle seemed amused by his comment. Nonetheless, he addressed Harrington. "Counsel, I would ask you to refrain from any extra-curricular comments. The jury is to disregard commentary by either of the lawyers as it is not evidence in this case."

"Sorry, Judge," Harrington smiled in response. "I guess I got carried away."

"Professor Braxton, I heard you mention in your qualifications that you had consulted with *Consumers' Review* for about five years in the 1990s, is that right?"

"From 1993 through 1998, yes."

"Would you tell the jury why your relationship with that publication was *severed*," he directed evenly.

Severed? I snuck a glance over my shoulder at Sandy. *What the hell is this all about*, my eyes questioned. She frowned. She didn't have a clue either.

"My relationship was not severed, as your question seems to suggest, Mr. Harrington. I left. I was told that they were reorganizing their automotive evaluation group and wanted to hire a full time auto engineer in-house to evaluate the performance and safety aspects of new vehicles being tested. My part-time consulting was being subsumed by the new hire."

"Sir," Harrington countered sharply, "isn't it true that you were *terminated* because you made a material error in the evaluation of the handling character-istics of a new production passenger car that Chrysler Motors had built and marketed under the name of *La Playa* Model?"

"That is not true Mr. Harrington," he answered, with a bit more emphasis than necessary. "If you are referring to the article that *Consumers' Review* pub-lished evaluating the *La Playa* model in which I consulted, I agree that a mate-rial error was made." Braxton turned and faced the jury in providing his expla-nation. "Chrysler Motors had just released a brand new model which it called the *La Playa*. The magazine decided to critically evaluate its overall perform-ance, including its front steering system, which was rather revolutionary at the time. There was another consultant by the name of Carl Thimble who was given the overall responsibility of evaluating its steering performance, including its safety aspects. He reported to the magazine that it had a dangerous 'over-steer' propensity, and the magazine reported that in the issue. They called it an unsafe vehicle in view of that oversteer problem. As it turned out, Mr. Thimble had not done his homework, and he was wrong. Its steering was fine. However, it was a major embarrassment, as you can imagine, to the publication, and a number of engineering consultants that were associated with that disaster were terminated. My job was to assess the suspension and dynamics of the vehicle and to report my findings to Mr. Thimble for his ultimate assessment. I re-ported to him that I found the vehicle to be satisfactory. Not sterling, by any means, but adequate to do the job. He actually test drove the vehicle and made his own, ultimate negative assessment which he later acknowledged as being wrong."

"Isn't it true, sir, that you received your 'termination notice' within two weeks of the magazine publishing a retraction and an apology for the story that you were a part of?"

"I received my notification that my services would no longer be necessary in that general time frame, that's true. But I resent your suggestion to me or to this court that there was any cause and effect relationship between that story and my departure from that publication!" It was the first time that I saw Braxton get angry.

"Well, *Consumers' Review* hasn't asked you to consult on even one item over the course of the last decade, have they?" Harrington asked rather smugly.

"No. I understand that they do everything in-house at this point."

"I see," he added gratuitously. He had succeeded in planting an insidious seed of doubt in the minds of the jury. Mission accomplished, no matter what Harrington said in his defense with respect to that issue. "Now, let me focus on another bit of your testimony that I find a bit troubling. This so-called 'rollover threshold' formula that you were emphasizing to the jury on direct, you know that 't over 2h' formula you referred to. Isn't it true, sir, that there is no S.A.E. standard at all that adopts that formula?"

Harrington was doing his damndest to refuse to address the witness by the respectful title of 'Doctor.'

"That is true. It is solidly present in the literature, however."

"Well, there's a lot of crazy stuff in the literature, isn't there doctor?"

"I don't consider that stability formula to be crazy, Mr. Harrington."

"Sir, isn't it true that any engineer can find just about any publication to publish any theory he wants to publish, both wacked-out and legitimate? Isn't that true?"

"I think you're overstating the case, but I don't deny that there's some truth to what you say. If an engineering theory is interesting to the average reader, and timely, there are a lot of publications that will be happy to publish it."

"But the S.A.E. the Society of Automotive Engineers, that's the foremost engineering authority recognized by responsible engineers for the publication and adoption of sound engineering and design principles in the entire world, isn't it?"

"That's correct."

"And *nowhere* in that recognized industry association's published data— *nowhere*—do you see *any* adoption of your so-called rollover threshold formula as any type of sanctioned design standard, do you?"

"No, you don't," Braxton conceded, evenly.

"And there isn't even an S.A.E. *recommended practice* that refers to, or sanctions that so-called rollover threshold, is there professor?"

"You are correct again."

"And for the jury's assistance, a recommended practice is a practice, procedure or engineering test which, while not quite a 'standard,' is recognized in the automotive industry as being a prudent and encouraged protocol to follow in connection with the design of motor vehicles. True?"

"Yes, that's the definition."

"And, so, we don't even see any *recommended practice* issued by the S.A.E., the most prestigious organization of automotive engineers in the world even suggesting that design engineers use or perform this little *rollover threshold* formula that you spent so much time talking to the jury about, do we?"

"No," Braxton answered evenly.

"And you're familiar with safety standards that are issued by the United States government, aren't you?"

"Yes, I am familiar with the Federal Motor Vehicle Safety Standards."

"Would you be so kind, Mr. Braxton to cite to this jury the specific Motor Vehicle Safety Standard that recognizes your so-called 'rollover threshold' formula as a legitimate predictor of, as you say, 'rollover propensities'?" Harrington pointed his theater glasses to the jury as he invited Braxton's response. He knew the response that was coming.

"There is no reference in the Federal Motor Vehicle Safety Standards, counsel, to that rollover indicator formula. However, as I'm sure you are aware, the federal standards are largely the product of intense lobbying efforts of the auto industry over the years. As a result, the existing standards are watered-down, toothless versions of what they were intended to provide as originally envisioned when they were first issued back in the 1960s."

Harrington stopped looking at his notebook and jumped on the morsel that Braxton had provided him with in his response.

"So, Professor Braxton," he asked with raised eyebrows and raised sarcasm, "you're now telling this jury that you're smarter and wiser than the entire U.S. Congress when it comes to safety standards, is that it?" He looked over at the jury, paying particular attention to the dry cleaning store juror. I suspect that he had sized him up as a potential foreman and was starting to curry his favor.

Braxton chuckled. "You take my comment out of context. All I'm saying is that it would be a drastic mistake, in my opinion, for anyone to assume that the federal government is up working late at night trying to legislate new and tougher safety requirements for the auto manufacturers to meet in order to better protect the everyday consumer. It just doesn't happen that way. The auto lobby is entirely too strong and deep-pocketed for that to happen."

"I see," he replied, meaning that he didn't. Nor did he hope that the juror saw. "So, it's your testimony that the motor vehicle safety standards mandated by Congress since 1967 in this country don't protect drivers and provide them with added safety, right?"

"No, they provide important safety aspects as to the design of motor vehicles. They just don't go far enough," Braxton responded, holding his ground.

"Well, toothless or not, if we do look at the federal safety standards, which our government has spent millions and millions of dollars developing over the years, they don't mandate, nor even recommend *any* type of 'stability threshold' formula of the type that you are advancing, do they, sir?"

"No, they don't."

"Thank you," Harrington said, tossing his Mount Blanc pen triumphantly onto the flat page of the open binder in front of him on the podium. He then walked away from the podium and over to his right where he stopped and stood directly in front of the jurors. Crossing his arms comfortably across his chest, and looking directly at the jurors, with his back to the witness, dismissively, he posed his next question. It was clear he was enjoying the part of the cat, toying with the mouse.

"So, *Professor*," he recapped sarcastically, making 'professor' sound like 'dope head,' "if the jury and I understand what your 'stability threshold formula' is, it's a *theoretical* formula that is *mentioned* in *some* engineering literature, which has neither been *sanctioned nor approved* by the U.S. Government, nor even by the highest ranking society of automotive engineers recognized in the entire world. Is that about it, in a nutshell?" As he asked the question, he rounded on the witness, for effect.

"Well, if you put it that way," Braxton struggled, not wanting to concede the connotation that Harrington was nicely creating, "I guess you're technically correct." The jury could see his discomfort. Braxton thought about it a moment, then qualified, "actually, I don't like the phrase you used that it is only 'mentioned in some engineering literature.' I think it's widely cited in the industry publications, Mr. Harrington."

Harrington ignored his belated attempt at distancing himself from his response. "Okay. Let's take your non-sanctioned, non-adopted, non-recommended theoretical formula for a moment. I have a couple of questions about it. Are you with me?"

"Fire away," Braxton answered evenly, ignoring the sarcasm woven in Harrington's question.

"If I understood what you told this jury, the utility vehicles produced in the industry have an industry 'stability threshold' of between point-nine and one-point-one Gs, is that correct?" Harrington wasn't using any notes for his cross. He had the numbers memorized. It was effective to watch, I begrudgingly admitted to myself. I doodled on my legal pad as he continued.

"You've got an excellent memory, Mr. Harrington."

"So that means that the entire auto industry is producing utility vehicles that have at least a minimum lateral stability threshold of point-nine Gs. Did I get that correct, too?"

"You did."

"Isn't it true that your non-sanctioned, non-adopted, non-recommended theoretical formula assesses the stability of a *rigid* vehicle on a roadway being subjected to certain lateral forces?"

"In rough terms, yes."

"But, in fact, Mrs. Hawkins' Mesa had non-rigid components designed into it as it drove down I-595 that afternoon of the unfortunate accident, right?"

"That is correct. It had both rigid and non-rigid components to it."

"And one of the non-rigid components designed into that Mesa was its suspension system, correct?" Harrington was taking a very aggressive but smooth and effective approach to the witness.

"I would agree that the Mesa was sprung on its wheels and body by virtue of a flexible suspension system."

"Sir, your answer to my question is 'yes'?" Harrington asked sharply. He was not about to lose control over the witness and let him stray in his responses.

"Yes," Braxton kowtowed.

"And the other non-rigid component that the Hawkins' Mesa had on it was a set of rubber tires, right?"

"It did."

"And, in fact, aren't tires one of your *big three* components making up a vehicle's stability system," he asked, mockingly, referring to Braxton's testimony during his direct examination by me.

"And Professor Braxton, when you told this jury that the Mesa, according to your calculations, had a so-called 'stability threshold' of only eight-point-eight Gs, you didn't tell them that the number *ignored* these other non-rigid components to my client's Mesa, did you?"

"Sir, I resent the implication of your question," Braxton said, suddenly injecting flint in his voice. "The literature specifically points out that one is to apply the stability threshold formula to the rigid components only, and that you are to ignore the non-rigid components like suspensions or tires."

"Well that *academic* exercise is well and good, but the Mesa that my client designed and manufactured and sold to Mrs. Hawkins, in fact, *did* have a suspension system designed into it and *did* have a tire system designed into it, didn't it?" He gave the emphasized words a steely edge, with just the right touch of righteous indignation.

"Yes, that's true, but you're missing the point."

Harrington went up to the clerk's table and sifted through the photos in evidence until he found the one he wanted. He walked over, stood in front of the equipment that projected onto a large overhead screen for the jury's view, enlargements of documents placed upon it. He placed the colored photo of the damaged Mesa, which the police took at the scene.

"I'm missing the point?" he queried, following up on Braxton's last response. "Those are rubber tires that are on that Mesa, aren't they?" He pointed to the two remaining tires that had not been burned.

"Yes, obviously, but—"

"And," he surgically cut, "your theoretical formula *ignores* the existence of those tires, doesn't it?"

"As I said before, that is the way the formula is set up."

Harrington exploded with his next question. "And isn't it true, sir, that if you *add in* the stability enhancements provided by the Mesa's suspension system and its tires, your theoretical equation, when applied to Mrs. Hawkins' Mesa will result in a number that is *well over* the point-nine minimum lower range parameter of the industry?" Harrington's entire demeanor suggested to the jury that he was helping them to uncover a great charade of false logic that was being perpetrated upon them by the witness.

"Mr. Harrington," the witness answered with growing irritation, "I can certainly add in the extra stability tolerance that the tires and the suspension provide to the vehicle's overall design if you want me to. And the addition of those items will undoubtedly result in its stability number exceeding point-nine. However, that is not the correct way to use the formula. The additional—"

"Professor," Harrington cut him off, "you've answered my question. I'm not interested in having you try to explain your inconsistent testimony to the jury. I'll let your attorney do that."

"Objection, Your Honor," I bellowed from my chair, "this isn't proper cross-examination. Mr. Harrington is simply arguing with the witness." Frankly, I was looking for an excuse to break Harrington's very effective rhythm.

Vaughn, who was resting comfortably back in his chair during the examination with his arms crossed over his chest, gave the appearance of an old weathered turtle resting on a sunny rock. I couldn't tell if he was asleep. While he wasn't, the hoods on the Turtle's eyes didn't even move when he spoke.

"This is cross-examination. A bit spirited, I'll agree, but cross-examination, nonetheless. Objection overruled."

Harrington continued the pummeling.

"Now, I also heard you criticize the Mesa's ground clearance. I believe you said that its nine-point-two inches is well above the ground clearance of the rest of the SUVs in its class. Did I quote your testimony correctly?"

"You did, except you forgot that I mentioned a single exception, the Koyo Klondike model."

"Yes, let's talk about the Klondike SUV that was marketed this year by Koyo Motors out of Japan. It also has a ground clearance of nine-point-two inches—just like my client's Mesa model, isn't that true, sir?"

"That's true, but—"

"So if the Mesa is defective, you're telling this jury that the Klondike is defective as well, aren't you?"

"No, I'm not saying that. The big difference between those two is the fact that the Klondike has a two inch wider track width. You didn't mention that fact, Mr. Harrington." he parried.

"And that two inch difference makes my client's Mesa defective yet doesn't render the Klondike defective. That's your expert opinion, isn't it, sir?" Harrington fired at the witness.

"It does, but I consider it a materially different design."

"It's a sport utility vehicle, isn't it, Professor?"

"Yes, but—"

"And the Mesa is a sport utility vehicle too, isn't it?" he asked with mock exasperation at the witness's logic.

"They're both utility vehicles in the broadest sense."

"Thank you." He looked over at the jury, making little attempt to conceal his scorn from the jurors. "And if I heard the rest of your testimony, you relied, to a great degree, upon the *expert* opinions, if I can call them that, of a Mr. Cargill and the accuracy of an eyewitness by the name of Mr. Abadin. Isn't that also true?"

"Let me put it to you this way, Mr. Harrington. Even without their testimony, my opinion would still remain the same. From a stability and rollover standpoint, the Mesa is defective and unreasonably dangerous. Its very geometry dictates that it will tip over at even modest speeds of fifty-five or better. I didn't need the testimony or observations of either of those two people to tell me that. What those two witnesses did do for me was to *confirm* what the geometry and the laws of physics already told me about the design of this vehicle. It's a bad design."

"But you did factor in the accuracy of their testimony in arriving at your opinions in this case, didn't you? Didn't I hear Mr. Culhane there," he said, pointing accusingly at me like a bad scene in an old Perry Mason rerun, "ask you if the basis of your opinions in this case included your reliance on their testimony?"

"I did."

Harrington was doing a nice job trying to put Braxton in the same leaky boat of credibility that those two prior witnesses were in.

"Dr. Braxton," Harrington said, finally using his proper title, "you would agree that *even the best and safest* designed utility vehicle will *always* roll over if it is sliding sideways and the leading wheels come in contact with a tripping mechanism, like a curb or a dirt rut, would you not?" Harrington had now gone back to using his most innocent and reasonable tone in asking this question to the witness.

"Yes, I agree that every vehicle will roll over if it is tripped while sliding sideways. No one can design a vehicle to prevent that from happening."

"And in this accident, you have not personally attempted to reconstruct exactly when the Mesa started its roll, did you?"

"No, I did not. I relied on the reconstruction opinions of Mr. Cargill who opined that the roll commenced, that is, the wheels of the Mesa started their lift-off, when the Mesa was sliding back to its left, while the entire vehicle was still on the flat, portion of the I-595 roadway, headed for the grassy median that separated eastbound lanes from westbound lanes."

Harrington smiled and looked at the jury for a brief moment before asking the next question. "Let's suppose that this jury doesn't believe Mr. Cargill's reconstruction opinion. Let's suppose that he screwed up on his math, or he just failed to account for the correct coefficient of friction. Whatever it is, let's suppose that the jury over there," he said pointing to them, "doesn't believe that the accident happened the way he says it did. Let's suppose, instead, that the jury believes that Mrs. Hawkins wasn't paying enough attention, that she was going somewhere in the neighborhood of seventy-five miles per hour at the time that the ladder fell in front of her, and that she made a series of very sharp, panicked steering inputs into the Mesa. Are you with me so far?"

"I follow you," Braxton said, hesitating as he did so.

"If she entered the grassy median sliding sideways, the two wheels on that leading side of her SUV would be digging into the soft earth in the median as they skid across that earth, correct?"

"That's correct," Braxton conceded. "It had just been raining, so the earth would have been soft."

"And you and I both know that two side-sliding wheels of her Mesa, under that scenario I just put to you, Doctor, would be digging into the earth and would be creating a 'rut,' that is, an increasing buildup of earth caused by the plowing side of the tires, right?"

Braxton's two hands tugged at the lapels of his tweed jacket, as he looked at Harrington and slowly considered the question. I could sense that pulling on his lapels was a habit he engaged in when he became nervous. The jury could sense it too. "That is true if we accept your hypothetical facts here," he finally agreed. "The heavy weight of that sliding vehicle, acting on the sliding tires on soft earth, would act to do just that—if, as you have asked me to assume, Mr. Harrington, the Mesa hadn't *already* been undergoing a rollover when it entered the grassy median." Braxton was politely reminding the jury that he was not conceding the accuracy of the factual assumptions that he was being asked to assume as correct.

"And if that Mesa were sliding sideways in that fashion on that grassy median, and if a rut were being created, *you're going to see a rollover occur*, aren't you, Professor?" he asked loudly, slapping his right palm sharply on the top of the podium for effect.

The jurors startled in response. Even The Turtle's massive head suddenly jiggled in response.

"Yes, under the assumptions that you have asked me to assume, you would likely get a rollover."

"And even the *safest, the most well-designed, SUV that you know of,* would roll over under those circumstances, isn't that true?"

"Under those set of assumptions—"

"Yes or no, sir!" Harrington ordered, in a loud, commanding voice.

"Yes," Braxton conceded. "Under those specific assumptions, that would be the likely result."

Harrington removed his glasses, raised both palms in mock disbelief and asked, "But you, sir, *haven't even test driven* the Mesa yourself before arriving at your opinions in this case that it is an unsafe and defective vehicle, have you?"

"No, I haven't," he finally admitted. His tail was between his legs, and the jury could sense it. As if a thought suddenly occurred, Braxton added, "I would have preferred to run stability tests, but one needs to run such tests correctly. However, Mr. Culhane told me," he said, with all of the heads of the jurors suddenly swiveling, in unison, to look at me, "that he and the Hawkins' family couldn't afford to perform those types of tests."

"Oh, well," Harrington injected, using the opportunity that Braxton's response just gave him, "we'll hear quite a bit about stability tests in my client's case, Professor. I can assure you of that. I have nothing more for this witness," he said dismissively as he collected his red cross-examination binder and headed back to his table.

I SPENT THIRTY minutes in re-direct examination with Dr. Braxton, attempting to shore up some of the damage which Harrington had done in his very effective cross. I decided to leave the *Consumers' Review* situation alone. I didn't want to leave the jury with a *me thinks thou protest too much* feeling.

The one critical area that I did address was the failure to include the non-rigid elements of suspension and tires in the rollover threshold formula, which Braxton had alluded to in cross but was cut off.

"Why is it that a design engineer is supposed to omit any increased stability advantages, which the non-rigid tires and suspension system provide, in applying the rollover threshold formula?" I asked.

"For safety reasons," he answered. "In applying the formula, you are attempting to be as conservative as possible in evaluating the stability, or anti-rollover, propensities of the basic utility vehicle itself. What you want to end up with is a basic, rigid vehicle which is, *by itself*, stable—without the crutches or assistance of the added stability forgiveness that the tires and suspension system add to the basic weight and geometry design of the vehicle. The additional stability of the tires is there to merely *augment* what should already be a basically stable, underlying design. That's why they are to be omitted."

"And if you apply that formula, without the … uh … fudging that Mr. Harrington is suggesting here on the final exam, will the basic design of the Mesa exceed the minimum stability threshold of point-nine Gs?"

"I object to Mr. Culhane's argumentative term," Harrington barked from his desk.

The Turtle leaned forward from the rock upon which he had been sunning. "Mr. Culhane, I think that remark is argumentative. The objection is sustained, and the jury is to disregard it in its entirety!" The Turtle was still pissed from our sidebar chat.

The x-ray tech crossed his arms across his chest and looked at me, disapprovingly.

I backed off and used my 'nice voice.' "If you apply the stability formula the way that you are *supposed to* apply it, without any of the suggested assumptions or suggested changes that Mr. Harrington was kind enough to suggest, does the Mesa meet the point-nine G industry average stability threshold that you spoke of earlier?"

"No, it does not," he answered, "it's below it."

"And in Mrs. Hawkins' case, did you find any basis to conclude that any 'forgiveness' that might have otherwise have existed in the Mesa's suspension and tires were used up, for lack of a better word, in this accident?"

"Very definitely, she was not driving an empty Mesa when she was forced to start swerving to avoid the stepladder that fell in front of her. The Mesa was being called upon to transport her, her son, and over six-hundred pounds of cargo in the form of the paint spraying equipment, boxes of paint and the boxes of Girl Scout cookies. When she started making sharp and sudden steering inputs into the Mesa's steering wheel, that cargo—because it was all above the Mesa's c.g., would have had a dramatic effect on taxing the inherent stability, or instability, of the Mesa itself. From everything I have seen, the forgiveness, or incremental stability, which the Mesa's suspension and tire system had to offer, would have been quickly and dramatically eaten up. Put simply, if the underlying Mesa had been stable, Mrs. Hawkins would have been able to control her vehicle, and the loss of control and subsequent rollover would not have occurred."

"Do you attribute the fire to the stability defect?"

"Unquestionably. It is direct cause and effect. If the Mesa had been stable, the rollover would not have occurred and the ensuing fire would also not have occurred."

"Thank you, sir."

Harrington had only one question for re-cross.

"Incidentally, Professor," he said, not even bothering to stand, "you're being paid by Mr. Culhane to come here and give your opinions, aren't you?"

"Yes. I am charging him for my time and my out-of-pocket expenses." His thick Massachusetts accent made his pronunciation of the word 'charging' sound like 'chaaawging.'

"That's what I figured," he said. "Nothing further."

Judge Vaughn excused the witness who left the courtroom, headed back to Massachusetts. He agreed to make himself available for our rebuttal case if I needed him after Global put on their defense case.

"The court stands in recess until one o'clock," Vaughn announced, looking at his watch. It was a few minutes to twelve and the judge was not one to miss a meal.

CHAPTER 41

"WHAT WAS THAT heated discussion at the side of the judge's bench?" Eric asked as he, Sandy and I quickly wolfed down sandwiches at my office over the lunch hour.

"I demanded a mistrial. A new trial with a new jury," I explained to him when he stared at me blankly. "I didn't care for his comment to the jury about their need to critically evaluate the expert credentials of my experts who take the stand."

"You had to be thick as a two-by-four not to realize that he was telling the jury that he didn't think much of Dr. Braxton's credentials," Sandy added as she removed the onions from her sandwich.

"That was my take, as well. That's why I made the motion," I explained, as I finished half of my sandwich and crumpled the remains in the waxy paper it was on and tossed it at the corner waste basket five feet away. It bounded off the rim and onto the carpet. *Figures.*

"What does all of that mean?" Eric asked, "I don't understand."

"If a judge commits a major error during the course of a jury trial, and a lawyer thinks that the error will prevent his client from getting a fair trial, he has the option of moving the court for a mistrial. If it is granted, the current trial is declared null and void, and a brand new one with a new jury is started fresh."

"And if that motion is denied," Eric asked, "what's the result?"

"A very pissed-off trial judge. Actually, you get a pissed-off judge, either way," I said. "They hate mistrial motions. That's what we have here, a pissed-off Turtle. I'm sorry that I didn't consult with you before I made the motion, but I knew that you would defer to my judgment anyway. It's just that the son of a bitch hasn't given us any serious favors at all in this case, and that crack to the jury about Braxton's credentials was the final straw. I wasn't letting him get away with it."

"I'm no expert, but it's pretty clear to me that he doesn't like our case much," Eric offered as he pushed his half-eaten sandwich away. His mood was down, and so was mine. As was Sandy's.

"Hey," I rallied, "so long as we can make it to the jury, we always have a shot." No one responded.

After a few minutes, Eric asked, breaking the gloomy silence, "who's going to be on the stand this afternoon?"

"I think it's time that the jury learned that the Mesa's instability is being experienced by other Mesa drivers as well," I said. "I'm going to be offering the videotaped depositions of the other five Mesa drivers that we took around the country a few months ago. If we can get them in, I think they will be extremely effective, especially the ones that also resulted in rollovers."

My qualification of 'getting them in' caught Sandy's ear. She looked over at me and, without any comment, simply raised both of her hands. Her first two fingers were crossed on each hand. She smiled.

"Are you ready with the video/DVD playback equipment for those video depositions" I asked her.

"Locked and loaded," she replied. "Who do you want to start with?"

"I'm going with Stafford, the guy who rolled the Mesa when he and his brother were coming back from deer hunting," I explained to Eric. "He's the guy who was rendered a quad as a result."

Sandy looked at her watch. "It's a quarter of one. We'd better hump."

"YOUR HONOR," I announced after lunch, "the plaintiffs call Mr. Brant Stafford to testify as our next witness, by videotape. He resides in Tennessee."

"I object on the grounds of relevance, Your Honor," Harrington stated, rising out of his seat. "I'll need a sidebar on this one." It was more a command than a request.

Vaughn looked at both of us with more than mild irritation. His dislike of our ever-increasing use of the sidebar tool was clearly not floating his boat. "Let's make it quick," he growled.

"Now what's the basis for your objection Mr. Harrington? We haven't even had the witness sworn in by videotape yet?" the Judge asked.

"Judge, the basis is relevance. Mr. Stafford is a man who was drunk and riding in the front seat of a Mesa in the hills of Tennessee last fall with his brother who was also drunk. His brother was driving the Mesa. We went to Tennessee and took the man's deposition. Mr. Culhane is going to try and offer that accident as some type of far-fetched evidence that the Mesa has a design defect. I submit that evidence of other accidents or incidents involving the same product are not the least bit relevant unless and until the proponent of the evidence provides the court with a *prima facie* showing that the two accidents are substantially similar in their accident details. As Your Honor knows," Harrington said, probably confident that The Turtle didn't have a clue what the law was on this point, "that's the law in Florida. Mr. Culhane simply can't make that *prima facie* showing. He just wants that jury to see a poor fellow sitting in a wheel chair who was also injured while occupying a Mesa in hopes that the jury will feel sorry and give his client a lot of money. That's totally improper, and that's why I felt it necessary to alert the court even before Mr. Culhane started running the videotape footage and started the prejudicial tears rolling," he concluded.

The Turtle, leaning over the side of his bench, turned to face me. The slits he had for eye openings narrowed even further as he listened to Harrington's comments. I don't think I could have passed a credit card between his eyelids. "Has Mr. Harrington accurately stated the reason that you want to offer this man's testimony by videotape?" His tone was one of challenge, not merely seeking to gather information.

"Yes and no. I'm offering it as circumstantial but relevant evidence that the Mesa is defective from a stability point of view. As this court knows from the case of *Halley v. Dustin Smith Yachting, Inc.*, evidence of similar product failures arising under substantially similar circumstances is absolutely admissible in Florida as evidence that the product is, indeed, defective and unreasonably dangerous. Here, Mr. Stafford's testimony is that he and his brother were driving at around fifty-five miles per hour when they hit a patch of ice on a road in northern Tennessee last winter. The Mesa that they were occupying, which is identical to the one that Mrs. Hawkins was driving, did exactly the same thing that hers did. It lost control and rolled over, all on a perfectly flat surface! I can assure you," I told Vaughn, "I'm not offering it for sympathy as he suggests. The fact that Mr. Stafford is in a wheel chair is simply a fact of life. It's the underlying behavior of the Mesa that is relevant. For the court to deny me the opportunity to present this highly relevant evidence to the jury would be extremely prejudicial. And that's why I'm offering it," I said with conviction. I did not want The Turtle to sense any backing down or hesitation on my part.

"Were those boys drinking like Mr. Harrington here says?" the Judge asked, fixating on that aspect immediately, like white on rice. Vaughn hated cases that involved alcohol. It was a throwback to the days when he had represented insurance companies before taking the bench.

"Yes. They both had alcohol in their systems, but that only goes to the weight of the evidence, not to its admissibility, your Honor. Global is certainly free to bring that fact out on cross-examination, as Mr. Harrington certainly did in the videotape."

The Turtle shook his head, emphatically. "Drinking and driving renders it dis-similar to this accident. It's not coming in," he flatly pronounced.

"But your Honor, the *Tripp* case," I said, handing him a copy of the case I had quickly pulled from my trial notebook, which I had carried with me to the sidebar, "emphasizes that unless alcohol is shown to have unequivocally played a causal role in the other accident, *to the exclusion of all other causes*, the other accident should come in. It is for the jury to sort through, not for the trial judge to make that determination!" I could not help but challenge him. The evidence of this case was vital, and if Harrington succeeded in keeping this one out, I foresaw the same result for the other accidents I wanted to offer.

Vaughn fumed. He didn't like his rulings questioned. "It's not coming in, I said. I consider the presence of alcohol to render Mr. ... what's that other driver's name in this videotape deposition we're talking about?" he asked with frustration.

"Stafford, Your Honor," Harrington quickly offered, like a dog bringing his master the evening paper.

The Turtle turned to face the court reporter, making sure she got every word of his ruling, for the record. "I consider the presence of alcohol to render Stafford's accident dissimilar to the Hawkins' case from a factual standpoint, and that's the last word I'm going to entertain on it. Is that understood Mr. Culhane? Don't question my rulings!"

"Your honor," I responded with building, but controlled, anger of my own, "you're the judge, I'm not. And while I certainly understand and respect that fact one hundred ten percent, I need to alert the court, on behalf of my client, that I have four other videotaped depositions of four other Mesa drivers who all will testify that their Mesas manifested the exact same unexpected loss of control when confronted with similar sudden road emergencies, just like Mrs. Hawkins experienced." I barged onward, as Vaughn listened. "Some ended up rolling over just like my client's Mesa did, while the others ended up losing control and running off the road and colliding with other objects. If there is going to be an objection to the admissibility of those other depositions as well, I want to know right now, so we can deal with them globally," I said.

"Judge," Harrington said smoothly, "they're all inadmissible for the same reason that you just ruled the Barton deposition inadmissible. They involve dissimilar conditions to the Hawkins' accident that is involved in this case. If you start allowing any of those other accidents in, we're going to end up trying the facts of those cases as well! That's ridiculous. These other accidents are all collateral evidence that does not belong in this case. We're here to try this case, not these four or five other cases."

Vaughn listened to the two of us go at it.

"Judge," I countered, "your pre-trial order also specifically ordered each side to file any motions to exclude depositions or witnesses three weeks prior to the commencement of trial. Global didn't file a single motion to exclude even one of my witnesses. My clients will be severely and irreparably prejudiced if you were to exclude these depositions from being heard by the jury. The evidence these other accidents provide is critical and extremely relevant!"

Vaughn finally took control. "Well, Mr. Culhane, while I'm not happy with Mr. Harrington here in failing to address his objections on my motion calendar before trial started, I'm not going to be hog-tied by the technicalities of any previous order I issued if it results in inadmissible evidence coming in." He thought for a moment. "Here's what I'm going to do. I'm going to call an hour recess and scan the written deposition transcripts of those other four witnesses you want to call," he said looking at me. "I'll let you know my ruling at that time. I understand how important this evidence is to you, but I'm not going to engage in trying those other four cases if they are not substantially similar in their facts. Do you understand?"

"Understood," I replied. Harrington nodded.

The Turtle turned to the jury. They were trying to figure out what was going on in the muffled heated exchange that they had been witnessing at the sidebar. "Ladies and gentlemen, the court needs to attend to a legal issue of some importance that has arisen with the lawyers. My apologies, but we're going to be taking a recess until two-fifteen to allow us to deal with those legal issues. Please re-assemble with the bailiff in the jury room at that time."

The jurors grabbed their personal belongings and exited. The Turtle took the four deposition transcripts Sandy brought up to me, which I handed to him, and waddled to his chambers.

"JESUS," SANDY SAID as she, Eric and I sat down with cups of coffee in the courthouse coffee shop awaiting his ruling. "He can't be serious about excluding those depositions from evidence, can he?"

I stirred cream into my Styrofoam cup of black coffee. "He's a loose, conservative cannon," I replied, "but it's going to be hard for even him to exclude all of those other depositions. They're just too similar. That's why Harrington is so worried about them getting into evidence. All we need is for the jury to hear even one or two other of those other accidents to realize that Jenny's rollover wasn't an isolated or freak accident. It's inherent in the design itself."

Eric sipped his hot coffee and said nothing. His concern over the judge's imminent ruling was obvious, and, I also reluctantly realized to myself, my lack of success in the first two days of trial didn't exactly elevate me to Clarence Darrow status.

"GENTLEMEN, I'VE REVIEWED the deposition transcripts in some detail during the break." Vaughn was back on the bench hunched over the transcripts that lay in a pile in front of him. The bailiff had not yet been ordered to bring the jurors back into the courtroom. "The case law on this issue points out that allowing evidence of other accidents in a products liability action is a matter for the trial court's broad discretion because of the great impact that such evidence can have on a jury. After reviewing the other depositions of these other four cases, I find them not sufficiently similar from a factual standpoint to allow them into evidence. Moreover, even if they had some tangential relevance, I find that, under Evidence Rule 90.403, it's outweighed by their tendency to confuse the jury. I have no intention of trying the details of those other accidents in this case. Accordingly, they aren't coming in." He handed the four transcripts to his clerk to mark as exhibits for the record.

I was momentarily stunned. "Your honor," I finally managed. "Do I understand that you are not permitting even *one* of these other accidents into evidence?"

"That's my ruling, counsel. My reasoning applies to all of them; they all suffer from the same deficiencies."

Eric, who had both elbows on the desk in front of him, put his head in the palm of his hands. His dejection was palpable. I felt it too.

I responded to the judge. I need to make my record for appeal purposes. "With all due respect, and I don't want to argue with Your Honor's ruling, but this evidence is absolutely essential to my client's case. All of those depositions meet the admissibility requirements of the *Halley* case, which I provided to the court. All of them involved the very same Mesa product. Two of them involved the same speed of approximately fifty-five miles per hour which the plaintiff has placed into evidence in this case, and those two also involved the driver having to react on a flat roadway to a sudden event that caused the drivers to swerve, like Mrs. Hawkins did, in order to avoid a collision with another object on the roadway. Indeed, in both of those two accidents, which I just mentioned, rollovers ensued, just as in the case of the Hawkins' vehicle. I must respectfully state that I am at a loss to understand how at least those two accidents would not be deemed 'substantially similar' from a factual standpoint so as to be admissible. For the sake of the record, I would ask that the court articulate its specific rationale for its findings of 'dissimilarity' on the record."

Judges hate to get painted into corners. Like a teenager trying to avoid homework, they do just about everything to prevent that from happening.

"I don't see a need to waste the court's time or that of the record getting into a long explanation of the court's reasoning, counsel," he snapped with irritation and finality. "Your case facts are materially different in the eyes of this judge from those that are presented in this case, and that's all that needs to be said. The transcripts of those depositions are already in the record, and that should be sufficient. Mr. Harrington's motion to preclude all of the videotaped witnesses is granted."

"Thank you, Your Honor," Harrington said as he sat back in his chair. Craige, I could see, was sporting a huge smirk in his chair off to the side. He was like the clichéd cat that had eaten the fucking canary, I fumed.

"Are you ready with your next witness, Mr. Culhane. I don't want to keep this jury waiting any longer this afternoon."

You reptilian son of a bitch. I knew that he could not have possibly meaningfully reviewed the transcripts in that short break to compare similarities. That was why he didn't want to explain his rationale on the record.

I wasted no time in my reaction to his ruling. "In view of your ruling, I have to again move for a mistrial, Your Honor."

"Denied," he ruled, this time without emotion, "call your next witness."

"I wasn't prepared for Your Honor's ruling," I said as evenly as I could. "I don't have another witness readily available this afternoon. I had planned to finish the day out playing those videotape depositions to the jury and to start my damage witnesses tomorrow morning."

The Turtle glared down at me through his Coke bottles. "Are you telling me that you don't have a live witness ready to go this afternoon?"

"Yes, that's what I'm saying. Mr. Harrington's late objection and motion *in limine* was not expected, nor was the breadth of your ruling. I can't possibly get my damage witnesses here until tomorrow morning. That's all I have left, damage witnesses," I added, looking for a lily pad upon which to jump. "I respectfully ask the court's indulgence until tomorrow morning in order to arrange for the balance of my damage witnesses to be here."

Harrington smelled blood in the water. "I strenuously object to that request," he added, piling on. "The defense is here and ready to proceed. We're both aware of the standing order that *if you run out of witnesses, you rest.* We're wasting both the court's valuable time and that of my client by not being able to proceed right now. If Mr. Culhane can't produce his next witness right now, I move they be stricken. He should have been prepared, especially since he knew full well that those other accidents were facially irrelevant and totally inadmissible." He was piling on with everything he had. I would probably have done the same, if the noose had been on his neck, instead of mine.

"Your Honor," I pleaded with some panic, "this is my clients' day in court. It's the only one that the Hawkins family will get. We're talking about a case involving a death and permanent injuries of catastrophic proportions to my client's family. Surely a recess of but a few hours left in this day, to resume full speed tomorrow morning, is not an unreasonable request." I sincerely meant it, and my voice reflected that fact.

For a moment, my sphincter was quivering like a tuning fork. Vaughn was notorious for dismissing cases when the plaintiff had failed to line up witnesses in a timely fashion. His mono-psychotic penchant for punctuality and speed was legendary around the courthouse. If he denied my motion and demanded that I put my damage witnesses on right now, I was in deep shit. Probably malpractice shit, to be more precise.

Vaughn looked over at the clock on the courtroom wall, then over at Harrington, and finally back down at me.

"I'm not happy about this, Mr. Culhane," he finally said, "but I'm going to grant your request. For the record," he said, looking pointedly, in turn, at Harrington, "I'm basing my ruling on the fact that Mr. Harrington failed to abide by my pretrial order and should have filed this motion in advance of the trial. Had he done so, in fairness to you and your client," Vaughn explained, with some regret, "I suppose you would have had your damage witnesses lined up now. However," he lectured, "I suggest that you do what you have to do to make sure this doesn't happen again in this trial, is that understood?"

"Perfectly, Your Honor." I breathed an internal sigh of relief.

He called the jury back in and informed them that the legal issues were going to take longer than had anticipated. He instructed them to return at nine a.m. sharp the next morning. They grumbled but accepted his ruling.

I was pissed and was shoving trial notebooks into my briefcase in anger when Harrington clasped his own large trial briefcase closed and walked past me, headed for the door. As he passed, he paused and leaned over close to me.

"You're fucked, my friend," he said quietly. There was a malevolent glee in his voice. "I gave you a golden chance to settle this case and put a chunk of cash in your pocket. Too bad. Consider the judge's adjournment as an executioner's reprieve, that's all." With that, he chuckled to himself and walked out of the room with the Global representative and his Hunt entourage in tow. They were all in the greatest of spirits.

I was fresh out of wise-ass comebacks. Eric had not moved in his seat from the moment of the judge's comments. His arms were in his lap, and it was as if a pin had let out all of his emotional air. He was pale and obviously distressed both by the judge's comments and by his demeanor. The devastating consequences of the judge's preclusion ruling on the depositions were obviously not lost on him either. I was also sure that he had heard Harrington's comments.

Sandy came over and sat on the edge of Harrington's table. The three of us were the only people left in the courtroom. After closing my briefcase, I sat back down at my own table, out of air.

"We're screwed, aren't we?" Eric finally asked. His voice was devoid of emotion.

I turned in my chair towards him. "Look, I'm not going to sugarcoat it. This was a disaster. I fully expected to get at least two of those depositions into evidence. However," I said, trying to look for something positive, "I still think the jury was listening to Dr. Braxton's opinions this morning. I think we scored some points. At the end of the day, it's all about what they think, and Braxton's opinion on defect and cause will get us to the jury."

Sandy sat with her arms crossed. Ever the independent-minded paralegal, she shook her head in disagreement. "We may get it to the jury, but they're having a tough time understanding all this technical stuff about c.g.s and inertia. I don't think they liked the point that Harrington brought out about Braxton's involvement in the incorrect article in *Consumers' Review*. And without evidence of those five other similar accidents, they're going to see this accident as a one off, not any overriding defect in the Mesa's design."

Eric sighed. "You warned me that this judge was conservative. I just didn't expect him to be so ... well ... so hostile in his attitude towards us. Where do we go from here?"

"All we're left with is our damage witnesses, Eric." I turned to Sandy. "Would you get on your cell right away to Cianciolo, Price, Avalos and Olive? Call them at home if you have to, but just make sure they know that we're going to need to move them up in their witness schedule. They need to be here tomorrow"

"They're going to scream about this schedule change," she warned.

"I don't give a shit," I barked in frustration, "just do what you have to, god dammit, to get them here tomorrow!"

Sandy winced at my tone.

"I'm sorry," I apologized, catching myself. "It's not your fault. I'm being an ass. Just do what you can to get them here, okay? We need them. I'm going with Dr. Olive first thing in the morning if he can make it. He'll make the biggest impact."

"Okay, I'll get it done," she replied. "We need a shot in the arm," she added.

More like a heart transplant, I quietly admitted to myself. We packed up our bags and left the courtroom.

CHAPTER 42

DR. STUART OLIVE was as effective as I hoped he would be. He presented the jury the next morning with the same level of sincere and genuine
care that I had witnessed when I had first observed him speaking with Eric in
the burn unit at Broward General Hospital the morning after the accident.

As the treating physician for Ryan, he took the jury through his severe
burn injuries. To explain the nature of the wounds, Olive was about to use the
enlarged, color photos of Ryan's burn injuries that Vaughn had previously ruled
during Eric's testimony could not be shown to the jury until they had been
'linked up.' I advised Vaughn of my intention to use the photos and of his earlier ruling. I could ill afford another blow from Vaughn, and I was doing my
best to stay on his good side, at least, to the extent he had one. Olive laid the
groundwork by explaining to the jury that it was his usual practice to take
photographs of all of his seriously injured patients for treatment purposes.
They allowed him and the treating staff to chart progress.

"Your honor," Harrington rose and objected, "I don't believe that the
predicate prima facie showing you required has been met. I also believe that
they're unnecessary and prejudicial under Rule 90.403," referring to the rule of
evidence in Florida that gives a trial judge wide latitude in precluding otherwise
relevant evidence if it contained inflammatory or emotional aspects that would
tend to unfairly affect the jury's ability to remain fair. It was a rule that judges
loved since it afforded them with discretion large enough to drive a tractor
trailer through, and, if used by the judge to exclude evidence, was rarely reversed on appeal. Harrington made his point efficiently and sat down.

I started to respond to Harrington's argument, but the Turtle beat me out
of the starting blocks with his own question to the witness.

"Dr. Olive, those photos are pretty graphic. I need to know, do you think you could make the points to the jury you need to make without actually showing them to the jury?"

The doctor nodded, understanding the Judge's concern. He was dressed in a navy blue sports coat, tan slacks, powder blue shirt and no tie. His salt and pepper hair added to his distinguished appearance. "I'm afraid I do need to use them if the jury is to fully appreciate not only the nature and degree of damage, but also the surgical treatment we've been required to do for Ryan. They also bear on the nature and extent of his future surgeries as well, both cosmetically and functionally. It's rather difficult to do that without being able to make reference to some of the photos themselves. In explaining burn injuries," he said, somewhat apologetically, "a picture truly is, unfortunately, worth a thousand words, Judge Vaughn." He could read Vaughn's name on the plaque that sat on the front of the judge's bench.

Vaughn liked the witness. I had primed Olive for questions from me. I didn't anticipate that The Turtle himself would jump into the fray with questions of his own. Olive handled them like a pro.

Vaughn surprised me at the ease in which he ruled on this point. It was a backhanded victorious evidentiary ruling, however.

"I'm going to permit him to show them to the jury," he announced. "They're necessary for the presentation of the doctor's testimony and opinions. However, I'm stating on the record that I am not necessarily finding that Mr. Culhane and his clients have made the prima facie showing that the record will reflect was the basis of my earlier ruling on these photos. I'm still reserving on that issue," he warned. It was intended to serve as a continued red flag to me that he was not impressed with the adequacy of my case and was reserving the right to throw it out at the close of my evidence. Not a good sign, and another shot over my bow. With that, Vaughn gave the jury a cautionary instruction that they were not to allow the shocking and graphic photographs of Ryan's injuries to influence their ultimate verdict on the liability issues in the case.

Vaughn's continued hostility to my case was troublesome. I tried to ignore it.

As The Turtle was instructing the jury, he had their complete attention. I casually turned my head to the right to look at Harrington seated at his defense table. He wasn't happy with the court's ruling, even with the cautionary instruction. I caught his eye. *Fuck you Bob*, I winked as payback for his earlier sarcastic *good luck* comment to me about getting the photos into evidence. The jury was paying attention to the judge and did not observe my exchange.

Dr. Olive proceeded to discuss Ryan's burn injuries with the jury. He asked permission, which Vaughn granted, to step down in front of the jury box itself so that he could display the enlarged photos as he spoke. The jury, both men and women alike, visibly cringed when they viewed Ryan's burns. Olive's photos were indeed worth a thousand words in the horrific pain, damage and disfigurement they depicted. Ryan's face and upper body had the appearance of a badly charred skin of a breast of chicken left on the barbeque entirely too long. The loss of his ear and nose appeared grotesque. The second series of photos Olive showed to the jury were taken after the initial debridement of the burned tissue, a procedure which the burn specialist described as horribly painful to the patient. It was a procedure that had to be repeated with regularity as needed.

"How painful is it to the patient, doctor?" I asked.

"Mr. Culhane, if it didn't have medical overtones and necessities, it would be considered torture. And that's not intended to be an exaggeration or a figure of speech."

The jurors winced.

The prior skin grafting he performed on Ryan was described. He also summarized the first stages that were only now underway for cosmetically re-fabricating an ear to replace the one that had been burned off. He explained that in the next month, he was about to use bone harvested and then whittled from Ryan's ribs in order to create the structure for a replacement ear. The whittled bone would be sewn into a skin pouch from new donor skin located on an unburned area of his stomach. If it took in the stomach area, it would be surgically attached to the area of his missing ear. It was a delicate, time-consuming, painful and expensive set of operative procedures. Success in that operative procedure, he noted, was a limited one and, even then, by no means guaranteed.

Olive was equally descriptive about the intense and painful operative and grafting procedures that were also planned for the rebuilding of Ryan's burned-off nose.

"Dr. Olive. How normal, if I can use that word, will Ryan look if your various planned surgeries are successful?"

He shook his head. "Normal and successful, as I alluded to a moment ago, are relative terms, as you must appreciate. They are not terms that I would use with this child's serious level of burn injuries, at least from the standpoint that most people think. Even the best results I can provide will still leave him with a hugely grotesque physical appearance. His appearance will always render him the subject of marked attention by the public. The best that we can do from a medical standpoint is to improve some of Ryan's function and to grossly improve his cosmetics."

"Dr. Olive, did Ryan sustain any burn-related damage to his lungs in this accident?"

"Yes. Based on the testing that I've had conducted on his pulmonary system, it appears that he ingested quite a bit of hot smoke before he was rescued from the vehicle. Some of his lung lining was scarred. He will always have some deficit in his full lung capacity and will always be at risk for pneumonia or emphysema. The little boy is a true fighter, but he's only begun his battles," he sighed. "I wish I could be more optimistic."

The chubby lady and the fast food employee on the jury were dabbing their eyes with Kleenex. The rest of the panel, though dry eyed, were visibly moved by the medical devastation related to them by Olive. As he finished, Eric couldn't handle the doctor's testimony any further. He quietly got up and walked out of the courtroom, leaving me alone at the podium. His control over his composure was losing its grip. It was his son's life and future that were being painfully outlined in graphic terms, which I was sure that Dr. Olive had never fully described to him before.

I ended my direct by obtaining his projections of the costs of future surgeries and follow-up medical care that would be required over the course of Ryan's life to deal with his injuries. The costs would likely be over seven hundred thousand dollars at today's costs.

"Thank you, doctor. Your witness," I said to Harrington.

It didn't take much to realize that the jury liked Dr. Olive. He was the type of doctor that you'd want treating your child should your child ever fall into Ryan's predicament. Recognizing that fact, Harrington asked only a few cursory questions. I didn't have any re-direct.

I put Dr. Natalie Avalos on as my next witness. Sandy had called her the night before at her home in Gainesville to inform her that we needed her a day earlier than planned. While caught with prior commitments, she nonetheless agreed to re-arrange her schedule and take the first morning plane into Ft. Lauderdale to testify. After having just heard Dr. Olive's testimony regarding Ryan's burn injuries, the jury needed to hear her opinions regarding the emotional and psychological injuries that the boy would face over the course of his life.

Eric did not return to the courtroom while she testified. He obviously couldn't handle what she had to say about his son.

A diminutive woman with large brown eyes and raven-black hair, Avalos made a great witness. Despite having been born in Cuba, she had mastered the English language to the point that one had to listen hard to detect an accent.

She explained her unique expertise, which was the treatment and assessment of the emotional injuries associated with burn injuries. She was the director of that department at Shands Hospital at the University of Florida, in Gainesville. Shands served as the major regional burn trauma center in the northern half of the state. As a result, she saw a lot of burn victims.

Like Olive, an immediate rapport developed between her and the jury. She was extremely professional and clinical, yet she coupled her approach with a refreshingly warm personal side. She took an interest in her patients. The fact that she had personally come down to Ft. Lauderdale to see Ryan on four different occasions was not lost on the jury.

"How many burn patients have you assessed and treated over your career, doctor?" I asked.

"I would estimate somewhere in the range of a thousand. Of that group, perhaps a third of that population had the severity of injuries that Ryan has."

She outlined her extensive publications in the field. They were numerous and impressive.

The essence of her testimony was that the Ryan Hawkins who left home with his mother on the afternoon of the accident no longer existed, nor did the man who would have developed from that child. Even as undefined as his young personality was on the day of the accident, she explained, it had been irreversibly altered forever by the burns which had ravaged his face and body. The resulting scars would cut deep into his soul and psyche. Those scars would define him.

"According to the studies that have been conducted, as well as my own observations with my own patients, there is a typical future profile for a child with the level and nature of burn injuries that Ryan has," she related. "He will be the subject of ridicule and isolation over the course of his life. He'll be laughed at by peers, viewed as beastly by strangers, and will begin to believe it himself. His confidence will be minimal. The stereotypical person with his facial injuries usually doesn't date, will likely never marry, and will lead a life of severe loneliness and depression. It is truly only the unique individual who can exhibit the will and inner strength to press forward and try to fit into what you and I would call normal socialization," she emphasized to the jury. "Unfortunately, with a few of my patients the depression associated with these injuries was simply too much to handle. They committed suicide. One was a fourteen-year-old boy."

I was glad that Eric had decided to leave the courtroom for her testimony.

After obtaining projected costs of periodic psychological counseling that Ryan would likely need to have over the course of his lifetime, which she put at one hundred fifty thousand dollars, I tendered the witness to Harrington.

As he did with his cross-examination of Dr. Olive, Harrington also played it low key in his cross of Dr. Avalos. The devastation of the injuries spoke for itself; he knew better than try to minimize them. He nibbled away at smaller points and ended. He was putting his marbles in the basket of 'no liability.'

The medical and damage testimony was moving quickly. After lunch, I called Paula Price to the stand to talk about the other 'forgotten plaintiff,' Sarah. I didn't want her injuries to get ignored with the significant focus I had been placing on Ryan's injuries. Price, in her 40s, was very professional, but a 'plain Jane' in the looks department, with red hair she wore in a bun. Her rather drab appearance, I felt, coupled with her excellent background and credentials, added to her credibility. She definitely did not appear as a hired gun

After qualifying her as an expert in the field of child psychology, I went directly to the meat of her opinions. She explained to the jury that she had first become involved with the Hawkins' family after the accident. She was asked to treat Sarah for her psychological response to the loss of her mother and the injuries to her brother. She had been seeing Sarah on a regular basis since that time to help her deal with her grief and loss.

"How is Sarah reacting to her loss?" I asked.

"Quite poorly. She blames herself for her mother's death. She had a very close and very positive relationship with her mother before her death, and she misses her intensely."

"Is this unusual behavior for a young girl of Sarah's age, that is, to blame herself for her mother's death?"

"No, it is actually quite common," Price answered. "However, we have an element in Sarah's case that is somewhat unique."

"What's that?"

"The fact that her mother was killed while on an errand for Sarah's Girl Scout Troop project. She was picking up some Girl Scout cookies, as I understand it. Sarah is aware of that and blames herself all the more as a result. It was only after about a dozen meetings with Sarah that she finally was willing to share her feelings with me about that. She sobbed heavily when she related that she had begged her mother to be the Girl Scout troop leader for this cookie project."

"How is Sarah's psychological condition now, and will it resolve itself in the future?"

She shook her head. "Sarah is a very devastated young girl. She has withdrawn into herself as a result of what has happened to her family. She is going through some very serious depression, even though, on the outside, she is really trying to be upbeat and positive for her dad and brother. I think that with the passage of time, she will improve," she offered, "but she will never get over it completely. In fact, over the course of my meetings with her, I've seen Sarah becoming a much more hardened child with a much more indifferent attitude about life."

"How so?"

"Sarah," she explained, "is an extremely bright girl. Before this accident, she was in her school's gifted program. She was given much more challenging schoolwork than the average students received." Price, being comfortable on the stand, had turned to speak directly to the jury. She possessed an easy rapport most witnesses, including experts, would never achieve, even after years of experience. "Her school records reflect that she excelled before this accident. In fact, she had straight As in each of the three years immediately preceding the death of her mother. She was also absent only a total of two sick days in that same three year period. Since the accident, her grades have dropped to Cs and Ds. That by itself is a very disturbing indicator. She's also been sick from school for twenty-two days this past school year alone. She doesn't want to talk about it. That's indicative of depression."

The witness took a small number of papers from a manila folder she had in front of her. "These are the assessment reports which her gifted teachers filled out on her for the three years prior to her mother's death," she said, referring to the pages in front of her. "They are glowing in their description of her cheerful and positive outlook and approach to her schoolwork. They emphasize her tendency to want to help out other students in her classes. She was also described as being a very social girl, with a great number of strong and diverse friends." She put the pages down and looked at the jury. "That is not the Sarah that I have come to know. Her present school assessment only echoes my opinion. She has been removed from the gifted program due to her lack of interest and motivation."

I needed to ask the question that I felt a lot of jurors think about: psychological injuries. "Ms. Price, are these psychological injuries that you've described to the jury real? I mean, aren't we just making matters worse for Sarah by dwelling on her emotional and psychological loss?"

"Mr. Culhane, Sarah's injuries are real. They're as real as her brother's injuries, although not as tangible or self-evident. As far as your question about her dwelling on her loss, I would say this: There are patients, I agree, who have a pre-existing psychological bent to want to dwell and fixate on a loss such as this, and who show little interest in getting on with their life. For those people, psychological counseling may have little benefit, although it should be tried. For those people, the loss of a mother, for example, could not fairly be said to completely cause their resulting emotional and psychological problems. Rather, the death only exacerbated a pre-existing problem. There are others, however, who did not have any pre-existing psychological baggage, if you will, before the loss event. These are people who are doing everything in their power to get on with their life, from a psychological point of view, after having suffered a loss. They want to move on. They need to move on. Yet, through no fault of their own, and despite their very best efforts to the contrary, they find themselves pulled back into depression and emotional malaise, which was caused totally—one hundred percent—by the loss event in question. Sarah fits into this latter group. By nature, she is a fighter. She will get better with time. She will get on with her life. But it will take an awful lot of time and a lot of emotional help for those scars and wounds to close to the point where she is able to move on. Her wounds, however, will never heal completely."

I ended on that note and tendered the witness for cross-examination.

Harrington spent a few moments conferring with the Global representative before beginning his cross. Unlike the other two damage witnesses for Ryan, Harrington felt that he could score points with an aggressive cross-examination of Price. He was aware of the same jury survey information I had regarding juror attitudes about psychological injury claims; they treated them with a great deal of suspicion and skepticism.

"Is it Dr. Price or Ms. Price?" he opened.

"It's Ms. Price. I do not have a doctorate," she answered.

Harrington frowned. "Are there doctoral degrees given in child psychology, which provide one with additional education and training in this area?"

"Yes, there are doctoral degrees in my area. Once I received my master's, I became involved in the clinical treatment end of the field and never found the time thereafter to obtain a doctorate."

"I assume that you've written and published in the area of psychological loss to children?" Again, he knew the answer to his question from the deposition he had taken from her.

"No, I've focused exclusively on the treatment end of the practice; in the trenches, so to speak."

"I see," he commented without enthusiasm.

"At the time that this accident happened, Sarah was eight years old, wasn't she?"

"That's correct, she's now nine," Price answered.

"You are familiar with the study undertaken and published by Dr. Ellen Blackstone dealing with the psychological changes in young adolescent girls, are you not?"

"Yes, I've read it."

"You would recognize that study as authoritative in your field, would you not?"

"Yes, I would. It's very good, very thorough."

"In fact, Dr. Blackstone was one of your college professors, wasn't she? She taught you some of the basic principles that you try to implement in your daily practice, isn't that correct?" Harrington casually glanced over at the jury for effect.

"Yes to both questions," she answered politely.

"Well, isn't it true that Dr. Blackstone's study found that even in the normal population of pre-teenage girls, those who have not suffered any catastrophe, like the death of a mother, roughly *eighteen percent* of those girls experienced *very drastic and disturbing changes* in their personalities as they went through their teen years?"

"That is what the study concluded, yes." She adjusted herself in the witness chair.

"So, isn't it true that some of the personality changes that you have observed in Sarah Hawkins may well be due to factors having absolutely nothing to do with this accident, that is, she just happens to fall within the eighteen percent group of these girls?" His tone was even but pressing.

Price held her ground. "No, I don't agree with that statement, and that certainly is not my opinion. Her present emotional and psychological problems are due to the accident."

Harrington walked back to his table and whipped a document out of the manila folder on his table. He made a big production for the jury as he walked over and handed a copy to the witness. He tossed a copy on my table as he passed on his way back to the examination podium.

"Well, didn't that student assessment I just hand you, which was conducted on Sarah by her own teacher *before* the accident, report that she was having periodic problems remaining focused, as her teacher put it, on her schoolwork? Go ahead and check the report in front of you if you'd like," he confidently suggested, nodding at the paper he had just handed her.

"Your Honor," I rose, "I object. This document was not disclosed as an exhibit by the defense in their pre-trial report. We've had absolutely no opportunity to address this document."

"Impeachment, Judge," Harrington quickly countered, "I'm not offering it into evidence, nor do I intend to."

Vaughn nodded in agreement at Harrington's last comment. "It is impeachment, so I'm going to overrule the objection. Go ahead and respond to the question, Ms. Price."

I sat down.

Price looked back from the judge to Harrington. "It does say that, but—"

"And isn't a lack of focus," Harrington drilled, "one of the very psychological problems that you still note in your reports regarding Sarah?" he asked, holding up one of the witness's written reports for the jury to see. You'd think that he was displaying O.J.'s bloody glove.

"Yes, I did say that, but it—"

"And isn't it true, Ms. Price," he now bludgeoned, "that Sarah's teacher would be in a much better position than you're in to know and appreciate what her *pre-accident* psychological make-up was?"

"I didn't see her until *after* the accident, if that's what you mean."

"That's precisely what I mean. You never saw her, spoke with her or even knew of her existence before this accident, did you?"

"That's true."

"So, when you tell the jury about how this accident *may* have adversely affected her, and how she *may* respond in the future, isn't it true that you're doing an awful lot of guesswork?"

His aggressive style rattled her. "I will concede that my opinions involve a certain degree of judgment on my part," she acknowledged.

"And part of your judgment involves educated guesswork, doesn't it?"

Stick to your guns, I mentally commanded. Of course, she didn't.

The witness considered for a moment before answering. "I suppose you could put it that way."

"Thank you for your candor," Harrington closed.

I spent fifteen minutes bringing out the points that Harrington had cut her off from making on cross. However, Harrington ended up getting the last word when Price started referring to clinical tests, which she had recently administered to Sarah, which confirmed her findings of traumatic-induced psychological problems on Sarah resulting from the Mesa accident.

"Wait a minute!" Harrington roared, as soon as Price started referring to those tests in response to my questions. "I took this witness's deposition, and she didn't say anything about conducting any tests! This is prejudicial. I move to strike any reference to this new area, Your Honor."

Vaughn's eyes ignited. He looked impatiently at the clock on the wall to his right and then over at me. This little firefight had lit his tinder. "Bailiff!" he barked impatiently, "Take the jury back to the jury room for a few moments while I handle this evidentiary matter. Ladies and gentlemen," he addressed the jury, "I'll call you back in when we are ready."

The Scarecrow bailiff, who had been sitting in his usual coma-like stupor on the other side of the courtroom, with his arms draped across his chest, and his legs stretched out before him, jumped from his chair at the judge's roar like he'd been jolted with stray voltage. He nodded wordlessly to Vaughn and immediately herded the jury out of the courtroom while the rest of us waited.

"Is that true?" The Turtle leaned forward and challenged the witness as soon as the jury was out the door. He ignored me altogether in his questioning of the witness.

"I'm sorry Judge, but is what true?" she responded.

"Testing! That's what we're talking about here, ma'am. Did you conduct testing after your deposition in this case was taken that you did not share with counsel for the defense?"

"Well, I did conduct testing after my deposition, but I certainly didn't intend to hide that testing from anyone," she said with some offense taken at the judge's insinuation. "I hadn't considered it necessary to conduct this testing earlier," she answered. "My decision to have Sarah undergo psychological testing was made after my deposition for reasons having nothing to do with this case. Sarah just wasn't getting any better, and I felt that I needed some objective indicators of her psychological problems for treatment purposes. The tests provide that information," she said defensively.

"Counsel," he now turned to me, scowling, like a man whose hemorrhoids were on fire, "why weren't these tests disclosed to Mr. Harrington prior to trial?"

"I wasn't even aware of them, judge, until last night when I prepared the witness for her testimony today. The tests were conducted only last week, and she obtained the complete written reports only a few days ago. Even I don't have a copy of the test results. They were performed by Ms. Price for treatment, not trial. And I wouldn't have even gone into them had defense counsel not pursued the cross-examination he did, Your Honor. Given those facts, it would be terribly unfair to my client if the jury was denied the opportunity to hear of their results."

"If you learned of them last night, why didn't you provide a copy of the written test results to Mr. Harrington this morning?" Vaughn fumed. "I don't see any excuse for that."

"Two reasons," I pleaded. "First, I wasn't required to. It's the *defendant's* obligation to obtain current treatment records up to the time of trial, not my obligation to spoon feed it treatment records. Global didn't do its job. Second, I didn't expect that the witness would even get into this area. You'll note that I asked her absolutely no questions about those tests in my direct exam, Judge. It was Mr. Harrington here, *not me*, who elicited her testimony regarding this recent testing. He asked the proverbial 'one too many questions' on cross, Judge, and he shouldn't be allowed now to cry 'prejudice' to this court."

"Well I disagree with your analysis, Mr. Culhane. I don't permit lawyers to try their cases in my courtroom by ambush," he ruled with ill temper. "I don't find your exhibit disclosure sufficient. Those tests should have been specifically identified and turned over so that the defense could evaluate them. They're prejudicial. Accordingly, I'm finding them inadmissible. Don't make any reference to them," he said to me, "and that goes for you too," he said, admonishing the witness sharply.

Finally exercising more discretion than valor, I shut up.

"Are you through with this witness, Mr. Culhane?" he asked, looking again at the clock on the wall.

You and your fucking fixation on tempus fugit, I thought to myself. The man might be the engineer on a train headed for hell, but he was damn well going to make sure he got there on time.

"Given your ruling, I am," I said.

"Good. Bailiff, bring in that jury and let's get this case moving."

The jury was escorted back into the courtroom and sat down, at which point The Turtle admonished them to completely ignore any reference the witness had made to tests or test results which she had alluded to in her testimony. He also advised them that I had finished with my re-direct with Ms. Price.

"Any re-cross, Mr. Harrington?" he inquired.

"Thank you, Your Honor," Harrington buttered as he rose from his chair, "but I've covered all that needs to be covered with this witness." He smiled confidently and sat down.

The witness was excused.

CHAPTER 43

MY LAST WITNESS was my economist and damage expert, Dr. Peter Cianciolo. A thin man, with the bulging eyes of a walleyed pike, Cianciolo was arrogant and expensive. He was also extremely bright and qualified.

With his dual doctorates in physical rehabilitation and economics, Cianciolo came across like he knew what he was talking about. He opined that over the course of his lifetime, Ryan's injuries, both burn and psychological, would result in him earning two-and-a-half million dollars less than what he would likely have earned without those injuries and disabilities.

Harrington's cross was short and sweet.

"Your entire economic opinions here are predicated on the *assumption* that Ryan will, indeed, suffer both physical and psychological problems and handicaps to such an extent that his work career, whatever it may be, will be adversely affected. Isn't that true?"

"Absolutely, it's an assumption, but it's going to happen," he answered, not giving Harrington any ground. "I've seen it occur time and time again in my consulting practice."

"Really? Are we talking about your litigation consulting practice where you charge two hundred fifty dollars an hour for your testimony?"

"No, I'm talking about my litigation consulting practice where I charge three hundred dollars an hour. You must have my old fee schedule," he said, not missing a beat in his reply. He held eye contact with Harrington and did not waiver.

Harrington looked through his tortoiseshell glasses over to the jury. "And you're charging three hundred dollars *an hour* to work on Mr. Culhane's case here, aren't you?"

"Actually, my regular rate is three hundred dollars an hour, as I mentioned, but when I testify, there is a four hour minimum, counsel, at three hundred fifty dollars an hour." Cianciolo was proud as punch of his billing rate.

"So, if I understand what you're telling us, you're getting *fourteen hundred dollars* today to come in and testify for Mr. Culhane in this case and give those opinions?" Harrington's voice was laced with mock surprise and shock.

"Yes, that's correct," the witness shot back in kind. "And," he added, looking directly at the jury to make his point, "that should not come as a surprise to you. I told you my rate at my deposition."

He was certainly on the arrogant side, I observed, but I hoped the jury appreciated his moxie as much as I did. He was not about to take any shit from any lawyer.

Harrington begged of sparring with him further. Not wanting to end up with a bloody nose, he sought to end the cross with a final question "Tell us, sir, exactly how much money did you make *consulting* in litigation cases last year?"

It should have been an easy question for Cianciolo to answer, concede and move on. It wasn't. Arrogantly, and feeling his oats, he bridled.

"I don't see where that's relevant," Cianciolo replied, looking at the judge for protection. I wasn't about to rescue him. It was proper cross. My repeated admonitions to Cianciolo over the phone last night not to alienate himself with the jury, or to antagonize Harrington, of course, went unheeded. I could only hope the jury accepted him for what he was: a smart-ass, but one who knew his stuff.

"It is relevant," Vaughn quickly ruled, without prompting from Harrington. "Answer the question."

"Uh ... I don't keep exact records like that in my head. It was a substantial sum. I work hard on a lot of cases."

Given this unexpected plum, Harrington didn't waste it.

"Come now, Dr. Cianciolo," Harrington said, returning to his table behind him to retrieve what looked like a deposition transcript, "didn't you give sworn deposition testimony only three months ago in the case of *Perkins v. Harley-Davidson* in which you testified that last year you earned *over* four hundred thirty thousand dollars from litigation consulting?" Harrington brandished the transcript like it was a revolver pointed at the witness.

Cianciolo shrugged his shoulders. "If that's what I testified to in that deposition, then that must be right," he answered.

"'If that's what I testified to in that deposition'?" Harrington repeated, mocking the witness's response. "You do tell the truth when you are under oath, don't you sir?"

"Of course I do."

"Sir, four hundred thirty thousand dollars is an awful lot of money, isn't it?"

"Yes. I've been fortunate."

"You certainly have," he said, looking again over at the jury for effect. "And every last one of the cases that you have *consulted* on in the last five years has been on behalf of a plaintiff. Isn't that true sir?"

"That's correct."

"Is that just a coincidence, sir?"

"No, not at all. The defense companies and their attorneys have their own favorite experts. You know it as well as I do, Mr. Harrington."

I kept my head down, doodling on a legal pad in front of me as if this was inane cross-examination. My mind, however, floated back to my freshman English class, and the only thing I remembered from the Greek classics: Everyone has a fatal flaw. Bright as he was, Cianciolo's flaw was that he was an arrogant ass.

"Favorite experts," Harrington repeated, "interesting phrase you used. That's exactly what you are in this case, isn't it, a favorite expert of the plaintiffs' lawyers?"

Cianciolo laughed out loud at the question. "Counsel, you've been around long enough to know me. I'm not a Casper Milquetoast. My opinions are entirely my own, and everybody who knows me knows that."

"Isn't it true, sir, that the *sole* reason that you're hired only by plaintiffs and paid *huge* sums of money is because plaintiffs' lawyers know that when they call on Dr. Peter Cianciolo, they know that he will take the stand, just like you're doing right now, and throw out huge boxcar damage numbers to a jury in order to recover huge damage verdicts?"

"I don't think that deserves a response."

I snuck a glance over at the jury. The x-ray tech with the tattoo sleeve looked like he was enjoying the wrestling match he was seeing.

"I see. Well," Harrington ended, "at three hundred dollars an hour— excuse me, at three hundred fifty dollars an hour," Harrington corrected himself, "I don't think we can afford to waste the time to ask you anymore questions. I have nothing more for this witness."

The hardware store owner on the jury broke open with a stifled laugh at Harrington's parting jab.

"THE PLAINTIFFS REST," I announced in front of the jury after Cianciolo had stepped down.

The Turtle looked at the wall clock. It was four o'clock.

"Do you have motions, Mr. Harrington?" he prompted. "I want to address them this afternoon. It's Friday, and I want them handled before Monday morning in this case."

"Yes I do."

Vaughn dismissed the jury for the day, explaining that the lawyers had to address certain legal motions outside their presence. He admonished them to be back on time first thing Monday morning.

CHAPTER 44

"THE DEFENDANTS MOVE for a directed verdict dismissing the plaintiffs' claims in this case," Harrington announced as soon as the last juror had exited the courtroom. Craige had moved his chair next to Global's table for the arguments. The Confederate also moved his next to Craige. Craige had the legal research memoranda and copies of cases for Harrington to use in his argument. I suspected that Craige wanted to be within easy reach of kissing Harrington's ass if The Turtle granted Harrington's motion.

"The plaintiffs have utterly failed to show any defect in the Mesa. As this court is aware, there must be a *prima facie* showing of defect, based upon some minimum level of non-speculative evidence before a case can be submitted to a jury for determination. Otherwise, the jury is left with pure conjecture."

Vaughn was sitting back in his chair. His arms were folded across his ample chest as he listened, nodding in agreement with Harrington's summary of the law.

"Here, the Hawkins' defect case is predicated on the defect opinion of Dr. Braxton. He opines that there is some type of stability defect in the Mesa. Yet his opinions, in turn, are based upon the accident happening like their other expert, Mr. Cargill, says it happened. And while Mr. Cargill refused to acknowledge it during cross-examination, it's clear, Your Honor, that his reconstruction opinions are clearly predicated, in turn, upon the supposed eyewitness testimony of Mr. Abadin that the rollover actually started while the Mesa was still on the road and not after it had started sliding sideways in the grassy median. The whole problem with that theory, however, is that Mr. Abadin's testimony doesn't support it! He clearly conceded during my cross-examination that he previously swore he was *three hundred feet* behind the Hawkins Mesa and that he isn't sure exactly what he saw when the accident occurred. The bottom line, Judge," he argued, "is that we have a house of cards built upon sheer conjecture, *not facts*. Consequently, the case should be dismissed here and now." He tossed his glasses on the legal pad on the table before him and sat down in his chair.

Contrary to typical protocol, The Turtle didn't wait for my response before he started in with his own observations.

"I'm troubled, Mr. Harrington. In a products liability case, I'm required to see some factual basis in the evidence to support the existence of the supposed defect. The plaintiff usually makes that factual showing in a products liability case such as this by presenting testing that his experts have conducted upon which the expert can base his opinions that the product is defective and unreasonably dangerous. Or," he said, adjusting his thick black glasses on the bridge of his nose, "the plaintiff is able to offer evidence to show that the accident couldn't have happened except for the presence of a defect in the product—a *res ipsa* type of case. Here," he said, leaning forward and paging through his yellow pad of his handwritten notes of witness testimony in front of him, "there are clear alternative explanations in the record for the cause of the Hawkins' accident that have nothing whatsoever to do with any 'defect' existing in the Mesa. For starters, it appears to me that there's a pretty good chance that Mrs. Hawkins could have been speeding here or could have simply lost control and flipped the utility vehicle after she was already on the grassy median. When you couple all of that with what I view as the inherently unreliable eyewitness testimony of this Abadin fellow, I don't see how I can allow this case to go to a jury. I'm inclined to grant Global's motion. What have I missed?" he asked, finally allowing me to respond.

I could feel Eric's panic as he looked sideways towards me. His panic was only a close second to mine. I rose and addressed Vaughn.

"With all due respect, your honor, Mr. Harrington has missed something in his analysis. That *something* is the law. While neither you nor Global are apparently impressed with the quality of my evidence, the fact of the matter is that a directed verdict is legally permissible only where there is a complete absence of *any evidence* in the record to support a finding of defect. That has been the law since day one, and was recently re-affirmed by the Fourth District Court of Appeals in *Bentley v. Trident Gear Company.*" I calmly stepped forward and handed him a copy of the *Bentley* case which I had pulled from my trial notebook. "As the *Bentley* court ruled, if there is *some evidence* of defect in the record, and the ultimate determination rests heavily on the credibility of the plaintiff's witnesses, it is not for the trial court to take the case away from the jury. It's the jury's function to make that determination after all the evidence is heard. While I respectfully disagree with Your Honor's analysis of my case, what I think I just heard you comment is that it really boils down to an issue of credibility of the evidence. So, unless this court is willing to rule that I have offered no evidence of defect, and that clearly is not the case, Global's directed verdict motion has to be denied. That's the law."

"So, you believe my hands are tied on this?" he asked me.

"Yes, Your Honor, if you're going to follow what is the clearly defined law in Florida on that issue."

"But your evidence, Mr. Culhane, with all due respect to your client," he said, nodding to Eric to soften the blow, "is gossamer thin. At best, it has the substance of rice paper. Don't I have the duty to dismiss it now?"

"Exactly," Harrington quickly piped up from his chair, "you're prohibited from allowing pure fantasy to go to the jury, Judge. You're the gatekeeper."

"You likened the strength of my evidence to that of rice paper, Your Honor," I persisted. "However, even evidence having the diameter of a *cobweb strand* is all that is required under Florida law to defeat a defendant's motion for directed verdict. You're hands are tied," I repeated, hoping to force him into the result I needed.

Vaughn frowned like a man whose underwear was three sizes too tight in exactly the wrong place. He sat back in his chair, grabbed the copy of the *Bentley* case I had given him and quietly re-read it. He then reviewed his handwritten notes of the evidence given by the witnesses. The rest of us waited quietly for his ruling. I had the impression he was scouring the case for any possible basis to throw the case out. Finally, after four or five long minutes, he spoke.

"Upon further reflection, I'm going to defer my ruling on Global's motion. Mr. Culhane, it looks like your reading of Florida law is correct. However," he sternly warned, "if the state of your defect evidence is the same at the close of Global's case as it is now, I'm granting the motion at that time. I'm not about to let the jury decide a case that is based on what appears to me to be fairy dust for evidence. Even the *Bentley* case doesn't sanction that result. Am I making myself clear, Mr. Culhane?"

Thank you, God. "Yes, Your Honor."

"All right," Vaughn continued, "I want everybody back here at nine a.m. sharp Monday morning. Mr. Harrington, I want Global ready to proceed with its defense case at that time." With that pronouncement, he slammed his gavel down and left the bench as I rose for his departure. As soon as he was gone, I slumped back into my chair next to Eric. We looked at each other and took a collective sigh of relief as the Global entourage harrumphed and packed its files to reload over the weekend for Monday morning's artillery siege of our case.

CHAPTER 45

"DAD'S NOT WITH us again," Erin announced. Liz and Anne both looked at me across the restaurant table, over the two remaining pieces of a large pizza in front of the four of us. Erin was working on a plate of pasta. We were eating at an outdoor restaurant overlooking the marina, off Seabreeze Boulevard.

"I'm sorry," I said, "I was thinking about something on the case."

My daughters looked at each other and laughed.

Liz and the girls *invited* me to go out for pizza with them that night after I got home from the trial. It was a rare Friday night; neither of the girls was babysitting nor doing something with their friends, so Liz suggested grabbing a pizza and catching a movie.

"Michael, you've got to let it go for tonight," Liz said, with irritation. "You're taking tonight off, remember?"

"You're right. I'm sorry. I was just thinking about the faces on a few of the jurors, that's all."

"What do you mean?" Anne asked as she picked the mushrooms off her piece and piled them on her plate. "Are they like making monkey faces at you, dad?" She teased and giggled as she said it. Erin and Liz joined in.

"Very funny," I laughed. Anne had recovered completely from the canal swim the two of us had taken. "No," I said more seriously, "what I meant is that I looked over at the jury at the end of the trial today. I caught two of them looking at me with kind of a scowl. I don't think they like my case much. It's got me worried, that's all."

"Well, you can't do anything about it tonight," Liz said. "And, besides, didn't you always tell me that it's a mistake to try and read the minds of the jurors?"

"Yeah, you're right," I said, dispelling my funk. "Anyway, I'm not dwelling on it tonight, am I?" I said, reaching over and giving Erin a 'horse bite' on her thigh. She squealed and laughed.

"Good, no more trial talk tonight," Liz added, grabbing another piece of pizza for herself.

"Now, this is not related to the trial," I said, raising my hand defensively, "but it came up during the trial today. I think that you'll find it interesting. It's really weird, though," I added, hoping to poke their curiosity.

"What?" Erin asked.

"Well, you know how the brain controls all of your sensations in your body?"

Erin looked at me, canting her head. "Yeah."

"Well, this doctor was on the stand trying to make a point about sensation in peoples' hands being controlled by the brain and its interaction with the eye. He was talking about Ryan's burn injuries," I said. "His point was that in some people, their brain is incapable of feeling complete sensation in the palm of their hands, for example, unless they can actually see their palm at the same time that it's being touched."

"I don't understand," Liz said.

"Let me show you the experiment that he showed the jury," I explained. "It was really weird. It will surprise you." I looked at Anne who was sitting directly across the table from me. "Put out your hand to me, palm side up. I'll show you what he showed us."

"Will it hurt?" she asked, ever the Doubting Thomas.

"Of course not. The doctor demonstrated it on me during trial. It's neat," I added.

She put out her right hand over the table between us. I turned it over so that it was palm side up and put my left hand underneath.

"Okay, close your eyes and tell me if you can tell how many of my fingers are touching your palm. It's going to be one, two or three fingers, okay? Ready?" I asked.

"This is supposed to be hard?" she mocked. She closed her eyes.

"Are you sure that your eyes are closed tight? The experiment won't work if you can see at all. It's some kind of brain thing," I cautioned her.

"Dad, they're closed tight," she replied. "This is dumb."

I looked over at Liz and Erin and brought my finger to my lips, signaling them to be quiet. I winked at them. Erin smiled as she realized what was about to happen.

"Now hold your palm out flat for a moment to let the blood supply even out," I instructed, as I quietly reached over with my right hand and grabbed the pile of squishy mushrooms on her plate that she had extracted from her pizza. "This is how the witness instructed. Now, tell me without looking, how many fingers I am laying in your palm," I directed.

With that I dropped a handful of the greasy mushrooms into her palm and, at the same instant, forced her hand closed with my left. Also now encompassing it within my right hand as well, I squished the greasy contents in her palm, not letting her open up her hand.

"Ahhhh ... yuck!!!" she exploded as her eyes instantly opened and she saw what was happening. Gelatinous, compressed mushrooms were squeezing out from between her fingers. "Dad!!" she yelled, causing the people at the tables around us to look over at the sudden noise and disturbance.

The three of us broke out laughing loudly at her as I finally let her hand go. She dropped the pasty remains on her plate with the same disgust as if they were the remains of squished night crawlers and grabbed a napkin, wiping off her palm.

"That, Sweet Pea, is payback for your monkey face comment," I smiled. I thought that Erin was going to wet her pants laughing, while Liz was running a close second. Anne, though disgusted, started laughing herself as she wiped her hand with a napkin.

"Let's get out of here," I suggested. We were still laughing and feeding off each other as we headed for the deck steps down to our car in the lot below.

I WAS IN my office the next morning, Saturday, working on cross examination points for Global's witnesses and writing briefs on two other cases that I had backing up due to the trial. There was a mess of mail and pleadings from other files that needed tending as well. Harrington surprised me by calling around eleven.

"I thought you'd be in," he said as soon as I answered, without introduction. "After Vaughn's comments to you and your client yesterday, I figured that you would be working double time to come up with a case since you haven't come up with one yet."

I recognized his voice immediately. "Well, what a pleasant surprise," I shot back. "I'm assuming you have a reason to bother me. I don't have time to spar with you."

"I'm not calling to spar. I'm calling at the specific direction of my client," he quickly pointed out.

"Oh, really? Tell me Bobby, what does my old pal Willis Cole want to threaten me with this time?"

"Don't get paranoid on us, Mikey," he shot back. "Cole instructed me to tell you that he's still willing to offer the Hawkins family a settlement of one hundred thousand dollars to resolve the case. It's going to cost us at least that much to bring in our experts next week to kick your ass around the court and to defend against the appeals that you will undoubtedly take when the case gets thrown out by Vaughn."

"Another settlement offer? I thought that you were through making settlement offers. Are the boys in Michigan getting a little nervous after all?" I bluffed. I wasn't expecting this kind of call and was still trying to tread water as I got my arms around the message being conveyed.

Harrington laughed benevolently. "Don't let your ego get in the way again, Mikey. It's a cost of defense offer. Don't get excited. It kills me to even make it, but it is the client's instruction. You see, unlike you, I try to follow Global's instructions and the authority they give me. If it was up to me, you wouldn't be getting even this offer. I'd continue the beating. In fact," he added, "do me a favor and reject this offer like you did the last one."

I decided I needed to get serious. "What exactly are the terms?" I asked.

"Very simple: Global pays your clients a hundred grand, and they execute general releases in favor of Global. A confidentiality order will be required, of course."

I waited a few seconds before responding. "While I don't think that Mr. Hawkins is going to waiver in his position, I'll pass it on to him. I'll get back to you."

"I need to hear back from you by the end of the day if you're going to accept. My experts are going to start coming in tomorrow afternoon, and Global doesn't want to spend the money on their air fares and travel time costs if your clients finally get smart and grab the money. Call me at home around five this afternoon if your client decides to take the offer. I'm going to a black tie event after that and won't be around. If I don't hear back from you by five today, I'm telling Cole you rejected it," he said curtly. He gave me his home number and hung up.

"IS OUR CASE really that bad?" That was Eric's first response when I called him at home an hour later to relay the settlement offer. I hesitated to call it a settlement offer at all; it was a capitulation offer. The amount was enough to cover the fifty-five thousand dollars in out-of-pocket costs that Eric and I had invested in the case, but it obviously left little more after my twenty-five percent fees were removed. "I mean, they offered us five hundred thousand dollars before the trial started. Now, it's down to one hundred thousand dollars. Are they that sure they're going to win?" I heard the television playing in the background of his call.

"Clearly they're confident," I answered honestly.

"Do they have reason to be?" he asked. He knew the answer as well as I did, but he apparently wanted to hear it from me.

I hesitated a full two seconds before replying. "Yeah, they do. I think you can see that we're certainly not scoring points with the judge, and I'm not sure we're faring any better with the jury from what I can see. And the problem, Eric," I said, reluctantly, "is that Global hasn't even started its case yet. They have some strong evidence coming at us."

"Are you suggesting that we take it?" It was the first time that I had heard Eric equivocating on pursuing the case.

I hesitated a moment before answering. "Let me put it to you this way. From an economic standpoint, taking the money would let us recover the out of pocket costs that we've both put into the case. I know that you have some of the insurance proceeds in the costs, and you'll need that money back for family costs. And," I continued, laying out the alternatives, "taking the offer would also remove the risk of losing and your having to pay Global's attorneys' fees for the offer of settlement you rejected. However, after taking out the costs and paying my reduced attorney's fees, there won't be anything left to speak of," I said. "That's the reality."

"Uh huh," he said, listening.

"On the other hand, you have to go back and ask yourself why you brought this lawsuit. You've told me time and time again that you didn't bring this case for the money. You brought it to force a jury to address the stability of the Mesa, and for them to tell you whether it's defective. If that's still your goal, then to hell with the offer. It's entirely your call, Eric, and I'm with you one hundred ten percent either way. You know that."

"Mike, do you think that we can win this case? Be honest with me."

"I can't say that. But let me pose the same question to you. You've sat through the trial. How would you vote if you were sitting on the jury so far? Be honest."

It was his turn to hesitate a moment before answering. "I'd probably have to conclude that we have some pretty shaky expert witnesses, and the eyewitness evidence isn't much better. I think we are in trouble." It was an honest response, and I respected his candor.

"Do you want to think it over for a few hours and call me back?" I asked.

"No, that's not necessary. I'm afraid I haven't done a smart thing yet in this case. No reason to start now," he said with a touch of humor in his voice. "Growing up, my dad always had a saying that 'there's an ass for every saddle.' I guess I'm the stupid or stubborn ass on this one."

I laughed. "Is that a 'no'?"

"That's a 'no.' I hope you understand."

"Enough said. In for a penny, in for a pound," I laughed. "I love your fight. I'll see you in my office around eight a.m. Monday morning."

"Mike?"

"Yeah?"

"Thanks for seeing this through with me. I'm proud to be your client."

"The feeling's mutual. I'll see you Monday."

CHAPTER 46

HARRINGTON CALLED OFFICER Martelli as his first witness out of the box on Monday morning. I knew I would have to face the guy and deal with his damaging accident report sooner or later. Later was now here.

When Martelli took the stand, his Oakley sunglasses were nowhere to be seen. Instead, he wore his best uniform, freshly pressed, and his charming, professional 'cop on the witness stand' demeanor. His weightlifter chest and arms bulged against the fabric of his shirt.

Harrington took him through his investigation and his accident report in great detail. I had to hand it to Martelli. He had spent enough time on the stand to know his audience and how to play to them. His deferential and polite attitude towards Harrington and The Turtle belied the nasty arrogant side, which Eric and I had witnessed when we first met him at the hospital the day after the accident. You would have thought the guy was running for office. Kiss the babies and no moving violation citations for anyone.

After an appropriate buildup lasting the better part of an hour regarding his investigation of the Hawkins accident, Harrington finally got to the home run questions.

"Based upon your experience and training in police accident investigation, did you ultimately arrive at a determination, Officer Martelli, as to the cause of this unfortunate accident?" Harrington asked.

"I did."

"And would you share your conclusions with us, sir?"

"This accident was caused by two factors. The first was the sudden appearance of the step ladder coming lose from the pickup truck in front of the Hawkins vehicle. The second, unfortunately, is one I see all too often: poor driver judgment and speeding on the part of the driver of the Mesa, Mrs. Hawkins."

"Meaning?"

"Her loss of control and the resulting rollover and fire were the direct result of her speeding, which I estimated to be approximately seventy-five miles per hour, and her severe and erratic steering inputs in attempting to steer clear of the ladder in front of her. If she had been observing the speed limit of fifty-five miles per hour when that ladder fell in front of her, or if she had not panicked and steered her vehicle with controlled steering into the grassy median, we wouldn't be here. The rollover accident and the resulting fire would not have happened."

I looked over at Eric His face was florid; he was seething. I hadn't seen him so angry since he and I had last met with Martelli at the hospital. I leaned over and whispered to him: "Keep your cool. It doesn't do anyone any good for the jury to see you go postal. Okay?"

Eric looked at me, breathed deeply and nodded.

"Officer, did you talk with anyone who you determined was an eyewitness to this accident?"

"I spoke with a ... Mr. Abadin," he said, looking at his field notes in front of him. "However, I did not find him to be reliable in his observations regarding any of the important details of what the Mesa's vehicle movements were in the seconds leading up to the loss of control and rollover. In effect, there were no eyewitnesses."

"I see. Thank you Officer Martelli," Harrington ended. "You've provided important information for the jury in this case. I have nothing further." He sat down at counsel's table.

"Good morning, Officer," I said as I approached the examining podium.

"Good morning," he replied, somewhat guardedly.

"You're only 28-years-old, aren't you?"

"Yes."

"How long have you been on the force?"

"Three years this coming January."

"And did I correctly hear you testify on direct examination that you're on the Motor Vehicle Homicide Team?"

"That's correct. I'm with Troop K out of Ft. Lauderdale. There are five of us on the team."

"Three years. Huh ... Isn't that rather quick for you to have gone from a beginning patrolman to being a member of the homicide team?"

"Uh ... its ... uh ... kind of quick, but I wanted the challenge, and I was lucky to get it so early in my career. Membership on the homicide team is based on aptitude and merit," he said smoothly.

I pulled a folder from the binder in front of me. "Aptitude and merit," I repeated. "Actually, wouldn't it be more accurate to say that your being a member of the homicide team is not so much a tribute to either your aptitude or your merit, but more of a tribute to your bloodlines?"

"I don't know what you're talking about," he replied, a bit too sharply.

"Well, would you tell the jury who heads up that homicide team for Troop K?"

"I don't see that has anything to do with my opinions in this case." A little sharper still and a little less collected in his demeanor. *Good.*

"Answer the question, sir."

"Objection," Harrington said, feigning boredom. "This is irrelevant."

"Overruled. This is cross, Mr. Harrington," Vaughn ruled.

"My father," he said somewhat more quietly.

"I'm sorry. I missed your response," I said, forcing him to repeat the point.

"I said that my father heads up the team," he said more loudly, with a tone of anger. His New Jerseyness was starting to peek out of his carefully controlled veneer.

"I see. Now you mentioned that getting on that team was a function of merit, isn't that what you said?"

"Yes, all applicants have to pass a rigorous test, counselor," he shot back. "I passed the test just like everybody else on the team."

I walked up to the witness stand carrying some papers. "Take a look at these for a second, will you?" I handed the papers to him. While he was looking at them, I walked over and dropped a copy onto Harrington's table. He hadn't seen them before either.

Martelli looked them over and then looked back at me.

"You are holding a copy of your test results for the homicide team exam you took, aren't you?"

"Yes."

"And I have also included the scores of the seven other officers who took that exam at the same time as you did for the one position that you were all competing for on the team, correct?"

"Where did you get these?" His calm, crafted demeanor was now completely gone. He had become instantly angry, and his face was getting red.

"Actually, the deal is that I'm the one that is supposed to be asking the questions, Officer, but, if you must know, Florida has a little law called The Sunshine Law. Ever heard of it before?"

"No," he said curtly.

"It's kind of an interesting law. It allows any private citizen to send a letter to any public entity, including police departments, and ask to see public records. I sent a letter to the highway patrol and asked to see your employment file. It's a public record. Are you with me?" I was playing with him, intentionally needling Joe Steroids to get the reaction I wanted.

He stared coldly at me, not saying a word.

"Well, the fact is," I continued, "according to these public records, you actually didn't do so hot on that merit test, did you?"

"I passed, counselor."

"That you did. You got a score of 73 didn't you?"

"Yes."

"Let's tell the jury what passing was, Officer Martelli."

"Seventy was passing," he mumbled.

"I see. Since we're discussing scores, would you tell the jury the name of the applicant, out of the seven who were taking that same exam, who got the lowest grade?"

There was ice in his eyes when he replied. He was not one for public humiliation. "Me," he finally said.

I casually looked over at the jury. I made eye contact with a few of them. "Can we assume that your father played a role in choosing which of the seven applicants was going to get the opening on the team?"

"My father was one of the people, yes. He picked the most qualified candidate, sir. That was me," he stubbornly persisted.

"Uh ... huh. Let's talk about your investigation of the Hawkins accident, Officer Martelli. Would you agree that this was not an easy accident to investigate?"

"What do you mean?"

"I mean, since you were dealing with a rollover and not much in the way of eyewitnesses—at least no *reliable* ones in your opinion—you had to essentially reconstruct this accident yourself in order to determine the Mesa's pre-accident speed, Mrs. Hawkins' steering behavior and generally what that Mesa did from the time that the step ladder came off the pickup truck until the fire started on the Mesa. Isn't that correct?"

"Yes, I did all that," he responded.

"When did you complete your analysis and reconstruction?"

He looked at the final accident report lying in front of him. "I signed the accident report ten days after the accident itself, so I'd say that I didn't complete looking at all the pieces of the puzzle until a day or two before I signed it."

"Did you keep an open mind to all possible causes of the accident until you had *completed* your analysis?"

"Of course."

"And that's what a good police officer is supposed to do, right?"

"Yes," he admitted.

"Sir, would you look at your field notes in front of you and tell us when it was that you met Mr. Hawkins there," I said, pointing to my client, "for the first time after the accident."

He took a moment and found the notation. "It was the morning after the accident, at the hospital."

"And I was with him at that time, wasn't I?"

"Yes."

"Sir," I said, emphasizing the words for effect, "Isn't it a fact that *less than twenty-four hours after the accident*, when you first spoke with Mr. Hawkins, you had *already made up your mind* that the accident, in your opinion, had been caused by speeding and erratic steering on the part of Mrs. Hawkins?"

"That's not true," he said emphatically.

"Sir, isn't it true that you told my client at the hospital, less than twenty-four hours after the accident, and before you had even performed any analysis of all the accident information, that Mrs. Hawkins was speeding and had caused this rollover herself!" I was harsh in my tone.

"If I said anything along those lines at that time, it would only have been *initial possibilities*, that's all," he shrugged. "Obviously, I had yet to do some of the reconstruction math involved to arrive at final determinations at that time. I did the math later, and it confirmed that possibility was, in fact, the correct cause."

"Where is your *math*, Officer? Show us in your field notes, or in the accident file for that matter, any calculations that you made of *the math* of this accident." I had seen his notes and the complete accident folder he had prepared for this accident at the time of his deposition three months earlier. There were no such calculations. None were set forth in the accident report either—only his raw ultimate conclusions that Jenny was speeding and steering recklessly.

He looked through the folder and his notes. "I don't see them. Sometimes I don't keep them after the accident report is prepared. That's obviously what happened here," he said dismissively.

"Come now, Officer Martelli, is it really your testimony that in a case as serious as this, where you were dealing with a death and a very serious burn injury, that you would *toss* your work papers out?" I asked incredulously.

"It happens."

"Really? Isn't it true that you didn't do the math at all; that you 'eyeballed' the accident and merely concluded that the Mesa driver was speeding and reckless in her driving actions?" I was convinced that was precisely what he had done. 'Doing the math' was more work than he wanted to put into the case, particularly since it was only a single vehicle accident.

"Objection, your honor," Harrington argued, "he's arguing with the witness."

"Sustained." The Turtle was quick with his ruling. He didn't cotton to the suggestion that a man in police uniform would engage in such conduct.

"Maybe this document might help," I offered. I pulled the last document from the sub-file in front of me and handed it to the witness. I walked over and laid a copy on Harrington's table.

"That's a copy of your daily work attendance for February and March of this year, isn't it?"

"I thought that this stuff is supposed to be private," he again said with irritation.

"It's that darn Sunshine Law again," I quipped. "The patrol gave me that one, too, from your personnel file. They really keep a lot of interesting stuff in there." The female Bubba Burger worker laughed at the exchange. As soon as Vaughn shot her a stern look, she immediately stopped. Vaughn's reproving look, however, didn't stop the juror with the pencil protector from chuckling as well.

"Officer Martelli, the Hawkins accident happened on Friday, February twenty-first of this year. According to your log there, you went on vacation starting the following Monday, the twenty-fourth, for an entire week. See that?" I asked, holding the log and walking towards him.

Martelli's pressure relief valve was starting to whistle. "I see that. What's your point!"

"Well, if you look at your final accident report in front of you, you'll see that it's dated and signed by you on the following Monday of the following week, March 3rd. That would be your first day back in the office from vacation, wouldn't it?"

"Yes. I obviously finished it that day, on the third. So what?" Joe Steroids was getting testier.

"You didn't work on this report while you were on vacation that week, did you?" That was a rhetorical question. As every juror knew damn well, no cop worked while on vacation. It was one of the rules in this world, without exception.

"I doubt it. I probably finished it on that first day back. Unlike lawyers, I don't take two hour lunches on my work days."

"So, you did *all* the mathematical calculations, and read *all* of the transcribed witness statements, and completed *all* your reconstruction analysis, and typed up *all* eleven pages of your single-spaced accident report in that one eight-hour shift on your first day back. Is that your testimony, sir?"

"That's right," he said, defiantly.

I merely nodded my head as he spoke. *And pigs can fly.*

I walked to the side of my podium and leaned on it, casually. "Incidentally, since you concluded that the rollover didn't start until the Mesa was on the grassy median, I assume that you took photographs of the deep dirt ruts that the Mesa's wheels would have made in the median, if that were true, right?"

He looked through the rather sparse stack of photographs that were in front of him. I knew that the file reflected that he had directed the assisting officer to only take approximately eight photos of the scene and vehicle—another indication that he didn't intend to perform an intensive investigation of the accident. I would have expected to see twenty-four to thirty-six digital photos of both the scene and the vehicle.

"I don't see that one. I must have neglected to capture those ruts on film. They were there, all right."

"Uh ... huh. Sir, isn't it true that the reason you have no photos of any ruts is because there were no ruts? They did not exist?"

"That's absolutely incorrect, counselor. They were there, big as life."

"If that's true," I shrugged, "they'd be pretty important to photograph for evidence and reconstruction purposes, wouldn't they?"

"Yes, but in the confusion of the fire truck, the ambulance and everything else that went on that night at the scene, I must have overlooked capturing them on film. It was a very active scene, and my first duty was public safety," he said, defensively.

"Well, if those wheel ruts were there, as you say, and were 'big as life,' can you tell me why there was absolutely no evidence of them in the ground when Mr. Cargill and I walked the accident scene and took these photographs of the median area within weeks of the accident?" I handed him the photographs of the accident scene taken by Cargill that had been received in evidence during the testimony of Cargill. The grass in those photos was smooth as a grassy billiard table, with no evidence of any plow marks that slide-slipping wheels would have supposedly made had the rollover started on the grass and not the roadway.

Joe Steroids glared at me. He was tiring of being challenged. "How do I know what happened to them? This is Florida. It rains a lot if you didn't notice. They were probably washed out or something."

At that point, Vaughn unexpectedly jumped into the fray. "Mr. Culhane, I'm instructing you to stop badgering this witness. The court finds that your questions are bordering on harassment."

I was momentarily stunned by his comments, especially since even Harrington had not registered an objection himself. Vaughn's old days as an insurance defense lawyer again made their uninvited appearance. He didn't like anyone attacking the integrity or competency of a law enforcement officer.

"Your Honor ..." I managed to say, "I don't think I fully understand the nature of your comments or your ruling. May we approach for a sidebar?"

"You may not. My comments are quite clear, as is my ruling. I suggest that you proceed with caution."

I fired a glance over at Harrington. He had the look of a guy who had unexpectedly found a fifty-dollar bill in an old pair of pants he had just put on after fishing them out of a dresser.

Vaughn's comments, made in full hearing of the jury, had not only broken my train of thought with the witness, but had also scalded my credibility with the jury.

"I have a motion to make, your honor. I need to make it now," I said evenly, but with unmistakable emphasis.

Vaughn was incensed at my new challenge. His eye slits narrowed, reflecting his stubborn fury at being challenged. "Gentlemen, I want to see both of you in chambers right now," he said with energy. He turned to the court reporter. "I want you as well to come in." The Turtle finally turned to the jury. "Ladies and gentlemen, please forgive me, but there are a few legal issues that I must deal with presently. We're going to take a ten-minute break. Please be back here promptly in ten minutes." The jurors nodded, confused at not knowing what was happening.

The court reporter grabbed her equipment and followed Harrington and me into the judge's chambers. We went through his door behind his chair.

We had no sooner sat down in his chambers than Vaughn unzipped his black robe and took his seat behind his desk. "You have a motion to make, Mr. Culhane?" he challenged, lighting up a short, black cigar about the size and width of his stubby fingers.

"I certainly do," I quickly replied, leaning forward in my chair, and speaking directly to the court reporter, to ensure that she got every word I said. "The comments you just made in front of that jury out there were not only uncalled for, Your Honor, but were incredibly prejudicial to my clients' case. I was well within the bounds of permissible cross-examination with that witness when you jumped in with your unfounded and unsolicited comments, and I vehemently object. I renew my prior motion for mistrial. This prejudice cannot be cured." I nodded at the reporter and leaned back in my chair.

"Are you through with your motion?" he responded. Pungent, gray cigar smoke now began filling his chambers. He made no effort to keep the smoke away from the attorneys.

"I am."

"Your motion is denied. And let me tell you something," he said, tapping the ash from the end of his cigar into his bullet casing of an ashtray, "I don't know where you think you're going with your case, but I am not about to let you try to bully a highway patrolman who is merely coming into my courtroom to do his job and testify about his accident investigation. Your desperation is not an acceptable excuse to try and assassinate that officer's good character by your innuendo." He drew heavily on the black cigar that he now firmly re-planted in his mouth.

"Judge Vaughn, I'm sorry, but I've got to take great issue with your com-ments, both personally and professionally. The officer's qualifications and competency are vitally at issue here and I've done nothing inappropriate, and I'm not about to be bullied either," I retorted, with controlled anger.

"*You're offended?* With all due respect, Mr. Culhane, I'm doing all I can to avoid dismissing your clients' case right now. While I'm certainly keeping an open mind," he said, careful to say the right things on the record, which the court reporter was dutifully taking down, word for word, "it appears to me that you are here to waste this court's time. I don't see any evidence to date of any defect, quite frankly, but I'm sticking by my prior ruling. I will wait to rule on Global's motion to dismiss your case until Global finishes putting on its de-fense evidence. But I caution you again, if you haven't established anything more substantial than what I've seen so far, I'm afraid your case will never see the jury room."

My Irish temper was about to erupt. However, I bit my tongue. More gasoline was not what this fire needed right now, and I wouldn't do anyone any good with my ass sitting in jail for contempt of court.

"This discussion is over, gentlemen," Vaughn stated dismissively as he took one last puff on the black stogie and put it out in his shell casing ashtray. "Be prepared to complete your cross of Trooper Martelli in five minutes, Mr. Culhane, and I caution you to conduct it properly," he warned. With that, he turned in his swivel chair and looked at pink message notes of telephone calls that his judicial assistant had left for him sitting on the table immediately be-hind him. We were dismissed.

"What did you want to talk to the judge about?" Eric asked as soon as I came out of chambers and sat down next to him. Sandy quickly came over and listened in too.

"I asked him to order a new trial. The son of a bitch has poisoned this jury as far as I'm concerned." I was still steamed.

"I assume he denied it?" he asked.

"Did President Clinton have sexual relations with that woman?" I replied.

As serious as the situation was, Eric still managed a laugh. "Well, I thought you scored points on Martelli. He's a damn liar as far as I'm concerned. He didn't spend any time analyzing the details of this accident, and I think the jury picked up on that."

"Let's hope so," I sighed. At that point, Vaughn came back out of his chambers and summoned the bailiff to bring back the jury.

I HAD NO further questions for Martelli after the jury came back. Not wanting to give my cross-examination any credibility in the eyes of the jurors, Harrington played cavalier and didn't bother posing any re-direct questions to Martelli. As he left the stand and walked passed me, I could feel his contained anger.

"The defense calls Dr. Lee Quarles," Harrington immediately announced after Martelli left the courtroom.

At the same time as Quarles came into the courtroom from the hall outside, so did Willis Cole. They must have been in the hall together, awaiting Quarles' call to the witness stand. As Quarles approached the front of the courtroom, Cole took a seat in the back. He stared at me without emotion as our eyes momentarily met.

Quarles was as confident and polished as I had remembered him from his deposition in the case. He smiled and nodded politely to the jury as he passed them on his way to the stand. His navy blue sports coat, gray dress slacks and conservative red tie went well with his light brown hair. He was as smoothly packaged, I conceded to myself, as Cargill wasn't.

The first thirty minutes of his testimony were spent by Harrington going over his vast experience and credentials in the field of accident reconstruction while he taught at Ohio State for twenty-two years. Harrington dwelled on Quarles' dozens of published articles on accident reconstruction techniques, as well as his textbook on techniques in the area. The sarcastic cockiness he displayed at his deposition had miraculously vanished.

He repeated the testimony he gave at his deposition; namely, that while he had originally been asked to perform his own independent reconstruction of the accident and to then generate a computer animation of that accident for the jury's understanding, he quickly abandoned the need to perform his own reconstruction when he determined that Trooper Martelli's reconstruction was eminently correct. Hence, he limited his work to the animation, which he said recreated what the actual accident looked like.

"I would like to share that animation with the jury here," he said, nodding towards them like they were old family to him. "It will aid them in understanding what happened here." It was Uncle George home from the war to share some stories with the nieces and nephews. He knew how to charm them.

"May I use your courtroom to show the computer animation, Your Honor"? he ass-kissed The Turtle.

"Be my guest," the judge invited, magnanimously. He obviously relished the fact that Quarles had the courtesy to ask his permission first.

I casually snuck a glance over at Sandy behind me. She rolled her eyes. *Please!!* they said.

At that point, Harrington turned and nodded to Craige behind him. Craige proceeded to wheel a large television and DVD player out of the corner of the courtroom behind him and quickly set it up in front of the judge and jury.

Harrington asked that the courtroom lights be turned down and popped in his DVD. He didn't need the lights turned down. I had viewed the video many times myself at home, and the clarity was just fine in normal daylight. However, Quarles wanted to give the video as much dramatic importance as possible. The drama was working. The jurors, I noted with concern, were all leaning forward, intent on getting a good view of the animation.

Quarles let it roll, narrating as it played.

Even I couldn't help but be impressed by the effective visual manner in which his animation dramatically depicted Martelli's reconstruction opinions. A scaled Mesa, appearing in the same forest green color as Jenny's, was shown traveling in the center lane of three interstate lanes. Quarles informed the jury that her Mesa, as they watched it, was traveling at seventy-five mph—twenty miles per hour faster than the posted speed limit, he added. Her Mesa was shown coming up behind a pickup truck in front of her carrying a stepladder on its rack. As we all watched, the ladder fell off the animated pickup, landing in the road directly in front of her Mesa. The Mesa's reaction, as depicted in the video animation, was an out-of-control, sharp turn to the right, followed by an equally sharp turn to the left, which culminated with the Mesa running onto the grassy median. Prior to entering the grassy median, the four wheels of the Mesa were depicted as never lifting from the asphalt roadway; there was no depiction of any tip whatsoever.

As the Mesa entered the green, grassy median nose first, it was depicted sliding sideways to its right. As it did so, little animated ruts of dirt were created on the right outside of the two passenger-side tires that were sliding sideways. The rollover began after approximately thirty feet of sliding. The Mesa underwent a three-quarters roll to its right, at which point its driver's side landed with great force on the cement pad in the median. It then completed another quarter roll, finally coming to rest upright on its four wheels. At that point, the video ended. Quarles had not recreated the fire.

"That, unfortunately," he said to the jury, "is exactly what happened in this accident. With my apologies to the Hawkins family," he said with solemnity, "it was a combination of human error and the laws of physics in the form of those two ruts of dirt created in the median by the sliding wheels that caused the trip levers that, in turn, caused the rollover and fire. It had nothing to do with any supposed defect in the Mesa."

Four or five of the jurors looked over at Eric and me for our reaction. I sat passively showing no facial response to his testimony. Eric, on the other hand, sat with his arms crossed on his chest. His face was again flushed, his eyes angry at the suggestion of human error.

"Your witness," Harrington said. He left the podium and sat down.

The lights were turned back on and Quarles looked over to me as I approached the podium.

"Dr. Quarles, I want to address your video in a moment, but I have a couple of preliminary matters I need to address with you first."

"Whatever you're comfortable with," he smiled graciously.

"Dr. Quarles, did I understand your testimony to say that you had originally started to do your own reconstruction but ..." I said, searching my handwritten notes of his testimony in front of me, "you 'quickly determined that Trooper Martelli's reconstruction opinions were eminently correct,' is that right?"

"That's correct."

"So, when you came to that point, as I understand it, you 'abandoned' your own initial reconstruction work-up in favor of adopting Trooper Martelli's. Did I get that right as well?"

"Yes," he nodded, "I didn't see the need to spend Global's money on completing a second reconstruction that was going to end up with the same opinions as Trooper Martelli had already determined."

"I see. Would you do me a favor and pull out of your file in front of you your own initial workup calculations of your own reconstruction that you started but did not finish?"

Quarles frowned at the stupid question. "Mr. Culhane, as I just stated, I saw no reason to do a reconstruction since Trooper Martelli's numbers appeared correct."

"I beg your indulgence, Dr. Quarles, but unless I was asleep at the switch, I thought I distinctly heard you say that you actually *started* your own reconstruction but *later abandoned* it when you determined that your initial numbers on the reconstruction were matching those of Trooper Martelli. Did I get that wrong?" I tried my best Colombo routine.

Quarles stared evenly at me for a split second before answering. "You've correctly restated my testimony. I still fail to see your point, however."

"Well, if you started your own preliminary workup and your own preliminary numbers, such as speeds and the like, and you then started matching them with Trooper Martelli's, as you say, I want you to show me your initial calculations that you compared with Martelli's. That's all I'm asking to see doctor," I said innocently.

"Well, there wasn't any need whatsoever to keep my own preliminary calculations after I saw that they were matching Trooper Martelli's numbers. I pitched them. They were unnecessary."

I paced ten feet from the podium, tapping my index finger to my mouth in thought. I paced back towards the podium and stopped half way, and looked at the witness. A thought came to me.

"How many cases are you presently working on for Global?"

He looked up at the ceiling in thought and then back at me. "Maybe twelve or so."

"*Twelve other cases?*" I asked in exaggerated disbelief.

"Yes," he said evenly.

"Well, how many more cases are you presently handling for the other auto manufacturers, both foreign and domestic?"

"That could be around another two dozen, I'd guess."

"I see," I said, looking over to the jury. "How many cases are you presently handling where you are doing a reconstruction for an injured plaintiff that is suing an auto company?"

"I can't think of any as I sit here."

"Sir, didn't you tell me in your deposition that in the last three years that you've been consulting for lawsuits that you've *never* consulted for a plaintiff against an auto manufacturer?"

"That's true, but I'd be happy to consult in such a case if I were presented with one that looked like it had merit," he adroitly jabbed. "They rarely do."

I ignored his riposte. "Would you tell me and the jury how much you were paid by all the auto companies last year for your consulting?" He had given me the information at his deposition.

"It was something in excess of five hundred thousand dollars, as I recall." To his credit, he said the number without hesitation and without embarrassment.

"I see," I said as I frowned and looked at him, scratching the brown hair on the back of my head. "Dr. Quarles, is it possible that the reason you threw out your preliminary reconstruction papers is because your numbers didn't square with Trooper Martelli's, that your numbers, in fact, showed that Jenny Hawkins wasn't speeding at all?"

"I object!" Harrington shouted from his chair, rising. "This is improper!"

"Sustained!" Vaughn exploded. "Mr. Culhane, I am ordering you to restrict your questions to those that have a basis in the record. I will not tolerate character assassination in this courtroom without a factual predicate being laid!"

"Your honor, there is—"

"Enough said!" The Turtle thundered, cutting me off from stating my position. "Ask your next question!"

I looked up at the judge for a moment and walked back the three feet to the podium.

"Let's spend a moment on your animation. Do I understand that you used a computer to assist in generating that cartoon?"

"It's not a cartoon, Mr. Culhane," he corrected, "it's a scientifically-based computerized animated illustration that accurately replicates this accident. And yes, I did feed the parameters from Trooper Martelli's accident reconstruction into the computer program to generate the visual re-creation which you and the jury saw."

"Doctor, in connection with computers, are you familiar with the phrase: 'garbage in, garbage out'?"

He chuckled. "Yes. I've heard it referred to before."

"And in twenty words or less, doesn't that phrase refer to the fact that a computer will only process the specific information that is fed into it by the person running the computer?"

"Yes, the accuracy of the results generated by the computer is dependent on the accuracy of the information and assumptions fed into it being correct and accurate. That's common sense."

"So, applying that concept to your computerized accident reconstruction, if the speed that you input into that computer for your cartoon—excuse me, your *animation*—was, say, only fifty-five miles per hour, your video would look different, correct?"

"Yes."

"And if the Mesa's wheels actually started lifting off the roadway while the Mesa was still on the roadway, your video animation would look a lot different than the one you showed us, wouldn't it?"

"You're answering your own question, Mr. Culhane. The answer is obviously yes to your new assumptions, but your assumptions are wrong," he added smoothly.

"Stay with me for a moment more, Doctor," I smiled politely. "If the Mesa actually *started* its tipping and roll while it was *still on the roadway*, well *before* it actually made it to the grassy median and supposedly created those so-called dirt wheel ruts, that would mean that your video animation would be dead wrong, wouldn't it?"

"I take issue with you. My animation is not wrong in any respect. I would agree, however, that if you were to ask me to change the assumptions that I fed into the computer to include the erroneous assumption that the roll started while the Mesa was still on the roadway, then, yes, it would look different than what I have demonstrated."

"Do you happen to have any photos of those so-called ruts in the median, Dr. Quarles?"

"You know that I don't counsel. As I understand it, in the frenzy of dealing with the Mesa occupants and securing accident data at the scene, Trooper Martelli forgot to photograph them at the scene."

"Doctor, if those ruts, in fact, existed only in the mind of Trooper Martelli, would that be yet another reason why they weren't photographed?"

"Objection! Mr. Culhane is arguing with the witness," Harrington fumed.

"I'll withdraw it," I said. "I have nothing more for this witness."

"Do you have any re-direct Mr. Harrington?"

"Absolutely none, your honor," he replied. He obviously thought that Quarles was Teflon during my cross-examination.

The Turtle looked up at the wall clock. It was eleven forty-five. Never one to miss a meal, he boomed: "Good. We're in lunch recess until one-thirty sharp."

CHAPTER 47

THE THREE OF us walked back to my office over the lunch break. It was a somber trip. Normally upbeat, Eric was particularly quiet. As we approached my building, he announced that he was going to take a walk along the New River. Not hungry, he said, he'd meet us back at the courtroom at one-thirty.

Sandy finally broke the silence between the two of us as we entered my building.

"You're certainly not out to extract any good testimony from any of Harrington's witnesses with sugar and cream," she quipped, keeping in stride with me as we walked through the lobby, headed for the bank of elevators.

"And what's that supposed to mean?" I asked testily, continuing to walk.

"Your cross-examination approach—don't you think you're being somewhat ... well ... too nasty with them?"

"No, I'm not. That's not my style when a witness is bullshitting me. You know my style," I said, shortly. "You know I'm usually not aggressive like that on cross-examination in front of a jury. But I'm a firm believer that if you're going to suggest to a jury that a witness is a liar, you should do it with your first question out of the box. No pussyfooting and no confusion."

"I know what you're saying," she added as we got to the elevator bank. "All I'm wondering is whether we're losing the jury in the process. I've been watching them Mike, and they're getting upset with your cross. I ... uh ... think they feel we're ... uh ... kind of grasping at straws. Do you know what I mean?" Unlike her, Sandy was struggling for words.

I turned to her with irritation. "Okay, get it out, goddammit, what's really bothering you?"

"What's bothering me? I'll tell you. I think you're too fucking hostile and aggressive in the way you're treating Global's witnesses, that's what. You're beginning to piss the jury off, and I think they're going to stop listening to our case. Is that direct enough for you?" she asked, leaning in towards me as she spoke. She was pissed as well.

"Look, don't you think I don't know that I'm running that risk. Juries hate lawyers to begin with, and they sure as hell hate asshole lawyers. But each case and each jury is different," I said, somewhat more defensively than I had hoped. "I've got to go with my gut instincts, Sandy, and my gut tells me that I've got to be right in the face of those experts. Velvet gloves and polished respectability isn't going to send the message that I need to send. Martelli is a lazy, lazy, lying son of a bitch who didn't do shit to accurately reconstruct this accident, and Quarles is a hired gun who grabbed on to Martelli's speed numbers and opinions because his own were in line with Cargill's!" The elevator arrived and opened, but we both ignored it. It closed.

"You really think that Quarles would take the stand and lie about his numbers?"

"Hell yes, I do. Are you nuts? He's at the feedbag of the auto companies. Wake up and smell the coffee!" I said, raising both hands in exasperation. "Don't think that over all the years that I represented Global I didn't wonder if they had retained experts around the country to raise their right hand and not tell the truth in a particularly troubling liability case. It never happened in any of my cases—at least none that I was aware of," I said honestly, "but I periodically would hear suggestions to that effect in connection with other cases Global tried around the country. I just passed them off as the sour grape allegations of whipped plaintiffs' attorneys. Now, I'm not so sure," I added.

She put her hand on my shoulder. "Look, I'm sorry if I sounded like I was jumping on you," she apologized. "It's just ... well ... I'm getting nervous that we're getting killed in there," she said, nodding her head back in the direction of the courthouse behind us. "The judge hates us, our case isn't all that persuasive and Global's witnesses are eating us alive. And the jury hasn't even seen their S testing video yet. Speaking selfishly, we can't afford to lose this case, Mike. With all the time that you've invested in this case, you've ignored the rest of your clients. They're not calling us with new cases if you haven't noticed."

"Thank you for reminding me," I replied. "Look, don't you think that I'm not nervous as hell myself? My practice is dog shit. My name is dog shit. I'm not getting cases worth a damn, and I'm running out of money. I lured you to quit your job and join me in this sinking boat," I lamented, shaking my head, "and to top off this little pity party, you apparently think I'm doing my damndest to screw up this trial and Eric's case. Well, for better or worse, I told Eric that I'd be here to see it through with him, and I will, goddammit, in the best way I know how." I sighed heavily.

She nodded and removed her hand.

"I'm going with my gut instincts on my cross-examination of their witnesses, Sandy. That's all I know, and that's what I've always done. Believe me, if I lose this case, I'm well aware of the consequences, to all of us, not to mention Eric and his family."

Sandy was somewhat taken aback by my candor and depressed outlook on the case and the potential consequences of a loss. She knew that it was not like me to see the glass of water as being half empty rather than half full. The next elevator arrived. We both looked at it then back at each other. "This probably isn't a good time to talk to you about all this," she said quietly, "I'll meet you back in the courtroom after lunch. I'm going for a walk myself." She turned and started walking in the opposite direction, leaving me standing there by myself.

"*Shit*," I quietly said in frustration to no one but myself. I wasn't hungry for lunch either.

CHAPTER 48

"HOW MANY MORE witnesses do you have to offer in your defense case?" Vaughn asked Harrington when we had reconvened in his courtroom after lunch. The jury had yet to be brought back by the scarecrow bailiff. The Turtle was into logistics.

"Actually, I had planned on calling Arthur Markov, the Global engineer who signed off on the Mesa design, but I don't think that will be necessary," he said. "The way the proof is going your honor," he said, smiling, "I've decided to send him back to Michigan. He's out in the corridor, but I'm going to release him if the court doesn't object. That would leave me with only one more witness, Dr. Murray Winchester."

"You're not going to be calling any witnesses on the issues of damages?"

"No, your honor, I'm hopeful that the court will be granting Global's renewed motion for a directed verdict after I finish with Dr. Winchester and close my defense case."

Vaughn nodded thoughtfully and looked over at me. "Do you have any objection to Mr. Markov being released as a trial witness, Mr. Culhane? I do note that while he's not under subpoena by you, he's also on your witness list. If you don't have any objection, then I'll order him released and free to return to Michigan."

"Judge, if you would allow me to make that decision at the close of the proceedings today, I would appreciate it. I'd like to see how Dr. Winchester goes," I answered.

"Your honor," Harrington whined, "this is really bordering on the ridiculous. Mr. Culhane should know his case well enough by now to know if he is going to need to call Mr. Markov in rebuttal, assuming that we even get to a rebuttal phase of this trial. Frankly, if he releases him now, Mr. Markov can catch a flight back to Detroit this afternoon. If you wait until the end of the day, he'll undoubtedly have to stay overnight here and catch a plane out in the morning. I'd like to avoid the extra cost and inconvenience for him."

That did it. "I think Mother Motors can afford to pick up the cost of a night's lodging, your honor," I countered, more sarcastically than I had intended. "After all, Mr. Harrington just acknowledged that he had originally planned on having Markov testify this afternoon. Since they planned on spending the money anyway, Judge, I just want a fair opportunity to assess the situation after I complete the cross of Winchester. That's all I'm asking," I pleaded, playing the part of the victim.

"You two can't seem to agree on anything," The Turtle grumbled. "I'm allowing Mr. Culhane the opportunity to let you know about Mr. Markov after the end of this afternoon." He looked over to Harrington and added: "Frankly, I want to give Mr. Culhane and his client every reasonable opportunity before I address your motions, Mr. Harrington."

Eric turned his head to look at me. He didn't miss the obvious message The Turtle was sending either. *Execution is hereby stayed until your case is closed ...*

"On an unrelated matter," Vaughn added, "I have a conference with the Chief Judge at four o'clock this afternoon. As a result, we're going to have to cut today's proceedings short if you're not wrapped up with Dr. Winchester at that time. Understood?" It was not really a question but a declaration.

We both nodded.

"Claude," he said to The Scarecrow, "bring in the jury."

'Claude'? I chuckled inwardly, having heard his first name for the first time. *If the shoe fits ...*

HARRINGTON DIDN'T WASTE much time with Winchester. After having the witness recount the details of his twelve years of active design experience at Global, as well as his seven years functioning on its product engineering analysis staff, he moved to the heart of his opinions.

"Sir, the allegation has been made in this courtroom by the plaintiff and his *experts*," he said with scoff woven into his tone, "that your company's Mesa model is defective and unreasonably dangerous in its design. Mr. Hawkins contends that it's unstable. Are those claims correct?"

"Absolutely not, it's a wonderfully stable vehicle. Its stability is superb."

"There has been criticism leveled by one of Mr. Culhane's experts, Dr. Braxton, regarding the height of the c.g. of the Mesa, are you aware of that?"

"Yes. I've read his deposition in this case, and you've summarized his trial testimony for me."

"Does Professor Braxton know what he's talking about?"

"Objection for the form of the question," I said, taking issue with Harrington's gilding of the lily.

"I'll rephrase it, your honor," Harrington offered magnanimously. "Is there merit to his opinions in that regard?"

"Not at all. They certainly don't fit this vehicle," he said, shaking his head dismissively at the same time. "May I explain?"

"Please do," Harrington encouraged.

"Let me preface my technical design comments by emphasizing to all of you," he said, turning in his witness chair and addressing the jury, "that every vehicle we build at Global is designed to be used in a safe and responsible manner. As a designer and manufacturer, we obviously can't control how a person drives our products once we have sold them. If they're driven in a reckless and unintended manner, well, we simply can't stop them from doing that. But the design only contemplates responsible driving." Three of the jurors, I couldn't help but notice, nodded in understanding. The only positive was that one of the alternate jurors was fighting to keep his fluttering eyes open, obviously clueless as to what the testimony was.

"If you were to compare the Mesa's c.g. height with that of all other sports utility vehicles out there in the industry, you would see that it is at the upper end of that range. But that's exactly where we want it to be since that higher c.g. is really another way of saying that we're giving the vehicle increased ground clearance distance. This is a utility vehicle," he emphasized. "Plain and simple, it's designed to be used off-road as well as on-road, and to be fully loaded at the same time. The extra couple of inches of ground clearance that we've designed into the Mesa allows it to clear stones, deep ruts and other objects when its driven off-road. Also, since its interior cargo area—when its back seats are folded down—is the largest in the SUV market, we had to make sure that when it was fully loaded with equipment or luggage, and its body was lowered on its springs due to that extra cargo weight, its underside would still have ample clearing distance when used off-road." He smiled warmly at the jury. "The last thing we want to hear from our customers is that they were hauling their family and their belongings on a vacation to Sedona and ended up getting their SUV high-centered, only to end up stranded in the middle of the desert."

Little Miss Chubby Juror smiled back at him.

Oh, please, I thought. *Shoot me now and be done with it.*

"So, from a design standpoint, are you saying that you *wanted* this higher riding height of the vehicle?"

"Yes, it's not only desired, it's absolutely necessary. Dr. Braxton ignores that functional user need altogether when he criticized the design of the Mesa. However," he added, gratuitously, uttering a line that I was sure Harrington spoon fed to him, "I can understand how someone who hasn't had any real-world automotive design experience would miss that."

Give me a break. "Judge Vaughn," I said, not even bothering to rise from my chair, "I'm requesting that you instruct the witness to refrain from adding his gratuitous remarks about Dr. Braxton." It was my small attempt to keep the weasel somewhat in check.

The Turtle looked over at me sitting in my chair, then back at Harrington. "Well, I suppose the witness probably shouldn't comment on the perceived strengths or weaknesses of your witnesses, Mr. Culhane." Turning to Winchester, Vaughn politely admonished him. "Dr. Winchester, the court asks that you not comment on the testimony of other witnesses. It might interfere with the jury's ability to make its own determination as to the credibility or qualifications of Mr. Culhane's experts."

Vaughn was treating him with velvet gloves. He liked him and was obviously impressed with his qualifications. He obviously didn't appreciate, or care, that he was Global's in-house, hired gun who testified for a living defending its products all around the country.

"I'm sorry, I apologize, sir," Winchester nodded to Vaughn.

Harrington continued. "Dr. Winchester, one of the things that Dr. Braxton told this jury is that he was concerned about something he referred to as a stability ratio. Are you aware of that term and concept?"

He chuckled lightly in response before answering.

"Yes, I'm very familiar with the term."

"Professor Braxton referred to it as a 'quick check' in the industry to determine the rollover propensities of a vehicle. Is that correct?"

"No," he said firmly, "the stability ratio that he referred to is not at all recognized in the auto industry as a serious predictor of the rollover characteristics or propensities of any given vehicle. Rather, it is merely a broad, generalized mathematical formula which is sometimes used by industry commentators as a *very rough way* of giving broad comparative stability characteristics. *In no way, shape or form,*" he emphasized, "is it, or should it be, used to predict or define whether any specific vehicle has any stability defect. That isn't what it was developed for."

"Are you saying that Professor Braxton is wrong in using it as a basis for evaluating the stability characteristics of the Mesa in this case?"

"Let me just say this," he offered, looking down and then at the jury, "in the hands of one who doesn't know or appreciate the function or usage of the stability ratio, it can easily be misunderstood and completely misapplied."

"Objection," I urged, "the witness is again offering personal homilies regarding the plaintiff's witnesses in violation of your recent admonition, Judge." Winchester's polished persona was getting under my skin.

"Overruled," The Turtle responded, almost predictably, "you're reading too much into his response, Mr. Culhane. Proceed Mr. Harrington," he said, hacking up a phlegmy obstruction in the process.

"Thank you," Harrington said. He canted his head, looking at the witness. "For the sake of argument, Dr. Winchester, let's spend a moment on this stability ratio matter that Professor Braxton brought up. He testified that the industry range for the stability ratio for utility vehicles of the type that the Mesa falls within is point-nine to one-point-one, and that the Mesa's ratio was point-eighty-eight. Was he right on those various numbers?"

"That part at least he got right, yes."

"Is the Mesa *defective*, or *rollover prone* because it is point-zero-two below the industry range?" Harrington was struggling in a patronizing way as he asked the question. He was letting the jury know that he was asking the question out of an obligation to dispel notions that Braxton had foolishly planted, rather than out of any serious engineering design concern he had for the Mesa.

"Clearly not, or it wouldn't have been sold by Global Motors. What Mr. Braxton ignored, or, probably, more likely, didn't fully appreciate," he added, "is that Global compensated for the increased c.g. elevation designed into the Mesa by adding an enhanced suspension system to the vehicle. We put front and rear stabilizing bars on the Mesa and stiffened its suspension package. We also used a little wider tire in the final design in order, again, to *augment* its stability characteristics. Frankly, that's the problem and the danger of using the stability ratio concept as a predictor of defects as Professor Braxton did. It completely ignores the fact that a vehicle's stability—its ability to avoid rollover—is not just a function of c.g. height and track width, which is all that the ratio addresses. Stability is the product of *an overall design system*, which includes suspension, tires and other components. We built the Mesa as a system at Global Motors."

Changing direction, Harrington finally moved into the area I was dreading: the results of the S testing performed by Global in Arizona. "Dr. Winchester, did you engage in any dynamic testing in this case?"

"We sure did," he said.

Again went the Hollywood glasses from Harrington's head into his hands, where he pointed them at the jury, for dramatic emphasis. "Could you explain to the jury what you did, and why?"

Like the practiced witness he was, Winchester, on cue, turned and faced the jury. He wanted 'a conversation' with them. All I could think of was Bill Clinton: "*I did not have sexual relations with that woman ...*"

"I was informed during the discovery phase of this case," he said, "that the experts retained by the plaintiff in this case, and his attorney, had expressed an opinion that Mrs. Hawkins was only traveling at around fifty-five miles per hour at the time of the accident, rather than the speed of seventy-five miles per hour that the state patrolman had determined she was going. I was further informed that they were of the opinion that the Mesa was defective from a rollover\stability standpoint because they claimed that it rolled over at that speed and that it shouldn't have. Well, I sat at my desk in Michigan and I decided that the best way for me to disprove their theory of defect would be to effectively rerun the very accident that occurred, using the plaintiff's own theories and an identical Mesa. And that's exactly what we did."

"How did you go about doing that?" Harrington asked. It was rehearsed well.

"We went out to a test facility in Arizona. We purchased a Mesa that was identical in every respect to the one that Mrs. Hawkins was driving at the time of her accident. Using information from our investigation, we outfitted that Mesa exactly like hers was. We put an anthropomorphic testing dummy in the driver's seat that was approximately the same weight as Mrs. Hawkins was, as well as an infant dummy in a child seat belted in the second-row seat, passenger side, to replicate the weight and location of her son at the time of the accident. We then loaded up the back of that Mesa with exactly the same objects that she was carrying at the time of the accident—eight cartons, each filled with four heavy gallons of paint, a paint compressor, and the same number of weighted boxes to reflect the boxes of Girl Scout cookies that she was carrying at the time. In all, including dummies and cargo, we loaded it with seven hundred sixty pounds of weight."

"Why did you put all of this heavy weight into the Mesa when you did your test?" Ever the inquisitive student, Harrington was milking this milk-engorged cow.

"The whole purpose of the test was to demonstrate, beyond a shadow of any doubt, that the test results could not be impeached or questioned by anyone. We were aiming to repeat the severe steering inputs which Mrs. Hawkins likely put into the Mesa at fifty-five miles per hour—their claimed speed," he added, nodding gratuitously towards Eric and me. "We wanted it to be weighted in an identical fashion to her Mesa so that we were truly testing the claimed rollover problems that the plaintiffs' experts said would appear at that speed under identical conditions. That's why we used the same heavy objects and weights in the back of the tested Mesa."

The dry cleaning juror nodded as he listened to the witness. He and the rest of the jurors were listening carefully.

At that point, Harrington walked over and dramatically pulled the blue cotton cover sheet off the large pile of items that had been placed in the corner next to him over the lunch hour. Sitting there were the large boxes of simulated cookies, the large boxes of heavy Sherwin Williams paint gallons, and a heavy steel air compressor.

"Are these the items that you had loaded in the exemplar Mesa when you ran your S tests?"

"They are," he said, energetically. "We had them shipped to your offices immediately after we finished the testing so that you would have them available to show to the jury."

Well, give you a fucking Boy Scout badge, I mentally fumed at the damage Winchester was doing. Global's presentation was killing our case.

Not one to give up on the theatrics when they were working in his favor, Harrington walked over and put his right foot on the steel compressor and pushed. It didn't budge. He made his point to the jury.

"Heavy?" he asked the witness.

"Heavy," Winchester responded.

"Okay. You have an identical Mesa, loaded with an identical load, identical replicated occupants, and a speed of fifty-five miles per hour, which is what the plaintiff's experts are claiming the speed was at the time of the accident. What did you do exactly in these tests?"

"We performed what the industry calls an S test," he responded. He proceeded to describe in great detail what the S test consisted of, including the heavy instrumentation and film footage focused on the Mesa to capture and quantify any stability anomalies.

After completing the description to orient the jury, Harrington was ready for the *coup de grâce*.

"Would you share those test results with us?" You would have thought that he was asking the witness to share a box of chocolates with the jury.

With that, Winchester asked for the playback equipment and large attached television to be wheeled forward from the corner of the courtroom where it had been sitting. Craige, ever-the-supplicant, immediately complied, pushing it forward into clear view for the jury.

Winchester turned on the player and narrated as the film footage started rolling. The jury saw the same S tests being performed that George Krueger had filmed at the Vehicle Testing Lab test facility from the mountainside outside of Arizona. The only difference was that the official VTL video used film footage shot by the VTL cameras, which were mounted closer to the test vehicle.

"As you can plainly see," Winchester narrated, as the jury followed along with the footage being played before them, "the Mesa is being subjected to severe steering inputs at fifty-five miles per hour, yet it doesn't show any tire lift from the asphalt roadway beneath it. Nor do you see any tipping or excessive lean in the body of the Mesa as the plaintiff's experts referred to. In short," he added, as the Mesa safely came to a rest after the test, "what you see is a very stable utility vehicle. If there had been a stability problem, you would have seen it being experienced in that film. You don't. It's a very stable vehicle. This accident was caused by speeding, inattentive driving and operator error. It wasn't caused by the Mesa." He was as comfortable and as casual as a mosquito in a nudist colony.

The Turtle was apparently impressed with the testing video he had seen. He put down his pen and stopped taking notes of the testimony. It was clear that he had heard all he needed to. While I tried to remain stoic in appearance, I couldn't help but feel that the jury felt the same way as The Turtle. The juror sitting at the end of the jury box closest to my table, whose family ran the hardware store, sat staring at me with his arms crossed on his chest in front of him. This was not good news. It was my experience in trying jury cases that if a juror was crossing his or her arms over their chest as I was making my pitch, they weren't buying it. The quality control supervisor looked at his watch. He had heard enough and wanted to get out of there.

Harrington looked up at Vaughn after the video equipment was moved out of the way.

"Judge, I don't see any reason for me to take up anymore of this jury's time. I have no further questions of the witness."

"Mr. Culhane?" The Turtle wheezed.

"Thank you," I said as I rose from my chair and stepped forward to the podium. Winchester appearance was similar to that of a Cheshire cat sitting in the sun in its owner's favorite living room chair. He was entirely comfortable with the world. He was at home, had eaten the family canary for breakfast and was entirely at peace with the world.

"Good afternoon, sir," I opened. I was out of bullets and decided to wing it.

"Good afternoon."

"As I listened to your direct exam, I heard you repeatedly use the word 'we' when you were describing the design considerations that went into the design of the Mesa. For example," I said, quoting from the yellow legal pad in front of me, "you said that when the Mesa was designed, '*we* intentionally designed it to have a greater ground clearance,' and that '*we* added an enhanced suspension package to the Mesa's design.' Do you remember using that 'we' word?"

"Yes," he said, frowning somewhat.

I scratched my chin and looked at him. "Isn't it true that you—Dr. Lee Winchester—didn't design a single bolt, nut or strut on the Mesa?"

"That's correct. I was speaking corporately, Mr. Culhane. I thought that was rather obvious."

"Corporately ...?" I repeated, raising my eyebrows. "Isn't it true that from a *corporate* standpoint, you're here to testify because you are the *corporate* in-house expert witness at Global Motors?"

He chuckled lightly before answering. "No, I'm afraid I don't see it that way. I do spend a great deal of time in court and in depositions defending our company's products against spurious product liability claims, but my opinions are my own. I call them as I see them."

"But being Global's in-house engineer to review and work with outside defense attorneys is what you do full time, isn't it sir?"

He hesitated a second before responding. "Yes."

I bulldozed. "And you've never come into a courtroom and told a jury: 'I am concerned about this particular Global model or product from a design or safety standpoint,' have you sir?"

"No. I haven't seen any suit that would have caused me to say that."

"How many cases do you presently have in your stable that you are personally defending on behalf of your employer?"

"Maybe sixty-five to seventy that I'm *consulting on*, not defending, as you say. It varies."

Vaughn was getting antsy in his chair.

"I'm just curious, Dr. Winchester, exactly whose idea was it to run that S test?" I couldn't resist asking out of curiosity since I knew full well that it had come from Harrington, via Craige.

"It was actually a joint decision."

"Involving whom?"

"Mr. Harrington, our attorney, as well as myself and Mr. Markov."

"Mr. Markov? How did he come to be involved in a litigation testing decision?" I was genuinely surprised to hear him mention that Markov had been involved since I knew from my prior representation of Global that general design engineers were intentionally kept isolated from the litigation end of the company. In fact, Global had always gone out of its way to keep them out of litigation when I had been defending them at Hunt.

"As you probably know from your discovery," Winchester replied, "Arthur Markov was the Chief Project Engineer at Global who was responsible for the completed Mesa vehicle design."

"I'm aware of that, but isn't that a little unusual, Mr. Winchester, to involve a design engineer like Mr. Markov in litigation testing decisions at Global?" I asked.

"I wouldn't call it unheard of. But after all, you're attacking the design which he signed off on. I think it was quite understandable for him to want to defend it against your claims in this case, Mr. Culhane."

"I can appreciate your sentiments, sir, but that wasn't my question. My question was actually pretty simple. Isn't it *unusual*, sir, for a general engineering design engineer to become involved in litigation testing?"

"I don't know. I don't keep track," he snapped in response. "It doesn't happen often, but it does happen."

"Well, let's see if we can approach this a little differently, sir," I said, unwilling to cede control over this discussion to Winchester. "Exactly how many cases have you been associated with over the last seven years that have involved the Product Engineering Analysis Group at Global? You just told us that you have around 70 right now."

"Well, it would be maybe four hundred to five hundred cases."

"In how many of those five hundred or so cases did you find a general design engineer from Global involved in *litigation* testing?"

"I can't say," he stubbornly persisted in his claimed ignorance.

"Name me one case that you have worked on at Global over all the years where that occurred before this case, sir."

He sat and looked over at Harrington for a moment before answering, obviously becoming increasingly irritated at my dogged questioning on this point. I wasn't about to let up. Right or wrong, I had always operated on the theory that it was important to let a hostile, adverse witness know who was in control of cross examination. It was a lot like paper training a dog. Sooner or later, the witness either gave in and started providing the information you requested, or he fought you on every point and risked looking either stupid or deceptive in the process. The trick was to keep the dog from peeing on your leg.

"I don't recall any," he finally conceded.

"Mmmmhuh," I said out loud, "tell me, how did you actually divide the testing responsibilities between yourself and Mr. Markov?"

"We both discussed performing an S test in this case, and we both discussed what test variables we would use, you know, speed, loading, steering input, and that type of thing."

"I noticed from the video of the S tests that you just showed the jury that you didn't use VTL test engineers to either set up the test or take part in the driving itself. Is that correct? You used Global engineers exclusively, right?"

"That's correct."

"Why is that?"

"Mr. Markov and I felt that we probably had greater expertise than VTL did in this type of testing. So, we decided to do it ourselves. The explanation is as simple as that. I couldn't actually make the testing event due to a conflict in my schedule. However, Mr. Markov attended."

The Turtle interrupted me. "How much more do you have with this witness, Mr. Culhane?" He wanted to get out of here, and he was obviously not impressed with my cross.

"Probably a half an hour, Your Honor," I responded, submissively.

He again looked at his wall clock and nodded at me to continue, apparently content that he would make his judicial meeting on time.

I needed to regain some momentum in my cross, if I ever had any, before I closed. Winchester was Global's last witness, and I needed to make a dent in his armor.

"Dr. Winchester, you said that this rollover was caused by human error, did I understand that correctly?"

"You did. That was the sole cause of this rollover."

I stood at the podium, with arms crossed over my chest, and looked up at the ceiling of the courtroom, as if an answer could be found there. I then looked at Winchester. "If the Mesa had a rollover problem in its design, wouldn't you agree that you would start to get reports of rollovers out in the real world from other Mesa drivers?"

"You would."

"And isn't' it true that Global has been informed of a number of other rollovers around the United States over the last year where Mesa drivers have claimed the exact same type of control problems as were involved in this case?"

"I strenuously object!" Harrington fired out of his chair. He walked two steps towards the judge's bench as he completed the objection. "Mr. Culhane is attempting, once again, to offer evidence, which you have previously ruled is inadmissible, Your Honor."

"Sidebar gentlemen!" The Turtle reluctantly barked. At the same time, he looked at the watch that pinched the end of his arm. We were fifteen minutes shy of his meeting with the chief judge, and he wasn't happy with the prospect of an evidentiary dispute throwing a wrench into his timetable.

"Where are you going with that line of questioning?" Vaughn asked me, trying to keep his voice low.

"Judge, the witness just testified that real world complaints and accidents of rollovers would be a potential indicator of any rollover problems in the Mesa. In view of that concession, I believe I'm entitled to go into the fact that Global has received not only complaints of other similar rollovers involving the Mesa, but also actual accidents."

Harrington piped up, "but you have ruled—"

"I know what I've ruled," The Turtle injected forcefully, glaring at Harrington before he looked back at me. "Mr. Culhane, we've been over these grounds once. I've already ruled those other accidents and suits are not relevant to the issues in this case. Are you proceeding in contravention of my prior ruling?" He was itching for a fight.

"Not at all, Your Honor," I said, politely. "You ruled that evidence inadmissible as part of my case in chief. However, this is entirely different. This is cross-examination of Global's own design expert. By acknowledging the relevance of other rollover accidents involving Mesas to the issue of whether the design itself has a rollover problem, the witness has opened the door to the admissibility of this line of questioning. It would be prejudicial for the court to prevent me from this critical line of questioning."

"That's faulty reasoning," Harrington charged. "He's created the 'open door' by his own predicate questions! I certainly didn't address other accidents in my direct examination of this witness."

"I agree," Vaughn stated. "I'm reiterating my earlier ruling Mr. Culhane. Other accidents and other lawsuits involving the Mesa are *verboten* ground. Stay out of that area. Am I making myself clear? Otherwise, you'll be needing a toothbrush for your overnight stay in jail on a contempt finding by this court. I simply won't have my orders ignored. Is that clear?" he repeated. He was the school-yard bully, and he meant me to know it.

"Clear as glass, Judge, but I must respectfully reiterate my objection. I think I'm entitled to elicit that evidence."

"Feel free to reiterate your objection till the cows come home if it makes you feel better, Mr. Culhane, but my ruling isn't going to change. Now, let's get this over with!" His flushed face showed his irritation with my questioning.

"The objection to the last question is sustained ladies and gentlemen," Vaughn announced as Harrington and I walked back to our positions. I glanced at Sandy as I walked back to the podium. She was biting her lip as she also recognized the significance of the court's adverse ruling; I wasn't getting the other rollover incidents into evidence for the jury's consideration. While convinced Vaughn's ruling was equally wrong this time as well, I recognized it was a decision that would stand on appeal since it involved a discretionary call. Judges won those types of calls, much like the "irrefutable evidence" that was required in a video replay to overturn a pass interference call in an NFL game.

Still reeling from his exclusionary ruling, I ended up fumbling around with Winchester for another five minutes to buy time. I didn't want to end my cross with Judge Vaughn's admonition to them being the last thing they heard. Unfortunately, my questions were largely ineffective, and I sat down.

For the same reason, Harrington didn't bother to ask the witness any questions in redirect. He wanted to end on the high that The Turtle's stern rejection of my case gave him. "The defense rests," he succinctly announced.

Like a five-year old at his birthday party itching to unwrap his birthday present, Vaughn wasted no time. He dismissed the jury for the day, informing them that he would see them back at ten a.m. the next morning instead of the usual starting time of nine o'clock.

"I will have some motions from the defense that I must deal with first thing in the morning, ladies and gentlemen. The lawyers and I will start at nine and be done by ten. Have a good evening." The jurors nodded back to the judge and were led out of the courtroom by The Scarecrow.

As soon as they were out, Vaughn addressed both of the attorneys. It was clear he was on a schedule to get out of the courtroom and on to his meeting with the Chief Judge.

"Be here at nine sharp," he ordered. "I intend to deal with Mr. Harrington's motion for a directed verdict at that time. Am I correct," The Turtle coached Harrington, "that your client will be reasserting that motion now that its case has been completed?"

"Absolutely, judge. It's more evident now than ever that there is absolutely no evidence to permit this case to proceed any further."

"I can tell both of you that, quite frankly, the court is strongly inclined to grant that motion. I'm disturbed by what I see as a complete lack of evidence that would even support a jury verdict should I let it go to the jury. We are dealing with what appears to be rank speculation based on what the court believes is the thoroughly discredited testimony of your experts, Mr. Culhane. However," he added, as he suddenly remembered his comments were on the record, "I'm keeping an open mind on this issue and will hear your respective arguments tomorrow." *Right.*

"May I comment Your Honor?" I asked.

"No, not this afternoon," he ordered. "I'm already late for my conference. Just be prepared to give me one concrete, *non-speculative* reason to permit you to proceed to put on a rebuttal case and let this case go to the jury. I've just told you of my predisposition in that regard."

Craige leaned over and whispered into Harrington's ear.

"Oh, yes, Your Honor," Harrington was reminded by Craige, "we still have the issue of Mr. Markov. I would ask that the court direct Mr. Culhane to let me know right now whether Mr. Markov is released from further trial attendance. He needs to get back to Detroit."

"I don't want him," I volunteered. He would only come in and pile on.

"Good. You both finally agree on something. We're making progress," The Turtle added. "I order Mr. Markov released and free to return to Michigan." Like an old plow horse smelling the oats in the barn, Vaughn sensed the imminent end of the trial and was suddenly in much better spirits. "Good evening, gentlemen." He pulled his corpulent, black-robed body from his leather, tall-backed chair and walked out the door leading to his chambers.

"I need to have a cigarette," Eric said to me after Vaughn had left the courtroom. He was as upset by the judge's comments as I was. He walked out of the courtroom by himself, leaving Sandy and me to collect our belongings for the day. He had taken up smoking since the trial began. He hadn't smoked for years. The pressure was getting to him.

Cole walked up to Harrington's table as we were collecting our notebooks. He spoke to Harrington in a voice that was obviously intended to be heard by me.

"Make sure that when the court directs a verdict for us that you go after every goddamn cent in fees and costs that we can get from that guy," he said, referring to Eric. "He had his chance to settle." His voice and demeanor were nasty.

"It will be my pleasure," Harrington chortled in response. "With the offer of judgment we served before trial, the court is going to give you a judgment against Hawkins for all the attorneys' fees and expenses you've paid us to defend the case."

"What kind of dollars are we talking about?" Cole asked, making no pretense that he intended the conversation to be private.

"I'd guess we're talking about four hundred thousand or so, all tolled."

"Well, this will be the only time that I'm glad you billed the shit out of me," Cole replied. They both laughed. They then grabbed their trial boxes, loaded up their dolly and left the courtroom.

"Look," Sandy said, leaning against Harrington's table after they were gone, "I'm sorry for my comments over lunch. I'm sure it came across as criticism, Mike. I didn't mean it as such, though."

"No, I'm the one that owes you the apology. I lost my cool and got thin-skinned in the process. I know you weren't criticizing me. We're both a little stressed out, I'd say."

"Fair enough," she conceded. "Enough said. What arguments do you have in mind to avoid Vaughn granting a directed verdict against us tomorrow morning?"

"Do you want the straight answer?" I asked.

"Not really, but I'd better know what it is."

I sighed. "I don't have a fucking clue. That's the answer," I said, throwing a crumpled up sheet of paper into a wastebasket ten feet away. Again, it missed, bouncing off the rim. *Son of a bitch!*

"Is there anything I can do to help tonight?" she asked.

"No. Thanks. I'm going to take some of the files home with me from the office and see if I can find some helpful case law and arguments. The problem is, I don't think that The Turtle is much interested in case law at this point. I'm afraid he's got his mind made up."

Eric said nothing. He merely nodded at the obvious.

Sandy didn't contradict me on that point either. We left the courtroom with our trial bags and boxes. We didn't talk on the way back to the office. Eric said his goodbyes outside of the courthouse and told us he would meet us in the morning. He was characteristically stoic but realistic as well. The tenor and content of Vaughn's comments hadn't been lost on him either.

CHAPTER 49

"WHO SHOT YOUR dog?" Liz quipped as she entered my study. It was after ten and I was looking over notes of the trial evidence and searching for case law on my laptop, hoping to come up with some novel arguments for to-morrow morning that I knew weren't there. I had been over the cases and the file a half dozen times since I had retreated to the study immediately after din-ner. There was no silver bullet for this one. No John Grisham ending this time, I thought dejectedly. My depressed mood was evident to Liz.

"It's the case, that's all. We're going to get thrown out of court tomorrow. The judge has already made up his mind." I sucked on a bottle of beer. It was my third since dinner, and I couldn't come up with a good reason to stop now. I was Irish, after all. I was entitled to black moods peppered with alcohol. Having sensed my dejection from my lack of engagement during dinner with her and the girls and having seen me retreat to my study immediately getting up from the table, I knew that she had come in to pick up my spirits.

She sighed and came over and sat down in the wing chair next to me. I was sitting on the carpeted floor. Parts of the file were strung out all over the carpet, in disarray, with my laptop to the side. That's symbolic, I mused to my-self. I had the remote control for the DVD player in my hand and was about to play the DVD that George Krueger had taken of the Global S tests when Liz had entered the room. I hadn't looked at it since the first time I had viewed it in the title insurance company's conference room. Since I felt like I was at-tending my own wake, I thought it only fitting that I look at the video that was the proverbial nail in my coffin.

"Is it that bad?"

"No, it's worse, for a lot of reasons," I said, putting the remote controller for the DVD player down on the carpet. "For starters, I'm not sure how Eric is going to take Vaughn's dismissal of our case tomorrow morning from an emotional standpoint. He's convinced himself that Jenny's death was caused by a stability problem in the Mesa. I'm convinced he's right too, but I guess it doesn't make a hell of a lot of difference what either of us thinks, at this stage. It's only The Turtle's opinion that counts, and he's hell bent on not letting it go any further."

"Eric's not going to take it well, is he?"

"That's an understatement. And add to that the fact that Global is going to be able to get Vaughn to enter a judgment on their rejected offer of judgment against Eric for at least three to four hundred thousand dollars. It'll ruin him financially."

"Michael, do you really think that if Global wins they'll pursue those kinds of costs from Eric. He doesn't have any money to collect from. It doesn't make any sense."

"It sure as hell does if vengeance is the motive," I said, almost to myself as I took another swig of beer. "That's what you're going to see from Global. They're going after Eric as blood payment for my going after Global. And you know what? They're right. I should have never taken this case for Eric. I think it's time to be honest with myself for a change. I did do it for selfish reasons. I did it more to get back at Hunt and get back at Global for what they did to me. I wasn't thinking about the consequences to my client." I took another long drink.

"Michael, you know that's not true!" There was now anger in her voice. "Eric wouldn't have anybody but you represent him, and you know it. Sometimes fate has a weird way of working, and that's all you're seeing here. This case wasn't meant to be won. They can't all be winners."

"Bullshit," I said without any emotion. "I've been sitting here thinking. I could have persuaded him to use another attorney to handle the case. But I wanted to do it," I said, finally turning to look up at her directly. "There's an old saying that says something about 'being careful what you ask for, because may just get it.' Well, I'm afraid I got exactly what I asked for. And Eric is going to pay for my bad judgment, not to mention the financial mess I've put us in as well."

"What are you talking about?"

"About the fact that I've been so fucking fixated on beating Harrington and Global that I've not been paying attention to developing other clients. Liz, I don't know what I'm going to do after this case is over. The fact of the matter is that my practice is in the toilet, and Vaughn is about to flush it. I'm running out of money to keep the doors open, and I'm plain out of great ideas about what to do about it. I bet the farm, our farm, on winning this case, or getting a decent settlement offer that Eric found acceptable. And neither one of those things is going to happen," I said flatly.

She got up from the wing chair and walked to the door where she turned and looked down at me sitting on the floor. "Michael, I'm going to go read in bed. I'm not about to sit in here and give you an audience so that you can feel sorry for yourself or question every decision you've made about Eric's case, your job or this family," she said evenly. "It doesn't become you. You made some decisions, and maybe they turned out to not be so great in hindsight, okay? But the fact of the matter is that I know you better than you know yourself sometimes, and you made the right ones. We'll do okay," she said without the same conviction she manifested only a few months ago. "Look, I don't need to live in this house, with all this ... this ... this stuff," she said, referring to our lifestyle. "I don't even need to live in South Florida. If you feel that you need to move and start up a practice someplace else, with a clean break from this whole area, you know that the girls and I will support it. If you decide you want to stay here and hook up with another law firm, we'll support that as well. But, Michael, the girls and I don't want to languish while you whip yourself with all this self-doubt, second guessing and self-pity. Losing that case is secondary to that, and one thing I can't stomach is self-pity."

With that, she opened the door and left the room, quietly closing the door behind her.

I sat there for a moment and stared at the closed door, angry at her words and angry at myself. She was right. As usual. But I didn't want to hear it right now. I angrily grabbed the bottle of beer, drained it and turned on the DVD player and the footage of the Global S Tests. *Fuck it. I'll deal with my problems later*, I thought as the video rolled.

Despite my comment, my depressive thoughts continued to drift back to the impending dismissal ruling by Vaughn a short twelve hours away. As I reflected, I absently watched the Krueger video. The film rolled on the TV screen in front of me as I both watched it and stewed over the case at the same time. Krueger's video had started just after the test crew had apparently finished setting up the forest green Mesa for the S tests since none of the vehicle preparation was caught on the video. Using the remote control, I fast forwarded Krueger's video until it got to the first test. I then let it play and leaned back against the front of the couch and watched my case get blown apart by each of the four successive tests. The body sway movement of the Mesa was quite noticeable, but the tires didn't lift from the asphalt skid pad roadway beneath. The last S test played, and I let the tape run as I was preoccupied with second thoughts of my stupidity in persuading Global to run these tests to begin with.

As I sat there, I wondered to myself if The Turtle would have let this case go to the jury if Global had elected to defend the case without running these S tests. I watched absent-mindedly as the Global test engineers on the screen in front of me went about performing their post-test breakdown of the cables, cameras and equipment.

"Fuck it," I said out loud to no one but myself, "I'm getting another beer."

As I started to get up, I suddenly froze, staring at the TV screen in front of me.

What the hell was that? I bent down, picked up the remote and hit the re-wind button. The picture on the screen rolled back images in reverse, at blurred speed. After a few seconds, I hit the play button. The playback picked up at a spot that captured the Global test crew engaged in the post-test breakdown efforts. I sat back down on the floor, intently now watching the footage I had only been half watching a moment ago. There it was, playing in front of me. *I didn't miss it!*

"Well I'll be a son of a bitch!" I said out loud. "Son of a bitch!" I said again, as I reran the footage and watched it yet one more time. The cobwebs from the beers I had consumed were instantaneously metabolized by the sudden rush of adrenaline that was now pumping like an out of control fire hose.

"I got 'em! I got 'em!" I whooped out loud, laughing at the same time.

The study door suddenly opened. Liz was standing there in her over-sized T-shirt nightie, looking at me, wild-eyed with concern. "What's the matter!" she asked quickly, with her voice full of concern. She was obviously thinking that I had finally gone over the edge.

I looked over at her and laughed heartily. "The fat lady hasn't sung on this trial yet, not by a long shot!"

I explained the situation to her in a hurried and excited fashion. As I talked, I furiously piled my entire file into the two banker's boxes I had used to lug them home from the office.

I kissed her on the mouth and headed for the door and to my office. "Don't wait up for me!" I yelled behind me.

In the car, I called Sandy's number at home. It was now close to eleven-thirty p.m. My call woke her up.

"Give my regrets to the guy lying next to you right now, but throw on some clothes and meet me down at the office in half-an-hour." I didn't bother with any introduction or preamble.

"What are you talking about? What's going on?"

"I'll tell you all about it when you get there." I hung up. I then grabbed my iPhone, looking at my list of contacts for the number I needed. Finding it, I put in the call to Miami. I was in luck. He was in too, although asleep like Sandy was. He agreed to meet me in his offices at two a.m. I thanked him profusely and hung up as I pulled into my parking spot outside my office building.

Ten minutes later, Sandy came through the office door. She had thrown on a sweatshirt and jeans. Her hair was pulled back in a ponytail, a scrunchie holding it together.

"What in the world is going on?" were her first words.

I quickly explained the situation to her as I was finishing up printing out the trial subpoenas I had prepared on the word processor after I got to the office.

"How did you miss it on Krueger's film footage?" she asked after I had finished explaining.

I shook my head. "I screwed up, that's how. I remember viewing Krueger's DVD when it came in. I viewed it down the hall, on the title company's VCR. As I recall, I was interrupted watching it by the secretary in that office. She told me that she had a closing lined up and they needed to use the office I was in. That was the same office that houses their DVD player. As a result, I stopped watching it and popped out the DVD since I had seen the four S tests, and the test crew in the film was just starting to do post-test clean up. I never saw any need to go back to view Krueger's video thereafter since we got much clearer film footage of those four S tests from Harrington shortly after that. I used his for viewing after that. It was a quirk that I happened to grab Krueger's copy to view tonight at home." I laughed, shaking my head.

"And Global didn't include any of this on the video of the tests they provided to us, did they?"

"Hell no, they turned their cameras off. We got lucky when Krueger left his running and caught it."

"Count us lucky on this one," she added.

"Dumb Irish luck," I scoffed as I pulled the final copies off the printer and quickly proofed them. "Good luck finally countering this dumb Irishman."

"I'm hoping that you know where Cole, Markov and Winchester are staying here in town. Harrington told the court that Markov wasn't going to be able to catch a flight back until tomorrow. I'm praying like hell they're all still here."

"All I know is that I overheard Cole tell Craige in the hall outside the courtroom during a break yesterday that he wanted some documents from Harrington on another case. He told Craige to have them brought over to him at the Hyatt Pier 66 Hotel to review. That's where I think they're all staying if they're still here," she answered.

I signed the trial subpoenas and made copies.

"For once we get a break in this case," I said as I signed. "It was only effective last January first that the Florida Supreme Court amended the rules to give lawyers, as officers of the court, the authority to now sign and issue trial subpoenas, without the need to get them issued by the Clerk's Office. Otherwise, we'd have had to wait until eight-thirty tomorrow morning to get the clerk's office to issue them. Markov would have been gone by then."

"Let's hope he didn't decide to catch a late flight out today anyway."

"Where is the 16 mm reel of film that Global produced of the Arizona S tests? I need to take it down to Miami tonight."

She went out to her desk and returned in a moment carrying the large reel in its plastic casing. It had been filed away by her desk where it had rested, untouched, since we had received it months ago from Harrington, along with the DVD that Harrington had provided of the four S Tests that Global had taken from a regular video camera. I had demanded that Global produce the 16 mm film but had not felt the need to analyze it after receiving and reviewing its DVD of the same four S tests. She laid the round plastic case on my desk as I handed her the subpoenas, ready for service on the Global employees.

She grabbed the subpoenas and headed for the door. "Wish me luck."

"Sandy?"

She stopped and turned, her blonde ponytail swaying as she whipped her head around. "Yeah?"

"Regardless of how this case comes out, thanks for standing by me."

She laughed. "I guess we're both plagued with the same bad judgment, huh?"

"Now, get your ass out of here!" I commanded with a laugh.

She laughed and left.

CHAPTER 50

NINE O'CLOCK CAME early the next morning. I had finally rolled home at six in the morning, three hours earlier. I passed on going to bed, opting, instead, for two slugs of concentrated Cuban coffee at a Cuban diner just off Las Olas that was open all night. The jolt of caffeine worked, although I probably didn't need much in the way of an artificial stimulant this morning.

The fireworks started immediately the moment that Sandy and I walked into the courtroom with Eric. I had called Eric and asked him to meet me at my office at eight o'clock. I explained the developments to him at that time, as well as the fact that Sandy had been successful in serving all three of the Global representatives around one a.m. that morning. She had dated one of the management executives of the Hyatt two years ago. *I should have guessed.* When the night front desk staff had refused to inform her of the room numbers of the Global employees, she called her friend up and finessed him into putting in a call to the front desk staff to obtain the room numbers.

"I'll have your law license for this!" Harrington charged the moment I entered the courtroom. The judge was not yet on the bench. I quickly scanned the courtroom. Sure enough, The Three Stooges, Cole, Markov and Winchester, were sitting in the first row of the spectator section, immediately behind the railing which separated that section from the tables of the lawyers in front of the railing. All three, particularly Cole, gave me an ugly glare as we walked towards our counsel table at the front of the courtroom.

"How dare you subpoena Mr. Cole. He's another lawyer in this case! And you damn well better have your toothbrush with you. I'm asking Judge Vaughn to hold you in contempt and throw you in jail for defying his order of yesterday afternoon releasing Mr. Markov and Dr. Winchester from further trial attendance. This is outrageous!"

Harrington walked menacingly towards me as he spoke. He stopped about a foot from me. For a moment, I thought he was going to take a swing at me. I don't think I had seen him ever quite so pissed off.

"Bobby, be my guest," I said, keeping my voice calm and even as I spoke. "Yell and scream to the judge. Be my guest," I repeated. "And go ahead and get your underwear all in a bundle in the process. I've got a few motions of my own that I will be making."
He wasn't expecting that comeback. He looked at me strangely. "What are you talking about?"

"Let me keep you in suspense. Let's both wait for Judge Vaughn." I put down my trial briefcase and the box of materials I was carrying with me. Eric put down the box he was carrying as well. He stood back, out of the crossfire between Harrington and me.

At that moment, Vaughn entered through his chambers' door.

"This honorable court is now in session, the Honorable Baylor T. Vaughn, presiding!" boomed The Scarecrow. "Silence is commanded!"

"Good morning ladies and gentleman," Vaughn mechanically said to all the lawyers and their client representatives and court staff as he sat down in his tall-backed leather chair. "I believe that the first order of business today is your renewed motion for directed verdict. Is that correct, Mr. Harrington?"

"It is your honor, although there is another matter, which I want to immediately bring to your attention. It involves a direct violation by Mr. Culhane of your order of late yesterday afternoon in which you *released* both Mr. Markov and Dr. Winchester from further attendance at this trial. Mr. Culhane, there," he said, pointing, as if Vaughn didn't know who Mr. Culhane was, "has taken it upon himself to wake those two Global employees up in the middle of the night last night at their hotel and have them served with trial subpoenas requiring their attendance at these proceedings this morning. He also served the same subpoena in the same manner on the Global in-house attorney who is in charge of all product liability cases in the United States, Mr. Willis Cole. I am outraged at his actions and the utter contempt he is demonstrating for your orders. I ask for immediate sanctions!" he thundered.

The Turtle's response was immediate and predictably direct. He leaned forward aggressively in his chair. Both arms were resting on top of the bench in front of him, his fingers laced together.

He looked at me for a full two seconds before saying anything, apparently not believing that his ruling releasing the two witnesses had been defied. "Has Mr. Harrington accurately restated what occurred last night, Mr. Culhane?"

"He has judge."

"Well you'd better have an explanation, counsel, for your actions. I'm in no mood to tolerate any contravention of my order, and I told you that yesterday when we broke for the day. It was clear and I think you understood it."

I rose from my chair and walked to the podium to address the judge. "Your Honor, I clearly understood and respected your Order. However, I have a very good reason for my actions. I didn't undertake them lightly, believe me. I would ask that the court defer ruling on Global's motion and, instead, allow me to proceed with my rebuttal case right now. I realize that you had ordered us to present arguments on Global's motion for directed verdict, but I've just become aware of evidence, *critical evidence*, which I believe takes pre-eminence over Global's motion. Once you hear it, I'm quite sure you will agree," I added.

Harrington ignited.

"This is ridiculous! Mr. Culhane knows full well that you are inclined to grant my motion to dismiss. That's what is behind this! I don't know if the court is aware of this, but Mr. Culhane is the godfather of the burned Hawkins boy. He's simply too close to this case and is now apparently trying to talk you into giving him yet another chance to put on more witnesses in his desperate attempt to keep you from dismissing his case. Enough is enough, Judge. There's no critical evidence. I ask that he be sanctioned and that my client's motion be granted. This case should not be permitted to proceed one moment longer!" Aiming directly at The Turtle's ego, he slammed his hand down on the table in front of him, "he's turning your court into a circus."

I jumped in with a full grovel; Vaughn needed to understand my sincerity.

"Judge, you've known me as a member of the Broward County Bar for over ten years now. I've tried cases in your courtroom during that time. You know me," I pleaded, raising both hands, palms up, "and you know that I'm a straight shooter." Walking towards the bench, I said, "I will represent to you that if you permit me to put Mr. Markov on the stand in front of the jury at this time, and if the evidence I elicit from him doesn't cause you to change your views about my clients' case, *we will voluntarily dismiss the case, with prejudice*," I said with emphasis. "My client will walk away and never take an appeal. That's how serious I am."

"But Judge Vau—"

The Turtle raised his beefy paw and immediately silenced Harrington in mid-stream.

"Counsel, I have it," he said to Harrington. He then turned his large bald head towards me. After quietly appraising me for a full two seconds, he finally spoke. "Mr. Culhane, I'll grant that I've never known you to be reckless or to try to pull any wool over me in the past. So, given your contemptuous violation of my order, you either have something I probably should listen to, or you have a death wish to be on your way to jail compliments of my finding you in contempt. I don't know which it is, but, either way, we're going to quickly find out," he announced. "I'm going to grant your request, but I do so with great reservation. And you had better have something good and relevant," he warned.

"Thank you judge," I said. I meant it. *There is a god and he has three chins!*

"If I find that you are playing tactical games with me, I will personally call The Florida Bar and lodge the ethic's complaint myself. Your problems with me will only be the beginning of your troubles. Do you understand me?"

"Yes, I do, judge. I accept those consequences."

Harrington fumed at the ruling as he looked back at his three client representatives in their front row seats.

"Bailiff, are the jurors here, by chance? They're not due 'till ten, but I've noticed that this group tends to arrive early."

"Yes," The Scarecrow answered. "The last one just arrived. They're all having coffee in the jury room."

"I'm sorry to interrupt, judge," I interjected, "but I need to ask you for one more order."

He looked down at me with equal measures of irritation and confusion written on his face. "And what's that?"

"I would ask that Mr. Cole and Dr. Winchester both be excluded from the courtroom while Mr. Markov is on the stand, and that they be further ordered not to speak with each other, nor make any telephone calls to anyone until after they are each finished testifying."

He narrowed his hooded eyes with puzzlement as he pondered my request. Gagging an in-house attorney like Cole from trial proceedings was not the norm. Not at all.

"This is a bit unusual, but I'll order it." Vaughn nodded to Harrington as he told him, "have Mr. Cole and Dr. Winchester sit outside of the courtroom and not speak to each other or to anyone else until they are called to the stand."

"I have to object," Harrington stated. However, even he appeared puzzled by the proceedings and by my requests.

"I understand," The Turtle said, "however, as I mentioned, Mr. Culhane is in the frying pan right now. The way the court sees it, he's either got something important for this jury, or he's going into the fire. I find no prejudice to Global since you've rested your case, so I'm going to overrule your objection." He then instructed the bailiff, "bring them in."

Harrington quickly slipped by the rail where he spoke quietly with Cole and Winchester. I could see that Cole was furious; his finger was jabbing at

Harrington's chest and his overall body language exuded anger. Winchester left the courtroom as they conversed. Cole finished with Harrington and left as well. Just as the jury filed in, Harrington returned to his table clearly looking upset from the exchange.

As Harrington returned to his seat at the adjoining table, a dark-haired Cuban gentleman entered the courtroom and took a seat in one of the audience benches. He was carrying a heavy square metal box. Upon seeing me, he nodded. I nodded back.

"Good morning, ladies and gentlemen," Vaughn said. "This morning, Mr. Culhane is going to be starting what we call his rebuttal case. It is his client's opportunity to put on evidence to respond to points brought out by the defendant in its defense case that closed yesterday afternoon. The plaintiff is given this opportunity because the plaintiff has the burden of proof." He turned his bald head towards me. "Proceed with your first rebuttal witness, Mr. Culhane."

"The plaintiffs call Mr. Arthur Markov," I said without hesitation.

The Brillo-haired Global engineer came forward, passed through the swinging wooden railing, was sworn in and took his seat in the witness chair.

"Mr. Markov, you are an engineer for Global Motors, aren't you?"

"Yes, I am. I'm in charge of—"

"You are the Project Engineer at Global who signed off approving the final design of the Mesa for production, aren't you?" My tone was direct and forceful.

"That's correct."

"And you are the Global engineer who directly supervised those four S tests that Dr. Winchester showed to the jury yesterday afternoon at the Vehicle Testing Lab facility outside Tempe, Arizona, correct?"

At the mention of the tests, he knew. And the look in his beady little eyes told me that he knew that I knew too.

"The ... uh ... the S tests that were done with the exemplar Mesa? Yes, I ... uh ... was one of the people involved in them."

"Mr. Markov. You were more than *one of the people involved*, weren't you? You were *the* person in charge of those tests, isn't that correct?"

He fidgeted a little in his chair before answering.

"The tests were discussed by a number of people, including Dr. Winchester and others, but I was the directing engineer on site if that's what you mean."

I started pacing back and forth behind the podium. I wanted him in the worst way.

"Tell us what you intended to show by those S tests, sir," I asked, playing out the rope.

"I'm ... not sure ... I understand what you mean."

"Tell this jury why your company spent forty-thousand dollars to conduct those S tests, sir. What message did you want this jury to come away with after viewing the video of those tests?"

"The message is rather straightforward, I think," he answered. "They ... they show the Mesa doesn't have any stability problem. That's why we ran them."

I ceased pacing side to side and walked, instead, a few paces towards Markov sitting in the witness chair. I stopped.

"Sir, you would agree that those S tests are very important in demonstrating how the Mesa's design behaves in response to sudden steering inputs, wouldn't you?"

"Yes. That's why we ran them as I just said." He looked over at Harrington with the slightest trace of nervousness.

"In fact, you ran those S tests to persuade this jury that the Mesa didn't have any propensity to tip or roll over, isn't that right?"

"Propensity? ... I'm not sure I'm following you," he said, suddenly treading water and buying time to avoid where I was going.

"Come now, Mr. Markov, you're an intelligent man. You know what the word 'propensity' means, don't you?"

"Of course. It means a natural tendency or inclination. But I still don't understand what you're driving at."

"Sir, you ran those S tests at fifty-five miles per hour using an identically equipped and loaded Mesa in order to persuade this jury that Jenny Hawkins' fully loaded Mesa, in particular, had no design propensity to tip or roll when it was subjected to sudden swerves and turns, just like she made to the Mesa, didn't you?"

I saw his Adam's apple move once as he swallowed before answering. "That's true."

"You falsified those tests, didn't you Mr. Markov?" I made the statement evenly and matter-of-factly.

"Objection!" Harrington shot out of his chair. "Objection! I want to be heard on this!"

I looked up at the judge. He looked at me for a moment, then over at the witness. Markov was intense and wide-eyed. The only adjective that could fairly describe his demeanor at that point was 'electric.'

To his credit, enough residue of The Turtle's old trial skills still existed to enable him to smell blood in the water. He recognized fear in the witness sitting before him. Fear that should not have been engendered by that question, if there was no truth to it. It piqued his curiosity.

"Overruled," he finally said, "we don't need a sidebar. Answer the question Mr. Markov," he directed, as he leaned forward, laced both hands together and put both robed elbows on the top of the bench before him. He apparently wanted a closer look at the witness.

"We did not falsify those tests, and I resent your allegations!" Markov fired back.

"Sir, I'm going to borrow Mr. Harrington's DVD player and television screen for a moment," I said as I walked over to the corner of the courtroom and pulled it forward in front of the jury, the witness and the judge. Sandy quickly jumped out of her chair, moved forward and plugged its extension cord into the wall's outlet. "I have a DVD of my own that I want you to see."

Sandy quickly returned to her seat as I turned it on. Markov didn't even attempt to now camouflage his concern. He looked expectantly to Harrington.

Taking his cue, Harrington jumped out of his chair, "I don't know what Mr. Culhane has there, Your Honor, but I can tell you that this DVD was not listed on the plaintiff's pre-trial catalog of exhibits. I object to its use here."

"Your Honor," I quickly argued, "the tape will speak for itself. As the court will see, there can be no claim of prejudice since Mr. Markov is in it. He'll be able to identify its authenticity."

Vaughn sat silently for a few seconds as he considered the objection and my response, pondering his ruling. "Overruled," he finally said, "I want to see where this goes."

I pulled the Krueger DVD out of my briefcase and popped it into the player. Taking the remote control in my right hand, I hit the play button. The TV screen showed the beginning of the Krueger footage. The camera captured the same four Global employees completing the same pre-test setup that the jury had seen on the Winchester video the afternoon before. The only difference was the camera angle and the fact that it was clear that the camera that took this footage was at a distance much further away and higher. It reflected Krueger's raised elevation from the mountainside.

"That's you there in that footage the jury is viewing, isn't it?" I asked, pointing to the video footage playing on the screen.

Markov just sat and stared at the footage. His face suddenly bore concern.

"Mr. Markov, I've posed a question to you. That's you, isn't it?"

"Where did you get this?" he asked.

"Sorry, sir, I get to ask the questions; your job is to give us truthful answers. That's you on that footage, isn't it?" I persisted.

The witness just sat and stared at the screen in front of him, transfixed.

"Respond to the question, sir," The Turtle directed.

"Yes ... yes ... that's me," he finally said. He again looked to Harrington, as if he could afford protection to him. Harrington, who had no basis for objection, simply watched the examination along with the jury. Puzzlement shown on his face. He was in the dark.

"These are the same S tests that were shown to the jury yesterday afternoon by Dr. Winchester, aren't they?"

The answer was self-evident; the jury could see for themselves that they were.

"Mr. Markov," I again interrupted his catatonic-like viewing of the screen in front of him. "Mr. Markov ..."

"Yes," he responded finally.

"Good. Let's just sit and watch your tests," I said, turning my head from the witness over to the jurors. All of the jurors had puzzled looks on their face, but they were all paying close attention to the footage running on the TV in front of them. Judge Vaughn quietly got up out of his chair and walked to the side of his bench closest to the jury and walked down the two steps to get a better view of what was showing on the TV screen.

Not a sound was heard in the courtroom as the footage played. When it reached a certain point after all four of the tests were completed, I hit the pause button. The tape froze in place on the screen in front of them.

"That's the spot where the footage Dr. Winchester showed the jury yesterday stopped, Mr. Markov. And that's the spot where your test cameras at Global *stopped shooting*, isn't it?" I asked, with emphasis.

He was literally breaking out in a sweat. His forehead was damp with a fine film of water. I thought witnesses only did that in novels, I reflected in passing.

"Sir!" I commanded sharply, "isn't that true?"

He nodded his head up and down, saying nothing.

"Now, let's keep playing this DVD footage and see what happened after you shut your Global cameras off."

I hit the pause button once again, and the footage picked back up where it had stopped. For the ensuing five minutes, the jury watched the film as three other Global test technicians removed film from the cameras and unbuckled cables. Then, the camera picked up Markov driving an open pickup truck and parking it next to the Mesa. He parked it on the far side and got out, permitting an unobstructed view from Krueger's video. His wooly head of hair, and his face beneath it, were unmistakable as he walked over to the hatchback of the Mesa and opened it. Reaching in, he grabbed one of the large boxes which, according to Winchester, was supposedly weighted to simulate the weight of a large container of boxed Girl Scout cookies. He grabbed a flap with one hand

and lifted it out at the same time that he reached in with his other hand and easily lifted out a second box and then effortlessly tossed them both into the open bed of the pickup.

The chubby female juror got it first and let out an audible gasp. A few of the others caught on as soon as Markov repeated the removal of two more 'weighted' cookie boxes. All of them finally got it, however, when, with one hand, he grabbed one of the cartons which supposedly contained four heavy gallons of Sherwin Williams' paint and, with no trouble, threw it into the bed of the pickup as well. While the boxes were real, there was nothing in them.

As Markov crawled into the back of the Mesa to remove the heavy 'air compressor' from within, I turned my head to look at Harrington. He sat back in his chair, in obvious shock at what he was seeing unravel before him. He had stopped making objections.

There on film was Markov easily carrying the air compressor, which supposedly weighed hundreds of pounds, over to the truck where he laid it into the bed with the rest of the items. It couldn't have weighed twenty pounds. It was undoubtedly built out of a dense Styrofoam and painted to simulate an old, heavy metal compressor.

As Markov was returning from the pickup to shut the rear hatch back of the Mesa, you could see him look up, directly at the camera. Even at the relatively long distance that Markov was from the camera taking the footage, the jury could make out first puzzlement on Markov's face, then realization, as he somehow discovered that he was looking at Krueger's camera pointed directly at him. It must have been a reflection from Krueger's camera lens or the metal tripod next to his RV that brought his eyes to look in the direction of the camera. He was obviously startled at recognition of the camera, and his reaction was captured on the footage now being watched by the jury.

At that point, Markov walked briskly over to a second pickup truck, a red one, climbed in and started driving towards a latched chain link exit gate off-camera. The next view, a minute later, was that of the same red pickup truck making its way up the road towards the camera. When the truck was only about fifty yards away, the view from the video camera suddenly whirled out of control for a second or two and then went black.

The whirling, I thought to myself, was old Krueger grabbing the tripod and hustling it and its mounted camera into the RV. He must have shut it off as he placed it inside the RV. There was no doubt in my mind that Markov had seen the camera and Krueger's efforts to hide it.

I turned to the witness. He was now ashen.

"Mr. Markov!" I said, intentionally cracking him to attention with a thunderous voice, "you falsified those S tests, didn't you?" My angry tone made clear that it was not really a question.

While his head looked up at me, his eyes weren't focused. He couldn't argue with the hard evidence staring all of us in the face. "Uh ... uh ... yes," he finally managed. His voice was so quiet that we could hardly hear him. He put his head down into the open palms of both of his hands and started crying. It was more like a whimper.

"Sir, look at me," I said angrily, "I'm not done yet!" My tone caused him to look up. His beady eyes were already red-rimmed.

Harrington made no effort to stem the bleeding. Like the jury, he appeared captivated at this sudden turn of events and at what he was hearing.

"You ran those S tests without carrying the approximately six hundred twenty pounds of cargo that Jenny Hawkins was actually carrying in her Mesa at the time of her accident, didn't you?"

He nodded slowly as his body showed complete resignation to the truth. He could not argue with the footage and was forced to concede. "No ... we didn't," he finally sighed. He again looked downward, with his head shaking back and forth.

"And you didn't run those tests at fifty-five miles per hour either, did you?"

"What ...?" he managed, unfocused.

"I said you didn't run those S tests at fifty-five miles per hour as Dr. Winchester told this jury yesterday, did you? You actually ran them at only fifty miles per hour, didn't you?"

His red-rimmed eyes stared blankly at me, either not comprehending my question or trying to gather his thoughts.

"Mr. Markov, I had the 16 mm film of those tests analyzed with a motion analyzer last night by a film lab expert in Miami," I said pointing to Raphael Cruz, the goateed Cuban-American sitting in the back of the courtroom. Mr. Cruz nodded to me and the jury as I made reference to him. "He counted the number of film frames per second that the Mesa travelled in the film, and, using the known distance between targeted reference points on the skid pad, he did the math and calculated the Mesa's test speed. Will it be necessary for me to put him on the stand to establish that, sir?"

Markov finally replied, with resignation. "No ... that won't be necessary ... we ran it at only fifty mile per hour."

To my right, I heard Harrington toss his pen onto the legal pad on the desk in front of him.

"And sir, *the reason* you falsified that test was because at fifty-five miles per hour, and with the *real* cargo load of six hundred twenty pounds that Jenny Hawkins was carrying that last afternoon of her life, your Mesa—the one that you, sir, signed off on for production approval—can become unstable when a sudden emergency steering input is introduced by the driver, isn't that true!" It was more a statement than a question. I took no mercy on him.

He nodded up and down, very slowly. "Yes ... yes," he finally managed, quietly.

"The Mesa has a propensity—a deadly propensity—to rollover, doesn't it?"

He again put his head down into the palms of both hands.

"Mr. Markov, I didn't get an answer to that question!" I now said viciously. I looked over at Eric as I finished the question. His face was red with pent-up anger. Sandy came over to kneel by the side of his chair, keeping him in check.

His answer could barely be heard above his quiet whimpering. "Yes ... it should never have been released for production." Then, with renewed focus, he looked up and angrily raised his voice as he spoke. "The company wouldn't listen to me!" he sobbed, suddenly trying to defend himself. "I told them that when it was heavily loaded, it couldn't hold its stability and control on the road if the driver was required to suddenly steer hard and fast. Its wheelbase was too narrow relative to its c.g. Our earlier stability testing at the proving grounds proved that, but they made me approve it," he managed between stifled sobs. "They wanted to get it to market on an accelerated schedule to compete with the new Japanese utility vehicle that just came out, but they wouldn't let me make the wheelbase changes that I begged for. I was told," he now said, between open sobs, "that I either had to approve it or lose my job. My son and daughter work at the company too," he cried in anguish. "I should have never done it. God forgive me," he said with self-pity.

There was a stunned silence that hung over the room for the moment. No one, not even me, expected that testimony.

I gave him no pity nor was I about to let up. His comment that the Mesa's wheelbase needed to be wider to make it 'stable' triggered the significance of a small fact I had noted in working up the case, which I did not appreciate until his present admission. "Mr. Markov!" I barked loudly, cutting through his sobbing self-pity and getting his attention, "we know that the manufacturer of the Powergrip AP tires on the Mesa specified a maximum tire pressure of thirty psi for the tires on that vehicle, yet Global's decal tag on its door jamb specified a maximum inflation of only twenty-six psi, isn't that true?"

He nodded quietly, still whimpering between sobs, "Yes."

"And *the reason* that Global did that was because removing four psi of air from a tire is a back door way of trying to increase a vehicle's wheel base, isn't it, because when you remove air from a tire, it flattens out and widens the tire's contact patch on the roadway which, in turn, causes its effective wheelbase to be increased, doesn't it!" It also was not intended to be a question.

"Yes, that is why we did it ... removing air pressure acted to increase its effective wheelbase. It wouldn't eliminate its inherent stability problem, but it would further limit the universe of problematic events in the real world."

"'Problematic events' ... 'problematic events'!" I bellowed, "Is that what you called them? Sir, your *problematic event* is what this jury and everybody else in this courtroom would simply call a *deadly rollover*, is it not! It's what killed Jenny Watson and broiled her son, is it not?" Again, it was not a question but a declarative statement.

Markov looked at me, then the jury and then up at the judge before starting to sob again. He then finally managed, "Yes, that was what the lower tire pressure was attempting to avoid."

"Well, you and your company's manipulations and your poor design caused Jenny Hawkins to lose her life and to burn her little baby boy, didn't they?" I said loudly and angrily as I slammed my right palm on the wooden podium's top.

Markov startled then merely nodded, sniffling in his self-pity.

"Is that a 'yes,' sir?" I asked angrily and loudly. "I want you to admit or deny it out loud and orally on this court's record!"

Judge Vaughn made no attempt to intervene.

"Yes," he finally managed quietly, as his shoulders moved up and down with each of his sobs.

"That was one of the *problematic events*, wasn't it?" I asked, with anger.

"Yes," he whimpered again.

My rage at his admissions was explosive. "Who in Global management knew of the rollover dangers of the Mesa?" I angrily asked.

Markov's demeanor suddenly went from self-pity to anger. "They all did, don't you see!" he lashed out in anger and anguish. "Everybody on the product safety committee knew it! I was called into a special meeting they had on the Mesa. I was told to shut up and sign off, that I was making a bigger deal out of this than I should," he whimpered, taking his white handkerchief out to blow his nose. "After that meeting, I was told to destroy all internal memos and erase all e-mail from the system that made any reference to the stability problem. I was told to re-title all the stability tests that my team conducted at the proving grounds to call them tire tests instead. Mr. Cole of the Legal Department was assigned to bury this ... Everybody was involved!"

I jumped on his testimony. "You're saying that Willis Cole, the Global in-house attorney who has been sitting in the back of this courtroom for the last few days knew all about this too?" I was as angry as I was stunned.

"Everybody!" Markov said fiercely. "Cole was with me at the S testing in Arizona; he was sitting off to the side in another truck. He never got out, but he saw it all. You don't see him on the camera film, but he was there. The S tests were his idea. God help me," he lamented. "And Winchester knew it too." With that, the witness lost all control. His sobbing became uncontrollable, with his shoulders rocking up and down.

The jury was as thunderstruck as I was. Vaughn had not left the place he had been standing while watching the test footage I had been displaying.

At that point I was suddenly hit by another thunderbolt. *Could the unthinkable have occurred?* "Mr. Markov ... Mr. Markov!" I thundered again, finally getting his attention.

"Objection, he's battering the witness," Harrington finally said, showing a little vigor. The air was out of his usually billowing sails.

"Overruled, counsel," Vaughn bellowed as he marched back up the two steps to ascend his chair, "we're going to hear this!"

I walked a few steps towards Markov as he sat in the witness chair. "The old man with the camera in the RV who took this film footage," I said, pointing to the TV screen, "he gave you his name, license plate number and the name of the motel where he was staying, didn't he?"

"Yes, he did. I knew that Cole would be furious when he found out that some old guy had filmed the tests, so I demanded that he tell me who he was and where he was staying. The old man was nervous, and so he told me."

"I want you to listen very carefully to the next question that I'm going to ask you," I said quietly. "Did you tell Mr. Cole about the cameraman on the hillside when you got back from scaring the cameraman off?"

He merely nodded his head up and down, refusing to look at the jury.

"And did you give Cole the man's name, license plate number and the name of the motel where he was staying?"

He was starting to sob anew. The witness was little more than Jell-O at this point, but I needed the answer to the last question.

"Did you, sir, did you tell Cole?"

"Yes," he sobbed, "I gave him all that information."

"*Oh my god,*" I said out loud to no one in particular as I realized the ramifications of what he had just said. "*Oh my god,*" I repeated more quietly to myself. *Cole had killed old George Krueger,* I suddenly realized. *That's why his RV was found going the wrong direction out of Tempe. And that's why his video card was gone from his camera. Cole had taken it.* I also knew that I would have to deal with that fact later.

"Are you okay, Mr. Culhane?" Vaughn suddenly asked as he saw my reaction to the testimony. There was surprising concern in his voice.

I just stood there at the podium looking absently at the witness as I tried to digest what I had just realized.

"Mr. Culhane," Vaughn repeated, showing uncharacteristic concern, "are you alright?"

His question snapped me out of it.

"Yes," I finally said after a moment. "Thank you."

The jury, whom I had momentarily forgotten about during my exchange with the witness, sat stern-faced and angry at what they had heard from him.

"I'm through with you," I finally said to the witness. I turned my back and walked back to my seat.

Harrington shook his head, motioning that he had no questions. He appeared shell-shocked at the testimony he had just heard, although he didn't realize the half of it.

Vaughn looked down at Markov with an angry fire in his eyes. "You," he ordered, pointing at the witness, "sit in the back of this courtroom and do not leave, do you hear me!" It was not a question.

Markov turned his head quickly at the Judge's booming voice. "Yes," he said, obediently. He dragged himself off the stand and quietly walked to the back of the courtroom where he sat down, his head lowered.

I looked directly at Eric next to me. His jaws were set in steel, trying to control his anger at the brutal revelations Markov had just made. His chest heaved up and down as his eyes burned holes in the judge's bench in front of him. He was doing all he could to prevent an explosion of rage. Sandy, I saw, who was still kneeling next to his chair, had his left hand between hers, attempting to soothe his emotions.

The jury members were now staring back and forth between Eric and the female Global trial representative sitting next to Harrington. For a person who played virtually no role in the courtroom thus far, she was now the target of openly hostile glares from the jury. Her confident demeanor had been utterly destroyed. She looked to be as upset about the testimony as everyone else in the courtroom. From all visual accounts, she obviously had no idea of the fraud her company had committed, nor of the fact that she had been sent to the trial as a false symbol of Global professionalism and caring.

Looking directly over at Harrington, I called my next witness: Cole. Without comment or push back, Craige rose from his chair and followed my direction that he bring Cole to the witness stand. The Boy Wonder walked past the swinging rail door, down the aisle and out of the courtroom door at the rear of the courtroom, to bring him in.

Ten seconds passed. Then twenty. Then thirty. As they passed, not a sound was evident in the courtroom except the rhythmic ticking back and forth of the pendulum on the wall clock as it swung back and forth. Vaughn was not about to call a recess.

After what seemed like five minutes, although closer to a minute, Craige finally returned, alone. Concern etched on his face, he quickly walked up the aisle, past the swinging railing where Harrington walked the few steps back to meet him. Craige leaned towards Harrington, whispering excitedly. Harrington's eyes widened, and his mouth perceptibly dropped as he listened. He nodded, turned and addressed the court.

"Judge Vaughn," he said sheepishly, "I must ask for a sidebar."

Vaughn looked at him with puzzlement and nodded. We both approached the side of the judge's bench.

"Where's Cole?" The Turtle demanded as soon as we both got there.

"That's the problem, your honor," Harrington responded, nervously looking over at me as well. It was a Harrington I hadn't seen before. "Uh ... it ... uh ... it appears that Mr. Cole must have misunderstood your instructions. Dr. Winchester informs my associate that Mr. Cole is on his way to the airport and is headed back to his office in Michigan."

"He's what!" The Turtle exploded. A couple of the jurors looked up at hearing the judge's raised and angry voice.

"He's gone, your honor," Harrington answered directly.

I didn't have a chance to jump in. I didn't need to. Vaughn beat me to it, again.

"Well, we'll just see about that!" He turned his massive, robed body to the jury, not even waiting for the lawyers to exit the sidebar. "Ladies and gentlemen, I have to apologize for the recess that I'm going to call right now. It seems that we have a ... an absent witness problem that I'm going to have to deal with. Please retire to the jury room. Rest assured, I'll call you back just as soon as I have a handle on the delay." He didn't even bother with a forced smile. He nodded at The Scarecrow who got out of his chair and ushered the jury out of the courtroom.

With agility and speed that I didn't think the big man had, Vaughn literally exploded out of his chair and walked down to his clerk's station to the far side of his bench, opposite the now-empty jury box. He grabbed the phone and dialed a number he apparently knew by heart.

"This is Judge Baylor T. Vaughn," he said with authority into the phone, "I have a witness who is under my order to be a material witness in my courtroom right now, and I'm told that he's headed over to the Ft. Lauderdale Airport to catch a plane back to Michigan right away. I'm ordering the Broward County Sheriff's Department to radio to your patrol squad at the airport. Find him, arrest him and bring him back to my courtroom immediately!"

He listened to the voice on the other end of the line, undoubtedly a deputy county sheriff who was questioning the department's legal authority to arrest a citizen at a public airport merely on the oral order of some judge without an arrest warrant. The Turtle cut his protestations short.

"I said do it! Consider this an oral *capias* if you need to, dammit, but just do it! We'll worry about the niceties of the paperwork later." After he provided the deputy with Cole's name and description, he slammed the phone down.

I could see that the old American Legion in him was not to be fooled with.

Finishing with that, he turned with full measure to Harrington.

"I want this on the record," he ordered, looking at the court reporter to make sure she was taking it all down. The red-headed woman, no longer chewing gum, nodded obediently. She poised her fingers in anticipation of getting down every word.

"Mr. Harrington, I want to know right now if you, or your co-counsel from Atlanta over there," he said glaring over at Aubrey Trenton III, "had any knowledge of what we just heard in this courtroom!"

"None, Your Honor, absolutely none!" Harrington immediately answered without any hesitation. His previously-smooth demeanor was in the trash can, and his Lauderdale tan was three shades lighter. I believed him.

"Nor I, Judge Vaughn!" Trenton echoed almost as quickly, rising out of his chair like a warmed Pop Tart out of a toaster. "I only get the information the client provides me, and this is all news to me."

"Either did I," said the Boy Wonder, nervously.

"And how about you, ma'am?" he said, now turning his cross hairs on the Global trial representative.

She looked like she was on the verge of tears. She just shook her head and quietly said she hadn't.

Vaughn turned to The Scarecrow. "Have Winchester put under arrest right now and held in the hall until further word from me," he ordered. The old bailiff jumped at the order and zipped through the swinging gates on the railing and out the door, calling another deputy on his police radio as he exited the courtroom.

I stepped forward. "Judge, based upon what we've all seen and heard this morning, I'm moving this court, *ore tenus*, to allow me to amend my pleadings in this case to assert a claim for punitive damages, if the jury is so inclined."

Harrington, though beaten up by the morning's proceedings, was still on his feet. "On behalf of my client, I must vigorously object. I realize that the evidence we've just heard is … well … is …"

"Try *criminal*," I suggested, sarcastically.

"… is terribly unfortunate," he continued, "but the prejudice to my client at this late date in the trial if you were to grant that motion would be monumental. I think the better avenue is for you to declare a mistrial and to grant a new trial."

"Your client, Mr. Harrington, is not getting any mistrial or any new trial, for that matter. It's getting exactly what it asked for when it hatched this plan to deceive me and my jury," he said angrily. "I'm granting the motion. Your complaint is deemed amended, Mr. Culhane, and punitives are going to the jury, gentlemen."

He ordered the attorneys not to leave his courtroom except to go to the bathroom if they had the need. He was determined to regain control over his courtroom and the trial. "I'm going to tell the bailiff to feed the jury a quick lunch, because we're proceeding as soon as Mr. Cole is brought back here!" He stormed off through his chambers' door, leaving Harrington and I just standing there.

EXACTLY SIXTY MINUTES later, Cole was escorted back into the courtroom by two huge Broward County deputy sheriffs. Not fighting their steely grip on his two arms, Cole was sporting a set of handcuffs, his arms behind him. His eyes were blazing with fury. His foulard tie was askew and his shirt wrinkled. He definitely had lost some of the *GQ* luster he had displayed when he first appeared in court earlier that morning. The deputies looked like they were thoroughly enjoying manhandling a lawyer for a change.

As soon as he was brought past the wooden railing up to the bench, the judge came out of his chambers, having been called by his clerk. He wasted no time getting to the meat of the matter as he plopped down into his high-backed leather chair.

"We're back on the record," he said to the court reporter, nodding emphatically to ensure that she was typing up the proceedings. She nodded back to let him know she had. He then looked up at Cole. "Mr. Cole, you violated not only the subpoena that commanded your presence in this courtroom today, but my specific instructions to wait in the hall! I'll deal with your contempt issues later, but right now you're going to take that witness stand and answer Mr.

Culhane's questions in this case! Now, straighten your tie, tuck in your shirt and get on that witness stand!" he boomed. His floating liver spots on his red-flushed bald head were back. He was livid.

"I have nothing to offer to this trial," he shot back angrily, challenging Vaughn's edict. "For god's sakes, I'm a lawyer and cannot be compelled to testify," he announced.

"Not for long are you a lawyer," Vaughn countered, "not after the facts that Mr. Markov shared with us. And, in the meantime, you *will* take that stand," Vaughan commanded. "If you want to take The Fifth, you're welcome to do so, but you're going to have to do it in front of this jury, and they may consider that in their deliberations."

For the first time Cole seemed to notice Markov who was still sitting in the audience benches behind the railing. One glance at the remains of Markov told Cole everything that he needed to know; Markov had spilled his guts, apparently confirming the suspicions which undoubtedly had fueled Cole's unsuccessful premature departure from the city. The expression in his eyes changed immediately, from hostility to fear—raw fear.

"Now, remove those cuffs," Vaughn instructed the burly deputies, and, turning to Cole, ordered, "and you then get on that stand! Bring in the jury as soon as we're ready," he commanded to The Scarecrow.

One of the deputies reached down and unlocked the cuffs. Cole rubbed his wrists and straightened his shirt and tie, more out of habit than anything else.

We all sat down as Cole reluctantly walked up and took the stand. Raw anger still shone in his face. The two deputies sat down in the first row of benches. The judge nodded and The Scarecrow fetched the jury.

The jurors came in, walked down the rows to their respective seats, and sat down. They registered shock at seeing Cole already on the stand. Their shock quickly turned to glares of thinly-veiled contempt for the witness.

Cole was sworn in. He fidgeted in the witness chair.

I didn't waste time.

"Mr. Cole, you're a lawyer, aren't you?"

"I am."

"And you chair the Global Motors Product Safety Committee, don't you?"

"I do."

"And you fabricated the S test' that your company presented yesterday to this jury, didn't you?"

It wasn't until that question was asked that it finally dawned on Cole just how deep the pile of shit was in which he was now standing.

He looked over at the judge and then at the jury before answering. "I decline to answer that question on the grounds that it may incriminate me." The Fifth Amendment. It didn't surprise me.

I knew that I wouldn't get anything more out of him from that point on. He was taking the Fifth, and there was way around it. However, I had to ask the question that had cut me like a knife when Markov told me that he had supplied Krueger's name and motel to Cole. I would never again get the chance.

"Mr. Cole," I asked quietly but directly. "Did you meet a George Krueger in Arizona on the evening those S test' were run?" The implication of what I was asking him was obvious to only Cole, myself, and possibly Sandy.

Cole stared at me without saying a word and then finally smirked. We both knew that he did. He was the only one ruthless enough to kill an old, defenseless man to protect his chance at the golden ring he had coveted so much, that of General Counsel at Global Motors—a position that public disclosure of the Mesa's stability defects, and his involvement in hiding those defects, would surely torpedo. I'm sure he believed he had contained the problem when he killed George Krueger that night after the old man had returned to his motel and Cole had secured what he mistakenly thought was the only videotape footage Krueger had taken. He never suspected that Krueger had any connection to this case or that the old man had duped a copy and Federal Expressed it to me on his way back to his motel in Arizona. He guessed wrong. Dead wrong. Gary Gilmore wrong.

Not a sound was heard in the courtroom over the relentless ticking of the regulator clock on the wall.

"I'm not saying another word without a lawyer," he finally snarled. It was straight out of a Hollywood movie. "That's all there is to it. I take The Fifth."

I looked him straight in the eye. He defiantly held my gaze. I sighed and slowly shook my head back and forth. The realization that I was facing George Krueger's murderer left me both saddened and angry.

"For once, you and I finally agree," I responded, "you have no more say in this case." I walked over and sat down, patting Eric on the knee as I did. He was emotionally exhausted as well.

Vaughn took charge at that point. "Deputies," he said to the two officers sitting in the front row, "please take this man under custody. I'll deal with that aspect after we conclude our civil trial this morning."

They walked up past the wooden rail. One of them walked up to the witness stand to escort Cole out of the witness box and out of the courtroom with the second deputy walking on the other side of Cole. He was unceremoniously escorted from the courtroom.

Harrington slumped back in his chair. He looked defeated, utterly and completely.

"Do you have any more witnesses you wish to call in rebuttal, Mr. Culhane?" Vaughn asked. Gone from his demeanor and tone was the hostile edge that I had experienced throughout the trial.

"No, Your Honor. I'm done," I said. "I rest." I didn't even bother to look at the jury. I was as shocked as they were at the sudden turn of events. Given those events, I felt no need no need to try to recall Dr. Winchester to the stand. I had made all the points I wanted to make.

To his credit, The Turtle didn't miss a beat.

"Ladies and gentlemen of the jury, the evidence in this case is now closed. We're going to be taking an hour break during which the attorneys and I are going to be finalizing the jury instructions and the verdict form. After that break, each of the attorneys is going to be making his final arguments to you on the evidence you have heard. I remind you that you are not to discuss this case in any respect until after you have heard the closing arguments and my final jury instructions."

He looked at the wall clock. "Bailiff, let's reconvene the jury here in one hour." With that, the jury filed out in silence.

As soon as the door to the jury room closed, I stood and addressed Judge Vaughn. "Your Honor, I have reason to believe that Mr. Cole murdered the man who shot the film footage I showed the jury this morning." Vaughn's eyes now widened as he heard that piece of new information. His eye slits were slits no more. Harrington's head shot up, wide-eyed as well, upon hearing my statement. Cole sat still, however, looking at me with defiance in his eyes.

Vaughn wasted no time in his response. After first looking over at Cole, he then addressed his judicial assistant. "Ms. Guerra, get the State Attorney on the line for me. I'll take it in my chambers. Deputies," he said, now addressing the two Broward County deputies who rose in unison from their first-row seats, "handcuff Mr. Cole here and take him into custody again. Do the same with that man sitting at the back of the courtroom," he said, pointing at Markov.

Perhaps already expecting the worst, Markov did not even react to that directive.

"We stand adjourned for the next hour," Vaughn then announced, banging his gavel on the bench for the first time since the trial started to make the point. He strode off the bench to chambers.

CHAPTER 51

AFTER APPROVING THE special verdict questionnaire that the jury would be answering, Vaughn ordered Harrington and me to commence our closing statements to the jury. Mine only lasted five minutes. I didn't even mention a damage figure to them. Harrington, to his credit, put aside the devastating developments earlier in the day and argued that while there might be 'some troubling questions' about the Mesa, I had failed to show that in this particular accident, there was any proven defect. "After all is said and done," he calmly stated, "Mr. Culhane's client has the burden of proof," referring to Eric sitting next to me. "Mr. Culhane didn't meet that burden. It was a terrible and horrific accident. No one denies that fact, but it was not an accident that was caused by any *proven* defect."

His words were as flat as an overnight beer left on the kitchen counter.

The jury deliberated for only an hour. It was the shortest jury verdict deliberation I had ever personally experienced. The jurors found the Mesa to be 'defective' and 'unreasonably dangerous.' They awarded the Hawkins family twenty-five million dollars in compensatory damages and two hundred fifty million dollars in punitive damages.

Harrington's only reaction when the verdict was read was to remove his show glasses, rest his right elbow on the table in front of him and rub both eyes with his right thumb and forefinger. The Global representative sitting next to him just shook her head. I wasn't sure if it was out of disbelief or candid acknowledgement of the appropriateness of the verdict, not only the liability issue, but also the amount of the award. I hoped it was the latter.

Upon hearing the verdict read out loud by the judge's clerk, Eric reached over and put his hand on my arm. I turned to look at him. His eyes were watering with tears. "It means nothing," he quietly said, almost whispering, "she's not coming back. She's gone." I leaned over and put my right arm around his shoulders and gave him a gentle hug. I was at a loss for words to console him.

"Thank you, Mike. Thank you for everything. I knew we were right about the Mesa."

I merely nodded. I had no momentous words to offer. I, too, was glad it was over.

EPILOGUE

LIZ AND I were lying side by side in the hammock in our backyard, enjoying New Year's Eve by ourselves. A mostly consumed bottle of champagne sat on the ground beside us. I had my right arm under her head and neck as we watched the second blue moon of the year that hung brilliant against the ink-black night sky above us.

"What's your New Year's resolution now that you're a fabulously rich plaintiff's lawyer?" Liz asked, laughing.

"Peace and quiet. That's all I want for the next few months. Peace and quiet."

"Isn't it going to seem a little boring now that all of the bar grievance charges against you have been dropped, your good name has been restored, and your practice suddenly has good clients—paying ones at that—beating your door down to have you represent them?" she teased.

"Yeah, I'm really going to miss the stress of being only days away from bankruptcy," I joked. "I guess I'll have to find some new hobbies. Maybe fast cars and hot women—or is it the other way around?"

She jabbed me in the side. "Just remember, hot stuff, that it's ninety/ten in any divorce—ninety percent is mine, and the rest of the crumbs are yours!"

I laughed. Then, turning reflective and serious, I added, "you know, it's hard to believe how this all turned out. The Mesa's been taken off the market, Cole is under arrest for murder, fraud and for hiring someone to run Annie and me off the road and into the canal, and other Global employees, including witnesses Winchester and Markov, are all facing criminal charges. Unbelievable. And to think that you and I are suddenly worth millions, to boot. Really unbelievable," I said, as I tilted my head forward and drained the last of the champagne from my glass.

"Why did Cole hire someone to try to run you into the canal?" she asked. "That made no sense." She was still raw from the emotional drain from the near drowning that Anne and I had experienced.

"The best the state attorney can figure," I replied, "is that while he probably wasn't trying to have us killed, he wanted to destroy my concentration for the trial. That's why he had it done the night before the trial was to start. He was incensed that we had not grabbed his settlement offer like the other four-rollover plaintiffs had done in the other Mesa accidents. He didn't want any chance of exposure of the Mesa's inherent stability problem that a trial might bring. He couldn't afford the risk, given what he personally had done to hide the design problems at Global, not to mention his involvement in the murder of our retired photographer, George Krueger. He just got in too deep."

"That terrible, terrible man. It just shows how little he really knew about you."

"And to think that barely a year ago, I was representing Global. It's a very strange world out there," I said, almost to myself.

"Speaking of strange," she suddenly asked, "what ever happened to that burned-out war veteran you were representing on that other case against Global for that bad seat? What was his name?" she asked as she struggled to recall it. There it was again, her inability to remember a case or client name. *It's reassuring that at least some things remain constant in life.*

"Rocky Watson," I finally said.

"Yes, that's the guy. Whatever happened to that case?" She leaned forward in the hammock and drained her glass of champagne as well.

I chuckled. "I guess I forgot to tell you about that, didn't I?"

"Yes, you did. So, what happened?"

"Well after Eric got his verdict, Global came begging to settle the case. I think I told you that Eric agreed to walk away from the two hundred fifty million dollars of punitive money awarded to him if Global agreed to pull the Mesa off the market, admit that it was defective and dangerous, and agreed to pay damages to all the families that had been injured by the Mesa to date, right, including more money to the families with which it had already settled."

"Yeah, you told me about that part. Frankly, I still think that Eric was too generous if you ask me," she offered, "but I suppose I can't blame him. He was never in it for the money, and his seventy-five percent share of the twenty-five million dollars will provide the financial protection and help that he and the kids need. And," she added, giggling, "your twenty-five percent share of that twenty-five million dollars is not too shabby either."

"Unbelievable," is all I could say, once again.

"But," she asked, refocusing, "what do all those discussions with Global have to do with Rocky Watson's case?"

I chuckled again as I thought about it anew. "That's the great part. When it came to signing all the settlement paperwork last week at the closing, Eric suddenly announced to Harrington that while the settlement was okay with Eric, Global still needed to get my consent as well since I was giving up my twenty-five percent contingent fee of the two hundred fifty million dollars. Harrington just about filled his pants when Eric told him that. He apparently figured there was no way I'd drop my contingent fee on that amount."

"So, what happened?" she asked, chuckling at the thought of Harrington's consternation—and his underwear.

"I told Harrington that I needed two things from Global before I would consent to the settlement. First, I demanded that Global publish a letter, on the front page of the Sunday business sections of both the *Miami Herald* and the Ft. Lauderdale *Sun Sentinel,* countersigned by King Avery, formally acknowledging that my departure from Hunt had been trumped up by Global and apologizing for that action. He hated to do it, but he had no choice. He made the call to the new general counsel at Global who agreed to it right away, as did Avery. They both want this case and its aftermath over and done with."

"Oh, so *that's* the genesis of those articles," she nodded, smiling, "I was wondering."

"Yup, and I loved every last bit of apologetic groveling they had to do," I replied. "Sweet revenge, I must admit."

"I *loved* those letters!" she added, energetically. "That French guy was right; 'revenge is a dish best served cold.'" She giggled, "So, what was your second condition?"

"Well," I grinned, "when Harrington had Global's new general counsel on the telephone to approve the first condition, I took the phone from Harrington and asked the Global GC to tell me the name of the most expensive sports car that Global presently sells. He told me that it was the 'Majesta.' It's a super luxury sports car that sells for around seventy-five thousand dollars."

"And?"

"I told the GC that the second condition to my approval of the settlement was that Global had to concede liability in Watson's county court suit against them, pay him the thirty-one hundred dollars it owed him for his damages, and deliver to him one of those Majesta models—a bright red one at that—titled in Watson's name, five years of pre-paid gas for Rocky, and a written apology signed by Global's Chairman for treating him like they did."

She laughed out loud, obviously feeling the champagne. "Did they go for it?"

"In a heartbeat. It's amazing how persuasive I can be when I dangle the release of a two hundred fifty million dollar judgment against Global in front of its GC!" I laughed. "I required them to give me the keys to the Majesta so that I could deliver the car to Rocky myself. I also bought him a new key ring with a 'semper fi' fob on it which I gave to him with the set of keys when I delivered the sports car to him. I suggested that he put away his Purple Heart medal in a safe place."

"His Purple Heart, what are you talking about?"

"His old key ring," I explained. "He actually drilled a hole in his Purple Heart medal and used it for a key-ring fob. While he won't admit it, I know how much that medal meant to him when he originally earned it. I wanted to make sure that he didn't lose it."

"And what did Watson have to say about getting a new car out of the deal?" she asked, turning her grinning face next to mine to look at me directly.

I laughed heartily before answering. "He said, and I quote, 'fuck me! I want my car in canary yellow!'"

Liz exploded in laughter, then, after a few seconds, cocked her head suggestively. "You know, that actually sounds like pretty good advice," she said, her voice now low, sexy and devilish.

"What do you mean, 'canary yellow'?" I asked.

"No, stupid, the other part," she said, smiling wryly.

We laughed together as we both simultaneously pitched our empty champagne glasses over our shoulders onto the grass and struggled to rip off each other's clothes in our suddenly-swaying hammock.

It's great to be alive, I thought.

THE END

CPSIA information can be obtained at www.ICGtesting.com
Printed in the USA
BVOW08s1114091015

421396BV00002B/3/P

R: less likely to smoke
D: more " " commit adultery
D: hardly " " ... be told how to vote by their clergy
D: hardly " " ... inject drugs, used crack
exercise about same
D: more overweight
R: say better mental health — D: more likely Prosac
author thinks no big difference between partisans
— but lots of little ones

R: paid more taxes by several thousands
R: more likely to believe free speech by controversial person
" " " ... continued books in library
R&D: same re muslim & Catholic — different prot. D: more against
more R: prohibited
D: 2x welfare

Made in the USA
Lexington, KY
12 April 2011

DEMOCRATS AND REPUBLICANS —
RHETORIC AND REALITY

DEMOCRATS AND REPUBLICANS — RHETORIC AND REALITY

COMPARING THE VOTERS IN STATISTICS AND ANECDOTES

JOSEPH FRIED

Algora Publishing
New York

Library of Congress Cataloging-in-Publication Data —

Fried, Joseph.
  Democrats and Republicans : rhetoric and reality / Joseph Fried.
     p. cm.
  Includes bibliographical references and index.
  ISBN 978-0-87586-603-1 (trade paper: alk. paper) — ISBN 978-0-87586-604-8 (hard
cover: alk. paper) — ISBN 978-0-87586-605-5 (ebook) 1. Party affiliation—United States.
2. Democratic Party (U.S.) 3. Republican Party (U.S. : 1854-) I. Title.

  JK2271.F75 2008
  324.273—dc22
                        2007050042

Front Cover: The cover illustration is the political cartoon, "They're Off, Again!" by
Clifford K. Berryman. It was first published on September 8, 1949 in the Washington
Star newspaper, and is now part of the Clifford K. Berryman Collection in the United
States Senate Collection of the Center for Legislative Archives of the National Archives,
in Washington, D.C.

Printed in the United States

For
Nina,
My wife, advisor, and best friend for nearly 40 years

*

For
My son, David,
Who has taught me more than he will ever realize

*

And for
My mother, Concetta Fried,
To whom I owe life, confidence, and common sense

TABLE OF CONTENTS

PREFACE   1

CHAPTER 1: LIFESTYLE DIFFERENCES   5

Introduction   5
   Do Republicans live on the edge?   5
   General excitement   5
Details   7
   Family, relationships, and sex   7
      Sex   7
      Marriage   11
      Children   16
      Family, Friends, Thugs and Activities 21
   Health and fitness   22
      Who Is Healthier?   22
      Healthy Habits   26
      Other Health Issues   33
   Religion   35
      Frequency of Attendance and Strength of Convictions 35
      Religion and Politics   36
      Religious Denominations   37
   Entertainment and leisure   37
      The Couch Potato Award   37
      Net surfing   41
      Reading Fine Books   41
      Holidays   42
   Family finances   44
      Income and Spending   44
      Investments   47
   Habitat   48
      Home Ownership   48
   Miscellaneous   49

Who Is More Likely To Gamble? 49
Gun Ownership 50
Hunting 52
Violence 52
Arrest Rates 54
Trivia 54
Conclusions 55

CHAPTER 2: WHO IS MORE INTELLIGENT, KNOWLEDGEABLE, AND EDUCATED? 57
Introduction 57
Details 59
Who has more civic and political knowledge? 59
Direct Testing 59
Interviewer Impressions 67
Time Spent Reading Or Watching Political News 68
Who has more scientific knowledge? 70
What Happens When Science Collides With Religion? 72
Who has more formal education? 73
High School Diplomas 73
Four-Year College Degrees 74
Graduate School Degrees 76
Who is more intelligent? 78
Interviewer Impressions 78
Tests Of Reasoning Ability (Or What's Your "Fruit IQ"?) 79
Word Tests 83
Analysis: Why Is There a Disparity? 84
What Factors Correlate With Education? 84
The Peculiar Relationship Between Party Identity And Political Ideology 86
Conclusions 88

CHAPTER 3: WHO IS THE BETTER "WORKING MAN"? 91
Introduction 91
The Better Working Man 92
Who is more likely to work for a living? 92
Who is the more valuable worker, and why? 95
Who works longer hours? 96
Who is the more educated worker? 100
The boss' opinion as indicated by supervisory assignments 101
Who has a better attitude? 105
Emotional stability 111
The Better Working Woman 112
Earnings and hours worked 112
Other factors related to women workers 116
Miscellaneous Work Factors for Men and Women 119
Work "prestige" 119
Type of work 122
Occupations 122
Private vs. Government vs. Self-Employment 124
Other work-related information 125
Union Membership 125
Miscellaneous 126
Conclusions 127

CHAPTER 4: WHO GIVES MORE TO CHARITY?   129

Introduction   129
   They Don't F$@#-ing Care!   129
Details   130
   Donations   130
      Who Is More Likely To Give?   130
      Who Writes the Larger Check?   134
   Volunteerism   139
Analysis: Why Some People Give More   142
   Income level   143
   Religious beliefs and political ideology 148
      The Impact Of Religion   149
      The Impact Of Political Ideology   150
Conclusions   152

CHAPTER 5: WHO PAYS MORE TAXES?   153

Introduction   153
   Red State Welfare Queens   153
Details   154
   Federal taxes   154
      Income Tax   154
      Other Federal Taxes   160
   State and local taxes   164
      Average Taxes Paid   164
      Median Taxes Paid   165
   Total taxes: federal, state, and local   166
      Total Without FICA Tax   166
      Total Taxes Including FICA   168
Conclusions   169

CHAPTER 6: WHO IS THE BETTER CITIZEN?   171

Introduction   171
   What Is "Good Citizenship"?   171
Details   172
   Who supports First Amendment rights?   172
      Tolerance For Controversial Speech   172
      Tolerance For Controversial Books And Literature 179
      Respect For The Right Of Assembly   181
   Who is more bigoted?   182
      With Regard To Jews   182
      With Regard To Other Religious Groups 183
      With Regard To Racial And Ethnic Groups 185
      Gays And Lesbians   185
   Who contributes more to society?   186
      Military Service   186
      Charitable Causes   189
      Helping The Environment   190
      Other Contributions   192
   Who is more likely to participate in the political process? 194
      Voting   194
      Political Campaigns, Rallies And Protests 195
      Directly Contacting Public Officials 197

Who is more likely to avoid negative social behavior? 198
  Who Gets The Felon Vote? 198
  Who Is More Likely To File For Bankruptcy? 198
  Who Is More Honest? 199
  Driving Over The Speed Limit 201
Conclusions 201

CHAPTER 7: WHO GETS MORE FROM SOCIAL SECURITY AND MEDICARE? 203

Introduction 203
  Dismantling the New Deal 203
  Caveats 204
Details 204
  Social Security 204
    Who Does Relatively Well in the Social Security System? 204
    Comparing Democratic Benefits To Republican Benefits 208
    One More Critical Factor: Young People Of Either Party Get Less. 212
  Medicare 214
    Everyone's A "Winner" — Except For Future Generations? 214
    Estimating Democratic Vs. Republican Medicare Benefits 216
    The Future Of Medicare Is Scary 216
Conclusions 218

CHAPTER 8: WHO GETS MORE WELFARE? 219

Introduction 219
  Democrats on Strike and Wal-Mart on Medicaid 219
Details 220
  Traditional (social) welfare 220
    What Is It, And How Much Does It Cost? 220
    Who Gets More Traditional Welfare? 221
    Has Welfare Been a Curse or a Benefit? 223
  Corporate welfare 223
    What Is Corporate Welfare, And How Much Does It Cost? 224
    Who Gets More Corporate Welfare? 226
Conclusions 227

CHAPTER 9: WHO IS HAPPIER, WHO IS MORE MISERABLE, AND WHY? 229

Introduction 229
  Do narrow, selfish goals lead to happiness? 229
Details 230
  Who is happier? 230
    Happiness in General 230
    Happiness With Regard To Specific Aspects Of Life 233
  Who is more miserable? 237
    Sadness And Depression 237
    Emotional Problems 238
  Why are there differences in happiness? 241
    Money 241
    Marriage 242
    Other Factors Correlating With Happiness 243
  Does cynicism lead to sadness? (a theory) 244
    Lack Of Trust 244
    The Inability to Control One's Destiny 247

"Capitalism Is Unjust"	253
Conclusions	257

CHAPTER 10: WHO GROWS UP TO BE A DEMOCRAT, AND WHO GROWS
UP TO BE A REPUBLICAN?   259

Introduction	259
Crossing Over	259
Details	260
How political viewpoints develop	260
As Children	260
As We Approach Adulthood	262
The "Strict Father" And "Nurturing Mother" Metaphors	264
Changes Later In Life	265
The parents of Democrats and Republicans	268
Was Dad in the Home?	268
How Much Education Did The Parents Have?	270
Employment Of The Parents	271
Parents' Occupational "Prestige"	274
Country Of Birth	275
Politics Of The Parents	276
Childhood life	277
Siblings	278
Religious Life	278
Family Income During Childhood	278
Where They Lived	280
Childhood Happiness	280
Childhood Miscellaneous	281
Conclusions	282

CHAPTER 11: DO DEVIANTS GROW UP TO BE REPUBLICANS?   283

Introduction	283
Details of a Seriously Flawed Study	286
The terms "liberal" and "conservative" are too vague.	286
Researcher assessments added circularity.	288
Did Democrats make the conservatives look bad?	291
A Curious Pattern	291
Researcher bias	297
Skewed Descriptions	297
Conclusions	299

CHAPTER 12: LESSONS TO BE LEARNED — IN MY OPINION   301

Introduction	301
Lots of Little Differences	301
Details	302
A lesson from Chapter 1: Delay having that first child	302
A lesson from Chapter 2: Make civics education mandatory	302
A lesson from Chapter 3: Work is the key to success	305
A lesson from Chapter 4: Open the wallet	306
A lesson from Chapter 5: Everyone should pay federal income tax	307
A lesson from Chapter 6: Clear up the confusion about free speech	308
A lesson from Chapter 7: Restructure SS and Medicare benefits	309
A lesson from Chapter 8 : All welfare is not the same	311

A lesson from Chapter 9: Be a happy-go-lucky Republican 312
A lesson from Chapter 10: Break the inter-generational cycle 313
A lesson from Chapter 11: Be careful with the terms "liberal" and "conservative" 315

APPENDIX A: DEMOGRAPHIC TRENDS OVER 50 YEARS 317

Part One: Relative Strength of Each Party in the Public 317
In general 317
Different age groups 318
Each gender 320
Racial and ethnic groups 321
Religious denominations 323
Married people 324
People in different occupations 325
College graduates 327
People in different family income brackets 327
People in the "political south" 330
People living in different communities 331

Part Two: The Composition of Each Political Party 332
Age
Gender 333
Race and ethnicity 335
Religious denominations 336
People who are married 338
Occupational categories 339
College students and graduates 340
People in different family income brackets 341
People in the "political South" 342
People in different communities 344

APPENDIX B: INFORMATION OVERFLOW AND ANALYSIS 345

APPENDIX C: INTERPRETING SURVEY DATA 359

APPENDIX D: A FEW NOTES ABOUT THE STATISTICS USED 361

APPENDIX E: THE SUPERIORITY OF THE DEMOCRAT–REPUBLICAN PARADIGM 362

APPENDIX F: SURVEY SOURCES USED 364

APPENDIX G: ACRONYMS AND ABBREVIATIONS 365

INDEX 367

PREFACE

Getting tired of books filled with political bombast and hot air? Here's an alternative. Within these pages you will find no unsupported views, only comprehensive and objective information. Questions about the constituents of America's two major political parties are answered in a straightforward, thorough, and easy-to-understand manner. Much of the information is presented graphically.

Most chapters have a theme, examining, for example, who pays more taxes, who is smarter, or who is the better citizen. The themes were not selected with the intent of making one political group look better than the other. Rather, they were chosen because they involve verifiable distinctions, distinctions which have two essential attributes:

- They relate to a person's actions, achievements, or specific preferences — not just general thoughts or wishes.
- They can be supported with credible evidence.

This concept can be illustrated with the following example: A verifiable distinction would exist if we had credible survey evidence showing that, during the last three months, Democrats were more likely than Republicans to give money to charity. A verifiable distinction would not exist if the evidence merely showed that Democrats were more likely to say that society should help the poor. In the former case we have a record of personal actions or achievements; in the latter case we simply have words.

The evidence in this book came from the survey results of large and well-respected nonpartisan organizations. Where possible, I used data from the General Social Survey (GSS) and the American National Election Studies (NES). GSS has been accumulating data since the early 1970s, and NES has been conducting its surveys since the early 1950s. Where more support was needed, I looked to surveys conducted by the Pew Research Center for the People and the Press (Pew), the Gallup Organization, the Institute for Public Policy and

Social Research, Harris Interactive, and other well-established research entities. In some instances, conclusions are supported by non-survey evidence. This is particularly true with regard to the chapters on taxes and Social Security. In all cases, however, credible sources are used, identified, explained, and referenced.[1]

In addition to comparison data, you will find lots of rhetoric in this book. There are numerous quotations from Democrats, Republicans, philosophers, comedians, pundits, actors, statesmen, and garden-variety fruitcakes. Some of this rhetoric will make you think, some will make you laugh, some will make you mad, and some will make you wince. There was no particular method (or objectivity) used in the selection of rhetoric; I simply chose the quotations that felt right to me.

No doubt some people will hate the book and feel it is mean-spirited, biased, or both. In anticipation of this reaction, let me give a brief defense. No matter how careful we try to be, comparisons are never completely fair, and one side (or both) will probably be slighted. Nevertheless, it would be a dull world if we did not make comparisons. More importantly, comparisons are needed to promote greater understanding and to facilitate progress in our lives. How else do we learn how the other guy thinks, and how else do we identify shortcomings so that solutions can be achieved? Speaking of solutions, Chapter 12 is filled with constructive lessons that, in my opinion, can be learned from the comparisons made throughout the book.

Have I been biased in selecting and presenting the comparison data? I hope not. I am not a political pundit; I am a CPA who has strived to present quantified information in a clear and balanced manner. This is a very transparent work, with sources and methods described in detail. Almost all source information is publicly available and, in nearly every case, relevant statistical information is provided. If a reader believes that I have erred, I hope he will contact me via the publisher so that the appropriate correction can be made.

Finally, I'd like to discuss a matter of potential controversy: the use of the Democrat–Republican paradigm. Some may wonder why this book makes comparisons based on party identification rather than political ideology (e.g., liberal versus conservative). I compare Democrats and Republicans because party identification is where the "rubber hits the road." In America, most of us support a candidate — with time, effort, money, or votes — based on his identification with one of the major political parties. In this manner, our political feelings are connected to tangible action of some sort. This is not true with regard to our ideological identifications such as "liberal" or "conservative."

In addition, the term "conservative" can be very misleading because it is not well understood. How many people realize that, during the last 35 years, 25 to 50 percent of all self-identified "conservatives" have been Democrats? And, how many realize that Democratic conservatives and Republican conservatives are as

---

1 The *General Social Survey* is conducted by the National Opinion Research Center (NORC), and the *National Election Studies* are produced by Stanford University and the University of Michigan. Please see Appendix F on page 364 for more information regarding survey sources used.

different as "night and day"? More discussion of these matters is found in Chapter 11 and in Appendix E.

I believe this is an informative, fair, and constructive book that can broaden your understanding of Democrats and Republicans. Also, it's pretty good if you just need some ammo for that next encounter with your brother-in-law.

Chapter 1: Lifestyle Differences

Introduction

> *Do Republicans live on the edge?*
>
> Live this day as if it will be your last. Remember that you will only find "tomorrow" on the calendars of fools. Forget yesterday's defeats and ignore the problems of tomorrow. This is it. Doomsday.
>
> — Og Mandino, American essayist and psychologist[2]

Now that you have been inspired by Mandino, prepare yourself for oodles of information about Democratic and Republican lifestyles — possibly more than you want. This is my everything-but-the-kitchen-sink chapter, and it contains trivia in addition to matters of consequence. It is a smorgasbord of the particulars that distinguish Democratic and Republican lifestyles.

Before getting to those details, however, consider the "bottom line:" Who leads the more exciting life? Surprisingly, it is Republicans. At least, that is what they think.

General excitement

When asked, "Do you find life exciting, pretty routine, or dull?" Republicans are consistently more likely to say that life is exciting. As seen in Figure 1, below, this tendency has existed for at least 30 years.

---

2 Og Mandino (attributed), "Thinkexist.Com."

Figure 1. "In general, do you find life exciting, pretty routine, or dull?" (General Social Surveys (GSS) conducted in 1975 through 2006, based on, left to right, 1946, 3026, 3650, 3233, 2319, and 3355 cases, with a confidence level of 99+% for all differences, and with relative proportions of, left to right, .85, .87, .82, .83, .82, and .88)[3][4]

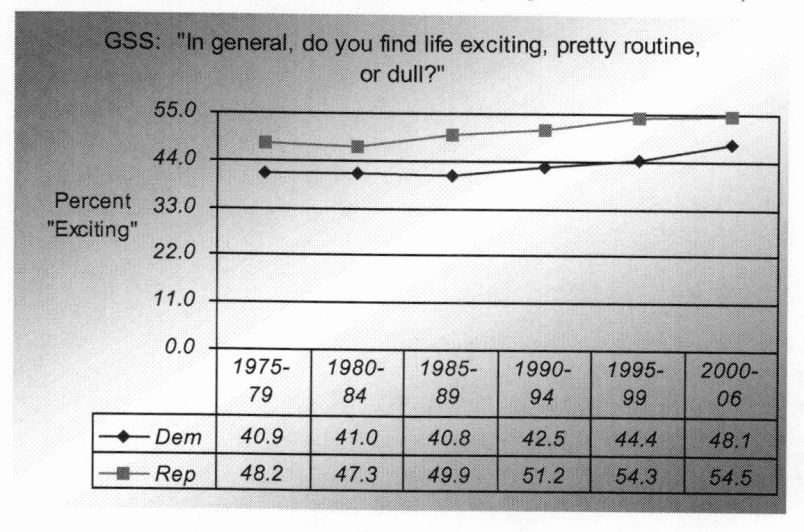

	1975-79	1980-84	1985-89	1990-94	1995-99	2000-06
◆ Dem	40.9	41.0	40.8	42.5	44.4	48.1
■ Rep	48.2	47.3	49.9	51.2	54.3	54.5

Figure 2. "How often would you say you have time on your hands that you don't know what to do with...?" (combined results of GSS surveys conducted in 1982 and 2004, based on, left to right, 575, 794, and 1369 cases, with a confidence level of 99+% for all columns, and with relative proportions of, left to right, .74, .78, and .77)

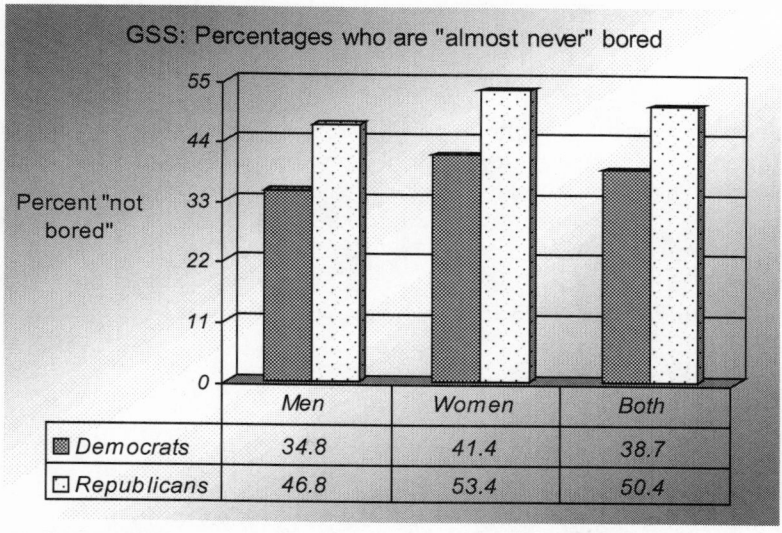

	Men	Women	Both
▦ Democrats	34.8	41.4	38.7
☐ Republicans	46.8	53.4	50.4

3 For the complete citation to the *General Social Survey*, and for appropriate acknowledgements and statements of limitations, please see Appendix F on page 364.

4 As explained in Appendix D, the relative proportion (RP) is simply the percentage of Democrats divided by the percentage of Republicans. For example, for the first column of Figure 1 it is 40.9% divided by 48.2%.

In addition, Republicans are less likely to be bored. Although equal percentages (about 26%) of Democrats and Republicans say they "always feel rushed even to do things [they] have to do," there seems to be a boredom gap for the other 74 percent. Republican men and women are more likely to say that they rarely have extra time they "don't know what to do with." See Figure 2, above.

Thus, Republicans are more apt to find life exciting, and less likely to be bored. With that matter settled, let's look deeper into the lifestyles microscope.

DETAILS

Family, relationships, and sex

Sex

Multiple Partners

Republicans tend to keep their shades drawn, although there is seldom any reason why they should. Democrats ought to, but don't.

— Anonymous (from a document published in the Congressional Record on October 1, 1974)

Figure 3. Percentage with 2 or more sex partners during the last 12 months (combined results of 6 GSS surveys conducted from 1996 through 2006, based on, left to right, 3662, 4910, and 8572 cases, with confidence level of 99+% for all columns, and with relative proportions of, left to right, 1.52, 1.63, and 1.41)

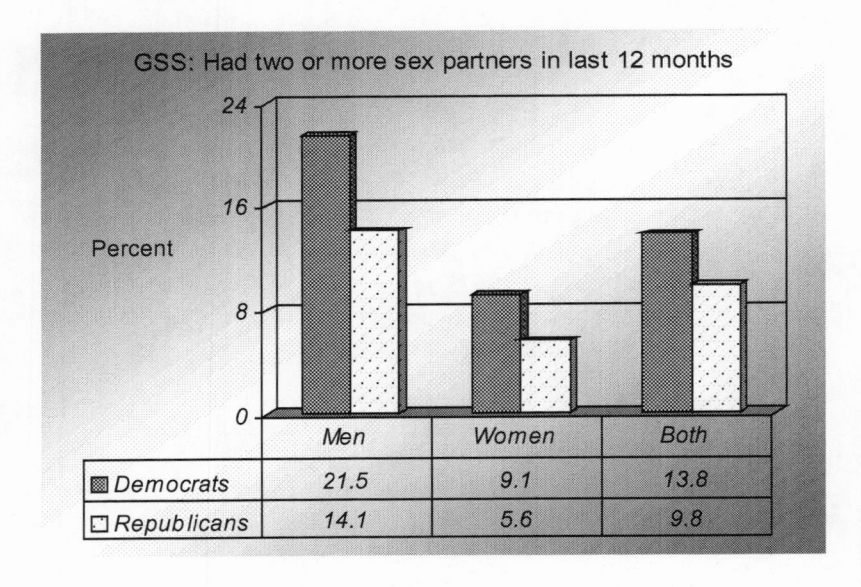

	Men	Women	Both
Democrats	21.5	9.1	13.8
Republicans	14.1	5.6	9.8

If Republicans lead more exciting lives, it is not in the area of sexual relations. The results of several GSS surveys, shown in Figure 3, tell us that Democrats are more likely to have multiple sexual partners.

Condoms

The multiple partners may explain the next statistic: Democrats are more likely to use condoms.

Figure 4. "The last time you had sex, was a condom used?" (combined results of 6 GSS surveys taken from 1996 through 2006, based on, left to right, 3557, 4636, and 8193 cases, with confidence level of 99+% for all three columns, and with relative proportions of, left to right, 1.40, 1.59, and 1.46)

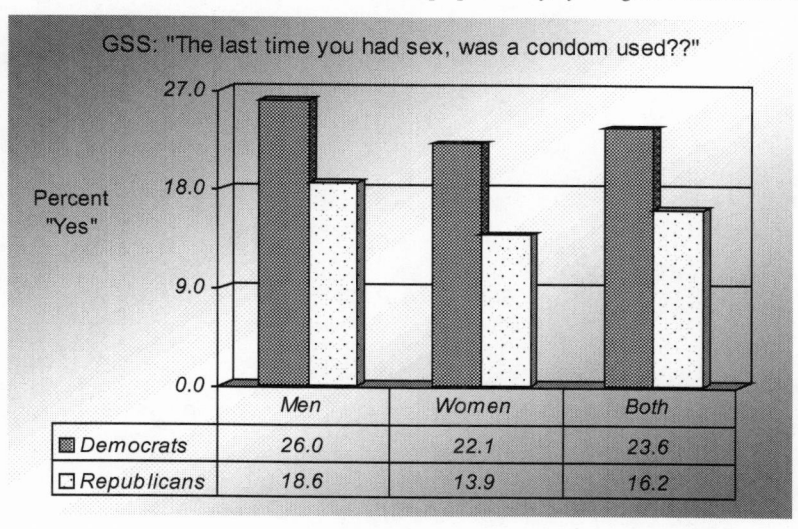

GSS: "The last time you had sex, was a condom used??"			
	Men	Women	Both
■ Democrats	26.0	22.1	23.6
□ Republicans	18.6	13.9	16.2

No Sex at All

Soon after the president and the president's defenders were claiming nightly that oral sex is not sex, the Washington Post reported on oral sex parties being held by local teenagers. The kids explained that the president said oral sex didn't count.

— Author and political activist Ann Coulter[5]

Although Democrats are more likely to have multiple partners, they are also a little more likely to have no sex at all (at least, nothing they consider to be sex).

The results shown in Figure 5 may explain why Democrats are less happy. (See Chapter 9.)

Figure 5. "How many sex partners have you had in the last 12 months?" (combined results of 6 GSS surveys conducted from 1996 through 2006, based on, left to right, 3662, 4910, and 8572 cases, with confidence level of 98% for men, 98% for women, and 99+% for both, and with relative proportions of, left to right, 1.19, 1.12, and 1.21)

---

5 Ann Coulter, "Toot in the Bush," in *Uexpress.com* (August 25, 1999), Retrieved September 1, 2006, from: http://www.uexpress.com/anncoulter/index.html?uc_full_date=19990825.

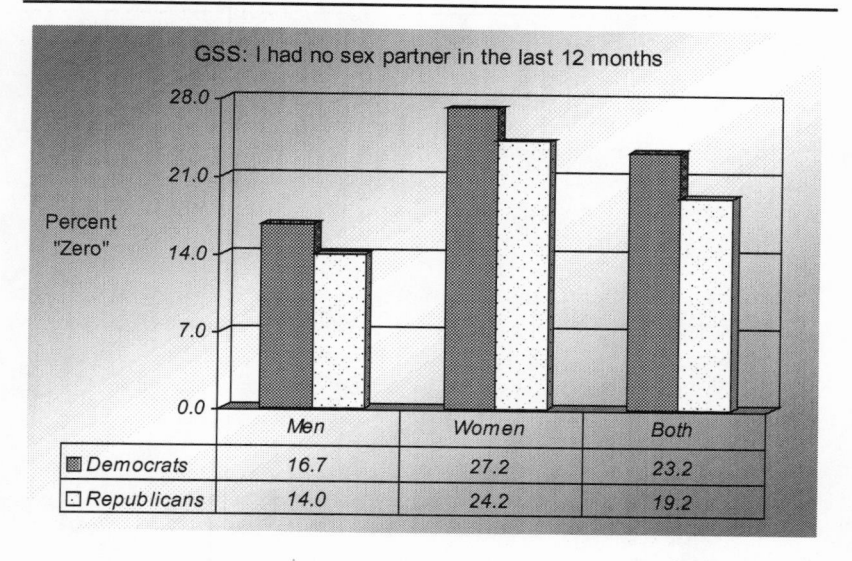

One Partner Only

At just about every stage of their lives, Republicans are more likely to have one, and only one, sexual partner.

Figure 6. Percentages who had exactly one sex partner during last 12 months (combined results of 6 GSS surveys conducted between 1996 and 2006, based on, left to right, 1333, 1829, 1865, 1376, 966, and 740 cases, with confidence level of, left to right, zero (i.e., no significance), 99+%, 99%, 99+%, 99+%, and 91% (marginal), with relative proportions of, left to right, n/a, .88, .94, .88, .83, and .86)

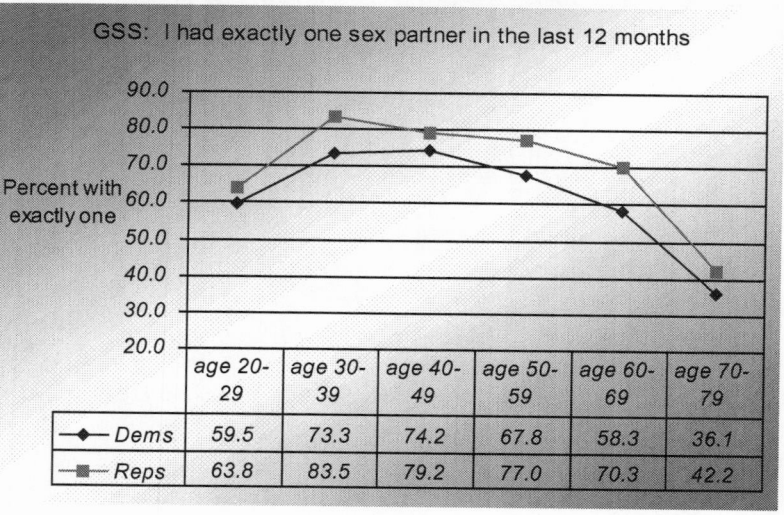

Gay Sex

One of the biggest un-kept secrets in Washington, DC is that closeted gay Republicans are everywhere — the White House, Republican Party organizations, the halls of Congress, the most influential law offices, and the most powerful lobbying firms in our nation's capitol.

— Columnist Brian van de Mark (4 weeks before the Mark Foley intern scandal became public, and a full year before the toe-tapping exploits of Senator Larry Craig)[6]

Among male Democrats and Republicans, there is a marked difference in the acknowledged rate of homosexual activity. This is evident from a review of Figure 7, which shows that a "gay gap" began to develop after the 1980s. The disparity might be attributable to gays leaving the GOP, or to an increased willingness on the part of Democrats to acknowledge gay sexual orientation.

Figure 7. (Asked of men) "Have your sex partners in the last 12 months been men?" (combined results of several GSS surveys conducted from 1988 through 2006, based on, left to right, 1147, 1941, and 1957 cases, with confidence level of, left to right, zero (i.e., no significance), 99+%, and 99+%, and with relative proportions of, left to right, n/a, 2.64, and 3.14)

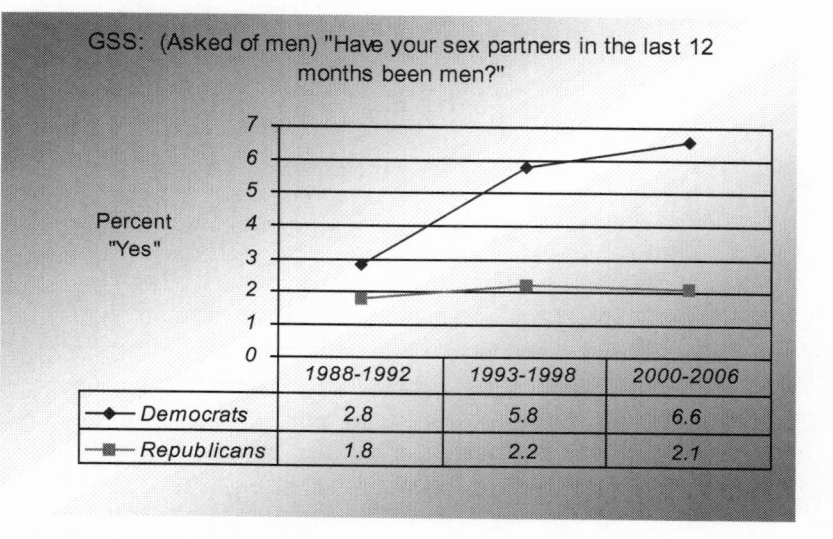

For women, there also is a statistically significant gay gap, albeit very tiny. By 2.6 to 1.7 percent, Democratic women are slightly more likely to have had sex with a female in the last year (6038 cases from 1988 through 2006, with 99% confidence level, and with a relative proportion of 1.53).

---

6 Brian van De Mark, "Gay Republicans - an Oxymoron?," in *Gay & Lesbian Times* (www.gaylesbiantimes.com, August 31, 2006), Retrieved September 1, 2006, from: http://www.gaylesbiantimes.com/?id=6206.

Sex Sundries

How did sex come to be thought of as dirty in the first place? God must have been a Republican.

— Will Durst, Political satirist[7]

Democratic males are a bit more likely than Republican males to engage in sex for money. See Table 1. For females there is no statistically significant difference. Less than 2 percent of women state that they have engaged in such conduct.

Table 1. Other surveys involving sex

Issue	Survey	Dem % "yes"	Rep % "yes"	No. of cases	Conf %	*RP
"Have you ever had sex with a person you paid or who paid you for sex? — males	8 GSS surveys from 1991 through 2006	17.8	13.9	5018	+99	1.28
"Do you or did you ... feel sexually attracted to someone of the same sex?"	2006 Harris Interactive survey	11.0	5.0	634	99	2.20

*RP is relative proportion, which is the Democratic % divided by the Republican %.

Marriage

If variety is the spice of life, marriage is the big can of leftover Spam.

— The late Johnny Carson, Comedian[8]

Marriage Rates

Republicans are now far more likely to be married, with a 9-point gap for men and a 20-point gap for women. This marriage disparity developed during the last 30 to 40 years, prior to which, marriage rates were similar. Male marriage rates are shown in Figure 8, below.

Figure 8. Are you married? (Men) (various surveys of the American National Election Studies (NES) conducted in 1952 through 2004, based on, left to right, 592, 2386, 2357, 2507, 2841, and 2047 cases, with no statistical significance for the 1952 through 1974 years, with 99% or more confidence level for the 1975 through 2004 years, and with relative proportions of, left to right, n/a, n/a, n/a, .94, .92, .86)[9]

---

7 Will Durst (attributed), "Brainyquote.Com."

8 Johnny Carson (attributed), "Quotationz.Com."

9 For the complete citation to the American National Election Studies (NES), and for appropriate acknowledgements and statements of limitations, please see Appendix F on page 364.

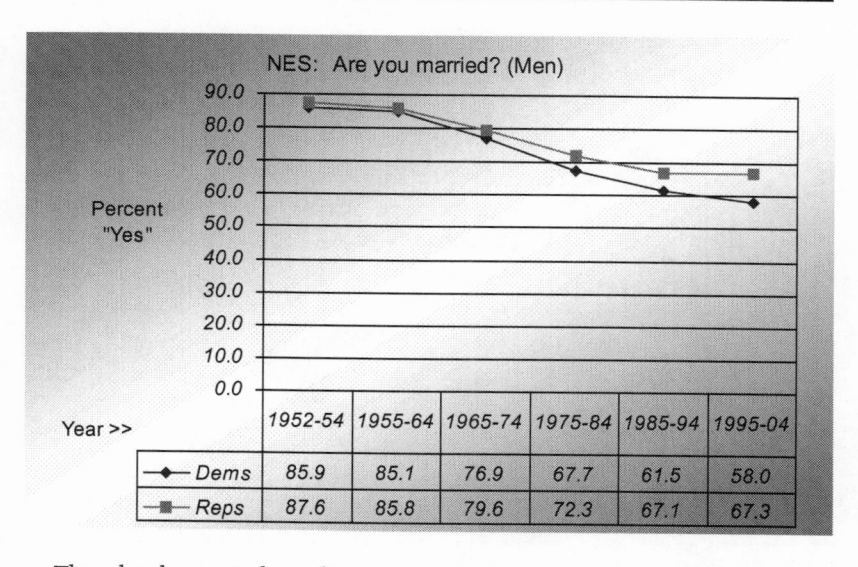

There has been a "rebound" in marriage rates among women — particularly Republican women. (See Figure 9, below.) Is this due to welfare reform (which was enacted in the mid-90s), to disenchantment with feminism, or to general frustration with the single life scene?

Figure 9. Are you married? (Women) (various NES surveys conducted in 1952 through 2004, based on, left to right, 735, 3035, 3344, 3694, 3751, and 2677 cases, with no statistical significance for the 1952 through 1954 years, and with 99% or more confidence level for the 1975 through 2004 years, and with relative proportions of, left to right, n/a, 1.10, .92, .86, .80, and .72)

NES: Are you married? (Women)	1952-54	1955-64	1965-74	1975-84	1985-94	1995-04
◆ Dems	71.0	74.7	58.1	51.2	46.8	50.0
■ Reps	71.1	67.8	63.2	59.4	58.2	69.9

Reasons Not Married

Don't marry for money; you can borrow it cheaper.

— Scottish proverb

There are three reasons Democrats are less likely than Republicans to be married, and each reason applies to both genders and to people in different age groups. First, they are more likely to have never married. This is particularly true for Democratic females.

Figure 10. People who never married (combined results of 5 NES surveys conducted from 1996 through 2004, based on, left to right, 2044, 1519, 2665, and 1915 cases, with confidence level of, left to right, 96%, 99+%, 99+%, and 99+%, and with relative proportions of, left to right, 1.18, 1.37, 1.94, and 2.32)

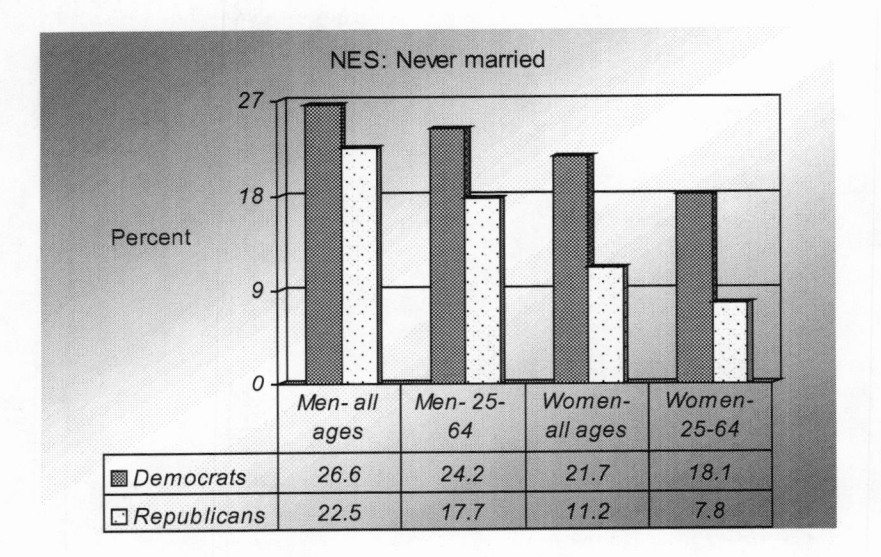

Democrats are also less likely to be married because of divorce or separation.

> We think there's a war that hasn't been discussed, and that's the Republican war on the American family.
>
> — Howard Dean, Former governor of Vermont, and Chairman of the Democratic National Committee[10]

The divorce divide is particularly pronounced among women.

---

10 Howard Dean interviewed on, "Face the Nation," (Transcript: CBS News, October 29, 2006).

Figure 11. People who are divorced or separated (combined results of 5 NES surveys conducted from 1996 through 2004, based on, left to right, 2044, 1519, 2665, and 1915 cases, with confidence level of 95%, 91% (marginal), 99+%, and 99+%, and with relative proportions of, left to right, 1.35, 1.33, 1.47, and 1.54)

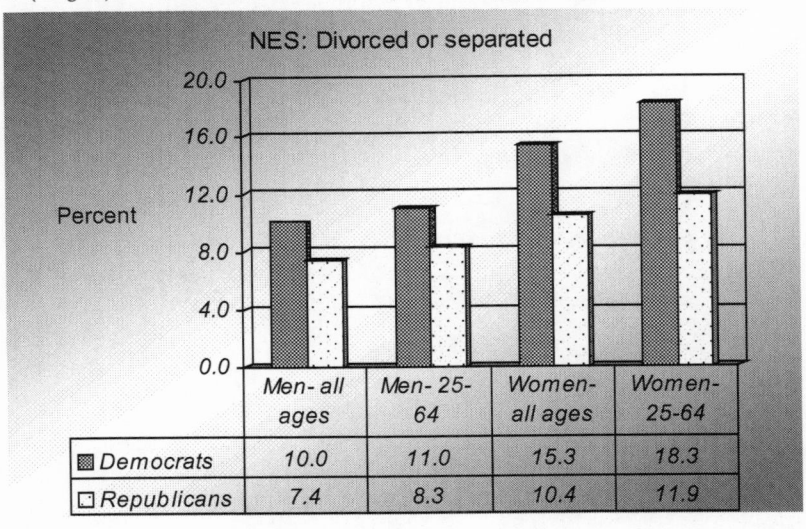

NES: Divorced or separated
Percent
20.0
16.0
12.0
8.0
4.0
0.0
Men- all ages
Men- 25-64
Women- all ages
Women- 25-64
Democrats 10.0 11.0 15.3 18.3
Republicans 7.4 8.3 10.4 11.9

Finally, Democrats are more likely to be unmarried because of the death of a spouse. This is the case even when we restrict the analysis to people aged 25 to 64 years. (See Figure 12, below.)

Figure 12. People who are widows/widowers (combined results of 5 NES surveys conducted from 1996 through 2004, based on, left to right, 2044, 1519, 2665, and 1915 cases, with confidence level of, left to right, 99+%, 98%, 99+%, and 98%, and with relative proportions of, left to right, of 2.04, 4.50, 1.53, and 2.00)

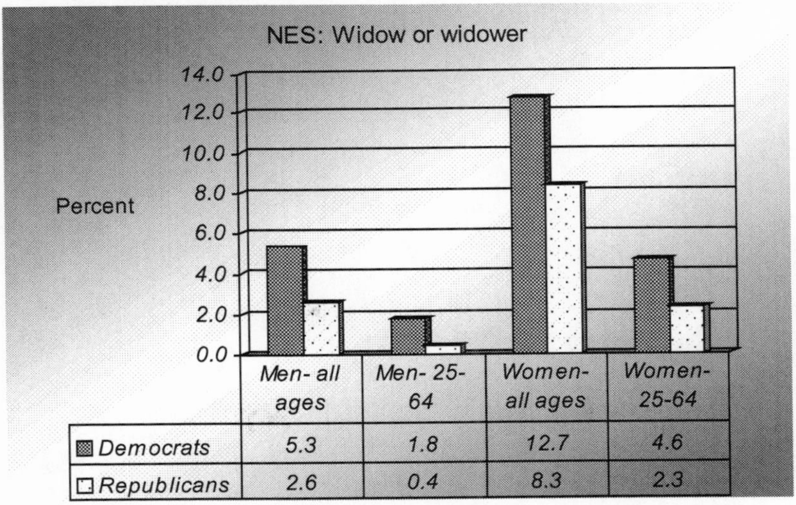

NES: Widow or widower
Percent
14.0
12.0
10.0
8.0
6.0
4.0
2.0
0.0
Men- all ages
Men- 25-64
Women- all ages
Women- 25-64
Democrats 5.3 1.8 12.7 4.6
Republicans 2.6 0.4 8.3 2.3

Premarital Sex

It isn't premarital sex if you have no intention of getting married.
— George Burns, Comedian[11]

Democrats are less likely to view premarital sex negatively. When asked if premarital sex is always wrong, GSS obtained the following results:

Figure 13. "If a man and woman have sex relations before marriage, do you think it is always wrong...?" (various GSS surveys conducted in 1986 through 2006, based on, left to right, 2848, 2542, 3283, and 2237 cases, with confidence level of at least 99% for all points, and with relative proportions of, left to right, .84, .81, .71, and .70)

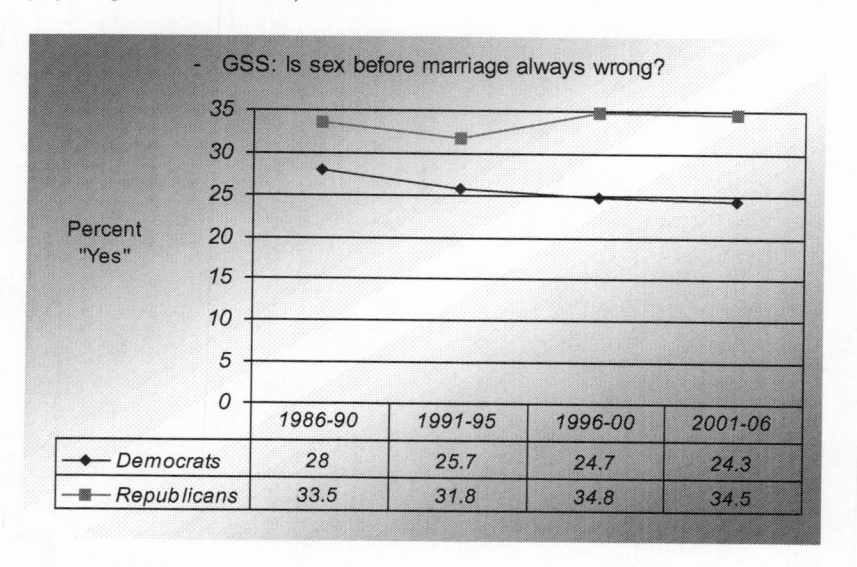

GSS: Is sex before marriage always wrong?

	1986-90	1991-95	1996-00	2001-06
Democrats	28	25.7	24.7	24.3
Republicans	33.5	31.8	34.8	34.5

Adultery

The best thing to do with the best things in life is to give them up.
— Movie star Doris Day[12]

Democrats are more likely to acknowledge having sex with others while married. Are they simply being more truthful than Republicans, or are they really more adulterous? If the latter is the case, this might explain the higher divorce rate.

Figure 14. Had sex with others while married? (9 GSS surveys conducted from 1991 through 2006, based on 3821 cases for men, 5584 cases for women, and 9405 for both, with confidence level of 99+% for all 3 columns, and with relative proportions of, left to right, 1.24, 1.44, and 1.26)

---

11 George Burns (attributed), "Lifestyles News," Retrieved April 3, 2007, from: http://www.lifestylesnews.com.
12 Doris Day cited in, "Columbia World of Quotations," (Columbia University Press, 1996).

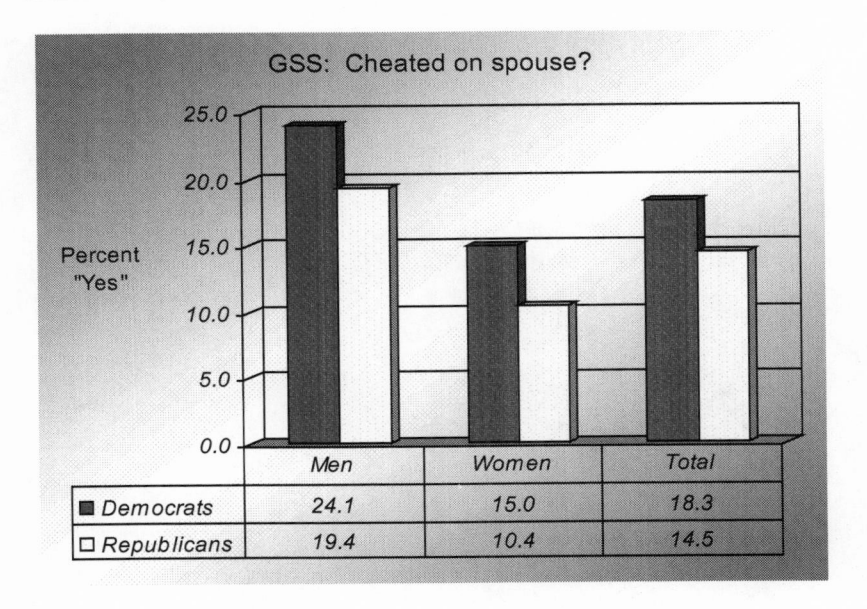

GSS: Cheated on spouse?	Men	Women	Total
■ Democrats	24.1	15.0	18.3
□ Republicans	19.4	10.4	14.5

Percent "Yes"

Children

Who Is More Likely To Have Children?

Democrats and Republicans are equally likely to have children. GSS surveys of 11,092 Democrats and Republicans, conducted from 1996 through 2006, show that the average Democrat has 1.94 children and the average Republican has 1.91 — a difference that is not statistically significant. If we limit the survey to Democrats and Republicans aged 30 years or less, the average Democrat has .57 children and the average Republican has .59, a difference that is still not significant.

Reality check — What about the so-called "fertility gap"?

In a much-discussed Op-Ed in the Wall Street Journal, Arthur C. Brooks (Professor at Syracuse University) noted that liberals are in danger of becoming politically disadvantaged due to the higher reproductive rate of conservatives.[13] Indeed, liberals do reproduce at a much lower rate than conservatives. However, as stressed in Chapter 11, the liberal-conservative paradigm must not be confused with the Democrat-Republican paradigm. For Democrats and Republicans there is procreation parity.

Although the likelihood of Democrats and Republicans having children is roughly equal, there is a large difference in the reproduction rate when we limit the analysis to unmarried Democrats and Republicans.

> Illegitimacy is something we should talk about in terms of not having it.
> — Vice President Dan Quayle[14]

---

13 Arthur C. Brooks, "The Fertility Gap," *Wall Street Journal*, August 22, 2006.
14 Vice President Dan Quayle (attributed), "The Quotations Page."

Unmarried Democrats are far more likely than unmarried Republicans to have children in the home, and this trend has existed since the 1950s.

Figure 15. Do you have a child under age 18 living in the household? (unmarried men and women) (various NES surveys conducted in 1955 through 2004, based on, left to right, 1170, 585, 1872, 2011, and 910 cases, with confidence level of 90% (marginal) for the far left difference and 99+% for all other differences, and with relative proportions of, left to right, 1.20, 2.01, 1.53, 1.35, and 1.77)

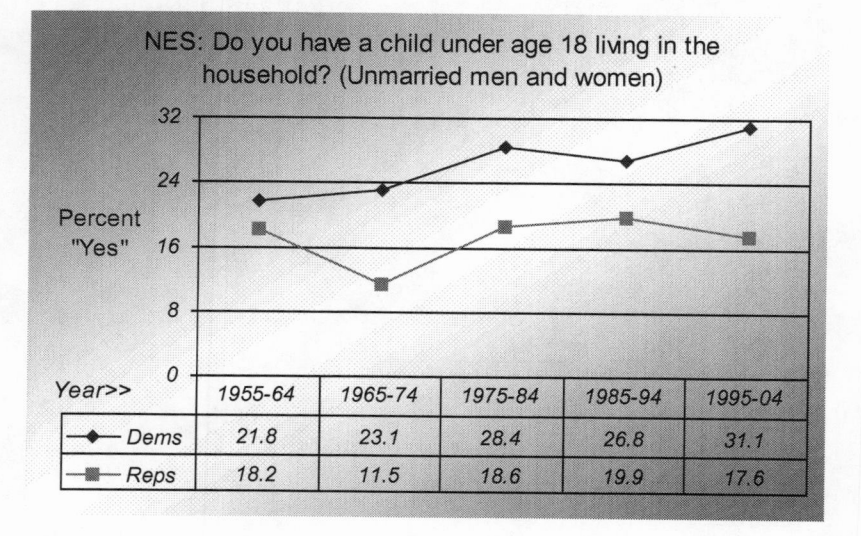

Year>>	1955-64	1965-74	1975-84	1985-94	1995-04
Dems	21.8	23.1	28.4	26.8	31.1
Reps	18.2	11.5	18.6	19.9	17.6

Just about all of the difference shown in Figure 15 is attributable to women. Unmarried Democratic and Republican men are about equally likely to have a child under age 18 in the home.

Children at What Age?

> The children of adolescents are more likely to be born prematurely and 50 percent more likely to be low-birth weight babies ... suffer poorer health ... child abuse or neglect ... [perform] more poorly on tests of cognitive ability ... drop out of high school. ... [T]he sons of young teen mothers are nearly three times more likely to be incarcerated than those born to adult mothers.
>
> — "Fact Sheet" on the web site of the FSU Center for Prevention & Early Intervention Policy[15]

It is widely acknowledged that babies born to teen parents are at greater risk with regard to a variety of health, social, and educational problems. Figure 16, below, shows the percentage of Democratic and Republican men, under the age of 50, who were aged 19 years or less when their first child was born. From this graphic, it is clear that Democratic males are almost twice as likely to have a

---

15 "The Children of Teen Parents - Fact Sheet," April 15, 2005, FSU Center for Prevention & Early Intervention Policy, Retrieved April 3, 2007, from http://www.cpeip.fsu.edu/resourceFiles/resourceFile_78.pdf.

child by the age of 19. The average difference in age, when the first child is born, is about 13 months.[16]

Figure 16. What was your age when your first child was born? (Men aged up to 50 years) (6 GSS surveys conducted from 1996 through 2006, based on 1543 cases, with overall confidence level of 99+%, and with a relative proportion of 1.97)

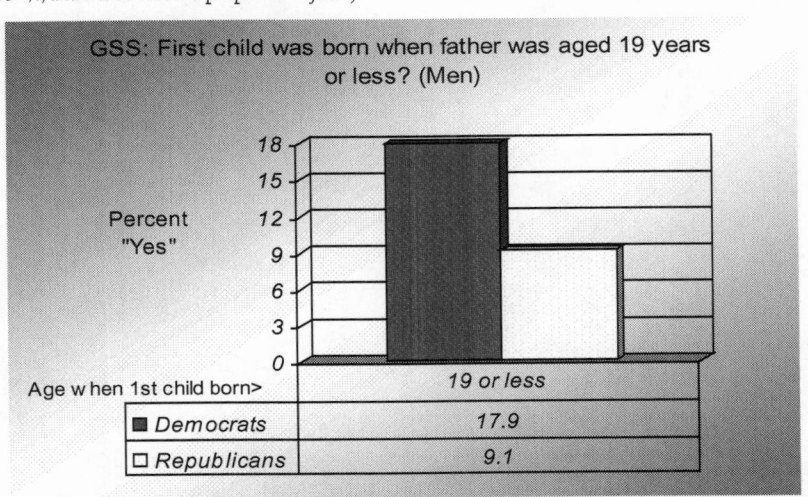

In Figure 17, below, we see a similar pattern for women. Democratic women are much more likely to procreate in their teenage years.

Figure 17. What was your age when your first child was born? (Women aged up to 50 years) (6 GSS surveys conducted between 1996 and 2006, based on 2412 cases, with overall confidence level of 99+%, and with a relative proportion of 1.64)

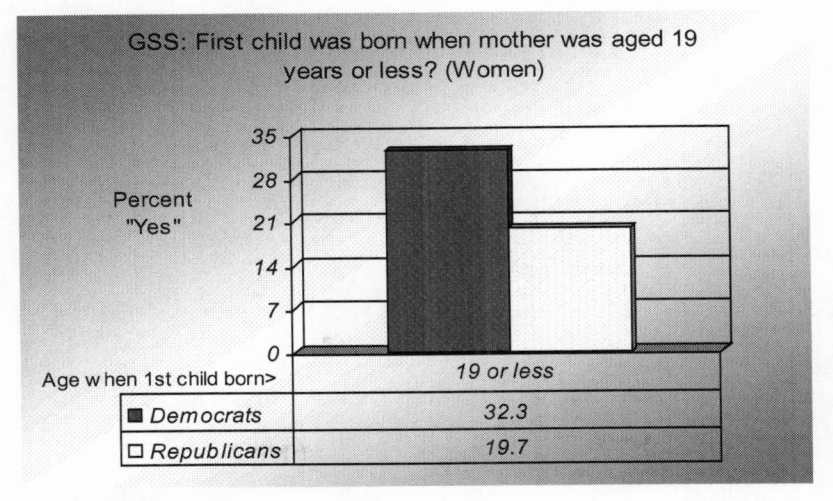

16 The analysis is limited to Democratic and Republicans aged
   50 years or less at the time of the surveys.

Democratic women are about 60 percent more likely to have children while still teenagers.[17] For women (under the age of 50), the average difference in the age of procreation is about 12.7 months.

Figure 18. Do you agree that it is sometimes necessary to discipline a child with a "good, hard spanking"? (5 GSS surveys conducted in 1998 through 2006, based on, left to right, 1837, 2582, and 4419 cases, with confidence level of 99+% for all columns, and with relative proportions of, left to right, .91, .93, and .91)

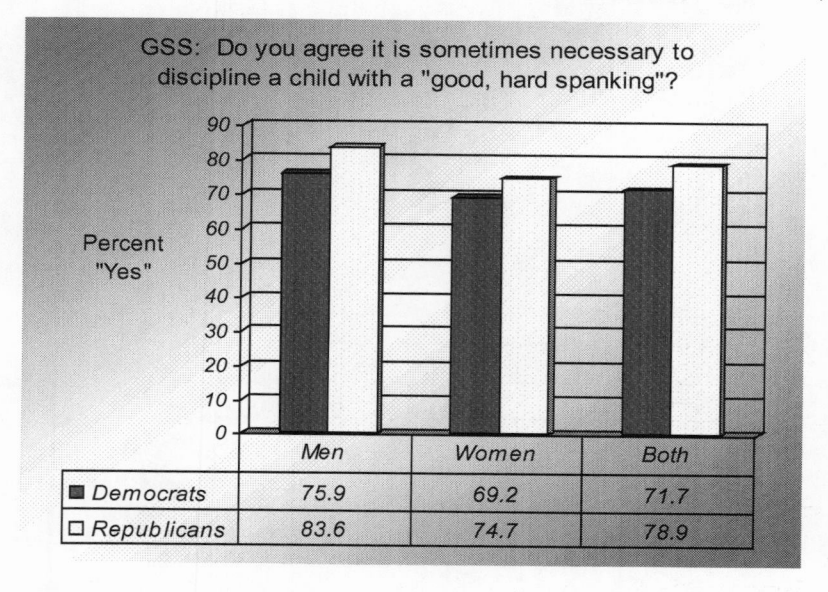

GSS: Do you agree it is sometimes necessary to discipline a child with a "good, hard spanking"?

Percent "Yes"

	Men	Women	Both
■ Democrats	75.9	69.2	71.7
□ Republicans	83.6	74.7	78.9

Spanking

A Democratic assemblywoman from Mountain View says she will submit a bill next week ... proposing that California become the first state in the nation to make spanking of children 3 years old and under a misdemeanor. Penalties could include child-rearing classes for offenders to one year in jail.

— Jennifer Steinhauer, January 21, 2007, the New York Times

Since 1986 the General Social Survey has been asking people if they believe in spanking. In most of those years the views of Democrats and Republicans were almost the same. However, a small divide has developed.

Computer Filters

Republicans are more likely to have use computer filters to prevent their children from viewing pornography on the Internet. The results in Figure 19 pertain to parents with computers in the home.

---

17 The analysis is limited to Democratic and Republicans aged 50 years or less at the time of the surveys.

Figure 19. "Does your home computer have a filter installed to prevent access to pornography ..." (Limited to parents) (2005 Pew News Interest Index, based on 242 cases, with confidence level of 96%, and with a relative proportion of .78)[18]

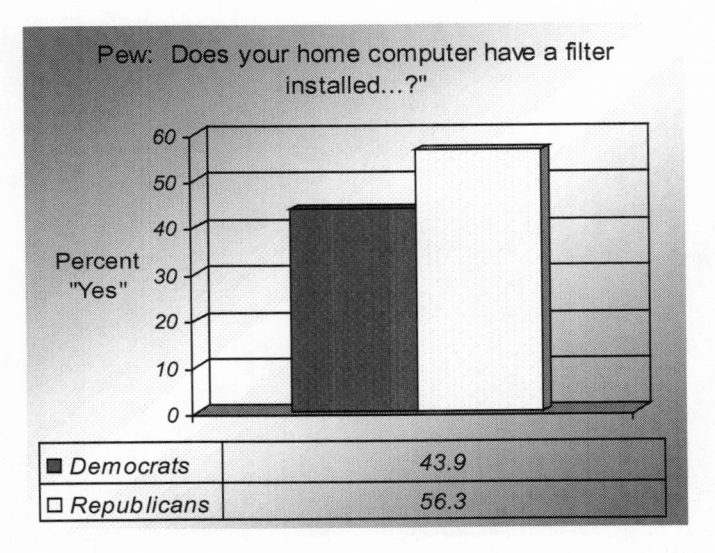

Figure 20. "Is this a religious or church affiliated school ...?" (2005 Pew Religion and Public Life Survey, based on 53 cases, with confidence level of 94% (marginal), and with a relative proportion of .79)

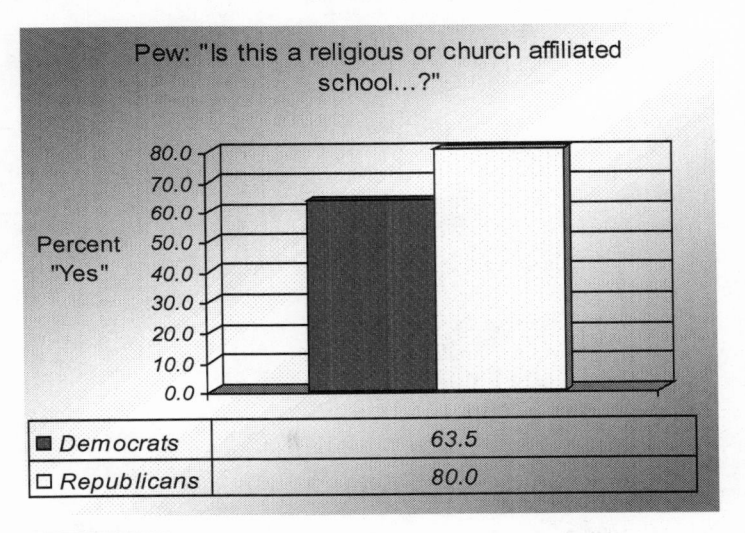

18 The Pew News Interest Index survey, and all "Pew" surveys in this book, was conducted and released to the public by the Pew Center for Research Center for the People & the Press, which is sponsored by the Pew Charitable Trusts. For appropriate acknowledgements and statements of limitations, please see Appendix F on page 364.

Private Schools

President-elect Bill Clinton, who has made improving public education a priority throughout his political career, announced today
that he was sending his daughter, Chelsea, to an expensive private
school attended by many children of Washington's power elite....

— Columnist Thomas L. Friedman[19]

Constituents of the two parties are equally likely to send their kids to private
schools according to a Pew 2005 Religion and Public Life Survey of 352 Democrats and Republicans. However, Republicans are significantly more likely to
send their kids to religiously-affiliated schools. See Figure 20, above.

Family, Friends, Thugs and Activities

Miscellaneous matters related to social activities and acquaintances are noted in Table 2, below.

Table 2. Miscellaneous issues related to family friends and activities

Issue	Survey	Dem % "yes"	Rep % "yes"	No. of cases	Conf %	*RP
Are you "acquainted with" one or more people in prison?	GSS 2006 survey	23.8	13.4	375	99	1.78
Have any of your close friends or relatives given their life while serving in the military?	Rasmussen November 2007	34.0	41.0	**1000	95	.83
Are you "acquainted with" one or more people in the military?	GSS 2006 survey	52.6	64.9	421	99	.81
Are you "acquainted with" one or more women "in a romantic relationship with a man to whom they are not married"?	GSS 2006 survey	69.6	54.9	361	+99	1.27
Are one or more of the women in your extended family "in a romantic relationship with a man to whom they are not married"?	GSS 2006 survey	45.6	34.0	300	96	1.34

19 Thomas Friedman, "The New Presidency," *The New York Times*, January 6, 2003, 1.

On a typical week day, do you contact 10 or more individuals (people you know) in person, on the telephone, via email, etc.?	GSS 2006 survey	58.6	**69.1**	823	+99	.85
Do you have a friend, colleague, or family member who is gay?	Pew Late March 2005 Political Typology Callback	**48.7**	39.0	708	+99	1.25
Do you have home schooling friends or family members?	Rasmussen August 2004	36.0	**50.0**	**1000	95	.72
Yesterday, did your family have a meal together?	Pew 2002 Biennial Media Consumption Survey	60.9	**67.7**	966	99	.90
Does your family discuss politics with a passion on holidays?	Rasmussen December 2007	13.0	**22.0**	**1000	95	.59
Do you discuss politics with family and friends?	Combined results of NES surveys from 1984 through 2004	64.0	**69.5**	12642	+99	.92

*RP is relative proportion, which is the Democratic % divided by the Republican %.

**Case numbers include independents and others in addition to Democrats and Republicans.

Health and fitness

Who Is Healthier?

The best activities for your health are pumping and humping.

— Arnold Schwarzenegger, Actor and Republican Governor of California[20]

General Health

Republicans seem to be healthier — or at least they think they are. As shown in Figure 21, below, this is true for both males and females.

Figure 21. "Would you say that your own health, in general, is excellent?" (24 GSS surveys conducted in 1972 through 2006, based on, left to right, 10278, 13974, and 24252 cases, with confidence level of 99+% for all columns and with relative proportions of, left to right, .84, .78, and .80)

---

20 Arnold Schwarzenegger (attributed), "Brainyquote.Com."

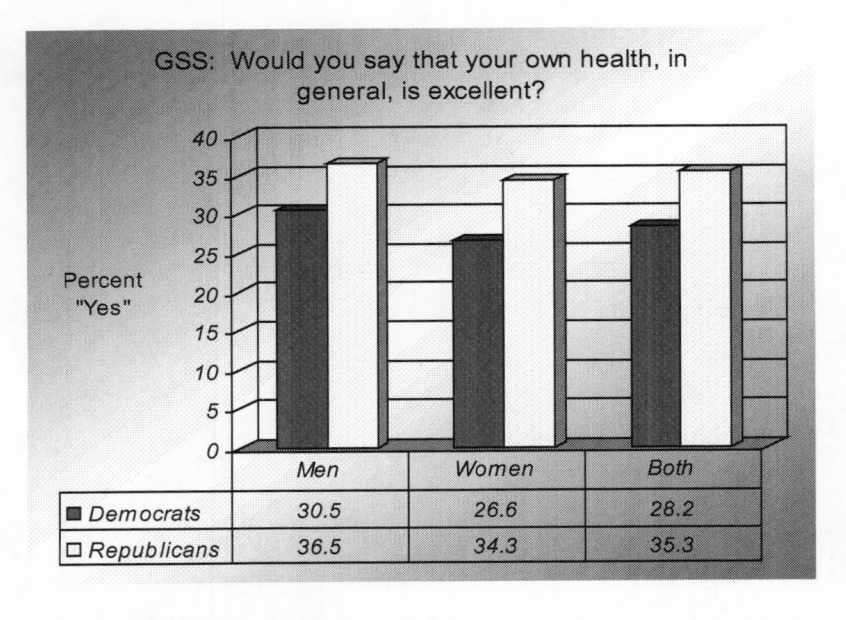

GSS: Would you say that your own health, in general, is excellent?

Percent "Yes"

	Men	Women	Both
■ Democrats	30.5	26.6	28.2
□ Republicans	36.5	34.3	35.3

A recent Gallup analysis shows a similar disparity, with Democrats being less likely to claim "excellent" health, by 27 to 35 percent.[21] In addition, Democrats are less likely to say that, during the prior 4 weeks, they had "a lot of energy" all or most of the time (62% to 71%),[22] and Democrats are more likely to state that poor health is a limiting factor in regard to "moderate activities, such as moving a table, pushing a vacuum cleaner, bowling, or playing golf" (15% to 5%).[23] Another survey found that Democrats were more likely to state they had a "condition that substantially limits one or more basic physical activities such as walking, climbing stairs, reaching, lifting, or carrying" (21% to 12%).[24] Among Democrats and Republicans who are not gainfully employed, Democrats are about twice as likely to say they are disabled (25% to 12%).[25]

21 Joseph Carroll, "Strong Majority of Americans in Good Physical and Mental Health," *The Gallup News Service* (December 8, 2006), Retrieved January 2, 2007, from Http://brain.gallup.com.

22 GSS 2000, based on 817 cases, with statistical significance of 99% and relative proportion of .87.

23 GSS 2000, based on 811 cases, with statistical significance of 99+% and relative proportion of 3.00.

24 GSS 2006, based on 1612 cases, with statistical significance of 99+% and relative proportion of 1.75.

25 GSS 2006 and 1998, based on 450 cases, with statistical significance of 99+% and relative proportion of 2.08.

The Long-Term Trends

Figure 22. "Would you say your own health, in general, is excellent ...?" (Combined results of 18 GSS surveys taken from 1977 through 2006, based on, left to right, 5069, 7316, and 6988 cases, with confidence level of 99+% for all categories, and with relative proportions of, left to right, .80, .82, and .79)

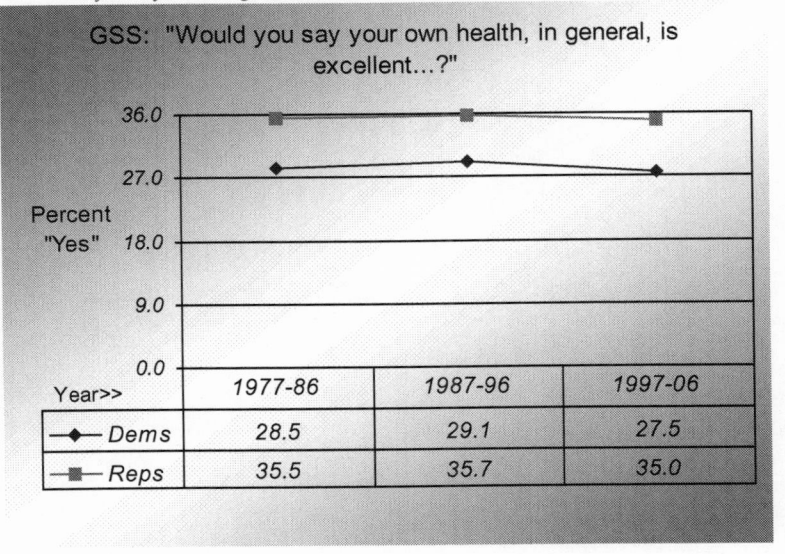

GSS: "Would you say your own health, in general, is excellent...?"

Percent "Yes"

Year>>	1977-86	1987-96	1997-06
Dems	28.5	29.1	27.5
Reps	35.5	35.7	35.0

The differences in reported health status have been consistent for at least 30 years, and could be due to several causes. Democrats might become less healthy because of lifestyle choices. For example, survey evidence (discussed elsewhere in this chapter) shows that Democrats are more likely to smoke and (possibly) to be overweight. Age, gender, and lack of health insurance coverage could be other factors. On the other hand, people may gravitate towards programs of the Democratic Party once they become ill. Yet again, Republicans may simply feel healthier due to a general sense of optimism (a trait discussed in Chapter 9).

General Health by Income Bracket

The first wealth is health.

— Ralph Waldo Emerson, 19th century American essayist[26]

When Democrats and Republicans are grouped by income bracket (in constant dollars), significant differences remain, but are diminished. For constituents of both parties, excellent health appears to increase significantly with income.

---

26 Ralph Waldo Emerson, "Columbia World of Quotations," (Columbia University Press, 1996).

Figure 23. "Would you say your own health, in general, is excellent ...?" (Combined results of 24 GSS surveys taken from 1972 through 2006, based on, left to right, 6377, 3267, 2782, 2879, 2377, and 6570 cases, with confidence level, left to right, of 99+%, zero, 99%, 99+%, 98% and 99%, and with relative proportions of, left to right, .70, n/a, .85, .80, .88, and .93)

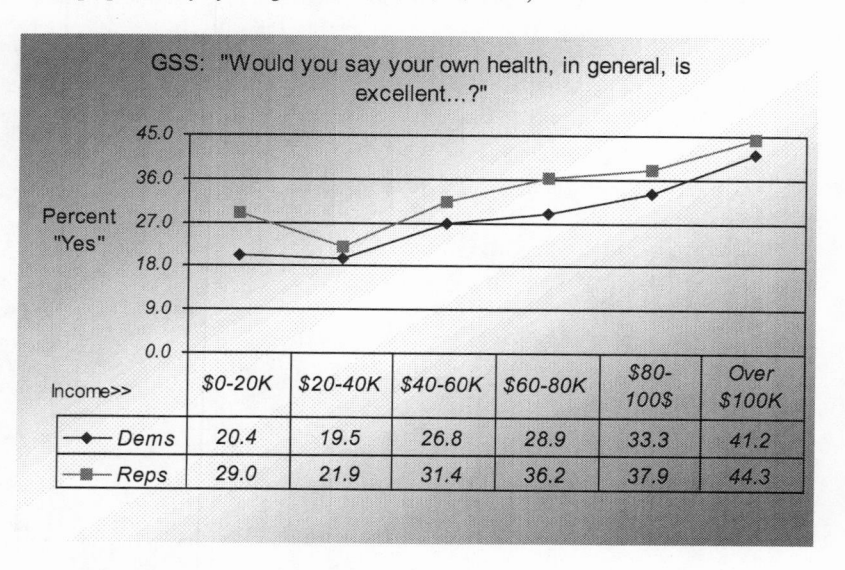

Income>>	$0-20K	$20-40K	$40-60K	$60-80K	$80-100$	Over $100K
Dems	20.4	19.5	26.8	28.9	33.3	41.2
Reps	29.0	21.9	31.4	36.2	37.9	44.3

Figure 24. Percentages of Democrats and Republicans with excellent mental health, based on self-assessments (4 consecutive Gallup surveys conducted in 2004 through 2007, based on 4014 total cases including independents, who are not shown, and with confidence level of at least 95% and a relative proportion of .64)

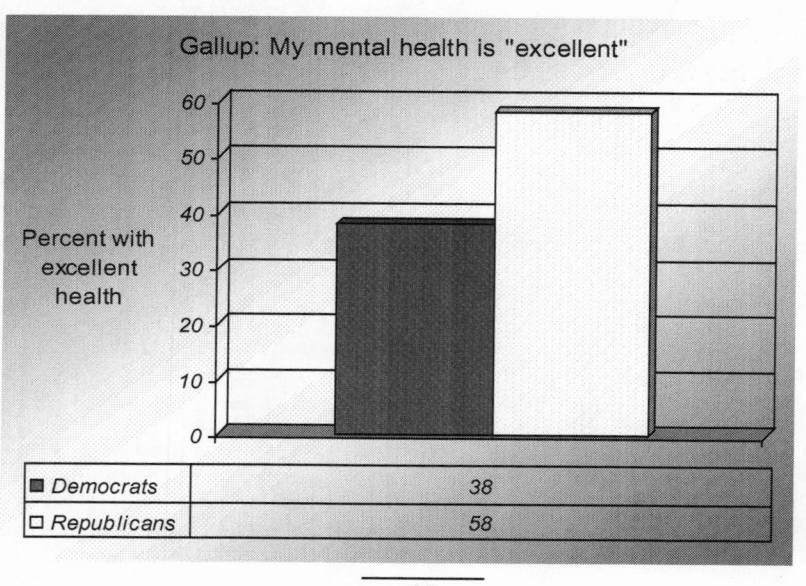

Democrats	38
Republicans	58

Mental Health

In November, 2007, Gallup reported that it had found a large disparity between the self-described mental health of Republicans versus Democrats and independents. The aggregate results of 4 consecutive surveys conducted in 2004 through 2007 showed that Republicans were far more likely to claim "excellent" mental health. The results are summarized in Figure 24, above.

Gallup also used multiple regression analysis in an effort to gauge the relationship between mental health and several variables, including party identification. Interestingly, the analysis showed that Republicans were more likely to report good mental health, even after controlling for the other variables, which included income, education, age, gender, race, marriage, and children.[27]

In addition, a 2006 GSS survey found that, by 17 to 11 percent, Democrats were more likely to say that they had "received treatment for a mental health problem."[28] And, by 9.8 to 6.4 percent, Democrats are more likely to have taken Prozac as treatment for depression and other disorders.[29]

Healthy Habits

Who Is More Overweight?

I'm not overweight. I'm just nine inches too short.

— The late Shelley Winters, Actress[30]

The available evidence is pretty slender, but it appears that weight control is more of a problem for Democrats than Republicans. At least, this was true for respondents of recent Michigan-based surveys. In a 2004 survey, Democrats were more likely to say they were overweight. See Figure 25, below.

Are Democrats really more overweight, or are they just more truthful and/or realistic about their weight? The results from another survey suggest that Democrats truly are more overweight. In a 2002 survey, respondents were asked for their individual heights and weights. The average results for men, by political party, are shown in Table 3, below. In addition, body mass calculations have been added. (Body mass is simply weight divided by height, using metric measures.) Generally, body mass numbers over 25 are considered potentially unhealthy. Using this standard, males of both political parties are overweight, but Democratic males are about 10 percent more so than Republican males.[31]

---

27 Frank Newport, "Republicans Report Much Better Mental Health Than Others," *The Gallup News Service* (November 30, 2007), Retrieved November 30, 2007, from Http://brain.gallup. com.

28 The results are based on 799 cases, with statistical significance of 98% and a relative proportion of 1.55.

29 The results are from the aggregate results of GSS surveys conducted in 1998 and 2006, based on 1478 cases, with 98% statistical significance and a relative proportion of 1.53.

30 Shelley Winters (attributed), "Brainyquote.Com."

31 If the survey population is adjusted to exclude minorities, Democratic male body mass drops slightly, to 28.5. This lowers the differential between Democrats and Republicans from

Figure 25. Are you overweight? (Michigan State of the State survey conducted in 2004, based on 242 cases for males, 341 cases for females, and 583 cases for both, with confidence level, left to right, of 94% (marginal), 99%, and 99+%, and with relative proportions of, left to right, 1.38, 1.45, and 1.42) [32]

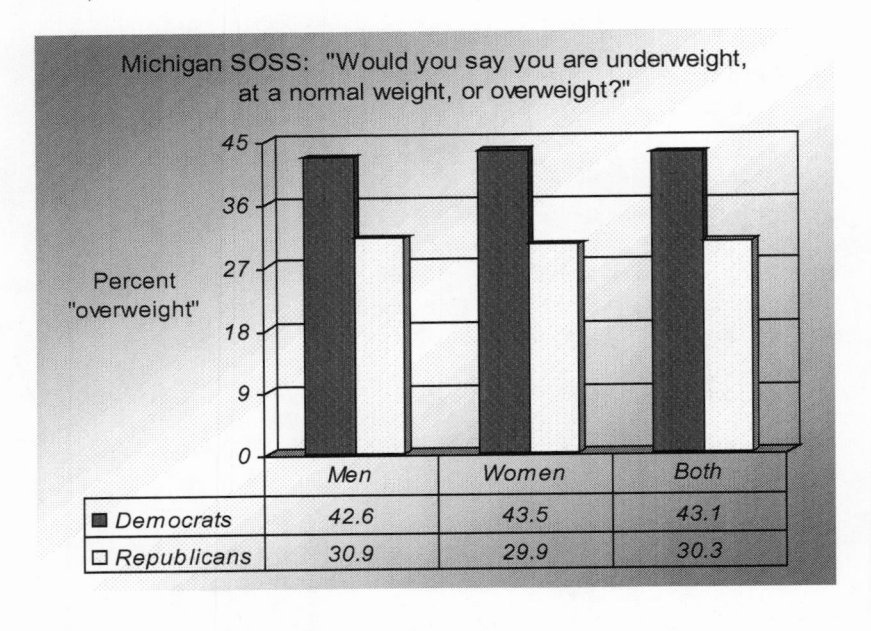

	Men	Women	Both
■ Democrats	42.6	43.5	43.1
□ Republicans	30.9	29.9	30.3

Table 3. What is your height and weight? (Men) (Michigan SOSS No. 26 conducted in summer, 2002, based on 194 cases, with confidence level of 95%)

Men	Height	Weight in lbs.	Body Mass Index*
Democrats	5' 9.9"	202.6	29.2
Republicans	5' 11.1"	189.8	26.4
Difference	–1.2"	12.8	2.8
Percentage excess		10.6%	

*25-30 is overweight; over 30 is obese.

The body mass of Republican women averages just below the "normal" limit of 25; however, Democratic women are about 12% heavier.[33]

10.6 percent to 8 percent, suggesting that weight control may be a little more of a problem among minority populations.

32 Michigan *State of the State* surveys are conducted by the Institute for Public Policy and Social Research (IPPSR), a nonprofit entity located within the Michigan State University. Please see Appendix F on page 364 for acknowledgements and limitations.

33 If the survey population is adjusted to exclude minorities, Democratic female body mass drops very slightly, to 27.5. This changes the body weight differential between Democrats and Republicans from 12% to 11% (essentially, no change).

Table 4. What is your height and weight? (Women) (Michigan SOSS No. 26 conducted in summer, 2002, based on 296 cases, with confidence level of 99+%)

Women	Height	Weight in lbs.	Body Mass Index*
Democrats	5' 4.4"	163.4	27.8
Republicans	5' 4.9"	148.0	24.8
Difference	−.5"	15.4	3.0
Percentage excess	12.1%		

*25-30 is overweight; over 30 is obese.

National Harris polls conducted in 2006 and 2007 also show that Democrats are slightly more likely to be overweight (by 58.6 to 53.6 percent); however, in the Harris surveys all of the statistically significant difference is attributable to women. The results, which are based on height and weight figures, are shown in Table 5, below.

Table 5. The percentages of women who are overweight or obese, based on height and weight measurements reported by respondents to Harris interviewers. For men, there was no statistically significant difference.

Surveys of women	% Overweight		No. of Cases	Conf %	*RP
	Dems	Reps			
Harris Feb. 2007	52.4	40.2	342	96	1.30
Harris Feb. 2006	54.0	40.4	354	98	1.34
Harris Jan. 2006	51.7	35.5	415	+99	1.46
Overall	52.7	38.4	1111	+99	1.37

*RP is relative proportion, which is the Democratic % divided by the Republican %.

The reason Democratic women are more likely to be overweight may be that they lack the time or inclination to cut back on eating. In a recent Harris survey, Democratic women were much less likely (by 51 to 72 percent) to report that they had reduced their food intake during the previous 30 days in an effort to shed pounds.[34] Here is another possibility: By 44 to 62 percent, Democratic women are less likely to drink caffeine beverages every day, according to a Georgia state survey conducted in 2007. Could this be linked to lower weight?[35]

It seems logical that Democrats might be slightly heavier, given the fact that, on average, they have less income than Republicans. Today's "fat cats" are more likely to be poorer people, as noted in an article published by a senior fellow with the National Center for Policy analysis (2003):

---

34 The results are from a Harris Interactive survey conducted in 2006, based on 216 cases, with a +99% confidence level and a relative proportion of .71.

35 The results are from a 2007 Georgia "Peach State" poll, based on 280 cases, with a 99% confidence level and a relative proportion of .71.

One of the more curious consequences of these trends is that the poor are now more likely to be obese than the wealthy. Indeed, obesity is now a problem in developing countries where starvation was the norm not too many years ago, according to the World Health Organization.[36]

Being overweight or obese diminishes the quality and length of life and has enormous implications for the cost of health care. In a recent research report, the Milken Institute estimated that America could eventually save over $300 billion annually, if it could get its obesity rate back to the level that existed just a few years ago, in 1998.[37] Some employers, struggling with rising health insurance costs, are now charging overweight employees an extra percentage of health insurance premiums. This is sure to be controversial, especially if obesity is more prevalent among the constituents of one major political party than the other.

Who Is to Blame for the Thick Thighs?

[M]organ Spurlock has invaded the [movie] theaters with his widely praised "Super Size Me," a wild jihadist tilt against the golden arches.... By gorging himself on vast quantities of the worst sludge on the McMenu — guess what? Spurlock gains 25 pounds ...
— Alex Beam, Boston Globe, May 11, 2004[38]

It is widely acknowledged that many poor people suffer from obesity; however, the causes are more controversial. Some people subscribe to a radical notion: Poor people, like most of us, don't use enough self-control with regard to the quantities they eat. Others attribute the bulging waistlines to a lack of nutritional information, a lack of money to buy healthy foods, a lack of playgrounds for poor children to play on, and/or the prevalence of enticing fast food restaurants. The truth may lie in between.

A Michigan survey asked respondents if they thought eating in fast food restaurants contributes to people becoming overweight. A majority of both constituencies answered, "Yes." However, Democrats were more likely to do so (Figure 26).

Who Exercises More?

Here, the evidence is conflicting. In a Pew Research Center poll conducted in 2002, respondents were asked if, during the prior day, they engaged in "some kind of vigorous exercise such as jogging, working out in a gym, or playing a racquet sport." By 38.8 to 34.3 percent Democrats were more likely than Republicans to respond in the affirmative (966 cases, with confidence level 96% and with a relative proportion of 1.13). However, a more recent Pew survey (conducted in 2004) found no statistically significant difference in the answers of Democrats and Republicans to this same question.

---

36 Bruce Bartlett, "Gaining Weight," in *Commentary* (National Center for Policy Analysis, April 23, 2003), Retrieved September 2, 2006, from: http://www.ncpa.org/edo/bb/2003/bb042303.html.

37 Ross DeVol and Armen Bedroussian, "An Unhealthy America: The Economic Burden of Chronic Disease," (October, 2007), Retrieved October 21, 2007, from: www.milkeninstitute.org.

38 Alex Beam, "A Super-Size Portion of Half Truths," in *Boston.com* (May 11, 2004), Retrieved September 2, 2006, from: http://www.boston.com/ae/food/articles/2004/05/11/a_super_size_portion_of_half_truths/.

Figure 26. "How much do you think eating in fast food restaurants contributes to people becoming overweight?" (Michigan State of the State survey conducted in 2003, based on, left to right, 208 and 320 cases, with confidence level of 99% for both differences, and with relative proportions of, left to right, 1.21 and 1.23)

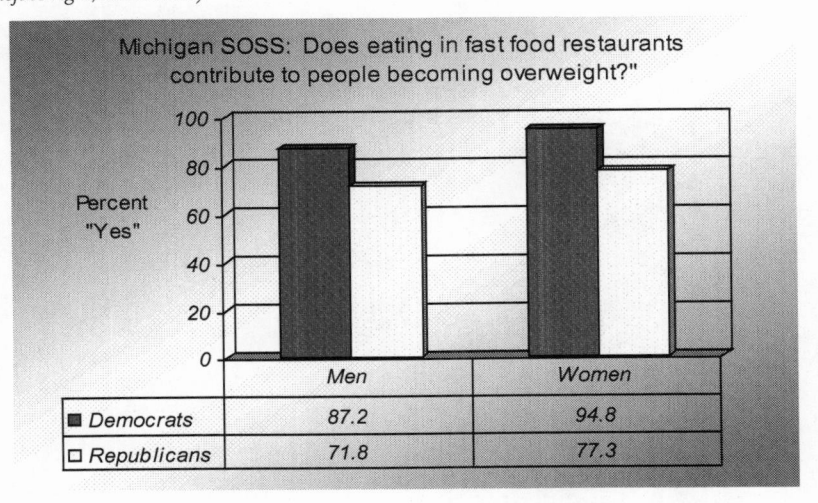

Who Is More Likely to Smoke Tobacco?

They're talking about banning cigarette smoking now in any place that's used by ten or more people in a week, which I guess means that Madonna can't even smoke in bed.

— Comedian Bill Maher[39]

All surveys suggest that Democrats are more likely to smoke. See Table 6, below.

Table 6. Surveys regarding smoking

Survey and Issue	Dem % "yes"	Rep % "yes"	No. of cases	Conf %	*RP
Pew survey 2005: "Do you smoke cigarettes on a regular basis?"	20.9	14.7	708	+99	1.42
Michigan SOSS 2004: "Have you smoked at least 100 cigarettes in your entire life?"	53.1	40.9	749	+99	1.30
Michigan SOSS 2003: "Do you now use any form of tobacco?"	32.8	25.6	712	96	1.28
GSS surveys conducted between 1977 and 1994: Do you smoke?	36.0	28.4	10695	+99	1.27

*RP is relative proportion, which is the Democratic % divided by the Republican %.

---

39 Bill Mahler (attributed), "Brainyquote.Com."

Who Wants to Ban Smoking?

It may surprise you to learn that Republicans are the activists when it comes to smoking bans, according to a survey released in July, 2005. Gallup reported: "Republicans are more likely than Democrats or independents to show increased support for smoking bans in restaurants, hotels and motels, and the workplace." The survey found that Republicans were more likely than Democrats to support restaurant smoking bans by 62 to 53 percent, hotel and motel smoking bans by 41 to 33 percent, and workplace bans by 47 to 37 percent. Perhaps Republicans support these restrictions because they are less likely to smoke.[40]

Who Is More Likely to Use Illegal Drugs?

> The historical record is that 19 years ago, I used marijuana once at a party ... in New Orleans .... It didn't have any effect on me. As a matter of fact, I never went back and revisited it.

— Former Republican Speaker of the House Newt Gingrich[41]

Only tiny percentages of Democrats and Republicans state that they have tried crack cocaine. However, Democrats comprise the majority of those who have tried the drug, according to the GSS surveys depicted in Figure 27, below.

Figure 27. "Have you ever used 'crack' cocaine?" (combined results of 4 GSS surveys conducted in 2000 through 2006, based on 2398 cases for men, 3158 cases for women, and 5556 cases for both, with confidence level of 97% for men, 99% for women, and 99+% for both, and with relative proportions of, left to right, 1.45, 1.74, and 1.50)

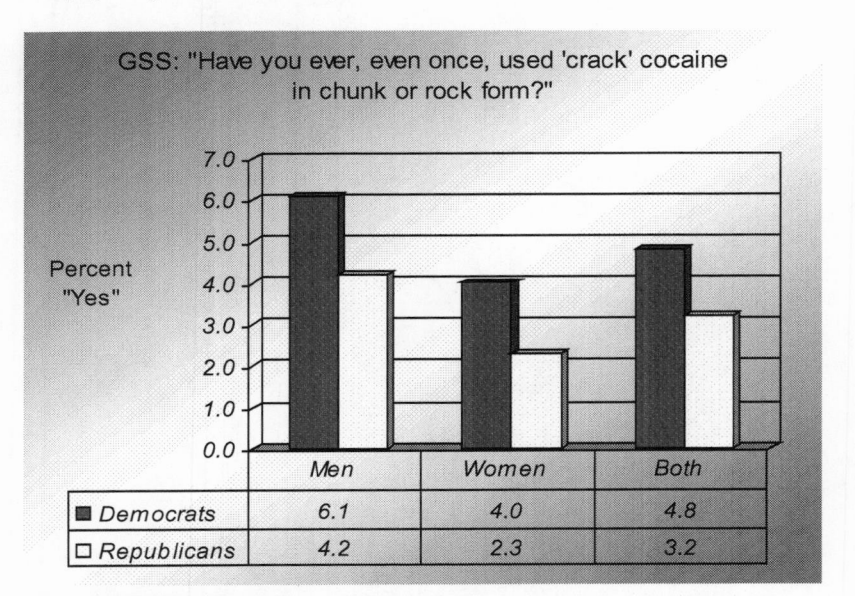

GSS: "Have you ever, even once, used 'crack' cocaine in chunk or rock form?"

Percent "Yes"

	Men	Women	Both
■ Democrats	6.1	4.0	4.8
□ Republicans	4.2	2.3	3.2

40 David Moore, "Increased Support for Smoking Bans in Public Places," *The Gallup News Service* (July 20, 2005), Retrieved January 31, 2007, from http://www.secondhandsmokesyou.com/ resources/one_news_article.php?id=98.

41 Jill Lawrence, "Speaker Gingrich," *AP*, November 28, 1994.

Even smaller percentages have taken illegal drugs by means of injection; however, Democrats again are slightly more likely to say they have done so.

Figure 28. [Not including doctor's prescriptions] "Have you ever, even once, taken any drugs by injection with a needle (like heroin, cocaine, amphetamines, or steroids)?" (combined results of 4 GSS surveys conducted in 2000 through 2006, based on 2401 cases for men, 3159 cases for women, and 5560 cases for both, with no statistical significance for men, 99% for women, and 90% (marginal) for both, and with relative proportions of, left to right, n/a, 2.08, and 1.29)

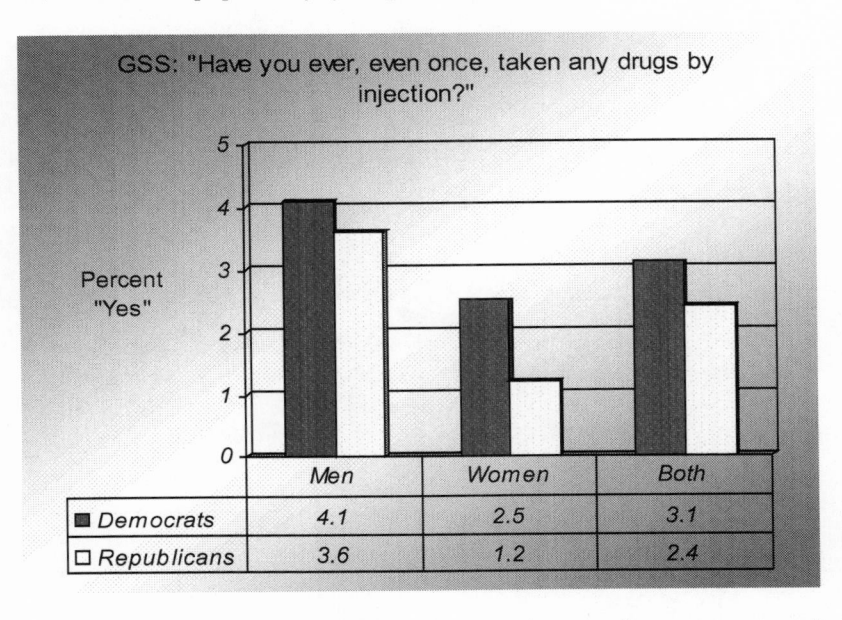

Republicans are just as likely as Democrats to have tried marijuana, according to a 1999 Gallup poll where 33 percent of Republicans and 31 percent of Democrats reported having experimented with the drug (statistically a tie).[42]

> Whenever a conservative is exposed as a "hypocrite" the behavior — Limbaugh's drug use, Bennett's gambling, whatever — <u>never</u> offends the Left as much as the fact that they were telling other people how to live. This, I think, is in part because of the general hostility the Left has to the idea that we should live in any way that doesn't "feel" natural.
>
> — Columnist Jonah Goldberg[43]

---

42 Jennifer Robison, "Who Smoked Pot? You May Be Surprised," *The Gallup News Service* (July 16, 2002), Retrieved August 21, 2004, from Http://brain.gallup.com. The results are based on a survey of 1000 adults aged 18 years or more (sampling error at 95% = plus or minus 3%).

43 Jonah Goldberg, "What Is a 'Conservative'?," in *National Review Online* (May 11, 2005), Retrieved August 14, 2006, from: http://www.nationalreview.com/goldberg/goldberg200505111449.asp.

Other Health Issues

Health Insurance

Democrats are less likely than Republicans to have health insurance, and this could explain why they seem particularly motivated to expand governmental programs in this area. See Figure 29, below.

Figure 29. Percentage without health insurance (NES 2004 Pre-election survey, based on 729 cases, with confidence level of 97%, and with relative proportion of 1.55)

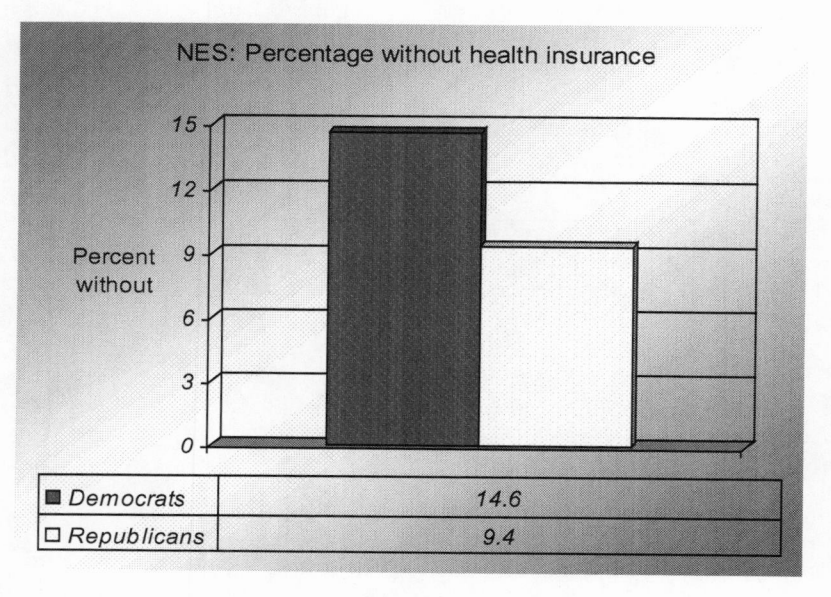

HIV Testing

By 40.5 to 33.8 percent, Democrats are more likely to have been tested for HIV, based on a 2006 GSS survey of 1433 men and women.[44]

Cleaner teeth and other important health matters

According to a 2001 ABC News poll:

> Republicans divide evenly on whether genetically modified foods are safe or unsafe. Independents rate them unsafe by a 20-point margin; Democrats by a 26-point margin.[45]

Other health-related issues are shown in Table 7, below.

---

44 The statistical significance is 99% and the relative proportion is 1.20.
45 The results are based on a sample of 1024 adults, with statistical significance of 95%.

Table 7. Miscellaneous health

Survey	Issue	Dem % "yes"	Rep % "yes"	No. of cases	Conf %	*RP
Harris 2006 Interactive survey	During the last 30 days have you cleaned your teeth 3 or more times in a single day?	40.0	61.0	334	+99	.66
Rasmussen 2006 survey	Do you belong to a health club?	13.0	22.0	**1000	95	.59
GSS surveys from 1998 through 2004	Are you a member of a sports group?	14.9	20.2	931	97	.74
1996 NBC, Wall St. Journal, via Roper	Do you use vitamins or supplements, or try to eat mostly organic foods?	48	55	1116	97	.87

*RP is relative proportion, which is the Democratic % divided by the Republican %.

**Case numbers include independents and others in addition to Democrats and Republicans.

Figure 30. "Aside from weddings and funerals, how often do you attend religious services ...? (February, 2007 Pew Survey, based on 910 cases, with confidence level of 99+%, and Phi of .25 for the series)

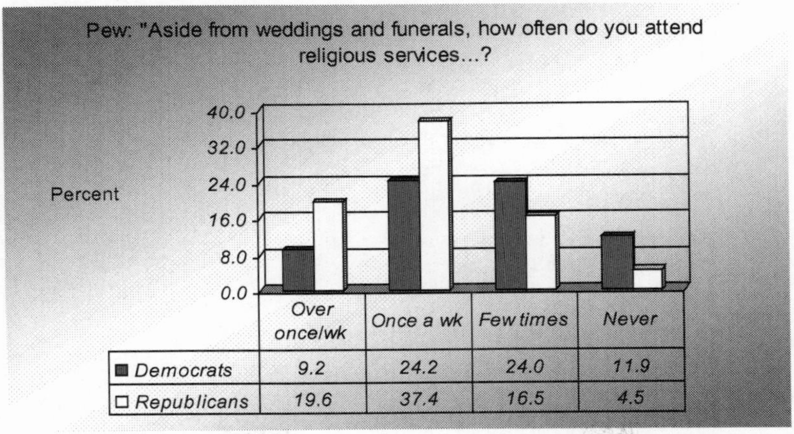

Pew: "Aside from weddings and funerals, how often do you attend religious services...?

	Over once/wk	Once a wk	Few times	Never
Democrats	9.2	24.2	24.0	11.9
Republicans	19.6	37.4	16.5	4.5

Religion

> My generation, faced as it grew with a choice between religious belief and existential despair, chose marijuana. Now we are in our Cabernet stage.

— Peggy Noonan, Republican political analyst and author[46]

Frequency of Attendance and Strength of Convictions

It appears that Republicans are more likely to attend religious services on a frequent basis. See Figure 30, above.

Other surveys addressing the issue of religious attendance are shown in Table 8, below.

Table 8. Other relevant surveys

Survey	Specific Issue	Dem % "yes"	Rep % "yes"	No. of cases	Conf %	*RP
Rasmussen March 2007	Do you attend a religious service every week or more frequently?	23.0	47.0	**1000	95	.49
Pew July 2005 Religion and Public Life Survey	Do you attend services once per week or more?	37.5	55.0	1288	+99	.68
Pew 1987-2003 Combined Values Surveys	Do you attend services once per month or more?	55.6	62.9	9475	+99	.88

*RP is relative proportion, which is the Democratic % divided by the Republican %.

**Case numbers include independents and others in addition to Democrats and Republicans.

Gallup surveys show that, by 66 to 57 percent, Republicans are more likely than Democrats to describe religion as being very important in their lives.[47] And, by 44.6 to 39.4 percent, Republicans are more likely to describe their religious convictions as "strong," according to several GSS surveys conducted during the last 10 years.[48] A 2006 Harris poll shows that Republicans are far more likely (by 92 to 73 percent) to say that, during the previous 30 days, they "felt the presence of God" in their lives.[49]

---

46 Peggy Noonan (attributed), "Brainyquote.Com."

47 Frank Newport, "An Abiding Relationship: Republicans and Religion," *The Gallup News Service* (June 14, 2007), Retrieved September 29, 2007, from Http://brain.gallup.com. The results are based on surveys conducted in 2004 through 2007, with statistical significance of at least 95%.

48 The GSS results are based on 8227 cases in surveys conducted from 1995 through 2004, with statistical significance of 99+% and a relative proportion of .88.

49 The Harris results are based on 370 cases, with a confidence level of 99+%, and with a relative proportion of .79.

According to a 2007 Rasmussen survey of 1000 adults (including all political parties), Republicans are more likely to believe that Jesus Christ actually walked the earth (by 91 to 76 percent), that Jesus Christ was the Son of God and died for our sins (by 89 to 71 percent), and that Jesus Christ rose from the dead (by 89 to 69 percent). A Rasmussen survey conducted in 2005 found that 77 percent of Republicans believed the literal truth of the Bible, versus just 59 percent of Democrats. Another Survey conducted by Rasmussen in 2005 found that 63 percent of Republicans claimed to pray "every day or nearly every day." Only 52 percent of Democrats made that same claim.[50]

Religion and Politics

Jihad Jesus Republicans need to understand that the separation of church and state has kept this country from getting into religious wars.

— Phillip Paulson, who (with the ACLU) has sued to remove the Mt. Soledad memorial cross[51]

Republicans are often accused of mixing religion and politics, however, the link between religion and politics may be stronger for Democrats.

Figure 31. Did your clergy encourage you to vote for a candidate or party? (NES post-election survey conducted in 2000, based on 803 cases, with confidence level of 99+%, and relative proportion of 2.94)

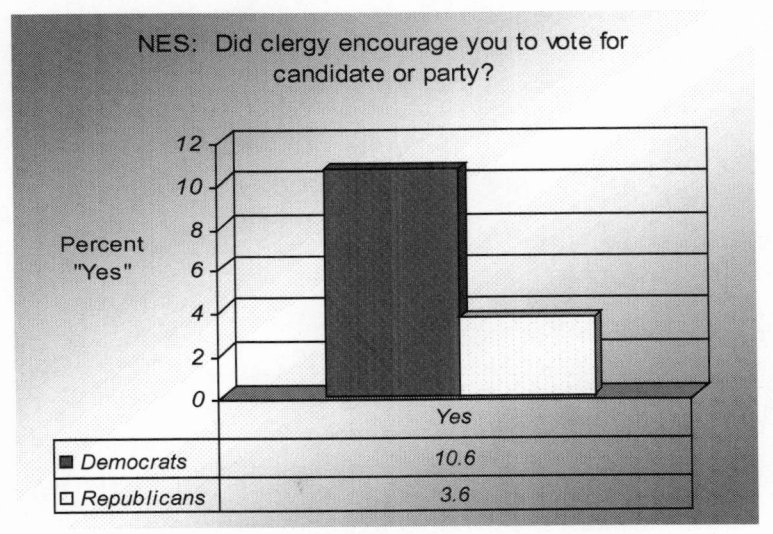

50 All Rasmussen survey responses have a confidence level of 95 percent or higher.
51 "Congress Gets into ACLU Cross Brouhaha," *WorldNetDaily*, Retrieved September 3, 2006, from http://www.worldnetdaily.com/news/article.asp?ARTICLE_ID=41617.

Religious Denominations
See Appendix A: Demographic Trends over 50 Years.

Entertainment and leisure

> We aren't in an information age; we are in an entertainment age.
>
> — Anthony Robbins, Motivational speaker and writer[52]

The Couch Potato Award

Time Spent Watching TV

Democrats consistently watch more television, as evident from Figure 32, below. They watch TV for an extra half hour (about) each day, or 3.5 extra hours per week. This disparity has been fairly steady for at least 25 years, and is true for both genders.

Figure 32. "On the average day, about how many hours do you personally watch TV?" (16 GSS surveys conducted between 1982 and 2006, based on 15064 cases, with confidence level of 99+%)

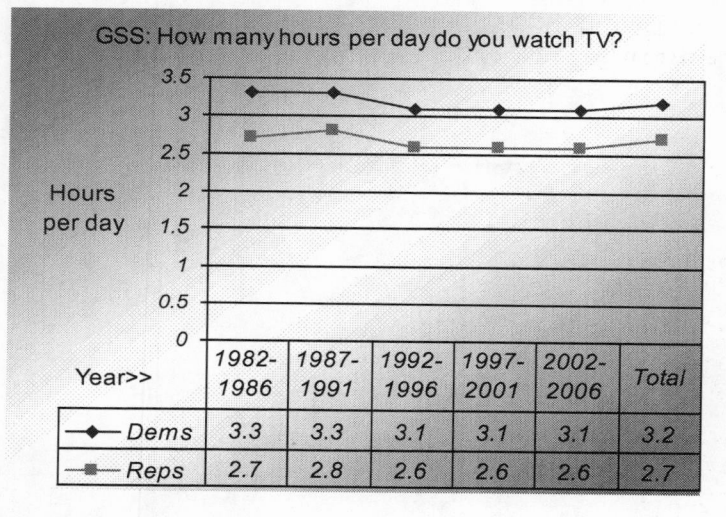

Year>>	1982-1986	1987-1991	1992-1996	1997-2001	2002-2006	Total
Dems	3.3	3.3	3.1	3.1	3.1	3.2
Reps	2.7	2.8	2.6	2.6	2.6	2.7

Table 9. Other relevant surveys

Survey and issue	Dem %	Rep %	No. of cases	Conf %	*RP
Rasmussen November 2007: Percentage watching more than 2 hours of TV in a typical day	34.0	24.0	**1000	95	1.42
Rasmussen November 2007: Percentage for whom Hollywood writers' strike has an impact on life	44.0	29.0	**1000	95	1.52

---

52 Anthony Robbins (attributed), "Brainyquote.Com."

Pew 2006 Biennial Media Consumption survey: Percentage watching TV for 4 hours or more per day (not counting news shows)	22.2	11.8	839	+99	1.88
Pew 2004 Biennial Media Consumption survey: Percentage watching TV for 4 hours or more per day (not counting news shows)	21.8	11.8	598	+99	1.85

*RP is relative proportion, which is the Democratic % divided by the Republican %.

**Case numbers include independents and others in addition to Democrats and Republicans.

TV Sex and Violence

The Republican-controlled FCC has, in the Bush years, already been heavy-handed in targeting what it deems broadcast speech too impure for you to hear.... From the ACLU to libertarian conservatives, predictions ... are dire.

— Doug Ireland, LA Weekly, March 24, 2005[53]

Republicans are more bothered than Democrats by adult language and sexual content on TV shows.

Figure 33. Does seeing adult language and sexual content on TV shows "bother you, personally"? (Pew News Interest Index survey conducted in March, 2005, based on, left to right, 484 and 979 cases, with confidence level of, left to right, 99+% and 97%, and with relative proportions of, left to right, .73 and .83)

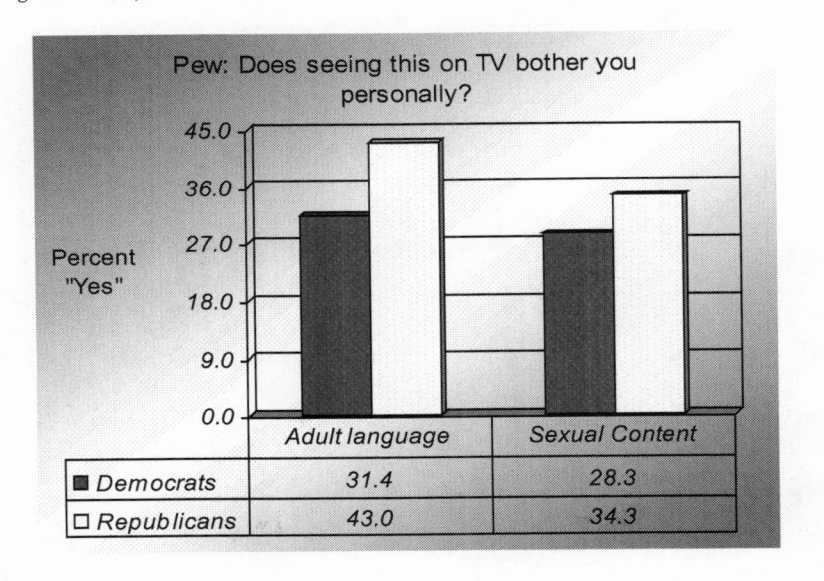

Pew: Does seeing this on TV bother you personally?

Percent "Yes"

	Adult language	Sexual Content
■ Democrats	31.4	28.3
□ Republicans	43.0	34.3

---

53 Doug Ireland, "Censor Alert," *LA Weekly*, March 24, 2005.

The following pair of Rasmussen surveys show that, while Republicans are more bothered by inappropriate sexual content on television shows, Democrats are much more concerned with TV violence.

Survey	Issue	Dem %	Rep %	No. of cases	Conf %	*RP
Rasmussen, June 2007	Sexual content is the biggest problem with TV	27.0	47.0	**1000	95	.57
Rasmussen, June 2007	Violence is the biggest problem with TV	55.0	32.0	**1000	95	1.72

*RP is relative proportion, which is the Democratic % divided by the Republican %.

**Case numbers include independents and others in addition to Democrats and Republicans.

Who Is More Likely to Watch an X-Rated Movie?

Both Democratic men and women outpace Republicans in regard to X-rated movies.

Figure 34. "Have you seen an X-rated movie in the last year?" (GSS surveys conducted between 1987 and 2006, based on, left to right, 4692, 6425, and 11117 cases, with confidence level of 99+% for all columns, and with relative proportions of, left to right, 1.26, 1.20, and 1.17)

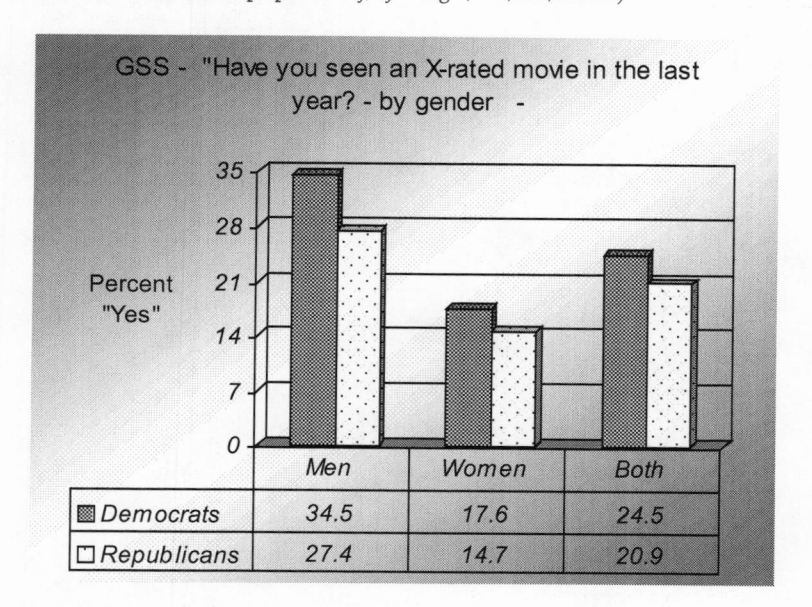

	Men	Women	Both
Democrats	34.5	17.6	24.5
Republicans	27.4	14.7	20.9

The X-rated movie gap extends to constituents in various age groups. See Figure 35, below.

Figure 35. "Have you seen an X-rated movie in the last year?" (GSS surveys conducted between 1987 and 2006, based on, left to right, 2117, 4566, and 4409 cases, with confidence level of 99+% for all columns, and with relative proportions of, left to right, 1.17, 1.18, and 1.42)

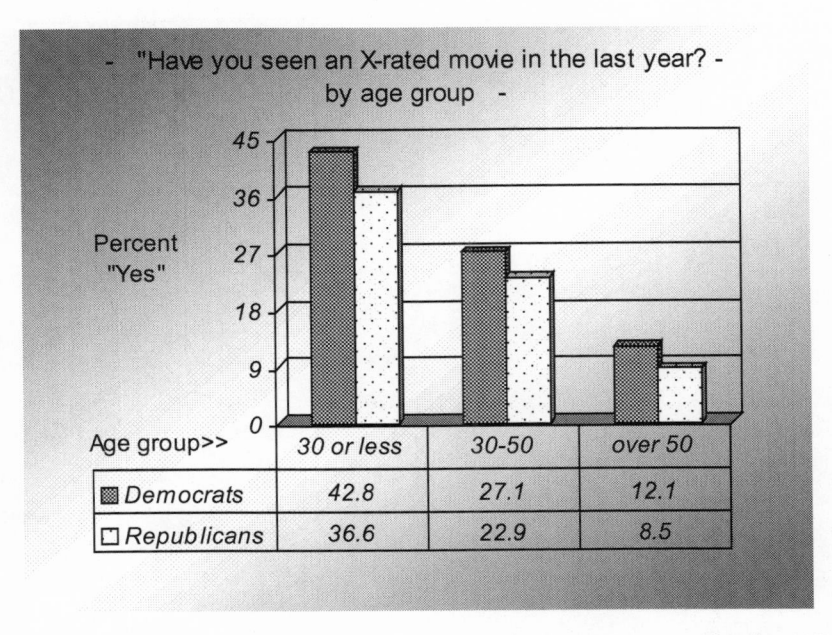

Figure 36. Did you "go online from home" yesterday? (Pew 2006 BMC survey, based on 1285 cases, with confidence level of 99+%, and with a relative proportion of .73)

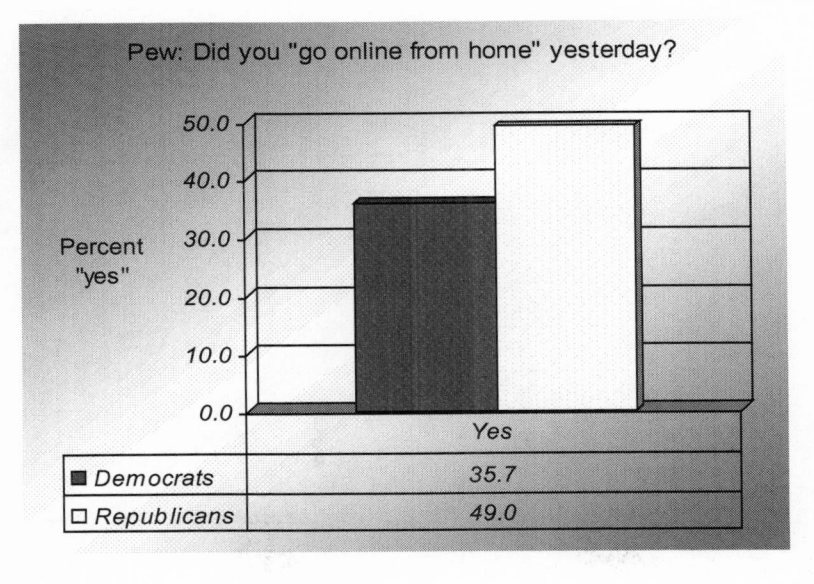

Net surfing

The Internet is not something you just dump something on. It's not a truck. It's a series of tubes. And if you don't understand, those tubes can be filled. And if they are filled, when you put your message in, it gets in line and it's going to be delayed by anyone that puts into that tube enormous amounts of material...

— Republican Senator Ted Stevens, giving a "technical" explanation of the Internet[54]

Republicans are more likely to use the Internet. (For what we can only speculate.) According to a 2006 Pew survey, 47 percent of Republicans had, on the prior day, used a computer to access the Internet from their homes. This was true for only 36 percent of Democrats. See Figure 36.

Privacy concerns are probably one reason Democrats use the Internet less frequently. A 2006 Michigan survey shows that, by 61.5 to 44.1 percent, Democrats worry more than Republicans about online privacy (included in Table 10, below).

Table 10. Various questions about computer and Internet usage

Survey	Issue	Dem %	Rep %	No. of cases	Conf %	*RP
Michigan 2006 SOSS	"... ever purchase anything online...?"	59.6	80.5	606	+99	.74
Michigan 2006 SOSS	"How concerned are you about privacy when you shop on-line?" (Percentage "Very concerned")	61.9	44.0	351	+99	1.41
Pew News Interest Index, June, 2005	Do you ever search the WWW, or send or receive e-mails?	62.6	73.9	938	+99	.84
Pew 2004 Political Typology	"Do you use a computer at your workplace, at school, at home, or anywhere else on at least an occasional basis?"	77.5	82.6	1303	+99	.94

*RP is relative proportion, which is the Democratic % divided by the Republican %.

Reading Fine Books

No entertainment is so cheap as reading, nor is any pleasure so lasting.

— Lady Mary Wortley Montagu, 18th century English aristocrat and writer[55]

---

54 Senator Ted Stevens cited in, "Internet 'Tubes' Speech Turns Spotlight, Ridicule onto Sen. Stevens," in *McClatchy Newspapers*, ed. Liz Ruskin (July 14, 2006).

55 Lady Mary Wortley Montagu cited in, "Columbia World of Quotations," (Columbia University Press, 1996).

Surveys conducted by Pew in 2006 and 2004 asked: "Not including school or work related books, did you spend any time reading a book yesterday?" In each case, around 37 percent of Democrats and Republicans answered affirmatively.[56] This may surprise some readers because a recent poll conducted by AP-Ipsos found that 34 percent of "conservatives" had not read a book in the last year, versus just 22 percent of "liberals."[57] However, as indicated in Chapter 11, we must not confuse Democrats and Republicans with liberals and conservatives. Historically, 25 to 50 percent of self-described conservatives are Democrats, and they tend to be at the lower end of the education scale. On the other hand, Republican conservatives are generally at the upper end of the education scale. For more information about these tendencies, please see page 291.

Holidays

In general, Republicans seem to value and enjoy holidays more than do Democrats. This is apparent from some of the survey results shown in Table 11.

Table 11. Surveys related to holidays

Issue	Survey	Dem %	Rep %	No. of cases	Conf %	*RP
Considers the holiday season (Christmas/ Hanukkah) to be joyous (versus stressful)	Rasmussen December 2007	39.0	61.0	**1000	95	.64
Considers the holiday season (Christmas/ Hanukkah) to be joyous (versus stressful)	Rasmussen December 2006	41.0	67.0	**1000	95	.61
Started holiday shopping as of the first week in December 2007	Rasmussen December 2007	44.0	63.0	**1000	95	.70
Started holiday shopping as of the first week in December 2006	Rasmussen December 2006	41.0	67.0	**1000	95	.61
Will decorate the house for the holidays	Rasmussen November 2007	62.0	77.0	**1000	95	.81
Will go Christmas caroling	Rasmussen November 2007	6.0	22.0	**1000	95	.27

56 For 2006 and 2004 the survey populations were 1285 and 973, respectively.

57 The AP-Ipsos poll was conducted between August 6 and 8th, 2007, and comprised 1003 cases with a marginal of error or plus or minus 3 percentage points.

Will attend religious service during the holidays	Rasmussen November 2007	54.0	**74.0**	**1000	95	.73
Will travel out of town for the holidays	Rasmussen November 2007	20.0	**34.0**	**1000	95	.59
Prefers saying "Merry Christmas" rather than "Happy Holidays"	Rasmussen December 2007	57.0	**88.0**	**1000	95	.65
Will have a Christmas tree	Rasmussen November 2006	59.0	**69.0**	**1000	95	.86
Will attend a Christmas party	Rasmussen November 2006	52.0	**73.0**	**1000	95	.71
Considers New Year's Day to be important holiday	Rasmussen December 2006	9.0	**15.0**	**1000	95	.60
Will attend a New Year's party	Rasmussen December 2006	23.0	**32.0**	**1000	95	.72
Believes that New Year's resolution will be kept	Rasmussen December 2006	44.0	**58.0**	**1000	95	.76
Considers July 4th to be important holiday	Rasmussen July 2006	53.0	**66.0**	**1000	95	.80
Will eat too much on Thanksgiving	Rasmussen November 2006	40.0	**57.0**	**1000	95	.70
Prefers turkey at Thanksgiving meal	Gallup, 2000	41.0	**50.0**	**1028	95	.82
Prefers stuffing at Thanksgiving meal	Gallup, 2000	**21.0**	15.0	**1028	95	1.4
Considers Veteran's Day to be one of the most important holidays	Rasmussen November 2007	39.0	**52.0**	**1000	95	.75
Will celebrate Veteran's Day	Rasmussen November 2007	35.0	**50.0**	**1000	95	.70

*RP is relative proportion, which is the Democratic % divided by the Republican %.

**Case numbers include independents and others in addition to Democrats and Republicans.

The Supreme Court has ruled that they cannot have a nativity scene in Washington, D.C. This wasn't for any religious reasons. They couldn't find three wise men and a virgin.

— TV host Jay Leno[58]

Family finances

Income and Spending

Of course, lifestyles are heavily influenced by the availability of money. In each of its surveys, American National Election Studies (NES) asks respondents to estimate total family income, before taxes, including salaries, wages, pensions, dividends, interest, etc. The NES survey results, over a 50-year time span, are presented on page 341, et seq. Those results, which are not repeated here, confirm the widely-held belief that Republicans have more total family income. Another survey indicates that the income differential results in a purchasing differential.

Figure 37. "Have there been times during the last year when you did not have enough money to buy... food, clothing, medical care, or gasoline? (Pew survey conducted in May, 2005, based on 969 cases for each column, with confidence level of 99+% for each column, and relative proportions of, left to right, 2.07, 1.94, 1.88, and 2.19)

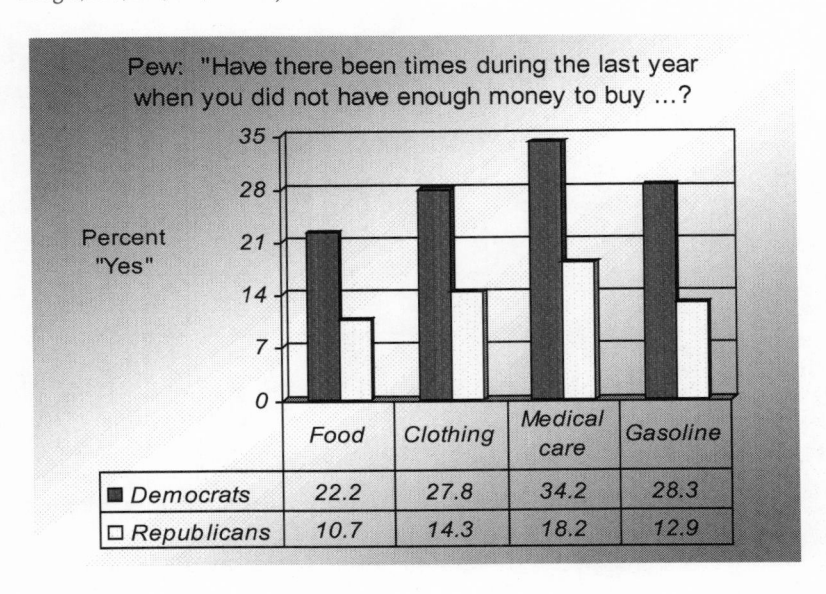

	Food	Clothing	Medical care	Gasoline
■ Democrats	22.2	27.8	34.2	28.3
□ Republicans	10.7	14.3	18.2	12.9

Indeed, Democrats are far less likely to indicate that they earn the money they need to live the kind of life they want. See Figure 38, below.

---

58 Jay Leno, "Brainyquote.Com."

Figure 38. "Do you now earn enough money to lead the kind of life you want, or not? (Pew survey conducted in May, 2005, based on 556 cases, with confidence level of 99+%, and relative proportion of .58)

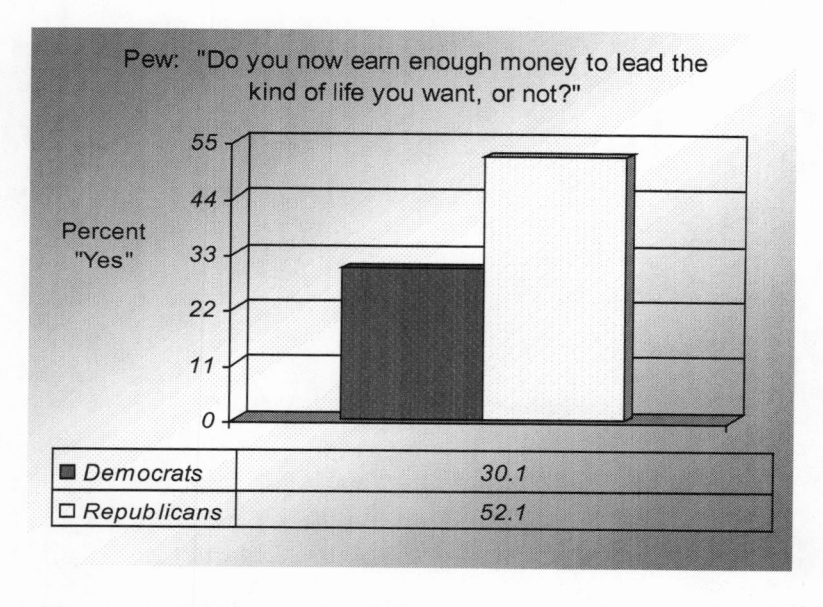

Figure 39. "Over the past 12 months, has there been a time when you or someone in your household has been without a job and looking for work, or not? (Pew survey conducted in May, 2005, based on 969 cases, with confidence level of 99+%, and relative proportion of 1.85)

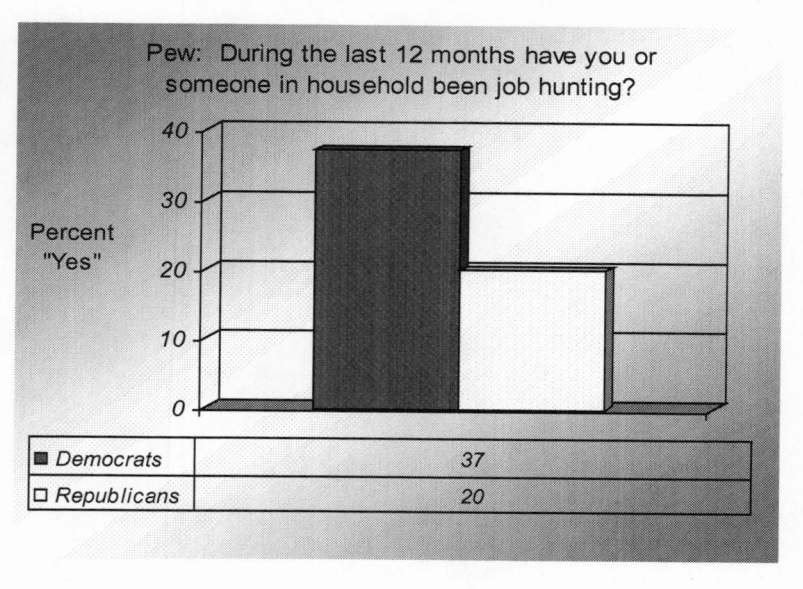

The root cause of the Democratic financial problem is probably unemployment (or underemployment). Democrats are significantly more likely to be out of work, as indicated in the same Pew survey, shown in Figure 39, above.

> I don't want to be a Republican. I just want to live like one.
> — Eugene Cervi, Newspaper publisher [59]

(Note: Extensive information about employment can be found in Chapter 3 and in Appendix A.)

Given these results, it is not surprising that Democrats are more likely to list lack of money and unemployment as their top financial problems. In a report issued in 2005, the Gallup Organization noted:

> The data show some slight variations by partisanship, with Democrats more likely than Republicans to say lack of money and unemployment are the top financial problems and Republicans more likely to not name any financial problems. These differences may result from Republicans being generally more likely to live in higher-income households than Democrats.[60]

The differences identified by Gallup are graphically displayed in Figure 40.

Figure 40. Most important financial problems by party affiliation (Gallup survey conducted in January-February, 2005, based on 2008 cases, with confidence level of 95% for each column).

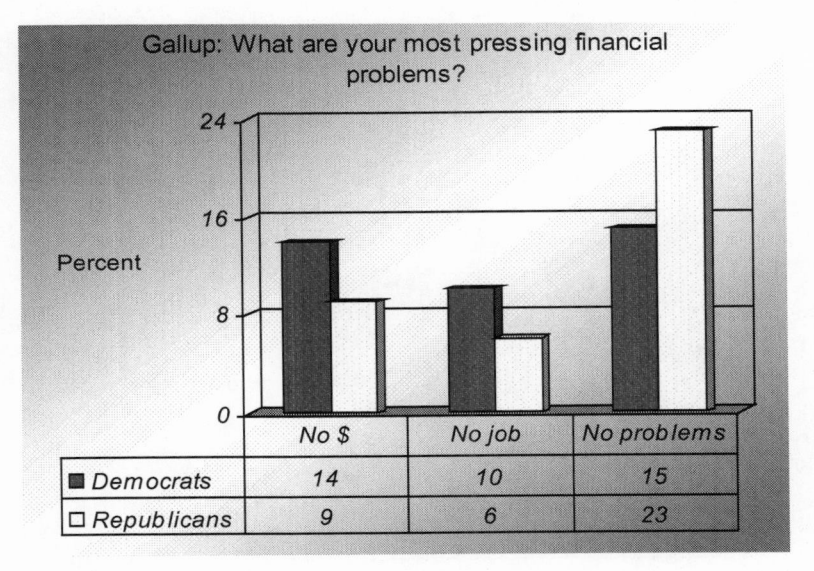

	No $	No job	No problems
■ Democrats	14	10	15
□ Republicans	9	6	23

59 Eugene Cervi (attributed), "Hearts & Minds," Retrieved August 17, 2004, from: http://www. heartsandminds.org/humor/fundemrep.htm

60 Joseph Carroll, "Americans' Financial Woes," The Gallup News Service (March 8, 2005), Retrieved August 5, 2006 from http://brain.gallup.com.

Investments

Stocks and Bonds

Republicans study the financial pages of the newspaper. Democrats put them in the bottom of the bird cage.

— Will Stanton, Unknown[61]

Republicans are more apt to trade stocks and bonds. This is reflected in a 2004 Pew Political Typology survey, the results of which are shown in Figure 41, below.

Figure 41. "Do you trade stocks or bonds in the stock markets?" (Pew survey conducted in July, 2004, based on 1303 cases, with confidence level of 99+%, and relative proportion of .72)

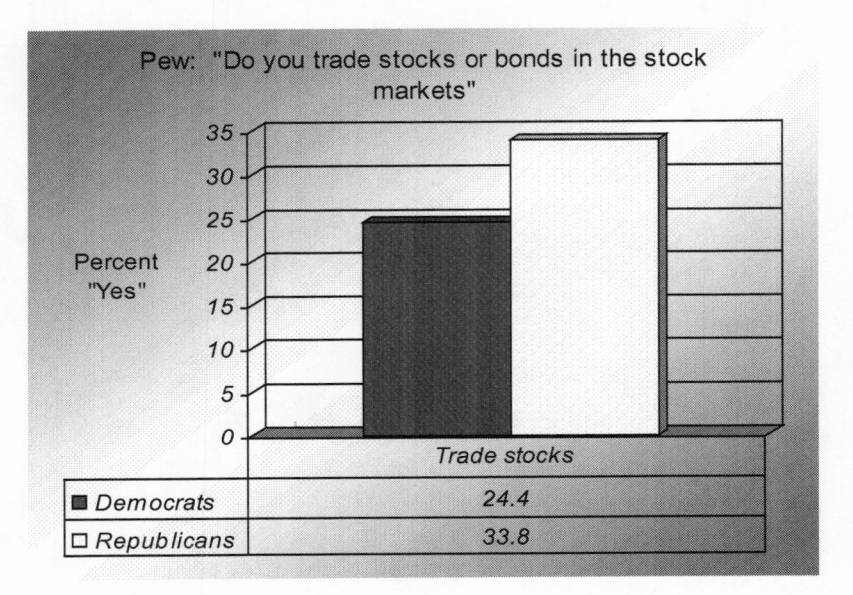

In a 2003 Pew survey, similar results were found, with 25.6 percent of Democrats and 39.4 percent of Republicans reporting that they trade stocks or bonds in the market. Republicans also invest larger sums. This can be deduced by their higher dividend and capital gain income. (See page 226.)

Retirement Planning

He gave a speech, then Kerry introduced his retirement plan — his wife, Teresa.

— TV host Jay Leno[62]

---

61 Will Stanton (attributed), "Quotationz.Com."

62 Jay Leno, "Tonight Show," in *About Political Humor*, Retrieved September 2, 2006, from: http://politicalhumor.about.com/library/jokes/blkerryjoke7.htm.

About 66 percent of Democrats and 77 percent of Republicans say that they have "a retirement plan or ... savings set aside for retirement...."[63] Over 80 percent of those amounts (for both Democrats and Republicans) are "in the stock market through stocks, mutual funds or a 401k plan."[64]

Democrats are much more likely to worry that they will not have enough retirement income. (See Figure 42, below.) Presumably, this concern has an impact on the average Democrat's lifestyle.

Figure 42. "How concerned are you, if at all, about not having enough money for your retirement?" (Pew survey conducted in May, 2005, based on 969 cases, with confidence level of 99+%, and relative proportion of 1.59)

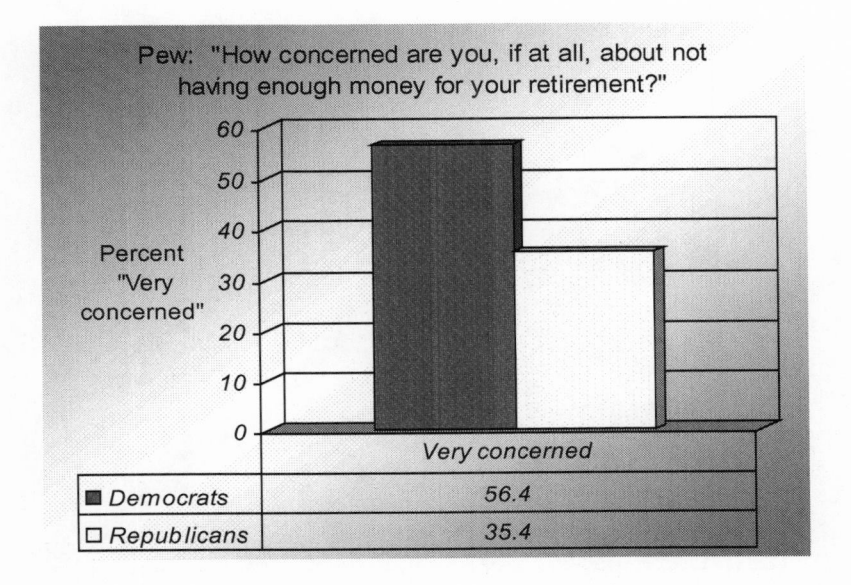

Habitat

Home Ownership

> A man builds a fine house; and now he has a master, and a task for life: He is to furnish, watch, show it, and keep it in repair, the rest of his days.
>
> — Ralph Waldo Emerson, 19th century American essayist[65]

Republicans are more likely to own their homes, and have been for at least 50 years.

---

63 2005 Pew News Interest Index survey, based on 737 cases, with statistical significance of 99+%, and with a relative proportion of .86.

64 2005 Pew News Interest Index survey, based on 549 cases.

65 Ralph Waldo Emerson, *Society and Solitude* (New York: Cosimo, 2005).

Figure 43. Do you own your home? (various NES surveys conducted in 1952 through 2004, based on, left to right, 1323, 1176, 4711, 6169, 6465, and 4699 cases, with confidence level of 99+% for all differences, and with relative proportions of, left to right, .88, .84, .85, .86, .89, and .89)

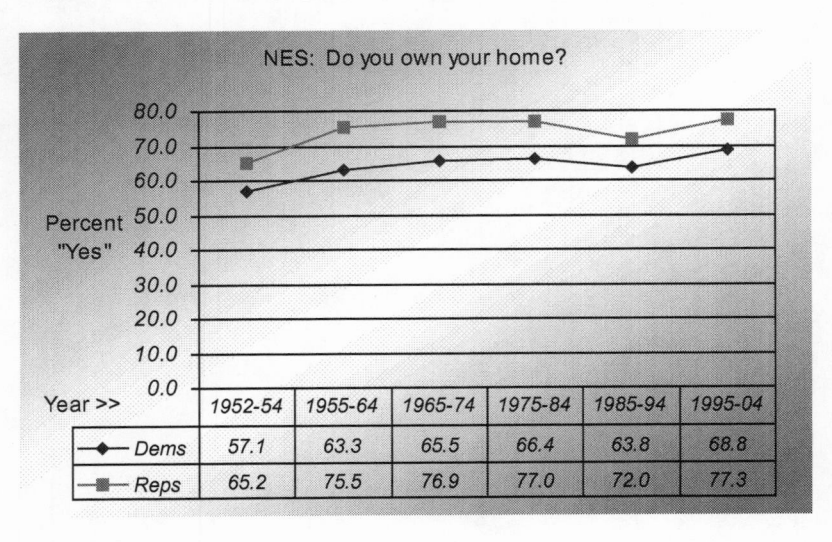

Miscellaneous

Who Is More Likely To Gamble?

Did you hear what [Bill] Bennett's lawyers said today? They said it wasn't gambling, but part of his Indian outreach program.

— TV host Jay Leno[66]

It appears that Democrats are a little more likely to gamble, but an exception might be sports-related betting.

Table 12. Surveys related to gambling

Survey	Issue	Dem % "yes"	Rep % "yes"	No. of cases	Conf %	*RP
Rasmussen September 2006	Have you ever bought a lot- tery ticket?	76.0	64.0	**1000	95	1.19
Rasmussen September 2006	Have you ever bet on a sports event or partici- pated in a sports betting pool?	30.0	37.0	**1000	95	.81

---

66 Jay Leno, "Tonight Show," (About: Political Humor), Retrieved July 28, 2006, from: http://politicalhumor.about.com/library/blrepublicanjokes.htm.

Gallup Poll December 2003	Did you gamble (in any one of several ways, including office pools, sports, and bingo) in last 12 months?	**68.0**	63.0	**1011	95	1.08
Time/CNN 1998	"Do you consider yourself a regular lottery player?"	**23.0**	15.0	474	97	1.53
Gallup/ CNN 1996	"During the last 12 months did you purchase a lottery ticket?"	**60.0**	49.0	633	99	1.22

*RP is relative proportion, which is the Democratic % divided by the Republican %.

**Case numbers include independents and others in addition to Democrats and Republicans.

Gun Ownership

A large gun gap has developed in recent years. Starting in the 1980s, ownership dropped sharply among Democratic males, while holding steady among Republican males.

Figure 44. "Do you happen to have in your home (or garage) any guns or revolvers?" (Men) (GSS surveys conducted between 1973 and 2006, grouped by decade, based on, left to right, 1664, 2693, 2312, and 1483 cases. The differences depicted by the graph points on the left side of the chart have no statistical significance. The differences depicted on the right side have a 99+% confidence level, with relative proportions of, left to right, .84 and .65)

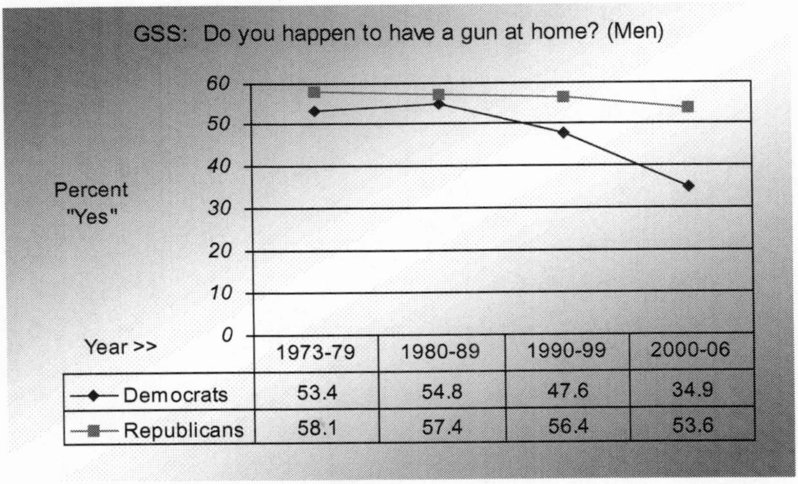

GSS: Do you happen to have a gun at home? (Men)

Year >>	1973-79	1980-89	1990-99	2000-06
Democrats	53.4	54.8	47.6	34.9
Republicans	58.1	57.4	56.4	53.6

Dick Cheney said he felt terrible about shooting a 78-year-old man, but on the bright side, it did give him a great idea about how to fix Social Security.

— Bill Maher, Comedian[67]

For women, there has always been a statistically significant difference, with Republicans being more likely to own a gun. During the last 30 years, ownership has dropped sharply for women of both political parties, but the drop has been greater for Democrats.

Figure 45. "Do you happen to have in your home (or garage) any guns or revolvers?" (Women) (GSS surveys conducted between 1973 and 2006, grouped by decade, based on, left to right, 2162, 3955, 3225, and 1867 cases, with 99+% confidence level for all depicted differences, and with relative proportions of, left to right, .83, .76, .72, and .65)

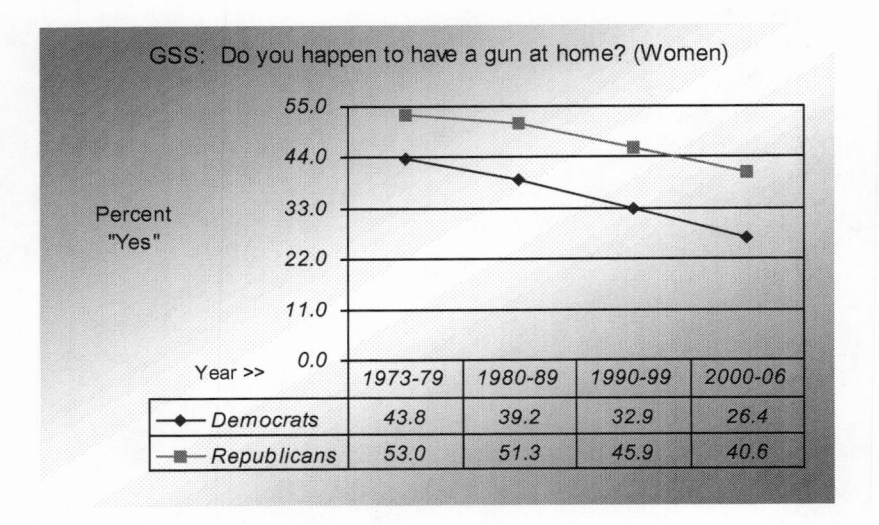

Table 13. A recent survey regarding gun ownership

Survey	Issue	Dem % "yes"	Rep % "yes"	No. of cases	Conf %	*RP
Rasmussen December 13, 2007	Does anyone in your house own a gun?	45.0	59.0	**800	95	.76

*RP is relative proportion, which is the Democratic % divided by the Republican %.

67 Bill Maher, in *About Political Humor*, Retrieved October 18, 2006, from: http://politicalhumor.about.com/od/cheneyshooting/a/cheneyshooting.htm.

**Case numbers include independents and others in addition to Democrats and Republicans.

Hunting

Surveys show that only about 2 percent of Democratic women and 4 percent of Republican women go hunting. On the other hand, sizeable percentages of men hunt — particularly Republican men. The trends for men are shown in Figure 46.

Figure 46. "Do you go hunting?" (Men) (18 GSS surveys conducted in 1977 through 2006, based on, left to right, 2071, 2902, and 1945 cases, with no statistical significance for the left column, and 99+% for the middle and right-side differences, and with relative proportions of, left to right, n/a, .88, and .64)

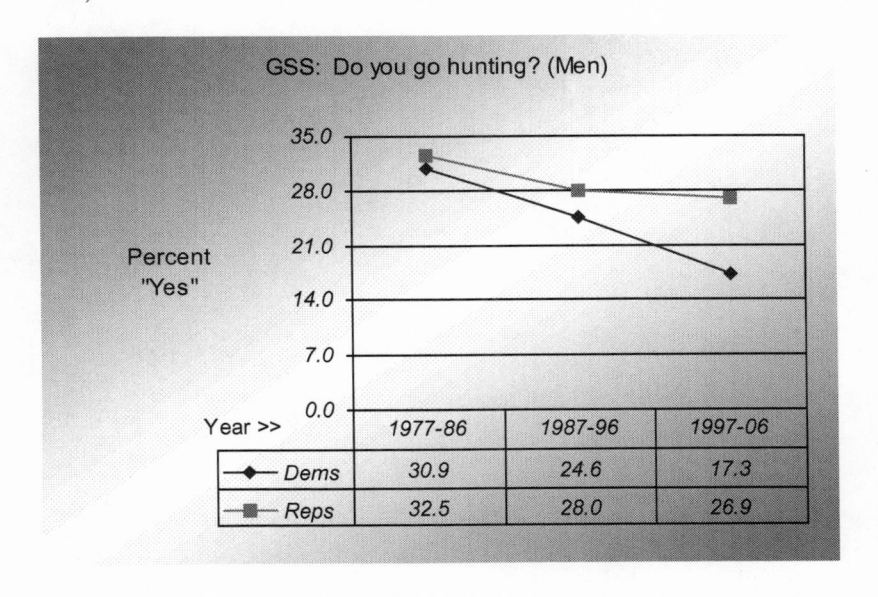

Year >>	1977-86	1987-96	1997-06
Dems	30.9	24.6	17.3
Reps	32.5	28.0	26.9

Violence

An interesting question was posed by a 1999 Michigan survey. Respondents were asked: "Has something ever happened that scared you so much that you thought about it for a long time?" Although there was not a clear difference in the responses of females, Democratic males were much more likely than Republican males to have been seriously scared. This is evident from a review of Figure 47.

Figure 48 may provide insights regarding the nature of those "scary" incidents. It appears that Democratic males (at least, those in Michigan) are much more likely to have been victims of serious physical attacks. This may simply reflect the fact that Democrats are more likely to live in high-crime urban communities.

Figure 47. Were you "scared so much you thought about it for a long time"? (Men) (1999 Michigan survey, based on 248 cases, with confidence level of 99+%, and with a relative proportion of 1.85)

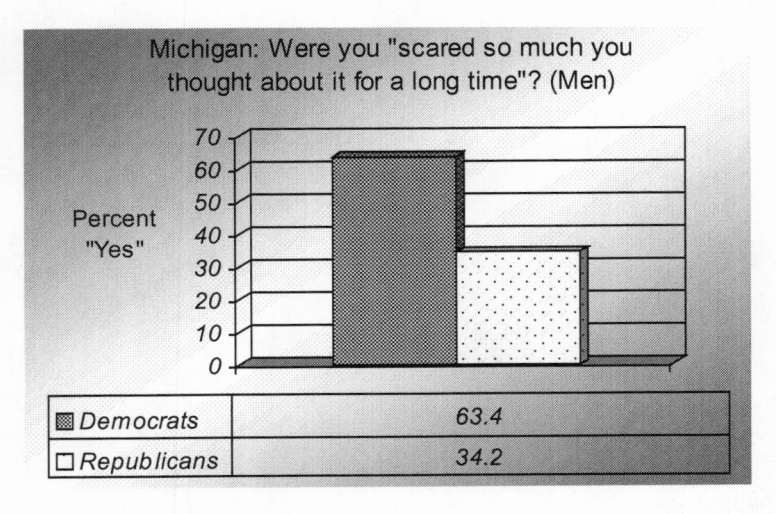

Figure 48. "Have you ever been the victim of a serious physical attack ... [other than sexual]?" (Men) (1999 Michigan survey, based on 248 cases, with confidence level of 99+%, and with a relative proportion of 2.44)

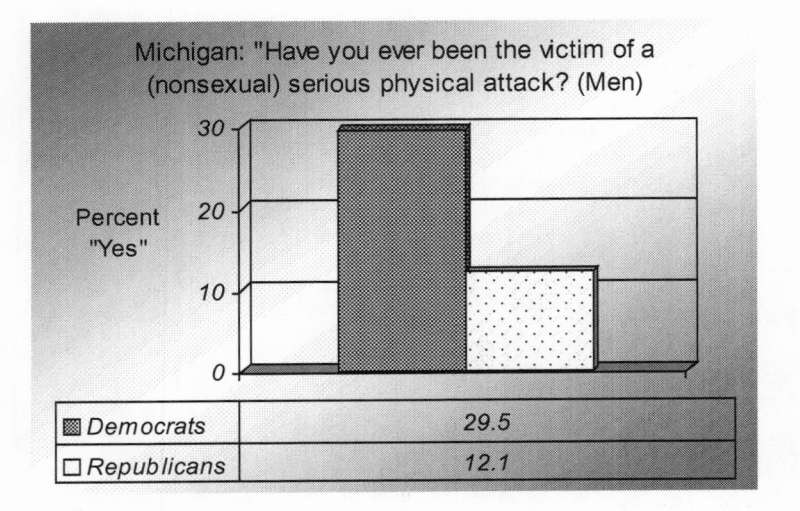

In addition, Democrats are a little more likely to have been threatened with a gun, or shot at. This is true for both genders. In general, the percentage of Democrats and Republicans threatened or shot at is astonishingly high — about 16 percent for Republicans and about 18 percent for Democrats.

Figure 49. "Have you ever been threatened with a gun, or shot at? (15 GSS surveys conducted between 1973 and 1994, based on 12498 cases, with confidence level of 99+% for each column, and with relative proportions of, left to right, 1.15, 1.34, and 1.16)

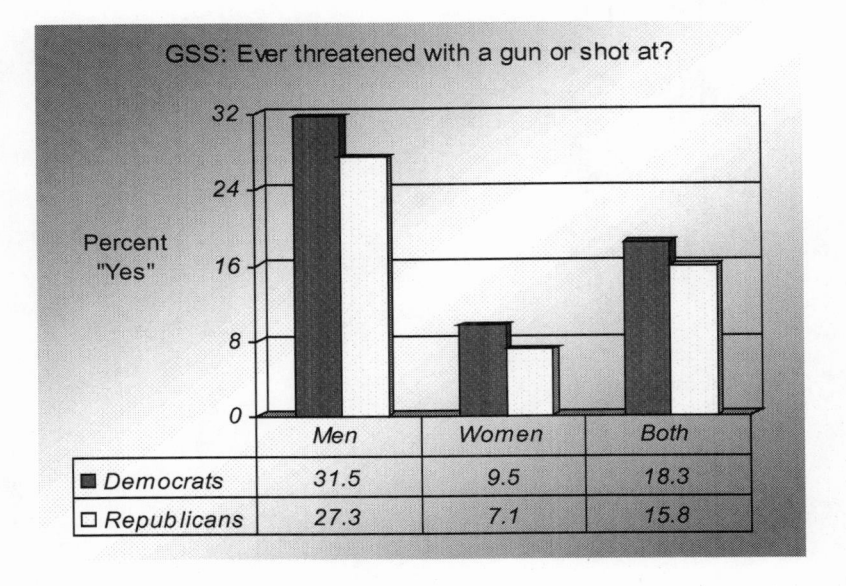

	Men	Women	Both
■ Democrats	31.5	9.5	18.3
□ Republicans	27.3	7.1	15.8

Arrest Rates

> Did you hear about the dyslexic cop from Utah that got arrested?
> He was handing out IUDs.
> — Anonymous[68]

In 1991 and 2004, GSS asked respondents if they had been arrested at any time since 1990. In those surveys (combined), Republicans were more likely than Democrats to state that they had been arrested, by 2 to .7 percent — a small but statistically significant difference. All of the difference in the arrest rates pertained to men.[69]

Trivia

Table 14. Miscellaneous trivia

Issue	Survey	Dem %	Rep %	No. of cases	Conf %	*RP
Owns a dog or cat	Eagleton Center for Public Interest NJ Poll 2003	44.7	61.3	238	98	.73

---

68 "Police Jokes", Retrieved April 19, 2007, from Aha Jokes: http://www.ajokes.com/jokes/2214. html.

69 1991 and 2004 GSS surveys, based on a total of 1528 cases, with statistical significance of 97%, and with a relative proportion of .35.

D   *R*

Displays the flag at home, work, or on car?	Pew 2005 Political Typology Callback	58.2	**76.2**	708	99	.76
Football is favorite sport	Penn, Schoen & Berland 2003	22.0	**31.0**	590	98	.71
Will watch football on New Year's Day	Rusmussen, December 2006	44.0	**55.0**	**1000	95	.80
Will watch football on Thanksgiving	Rusmussen, November 2006	48.0	**58.0**	**1000	95	.83
"Country" is favorite radio format	Penn, Schoen & Berland 2003	14.0	**21.0**	590	96	.67
Likes to travel abroad	Penn, Schoen & Berland 2003	**52.0**	40.0	590	99	1.3
First child is a female	GSS 1994	42.6	**52.5**	738	99	.81
Felt "in touch with someone who had died"	4 GSS surveys from 1984 through 1991	**42.5**	36.7	3325	+99	1.16

*RP is relative proportion, which is the Democratic % divided by the Republican %.
**Case numbers include independents and others.

Last, and least, an Eagleton New Jersey survey found that Democrats were more likely to exclusively drink bottled water by 61 to 50 percent. The significance of this fact is left for the reader to ponder.[70]

CONCLUSIONS

This chapter compares Democrats and Republicans with regard to various aspects of lifestyle. A few conclusions are listed below:

Sex, Marriage, and Family

- Democrats are more likely to have multiple sex partners, but are also more likely to have no sex partners.
- Since the 1980s a "gay gap" has developed among men, with Democrats more likely to say they have engaged in gay sex.
- There has been a growing "marriage gap" since the 1960s. Democrats are less likely to be married because they never married, married and became divorced, or married and became widowed.
- Democrats are more likely to engage in adultery.
- On average, Democrats have their first child at a significantly younger age.

---

70 Ibid, Poll No. 143c, questions qen7 and qd2, May, 2003, based on 555 cases, with 98 percent confidence and a relative proportion of 1.22.

- Democrats and Republicans are about equally likely to have minor children in the household, even though Democrats are less likely to be married when they have those children.

Health

- Republicans report that they are healthier, and this has been true for decades. It is particularly true with respect to mental health.
- Republicans are less likely to smoke tobacco, and more likely to want to ban smoking in public places.
- On the whole, it appears that Democrats are a little more likely to be overweight.
- Democrats are less likely to have health insurance.

Religion

- Although Republicans attend religious services more frequently, survey evidence suggests that Democrats are more likely to be told how to vote by their clergy.
- Republicans are more likely to believe the Bible, literally, and to believe that Jesus Christ was the son of God, and died for our sins.

Entertainment and Leisure

- Democrats watch about 3.5 hours more TV per week than do Republicans.
- Republicans spend more time going "online" from home.
- Republicans are far more likely to perceive that holidays are important and joyous occasions.

Other

- Democrats are more likely to get news from the major networks, while Republicans get it from radio and online sources. They are equally likely to read books.
- A shortage of money is of much more concern to Democrats, and more likely to affect purchase decisions with regard to food, clothing, medical care, and gasoline.
- Republicans are more apt to own their homes, and to keep guns in those homes.

Chapter 2: Who Is More Intelligent, Knowledgeable, and Educated?

Introduction

George Bush, The Chimp

George Bush resembles a chimp in various ways which I will now enumerate: the size of his ears, his intelligence, the look of confusion on his face. Further, democrats are smarter than republicans, and would perform more ably in high positions of governmental power ... [G]iven the facts, I draw the conclusion that Kerry will win the election.

— Blogger named Hildago[1]

Partisans from each side hurl insults; a favorite target for Democrats is the mental acuity of Republicans. In the run-up to the 2004 presidential election, the Internet was filled with proclamations that people in the Democratic "blue states" have higher IQs than those living in the Republican "red states." Many touted a Gallup poll showing that Republicans and less educated people supported the war in Iraq, while Democrats and well-educated people opposed it.[2]

Another survey, conducted in late 2004, showed that nearly half of Bush supporters theorized that Saddam Hussein had weapons of mass destruction and

---

1 Hildago (pseudonym), "Bush & Kerry Round Three: Doin' Damage in Gammage," October 13, 2004, MetaFilter Community Weblog, Retrieved March 11, 2007, from http://www.metafilter.com/36234/Gammage-Auditorium-ASU-that-is.

2 David W. Moore, "War Support and the Education Gap," *The Gallup News Service* (February 11, 2003), Retrieved November 11, 2004, from Http://brain.gallup.com.

provided support to al Qaeda, prior to the U.S. invasion.[3] To most Democrats, these Republican beliefs were irrefutably wrong and were evidence of ignorance, or worse. After the 2004 election, ABC News correspondent Carole Simpson seemed to imply that those voting for Bush lacked basic intelligence: "I look at the election, and I'm going, 'Well, of course our kids are not bright about these things because their parents aren't'"[4]

Simpson's point was suggested by others, albeit in gentler terms. One columnist wrote:

> It has been said that Democrats tend to be too complex and wordy, but they establish realistic and principled platforms. Republicans, on the other hand, generally are said to be superior at conducting campaigns and coming into power.[5]

A psychology professor said it this way:

> Democrats tend to be more intellectual than Republicans, and to focus more on giving good arguments. ... I see Republican candidates making bad arguments and short-sighted policies, but they skillfully press people's moral buttons and they win elections.[6]

Even Republicans may feel intellectually inferior, given that the college crowd leans sharply leftward. It is certainly the case with faculty members. A 1999 survey of 1,643 teachers at 183 four-year colleges found a 5 to 1 ratio of Democrats to Republicans. A 2005 study found an 8 to 1 ratio of Democrats to Republicans at Stanford and a 10 to 1 ratio at Berkeley. And, after studying the political orientation of Ivy League professors, pollster Frank Luntz reported: "Just 6 percent of Ivy League professors would describe themselves as either conservative or somewhat conservative, and only 3 percent consider themselves to be Republicans. So much for diversity."[7]

> Leftists own higher education. At the University of Colorado, 94 percent of the liberal arts faculty are registered Democrats. Of the 85 English professors, zero are registered Republicans. ... Ensconcing their own in our institutions of higher learning has given the left's "Conservatives are stupid" theory a self-created syl-

---

3 Program on International Policy Attitudes of the University of Maryland cited by Alan Wirzbicki, "Divide Seen in Voter Knowledge," in *Boston Globe* (Boston: October 22, 2004), Retrieved January 11, 2005, from: http://www.boston.com/news/nation/washington/articles/2004/10/22/divide_seen_in_voter.

4 "National Press Club Forum," (C-span, November 22, 2004), Retrieved January 13, 2005, from: http://www.mrc.org/notablequotables/2004/nq20041122.asp.

5 Tim Botkin, "Lessons from Our Mud-Slinging Election Season," *Sun Newspaper Online* (November 1, 2004), Retrieved November 10, 2004, from http://www.thesunlink.com.

6 Jonathan Haidt, "Intuitive Ethics: Advice for Democratic Candidates," 2004, Faculty Web Page, Retrieved November 10, 2004, from http://faculty.virginia.edu/haidtlab/articles/haidt.advice-for-democrats.doc.

7 Frank Luntz, "Inside the Mind of an Ivy League Professor," in *FrontPageMagazine.com* (August 30, 2002), Retrieved December 22, 2007, from: http://www.frontpagemag.com/articles/Read.aspx?GUID={08DE7057-EA18-4775-B58A-D7A361431936}.

logism. Professors are smart. Professors are leftists. Ergo, leftists
are smart.

— Marianne M. Jennings, Professor at Arizona State University[8]

Are Republicans less educated and more ignorant than Democrats? To the
contrary, the opposite is the case, and the supporting evidence is substantial and
consistent. In addition, there is some evidence suggesting that, as a group, Republicans may have a bit more "apparent intelligence" than Democrats.[9]

DETAILS

Who has more civic and political knowledge?

Direct Testing

In a Cato Policy Analysis, general political knowledge was assessed on
the basis of responses to a survey conducted by the American National Election Studies (NES). In total, 31 questions and responses were considered. They
didn't require Einstein-like reasoning skills; rather, the questions were "basic in
nature." For example, people were asked to name candidates for the House of
Representatives from their congressional districts, and to identify the political
offices of prominent people in government. They were also asked who controlled
the Senate and the House of Representatives, who was more likely to support
gun control (Gore or Bush), and whether U.S. crime rates had increased or decreased between 1992 and 2000. The average respondent answered only 14.4 of
the 31 questions correctly.[10]

> The arrogance of this C student!
>
> — Actress Barbara Streisand (referring to President George W.
> Bush in a blog posting replete with her own misspellings)[11]

Although the Cato Policy Analysis did not include a breakdown of scores
based on political party alignments, the author of the study, Professor Ilya Somin

---

8 Marianne M. Jennings, "Are Conservatives Dumb?," in *Jewish World Review* (June 17, 2004),
Retrieved October 17, 2007, from: http://www.jewishworldreview.com/cols/jen-
nings061704.asp.

9 Is it possible that Republicans are poorly represented in academia because they have fewer
professional accomplishments? After studying 1643 faculty members from 183 colleges and
universities, researchers concluded: "[E]ven after taking into account the effects of professional accomplishment, along with many other individual characteristics, conservatives
and Republicans teach at lower quality schools than do liberals and Democrats. This suggests that complaints of ideologically-based discrimination in academic advancement deserve serious consideration and further study." (Rothman, Lichter, and Nevitte, "Politics
and Professional Advancement Among College Professors," *The Forum 3*, no. 1 (2005).

10 Ilya Somin, "When Ignorance Isn't Bliss - How Political Ignorance Threatens Democracy,"
Policy Analysis of the Cato Institute no. 525 (September 22, 2004).

11 Mike Baron, "Barbra Streisand: Man-Eater Who Can't Spell," in *Post Chronicle* (March 27, 2006),
Retrieved March 14, 2007, from: http://www.postchroncile.com/news/entertainment/
tittletattle/printer.

of the George Mason School of Law, was kind enough to provide one to me.[12] The breakout he prepared is shown in Figure 50, below.

Figure 50. Number of correct answers out of a potential of 31 (Ilya Somin's analysis of NES 2000 political knowledge questions. Case numbers vary with questions asked.)

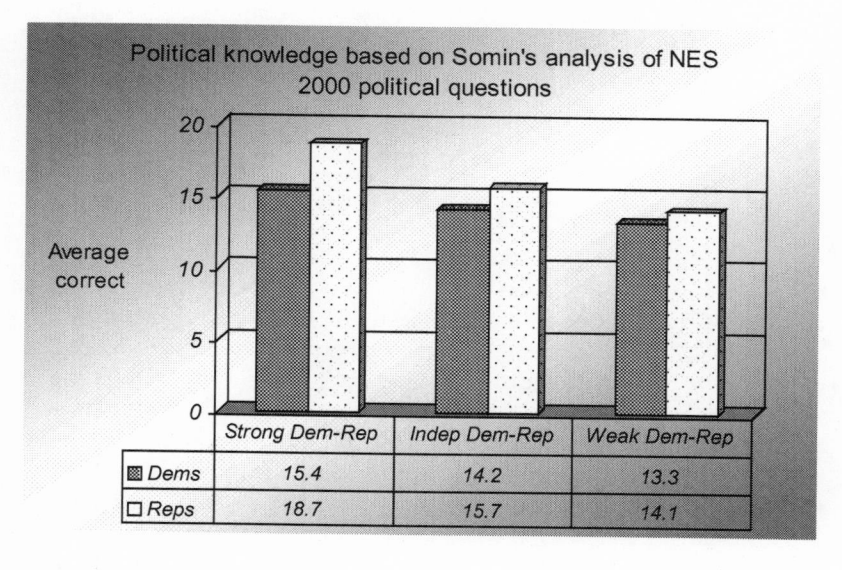

Two observations can be made based on Somin's results: First, people with stronger convictions, regardless of party affiliation, tend to have more knowledge of basic, political facts. For example, a "strong" Democrat tends to have more political knowledge than does a "weak" Democrat. This makes sense, since people with strong convictions probably follow political news stories more closely.

The second observation is that the average Republican seems to have more political knowledge than does the average Democrat. On average, Democrats answered 14.4 questions correctly, while Republicans answered 16.3 correctly (weighted averages of the 3 columns). These results suggest that Democrats may only have 88 percent of the general political knowledge possessed by Republicans.[13]

> I don't want to lay the blame on the Republicans for the Depression. They're not smart enough to think up all those things that have happened.
>
> — Humorist and author Will Rogers[14]

That is only one test, so it must be taken with a grain of salt. However, similar questions have been asked in multiple NES studies, involving numerous cases

---

12 Ilya Somin, e-mail letter to author, November 29, 2004.
13 The calculation is 14.4/16.3 = 88.3%.
14 Arthur Power Dudden, "The Record of Political Humor," *American Quarterly* 37, no. 1 (1985).

and spanning several years. The results are consistent: Democrats are significantly less likely to give correct answers. A summary of the results is presented in Table 15, below.

Table 15. Political questions asked in several NES surveys

Question	No. of cases	Range of test years	Percent correct		Conf %	RP
			Dems	Reps		
Which party had the most Congressmen in Washington before the election this/last month?	22843	21 surveys from 1958 to 2004	55.6	64.8	+99	.86
Which party elected the most Congressmen in the election this/last month?	12252	12 surveys from 1958 to 1984	52.5	58.4	+99	.90
Which party had the most members in the U.S. Senate before the election?	11896	11 surveys from 1982 to 2004	48.6	58.2	+99	.84
Can you name the candidate who ran in this state for U.S. Senate?	5323	7 surveys from 1978 to 1992	39.9	47.9	+99	.83
Name a candidate in the November elections from this district for the House of Representatives?	13544	12 surveys from 1978 to 2000	25.2	30.6	+99	.82
Average percentage correct			44.4	52.0		
Overall proportion (Dem % divided by Rep %)			85.4%			

On average, Democrats were about 85 percent as likely to correctly answer these questions. (See bottom line of Table 15, above.)

> Ignorance is no excuse, it's the real thing.
> — Epigrammatist Irene Peter[15]

Very similar results can be gleaned from the results of a "Multi Investigator Study" conducted in 1998 and 1999.[16] (See Table 16, below.)

15 Irene Peter (attributed), "Womens Media.Com," Retrieved March 14, 2007, from: http://www.womensmedia.com/new/quote-theme-ignorance.shtml.

16 The Multi Investigator Study was a national telephone survey conducted by the Survey Research Center of the University of California at Berkeley, and funded by the National

Table 16 – *Political knowledge questions asked in the 1998-1999 Multi Investigator Study*

Question	No. cases	Survey years	Percent correct		Conf %	*RP
			Dems	Reps		
Which party has the most members in House of Representatives?	544	1998–1999	72.0	79.6	96	.90
What majority is required for an override of a presidential veto?	578	1998–1999	51.0	64.3	+99	.79
Average percentage with correct answers			61.5	72.0		
Overall proportion (Dem % divided by Rep %)			85.4%			

*RP is relative proportion, which is the Democratic % divided by the Republican %.

Other data also suggest that Republicans have, on the whole, more political knowledge than Democrats. In March, 2000, the Gallup Organization surveyed 1024 Democrats, independents, and Republicans to see how many could identify the two presidential candidates (Bush and Gore). The results of this survey, with respect to Democrats and Republicans, are depicted in Figure 51, below.[17]

Figure 51. Who are the presidential candidates? (Gallup poll taken in March, 2000, based on total sample of 1024, including independents, with confidence level of at least 95% and with a relative proportion of .85)

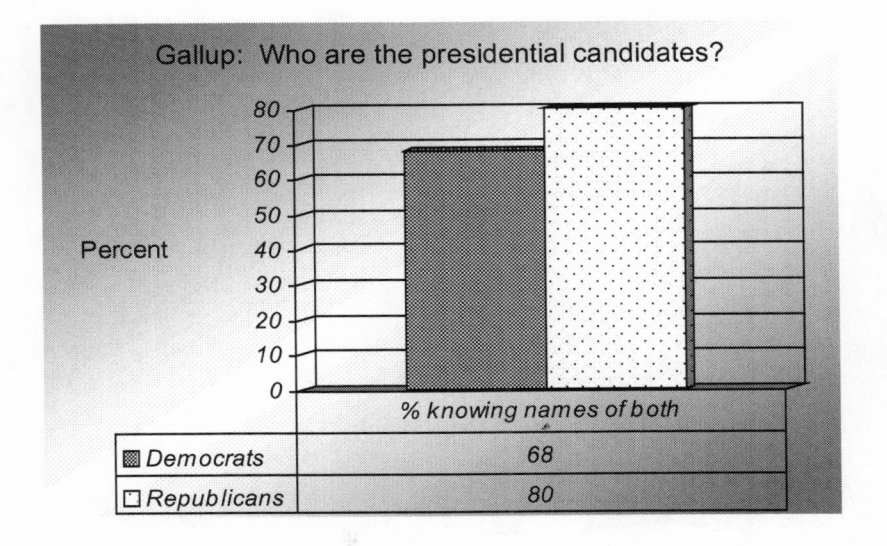

Science Foundation.

17 David W. Moore, "One in Five Americans Unaware That Either Bush or Gore Is a Likely Presidential Nominee," *The Gallup News Service* (March 22, 2000), Retrieved November 11, 2004, from Http://brain.gallup.com.

The percentage of Democrats who answered correctly (68%) was only 85 percent as great as the percentage of Republicans answering correctly (80%).

> The myth of the "dumb" Republican is no more rational than a cultural belief in voodoo or rain dances. It keeps not raining, but the people still believe in it.
>
> — Author and political pundit Ann Coulter[18]

In September, 2003, a "history test" was administered to Democrats and Republicans (and others) by the Gallup Organization. Some of the questions included:

How many senators does each state have?
What is the name of the National Anthem?
Who was the first president of the United States?
Who gave the Gettysburg Address?
Who wrote the "Letter from Birmingham Jail"? (Martin Luther King, Jr.)
Who is the Chief Justice of the Supreme Court?

The results were summarized by the Gallup Organization:

> In general, Republicans outscored Democrats on most of the 10 questions asked. However, this difference likely results from the fact that Republicans tend to be better-educated than Democrats are.[19]

A total of 681 Democrats and Republicans took the 10-question Gallup quiz. On average, Democrats were only 87.5 percent as likely to get the correct answer.

> If liberals were prevented from ever again calling Republicans dumb, they would be robbed of half their arguments. To be sure, they would still have "racist," "fascist," "homophobe," "ugly," and a few other highly nuanced arguments in the quiver. But the loss of "dumb" would nearly cripple them."
>
> – Author and political pundit Ann Coulter[20]

In a 2004 NES survey, respondents were also asked to identify four prominent political figures. The percentage of Democrats and Republicans correctly identifying the people is depicted in Figure 52, below. On average, Democrats were correct 43.2 percent of the time, while Republicans were correct 53.4 percent of the time. In other words, Democrats answered correctly about 81 percent as often as did Republicans.[21]

---

18 Ann Coulter, *Slander* (New York: Crown, 2002), 123.
19 George H. Gallup Jr., "How Many Americans Know U.S. History? Part I," *The Gallup News Service* (October 21, 2003), Retrieved November 11, 2004, from Http://brain.gallup.com.
20 Coulter, *Slander*, 127.
21 The calculation is 43.2/53.4 = 81%.

Figure 52. Can you identify this person? (2004 NES survey, based on 740 cases for all columns, with confidence level of 97% for the left-side column and 99+% for all other columns, and with relative proportions of, left to right, .62, .92, .76, .71, and .81)

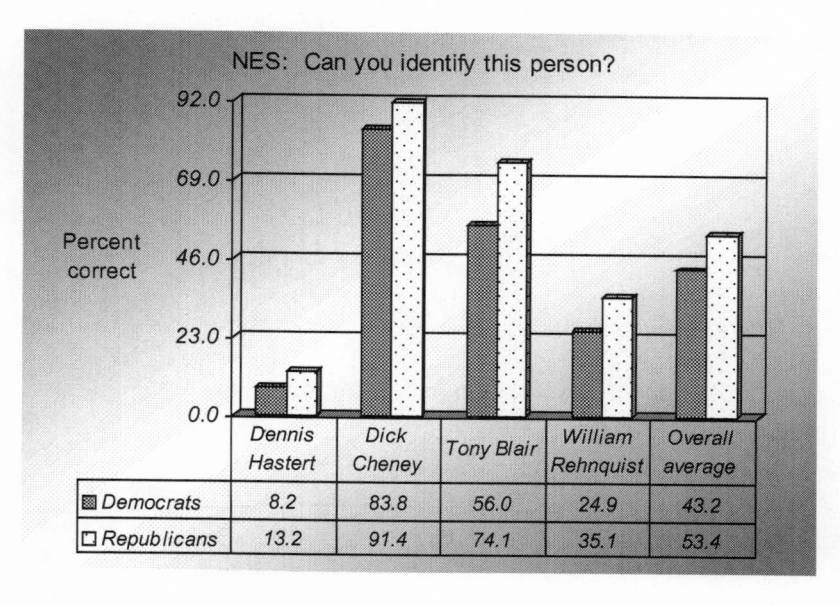

	Dennis Hastert	Dick Cheney	Tony Blair	William Rehnquist	Overall average
▨ Democrats	8.2	83.8	56.0	24.9	43.2
▢ Republicans	13.2	91.4	74.1	35.1	53.4

When I listen to the Republicans in Congress on foreign policy, there's such an "I'm stupid and proud of it" attitude.

— Thomas L. Friedman, Columnist, speaking on Face the Nation in 1999[22]

Democrats may now be closing the political knowledge gap, according to Pew surveys conducted in 2000 through 2007. The Pew surveys included many questions directly related to political knowledge, and these are shown in Table 17, below. Although Democrats were only about 88 percent as likely to give correct answers (see bottom-line results), a careful review of the table reveals an interesting pattern. In the Pew surveys conducted in 2000 through 2006 Democrats were only about 82 percent as likely to give correct answers, but that percentage increased to about 96 percent for questions asked in early 2007. This 96 percent rate is far higher than for any other series of political questions I came across, and may reflect the political interest and enthusiasm Democrats had in the wake of the 2006 congressional elections. Democrats did particularly well with regard to questions about Iraq and the new Democratic leadership. Note that Table 17 does not include a few questions for which there was no statistical difference, and if those questions were added, the gap would probably narrow slightly. [23]

---

22 Thomas L. Friedman quoted by Ben Stein and Phil DeMuth, "Can America Survive?," (Carlsbad:New Beginnings Press, 2004), 124.
23 Please see Appendix F on page 364 for more information regarding this survey source.

Table 17. Political questions asked in recent Pew surveys

Pew Survey	Question	Percent correct		Conf %	*RP
		Dems	Reps		
Feb 2007 922 cases	Who is Arnold Schwarzenegger? (Governor of California or actor)	91.5	**97.5**	+99	.94
Feb 2007 922 cases	Who is Barack Obama? (presidential candidate or Democratic leader)	**68.6**	60.7	+99	1.13
Feb 2007 922 cases	Who is Nancy Pelosi? (Speaker, San Francisco politician, Democratic leader)	49.6	**54.9**	98	.90
Feb 2007 922 cases	Who is Harry Reid? (Senate majority leader, senator, or Democratic leader)	13.7	**16.7**	**93	.82
Feb 2007 922 cases	Who is the United States Vice President? (Dick Cheney or Richard Cheney)	70.9	**79.2**	+99	.90
Feb 2007 922 cases	Who is your state governor?	66.8	**72.5**	99	.92
Feb 2007 922 cases	Who is the President of Russia? (Putin or Vladimir Putin)	35.2	**40.1**	97	.88
Feb 2007 922 cases	Does the Iraq "surge" strategy call for an increase or decrease in troops? (increase)	**90.7**	88.3	**91	1.03
Feb 2007 922 cases	Which party has a majority in the U.S. House of Reps? (Democratic Party)	79.4	**82.8**	**94	.96
Feb 2007 922 cases	In Iraq, have there been more civilian deaths or more troop deaths? (more civilian)	71.8	**75.3**	**92	.95
Feb 2007 922 cases	Who is the former mayor of NYC who may run for president? (Rudolph Giuliani)	61.5	**68.1**	99	.90
Feb 2007 922 cases	Bush's surge plan calls for an increase of about how many troops? (20,000, at the time)	**72.6**	67.0	99	1.08
June 2006 1285 cases	Who is the current Secretary of State? (Condi or Condoleeza Rice)	42.5	**46.1**	**93	.92
June 2006 1285 cases	Who is the president of Russia (Putin or Vladimir Putin)	30.3	**36.5**	+99	.83
Dec 2004 1303 cases	When is Iraq scheduled to hold its first election? (this winter)	53.5	**61.5**	+99	.87

June 2004 1964 cases	What terrorist group struck the U.S.A. on September 11, 2001? (al Qaeda)	61.9	**73.7**	+99	.84
June 2004 1964 cases	Which political party has a majority in the House of Representatives?" (Republicans)	57.7	**65.5**	+99	.88
Jan 2003 – 759 cases	What Senate majority leader resigned due to his controversial comments? (Lott)	46.2	**50.9**	**92	.91
June 2002 643 cases	Who is the current Secretary of State? (Powell or Colin Powell)	47.3	**58.2**	+99	.81
June 2002 1910 cases	Do you happen to know the name of the new European currency? (Euro)	38.7	**53.5**	+99	.72
June 2002 1910 cases	When was the state of Israel was created? (1852, 1948, or 1960?" (1948)	36.3	**49.4**	+99	.73
June 2002 641 cases	Who is the current Secretary of Defense? (Rumsfeld or Donald Rumsfeld)	27.8	**35.2**	+99	.79
June 2002 626 cases	Who is the current vice president of the United States?" (Dick/Richard Cheney)	58.8	**70.7**	+99	.83
Jan 2002 738 cases	Which Latin America country has been in a political/economic crisis lately? (Argentina)	22.7	**29.2**	+99	.78
June 2001 419 cases	What political party has a majority in the U.S. Senate? (Democrats)	52.5	**68.6**	+99	.77
April 2001 381 cases	Did Senate vote for a larger or smaller tax cut than proposed by Pres. Bush? (smaller)	40.0	**55.0**	+99	.73
April 2001 381 cases	Did the Senate pass the McCain-Feingold campaign finance reform bill? (yes)	18.9	**26.6**	97	.71
April 2001 381 cases	Was Slobodan Milosevic (former Yugoslavian president) arrested? (yes)	44.7	**52.8**	95	.85
April 2001 381 cases	Did President Bush propose to increase or decrease the education budget? (increase)	55.6	**65.2**	98	.85
July 2000 1243 cases	Which candidate proposed Social Security private investment accounts? (Bush)	25.5	**35.3**	+99	.72

July 2000 1243 cases	Which candidate proposed reducing U.S. nukes unilateral, if necessary? (Bush)	14.6	**22.1**	+99	.66
July 2000 1243 cases	Which candidate proposed using Medicare surplus to protect the program? (Gore)	**31.3**	27.6	95	1.13
June 2000 1897 cases	Who is Alan Greenspan? (Federal Reserve Chairman)	41.3	**55.7**	+99	.74
June 2000 1897 cases	Did the Federal Reserve recently cut interest rates? (raised rates)	52.6	**64.9**	+99	.81
Average percentage with correct answers		49.2	**56.1**		
Overall proportion (Dem % divided by Rep %)		**87.7%**			

*RP is relative proportion, which is the Democratic % divided by the Republican %.
**Marginally significant

> Eighty percent of Republicans are just Democrats who don't know what's going on.
>
> — Robert Kennedy, Jr., Environmental lawyer and political pundit[24]

Reality check — Neither constituency does well

Although Republicans have the edge with regard to basic political knowledge, there is plenty of ignorance in both constituencies. Apparently, the American educational system is not preparing us to assume our citizenship responsibilities. The dismal state of civics education was addressed in a forum held by the Center for Public& Nonprofit Leadership. One participant noted:

> The schools no longer teach civics, and if you have kids yourself, you probably understand that. Only about 10 percent of public schools teach civics. ... How do you teach people what they should know about being engaged in civic life, about how they can, in fact, change the policy framework? Many do not understand how the city council works, and do not understand how the state legislature works and, in fact, do not even know how to vote.[25]

Interviewer Impressions

> Better to remain silent and be thought a fool, than to speak and remove all doubt.
>
> — President Abraham Lincoln[26]

---

24 Greg Esposito, "RFK Jr. Rips President Bush for Environmental Policy," *The Roanoke Times* (2007), Retrieved February 28, 2007, from http://www.roanoke.com/news/nrv/wb/106349.

25 Geri Mannion, "Nonprofit Voter Engagement Initiatives: Expanding the Electorate, Inspiring Participation," in *Issues Forum*, ed. Center for Public & Nonprofit Leadership (Georgetown University, May 1, 2006), Retrieved April 19, 2007, from: http://cpnl.georgetown.edu/doc_pool/NonprofitVoterEngagement%20InitiativesTranscript.pdf.

26 Abraham Lincoln as cited by Daniel E. Cummins, "Lincoln Logs of Wisdom," (Lawjobs.com, 2006), Retrieved March 24, 2007, from: http://www.law.com/jsp/law/careercenter/lawAr-

---

In several surveys, NES asked its interviewers to assess each respondent's "general level of information about politics and public affairs." This was done by categorizing the level of knowledge as "very high ... fairly high ... average ... fairly low [or] very low." Figure 53, below, shows the percentages of Democrats and Republicans who were categorized as having a "very high" or "fairly high" level of knowledge in the 5 NES surveys conducted in 1996 through 2004. On average, 40.4 percent of Democrats and 54.3 percent of Republicans received these ratings for the 5 year period, in aggregate. This means that Democrats were about 74 percent as likely as Republicans to be judged as having a very or fairly high level of knowledge.[27]

Figure 53. Interviewer's assessment of respondents' "general level of information about politics and public affairs" (assessments made in 5 consecutive NES pre-election surveys conducted in 1996 through 2004, based on, left to right, 1101, 814, 1068, 970, and 707 cases, with confidence level of 99+% for all differences, and with relative proportions of, left to right, .70, .73, .67, .85, and .73)

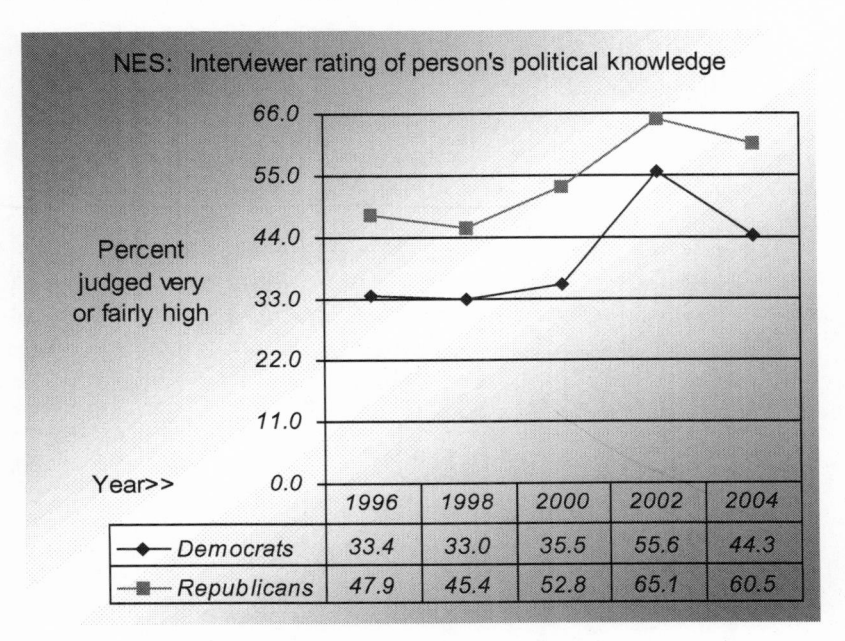

NES: Interviewer rating of person's political knowledge

Year>>	1996	1998	2000	2002	2004
Democrats	33.4	33.0	35.5	55.6	44.3
Republicans	47.9	45.4	52.8	65.1	60.5

Time Spent Reading Or Watching Political News

Half the American people never read a newspaper. Half never vote for President — the same half?

— Novelist Gore Vidal[28]

---

ticleCareerCenter.jsp?id=1171015369928.

27 The calculation is 40.4/54.3 = 74.4%.

28 Gore Vidal quoted by Herbert Mitgang, "Books of the Times: One Affair with Movies and One of Sacrifice," in *New York Times* (NY: September 23, 1992).

By analyzing the cumulative results of numerous surveys of the American National Election Studies, we can determine that Republicans, over the long haul, have been slightly more likely to read about or watch programs about specific political candidates and campaigns.

Table 18. NES cumulative surveys: Questions reflecting on one's diligence in following political activities

Question	No. of cases	Range of test years	Percent "Yes"		Conf %	*RP
			Dems	Reps		
Did you watch the campaign on TV?	20139	19 surveys from 1952 to 2004	78.1	80.6	+99	.97
Did you hear about campaign on the radio?	18363	17 surveys from 1952 to 2004	43.9	47.4	+99	.93
Did you read about campaign in magazines?	16027	15 surveys from 1952 to 2004	30.3	39.2	+99	.77
Did you read about the campaign in newspapers?	19608	19 surveys from 1952 to 2004	69.2	74.8	+99	.93
Average percentages			55.4	60.5		
Overall proportion (Dem % divided by Rep %)			91.6%			

*RP is relative proportion, which is the Democratic % divided by the Republican %.

Based upon the NES survey results (Table 18, above) we might conclude that, on average, Democrats are about 92 percent as likely as Republicans to pay attention to political campaigns and candidates. However, recent survey information suggests that Republican interest in political news has waned since 2004, and there is now a rough parity in the political news appetites of Democrats and Republicans. In a Biennial News Consumption survey, released in July 2006, Pew found that Democrats and Republicans are equally likely to have "high interest" in "hard news," defined as political, international, and business news. Perhaps the drop in Republican news interest between 2004 and 2006 was caused by the GOP's loss of control of Congress, or by the discouraging news from Iraq, prior to the security improvement resulting from the military "surge."

It is also important to realize that, with the exception of Fox News, certain radio political talk shows (such as Rush Limbaugh), and Internet news, Democrats are more likely to watch and listen to most general news programming, including National Public Radio, CNN, PBS, the broadcast evening news shows, and local news shows.

Reality check — The impact of perceived media bias

> So you look at what's happened to the liberal media in the last few months and years, Jayson Blair, the New York Times, lying about circulation at Newsday and all these other newspapers, CBS running with bogus [Bush's National Guard] documents. The list is expanding. The old media is losing credibility and audience by refusing to acknowledge that and clean up its act.
>
> — Author and radio talk show host Rush Limbaugh[29]

Media preferences, discussed above, may be driven by concerns about media bias. Republicans are much more skeptical regarding the accuracy and fairness of reporting by major news organizations. This phenomenon was described by Pew in one of its 2006 reports:

> Republicans express less confidence than Democrats in the credibility of nearly every major news outlet, with the exception of Fox News Channel. Among TV and radio sources, the partisan gap is particularly evident for the NewsHour with Jim Lehrer and NPR — Democrats are twice as likely as Republicans to say they believe all or most of what these outlets report, placing them among the *most* credible sources for Democrats, and among the *least* credible for Republicans.[30]

However, Republicans don't always want objective news coverage. When it comes to the "War on Terror," Republicans are more likely to want pro-American news coverage rather than neutral news coverage. This was the expressed view of 33.5 percent of surveyed Republicans, versus 19.5 percent of surveyed Democrats.[31]

Who has more scientific knowledge?

> The Bush administration has declared war on science. In the Orwellian world of 21st century America, two plus two no longer equals four where public policy is concerned, and science is no exception. When a right-wing theory is contradicted by an inconvenient scientific fact, the science is not refuted; it is simply discarded or ignored.
>
> — Howard Dean, Chairman of the Democratic National Committee[32]

In 2006, GSS asked several questions designed to assess scientific knowledge. With regard to very simple questions (i.e., idiot level), there was no significant difference in the likelihood that Democrats and Republicans would answer

29 Rush Limbaugh, "Final Days of Elite Media Empire," (Radio show transcript:Rushlimbaugh. com, September 10, 2004).

30 "Online Papers Modestly Boost Newspaper Readership," *Pew Research Center Survey Reports* (July 30, 2007), Retrieved December 19, 2007, from http://people-press.org/reports/pdf/282. pdf.

31 Pew News Interest Index survey dated June 26, 2005, based on 938 cases, with 99+% significance, and relative proportion of .58.

32 Howard Dean, "Bush's War on Science," *Common Dreams News Center* (July 5, 2004), Retrieved August 3, 2007, from http://www.commondreams.org/views04/0705-04.htm.

correctly. For example, both groups were about equally likely to know that electrons are smaller than atoms (73% correct), the earth goes around the sun (81% correct), and the center of the earth is very hot (94% correct).

There were a few tougher questions, however, and on those Republicans were more likely to answer correctly. These are shown in Table 19, below.

Table 19. GSS 2006 survey: Basic science questions

Question	No. of cases	Percent correct		Conf %	*RP
		Dems	Reps		
Is it true that "all radioactivity is man-made?	920	80.6	**88.1**	+99	.91
Do "antibiotics kill viruses as well as bacteria"?	996	56.4	**69.3**	+99	.81
Do "lasers work by focusing sound waves"?	685	64.1	**74.9**	+99	.86
Is astrology scientific?	1058	63.0	**77.9**	+99	.81
Average percentages		66.0	**77.6**		
Overall proportion (Dem % divided by Rep %)	85.1%				

*RP is relative proportion, which is the Democratic % divided by the Republican %.

Figure 54. Is it true that…? (GSS survey conducted in 2006, based on, left to right, 940 and 741 cases, with confidence level of 99+% for each column, and relative proportions of .1.34 and 1.40)

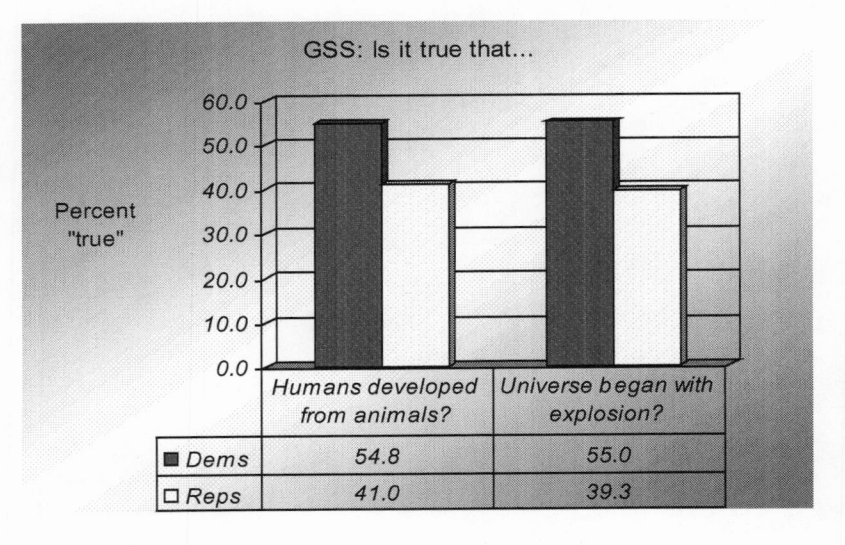

What Happens When Science Collides With Religion?

> Republicans don't believe in the imagination, partly because so few of them have one, but mostly because it gets in the way of their chosen work, which is to destroy the human race and the planet.

— Columnist Michael Feingold[33]

Republicans are sometimes accused of being anti-science, and there may be some truth to that charge with regard to certain questions that force a choice between science and religion. Responses to two such questions, involving evolution and the "big bang" theory of the universe, are shown in Figure 54. In each case we see that Republicans are more likely to reject the consensus position of the scientific community.

A Gallup survey, conducted in June, 2007, confirms the results pertaining to evolution. By 57 to 30 percent, Democrats were more likely to state that they believed in evolution. Most of the Republicans who rejected the theory cited religious beliefs as the reason.[34]

Figure 55. Do you have (at least) a high school diploma? (Men) (NES surveys conducted in 1956 through 2004, based on, left to right, 2371, 2343, 2490, 2786, and 2042 cases, with confidence level of 99+% for all differences, and with relative proportions of, left to right, .78, .79, .78, .84, and .90)

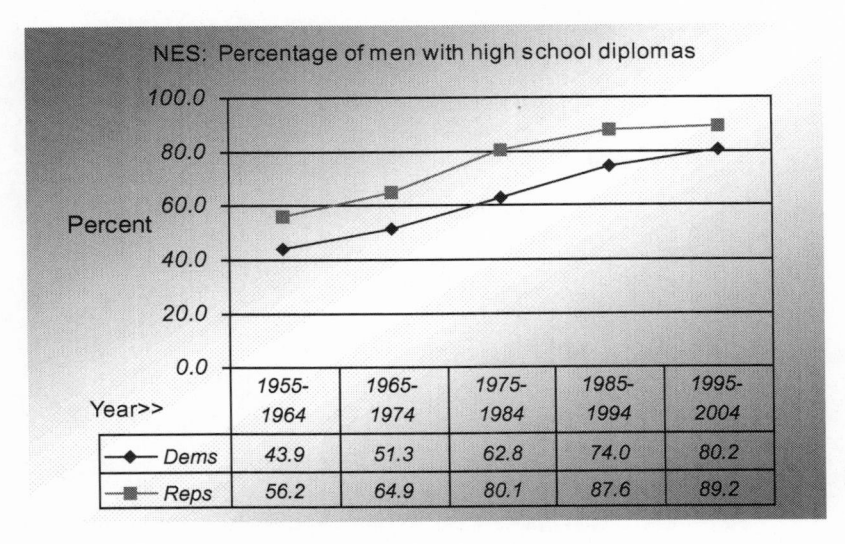

NES: Percentage of men with high school diplomas

Year>>	1955-1964	1965-1974	1975-1984	1985-1994	1995-2004
Dems	43.9	51.3	62.8	74.0	80.2
Reps	56.2	64.9	80.1	87.6	89.2

33 Michael Feingold, "Foreman's Wake-up Call," *Village Voice* (January 21-27, 2004), Retrieved December 8, 2006, from http://www.villagevoice.com.

34 Frank Newport, "Majority of Republicans Doubt Theory of Evolution," *The Gallup News Service* (June 11, 2007), Retrieved July 30, 2007, from Http://brain.gallup.com. The results were based upon a survey of 1,007 adults.

Who has more formal education?

> Education's purpose is to replace an empty mind with an open one.
> — Publisher Malcolm S. Forbes[35]

High School Diplomas

NES has been collecting data regarding diploma and degree attainment for more than 5 decades, and during that time Republicans have been more likely than Democrats to earn high school diplomas. Figure 55 shows the 50-year trend lines for men.

As shown in Figure 56, below, there has been a similar diploma disparity for women.

Figure 56. Do you have (at least) a high school diploma? (Women) (NES surveys conducted in 1956 through 2004, based on, left to right, 3017, 3332, 3682, 3690, and 2667 cases, with confidence level of 99+% for all differences, and with relative proportions of, left to right, .82, .79, .84, .88, and .90)

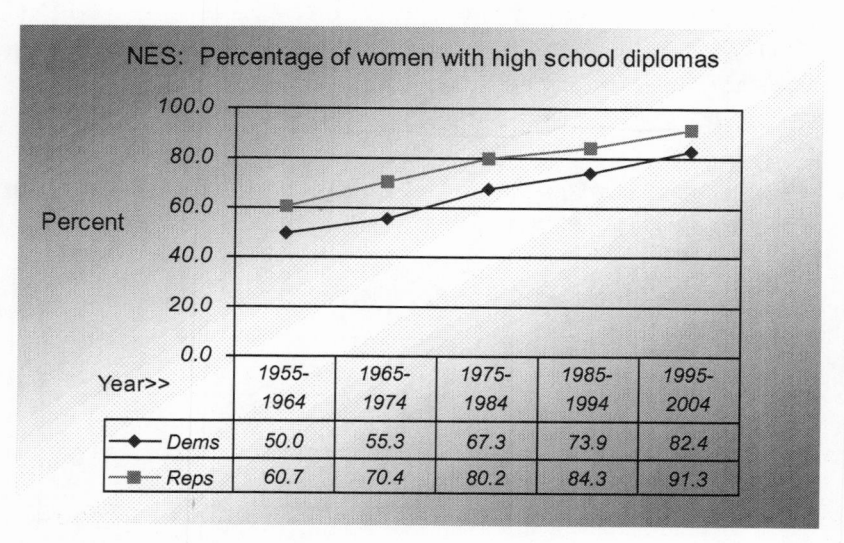

> Brains, you know, are suspect in the Republican Party.
> — Author and journalist Walter Lippmann[36]

By the way, contrary to popular perceptions, women are not less likely than men to have a high school diploma, and this has been true for at least 50 years.

---

35 Malcolm Forbes (attributed), "Quotations on Teaching, Learning, and Education," (National Teaching & Learning Forum), Retrieved March 27, 2007, from: http://www.ntlf.com/html/lib/quotes.htm.

36 Walter Lippman (attributed), *Simpson's Contemporary Quotations* (1988).

Compare the high school graduation rates for men (Figure 55) to the percentages for women (Figure 56).

Surveys conducted by other organizations also show a Republican high school diploma advantage. For example, GSS surveys are show this tendency. (See Appendix B 1.) And, in a report entitled, "Who are the Democrats," Gallup notes:

> Although both Democrats and Republicans have equal numbers of Americans at the upper end of the educational spectrum — that is, with post graduate degrees — Democrats are more likely than Republicans to be in the category of those with only high school educations or less.[37]

Thus, there is agreement by all major survey entities: Republicans are more likely to have, at the least, a high school diploma.[38]

Four-Year College Degrees

> College-bred is a four-year loaf, using dad's dough, coming out half-baked, with a lot of crust.

> — Anonymous[39]

Although the Gallup Organization explicitly commented on the disparity in high school diplomas, it did not address the significant gap in 4-year college degrees. Republican males have dominated at this level (Figure 57).

Figure 57. Do you have a 4-year college diploma (at the least)? (Men) (NES surveys conducted in 1955 through 2004, based on, left to right, 2371, 2343, 2490, 2786, and 2042 cases, with confidence level of 99+% for all differences, and with relative proportions of, left to right, .45, .48, .51, .60, and .63)

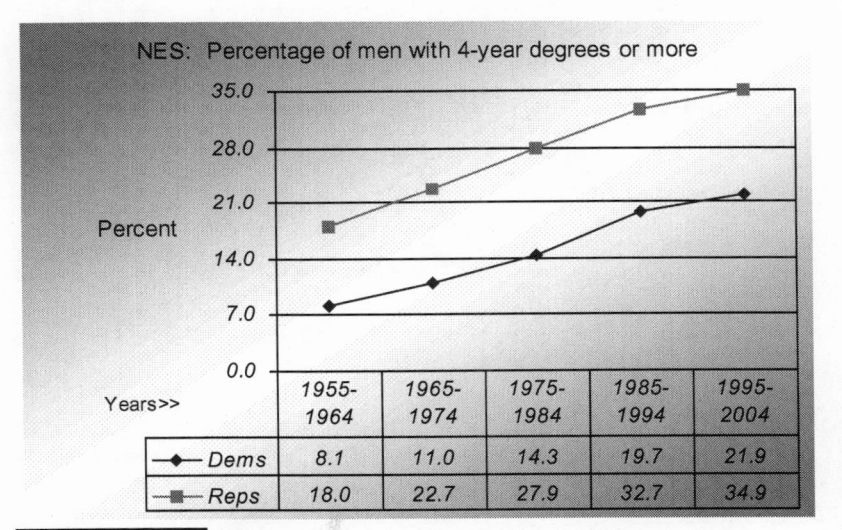

NES: Percentage of men with 4-year degrees or more

Years>>	1955-1964	1965-1974	1975-1984	1985-1994	1995-2004
Dems	8.1	11.0	14.3	19.7	21.9
Reps	18.0	22.7	27.9	32.7	34.9

37 Frank Newport, "Who Are the Democrats?," *The Gallup News Service* (August 11, 2000), Retrieved March 13, 2006, from Http://brain.gallup.com.

38 . For GSS surveys pertaining to high school graduation rates, see Appendix B 1.

39 "Quotationz.Com."

The 4-year college degree gap is smaller for women, but still significant, according to NES (Figure 58). Important note: GSS surveys show a much smaller disparity in the attainment of 4-year degrees by Democratic and Republican women. In fact, GSS shows virtually no gap in recent years. Please see Figure 284 on page 347.

Figure 58. Do you have a 4-year college diploma (or higher degree)? (Women) (NES surveys conducted in 1955 through 2004, based on, left to right, 3017, 3332, 3682, 3690, and 2667 cases, with confidence level of 99+% for all differences, and with relative proportions of, left to right, .66, .49, .66, .74, and .74)

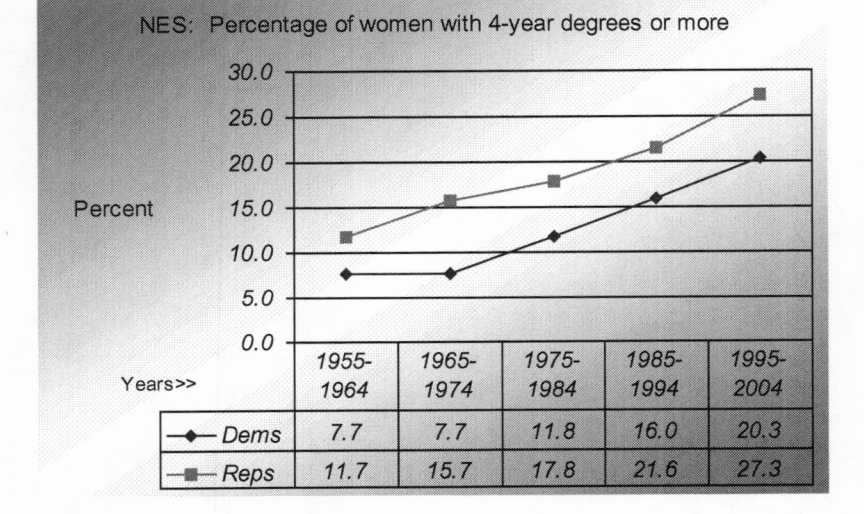

NES: Percentage of women with 4-year degrees or more				
Years>>	1955-1964	1965-1974	1975-1984	1985-1994	1995-2004
Dems	7.7	7.7	11.8	16.0	20.3
Reps	11.7	15.7	17.8	21.6	27.3

What a waste it is to lose one's mind. Or not to have a mind is being very wasteful. How true that is.

— Vice President Dan Quayle[40]

It is interesting to note (by comparing Figure 57 with Figure 58) that Republican males have earned 4-year college degrees at a significantly higher rate than Republican females. On the other hand, Democratic men and women have earned college degrees at approximately the same rate. GSS and Pew surveys on 4-year college degrees attainment rates can be found in Appendix B 2.

Reality check — Are college campuses infested with Republicans?

You may be wondering why more Republicans have college degrees, yet the student bodies of colleges seem to lean to the political left. It is truly not a mystery. Although college students tend to be Democrats (or liberals of some sort), many eventually become Republicans (or conservatives of some type) after they graduate, get jobs, and start their families. This explanation is supported

---

40 Elizabeth Knowles, ed., *Oxford Dictionary of Twentieth Century Quotations* (Oxford: Oxford University Press, 1998), 258.

by survey evidence, discussed on page 266, suggesting that Democrats are more likely to become Republicans, than vice versa. Also, when it comes to earning advanced (graduate school) degrees, there is a rough parity between Democrats and Republicans.

Graduate School Degrees

A university is what a college becomes when the faculty loses interest in students.

— Poet John Ciardi[41]

NES also shows a small but significant difference between Democratic and Republican men with regard to advanced university degrees, with Republican males having the edge.

Figure 59. Do you have a graduate college degree? (Men) (NES surveys conducted in 1955 through 2004, based on, left to right, 2371, 2343, 2490, 2786, and 2042 cases, with confidence level of, left to right, 99+%, 99+%, 97%, zero (not significant), and 99+% for all differences, and with relative proportions of, left to right, .29, .55, .73, n/a, and .89)

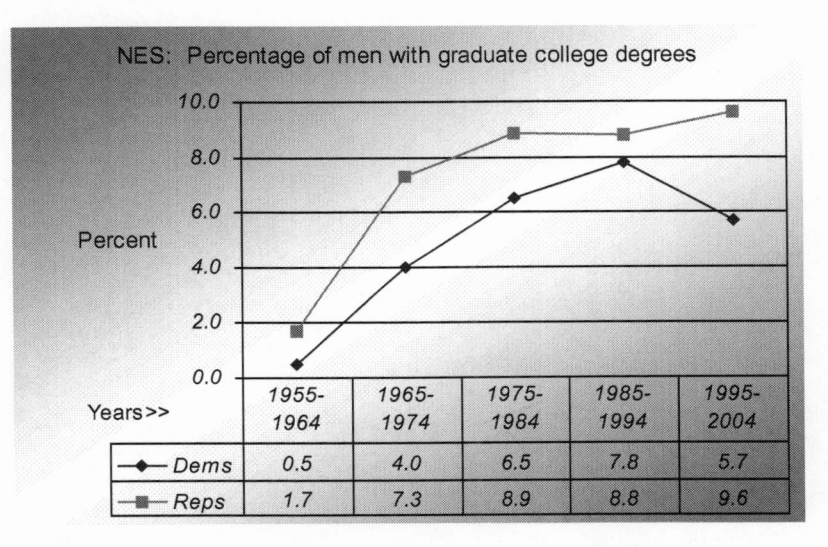

With regard to women, however, NES shows no difference in the rate of attainment of advanced degrees. None of the differences in Figure 60, below, is significant.

Figure 60. Do you have a graduate college degree? (Women) (NES surveys conducted in 1955 through 2004, based on, left to right, 3017, 3332, 3682, 3690, and 2667 cases, with no statistical significance for any of the differences depicted)

---

41 John Ciardi cited by W.W. Betts. Jr. in, "Hermes and Apollo," *Peabody Journal of Education* 48, no. 1 (1970): 49.

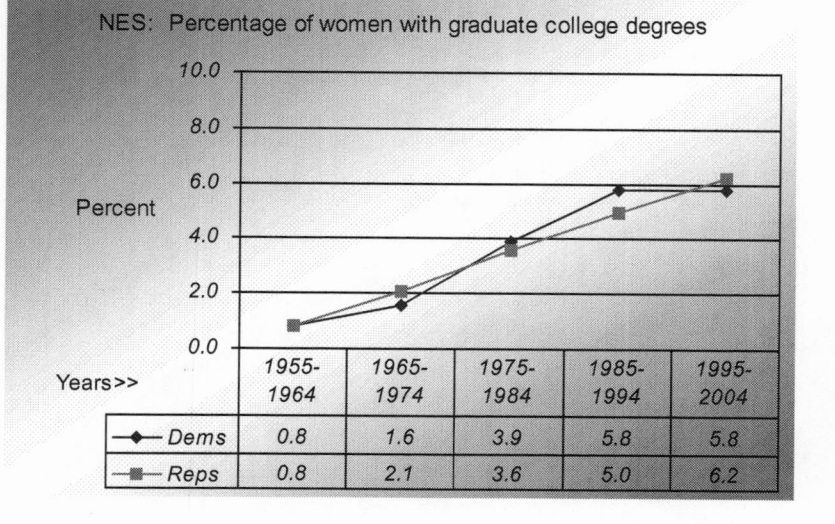

NES: Percentage of women with graduate college degrees

Years>>	1955-1964	1965-1974	1975-1984	1985-1994	1995-2004
Dems	0.8	1.6	3.9	5.8	5.8
Reps	0.8	2.1	3.6	5.0	6.2

I never meant to say that the Conservatives are generally stupid. I meant to say that stupid people are generally Conservative. I believe that is so obviously and universally admitted a principle that I hardly think any gentleman will deny it.

— John Stuart Mill, English philosopher and economist[42]

Figure 61. Do you have a graduate school degree? (Women) (GSS surveys conducted in 1977 through 2006, based on, left to right, 3017, 3332, and 3682 cases, with confidence level of, left to right, zero, 99% and 99+%, and with relative proportions of, left to right, n/a, 1.37, and 1.42)

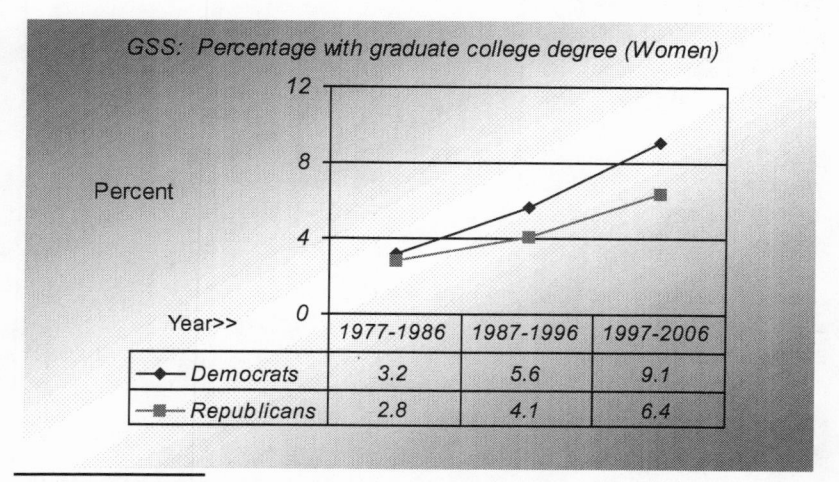

GSS: Percentage with graduate college degree (Women)

Year>>	1977-1986	1987-1996	1997-2006
Democrats	3.2	5.6	9.1
Republicans	2.8	4.1	6.4

---

42 John Stuart Mill in, "Letter to the Conservative MP, Sir John Pakington (March, 1866)," (Spartacus Educational), Retrieved April 8, 2007, from: http://www.spartacus.schoolnet. co.uk/PRmill.htm.

In most cases, GSS survey results are similar to NES results; however, that is not the case with regard to the attainment of graduate school degrees by women. GSS surveys show that, during the last 30 years, Democratic women have pulled ahead of Republican women, and now are more likely to earn an advanced degree. These results are shown in Figure 61, above.

Thus, we can conclude that Republicans have had a small but consistent advantage with regard to formal education for several decades, with one exception: the attainment of graduate school degrees by women. NES surveys show that Democratic and Republican females have been equally likely to earn advanced college degrees during the last 50 years. And, in conflict with the NES results, GSS surveys show that Democratic women have already overtaken their Republican complements with regard to the attainment of advanced degrees.

Who is more intelligent?

> Intelligence recognizes what has happened. Genius recognizes what will happen.
>
> — Poet John Ciardi[43]

Interviewer Impressions

We noted that NES interviewers are asked to give an overall ranking to the political knowledge of each respondent. Likewise, they are asked to give an assessment of the "apparent intelligence" of each survey participant. Of course, the interviewers are not trained psychologists administering IQ tests, so we must add a large grain of salt when utilizing this information. Nevertheless, it is entirely possible that an interviewer would have a feel for the alertness and mental quickness of a participant, after asking him/her many questions over an extended period of time.[44]

The assessments made during each pre-election survey conducted in 1996 through 2004 are summarized in Figure 62, below, and the percentages of Democrats and Republicans judged to have "fairly" or "very high" intelligence are shown. The differences are quite large. On average (for the 5 surveys in aggregate), 48.8 percent of Democrats were rated fairly or very high in intelligence, whereas 64.4 percent of Republicans were given that assessment. Expressed another way, Democrats were about 76 percent as likely to be judged to have fairly or very high intelligence.[45]

Figure 62. Interviewer's concluding assessment of "apparent intelligence" (consecutive NES pre-election surveys conducted in 1996 through 2004, based on, left to right, 1099, 814, 927, 970, and 707 cases, with confidence level of 99+% for all 5 differences, and relative proportions of, left to right, .71, .71, .74, .83, and .78)

---

43 John Ciardi (attributed), "Simpson's Contemporary Quotations," (Houghlin Mifflin Company, 1988).

44 NES conducts "face-to-face" survey interviews in all presidential election years. Often these sessions last for more than an hour.

45 The calculation is 48.8/64.4 = 75.8%.

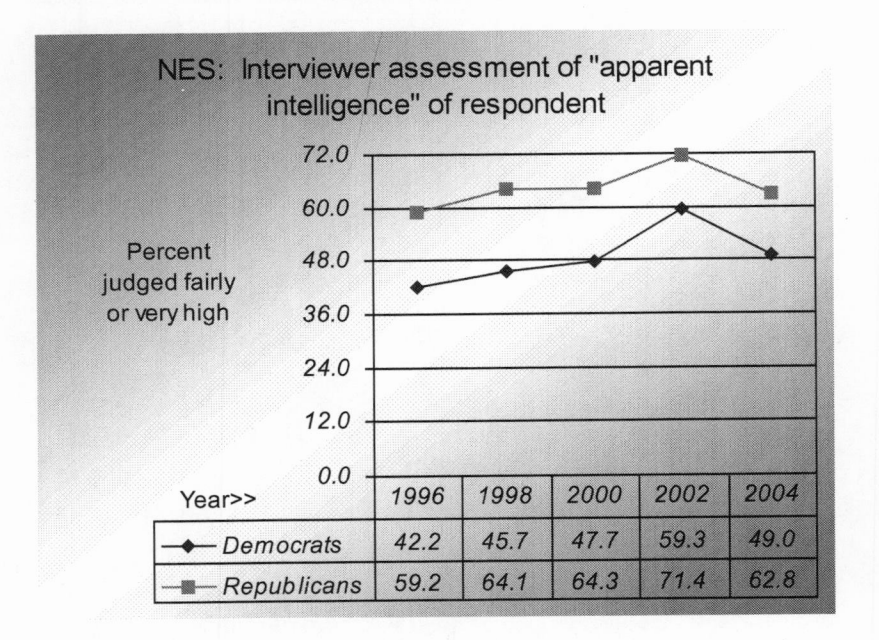

Tests of Reasoning Ability (Or What's Your "Fruit IQ"?)

I had a lot of experience with people smarter than I am.
— President Gerald Ford[46]

Figure 63. "In what way are an orange and a banana alike?" (GSS survey conducted in 1994, based on 1872 cases, with confidence level of 99+%, and with a relative proportion of .92)

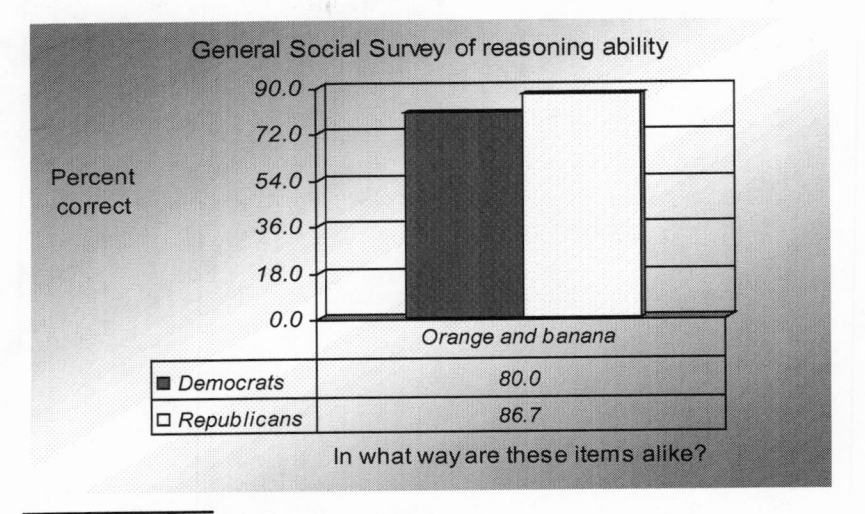

---

46 President Gerald Ford (attributed), "Brainyquote.Com."

Do Democrats and Republicans differ in their ability to reason? I could not find an abundance of information addressing that subject but, in 1994, the General Social Survey asked respondents 8 questions that could be used to test reasoning ability. Statistically significant differences were found with regard to 6 of the 8 questions, and in each of those cases the Republican respondents were slightly more likely to answer correctly. The results for the six questions are shown in charts below. Unfortunately, the answer options were not published by GSS.

> I won't insult your intelligence by suggesting that you really believe what you just said.
>
> — William F. Buckley, Author and political commentator[47]

Most people had no difficulty with the question about fruit (Figure 63). The question about an egg and seed (Figure 64) was more difficult — especially for Democrats.

Figure 64. "In what way are an egg and seed alike?" (GSS survey conducted in 1994, based on 1745 cases, with confidence level of 99+%, and with a relative proportion of .73)

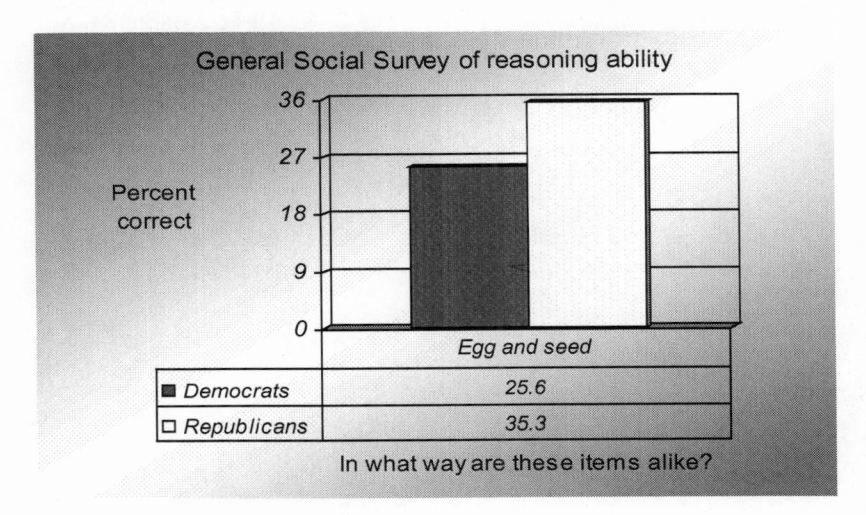

Almost everyone had difficulty with regard to "work and play." The correct answer rate was in single digits for constituents of either party (Figure 65).

> "Weird" may have been okay during my upbringing, but "stupid" most emphatically was not. And Republican affiliation seemed to my parents to represent the most glaring and appalling example of stupidity.
>
> — Michael Medved, Author and radio talk show host[48]

---

47 William F. Buckley (attributed), "Thinkexist.Com."
48 Michael Medved, *Right Turns*, 1st ed. (New York: Random House, 2004), 41.

Figure 65. *"In what way are work and play alike?" (GSS survey conducted in 1994, based on 1782 cases, with confidence level of 96%), and with a relative proportion of .69)*

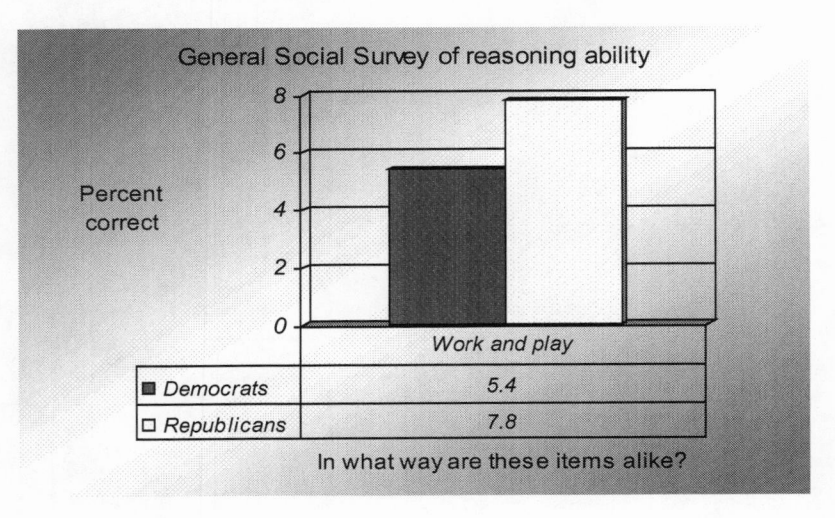

A majority correctly answered a question about animals.

Figure 66. *"In what way are a dog and a lion alike?" (GSS survey conducted in 1994, based on 1865 cases, with confidence level of 98%, and with a relative proportion of .93)*

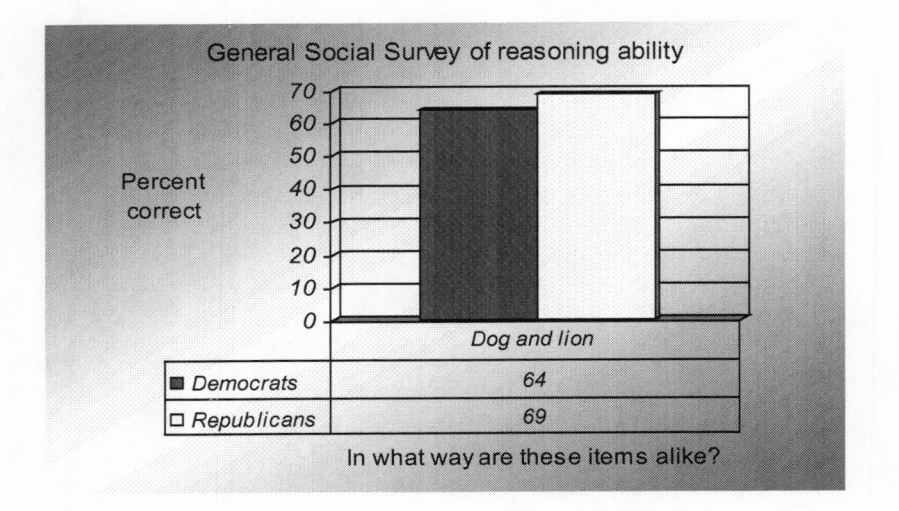

Only half of Republicans and even fewer Democrats correctly answered the following question about anatomy.

Figure 67. "In what way are an eye and ear alike?" (GSS survey conducted in 1994, based on 1840 cases, with confidence level of 96%, and with a relative proportion of .91)

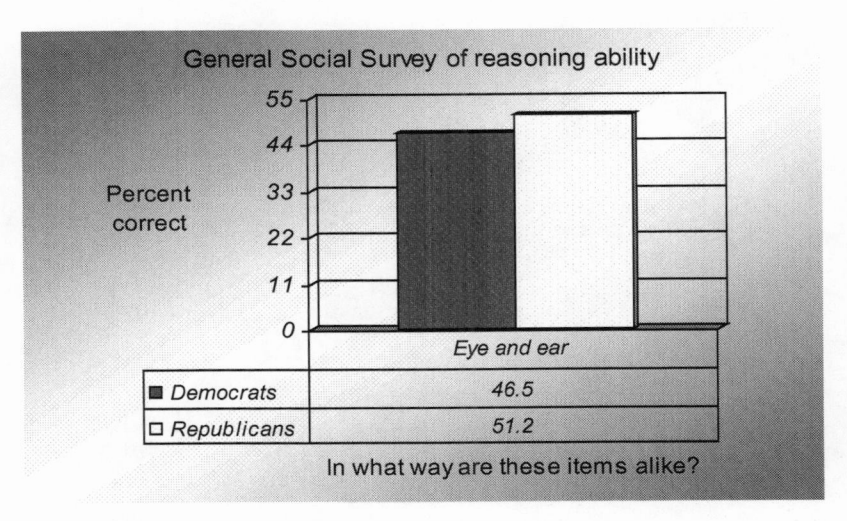

Finally, almost everyone struck out with respect to "praise and punishment."

Figure 68. "In what way are praise and punishment alike?" (GSS survey conducted in 1994, based on 1689 cases, with confidence level of 91% (marginal), and with a relative proportion of .79)

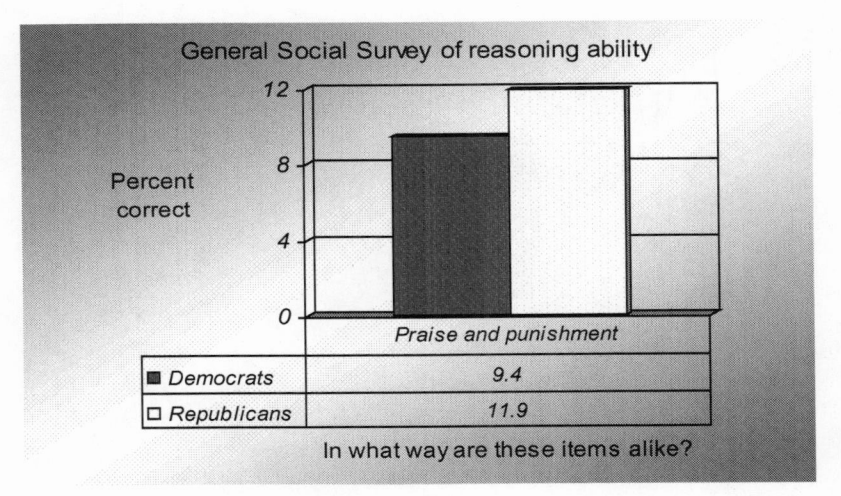

If we combine the results for these 6 questions, we find that, on average, Democrats answered correctly only about 88 percent as often as Republicans. More appropriately, however, we should use the results of all 8 questions, including

the 2 for which there was no statistically significant difference. In that case, the Democrats were about 90 percent as likely to correctly answer the questions.

Word Tests

> Ideas improve. The meaning of words participates in the improvement.
>
> — French writer and film maker Guy Debord[49]

The General Social Survey also tested the word comprehension of participants in several surveys conducted during the last 30 years. Respondents were asked to guess the correct (or most nearly correct) meaning of 10 words, by associated each of them with another listed word with a similar meaning. The results of those tests, for males, are depicted in Figure 69, below. Republican males have consistently scored higher on this test; however, the gap is closing quickly.

Figure 69. What is the meaning of these 10 commonly-used words? Results equal the percentage of correct answers for men. (GSS surveys conducted in 1977 through 2006, based on, left to right, 2916, 6596, and 3258 cases, with confidence level of at least 99% for each column.)

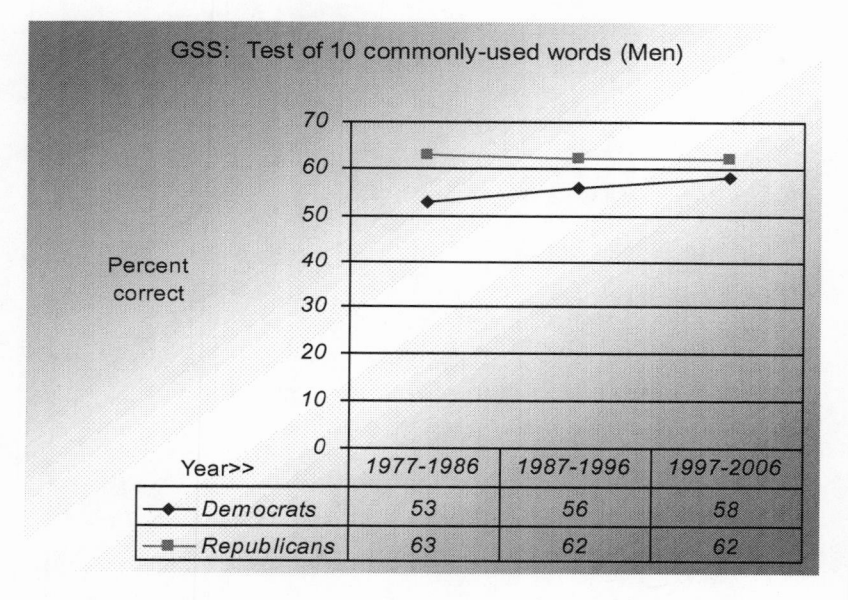

With regard to women, we see similar results. Although Republican women have consistently outscored Democratic women, the differential is getting smaller.

---

49 Guy Debord (attributed), "Columbia World of Quotations," (Columbia University Press, 1996).

Figure 70. What is the meaning of these 10 commonly-used words? Results equal the percentage of correct answers for women. (GSS surveys conducted in 1977 through 2006, based on, left to right, 1774, 3906, and 1895 cases, with confidence level of at least 99% for each column.)

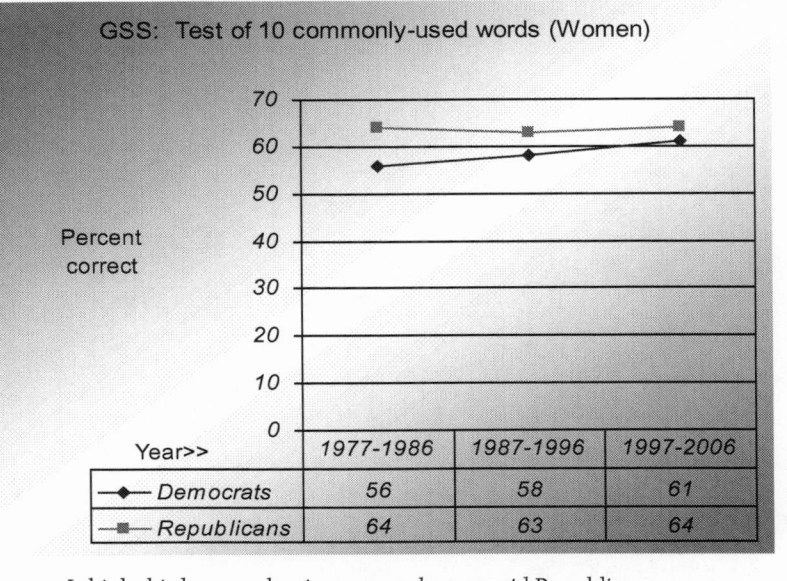

I think this last year has just proven how stupid Republicans are.

— Comedian Margaret Cho[50]

ANALYSIS: WHY IS THERE A DISPARITY?

What Factors Correlate With Education?

The average Republican has had a discernable education and knowledge advantage, and may have the edge with regard to reasoning and vocabulary skills.[51] Why is this? In the remainder of the chapter, we consider one of the above factors (the number of years of schooling), and determine if it correlates with traits commonly thought to distinguish Republicans from Democrats. Specifically, we consider the relationship between the average years of education and each of the variables in Table 20, below.

The Thirty-Year Analysis

Using basic statistics and 30 years of GSS survey data it is possible to test the relationship between each factor and the number of years of schooling. Details of

---

50 Margaret Cho as quoted in, "Hollywood Vs. America: Moveon Stays on Bush-Hitler Theme," *WorldNetDaily*, Retrieved March 14, 2007, from http://worldnetdaily.com/news/.

51 With regard to education and political knowledge, numerous and large surveys allow us to reach firm conclusions. However, with regard to reasoning and vocabulary skills relevant survey results are limited, and firm conclusions should be avoided.

the underlying multiple regression analysis are shown in Appendix B 3. We find that education is strongly correlated with income, health, and, to a lesser extent, race. Specifically, having higher income, having good health, and being white are factors that correlate positively with more years of schooling. Surprisingly, there is a moderate and *negative* correlation between years of education and marriage. That is, being married correlates with less education.

Table 20. Variables commonly thought to distinguish Republicans from Democrats

Variable	Specific question used in this analysis
Income	Is family income at least $50,000 (in 2006 dollars)?
Health	Is respondent's health good or excellent?
Race	Is respondent white?
Marital status	Is respondent married?
Political views	Is respondent a conservative (moderate to strong)?
Religiosity	Does respondent claim to have strong religious convictions?
Gender	Is the respondent a man?

The top row of Table 21, below, shows the 30-year Democrat-Republican education gap, if no other variables are considered. The next 3 rows show the gap if we control each of the factors found to significantly and positively correlate with education.

Table 21. Democratic and Republican years of education, in light of various correlating factors — 30 year analysis

Thirty year analysis Survey population limited to:	Ave. yrs. of school Dems	Ave. yrs. of school Reps	Gap in years	No. of cases	Conf %
All respondents (no limitation)	12.57	13.39	–.82	27188	+99
Just those earning over $50000/year	13.83	14.22	–.39	10725	+99
Just those in good or excellent health	13.11	13.69	–.58	14747	+99
Just those who are white	12.70	13.46	–.76	21759	+99
All of the 3 factors, above	14.09	14.30	–.21	5746	+99

As we would expect, the education gap between Democrats and Republicans (.82 years), shown on the top line, decreases when we control for income, health, or race. When we control for all 3 factors in combination, the Democratic educational deficit is cut from .82 years to just .21 years. That remaining amount (.21 years) could be called the unidentified "Republican educational factor" that existed during the last 30 years.

My guess is more reporters probably vote Democrat than Republican — just because I think reporters are smart.

— TV personality Jerry Springer[52]

A Nine Year Analysis Produces Different Results

I prepared an alternative analysis that is limited to more recent years, from 1998 through 2006. Details of the underlying multiple regression analysis are shown in Appendix B 4 on page 348. Again, education was found to positively correlate with higher income, good health, and race; and was found to negatively correlate with marriage. The impact of each significant and positively-correlating factor is shown in Table 22, below.

Table 22. Democratic and Republican years of education, in light of various correlating factors — 9-year analysis

Nine-year analysis Survey popula- tion limited to:	Ave. yrs. of school Dems	Ave. yrs. of school Reps	Gap in years	No. of cases	Conf %
All respondents (no limitation)	13.37	13.88	–.51	9305	+99
Just those earning over $50000/ year	14.63	14.57	.06	3878	*
Just those in good or excellent health	13.72	14.12	–.40	5420	+99
Just those who are white	13.55	13.96	–.41	7197	+99
All of the 3 fac- tors, above	14.73	14.64	.09	2144	*

In the 9-year analysis we find that controlling for the income difference is, by itself, sufficient to eliminate the Republican advantage. The advantage is also eliminated when all 3 correlating factors are combined. In other words, there is no longer a "Republican educational factor."

The Peculiar Relationship Between Party Identity and Political Ideology

Too Dumb To Know Which Party Is Which?

I'm a meathead. I can't help it, man. You've got smart people and you've got dumb people.

— Actor Keanu Reeves[53]

---

52 Jerry Springer (attributed), "Brainyquote.Com."

53 Keanu Reeves cited in, "Dumb Beau," in *Guardian Unlimited*, ed. John Patterson (U.K.), Retrieved April 1, 2007, from: http://film.guardian.co.uk/features/featurepages/0,,957479,00. html#article_continue.

If we analyze the educational achievements of "conservatives," grouped together without regard to political party, we find only small correlation between years of education and conservatism (generally a positive correlation). However, when we break-out conservatives by political party, the results are quite different: Conservative Republicans tend to be the most educated, while conservative Democrats are likely to be the least educated. A similar pattern is evident for liberals: Democratic liberals tend to have more education than the Republican liberals. This peculiar pattern is depicted in Figure 71, which shows educational attainment for a 30-year period extending from 1975 through 2006. Are liberal Republicans and conservative Democrats so uneducated that they don't realize they are in the wrong party?

Figure 71. What is your "highest year of school completed"? (GSS surveys conducted in 1977 through 2006 of, left to right, 599, 2845, 2998, 8644, 4023, 4095, and 875 cases, with confidence level of at least 99+% for all differences except the one designated "Slightly liberal," for which there is 95% confidence level)

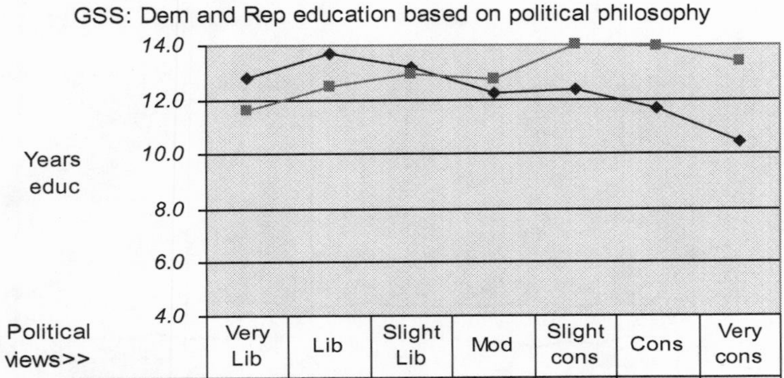

GSS: Dem and Rep education based on political philosophy

Political views>>	Very Lib	Lib	Slight Lib	Mod	Slight cons	Cons	Very cons
Dems	12.9	13.7	13.2	12.2	12.4	11.7	10.4
Reps	11.6	12.5	13.0	12.8	14.0	13.9	13.4

The difference in educational achievement between conservative Democrats and Republicans is particularly great, and can be quantified by comparing the educational achievements of Democrats and Republicans while controlling for their degree of "conservatism." This is done in Table 23, below.

The second row of Table 23 is illuminating. It shows that Democrats who are conservative have, on average, much less education than other Democrats (11.96 years versus 12.57 years). On the other hand, Republicans who are conservatives have much more education than other Republicans (13.92 years versus 13.39 years). Putting these two tendencies together, there is a difference of nearly 2 years between the educational achievements of conservative Democrats and conservative Republicans (11.96 years versus 13.92 years). I found no demograph-

ic variable, or combination of variables, that produces an educational gap this large. If political scientists fail to take heed of this fact, the generalizations they make about conservatives or liberals are apt to be misleading. This is particularly important with regard to conservatives because 25 to 50 percent of all self-identified "conservatives" in the United States are Democrats. Please see Chapter 11 for additional discussion of this phenomenon.

Table 23. A quantification of the large educational difference between conservative Democrats and conservative Republicans

30-year analysis Survey population limited to:	Ave. yrs. of school Dems	Ave. yrs. of school Reps	Gap in years	No. of cases	Conf %
All respondents (no limitation)	12.57	13.39	−0.82	27188	+99
All respondents who are conservative	11.96	13.92	−1.96	8982	+99

> Human beings only use ten percent of their brains. Ten percent! Can you imagine how much we could accomplish if we used the other sixty percent?
>
> — Comedian Ellen Degeneres[54]

CONCLUSIONS

Republicans are more likely to correctly answer questions related to basic political knowledge and, in some cases, scientific knowledge. However, where the scientific knowledge conflicts with religious beliefs, Republicans are less likely to give the answers that most scientists would provide.

There is some information suggesting that Republicans are more likely to correctly identify analogous relationships and the meanings of words. Also, survey interviewers are much more likely to give high marks to Republicans for political knowledge and "apparent intelligence."

During the last 50 years, Republicans have been more likely to earn high school diplomas, 4-year college degrees, and, with regard to men, graduate school (advanced) degrees. Depending upon the survey source, Democratic women have recently equaled or significantly exceeded Republican women with regard to the attainment of advanced college degrees.

Higher family income, good health, and being (racially) white are factors which correlate positively with educational achievement (measured by years of schooling). In fact, they seem to explain most or all of the Republican educational advantage. On the other hand, marriage correlates negatively with educational achievement.

---

54 "Ellen Degeneres: The Beginning" (2000), Retrieved March 14, 2007, from IMdb: http://imdb.com.

There is only a small correlation between political orientation (conservative versus liberal) and education. However, a more meaningful analysis requires that we distinguish conservatives and liberals by political party. Republican conservatives and Democratic liberals are far more educated than Democratic conservatives and Republican liberals. They are at opposite ends of the educational spectrum.

Finally, the ability of someone to make sound judgments depends upon more than college diplomas and hours spent reading the newspaper. People learn valuable lessons in the home and from their personal and economic successes and failures. And, even when they have complete command of the facts, people can fail to reach the proper conclusions, due to their own lack of objectivity.

At the beginning of this chapter, it was noted that, shortly before the 2004 Presidential election, nearly half of surveyed Republicans believed that Saddam Hussein had weapons of mass destruction before the U.S. invasion. In addition, more than half of these Republicans thought that Hussein provided support to al Qaeda. Is this an indication of Republican ignorance or stupidity? Perhaps, it is. However, it could also be evidence of party constituents faithfully supporting their candidate in the heat of a political campaign. Or, it could be evidence that many Republicans thought weapons were removed just prior to the invasion, and that ties to al Qaeda were concealed. (And, neither belief can be proven false.)[55] The point is that a fair analysis of education and intelligence cannot be made on the basis of controversial questions raised in the midst of a political campaign. As shown in this chapter, however, it is possible to make a sound assessment, if it is based upon comprehensive and non-controversial survey data.[56]

---

55 After the Iraq Survey Group's "final" report (dated September 30, 2004), an Addendum was issued, in March 2005, to report findings related to the possible movement of weapons to Syria. The Addendum stated: "There was evidence of a discussion of possible WMD collaboration initiated by a Syrian security officer, and ISG [the Iraq Study Group] received information about movement of material out of Iraq, including the possibility that WMD was involved. In the judgment of the working group [formed by ISG to investigate], these reports were sufficiently credible to merit further investigation. ISG was unable to complete its investigation [due to violence] and is unable to rule out the possibility that WMD was evacuated to Syria before the war." In the subsequent year (2006), a former Iraq Air Force officer, George Sada, publicly declared (without providing evidence) that WMD were transported to Syria via trucks and modified commercial passenger planes during 2002. This allegation has not been confirmed or disproven, but it is compatible with testimony reported by the Iraq Survey Group indicating that, until December, 2002, Sadam Hussein told his military generals that he had WMD. According to Sada, the WMD were shipped to Syria only because of the imminence to the U.S. invasion. This is also the conclusion of some members of Israeli Intelligence. We may never have definitive proof that resolves this controversy. (See Iraq Survey Group Final Report, the Group's Addendum, and Georges Sada, *Sadam's Secrets* (Brentwood (TN): Integrity Publishers, 2006), 250-61.)

56 Another controversial political question has to do with Iraq casualty estimates. When asked (in 2005) how many U.S. soldiers have been killed in Iraq, Democrats were less likely to give the "correct" number because they tended to overestimate the amount. Perhaps they did this out of ignorance, perhaps they did it because they thought the government understated casualty figures, or maybe they did it because they were angry at President Bush. In any event, the failure of Democrats to answer the question accurately does not necessarily reflect simple ignorance. For this reason, the Iraq casualty question was omitted from this chapter.

Chapter 3: Who Is the Better "Working Man"?

Introduction

> At the Bush White House, the working man is the forgotten man.
>
> — Senator Robert Byrd, Democrat of West Virginia[1]

> In Congress, the battles were fierce because Republicans tried to leave working people behind.
>
> — David Bonior, former Democratic Rep. of Michigan[2]

> A working person who votes for Bush is like a chicken who votes for Colonel Sanders.
>
> — Robert Reich, former U.S. Secretary of Labor[3]

For some people references to the "working man" or "working people" are part of the daily vernacular, and their words often imply that Democrats believe in helping working people while Republicans oppose them. This may lead some

---

1 Senator Robert Byrd as quoted by Nick Anderson, "Race for the White House," *Los Angeles Times*, October 12 2004.

2 David Bonior as cited in, "Democrats: GOP Forsaking Working Class," (CNN.com, December 29, 2001), Retrieved December 6, 2004, from: http://archives.cnn.com/2001/ALLPOLITICS/12/29/democrats.radio/index.html.

3 Robert Reich as quoted by Candice Rainey, "Do Celebrity Plugs Translate to Votes?," (2004), Retrieved December 7, 2004, from http://us.gq.com/culture/general/articles/040928plc0_02.

to assume that Democrats are working people, and Republicans are not. But, is this true?

To answer the question, we must make two determinations: Who is more likely to work for a living and, among those working, who is the more valuable worker, and why? Given the historical differences in the nature of work done by men versus women, this analysis is best done one gender at a time.

After the separate male and female analyses, this chapter contains some general information on occupational types and job "prestige." Yes, it is possible to estimate, in an objective and quantified manner, the relative cachet of the work we do.

THE BETTER WORKING MAN

Who is more likely to work for a living?

> The Democrats were "the party of the working man" decades ago, but now the Republicans are.
>
> — Peggy Noonan, Republican political analyst and author[4]

Republican men are more likely than Democratic men to work outside of the home, and those who do are likely to work longer hours. In Figure 72, below, employment rates of Democratic and Republican men are shown for 6 time periods in years 1952 through 2004. The source is the American National Election Studies (NES).

Figure 72. Are you currently employed (Men of all ages)? (NES surveys conducted in 1952 through 2004, based on, left to right, 592, 1955, 1964, 2507, 2841, and 2047 cases, with no statistical significance for the 3 differences on the left side of the chart, and a 99+% confidence level for the remaining differences. For the right-side differences the relative proportions are, left to right, .90, .87, and .87.)

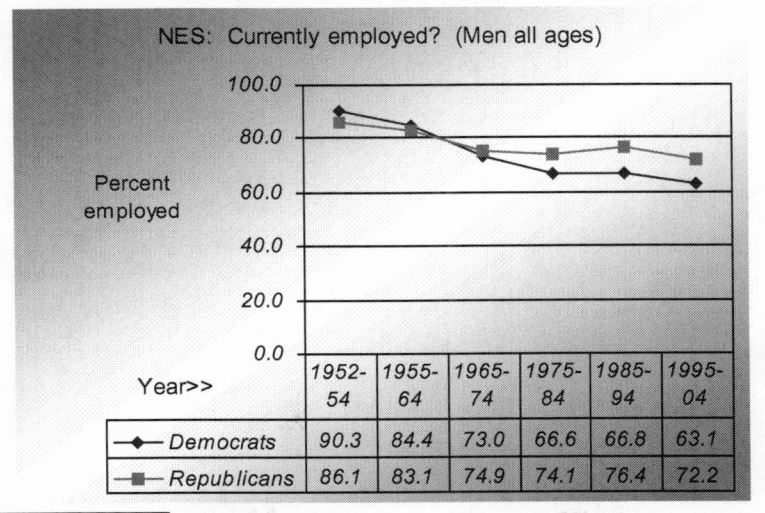

NES: Currently employed? (Men all ages)

Year>>	1952-54	1955-64	1965-74	1975-84	1985-94	1995-04
Democrats	90.3	84.4	73.0	66.6	66.8	63.1
Republicans	86.1	83.1	74.9	74.1	76.4	72.2

4 Peggy Noonan as quoted by Chuck Noe, "Noonan: Why Democrats Become Republicans," in *NewsMax.com* (October 7, 2004), from: http://www.newsmax.com.

An interesting trend is displayed: Forty or fifty years ago, Democratic men were at least as likely as Republican men to be employed. Now, Democratic men are much less likely to be in paid employment (just 88 % as likely during the last 30 years).

> A recession is when your neighbor loses his job. A depression is when you lose yours. A recovery is when Jimmy Carter loses his.

> — President Ronald Reagan[5]

If we limit our analysis to men aged 22 to 65 years — the traditional working age — we see a disparity that is similar, but slightly smaller. Among men of this age range the Democratic employment rate has been about 91 percent of the Republican rate during the last 30 years. See Figure 73, below.

Figure 73. Are you currently employed (Men aged 22 to 65 years)? (NES surveys conducted in 1952 through 2004, based on, left to right, 515, 1648, 1536, 1930, 2231, and 1628 cases, with no statistically significant difference for the left-side differences, and with a 99+% confidence level for the remaining differences. For the statistically significant differences the relative proportions are, left to right, .91, .92, and .91.)

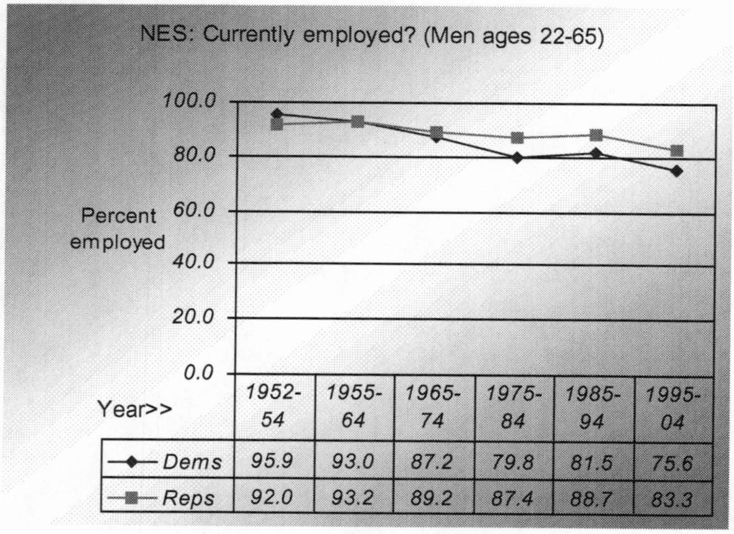

NES: Currently employed? (Men ages 22-65)

Year>>	1952-54	1955-64	1965-74	1975-84	1985-94	1995-04
—◆— Dems	95.9	93.0	87.2	79.8	81.5	75.6
—■— Reps	92.0	93.2	89.2	87.4	88.7	83.3

The General Social Survey (GSS) also shows an employment gap — but in a different way. It asks men and women how many weeks they worked in the prior year, including paid vacations and sick leave. It appears that Republicans men, aged 22 to 65 years, worked about 3.3 more weeks each year than their Democratic counterparts, between 1994 and 2006.

---

5 Ronald Reagan cited by Brendan Miniter, "The Western Front: Senator No-Show," in *Wall Street Journal* (New York: 2004), Retrieved August 18, from: http://www.opinionjournal. com/columnists/bminiter/?id=110005490.

Figure 74. *"How many weeks did you work either full-time or part-time not counting work around the house? (Include paid vacation and sick time.)" (GSS surveys conducted from 1994 through 2006, limited to men aged 22 to 65 years, based on 4103 cases, with confidence level of 99+%)*

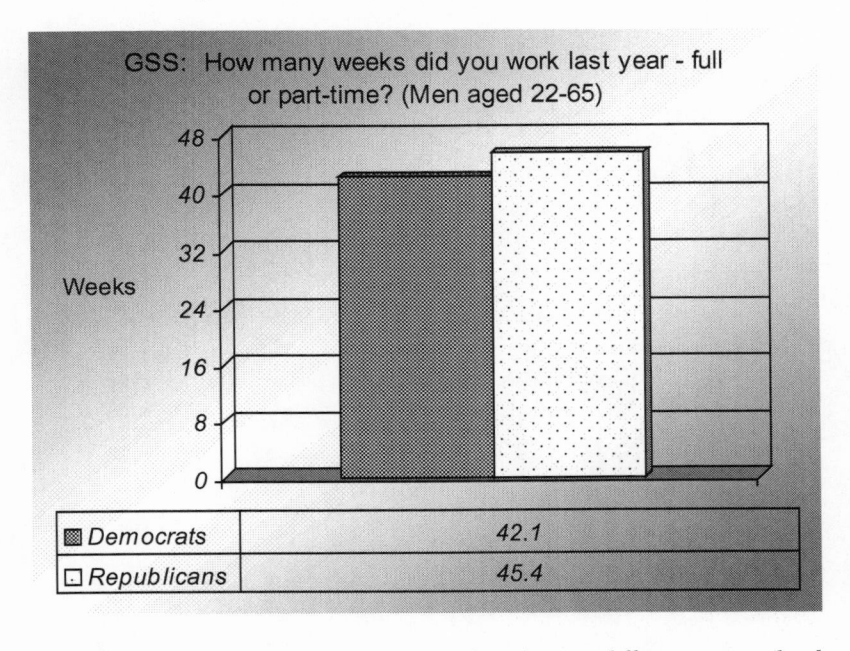

▨ *Democrats*	42.1
☐ *Republicans*	45.4

The employment gap does not necessarily indicate a difference in work ethics, as there are legitimate reasons why an individual might be unemployed. He could be retired after many years of hard work, he could be disabled, he could be a student too young to work, or he could be laid off from employment — through no fault of his own.

Why Democratic males are less likely to be employed

> I have never worked a f---ing day in my life.
> — Democratic Congressman Patrick Kennedy[6]

The General Social Survey (GSS) tracks work status using the 7 categories that are shown in Table 24, below. We see that the employment rate differential is generally linked to factors that are (presumably) unavoidable, such as being unemployed (row 3) or being disabled (row 7). On the other hand, there are a few "lifestyle" choices that also contribute to the employment disparity. These could be characterized as avoidable but legitimate reasons for not being employed. They are found in row 2 (vacation, sick time or strike time), row 4 (retirement by age 65), and row 6 ("keeping house").

---

6 Lloyd Grove, "Rep. Patrick Kennedy: I've Never Worked a (Bleeping) Day in My Life," in *Jewish World Review* (June 30, 2003), Retrieved August 29, 2006, from: http://www.jewish-worldreview.com/0703/grove063003.asp.

Table 24. *Employment status of Democratic and Republican males, aged 22 to 65 years, during the period 1977 through 2006. The differences on the individual rows are not necessarily significant; however the confidence level of the overall cross tabulation (Democratic vs. Republican) is 99+%, and the overall strength of association (Phi) is .11.*

Row	Work status of Men	Dem %	Rep %	Differ-ence
1	Working	78.4	85.9	−7.5
2	Vacation, illness, or strike time	2.9	2.6	0.3
3	Laid off, unemployed	5.4	2.5	2.9
4	Retired	6.9	4.9	2.0
5	Student	1.8	1.8	0.0
6	"Keeping house"	1.4	.7	0.7
7	Other, including disability	3.2	1.6	1.6
	Total	100	100	0.0

Thus, it is clear that modern Democratic males are less likely than their Republican complements to be in paid employment; however, legitimate reasons may justify all or most of the disparity. Therefore, in our quest to determine the "better working man" we will have to focus on a second criterion: Among those who are employed, who is the more valuable worker?

Who is the more valuable worker, and why?

> They say hard work never hurt anybody, but I figure why take the chance.
>
> — President Ronald Reagan[7]

In each of its surveys, the GSS asks respondents to estimate their occupational earnings. Based on the surveys conducted in 1998 through 2004 it is possible to estimate the average earnings for all Democratic and Republican men of working age (assumed to be 22 to 65 years old). These earnings are depicted in Figure 75, below:

As shown in Figure 75, the average working Democratic male (aged 22 to 65 years) earned salary and/or wages that were about $10,400 less per year than his working Republican counterpart (i.e., 18% less.) The median wages (versus average wages) were about $40,200 and $48,500 for Democratic and Republican men, respectively, in 2007 dollars.

> I have ways of making money that you know nothing of.
>
> — John D. Rockefeller, American industrialist[8]

---

7 John C. Hopwood. (2007), "Biography for Ronald Reagan", Retrieved March 16, 2007, from IMdb: http://imdb.com/name/nm0001654/bio.
8 John D. Rockefeller (attributed), "Brainyquote.Com."

Figure 75. Average earnings reported by Democratic and Republican men aged 22 to 65 years (calculated using wage distributions from GSS surveys in 1998-2004, based on 1862 cases, with confidence level of mean differences of 99+%). The amounts were adjusted by the Consumer Price Index to reflect inflation between the survey years and 2007.

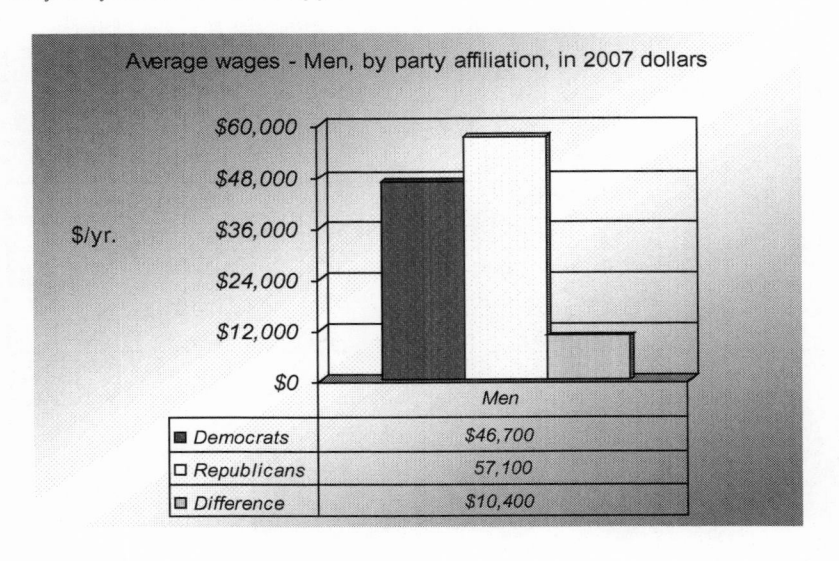

Theoretically, in a free market economy the employees who are paid more are considered (by employers and economists) to be more valuable workers; however, many people distrust decisions made in the market place. They point to "glass ceilings," "silver spoons," "old boys clubs," luck, and outright discrimination as factors that contribute to pay inequities. These skeptics conclude that some people — the working people — truly earn their wages, while others do not. To satisfy such skeptics we must justify the pay differences, and that is what we do in the remainder of this chapter. We compare Democratic and Republican men in the context of 5 assessment criteria: work hours, the amount of education brought to the job, the boss' opinion as manifested by supervisory assignments, expressed work attitudes, and emotional stability. Using that approach, we identify the better "working man."

Who works longer hours?

> [T]he Republican's and corporate America's vision ... is that the rich get richer and everyone else fights for the crumbs, everyone else has to work harder, work longer hours....
>
> — Film producer Michael Moore[9]

---

9 Michael Moore as cited in, "Countdown with Keith Olbermann," (In video clip:MSNBC, November 6, 2007), Retrieved November 7, 2007, from: http://www.msnbc.msn.com/id/3036677/.

When the GSS quizzes respondents concerning their employment status, it asks those who are currently working to estimate the hours they worked during the prior week. Figure 76, below, shows the estimated hours worked by male Democrats and Republicans aged 22 to 65 years, who were actively working when surveyed by GSS (at various times in 1993 through 2006). The differences depicted for the separate years are not, in themselves, statistically significant, and are provided merely to show that the Republican work-hour advantage may be fairly constant, over time.

Figure 76. Average hours/week worked by men aged 22 to 65 years (GSS surveys conducted in 1991 through 2004, based on aggregate sample size of 3927, with overall confidence level of 99+%)

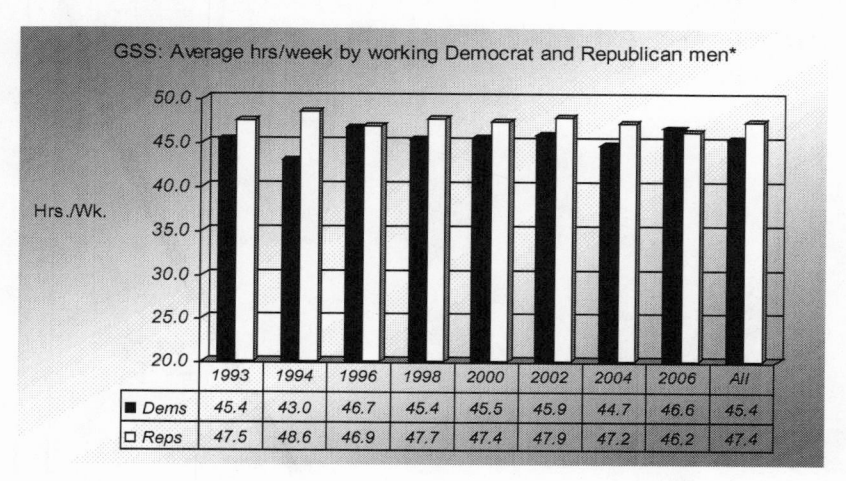

*Differences depicted for individual years are not statistically significant. Confidence level of the "All" column is 99+%.

On the other hand, the difference shown in the "All" column, on the right side of Figure 76, has a confidence level of 99+ percent. It shows that the average employed Democratic male worked about 45.4 hours per week for his paycheck, while the average employed Republican male put in about 47.4 hours — an excess of 2 hours.

> A lot of [Republicans] have never made an honest living in their lives.
>
> — Howard Dean, DNC Chairman[10]

---

10 Stephen Dinan and Amy Fagan, "Dean Hits GOP on 'Honest Living'," *Washington Times*, June 3, 2005.

Reality check — NES shows a larger difference

NES also asked currently-employed respondents to estimate average weekly work hours in surveys conducted in 1996, 1998, 2000, and 2004. In total, 1082 male Democrats and Republicans, aged 22-65 years, were surveyed in those years. Democrats averaged 45.1 hours per week, while Republicans averaged 48.9 hours per week — a statistically significant difference (99+%) of about 3.8 hours. However, in the remainder of this chapter, we use the more conservative difference of 2 hours, reflected in the GSS surveys conducted in 1993 through 2006.[11]

Being Republican Means Longer Work Hours?

What are the Republican traits that correlate with the tendency to work more hours? I analyzed several variables including income, health, race, marital status, political philosophy, religiosity, and education level. Only one of those variables correlated significantly with hours worked: level of income.[12] In other words, people who earn more work longer hours.

Figure 77. Average and median hours worked by all men (including Democrats and Republicans), aged 22 to 65 years, by earnings level (GSS surveys conducted in 1991 through 2004, based on, left to right, sample sizes of 1830, 1462, 1442, and 536, and with confidence levels of at least 95%)

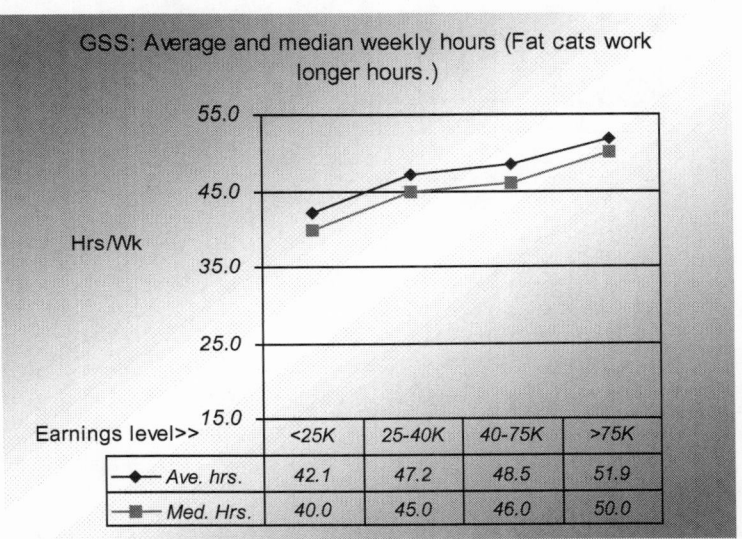

The link between work hours and income is clearly seen in Figure 77, which shows the average and median hours worked by men of differing wage levels. The "fat cats," earning over $75,000 per year, worked nearly 10 hours more each week

---

11 The NES hours gap may be larger than the GSS gap because NES asks for the work hours of anyone who is "working now/temporarily laid off (in combination with any other status)." In other words, it includes people who may be working while retired, while in school, while disabled, etc.

12 To see the results of a multiple regression analysis, please go to Appendix B 6.

than the men earning under $25,000 per year. This was true for both average and median hours worked, and it was true for Democrats as well as Republicans.

Two Hours Per Week Can Make A Big Difference

There are no gains, without pains.

— Benjamin Franklin, Author, politician, scientist, philosopher[13]

We know there is a correlation between hours worked and income, and that employed Republican men work about 2 hours per week more than employed Democratic men. The financial implications of this differential are significant. Even if we assume identical pay rates at the U.S. hourly average, a difference of 2 hours per week could let the Republican male safely accumulate an additional $170,000 in his IRA (retirement account), in today's dollars. See Figure 78, below, where the column on the right side depicts the Republican's eventual IRA balance, and the smudge on the left depicts the Democrat's expected balance.[14] For a husband and wife who both work an extra two hours per week, the additional accumulated wealth could easily exceed $300,000.

Figure 78. Work hours can translate to differences in accumulated wealth! (calculation of present value based on the overall difference in hours shown in Figure 76, times the average male wage rate of $19.57, invested in an IRA for 40 years at after inflation rate of 3%)[15]

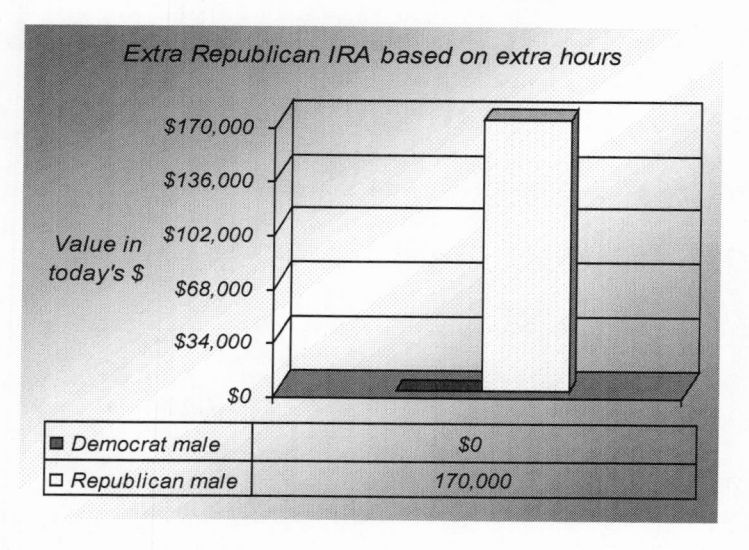

---

13 Benjamin Franklin, *The Way to Wealth*, 1986 ed. (Bedford, MA: Applewood Books, 1757).
14 If we used the NES 3.8 hour differential, the IRA disparity could be as much as $300,000.
15 See Appendix B 5 for the calculation of the average male hourly rate.

The two-hour-per-week work difference explains much of the Republican wage advantage, and that is good: Work and effort should make a difference. Wealth accumulation should not be based on contacts, "old boys clubs," or luck. However, this hours gap does not explain the entire Democrat-Republican earnings differential. Democratic men work 95.8 percent as many hours as do Republican men;[16] yet they earn only 81.8 percent as much as the Republicans.[17] In other words, there is an 18.2 percent gap in earnings while there is only a 4.2 percent gap in hours worked. There must be other factors in play.

Who Is the More Educated Worker?

> An educated workforce is the foundation of every community and the future of every economy.
>
> — Brad Henry, Democratic Governor of Oklahoma[18]

In Chapter 2 we noted that, on the whole, Republicans are a little more educated than Democrats. This is particularly true for males. During the last decade, Republicans males have been 10 percent more likely to have high school diplomas (Figure 55 on page 72), and 60 percent more likely to have 4-year college degrees (Figure 57 on page 74).

One way we can estimate the impact of education on wages is by focusing on the value of these educational diplomas and degrees. Figure 79, below, shows the percentages of working Democratic and Republican males, aged 22 to 65 years, at two ends of the educational spectrum: those without high school diplomas and those with 4-year college degrees.

Figure 79. Educational differences between working Democratic and Republican men aged 22-65 years (GSS surveys conducted in 2000 through 2004, based on a sample size of 1432, with differences that are at least 99% statistically significant, and with relative proportions of, left to right, 1.96 and .66)

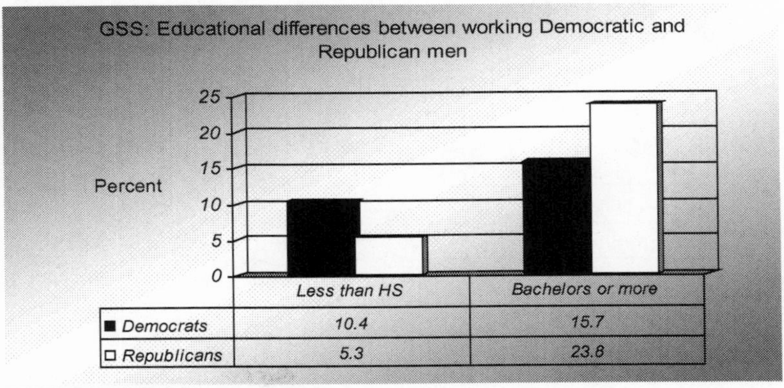

GSS: Educational differences between working Democratic and Republican men

	Less than HS	Bachelors or more
■ Democrats	10.4	15.7
□ Republicans	5.3	23.8

---

16 The calculation is 45.4/47.4 = 95.8%.

17 The calculation is $46700/$57100 = 81.8%.

18 "State of the State Address," 2005, Office of Governor Brad Henry Web Site, Retrieved March 17, 2007, from http://www.ok.gov/governor/stateofthestate2005.php.

The first column in Figure 79 shows that a Democratic male is about twice as likely to have less than a high school diploma, and the second column shows that a Republican male is far more likely to have a 4-year college degree.

The Dollar Value of Education

> Education today, more than ever before, must see clearly the dual objectives: Education for living and education for making a living.
>
> — James Mason Woods (Position unknown)[19]

It is possible to estimate the impact of these educational differences on wages, and this is done in Appendix B 7 on page 350. However, the bottom-line result is that, all other factors being equal (e.g., equal work hours), we'd expect the average Democrat to earn about $51,500 and the average Republican to earn about $56,300. The $4,800 difference equals about 8.5 percent, and that is the amount of the wage gap that may be attributable to educational differences.[20]

The 8.5 percent calculated above is equal to almost half of the total 18.2 percent wage gap (first discussed on page 95). When we add the 8.5 percent to the wage disadvantage attributable to the shortfall in Democratic work hours (4.2%, as calculated on page 95), we find that these two factors — less education and fewer work hours — could explain about 70 percent of the Democrat-Republican wage disparity.

The Boss' Opinion As Indicated by Supervisory Assignments

> Suck up to the boss from day one. If he's stupid, tell him he's smart. If she's fat and ugly, tell her she's hot. If he's weak and ineffectual, tell him he's a powerhouse.
>
> — Online tabloid[21]

We have seen that Republican males tend to work more hours and have more education than Democratic males, and those two factors explain a lot of the Republican earnings advantage. However, there is another way to gauge the relative worth of Democratic and Republican male workers: the boss's opinion.

An employer indicates his assessment of a worker's value in two tangible ways: by the amount of compensation and by the amount of responsibility he gives to the worker. As noted, Republicans are generally paid more, and in a free market system economists believe that additional wages usually indicate additional labor value. Likewise, Republicans are more apt to be given supervisory responsibilities — both formal and informal. This is significant because it is generally assumed that employers promote the workers who have superior technical

---

19 James Mason Wood (attributed), "The National Teaching & Learning Forum," Retrieved March 16, 2007, from: http://www.ntlf.com/html/lib/quotes.htm.

20 The calculation is (56300-51500)/56300 = 8.5%.

21 "How to Get the Most out of Your New Job," in *Weekly World News Online* (August 2, 2004), Retrieved March 16, 2007, from: http://unitethecows.com/.

and managerial skills. Thus, by looking at supervision rates, we learn what the boss thinks, so to speak.

> Opportunity is missed by most people because it is dressed in over-alls and looks like work.

— Thomas A. Edison, Inventor and businessman[22]

On several occasions in 1972 through 2006, the GSS asked workers if they supervised other employees as part of their job duties. The results (for male employees aged 22 to 65 years) are displayed in Figure 80, below.

Figure 80. Percentage of Democratic and Republican male supervisors aged 22 to 65 years (GSS surveys conducted in 1972 — 2006, based on 5223 cases, with confidence level of 99+%, and with a relative proportion of .89)

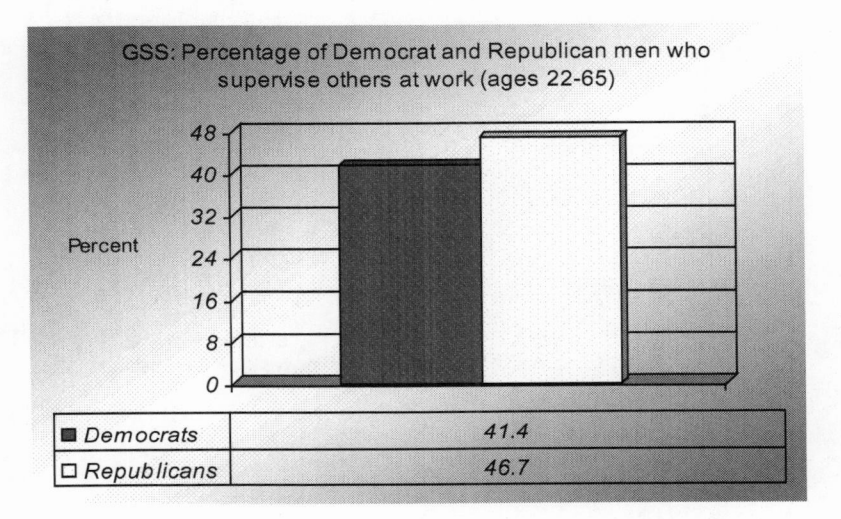

As shown in Figure 80, Republican males are only slightly more likely than Democratic males to supervise other workers on the job. A closer look, however, reveals a more complex pattern with much larger differences.

With Older Workers The Supervision Gap Is Larger

> To supervise men, you must either excel them in their accomplish-ments, or despise them.

— Benjamin Disraeli, 19th century British Prime Minister and novelist[23]

---

22 Gerald Beals, "Thomas Edison 'Quotes'," Retrieved April 1, 2007, from: http://www.thomasedison.com/edquote.htm.

23 Paul Elmer More, "Disraeli and Conservatism," in *Shelburne Essays*, Retrieved April 1, 2007, from: http://jkalb.freeshell.org/more/disraeli.html.

If we just consider the younger workers, aged 25 to 45 years, there is no statistical difference in the supervision rates. As workers get older, however, a significant gap develops. As shown in Figure 81, below, 50.9 percent of Republican
males aged 45 to 65 years supervise others in the workplace, whereas only 40.4
percent of their Democratic counterparts are supervisors. Expressed another
way, Democratic men in this age range are only about 79 percent as likely to
supervise.[24]

*Figure 81. Percentage of Democratic and Republican male supervisors aged 45 to 65 years
(various GSS surveys conducted in 1972–2006, based on 1948 cases, with confidence level of 99+%,
and of .79)*

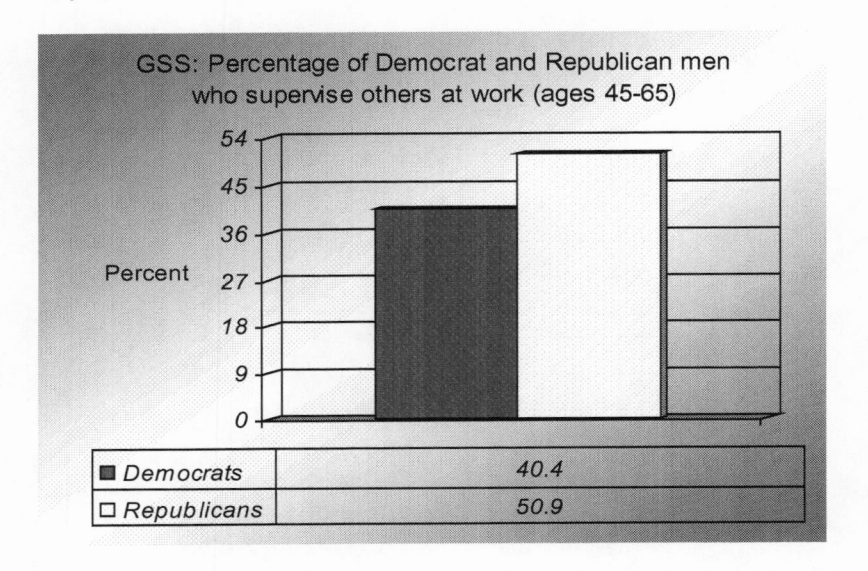

It is important to note that these statistics exclude owner-employees. We
are talking about employees who acquire their responsibilities through promotions — not stock purchases.

With Formal Management Positions The Gap Is Even Larger

Executive ability is deciding quickly and getting somebody else to
do the work.

— John G. Pollard, Former Democratic Governor of Virginia[25]

If we look at workers in formal positions requiring managerial duties, we
see a more significant difference between male political constituencies. Figure
82, below, shows the percentages of Democratic and Republican men serving

---

24 The calculation is 40.4/50.9 = 79%.
25 John G. Pollard (attributed), "Quotationz.Com."

as general, production and operating department managers based upon the aggregate results of GSS surveys conducted in years 1988 through 2006. The gap is substantial, even though we are considering men of all ages.

Figure 82. Percentage of Democratic and Republican men working in formal management positions (GSS surveys conducted in 1988 through 2006, based on 4370 cases, with confidence level of 99+%, and with a relative proportion of .58)

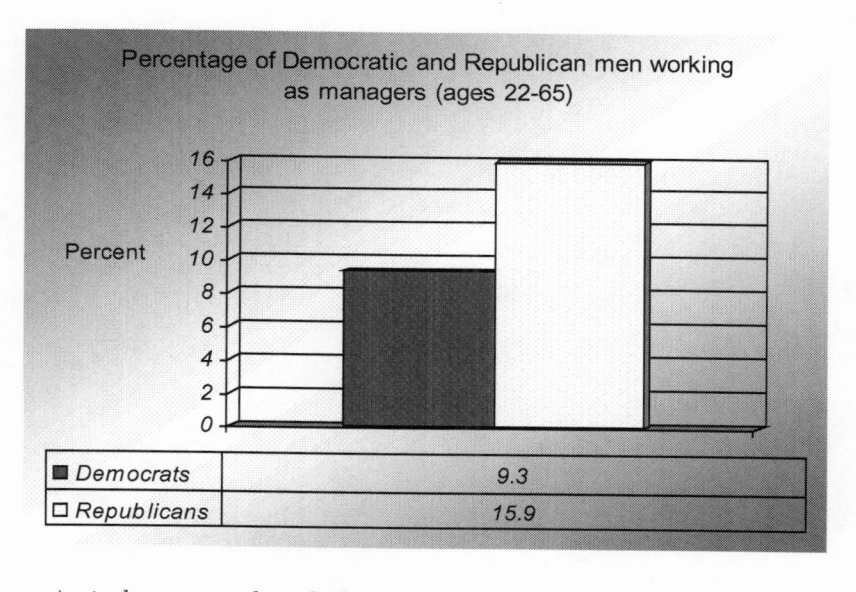

Again, however, a closer look at these numbers reveals a more complicated pattern. For men under age 35, there is no statistically significant difference with regard to the percentages working in formal management positions. However, as men get older, a larger difference develops, as is evident in Figure 83, below.

The chart shows us that the gap between Democratic and Republican men, which is statistically insignificant until age 35, grows until workers are between 61 and 65 years old. At that age, the percentage of men working in management declines for both Democrats and Republicans. Again, it should be noted that these are not business owners — they are employees who (presumably) were promoted to managerial positions.

Figure 83. Percentage of Democratic and Republican men working in formal management positions, by age ranges (GSS surveys conducted in 1988 through 2006, based on, left to right, 691, 600, 525, 387, 324, 173, and 2700 cases, with confidence level of 99+% for all columns except the age 61-65 column, which is 93% (marginal), and with relative proportions of, left to right, .46, .50, .46, .34, .35, .46, and .44)

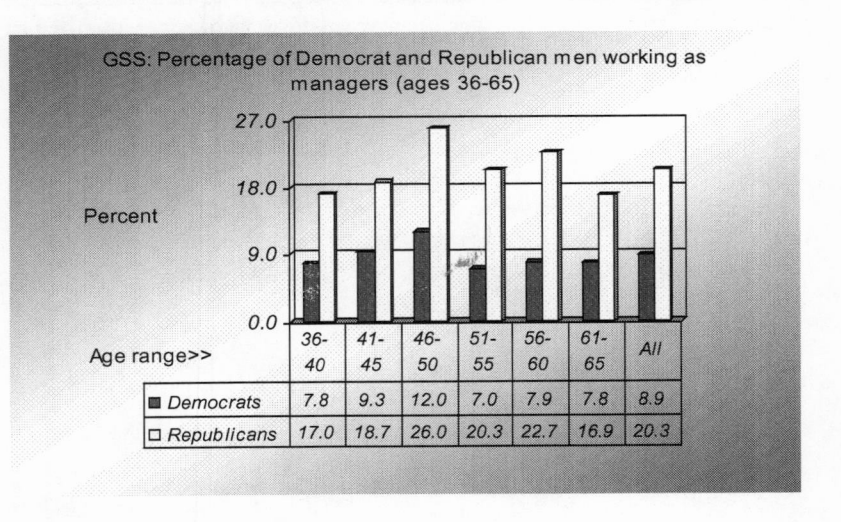

Age range>>	36-40	41-45	46-50	51-55	56-60	61-65	All
■ Democrats	7.8	9.3	12.0	7.0	7.9	7.8	8.9
□ Republicans	17.0	18.7	26.0	20.3	22.7	16.9	20.3

> In a hierarchy every employee tends to rise to his level of incompetence.
> — Educator and author Lawrence J. Peter[26]

Thus, we can conclude that, among middle-aged and older workers, there is a considerable gap in the percentage of Democrats and Republicans who are given the responsibility of supervising others. Undoubtedly, this is another factor accounting for the earnings gap. It may indicate that "the boss" has a higher opinion of the average Republican than his Democratic counterpart. In addition, it suggests that Republicans have, on average, more important employment responsibilities that justify their earnings advantage.

Reality check — Which came first: the chicken or the egg?

Do Republicans have work or character qualities that increase the likelihood of their becoming managers? Or, is it the other way around? When people become supervisors they change into Republicans because they a) make more money, or b) see things from the perspective of business?

Who Has A Better Attitude?

> Motivation determines what you do. Attitude determines how well you do it.
> — Novelist Raymond Chandler[27]

If you were an employer interviewing candidates for a new job opening, you'd probably ask several questions designed to appraise their general feelings

---

26 Lawrence J. Peter (attributed), "New Dictionary of Cultural Literacy," (Houghton Mifflin Company, 2002).
27 Raymond Chandler (attributed), "Brainyquote.Com."

about work, expectations regarding the new employment, and potential dedica-tion and loyalty as employees. These are also questions that have been asked in some of the surveys conducted by GSS and others. When we sort the questions and answers by the political party of each respondent, we find that there are sta-tistically significant attitudinal differences between Democratic and Republican males.

Republican men are more likely to state that they are "very satisfied" with their jobs. This may indicate that they have more positive attitudes; however, it could also indicate that they have jobs that are truly more satisfying. See Figure 84, below.

Figure 84. "All in all, how satisfied would you say you are with your job?" (GSS surveys con-ducted in 2002 and 2006, based on 981 cases, with overall confidence level of +99%, and a relative proportion of .76)

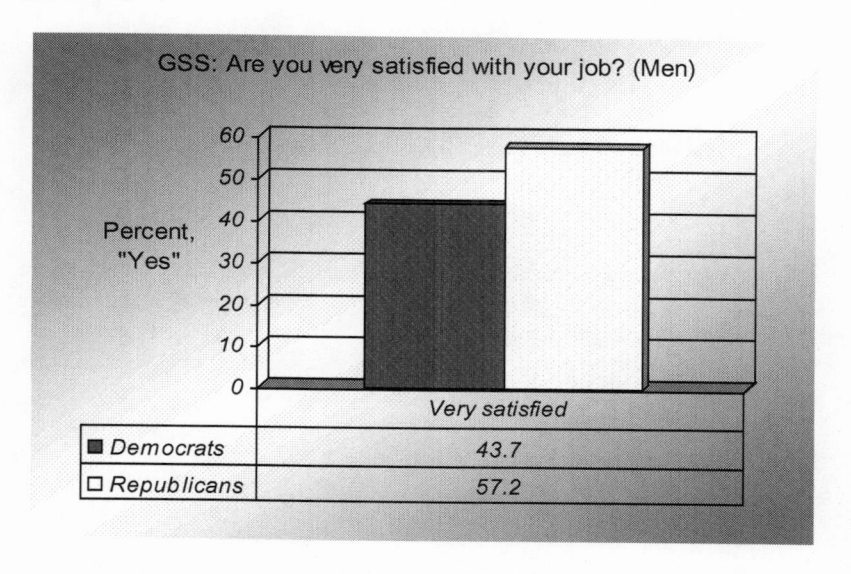

Our environment, the world in which we live and work, is a mirror of our attitudes and expectations.

— Self-improvement author Earl Nightingale[28]

Republican men are also more likely to "strongly agree" that they are "proud to be working for" their employers. That is something any boss loves to hear. See Figure 85.

---

28 Earl Nightingale (attributed), "Quotationz.Com."

Figure 85. Do you strongly agree with the statement, "I am proud to be working for my employer"? (GSS surveys conducted in 2002 and 2006, based on 974 cases, with confidence level of 99+%, and with a relative proportion of .76)

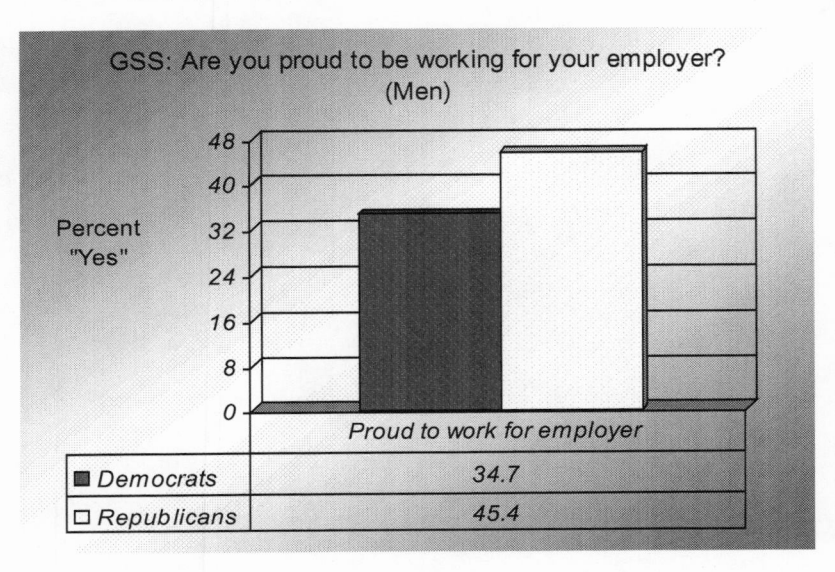

Surveys spanning a 30-year period indicate that Democratic men would be more likely to quit working if they could swing it, financially. Does this reflect an inherent difference in work ethic, or simply a tendency for Democrats to work in less rewarding jobs?

Figure 86. If you were rich would you stop working? (GSS surveys conducted in 1975 through 2004, based on, left to right, 1320, 1914, and 1383 cases, with confidence level of, left to right, 99+%, 99%, and 98%, and with relative proportions of, left to right, .1.50, 1.22, and 1.21)

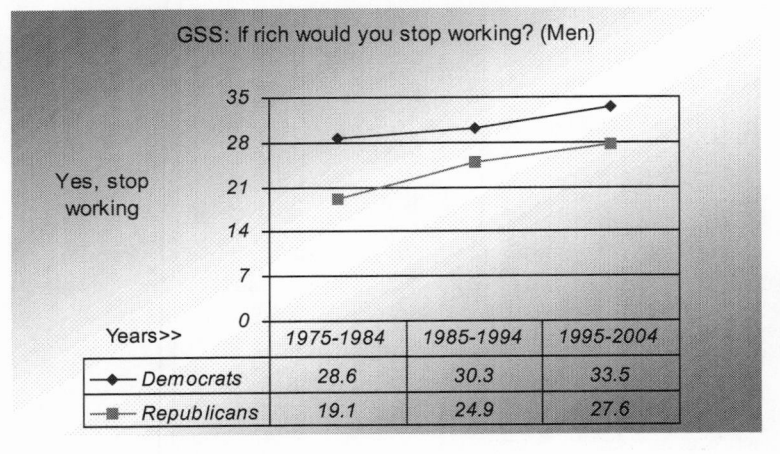

In addition, Democratic men may be a little more likely to leave work early or stay at home because they are dissatisfied with their jobs. This is shown in Figure 87, below, which is based on a 2004 GSS survey.

> Take this job and shove it, I ain't working here no more. ... You better not try to stand in my way as I'm walking out the door.
>
> — Singer Johnny Paycheck[29]

Figure 87. During the past 3 months did you ever stay home or leave work early because you were unhappy about your job? (GSS 2004 survey, based on 573 cases, with confidence level of 99%, and with a relative proportion of 1.66)

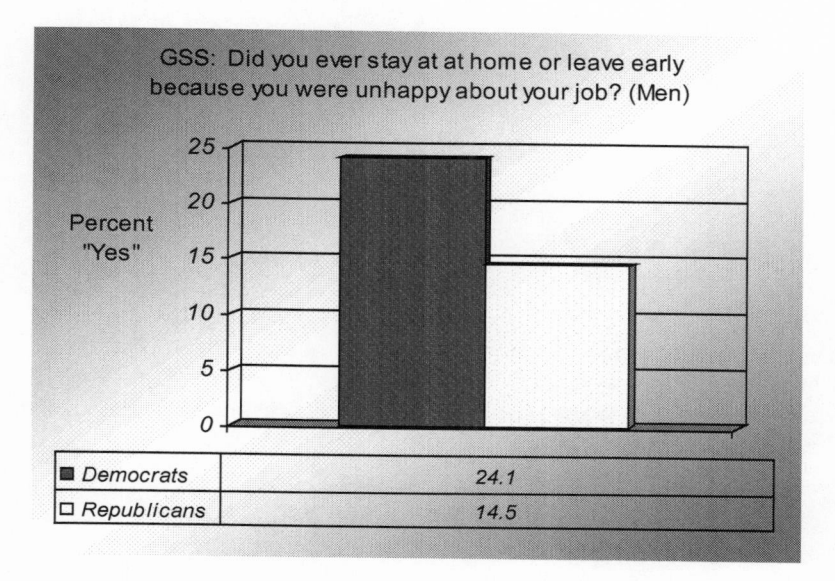

According to a 2006 GSS survey, Democratic men are more likely to reject the proposition that they take a pay cut, or travel greater distances, to avoid unemployment (Figure 88, below). This could be a sign of a poor attitude.

> There is joy in work. There is no happiness except in the realization that we have accomplished something.
>
> — Industrialist Henry Ford[30]

Republican men are more likely to "strongly agree" that they would work harder than required in order to help their employer succeed (Figure 89, below).

---

29 Johnny Paycheck song lyrics cited in, "Lyricskeeper.Com," Retrieved March 17, 2007, from: http://www.lyricskeeper.com.

30 Henry Ford (attributed), "Brainyquote.Com."

Figure 88. Percentage disagreeing with this statement: "In order to avoid unemployment I would be willing to ..." (GSS survey conducted in 2006, based on 271 cases, with confidence level of, left to right, 99% and 99%, and with relative proportions of 1.69 and 1.76)

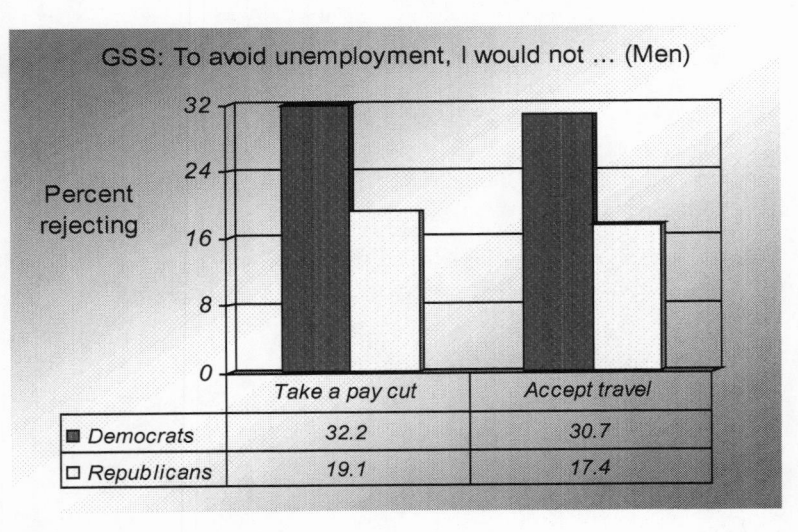

Figure 89. I am willing to work harder than I have to help my employer. (GSS surveys conducted in 1998 and 2006, based on 481 cases, with a confidence level of 99%, and with relative proportion of .70)

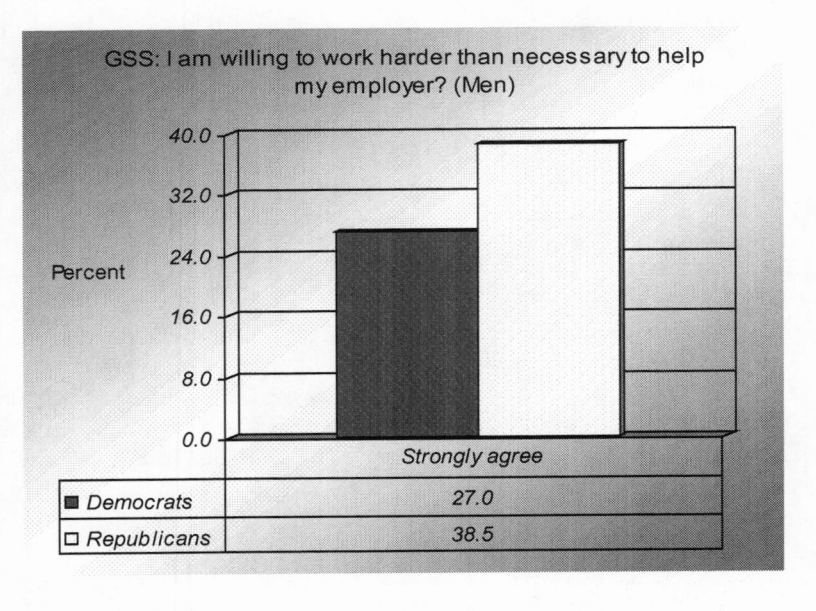

Many Americans suffer from what I call the "union mentality," an eagerness to do everything in their power to shortchange their employer.

— Author and radio talk show host Mike Gallagher[31]

Finally, Democratic men appear to be less proactive in solving problems at work. In a 2006 GSS survey, respondents were asked, "If you were to see a fellow employee not working as hard or well as he or she should..." what actions would you take? Democratic men were more likely than Republican men to indicate that they would not discuss the problem with the co-worker or with the supervisor.

Figure 90. If I saw an employee who was not working as hard or well as he could, it is "not at all likely" that I would ... (GSS surveys conducted in 2002 and 2006, based on, from left to right, 942 and 854 cases, with a confidence level of 99%, and with relative proportions of, left to right, 1.42 and 1.33)

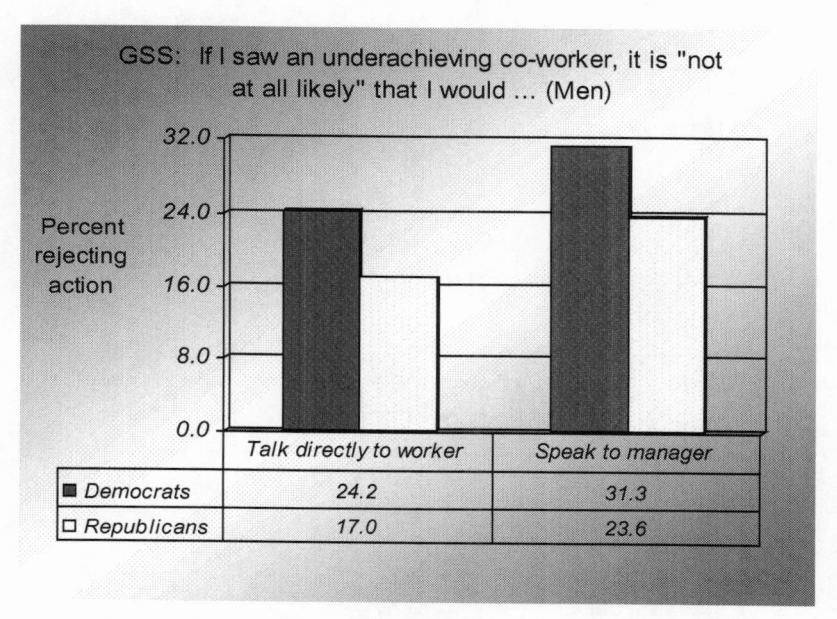

GSS: If I saw an underachieving co-worker, it is "not at all likely" that I would ... (Men)

Percent rejecting action

	Talk directly to worker	Speak to manager
■ Democrats	24.2	31.3
□ Republicans	17.0	23.6

To summarize the issues related to attitude, there are survey data suggesting that Democratic males might be less satisfied with their jobs, less proud of their employers, less willing to help their employers succeed, less willing to take a pay cut to avoid unemployment, and less pro-active in addressing work problems. A higher percentage of Democratic men would quit working if they could afford to, financially, and Democrats are slightly more likely to take time off from work for inappropriate reasons. These results suggest that Republicans might have, on average, attitudes more valued by employers.

---

31 Mike Gallagher, *Surrounded by Idiots* (New York: Thumper Communications, Inc., 2005), 210.

Emotional Stability

> Snow was falling as Edmund Muskie spoke, and he claimed that
> the drops on his cheeks were actually melted snowflakes. That did
> him no good. The Union Leader declared that crying proved he
> "lacked stability"...
>
> — Journalist Robert Fulford[32]

In a 2000 GSS survey, respondents were asked whether, during the previous
4 weeks, "emotional problems (such as feeling depressed or anxious)" interfered
with work. Democratic males were significantly more likely to state that there
was such interference. (See Figure 91.)

*Figure 91. "During the past 4 weeks, have you had ... the following problem ... as a result of any
emotional problems (such as feeling depressed or anxious)"? You "didn't do work or other activities
as carefully as usual"? — (Men) (GSS survey conducted in 2000, based on 345 cases, with confidence
level of 99+%, and a relative proportion of 4.71)*

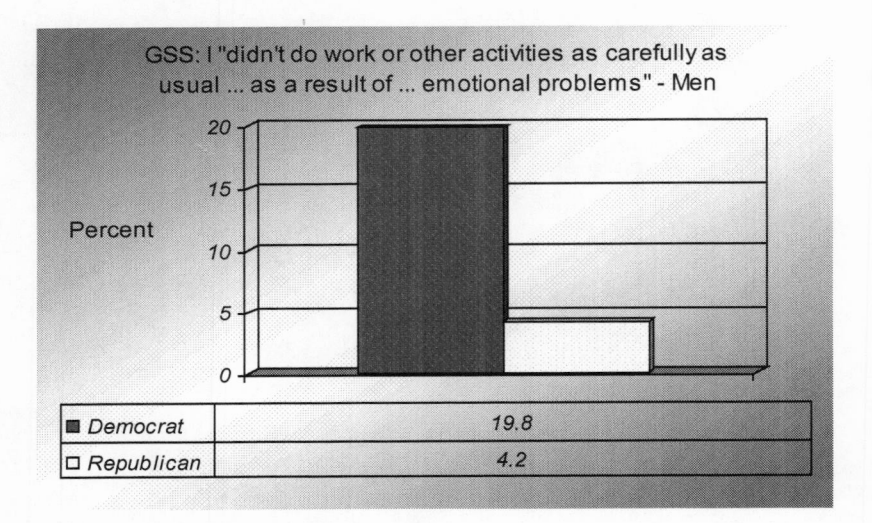

The GSS results are supported by other Gallup and GSS surveys (shown on
page 26) that show Democrats are more likely to state that they have poor mental health, and that they have been treated for mental health problems.

> Last week I told my psychiatrist, "I keep thinking about suicide."
> He told me from now on I have to pay in advance.
>
> — Comedian Rodney Dangerfield[33]

---

32 Robert Fulford, "Male Crying: Now It's Mandatory," *National Post*, May 7, 2002.

33 "Rodney Dangerfield Jokes", Retrieved October 26, 2006, from Ringsurf.com: http://www.
ringsurf.com/info/people/celebrities_in_the_news/Rodney_Dangerfield/.

If the mental health of Democrats and Republicans differs, as suggested by these surveys, and the difference has an impact on work performance, we may have identified an additional factor that explains the Democrat-Republican male compensation gap.

THE BETTER WORKING WOMAN

Earnings and hours worked

During the years 1998 through 2006, the likelihood of Democratic and Republican women being in paid employment was about the same (around 69%), as was their average occupational earnings. However, there was a significant difference in the average weekly work hours. As indicated in Figure 92, below, the disparity in work hours developed after the mid-1990s. Democratic women now work about 1.5 hours more per week (in paid employment) than their Republican sisters.

Figure 92. Percentage of Democratic and Republican women, aged 22-65 years, working at paid jobs (GSS surveys in 1991-2006, based on, left to right, 1737 and 2771 cases, with confidence level of 99% for the right-side difference, and no statistical significance for the left-side difference)

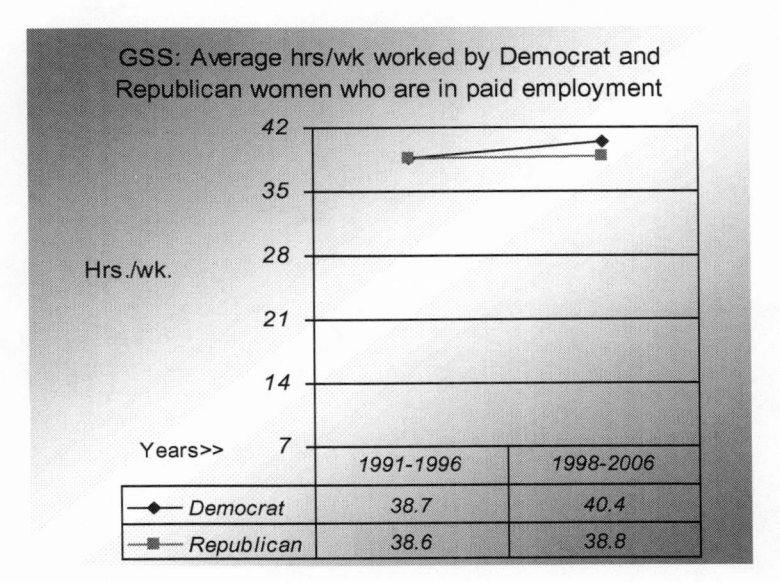

... I don't know that [Laura Bush] has ever had a real job — I mean, since she's been grown up.

— Teresa Heinz Kerry, wife of Democratic Senator John Kerry[34]

---

34 "The Real Running Mates," *USAtoday.com* (October 19, 2004), Retrieved March 17, 2007, from http://www.usatoday.com/news/politicselections/2004-10-19-teresa_x.htm.

Why do Democratic women work longer hours than Republican women? There are probably several reasons. First, Democratic women are less likely to be married, and unmarried women — regardless of party — tend to work longer hours outside of the home. The growing "marriage gap" among women of working age is displayed in Figure 93, below:

Figure 93. Marital status of Democratic and Republican women aged 22 to 65 years (GSS surveys in 1977-2006, based on, left to right, 3566, 4363, and 4065 cases, with confidence level of 99+% for all differences, and with relative proportions of, left to right, .89, .79, and .73)

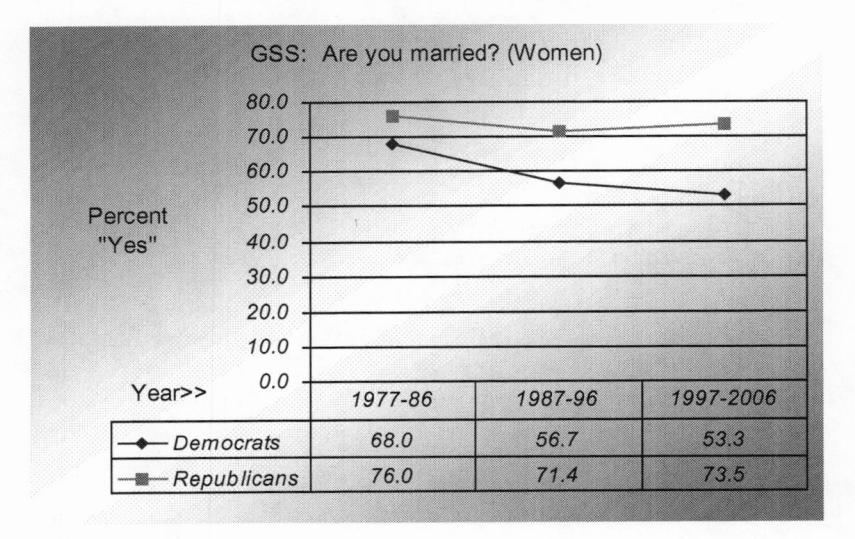

Reality check — Less married doesn't mean fewer children

If you're visualizing unmarried Democratic women who are unencumbered by the responsibilities of parenthood, you may want to consult Figure 94, below. It shows that Democratic women are nearly as likely as Republican women to have children in the household — despite their relatively low marriage rate. (The difference shown in the chart is not statistically significant.) This means that Democratic women are probably working more outside of the home, even though they have as many or more responsibilities within the home.

A second factor explaining why Democratic women work more hours might be a different philosophy regarding child rearing.

> Republicans understand the importance of bondage between a mother and child.
>
> — Vice President Dan Quayle[35]

---

35 Dan Quayle (attributed), "Quotationz.Com."

Figure 94. Percentage of women, aged 22-65 years, with children in the household (GSS surveys in 1991 through 2006, based on 6574 cases. The difference is not statistically significant.)

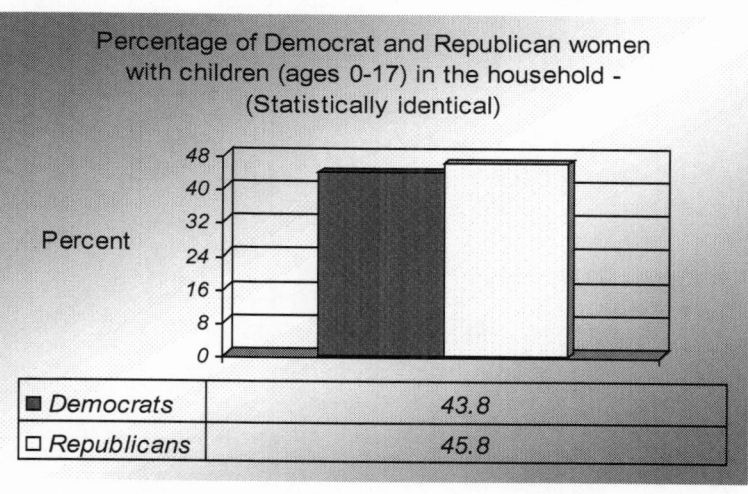

Periodically, the General Social Survey (GSS) asks whether women should work outside the home in various circumstances, and most Democratic and Republican women respond by saying a woman should work if there is no child in the home. However, the views diverge when the hypothetical scenario includes a preschooler in the home. In that case, Republican women are much less likely to agree that the woman should work.

Figure 95. Should a woman work outside the home "when there is a child under school age"? (GSS surveys in 1988, 1994, and 2002 of women aged 22-65 years, based on 1021 cases, with confidence level of 99+%, and with a relative proportion of .1.40)

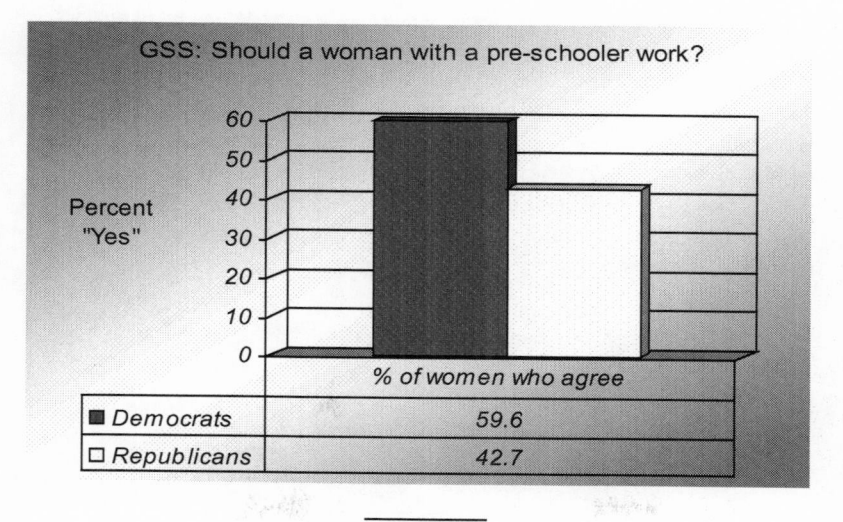

The results shown in Figure 95, above, are not surprising since Democratic women are less inclined to believe that preschool children suffer when the mother works outside of the home. The aggregate results of several GSS surveys, conducted in years 1997 through 2006, show that, by 69.8 to 59.3 percent, Democratic women are more likely than Republican women to disagree that "a preschool child is likely to suffer if his or her mother works."[36]

Is Housework Fulfilling?

I hate housework! You make the beds, you do the dishes — and six months later you have to start all over again.

— Comedian Joan Rivers[37]

Another possible factor accounting for the difference in female work hours is the attitude of women with regard to housework. In 1988, 1994, and 2002 the GSS asked women: "Do you agree or disagree...being a housewife is just as fulfilling as working for pay?" Republican women were more likely to agree, as evident in Figure 96, below.

Figure 96. Is housework fulfilling? (GGS surveys conducted in 1994 and 2002 of women aged 22-65 years, based on 769 cases, with confidence level of +99%, and with a relative proportion of .77)

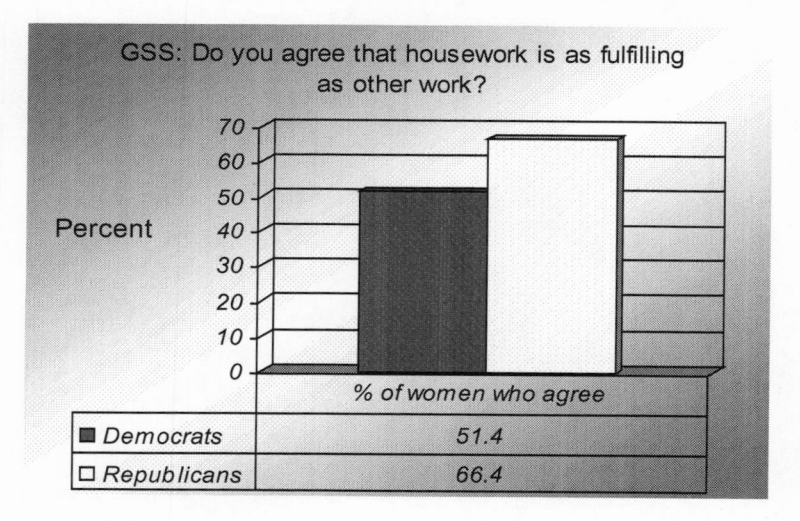

Last, but probably most important, financial need could explain the fact that Democratic women work longer hours outside of the home. We can deduce that the average Democratic woman has a lower pay rate than her Republican coun-

---

36 GSS surveys of 1942 women aged 22-65 years, with statistical significance of 99+% and a relative proportion of 1.82

37 Joan Rivers (attributed), "Quotationz.Com."

terpart, since she works about 1.5 extra hours per week to get (approximately) the same wages. This lower pay rate may be explained by the fact that a Demo-cratic woman is a little less likely to have a 4-year college degree.[38] In addition, Democratic women generally have less family income, even though their own occupational earnings are comparable to those of Republican women. The family income differential is shown in Figure 97, below, and is probably attributable to the fact that Democratic women are less likely to be married.

Figure 97. Percentage of women, aged 22-65 years, with family incomes over $50,000 per year (GSS surveys conducted in 1998 through 2006, based on 3679 cases, with confidence level of 99+%, and with a relative proportion of .79)

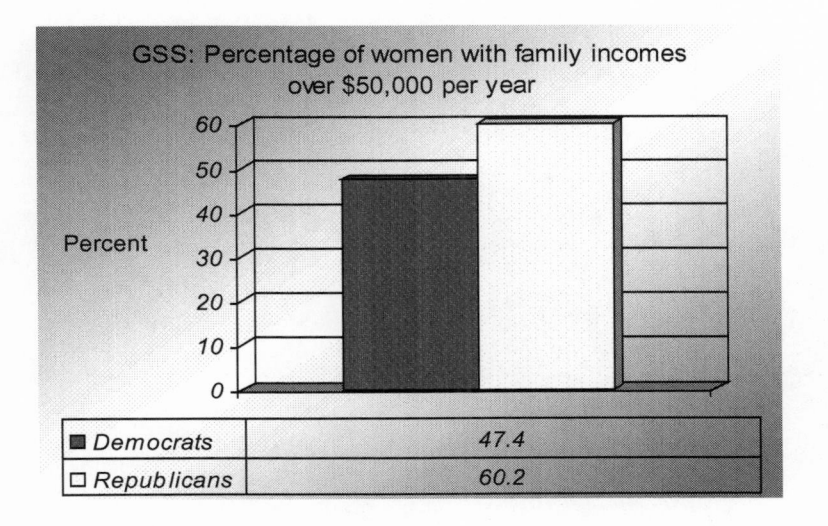

The lower wage rates and the smaller family incomes put Democratic women under greater financial pressure, and this financial pressure increases the need for them to work longer hours.

Other factors related to women workers

> To find joy in work is to discover the fountain of youth.
> — Author Pearl S. Buck[39]

In the case of men, there were significant differences with regard to work-attitudes and emotions, and this was also true for women, but to a lesser degree.

---

38 However, Democratic women are as likely, or more likely, to have an advanced (graduate) university degree.

39 Pearl Buck quoted by Frank McDonough, "Another View: You'll Just Know When It's Time to Go," (May 6, 2003), Retrieved March 17, 2007, from http://www.gcn.com/print/22_12/22144-1.html.

Republican women — like Republican men — are a little more likely to say they are "very satisfied" with their jobs.

Figure 98. "All in all, how satisfied would you say you are with your job?" (Women) (GSS surveys conducted in 2002 and 2006, based on 1106 cases, with overall confidence level of 96%, and a relative proportion of .89)

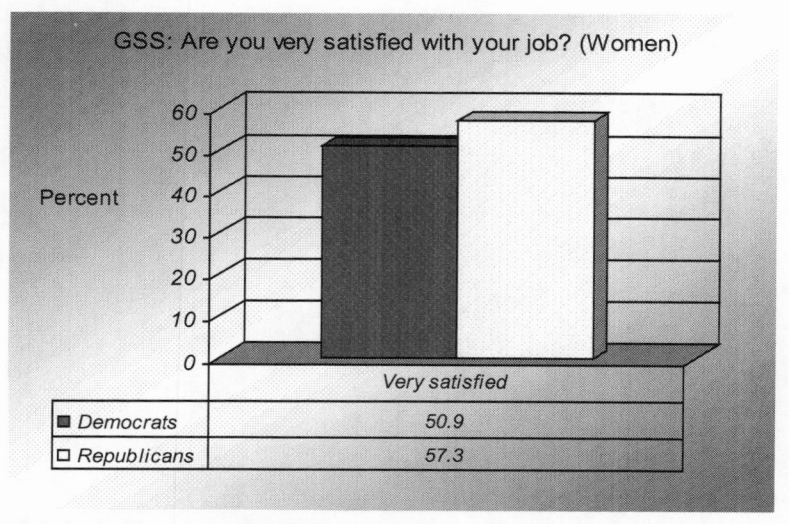

Democratic women are more likely to reject pay cuts in order to avoid unemployment. See Figure 99.

Figure 99. Percentage disagreeing with this statement: "In order to avoid unemployment I would be willing to accept a position with lower pay." (GSS survey conducted in 2006, based on 265 cases, with confidence level of 95%, and relative proportion of 1.48)

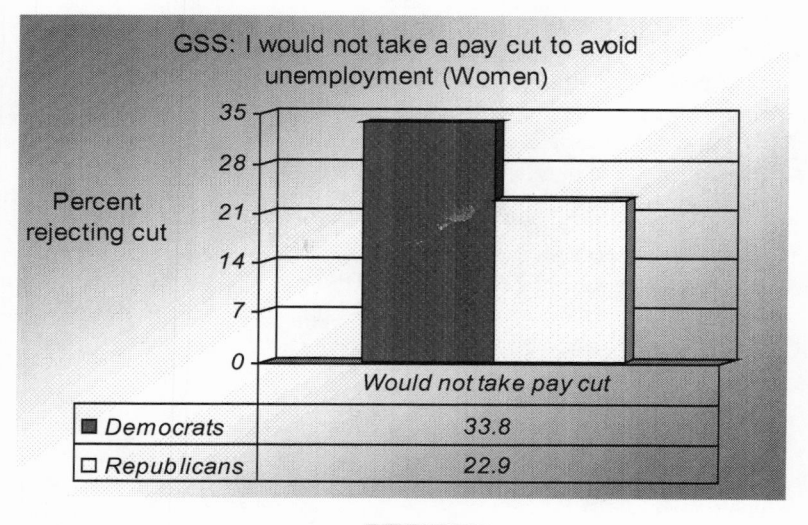

In addition, it appears that a Democratic woman would be less likely than her Republican counterpart to talk to an underachieving employee, or about the underachieving employee to the boss.

Figure 100. If I saw an employee who was not working as hard or well as he could, it is "not at all likely" that I would ... (GSS surveys conducted in 2002 and 2006, based on, from left to right, 1073 and 1025 cases, with a confidence level of 98% and 93% (marginal), and with relative proportions of 1.23 and 1.19)

	Talk directly to worker	Speak to manager
Democrats	35.5	31.9
Republicans	28.8	26.7

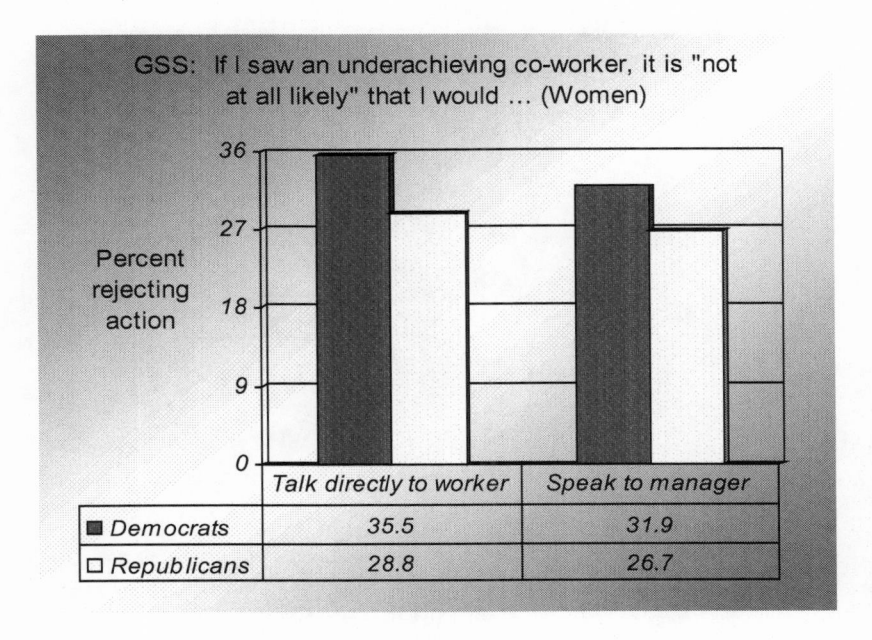

Democratic women are also a bit more likely than Republican women to say that emotions have negatively affected the quality of their work.

Notably, no statistically significant difference was found regarding the attitudes of Democratic and Republican women with respect to their pride in their employers, their willingness to work harder to help their employers, or the likelihood that they would quit their jobs if they could afford to do so, financially.

Figure 101. "During the past 4 weeks, have you had ... the following problem ... as a result of any emotional problems (such as feeling depressed or anxious)"? You "didn't do work or other activities as carefully as usual"? — (Women) (GSS survey conducted in 2000, based on 471 cases, with confidence level of 97%, and a relative proportion of 1.64)

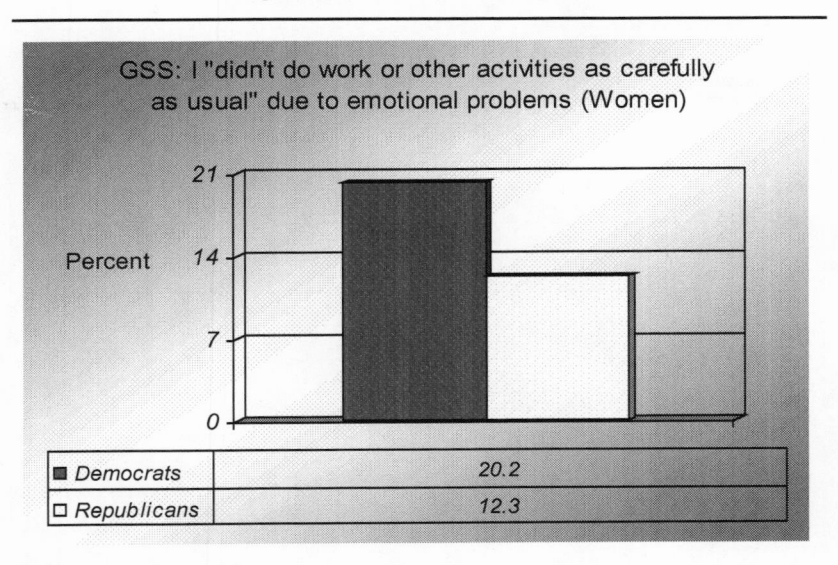

GSS: I "didn't do work or other activities as carefully as usual" due to emotional problems (Women)

■ Democrats	20.2
□ Republicans	12.3

MISCELLANEOUS WORK FACTORS FOR MEN AND WOMEN

Work "prestige"

> Let's face it, we all have egos. You might not be able to give people huge salary increases, but here is a lot you can do by giving them better titles, access to new perks, etc.
>
> — Bob Rosner, Author and columnist[40]

The National Opinion Research Center (NORC), an organization based at the University of Chicago, developed a system for rating the "prestige" of various occupations. To develop the system, survey respondents were asked to evaluate the prestige of each occupation and assign to it a numerical ranking. Those numerical scores were averaged and summarized in a table of "prestige" scores. A few of the scores are presented in Table 25, below.

GSS uses the NORC system to assign a prestige score to the each of the occupations identified in its surveys. Figure 102, below, shows the mean prestige scores for male Democrats and Republicans. The lowest score possible is 17 and the highest is 86. There has been a small but significant difference between Democratic and Republican men since 1988, when the current index was developed.

> Never make friends with people who are above or below you in status. Such friendships will never give you any happiness.
>
> — Chanakya, Indian politician and writer[41]

---

40 Bob Rosner, "Working Wounded: High Maintenance Help," in *ABC News* (August 25, 2006), Retrieved January 31, 2007, from: http://abcnews.go.com/Business/CareerManagement/story?id=2379097.

41 Chanakya (attributed), "Brainyquote.Com."

Table 25. NORC/GSS occupational "prestige" scores, as last updated in 1989 (Scores range from a low of 17 to a high of 86.)

Occupation	Score	Occupation	Score
Physicians	86	Police detectives	60
Attorneys	75	Actors and directors	58
College professors	74	Statisticians	56
Physicists & astronomers	73	Kindergarten teachers	55
Architects	73	Librarians	54
Aerospace engineers	72	Dental hygienists	52
Judges	71	Real estate sales people	49
CEOs	70	Funeral directors	49
Psychologists	69	Musicians	47
Clergy	69	Photographers	45
Pharmacists	68	Receptionists	39
Registered nurses	66	Recreation workers	38
Athletes	65	Artists and performers	36
Accountants/auditors	65	Car sales people	34
Mechanical engineers	64	Hotel clerks	32
Authors	63	Baby sitters	29
Veterinarians	62	Shoe sales people	28
Sociologists	61	Bill collectors	24
Airplane pilots	61	Messengers	22
Legislators	61	Door-to-door sales people	22
Physicians' assistants	61	Newspaper sales people	19

Figure 102. Average occupational prestige scores for Democratic and Republican men (GSS surveys conducted in 1988 through 2006, based on, left to right, 2000, 2205, and 3198 cases, with confidence level of 99+% for all differences)

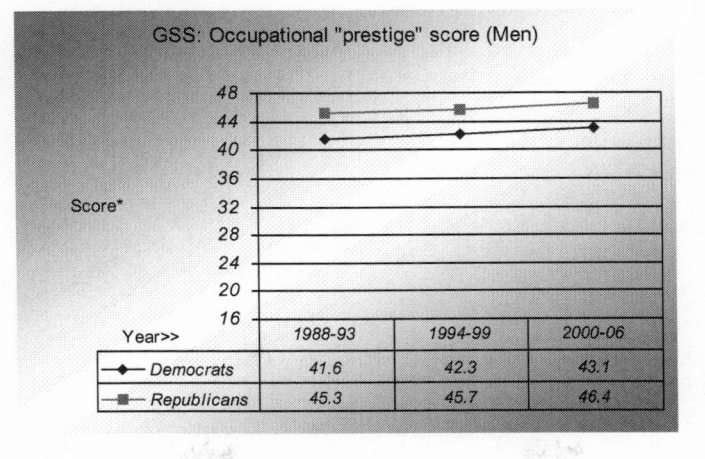

GSS: Occupational "prestige" score (Men)

Year>>	1988-93	1994-99	2000-06
Democrats	41.6	42.3	43.1
Republicans	45.3	45.7	46.4

With regard to women there are a few interesting phenomena. First, women of both parties have increased the prestige of their work substantially, as compared to men. Second, the prestige advantage held by Republican women, just a few years ago, has been cut in half. Finally, Democratic men hold jobs with substantially less prestige than women of either political party. (Compare the most recent prestige rating for Democratic men, shown in Figure 102, with the most recent prestige ratings for women, shown in Figure 103, below.)

Figure 103. Average occupational prestige scores for Democratic and Republican women (GSS surveys conducted in 1988 through 2006, based on, left to right, 2713, 2931, and 4103 cases, with confidence level of 99+% for all differences)

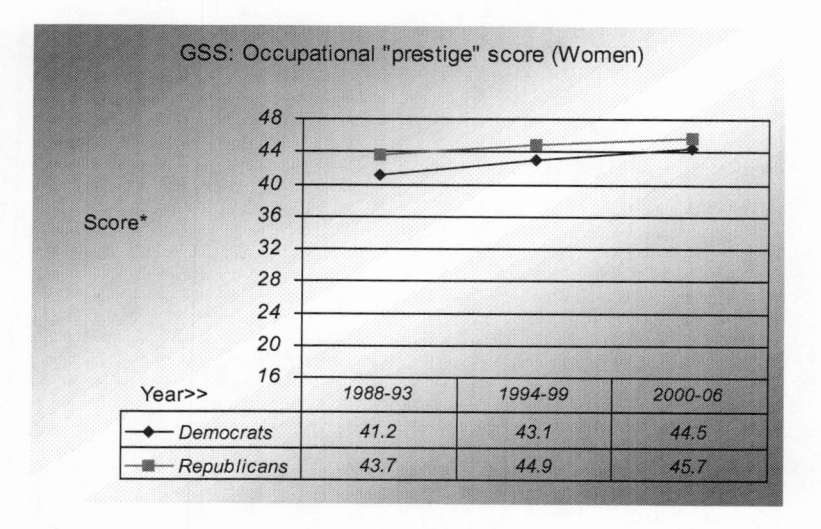

Year>>	1988-93	1994-99	2000-06
◆ Democrats	41.2	43.1	44.5
■ Republicans	43.7	44.9	45.7

*The lowest score possible is 17, and the highest is 86.

Reality check – Prestige is in flux

The NORC prestige rankings were produced in 1989, and it is very likely that some professions would now be judged differently. In 2006, a Harris Interactive survey asked respondents to give their prestige rankings for 23 different professions. The five most prestigious fields for Democrats were, in rank order, firefighter, medical doctor, nurse, teacher, and scientist. For Republicans the top spots were firefighter, medical doctor, military officer, scientist, and nurse. The least prestigious occupations, for Democrats, were real estate agent, followed by actor, stockbroker, business executive, and union leader. For Republicans, the least prestigious jobs were actor, real estate agent, union leader, journalist, and stockbroker.

Type of work

Occupations

> At the age of six I wanted to be a cook. At seven I wanted to be Napoleon. And my ambition has been growing steadily ever since.

> — Salvador Dali, Spanish artist[42]

Over the years, Republican men have dominated the professional and managerial jobs.

Figure 104. Are you a professional or managerial worker? (Men) (various NES surveys from 1952 through 2004, based on, left to right, 584, 1938, 1918, 2458, 2773, and 1561 cases, with significance of 99+% for all points on chart, and with relative proportions of, left to right, .56, .64, .64, .60, .70, and .67)

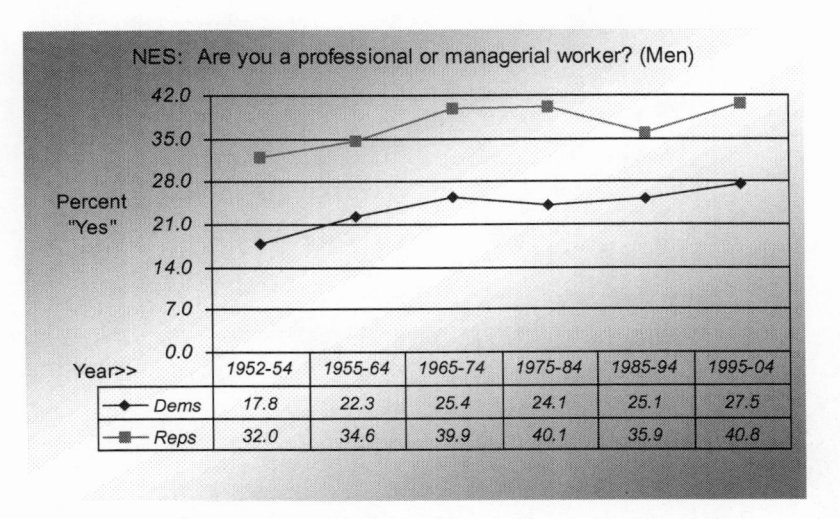

Year>>	1952-54	1955-64	1965-74	1975-84	1985-94	1995-04
Dems	17.8	22.3	25.4	24.1	25.1	27.5
Reps	32.0	34.6	39.9	40.1	35.9	40.8

Democratic men have held sway in the skilled, semi-skilled, and service sectors.

> Ashamed of work! Mechanic, with thy tools? The tree thy axe cut from its native sod, and turns to useful things — go tell to fools — was fashioned in the factory of God.

> —From the poem "Labor," by Frank Soule[43]

Figure 105. Are you a skilled, semi-skilled, or service worker? (Men) (various NES surveys from 1952 through 2004, based on, left to right, 584, 1938, 1918, 2458, 2773, and 1561 cases, with significance of 99+% for all points on chart, and with relative proportions of, left to right, 1.36, 1.35, 1.43, 1.57, 1.40, and 1.58)

---

42 Salvador Dali (attributed), "Quotationz.Com."
43 Frank Soule, "Labor," in *California Magazine* (San Francisco:Hutchings & Rosenfield, 1858), 521.

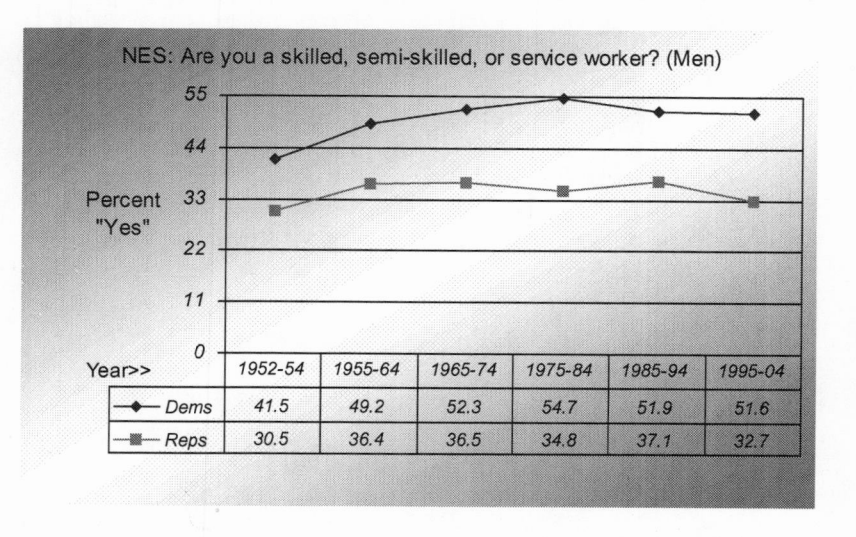

Until recent years, Democratic men have also been more likely to hold un-skilled labor jobs; however, there is no longer a statistically significant differ-ence. In either case, only about 4 percent of men now perform this type of work.

Figure 106. Are you a laborer (except for farm workers)? (Men) (various NES surveys from 1952 through 2004, based on, left to right, 584, 1938, 1918, 2458, 2773, and 1561 cases, with signifi-cance of 99+% for all points on chart except the "1995-04" column, which is not statistically signifi-cant, and with relative proportions of, left to right, 2.2, 1.77, 2.26, 2.03, 1.6, and n/a)

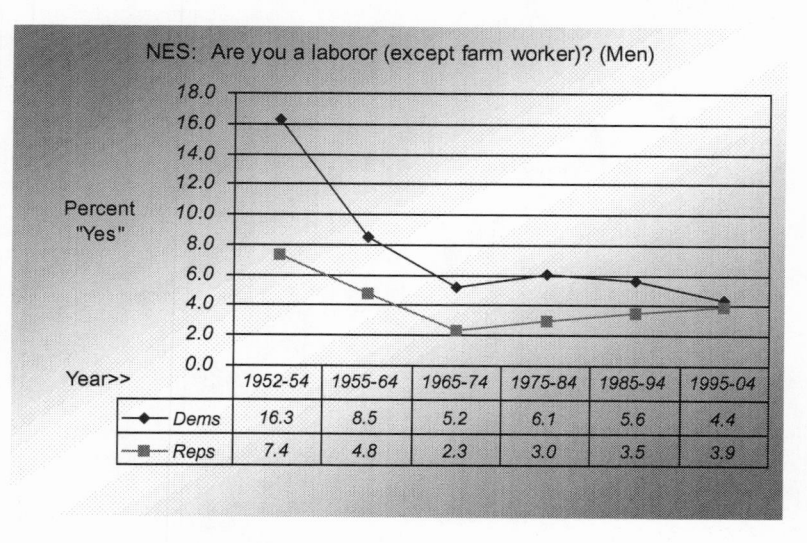

Since 1952 (or sooner), the percentages of Democrats and Republicans doing clerical, sales and farm-related work have been roughly equal (not shown in any graph).

For women, the job disparities are smaller. In the 10-year span from 1995 through 2004, almost equal percentages of Democratic and Republican women worked as professionals (29.6% of Democrats vs. 30.8% of Republicans). Democratic women were significantly more likely to hold skilled, semi-skilled or service jobs (29.6% vs. 14.9%), and Republican women were slightly more likely to hold clerical and sales jobs (34.2% vs. 29.0%). Less than 1 percent of women from either party were laborers.

Private vs. Government vs. Self-Employment

A bureaucrat is a Democrat who holds some office that a Republican wants.

— Vice President Alben W. Barclay (1949-1953)[44]

Democrats are more likely to work for the government, rather than a private employer, however, the gap has closed sharply in recent years.

Figure 107. "Are you employed by the federal, state, or local government?" (combined results of GSS surveys conducted in 1985-1986 and in 2000-2006, based on, left to right, 1888 and 7301 cases, with confidence level of 99+%, and with relative proportions of 1.77 and 1.17)

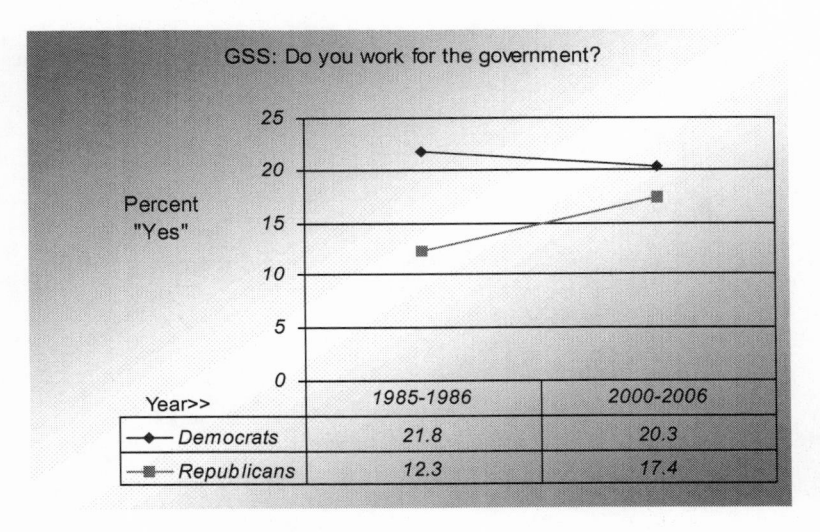

Another survey addressing this issue is shown in Table 26, below.

---

44 Vice President Alben W. Barkley (attributed), "The Quotations Page."

Table 26. Other relevant surveys

Survey and Issue	Dems	Reps	No. of cases	Conf %	RP
NES 2004 survey: "Were you (are you) employed by a federal, state or local government?"	**31.8**	20.8	547	+99	1.53

Republicans are more likely to be self-employed. Figure 108, below, shows the trend since 1972.

Figure 108. "Are you self-employed...?" (various GSS surveys conducted from 1972 through 2004, based on, left to right, 4385, 2629, 4842, 4884, 4477, 3101, and 3354 cases, with significance of 99+% for all points on chart, and with relative proportions of, left to right, .61, .72, .59, .60, .73, .72, and .68)

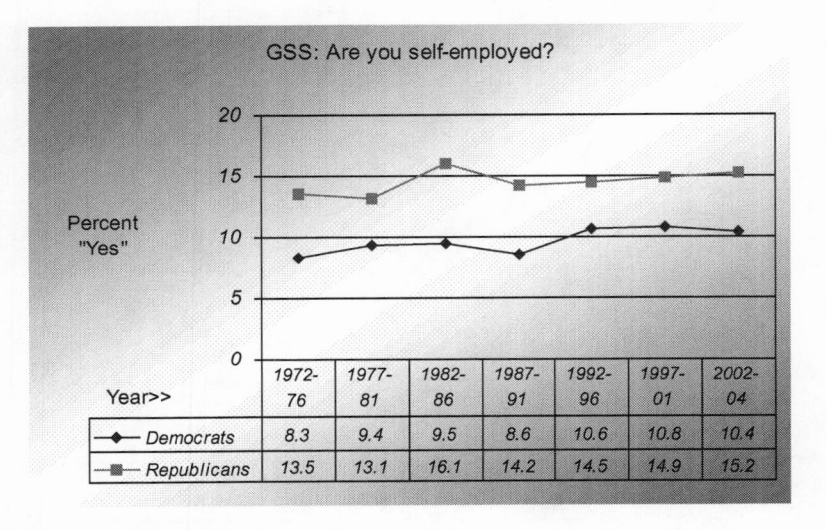

Other work-related information

Union Membership

> No king on earth is as safe in his job as a Trade Union official. There is only one thing that can get him sacked; and that is drink. Not even that, as long as he doesn't actually fall down.
>
> — George Bernard Shaw, Irish playwright[45]

A Democrat of either gender is more likely to have a labor union member in the household; however, the Democrat-Republican gap has narrowed slightly.

---

45 George Bernard Shaw (attributed), "Columbia World of Quotations," (Columbia University Press, 1996).

The trend for more than 50 years is shown in Figure 109, below. Note the sharp decline in membership for constituents of either party.

Figure 109. Does someone in your household belong to a labor union? (various NES surveys from 1952 through 2004, based on, left to right, 2151, 4439, 5640, 6161, 6563, and 4703 cases, with significance of 99+% for all points on chart, and with relative proportions of, left to right, 1.48, 2.06, 1.77, 1.87, 1.67, and 1.70)

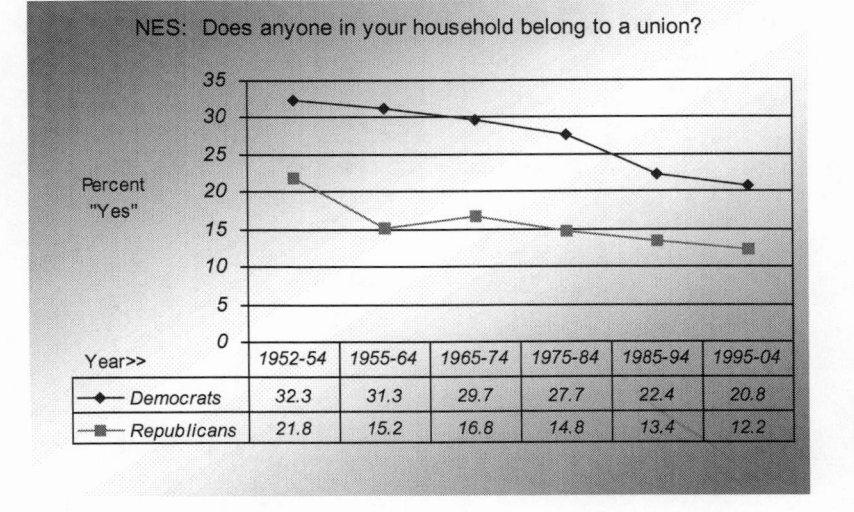

NES: Does anyone in your household belong to a union?

Year>>	1952-54	1955-64	1965-74	1975-84	1985-94	1995-04
Democrats	32.3	31.3	29.7	27.7	22.4	20.8
Republicans	21.8	15.2	16.8	14.8	13.4	12.2

Miscellaneous

Table 27. Other relevant surveys

Issue	Survey	Dems	Reps	RP	No. of cases
Are you a "workaholic"?	Penn, Schoen & Berland 2003	10.0	20.0	.50	590
"Generally work as a team"	Penn, Schoen & Berland 2003	56.0	34.0	1.65	590
"Fax, cell phones, e-mail, internet chang-ing my work"	Penn, Schoen & Berland 2003	38.0	68.0	.56	590

NOTE: Additional employment-related information can be found in Appendix A at pages 325 and 339.

> After many years of trying to find steady work I finally got a job as a historian. Then I realized there was no future in it.
>
> — Anonymous[46]

---

46 "Job Jokes," Retrieved August 8, 2007, from: http://www.analyticalq.com/humor/jobs.htm.

CONCLUSIONS

The "Working Man" award goes to ...

Republicans. Prior to 1970, Democratic and Republican men were about equally likely to be employed. Since that time, however, a gap has grown, and Republican men are now significantly more likely to be employed.

Republican males earn more than Democratic males, and there are a few factors that may explain, and even justify, the earnings gap. Employed Republican males:

- Work longer hours than do employed Democrats
- Are more likely to have higher education degrees
- Are more likely to be promoted to supervisory positions, implying that they have greater technical and/or managerial skills and greater job responsibility. This assumes, however, that they didn't become Republicans after their promotions.
- Have work-related attitudes that are, presumably, more valued by employers
- Might be less likely to let emotional problems interfere with work

From all of this, we could conclude that it is the Republican who is the better "Working Man."

The "Working Woman" award goes to ...

Democrats. Although there is no statistically-significant difference in the occupational earnings of Democratic and Republican women, Democratic women now average about 1.5 extra hours of work (outside of the home) per week. The extra hours worked may be the result of greater financial need or may simply reflect the fact that Democratic women are more likely to be unmarried (even though they are almost as likely to have children in the household). The longer work-week may also reflect greater Democratic acceptance of the appropriateness or even desirability of working with pre-school children in the home.

The work-related attitudes of Democratic and Republican women vary less than for men. However, Republican women generally express more positive statements regarding their jobs and employers.

Other Work-Related Information

Republicans are much more likely to work in professional, managerial, or self-employed positions; and they are more likely to work in "prestige" jobs.

A higher percentage of Democrats are in government jobs, and in unions.

CHAPTER 4: WHO GIVES MORE TO CHARITY?

INTRODUCTION

They Don't F$@#-ing Care!

> Wake up America! We left-wingers care about people and justice. The Republicans only care about money.
>
> — Blogger named "F--k Bush"[1]

> The Republicans don't care about the working poor — they don't know any.
>
> — James Carville, Democratic consultant and pundit[2]

> [T]he compassionate conservative Republicans DON'T CARE ABOUT YOU OR ME. THEY DON'T F$@#ING CARE.
>
> — Columnist Alan Bisbort[3]

The above-stated views are extreme, but not rare. Many Americans seem to believe that Republicans care mostly about money, while Democrats care more about helping people. However, the evidence does not support those assertions — at least, not with respect to charitable donations.

---

1 F--k Bush (pseudonym), October 8, 2004, HaloScan.com blog, Retrieved March 17, 2007, from http://www.haloscan.com/comments/.

2 Joan Walsh, "James Carville," *Salon.com* (March 11, 2002), Retrieved March 17, 2007, from http://dir.salon.com/story/people/feature/2002/03/11/carville/index.html?pn=1.

3 Alan Bisbort, "Compassionate Cancer," *AmericanPolitics.com* (May 8, 2003), Retrieved October 28, 2004, from http://www.americanpolitics.com/20030508Bisbort.html.

Republicans are more likely to give both time and money to charities and other nonprofit organizations. The amounts contributed by Republicans tend to be much larger, and this is partly explained by the higher income earned by the average Republican. However, religiosity and political conservatism are two additional factors that seem to correlate significantly with the tendency of Republicans to give more.

DETAILS

Donations

Who Is More Likely To Give?

[W]ealth isn't bad ... and rich Republicans aren't greedy. To the contrary, wealth makes it possible to make a difference in the world.

— Wayne Allyn Root, explaining the thesis of his book, Millionaire Republican.[4]

Figure 110. Did you donate? (aggregate results of 16 surveys conducted by various entities in 1992 through 2006)

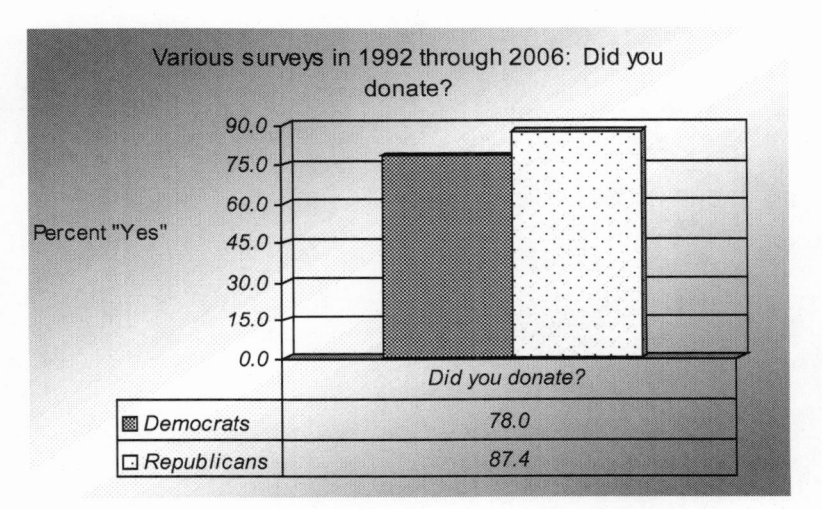

With no apparent exceptions, major surveys indicate that Republicans are more likely than Democrats to contribute both time and money to charities. In addition, the amounts Republicans donate tend to be much larger — even when income levels are held constant. In this chapter we quantify the differ-

---

4 "Millionaire Republican," Promotional Web site, Retrieved April 19, 2007, from http://www.millionairerepublican.com/home/charity.php.

ences and try to explain why Republicans appear to give and volunteer more than Democrats.

Figure 110 shows the combined results of 16 surveys taken by various organizations in 1992 through 2006.[5]

The results of the 16 individual surveys, summarized in Figure 110, are itemized in Table 28, below. For a more detailed description of the survey, and the actual question asked, please see Appendix B 8.

Table 28. Percentage of Democrats and Republicans who reported that they made a donation, or had made one in the prior year

Row No.	Survey/Date (Did you donate in prior year?)	Dem %	Rep %	No. of cases	Conf %	*RP
1	Michigan SOSS — 2006	79.2	95.5	546	+99	.83
2	Harris Interactive survey — 2006	62.9	77.3	374	+99	.81
3	Michigan SOSS — 2005	81.1	96.1	577	+99	.84
4	NES — 2004	75.8	81.9	649	94 (marg)	.93
5	GSS — 2004	78.7	85.7	842	99	.92
6	Mich. SOSS — 2003	80.6	87.6	555	97	.92
7	Community Foundation Trends Survey (CFTS) — 2002/ 2003	82.7	87.7	**2404	95	.94
8	NES — 2002	77.7	86.0	855	+99	.90
9	GSS — 2002	79.1	85.4	815	98	.93
10	Mich. SOSS — 2001	83.8	92.4	586	+99	.91
11	Individual Philanthropy Patterns Survey — 2000	77.0	87.0	**2545	95	.89
12	NES — 2000	77.6	86.7	928	+99	.90
13	Mich. SOSS — 1999	77.2	85.4	723	+99	.90
14	GSS — 1996***	67.2	82.6	875	+99	.81
15	NES — 1996	78.8	91.0	855	+99	.87
16	Economic Values — 1992	73.3	80.7	1340	+99	.91
17	Average percentage	77.0	86.8			
18	Overall proportion (Dem % divided by Rep %)	88.7%				

*RP is relative proportion, which is the Democratic % divided by the Republican %.
**Case numbers include independents in addition to Democrats and Republicans.
***Includes work-related entities such as labor unions.

5 All survey results available to the author indicate that a higher percentage of Republicans make donations; however, the Republican excess shown by one survey (2002 Michigan SOSS) was not statistically significant. For that reason, those results are not included in Figure 110 or in Table 28.

The bottom line of Table 28 shows that the average Democrat is about 89 percent as likely as a Republican to say he has contributed to charity.

> I don't know what compassionate conservative means. Does it mean cutting kids out of after school programs? Does it mean drilling in the arctic wildlife refuge?
>
> — Democratic Senator John Kerry[6]

How Much of "Charity" Giving is Church Giving?

Since Republicans are more likely to regularly attend religious services (see page 35), one might assume that church giving accounts for most of the donation disparity. However, this does not appear to be the case. Three of the surveys listed in Table 28 asked respondents to distinguish between their donations to religious versus secular charities. One of these, the 1996 GSS survey shown in the Table on line 14, is depicted in Figure 111, below.

Figure 111. Did you or your family donate "money or other property for charitable purposes" in the past 12 months? (1996 GSS survey, based on 875 cases, with confidence level of 99+% for all differences, and with relative proportions of, left to right, .81 and .83)

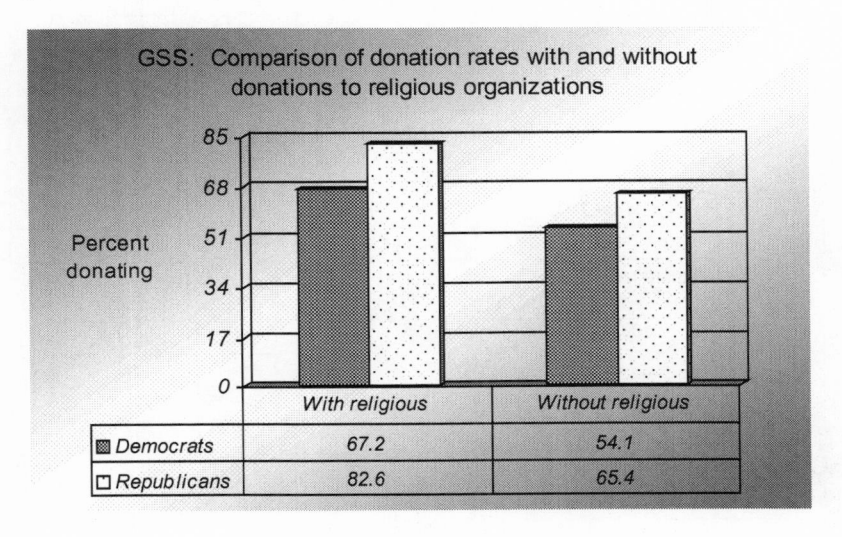

The columns on the left side of Figure 111 show the rate of giving when religious entities are included, and the columns on the right side show the rate of giving when religious entities are excluded. When we exclude the religious organizations the donation percentages drop for both Democrats and Republicans; however, the relative ratio between them is only slightly changed. According to the 1996 GSS survey, Democrats are about 81.4 percent as likely as Republicans

---

6 Anne Q. Hoy, "Kerry Clowns around on 'Daily Show'," *Chicago Tribune*, August 25, 2004.

to donate if religious groups are included,[7] and about 82.7 percent as likely to donate if religious groups are excluded.[8]

> The Republicans could care less about these [poor] families. It is the grassroots Democrats who do the fighting for those who can't fight for themselves.

— Columnist Mark W. Brown[9]

Results from the 2006 and 1999 Michigan surveys (lines 1 and 13 in Table 28) are displayed in Figure 112, below. Again, when religious organizations are excluded the donation percentages drop for both Democrats and Republicans, but the relative ratios between Democrats and Republicans are only slightly changed. The ratio of contributing Democrats to contributing Republicans changes from about 83 percent to 84 percent for 2006, and from about 90 percent to 88 percent for 1999.

Figure 112. Did you or your family donate "money or other property for charitable purposes" during the past 12 months? (2006 and 1999 Michigan SOSSs, based on, left to right, 546, 551, 722, and 723 cases, with confidence level of 99+% for each comparison, and with relative proportions of, left to right, .83, .84, .90, and .88)

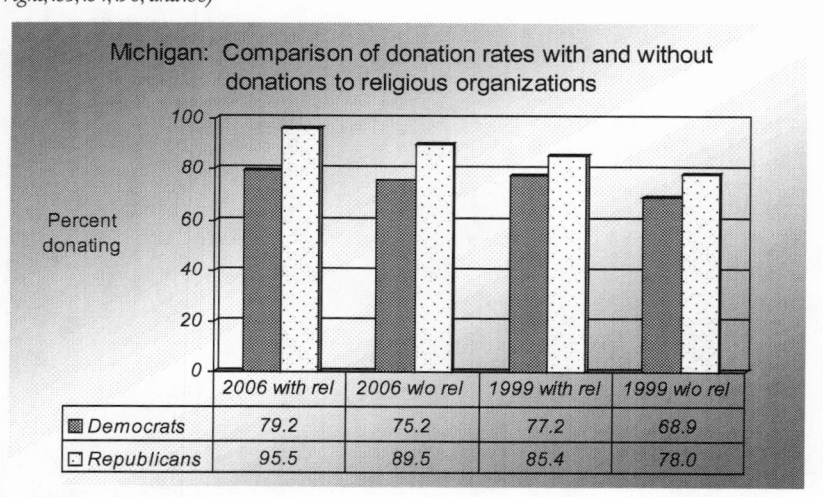

Michigan: Comparison of donation rates with and without donations to religious organizations			
	2006 with rel	2006 w/o rel	1999 with rel	1999 w/o rel
Democrats	79.2	75.2	77.2	68.9
Republicans	95.5	89.5	85.4	78.0

> Bush Republicans have become the transvestites of the political world. They can put a dress and makeup on, make themselves all pretty, and promise to care about the poor ... but behind the mascara, cheap perfume, and come-hither looks, they're the same guys ...

— Arianna Huffington, Author and political commentator[10]

---

7 The calculation is 67.2/82.6 = 81.4%.

8 The calculation is 54.1/65.4 = 82.7%.

9 Mark W. Brown, "Finding My Place," in *Democratic Underground.com* (June 3, 2003), Retrieved August 28, 2006, from: http://www.democraticunderground.com/articles/03/06/p/03_place.html.

10 Arianna Huffington, *Fanatics and Fools* (New York: Hyperion, 2004), 153.

The above findings are not surprising in light of the 2000 Social Capital Community Benchmark Survey — a large national survey of 29,233 cases. After analyzing the survey results, Arthur C. Brooks, a professor at Syracuse University, concluded than religious people are more likely to give to secular as well as religious causes:

> Religious people are more generous than secular people with nonreligious causes as well as with religious ones. While 68 percent of the total population gives (and 51 percent volunteers) to nonreligious causes each year, religious people are 10 points more likely to give to these causes than secularists (71 percent to 61 percent) and 21 points more likely to volunteer (60 percent to 39 percent).[11]

If Republicans participate more frequently in religious activities than do Democrats (and the available data suggest that they do), and religious people are more likely to contribute time and money to secular as well as religious causes, we should not be surprised to find (as we do) that Republicans are more likely to donate than Democrats — even with respect to secular causes.

Who Writes the Larger Check?

> We have things ass-backward here in America.... We constantly hear calls to those who've been the most blessed to "give back something;" that is utter nonsense. It is the thief who should be giving something back because he's produced nothing, whereas the Bill Gates's of the world have already served their fellow man by making life easier for all of us and making jobs in the process.

— Economist Walter Williams[12]

Figure 113. "[H]ow much do you and/or other family members contribute to charitable organizations each year?" (Michigan SOSS 42 conducted in 2006, based on 384 respondents, with confidence level of 99+%)

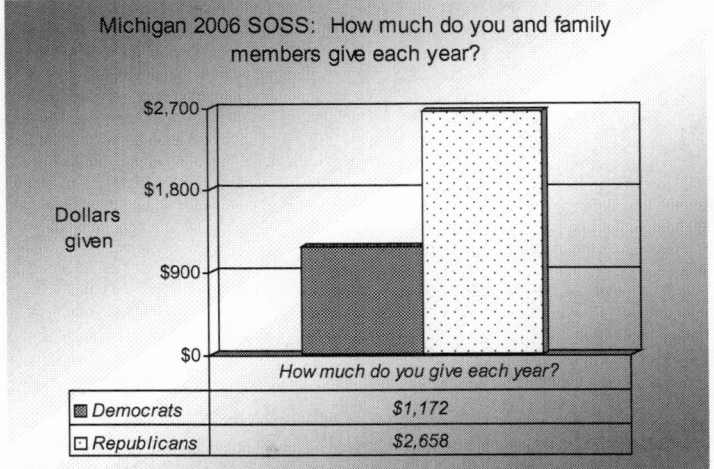

11 Arthur C. Brooks, "Religious Faith and Charitable Giving," *Policy Review* (October and November, 2003): 43.
12 Walter Williams, (Destiny Magazine, July 1995).

With regard to the amount of the donations, the differences between Democrats and Republicans are very great. Several surveys suggest that Republicans, on average, contribute significantly larger amounts. One of the more recent dollar-quantified surveys is the Michigan State of the State Survey, conducted in 2006. Overall charitable giving averages are shown in Figure 113, above.

The Michigan survey suggests that the average Republican may give more than twice as much to charity as his Democratic counterpart. Similar disparities were found in all other dollar-quantified surveys reviewed. Results of those surveys are shown in Figure 114, below.

Figure 114. How much do you and/or other family members contribute to charitable organizations each year? (Michigan SOSS surveys conducted in 2005 and 2003, Community Foundation Trends Survey conducted in 2002-2003, Individual Philanthropy Patterns Survey conducted in 2000, Michigan SOSS 19 conducted in 1999, and GSS conducted in 1996, based on, left to right, 411, 360, 2404, 2545, 464, and 576 cases, with confidence level of mean differences ranging from 95 to 99%) Note: The case numbers for the Community Foundation Trends Survey and Individual Philanthropy Patterns Survey include independents as well as Democrats and Republicans.

Various surveys: Average amounts donated by those who at least gave something

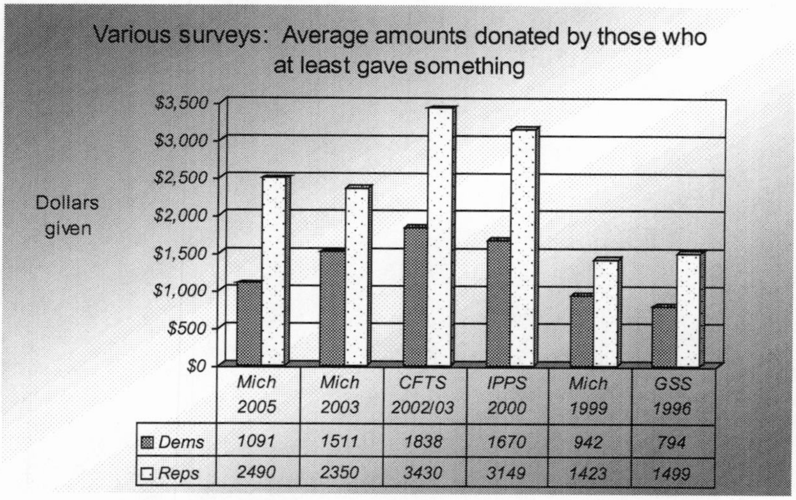

	Mich 2005	Mich 2003	CFTS 2002/03	IPPS 2000	Mich 1999	GSS 1996
Dems	1091	1511	1838	1670	942	794
Reps	2490	2350	3430	3149	1423	1499

Yet again, President Bush and Republicans in Congress are stealing from the poor to give to the rich. Does their shame know no bounds?

— Democratic Congressman Pete Stark[13]

Although the disparities shown in Figure 113 and Figure 114 are large, they are understated because they do not reflect the Democrats and Republicans who

---

13 "Stark Attacks Republicans for Stealing from the Poor and Giving to the Rich," May 10, 2006, Congressman's Web page, Retrieved March 17, 2007, from http://www.house.gov/stark/news/109th/pressreleases/20060510_Stealing.htm.

gave nothing at all. To get the bottom-line, per capita contribution amounts, we need to multiply the amount given according to each survey by the rate of giving for that survey (found in Table 28, on page 131). Those adjustments slightly increase the donation gap because Democrats tend to give smaller amounts and are more likely to give nothing at all. Adjusted per capita contribution amounts are shown in Figure 115, below.[14]

Figure 115. Annual donation amounts of those who made contributions (per Figure 113 and Figure 114), multiplied times the percentages who at least gave something (per Table 28)

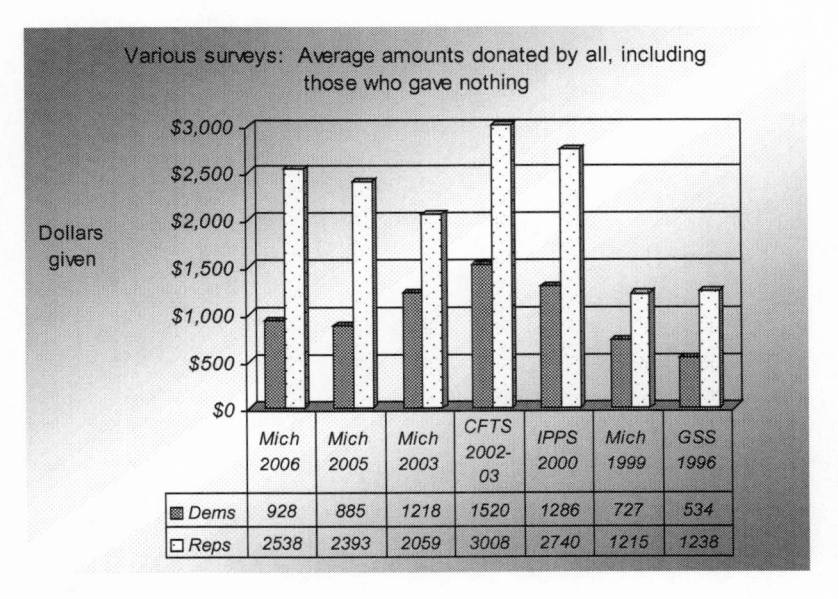

These same results are displayed in Table 29, below. On the bottom line we see the aggregate results of all dollar-quantified surveys. On average, Democrats seem to give less than half as much as Republicans.

Table 29. Figure 115 results in tabular form. These are average amounts given by all, including those who gave nothing at all.

Average amounts donated, including those who gave nothing Survey/Date	Dem Amt.	Rep Amt.	Conf of <u>amt.</u> of giving	Conf of <u>rate</u> of giving
Michigan SOSS 2006	$928	$2538	+99	99
Michigan SOSS 2005	885	2393	+99	99
Michigan SOSS 2003	1218	2059	+99	97

---

14 This was calculated by multiplying frequency of giving times the average amount given.

CFTS 2002/03	1520	3008	95	95
IPPS 2000	1286	2740	95	95
Michigan SOSS 1999	727	1215	+99	+99
GSS 1996	534	1238	+99	+99
Averages	$1014	$2170		
Overall proportion (Dem amt. divided by Rep amt.)	46.7%			

In most Democrats' minds, conservative Republicans do not care if children go to bed hungry, and they are racist, intolerant, regard women as inferior, are stingy and mean spirited ...

— Author and radio talk-show host Dennis Prager[15]

Average Vs. Median

Figure 116. How much do you and/or other family members contribute to charitable organizations each year? — MEDIAN amounts (Michigan SOSS surveys conducted in 2006, 2005, 2003, and 1999, and GSS conducted in 1996, based on, left to right, 384, 411, 360, 464, and 576 cases)

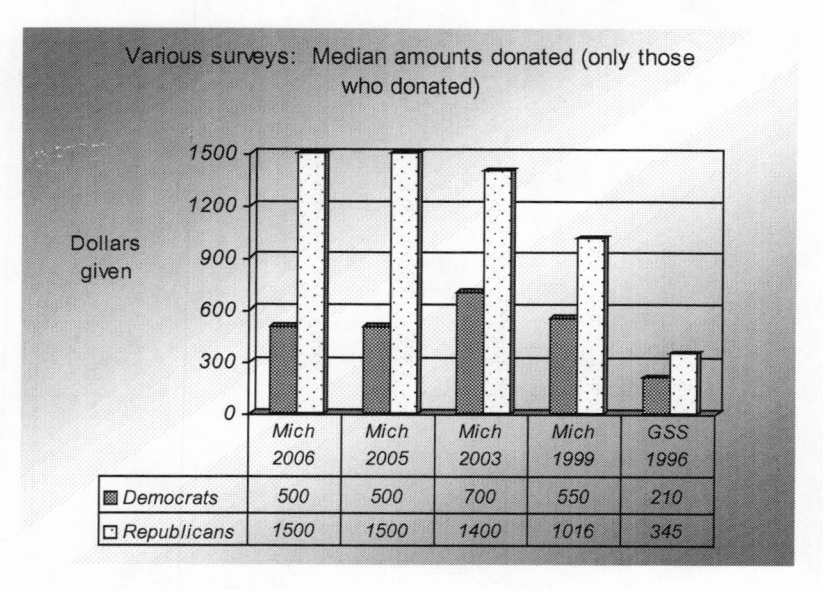

Averages can be misleading, since the large donations of a few can raise the mean to misleading heights. Figure 116 shows some of the same surveys included in Figure 115; however, median contribution amounts are shown instead of aver-

15 Dennis Prager, "Why the Left Fights," in *FrontPageMagazine.com* (July 6, 2005), Retrieved March 17, 2007, from: http://www.frontpagemag.com/Articles/ReadArticle.asp?ID=18665.

age contribution amounts.[16] Of course, the medians represent the midpoints of contribution values. That is, there are equal numbers of contributors who give more and less than these amounts. Republican gifting is still much greater, even when measured by median amounts. This means that the tendency of Republicans to donate larger amounts is probably fairly widespread (involving large percentages of Republicans), and is not attributable to the very large gifts of a few ultra-rich Republicans.

The donations disparity is particularly surprising given that Democrats are much more likely to advocate support for the needy. This is shown in many surveys, one of which is depicted in Figure 117, below.

Figure 117. How important is it "to help people in America who are worse off than yourself"? (GSS survey conducted in 2004, based on 929 cases, with confidence level of 99+%, and with a relative proportion of 1.31)

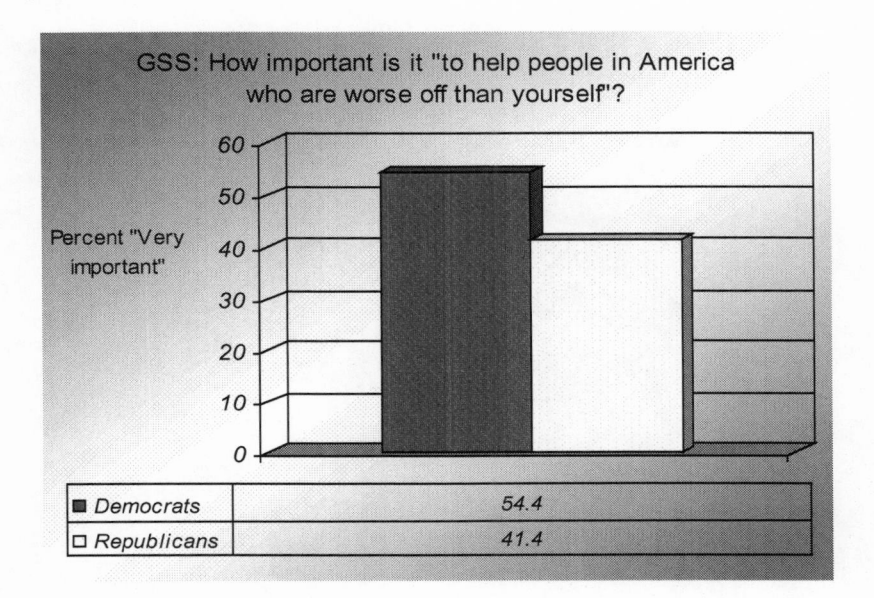

Do Republicans Diss the Homeless?

A man who sees another man on the street corner with only a stump for an arm will be so shocked the first time he'll give him sixpence. But the second time it'll only be a three penny bit. And if he sees him a third time, he'll have him cold-bloodedly handed over to the police.

— German poet Bertolt Brecht[17]

---

16 The CFTS and IPPS surveys were excluded because median information was not available for those surveys.

17 Bertolt Brecht, "Three Penny Opera," (1928).

Although Republicans generally donate more than their Democratic counterparts, they are less likely to give money to people on the street. In a 1996 General Social Survey of 864 Democrats and Republicans, 40 percent of Democrats reported that they gave money, food, or clothing to "homeless or street people," whereas only 33 percent of Republicans reported making such contributions (confidence level = 97%). These results were affirmed in 2004 and 2002 GSS surveys of a total of 1653 Democrats and Republicans, in which 68 percent of Democrats reported giving food or money to the street people, but only 61 percent of Republicans reported making such donations (confidence level = 99+%). It appears that Democrats are more likely to give aid to homeless "street people."

Volunteerism

There Is A Significant Difference

Of course, the general tendency of Republicans to give more, and to give more often, could relate to the fact that they have more money to give. Income level might be what statisticians call an "intervening variable" (the link) in the causal chain between the independent variable (political party) and the dependent variable (level of charitable activity). Income level and other intervening variables are discussed in some detail later in this chapter. However, it is obvious that higher levels of earnings do not entirely explain differences in charitable giving because, even when it comes to volunteering, Republicans still outpace Democrats significantly.

> Behold I do not give lectures or a little charity. When I give I give myself.
> — American poet Walt Whitman[18]

Table 30, below, displays the results of several surveys that asked participants whether they recently performed volunteer work. In some cases, the volunteerism was specifically linked to charity work, and in other cases, the respondent might have construed the question to include political or union-related work. Excerpts from the questions are provided. In all cases, Republicans were more likely to have volunteered their time. The table's bottom line shows overall volunteerism rates of 42.5 percent and 53.7 percent for Democrats and Republicans, respectively.

Democrats were only about 79 percent as likely as Republicans to have participated in volunteer causes. The overall results of Table 30 are charted in Figure 118, below, following the table.

---

18 Walt Whitman, "Song of Myself," (1855).

Table 30. *Percentage of Democrats and Republicans who volunteered for charities or other types of organizations (various surveys, as noted)*

Row No.	Survey/Date***	Dem % "yes"	Rep % "yes"	No. of cases	Conf %	*RP
1	Michigan SOSS #42 — 2006: "Last year … did you volunteer for any type of organization?"	40.1	**64.9**	551	+99	.62
2	Michigan SOSS #38 — 2005: "Last year … did you volunteer for any type of organization?"	43.7	**56.6**	580	+99	.77
3	NES — 2004: "Were you able to devote time to volunteer work in last 12 months?"	35.5	**46.4**	643	+99	.77
4	GSS — 2004 and 2002: "During the last 12 months" have you "done volunteer work for a charity"?	47.8	**52.0**	1660	**92	.92
5	Michigan SOSS #32 — 2003: "This year, have you volunteered for any type of organization?"	46.0	**53.2**	560	**91	.86
6	NES — 2002: "Were you able to devote time to volunteer work in last 12 months?"	36.4	**48.9**	854	+99	.74
7	Michigan SOSS #22 — 2001: During the past 12 months, did you volunteer for any type of organization?"	48.6	**57.3**	584	96	.85
8	Pew (via Roper) — 2000: In last year, have you "done any volunteer work for any church, charity, or community group"?	55.0	**65.0**	591	98	.85

9	Michigan SOSS #19 — 1999: "During the past 12 months did you volunteer for any type of organization?"	42.1	**59.0**	723	+99	.71
10	Pew (via Roper) — 1997: In last year, have you In last year, have you "done any volunteer work for any church, charity, or community group"?	51.0	**63.0**	626	98	.81
11	General Social Survey (GSS) — 1996: Have you done volunteer work in any of several different types of charities? (Specifically includes labor unions, but not political organizations.)	52.6	**65.0**	876	+99	.81
12	NES — 1996: "Were you able to devote any time to volunteer work in the last 12 months?"	38.8	**50.8**	859	+99	.76
13	Economic Values Survey — 1992: "Do you, yourself, happen to be involved in any charity or social service activities...?"	25.7	**30.2**	1340	+99	.85
14	Economic Values Survey — 1992: "In the past year, have you donated time to a volunteer organization?"	32.2	**39.9**	1340	+99	.81
15	Average percentages reporting that they volunteered	42.5	**53.7**			
16	Overall proportion (Dem % divided by Rep %)	79.1%				

*RP is relative proportion, which is the Democratic % divided by the Republican %.

**Statistical significance is marginal

***See Appendix F for general information regarding survey source.

Figure 118. Overall percentages of Democrats and Republicans who volunteered for charities or other types of organizations (various surveys, as noted in Table 30, above)

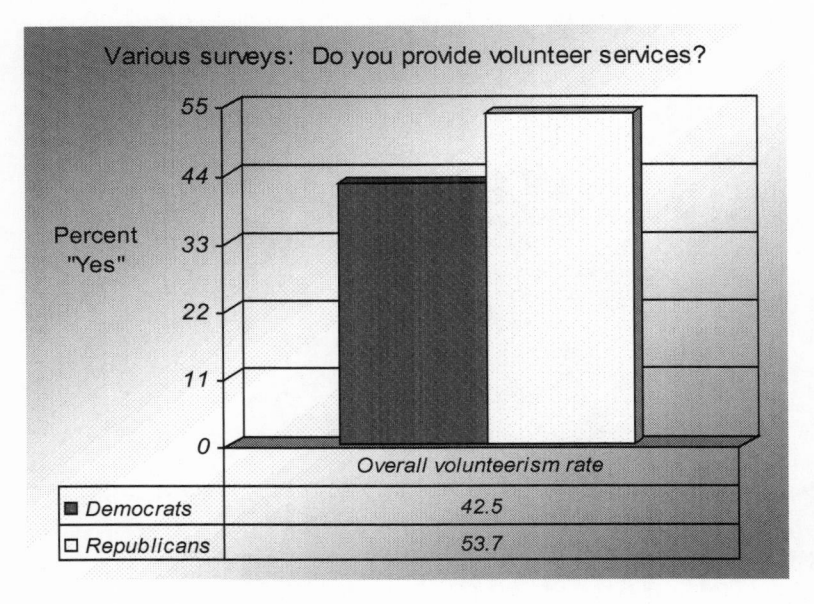

ANALYSIS: WHY SOME PEOPLE GIVE MORE

> If Democrats are more eager to spend "government" money than Republicans are ... does this mean that Democrats are more "generous? Or does it mean that Republicans are more apt to think of government as spending *their* money, while Democrats think of it as *other people's*?
>
> — Columnist James Taranto[19]

As noted, one might assume that the average Republican donates more to charity simply because he has more income than his Democratic counterpart. However, the disparity in volunteerism raises doubts about that assumption. A careful analysis suggests that, while level of income correlates with the amount of giving, other factors may be just as important.

In the remainder of this chapter, three intervening factors, including income level, are analyzed. The goal is to ascertain why Republicans give more money and time to charity.

It is commonly assumed that Republicans:

- have more income
- are more conservative
- attend religious services more frequently

---

19 James Taranto, "Liberals Are Racist, Study Suggests - 2," *Wall Street Journal*, June 23, 2006.

Each of these 3 factors is reviewed below:

Income level

> A check or credit card, a Gucci bag strap, anything of value will do.
> Give as you live.
>
> — Jesse Jackson, Democratic civil rights activist[20]

On average, Republicans earn more than Democrats earn, and their higher incomes give them the ability to donate more. In addition, higher incomes give Republicans a greater tax incentive related to charitable giving. This begs the question: Does the difference in income, between Democrats and Republicans, account for the difference in the amount of charitable giving? Yes, but only to a limited degree.

With regard to 5 of the surveys discussed in this chapter it is possible to break out the amount of donations by the income level of the survey respondents. By so doing, and by using statistical weighting to equalize the number of Democrats and Republicans at each income level, we can determine whether the differences in charitable giving of Democrats and Republicans are caused by income differences.

Figure 119. "[H]ow much do you and/or other family members contribute to charitable organizations each year?" (Michigan SOSS no. 42 conducted in 2006, based on total of 369 respondents. Only columns marked with an asterisk are individually statistically significant.)

Mich SOSS 2006: Average amounts given by those who gave

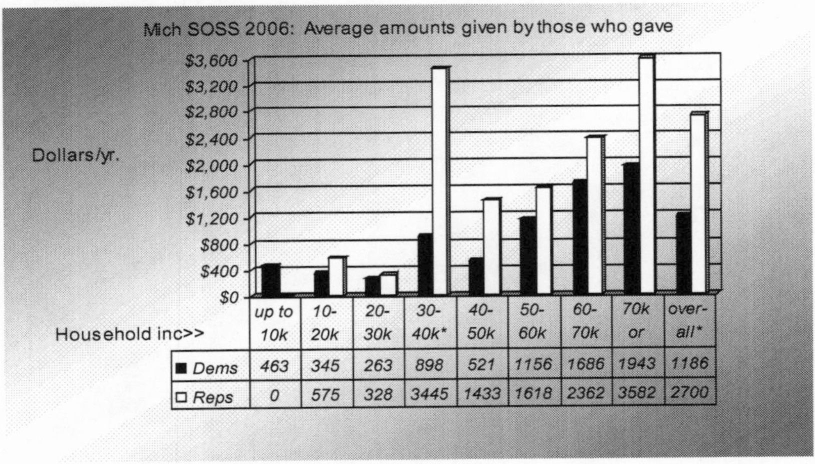

Household inc>>	up to 10k	10-20k	20-30k	30-40k*	40-50k	50-60k	60-70k	70k or	over-all*
■ Dems	463	345	263	898	521	1156	1686	1943	1186
□ Reps	0	575	328	3445	1433	1618	2362	3582	2700

*Differences depicted in columns marked with asterisks are statistically significant. The amounts in the "overall" column differ somewhat from those shown in Figure 113, due to fact that a few people represented in Figure 113 did not answer the income question, and thus are excluded from these results.

20 Jesse Jackson cited in, "Columbia World of Quotations," (Columbia University Press, 1996).

The results for the 2006 Michigan SOSS are shown in Figure 119. We saw the overall results of this survey in an earlier graphic (Figure 113); however, this time the amount of charitable giving is grouped by the total family income of each survey respondent. Although there seems to be a large donations gap within each income range, those differences must be viewed with skepticism due to the relatively small sample sizes and large standard deviations. Only a few columns (marked with asterisks) depict mean differences that are statistically significant. The "overall" column on the far right side of the chart shows a large and statistically significant difference, but it represents all Democrats and Republicans reporting income, without consideration of income level. In other words, part of the overall difference is attributable to the fact that Republicans have higher incomes.

How Do We Compare the Donations of People with Similar Incomes?

A bone to the dog is not charity. Charity is the bone shared with the dog, when you are just as hungry as the dog.

— Author Jack London[21]

Figure 120. A comparison of the overall amount of donations shown in Figure 119 to the estimated average amount of donations that would have been made if equal numbers of Democrats and Republicans were represented within each income category. Both differences (unadjusted and adjusted) are 99+% statistically significant. For more information regarding the calculation procedures, see Appendix B 9.

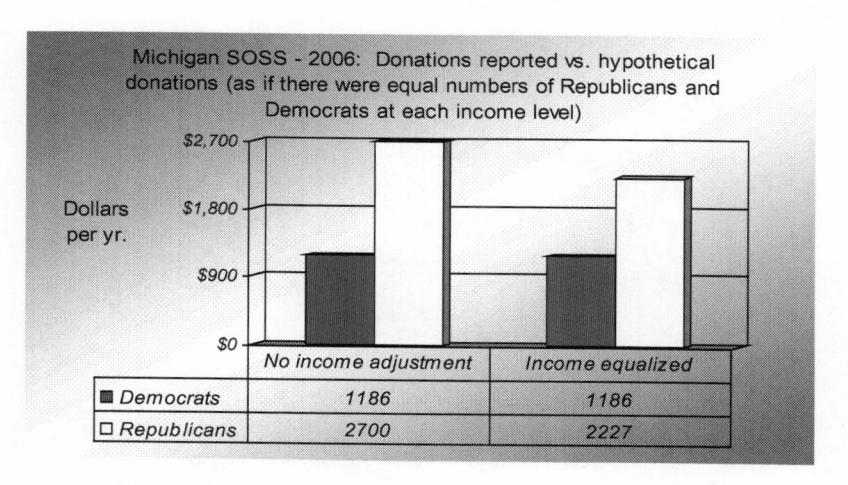

To determine whether Democrats and Republicans at similar income levels donate significantly different amounts, an additional calculation is required. The calculation method is described in Appendix B 9, and the results of that calculation are displayed in Figure 120. The left-side columns of Figure 120 are

21 Jack London (attributed), "The Quotations Page."

the same as the "overall" columns shown on the right side of Figure 119. That is, they simply depict the average amounts donated by Democrats and Republicans, without consideration of income level. However, on the right side of Figure 120, the Republican column depicts the hypothetical amount donated by the average Republican — assuming that the number of Republicans within each income range is identical to the number of Democrats in that income range. In other words, the Republican case numbers for each income category have been statistically weighted to make them proportional to the Democratic case numbers for the same income category.

Note that the donation disparity is only partly reduced. According to the unadjusted survey figures (on the left side) Democrats gave about 44 percent as much as Republicans (1186/2700 = 43.9%). The amounts adjusted to equalize income (on the right side) show a disparity that is only partly reduced, with Democrats donating about 53 percent as much as Republicans (1186/2227 = 53.3%). Thus, the gap was lessened, but a very large disparity remains.

> Earn as much as you can. Save as much as you can. Invest as much as you can. Give as much as you can.
>
> — American Reverend John Wellesly[22]

Figure 121 "[H]ow much do you and/or other family members contribute to charitable organizations each year?" (Michigan SOSS 38 conducted in 2005, based on total of 386 respondents. Only columns marked with an asterisk are individually statistically significant.)

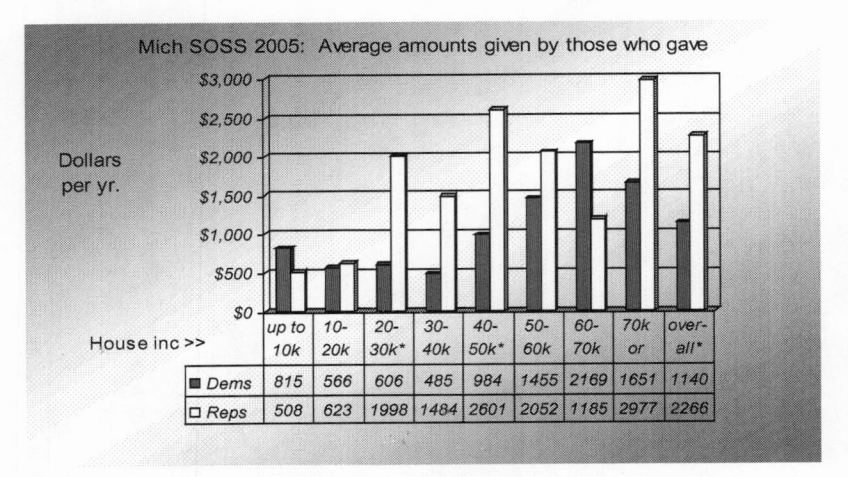

Mich SOSS 2005: Average amounts given by those who gave								
House inc >>	up to 10k	10- 20k	20- 30k*	30- 40k	40- 50k*	50- 60k	60- 70k	70k or	over- all*
■ Dems	815	566	606	485	984	1455	2169	1651	1140
□ Reps	508	623	1998	1484	2601	2052	1185	2977	2266

* Differences depicted in columns marked with asterisks are statistically significant. The amounts in the "overall" column differ somewhat from those shown in Figure 114 on page 135 due to fact that a few people represented in Figure 114 did not report income, and thus are excluded from these results.

---

22 Rev. John Wellesly as cited in, "Why Investors Face a Difficult Balancing Act," in *Telegraph.co.uk* (February 24, 2007), Retrieved March 20, 2007, from: http://www. telegraph.co.uk/money/main.jhtml?xml=/money/2007/02/24/cmsave24.xml.

Figure 121, above, shows the results for another survey: the Michigan SOSS conducted in 2005. Each set of columns shows the average donations made by people at a particular income level and, once again, Republicans seem to give more in almost every case. Again, however, we must be skeptical of the results, due to the small samples and large standard deviations associated with each separate column. (Although the "overall" column on the right side of Figure 121 is statistically significant, it doesn't depict Democrats and Republicans at similar income levels.)

> Just because someone's Republican doesn't mean that they don't also, you know, have the capacity to understand or care about children.

— Actress Angelina Jolie[23]

As we did with the 2006 Michigan survey, we can adjust the results so they depict the donations made by people of like income. This is done in Figure 122, where the Republican amounts, depicted on the right side of the chart, are hypothetical amounts that are predicated on the assumption that there are equal numbers of Democrats and Republicans at each level of income.

Figure 122. A comparison of the overall amount of donations shown in Figure 121 to the estimated average amount of donations that would have been made if equal numbers of Democrats and Republicans were represented within each income category. Both differences (unadjusted and adjusted) are 99+% statistically significant. For more information regarding the calculation procedures, see Appendix B 9.

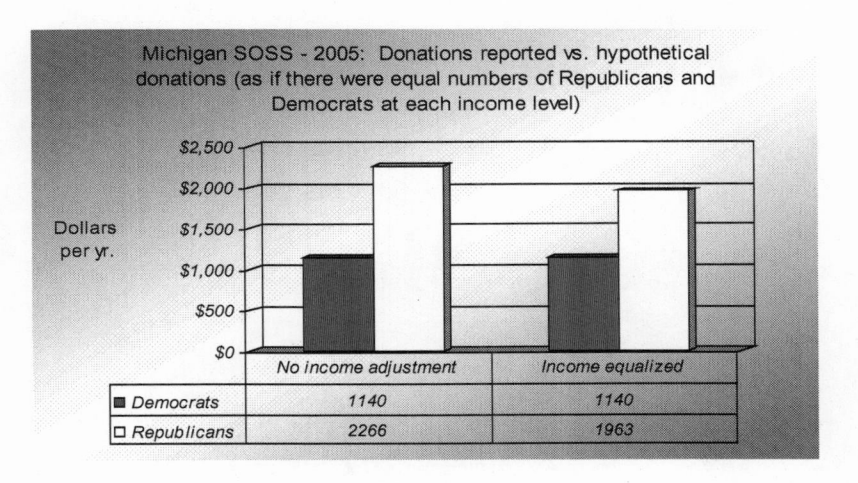

Yet again, we see that equalizing the numbers of Democrats and Republicans within each income range reduces, but does not eliminate, the disparity. For this

23 Angelina Jolie interviewed on, "Anderson Cooper 360 Degrees," (Transcript: CNN, June 20, 2006), Retrieved March 20, 2007, from: http://transcripts.cnn.com/TRANSCRIPTS/0606/20/acd.01.html.

particular survey, the Democratic average donation amount, as a percentage of the average Republican donation amount, changes from 50 to 58 percent.

> The leftist media often portrays conservatives as mean, cruel and insensitive to the plight of the downtrodden. But, as the tax returns of multi-millionaires Dick Cheney and Al Gore prove, the media image is false. The Vice President gives millions to charity, Mr. Gore very little.

— Bill O'Reilly, Author and radio talk show host[24]

There are three other surveys for which we can prepare the same analysis: the Michigan SOSSs conducted in 2003 and 1999, and the GSS conducted in 1996. The results for those surveys, along with those for the 2006 and 2005 Michigan surveys, are shown in Table 31.

Table 31. Democratic contributions as a percent of Republican contributions, after weighting so that equal numbers of Democrats and Republicans are in each income range

Survey	Dem contributions as % of Rep contributions	
	Not adjusted for income	Adjusted to have equal numbers within income ranges
Michigan SOSS 2006	43.9	53.3
Michigan SOSS 2005	50.3	58.1
Michigan SOSS 2003	61.1	69.0
Michigan SOSS 1999	66.2	76.2
GSS1996	52.6	57.1
Average percentage	54.8%	62.7%

In Table 31 we see that Democratic contributions increase when an attempt is made to equalize income; however, Democratic contributions remain far below those of Republicans (just 62.7%).[25] This suggests that other factors, in addition to income, must account for the disparity in charitable giving.

Reality check — Can we really test the impact of income?

As noted, in each instance a significant charity gap remains, even after weighting the case numbers to ensure equal numbers of Democrats and Republicans at each income level. However, if we could reduce the size of the income ranges (e.g., to ranges of just one or two thousand dollars) we would expect the donation gap to get even smaller. That said, it seems very likely that a significant donation gap would remain. This can be demonstrated by the following

---

24 Bill O'Reilly, "Charity: It's the Right Thing to Do," November 30, 2006, Personal Web page, from http://www.billoreilly.com/site/product?printerFriendly=true&pid=20684&said=null&satype=null.

25 I have estimated the per-person donations gap to be about $785, on average, stated in 2007 dollars. In aggregate, this charity gap may exceed $50 billion per year. Please see Table 54 on page 307 for the details.

experiment. If we combine the results in the last 5 surveys discussed (Michigan 2006, 2005, 2003, 1999, and GSS 1996) we find that Republicans with total family incomes of $30,000 to $50,000 seem to donate more than Democrats earning $50,000 to $70,000. The average donation amount for the 244 Republicans earning between $30,000 and $50,000 was $1670, while the average donation amount for the 239 Democrats earning between $50,000 and $70,000 was just $1413. It seems that the lower income Republicans give as much or more than the relatively more affluent Democrats.

Religious beliefs and political ideology

> Charity is the scope of all God's commands.
>
> — St. John Chrysostom, Christian bishop from the 4th and 5th centuries[26]

Income can only explain part of the difference in the rates of charitable giving by Democrats and Republicans. This begs the question: What other factors relate to the tendency of Republicans to give more?

The Gianneschi Paper

In a mid-2000 survey conducted by the Social Science Research Center at California State University, Fullerton, 556 randomly-selected residents of Orange County, CA were queried on their charitable activities, income levels, religious activities, political party affiliation, and political ideology (e.g., conservative, liberal, etc.). Based on the results of that survey, the Gianneschi Center for Nonprofit Research issued a comprehensive paper containing several interesting conclusions, some of which are relevant to the central themes of this chapter. For example, it was noted that Republicans tend to give more to charity, and that income level does not seem to be the reason. The report stated:

> There is a significant association ... between [political] party and the value of annual giving" even though "the relationship between party affiliation and total annual household income in Orange County is not statistically significant.[27]

In other words, Democrats and Republicans in Orange County have similar incomes, yet they have significantly different tendencies with regard to charitable contributions.

It was also noted that the biggest gap between Democrats and Republicans pertains to the amount that is given (versus the percentage who give). Specifi-

---

26 St. John Chrysostom as cited in, "Communicating Christ Cross-Culturally," (Church of the Nazarene, 2002).

27 Gregory Robinson and Kathleen Costello, "Patterns of Giving: A Preliminary Study of Ethnic, Political and Religious Differences among Donors in Orange County (Ca)," (Gianneschi Center for Nonprofit Research, 2001), 15, from: http://www.fullerton.edu/gcnr/Patterns.pdf.

cally, the survey found a "high proportion of Republicans (37.9%) compared to Democrats (23.6%) ... that donate $1,000 or more per year." [28]

Why do Republicans give larger amounts to charity? The Gianneschi report concluded:

> Both political party and ideology, and the characterization of religious beliefs and religious activity are significantly associated with giving. The findings indicate that Republicans and political conservatives are the groups most likely to give at the highest levels; as are those defining themselves as religious conservatives/fundamentalists and those most active in the practice of their religious/spiritual development.[29]

These two factors, religiosity and political ideology, are addressed below.

The Impact Of Religion

> Religion was nearly dead because there was no longer real belief in future life; but something was struggling to take its place —service — social service — the ants' creed, the bees' creed.
>
> — John Galsworthy, English novelist and playwright[30]

The Gianneschi paper addressed two dimensions of religious practice: the nature of the religious beliefs and the frequency of religious activity. Regarding the nature of religious beliefs, the paper concluded:

> A significantly larger proportion of fundamental/conservatives (31.1%) donate $1,000 or more ... than do [religious] moderates (23.5%) or [religious] liberals (18.4%).... [I]t appears that [religious] conservatives are more likely to donate larger amounts.[31]

Unfortunately, I could not find survey data indicating whether Republicans are religiously more conservative than Democrats. (Although one suspects that they are.) However, there is considerable survey information showing that Republicans, on the whole, attend religious services more frequently. This dimension of religiosity is also addressed by the Gianneschi paper:

> [T]here is a linear <u>decrement</u> in the proportion that gives more than $1,000 annually as one moves from the [religiously] "Very Active" (39.9%) to the [religiously] "Not Very Active" (11.1%). ... Clearly, activity in the pursuit of religious or spiritual practice is strongly related to the value of annual giving.[32]

---

28 Ibid.

29 Ibid., 18.

30 John Galsworthy cited in, "Columbia World of Quotations," (Columbia University Press, 1996).

31 Robinson and Costello, "Patterns of Giving: A Preliminary Study of Ethnic, Political and Religious Differences among Donors in Orange County (Ca)," 16.

32 Ibid., 17.

Similar conclusions were reached by Arthur C. Brooks, a professor at the University of Syracuse. In an article in the Oct/Nov 2003 issue of "Policy Review," Mr. Brooks stated his findings with regard to his analysis of the Social Capital Community Benchmark Survey, conducted in 2000:

> The differences in charity between secular and religious people are dramatic. Religious people are 25 percentage points more likely than secularists to donate money (91 percent to 66 percent) and 23 points more likely to volunteer time (67 percent to 44 percent). [33]

The importance of religion is clearly evident in other survey data. The Individual Philanthropy Patterns Survey, conducted in 2000, found that people who attended church at least once per week gave more than twice as much to charity as those who attended on a less-frequent basis ($2,429 versus $1,124). A similar pattern was noted in the Community Foundation Trends Survey, conducted during 2002. Those who attended church at least once per week gave $2,851, while those attending less often gave only $1,331.

The Impact of Political Ideology

> The conventional wisdom runs like this: Liberals are charitable because they advocate government redistribution of money in the name of social justice; conservatives are uncharitable because they oppose these policies. But note the sleight of hand: Government spending, according to this logic, is a form of charity.
>
> –Author Arthur C. Brooks[34]

Generally, Republicans are more likely than Democrats to classify themselves as "conservative," and, as noted, the Gianneschi paper found that political conservatism positively correlates with charitable giving. The methods used and conclusions reached are described in the paper:

> Respondents characterized their political ideology on a five-point scale ranging from "Very Liberal" to "Very Conservative. ... The clearest effect is that 19.77 percent of those that self-identify as "Very Liberal" or "Somewhat Liberal" report contributing $1,000 or more per year compared to 31.73 percent of respondents that characterize their political ideology as "Somewhat Conservative" or Very Conservative." In other words, political conservatives are more likely to donate larger amounts than are liberals.[35]

The link between charitable giving and political ideology is also evident in the Michigan surveys cited earlier in this chapter. Using data from the 2005 Michigan SOSS, we see a very strong relationship between the average amount of charitable donations and the political ideology of the donor. (See Figure 123, below.) These results are limited to households with total income between $40,000 and $50,000 per year, so income should not be a major factor.

---

33 Brooks, "Religious Faith and Charitable Giving," 41.

34 Arthur C. Brooks, *Who Really Cares: The Surprising Truth About Compassionate Conservatism* (New York: Basic Books, 2006), 20.

35 Robinson and Costello, "Patterns of Giving: A Preliminary Study of Ethnic, Political and Religious Differences among Donors in Orange County (Ca)," 15.

Figure 123. The effect of political ideology on the value of charitable contributions (Michigan SOSS conducted in 2005, based on 55 cases, with confidence level (ANOVA F-statistic) of 99+%)

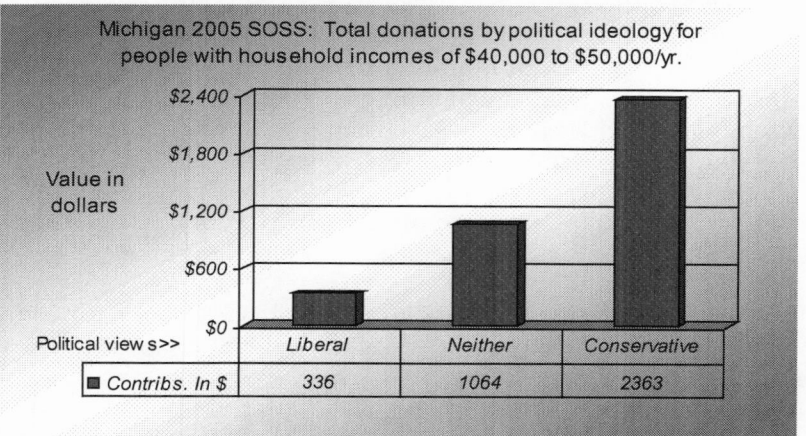

The modern conservative is engaged in one of man's oldest exercises in moral philosophy; that is, the search for a superior moral justification for selfishness.

— John Kenneth Galbraith, Keynesian economist[36]

We see the very same trend in the 2003 and 2006 Michigan SOSSs, which are combined in Figure 124, below.

Figure 124. The effect of political ideology on the value of charitable contributions (Michigan SOSSs conducted in 2006 and 2003, based on 129 cases. Confidence level not measured, but presumed to be in excess of 99%, given the much larger sample size than the very significant and similar pattern depicted in Figure 123.)

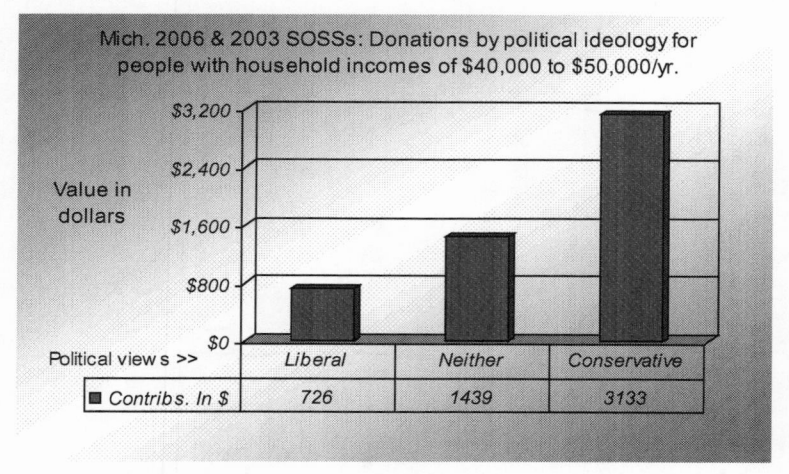

36 Amitabh Pal, "Meeting John Kenneth Galbraith," *The Progressive* (May 2, 2006), Retrieved March 21, 2007, from http://progressive.org/.

Reality check — How do liberals explain the lack of giving?

I'd like to offer a personal perspective regarding the liberal lack of giving. My father, Floyd Fried, was a steadfast liberal for all of his life. He was a generous man, and upon his death left significant sums to charities. However, during his life I heard him rail against the general concept of charities. In his mind, they were tools of the rich, designed to forestall needed action by the government. Like many liberals, my father felt that needy people deserved to have guaranteed entitlements.

I believe that my father was, at the least, partially wrong about charities, and he implicitly acknowledged this when he drafted his final will and testament. Why didn't he leave his money to the federal government to reduce the national debt, or to the State of New York to help pay the salaries of its many employees? He left nothing to government, I think, because he felt the charities he selected could use the money more effectively, and with greater focus on the goals that were particularly important to him.

Not all charities are well-conceived or managed. However, many are efficient entities that can adroitly address important needs that are not well handled at the governmental level. For this reason, we need our charities, and we need to support them, regardless of political ideology.

> I would say to myself Democrats care about the poor and Republicans don't, and how can I join the party that doesn't care about the poor. I finally came to the conclusion that we care about the poor more.
>
> — Rudy Giuliani, former Republican Mayor of New York City.[37]

CONCLUSIONS

Survey data consistently show that Republicans are more likely than their Democratic counterparts to donate time and money to charity. In addition, the average and median amounts given by Republicans tend to be significantly larger. These tendencies can be explained by analyzing the demographic differences between Republicans and Democrats.

Although income level positively correlates with charitable giving, it is not the only important factor. People who frequently attend religious services or who are religiously conservative tend to give more time and money to charitable causes. In addition, people who have politically conservative views are much more likely to donate to charity. All of these traits — higher income, religiosity, and political conservatism — are more prevalent among Republicans than Democrats. Therefore, it is likely that they are the important "intervening variables" that explain the significant difference in charitable giving and volunteerism between Democrats and Republicans.

---

37 "Giuliani Keys on the Economy and Taxes," *Associated Press via MSNBC.com* (February 27, 2007), Retrieved March 21, 2007, from http://www.msnbc.msn.com/id/17360348/.

CHAPTER 5: WHO PAYS MORE TAXES?

INTRODUCTION

Red State Welfare Queens

The same red states who voted to reelect the Chimperor are net tax recipients. They get more than they pay. ... In other words — most of the folks who represent the Red States and those in the red states who voted for the chimp are Red State Welfare Queens....

— Anonymous blogger[1]

Every year, the Tax Foundation, a non-partisan tax research organization, compares the federal taxes paid by residents of each of the 50 states to the respective amounts of federal spending in those states. Generally, these comparisons show that the red states (ones that lean Republican) are net beneficiaries, while the blue states (those that generally vote Democratic) get short-changed. For example, the newly-red state of New Mexico receives nearly $2 in federal spending for each $1 dollar in federal taxes paid by its residents. On the other hand, New Jersey receives just 57 cents in federal spending for every dollar of federal taxes paid by its residents.

These comparisons cause some Democrats to believe that the blue states are being cheated by the red states. In other words, Democrats are being cheated by Republicans. However, a spokesman for the Tax Foundation suggests that the differences in federal spending are modest, and understandable:

---

1 "Red State Welfare Queens," June, 2005, Political Web site, Retrieved March 21, 2007, from http://demopedia.democraticunderground.com/.

> Spending does lean red, but the reason is demographic, not political. Most federal money is spent on retirees, especially Social Security and Medicare. And of course, the elderly have been moving south and west for years. Every large blue state saw its elderly population depleted during the late 1990s.[2]

In other words, federal spending is higher in the red states primarily because people tend to move to the red states just as they start to collect Social Security and Medicare.

We can't blame Republicans for the disparity in federal spending because they are not responsible for retirees moving to the Sun Belt. However, spending is only half of the story: What about the amount of taxes collected? Does the government collect more from people in the blue states than from people in the red states? The answer is "yes," and the reason is obvious: People in blue states tend to earn more than people in red states. However, this does not mean that Democrats pay more taxes than Republicans. To the contrary, the average Republican pays far more taxes than does the average Democrat — in absolute dollars and as a percentage of income. This is generally true for all types of taxes and at all governmental levels (federal, state, and local).

DETAILS

Federal taxes

Income Tax

> The taxpayer — That's someone who works for the federal government but doesn't have to take the civil service examination.
>
> — President Ronald Reagan[3]

Figure 125, below, shows estimated annual federal income tax amounts paid by men and women in 2003. We see that, on average, Republican men paid about 70 percent ($2,900) more in federal income tax than did Democratic men, Republican women paid about 53 percent ($1,700) more than Democratic women, and, on a gender-neutral basis, Republicans paid about 62 percent ($2,300) more.[4]

Figure 125. Estimated average federal income tax paid, calculated by multiplying the percentage of Democrats and Republicans in each income quintile (based on General Social Survey results) times the Congressional Budget Office (CBO) 2003 tax rates and income amounts for the respective quintiles

---

2 William Ahern, "Blue States: Ready for a Less Progressive Tax Code?," in *Commentary* (Tax Foundation, December 15, 2004), Retrieved July 5, 2005, from: http://www.taxfoundation. org/news/show/75.html.

3 President Ronald Reagan, October 27, 1964, Conservativeforum.org, Retrieved March 21, 2007, from http://www.conservativeforum.org/authquot.asp?ID=12.

4 Note: Most of the figures in this chapter are for 2003 amounts. To adjust these amounts for the inflation that took place between 2003 and 2007, add about 15 percent.

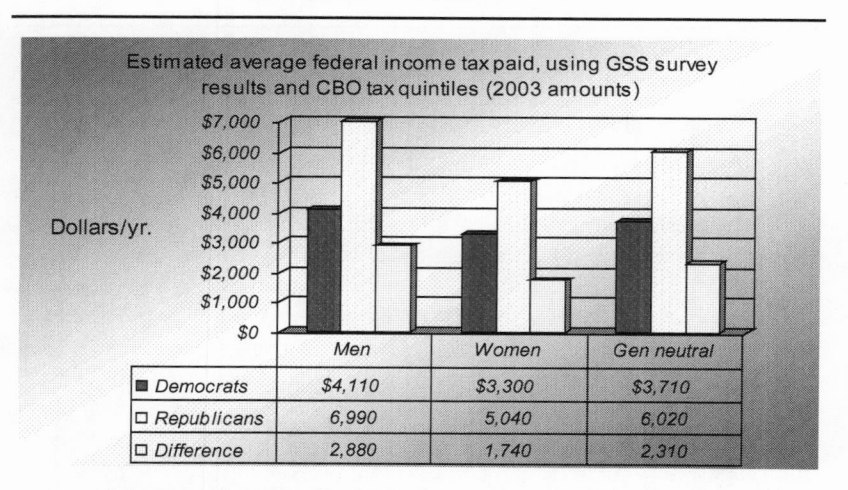

Estimated average federal income tax paid, using GSS survey results and CBO tax quintiles (2003 amounts)

Dollars/yr.

	Men	Women	Gen neutral
■ Democrats	$4,110	$3,300	$3,710
□ Republicans	6,990	5,040	6,020
□ Difference	2,880	1,740	2,310

[The Republicans] will take food out of the mouths of children in order to give tax cuts to the wealthiest.

— Democratic House Majority Leader Nancy Pelosi[5]

The calculation of these amounts is explained in detail in Appendix B 10, and is extremely exciting if you are an accountant. For other readers, however, the following general overview is more than sufficient. The Congressional Budget Office (CBO) periodically releases a publication entitled, "Historical Effective Federal Tax Rates," and it provides the effective individual federal tax rates for taxpayers in 5 different household income levels (quintiles). The 2003 average tax rates are shown in Figure 126, below.

Figure 126. Federal individual income tax rates for 2003 by household income quintile, per CBO's Historical Effective Federal Tax Rates, released in December, 2005

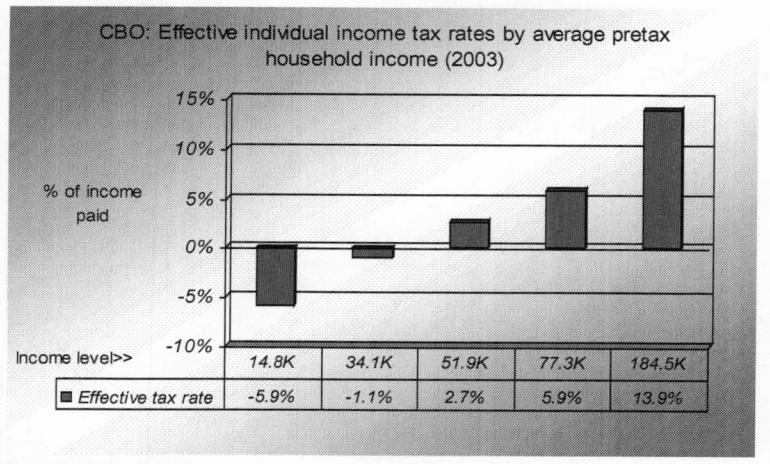

CBO: Effective individual income tax rates by average pretax household income (2003)

% of income paid

Income level>>	14.8K	34.1K	51.9K	77.3K	184.5K
■ Effective tax rate	-5.9%	-1.1%	2.7%	5.9%	13.9%

---

5 Sue Kirchhoff and Richard Wolf, "Rift Appears in GOP over Cutting Taxes and Spending," *USA Today*, November 13 2005.

> A little history. Congress and the courts repelled the first attempt to impose an income tax, ruling it unconstitutional. Only after state legislatures amended the Constitution, in 1913, did Congress impose the federal income tax. The initial tax rate? One percent.
>
> — Larry Elder, Radio talk show host[6]

The effective average tax rates are negative for the lower 2 quintiles (i.e., people whose household income is in the lower 40%). This is primarily due to the Earned Income Tax Credit (EITC), which is a refundable credit designed to give assistance (a form of welfare) to lower-income working people. When we cite the amount of taxes paid by low-income taxpayers, we are really citing a net number: taxes paid by poor people who don't qualify for the EITC, net of the EITC received by others who do qualify for the credit. It would be preferable to separate the amounts, and to consider the EITC in Chapter 8. However, the available data are not conducive to estimating the EITC component, so net amounts are used in this analysis.

Figure 127, below, shows dollar amounts instead of rates. Obviously, 60 percent of Americans paid little or nothing in 2003; almost all federal income tax was paid by about 40 percent of the population. In fact, people in the lowest 20 percent of the income range "paid" a negative tax in the amount of more than $850 per year. (In other words, they were paid by the government.) Again, this was due to the massive EITC program.

Figure 127. Federal individual income tax amounts for 2003 by household income quintile, per CBO's Historical Effective Federal Tax Rates, released in December, 2005. Computed by multiplying the CBO rate per quintile times the CBO average household income per quintile.

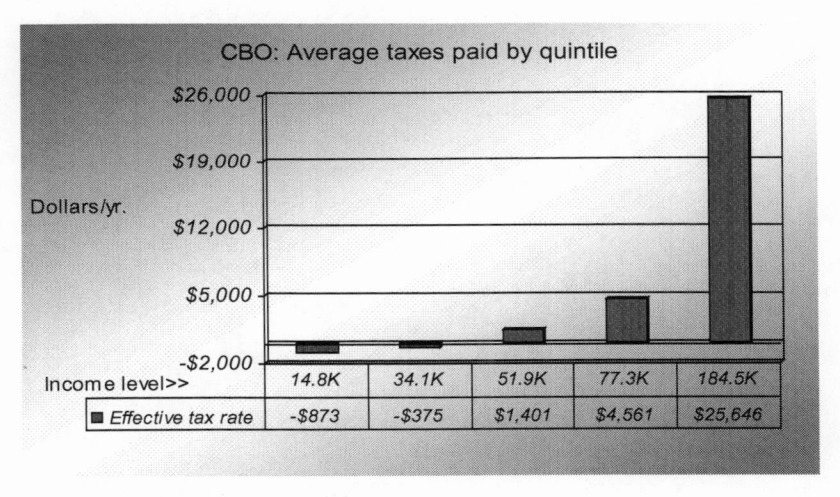

CBO: Average taxes paid by quintile					
Income level>>	14.8K	34.1K	51.9K	77.3K	184.5K
■ Effective tax rate	-$873	-$375	$1,401	$4,561	$25,646

---

6 Larry Elder, *Ten Things You Can't Say in America* (New York: St. Martin's Press, 2000), 212-13.

The Government that robs Peter to pay Paul can always depend upon the support of Paul.

— George Bernard Shaw, Irish playwright[7]

Reality check — By definition, tax cuts are for taxpayers!

As evident in Figure 127, many Americans pay little or no federal income tax — a point that seems to elude many so-called tax "experts." They seem surprised and incensed by tax reduction plans that give larger tax cuts to high-income than low-income Americans. Yet, simple logic tells us that we can't cut the tax burden of someone who pays no taxes.

For example, after President Bush announced his initial tax cutting proposals (early in his administration), the Center on Budget and Policy Priorities made the following shocking discovery:

> Based on an examination of the most recent Census data, [our analysis] finds that the President's tax-cut proposals would provide no benefit to nearly one in every three U.S. families[8]

What the Center failed to state was that no federal income tax cut plan — Bush's or any other — could possibly provide a reduction in taxes to more than two thirds of Americans. That's because federal income tax is not paid by about a third of the American households that have income. "Tax reductions" for those Americans would be, in reality, a distribution of welfare.

The percentage of non-paying Americans has grown rapidly in recent years. The Tax Foundation reports that, since 1985, the percentage of zero-liability tax returns has nearly doubled. If that trend continues, a potentially tyrannical situation might develop, as noted by the Heritage Foundation:

> Are we close to a tipping point where the non-taxpaying class is larger than the group who pays taxes? Are we nearing the point of government dependency that threatens the American Republic left by our Founding Fathers?[9]

The Relationship of Federal Income Tax to Household Income

Of course, we would expect Republicans to pay more income tax because they earn more income. Average 2003 household pretax income for Democrats and Republicans, based on CBO estimates, is shown in Figure 128.

Figure 128. Estimated 2003 average total pretax household income, calculated by multiplying the percentage of Democrats and Republicans in each income quintile times the CBO income amount for that quintile.

---

7 George Bernard Shaw cited in, "Columbia World of Quotations," (Columbia University Press, 1996).

8 "Bush Tax Plan Offers No Benefits to One in Three Families," (Center on Budget and Policy Priorities, February 7, 2001), Retrieved July 6, 2005, from: http://www.cb99.org/2-7-01leftoutshort.htm.

9 "The American Political Experiment: What the 2005 Index of Dependency Tells Us," in *Press release advertising tax seminar* (Heritage Foundation, June 13, 2005).

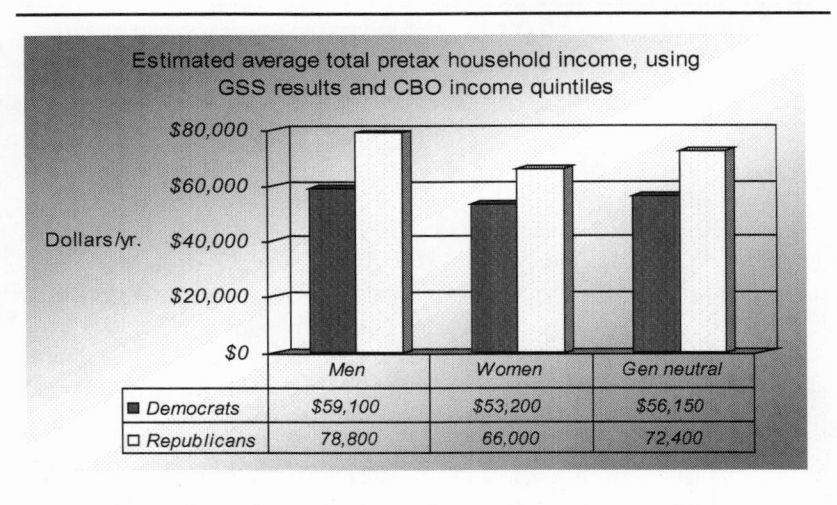

I am in favor of cutting taxes under any circumstances and for any
excuse, for any reason, whenever it's possible.
— Economist Milton Friedman[10]

Although the Republican income advantage is substantial, it is not as large,
percentage-wise, as the tax excess. The excess of taxes paid and income made by
Republicans (in 2003) is shown in Figure 129, below. This chart simply shows
that our progressive tax system is alive and well. It also may explain why Democrats and Republicans often have different perspectives regarding tax rates.

*Figure 129. A comparison of the excess of Republican 2003 federal income taxes paid (Figure
125) to the excess of Republican 2003 pretax household income earned (Figure 128). Both excess
amounts are expressed as percentages.*

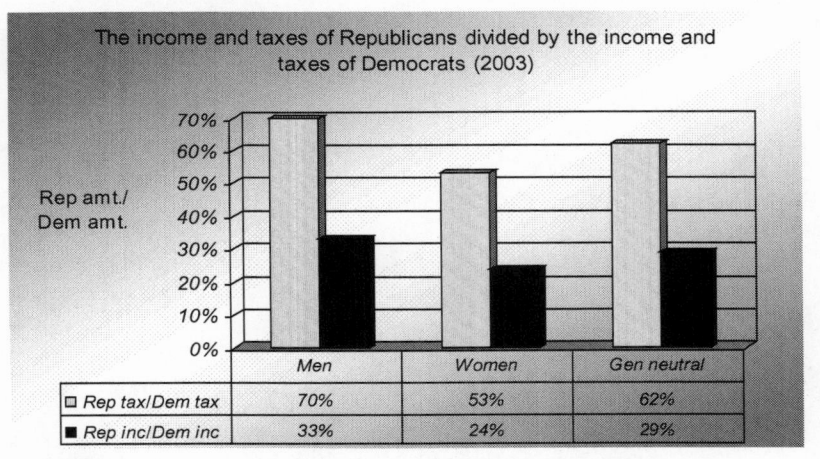

10 Milton Friedman as cited by Gerald Prante, "Economics Community Mourns the Loss of
   Milton Friedman," (The Tax Foundation, November 21, 2006), Retrieved March 22, 2007,
   from: http://www.taxfoundation.org/news/show/2016.html.

Average Federal Tax For Median Incomes

> Many of you are buckling beneath high-interest debts, insane taxes, and mortgages.... Islam has no taxes and only limited alms that stand at 2.5 percent.

— Terrorist and flat-tax advocate Osama bin Laden[11]

"Average" can be a poor indication of "typical" when it comes to taxes. Wealthy people (who are more likely to be Republicans) pay a great deal of tax, and this raises the Republican tax average substantially. On the other hand, many people pay no tax whatever. These people tend to be Democrats, and this significantly lowers the Democratic average. For these reasons, a better representation of "typical" might be the average taxes paid by people with median incomes (incomes above and below which there are equal numbers of people).

Figure 130. Estimation of 2003 average federal income tax paid by a median-income Democrat and a median-income Republican, by gender (GSS survey results from 1998 through 2004 and CBO quintiles for pretax household income and federal tax, based on 2648 cases for men and 3358 cases for women)

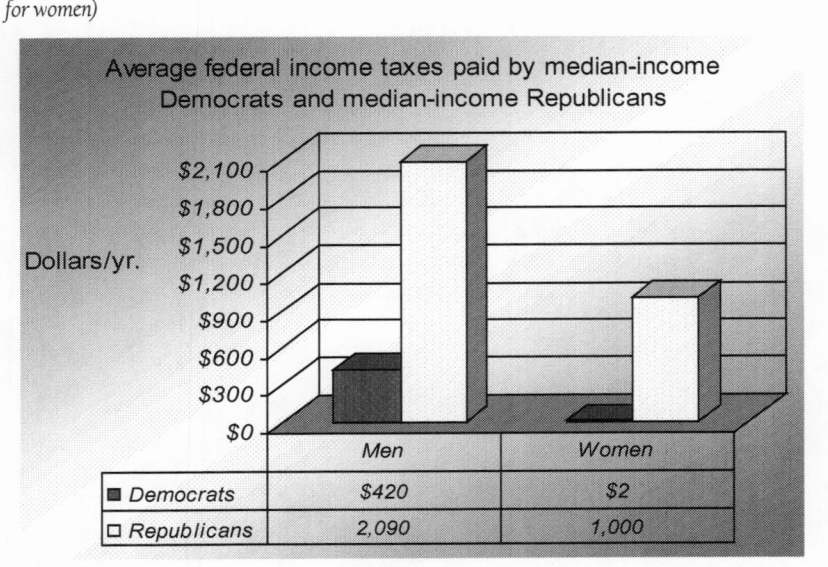

> Today, under George W. Bush, there are two Americas, not one.... One America that pays the taxes, another America that gets the tax breaks.

— Democratic Senator John Edwards[12]

---

11 Daniel Kimmage. (September 11, 2007), "Terrorism: Bin Laden Video Represents "Distilled Lunacy" Of Two Cultures", Retrieved September 25, 2007, from Radio Free Europe/ RL, Inc.: http://www.rferl.org/featuresarticle/2007/09/7996EEF9-910C-4E1D-86D2-9E56A1902E8C.html.

12 John Edwards as cited by Michael Duffy, "The Natural," in *Time.com* (July 11, 2004), Retrieved March 21, 2007, from: http://www.time.com/time/printout/0,8816,662792,00.html.

In Figure 130, above, we see that a person with 2003 median Democratic income had a very different tax liability than a person with median Republican income. Federal income tax associated with the Democratic median ranged from about zero to $400, depending on gender. Federal tax related to the Republican median income ranged from around $1,000 to $2,000. Although these gaps are less, dollar-wise, than the average tax differences shown in Figure 125, they may be large enough to account for the attitudinal divergence between Democrats and Republicans with respect to the federal income tax. The estimation of median tax amounts is explained in Appendix B 11 on page 390.

A very brief history of the United States income tax

In 1895, the Supreme Court ruled that the income tax was unconstitutional under Article I of the Constitution, which barred most taxes that were not apportioned in accordance with the population of each state. The impact of the Supreme Court's decision did not last long. Populists argued that the income tax was needed as a source of revenue and as a tool of social justice. Public demands for the income tax grew very strong "amid a frenzy of 'soak the rich' rhetoric...."[13] By 1913, Congress was given the power to impose an income tax by the 16th Amendment to the Constitution.

Initially, less than 1 percent of the population paid the new income tax, and rates ranged from 1 to 7 percent. Just 5 years later, however, the top rate was pushed to 77 percent, and it grew to 94 percent during World War II. Thereafter, tax rates began to fall, reaching their low points during the Reagan presidency. At that time, the top tax rate was 28 percent. During the Clinton presidency the top rate was increased to about 40 percent, and under the George W. Bush presidency it now stands at about 35 percent.

Other Federal Taxes

Excise Taxes

Most consumers would be shocked to learn how much they ultimately pay in taxes on their beverage of choice. ... If all the taxes levied on the production, distribution and retailing of beer are added up, they amount to an astonishing 44% of the retail price!

— The Beer Institute, an organization representing American breweries[14]

Although the United States constitutional definition of excise tax includes a tax on any "event," including the receipt of income or the purchase of a product, the commonly understood (and IRS) definition of excise tax is limited to those taxes that are paid on the purchase of certain products and services. These in-

---

13 Larry P. Arnn and Grover Norquist. (April 15, 2003), "Repeal of the 16th Amendment", Retrieved September 25, 2007, from The Claremont Institute: http://www.claremont.org/publications/pubid.477/pub_detail.asp.

14 "Beer Tax Facts," (The Beer Institute), from: http://www.beerinstitute.org/BeerInstitute/files/ccLibraryFiles/Filename/000000000275/beertaxfacts.pdf.

clude, among other things, gasoline, cigarettes, tires, certain sports equipment, telecommunication services, and air transportation. We sometimes pay excise taxes directly, but often the taxes are buried in the cost of products and services acquired.

There are two functions served by the use of excise taxes: to raise revenue for the federal government, and to discourage certain behaviors, such as smoking and alcohol consumption. Most excise taxes are proportional to purchases, but regressive to income. To prepare its reports, CBO distributes federal excise taxes to households "according to their consumption of the taxed good or service." As a percentage of income, excise taxes equal about 2.3 percent of income for people in the lowest quintile of household income, but only about .5 percent for those in the highest quintile of household income.

Federal Corporation Income Tax Attributed To The Owner

The whole idea of our government is this: If enough people get together and act in concert, they can take something and not pay for it.

— P.J. O'Rourke, American political satirist[15]

Figure 131. Estimated average 2003 federal income, excise, and imputed corporation taxes paid, calculated by multiplying the percentage of Democrats and Republicans in each quintile times the CBO tax rates and income amounts for the respective quintiles

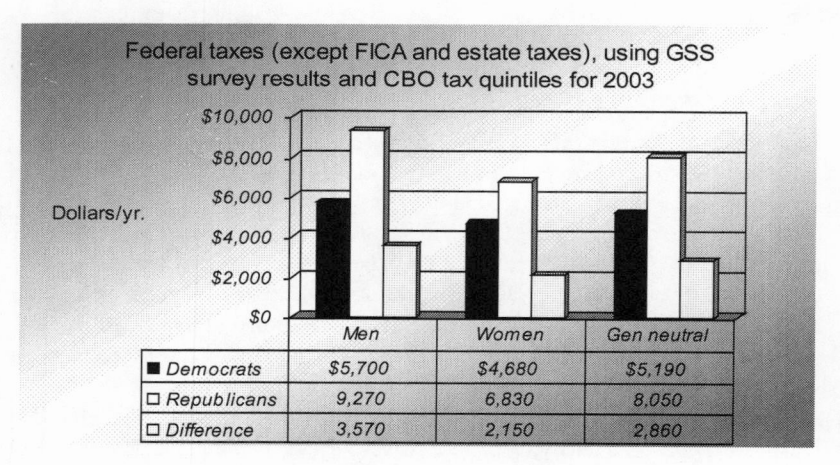

Profitable corporations generally pay a federal income tax, and this tax is indirectly paid by the shareholders of the corporation via lower dividends.[16] When it prepares its individual tax burden reports, CBO distributes corporate income tax to households "according to their share of capital income." It is a progressive

15 P. J. O'Rourke, *Parliament of Whores* (New York: Grove Press, 2003), 232.
16 A profitable corporation does not pay federal income tax if it elects to have each shareholder directly pay tax on his or her share of profits. Also, a profitable corporation may not pay taxes if it qualifies for certain incentive credits, which are intended to promote new energy technologies, the hiring of disadvantaged workers, etc.

tax that ranges from .3 percent of income for people in the lowest income quintile, to 3.4 percent for those in the highest income quintile.

Using the same methods and sources already discussed with regard to federal income taxes (i.e., GSS survey results and CBO quintiles), we can expand our tax estimate to add federal excise taxes and corporation income tax. These taxes, combined with the federal individual income tax, are shown in Figure 131, above.

As indicated in Figure 131, in 2003 the average Republican (on a gender-neutral basis) paid about 55 percent ($2,860) more in federal income, excise, and imputed corporation taxes than did the average Democrat.[17]

Estate Tax

> When we were at peace, Democrats wanted to raise taxes. Now there's a war, so Democrats want to raise taxes. When there was a surplus, Democrats wanted to raise taxes. Now that there is a mild recession, Democrats want to raise taxes.
>
> — Author and political pundit Ann Coulter[18]

The analysis in this chapter does not include federal estate ("death") tax, which affects a small minority of Americans who are usually fairly wealthy. Intuitively, we might assume that the people who pay estate tax are (or were) more likely to be Republicans. However, I have no factual basis for that hunch.

My Long-Winded FICA "Tax" Caveat

Before we complete our federal tax estimate by adding FICA (Social Security and Medicare payroll taxes), a lengthy caveat must be given. For the following reasons, FICA "taxes" are not taxes in the normal sense, and are best evaluated separately, net of anticipated benefits:

People who do not contribute to Social Security or Medicare are not eligible to participate.[19] This is normally not the case for a tax, which is defined as "a charge usually of money imposed by authority on persons or property for public purposes."[20] These "public purposes," such as national defense, highway improvements, environmental protection, public schools, and police protection, are available to everybody, whether or not they pay the tax.

About 5 million of America's 145 million workers do not participate in Social Security. Instead of paying payroll "taxes," these state and local government workers make "contributions" to their alternative retirement plans — many of which are like 401k plans. Upon retirement, most of these people get back every nickel of "contributions" — plus earnings. If the Social Security payroll "tax"

---

17 The calculation is $8,050/$5,190 = 155%.

18 Ann Coulter, "Put the Tax Cut in a Lock Box," in *Jewish World Review* (February 21, 2002), Retrieved March 22, 2007, from: http://www.jewishworldreview.com/cols/coulter022102.asp.

19 However, in certain limited circumstances the close relatives of participating workers are also given coverage.

20 The definition is from the Merriam Webster's Collegiate Dictionary — Tenth Edition.

were a tax in the normal sense, the federal government could not allow 5 million government workers to evade that tax by putting their money into these alternative, 401k-type investments.

This is the most important point. Even if we were to classify Social Security and Medicare contributions as "taxes," a balanced analysis would require that we report those taxes net of anticipated individual benefits. In other words, we'd have to reduce the so-called tax by the present value of the expected monthly cash retirement benefits (or, the estimated value of the Medicare insurance). It is intellectually and economically dishonest to credit people with paying Social Security and Medicare "tax," while disregarding the offsetting retirement and health insurance benefits. And, when we count those benefits, there no longer is a tax for many people.

> The principal purpose of the Democratic Party is to use the force of government to take property away from the people who earn it and give it to people who do not.

> — Neal Boortz, Author and radio talk show host[21]

In short, the inclusion of Social Security and Medicare contributions in tax calculations makes no sense — especially if there is no offset for the expected monthly cash benefits and medical insurance. For all of these reasons, FICA "taxes" and the offsetting benefits are considered separately, in Chapter 7. However, for those who insist on mixing apples with oranges, FICA is also added to other federal taxes in Figure 132.

Figure 132 — Estimated average federal income, excise, imputed corporation taxes paid, and FICA tax, calculated by multiplying the percentage of Democrats and Republicans in each quintile times the CBO tax rates and income amounts for the respective quintiles

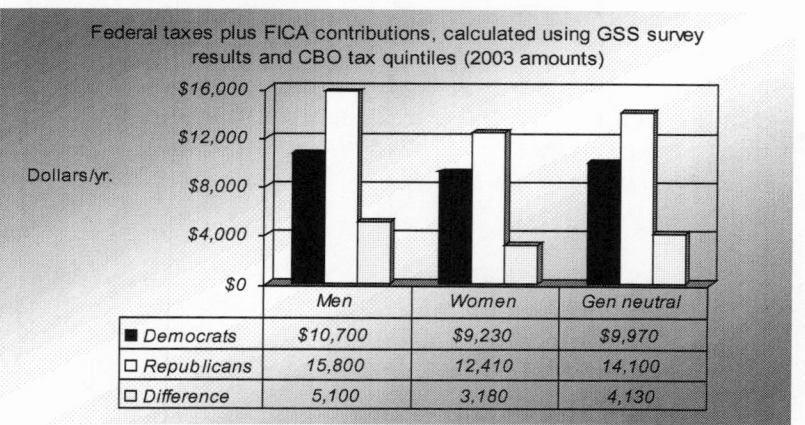

	Men	Women	Gen neutral
■ Democrats	$10,700	$9,230	$9,970
□ Republicans	15,800	12,410	14,100
□ Difference	5,100	3,180	4,130

---

21 Neil Boortz (attributed), "Thinkexist.Com."

In Figure 132 we see that, in 2003, the average Republican man paid about 48 percent ($5,100) more than his Democratic counterpart in total federal taxes, including FICA contributions.[22] The average Republican woman paid about 34 percent ($3,200) more than her counterpart. On a gender-neutral basis, the excess paid by Republicans was about 41 percent ($4,100).

Reality check — Did FDR think FICA was a "tax"?

According to Larry DeWitt, a Social Security Administration historian, the Social Security program was designed so that each worker would contribute to the "old age reserve account." There was the "clear idea that this account would then be the source of monies to fund the workers' retirement."

Unlike a tax in the normal sense, "the contributions established an 'earned right' to the eventual benefits." This was extremely important to President Roosevelt, who "strenuously objected to any attempt to introduce general revenue [tax] funding into the program." FDR stated:

> We put those payroll contributions there so as to give the contributors a legal, moral, and political right to collect their pensions and unemployment benefits.[23]

Thus, there is an undeniable connection between an individual's payment of the payroll tax and his moral and political (but not legal) right to collect benefits. This distinguishes the payroll "tax" from other taxes.

State and local taxes

> The tax systems of most states already are significantly regressive — that is, they take a larger proportion of the income of lower-income families than the income of more affluent families.
>
> — The Center on Budget and Policy Priorities[24]

Average Taxes Paid

State and local taxes comprise income, sales, excise, and property taxes. Estimating the amount paid by Democrats versus Republicans was no easy task, and required separate calculations for people aged 65 or more years, and for people under the age of 65. These two estimates were then combined into a weighted average by the proportion of people in those two age groups. The details of the sources and calculation methods used are given at Appendix B 12. Figure 133, below, shows the overall results. We see that, the average Republican paid significantly more state and local income, sales, excise, and property taxes than did the average Democrat. However, the disparity was smaller than the federal tax

---

22 This does not include the federal estate ("death") tax.

23 Historian Larry DeWitt, "The 1937 Supreme Court Rulings on the Social Security Act," 1999, Social Security Administration, Retrieved August 13, 2006, from http://www.ssa.gov/history/court.html.

24 "State Tax Systems Are Becoming Increasingly Inequitable," January 15, 2002, Center on Budget and Policy Priorities, Retrieved October 12, 2006, from http://www.cbpp.org/1-15-02sfp-pr.htm.

differential, whether measured in absolute dollars or as a percentage. This is because some state and local taxes are either "proportional" or regressive, rather than progressive.[25] Republican men paid about 33 percent more, Republican women paid about 26 percent more, and, on a gender-neutral basis, Republicans paid about 30 percent more state and local taxes than did their Democratic counterparts.

Figure 133. Estimate of state and local income, sales, excise, and property tax, based on GSS survey data for 1998 through 2004, 430 separately calculated tax returns, Social Security data, and information published by the Tax Policy Center. A detailed explanation of the calculation is available at Appendix B 12.

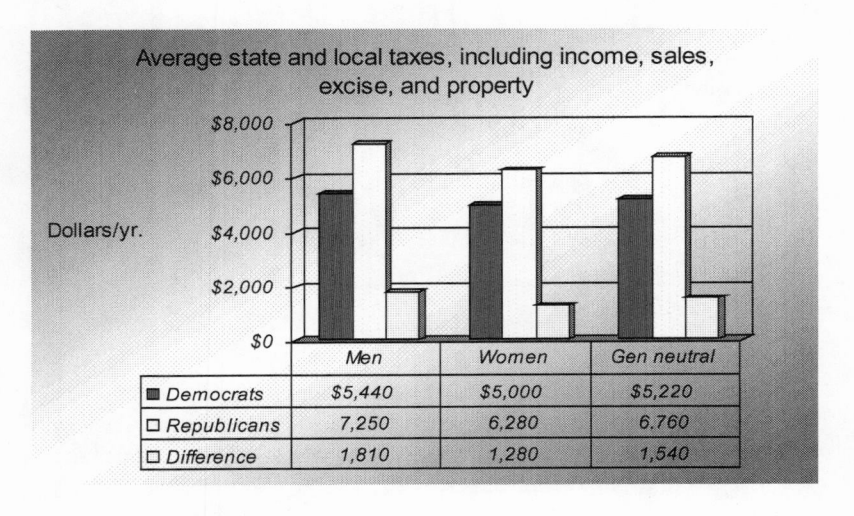

Income taxes are progressive.... Other taxes, like sales taxes, property taxes and payroll taxes aren't progressive, that is, everyone pays the same rate regardless of income. We have that mix so that most people pay at least some tax. Otherwise the tax users would pick the taxpayers clean. That's called socialism.

— Mike Rosen, Radio talk show host[26]

Median Taxes Paid

It is difficult to provide a meaningful estimate of the average state and local taxes paid by a median-income Democrat or a median-income Republican because multiple data sources were used for the different groups of taxpayers (e.g.,

25 "Proportional" taxes are those that increase proportionally to income. For example, a man earning ten times more than his neighbor would pay ten times the income tax. People often mislabel the proportional tax as a "flat" tax — which falsely implies that everyone pays the same amount of tax, regardless of income. Progressive taxes increase at a rate that is faster than the increase in income, and regressive taxes increase at a rate that is slower than the increase in income.

26 Mike Rosen, "Lowdown on Higher Taxes," April 26, 2005, Sean Hannity Web site, Retrieved December 8, 2006, from http://www.hannity.com/forum/showthread.php?t=3981.

for those over age 64 and those under age 65). However, if we limit the results to those under the age of 65, meaningful estimates are possible. These are presented in Figure 134, below.

Figure 134. Median differences for total state and local taxes for people under age 65, based on GSS survey data for 1998 through 2004, and Tax Policy Center tax amounts by income quintile

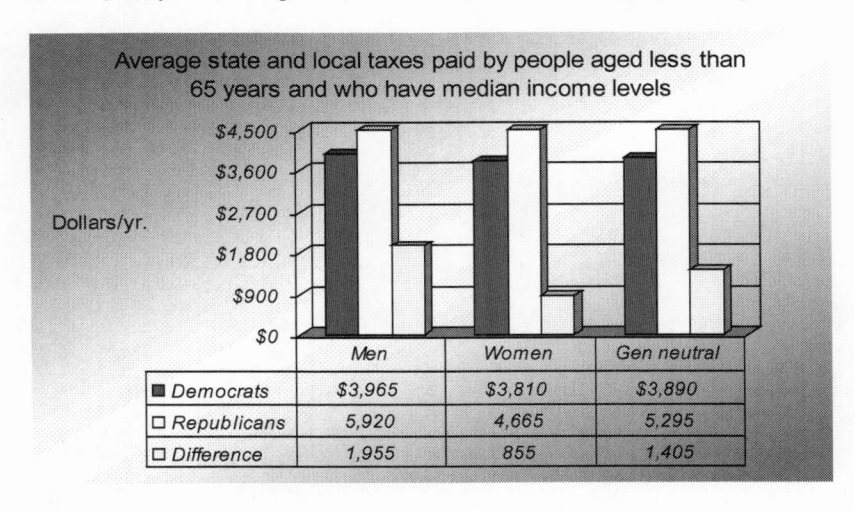

We see that the median ("typical") Republican man paid about 49 percent more than the median Democratic man, and the median Republican women paid about 22 percent more than her Democratic counterpart. On a gender-neutral basis, the difference was about 36 percent.

Total taxes: federal, state, and local

> [I]n liberal eyes, the Republican — conservative preference for lowering taxes can only emanate from selfishness and apathy toward the poor.
>
> — Radio talk-show host Dennis Prager[27]

Total Without FICA Tax

The total taxes paid by Democrats and Republicans are simply all of the amounts presented heretofore, and they are summarized in Figure 135. FICA taxes are not included in this estimate; however, they are added in a subsequent graphic.

Figure 135 shows that the average Republican man paid about 48 percent ($5,380) more in total taxes than did the average Democratic man, while the average Republican woman paid about 35 percent ($3,420) more than her Democratic counterpart. The gender-neutral difference was about 42 percent ($4,400).

---

27 Prager, "Why the Left Fights."

Figure 135. Estimate of total average taxes paid. This is simply the combination of federal tax amounts in Figure 131 and the state and local tax amounts in Figure 133.

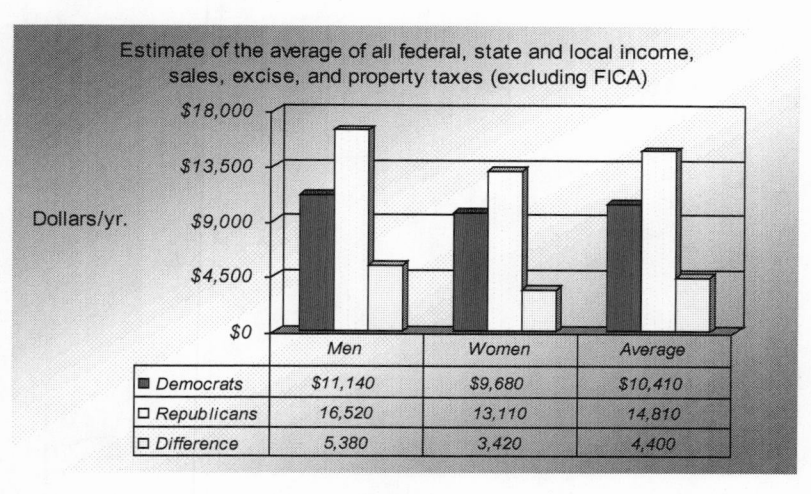

	Men	Women	Average
■ Democrats	$11,140	$9,680	$10,410
□ Republicans	16,520	13,110	14,810
□ Difference	5,380	3,420	4,400

Who Pays More Tax In Proportion To Income?

Republicans believe every day is the Fourth of July, but the Democrats believe every day is April 15th.

— President Ronald Reagan[28]

The differences above are almost entirely due to the fact that Republicans, on average, have more per capita income. That is, they are likely to have greater income in proportion to the size of the household. The excess of Republican income, however, is not proportionally as great as the excess of taxes paid, as can be seen in Figure 136, below. Note: This chart is similar to Figure 129; however, it includes state and local, as well as federal taxes.

28 President Ronald Reagan (attributed), "Quotationz.Com."

Figure 136. A comparison of the excess of Republican 2003 federal, state, and local taxes paid (Figure 135) to the excess of Republican 2003 pretax household income earned (Figure 128). Both excess amounts are expressed as percentages.

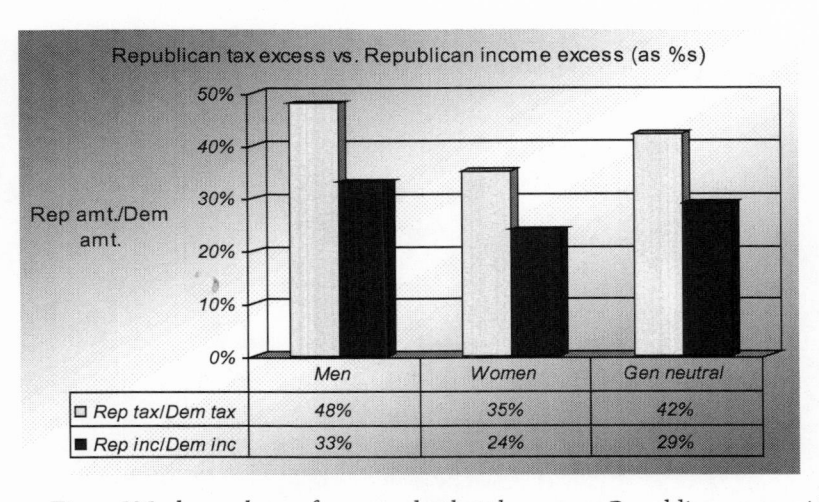

	Men	Women	Gen neutral
☐ Rep tax/Dem tax	48%	35%	42%
■ Rep inc/Dem inc	33%	24%	29%

Figure 136, above, shows, for example, that the average Republican man paid 48 percent more in taxes, but collected only 33 percent more in household income (than the average Democratic man). For Republican women, a similar, albeit less pronounced, differential is evident.

Total Taxes Including FICA

I can remember way back when a liberal was one who was generous with his own money.

— Will Rogers, Humorist and author[29]

In my opinion, Figure 135 displays the most meaningful federal, state, and local tax totals. However, for readers who want to see the impact of FICA tax on this analysis, they are included in Figure 137, below.

As expected, Figure 137 shows that Republicans pay more FICA tax than do Democrats (by virtue of having higher earnings). However, the inclusion of FICA slightly narrows the percentage tax gap between Democrats and Republicans. For example, with the inclusion of FICA tax the percentage of excess taxes paid by Republican men and women (on average) was 37.5 percent — which is a little lower than the amount shown in Figure 136 (42%).

---

29 "Election Wisdom from Will Rogers," in *Virginian-Pilot*, ed. Richard W. Reeks (Landmark Communications, Inc., October 25, 1996).

Figure 137. All taxes shown in Figure 135 plus FICA

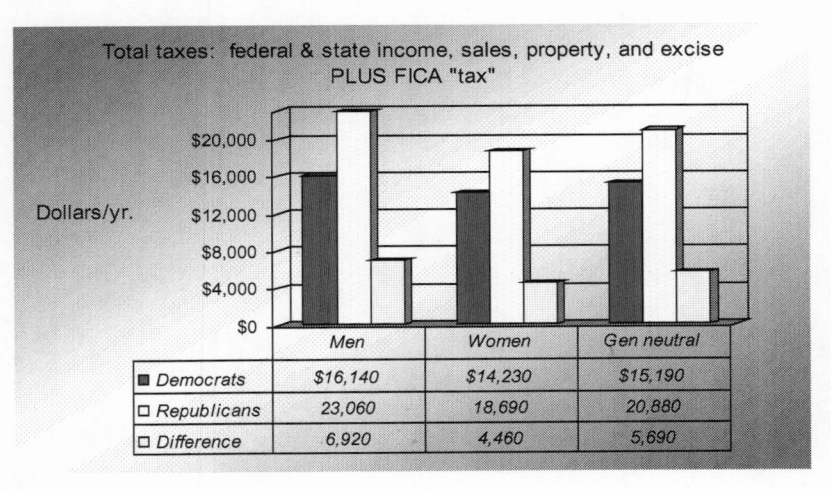

Total taxes: federal & state income, sales, property, and excise PLUS FICA "tax"

Dollars/yr.	Men	Women	Gen neutral
■ Democrats	$16,140	$14,230	$15,190
□ Republicans	23,060	18,690	20,880
□ Difference	6,920	4,460	5,690

This may be all Bush is really good for, for me. I want some money back. I would like a little bit of it.

— Comedian Whoopi Goldberg[30]

CONCLUSIONS

If we include the effects of the Earned Income Tax Credit (EITC), people in the lowest 2 quintiles (i.e., the lowest 40%) pay, on average, a "negative" federal income tax. Another 20 percent of the income-earning population pays almost nothing. For these reasons, it is never possible to give federal income tax cuts to everyone.

For 2003, the average Republican (on a gender-neutral basis) paid about 62 percent ($2,300) more federal income tax per year than did the average Democrat, and about 42 percent ($4,400) more of all types of federal, state, and local taxes, except for FICA.[31] If we add FICA taxes, the average Republican paid about 37.5 percent ($5,700) more than that paid by the average Democrat.

There is also a significant differential between the tax amounts paid by Republicans and Democrats with median income, and estimates of these amounts are provided in the chapter.

---

30 Whoopi Goldberg speaking on, "Tonight Show " (Transcript: NBC, April 9, 2001), Retrieved March 22, 2007, from: http://www.acmewebpages.com/whoopi/interviews/leno04092001. htm.

31 The gap is nearly $5700 if Social Security and Medicare tax are considered. However, I believe that FICA is not a true "tax," and should be considered separately — net of estimated SS and Medicare benefits.

Although it is no surprise that the average (and median) Republican pays more in taxes (of all types) than does his Democratic counterpart, we rarely or never see these tax differentials quantified. Whether these differentials are the economically or ethically "correct" amounts is beyond the purview of this book.

CHAPTER 6: WHO IS THE BETTER CITIZEN?

INTRODUCTION

What Is "Good Citizenship"?

> The first requisite of a good citizen in this republic of ours is that he shall be able and willing to pull his own weight.
>
> — President Theodore Roosevelt[1]

> [A radical] is not a bad citizen turning to crime; he is a good citizen driven to despair.
>
> — H. L. Mencken, American journalist and social critic[2]

> The test of good citizenship is loyalty to country.
>
> — Bainbridge Colby, Secretary of State for President Woodrow Wilson[3]

---

1 President Theodore Roosevelt as cited by Richard C. Harwood, "Able, but Willing?," in *The Tampa Tribune* (2000).

2 H.L. Mencken as cited by Mark Lowry in, "Best Way to Defeat Bushite Coup's Attack on America, Democracy and Freedom," in *American Chronicle* (March 11, 2007), Retrieved March 23, 2007, from: http://www.americanchronicle.com/articles/viewArticle. asp?articleID=21946.

3 Colby Bainbridge (Secretary of State under Woodrow Wilson) in his speech, "Loyalty," (The Authentic History Center, 1918), Retrieved March 23, 2007, from: http://www.authentichistory.com/audio/wwl/1918_Colby_Bainbridge-Loyalty.html.

Everyone seems to admire good citizenship but we don't necessarily agree on the qualities that define it. Are they hard work, sacrifice, loyalty, political activism, conservation of resources, adherence to the law, or something else? In this book, no attempt is made to define "good citizenship." Rather, Democrats and Republicans are measured against some of the standards that are commonly associated with good citizenship, and for which appropriate survey data are available. It is hoped that the information in this chapter will enable each reader to evaluate and compare Democratic and Republican "citizenship" based on the factors that are most relevant, in his or her judgment.

DETAILS

Who supports First Amendment rights?

> The good citizen always has easy access to a copy of the United States constitution and the Declaration of Independence. ... These documents should be read, studied, learned, understood, and appreciated.
>
> — "On the Nature of Good Citizenship in a Democratic Society" by Winfield H. Rose[4]

Tolerance For Controversial Speech

The first amendment to the Constitution states that Congress shall make no law ... abridging the freedom of speech. ..." Which constituency, Democratic or Republican, is more likely to support and respect this important constitutional right? Does it depend on who is doing the speaking?

On several occasions from the mid-1970s through 2006, the General Social Survey (GSS) questioned respondents concerning hypothetical free-speech situations. Some questions involved speech by people associated with the "right" side of politics, while others involved people normally associated with the "left" side of politics. Figure 138, below, summarizes the responses of Democrats and Republicans when asked if a racist should be allowed to speak in their communities. Republicans were more a little more likely to say they would allow the racist speech.

> One of the curious things about censorship is that no one seems to want it for himself. We want censorship to protect someone else; the young, the unstable, the suggestible, the stupid. I have never heard of anyone who wanted a film banned because otherwise he might see it and be harmed.
>
> — Edgar Dale, Educator[5]

---

4 Winfield H. Rose, "On the Nature of Good Citizenship in a Democratic Society," January, 1999, Personal Web site, Retrieved July 4, 2006, from http://campus.murraystate.edu/academic/faculty/winfield.rose/goodcit.html.

5 Edgar Dale (attributed), "Quotations Site," in *BellaOnline*, ed. Danielle Hollister, Retrieved March 23, 2007, from: http://www.bellaonline.com/articles/art35627.asp.

Figure 138. If a person wanted to speak in your community, "claiming that Blacks are inferior, should he be allowed to speak, or not?" (GSS surveys conducted from 1976 through 2006, based on, left to right, 6803, 9418, and 16221 cases, with confidence level of, left to right, 99+%, 95%, and 99+%, and with relative proportions of, left to right, .90, .96, and .92)

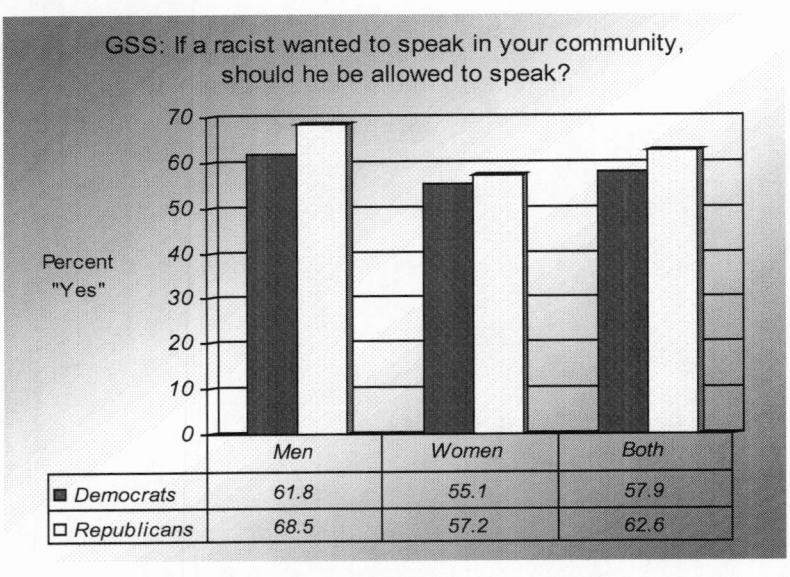

	Men	Women	Both
■ Democrats	61.8	55.1	57.9
□ Republicans	68.5	57.2	62.6

Figure 139. Should a person who is "against all churches and religion" be "allowed to speak in your community? (several GSS surveys conducted 1977 through 2006, based on, left to right, 6882, 9515, and 16397 cases, with confidence level of 99+% for all columns, and with relative proportions of, left to right, .88, .94, and .91)

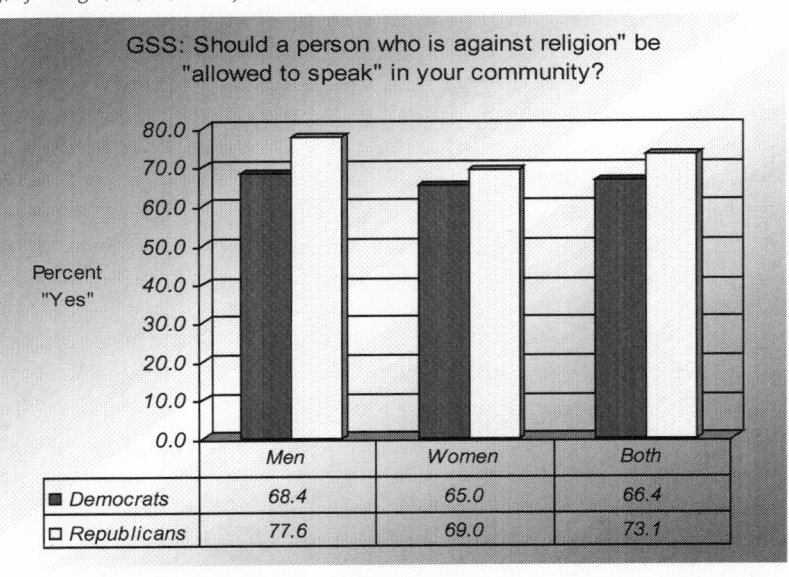

	Men	Women	Both
■ Democrats	68.4	65.0	66.4
□ Republicans	77.6	69.0	73.1

Interestingly, Republicans were also more likely to express tolerant views for speech advocating positions presumed to be contrary to their own values. An example is shown in Figure 139, above, which summarizes views regarding someone who is "against all churches and religion."

These and the results from all similar GSS questions (regarding speech by homosexuals, Communists, and anti-militarists) are summarized in Table 32. Republicans were slightly more likely to express tolerance in each instance.

Table 32. *Views of Democratic and Republican men and women concerning the right to free speech in their communities, based on GSS surveys conducted in 1977 through 2006*

Allow speech in your community by person who is ...	Dems	Reps	No. of cases	Conf %	*RP
Racist	57.9	62.6	16221	+99	.92
Against all churches and religion	66.4	73.1	16397	+99	.91
Communist	59.7	65.4	16150	+99	.91
Homosexual	74.3	75.8	16090	98	.98
For letting military run country	56.5	62.3	16245	+99	.91

*RP is relative proportion, which is the Democratic % divided by the Republican %.

What Are The Trends?

> You know it's ironic that we're fighting for democracy in Iraq because we ultimately aren't celebrating democracy here. Because anybody who has anything to say against the war or against the president or whatever — is punished, and that's not democracy — it's people being intolerant.

—Popular singer Madonna Ciccone[6]

The data above comprise the aggregate results from extended time periods, spanning about 30 years. Have these attitudes been changing during that time? The answer can be found in the following four graphics, each of which breaks out the attitudes of Democrats and Republicans into three 10-year periods. Note: There is no trend breakout for views regarding homosexuals because, when reduced to 10-year periods, there is no statistically-significant difference in the expressed views of Democrats and Republicans.

First, we see the views regarding racists, and their right to speak. In each 10-year time span, Republicans have been more likely to express tolerance for having racists speak in their communities. See Figure 140.

Figure 140. *If a person wanted to speak in your community, "claiming that Blacks are inferior, should he be allowed to speak, or not?"* — *30-year trend (GSS surveys conducted various times from*

---

6 "Madonna Talks Democracy," in *SFGate.com* (April 15, 2003), Retrieved March 23, 2007, from: http://www.sfgate.com/cgi-bin/article.cgi?file=/gate/archive/2003/04/15/ddish.DTL.

1977 through 2006, based on, left to right, 4955, 6836, and 4430 cases, with confidence level of 99+% for all differences, and with relative proportions of, left to right, .92, .94, and .93)

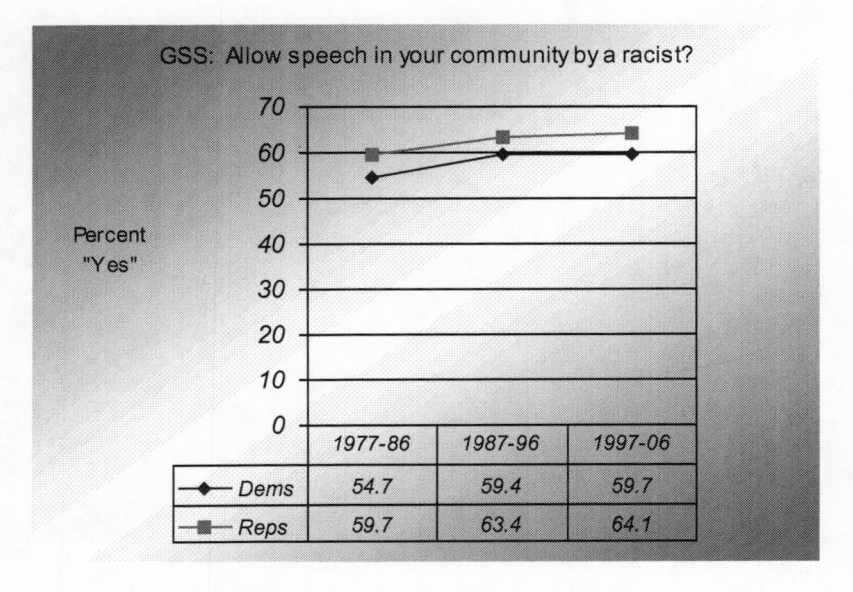

The atmosphere in my country is poisonous, intolerable for those of us who are not right-wing....

— Actress Jessica Lange[7]

In the next graphic (Figure 141) we see a general increase, during the 30 years, in tolerance for speech that is critical of religion. Nevertheless, there remains a tolerance gap between Democrats and Republicans. Republicans seem to be more accepting of anti-religious speech, even though they are generally assumed to be more religious.

Liberals claim to want to give a hearing to other views, but then are shocked and offended to discover that there are other views.

— William F. Buckley, Jr., American author and journalist[8]

Figure 141. Should a person who is "against all churches and religion ... be allowed to speak in your community, or not?" — 30-year trend (GSS surveys conducted various times from 1977 through 2006, based on, left to right, 5034, 6911, and 4452 cases, with confidence level of 99+% for all differences, and with relative proportions of, left to right, .88, .95, and .91)

7 Jessica Lange as cited by James H. Hansen, "Radical Road Maps," (Nashville: WND Books, 2006), 197.

8 William F. Buckley (attributed), "Conservativeforum.Org," Retrieved March 23, 2007, from: http://www.conservativeforum.org/quotelist.asp?SearchType=5&Interest=15.

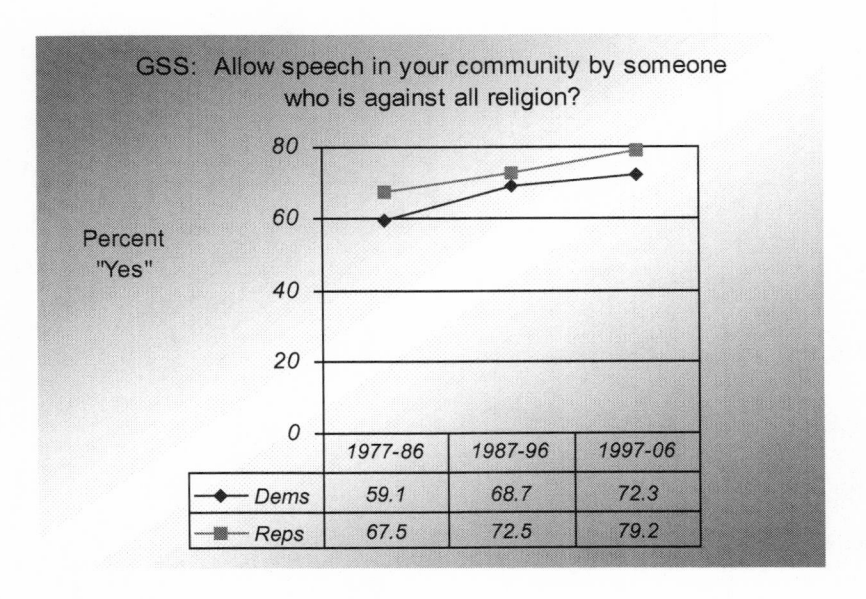

Figure 142. Should a person who is an "admitted Communist ... be allowed to speak in your community, or not? — 30-year trend (GSS surveys conducted from 1977 through 2006, based on, left to right, 4919, 6832, and 4399 cases, with confidence level of 99+% for all differences, and with relative proportions of, left to right, .92, .95, and .90)

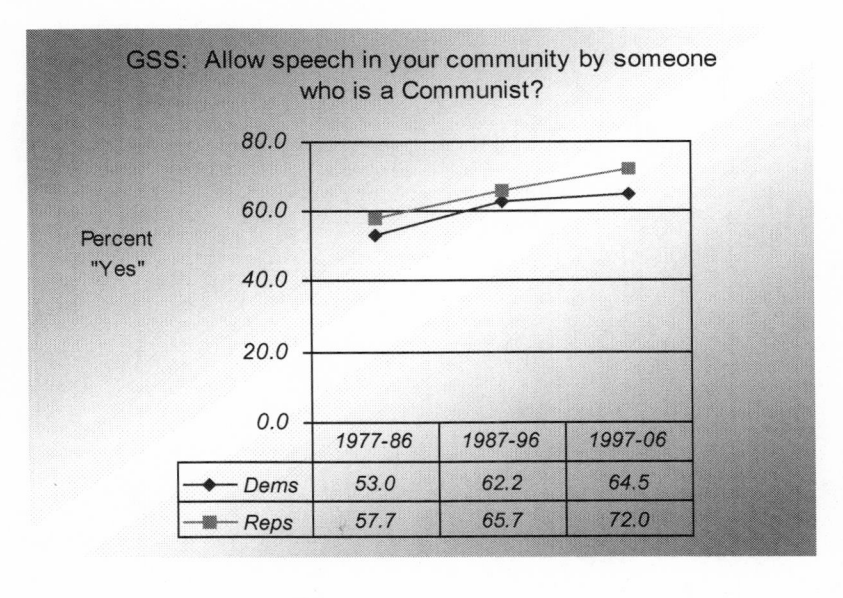

Tolerance for speech by Communists has grown sharply within both constituencies. This may be partly due to the end of the "cold war." Although Republicans have a reputation for being particularly critical of communism, during the last 30 years they have expressed more willingness to allow Communists to speak in their own communities. These trends are reflected in Figure 142, above.

The final trend analysis has to do with militarists. Not surprisingly (given all the other results) Republicans have been more willing than Democrats to allow speech by militarists.

Figure 143. Should a person "who advocates doing away with elections and letting the military run the country ... be allowed to speak [in your community] or not?" — 30-year trend (GSS surveys conducted various times from 1977 through 2006, based on, left to right, 4968, 6845, and 4432 cases, with confidence level of 99+% for all differences, and with relative proportions of, left to right, .91, .92, and .92)

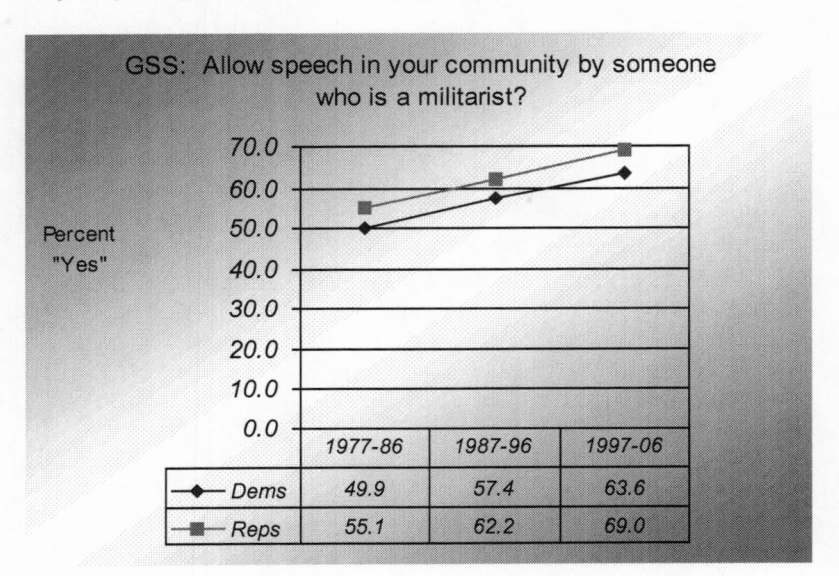

	1977-86	1987-96	1997-06
Dems	49.9	57.4	63.6
Reps	55.1	62.2	69.0

The hypocrisy of it is palpable. The left-wing thought police are forever paying lip service to the ideals of free expression, but they are the first ones in line to place restriction on it for those with whom they disagree.

— Rush Limbaugh, Author and radio talk show host[9]

Reality check — The real life implications for free speech

Talk is cheap. Republicans may express more tolerance of controversial speech, but are they truly more tolerant? Do their claims of tolerance have real life implications that are measurable? To test this theory I conducted the fol-

---

9 Rush Limbaugh, *See, I Told You So* (New York: Pocket Books, 1993), 228.

lowing, highly scientific experiment in July 2006: First, I "Googled" the three-word phrase, "prevented from speaking."[10] Then, I scanned the first 100 articles retrieved from that Google search, looking for instances where it was claimed that a person was seriously harassed while speaking (e.g., pie thrown in face, subject to constant loud shouting and/or threats), or "prevented from speaking" (e.g., speech was cut short or cancelled). Finally, I classified the person by his apparent political orientation (Conservative and/or Republican vs. Liberal and/or Democrat). I have not confirmed the veracity of these claims or the motives and political orientation of the parties. The results are listed below, for your own evaluation.

Harassed or prevented from speaking (per review of the first 100 Google results for "prevented from speaking")	
Conservative and/or Republican speaker	Liberal and/or Democratic speaker
Pat Buchanan, Conservative commentator and author	Ward Churchill, Professor and critic of U.S. foreign policy
Ann Coulter, Conservative commentator and author	
Dan Flynn, Author of a book critical of Mumia Abu Jamal (convicted cop-killer)	
Alexander Haig, Secretary of State under the Reagan Administration	
David Horowitz, Conservative commentator and author	
William Kristol, Conservative commentator and editor	
Henry Kissinger, Secretary of State under Richard Nixon	
Jeane Kirkpatrick, Former Ambassador to the U.N.	
Michelle Malkin, Conservative commentator and author	
Daniel Pipes, Bush appointee to U.S. Institute of Peace	
Caspar Weinberger, Secretary of Defense under Ronald Reagan	

In total, eleven conservatives/Republicans claimed to be "prevented from speaking" or seriously harassed, versus one liberal/Democrat. That same Google search also revealed that the following conservative foreign leaders were allegedly seriously harassed or prevented from speaking at universities in the United States: Nathan Sharansky (Israeli Minister), Benjamin Netanyahu (former Israeli Prime Minister), and Adolfo Calero (Nicaraguan resistance leader during the 1980s).

---

10 I simply made up the phrase. It was the only one I tested.

Readers are encouraged to conduct their own "Google test" to see if these results can be replicated.

Are Democrats Conflicted About Free Speech?

We forbid any course that says we restrict free speech.

— Dr. Kathleen Dixon, Director of Women's Studies, Bowling Green State University[11]

We might conclude from the survey evidence (and from the "scientific" Google search) that Republicans are more likely to tolerate free speech by controversial figures. If true, why is it so? There is an interesting theory advanced by John Leo, a columnist and contributing editor at U.S. News & World Report. He notes that on many college campuses (which generally tilt leftward) free speech has almost become unacceptable behavior.

> A whole vocabulary has sprung up to convert free expression into punishable behavior: hate speech, verbal assault, intellectual harassment, and nontraditional violence, a fancy term for stinging criticism. ...

> Protestors and half the faculty take an impassioned pro-brown shirt stance, arguing that the so-called offense was an understandable reaction to hate speech and great psychic injury. They refer here to the pain of being exposed to ideas they don't agree with.[12]

In the view of Mr. Leo, some college students and faculty feel that conservative ideas are so hateful and so dangerous that it is OK — and even necessary — to prevent those ideas from being expressed.

Tolerance For Controversial Books And Literature

GSS surveys conducted during the last 30 years show that Democrats are a little more likely to advocate the removal, from their community libraries, of books written by people with controversial perspectives. The hypothetical authors are from the same 5 categories we considered with respect to free speech: racists, atheists, Communists, homosexuals, and militarists. The percentages of Democrats and Republicans who would have books removed are presented in Table 33, below:

> [I]f you're burning a Harry Potter book you need some serious counseling, you don't get it, you're missing the whole point.

— Actor Michael Berryman[13]

---

11 Larry Elder, "The Politically Incorrect Professor," in *Jewish World Review* (September 29, 2000), Retrieved February 18, 2007, from: http://www.jewishworldreview.com/cols/elder092900.asp.

12 John Leo, "Ivy League Therapy," in *Jewish World Review* (March 27, 2001), Retrieved July 8, 2006, from: http://www.jewishworldreview.com/cols/leo032701.asp.

13 Michael Berryman (attributed), "Brainyquote.Com."

Table 33. *Views of Democratic and Republican men and women concerning whether books should be removed from the public library, based on GSS surveys conducted in 1977 through 2006*

Remove book from your public library if author is a person who ...	Dem % "yes"	Rep % "yes"	No. of cases	Conf %	*RP
"believes that Blacks are genetically inferior"	39.0	33.7	16065	+99	1.16
"is against churches and religion"	36.1	31.3	16131	+99	1.15
"admits he is a Communist"	39.6	33.8	15977	+99	1.17
"admits that he is a homosexual"	36.8	33.8	16061	+99	1.09
"advocates letting ... the military run the country"	41.5	35.4	16078	+99	1.17

*RP is relative proportion, which is the Democratic % divided by the Republican %.

What Are The Current Trends?

For the most part, surveys conducted during the last 10 years show a similar pattern, with Republicans being a bit more tolerant of controversial books within their community's public library. However, Democrats and Republicans now have the same outlook with regard to books written by homosexuals.

Figure 144. *Would you favor removing this person's book from the public library? (the aggregate results of GSS surveys conducted from 1997 through 2006, based on, left to right, 4378, 4388, 4364, 4377, and 4378 cases, with confidence level of 99% for all differences except with respect to homosexuals (not significant), and with relative proportions of, left to right, 1.16, 1.16, 1.21, 1.03, and 1.12)*

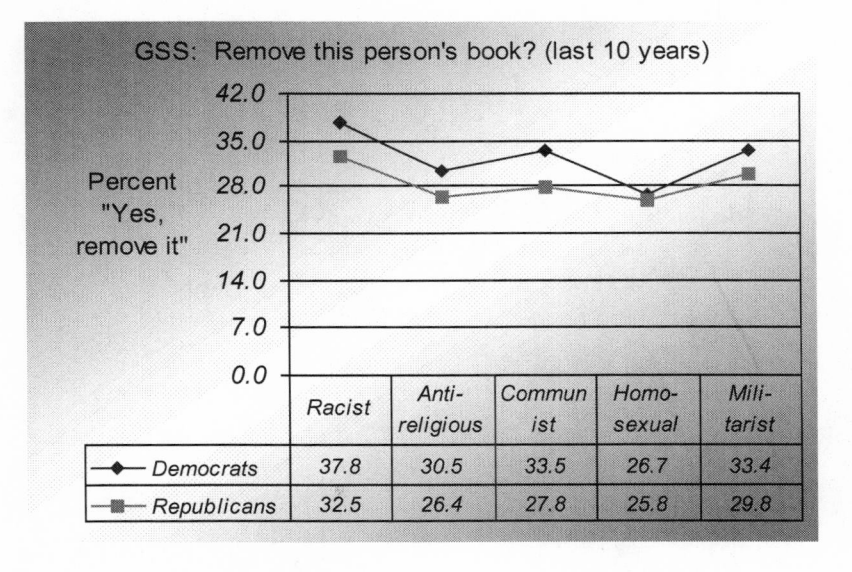

They have expelled Huck from their library as "trash and only suitable for the slums." That will sell us 25,000 for sure.

— Author Samuel Clemmons ("Mark Twain"), writing to his editor after the Concord Public Library banned his book, Huckleberry Finn.[14]

Respect For The Right Of Assembly

The "right of people peaceably to assemble" is guaranteed by the first Amendment to the U.S. Constitution. In Figure 145, below, we see that Democrats and Republicans have slightly different views with respect to this constitutional right. Most Republicans would "definitely not" allow the assembly of "people who want to overthrow the government by force...." A slightly smaller percentage of Democrats feel that way. On the other hand, Republicans are a little more willing to allow assembly by racists and religious extremists.

Figure 145. Should these people "be allowed to hold public meetings"? (GSS surveys conducted in 2004, based on, left to right, 918, 924, and 907 cases, with confidence level of, left to right, 95%, 97%, and 98%, and with relative proportions of, left to right, .87, 1.20, and 1.63)

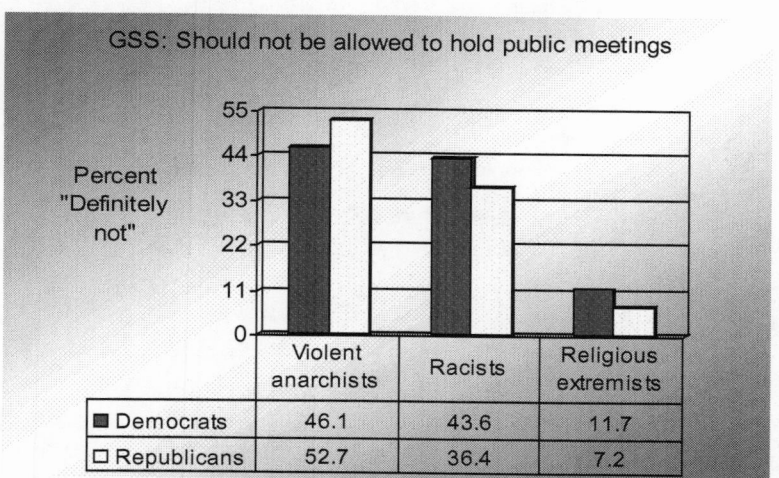

In summary, a higher percentage of Republicans express tolerant viewpoints with regard to controversial speech and books within their communities, and this tendency has existed for at least 30 years. They are slightly more willing to let racists and religious fanatics meet publicly, but most Republicans would bar meetings by those advocating the violent overthrow of the government.

Liberals are stalwart defenders of civil liberties — provided we're only talking about criminals.

— Author and political activist Ann Coulter[15]

14 Samuel Clemens as quoted in, "Twain Classics Have Often Been Banned," (Star-Gazette. com, February 15, 2004), Retrieved October 5, 2007, from: http://www.stargazettenews. com/newsextra/marktwain/021504_2.html.

15 Ann Coulter, "Mothers against Box Cutters Speak Out," in *Jewish World Review* (October 18, 2001), Retrieved March 24, 2007, from: http://www.jewishworldreview.com/cols/coulter101801.asp.

Who is more bigoted?

This section is presented with reticence because negative attitudes about people do not necessarily translate into negative treatment of those people. That concern notwithstanding, Democrats and Republicans seem to have statistically significant differences in their personal feelings towards some groups of people, identified by religion, race and ethnicity, and sexual orientation.

With Regard To Jews

To some it may be surprising to learn that Republicans are (now) less likely than Democrats to express anti-Semitic views. In a report issued in 2003 (based on a survey of 1013 individuals conducted in 2002), the Institute for Jewish & Community Research stated: "On nearly all variables, Democrats held more anti-Semitic beliefs than Republicans, reversing a historical trend." For example, "Republicans are less likely to view Jews as selfish (12%) than Democrats or independents (20% each)." The report also noted that Republicans are less likely to subscribe to the belief that Jewish control of the media contributes to our failure to get the "whole truth in some stories." Only 16 percent of Republicans expressed this view, versus 28 percent of Democrats and 26 percent of independents.

> A great many people think they are thinking when they are really rearranging their prejudices.
>
> — William James, American philosopher and psychologist[16]

Figure 146. How do you feel about Jews? (GSS survey conducted in 2004, based on 513 cases, with confidence level of 99+%, and relative proportion of 2.33)

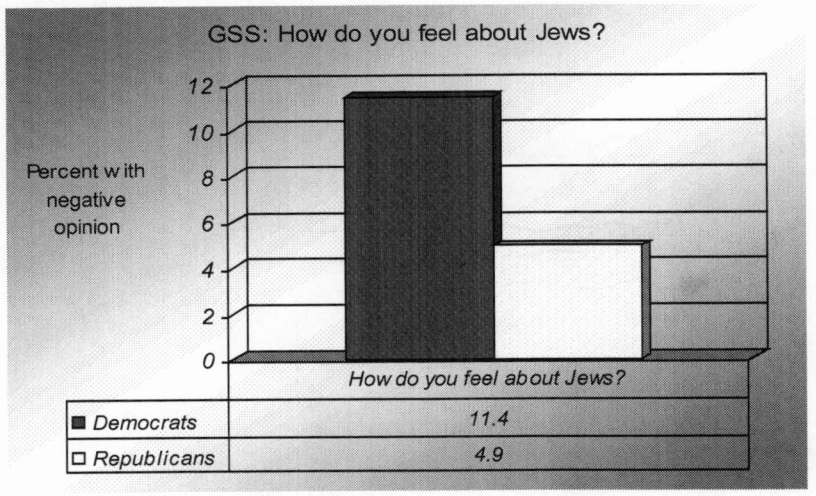

16 William James (attributed), "The Quotations Page."

These findings are not surprising in light of a 2004 General Social Survey (GSS). Respondents were asked if they felt "warm or cold" towards different religious groups, and so indicated by giving a number between zero and 100 on a "feelings thermometer." In Figure 146, above, we see that Democrats were more likely than Republicans to express negative feelings (i.e., "temperatures" below 50 degrees) in regard to Jews.

Note: The disparity in Democratic and Republican feelings regarding Jews is a recent phenomenon. The same thermometer was used by GSS in 1986, 1988, and 1989 and, during those years, statistically significant differences were not found.

With Regard To Other Religious Groups

GSS also used its "thermometer" to gauge feelings about Protestants, Catholics, and Muslims. There was no significant difference in the likelihood of negative views being expressed regarding Catholics and Muslims, but there was with regard to Protestants. Democrats were more likely to view Protestants in a negative light (by 8.3% to 2.4%).[17]

> Bigot — a person who wins an argument with a liberal.

> — Rush Limbaugh, Author and radio talk show host[18]

Figure 147. How do you feel about ...? (NES surveys conducted in years from 2000 through 2004, based on, left to right: 2255, 1664, and 2336 cases, with confidence level of, left to right, 98%, 99%, and 99+%, and with relative proportions of, left to right, 1.53, 1.81, and 1.77.)

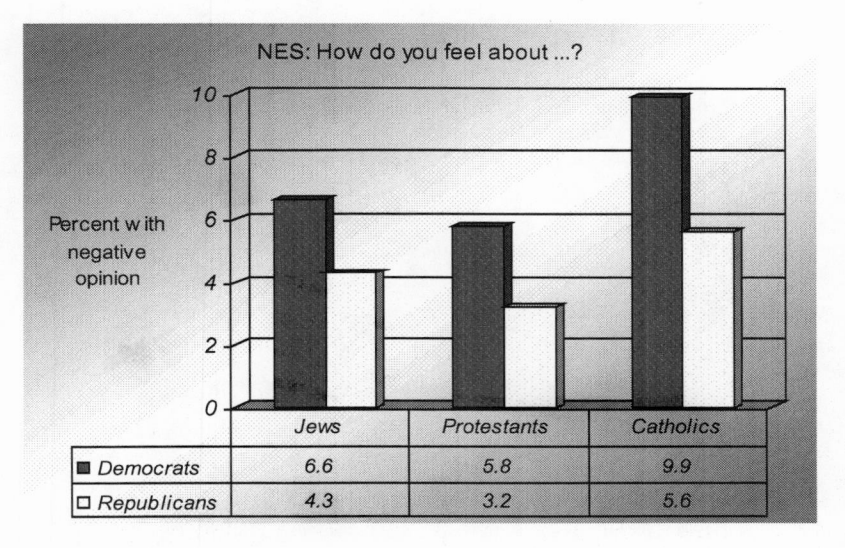

	Jews	Protestants	Catholics
■ Democrats	6.6	5.8	9.9
□ Republicans	4.3	3.2	5.6

NES: How do you feel about ...?

Percent with negative opinion

17 GSS survey conducted in 2004, based on 514 cases, with statistical significance of 99+%, and with relative proportion of 3.46.
18 Rush Limbaugh (attributed), "Thinkexist.Com."

NES is another organization that uses "thermometers" to assess feelings regarding various groups. Democrats are substantially "colder" with regard to Christian Fundamentalists —by 30.6 to 19.8 percent.[19] In addition, Democrats are slightly more negative regarding Jews, Protestants, and Catholics. The feelings towards those 3 groups are depicted in Figure 147.[20]

> ... I have reluctantly concluded that I was wrong. The far right does not have a monopoly on bigotry and hatred and sanctimony.
>
> — Lanny J. Davis, Special counsel to President Bill Clinton[21]

The Gallup Organization does not use "thermometers" to measure feelings towards members of different groups, but in August 2006 it conducted a survey to measure the degree of *positive* feelings of 1001 Democrats and Republicans towards followers of various religions.[22] The religious groups considered were:

Jews
Catholics
Methodists
Baptists
LDS/Mormons
Muslims
Evangelical Christians
Fundamentalist Christians
Atheists
Scientologists

Gallup concluded:

> Democrats have less positive views towards a number of religious groups in America. ... The gap between the percent of Democrats and Republicans who have a positive image of the religious groups extends across Jews, Catholics, Baptists, Methodists, Mormons, Evangelical Christians, and Fundamentalist Christians.

On the whole, Democrats were only 72 percent as likely as Republicans to have warm feelings for the groups identified by Gallup (above). The only specific category for which Democrats had warmer feelings was atheists.[23]

---

19 NES surveys conducted in 2000, 2002, and 2004, based on 2117 cases, with statistical significance of 99+%, and with a relative proportion of 1.55.

20 The NES results are based on surveys conducted in the years 2000, 2002, and 2004, except for those pertaining to Protestants, which were only asked in 2000 and 2002.

21 Lanny J. Davis, "Liberal Mccarthyism," *Wall Street Journal*, August 8, 2006.

22 The 1001 Democrats and Republicans included independents who "leaned" towards the Democratic or Republican parties.

23 Frank Newport, "Democrats View Religious Groups Less Positively Than Republicans," *The Gallup News Service* (September 7, 2006), Retrieved January 2, 2007, from Http://brain.gallup.com.

With Regard To Racial And Ethnic Groups

> [T]here isn't a day that goes by without Democrats effectively us-
> ing the race card against their opponents in every political debate
> ranging from education to border security to the courts. It's time
> for conservatives, Republicans in Washington and minorities with
> half a brain to call their bluff.

— Author and columnist Michelle Malkin[24]

Republicans are often accused (by Democrats and people in the media) of harboring intolerance towards racial and ethnic groups. However, those alleged tendencies are not evident in the results of the major surveys reviewed by this author.

NES uses its "feeling thermometers" with respect to four ethnic/racial groups: whites, blacks, Hispanics, and Asian-Americans. The aggregated results for years 2000 through 2006 did not show a statistically significant difference in attitudes expressed by Democrats and Republicans.

In 2002, GSS asked respondents "how warm or cool" they felt towards each of those same four ethnic/racial groups. The proportion of Democrats and Republicans expressing negative views did not differ to a statistically significant degree, except with respect to whites. Slightly more Democrats had negative feelings towards whites (8.1% to 3.8%).[25]

Gays And Lesbians

Figure 148. How do you feel about gays and lesbians? (combined results of NES surveys conducted in 2000, 2002, and 2004, based on 2324 cases, with confidence level of 99+%, and relative proportion of .63)

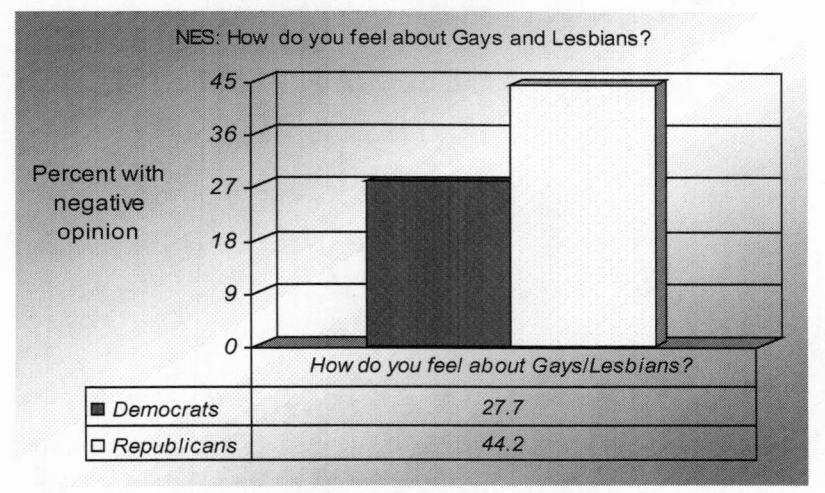

	How do you feel about Gays/Lesbians?
■ Democrats	27.7
□ Republicans	44.2

---

24 Michelle Malkin, "The 'D' Stands for Demagogue," (Jewish World Review, January 18, 2006), Retrieved April 2, 2007, from: http://www.jewishworldreview.com/michelle/malkin011806.php3.

25 GSS survey conducted in 2002, based on 1677 cases, with statistical significance of 99+%, and with relative proportion of 2.13.

Republicans are far more likely than Democrats to express negative feelings about gays and lesbians, judging by the results of recent NES surveys. See Figure 148, above.

> I was going to have a few comments on the other Democratic presidential candidate, John Edwards, but it turns out you have to go into rehab if you use the word 'faggot.'
>
> — Author and political activist Ann Coulter[26]

Who contributes more to society?

Military Service

In a 2004 GSS survey, Democrats and Republicans were asked:

> There are different opinions as to what it takes to be a good citizen. As far as you are concerned personally ... how important is it to be willing to serve in the military at a time of need?

In response to the questions, Republicans were much more likely to state that it is "very important." The views express, by party and gender, are shown in Figure 149, below.

Figure 149. How important is it to serve in the military when needed? (2004 GSS survey based on 414 cases for males, 507 cases for females, and 921 cases for both, with confidence level of 99+% for males, females, and both, and with relative proportions of, left to right, .68, .56, and .59)

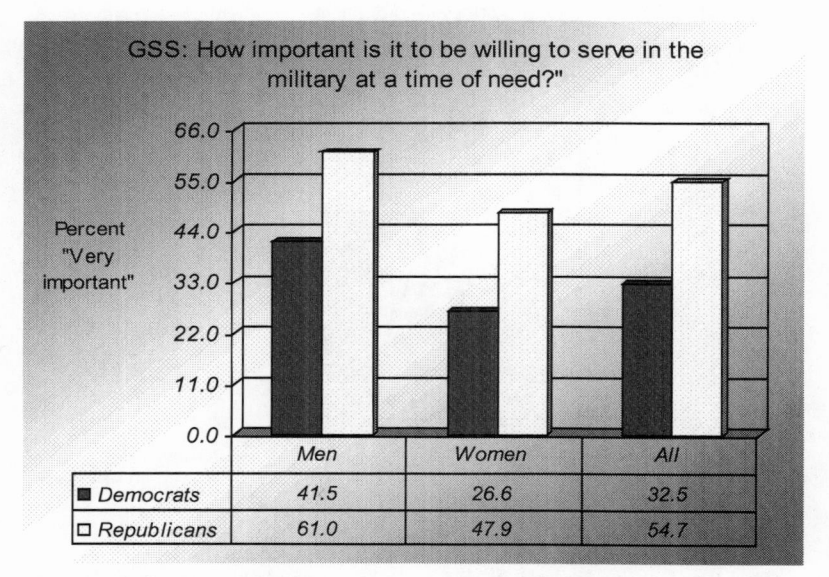

	Men	Women	All
■ Democrats	41.5	26.6	32.5
□ Republicans	61.0	47.9	54.7

26 Ann Coulter, "John Edwards Breaks Silence on Coulter's 'Faggot' Barb," *Foxnews.com* (March 5, 2007), Retrieved April 2, 2007, from http://www.foxnews.com/story/0,2933,256526,00.html.

Are these Republican beliefs reflected in actual service? Probably, but the record is mixed.

> When it was their turn to serve, where were they? AWOL, that's where they were. The lead chicken hawk against Senator Kerry is the vice president of the United States. What nerve!

— Democratic Senator Frank Lautenberg[27]

A 2004 ABCNEWS poll asked 629 Democrats and Republicans if they were military veterans. Almost identical percentages of Democrats and Republicans responded in the affirmative. However, that result was contradicted by a 2005 Pew Religion and Public Life Survey:

Figure 150. Are you a veteran of the armed forces?" (2005 Pew survey based on 1288 cases, with confidence level of 99+%, and with a relative proportion of .64)

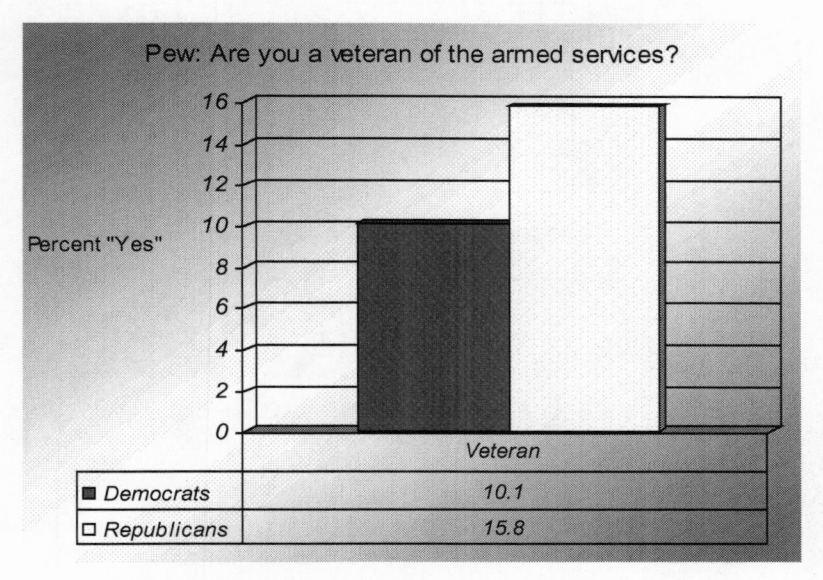

In Louisiana, President Bush met with over 15,000 National Guard troops. Here's the weird part — nobody remembers seeing him there.

—Comedian Craig Kilborn[28]

Only a tiny percentage of the constituents of either party are serving in the military at any given point in time. However, the results of several NES surveys, conducted in 1990 through 2004, suggest that Republicans are more likely to be

---

27 James G. Lakely, "Cheney Emerges as Attack Magnet," *Washington Times*, April 29, 2004.

28 Craig Kilborn, "AWOL Bush Jokes," in *ABOUT: Political Humor*, ed. Daniel Kurtzman, Retrieved April 2, 2007, from: http://politicalhumor.about.com/library/blbushawoljokes. htm.

serving as current members of the armed forces. The survey results are depicted in Figure 151, below. None of the surveyed women — Democratic or Republican — was currently serving as a member of the armed forces. The results below are limited to males.

Figure 151. Are you a "current member of the armed forces"? (Men only) (NES surveys conducted from 1990 through 2004, based on 3280 cases, with confidence level of 99%, and relative proportion of .38)

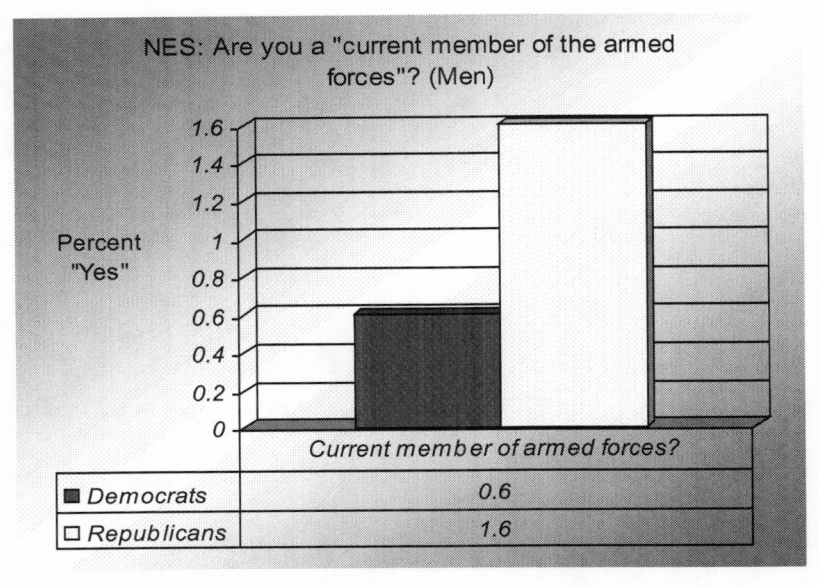

...Cliff May, who now works as the president of the Foundation for the Defense of Democracies ... called the "chicken hawk" theory a "wrong and rather cheap argument. In the United States, we have civilian control of the military and that's probably a good idea."

—Terry M. Neal, Washingtonpost.com[29]

We can also consider this matter from the opposite perspective: the party preference of active members of the military. With respect to a 2004 survey of 655 adults who had served on active duty, the Annenberg Public Policy Center noted:

> Forty-three percent [of respondents] called themselves Republican, 19 percent called themselves Democrats and 28 percent said they were independents.[30]

29 Terry M. Neal, "Chickenhawk Vs. Chicken Little," *Washington Post*, September 6, 2002.
30 "Service Men and Women Upbeat on Bush," in *National Annenberg Election Survey Report* (Annenberg Public Policy Center, October 15, 2004), Retrieved March 17, 2006, from: www.naes04.org.

And, the New York Times reported:

> Various studies in the past have found that overall, military personnel and their families vote at least 2 to 1 Republican; in some subsets, like elite officers, the ratio is as high as 9 to 1.[31]

Among the professional military, Republicans clearly dominate. This is evident from the results of surveys performed by *the MilitaryTimes* magazine.

Figure 152. "In politics today, do you consider yourself a ..." (Military Times survey conducted November 14, 2006, based on 1215 cases randomly selected from the magazine's list of active-duty subscribers, with confidence level of at least 95%)

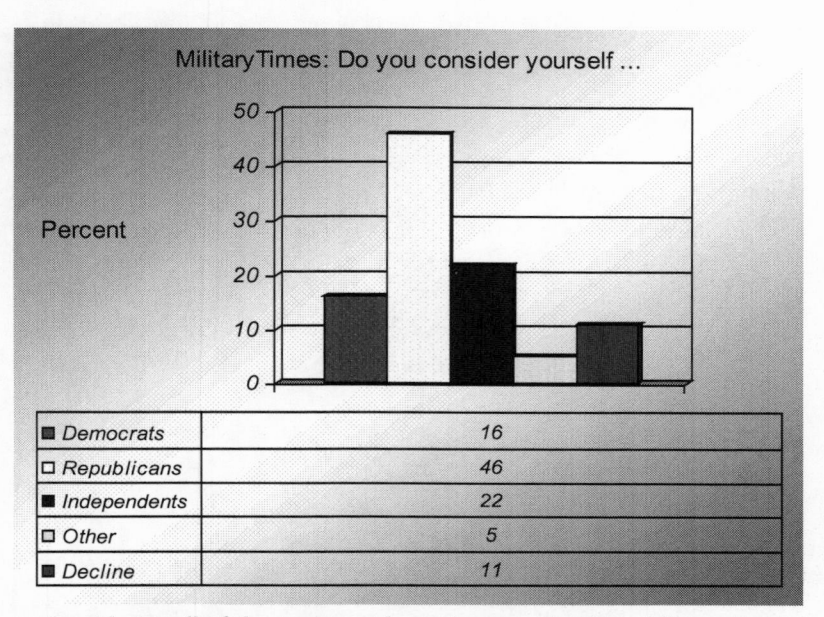

Democrats	16
Republicans	46
Independents	22
Other	5
Decline	11

Considering all of the survey evidence, it seems that Republicans are more likely than Democrats to be serving, or to have served, in the military.

Charitable Causes

> Be of service. Whether you make yourself available to a friend or co-worker, or you make time every month to do volunteer work, there is nothing that harvests more of a feeling of empowerment than being of service to someone in need.
>
> — Gillian Anderson, American actress[32]

A detailed discussion of charitable donations and volunteerism is found in Chapter 4. Those results are not replicated here; however, no assessment of

---

31 Elisabeth Rosenthal, "Among Military Families, Questions About Bush," *The New York Times*, April 11 2004.

32 Gillian Anderson (attributed), "Brainyquote.Com."

citizenship would be complete without some reflection on this issue. Survey evidence suggests that Republicans are more likely than Democrats to donate to charities, and to donate larger amounts. This appears to be the case even when income levels between Democrats and Republicans are controlled. In addition, Republicans are more likely to state that they have volunteered for charitable causes.

Helping The Environment

Gas-Guzzling SUVs

"The blame for the world's higher temperature rests on gas guz-zling vehicles."

— Democratic Senator Barack Obama, who drove off in an SUV shortly after making the statement at a town hall meeting.[33]

By 53 to 37 percent, Democrats are more likely than Republicans to state that it is "very important" for SUV drivers to switch to more fuel-efficient vehicles. In addition, 39 percent of "liberal Democrats" state that they have purchased a car that gets better mileage. This is only true of 20 percent of "conservative Republicans." These words are backed up by deeds according to a Pew 2003 "Religion and Public Life" survey. It shows that Democrats are much less likely to own a sports utility vehicle.

Figure 153. Do you own an SUV? (2003 Pew survey, based on 1226 cases, with confidence level of 99+% and relative proportion of .55)

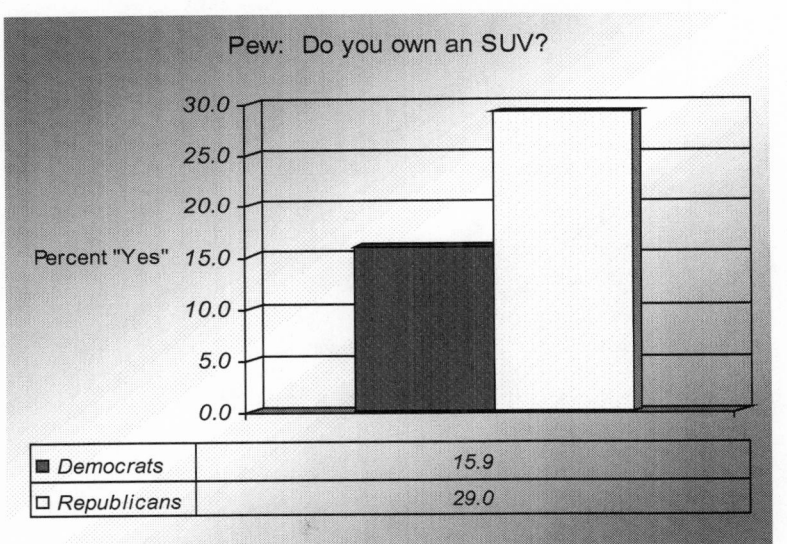

33 "Obama Preaches Fuel Efficiency from the Back Seat of an Suv," in *The Illinois Review* (LaComb, Dennis, August 16, 2006), Retrieved April 2, 2007, from: http://illinoisreview.typepad.com/illinoisreview/2006/08/obama_preaches_.html.

Recycling

What's most curious about recycling is that it seems bulletproof to criticism. A few years ago, The New York Times Magazine ran an article exposing curbside recycling as a sham. Turns out there are much more efficient market systems that would dispose of our trash without all that individual participation.

— Jack Hitt, American author[34]

There is one thing that Democrats and Republicans seem to agree on: the need for recycling waste. A 2006 survey conducted by the Opinion Research Corporation showed that about 70 percent of Democrats and Republicans utilized curbside recycling programs. In addition, about 95 percent of each constituency stated that recycling was, at the least, "somewhat important." In a 2003 Gallup survey, respondents were asked if they had "voluntarily recycled newspapers, glass, aluminum, motor oil or other items." Again, approximately equal percentages of Democrats and Republicans (about 90 percent) said that they had recycled.[35] Questions regarding recycling efforts were also asked in 3 GSS surveys in 1993, 1994, and 2000. The combined results of those surveys also show no statistically significant difference between Democrats and Republicans with regard to recycling.

Other Environmental Efforts

Although the record is mixed, it appears that Democrats are more likely to volunteer in support of environmental causes. A 2003 Gallup survey showed that Democrats were no more likely to have "been active in a group or organization that works to protect the environment."[36] And, on the basis of a mail survey of 623 residents of central Pennsylvania, it was concluded (in 2002):

> Although Democrats are more likely to support government mitigation programs, party identification accounts for much less variance than either cognitive or economic measures. Partisan identification has almost no impact on voluntary actions.[37]

However, those results are out of sync with surveys conducted by GSS and by the State of Michigan. The results of the GSS surveys, conducted in 1993, 1994, and 2000, and the results of Michigan surveys, conducted in 1999, 2003, and 2005, are shown in Figure 154, below.

Figure 154. Do you participate in a group dedicated to helping the environment? (GSS surveys conducted in 1993, 1994, and 2000, and Michigan SOSS surveys conducted in 1999, 2003, and 2005, based on, left to right, 2610 and 1060 cases, with confidence level of 99+%, and relative proportions of, left to right, 1.47 and 1.83)

---

34 Jack Hitt, "A Gospel According to the Earth," *Harpers*, July 2003.

35 "The Environment," in *Gallup Poll Social Series* (Gallup Organization, March, 2003), 363.

36 Ibid., 338.

37 Robert E. O'Connor, Richard J. Bord, and Brent Yarnal, "Who Wants to Reduce Greenhouse Gas Emissions?," *Social Science Quarterly* 83, no. 1 (March, 2002): 10.

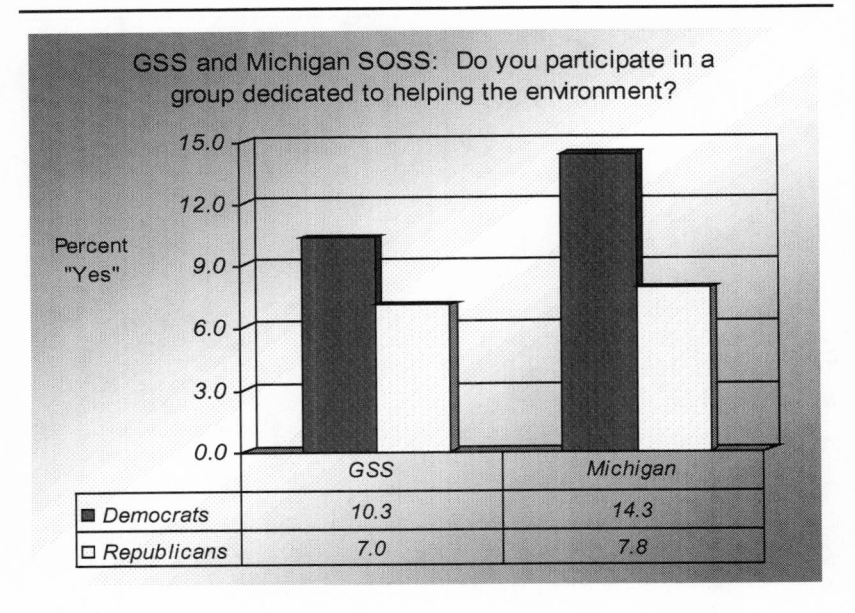

Democrats are also more likely to have reduced their "household use of energy" in an effort to help the environment, according to a 2003 Gallup survey of 323 Democrats and Republicans (82% to 72%).[38]

Thus, with regard to the environment, we might conclude that Democrats are more likely to drive environmentally-friendly vehicles, participate in environmental organizations, and reduce home energy usage. On the other hand, the evidence does not suggest that they are more likely to recycle.

Other Contributions

Blood Donations

A brave man's blood is the best thing in the world when a woman is in trouble.

— Abraham Van Helsing, the fictional character from Dracula.[39]

It seems that the donation of blood might be a good indicator of civic responsibility. After all, wealth is not a requirement for blood donations. I found two surveys addressing this subject, and they suggest that Republicans are a little more likely to contribute to the blood bank. The combined results are shown in Figure 155, below.

Figure 155. During the last 12 months have you donated blood? (2 GSS surveys conducted in 2002 and 2004, based on 1660 cases, with confidence level of 95% for men, no statistical significance for women, overall significance of 99%, and with relative proportions of, left to right, .77, .79, and .76)

38 "The Environment," 368.
39 Bram Stoker, *Dracula* (New York: Bantam Books, 1981).

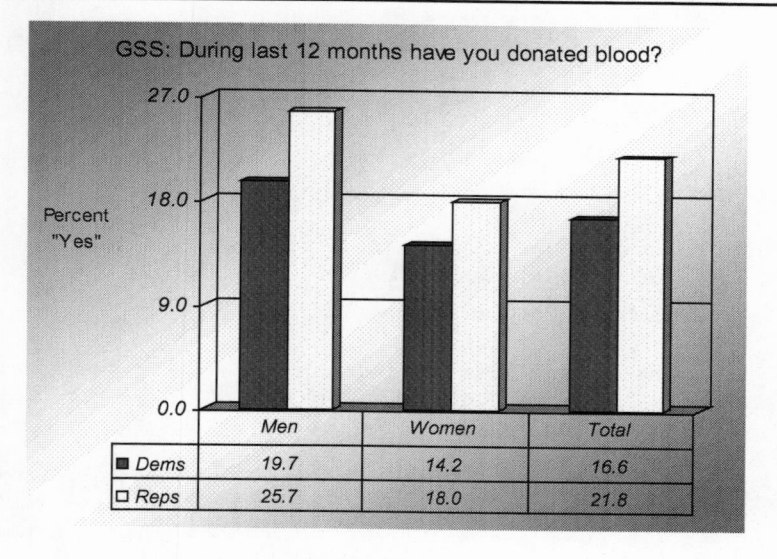

Jury Duty

A jury consists of twelve persons chosen to decide who has the better lawyer.

— Robert Frost, American poet[40]

Figure 156. "If you were selected to serve on a jury, would you be happy to do it or would you rather not serve?" (NES surveys conducted in 1996 and 2000, based on, left to right, 857 and 899 cases, with confidence level of 94% (marginal) for 1996 and 99+% for 2000, and relative proportions of, left to right, .90 and .85)

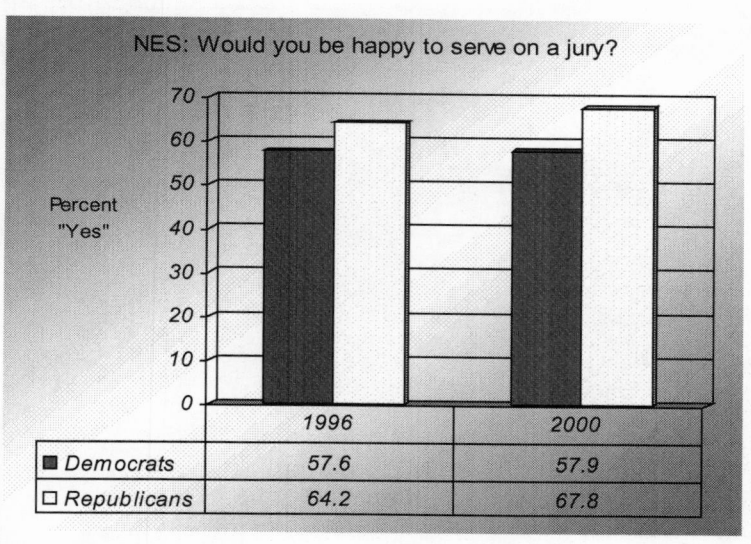

40 Robert Frost (attributed), "The Quotations Page."

I was able to find two surveys addressing this issue, conducted by NES in 1996 and 2000. Respondents were asked: "If you were selected to serve on a jury, would you be happy to do it or would you rather not serve?" Republicans were more likely to indicate a willingness to serve. See Figure 156, above.

Who is more likely to participate in the political process?

Voting

> Bad officials are the ones elected by good citizens who do not vote.
>
> — George Jean Nathan, American drama critic[41]

As generally assumed, Republicans are more likely to vote in presidential elections. This fact is apparent in the results of 50 years of NES surveys, which are summarized, by decade, in Figure 157.

Figure 157. Did you vote in the presidential election? (Several NES surveys conducted between 1952 and 2004, based on, left to right, 2605, 3149, 4508, 6098, 5856, and 2776 cases, with confidence levels of 99% for all differences, and with relative proportions of, left to right, .88, .90, .83, .92, .94, and .86)

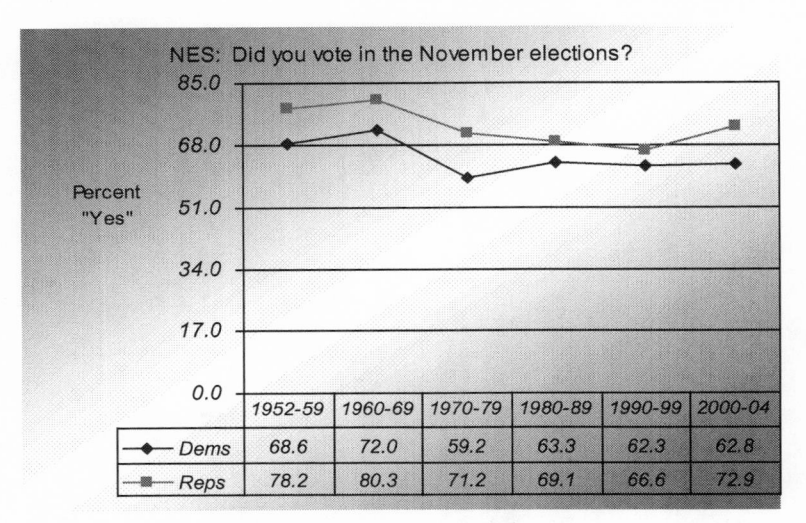

	1952-59	1960-69	1970-79	1980-89	1990-99	2000-04
Dems	68.6	72.0	59.2	63.3	62.3	62.8
Reps	78.2	80.3	71.2	69.1	66.6	72.9

GSS surveys show a similar pattern, but with slightly smaller disparities. To see the GSS results, go to Appendix B 15 on page 357.

> Well, Republicans, I guess, can do that [vote]. ... But for ordinary working people, who have to work eight hours a day, they have kids, they got to get home to those kids, the idea of making them stand for eight hours to cast their ballot for democracy is wrong.
>
> — Howard Dean, Chairman of the Democratic National Committee[42]

---

41 George Jean Nathan (attributed), "The Quotations Page."
42 Dinan and Fagan, "Dean Hits GOP on 'Honest Living'."

Reality check — Should we necessarily encourage people to vote?

Conservative columnist Jonah Goldberg wonders if we have our priorities wrong when we encourage the uninformed (of either political party) to vote:

> Maybe the emphasis on getting more people to vote has dumbed-down our democracy by pushing participation onto people uninterested in such things. Maybe our society would be healthier if politicians aimed higher than the lowest common denominator.... Perhaps cheapening the vote by requiring little more than an active pulse (Chicago famously waives this rule) has turned it into something many people don't value. ...
>
> Instead of making it easier to vote, maybe we should be making it harder. Why not test people about the basic functions of government? Immigrants have to pass a test to vote; why not all citizens?[43]

According to Goldberg, if we "threaten to take the vote away from the certifiably uninformed," we will send the message that voting is a valued accomplishment. Ironically, that could lead to a boost in voter turnout.

Political Campaigns, Rallies And Protests

A recent Michigan survey suggests that Democrats are more likely to volunteer for a political organization or campaign. (See Figure 158, below.)

Figure 158. Last year, did you volunteer for "a political organization or campaign (such as the Democratic or Republican parties)"? (2005 Michigan SOSS, based on 297 cases, with statistical significance of 99+%, and with a relative proportion of 2.23)

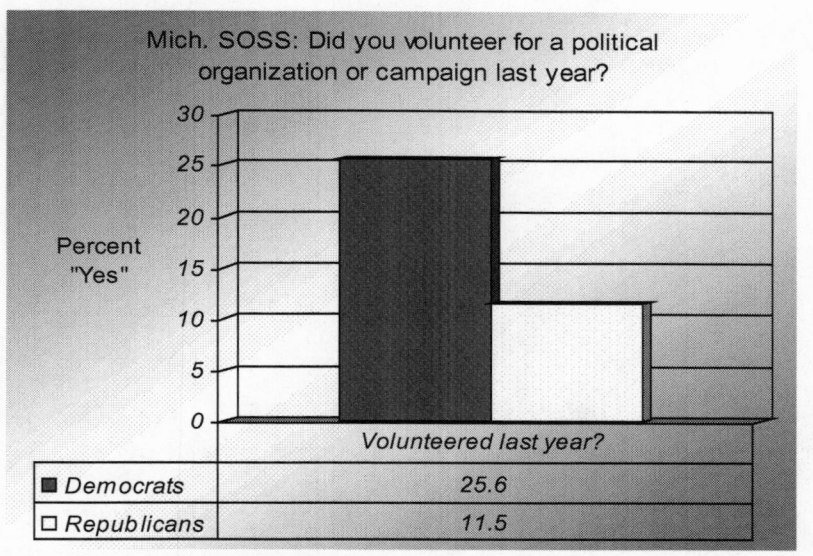

Two questions on the 2004 GSS survey address related subjects. Respondents were asked if they "took part in a demonstration" or "attended a political meeting or rally." Again, Democrats were more likely to answer in the affirmative.

---

43 Jonah Goldberg, "Too Uninformed to Vote?," *Los Angeles Times*, July 31, 2007.

Figure 159. Last year, did you take part in a demonstration or attend a political meeting or rally? (GSS survey conducted in 2004, based on, left to right, 927 and 929 cases, with confidence level of, left to right, 99% and 99+%, and with relative proportions of, left to right, 2.02 and 1.58)

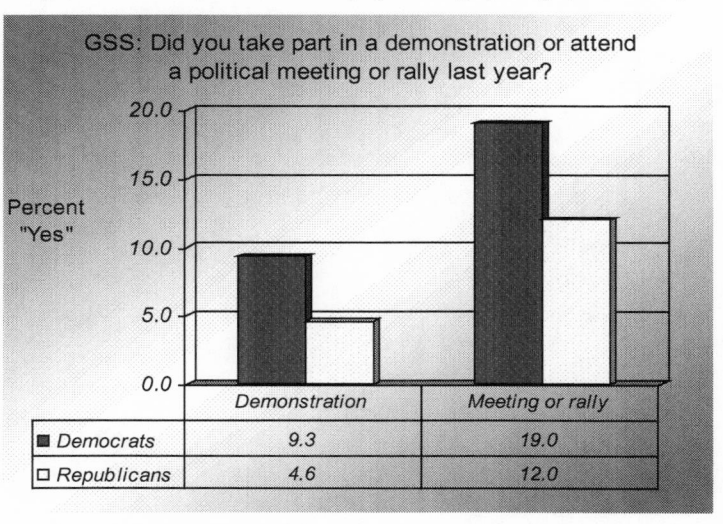

Say you want a revolution, we better get on right away. Well you get on your feet, and out on the street, singing Power to the People!

— Popular song-writer John Lennon[44]

Protest rallies and marches were the topic of a 2002 GSS survey. In Figure 160, below, we see that Democrats dominate in this area, regardless of gender.

Figure 160. Over the past 5 years have you joined a protest, rally or march? (GSS survey conducted in 2002, based on, left to right, 343, 519, and 862 cases, with confidence levels of, left to right, 97%, 95%, and 99+%, and with relative proportions of, left to right, 2.41, 2.22, and 2.24)

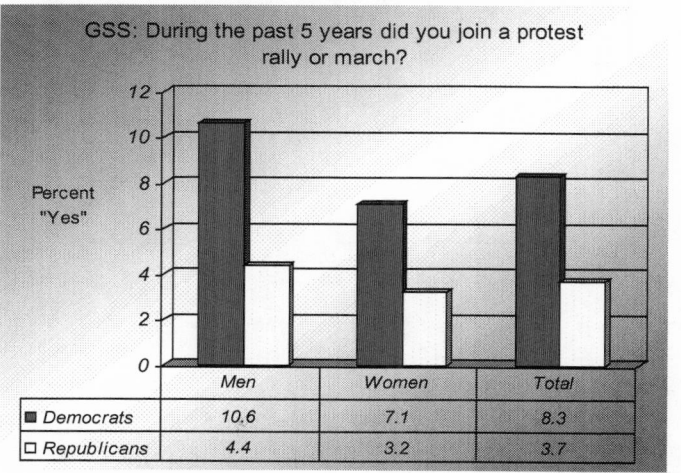

44 John Lennon, "Power to the People (Song)," in *Oldielyrics.com*.

Directly Contacting Public Officials

> If you think you're too small to have an impact, try going to sleep with a mosquito.
>
> — Philip Elmer-DeWitt, Science and Technology writer[45]

In 2004, NES asked respondents if they had contacted the government to express views regarding a public matter. Republicans were a little more likely to indicate that they had.

Figure 161. "During the past twelve months, have you telephoned, written a letter to, or visited a government official to express your views on a public issue?" (2004 NES survey, based on 643 cases, with confidence level of 96%, and relative proportion of .73)

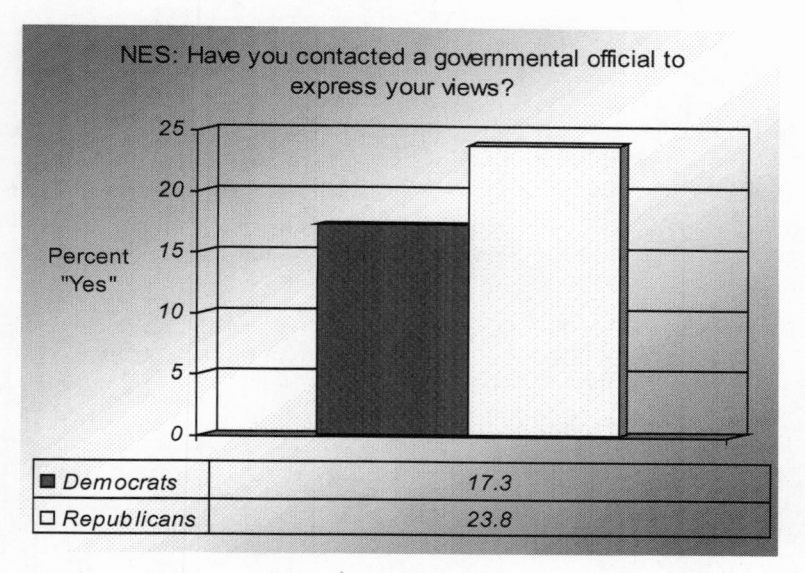

These results are supported by a 2004 GSS survey, where people were asked if they had ever "contacted, or attempted to contact, a politician or a civil servant to express [their] views." By 48.9 to 41.2 percent Republicans were more likely to have done so.

Reality check — There was no statistically significant difference for:

- Contacting or appearing in the media to express a view. (About 16% did it.)
- Joining an Internet political forum. (About 9% did it.)
- Boycotting products for political reasons. (About 40% did it.)
- Signing a petition. (About 70% did it.)[46]

---

45 Philip Elmer-DeWitt, "Anita the Agitator," *Time Magazine*, January 25, 1993.
46 Based on GSS surveys conducted in 2004, and involving about 930 cases.

Who is more likely to avoid negative social behavior?

The flip side of ethical behavior is the avoidance of negative social behavior, which can include a wide variety of improper conduct, from littering all the way up to murder and mayhem. There are few (if any) surveys that question participants with regard to such matters; however, it was possible to glean some information with respect to felonies and bankruptcy.

Who Gets The Felon Vote?

> You could abort every black baby in this country, and your crime rate would go down. That would be an impossible, ridiculous and morally reprehensible thing to do, but your crime rate would go down.
>
> — William Bennett, former Secretary of Education under President Reagan[47]

Although social surveys are useless for detecting felony rates among Democrats and Republicans, an academic analysis of this subject has been performed. Two professors of sociology, Christopher Uggen and Jeff Manza, estimated felon voting preferences by analyzing the demographic makeup of felons (e.g., race, gender, and economic background) and applying the voting preferences associated with that demography. Based upon their research and analysis, published in 2002, they concluded:

> [T]he survey data suggest that Democratic candidates would have received about 7 of every 10 votes cast by the felons and ex-felons in 14 of the last 15 U.S. Senate election years.[48]

Assuming they are right, we could conclude that 70 percent of felons were Democrats when they committed their crimes, or we could speculate that there is something about the judicial process and/or incarceration that makes turns criminals into Democrats.

Who Is More Likely To File For Bankruptcy?

> Capitalism without bankruptcy is like Christianity without hell.
>
> — Former astronaut Frank Borman[49]

Bankruptcy is painful for the debtor, and it is costly for society. The unpaid debts of the bankrupt result in losses to his private and/or public creditors, and those losses get absorbed by society, as a whole. The combined results of 2 GSS

---

47 Brian Faler, "Bennett under Fire for Remark on Crime and Black Abortions," *Washington Post*, September 30, 2005, 5.

48 Christopher Uggen and Jeff Manza, "Democratic Contraction? Political Consequences of Felon Disenfranchisement in the United States," *American Sociological Review* 67, no. 1 (2002): 786.

49 Frank Borman, "The Growing Bankruptcy Brigade," *Time Magazine*, October 18, 1982.

surveys — taken in 1991 and 2004, suggest that Democrats file for bankruptcy at a slightly higher rate than Republicans. Like most of the survey results in this book, these can be viewed from two perspectives: On the one hand, we have to conclude that bankruptcy is a very slim likelihood for either constituency. On the other hand, these results suggest that a large majority of personal bankruptcies involve Democrats.

Figure 162. During the last year did you declare bankruptcy? (GSS surveys conducted in 1991 and 2004, based on 1528 cases, with confidence level of 97%, and with a relative proportion of 3.2)

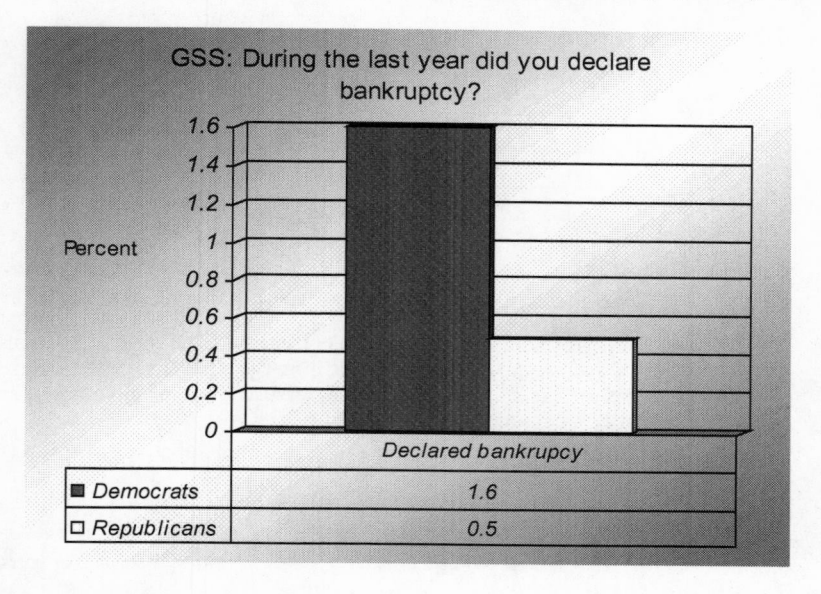

Who Is More Honest?

> Honesty is the best policy — when there is money in it.
>
> — Author and humorist Samuel Clemens ("Mark Twain")[50]

I found only a few surveys quizzing Democrats and Republicans regarding their honesty in certain hypothetical situations. The responses show that a higher percentage of Democrats than Republicans say it is acceptable to cheat with respect to taxes and government benefits. Of course, it could be that Republicans are so dishonest that they won't admit how dishonest they are.

Figure 163. It is not wrong or only slightly wrong to conceal part of my income to save taxes, or to give the government false information to get benefits (aggregate results of GSS surveys conducted in 1991 and 1998, based on 1598 cases, with confidence level of, left to right, 99+% and 98%, and with a relative proportions of, left to right, 1.34 and 2.13)

---

50 "Mark Twain Quotations," (March 30, 1901), Retrieved April 2, 2007, from: http://www. twainquotes.com/Honesty.html.

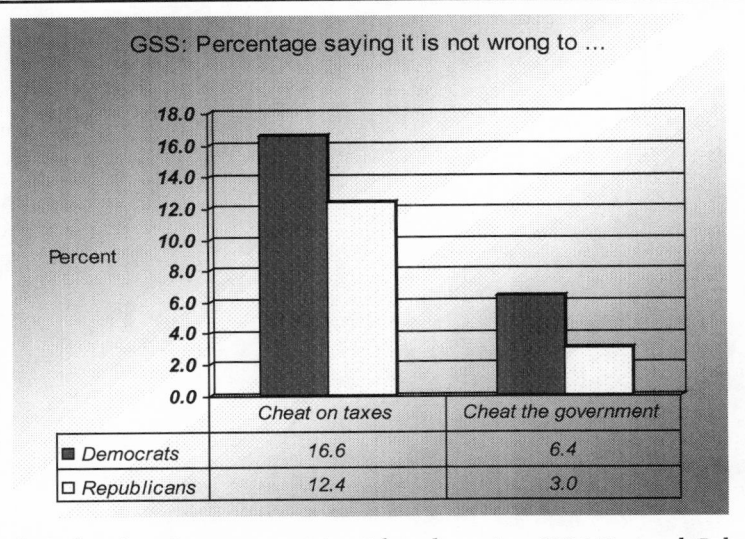

The only other "honesty" question I found was in a 2006 National Cultural Values Survey. Respondents were given this hypothetical moral dilemma:

> You are out to dinner with a group of friends. When the check arrives you notice that several items are missing from the bill. Your friends say you should just pay the bill, and that it's the restaurant's own fault for making the mistake. What would you do?

The responses suggest that Democrats would be more likely to pay the lower (incorrect) bill. See Figure 164.

Figure 164. I would go along with my friends and cheat the restaurant (National Cultural Values Survey conducted in December, 2006 by the Cultural and Media Institute, based on 2000 cases, with confidence level of 95% and with relative proportion of 1.65)

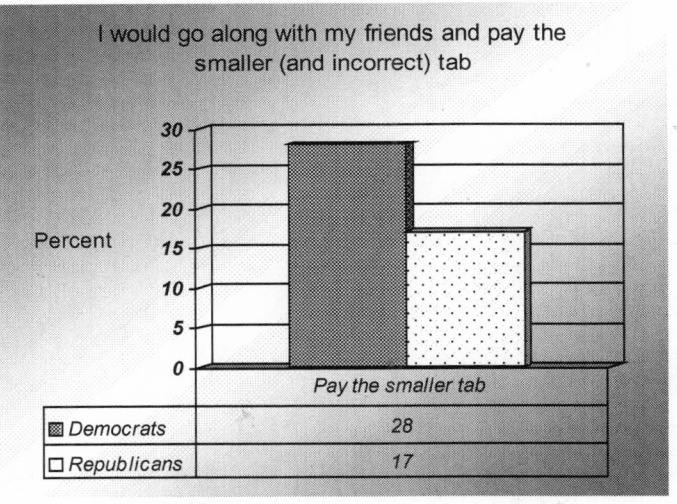

I like to do my principal research in bars, where people are more likely to tell the truth or, at least, lie less convincingly than they do in briefings and books.

— P.J. O'Rourke, American political satirist[51]

Driving over the speed limit

Republicans truly live in the fast lane. By 50 to 38 percent they are more likely to "often drive over the speed limit."[52]

Conclusions

This chapter has presented statistical comparisons concerning bigotry, support for first amendment rights, contributions to society, political participation, and the avoidance of negative social behavior. Survey evidence indicates that there are statistically significant differences between Democrats and Republicans in each of these areas. Specifically, the survey results indicate:

Democrats have slightly more unfavorable views regarding whites and most religious groups, and Republicans express much more negativity regarding gays and lesbians. The unfavorable views regarding racial and ethnic groups do not differ to a statistically significant degree.

Democrats express less tolerance for controversial speech and books in their communities, and have done so for decades. They are also more likely to state that public meetings by racists and religious extremists should not be permitted. Republicans are more likely to bar meetings by those advocating the violent overthrow of the government.

It appears that Republicans are more likely to participate in the military, charitable activities, jury duty, and voting. Their statements indicate that they are more likely to directly contact public officials to express their views.

Surveys indicate that Democrats are more likely to participate in environmental organizations, to participate in political campaigns, protests and boycotts, and to not drive SUVS.

Academic research suggests that a higher percentage of convicted felons are Democrats, although this constitutes a very tiny percentage of Democrats as a whole (of course). In addition, survey evidence suggests that Democrats are slightly more likely to have gone through bankruptcy.

There are a couple of surveys showing that Democrats are more likely to state that they would engage in dishonest conduct in certain situations.

As noted in the introduction, it is left to the reader to determine the specific elements that comprise the "good citizen." Some of the items addressed herein may not be included within your definition, and some of the elements in your definition may be omitted here. If so, this was due to author oversight or, more likely, a lack of relevant survey data.

---

51 P. J. O'Rourke, *Holidays in Hell* (London: Picador, 1989), 212.

52 The results are from a 2004 Harris survey, based on 635 cases, with a confidence level of 99+%, and with a relative proportion of 1.32.

CHAPTER 7: WHO GETS MORE FROM SOCIAL SECURITY AND MEDICARE?

INTRODUCTION

Dismantling the New Deal

> Since the days of Barry Goldwater, the Republican right has really wanted to dismantle Social Security. And now they have a degree of political dominance that lets them push it to the top of the agenda....

— Economist Paul Krugman[1]

> With special interests, not seniors, in mind, Republicans designed a [prescription drug] bill that will dismantle Medicare. For the sake of our seniors, we must dismantle this cruel hoax of a bill.

— Democratic Congresswoman Nancy Pelosi[2]

It is not clear that most Republicans want to dismantle Social Security and Medicare (as claimed by some), but many of them criticize the effectiveness and funding of these programs. They do this more than Democrats, so we might assume that Republicans are less likely to derive significant benefits from these entitlements. However, this is not the case. The average Republican, retiring now or during the next 40 years, can expect to get a net benefit (i.e., an investment

---

1 Paul Krugman, "The Fake Crisis," in *Rollingstone* (January 13, 2005), Retrieved January 27, 2006, from: http://www.rollingstone.com/politics/story/6822964/the_fake_crisis/.

2 Congresswoman Nancy Pelosi, "For the Sake of Our Seniors, We Must Dismantle This Cruel Hoax of a Medicare Bill," January, 2004, Pelosis Web site, Retrieved January 28, 2006, from http://www.house.gov/pelosi/press/releases/jan04/Medicare012804.html.

return) on his Social Security and Medicare tax dollars that is at least as high as that of his Democratic counterpart.

Caveats

Economics And Demographics May Change

The amounts shown in this chapter are predicated on the assumption that several demographic and economic factors remain constant over an extended time period. The results will change if the presumed real interest rate proves to be unrealistic, or if there are significant changes in the percentage of Democrats and Republicans who are male, female, married and working. In addition, it is assumed that the Social Security and Medicare programs remain solvent, and there is no restructuring of benefit or tax rates. (Of course, there is great public concern about the solvency of these programs, and this is why many Republicans — and Democrats — feel that program reform is required.)

Average Isn't Typical

In the case of Social Security and Medicare, averages mask huge variations in benefits, attributable to income level, gender, age, marital status, the distribution of wages among members of the household, and the year of retirement. In many cases, the variations seem arbitrary and inequitable. A meaningful analysis of these programs requires awareness of these factors, some of which are described below.

DETAILS

Social Security

> A leading Republican said Sunday that President Bush is so worried about Social Security that he is only able to sleep ten hours a night.
>
> — Comedian Tina Fey[3]

Who Does Relatively Well in the Social Security System?

Compared To Others, Women And The Poor Do Well

As noted, the value of net benefits varies sharply, depending on certain demographic factors. Indeed, it would be fair to say that the Social Security system has some "winners" and many "losers."

Social Security benefit rates are not adjusted for gender longevity differences so women usually collect far more benefits than do men. In addition, people with lower wage incomes usually get benefits that are much higher in proportion to the FICA taxes they pay.

---

3 Comedian Tina Fey as cited in, "Saturday Night Live," (Transcript: NBC, February 19, 2005), Retrieved March 23, 2007, from: http://snltranscripts.jt.org/04/04mupdate.phtml.

The importance of these two factors — gender and wage level — is clearly evident from an inspection of Figure 165, below, which depicts the net lifetime Social Security benefits of single men and women with varying levels of wage income. Information used in the chart (and subsequent charts) was derived from a Web-based Social Security benefits calculator created by economists C. Eugene Steuerle and Adam Carasso of the Urban Institute. [4]

Figure 165. The information is from a table of net lifetime transfers (benefits minus taxes) prepared by C. Eugene Steuerle and Adam Carasso of the Urban Institute. These are the average net benefits of single men and women turning 65 in years 2005 through 2045.

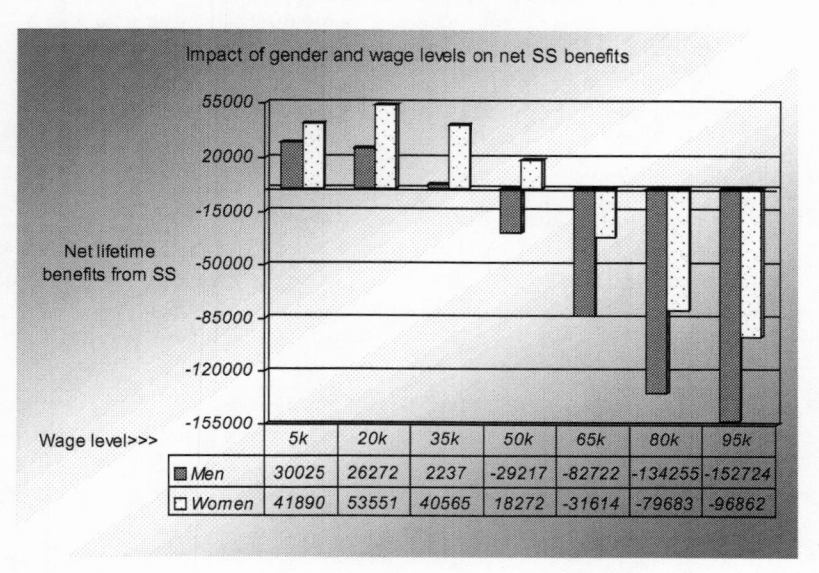

Social Security is not in crisis. It's a crisis the president's created. Period.

— Democratic Senator Harry Reid[5]

The columns represent estimated net lifetime benefits from Social Security (total estimated benefits less total estimated taxes paid, in today's dollars). Both men and women with higher wage levels (towards the right side of the chart) have much lower net lifetime Social Security benefits than those at the lower wage levels. In fact, these columns depict very negative amounts, signifying that

4 C. Eugene Steuerle and Adam Carasso, "The USA Today Lifetime Social Security and Medicare Benefits Calculator," (Urban Institute, October 1, 2004), from: http://www.urban.org/publications/900746.html. NOTE: The calculator does not include the value or cost of the Social Security disability program.

5 Senator Harry Reid as cited in, "Judy Woodruff's inside Politics," (Transcript: CNN, March 3, 2005), Retrieved March 23, 2007, from: http://transcripts.cnn.com/TRANSCRIPTS/0503/03/ip.01.html.

middle and upper-class single workers lose substantial sums by participating in Social Security. It is also evident that matters are even worse for men — no matter what the level of wage income. Because they don't live as long as women (on average) and because there are no significant early payout options provided by Social Security, men generally get lower benefits than women.

We might say that women are Social Security "winners;" however, this is only with respect to the benefits paid by Social Security to men. Comparisons with private retirement accounts, or with state and local government pension plans, could lead to a different conclusion.

> According to a study by researchers at Harvard University, virtually every woman-single, divorced, married, or widowed-would be better off financially under a system of fully private retirement accounts
>
> — Michael Tanner, Director of Health and Welfare studies at the libertarian CATO Institute[6]

Married Workers With Stay-At-Home Spouses Are Social Security Winners

Based on a review of Figure 165, one would assume that Republicans do very poorly in the Social Security system because the average Republican is more likely to be male, and is more likely to have high wages. However, this is not the case, due to a very important offsetting factor: The Republican worker is more likely to have a stay-at-home spouse.

In 1939, four years after the enactment of Social Security, the program was changed to provide generous spousal and survivor benefits to workers with stay-at-home spouses. The workers get these extra benefits, even if they are wealthy. In fact, the more a worker earns, the greater his extra (spousal and survivor) benefits will be.

Figure 166, below, shows the net benefits of a worker with a stay-at-home spouse, assuming various wage levels (the same wage levels depicted in Figure 165). Two significant factors are evident: First, every column in Figure 166 depicts a net benefit that is higher than any column in Figure 165. In other words, the average married person (with a stay-at-home spouse) gets a greater benefit per FICA tax dollar paid than does the average single person — no matter what the gender or wage level. Second, there is only limited progressivity among married workers with stay-at-home spouses. Review Figure 166 carefully: The net benefits drop as the wage levels increase from $50,000 to $95,000; however, they increase as the wage levels grow from $5,000 to $50,000. In fact, net benefits are lowest for those earning just $5,000 per year. (These people get smaller benefits per FICA tax dollar paid.)

---

6 Michael Tanner and Darcy Olsen, "Increasing Social Security," in *PBS Online Newshour Forum* (December 1998), Retrieved August 30, 2006, from: http://www.pbs.org/newshour/forum/december98/socsec2.html.

Figure 166. The information is from a table of net lifetime transfers (benefits minus taxes) prepared by C. Eugene Steuerle and Adam Carasso of the Urban Institute. These are the average net benefits of married people (with non-working spouses) turning 65 in years 2005 through 2045.

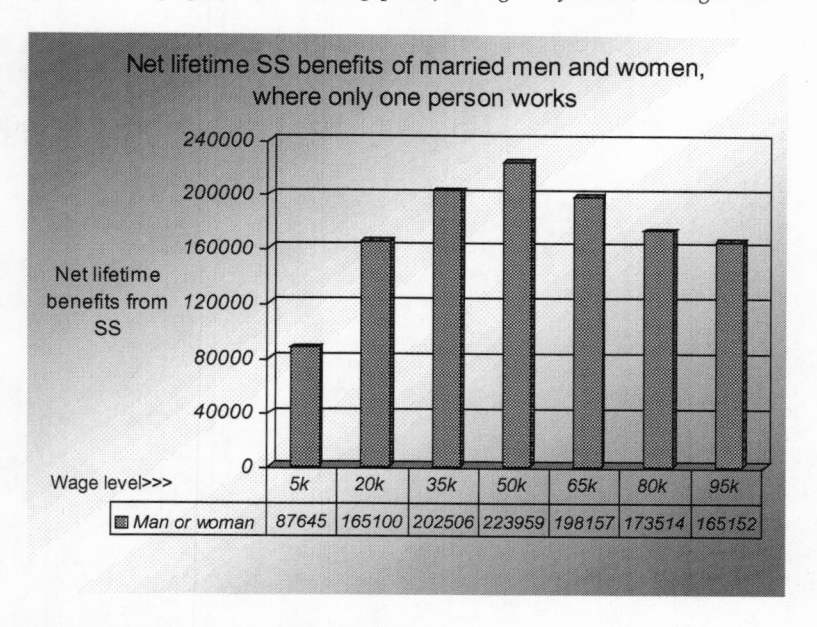

Republicans know that people will get a better return on their [Social Security] money if they are allowed to invest it in things that bring a larger return rather than investing it in the phony promises of government and in the patronage system of politicians. ... Republicans trust the people. Democrats trust the government.

— Alan Keyes, Former diplomat and Republican presidential aspirant[7]

Bill Gates Is A Social Security Winner?

The current system of spousal and survivor benefits results in huge transfers of wealth from low-income workers to high-income workers. It is likely, for example, that Bill Gates will get a higher rate of return from Social Security (assuming his wife has no wage income) than the two-earner married couple earning just $40,000 per year (together). Some people feel that marital benefits should be "means tested;" however, politics seems to prevent candid public discourse regarding this topic. For an in-depth analysis, refer to my book, *How Social Security Picks Your Pocket* (Algora Publishing, 2003).

Figure 167, below, is simply a combination of Figure 165 and Figure 166. In other words, one graph has been placed on top of the other. Now we see that the "average" masks huge variations in a patch quilt benefit structure. For example,

7 Alan Keyes, "The Key to Republican Victory," in *WorldNetDaily* (March 19, 1999), Retrieved March 23, 2007, from: http://www.worldnetdaily.com/news/article. asp?ARTICLE_ID=18658.

a worker making $95,000 per year could be one of the biggest "winners," if he is married to a stay-at-home spouse. His expected net benefit would be more than $160,000. On the other hand, if he remains single he can expect a net benefit of negative $150,000. (In other words, he would end up subsidizing the system.) That should be sobering information for any confirmed bachelor.

Figure 167. This chart combines the information in Figure 165 and Figure 166. Note the wide variances in net benefits for people at any given level of income — particularly at the upper earnings levels.

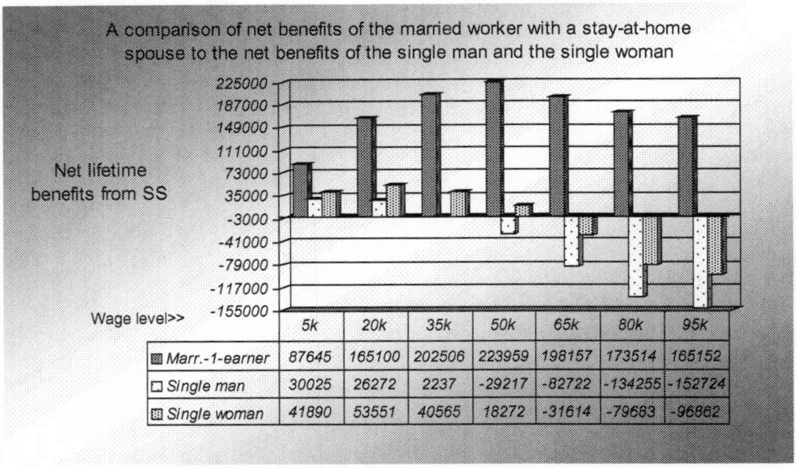

A comparison of net benefits of the married worker with a stay-at-home spouse to the net benefits of the single man and the single woman

Wage level>>	5k	20k	35k	50k	65k	80k	95k
Marr.-1-earner	87645	165100	202506	223959	198157	173514	165152
Single man	30025	26272	2237	-29217	-82722	-134255	-152724
Single woman	41890	53551	40565	18272	-31614	-79683	-96862

The Democrats cannot be bribed, cajoled or threatened into voting for Social Security reform — it can't happen.

—GOP strategist Grover Norquist[8]

Comparing Democratic Benefits To Republican Benefits

Now that we have reviewed the basic benefit structure of Social Security, we can use these findings to estimate the expected net benefits of Democrats and Republicans. As noted, economists C. Eugene Steuerle and Adam Carasso of the Urban Institute designed a Web-based Social Security benefits calculator that can be used to estimate the total lifetime value of benefits as opposed to the total lifetime cost of payroll taxes.[9]

Using the calculator, net benefits can be estimated separately for single males, single females, one-earner married couples, and two-earner married couples. In addition, separate calculations can be made for people in different wage

---

8 Grover Norquest as quoted by Michael Abramowitz, "President Remains Eager to Cut Entitlement Spending," in *Washington Post* (August 11, 2006), Retrieved March 23, 2007, from: http://www.washingtonpost.com/wp-dyn/content/article/2006/08/10/AR2006081001508_pf.html.

9 Steuerle and Carasso, "The USA Today Lifetime Social Security and Medicare Benefits Calculator."

brackets (by $5,000 increment) and for people in of different age brackets (i.e., people reaching age 65 in years 1975 through 2045, by 5-year intervals). Other parameters and assumptions used in the calculator are noted in Appendix B 13.

To estimate the net benefits of the average Democrat or Republican, we simply determine the percentage of Democrats and Republicans within each of the major parameters used by Steuerle and Carasso. This was done in a two-step process, using demographic information obtained from General Social Survey (GSS) surveys conducted over a 14-year period spanning 1991 through 2004. It's pretty boring, but I feel compelled to provide a brief overview of the calculation process. If you want to skip the calculation overview and get to the results, please advance to the bottom line of Table 35.

Net Benefits for Each Type of Beneficiary

> The deceptive marketing of Social Security has been deliberate, carefully designed to prevent the American public from realizing that Social Security is simply a pay-as-you-go welfare system. As Arthur Altmeyer, Roosevelt confidante and first Social Security commissioner, said, "Every effort was made to use terminology that would inspire confidence rather than arouse suspicion."

— Political scientist and author James L. Payne[10]

Lifetime net benefit amounts were determined, by political party, for each major category of benefit recipient. These net benefit amounts are shown in Table 34, below. For this step, the differences between the Democratic and Republican columns are entirely attributable to differences in the average levels of wage income of Democrats and Republicans. The impact of the varying wage levels on each category is explained in the "Comments" column of the table.

Table 34. Total average net SS benefit amounts for various categories of beneficiaries. The slight differences in the amounts for Democrats and Republicans (in each row) are attributable to differences in wage levels, the impact of which is explained in the "Comments" column.

Type of beneficiary	Net benefits ($)		Comments
	Dems	Reps	
Married – spouse works full-time	41,500	37,100	For two-earner couples, net benefits are progressive. Therefore, Republicans (who generally earn more) get less. (Note: These are the benefits for each man or woman in the couple.)
Married man – spouse works part-time or less	188,500	190,700	For one-earner couples, benefits are regressive up to about $50,000; thereafter they are progressive. It appears that Republicans get slightly more.

10 James Payne, "How America Drifted from Welfare To "Entitlement"," (The American Enterprise March, 2005), 26, Retrieved March 23, 2007, from: http://www.taemag.com/docLib/20050131_Payne.pdf.

Married woman –spouse works part-time or less	186,000	192,800	Same as above.
Single man	–2,200	–7,300	For single men, benefits are progressive. Therefore, Republican men (who generally earn more than Democratic men) get less.
Single woman	39,600	40,700	Benefits are progressive; however, there is no statistically significant difference in the earnings of Democratic and Republican single women. Therefore, the benefits are essentially the same. In either case, the benefits are much greater than for single men, due to the greater longevity of women.

The dimensions of the conservative campaign to destroy Social Security — and dismantle the New Deal — are now heaving into view. Determined to achieve the victory that has eluded them for more than 70 years, George W. Bush's aides and allies are building a very big, very ugly propaganda juggernaut.

— Columnist Joe Conason[11]

Weighted Average Of Net Benefits, By Political Party

The figures shown in Table 34, above, were multiplied times the percentages of Democrats and Republicans within each category, as shown in Table 35, below.

Table 35. Average estimated net benefits for Democrats and Republicans turning 65 in years 2005 through 2045, calculated as an average of the net benefits for all categories of beneficiaries, weighted to reflect the percentage of Democrats and Republicans in each category.

	Democrats			Republicans		
Type of beneficiary	% in category *	Dollar amount per Table 34	% times dollar amt.	% in category *	Dollar amount per Table 34	% times dollar amt.
Married and both work full-time	0.36	41,500	14,940	0.43	37,100	15,953
Married and spouse works part-time or not at all — men	0.10	188,500	18,850	0.20	190,700	38,140

11 Joe Conason, "Beware the Coming Propaganda Juggernaut," (Salon.com, February 25, 2005), Retrieved January 27, 2006, from: http://dir.salon.com/story/opinion/conason/2005/02/25/propaganda/index.html.

Married and spouse works part-time or not at all— women	0.02	186,000	3,720	0.02	192,800	3,856
Single men	0.19	-2,200	- 418	0.19	-7,300	-1,387
Single women	0.33	39,600	13,068	0.16	40,700	6,512
Total	1.00		$50,160	1.00		$63,074

*Confidence level of numbers in this column is 95% or greater.

The bottom line of Table 35 shows us that, during his lifetime, the "average" Republican will get nearly $13,000 more in total net benefits than will the "average" Democrat.[12] Given the many economic and demographic assumptions used, we should take the $13,000 difference with a large grain of salt. However, it is fair to say that, as a group, Republicans are at least as likely to benefit from Social Security as are Democrats.

> In years past ... Democrats and Republicans might have had a reasonable debate over whether to partially privatize Social Security. Today, though, all chance for a civil debate on the merits of the issue is lost, giving way to the politics of fear.

> — Sean Hannity, Author and TV talk show host[13]

A Gender-Neutral Calculation

As noted, Republicans comprise a higher percentage of males than do Democrats. Does this affect the results? Yes, but only to a minor degree, as can be seen in Table 36, below.

Table 36. Estimated SS net benefits for people turning 65 in years 1975 through 2045 — gender neutral.

Gender	Dems	Reps
Males	$48,500	$65,000
Females	47,500	53,000
Gender neutral (average)	$48,000	$59,000

The gender neutral amount, shown in the bottom row of Table 36, above, represents the amount of benefits received by the average Democrat and Republican, assuming that each party comprises equal numbers of men and women. These estimated amounts are not much different than the bottom-line amounts in Table 35.

Whether we use the amounts calculated in Table 35, or the gender-neutral amounts shown in Table 36, the average Republican can expect to get net life-

12 The calculation is $63,074-$50,160 = $12,914.
13 Sean Hannity, *Let Freedom Ring*, 1st Edition ed. (New York: HarperCollins, 2002), 275.

time Social Security benefits that are as much or more than the average Democrat. This suggests that the overall Social Security benefit structure is not progressive, and that Republicans, on the whole, have as much to lose as Democrats from any "dismantling" of the system.

One More Critical Factor: Young People of Either Party Get Less

When Social Security began, the payroll tax was just 2 percent of income. Now it's 12.4 percent. ... Twenty-five-year-old workers can expect a return of minus 0.64 percent — they actually lose money.

— Edwin Feulner, President of Heritage Foundation and Doug Wilson, Chairman of Townhall.com[14]

Before leaving the subject of Social Security, a comment is required regarding the impact of a person's retirement date on the amount of his net lifetime benefits. Generally, people who retire sooner get more than those who retire later. For example, a person who retired in 2005 can expect to get significantly greater net lifetime Social Security benefits than a person retiring in 2045. This is due to the fact that payroll taxes were relatively modest until recent years. As a result, younger workers have paid and will pay more in payroll tax to get their benefits than did older workers. This fact is evident from a review of Figure 168, below, which compares expected benefits for men at differing wage levels, assuming two different retirement dates: 2005 and 2045. The man retiring in 2045 gets substantially less than does the man retiring in 2005, no matter what the wage level.

Figure 168. The information is from a table of net lifetime transfers (benefits minus taxes) prepared by C. Eugene Steuerle and Adam Carasso of the Urban Institute. These are the average net benefits of single men who turn 65 in 2005 and in 2045.

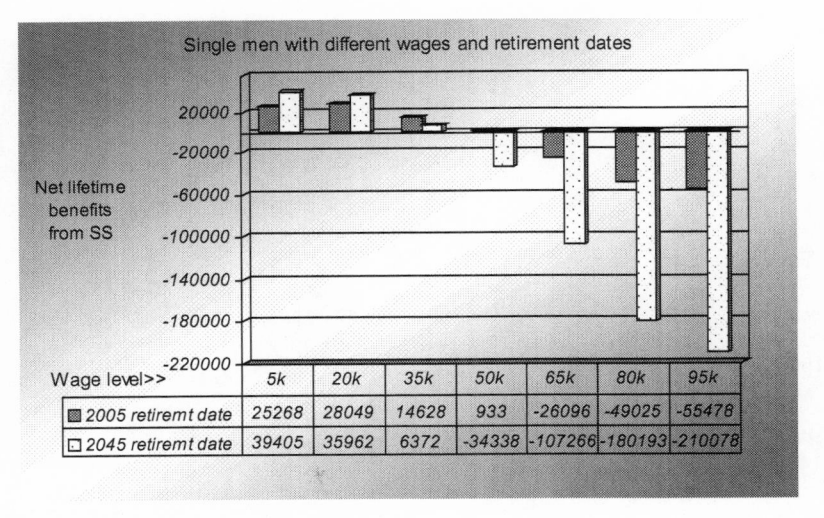

Wage level>>	5k	20k	35k	50k	65k	80k	95k
▨ 2005 retiremt date	25268	28049	14628	933	-26096	-49025	-55478
☐ 2045 retiremt date	39405	35962	6372	-34338	-107266	-180193	-210078

---

14 Edwin Feulner and Doug Wilson, *Getting America Right* (New York: Crown Forum, 2006), 79.

> Seniors tend to be opposed to change, and they don't, for under-
> standable reasons, care about Social Security's dismal rate of return
> for workers who will retire decades from now. Fine. Preserve the
> current system for seniors, but let young workers experiment with
> private accounts
>
> — Rich Lowry, Author and columnist.[15]

Does this factor affect the members of one political party more than another? It probably is not a significant factor because the age distribution of Democrats and Republicans is fairly equal. It does mean, however, that there are two key problems facing future Social Security recipients: a dismal rate of return on their Social Security contributions, and funding problems that may force a reduction in those meager benefits. Add to these the inequitable patch quilt benefit struc-ture (discussed on page 207) and there is plenty to justify reform of this retire-ment system.

Who gets the very best deal from Social Security?

How would you like to receive $45,000 for each one dollar you put into your retirement plan? Sound too good to be true? It's not. In 2003 and 2004, 7 tiny Texas school districts ran special programs where thousands of retiring teachers were hired to work for just a single day as "custodians" or "clerks." On average, the one-day workers earned wages of about $40, on which they paid only $2.50 in FICA tax. For many of the teachers, that was the only FICA tax they paid during their entire careers. However, due to a loophole in the law (since closed), these one-day cleaners and clerks could each receive, on average, about $113,000 in retirement benefits (in today's dollars). In to-tal, this could cost the Social Security trust fund over $2 billion dollars.

Although the loophole was considered to be legal, the way the school districts exploited it was not. This author first identified the potentially fraudulent nature of these work programs in his book *How Social Security Picks Your Pocket* (Algora Publishing, 2003). Later, he confirmed that some of the school districts weren't really paying anything to their one-day workers: Ef-fectively, these were sham transactions where the workers paid themselves via special "processing fees" that were given to the school districts in ad-vance of their work days. In addition, many of the districts were violating signed Social Security agreements by extending the Social Security coverage to workers in part-time positions. These allegations were presented to the Inspector General of Social Security, who launched a major audit that con-cluded in January, 2007. The findings confirmed the author's suspicions:

> We identified 20,248 individuals who were employed as 1-day work-
> ers by the 7 school districts.... Over their lifetimes, they will potentially re-
> ceive about $2.2 billion in spousal benefits.... We found that individuals
> employed as 1-day workers by the seven Texas school districts did not ap-

---

15 Rich Lowry, "Young People Be Damned," in *National Review Online* (December 7, 2004), Retrieved December 8, 2006, from: http://www.nationalreview.com/lowry/low-ry200412070848.asp.

pear to meet the requirements to receive a GPO exemption [the loophole]. This occurred because of the questionable nature of these individuals' employment. We also found that five of the school districts did not have the authority to provide these individuals Social Security coverage.[16]

Case closed? Not so fast. Thus far, the Social Security Administration has taken no action to cut off benefits to these 20,248 jani-teachers, and has imposed no penalties on the districts that operated the shady hiring programs. The OIG audit report is at http://www.ssa.gov/oig/ADOBEPDF/A-09-06-26086.pdf.

Medicare

Everyone's A "Winner" — Except For Future Generations?

I care about our young people, and I wish them great success, because they are our Hope for the Future, and some day, when my generation retires, they will have to pay us trillions of dollars....

—Dave Barry, American writer and humorist.[17]

Gender and wage levels affect Medicare benefits in the same way they impact Social Security benefits: Woman tend to get higher net benefits than men (because they live longer), and workers with low wages tend to get higher net benefits than those with higher wages (because they get the same benefits even though they pay less payroll tax). Unlike Social Security, however, there are no apparent "losers" (except for future generations who will probably have to pay for these benefits via legislated tax hikes).

Every beneficiary, regardless of gender or wage level, can expect to get a substantial net lifetime Medicare benefit. This is evident by reviewing Figure 169, below. By way of comparison, consider Figure 165. There, many people (at the higher income levels) received sharply negative "benefits."

As was the case with Social Security, one would expect Republicans to get lower net lifetime Medicare benefits because the average Republican is more likely to be male and to have higher wages. Again, however, this is not the case, due to the fact that the Republican worker is more likely to have a stay-at-home spouse.

Figure 169. Net lifetime Medicare benefits for single men and women at various income levels. The information is from a table of net lifetime transfers (benefits minus taxes) prepared by C. Eugene Steuerle and Adam Carasso of the Urban Institute. These are the average net benefits of single men and women who turn 65 in years 2005 through 2045.

---

16 Office of Inspector General, "Government Pension Offset Exemption for Texas School Districts' Employees," ed. Social Security Administration (January 2007), from: http://www.ssa.gov/oig/ADOBEPDF/A-09-06-26086.pdf.

17 Dave Barry, "Kids, Please Be Spank to Your Elders," in *Daily Athenaeum* (West Virginian University, 1998), Retrieved March 23, 2007, from: http://www.da.wvu.edu/archives/000509/news/000509,04,03.html.

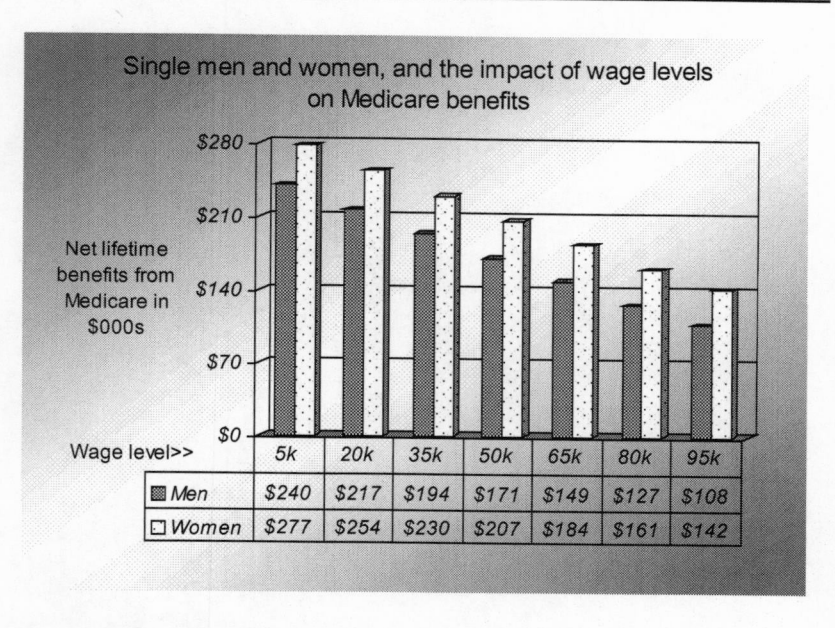

Single men and women, and the impact of wage levels on Medicare benefits

Net lifetime benefits from Medicare in $000s

Wage level>>	5k	20k	35k	50k	65k	80k	95k
■ Men	$240	$217	$194	$171	$149	$127	$108
□ Women	$277	$254	$230	$207	$184	$161	$142

We believe in Medicare; they don't. They brag about voting to kill Medicare or to prevent it from being created 30 years ago. We believe it was an enormously important achievement.

— Mike McCurry, Whitehouse spokesman during the Clinton presidency[18]

With regard to Medicare, a man or woman with a stay-at-home spouse gets benefits that are approximately twice those of the single worker or of the person in a two-earner marriage. This is evident from a review of Figure 170, below, which compares the average benefits that would go to a man or woman with a stay-at-home spouse to those of a single, working woman. The single woman's net benefits never come close to those of the man or woman with the stay-at-home spouse. In fact, the poorest single woman gets far less in net benefits ($277,000) than does the wealthiest person married to a stay-at-home spouse ($393,000). Effectively, the system transfers wealth from poorer workers to wealthier workers.

Figure 170. The information is from a table of net lifetime transfers (benefits minus taxes) prepared by C. Eugene Steuerle and Adam Carasso of the Urban Institute. These are the average net benefits of single women and a married person with a non-working spouse, who turn 65 in years 2005 through 2045.

---

18 Press Secretary Mike McCurry, "White House Press Briefing," October 26, 1995, Retrieved March 23, 2007, from http://www.ibiblio.org/pub/archives/whitehouse-papers/1995/Oct/1995-10-26-Press-Briefing-by-Mike-McCurry.

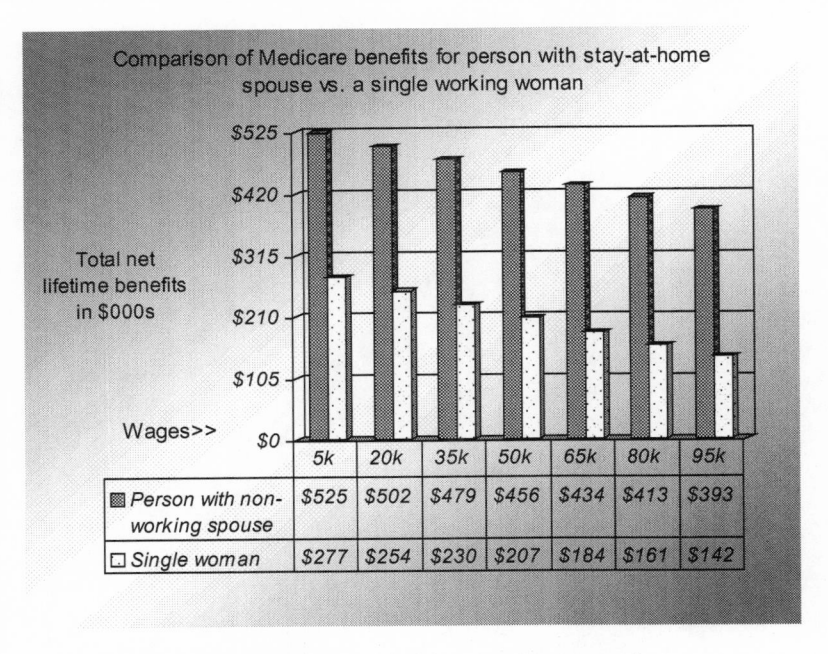

Comparison of Medicare benefits for person with stay-at-home spouse vs. a single working woman

Wages>>	5k	20k	35k	50k	65k	80k	95k
Person with non-working spouse	$525	$502	$479	$456	$434	$413	$393
Single woman	$277	$254	$230	$207	$184	$161	$142

Estimating Democratic vs. Republican Medicare Benefits

> Republicans have made their intentions clear from the beginning — they want to kill Medicare.
>
> — Democratic Congresswoman Nancy Pelosi[19]

The Medicare benefit estimates in this chapter were derived from tables created by Economists C. Eugene Steuerle and Adam Carasso. As we did with regard to Social Security benefits, we can use the Steuerle/Carasso tables to estimate total lifetime net Medicare benefits for single males, single females, one-earner married couples, and two-earner married couples. In addition, we can use the information to calculate benefits for people with differing wage histories, and with different retirement dates.

By using a two-step estimation process, similar to that used for estimating Social Security net benefits, we find that average Medicare net benefits are about the same for Democrats and Republicans — $231,000 and $245,000, respectively. The calculation of these amounts is shown in Appendix B 14.

The Future of Medicare Is Scary

> I reject the notion that Republicans are trying to kill Medicare. I think that is ridiculous. I don't think there is any indication that is

---

19 "Pelosi: AARP Letter Confirms That House Republican Medicare Prescription Drug Bill Is Another Empty Promise," July 15, 2003, Retrieved March 23, 2007, from http://www.house. gov/pelosi/press/releases/July03/prAARPletter071503.html.

the cased, never has been, but it is party of the political mantra that we hear over and over again.

— Republican Senator Bob Bennett[20]

Finally, we need to address the issue of retirement date. Do retirees in 2005 get about the same net lifetime Medicare benefits as those retiring in 2045? The answer is no. The man retiring in 2045 will get far *more* net Medicare benefits than the man retiring in 2005, as is evident from a review of Figure 171, below. If you will recall, Figure 168 (on page 212) shows dramatically different results with regard to Social Security benefits. In that case, the person retiring in 2045 would receive far less in net benefits. In fact, he would have a large loss.

Figure 171. The information is from a table of net lifetime transfers (benefits minus taxes) prepared by C. Eugene Steuerle and Adam Carasso of the Urban Institute. These are the average net Medicare benefits of single men who turn 65 in 2005 and in 2045.

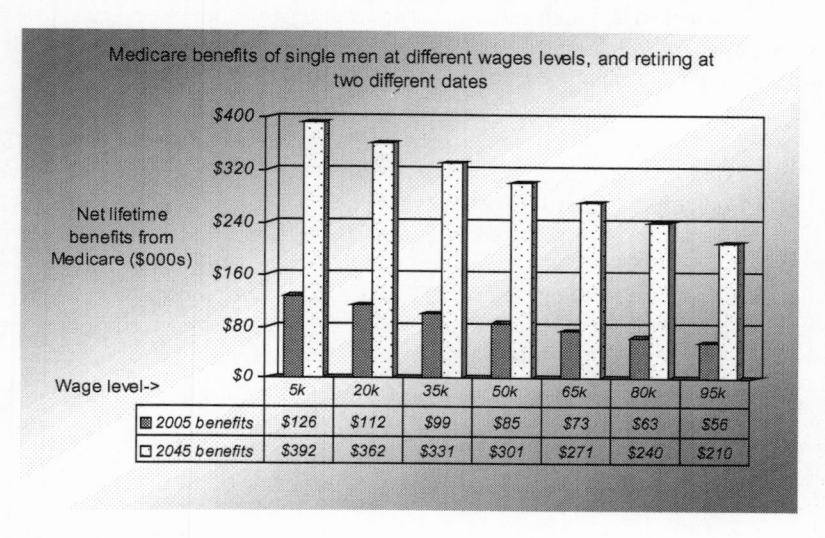

As was true with Social Security, however, retirement dates do not significantly impact our estimations of net benefits because the ages of Democrats and Republicans do not vary significantly. Of course, one day we will have to figure out how to pay for all of these unfunded benefits. One solution would be to means-test Medicare benefits; another would be to raise payroll and/or income taxes. Either solution is more likely to adversely affect Republicans because they tend to have higher earnings, which would make them more susceptible to means testing plans, or tax increases. Perhaps Republicans instinctively suspect this and, consequently, are more eager to reform the system.

---

20 Senator Bob Bennett in debate of, "Medicare Prescription Drug, Improvement, and Modernization Act of 2003," (Transcript: Senator's Web site, November 22, 2003), from: http://bennett.senate.gov/press/record.cfm?id=226106.

I'm too young for Medicare and too old for women to care.

— Kinky Friedman, Humorist, singer, and politician[21]

CONCLUSIONS

Generally, low wage earners and women, two major constituencies of the Democratic Party, get above-average net benefits from Social Security. However, high-earning married people with stay-at-home spouses (prevalent among Republican ranks) get the highest net benefits of all, due to lucrative spousal and survivor benefits. The net result of these factors is a rough parity between the parties, with the "average" Republican getting the same or slightly higher total net benefits than the "average" Democrat. For our purposes, total net benefits are the excess of lifetime benefits received over lifetime payroll taxes paid in today's dollars, assuming a conservative real interest rate of 2 percent.

Like Social Security, Medicare favors low earners and women (two Democratic constituencies) and high-earning married workers with stay at home spouses (a Republican constituency). Medicare total net benefits are roughly the same for the average Democrat and Republican — around $235,000 to $245,000.

Unlike Social Security, Medicare doesn't have benefit winners and losers. Instead, it has winners and huge winners. The Medicare benefit structure is such that everyone can expect to gain from the system — that is, everyone except the future generations that will have to pay for it.

It is important to understand that the averages discussed in this chapter mask the great variances — inequities — built into the benefit formulas. Those inequities, and the looming insolvency issues, should compel Democrats and Republicans, alike, to search for ways to improve the systems. A good starting point would be to eliminate or, at least, "means test," spousal and survivor benefits.

---

21 Kinky Friedman (attributed), "Brainyquote.Com."

CHAPTER 8: WHO GETS MORE WELFARE?

INTRODUCTION

Democrats on Strike and Wal-Mart on Medicaid

What would we do without Democrats working? Who would make the $5 coffees at $tarphucks, who would teach the incoming freshmen how to hate the US? Would [a day without Democrats] mean *Democrats on welfare* would strike against welfare so they would get out and work?

— Blogger named Spobot[1]

Wal-Mart gets Medicaid. Lockheed-Martin gets food stamps. Everyone knows that Halliburton is on the dole.... If checks from us didn't arrive in corporate mailboxes at the first of each month, we would immediately see what a joke American "capitalism" is.

— Columnist Jane Stillwater[2]

In this chapter we define "welfare," determine its cost, and roughly estimate who — Democrats or Republicans — collects more welfare dollars. Necessarily, the definitions are subjective and the estimates are crude. Nevertheless, reasonably fair conclusions can be reached. As usual, sources and methods are presented so that the user can assess their validity.

---

1 Spobot (pseudonym), November 3, 2004, Sgt Grit's Marine Forum, Retrieved February 26, 2006, from http://www.grunt.com/forum/topic.asp.

2 Jane Stillwater, "How Come Lockheed Gets Food Stamps and We Don't," *Novakeo.com* (February 15, 2005), Retrieved February 26, 2006, from http://novakeo.com/?p=98.

The average Democrat probably collects about twice as much "traditional (social) welfare" as does the average Republican. On the other hand, Republicans are more likely to benefit from "corporate welfare."

DETAILS

Traditional (social) welfare

What Is It, And How Much Does It Cost?

> [W]hen [John] Kerry was running for re-election, he uncorked a priceless rib-ticker about his opponent, Massachusetts Governor Bill Weld. "This guy ... takes more vacations than the people on welfare." Is that a Hoot? And yet, believe it or not, some people didn't think it was funny.
>
> — Columnist Jeff Jacoby[3]

In November, 2003, the Congressional Research Service (CRS) of the Library of Congress issued a report describing our public welfare system:

> More than 80 benefit programs provide aid — in cash and non-cash form — that is directed primarily to persons with limited income. Such programs constitute the public "welfare" system, if welfare is defined as income-tested or need-based benefits.[4]

The report described a network of 80 different programs involving total payments (in FY 2002) of $522.2 billion: $373.2 billion in federal funds and $149 billion in state and local funds. The 80 assistance programs are found within the following broad categories:

- Medical aid, such as Medicaid
- Cash aid, such as Supplemental Security Income (SSI)
- Food aid, such as Food Stamps and free school lunch programs
- Housing aid, such as Section 8 low-income housing assistance
- Educational assistance, such as Head Start and Pell Grants
- Services, such as the Emergency Food and Shelter Program
- Job and training programs such as Job Corps and Welfare-to-Work grants
- Energy assistance, such as the Low-Income Home Energy Assistance (HEAP) program

> Most women are one man away from welfare.
>
> — Feminist Gloria Steinem[5]

---

3 Jeff Jacoby, "Heard the One About Kerry's Sense of Humor?," *The Boston Globe* (September 12, 2004).

4 Vee Burke, "Cash and Noncash Benefits for Persons with Limited Income: Eligibility Rules, Recipient and Expenditure Data, Fy2000-Fy2002," ed. Congressional Research Service, CRS Report for Congress (The Library of Congress, 2003), from: http://www.opencrs.com/rpts/RL32233_20031125.pdf.

5 "Gloria Steinem Quotes," in *About: Women's History*, ed. Jone Johnson Lewis, Retrieved March 23, 2007, from: http://womenshistory.about.com/cs/quotes/a/qu_g_steinem.htm.

Most of these programs target very needy Americans; however, one suspects that some may also be used by significant numbers of middle-class Americans. For example, Pell Grants are mostly used by families with very low income (under $20,000); however, the grants can be used by families earning substantially more. In addition, certain programs, such as veteran medical benefits, simply do not fit the common perception of "welfare." And, finally, some benefits, such as the Earned Income Tax Credit, are distributed in the form of tax reductions, and in this book, such benefits are considered to be offsets to taxes paid, in Chapter 5. The cost of items such as these must be subtracted from the CRS welfare estimate ($522.2 billion) before we attempt to estimate who gets most of the benefits from programs we typically consider to be "welfare." This is done in Table 37, below.

Table 37. FY 2002 traditional (social) welfare expenditures

Total federal and state/local expenditures for income-tested benefits	$522.2
Less certain education assistance	−20.2
Less tax credits (primarily the Earned Income Tax Credit)	−32.9
Less certain veteran medical and dependent benefits	−5.1
Less other benefits	−4.7
Adjusted amount of welfare expenditures	$459.3

In Table 37, above, we see that the $522.2 billion figure has been reduced to $459.3 billion, and this is the amount that can be allocated on the basis of income levels.

Who Gets More Traditional Welfare?

[C]ompassion is defined not by how many people are on the government dole but by how many people no longer need government assistance.

— Rush Limbaugh, Author and radio talk show host[6]

Table 38, below, presents the results of surveys that asked Democrats and Republicans whether they receive or received "Medicaid," "cash assistance," "Food Stamps," "SSI," or "welfare." When these statistically significant results are averaged, we find that Democrats seem to be about twice as likely to receive welfare assistance.

If total welfare expenditures are about $459 billion (Per Table 37), and Democrats are twice as likely to get welfare, we can roughly guesstimate that, as a group, Democrats get about $150 billion more in welfare than Republicans (using basic math and the simplifying assumption that there are equal numbers of Democrats and Republicans).[7]

---

6 Rush Limbaugh, *The Way Things Ought to Be* (New York: Pocket, 1993), 2.

7 In reality, there are usually more people that identify with the Democratic Party than the Republican Party, and this means that the welfare gap is larger than the estimate presented

Table 38. Various surveys pertaining to welfare benefits

Row	Survey and Issue	% of Dems receiving aid	% of Reps receiving aid	No. of cases	Conf %	*RP
1	GSS 2006 and 1998 (If not currently working for pay, "what is your main source of economic support"?) (percentage saying "welfare")*	10.4	5.1	492	99	2.04
2	Michigan State of the State Survey #27, 2002 ("ever received cash assistance?")	24.8	10.5	577	+99	2.36
3	NES PreElection Survey, 2002 (currently receive Medicaid benefits?)	8.2	3.3	946	+99	2.48
4	Pew Religion & Public Life Survey, 2002 ("ever received welfare?")	18.3	12.1	1247	+99	1.51
5	NES PreElection Survey, 1992 (currently receive Medicaid benefits?)	10.8	5.3	1488	+99	2.04
6	1986 General Social Survey (ever received AFDC, general assistance, SSI, or food stamps?)	23.0	10.0	957	+99	2.30
7	Average percentages	15.9	7.7			
8	Overall proportion (Dem % divided by Rep %)	**206.5%				

*RP is relative proportion, which is the Democratic % divided by the Republican %.

**The disparity is slightly understated since Democrats are a little less likely to be currently employed.

in this chapter. Also note that these are 2002 values, and would be about 16% higher if restated into 2007 dollar values.

222

Reality check: Has Welfare been a curse or a benefit?

Bill ... attacked the worst aspects of the Republican Contract, such as the welfare bill, as "weak on work and tough on kids."

— Democratic Senator Hillary Clinton, describing her husband's political strategies with respect to welfare reform[8]

Although Democrats receive more welfare dollars than do Republicans, they are not necessarily receiving more help. After welfare reform was enacted in the mid-1990s, a new understanding emerged: For many, welfare was never help at all — it was a curse.

Ron Haskins, an expert on welfare programs, describes the early predictions regarding reform:

> It would be difficult to exaggerate the predictions of doom hurled against the Republican welfare reform bill ... [Critics of welfare reform] claimed that it "attacked," "punished" and "lashed out at" children. Columnist Bob Herbert said the bill conducted a "jihad" against the poor. Sen. Frank Lautenberg said poor children would be reduced to "begging for money, begging for food, and ... engaging in prostitution."

Despite the dire predictions, the results of welfare reform seem to be extremely positive. According to Haskins:

> In the decade that has passed since the 1996 reforms, the welfare rolls have plummeted by nearly 60 percent, the first sustained decline since the program was enacted in 1935. Equally important, the employment of single mothers heading families reached the highest level ever.[9]

With that increase in employment, there has been a steady augmentation of earnings and a marked decrease in black-child poverty and poverty among female-headed families.

We can't give welfare reform the credit for all of these improvements but it most likely had a positive impact by motivating people to help themselves. Perhaps this thought was expressed most succinctly by Robert J. Samuelson, a columnist for the Washington Post: "[W]hat people do for themselves often overshadows what government does for them."[10]

Corporate welfare

To the Honorable Secretary of Agriculture
Washington, D.C.
Dear Sir:

Our competitor, P. Gish Farm Corporation, received over $1 million from the government for not raising hogs. So, we'd like to go into the "not raising hogs" business next year.

What I want to know is, in your opinion, what is the best kind of farm not to raise hogs on, and what is the best breed of hogs not

---

8 Hillary Clinton, *Living History* (New York: Simon & Shuster, 2003), 288.

9 Ron Haskins, "Welfare Check," *Wall Street Journal*, July 27 2006. Mr. Haskins is the author of the book, *Work OverWelfare* (Brookings Institution Press, 2006).

10 Robert J. Samuelson, "Lessons of Welfare Reform Success," *Washington Post*, August 2, 2006.

to raise? We would prefer not to raise razorbacks, but if that is not a good breed not to raise, then we will just as gladly not raise Yorkshires or Durocs.

Sincerely,

— J. P. Fleecem, CEO, Oink Oink, Inc.[11]

What Is Corporate Welfare, And How Much Does It Cost?

According to the libertarian think tank, Cato Institute:

> Corporate welfare consists of government programs that provide unique benefits or advantages to specific companies or industries. Corporate welfare includes programs that provide direct grants to businesses, programs that provide indirect commercial support to businesses, and programs that provide subsidized loans and insurance.[12]

The specific agencies distributing these funds are listed in Table 39, below.[13]

Table 39. Per Cato "Handbook for Congress," based on the Budget of the United States for FY2003.

Federal Department	FY 2002 expenditures in billions
Agriculture	$35.0
Health & Human Services	9.1
Transportation	10.7
Energy	5.9
Housing and Urban Development	7.8
Defense	4.0
Interior	2.0
Commerce	2.0
All other agencies	16.1
Total	$92.6

11 Loosely based upon an anonymous letter posted on the Internet

12 *Cato Handbook for Congress: Policy Recommendations for the 108th Congress*, ed. Edward Crane and David Boaz (Washington: Cato Institute, 2003), 338. NOTE: Cato does not include corporation tax credits in its calculation — and it should not for two very good reasons: When we calculate the amount of tax paid by corporations and their shareholders, we use the net amount paid — after any "welfare" credits. (Indeed, we used the net tax amounts in the tax chapter of this book.) Were we to also treat those tax credits as welfare, we'd effectively be double-deducting the same amounts. In addition, to treat corporate tax credits as corporate welfare is inconsistent with how we compute traditional (social) welfare. Millions of Americans get exemptions and credits for children, education, rehabilitation of old houses, etc. Yet, those credits are never added into the traditional welfare tally.

13 Ibid., 339.

As shown in the table, the total 2002 federal corporate welfare expenditures, according to Cato, were about $93 billion.

> All I want to say is that Republicans are always worried about welfare, welfare for poor people. They never talk about *welfare for the rich*, education, that George Bush got into Yale. How did he get into Yale?

— Joy Behar, Co-host of the television talk show, "The View"[14]

Reality check — Is it real "welfare" or public policy welfare?

The libertarian Cato Institute has an expansive definition of "corporate welfare." For example, it regards federal agricultural and energy research as "welfare" because the research may ultimately prove useful and profitable to businesses. Of course, that same research may lead to findings that benefit individuals in their homes and in their daily routines. Would it be logical, therefore, to also classify agricultural and energy research as welfare for individuals (similar to food stamps, SSI, or TANF)?

Cato also includes, in its welfare tally, governmental loan guarantees and risk insurance for corporations that invest in third world countries, or in other expensive and risky ventures. In some cases, however, that is not truly welfare, in the normal sense of the word. Rather, it is the compensation we must pay to businesses (or individuals) that incur unusual risks and costs in order to fulfill an important public policy need.

The above concerns notwithstanding, Cato's estimate of $93 billion has been used here without modification, to avoid the introduction of additional subjectivity into this analysis.

To Cato's estimate of federal corporate welfare we need to add the assistance provided by state and local governments. Although this component is very difficult to determine, two independent sources have (roughly) estimated it to be around $50 billion per year. These sources and their estimates are described by Alan Peters and Peter Fisher, two University of Iowa professors, in a report issued in 2004.

> In a recent study, Thomas (2000) estimates conservatively that total state and local expenditures on economic development incentives were around $48.8 billion in 1996. In an ongoing study of incentive expenditures using a variety of methods and using a conservative definition of economic development, we estimate a likely top-end annual state and local number of around $50 billion.[15]

---

14 Joy Behar as cited in, "Real Time with Bill Maher," (Transcript: HBO, September 16, 2005), Retrieved February 26, 2006, from: http://www.safesearching.com/billmaher/print/t_hbo_realtime_091605.html.

15 Alan Peters and Peter Fisher, "The Failures of Economic Development Incentives," *Journal of the American Planning Association* 70, no. 1 (Winter, 2004): 28.

By adding the state and local estimate of $50 billion to Cato's federal estimate of $93 billion, we get a total of around $143. This is the estimated corporate welfare distributed by federal, state, and local governments.

Who Gets More Corporate Welfare?

> Ronald Reagan memorably complained about "welfare queens," but he never told us that the biggest welfare queens are the already wealthy. Their lobbyists fawn over politicians, giving them little bits of money — campaign contributions, plane trips, dinners, golf outings — in exchange for huge chunks of taxpayers' money.
>
> — John Stossel, Author and TV commentator[16]

When a corporation gets "welfare," there are many parties who benefit, including creditors, employees, and investors. However, for the sake of simplicity, we assume here that all of the benefits accrue to the shareholders (an assumption that tends to shift more of the estimated corporate welfare towards Republicans). Therefore, we only need to figure out how much of America's corporate stock is owned by the average Democrat vs. the average Republican. This can be done in the following way: A table published by the Tax Policy Center (TPC) breaks out estimated qualifying dividends and capital gain income by household income level.[17] With the use of GSS survey data (1998-2004) we can determine the percentage of Democrats and Republicans in each of those TPC income ranges and, in turn, determine the amount of dividend and capital gain income earned by the "average" Democrat versus the "average" Republican. Using this procedure, we find that the average Republican earned about $3,500 in dividends and capital gains, while the average Democrat earns only about $2,100.[18]

It seems reasonable to assume that the relationship between these amounts of investment income correlate closely with the relationship between the amounts of stock owned, and in turn with the amount of corporate welfare. This implies a $35 billion corporate welfare differential in favor of Republicans, assuming equal numbers of Democrats and Republicans. (I.e., Democrats get about $54 billion in corporate welfare and Republicans get about $89 billion — a difference of $35 billion.)[19]

> Corporate welfare-the enormous and myriad subsidies, bailouts, giveaways, tax loopholes, debt revocations, loan guarantees, and other benefits conferred by government on business-is a function of political corruption.
>
> — Consumer activist, Ralph Nader[20]

---

16 John Stossel, "Confessions of a Welfare Queen," (ReasonOnline, March, 2004), Retrieved August 30, 2006, from: http://www.reason.com/0403/fe.js.confessions.shtml.

17 Table T05-0009, published on the TPC Web site in 2005. This table was produced using the Urban-Brookings microsimulation tax model.

18 The GSS survey was based on a total of 6010 men and women. The statistical significance of the overall GSS distribution difference was 99+%, with Phi of .20.

19 These amounts would be about 16% higher if restated into 2007 dollar values.

20 Ralph Nader, *Cutting Corporate Welfare* (New York: Seven Stories Press, 2000), 13.

CONCLUSIONS

Traditional (or social) welfare is defined as "income-tested or need-based benefits." There are over 80 different traditional welfare programs, which cost the federal, state, and local governments over $520 billion in 2002. Of that amount, I have estimated that about $460 billion was distributed to low-income Americans in the form of direct assistance and another $33 billion was distributed in via the Earned Income Tax Credit (EITC). We considered the EITC in Chapter 5 (as an offset to taxes paid) so it would be redundant to consider it again (as a welfare benefit) in this chapter.

Survey evidence suggests that Democrats are twice as likely as Republicans to be on welfare, or to have been on welfare. By implication, this means that, of the $460 billion in direct welfare assistance distributed in 2002, Democrats probably received about $150 billion more than did Republicans. Here, we are using the simplifying assumption that there are equal numbers of Democrats and Republicans. (The actual amount distributed to Democrats would be larger because there are usually more Democrats than Republicans.).

It is estimated that, in 2002, the federal government spent about $93 billion in corporate direct and indirect subsidies. In addition, state and local governments are estimated to spend about $50 billion each year on corporate assistance. These corporate welfare payments are more likely to benefit Republicans than Democrats because Republicans are more likely to own corporate stock. If we assume that all corporate welfare benefits accrue to the corporate investors (and not to the employees or creditors of the corporation), we would expect Republicans to get $35 billion more corporate welfare than Democrats would get. Again, we assume equal numbers of Democrats and Republicans. (The actual amount distributed to Republicans would be smaller, since there are usually fewer Republicans than Democrats.)

Often, there is a thin line separating real welfare from public policy welfare. This is particularly the case when we compensate an individual or business for undertaking a project that has multiple beneficiaries.

CHAPTER 9: WHO IS HAPPIER, WHO IS MORE MISERABLE, AND WHY?

INTRODUCTION

Do narrow, selfish goals lead to happiness?

> I hypothesize that Republicans, as a group, may be happier because ... compared with Democrats and Independents, their main goals are narrower and more selfish, and thus more easily obtained.

— Matt Vidal, Op-Ed, CommonDreams.org, 2006[1]

All surveys suggest that Republicans are happier than Democrats, but the reasons for this tendency are not entirely clear. There are many characteristics associated with happiness, such as being married, wealthy, religious, and better educated; and those traits are more prevalent among Republicans than Democrats. However, even after controlling for all obvious factors, Republicans seem to be happier than Democrats.

At the end of this chapter, I offer my own hypothesis of the factors contributing to the bliss disparity. I argue that Democrats are less happy than Republicans due, in part, to a certain type of Democratic cynicism, identifiable in survey results. This cynicism comprises three distinct elements:

1. A general lack of trust in other people
2. A sense that destiny can not be controlled
3. A belief that capitalism is inherently unjust.

Each element is addressed in detail, and supported by reference to survey evidence.

---

1 Matt Vidal, "Republican Bliss: The Selfish Road to Happiness," *Common Dreams News Center* (April 6, 2006), Retrieved April 20, 2006, from http://www.commondreams.org/views06/0406-30.htm.

DETAILS

Who is happier?

Happiness in General

On the radio show I've hosted since 1996, no subject provokes more
anger from callers across the country than my contention that conservatives aren't just more astute and practical than their liberal
counterparts, they are also happier, more fulfilled in their lives and
their work.

— Michael Medved, Author and radio talk show host[2]

Republicans are more likely than Democrats to state that they are "very happy," a fact that is reflected in several Gallup surveys conducted in 1996 through
2003. The results of those surveys are shown in Figure 172, below. Note that the
2001 survey (depicted in the middle of the graph) was taken 2 months after the
attack on the World Trade Center, and may account for that year's sharp dip in
happiness, for both Democrats and Republicans.

*Figure 172. Are you "very happy"? (Gallup polls conducted in 1996 through 2003, based on,
left to right, total sample sizes (including non-Democrats and non-Republicans) of 979, 1052, 1005,
1001, and 1011, with confidence levels of 95% or more, and with relative proportions of, left to right,
.96, .85, .88, .78, and .81)*

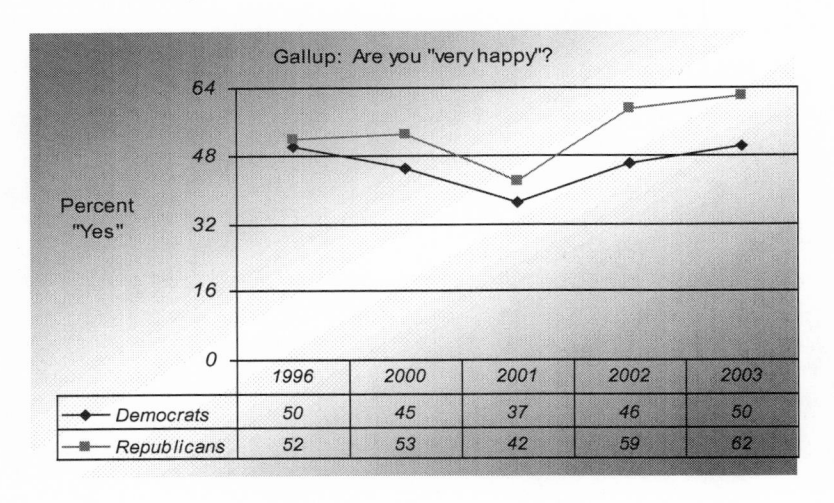

The Gallup Organization states that the happiness gap has been fairly
consistent:

---

2 Medved, *Right Turns*, 229.

Why Republicans are happier is not clear, but the result has been the same in nearly every asking of this measure since 1996, including one reading under former President Bill Clinton, a Democrat, and three under Republican President George W. Bush. Only in 1996 did Republicans and Democrats express about equal levels of happiness.[3]

Actually, the contentment chasm developed long before 1996. In each of the 25 surveys conducted by the General Social Survey (GSS) since its inception in 1972, Republicans were more likely to state that they were "very happy." The disparity existed in years when Republicans were in and out of control of the federal government, and it has existed for both men and women. For men, see Figure 173.

Everyone knows that a happy Republican is an annoyed Republican. Being perpetually pissed off about everything is at the very heart of Republicanism today.

— Linwood Barclay, Columnist for the Toronto Star[4]

Figure 173. Would you say that you are very happy...?" (Men) (25 GSS surveys taken from 1972 through 2006, based on, left to right 2184, 1173, 2061, 2112, 1963, 1381, and 1460 cases, with confidence level of, left to right, 99+%, 95%, 99%, 98%, 99%, 97%, and 99+%, and with relative proportions of, left to right, .82, .86, .83, .86, .84, .84, and .73)

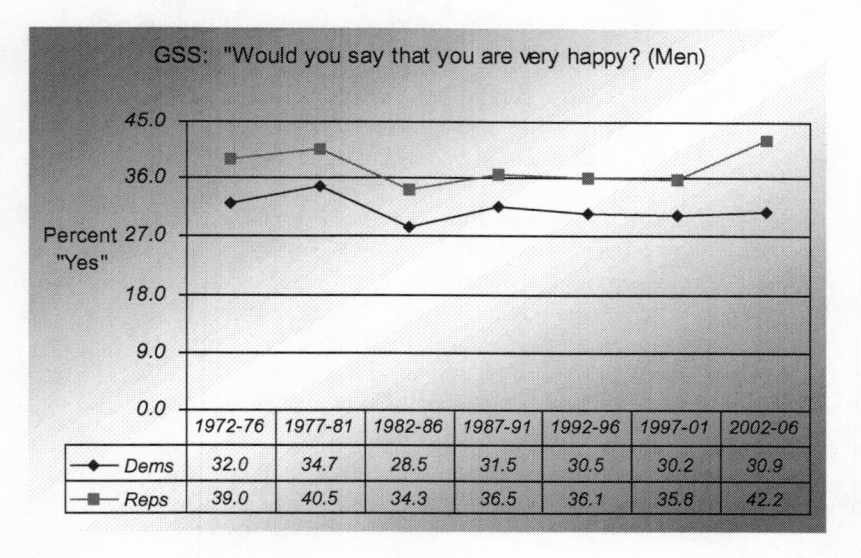

	1972-76	1977-81	1982-86	1987-91	1992-96	1997-01	2002-06
Dems	32.0	34.7	28.5	31.5	30.5	30.2	30.9
Reps	39.0	40.5	34.3	36.5	36.1	35.8	42.2

---

3 Lydia Saad, "A Nation of Happy People," *The Gallup News Service* (January 5, 2004), Retrieved August 20, 2004, from Http://brain.gallup.com.

4 Linwood Barclay, "An Annoyed Republican Is a Happy Republican," *Toronto Star*, August 30, 2004.

Figure 174 shows an even larger disparity among women. Again, Republicans have claimed to be happier for at least 35 years.

Figure 174. "Would you say that you are very happy...?" (Women) (25 GSS surveys taken from 1972 through 2006, based on, left to right, 2693, 1681, 3065, 3037, 2737, 1882, and 1948 cases, with confidence level of, left to right, 99+%, 83% (not significant), 99+%, 99%, 99+%, 99+%, and 99+%, and with relative proportions of, left to right, .77, n/a, .74, .73, .69, .83, and .79)

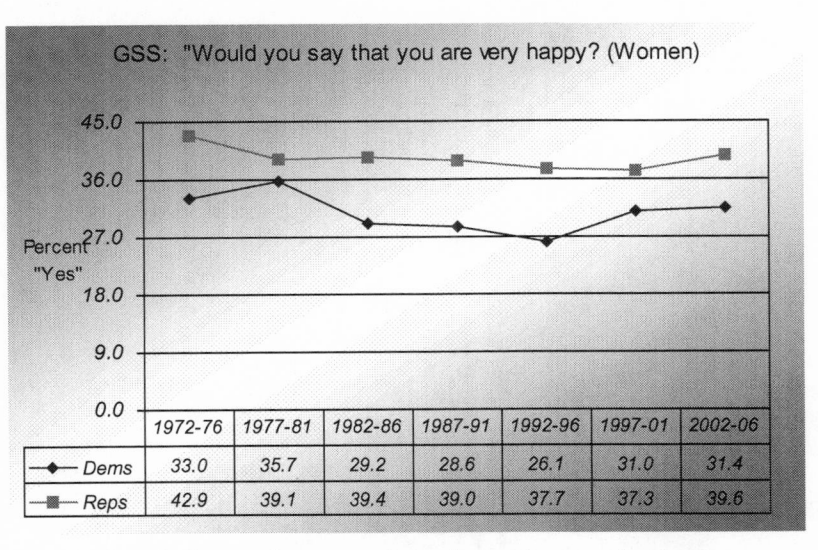

	1972-76	1977-81	1982-86	1987-91	1992-96	1997-01	2002-06
◆ Dems	33.0	35.7	29.2	28.6	26.1	31.0	31.4
■ Reps	42.9	39.1	39.4	39.0	37.7	37.3	39.6

[Y]ou look around your country today, at the squandered promises, the unfulfilled promises, and you can't sit back and sing "Be Happy," you know, that song, "Be Happy, Don't Worry...."

— Katrina vanden Heuvel, Editor of "The Nation"[5]

A similar glee gulf is apparent from several surveys conducted by the Pew Research Center for the People and the Press (Pew). The results of Pew's November, 2005 survey are shown in Figure 175, below, and those results show that Republicans are more likely than Democrats or independents to state that they are "very happy."

A general summary of various Pew surveys is found in a report entitled, "Are We Happy Yet?" In that report, Pew notes that Republicans were found to be happier in all of its recent surveys:

> Pew surveys since 1991 also show a partisan gap on happiness; the current 16 percentage point gap [for the November, 2005 survey] is among the largest in Pew surveys, rivaled only by a 17 point gap in February 2003."[6]

---

5 Katrina Vanden Heuval, "ABC's This Week," (Transcript: The LIberal Oasis Blog, February 19, 2006), Retrieved April 2, 2007, from: http://www.liberaloasis.com/archives/021906. htm.

6 Pew, "Are We Happy Yet?," in *Social Trends Report* (The Pew Research Center, February 13, 2006), 5.

Figure 175. Percentage very happy by party identification (Pew survey conducted in October and November, 2005, based on 3014 interviews with people of all political orientations, and with confidence level of 95%)

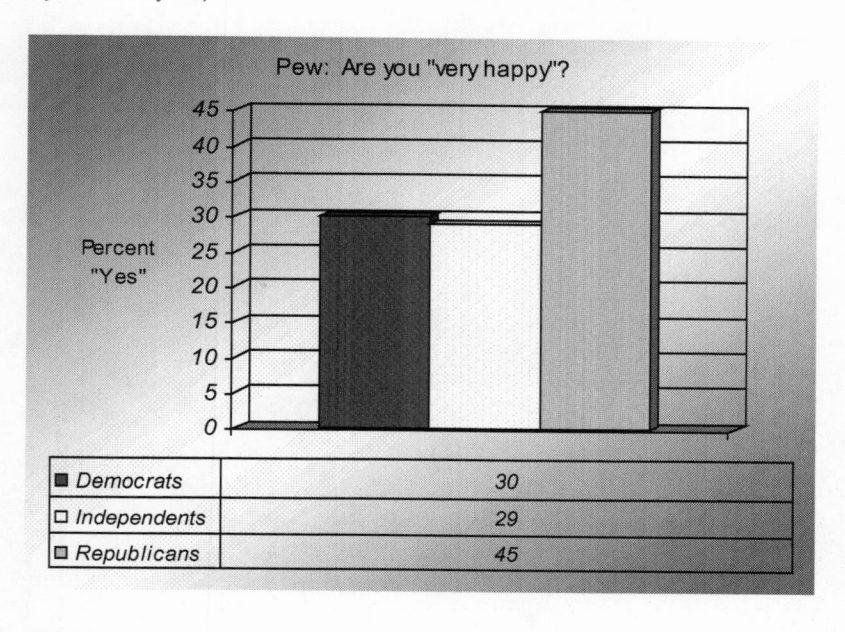

Pew: Are you "very happy"?
Percent "Yes"
45
40
35
30
25
20
15
10
5
0
Democrats 30
Independents 29
Republicans 45

Other surveys addressing the subject of happiness are shown in Appendix B 16 on page 358.

Happiness With Regard To Specific Aspects Of Life

Marriage

> The most happy marriage I can imagine to myself would be the union of a deaf man to a blind woman.
>
> — Samuel Taylor Coleridge, English poet and philosopher[7]

Republicans appear to be happier with regard to certain aspects of their lives, one of which is marriage. As seen in Figure 176, below, this is true for both genders.

Figure 176. "Would you say that your marriage is very happy?" (combined results of 25 GSS survey taken from 1973 through 2006, based on, left to right, 7343, 8449, and 15792 cases, with confidence level of at least 99% for all three columns, and with relative proportions of, left to right, .94, .88, and .91)

7 *The Times Book of Quotations*, (Glasgow: Harper Collins, 2000), 452.

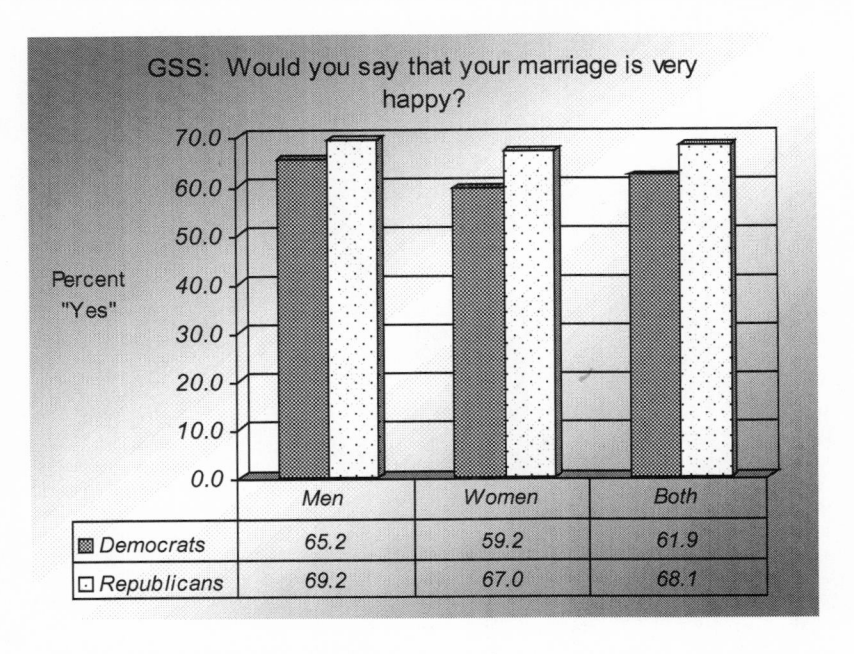

The difference in marital bliss has been fairly constant during the last three decades. See Figure 177.

Figure 177. "Taking all things together, how would you describe your marriage?" (several GSS surveys taken from 1977 through 2006, based on, left to right, 4714, 5215, and 3271 cases, with confidence level of at least 99% for all three columns, and with relative proportions of, left to right, .93, .88, and .90)

GSS: "How would you describe your marriage?"			
Percent "Very happy"	1977-1986	1987-1996	1997-2006
Democrats	62.9	59.3	60.5
Republicans	67.9	67.1	67.5

Happiness is having a large, loving, caring, close-knit family —in another city.

— Comedian George Burns[8]

Finances

They say that money doesn't buy happiness, but don't believe it! Republicans tend to have higher incomes, and they also tend to have warm and fuzzy feelings about financial matters, as shown in Table 40.

Table 40. Surveys dealing with the satisfaction of Democrats and Republicans regarding aspects of their financial condition

Survey	Issue	Dems	Reps	No. cases	Conf %	*RP
GSS surveys conducted 26 times in 1972 through 2006.	Are you satisfied "with financial condition"? (% answering "satisfied")	27.6	38.4	29465	+99	.72
Pew News Interest Index survey — May, 2005	"Do you now earn enough money to lead the kind of life you want, or not?"	30.0	52.1	556	+99	.58
(same as above)	"How concerned are you, if at all, about going too deeply into debt? (Percentage who responded, "very concerned")	46.7	29.5	969	+99	1.58

*RP is relative proportion, which is the Democratic % divided by the Republican %.

Work

Busy people are happy people whether they want to admit it or not.

— Terry Paulson, Psychologist and organizational advisor[9]

Democrats are less satisfied with their jobs, and much more worried about losing them. See Table 41, below.

---

8 George Burns (attributed), "Brainyquote.Com."

9 Terry Paulson, "Ten Sure Fire Ways to Fail as a Manager," 2006, from http://terrypaulson.typepad.com/leaderline/difficult_people/index.html.

Table 41. *Surveys dealing with the employment satisfaction of Democrats and Republicans*

Survey	Issue	Dems	Reps	No. of cases	Conf %	*RP
GSS survey — 2006	"All in all, how satis-fied would you say you are with your job?" (% answering "very satisfied")	47.8	57.1	2087	+99	.84
Pew News Interest Index survey — May, 2005	"How concerned are you, if at all, about losing your job or taking a cut in pay? (% responding "very concerned")	37.5	21.9	969	+99	1.71

*RP is relative proportion, which is the Democratic % divided by the Republican %.

Age

Thomas Jefferson once said, "We should never judge a president by his age, only by his works." And ever since he told me that I stopped worrying.

— President Ronald Reagan at age 73[10]

Within every 5-year age interval between 18 and 82, Republicans are more likely to say that they are "very happy." This trend even extends beyond age 82; however, at that point the sample sizes get pretty small — for obvious reasons. The figures in Figure 178, below, reflect a 33-year period from 1973 through 2006.

Figure 178. *"Would you say that you are very happy?" (combined results of 25 GSS survey taken from 1973 through 2006, based on, left to right, 1620, 2708, 3029, 3054, 2828, 2567, 2384, 2193, 2133, 1944, 1775, and 1426 cases, with confidence level of at least 99% for all columns except the youngest (96%) and the oldest (95%), and with relative proportions ranging from .66 to .87)*

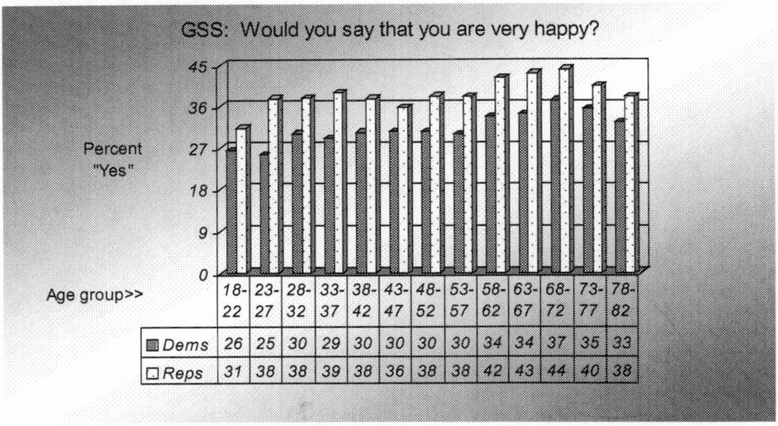

GSS: Would you say that you are very happy?

Age group>>	18-22	23-27	28-32	33-37	38-42	43-47	48-52	53-57	58-62	63-67	68-72	73-77	78-82
Dems	26	25	30	29	30	30	30	30	34	34	37	35	33
Reps	31	38	38	39	38	36	38	38	42	43	44	40	38

10President Ronald Reagan, *Simpson's Contemporary Quotations* (1984).

Who is more miserable?

Sadness And Depression

> There is no greater pain than to remember a happy time when one is in misery.

— Durante Degli Alighieri (Dante), 13th Century Italian poet[11]

Since Democrats are less happy, it is not surprising to learn that they are more likely to be sad and depressed. This is indicated by the results of a 2004 GSS survey, shown in Figure 179, below.

Figure 179. Are you "a person who often feels sad and blue"? (2004 GSS Survey, based on , left to right, 670, 840, and 1510 cases, with confidence level of, left to right, 99%, 96%, and 99+%, and with relative proportions of, left to right, 1.62, 1.39, and 1.50)

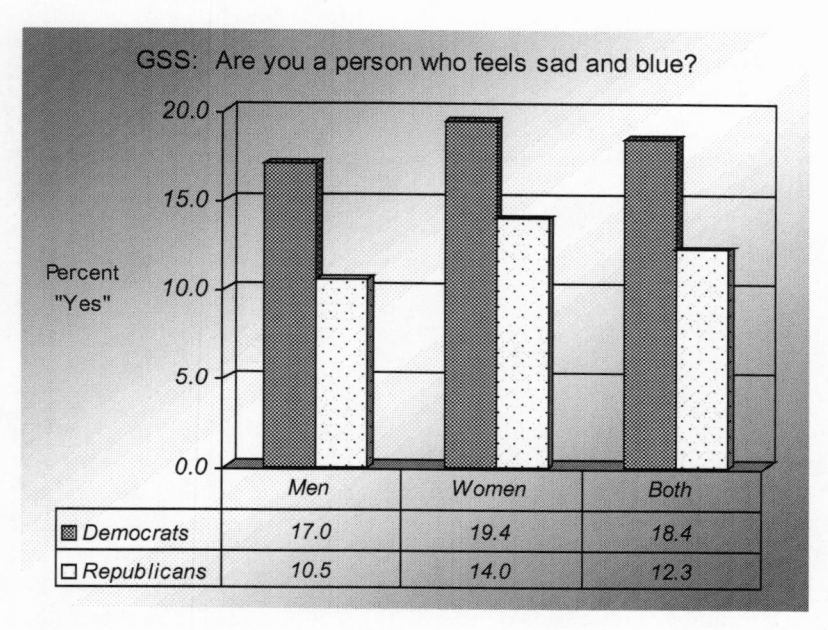

Similar results were indicated in all of the other relevant surveys found, which are shown in Table 42.

---

11 Elizabeth Knowles, ed., *Oxford Dictionary of Quotations*, 5th ed. (Oxford: Oxford University Press, 1999), 249.

Table 42. Various surveys regarding "the blues"

Surveys and Dates	Dem % "yes"	Rep % "yes"	No. of cases	Conf %	*RP
Harris Interactive 2006: During the past 30 days have you "felt very sad throughout most of [a] day"?	32.7	14.8	371	+99	2.21
GSS 2000: During the last 4 weeks, have you felt "downhearted and blue" some or all of the time?	30.4	23.5	817	97	1.29
Michigan 1999 State of the State: In the past month were you depressed some or all of the time?	38.1	23.6	635	+99	1.61
GSS 1996: During the last 7 days have you felt "sad" on some days?	64.2	57.5	899	96	1.12
GSS 1996: During the last 7 days were there times when you "felt that you couldn't shake the blues"?	49.9	37.0	901	+99	1.35

*RP is relative proportion, which is the Democratic % divided by the Republican %.

Emotional Problems

> According to the Boca Raton News, Bush's victory has triggered psychological disorders in this tiny South Florida Democratic community.... [W]hen some 20 Kerry voters met for their first therapy session ... the group's rage became uncontrollable.
>
> — NewsMax.com[12]

It's normal to have emotions, but if they go unchecked and interfere with normal, desirable activities, the consequence can be misery. Surveys show that emotions may be more of a problem for Democratic males than Republican males. Respondents were asked if emotions affected the amount they accomplished during the previous 4 weeks (Figure 180, next page, top). Note: For women there was not a significant difference.

Emotions and the quality of work were the subject of another survey question. In this case, Democratic males and females were both more likely to say that "emotional problems ("such as feeling depressed or anxious") affected performance. (See Figure 181, next page, bottom.)

Figure 180. "During the past 4 weeks ... as a result of any emotional problems (such as feeling depressed or anxious)" have you "accomplished less than you would like"? (GSS survey conducted in 2000, based on, left to right, 346, 471, and 817 cases, with confidence level of, left to right, 94%, 79% (not significant), and 95%, and with relative proportions of, left to right, 1.68, n/a, and 1.33)

---

12 "Group Therapy 'Screaming Epithets' at Bush," in *NewsMax.com* (December 5, 2004), from: http://www.newsmax.com/archives/ic/2004/12/5/113802.shtml.

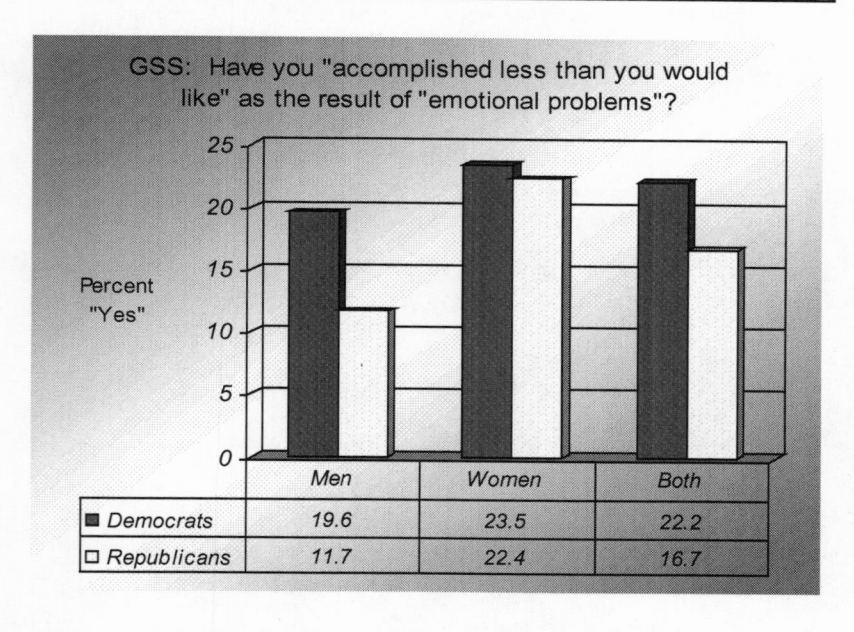

Figure 181. "During the past 4 weeks ... as a result of any emotional problems (such as feeling depressed or anxious)" have you performed less carefully than usual? (GSS survey conducted in 2000, based on, left to right, 345, 471, and 816 cases, with confidence level of, left to right, 99+%, 97%, and 99+%, and with relative proportions of, left to right, 4.71, 1.64, and 2.56)

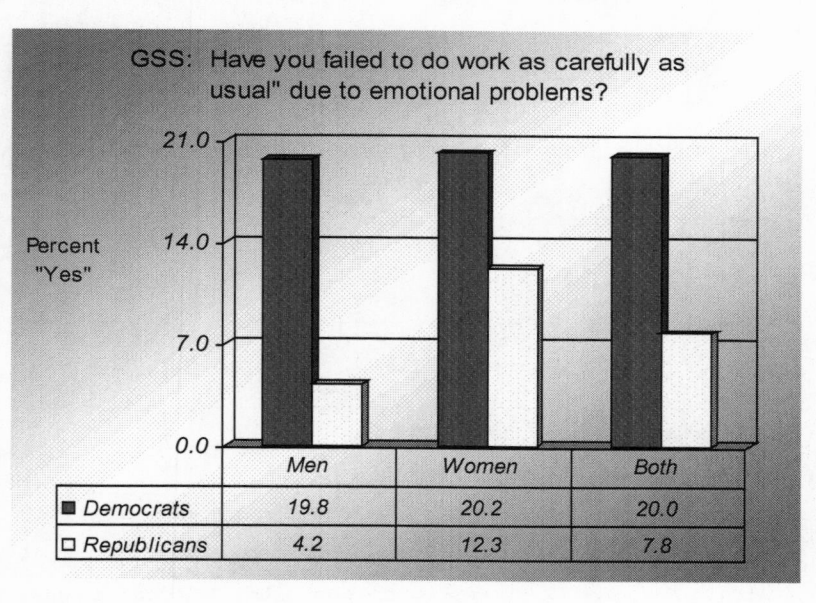

It's a real conflict for me when I go to a concert and find out some-body in the audience is a Republican or fundamental Christian. It can cloud my enjoyment. I'd rather not know.

— Popular singer Linda Ronstadt[13]

A 1996 GSS survey asked respondents: "On how many days in the past 7 days have you ..." [been anxious, been worried, or been fearful]? In each case, the aver-age number of days was higher for Democrats. (See Figure 182, below.)

Figure 182. "On how many days in the past 7 days have you ... ?" (GSS survey taken in 1996, based on surveys, left to right, of 894, 900, and 899 Democrats and Republicans, with confidence level, left to right, of 98%, 95%, and 99%)

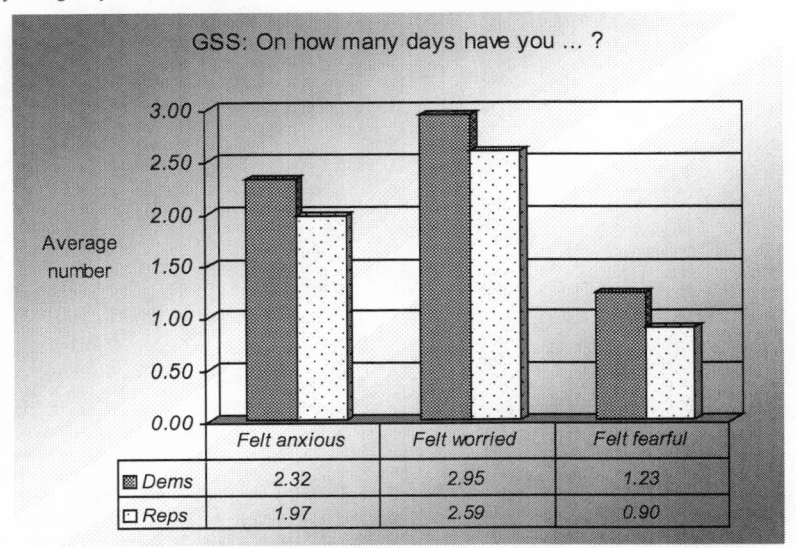

The results of other surveys involving mental health are shown in Table 43.

Table 43. Miscellaneous surveys regarding mental health

Survey	Issue	Dem % "yes"	Rep % "yes"	No. of cases	Conf %	*RP
Harris 2004	Are you or have you been diagnosed with depression?	22.8	15.5	642	98	1.47
GSS 1996	Have you ever felt you were "going to have a nervous breakdown"?	25.6	20.4	869	93 marg	1.25

*RP is relative proportion, which is the Democratic % divided by the Republican %.

---

13 Marc A. Levin, "Off Their Rockers for Kerry," in *The Austin Review* (August, 2004), Retrieved April 2, 2004, from: http://www.austinreview.com/archives/2004/08/off_their_rocke_1. html.

Why are there differences in happiness?

> One of the indictments of civilizations is that happiness and intelligence are so rarely found in the same person.

— William Feather, American author and publisher[14]

Survey evidence, by itself, can not determine what causes happiness (or anything else); however, it can be used to identify correlating factors. The factors that seem to correlate with happiness are identified below.

Money

Republicans are likely to have higher income, and that variable correlates positively with happiness. Gallup acknowledges the relationship, but dismisses the notion that it explains the entire happiness differential:

> Even when accounting for partisan differences in ... household income, Republicans are significantly more likely than Democrats and independents to be very happy.

We can test Gallup's assertion by analyzing 34 years of GSS survey data, grouped by income level (expressed in 2006 dollars). In Figure 183, below, we see the percentages of happy Democrats and Republicans in each of 6 income ranges.

Figure 183. "Would you say that you are very happy...?" (26 GSS surveys taken from 1972 through 2006, based on, left to right, 5805, 6358, 5195, 3633, 2040, and 3652 cases, with confidence level of 99% for all differences, with relative proportions of, left to right, .76, .80, .91, .86, .86, and .85)

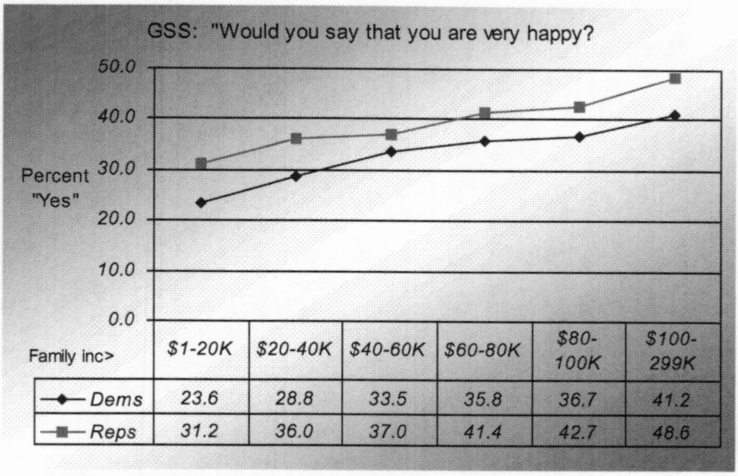

GSS: "Would you say that you are very happy?

Family inc>	$1-20K	$20-40K	$40-60K	$60-80K	$80-100K	$100-299K
Dems	23.6	28.8	33.5	35.8	36.7	41.2
Reps	31.2	36.0	37.0	41.4	42.7	48.6

We learn two things by analyzing Figure 183: More money does mean more happiness, and, at any given income level, Republicans seem to be happier than Democrats.

---

14 William Feather (attributed), "The Quotations Page."

Having more money does not insure happiness. People with ten million dollars are no happier than people with nine million dollars.
— Hobart Brown, American sculptor[15]

Reality check — Does happiness continue to rise as income goes up?
If we were to extend our analysis into even higher income levels (beyond $299,000), would overall happiness continue to increase? The experts would have us believe that it would not. Psychologists seem to feel that the positive correlation between income and happiness gets smaller — not larger — as we get into higher income ranges. This is stated succinctly by F. Heylighen, co-director of the Center "Leo Apostel" for transdisciplinary research:

> It is interesting to note that the correlation between purchasing power and happiness becomes less important for more wealthy societies, implying that once the basic material needs of nutrition and shelter are satisfied, further prosperity adds little to happiness.[16]

Marriage

All marriages are happy. It's the living together afterward that causes all the trouble.

— Author Raymond Hull[17]

Figure 184. "Would you say that you are very happy...?" (married only) (combined results of 25 General Social Surveys taken from 1972 through 2004, based on, left to right, 7405, 8368, and 15773 cases, with confidence level of 99% for all differences, and with relative proportions of, from left to right, .88, .83, and .85)

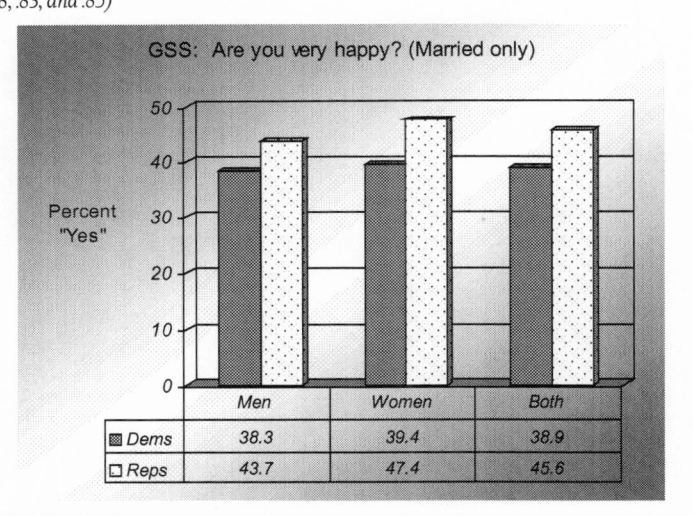

	Men	Women	Both
Dems	38.3	39.4	38.9
Reps	43.7	47.4	45.6

---

15 Hobart Brown (attributed), "The Quotations Page."
16 F. Heylighten. (July 29, 1999), "Happiness", Retrieved April 2, 2007, from Principia Cybernetica Web: http://pcp.lanl.gov/HAPPINES.html.
17 Raymond Hull (attributed), "The Quote Garden," Retrieved April 2, 2007, from: http://www.quotegarden.com/marriage.html.

Marriage is another factor that positively correlates with happiness, according to Gallup and other survey organizations. Like income, however, it explains only a small part of the happiness divide.

As we did for income, we can use GSS data to test the impact of marriage on the happiness gap. In Figure 184, above, we see the combined GSS results for all 25 surveys conducted in 1972 through 2004, limited to Democrats and Republicans who are married.

Note that, even when marital status is controlled, Republican men and women seem to be significantly happier than Democratic men and women.

Other Factors Correlating With Happiness

Happiness is good health and a bad memory.

— Actress Ingrid Bergman[18]

The Pew report, "Are We Happy Yet" (previously referenced), identified several additional correlating factors. These are listed in Table 44, below.

Table 44. Miscellaneous factors that correlate with happiness, according to Pew.

More happy	Less happy
Healthy	Unhealthy
Conservative	Liberal
Middle aged or older	Young*
Better educated	Poorly educated
Religious	Not religious
White or Hispanic	Black
Sunbelt resident	Northern resident

*No, this is not a mistake. Younger people, especially younger men, tend to be less happy, according to Pew.

Just about every happiness trait shown in Table 44 is a factor typically associated with Republicans rather than Democrats. This caused Pew to broach the question: "[I]s being a Republican really a predictor of happiness, independent of all other factors?" Using multiple regression analysis, Pew concluded that it is. In other words, even if we were to equalize all the correlating factors mentioned heretofore, Republicans would probably still be happier than Democrats to a statistically significant degree.[19] Perhaps the GOP should consider the campaign slogan, "Vote Republican — it will make you happy!"

> [O]f course Republicans are happier — that's what happens when you refuse to face reality and only want to hear "the good news" and your head is stuck up your ass.
> — Blogger named "ImpeachW," posted on the Majority Report Radio show blog[20]

---

18 Ingrid Bergman (attributed), "Brainyquote.Com."

19 Multiple regression analysis is a statistical technique that can be used to test the relationship between a dependent variable and several independent variables.

20 ImpeachW (pseudonym), "Majority Report," March 15, 2006, Bluestateblogs.com, Retrieved April 3, 2007, 2007, from http://www.bluestateblogs.com/majorityreport/archives/2006/03/

Does cynicism lead to sadness? (a theory)

We have established that Republicans are happier than Democrats, and listed several factors correlating with that happiness. Yet, even after Pew controlled for every known factor, a happiness gap remained. What is the missing "X" factor?

Surveys show that Democrats are more likely to have the following three traits, and I would argue that each of these correlates negatively with happiness:

- A lack of trust in others
- A sense that one can not control his or her own destiny
- A feeling that the capitalist economic system is unjust.

These three traits, comprising what I call "Democratic cynicism," warrant detailed analysis.

Lack of Trust

It's still trust but verify. It's still play — but cut the cards. It's still watch closely. And don't be afraid to see what you see.

— Ronald Reagan, President, in his formal farewell address after two terms in office[21]

Figure 185. "Generally speaking, would you say that most people can be trusted or that you can't be too careful in life?" (several GSS surveys conducted in 1972 through 2006, based on, left to right, 3915, 1853, 2378, 3916, 3099, 2464, and 3348 cases, with confidence level of at least 99% for all differences, and with relative proportions of, left to right, 1.32, 1.19, 1.27, 1.24, 1.08, 1.15, and 1.19)

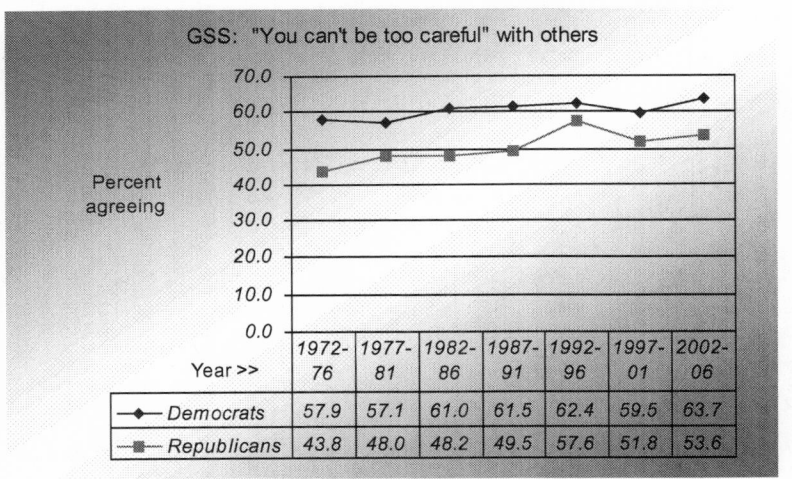

GSS: "You can't be too careful" with others							
Year >>	1972-76	1977-81	1982-86	1987-91	1992-96	1997-01	2002-06
Democrats	57.9	57.1	61.0	61.5	62.4	59.5	63.7
Republicans	43.8	48.0	48.2	49.5	57.6	51.8	53.6

hour_one_wednes_66.php.

21 President Ronald Reagan, "Farewell Address to the Nation," (Ronald Reagan Presidential Foundation, January 11, 1989), Retrieved September 16, 2006, from: http://www.reagan.utexas.edu/archives/speeches/1989/011189i.htm.

I was very surprised to find that, year-in and year-out, Democrats seem to be far less trusting of their fellow citizens than are Republicans. In Figure 185, we see this pattern for the 35-year period from 1972 through 2006, based on GSS surveys. (1972 was the first year GSS conducted surveys.) Respondents were asked whether most people can be trusted or "you can't be too careful in life." In each case, Democrats were much more likely to reject the notion that most people can be trusted.

Figure 186, below, also shows a 30-year trend, based on GSS surveys. This time, the question was slightly different: "Do you think most people would try to take advantage of you if they got the chance ...?" Again, Democrats leaned towards the more cynical response.

Figure 186. "Do you think most people would try to take advantage of you if they got a chance, or would they try to be fair?" (several GSS surveys conducted in 1975 through 2004, based on, left to right, 2803, 2822, 3557, 3228, 2260, and 2165 cases, with confidence level of at least 99% for all differences, and with relative proportions of, left to right, 1.44, 1.34, 1.33, 1.26, 1.27, and 1.16)

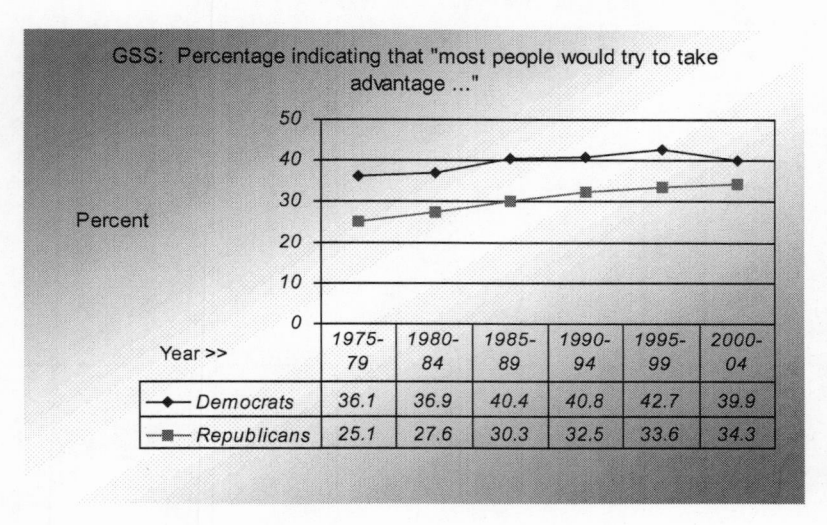

GSS: Percentage indicating that "most people would try to take advantage ..."

Year >>	1975-79	1980-84	1985-89	1990-94	1995-99	2000-04
Democrats	36.1	36.9	40.4	40.8	42.7	39.9
Republicans	25.1	27.6	30.3	32.5	33.6	34.3

Love all, trust a few.

— Shakespeare[22]

Other surveys pertaining to trust are identified in Table 45, below, and each shows a similar result.

We should not assume that Democrats have innate psychological characteristics that distinguish them from Republicans. Perhaps they live and work among less trustworthy people, which would make their lack of trust understandable and appropriate. Whatever the cause, however, this lack of trust probably correlates negatively with happiness.

22 William Shakespeare, *All's Well that Ends Well*, Act 1 Scene 1.

Table 45. Other surveys addressing the issue of trust

Survey and Issue	Dems	Reps	No. of cases	Conf %	*RP
GSS survey conducted in 2006: Percentage strongly agreeing that "If you are not careful, other people will take advantage of you."	**39.5**	32.7	820	96	1.21
Harris Interactive conducted in 2002: Do you trust "the ordinary man or woman to tell the truth, or not"? (percentage "yes")	64.0	**80.5**	290	+99	.80
NES cumulative surveys from 1996 through 2004: Percentage indicating that most people can not be trusted, so "you can't be too careful."	**58.0**	50.5	4394	+99	1.15
NES cumulative surveys from 1996 through 2004: Percentage indicating that "most people would take advantage you if they got a chance."	**39.3**	31.5	3950	+99	1.25
NES cumulative surveys from 2000 through 2004: Percentage indicating that people are "mostly just looking out for themselves."	**37.5**	31.4	2021	+99	1.19
Several GSS surveys conducted in 1972 through 2006 (combined results): "Would you say that most of the time people ... are mostly just looking out for themselves?" (percentage "yes")	**47.0**	39.0	20068	+99	1.21
GSS survey conducted in 2004: During the last 12 months how often did "other people take credit for [your] work or ideas"? (Percentage responding "often" or "sometimes")	**29.5**	21.2	1142	+99	1.39
GSS 2004: During the last 12 months at work how often did people "put [you] down ..."?	**16.8**	11.7	1144	99	1.44

*RP is relative proportion, which is the Democratic % divided by the Republican %.

> Someone who thinks the world is always cheating him is right. He is missing that wonderful feeling of trust in someone or something.
>
> — Social Writer Eric Hoffer[23]

The link between trust and happiness has been described by researchers comparing the happiness of citizens of different countries. These findings were summarized by Economist Richard Layard in his book about happiness:

23 Eric Hoffer (attributed), "Brainyquote.Com."

As social beings, we want to trust each other. The average happiness in one country compared with another can be largely explained by six key factors ... [the first of which is] the proportion of people who say that other people can be trusted...[24]

Trust and happiness have also been linked to each other by studying the chemical, oxytocin (not to be confused with the addictive pain-killer, "oxycontin"). Scientists have observed that oxytocin seems to promote trust which, in turn, leads to happiness. As one neuroscientist put it: "So, oxytocin is not a happiness chemical, but a brain tool for building trust ... and we feel happiest in learning to trust each other."[25] From this we might speculate that Democrats are less happy because they are less trusting.

Trust in a bottle?

In Nature Journal, it was reported that a Swiss-led research team produced "a potion that, when sniffed, makes people more likely to give their cash to someone to look after." The potion was tested by a Swiss-led research team on volunteers playing an investment game for real money. Of 29 subjects given the potion, 13 handed over all of their money during the "game." Of the 29 volunteers given a placebo, only 6 gave up their money.

What was the potion's magic ingredient? Oxytocin.[26]

The Inability to Control One's Destiny

You got to control your own destiny. You got to keep writin' different stuff. Keep switchin' up and never do the same thin' too many times.

— Chris Tucker, American actor and comedian[27]

A GSS survey conducted in 2000 indicates that Democrats are less likely to feel that they have "a great deal" of "control over the way their lives turn out ..." (Figure 187, below). Although the results are for both men and women, most of the difference is attributable to men.

Let's analyze this "control" issue in much more detail. Common sense tells us that insecurities about control can be indirectly revealed, in the following forms:

- A general lack of optimism
- A belief that much of success in life is due to luck
- A belief that you need "connections" to get ahead in life
- A lack of confidence in one's own abilities and worth

---

24 Richard Layard, *Happiness: Lessons from a New Science* (New York: Penquin Press, 2005), 226.

25 Walter J. Freeman, "Happiness Doesn't Come in Bottles," *Journal of Consciousness Studies* 4 (May 24, 1996): 67-71.

26 Michael Hopkin, "Trust in a Bottle," in *Nature* (June 1, 2005), Retrieved October 6, 2007, from: http://www.nature.com/news/2005/050531/full/news050531-4.html.

27 Chris Tucker (attributed), "Brainyquote.Com."

Figure 187. Do you have a "great deal" of "freedom of choice and control ... over the way your life turns out? (GSS survey conducted in 2000, based on 801 cases, with confidence level of 97%, and with a relative proportion of .80)

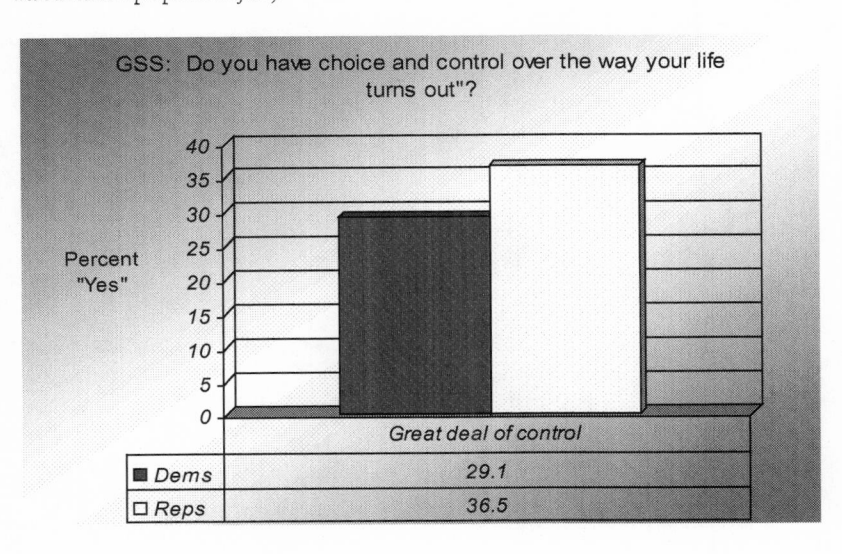

In aggregate, these traits and beliefs effectively constitute a sense of fatalism that could cause one to doubt his or her ability to control destiny. Survey evidence shows significant differences between Democrats and Republicans with regard to each of these four "control" factors, which are separately addressed below.

A General Lack of Optimism Leads to a Lack of Control

> There's so much to enjoy, so much to learn, so much to experience.
> ... To sit around and be enmeshed in a whole bunch of suffering,
> self-imposed and self-created ... that's where the American left is.
> When you get in that cycle, there's nothing optimistic. ...
>
> — Rush Limbaugh, Author and radio talk show host[28]

Democratic men and women are less likely than Republicans to feel optimistic, according to GSS survey results. Some of these are displayed in Figure 188, below.

Figure 188. I am not always optimistic about my future (GSS survey taken in 2004, based on, left to right, 670, 837, and 1507 cases, with confidence level of, left to right, 99+%, 98%, and 99+%, and with relative proportions of, left to right, 1.97, 1.46, and 1.68)

---

28 Rush Limbaugh as cited in, "Rush Limbaugh Radio Show," (transcript: August 31, 2006), Retrieved September 1, 2006, from: http://www.rushlimbaugh.com.

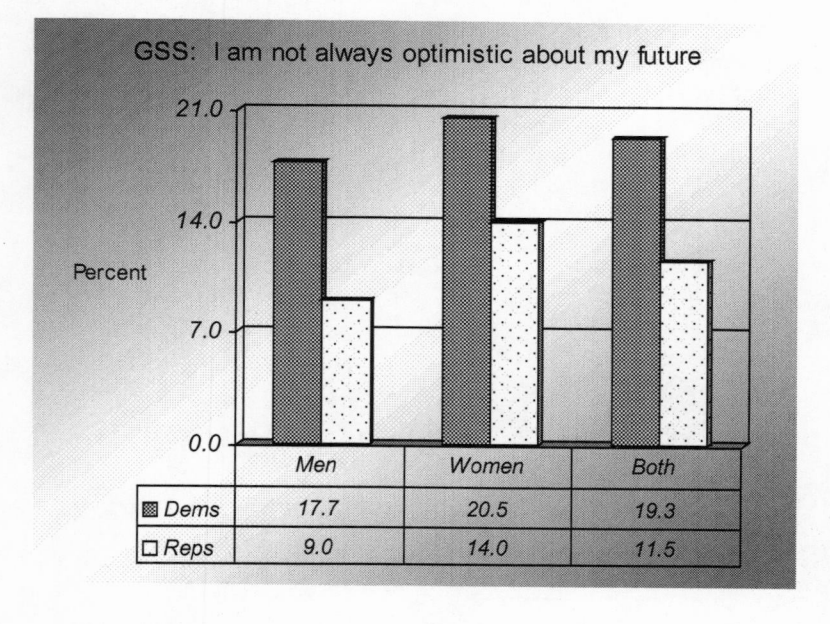

Other surveys showing an optimism gap are displayed in Table 46, below.

Table 46. Surveys addressing the issue of optimism

Survey and Issue	Dems	Reps	No. of cases	Conf %	*RP
NES Pilot Survey, 2006: Percentage indicating they are "very optimistic" about their futures.	36.8	**52.3**	240	97	.70
GSS survey conducted in 2004: Percentage indicating that "I hardly ever expect things to go my way."	**24.7**	13.7	685	+99	1.80
GSS survey conducted in 2004: Percentage indicating that "I rarely count on good things happening to me."	**32.0**	20.4	683	+99	1.57

*RP is relative proportion, which is the Democratic % divided by the Republican %.

Luck

Success is simply a matter of luck. Ask any failure.

— Earl Wilson, Major-league ball player[29]

---

29 Earl Wilson (attributed), "Thinkexist.Com."

The second control indicator is one's belief in the importance of luck. Democrats are much more likely than Republicans to ascribe success in life to chance, good fortune, and/or accident. By implication, some Democrats may be discounting the role that hard work, intelligence, and determination play in getting ahead.

Figure 189, below, shows the aggregate results of several Pew surveys conducted in 1987 through 2003, and these show a large difference between Democrats and Republicans with regard to attitudes about luck.

Figure 189. Percentage agreeing that "success in life is pretty much determined by forces outside of our control" (Pew surveys conducted in 1987 through 2003, based on 14192 cases, with confidence level of 99+%, and with a relative proportion of 1.43)

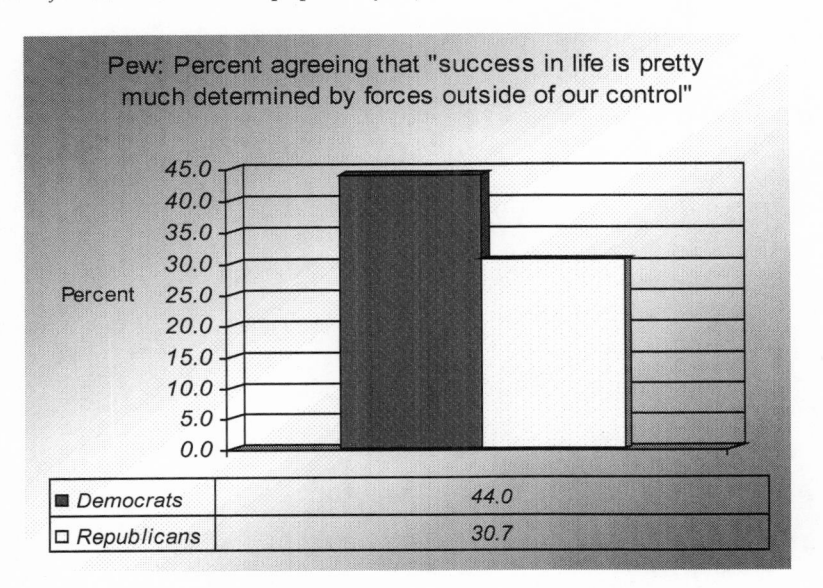

The results of similar survey questions are shown in Table 47, below. All of the surveys support the notion that Democrats are more likely to see their fortunes tied to luck (and bad luck at that).

Table 47. Other surveys results related to the issue of luck

Survey and Issue (percentage agreeing)	Dems	Reps	No. of cases	Conf %	*RP
GSS — 2006: "The most important reason why people get ahead" is "lucky breaks and help from other people"	26.5	10.3	416	+99	2.57
Pew 1987 through 2003 Combined Values Surveys: "Hard work offers little guarantee of success."	38.2	27.4	16115	+99	1.39

GSS — 1996: "Most of my problems are due to bad breaks." (agree or not sure)	31.3	16.2	901	+99	1.93
GSS — 1993: "How somebody's life turns out ... it's just a matter of chance."	23.7	15.9	1004	+99	1.49

*RP is relative proportion, which is the Democratic % divided by the Republican %.

"Connections"

Only in an election year ruled by fiction could a sissy who used Daddy's connections to escape Vietnam turn an actual war hero into a girlie-man

— Frank Rich, Columnist (referring to President Bush and Senator Kerry during the 2004 election campaign) [30]

There is a third reason why people may not feel in control of their destinies: The belief that "connections" are necessary for getting ahead in life. Democrats are more apt to feel it is "very important" or "essential" to "know the right people," has shown in Figure 190, below.

Figure 190. Percentage indicating that "knowing the right people" is "very important" or "essential ... for getting ahead in life." (combined results of GSS surveys conducted in 1987 and 2000, based on 1741 cases, with confidence level of 99+%, and with a relative proportion of 1.33)

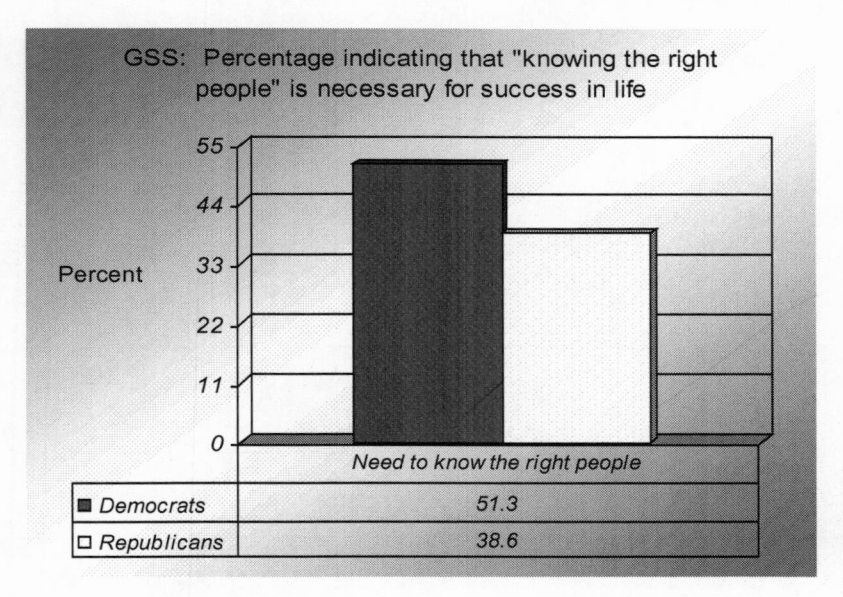

In addition, Democrats are more likely to believe that it is "very important" or "essential" to come from a wealthy background in order to succeed.

---

30 Frank Rich, "How Kerry Became a Girlie-Man," *New York Times*, September 5, 2004, 1.

Figure 191. Percentage indicating that it is very important or essential to come "from a wealthy family" for "getting ahead in life" (combined results of GSS surveys conducted in 1987 and 2000, based on 1697 cases, with confidence level of 99+%, and with a relative proportion of 1.69)

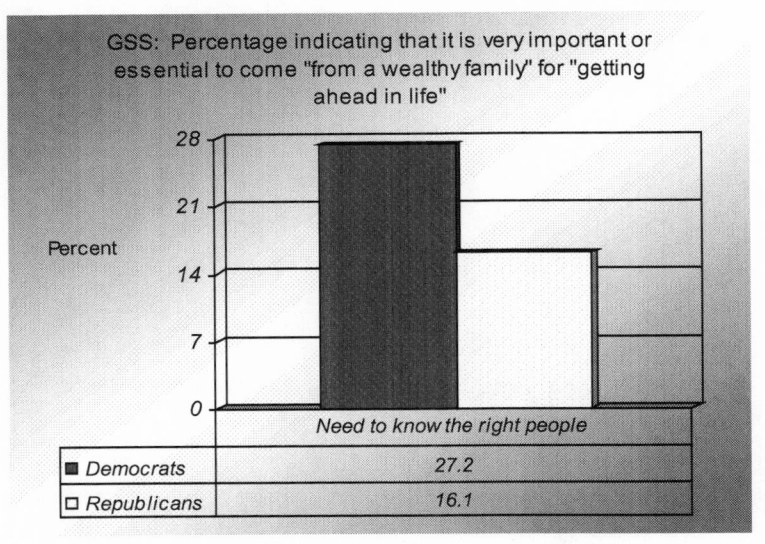

Confidence In One's Own Abilities

No one can make you feel inferior without your consent. Never give it.

— Eleanor Roosevelt[31]

The fourth and final factor related to the issue of control may be a lack of self-confidence. Both male and female Democrats are less likely than Republicans to say they are satisfied with themselves. See Figure 192.

Democratic males, in particular, seem to suffer from a serious lack of self-assurance. See Table 48, below.

Table 48. Surveys addressing the issue of self-esteem (Men only)

Survey and Issue (Men only)	Dem %	Rep %	No. of cases	Conf %	*RP
GSS survey conducted in 2004: "At times I think I am no good at all." (percentage agreeing)	22.6	11.0	668	+99	2.05
GSS survey conducted in 2004: "I wish I could have more respect for myself." (percentage agreeing)	27.8	21.4	667	95	1.30

*RP is relative proportion, which is the Democratic % divided by the Republican %.

---

31 Knowles, ed., *Oxford Dictionary of Twentieth Century Quotations*, 267.

Figure 192. Do you agree with the statement, "On the whole I am satisfied with myself"? (GSS survey taken in 2004, based on survey of 670 Democrats and Republicans, with confidence levels of at least 99%, and with relative proportions of, left to right, 2.41, 1.79, and 2.06)

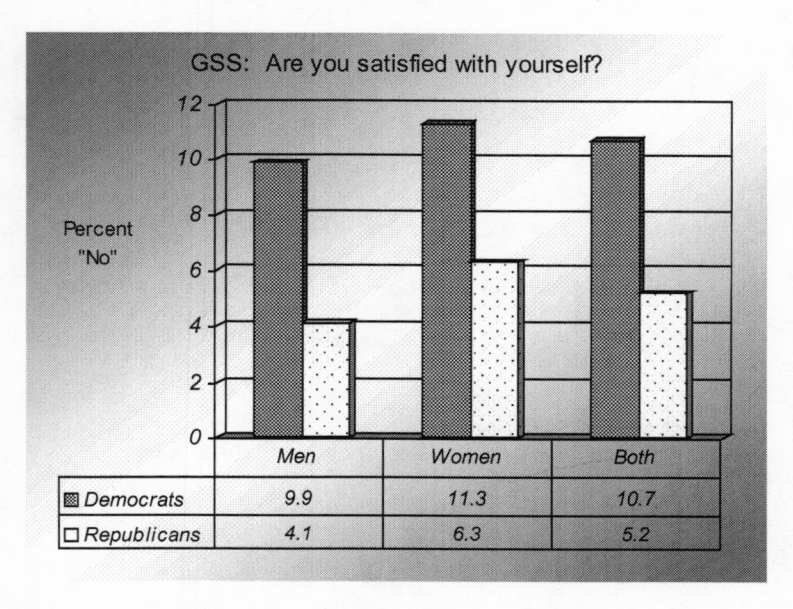

For all four reasons — the general lack of optimism, the feeling that life is heavily subject to luck, the belief that connections are needed to succeed in life, and the lack of self confidence — the average Democrat is more likely to feel that he can not control his own destiny. How does that relate to happiness?

Most psychologists believe that a feeling of control is an essential ingredient of happiness. Psychologist Daniel Gilbert put it this way:

> The fact is that human beings come into the world with a passion for control, they go out of the world the same way, and research suggests that if they lose their ability to control things at any point between their entrance and their exit, they become unhappy, helpless, hopeless, and depressed.[32]

"Capitalism Is Unjust"

> The Democratic Party has so successfully exploited class envy that people hold the wealthy and successful in contempt. The Democrats are breeding resentment. They have many people believing that anybody who is doing well is a cheater, a crook, selfish, and/or doing something unfair and unjust.
>
> — Rush Limbaugh, Author and radio talk show host[33]

---

32 Daniel Gilbert, *Stumbling on Happiness* (New York: Alfred A. Knopf, 2006), 21.
33 Limbaugh, *See, I Told You So*, 16.

We have discussed two of the three elements related to my hypothesis of Democratic cynicism: lack of trust and feeling out of control. There may be a third factor: the belief that the American socio-economic system is unjust.

Democrats are much more likely than Republicans to see a society that is divided into "haves" and "have-nots." A Pew 2005 survey asked:

> Some people think of American society as divided into two groups, the "haves" and the "have-nots," while others think it is incorrect to think of America that way. Do you, yourself, think of America as divided into haves and have-nots, or don't you.

The survey results, shown in Figure 193, below, indicate that far more Democrats than Republicans see an America that comprises two distinct classes.

Figure 193. "Do you, yourself, think of America as divided into haves and have-nots ...?" (Pew survey conducted in 2005, based on 708 cases, with confidence level of 99+%, and with a relative proportion of 2.71)

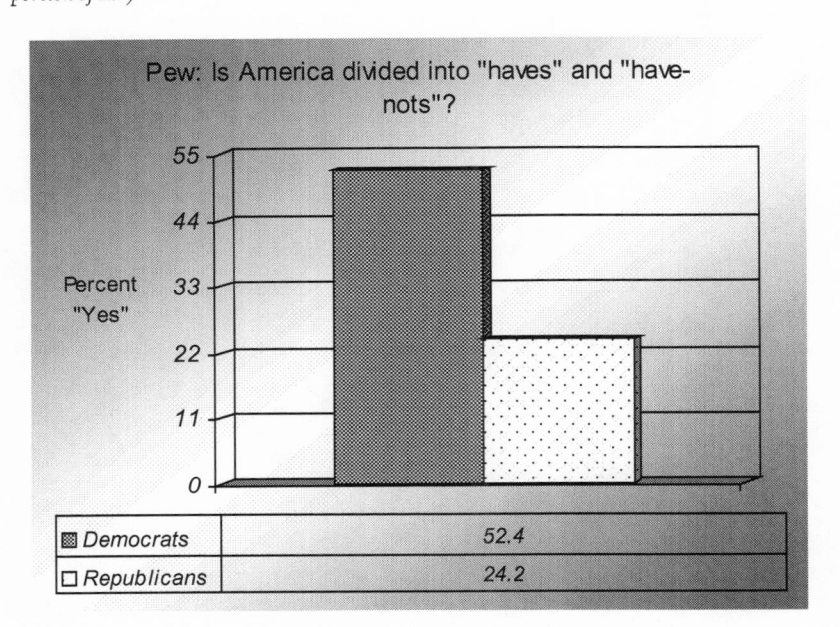

> Today, under George W. Bush, there are two Americas, not one: One America that does the work, another that reaps the reward.
>
> — Democratic Senator John Edwards[34]

In addition, Democrats are much more likely than Republicans to be concerned with the income gaps that occur in capitalist societies, and to believe that

---

34 Senator John Edwards, "Two Americas Speech Delivered in Des Moines, Iowa," December 29, 2003, Campaign Web site, from http://www.johnedwards2004.com/page.aspid?+481.

the government should reduce those disparities. A review of Figure 194 shows this to be true, even when we control for income level.[35]

Figure 194. The "government in Washington ought to reduce the income differences between the rich and the poor ..." (several GSS surveys conducted in 1998 through 2004, based on, left to right, 768, 815, and 184 cases, with confidence level of at least 99% for all differences, and with relative proportions of, left to right, 1.77, 1.92, and 2.68)

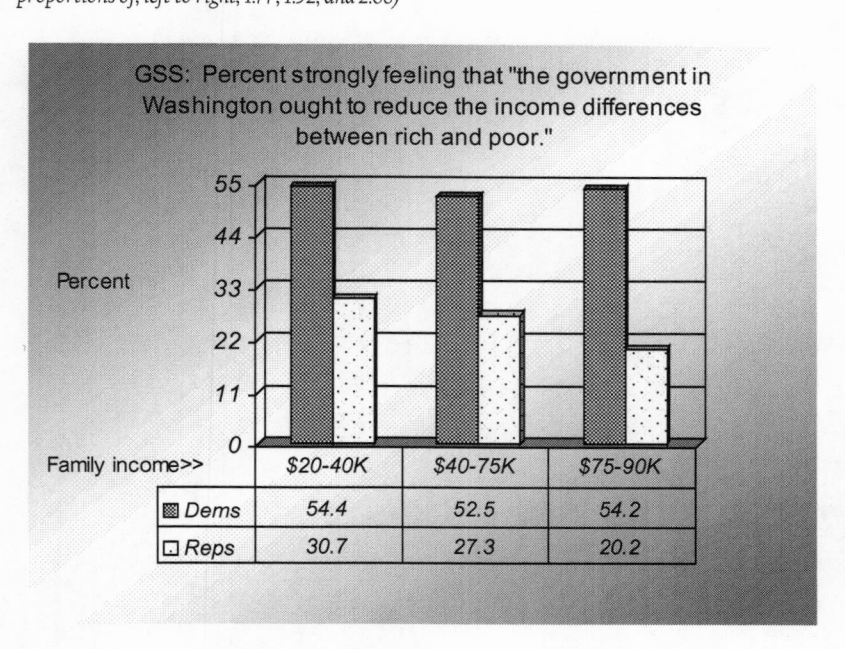

GSS: Percent strongly feeling that "the government in Washington ought to reduce the income differences between rich and poor."

Family income>>	$20-40K	$40-75K	$75-90K
Dems	54.4	52.5	54.2
Reps	30.7	27.3	20.2

The left wants control. They want to decide the allocation of resources, instead of living with the mess made by capitalism and the open market, with its arbitrary and unfair winners and losers.

— Ben Stein and Phil DeMuth, Can America Survive? (New Beginnings Press, 2004)[36]

The Democratic dislike of income gaps has existed for many years, and persists despite a dramatic overall increase in per capita prosperity. This is evident from a review of Figure 195, below. Here, we see the percentages of Democrats and Republicans who indicated strong support for having the federal government reduce the income gap. Among Democrats the support is especially high, and reaches 60 percent in years 2002-2006 — despite the fact that per capita

---

35 People were asked to indicate the strength of their feelings on a scale of 1 to 7, with 1 meaning that they strongly believed that government should reduce differences between rich and poor, and 7 meaning that they did not. Figure 194 shows those assigning a 1, 2, or 3 to the issue.

36 Ben Stein and Phil DeMuth, *Can America Survive?* (Carlsbad: New Beginnings Press, 2004), 142.

income rose by 50 percent between 1977 (shown at the left side of the graph) and 2006 (shown at the right side).[37]

Figure 195. Do you support the idea that the "government in Washington ought to reduce the income differences between the rich and the poor"? (GSS surveys conducted between 1977 and 2006, based on, left to right, 1339, 2855, 3840, 3053, 2162, and 2213 cases, with confidence level of 99+% for all differences, and with relative proportions of, left to right, .1.61, 1.66, 1.55, 1.94, 1.77, and 2.03)

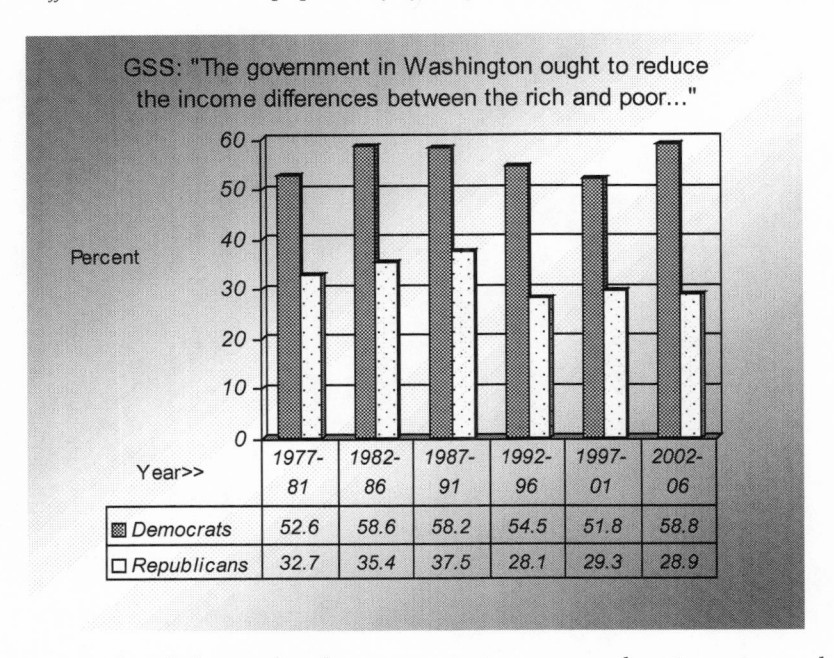

Year>>	1977-81	1982-86	1987-91	1992-96	1997-01	2002-06
Democrats	52.6	58.6	58.2	54.5	51.8	58.8
Republicans	32.7	35.4	37.5	28.1	29.3	28.9

Pew identified a similar phenomenon in its report on happiness. It noted that, during recent decades, "average annual per capita income in this country has more than doubled in inflation adjusted dollars ... But in the aggregate, we're no happier." This led Pew to conclude that "What matters on the happiness front is not how much money you have, but whether you have more (or less) at any given time than everyone else."[38]

If the Democratic concern about income gaps is based solely on humanitarian, economic, or academic beliefs (and it often is, no doubt), it is not a "happiness" issue. However, if the concern relates to personal comparisons with the income of peers and colleagues (E.g., my neighbor earns more they I do, and it bothers me.), it can be a very significant problem, leading to unhappiness.

---

37 People were asked to indicate the strength of their feelings on a scale of 1 to 7, with 1 meaning that they strongly believed that government should reduce differences between rich and poor, and 7 meaning that they did not. Figure 195 shows those assigning a 1, 2, or 3 to the issue.
38 Pew, "Are We Happy Yet?," 4.

What is a Communist? One who has yearnings for equal division of unequal earnings.

— Ebenezer Elliot, English poet[39]

Excessive concern with the achievements of others can be destructive and even pathological. Lyubomirsky observes that some "unhappy people actually feel better if they do poorly on a test but someone else did worse than if they performed excellently but another person did better." This same phenomenon has been observed in relation to income levels. Psychologists Hill and Buss describe this tendency, which is known as "relative poverty:"

> People who earn $40,000 a year may be happy or sad. But they are far more likely to be satisfied with their income if their co-workers earn $35,000 than if they earned $60,000 a year (Frank, 1999). Individuals appear to be satisfied with their incomes only if they are better off than those with whom they compare themselves. So pervasive is this effect that economists have given it its own name. *Relative poverty* describes individuals who are not objectively poor, but feel poor compared to everyone else.[40]

Hill and Buss note that "relative poverty" can lead to "negative feelings," which interfere with happiness. Psychologists state that happy people are more concerned with their own performance, and less concerned with how they "stack up" to others. Psychologist Sonja Lyubomirsky notes: "Happy people don't ruminate. They concentrate on inner personal standards. If they think much about a better performance of another person, it is typically to learn something from it to make themselves better."[41] Her advice: Avoid comparisons that can sap your energy and happiness.

Like it or not, income gaps are inherent in the capitalist economic system. Possibly, Democrats put their happiness at risk by focusing on "gaps" rather than on the growth of their resources and accomplishments, in absolute terms.

It's not enough to succeed. One's friends must fail.

— Gore Vidal, American novelist[42]

Conclusions

The evidence is overwhelming: Republicans are more likely to state that they are very happy, and the Republican happiness advantage extends to work, finances, and various aspects of personal life. Republicans are also less depressed, and less likely to let emotions negatively affect their lives.

39 Knowles, ed., *Oxford Dictionary of Quotations*, 298.

40 Sarah E. Hill and David M. Buss, "Envy and Positional Bias in the Evolutionary Psychology of Management," *Managerial and Decision Economics* 27 (2006): 131-43.

41 Sonja Lyubomirsky cited by Bob Condor, "In Pursuit of Happiness," in *Chicago Tribune* (December 9, 1998).

42 Gore Vidal as cited in, "Why You Think You'll Never Stack Up," ed. Carlin Flora (Psychology Today, 2005).

Being Republican is associated with several "intervening variables" that are known to correlate with happiness. For example, being Republican correlates with higher income and the increased likelihood of marriage and good health — factors associated with happiness. No doubt, these variables explain a lot of the happiness gap; however, there is evidence suggesting that Republicans are significantly happier — even when all obvious correlating factors are controlled.

We considered an additional factor that may relate to Democratic unhappiness — what I term, "cynicism." Surveys indicate that Democrats are more cynical than Republicans in three ways: They tend to be less trusting of other people, they feel less control over their destinies, and they seem more concerned with the income disparities generally associated with the capitalist economic system. It was postulated that each of the three traits could contribute to the happiness disparity.

CHAPTER 10: WHO GROWS UP TO BE A DEMOCRAT, AND WHO GROWS UP TO BE A REPUBLICAN?

INTRODUCTION

Crossing Over

> I have gone from a Barry Goldwater Republican to a New Democrat, but I think my underlying values have remained pretty constant: individual responsibility and community.
>
> — Democratic Senator Hillary Clinton[1]

> I became a Republican to make come to life the ideals I had as a Democrat. I believe in equality and social justice. The key to justice and equality is for mom and dad to have a job.
>
> — Republican Senator Norm Coleman[2]

What causes a person to identify with a particular political party, or to change his allegiance from one party to another? In this chapter we examine some of the leading theories offered by political scientists, and identify the constituency that is more likely to change its "political stripes." We also compare and contrast the early childhoods of Democrats and Republicans, with particular focus on the parents who raised them. Some of the factors considered include childhood economics and happiness, and parental education, occupational prestige, and political viewpoints.

---

[1] "Hillary Clinton's Education," Hillary Rodham Clinton Web page, Retrieved April 7, 2007, from http://www.hillary-rodham-clinton.org/education.html.

[2] Senator Norm Coleman as quoted in, "GOP Senator Works to Rally Jewish Support for Bush," *Associated Press via Freerepublic.com* (June 13, 2003), Retrieved October 27, 2006, from http://www.freerepublic.com/focus/f-news/928866/posts.

The survey evidence suggests that the distinguishing values and characteristics of Democrats and Republicans, such as income levels, job prestige, educational attainment, and marriage stability, were also discernable in their parents.

DETAILS

How political viewpoints develop

> Rush Limbaugh will "lose his fortune and become destitute. Forced on welfare, Rush will become a Democrat."
>
> — News reporter Eugene Emery, quoting a 1995 National Examiner prediction[3]

As Children

Most children have already developed partisan inclinations. According to political scientist Donald R. Kinder:

> Children may be naïve and poorly informed when it comes to politics, but they are far from innocent. They express strong attachment to the nation. They think of themselves, proudly, as partisans of one party or the other. They believe that their country and its way of life are best.[4]

Political scientists state that the initial development of our political identities is almost always tied to the political leanings of our parents.

> Though expressed partisanship is not always meaningful among the very young ... by adolescence, most children have a partisan identification connected to political preferences in the same manner as adults, though not always as strongly. Among those children who have a partisan preference, nearly all share it with their parents.[5]

This link between the political views of parents and children exists for two obvious reasons: Parents are usually the most salient initial influences on the development of their children and the "parent and child will often occupy similar positions in the social structure and thus parental experience is likely to be relevant to the child's future adult life."[6]

> The first election campaign that I remember took place in 1956, with my mother patiently explaining that Adlai Stevenson de-

---

3 Eugene Emery, "Psychics Strikes out (Again) in 1995," December 1995, Committee for Skeptical Inquiry, Retrieved October 22, 2006, from http://www.csicop.org/articles/psychic-predictions/1995.html.

4 Donald R. Kinder, "Politics and the Life Cycle," *Science* 312 (June 30, 2006): 1905.

5 Christopher H. Achen, "Parental Socialization and Rational Party Identification," *Political Behavior* 24, no. 2 (June, 2002): 152.

6 Ibid.: 155.

served to be president because he was an intellectual and Ike was
a dummy.

— Michael Medved, Author and radio talk show host[7]

Recently, a third and more controversial factor — genetics — has been offered to explain the correlation between the political perspectives of parents and children. Kinder summarizes the preliminary findings:

> A number of studies have compared the political views expressed by monozygotic twins (who share an identical genetic inheritance) to the views expressed by dizygotic twins (who develop from two separate eggs fertilized by two separate sperm). ... The results suggest that adult political beliefs — on the death penalty, say, or on school prayer — have a sizable genetic component.[8]

In one of those gene-related studies, researchers studied data pertaining to 8,000 sets of twins, including their opinions regarding 28 "political" issues. They concluded that, in each case, genetics appeared to be a statistically significant factor. This was particularly true with regard to views on property taxes and school prayer.[9]

Why they became Democrats

Not so many years back, I was a rather close-minded (is there another type?) conservative Republican. Then, the light came on, and I realized, "This is bulls***. Why did I buy into this philosophy all these years?" ... Every time they said they stood for a principle — they did the exact opposite.

— Blogger Mark in LA

I was a Republican until I got to New York and had to live on $18 a week. It was then that I became a Democrat.

— The late Julia Child, Master Chef and author

When I began to admit to myself that I had gay tendencies was when I became a Democrat ... My values could no longer align with a group of people that hated me openly.

— Blogger JakeHalsted

[I] became a Democrat because of this [George W. Bush] Administration and its preference for using military force.

— General Wesley Clark

Ronald Reagan ... is the primary reason why I became a Democrat. ... I never hated Reagan the man, but I did despise his policies. I never thought he was evil, but I did think he had a major mean streak.

— Blogger Azael

---

7 Medved, *Right Turns*, 41.
8 Kinder, "Politics and the Life Cycle," 1905.
9 Erin O'Donnell, "Twigs Bent Left or Right," *Harvard Magazine* 108, no. 3 (Jan-Feb, 2006).

As We Approach Adulthood

Although the correlation between the political views of parent and child can remain high for decades, there is usually some divergence beginning in late adolescent and early adulthood. There are at least three reasons for this: the impact of major world events, peer pressure during college years, and a "rational reevaluation" process based on the different needs and views of the child. Some of the major events that have shaped political viewpoints for decades are the Great Depression, World War II, Viet Nam, and the Civil Rights changes that have taken place since the 1960s.

> Vietnam radicalized me. It caused me to awaken.
>
> — Thom Hartmann, Air America radio talk show host, explaining how he changed from a Goldwater Republican to a liberal Democrat.[10]

The most significant of these events was probably the Great Depression, which led to the New Deal, Social Security, and decades of Democratic popularity.[11] Could an event such as the September 11th al Qaeda attack lead to a long-term change in the political landscape? It is doubtful, according to Radcliffe fellow J. Russell Muirhead:

> If an event impoverishes large numbers of the electorate, like the Great Depression, or slaughters large numbers of the electorate, like the Civil War, or introduces lots of new people into the electorate by enfranchising people who had previously been disenfranchised, like the Voting Rights Act, then the event has a lasting impact. Events that affect our moods or our passions may have consequences for policies, but those consequences last only as long as the mood. September 11 affected our mood, but it didn't change the demographic character of the country.[12]

Of course, Muirhead's conclusion is premised on the assumption that the 911 attack has simply created a bad "mood" that will eventually dissipate. If it turns out to be the first battle in a lengthy and costly war against Islamic radicalism, as assumed by many, the political implications could be far-reaching. This would be particularly true if the war necessitated the resumption of a military draft.

As noted, there are two additional factors that lead young adults to politically separate from their parents: peer pressure and "rational reevaluation." These factors were considered by political scientist Alan Abramowitz after he reviewed 521 interviews that had been conducted (in 1983) with undergraduate students at the State University of New York at Stony Brook. Abramowitz noted that "there was a much higher rate of political defection among students from Republican families than among students from Democratic families," and he attributed

---

10 "Thom Hartmann Brings Context to Today's Political Frays," February 7, 2006, Buzz Flash Political Web site, Retrieved October 27, 2006, from http://www.buzzflash.com/.

11 Kinder, "Politics and the Life Cycle," 1906.

12 J. Russell Muirhead as cited by Erin O'Donnell, "Twigs Bent Left or Right," *Harvard Magazine* 108, no. 3 (Jan-Feb, 2006).

the tendency, in part, to a liberal atmosphere at the school. He reasoned that the liberal environment produced a peer pressure that put Republican views on the defensive, and made it difficult for students to maintain allegiance to the GOP.

> At Bowling Green University, a Spanish language professor ... reserves a ritual ten minutes or 20 percent of his class time in every class .This time is devoted to what he calls a "political parenthesis," by which he means a class segment in which he allows himself to indulge in tirades against Republicans, George Bush, the war in Iraq, and conservatives generally.
>
> — Author and political activist David Horowitz[13]

Abramowitz also concluded that some students simply found more relevance in the liberalism espoused by the Democratic Party. For such students, the move away from the Republican Party was attributable to a "rational reevaluation" of their personal needs, desires, and values.[14]

Given these findings by Abramowitz, you may assume that most young adults are less likely than their parents to identify with the Republican Party. However, this has not always been the case. By analyzing data from the American National Election Studies (NES) (as displayed in Appendix A) we see that young adults were least likely to support the GOP prior to 1985, but have been one of the most supportive age groups since that time.

Figure 196. Party affiliation of different age groups for two time periods: 1952 through 1984, and 1985 through 2004. This information was derived from the NES survey results displayed in Appendix A.

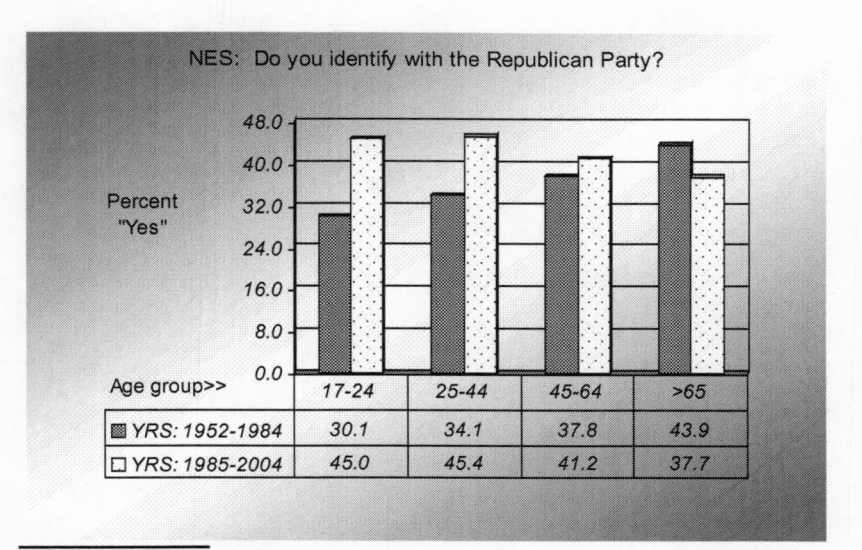

Age group>>	17-24	25-44	45-64	>65
▨ YRS: 1952-1984	30.1	34.1	37.8	43.9
☐ YRS: 1985-2004	45.0	45.4	41.2	37.7

13 David Horowitz, "Bowling Green Barbarians," *Students for Academic Freedom* (April 3, 2005), Retrieved September 14, 2007, from http://cms.studentsforacademicfreedom.org.
14 Alan I. Abramowitz, "Social Determinism, Rationality, and Partisanship among College Students," *Political Behavior* 5, no. 4 (1983): 353, 56-57.

Figure 196 ends with the year, 2004, and since that time, the Republican Party has not been doing well with young voters. A 2006 Pew Survey found:

> Young people today are much more likely to identify or lean Democratic rather than Republican, especially compared with the GenXers and late Baby Boomers who are in their 30s and 40s today. For example, among 18-24 year olds in Pew surveys over the past year and a half, fully 51 percent say they are Democrats ... [but] just 37 percent are Republicans or lean to the GOP.[15]

Thus, the future of the GOP is unclear.

> Young Americans have become so profoundly alienated from Republican ideals on issues including the war in Iraq, global warming, same-sex marriage and illegal immigration that their defections suggest a political setback that could haunt Republicans.
>
> — Columnist Carla Marinucci[16]

The "Strict Father" And "Nurturing Mother" Metaphors

An interesting explanation for the development of political beliefs has been offered by George Lakoff, a cognitive linguist. He believes that people frequently use metaphors to help them simplify and understand the complexities of life. In the case of politics the metaphors involve parental styles and values. More specifically, people see the nation as the parent and the citizen as the child. According to Lakoff, a Republican is more likely to believe that the nation should govern as a "strict father," who instills discipline in his child (citizen) in order to help her become a responsible adult who makes prudent financial and moral choices. On the other hand, a Democrat is more likely to see that nation as a "nurturing mother," who works to keep an essentially good child (citizen) away from harmful and corrupting factors such as discriminatory employers, greedy retailers, polluting industries, and social injustice. Expressed another way, Lakoff believes that, to a degree, Democrats and Republicans make political choices on the basis of their recollections and appreciation of the parent-child interactions that existed when they were growing up.[17]

> The father is always a Republican toward his son, and his mother's always a Democrat.
>
> — Robert Frost, American poet[18]

---

15 Scott Keeter, "Politics and The "Dotnet" Generation"," *PewResearchCenter Publications* (May 30, 2006), Retrieved September 3, 2007, from http://pewresearch.org/pubs/27/politics-and-the-dotnet-generation.

16 Carla Marinucci, "Poll: Young Voters Disenchanted with Republican Party," *SFGate.com* (August 27, 2007), Retrieved September 3, 2007, from http://sfgate.com/cgi-bin/article.cgi?f=/c/a/2007/08/27/MNMIRNDUK.DTL&tsp=1.

17 George Lakoff. (1995), "Metaphor, Morality, and Politics, Or "Why Conservatives Have Left Liberals in the Dust"", Retrieved September 13, 2007, from George Lakoff: http://www.wwcd.org/issues/Lakoff.html.

18 Robert Frost (attributed), "Simpson's Contemporary Quotations," (Houghlin Mifflin Company, 1988).

Reality check — Do we have it backwards?

Do our values determine our political identities, or do our political identities determine our values? A political scientist, Paul Goren, compared the stability of our partisan identities with the stability of our beliefs in four core principles: equal opportunity, limited government, traditional family values, and moral tolerance. In essence, he found that we are more likely to adhere to our partisan beliefs than to adhere to our values:

> [P]artisan identities are more stable and resistant to change than abstract beliefs about equal opportunity, limited government, traditional family values, and moral tolerance.... [P]arty identification systematically constrains beliefs about equal opportunity, limited government, and moral tolerance. This influence, while far from overwhelming, is substantively meaningful, and therefore, can produce genuine shifts in value preferences over extended periods of time.[19]

How does this happen? Citing other researchers, Goren states:

> Party identification 'raises a perceptual screen through which the individual tends to see what is favorable to his partisan orientation. The stronger the party bond, the more exaggerated the process of selection and perceptual distortion will be.' Hence, partisan bias 'plays a crucial role in perpetuating and reinforcing sharp differences in opinion between Democrats and Republicans.[20]

This makes sense. We have all seen Democrats and Republicans behave hypocritically — changing their positions when it serves the partisan interest.

Changes Later In Life

After young adulthood, our political views continue to change, albeit at a slower pace. The changes may be triggered by the transitions we make from student to employee, from child to parent, from tenant to home owner, etc. Some assume that we change our political beliefs as we acquire wealth, but the evidence is murky. According to Harvard professor D. Sunshine Hillygus:

> Researchers have found that even though a lot of people vote on the basis of the economy, they're generally thinking of the economy of the country, rather than their own economic situation. They might think, "If the economy of the country improves, then that's going to have a trickle-down effect and improve my own economic situation." But to say, "I earn $200,000, and if I elect the Republicans, I might get a tax cut"? — that doesn't appear to be part of the decision-making process.[21]

---

19 Paul Goren, "Party Identification and Core Political Values," *American Journal of Political Science* 49, no. 4 (October 2005): 892.

20 Paul Goren citing Angus Campbell et al. and Larry Bartels in "Party Identification and Core Political Values," *American Journal of Political Science* 49, no. 4 (October 2005): 883.

21 D. Sunshine Hillygus as cited by Erin O'Donnell, "Twigs Bent Left or Right," *Harvard Magazine* 108, no. 3 (Jan-Feb, 2006).

Is aging generally accompanied by a move towards the left or right? Donald R. Kinder and other political scientists state that it is not,[22] but the survey data available to me indicate that, until now at least, it is much more likely that a Republican was once a Democrat than vice versa.

This fact is evident from the results of a 2005 PEW survey, shown in Figure 197, below.

Figure 197. "Has there ever been a time when you have thought of yourself as" [a member of the opposing major political party]? (2005 PEW Political Typology Callback Survey, based on 784 cases, with confidence level of 99+%, and with a relative proportion of .52)

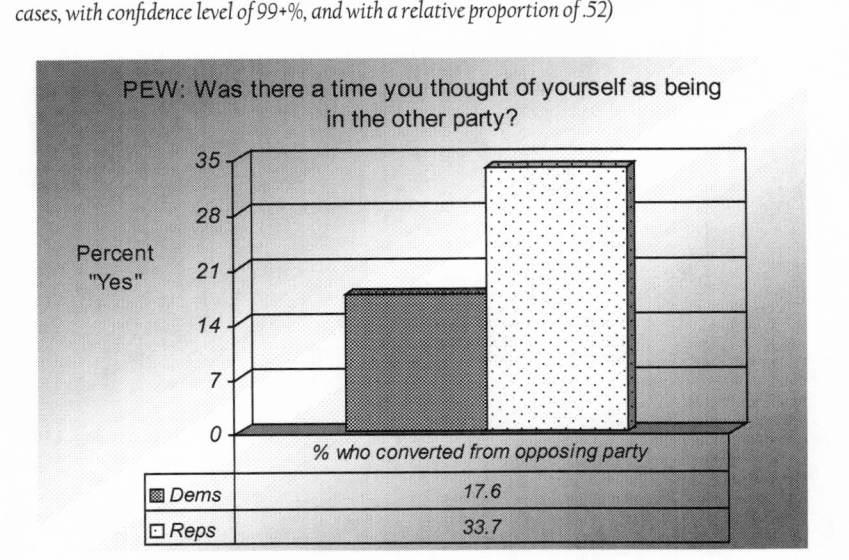

In addition, Republicans are a bit more likely, by 50.6 to 45.7 percent, to be former independents.[23]

> Yes, [I share blame for the recession] because for many years I was a Democrat.
>
> — President Ronald Reagan.[24]

This is not a short-term trend. From 1952 through 1980, the GSS asked respondents if they had always voted for the same political party, or had voted for a different party. The results of these surveys, by political orientation, are shown for 3 different decades in Figure 198, below. Although the results don't identify the "other party," it seems reasonable to assume that more Republicans used to vote as Democrats (the "other party") than vice versa.

---

22 Kinder, "Politics and the Life Cycle," 1906.

23 The results are based on 2005 PEW Political Typology Callback Survey of 603 cases, with overall statistical significance of 99+%.

24 Dan Rather, "Ronald Reagan, Master Storyteller," (CBS News, June 7, 2004), Retrieved April 7, 2007, from: http://www.cbsnews.com/stories/2004/06/07/48hours/main621459. shtml.

Figure 198. "Have you always voted for the same party ...? (various NES Surveys conducted from 1952 through 1980, based on, left to right, 3899, 4408, and 4394 cases, with confidence level of 99+% for each column, and with relative proportions of, left to right, .86, .77, and .87)

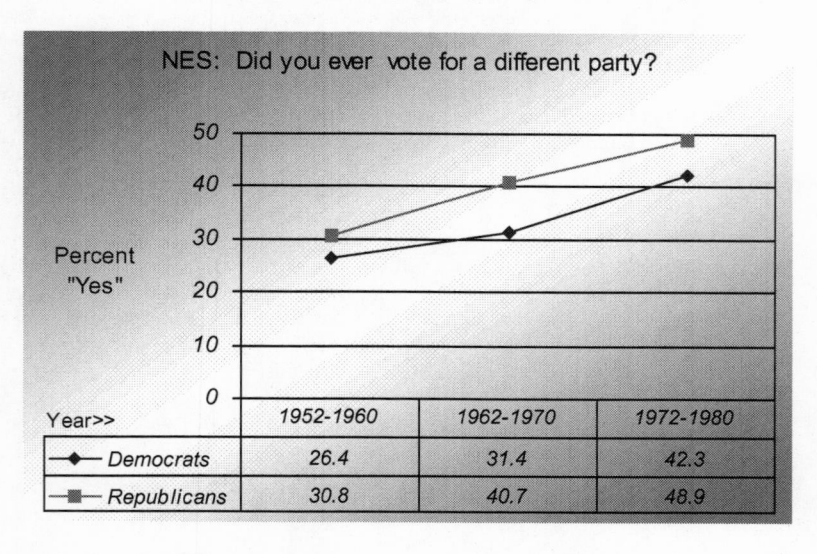

Year>>	1952-1960	1962-1970	1972-1980
◆ Democrats	26.4	31.4	42.3
■ Republicans	30.8	40.7	48.9

Is the movement away from the Democratic Party attributable to the wisdom we acquire as we age (the likely Republican explanation), or because we become corrupted by wealth (the likely Democratic explanation)? More likely, it is due to the fact that, prior to 1985, a very high percentage of young adults started off as Democrats, so there was really only one directional change they could make. In addition, many southern Democrats became Republicans during the 1960s and 70s. Undoubtedly, that was also a factor.

Why they became Republicans

As a small business owner, I remember coming home from work exhausted after a 10-plus-hour, hot-as-hell, July 1979 day at my then-struggling manufacturing business, arriving just in time for the 6:00 PM ... lecture from a stern-faced Jimmy Carter — the one where he told us that everything was our fault because we had a bad attitude. At that moment I became a Republican. — Joe Sherlock, Mechanical Engineer and consultant

I became a Republican when a very wise young lady asked me how I could remain a Democrat when I didn't agree with what they stood for and did agree with what the Republicans supported. — Republican Senator Jesse Helms[25]

[H]umphrey was talking about more government is the solution, protectionism, and everything he said about government involvement sounded to me more like Austrian Socialism. Then when I heard Nixon talk about it, he said open up the borders, the consumers should be represented there ul-

---

25 Senator Jesse Helms (attributed), "Brainyquote.Com."

timately and strengthen the military and get the government off our backs....
That's how I became a Republican. — Governor Arnold Schwarzenegger

The more I listened to Rush [Limbaugh], the more he made sense to me.
I can't say I agree with everything Rush says, but I love the way he frames
an issue. I have been listening to him since '92 or '93, and the only "preaching" I remember was for self-reliance and the 3 "Fs" (Family, Friends, and
Faith), as opposed to reliance on government! The logical extension of this
is to defeat the Democrats, and this is how I became a Republican, thanks
to Rush Limbaugh. — Blogger Chris Leavitt

[M]y final and emotional break with my remaining Left-wing friends
didn't come until the fall of Saigon and the bloody denouement in Cam-
bodia. ... I felt that those of us who had participated in the anti-war movement had a moral obligation to admit that we had been profoundly wrong
concerning the postwar future of Southeast Asia and the nature of the Viet-
namese and Cambodian Communists. ... After that, it was as though a spell
had been broken. I began to view things in a wholly different light. — Michael Medved, Author and radio talk show host[26]

The parents of Democrats and Republicans

When you have a good mother and no father, God kind of sits in.
It's not enough, but it helps.

— Dick Gregory, Civil rights leader and comedian[27]

Some of the major sociological surveys have asked thousands of people questions regarding the education, occupations, and political leanings of their parents. When we analyze these data, we find that many of the differences between
today's Democrats and Republicans were the same differences that distinguished
their parents.

Was Dad in the Home?

In Figure 15 on page 17, we saw that unmarried Democrats are more likely
to have children in the household. This tendency was also found in the previous
generation. In Figure 199, below, we see that more than one in every five Democrats surveyed in 1997 through 2006 was raised in a fatherless home.

The relatively high number of Democratic homes with absent fathers could
be a confirmation of Lakoff's "strict father" and "nurturing mother" metaphors,
discussed earlier. Is it possible that the absence of a father leaves children in
the more "nurturing" care of the mother, and that leads to a creation of a future
Democrat? In other words, does a fatherless home cause people to become Democrats? Or, is the fatherless home simply a reflection of the high value Democrats
place on independent conduct by women?

---

26 Michael Medved, *Second Thoughts: Former Radicals Look Back at the Sixties*, ed. Peter Collier and
David Horowitz, 1st ed. (Lanham: Madison Books, 1989).
27 Dick Gregory cited in, "God Bless the Children - Quotes from 18 Wisdom Speakers," *Essence
Magazine*, May, 1995.

Figure 199. At age 16, father was absent from home (GSS surveys conducted in 1977 through 2006, based on, left to right, 8038 cases, 9932 cases, and 8506 cases, with confidence level of 99+% for all categories, and with relative proportions of, left to right, 1.39, 1.55, and 1.62)

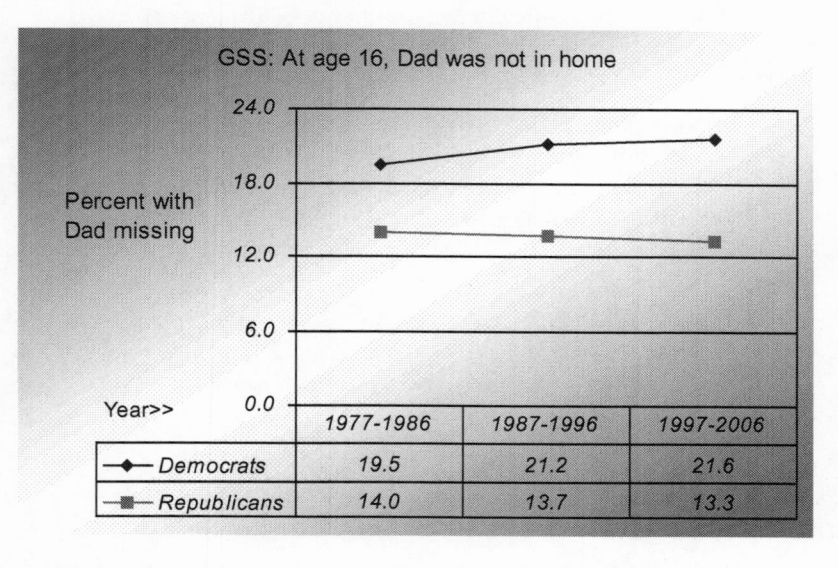

GSS: At age 16, Dad was not in home			
Year>>	1977-1986	1987-1996	1997-2006
Democrats	19.5	21.2	21.6
Republicans	14.0	13.7	13.3

Figure 200. Did your parents have serious marital problems? Did they divorce before you were age 18? (1999 Michigan SOSS, based on, left to right, 622 and 637 cases, with confidence level of 99% and relative proportions of, left to right, 1.53 and 1.62)

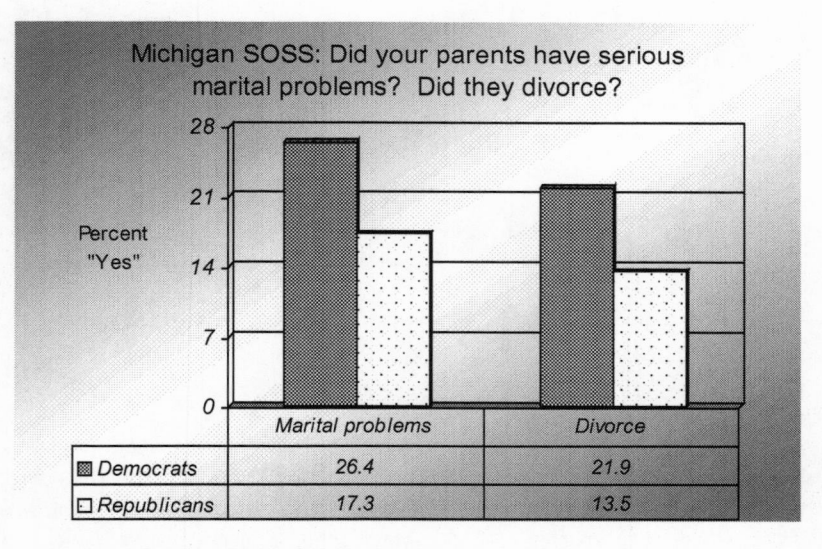

Michigan SOSS: Did your parents have serious marital problems? Did they divorce?		
	Marital problems	Divorce
Democrats	26.4	21.9
Republicans	17.3	13.5

A reason for the absent fathers might be marital discord or divorce. It appears, based on a 1999 Michigan State of the State (SOSS) survey, that the par-

ents of Democrats are less likely to have had successful marriages (Figure 200). Of course, we saw this same tendency in the current generation of Democrats. (See Figure 11 on page 14.)

> My wife and I were happy for twenty years. — Then we met.
>
> — The late Rodney Dangerfield, Comedian[28]

How Much Education Did The Parents Have?

The education gap we see in today's generation of Democrats and Republicans existed between their parents. Figure 201 shows the disparity and trend with respect to the fathers of Democrats and Republicans, based on results from the General Social Survey (GSS). The percentage with high school diplomas is compared.

Figure 201. Did Dad have a high school diploma (or higher degree)? (GSS surveys, conducted from 1972 through 2006, based on, left to right, 3712, 2205, 4011, 4156, 3636, 2505, and 4147 cases, with confidence level of 99+% for all differences, and with relative proportions of, left to right, .62, .76, .69, .67, .80, .81, and .89)

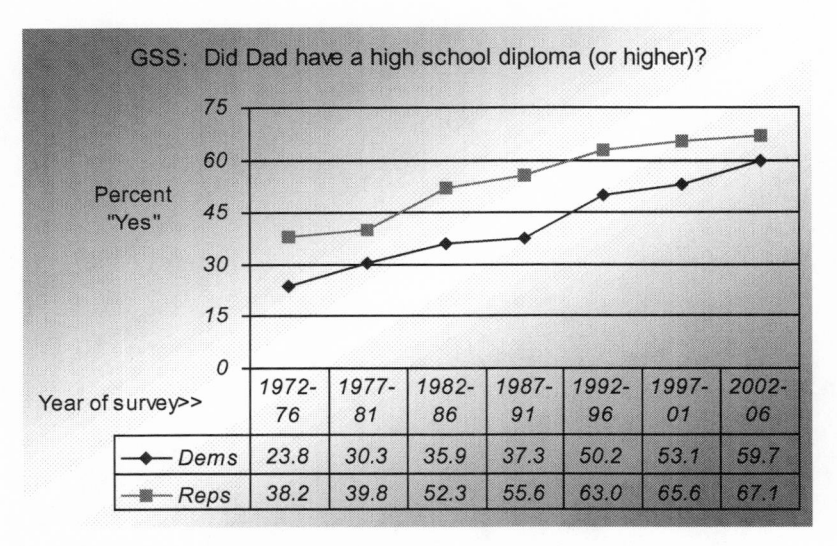

Year of survey>>	1972-76	1977-81	1982-86	1987-91	1992-96	1997-01	2002-06
Dems	23.8	30.3	35.9	37.3	50.2	53.1	59.7
Reps	38.2	39.8	52.3	55.6	63.0	65.6	67.1

> I've never been jealous. Not even when my dad finished the fifth grade a year before I did.
>
> — Comedian Jeff Foxworthy[29]

Figure 202, below, shows the same information with respect to mothers. Again, there is a significant gap, with the mothers of Republicans likely to have more education. Interestingly, the mothers of both Democrats and Republicans were more likely to have high school diplomas than were the fathers.

---

28 Rodney Dangerfield (attributed), "The Quotations Page."
29 Jeff Foxworthy as cited in, *Squeaky Clean Comedy* (New Jersey: Andrews McMeel, 2005).

Figure 202. Did Mom have a high school diploma (or higher degree)? (GSS surveys, conducted from 1972 through 2006, based on, left to right, 4125, 2512, 4643, 4724, 4214, 2943, and 4751, with confidence level of 99+% for all differences, and with relative proportions of, left to right, .72, .80, .70, .70, .80, .79, and .88)

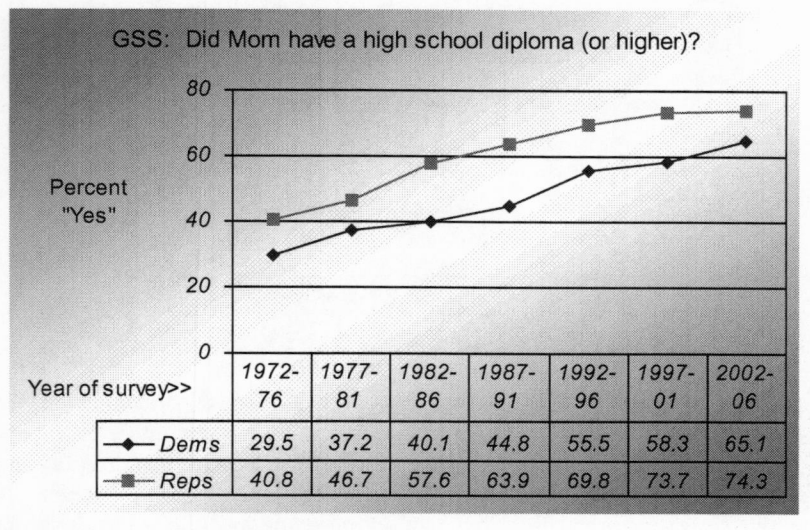

GSS: Did Mom have a high school diploma (or higher)?

Year of survey>>	1972-76	1977-81	1982-86	1987-91	1992-96	1997-01	2002-06
—◆— Dems	29.5	37.2	40.1	44.8	55.5	58.3	65.1
—■— Reps	40.8	46.7	57.6	63.9	69.8	73.7	74.3

Employment Of The Parents

I grew up in a home where my father was a janitor. I'm used to having bills last till Friday when the paycheck only lasted till Thursday

— Gary Bauer, former Republican presidential aspirant[30]

Republicans are more likely to have dads who held management, professional, technical/sales jobs while they were growing up. In particular, the dads of Republicans are more likely to have worked in the areas of administration, personnel, training, labor relations, engineering, and sales. Democratic dads are more likely to have worked in farming and labor occupations as machine operators, assemblers, truck drivers, construction workers, and farm hands. In the service and trade craft occupations, the overall percentages are about equal. The major categories, and the percentages of Democratic and Republican dads who worked in each, are shown in Figure 203, below. (The service and trade craft occupations are not depicted due to a lack of confidence level.) Of course, these same occupational distinctions were found in the current generation of Democrats and Republicans.

Figure 203. When you were growing up, what was Dad's occupation? (various GSS surveys conducted in 1988 through 2004, based on 12675 cases, with overall confidence level of 99+%, and a Phi association of .14 for the entire sequence)

30 Gary Bauer, "Online Newshour," (Transcript: PBS, October 29, 1999), Retrieved September 4, 2006, from: http://www.pbs.org/newshour/bb/politics/gop_debate_10-29.html.

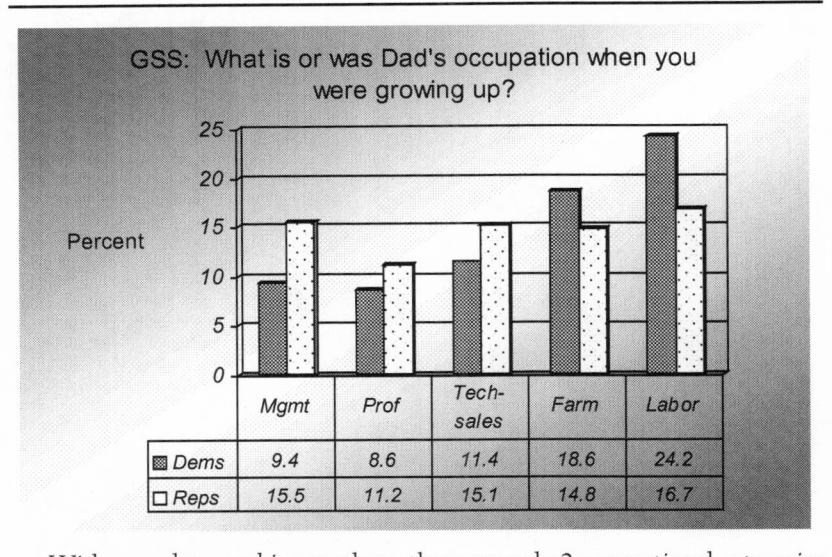

With regard to working mothers, there are only 2 occupational categories with significant differences. The moms of Republicans are more likely to have worked in technical/sales jobs — particularly in the fields of bookkeeping and secretarial services. The mothers of Democrats are liable to have worked in the service sector — especially in nursing and cleaning jobs. The percentages of women who work in those two general fields is shown in Figure 204.

Figure 204. What was Mom's occupation when you were growing up? (various GSS surveys conducted in 1988 through 2004, based on 5954 cases, with overall confidence level of 99+%, and a Phi association of .13 for the sequence)

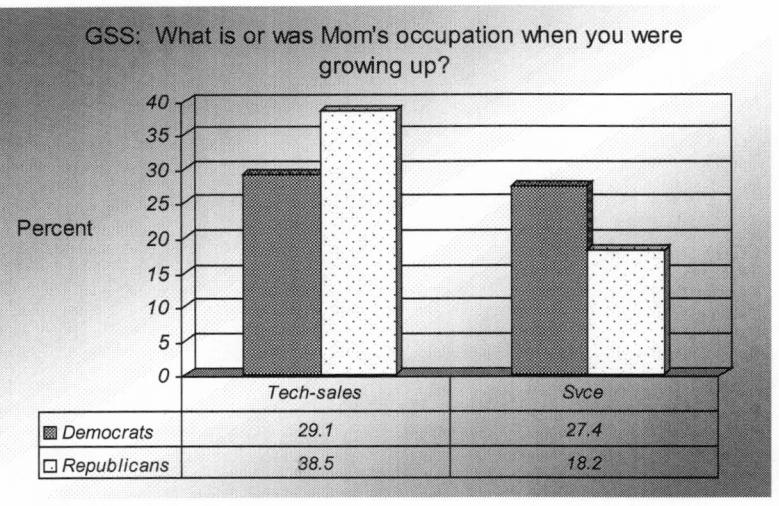

> I just knew then that I had been a lazy Democrat and I never looked back. I became a Republican.
>
> — Winsome Earle Sears, Republican member of the Virginia House of Delegate, describing her reaction to the Dukakis presidential campaign[31]

Mothers of Democrats and Republicans are about equally likely to have been self-employed. For fathers, however, there is a small difference that is statistically significant. By 34.5 to 29.7 percent, the fathers of Republicans are a little more likely to have owned their own businesses.[32] This disparity has been fairly consistent over the last 30 years or more.

Mom Worked With Preschooler

Some survey evidence suggests that the mothers of Democrats are more likely to have worked outside of the home before their children reached school age.

According to 4 GSS surveys taken in the early 1990s, Democrats are more likely to recall that, prior to beginning first grade, their mothers worked outside of the home.

Figure 205. After I was born, and before I started 1st grade, Mom worked for at least 1 year outside of home. (4 GSS surveys, conducted in 1990 through 1994, based on 1903 cases, with confidence level of 99+%, and with a relative proportion of 1.22)

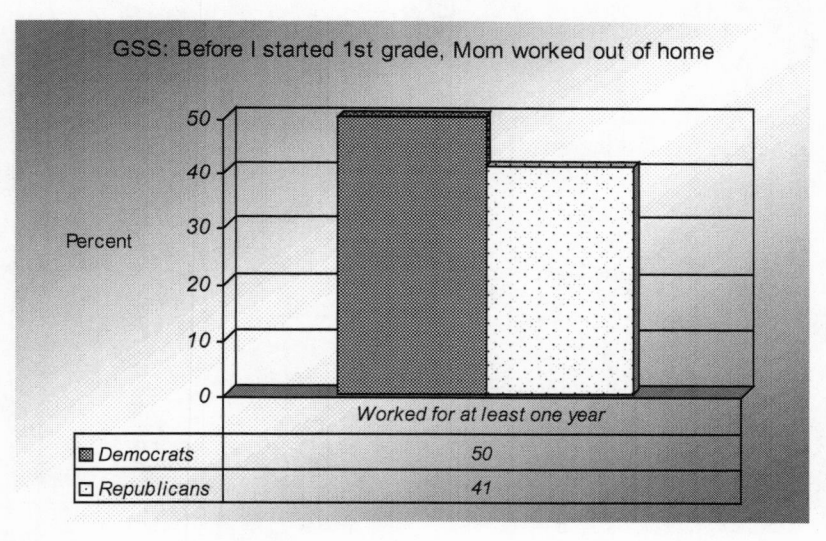

31 John H. Fund, "A Winsome Politician," *Wall Street Journal*, November 8, 2001.

32 GSS surveys conducted between 1972 and 2004, based on 24,897 cases, with confidence level of 99+ percent and with a relative proportion of 1.16.

Parents' Occupational "Prestige"

> Prestige is the shadow of money and power. Where these are, there it is.

— C. Wright Mills, American sociologist[33]

As noted in an earlier chapter, the National Opinion Research Center (NORC), a research organization based at the University of Chicago, developed a system for rating the "prestige" of various occupations. The scores, which range from a low of 17 to a high of 86, were averaged and summarized in a table of "prestige" scores.

GSS uses this rating system to assign a prestige score to the each of the occupations identified in its surveys. Figure 206, below, shows the mean prestige scores for the dads of Democrats and Republicans. There has been a small, but significant difference since 1988, when the most recent index was developed. Like their children, the parents of Republicans generally had more prestigious jobs than their Democratic contemporaries.

Figure 206. Average occupational prestige scores for the fathers of Democrats and Republicans (GSS surveys conducted in 1988 through 2004, based on, left to right, 4231, 4356, and 4088 cases, with confidence level of 99+%)

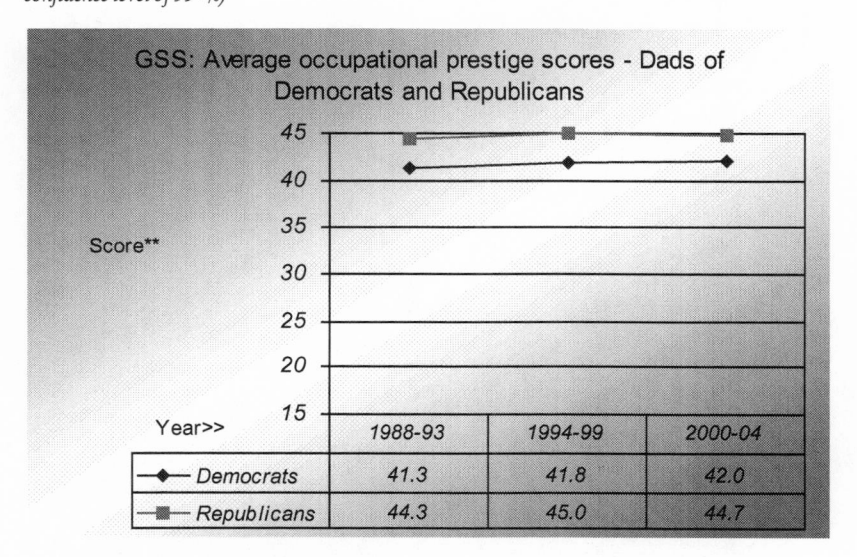

GSS: Average occupational prestige scores - Dads of Democrats and Republicans			
Year>>	1988-93	1994-99	2000-04
—♦— Democrats	41.3	41.8	42.0
—■— Republicans	44.3	45.0	44.7

**The minimum possible score is 17 and the maximum is 86.

In 1994, GSS began accumulating information regarding the occupations of the mothers of its respondents. In Figure 207 we see that the mothers of Republicans generally worked in slightly more prestigious jobs than did the mothers of Democrats.

---

33 C. Wright Mills (attributed), "Quotationz.Com."

Figure 207. Average occupational prestige scores for the mothers of Democrats and Republicans (GSS surveys conducted in 1988 through 2004, based on, left to right, 2992 and 2962 cases, with confidence level of 99+%)

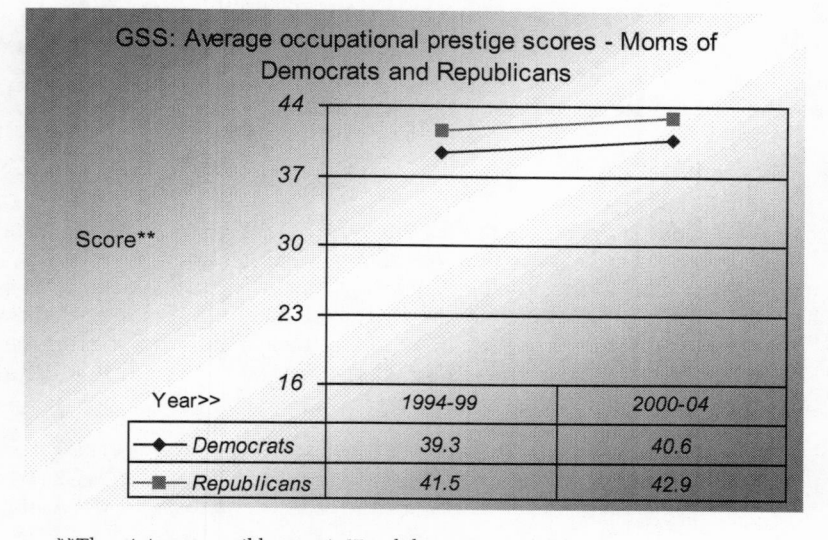

Year>>	1994-99	2000-04
◆ Democrats	39.3	40.6
■ Republicans	41.5	42.9

**The minimum possible score is 17 and the maximum is 86.

Country of Birth

Figure 208. "Were both your parents born in this country? (various NES surveys conducted in 1952 through 2004, based on, left to right, 1327, 2610, 6245, 6578, 6572, and 2877 cases, with no statistically significant difference for the 4 differences on the left, and significance of 99% for the 2 differences on the right side, and relative proportions of 1.24 and 1.38 for the 2 right-side differences)

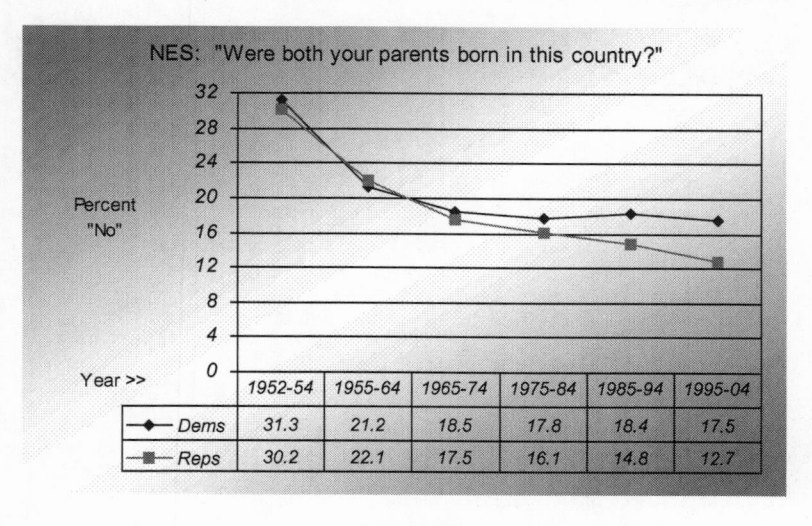

Year >>	1952-54	1955-64	1965-74	1975-84	1985-94	1995-04
◆ Dems	31.3	21.2	18.5	17.8	18.4	17.5
■ Reps	30.2	22.1	17.5	16.1	14.8	12.7

It's unclear. And I've looked at this issue, I've talked to my parents about it, and it's just not clear.

— Former Attorney General Alberto Gonzales, describing the citizenship status of his grandparents[34]

It appears that Democrats are a little more likely to have parents who were born in a country other than the U.S. or Canada, as indicated in Figure 208. This disparity has developed during the last 20 to 30 years. Overall, however, there has been a sharp decline in foreign-born parents for constituents of either political party.

Politics of the Parents

During a 40 year period from 1952 through 1992, NES queried respondents 11 times regarding the political leanings of their fathers. As can be seen in Figure 209, below, a minority of children changed from the party of their fathers; however, those who did were more likely to be Republicans than Democrats. The significance of this pattern is hard to assess. It may simply indicate that the Democratic Party was so popular during the depression and World War II era that most people's parents were Democrats.

Figure 209. Democrats with Republican fathers, and Republicans with Democratic fathers (various NES surveys conducted in 1952 through 1992, based on, left to right, 2714, 2263, 4542, 2387, and 2774 cases, with a 99+% statistically significant difference for all differences, and with relative proportions of, left to right, .67, .51, .42, .40, and .37)

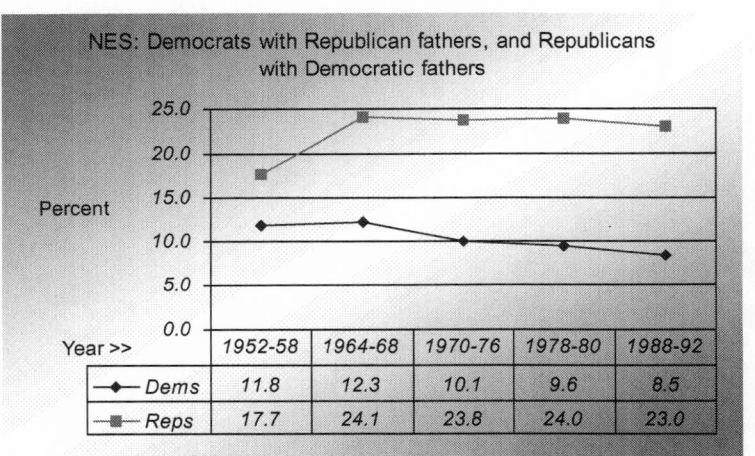

NES: Democrats with Republican fathers, and Republicans with Democratic fathers

Year >>	1952-58	1964-68	1970-76	1978-80	1988-92
Dems	11.8	12.3	10.1	9.6	8.5
Reps	17.7	24.1	23.8	24.0	23.0

I will f---ing find you and I will f---ing hurt you.

— Tim Robbins, who was angry when a reporter wrote that his mother-in-law is a Republican[35]

34 Attorney General Alberto Gonzales, "The Situation Room with Wolf Blitzer," (Transcript: Newsmax.com, May 17, 2006), Retrieved October 27, 2006, from: http://www.newsmax.com/archives/ic/2006/5/17/91751.shtml.

35 Lloyd Grove, "Verbatim," *Washington Life Magazine* 2003.

A similar pattern is seen in a 1999 Pew survey, where 26 percent of Republicans had parents who were Democrats, and only 12 percent of Democrats had parents who were Republicans.[36].

> You have to have been a Republican to know how good it is to be a Democrat.
>
> — Former First Lady Jacqueline Kennedy Onassis[37]

Many sociologists believe that the mother has more influence on the child's eventual political orientation:

> [R]esearch performed in America, Jamaica and Japan shows that ... the mother is more effective in the child's political socialization. (Yesilorman, 2005)[38]

Nevertheless, survey evidence suggests that children are just as likely to shun the mother's political party as they are to shun their dad's political party. This is evident when one compares Figure 210, below, to Figure 209, above. The amounts and patterns are similar. Again, more recent data are unavailable.

Figure 210. Democrats with Republican mothers, and Republicans with Democratic mothers (various surveys of the American National Election Studies conducted in 1952 through 1992, based on, left to right, 2714, 2263, 4543, 2387, and 2775 cases, with 99+% statistical significance for all differences, and with relative proportions of, left to right, .60, .60, .41, .38, and .36)

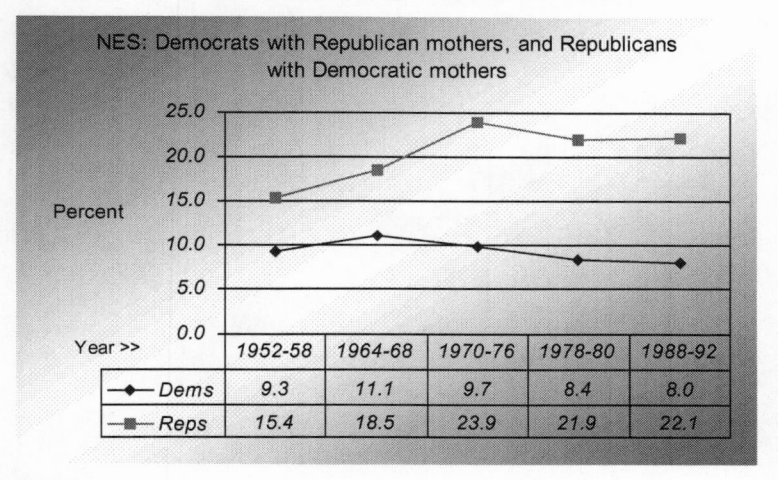

Year >>	1952-58	1964-68	1970-76	1978-80	1988-92
Dems	9.3	11.1	9.7	8.4	8.0
Reps	15.4	18.5	23.9	21.9	22.1

Childhood life

> The four stages of man are infancy, childhood, adolescence, and obsolescence.
>
> — Art Linkletter, TV performer and motivational speaker[39]

---

36 Pew July 1999 Typology survey, based upon 2301 cases.

37 "Why I Am a Democrat," San Diego County Democratic Party, Retrieved October 27, 2006, from http://www.sddemocrats.org/why_demo.html.

38 Mehtap Yesilorman, "Do Families Lose Their Political Efficacy or Not?," *Bilig*, no. 32 (Winter 2005): 110.

39 Knowles, ed., *Oxford Dictionary of Quotations*, 469.

Siblings

So far, we have seen that tendencies in the current generation of Democrats and Republicans were also evident in the generation of their parents. Here is an exception. As noted in Figure 211, Democratic families used to be larger than Republican families — at least with respect to children. Today, however, Democrats and Republicans are averaging about the same number of children (See page 16 for information regarding the family size of the current generation of Democrats and Republicans.)

Figure 211. How many brothers and sisters did you have when you were a child? (25 GSS surveys, conducted from 1972 through 2004, based on, left to right, 3013, 3834, 4045, 5276, 4853, 3459, 5062, and 29542 cases, with confidence level of 99+%)

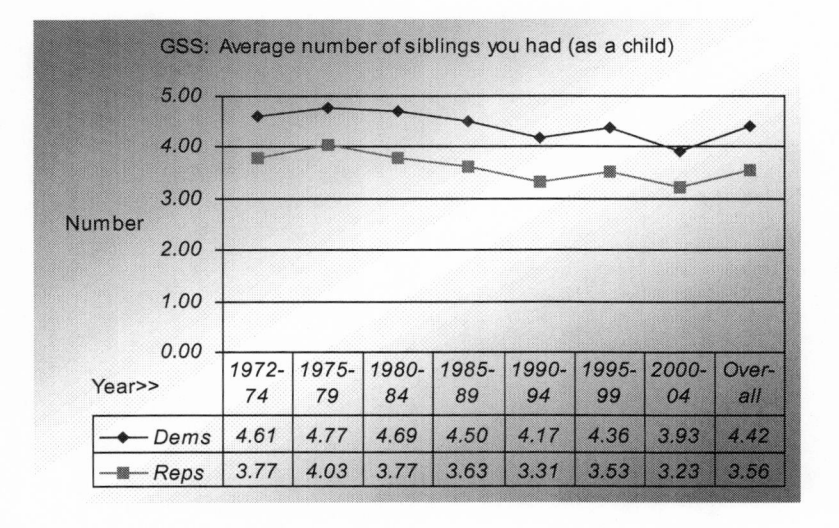

Year>>	1972-74	1975-79	1980-84	1985-89	1990-94	1995-99	2000-04	Over-all
Dems	4.61	4.77	4.69	4.50	4.17	4.36	3.93	4.42
Reps	3.77	4.03	3.77	3.63	3.31	3.53	3.23	3.56

Religious Life

As youngsters, Republicans were a bit more likely to be raised as Protestants (65% to 56%), while Democrats were more likely to be raised as Catholics and Jews (31% to 27% and 3.5% to 1%, respectively).[40]

Family Income During Childhood

> My family got all over me because they said Bush is only for the rich people. Then I reminded them, "Hey, I'm rich."
>
> — Charles Barclay, Professional basketball star[41]

Income level is another attribute passed from one generation to another. Although approximately equal numbers of Democrats and Republicans recall having "average" income when they were aged 16 years (about 50%), Democrats are more likely to report sub-average income.

---

40 The results are based on GSS surveys in 1995-2004 of 8511 cases, with 99+% statistical significance for all differences, and relative proportions of 1.16, 1.15, and 3.5.
41 Charles Barkley (attributed), "Brainyquote.Com."

Figure 212. "Thinking about the time when you were 16 years old, compared with American families in general then, would you say your family income was below average?" (various GSS surveys conducted in 1992 through 2004, based on, left to right, 7825, 9153, and 2718 cases, with confidence level of 99+% for each difference, and with relative proportions of, left to right, .1.38, 1.47, and 1.19)

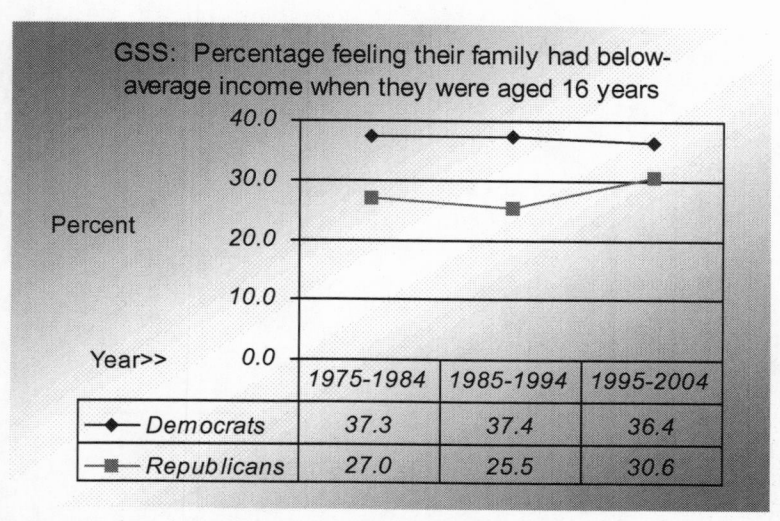

Year>>	1975-1984	1985-1994	1995-2004
Democrats	37.3	37.4	36.4
Republicans	27.0	25.5	30.6

Conversely, relatively few Democrats state that their family income (at age 16) was above average. The figures are shown in Figure 213, below.

Figure 213. "Thinking about the time when you were 16 years old, compared with American families in general then, would you say your family income was above average?" (various GSS surveys conducted in 1992 through 2004, based on, left to right, 7825, 9153, and 2718 cases, with confidence level of 99+% for each difference, and with relative proportions of, left to right, .58, .61, and .71)

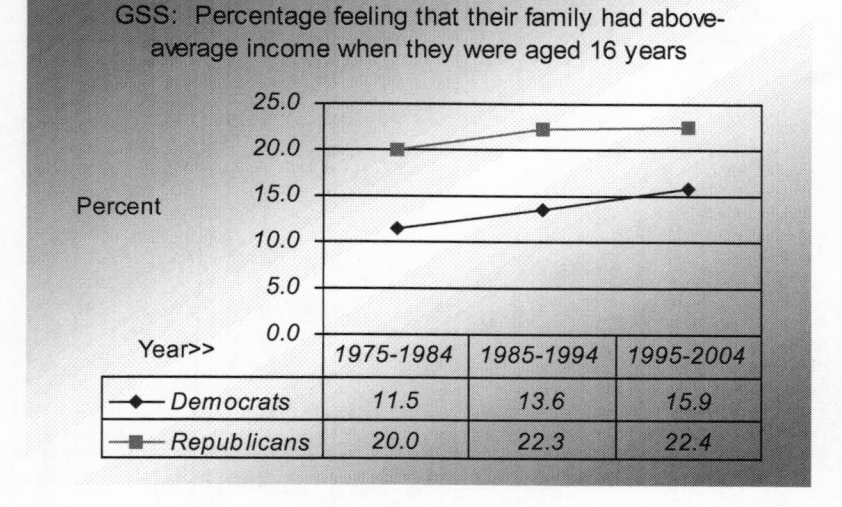

Year>>	1975-1984	1985-1994	1995-2004
Democrats	11.5	13.6	15.9
Republicans	20.0	22.3	22.4

Where They Lived

When I was a kid my parents moved a lot, but I always found them.

— The late Rodney Dangerfield, Comedian[42]

Republicans are more likely to have moved from their childhood cities of residence. The reasons for this disparity are not clear. It is probably partly due to the higher college attendance rates among Republicans, which could have led to post-graduate relocations.

Figure 214. "When you were 16 years old, were you living in this same city?" (combined results of 25 GSS surveys, conducted from 1972 through 2004, based, left to right, on 4731, 2801, 5122, 5164, 4700, 3279, 3467, and 29264 cases, with confidence level of 99+% in all cases, and with relative proportions of, left to right, 1.14, 1.06, 1.23, 1.17, 1.11, 1.13, 1.19, and 1.16)

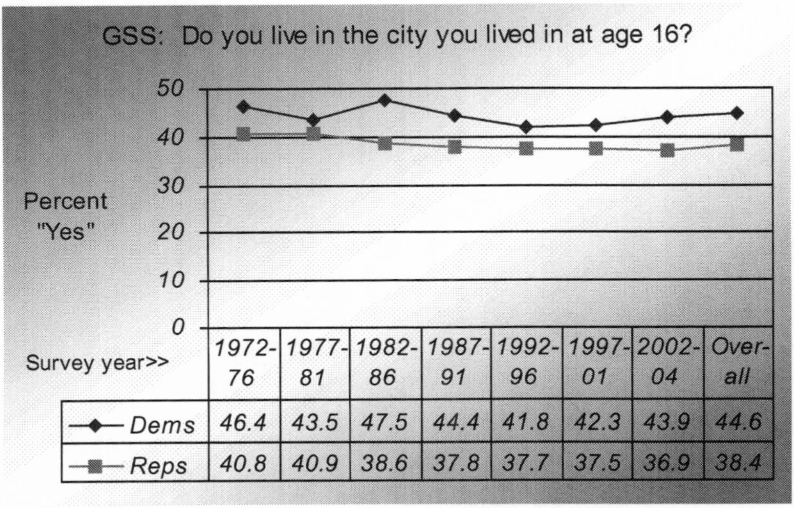

GSS: Do you live in the city you lived in at age 16?							
Survey year>>	1972-76	1977-81	1982-86	1987-91	1992-96	1997-01	2002-04	Over-all
Dems	46.4	43.5	47.5	44.4	41.8	42.3	43.9	44.6
Reps	40.8	40.9	38.6	37.8	37.7	37.5	36.9	38.4

Predictably, Democrats were, as 16-year-olds, more likely to live in the large cities, with populations of 250,000 or more. Democrats and Republicans were equally likely to live in small cities, and Republicans were a little more likely to live in towns, on farms, and in the country.

Childhood Happiness

Those who seek happiness miss it, and those who discuss it, lack it.

— Holbrook Jackson, British journalist[43]

---

42 Dangerfield (attributed), "The Quotations Page."

43 Holbrook Jackson (attributed), "Happiness Quotes," (Josephson Institute of Ethics), Retrieved April 7, 2007, from: http://www.josephsoninstitute.org/quotes/quotehappiness. htm.

In response to a question on the 1992 Economic Values Survey, Republicans were slightly more likely to indicate that they had very happy childhoods.

Figure 215. "Thinking back to your childhood, how happy were you then? Would you say very happy...?" (1992 Economic Values Survey, based on 1340 cases, with confidence level of 97%, and with a relative proportion of .89)

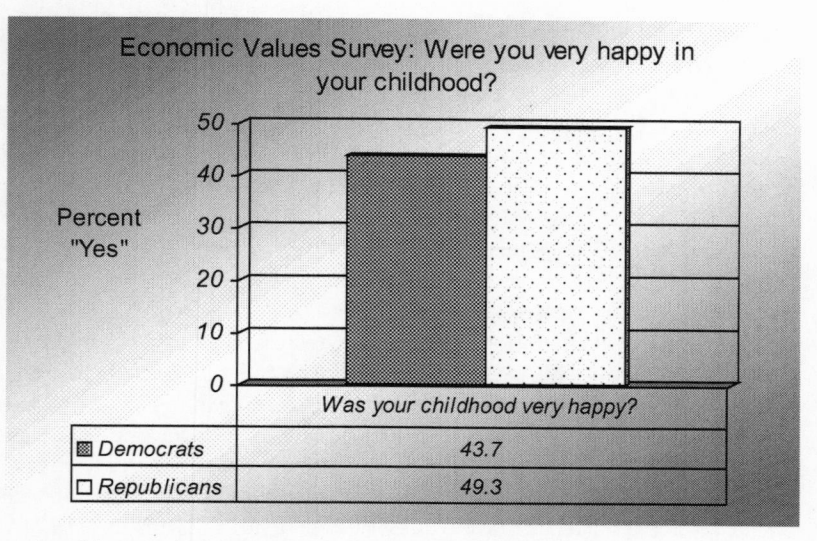

In addition, there is some evidence suggesting that, among young adults, Republicans tend to be happier than Democrats. A 2007 unpublished Northern Kentucky University study of about 60 students, aged 19 to 21 years, reported: "Our research is perhaps the first to show that the higher level of well-being of Republicans can be observed as early as the first few years of college."[44]

Childhood Miscellaneous

Table 49. Other

Question	Survey	Dem % "yes"	Rep % "yes"	No. of cases	Conf %	*RP
When you were a child, did you and your family have dinner together regularly?	Eagleton New Jersey Poll, 2004	77	89	469	+99	.87
When you were a child, did you and your family have regular vacations together?	Eagleton New Jersey Poll, 2004	37	56	469	+99	.66

*RP is relative proportion, which is the Democratic % divided by the Republican %.

---

44 Alyssa Rowland and David E. Hogan, "A Comparison of Well-Being in Republicans, Democrats and Independents," (Northern Kentucky University, 2007).

CONCLUSIONS

Most children have rudimentary political beliefs, loosely based upon the views of their parents. They have similar views because their parents are salient initial influences, and because they share common positions within the social structure. Some political scientists believe that genetics may also be a factor, based upon studies of identical twins.

As children approach young adulthood, a divergence of political perspectives often takes place due to the impact of major world events (such as the Great Depression or Viet Nam), peer pressure in college, and a "rational reevaluation" based upon the unique perspectives of the child versus the parent.

Until 1985, young adults were much less likely than other age groups to identify with the Republican Party. However, the opposite was the case between 1985 and 2004. More recent surveys (2006 and 2007) suggest that young people are avoiding the GOP once again.

Survey evidence suggests that Republicans are more likely to be ex-Democrats than vice versa. The reasons are not clear.

Many of the characteristics distinguishing the current generation of Democrats and Republicans were also evident in their childhood homes and among their parents. Republicans may be slightly more likely than Democrats to state that they had happy childhoods, that their fathers lived in the household, and that their mothers did not work outside of the home when they were young.[45] The parents of a Republican child are more likely to have been affluent and well-educated, and more likely to have avoided divorce or other marital discord.

Republican fathers are more likely than their Democratic counterparts to have worked in relatively "prestigious" occupations in professional, managerial, or technical fields. The mothers of Republicans are more likely to have worked in sales or technical jobs.

A change from the previous generation concerns family size. Whereas Democratic families used to have more children than Republican families, in recent years the number of children is likely to be about the same.

---

45 The survey regarding happiness was conducted in 1992, and may not be representative of the feelings of Democrats and Republicans of other eras.

CHAPTER 11: DO DEVIANTS GROW UP TO BE REPUBLICANS?

INTRODUCTION

Ruminative 3-year-olds

Remember the whiny, insecure kid in nursery school, the one who always thought everyone was out to get him, and was always running to the teacher with complaints? Chances are he grew up to be a conservative.

— Columnist Kurt Kleiner, commenting on report in Journal of Research into Personality.[1]

In 2006, some Berkeley psychology professors reported the results of a 20-year longitudinal study of 95 "conservatives" and "liberals," which commenced when the subjects were just 3 years old. Professor Jack Block and his associates concluded that the 3-year-olds who eventually became liberals were:

... resourceful and initializing, autonomous, proud of their blossoming accomplishments, confident and self-involving ... bright, competitive, and as having high standards [and exhibited] self-assertiveness, talkativeness, curiosity, openness in expressing negative feelings and in teasing ...[2]

On the other hand, the researchers judged the future conservatives to be:

... visibly deviant, feeling unworthy and therefore ready to feel guilty, easily offended, anxious when confronted by uncertainties, distrustful of others, ruminative, and rigidifying when under stress ... indecisive and vac-

---

1 Kurt Kleiner, "How to Spot a Baby Conservative," *Toronto Star*, March 19, 2006.
2 Jack Block and Jeanne H. Block, "Nursery School Personality and Political Orientation Two Decades Later," *Journal of Research in Personality* 40, no. 5 (2006): 6.

illating, easily victimized, inhibited, fearful, self-unrevealing, adult-seeking, shy, neat, compliant, [and] anxious when confronted by ambiguity ...[3]

It's worth noting that these kids were practically toddlers when they were assessed to have these psychological traits. At that young age, some of us had different priorities — such as talking and potty training.

What happened to the little kids when they became 23-year-old adults? In some respects, the liberal-conservative chasm grew even larger. Whereas the conservatives were "uncomfortable with uncertainty" and "emotionally bland," the liberals were judged to be "introspective, life contemplative, esthetically responsive ... vital, motivationally aware, perceptive, fluent," and god-like. (OK, I added the last trait.) In addition, the psychologists found that being liberal "correlates positively with intelligence," and the liberal men and women, at age 23, had significantly higher IQs.[4] Professor Block will not be asked to speak to the Heritage Foundation any time soon.

> The more they talk, the more being called a Liberal sounds like a compliment.
>
> — Douglas Giles, ProgressiveThought.net, 1997

Why analyze the Berkeley study?

In this odd-ball chapter, which doesn't fit the format of any other, we simply analyze one academic study and its many defects. It may seem that we are straying from our topic since the academic study does not directly concern Democrats and Republicans. However, there are good reasons to go through this analytical exercise:

- It demonstrates why this book is based upon Democrat-Republican comparisons rather than the oft-used, but less meaningful, liberal-conservative paradigm.
- It shows that Democratic conservatives are the polar opposites of Republican conservatives. Democratic conservatives generally have the least amount of education, while Republican conservatives tend to have the most.
- It helps us reconcile the findings in this book (concerning Democrats and Republicans) to the dissimilar findings in the study (concerning liberals and conservatives).
- It reminds us to beware of academic studies that are light on data and heavy on interpretations, assumptions, and analysis.

If you've been reading this book in the normal order, you know that Republicans are just as (or more) politically well-informed, educated, happy, and successful in business and personal life as are Democrats. In addition, there are survey data suggesting that Republicans were, as adolescents, at least as happy Democrats, as adolescents. (See page 281.)

---

3 Ibid.: 8.
4 Ibid.: 9-10.

Why are the findings of this book in conflict with the Berkeley results? There are two reasons. First, generalities about liberals and conservatives are never fully applicable to Democrats and Republicans. Second, the Berkeley study was so severely flawed that its conclusions are not applicable, for any purpose and to any degree. The truth of these statements will become apparent as we diagnose each aspect of this classic example of academic "smoke and mirrors."

Flawed research and reporting

Experiments with laboratory rats have shown that, if one psychologist in the room laughs at something a rat does, all of the other psychologists in the room will laugh equally. Nobody wants to be left holding the joke.

— Garrison Keillor, American humorist and author[5]

The Berkeley study was flawed in regard to design, execution, and reporting:

1. In part, the study relied on the self-identifications of the participating subjects. Self-identifications are fine when everyone agrees on the definitions used. However, for the liberal-conservative paradigm self-identifications are not useful because the terms "conservative" and "liberal" (as used in the United States) are vague and subjective, and convey different meanings to different people.

2. Recognizing the problem identified in item 1, above, the Berkeley researchers supplemented the self-identifications with their own assessments of each participant's degree of liberalism and conservatism. That was a huge mistake that added circularity to the study. The final results of the study were preordained by the assessments made by the Berkeley crew.

3. The study failed to recognize and report that it included a disproportionally high percentage of Democratic conservatives versus Republican conservatives. These two categories of conservatives are not interchangeable. In addition, the study incorrectly assumed a linear relationship between the personality traits of the participants and their degree of liberalism or conservatism. More likely, there is a U-shaped relationship. These mistakes led to false conclusions.

4. Researcher bias may have skewed the jargon used to describe psychological and social traits of liberals and conservatives. In addition, important traits were selectively included in and excluded from the study's final summary, giving a false impression of study results.

A full discussion of each deficiency follows:

---

5 Garrison Keillor, *We Are Still Married: Stories and Letters* (New York: Penquin, 1990), Introduction.

DETAILS OF A SERIOUSLY FLAWED STUDY

The terms "liberal" and "conservative" are too vague.

> Have the adjectives — and nouns — "liberal" and "conservative"
> become meaningless? Not quite. But almost. Inflation first weak-
> ened, then liquefied much of their meaning.
>
> — John Lucas, Author[6]

In America few people vote for candidates of the Conservative Party or Liberal Party, so there are no widely-held, institution-related definitions of the terms.
Unlike the terms "Democrat" and "Republican," we can't link the meanings of
"liberal" and "conservative" to party platforms or political candidates (with rare
exceptions). That forces us to use our own, individual definitions.

A huge number of Democrats describe themselves as "conservative." Figure
216, below, shows General Social Survey (GSS) results for Democrats. They were
asked if they thought of themselves as liberal, moderate, or conservative. (The
results for moderates are not shown.)

*Figure 216. Do you think of yourself as liberal or conservative? (Democrats surveyed by vari-
ous GSS surveys conducted in 1972 through 2006, based on, left to right, 2952, 5112, 4417, 3170, and
15476 cases)*

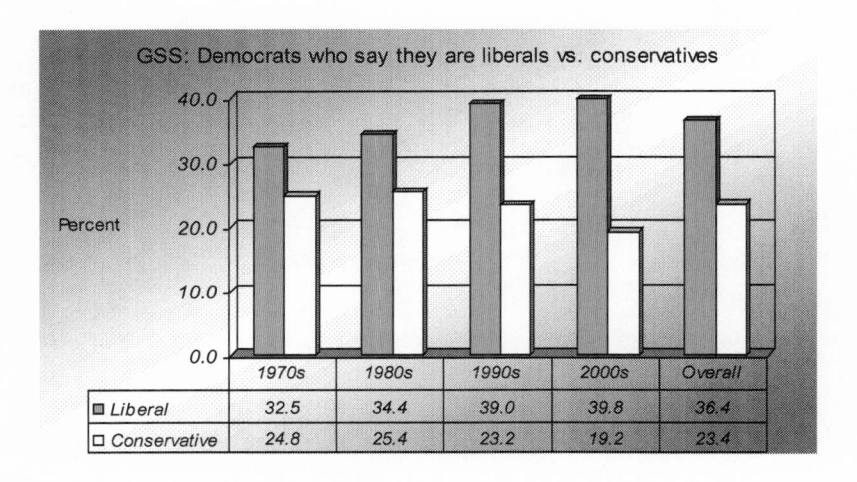

	1970s	1980s	1990s	2000s	Overall
■ Liberal	32.5	34.4	39.0	39.8	36.4
□ Conservative	24.8	25.4	23.2	19.2	23.4

In the "Overall" column, on the right side of the chart, we see that, during the
last 30 years, for every 3 Democrats identifying as liberal there were about 2 who
felt they were conservative. Do these Democrats really reflect the typical image
of a conservative? Do they reflect your vision of a conservative?

---

6 John Lucas, "What Is Left? What Is Right? Does It Matter?," *The American Conservative* (August
28, 2006), Retrieved October 19, 2006, from http://www.amconmag.com/2006/2006_08_28/
index1.html.

Before answering, consider a couple of surveys involving recent presidential elections. In 1988, NES asked Democrats to classify themselves as "liberal," "moderate," or "conservative." In that particular survey, more Democrats said they were conservative than liberal or moderate (45% conservative, 17% moderate, and 34% liberal). However, the overwhelming majority of Democrats (83%) said they would be voting for Michael Dukakis rather than George H. Bush. Of those describing themselves as conservative, 77 percent said they would be voting for Dukakis.

The same pattern held in 1996 with regard to the Clinton-Dole race. Far more Democrats claimed to be conservative than liberal or moderate, but nearly all Democrats (about 94%) said they would be voting for Clinton, rather than Dole. This included 96 percent of the Democrats claiming to be "conservative." These results are revealing because most people would probably say that Bush (the elder) was more conservative than Dukakis, and Dole was more "conservative" than Clinton.

> What is a "Conservative"...? It all depends on what you're conserving. A true revolutionary in a truly decent and humane society is almost surely going to be a fool, an ass, a tyrant, or, most likely, all three. A conservative in a truly evil regime is even more likely to be the same.
>
> — Jonah Goldberg, Columnist[7]

This doesn't mean there is a "correct" definition or an "incorrect" definition of conservative, and it doesn't mean that a Democrat can't be one. Rather, it means that we each have our own definition, and this fact can undermine the validity of conclusions about self-identified conservatives. For example, a person might think of himself as conservative because he is easily embarrassed by nudity or likes old-fashioned movies. Yet, that same individual might believe in socialized medicine, unilateral disarmament, and redistribution of wealth via the tax code.[8]

The term "liberal" is also subject to varying interpretations. The proportion of Republicans saying they are liberal is shown in Figure 217, below. Although it is substantially less than the proportion of Democrats claiming to be conservative, it is significant.

Figure 217. Do you think of yourself as liberal, moderate, or conservative? (Moderates are not shown.) (Republicans surveyed by various GSS surveys conducted from 1972 through 2006, based on, left to right, 1582, 3338, 3670, 2537, and 11127 cases)

---

7 Goldberg, "What Is a 'Conservative'?."

8 Many Democrats see themselves as "conservatives," and many also regard their political leadership to be conservative. In a 1998-1999 Multi Investigator Study, 661 Democrats and Republicans were asked: "In general, thinking about the political parties in Washington, would you say Democrats are more conservative than Republicans, or Republicans are more conservative than Democrats?" By 52.4 to 47.6 percent, Democrats perceived the Democratic Party to be more conservative than the Republican party. Only 16.1 percent of Republicans shared that view.

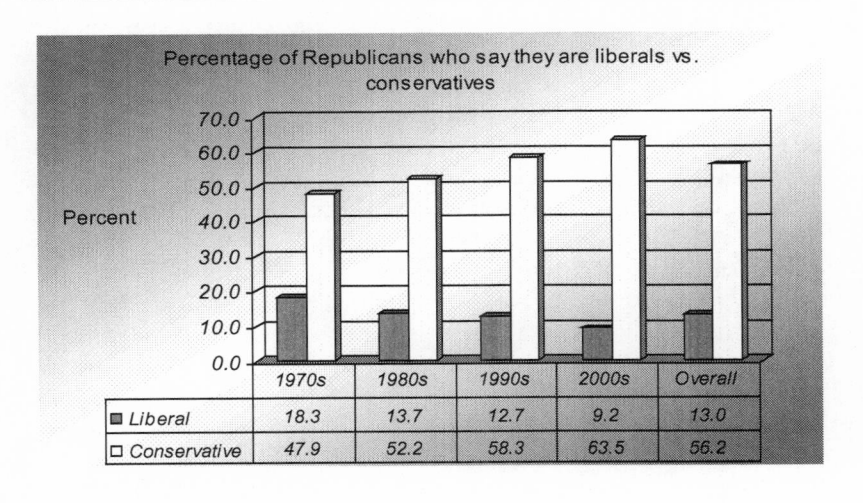

	1970s	1980s	1990s	2000s	Overall
■ Liberal	18.3	13.7	12.7	9.2	13.0
□ Conservative	47.9	52.2	58.3	63.5	56.2

We don't know why some Republicans think they are liberals. Perhaps they feel liberal because they are friendly, caring, flexible, and "people-oriented." Yet, those same Republicans might advocate repeal of the estate tax, welfare cuts, and an aggressive and militaristic foreign policy.

The bottom line is this: Although the terms "liberal" and "conservative" are a pervasive and indispensable part of our language, we must be cautious when making broad generalizations on the basis of those terms.

> [T]he terms conservative and liberal will continue to be used and misused as we, who doubt we are a part of either, stumble in the swamp, looking for a solid place to put our feet.
>
> — Nicholas von Hoffman, Newspaper columnist and author[9]

As discussed below, the Berkeley researchers tried to supplement the self-identifications with their own standardized definitions of "liberal" and "conservative." Unfortunately, this just made matters worse.

Researcher assessments added circularity.

Many sociologists, political scientists, and psychologists know that there is a problem with having people self-identify as liberals or conservatives, and the authors of the Berkeley study were not exceptions. Unfortunately, their attempt to remedy the problem made matters much worse.

Although participants in the Berkeley study were classified as liberals or conservatives based upon self-identifications, they were also classified by the researchers on the basis of their responses to standard measurement devices, such

---

9 Nicholas von Hoffman, "What Is Left? What Is Right? Does It Matter?," *The American Conservative* (August 28, 2006), Retrieved October 19, 2006, from http://www.amconmag.com/2006/2006_08_28/index1.html.

as the Kerlinger Liberalism Scale, the Kerlinger Conservatism Scale, and Mc-Closky's "Dimensions of Political Tolerance. By examining these measurement devices we can readily see the pitfalls inherent in their usage.

Kerlinger, for example, created lists of words or phrases designed to elicit positive or negative reactions, depending upon one's political ideology.[10] One Kerlinger phrase is "government price controls." Presumably, a liberal would respond positively to that phrase, and a conservative would not.

Another phrase is "law and order" — designed to get a positive reaction from conservatives. Some of the other Kerlinger words and phrases, used in the Berkeley research, are shown in Table 50.

Table 50. Phrases from Kerlinger's "Referent Scale" (REF-IX, 1984)

Kerlinger's exact word or phrase	Feeling positive about the phrase suggests you are a:
"Moral standards"	Conservative
"Social stability"	Conservative
"Authority"	Conservative
"Freedom"	Liberal
"Law and order"	Conservative
"Social Status"	Conservative
"Social Change"	Liberal
"Sexual freedom"	Liberal

There is a problem with using such listings (as in Table 50): The ultimate conclusions about conservatives and liberals are pre-ordained at the moment participants are categorized by the researchers.

> Circularity: The reason I keep insisting that there was a relationship between Iraq and Saddam and al Qaeda [is] because there was a relationship between Iraq and al Qaeda.
>
> — President George W. Bush[11]

In Table 51, below, we see the same Kerlinger words and phrases used to classify subjects as being either liberal or conservative. However, there is an additional column showing some of the conclusions reached in the Berkeley study. Aren't they a surprise?!

---

10 Fred N. Kerlinger, *Liberalism and Conservatism* (New Jersey: Lawrence Erlbaum Associates, 1984).

11 David E. Sanger and Robin Toner, "Bush and Cheney Talk Strongly of Qaeda Links with Hussein," *The New York Times*, June 18 2004.

Table 51. The connection between the Kerlinger phrases used to classify participants as "conservative" or "liberal," and the final conclusions of the Berkeley study

What goes in »»»»		Dictates what comes out
If you liked this phrase …	You were classified by Berkeley researchers as a:	Which led the researchers to this astonishing conclusion:
Moral standards	Conservative	A conservative: "Is moralistic and self-righteous;" "Judges self, others in conventional terms;" "Makes moral judgments"
Social stability	Conservative	A conservative: "Is uncomfortable with uncertainty"
Authority	Conservative	A conservative: "Is power oriented"
Freedom	Liberal	A liberal: "Tends to be rebellious, nonconforming"
Law and order	Conservative	A conservative: "Behaves in an ethically consistent manner"
Social Status	Conservative	A conservative: "Compares self to others"
Social Change	Liberal	A liberal: "Tends to be rebellious, nonconforming"
Sexual freedom	Liberal	A liberal: "Enjoys sensuous experiences"

The conclusions shown on the right side of the table could be predicted by the words and phrases used in the classification process (left 2 columns of the table). For example, if we classify, as "conservative," participants who feel favorably about "Moral standards," we should not be surprised to find that these conservatives (as we just defined and selected them) tend to "make moral judgments." And, if we classify as conservative, those who feel positively towards "Social status," should we not expect to find that these conservatives (as we just defined and selected them) "compare [themselves] to others"? The study simply spits out the very same stereotypes put into it. The circularity of the process is illustrated in Figure 218, below.

In short, the use of these measurement devices added a large degree of circularity to the Berkeley study.

> If goodness is a defining attribute of God, then God cannot be used to define goodness. If we do so, we are guilty of circular reasoning.

> — Minister Ray Cotton[12]

---

12 Ray Cotton, "Morality Apart from God: Is It Possible?," *Probe Ministries International* (1997), Retrieved November 30, 2007, from http://www.leaderu.com/orgs/probe/docs/god-ethi.html.

Figure 218. The circularity inherent in the use of measurement "scales"

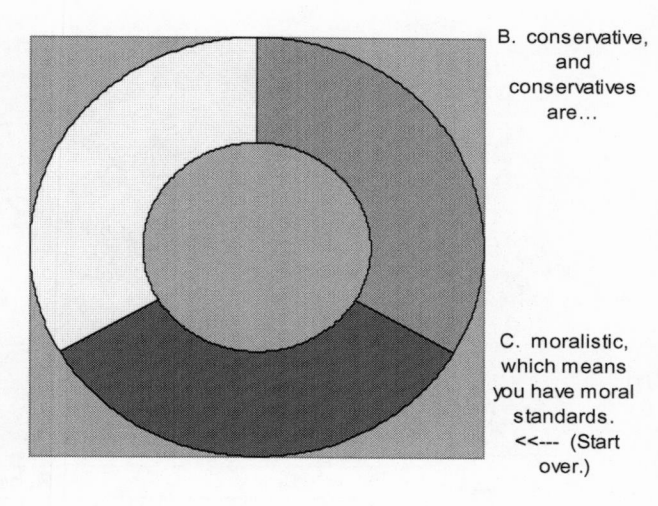

START
A. Moral
standards
make you
a...-->>

B. conservative,
and
conservatives
are...

C. moralistic,
which means
you have moral
standards.
<<--- (Start
over.)

Reality check — What did the Professor say about this?

Professor Block disagreed that the study suffered from definitional vague-
ness. He told me that the tests administered to the 23-year-olds in the study
were specifically designed by social scientists to measure "relatively liberal or
relatively conservative inclinations." He also noted that the several indices used
were standardized and averaged to produce an overall result that was more valid
than any single indicator.[13]

Block also disagreed with the circularity criticism. He pointed out that it is
important to distinguish between what one says about himself and the opinions formed by qualified assessors on the basis of various interactions with that
person.

Did Democrats make the conservatives look bad?

A Curious Pattern

In Chapter 2 there is a discussion of political ideology and its correlation
with education level achieved. As noted, there is no clear association between
political philosophy and educational level, in general; however, there is a curious
pattern involving conservative Democrats and liberal Republicans. A chart from
page 87 is reproduced below.

*Figure 219, replicating Figure 71: What is your "highest year of school completed"? (GSS sur-
veys conducted in 1977 through 2006 of, left to right, 599, 2845, 2998, 8644, 4023, 4095, and 875*

---

13 Jack Block, e-mail letters to author, 2005 and 2006.

cases, with confidence level of at least 99+% for all differences except the one designated "Slightly liberal," for which there is 95% confidence level)

GSS: Dem and Rep education based on political philosophy

Political views>>	Very Lib	Lib	Slight Lib	Mod	Slight cons	Cons	Very cons
Dems	12.9	13.7	13.2	12.2	12.4	11.7	10.4
Reps	11.6	12.5	13.0	12.8	14.0	13.9	13.4

Years educ — axis values: 14.0, 12.0, 10.0, 8.0, 6.0, 4.0

Legend: Dems — Reps

Look carefully at the chart and you will notice that liberal Democrats tend to have more education than liberal Republicans, while conservative Republicans tend to have more education than conservative Democrats. The gap on the conservative side of the graph (the right side) is particularly large. In fact, Republican conservatives have more education than any other segment, while Democratic conservatives have less education than any other segment.

> Seeing ignorance is the curse of God, Knowledge the wing where-with we fly to heaven...
>
> — William Shakespeare, King Henry the Sixth, Act 4, Scene 7

The pattern shown above can be found in several other data sources pertaining to education and intelligence. In Figure 220, below, we see percentages of liberals and conservatives with high school diplomas. These ideological groups are further divided by party affiliation. On the left side of the graphic we see the percentages of liberals who have acquired high school diplomas (or higher degrees). Note that Democratic liberals are more educated than Republican liberals. On the right side of the chart, we see similar information for conservatives. We find that Republican conservatives are much more educated than Democratic conservatives. In fact, Democratic conservatives are only 73 percent as likely as the Republican conservatives to have a high school diploma (65.6/89.8 = 73%).

Figure 220. Percentage of liberals and conservatives with at least a high school diploma, broken out by political party identification (GSS surveys conducted in 1977 through 2006, based on, left to right, 3443 and 4967 cases, with confidence level of at least 99%, and with relative proportions of, left to right, 1.08 and .73)

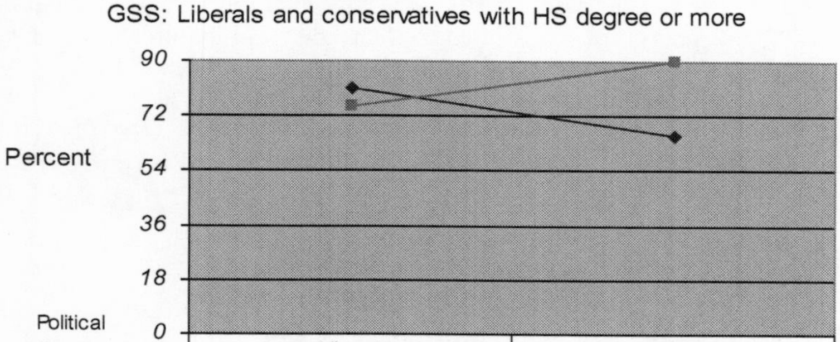

GSS: Liberals and conservatives with HS degree or more

Political views>>	Liberal	Conservative
Dems	80.8	65.6
Reps	75.1	89.8

Figure 221, below, also illustrates this phenomenon. We see one of the analytical questions first presented in Chapter 2. This time, however, the results are broken out by political ideology as well as party identification. Liberal Democrats and conservative Republicans were the most likely to correctly answer the question: "How are an egg and seed alike?"

Figure 221. "How are an egg and seed alike?" (GSS survey conducted in 1994, based on. left to right, 243 and 384 cases, with confidence level of, left to right, 98% and 99+%, and with relative proportions of, left to right, 2.70 and .37)

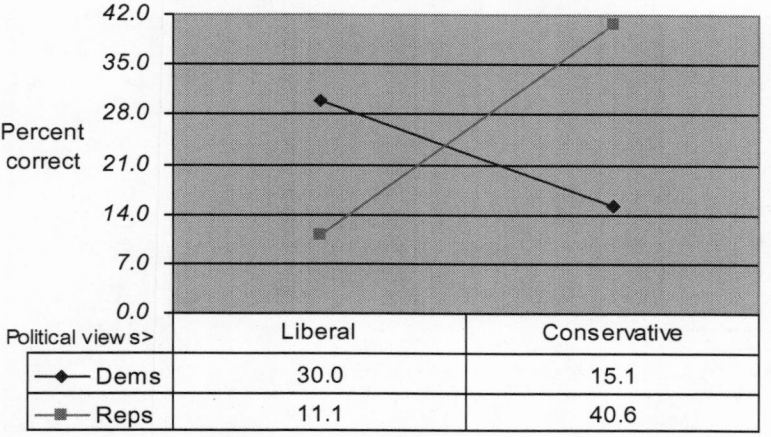

GSS: How are an egg and seed alike?

Political views>	Liberal	Conservative
Dems	30.0	15.1
Reps	11.1	40.6

> A conservative is a man who sits and thinks, mostly sits.
> — President Woodrow Wilson[14]

A final and very compelling example of this phenomenon is offered. As noted in Chapter 2 (page 78), NES interviewers are usually asked to give an assessment of the "apparent intelligence' of each survey participant. In Figure 222, below, we see a summary of the assessments made in each of the surveys taken in 1996 through 2004. This graphic is limited to Democrats and Republicans who self-identified as "conservatives." (No liberals are included.)

Figure 222. NES interviewer's assessment of apparent intelligence (NES surveys conducted in 1996 through 2004, based on. left to right, 411, 289, 590, 379, and 272 cases, with confidence level of 99+% for all differences, and with relative proportions of, left to right, .58, .51, .59, .70, and .51)

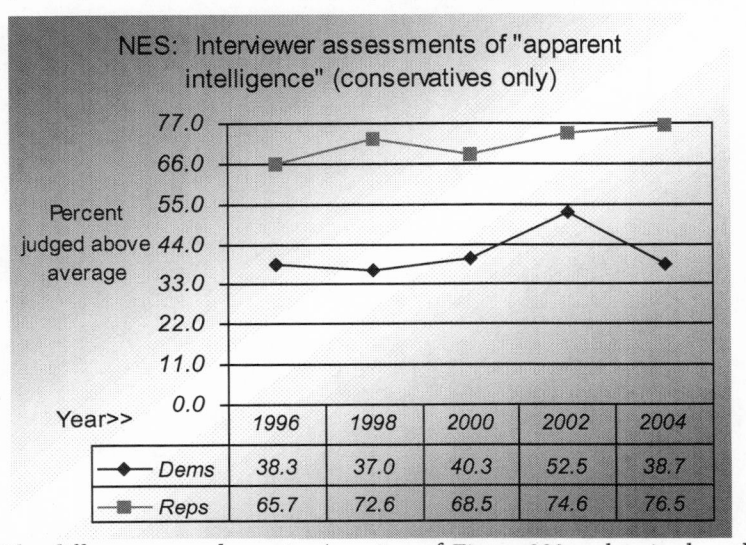

The differences are dramatic. A review of Figure 222 makes it clear that Democratic and Republican conservatives are as different as night and day. Most Republican conservatives were judged to have above-average intelligence, but only a minority of Democratic conservatives was given this rating. Because the "conservatives" analyzed in the Berkeley study all came from a Democratic community, the study's conclusions about conservatives are suspect.[15]

A U-Shaped Relationship

> The swing voters — I like to refer to them as the idiot voters because they don't have set philosophical principles. You're either a liberal or you're a conservative if you have an IQ above a toaster.
>
> — Author and political activist Ann Coulter[16]

---

14 President Woodrow Wilson (attributed), "The Quotations Page."

15 A 2005 analysis of Berkeley faculty found a 10 to 1 ratio of registered Democrats to registered Republicans.

16 John Hawkins, "RWN's Favorite Ann Coulter Quotes," (Right Wing News, September 4, 2004), Retrieved April 6, 2007, from: http://www.rightwingnews.com/quotes/coulter.php.

In Figure 220, we compared liberal and conservative educational achieve-ment, and we broke out the results by party affiliation. That chart is reproduced here (as Figure 223), with two changes: The educational achievements of politi-cal independents have been added, and the results are all shown on a single line (instead of two lines).

Figure 223. Percentage of liberals and conservatives with at least a high school diploma, broken out by political party identification and political ideology (GSS surveys conducted in 1975 through 2004, based on, left to right, 2911, 1722, 532, 1523, 1775, and 3444 cases, with overall confidence level of the sequence of 99+%)

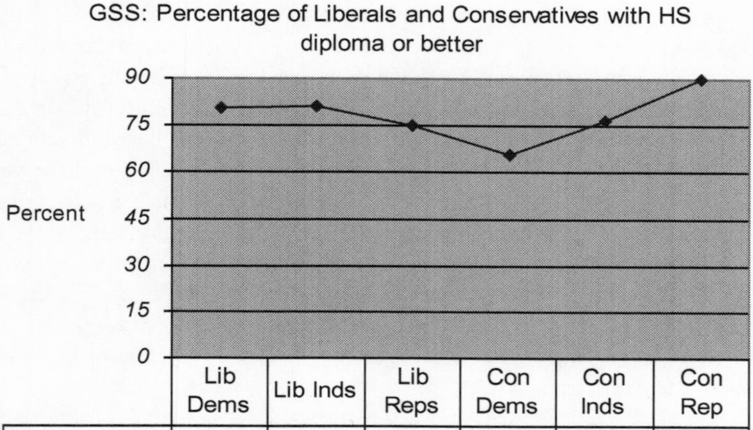

GSS: Percentage of Liberals and Conservatives with HS diploma or better

	Lib Dems	Lib Inds	Lib Reps	Con Dems	Con Inds	Con Rep
Ideol/Pty	80.8	81.4	75.1	65.6	76.7	89.8

By putting all results on a single line, the "U-shaped" relationship is apparent. If we assume that the most ardent liberals are the Democratic liberals and the least ardent liberals are the Republican liberals, then it appears that education declines as the intensity of the liberal commitment declines. On the other hand, it seems that the level of education increases among those who are increasingly more conservative (i.e., as we move from conservative Democrats to conservative Republicans).[17]

The importance of the U-shaped relationship, shown in Figure 223, can not be overstated. If we didn't see the right side of the chart, we would almost surely reach a false conclusion. For example, if our sample contained only a "few par-ticipants tilting towards conservatism" (as was true with the Berkeley study), we would falsely conclude that people who are more conservative are likely to have less education. That conclusion would be ironic, since conservatives are likely to have the most education.

---

17 Credit for recognizing the potential significance of the U-shaped relationship must be given to Jim Lindgren, a law professor at Northwestern University. Posting on The Volokh Conspiracy (www.Volokh.com, March 23, 2006), Lindgren noted that the Berkeley study could be seriously flawed if the liberal-conservative continuum was not linear.

Indeed, this is probably what happened in the Berkeley study, which comprised two groups of unequal size: a huge group of liberals/moderates and a few people leaning towards conservatism.[18]

> To be conservative requires no brains whatsoever. Cabbages, cows and conifers are conservatives, and are so stupid they don't even know it. All that is basically required is acceptance of what exists.
>
> — British journalist Colin Welch[19]

Reality check — How do we know there were few or no conservatives?

In their report, the Berkeley researchers concede that most of the 95 participants were either liberal or moderate, with "relatively few participants *tilting toward* conservatism" (emphasis added). And, in recent e-mail correspondence, Professor Block indicated that participants were simply rank-ordered along a liberal/conservative continuum. He added that the researchers did not "breakout" the participants into liberal or conservative categories, so he could not readily identify the number of conservatives who participated (assuming there were any). Given the expansive and controversial claims made by the Berkeley group, it is amazing that no effort was made (apparently) to ascertain that an adequate number of conservatives was included among the participants (or that *any* were included). It is possible that the continuum described by Block merely stretched from liberals to moderates, without extending to conservatives.[20]

In addition, Columnist Michelle Malkin reported, and Professor Block apparently confirmed, that many of the study participants were children of faculty and staff at UC at Berkeley – noted as a liberal university.[21] It seems highly doubtful that the 23-year-old child of a Berkeley professor would be wearing a George W. Bush campaign button.[22]

When the possibility of a U-shaped relationship was raised with Professor Block, he maintained that the analysis was linear; however, he also seemed to concede that he had not tested this belief, stating that the samples were "too small to have enough statistical power to test that U-shape hypothesis." Block

---

18 Block and Block, "Nursery School Personality and Political Orientation Two Decades Later," 4.

19 Colin Welch (attributed), "Columbia World of Quotations," (Columbia University Press, 1996).

20 Block's statements to me are in conflict with a statement he (allegedly) made to online columnist Justin Berton in April, 2006. When Berton asked Block if his conclusions were based upon the experiences of a handful of conservatives, Block responded "absolutely wrong." See *Growing up Right* by Justin Berton in the East Bay Express at http://www.eastbayexpress.com/news/growing_up_right/Content?oid=290796.

21 The Berkeley faculty have a ten to one ratio of Democrats to Republicans according to a voter registration study performed in 2005 by Daniel B. Klein, Associate professor of economics at Santa Clara University (http://lsb.scu.edu/~dklein/)

22 Credit for identifying the venue of the study, the small number of conservatives, and the likely impact of these facts on the study results must be given to Michelle Malkin ("Who are the Whiny Kids?," www.Michellemalkin.com, March 23, 2006).

pointed out that the analysis used "reliable observational data" - both when the subjects were in nursery school and when they were young adults. He also said that comparing the two sets of data produced surprising findings, "which many have over interpreted and apparently found threatening...."[23]

Researcher bias

Skewed Descriptions

> Argument now masquerades as conversation. Spin, the political columnist E.J. Dionne wrote recently, "obliterates the distinction between persuasion and deception."
>
> — Malcolm Gladwell, The New Yorker, July 6, 1998

Is the glass half empty, or half full? It depends upon who is taking the drink. Similarly, the specific findings of the Berkeley study can be viewed as negative or positive, depending upon one's ideological perspective. Table 52, below, shows all of the Berkeley findings for conservative young men aged 23 years. The first finding is obvious, and adds no useful information. The other 7 findings seem to have negative connotations.[24]

Table 52. Specific findings of the Berkeley study for conservative men

Specific findings for conservative men from the Berkeley study (Most have negative connotations.)
"Favors conservative values"
"Uncomfortable with uncertainty"
"Behaves in sex-typed manner"
"Judges self, others in conventional terms"
"Tends to proffer advice"
"Makes moral judgments"
"Compares self to others"
"Is power oriented"

You will find the same 8 findings in Table 53, below; however, this time I have provided my own more positive "spin."

Conversely, the positive study findings for liberal men can be reworded to give them a negative "spin." For example, the finding that liberal men are "introspective, concerned w/self" can be recast as "self-centered." And, the finding that liberal men are "concerned w/philosophical problems" can be re-phrased to indicate that they get "bogged down with impractical considerations." This begs the question: Does the Berkeley study tell us anything at all about liberals

---

23 Block.

24 Block and Block, "Nursery School Personality and Political Orientation Two Decades Later," 9.

and conservatives? Or, does it simply tell us about the ideological biases of a few Berkeley researchers?

Table 53. Specific findings of the Berkeley study for conservative men, compared to my "more positive" expressions

Specific findings for conservative men (verbatim from the Berkeley study)	My more positive expression for the finding
"Favors conservative values"	(No comment, since the finding is obvious)
"Uncomfortable with uncertainty"	Interested in resolving uncertainties
"Behaves in sex-typed manner"	Comfortable with sexual identity
"Judges self, others in conventional terms"	Uses established norms to make realistic judgments
"Tends to proffer advice"	Willing to give helpful advice
"Makes moral judgments"	Strives to be a moral person
"Compares self to others"	Displays healthy competitive spirit
"Is power oriented"	Respects authority

interesting

Skewed Summary

There is but one art, to omit.

— Robert Louis Stevenson, Scottish novelist and poet[25]

Notwithstanding, the Berkeley study did report a few positive findings with regard to conservative young women, and it offered a handful of negative findings pertaining to liberal women. For some reason, however, none of those findings made it to the final study summary. For example, the detail indicated that conservative women were "ethically consistent" and liberal women were "self-dramatizing, histrionic," yet those findings did not get into the study summaries. Here is the entire summary for liberal women. Where is the reference to "self-dramatizing, histrionic"?

> At age 23, relatively Liberal young women are assessed independently as: vital, motivationally aware, perceptive, fluent, bright, with extensive and esthetic interests, somewhat non-conforming.

Here is the entire summary for conservative women. Where is the reference to "ethically consistent"?

> Relatively Conservative young women were characterized as: conservative, uneasy with uncertainties, conventional, as sex-typed in their personal behavior and social perceptions, emotionally bland, appearing calm, and candid but also somewhat moralistic.[26]

25 Robert Louis Stevenson, *The Letters of Robert Louis Stevenson: Volume One, 1984– April 1874* (London: Yale University Press, 1994).

26 Block and Block, "Nursery School Personality and Political Orientation Two Decades Later," 9.

It seems that the researchers had a point to make, and didn't want any incon-venient findings to get in the way of that point.

> Personally, I don't like the terms "liberal" and "conservative." I find them simplistic and largely meaningless.

> — Joseph Farah, Editor and CEO, World Net Daily[27]

CONCLUSIONS

Making generalizations about "liberals" and "conservatives" is fraught with peril. Self-identifications are unreliable and misleading because each of us de-fines these terms differently. Further, classifying people in accordance with es-tablished definitional yardsticks leads to preordained, circular results. For these reasons, I believe that the Democrat-Republican paradigm leads to more mean-ingful comparisons.

In terms of education and intellectual ability, it appears that Republican lib-erals are quite different from Democratic liberals, with the Democrats generally being more successful. On the other hand, Republican conservatives tend to have far more education and intellectual ability than their Democratic complements.

The Berkeley study was probably doomed to failure because it overlooked the above factors. In addition:

1. The researchers incorrectly assumed a linear relationship between the personality traits of the participants and their degree of liberalism or conservatism. In fact, there is probably a U-shaped relationship. In addition, the study's population comprised a large number of liberals and moderates, a small number of conservative "leaners," and few if any strongly conservative participants. These two factors — the U-shaped relationship and the small number of conservatives — probably led to false conclusions.

2. There was "spin" in the jargon used to describe individual psychological/social factors. Neutral or positive traits were converted to negative traits by the choice of adjectives used.

3. The study summaries excluded positive conservative traits and negative liberal traits. These omissions raise questions regarding the objectivity of the researchers involved in the study.

---

27 Joseph Farah, "Why Liberal Read More Books," *WorldNetDaily* (2007), Retrieved October 2, 2007, from http://www.worldnetdaily.com/news/article.asp?ARTICLE_ID=57290.

Chapter 12: Lessons to be Learned — In My Opinion

Introduction

Lots of Little Differences

> Nothing is particularly hard if you divide it into small jobs. There are no big problems; there are just a lot of little problems.
>
> — Henry Ford, Industrialist[1]

I'd like to propose a corollary to those wise words of Henry Ford: There are no big differences distinguishing Democrats from Republicans; there are just a lot of little differences. But, little differences add up. Although it appears that the average Republican is happier, more prosperous, and (arguably) more successful than his Democratic complement; this is not necessarily due to a "big difference" in lifestyles, abilities, or opportunities.[2] Rather, it may be (partly) attributable to several small choices made differently by Democrats and Republicans. Some of these are basic choices that are available to most Americans.

Of course, some people are victimized by forces beyond their control. For example, no woman decides to become a widow (with a few notable exceptions), and people don't choose to be victimized by discrimination, disability, or illness. However, it seems that the cumulative effect of decisions regarding marriage, children, education, work, etc. critically affects the quality of life for Democrats and Republicans, and their descendants. It may even account for their different political philosophies.

---

1 Henry Ford (attributed), "The Quotations Page."

2 The argument for Republicans being "more successful" would be based on their attainment of higher educational levels, occupations with higher "prestige" scores and more supervisory responsibility, and lower incidents of marital discord and divorce.

In this chapter we revisit each of the preceding chapters to see what lessons can be learned. These are lessons that pertain to Democrats, Republicans, educators and legislators.

Finally, there have been few personal opinions in this book, heretofore (Chapter 9, "Happiness," being a major exception). The goal was to let the numbers "do the talking." However, the muzzle is now gone so be prepared for large doses of hypothesis, conjecture, and righteous opinion.

DETAILS

A lesson from Chapter 1: Delay having that first child

> Clearly, preventing teen pregnancy is a highly effective and efficient way to reduce poverty and improve overall child and family well-being.
>
> — National Campaign to Prevent Teen and Unplanned Pregnancies

One of the most significant lifestyle differences between Democrats and Republicans is the age of procreation. On average, Democrats are about 13 months younger than Republicans when they start having children.[3] In addition, Democratic women are about 60 percent more likely than Republican women, and Democratic men are about twice as likely as Republican men, to have children during their teen years.

At the beginning of this chapter we discussed the many choices that are made differently by Democrats and Republicans — choices which can ultimately result in significant differences in happiness and prosperity. This is one of those choices.

Teenagers who have children put their own educations, careers, and financial futures at risk. In addition, they put their children at great risk. Studies show that those children are more likely to have health problems, to live in poverty, to be abused, to drop out of school, and get into trouble with the law.

Few people are forced to start having children at a young age, regardless of their income level or social standing. The Democratic Party, in particular, should directly help its constituents by forcefully delivering this message to them.

A lesson from Chapter 2: Make civics education mandatory

> As long as I live, I will never forget that day 21 years ago when I raised my hand and took the oath of citizenship.... I was so proud that I walked around with an American flag around my shoulders all day long.
>
> — Arnold Schwarzenegger, Actor and Republican Governor of California[4]

---

3 Considering Democratic and Republicans aged 50 years or less at the time of the surveys.
4 "Text of Arnold Schwarzenegger's Speech," in *Associated Press* (Boston.com, 2004), Retrieved August 31,, from: http://www.boston.com/news/politics/conventions/articles/2004/08/31/text_of_arnold_schwarzeneggers_speech/.

Many Democrats and Republicans are woefully ill-informed about government, current events and political matters. In Figure 224, below, we see the percentages of Democrats and Republicans who could not correctly answer simple questions about current events and government. In 2004 they were asked to name the terrorist group that attacked the United States on September 11, 2001 (al Qaeda). In 2006 they were asked to identify the Secretary of State (Condoleeza Rice), and in 2007 they were asked to identify the president of Russia (Vladimir Putin).

Figure 224. Do you know the name of ... (Pew surveys. See Table 17.)

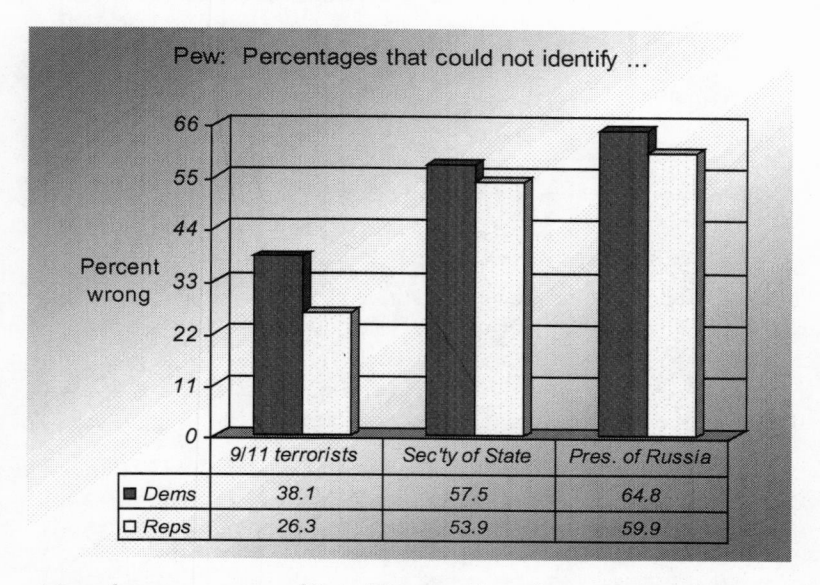

More than one-quarter of Republicans and nearly 40 percent of Democrats did not know the name of the 911 terrorist organization. Over half of Democrats and Republicans could not identify the Secretary of State, and nearly two thirds could not name the president of Russia. These figures suggest that many Americans do not feel it is their civic duty to be informed. Let's just hope that they don't' vote.

Formal Education Hasn't Helped
Figure 225, below, is a replica of Figure 56. It shows that a woman today is 50 or 60 percent more likely to have a high school diploma than the woman of 50 year ago. A similar trend exists for men.

Figure 225. Do you have (at least) a high school diploma? (Women) (NES surveys conducted in 1956 through 2004, based on, left to right, 3017, 3332, 3682, 3690, and 2667 cases, with confidence level of 99+% for all differences, and with relative proportions of, left to right, .82, .79, .84, .88, and .90)

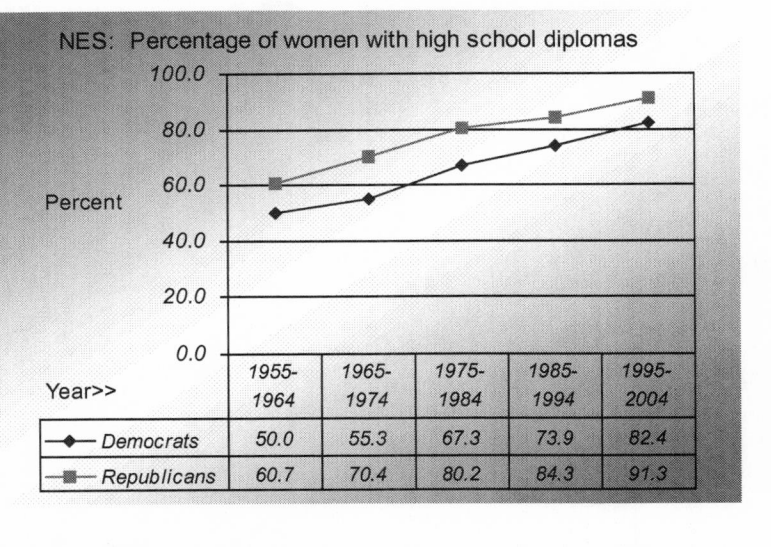

Despite the dramatic increase in the percentage of people with high school diplomas, Democrats and Republicans have not improved their knowledge of civic affairs. For example, in Figure 226, below, we see the percentages of Democrats and Republicans (combined) who could correctly name the political party that held the House majority. In the 2000s, respondents were a little less likely to get the correct answer than in any other decade.

Figure 226. Do you know who held the House majority prior to the most recent election? (Democrats and Republicans combined in several NES surveys conducted in 1952 through 2004, based on, left to right, 1382, 4281, 4603, 5616, 5529, and 2385 cases)

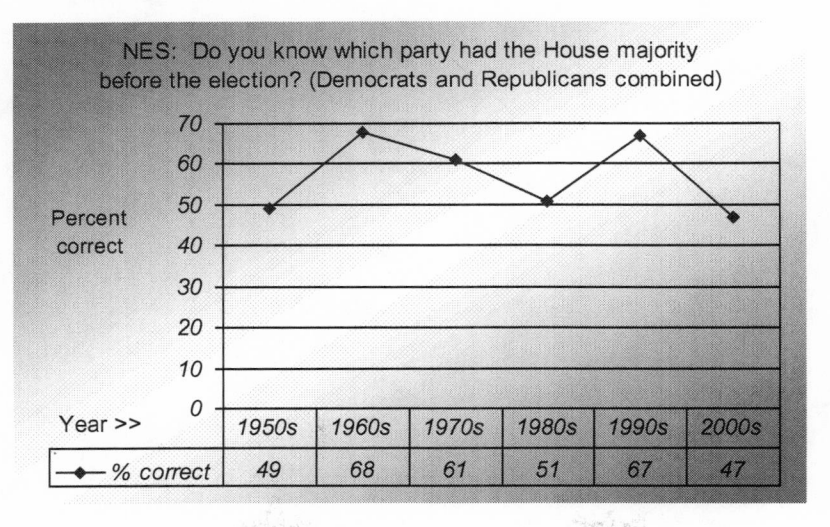

Detailed civics courses should be a mandatory part of the curricula of our nation's elementary and secondary schools, and our colleges. The objectives of such courses should be two-fold: to instill a sense of civic responsibility (to be informed, to vote, etc.), and to give students some of the basic facts needed to carryout those responsibilities. In addition to teaching about the Constitution, the structure of our government, the process of enacting laws, and the role of political parties, these courses should inform students about key societal systems related to the political processes. These include the role of the press and the workings of our economy. Many people are particularly confused by economic concepts. They toss around terms such as "corporations," "revenues," "profits," "write-offs," "loopholes," etc, but they don't know what those terms actually mean. A good citizen must know.

A lesson from Chapter 3: Work is the key to success

> In this country, you can succeed if you get educated and work hard.
> Period. Period.
>
> — Bill O'Reilly, Author and radio talk show host [5]

Between 1977 and 2006, the overall unemployment/laid off rate for Democratic males was 5.4 percent — twice as high as the 2.5 percent rate for Republican males. (See Table 24.) In addition, Democratic men were more likely to miss work due to vacation, illness, strikes, or "keeping house."[6]

The actual work gap was larger because, among men who were employed, Republicans put in 2.0 to 3.8 more hours of work per week (depending on the survey source used). There is a strong and direct correlation between hours worked and total earnings. Thus, the financial impact of the higher rate of employment and the extra hours worked by Republican men is huge. This accounts for much of the prosperity gap between Democrats and Republicans.

It is important for Democratic men to try to close this work gap. Let's assume that Democrats are just as motivated as Republicans in finding jobs, keeping jobs, and working longer hours. If that is the case, Democratic men must be less desirable workers in the eyes of their employers or potential employers. This could be the result of some form of discrimination in the workplace (race, ethic, or age-related), but it also relates, undoubtedly, to the much higher education drop-out rate among Democratic males. And, no employer can be blamed for that.

In Figure 227, below, we see that Democratic men are far less likely than Republican men to have a 4-year college degree.

Part of this gap could be attributable to the high cost of college education; however, there is also a significant gap with respect to high school education — the kind that is free everywhere in this country.

A difference in attitudes could also explain part of the employment gap between Democratic and Republican males. We know, intuitively, that attitudes

---

5 MediaMatters.org, *Misstating the State of the Union* (New York: Akashic Books, 2004).
6 The source is Table 24 on page 95.

can affect employment success. We also know, on the basis of surveys identified in the "Working Man" chapter (Chapter 3), that Republican men seem to
express attitudes that are more highly-valued by employers. They state that they
are more satisfied with their jobs, more proud of their employers, more willing
to help their employers succeed, and willing to take pay cuts and travel longer
distances to avoid losing their jobs.

Figure 227. A replica of Figure 55 on page 72

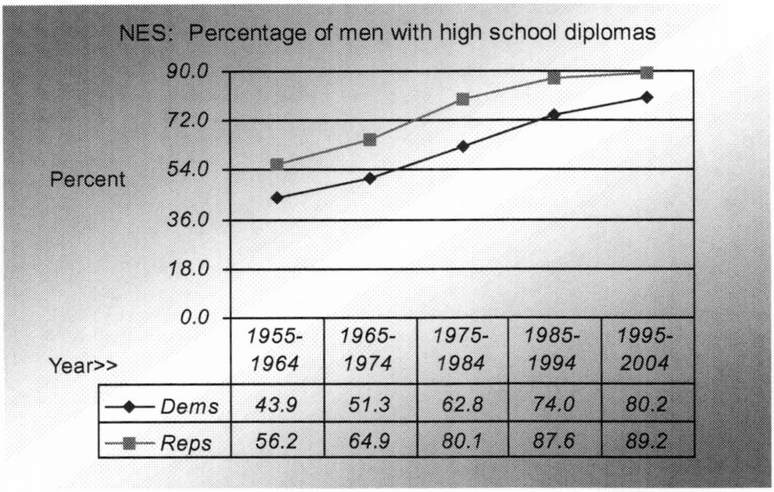

NES: Percentage of men with high school diplomas

Year>>	1955-1964	1965-1974	1975-1984	1985-1994	1995-2004
Dems	43.9	51.3	62.8	74.0	80.2
Reps	56.2	64.9	80.1	87.6	89.2

Adopting these attitudes and achieving higher education levels may be
two of the keys that Democratic males need to improve their employment
circumstances.

Reality check — Is there another factor affecting employment?
Are Republicans more willing to relocate in order to get a job? In Figure 214
on page 280 we saw that Republican men are significantly more likely to have
relocated from their childhood homes. Although there could be several reasons
for this (e.g., moving due to marriage or college attendance), one reason for the
relocation might be the pursuit of employment. This is mere speculation because
surveys asking about the reasons for relocation could not be located.

A lesson from Chapter 4: Open the wallet

Charity should begin at home, but should not stay there.

— Phillips Brooks, American clergyman[7]

Our federal, state and local governments have useful roles to play in solving many of society's problems. Nevertheless, it is not enough to simply wait for

7 Phillips Brooks (attributed), "Brainyquote.Com."

governmental action. Democrats should consider giving more time and money to charity. If they did, there would be tens of billions of additional dollars, each year, for the specific needs identified by Democrats.

Table 54, below, shows the bottom-line results from 5 of the surveys discussed in Chapter 4. Displayed are the donations made by the average Democrat and Republican who are within the same income bracket. In the right-side columns we see these amounts stated in 2007 amounts (using the change in the Consumer Price Index per the Bureau of Labor Statistics). The dollar difference, based on these 5 surveys, is $785.

Table 54. The dollar-amount of donations made by Democrats and Republicans who are within the same income brackets

Survey and Date	Unadjusted $		2007 $	
	Dems	Reps	Dems	Reps
Michigan State of the State (SOSS) 2006	1186	2227	1233	2316
Michigan State of the State (SOSS) 2005	1140	1963	1231	2120
Michigan State of the State (SOSS) 2003	1513	2193	1725	2500
Michigan State of the State (SOSS) 1999	942	1236	1187	1557
General Social Survey 1996	805	1410	1079	1889
Averages			$1291	$2076
Excess of Rep contributions			$785	

If each of the estimated 72 million registered Democrats matched Republican gifting rates by donating (on average) another $785 to charity every year, over $56 billion would be raised — each year — for goals and aspirations specifically selected by Democrats. That money could be used for minority lending programs, scholarships, urban renewal loans, research involving stem cells and AIDS, alternative energy sources, and global warming. What's more, the money would not be used to fund government budgets that don't coincide with Democratic objectives (e.g., military conflict spending?)

A lesson from Chapter 5: Everyone should pay federal income tax

> I'm proud to pay taxes in the United States; the only thing is, I could be just as proud for half the money.
>
> — The late Arthur Godfrey, TV and radio broadcaster[8]

The following opinion may shock you: Almost everyone in America — even those on welfare — should pay at least some federal income tax. This is essential

---

8 Arthur Godfrey (attributed), "Brainyquote.Com."

if we want people to care about the efficient and effective management of government programs. It is also basic human psychology: If you don't pay for something you don't pay attention to it, and you don't appreciate it. This is precisely why health insurance companies have learned to require that their customers pay, at the minimum, nominal "co-payments."

Important note: I am not advocating a reduction in aid to the poor — only a change in the way we give that aid. Welfare should not be distributed via tax reductions or by means of offsets to federal taxes, such as the Earned Income Tax Credit. Netting benefits against taxes only serves to confuse people about the true cost of federal programs, and the true cost of welfare assistance. It is better to give the full amount of aid directly to those who show need. They, in turn, should be asked to pay back some of those funds to help finance federal programs.[9]

In some cases, the federal income tax levied would have to be nominal, and in other cases we might have to accept the tax in the form of services rendered. This could be the case for unemployed taxpayers. Either way, however, taxpayers would gain a sense of civic concern and pride, and would become keenly interested in controlling government waste. And, here is a side benefit: If everyone paid income tax, everyone would get to participate in subsequent tax rate cuts. Perhaps this would put an end to the old mantra: "Tax cuts are only for the rich."

Reality check — Don't the poor pay other types of taxes?

Almost everyone pays some form of sales tax but it is generally used to fund state and local programs. Most workers pay FICA tax, but it is contributed in anticipation of a monthly cash retirement benefit. (And, the Medicare health insurance benefit will greatly exceed any Medicare taxes paid.) We may be overcharging the poor with regard to certain taxes, such as the excise taxes paid on gasoline and alcohol. (And, perhaps these taxes should be reduced.) Nevertheless, federal income taxes should be paid by all, so that everyone participates in the support of our national defense, federal courts, federal highways, disaster relief, EPA, health research, parks, etc.

A lesson from Chapter 6: Clear up the confusion about free speech

> It is a paradox that every dictator has climbed to power on the ladder of free speech. Immediately on attaining power each dictator has suppressed all free speech except his own.

— President Herbert Hoover[10]

Survey evidence suggests that Democrats are less tolerant than Republicans with respect to free speech by controversial figures. This may be due to moral

---

9 As a practical matter, the payment of taxes would probably be made (largely) via withholding from the welfare check.

10 As cited in Joslyn Pine, *Wit and Wisdom of the American Presidents: A Book of Quotations* (New Jersey: Courier Dover, 2000).

confusion regarding legitimate protest vs. suppression of so-called "hate speech." Columnist John Leo notes that, on many college campuses, free speech has almost become unacceptable. He explains that some college students and faculty feel that conservative ideas are so hateful and so dangerous that it is OK — and even necessary — to prevent those ideas from being expressed:

> Universities tell students they have a right not to be harassed by hostile speech. Well, sure. Nobody should be harassed. But the connection between harassment and speech is made so relentlessly on campus that many students think they have a right not to be offended. Real debate fades as ordinary argument is depicted as a form of assault.[11]

While it is perfectly acceptable, and possibly desirable to express views through protest, that protest should never become a vehicle for the stifling of free speech. This is a lesson that many Democrats, and Republicans, still need to learn.

A lesson from Chapter 7: Restructure SS and Medicare benefits

> Social Security is a government program with a constituency made up of the old, the near old and those who hope or fear to grow old. After 215 years of trying, we have finally discovered a special interest that includes 100 percent of the population. Now we can vote ourselves rich.
>
> — P.J. O'Rourke, American political satirist[12]

On the whole, Republicans are probably getting a slightly larger net benefit from Social Security and Medicare than are Democrats. In other words, for every dollar they put into Social Security or Medicare, Republicans get back a little bit more than do Democrats, in the form of benefits. This makes no sense because the Social Security and Medicare systems are supposed to have progressive benefit structures (favoring workers with lower wages), and the average Republican earns substantially more than the average Democrat. Dramatic reform of the core benefit structures of Social Security and Medicare is warranted.

The major problem has to do with spousal and survivor benefits, which tend to make the programs costly and regressive. This is illustrated in Figure 228, below, which compares the net benefits of a single man earning $50,000 to a married man (with a stay-at-home spouse) earning $95,000.

Remember, these are net benefits, and represent the excess of benefits received over payroll taxes paid. In this example, we have effectively taken about $30,000 from the middle-class worker while shifting $165,000 to the upper-class worker. This $195,000 differential is absurd and shameful, and it completely undermines the progressive nature of Social Security. It also explains why higher income Republicans tend to benefit more from Social Security than do Demo-

---

11 Leo, "Ivy League Therapy."
12 O'Rourke, *Parliament of Whores*, 220.

crats, even though the system is supposed to be progressive: Republicans are more likely to get marred and have stay-at-home spouses.

Figure 228. Net Social Security benefits of a single man earning $50,000 vs. a married worker earning $95,000 (and having a stay-at-home spouse). This graphic, which is based on Figure 167 on page 208, shows that the system is regressively distributing wealth from the middle class worker to the relatively wealthy worker.

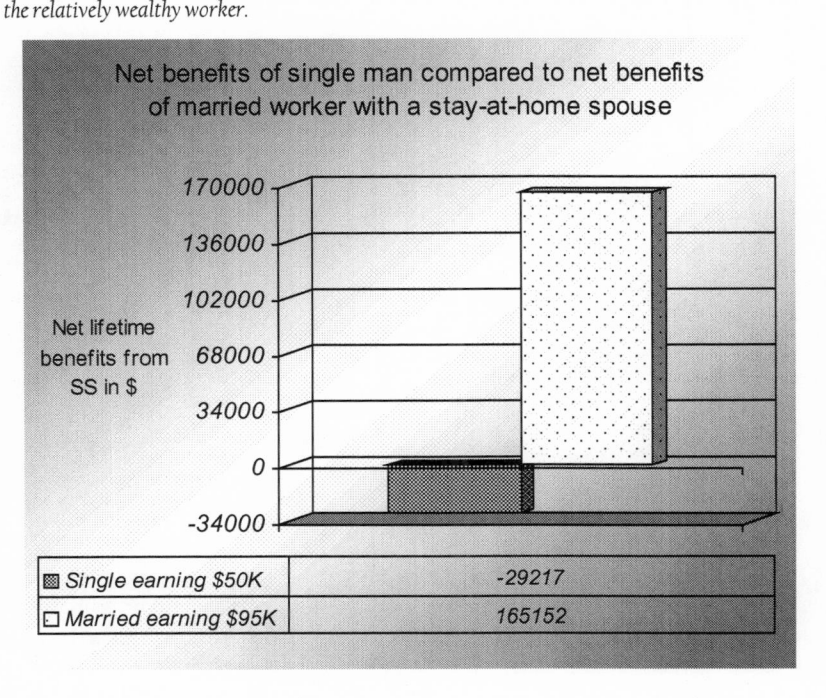

A similar illustration can be made with respect to Medicare. In Figure 229, below, we see that there are two problems with respect to the benefit structure: The net benefits are regressive and the net benefits are, for single and married people, far too high to be sustainable. Future generations are going to be stuck with dramatic increases to the payroll tax unless benefits (and the underlying medical costs) are contained.

The Bush administration may have erred, politically and substantively, by emphasizing private retirement account options while neglecting reform of the core Social Security benefit structure. Spousal and survivor benefits should be eliminated and replaced, in the case of low-income retirees, with an expanded Supplemental Security Income program (SSI). Alternative remedies might include reducing spousal and survivor benefits while increasing the benefits of single workers, or "means testing" spousal and survivor benefits so they are reduced or eliminated for retirees with relatively high incomes.

Figure 229. Net Medicare benefits of a single working woman vs. a married worker with a stay-at-home spouse (based on Figure 170 on page 215). Note that the wealthier worker derives the greater net benefit.

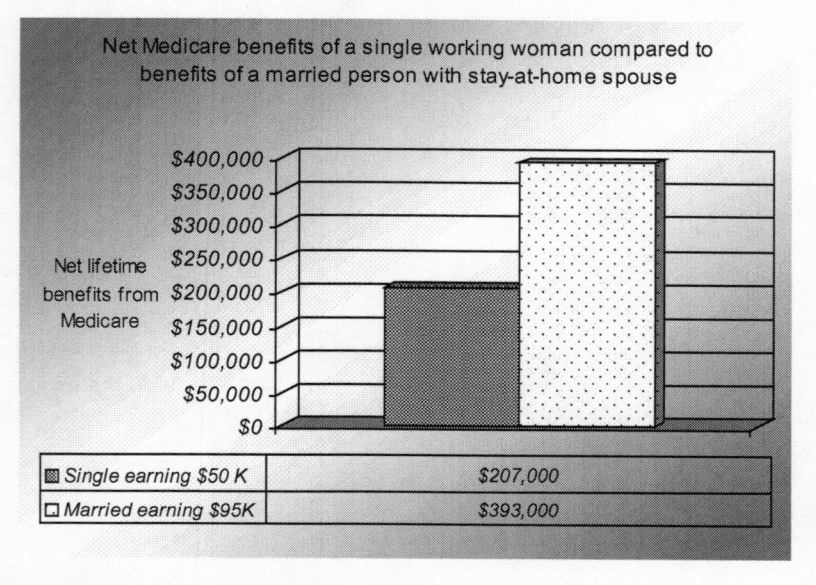

▩ Single earning $50 K	$207,000
☐ Married earning $95K	$393,000

A lesson from Chapter 8 : All welfare is not the same

> Welfare distorts behavior, makes one less personally responsible and reduces the role of private charity. This principle [also] applies to corporate welfare.
>
> — Larry Elder, Radio talk show host[13]

There is real welfare and there is "public policy" welfare, and it is important to know the difference. Real welfare is the support we give to people so they can eat, stay warm, and stay healthy. Public policy welfare is entirely different. If we give a moderate tax credit to an individual to encourage him to buy an experimental electric car (that he would not otherwise buy), we have not given welfare — provided the tax credit is appropriately designed. Rather, we have compensated someone for taking a risk in an effort to help preserve society's supply of energy.

The same is true with respect to corporate welfare. If we give federal loan guarantees to a business to keep it from closing its doors, that is probably real corporate welfare. On the other hand, if we give tax incentives to businesses that try out perilous new foreign markets or that take a chance on risky inner city investments, that is public policy welfare, designed (we hope) to further some national objective. In those instances, we are simply compensating the businesses for the extra risks and expenses they are undertaking.

---

13 Larry Elder (attributed), "Brainyquote.Com."

Real welfare is often essential — especially for individuals in need. There are also times when a government must encourage behaviors that are in the long-term interests of the nation. This is particularly true with respect to long-term endeavors such as pollution control, resource conservation, and the development of alternative energy supplies.

The line separating real welfare from public policy welfare can get pretty thin, but it is important to keep them separate, and to know when and where each type of "welfare" is appropriately used.

A lesson from Chapter 9: Be a happy-go-lucky Republican

> Maybe if I work hard enough at it I can learn to live like a Republican for the next few years, say "I got mine" and screw everyone else.

— Actor Alec Baldwin[14]

If Democrats want to lead happier lives, they should consider being more like Republicans. That's because many of the characteristics of Republicans are more likely to correlate with happiness. Some of these traits are included in Table 55, below.

Table 55. A few of the "happiness" factors discussed in Chapter 9.

Row	More happy is being...	Less happy is being...
1	Wealthier	Poorer
2	Well-educated	Poorly educated
3	Married	Single
4	Healthy	Unhealthy
5	Concerned with individual achievements	Concerned with social comparisons
6	Religious	Not religious
7	Trusting of others	Not trusting of others

My "let them eat cake" advice may seem Pollyannaish, but further reflection may change your mind. Many of these factors are interrelated and achievable by almost anyone. For example, one of the keys to happiness is wealth (row 1), and one of the keys to building wealth is education (row 2) — itself a factor that correlates with happiness. As noted in Chapter 2, Democrats are significantly more likely to drop out of school before getting a high school diploma. It is likely that in most cases there is no good reason for dropping out of school — especially a free, public high school. That is simply a poor choice that can lead to a less happy life.

Marriage (row 3) is another factor that correlates with happiness and also relates to prosperity. Two people can generally live more inexpensively than one, so people who get married and stay married tend to become wealthier. Marriage

---

14 Ingrid Randoja, "Alec Baldwin," *NOW* 20, no. 16 (December 21-27, 2000).

is, of course, a choice that is available to almost everyone — regardless of socio-economic class.

Another factor relating to happiness is good health (row 4). No one can be guaranteed good health, but we can greatly improve our odds by not smoking tobacco and by not being overweight. Survey evidence indicates that Democrats are significantly more likely to smoke, and may be more overweight than Republicans. Although some may have addictions and metabolic disorders, important decisions regarding smoking and eating can be made by most or all of us.

Row 5 has to do with two different ways people measure their own achievements: by comparison with what they once had, or by comparison with what others have. Psychologists feel that happy people are more concerned with their own progress, while less happy people tend to compare what they have achieved to the accomplishments of others. Possibly, some of the concern regarding income gaps (as opposed to absolute income levels, which are generally increasing) may be hazardous to happiness. If the concern is academic or moral in nature, there should be no "happiness" issue. However, if the concern over income gaps involves personal comparisons, it may be very destructive.

The two factors in rows 6 and 7 are related to happiness and related to each other. Presumably, a person of religious faith is also a trusting person. Psychologists say that trust is a factor that correlates with happiness.

Finally, it should not be assumed that happiness is simply one of the end results of success: It can also be a means for achieving success. After reviewing 225 studies involving 275,000 people, Psychologist Sonja Lyubomirsky concluded:

> Our review provides strong support that happiness, in many cases, leads to successful outcomes, rather than merely following from them, and happy individuals are more likely than their less happy peers to have fulfilling marriages and relationships, high incomes, superior work performance, community involvement, robust health and even a long life.[15]

A lesson from Chapter 10: Break the inter-generational cycle

> Children who live in poverty tend to live in a continuous cycle passed on from one generation to the next.
>
> — United States Department of Agriculture[16]

Recently, there was an interesting article in the New York Times regarding the relative affluence of blacks in Queens, New York. It seems that black median incomes have surpassed white median incomes in Queens — something that has not happened in any other county of significant size in the country. How did it happen? One factor was the creation of two-parent black homes, largely by immigrants from the West Indies:

---

15 Sonja Lyubomirsky, "The Benefits of Frequent Positive Affect: Does Happiness Lead to Success?," *Psychological Bulletin* 131, no. 6 (December 2005).

16 "The Impact of Poverty on Learning: Implications for the Classroom," June 22, 2006, United States Department of Agriculture, Retrieved April 8, 2007, from http://www.csrees.usda.gov/nea/family/in_focus/communities_if_poverty.html.

> The gains among blacks in Queens, the city's quintessential middle-class borough, were driven largely by the growth of two-parent families and the successes of immigrants from the West Indies.... They're married-couple families living the American dream in southeast Queens....
>
> Immigrants helped propel the gains among blacks. The median income of foreign-born black households was $61,151, compared to $45,864 for American-born blacks. The disparity was even more pronounced among black married couple.[17]

The other factor leading to the Queens success story was the great respect and appreciation shown by black immigrants for the American educational system, and for the benefits it could afford. According to a Jamaican immigrant:

> When immigrants come here, they're not accustomed to social programs ... and when they see opportunities they had no access to — tuition or academic or practical training — they are God-sent, and they use those programs to build themselves and move forward.[18]

I would argue that the best part of this story was not even mentioned in the New York Times article: By pulling themselves up, the blacks of Queens have greatly improved the odds that their children will also lead happy, productive, and successful lives.

In Chapter 10 we saw that many of the differences between today's Democrats and Republicans also existed between their respective parents. For example, Democrats are more likely than Republicans to have marital problems, to raise children in 1-parent homes, to have less education, to work in less prestigious jobs, and to earn less income. Likewise, the parents of Democrats were more likely than the parents of Republicans to have the same tendencies.

Clearly, the choices made by one generation have good or bad consequences for the next generation. Even if we don't care about our own happiness and success (and most of us do), as parents we have an obligation to give our children every opportunity to move ahead into happy and successful lives.

Most of the black immigrants in Queens came to the United States recently — in the 80's and 90's. By making wise choices they have already greatly improved their lives, and have greatly improved the chances that their children will lead healthy, happy, and productive lives. As stated at the beginning of this chapter: "[T]he cumulative effect of decisions regarding marriage, children, education, work, etc. critically affects the quality of life for Democrats and Republicans, and their descendants."

---

17 Sam Roberts, "Black Income Surpass Whites in Queens,"
   The New York Times, October 1, 2006.
18 Ibid.

A lesson from Chapter 11: Be careful with the terms "liberal" and "conservative"

> In this era of a big-spending Republican administration, the differences between conservatives and liberals have shrunk so much, it's hard to tell who's who.

— John Stossel, Author and television commentator[19]

No one is born with an "L" or "C" stamped on his forehead, and few people (in the United States) actively campaign or vote for liberals or conservatives, or take other observable actions on their behalf. To determine who is a liberal and who is a conservative we usually rely on self-identifications, based upon varying individual definitions.

Unfortunately, people do not always say what they really believe, or even know what they really believe. With regard to liberalism and conservatism, everyone seems to have a unique definition. A person may feel conservative because he is prudish, wants lower taxes, opposes abortion, favors recitation of the Pledge of Allegiance in schools, wants to hunt with a shot gun, or because of some combination of the above. A person may feel liberal because he is a "people person," wants national health care, is opposed to war, wants the government to "stay out of the bedroom," or believes in a combination of those ideals.

In an attempt to clarify the definitions of liberal and conservative a researcher could be tempted to ignore self-classifications altogether, opting instead for standardized definitions. This only makes matters worse, however, by interjecting research bias and circularity into the process.

There is another problem with liberal vs. conservative comparisons: In terms of education and intellect, Democratic liberals differ starkly from Republican liberals, and the same is true for Democratic and Republican conservatives.

This author believes that more objective and meaningful comparisons can be made on the basis of political party identification. Please see Appendix E for more discussion of this matter.

---

19 John Stossel, "It's Hard to Tell a Conservative from a Liberal," *RealClearPolitics. com* (September 20, 2006), Retrieved April 8, 2007, from http://www.realclearpolitics.com/articles/2006/09/its_hard_to_tell_a_conservativ.html.

Appendix A: Demographic Trends over 50 Years

Part One: Relative Strength of Each Party in the Public

In this section you will find the percentages of the public and key demographic groups who identify as Democrats versus Republicans. Columns add to 100% because other groups, such as independents, are not included.

In general

Figure 230. Party identification — (combined results of several surveys of the American National Election Studies (NES) conducted from 1952 through 2004, based on, left to right, 2168, 5421, 5701, 6201, 6592, and 4724 cases)

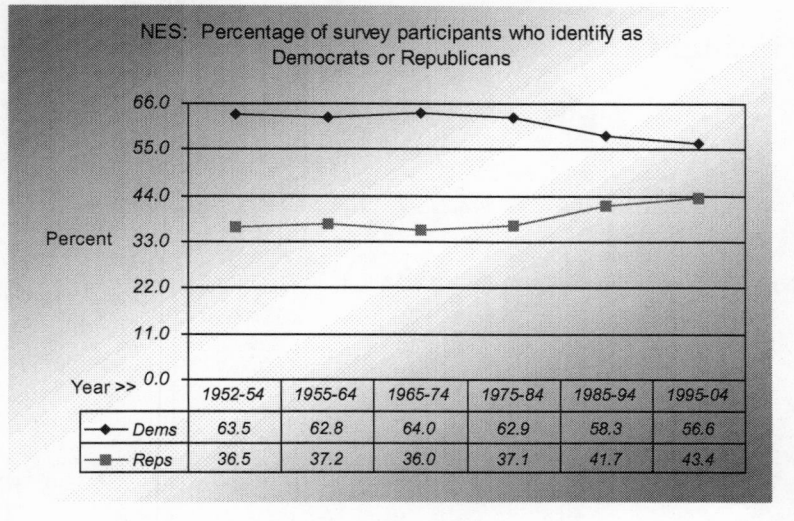

NES: Percentage of survey participants who identify as Democrats or Republicans

Year >>	1952-54	1955-64	1965-74	1975-84	1985-94	1995-04
Dems	63.5	62.8	64.0	62.9	58.3	56.6
Reps	36.5	37.2	36.0	37.1	41.7	43.4

During the last 50 years, there has been a small increase in the percentage of the general public that identifies as Republican, as opposed to Democratic. However, there is still a large disparity, with Democrats having the advantage. Figure 230 ends with the year 2004. Since that time, the Democratic advantage has increased, with nearly 3 self-identified Democrats for every 2 self-identified Republicans, according to Pew surveys taken in early 2007. [1]

Different age groups

In Figure 231, below, we see that Democrats generally lost ground with the 17 to 24-year-old age group, until the 1985-94 decade. Since that time, however, it appears that a Democratic "rebound" has been taking place.

Figure 231. Party identity over years, for the 17-24 age group — (combined results of several NES surveys conducted from 1952 through 2004, based on, left to right, 83, 236, 465, 641, 557, and 314 cases)

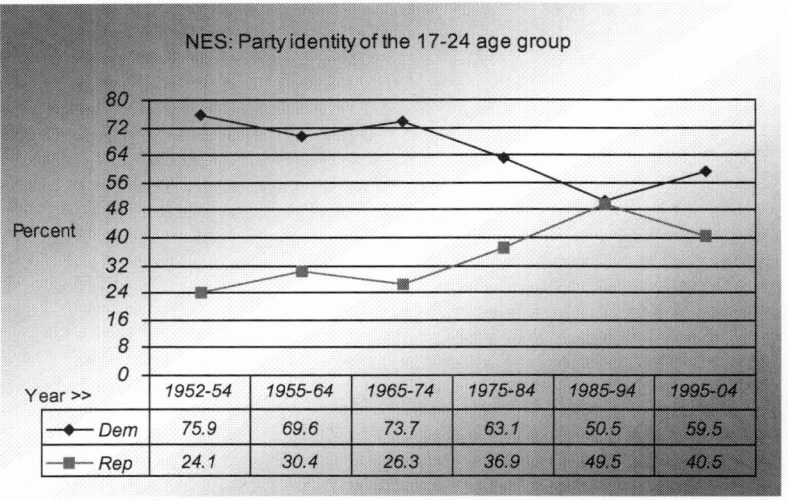

With respect to the 25- to 44-year-old age group, shown in Figure 232, below, the trend has been steadily to the benefit of Republicans. The gains of Republicans with regard to this group exceed the gains of Republicans with respect to the population in general.

Figure 232. Party identity over years, for the 25-44 age group — (combined results of several NES surveys conducted from 1952 through 2004, based on, left to right, 620, 2333, 1974, 2358, 2860, and 1809 cases)

---

1 "Trends in Political Values and Core Attitudes: 1987-2007," *Pew Research Center Survey Reports* (March 22, 2007), Retrieved October 27, 2007, from http://people-press.org/reports/pdf/312.pdf.

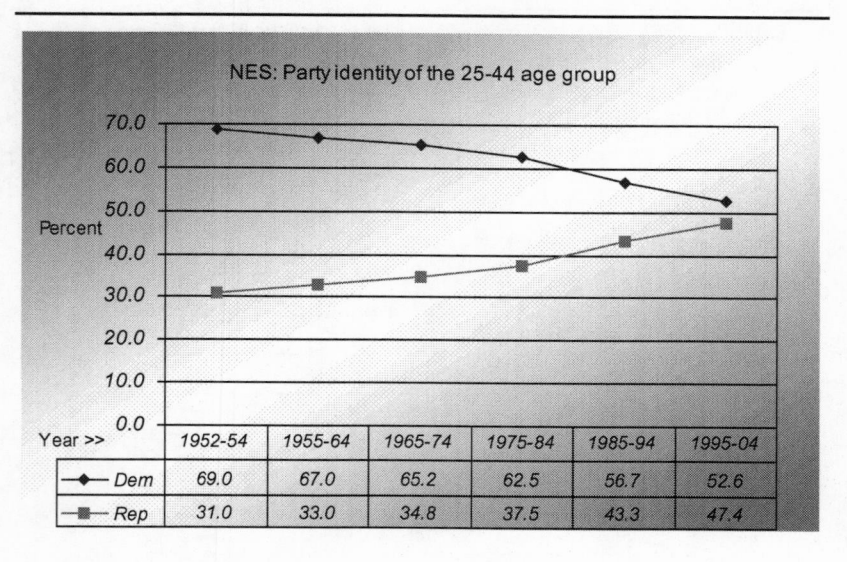

Year >>	1952-54	1955-64	1965-74	1975-84	1985-94	1995-04
—◆— Dem	69.0	67.0	65.2	62.5	56.7	52.6
—■— Rep	31.0	33.0	34.8	37.5	43.3	47.4

Figure 233 shows the age 45 to 64 year-old-age bracket, where Democrats have maintained a sizable advantage. This includes the all-important "baby boomer" group, which is represented within the 1995-04 column, on the right side of the chart.

Figure 233. Party identity over years, for the 45-64 age group — (combined results of several NES surveys conducted from 1952 through 2004, based on, left to right, 426, 1950, 2067, 1891, 1714, and 1631 cases)

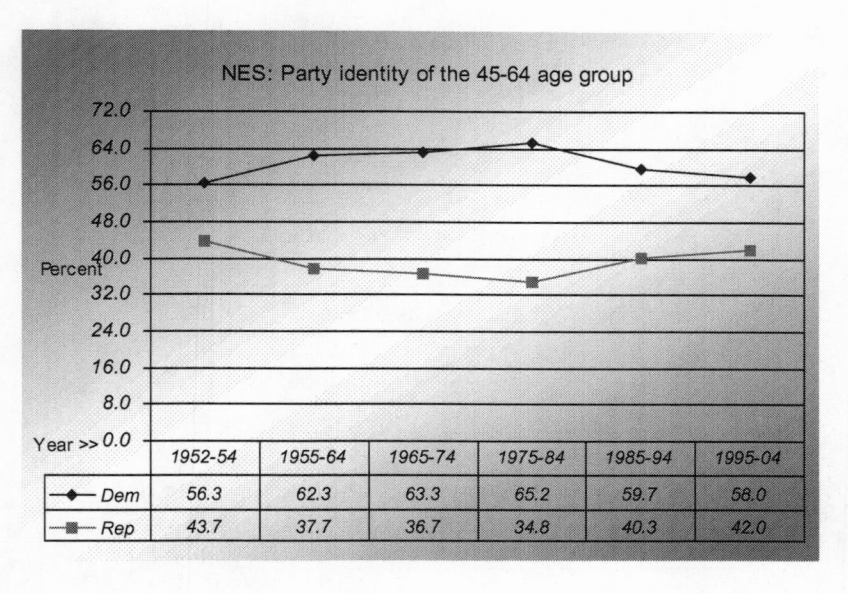

Year >>	1952-54	1955-64	1965-74	1975-84	1985-94	1995-04
—◆— Dem	56.3	62.3	63.3	65.2	59.7	58.0
—■— Rep	43.7	37.7	36.7	34.8	40.3	42.0

Republicans once had parity with Democrats with respect to the people aged over 65 years. That was in the days of Dwight D. Eisenhower. Since then, Democrats have gained among senior citizens, despite the overall population shift in favor of Republicans (shown in Figure 230). This age group is shown in Figure 234.

Figure 234. Party identity over years, for the over 65 age group — (combined results of several NES surveys conducted from 1952 through 2004, based on, left to right, 176, 880, 1155, 1278, 1458, and 952 cases)

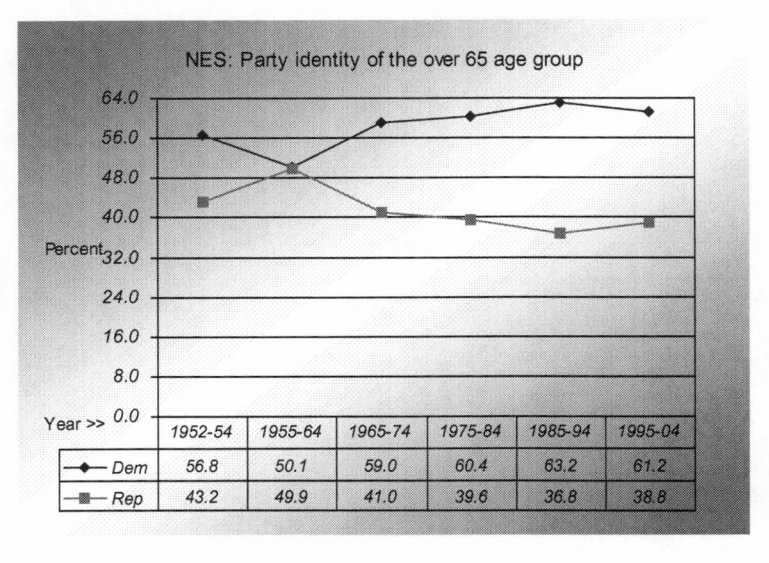

NES: Party identity of the over 65 age group

Year >>	1952-54	1955-64	1965-74	1975-84	1985-94	1995-04
Dem	56.8	50.1	59.0	60.4	63.2	61.2
Rep	43.2	49.9	41.0	39.6	36.8	38.8

Each gender

Figure 235. Percentages of Men who identify as Democrats or Republicans (several NES surveys conducted in 1952 through 2004, based on, left to right, 989, 2386, 2357, 2507, 2841, and 2047 cases)

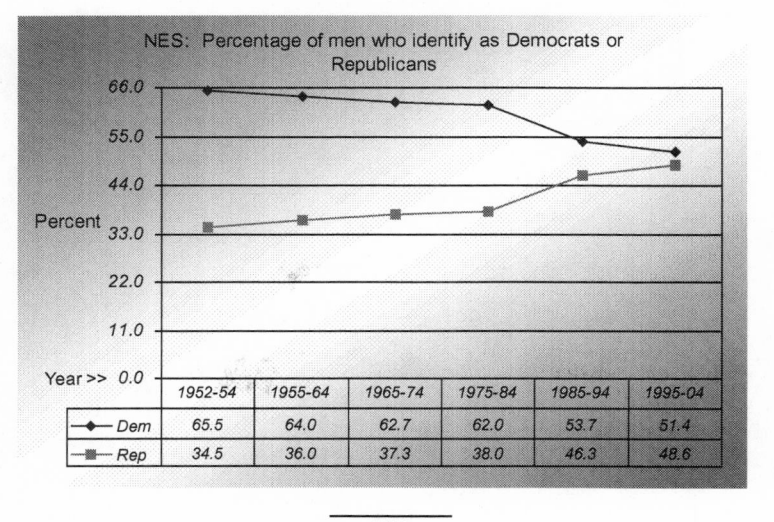

NES: Percentage of men who identify as Democrats or Republicans

Year >>	1952-54	1955-64	1965-74	1975-84	1985-94	1995-04
Dem	65.5	64.0	62.7	62.0	53.7	51.4
Rep	34.5	36.0	37.3	38.0	46.3	48.6

Republicans have had steady increases among men for at least 50 years. These gains, which exceed the gains of Republicans in the general population, are shown in Figure 235, above.

With regard to women there has been a gender gap for a long time. It reached its peak during the Viet Nam and feminist days of the late '60s and early '70s.

Figure 236. Percentages of women who identify as Democrats or Republicans (several NES surveys conducted in 1952 through 2004, based on, left to right, 1179, 3035, 3344, 3694, 3751, and 2677 cases)

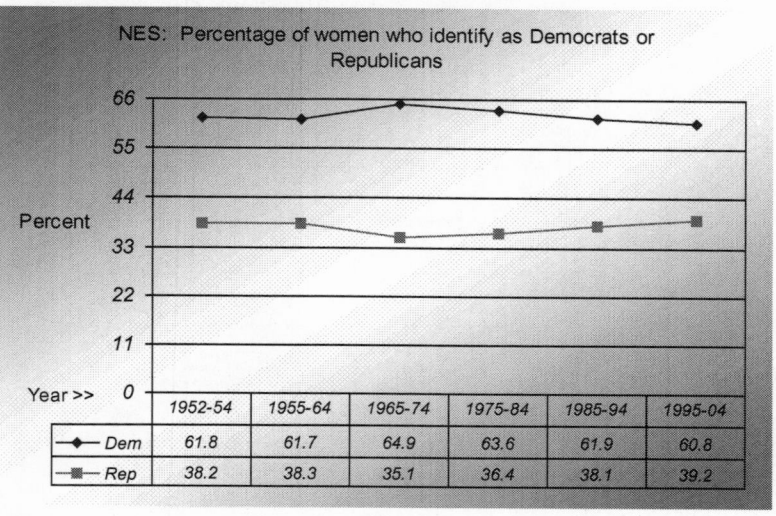

NES: Percentage of women who identify as Democrats or Republicans

Year >>	1952-54	1955-64	1965-74	1975-84	1985-94	1995-04
Dem	61.8	61.7	64.9	63.6	61.9	60.8
Rep	38.2	38.3	35.1	36.4	38.1	39.2

Racial and ethnic groups

Figure 237. Percentages of Whites who identify as Democrats or Republicans (several NES surveys conducted in 1952 through 2004, based on, left to right, 1977, 4936, 4944, 5075, 4958, and 3492 cases)

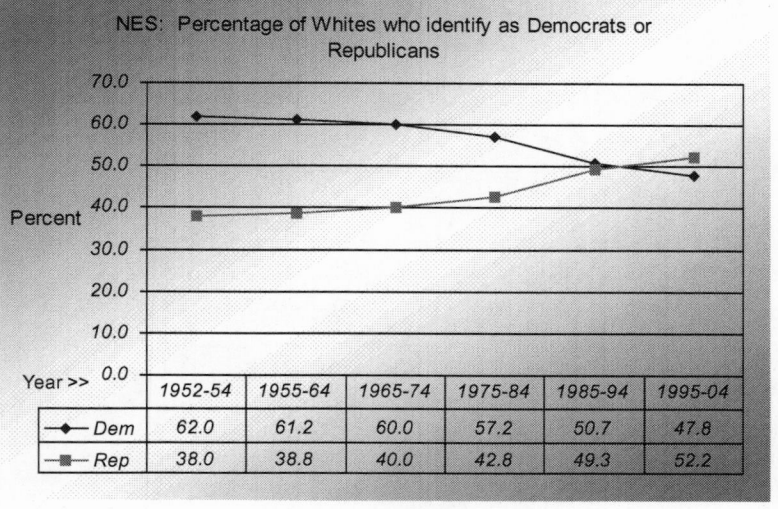

NES: Percentage of Whites who identify as Democrats or Republicans

Year >>	1952-54	1955-64	1965-74	1975-84	1985-94	1995-04
Dem	62.0	61.2	60.0	57.2	50.7	47.8
Rep	38.0	38.8	40.0	42.8	49.3	52.2

As shown in Figure 237, above, most of white America has identified with the Republicans for the last 10 to 20 years.

Black America was solidly Republican until the New Deal days of FDR. Since then, a large majority has been Democratic. That majority grew even larger during the Civil Rights legislative battles of the mid-1960s. See Figure 238, below.

Figure 238. Percentages of Blacks who identify as Democrats or Republicans (several NES surveys conducted in 1952 through 2004, based on, left to right, 180, 452, 641, 762, 956, and 648 cases)

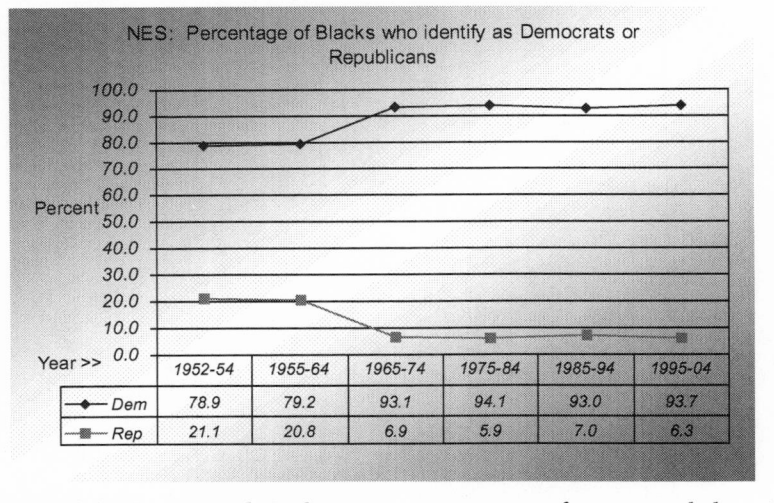

NES didn't keep records with respect to Hispanic preferences until about 30 years ago. At that time 4 out of 5 Hispanics considered themselves to be Democrats. Now the ratio is a little over 2 out of 3. The trend is shown in Figure 239, below.

Figure 239. Percentages of Hispanics who identify as Democrats or Republicans (several NES surveys conducted in 1975 through 2004, based on, left to right, 189, 381and 309 cases)

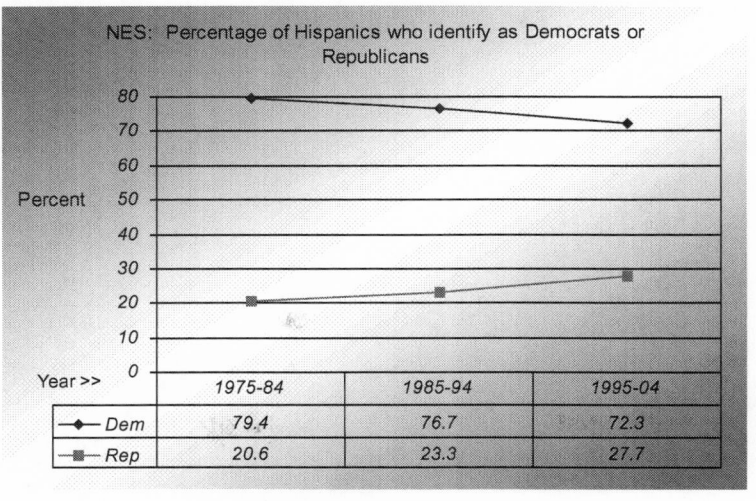

Religious denominations

Although more Protestants consider themselves to be Democratic than Republican, the gap has always been a bit smaller than it has been for the population, in general. This can be seen by comparing Figure 240, below, with Figure 230.

Figure 240. Percentages of Protestants who identify as Democrats or Republicans (several NES surveys conducted in 1952 through 2004, based on, left to right, 1613, 3943, 4062, 4069, 4172, and 2766 cases)

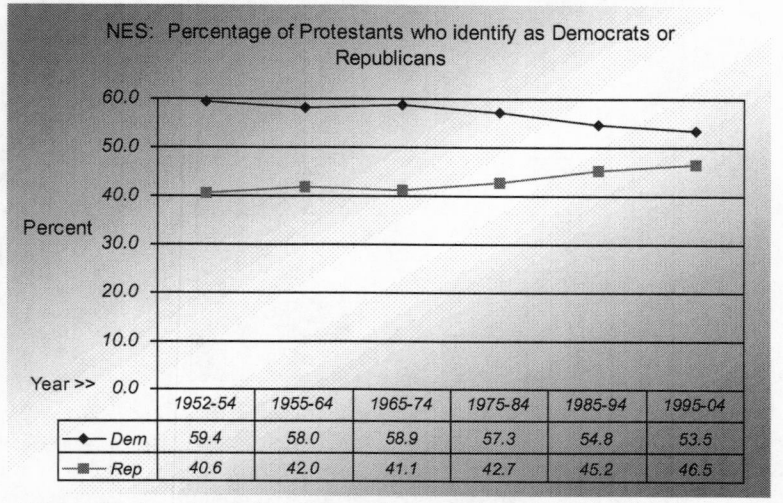

NES: Percentage of Protestants who identify as Democrats or Republicans						
Year >>	1952-54	1955-64	1965-74	1975-84	1985-94	1995-04
Dem	59.4	58.0	58.9	57.3	54.8	53.5
Rep	40.6	42.0	41.1	42.7	45.2	46.5

Democrats have lost a lot of ground among Catholics, but they have always held an advantage.

Figure 241. Percentages of Catholics who identify as Democrats or Republicans (several NES surveys conducted in 1952 through 2004, based on, left to right, 437, 1129, 1258, 1512, 1591, and 1249 cases)

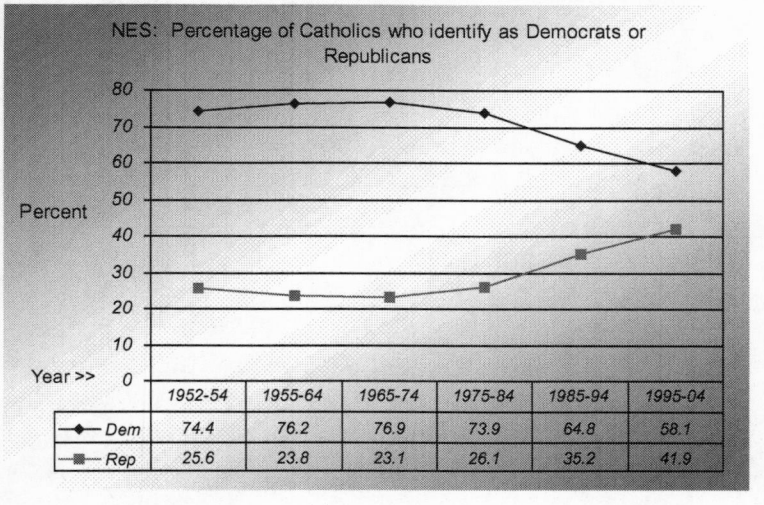

NES: Percentage of Catholics who identify as Democrats or Republicans						
Year >>	1952-54	1955-64	1965-74	1975-84	1985-94	1995-04
Dem	74.4	76.2	76.9	73.9	64.8	58.1
Rep	25.6	23.8	23.1	26.1	35.2	41.9

The percentage of Jews who consider themselves to be Democrats is higher than for any other group except Blacks. See Figure 242, below.

Figure 242. Percentages of Jews who identify as Democrats or Republicans (several NES surveys conducted in 1952 through 2004, based on, left to right, 62, 161, 139, 164, 116, and 123 and 2576 cases)

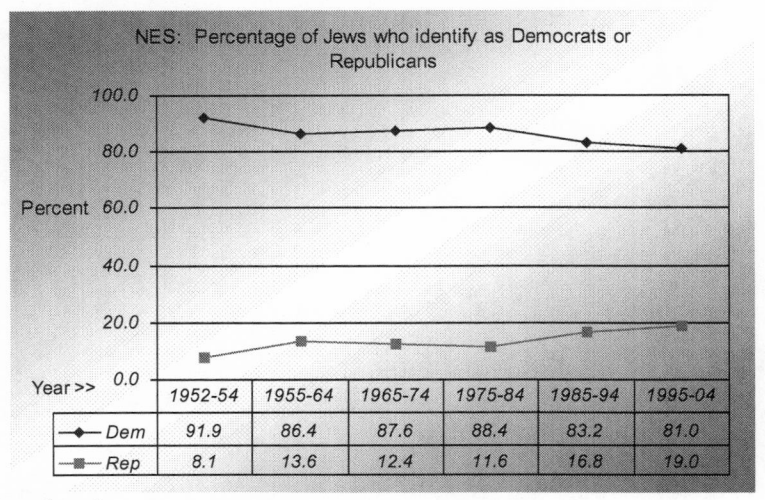

NES: Percentage of Jews who identify as Democrats or Republicans

Year >>	1952-54	1955-64	1965-74	1975-84	1985-94	1995-04
Dem	91.9	86.4	87.6	88.4	83.2	81.0
Rep	8.1	13.6	12.4	11.6	16.8	19.0

Married people

Marriage may effectively serve as a "filter" that separates relatively conservative people from more liberal people. That could explain why married people are more likely to be Republicans than are married and unmarried people, considered as a whole. See Figure 243, below.

Figure 243. Percentages of married people (living with spouse) who identify as Democrats or Republicans (several NES surveys conducted in 1952 through 2004, based on, left to right, 1034, 4239, 3881, 3756, 3675, and 2590 cases)

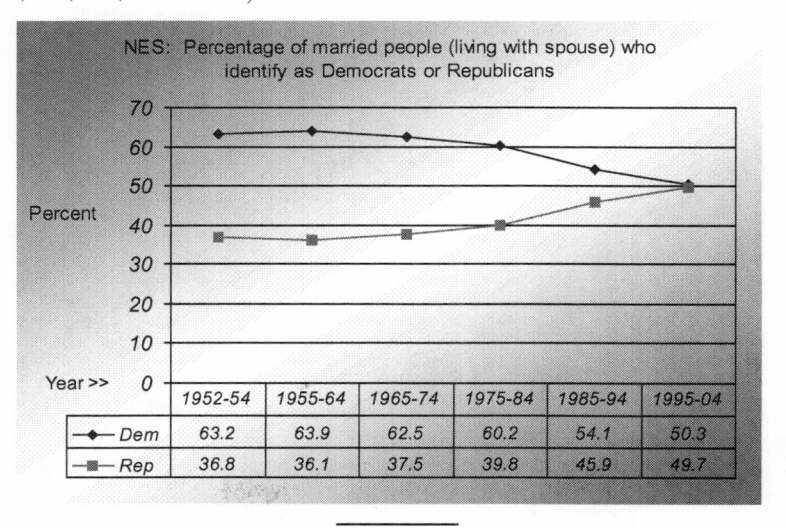

NES: Percentage of married people (living with spouse) who identify as Democrats or Republicans

Year >>	1952-54	1955-64	1965-74	1975-84	1985-94	1995-04
Dem	63.2	63.9	62.5	60.2	54.1	50.3
Rep	36.8	36.1	37.5	39.8	45.9	49.7

People in different occupations

Although more professionals and managers consider themselves to be Democratic, versus Republican, the difference is far less than for the population in general.

Figure 244. Percentages of professionals and managers who identify as Democrats or Republicans (several NES surveys conducted in 1952 through 2004, based on, left to right, 190, 734, 934, 1414, 1742, and 1012 cases)

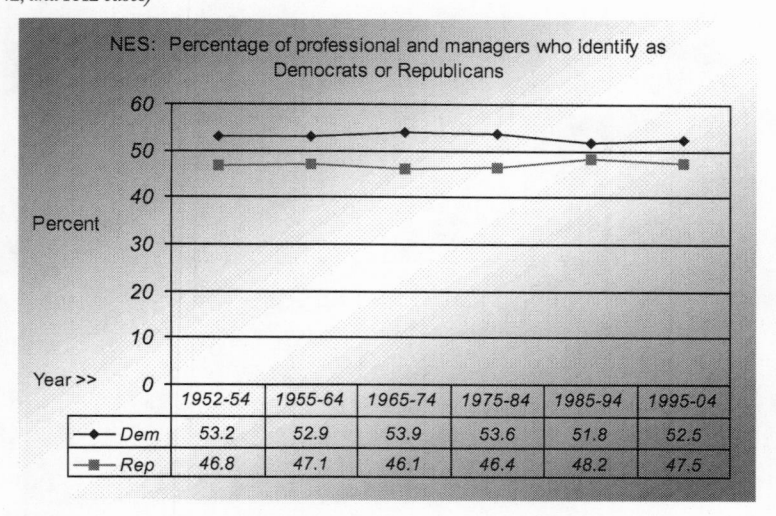

NES: Percentage of professional and managers who identify as Democrats or Republicans

Year >>	1952-54	1955-64	1965-74	1975-84	1985-94	1995-04
Dem	53.2	52.9	53.9	53.6	51.8	52.5
Rep	46.8	47.1	46.1	46.4	48.2	47.5

The Democratic advantage with respect to clerical and sales workers is a bit smaller than it is among the population at large.

Figure 245. Percentages of clerical and sales workers who identify as Democrats or Republicans (several NES surveys conducted in 1952 through 2004, based on, left to right, 139, 531, 660, 1088, 1379, and 860 cases)

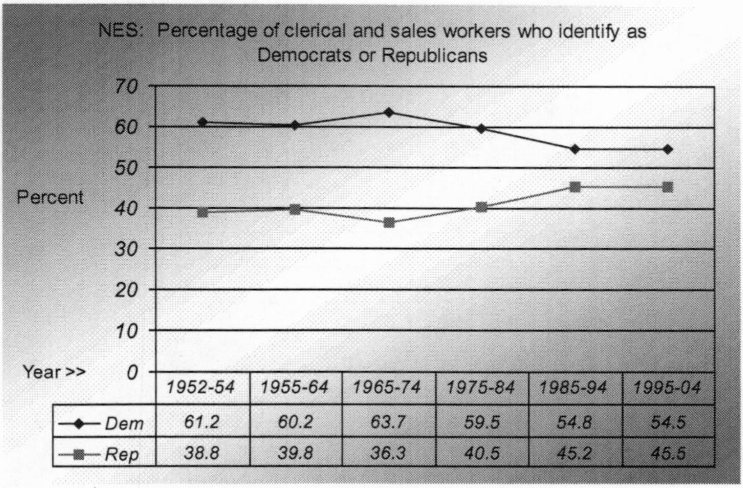

NES: Percentage of clerical and sales workers who identify as Democrats or Republicans

Year >>	1952-54	1955-64	1965-74	1975-84	1985-94	1995-04
Dem	61.2	60.2	63.7	59.5	54.8	54.5
Rep	38.8	39.8	36.3	40.5	45.2	45.5

It is not surprising to see a strong Democratic advantage among skilled, semi-skilled, and service workers, since many of these workers are unionized. In the '80s, some of these workers became Republicans because, perhaps, of the popularity of President Ronald Reagan. However, since then, the gap has grown larger again. These trends are shown in Figure 246, below.

Figure 246. Percentages of skilled, semi-skilled, and service workers who identify as Democrats or Republicans (several NES surveys conducted in 1952 through 2004, based on, left to right, 272, 1215, 1463, 2032, 2133, and 1012 cases)

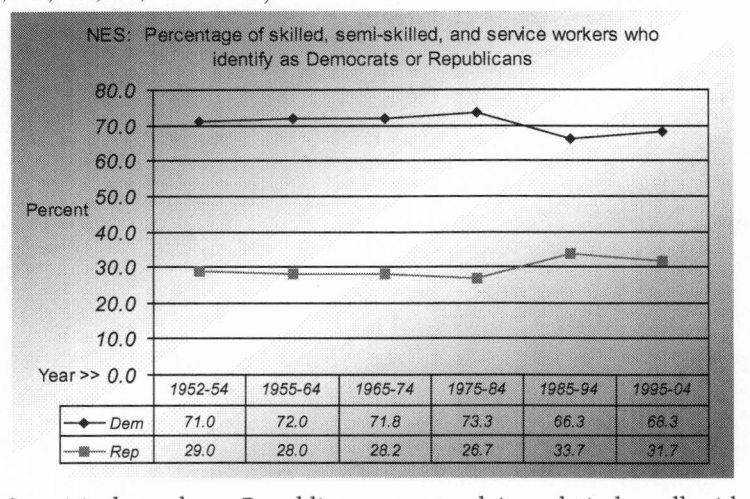

NES: Percentage of skilled, semi-skilled, and service workers who identify as Democrats or Republicans

Year >>	1952-54	1955-64	1965-74	1975-84	1985-94	1995-04
Dem	71.0	72.0	71.8	73.3	66.3	68.3
Rep	29.0	28.0	28.2	26.7	33.7	31.7

Surprisingly, perhaps, Republicans are now doing relatively well with respect to laborers. This is partly due to the inclusion of farmers and farm workers, who tend to be more conservative than city laborers.

Figure 247. Percentages of laborers, farmers and farm workers who identify as Democrats or Republicans (several NES surveys conducted in 1952 through 2004, based on, left to right, 236, 488, 303, 347, 371, and 135 cases)

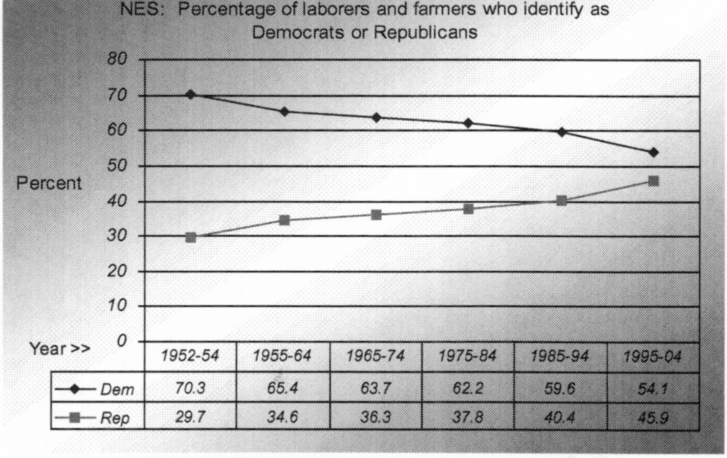

NES: Percentage of laborers and farmers who identify as Democrats or Republicans

Year >>	1952-54	1955-64	1965-74	1975-84	1985-94	1995-04
Dem	70.3	65.4	63.7	62.2	59.6	54.1
Rep	29.7	34.6	36.3	37.8	40.4	45.9

College graduates

The Republican advantage among people with college or advanced degrees is very strong when we consider that Democratic advantage among the population in general. Contrast the trends shown in Figure 248, below, with those shown in Figure 230.

Figure 248. Percentages of people with a college or advanced degree who identify as Democrats or Republicans (several NES surveys conducted in 1952 through 2004, based on, left to right, 118, 547, 685, 1008, 1450, and 1490 cases)

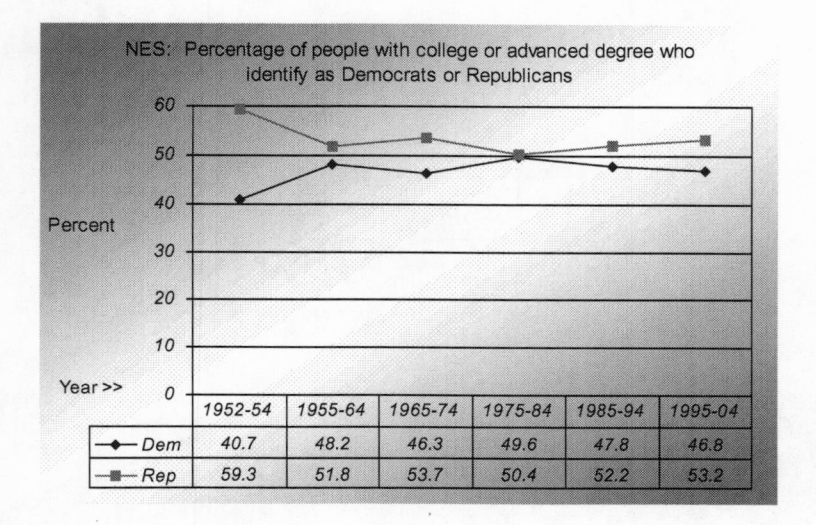

Year >>	1952-54	1955-64	1965-74	1975-84	1985-94	1995-04
Dem	40.7	48.2	46.3	49.6	47.8	46.8
Rep	59.3	51.8	53.7	50.4	52.2	53.2

People in different family income brackets

NES asks its respondents this question, or a similar question, in each survey:

> Can you give us an estimate of your total family income in 20XX before taxes? This figure should include salaries, wages, pensions, dividends, interest and all other income for every member of your family living in your house in 20XX.

Using this information, respondents are placed within the following income ranges: zero to 16th percentile, 17th to 33rd percentile, 34th to 67th percentile, 68th to 95th percentile, and 96th to 100th percentile. These ranges, and the percentage of Democrats and Republicans in each one, are graphically depicted in the following 5 charts.

The correlation between party identity and family income is strong. By 70 to 30 percent, people with family incomes in the lowest 16 percent of the population favor the Democrats.

Figure 249. Percentages of people with family incomes in the 0 to 16th percentile who identify as Democrats or Republicans (several NES surveys conducted in 1952 through 2004, based on, left to right, 424, 940, 1013, 882, 1017, and 525 cases)

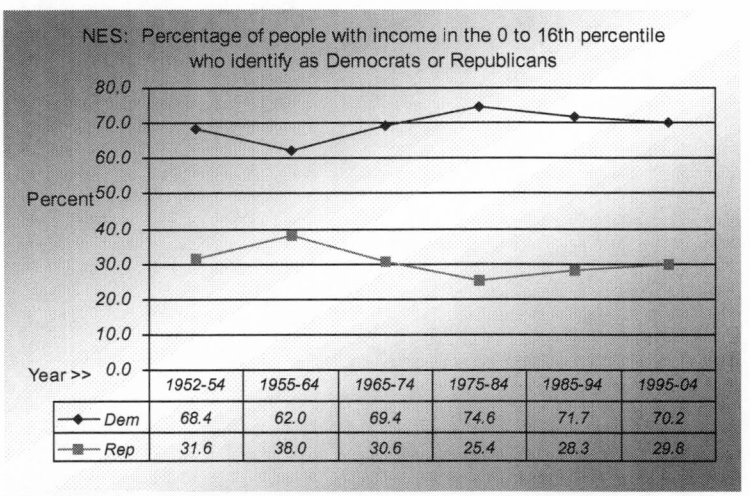

The gap is just slightly smaller for those with family incomes in the 17th to 33rd percentiles. See Figure 250, below.

Figure 250. Percentages of people with family incomes in the 17th to 33rd percentile who identify as Democrats or Republicans (several NES surveys conducted in 1952 through 2004, based on, left to right, 303, 953, 792, 1046, 992, and 655 cases)

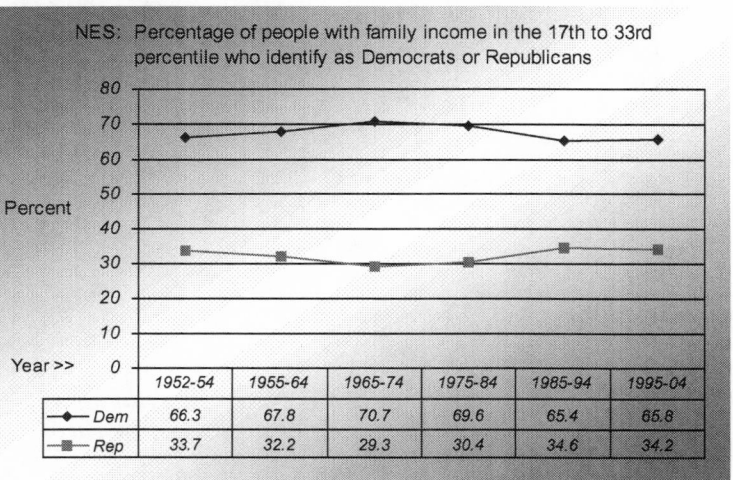

We still see a strong Democratic advantage when we consider people with family incomes ranging from the 34th percentile to the 67th percentile. The gap is a bit larger than for the population in general.

Figure 251. Percentages of people with family incomes in the 34th to 67th percentile who identify as Democrats or Republicans (several NES surveys conducted in 1952 through 2004, based on, left to right, 564, 1580, 1893, 1753, 2022, and 1084 cases)

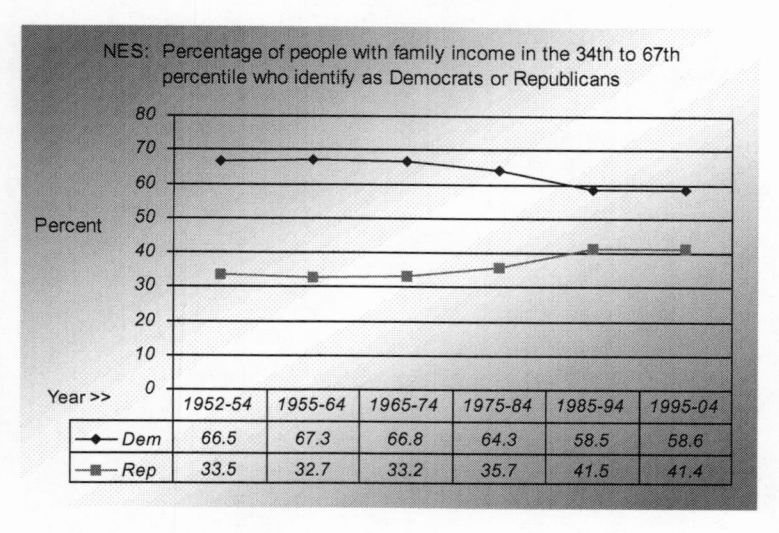

For people with incomes in the 68th percentiles and higher, Republicans have parity or an advantage. This is a fairly recent phenomenon which has taken place during the last 20 years.

Figure 252. Percentages of people with family incomes in the 68th to 95th percentile who identify as Democrats or Republicans (several NES surveys conducted in 1952 through 2004, based on, left to right, 723, 1457, 1532, 1484, 1747, and 850 cases)

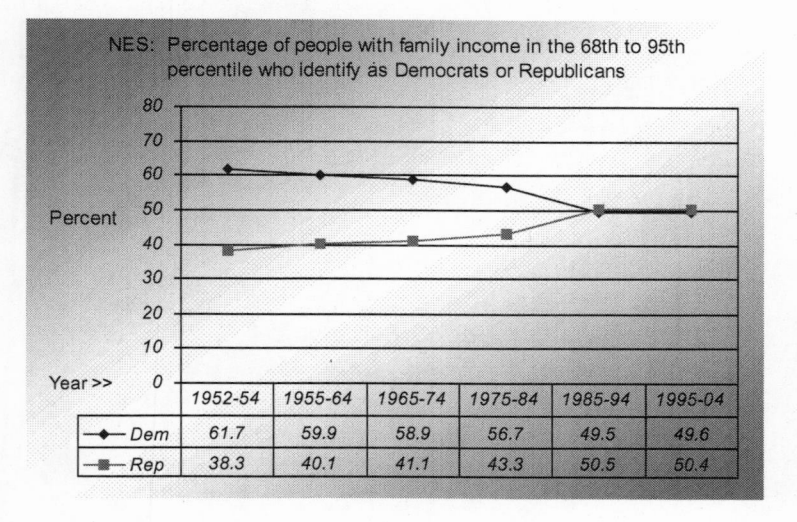

Among those with family incomes in the top 5 percent, the Republican advantage is huge. This may be due to the fact that this small segment of the population pays about 50 percent of the federal income tax, and is attracted to the normal Republican advocacy of lower tax rates.

Figure 253. Percentages of people with family incomes in the 96th to 100th percentile who identify as Democrats or Republicans (several NES surveys conducted in 1952 through 2004, based on, left to right, 93, 308, 267, 352, 264, and 248 cases)

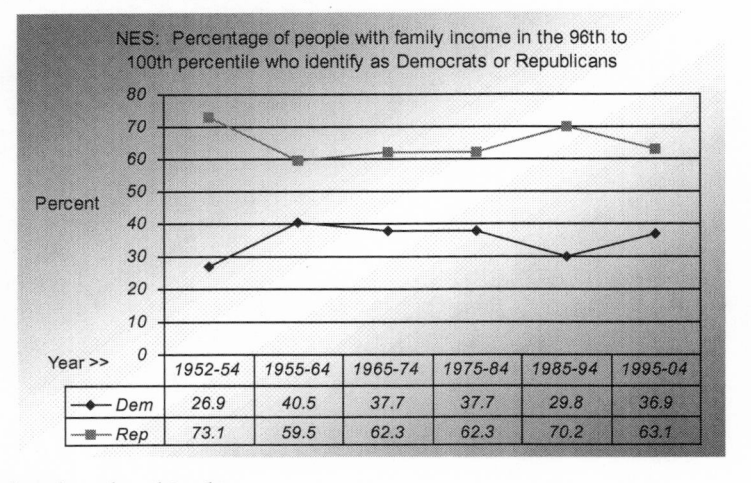

NES: Percentage of people with family income in the 96th to 100th percentile who identify as Democrats or Republicans

Year >>	1952-54	1955-64	1965-74	1975-84	1985-94	1995-04
Dem	26.9	40.5	37.7	37.7	29.8	36.9
Rep	73.1	59.5	62.3	62.3	70.2	63.1

People in the "political South"

Although Democrats still hold a small advantage in the "old South" (the original 11 succession states), the advantage has dramatically decreased during the last 50 years. If the trend continues, Republicans will reach parity in about 10 years.

Figure 254. Percentages of people living in the "old South" who identify as Democrats or Republicans (several NES surveys conducted in 1952 through 2004, based on, left to right, 324, 1392, 1484, 1804, 2100, and 1618 cases)

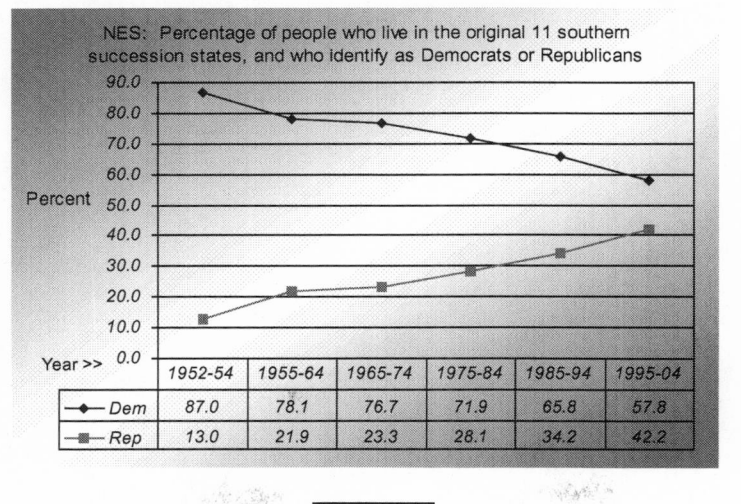

NES: Percentage of people who live in the original 11 southern succession states, and who identify as Democrats or Republicans

Year >>	1952-54	1955-64	1965-74	1975-84	1985-94	1995-04
Dem	87.0	78.1	76.7	71.9	65.8	57.8
Rep	13.0	21.9	23.3	28.1	34.2	42.2

People living in different communities

The final 3 graphs, for this section, address the party identification of people living in different types of communities. Figure 255, below, shows that more than 70 percent of people living in the central cities consider themselves to be Democrats.

Figure 255. Percentages of people who live in the central city who identify as Democrats or Republicans (several NES surveys conducted in 1952 through 2004, based on, left to right, 694, 1567, 1691, 1828, 1725, and 712 cases)

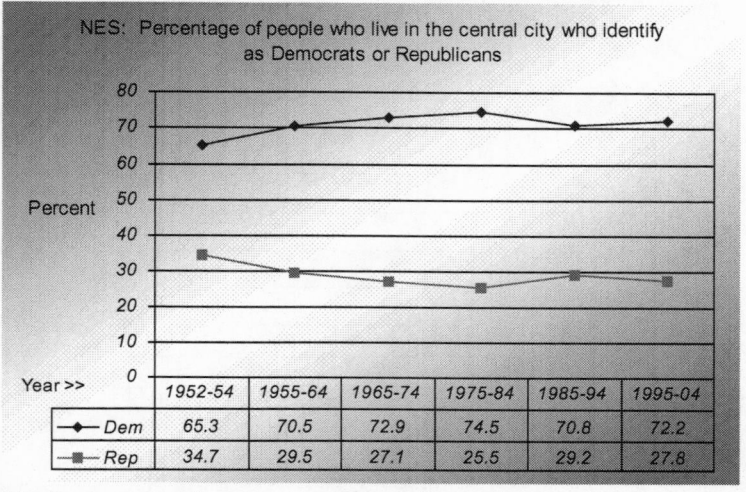

The Democratic advantage is much smaller in the suburbs and rural areas. During the last 10 years, roughly equal numbers of suburbanites have considered themselves to be Republicans and Democrats.

Figure 256. Percentages of people who live in the suburbs who identify as Democrats or Republicans (several NES surveys conducted in 1952 through 2004, based on, left to right, 661, 1849, 1904, 2404, 2725, and 950 cases)

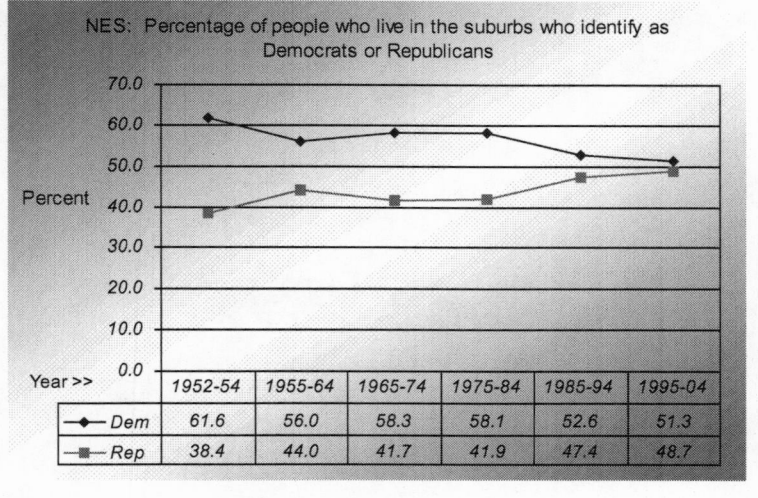

For about 4 decades, Republicans gained among people living in small towns and rural areas, however, that trend has reversed during the last 10 years. This may be due to the significant number of big city retirees moving south to smaller retirement communities.

Figure 257. Percentages of people who live in rural areas and small towns who identify as Democrats or Republicans (several NES surveys conducted in 1952 through 2004, based on, left to right, 813, 2823, 2650, 2346, 2122, and 803 cases)

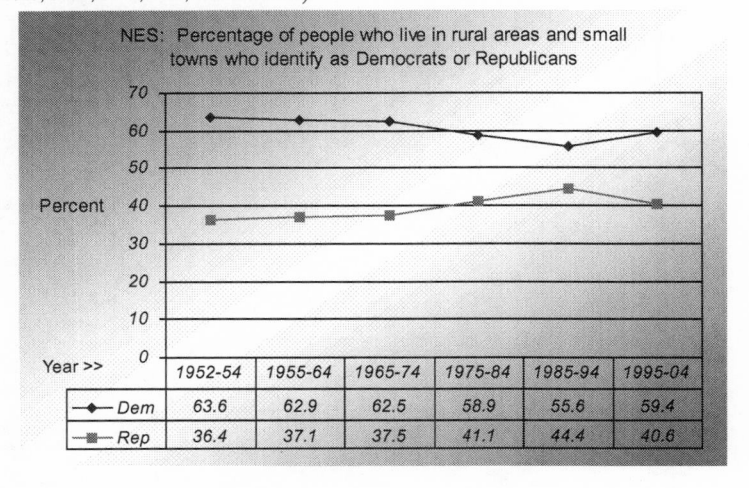

Year >>	1952-54	1955-64	1965-74	1975-84	1985-94	1995-04
Dem	63.6	62.9	62.5	58.9	55.6	59.4
Rep	36.4	37.1	37.5	41.1	44.4	40.6

PART TWO: THE COMPOSITION OF EACH POLITICAL PARTY

In this section, you will find the composition of each party with respect to:

Age

Figure 258. Age breakout of the parties — Democrats (combined results of several NES surveys, conducted from 1952 through 2004, based on, left to right, 1365, 3902, 3970, 4116, 3829, and 2615 cases)

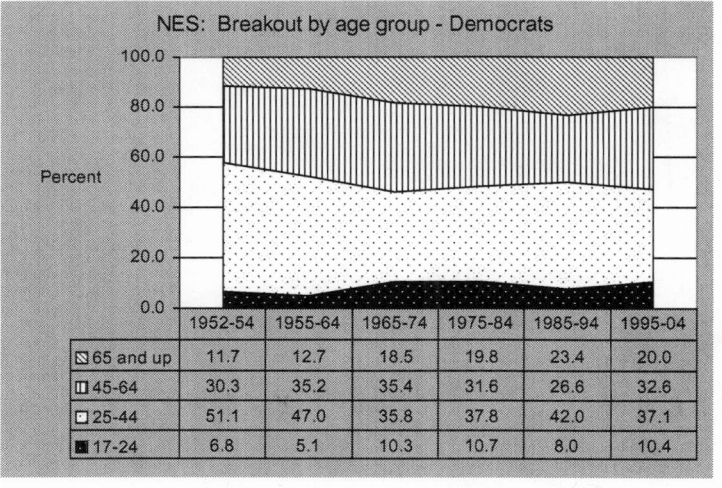

	1952-54	1955-64	1965-74	1975-84	1985-94	1995-04
65 and up	11.7	12.7	18.5	19.8	23.4	20.0
45-64	30.3	35.2	35.4	31.6	26.6	32.6
25-44	51.1	47.0	35.8	37.8	42.0	37.1
17-24	6.8	5.1	10.3	10.7	8.0	10.4

Each political party is broken out by the proportion of people within 4 different age groups. In Figure 258, above, we see a general increase in the percentage of Democrats who are over age 65, and a general decline in the percentage of Democrats who are ages 25 to 44.[2]

In Figure 259, below, the same information is displayed with regard to Republicans. It is apparent that Republicans have not gained among the elderly, despite the overall aging of the population. In 1952-54 about 16.5 percent of Republicans were over age 65, and the same percentage exists today. Republicans have, however, done well with the 25 to 44 age group, a group that now comprises nearly 44 percent of Republicans (versus just 41% of the general survey population).

Figure 259. Age breakout of the parties — Republicans (combined results of several NES surveys, conducted from 1952 through 2004, based on, left to right, 776, 2315, 2229, 2424, 2739, and 2005 cases)

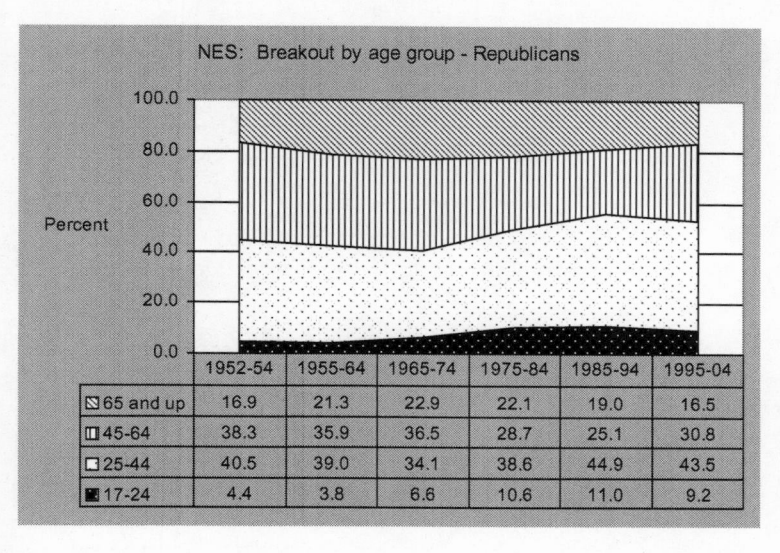

	1952-54	1955-64	1965-74	1975-84	1985-94	1995-04
▨ 65 and up	16.9	21.3	22.9	22.1	19.0	16.5
▯ 45-64	38.3	35.9	36.5	28.7	25.1	30.8
▢ 25-44	40.5	39.0	34.1	38.6	44.9	43.5
▪ 17-24	4.4	3.8	6.6	10.6	11.0	9.2

Gender

The modern "gender" gap started in the '60s and '70s, and has become a major political factor for each party during the last 20 to 30 years. In Figure 260, below, we see that, during the last 20 years, men have comprised nearly 50 percent of Republicans, but only 40 percent of Democrats. This might mean that Republicans need to adopt policies and platforms that appeal equally to the genders, while Democrats may find it more advantageous to adopt distaff policies and messages.

---

2 During those same years, the over 65 age group, *as a percentage of the general survey population*, changed from 13 to 16%; and the 25 to 44 age group changed from 48 to 41% of the general survey population.

Figure 260. The composition of each party with respect to males — (combined results of several NES surveys conducted from 1952 through 2004, based on, left to right, 989, 2748, 2571, 2652, 2848, and 2060 cases)

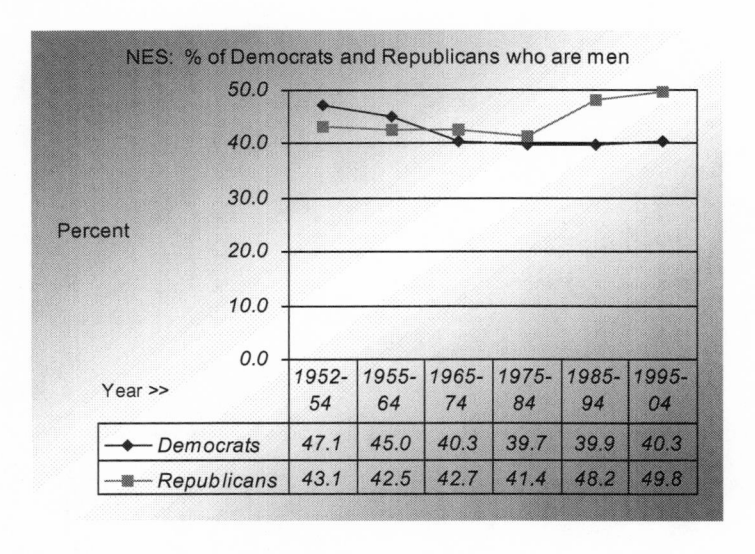

NES: % of Democrats and Republicans who are men						
Year >>	1952-54	1955-64	1965-74	1975-84	1985-94	1995-04
Democrats	47.1	45.0	40.3	39.7	39.9	40.3
Republicans	43.1	42.5	42.7	41.4	48.2	49.8

Of course, the gap is reversed with regard to women. In Figure 261, below, we see that about 60 percent of Democrats are women, while only about 50 percent are Republicans.

Figure 261. The composition of each party with respect to females — (combined results of several NES surveys conducted from 1952 through 2004, based on, left to right, 1179, 3491, 3674, 3925, 3724, and 2576 cases)

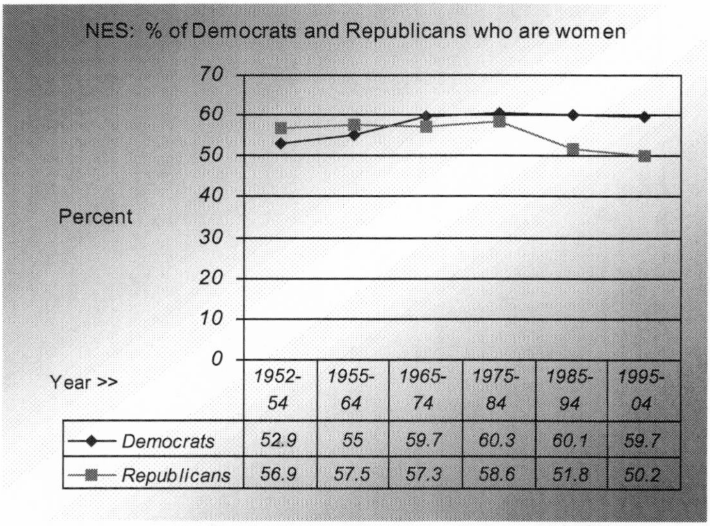

NES: % of Democrats and Republicans who are women						
Year >>	1952-54	1955-64	1965-74	1975-84	1985-94	1995-04
Democrats	52.9	55	59.7	60.3	60.1	59.7
Republicans	56.9	57.5	57.3	58.6	51.8	50.2

Race and ethnicity

Figure 262 shows the percentage of Democratic constituents broken out by race over the last 50 years. Blacks now comprise about one quarter of all Democrats, Hispanics about 10 percent, and other minorities about 5 percent.

Figure 262. Race breakout — (Democrats) (combined results of several NES surveys, conducted from 1952 through 2004, based on, left to right, 1377, 3915, 3999, 4141, 3831, and 2624 cases)

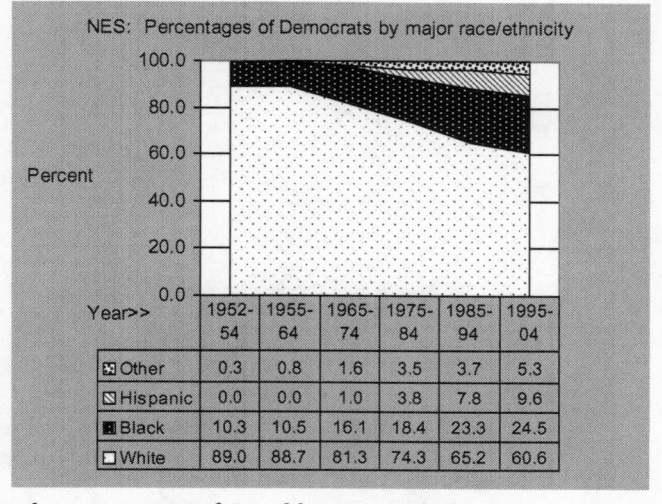

Only about 2 percent of Republicans are Black, a percentage that is less than half that of Hispanics. During the last 10 years, Whites have remained the overwhelming majority of Republicans, comprising about 86 percent. That is far higher than the Democratic percentage, which is only about 61 percent.

Figure 263. Race breakout — (Republicans) (combined results of several NES surveys, conducted from 1952 through 2004, based on, left to right, 791, 2324, 2246, 2439, 2741, and 2010 cases)

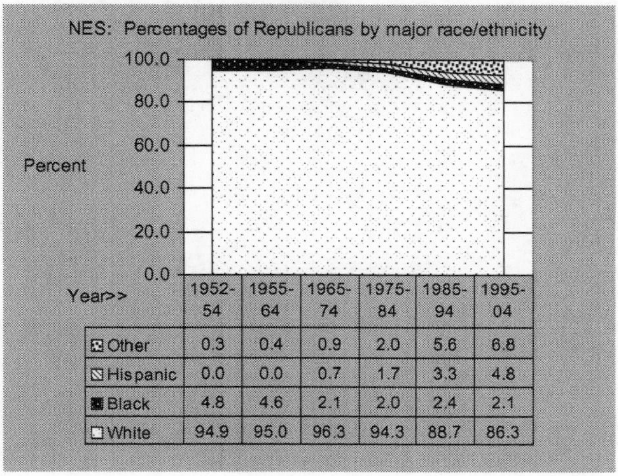

NES: Percentages of Republicans by major race/ethnicity

Year>>	1952-54	1955-64	1965-74	1975-84	1985-94	1995-04
Other	0.3	0.4	0.9	2.0	5.6	6.8
Hispanic	0.0	0.0	0.7	1.7	3.3	4.8
Black	4.8	4.6	2.1	2.0	2.4	2.1
White	94.9	95.0	96.3	94.3	88.7	86.3

Religious denominations

There are some statistically significant differences in religious identification. Protestants comprise a declining percentage of both Democrats and Republicans; however, they remain a larger percentage among Republicans.

Figure 264. The percentage of each party that is Protestant (combined results of several NES surveys, conducted from 1952 through 2004, based on, left to right, 1613, 4552, 4426, 4319, 4141, and 2694 cases)

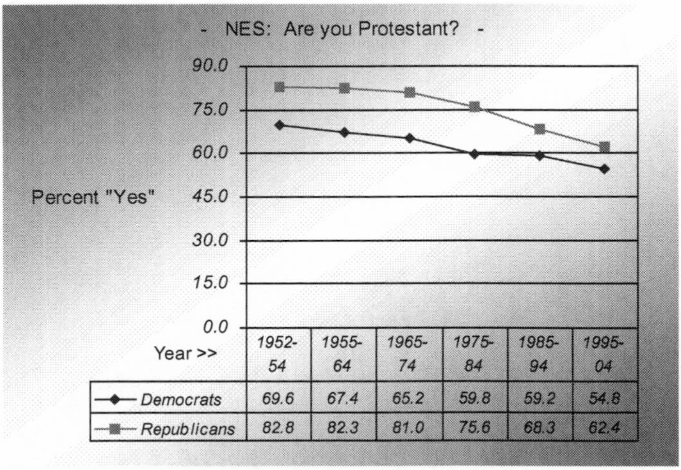

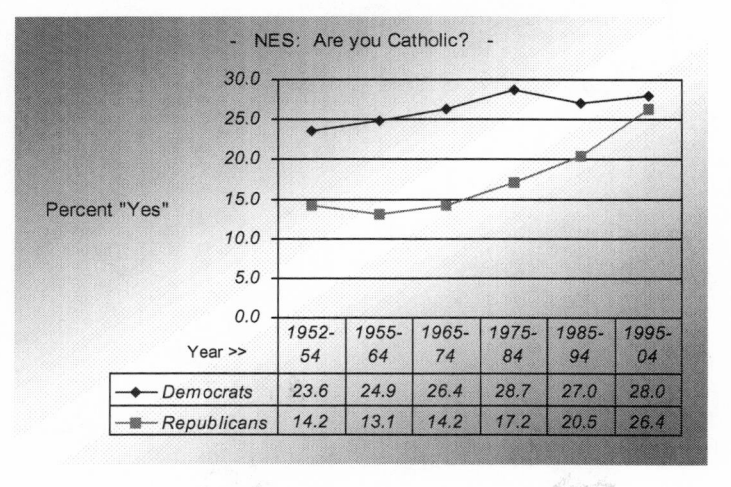

Catholics have grown as a percentage of both Democrats and Republicans; however, the percentage growth has been far larger for Republicans. Now, Catholics comprise nearly equal percentages of each of the two political parties.

Figure 265. The percentage of each party that is Catholic (combined results of several NES surveys, conducted from 1952 through 2004, based on, left to right, 437, 1279, 1374, 1608, 1598, and 1266 cases)

Jews comprise a slightly smaller percentage of Democrats, having dropped from about 4 to 3 percent. The percentage of Republicans who are Jewish has held fairly even at just below 1 percent.

Figure 266. The percentage of each party that is Jewish (combined results of several NES surveys, conducted from 1952 through 2004, based on, left to right, 62, 177, 161, 173, 113, and 100 cases)

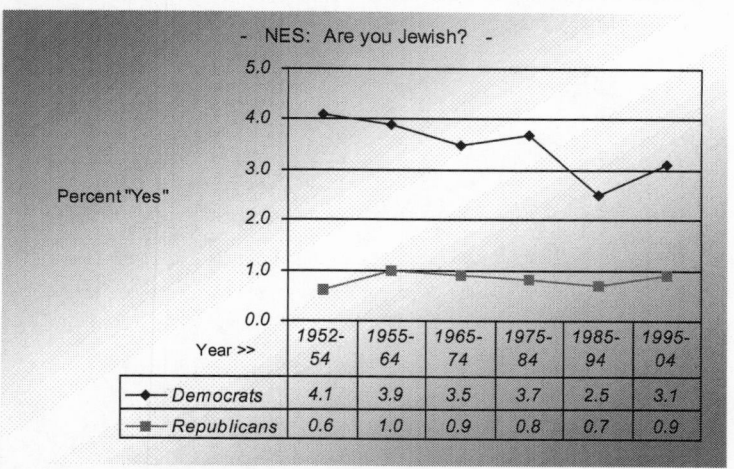

For both political parties there has been a large increase in the percentage of constituents who are either not religious or belong to another religion (e.g., Islam). The percentages for the last decade are 14 and 10 for Democrats and Republicans, respectively.

Figure 267. The percentage of each party that is another religion, agnostic, or refuses to answer (combined results of several NES surveys, conducted from 1952 through 2004, based on, left to right, 50, 139, 256, 442, 682, and 530 cases)

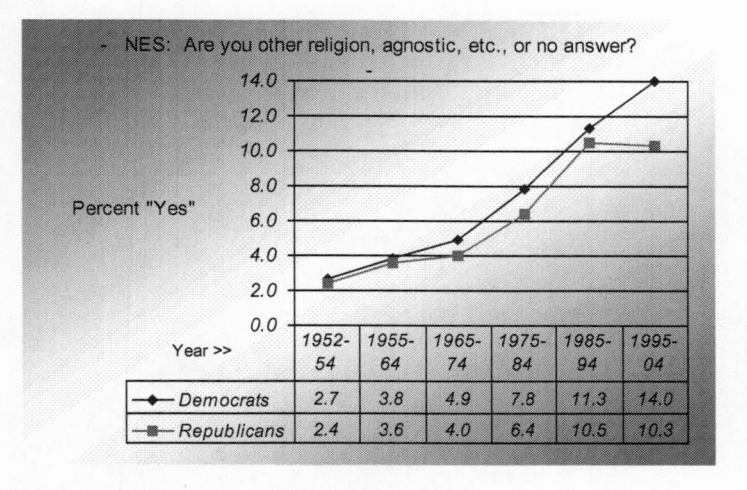

People who are married

This topic was covered in "Lifestyles" (Chapter 1). The following chart, showing the percentages of Democrats and Republicans who are married, is a reproduction of Figure 8.

Figure 268. Are you married? (Men) (various NES surveys conducted in 1952 through 2004, based on, left to right, 592, 2748, 2571, 2653, 2847, and 2059 cases)

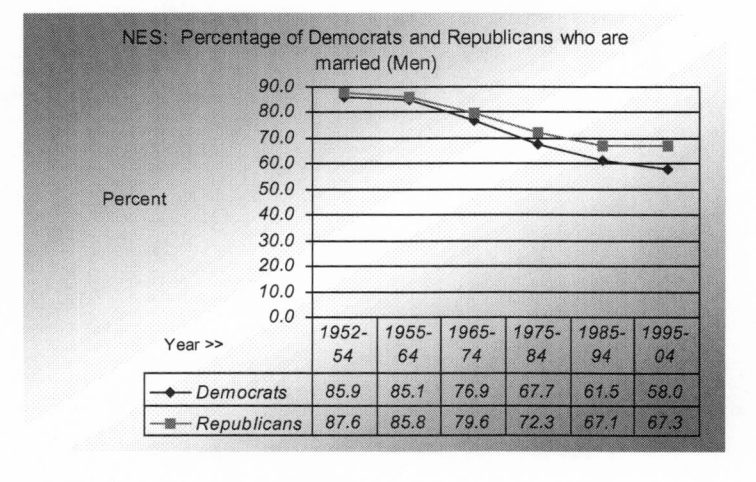

Year >>	1952-54	1955-64	1965-74	1975-84	1985-94	1995-04
Democrats	85.9	85.1	76.9	67.7	61.5	58.0
Republicans	87.6	85.8	79.6	72.3	67.1	67.3

The following chart, pertaining to married women, is a reproduction of Figure 9, shown on page 12. It is interesting to note a "rebound," so to speak in marriage rates among women (but, not among men). Could this be partly due to welfare reform (which was enacted in the mid-90s)?

Figure 269. Are you married? (Women) (various NES surveys conducted in 1952 through 2004, based on, left to right, 735, 3491, 3674, 3925, 3724, and 2576 cases)

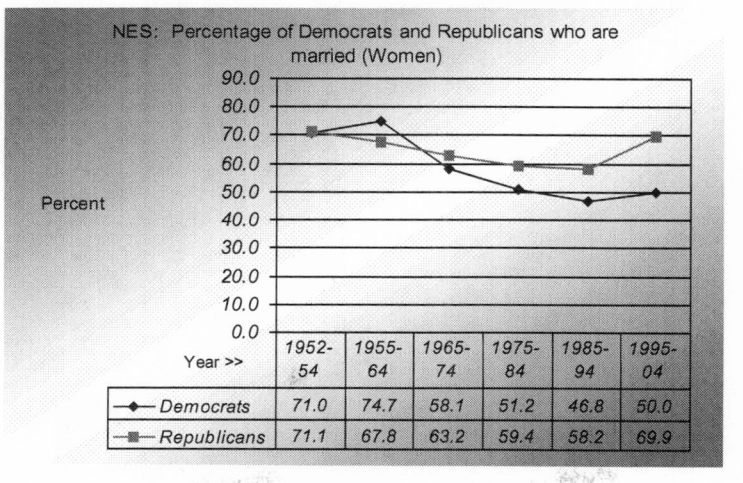

Year >>	1952-54	1955-64	1965-74	1975-84	1985-94	1995-04
Democrats	71.0	74.7	58.1	51.2	46.8	50.0
Republicans	71.1	67.8	63.2	59.4	58.2	69.9

Occupational categories

The figures below show the percentages of Democrats and Republicans in various occupational categories. The percentages do not add to 100 percent because homemakers and military personnel are not shown. By far, skilled, semi-skilled, and service workers comprise the largest proportion of Democrats (over one third). Professionals and managers come in second at about 27 percent.

Figure 270. What is your occupational category? (Democrats) (various NES surveys conducted in 1952 through 2004, based on, left to right, 841, 3318, 3415, 4139, 3833, and 2129 cases)

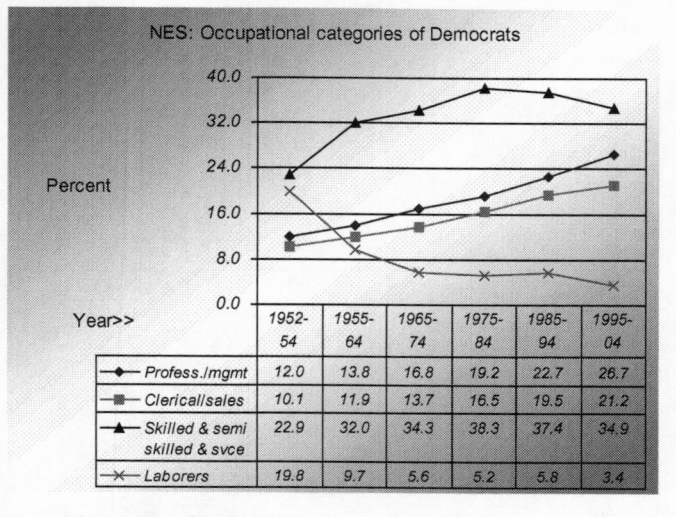

	1952-54	1955-64	1965-74	1975-84	1985-94	1995-04
Profess./mgmt	12.0	13.8	16.8	19.2	22.7	26.7
Clerical/sales	10.1	11.9	13.7	16.5	19.5	21.2
Skilled & semi skilled & svce	22.9	32.0	34.3	38.3	37.4	34.9
Laborers	19.8	9.7	5.6	5.2	5.8	3.4

For Republicans, professionals and managers are the largest group (about 33%), while clerical and sales workers account for the next largest segment (about 24%).

Figure 271. What is your occupational category? (Republicans) (various NES surveys conducted in 1952 through 2004, based on, left to right, 486, 1957, 1929, 2439, 2740, and 1562 cases)

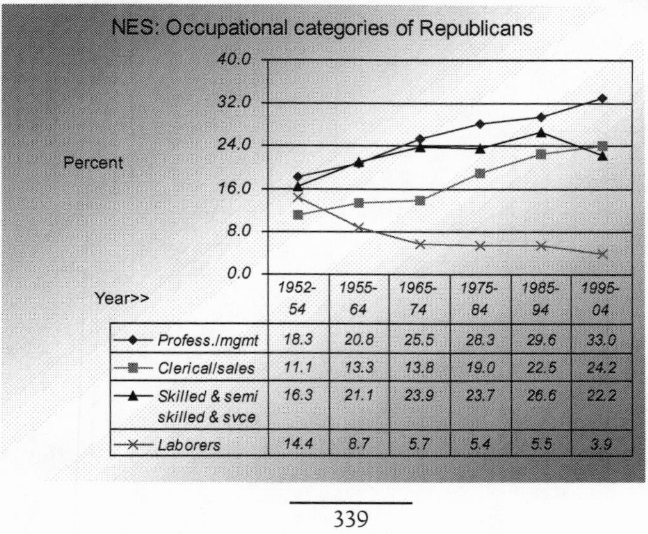

NES: Occupational categories of Republicans

	1952-54	1955-64	1965-74	1975-84	1985-94	1995-04
Profess./mgmt	18.3	20.8	25.5	28.3	29.6	33.0
Clerical/sales	11.1	13.3	13.8	19.0	22.5	24.2
Skilled & semi skilled & svce	16.3	21.1	23.9	23.7	26.6	22.2
Laborers	14.4	8.7	5.7	5.4	5.5	3.9

College students and graduates

Displayed in this section are the 50-year trends for Democrats and Republicans with at least some college education. A review of Figure 272 shows that Republicans have been more likely to have some college training for several decades. However, as noted in Chapter 2, recent trends show a narrowing of the education gap. The amounts depicted here represent Democrats and Republicans of both genders and of all ages. For additional comparison information see Chapter 2.

Figure 272. Do you have at least some college education?? (various NES surveys from 1952 through 2004, based on, left to right, 2168, 6239, 6245, 6580, 6573, and 4635 cases)

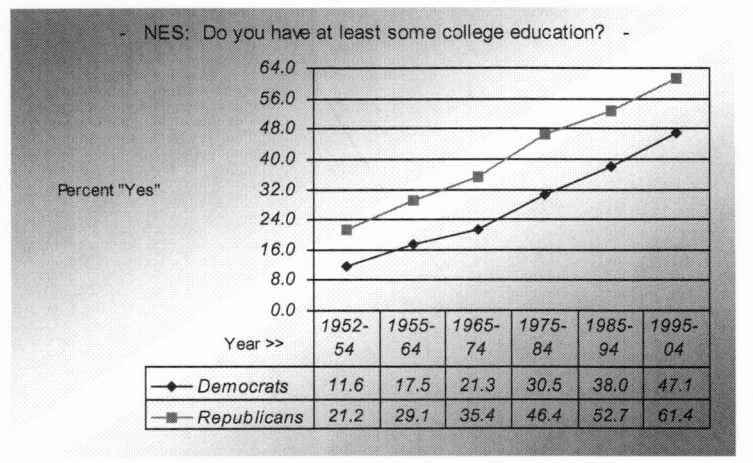

Republicans have also been more likely to have college and advanced degrees. Again, however, this disparity is narrowing in very recent years.

Figure 273. Do you have a college or advanced degree? (various NES surveys from 1952 through 2004, based on, left to right, 2168, 6239, 6245, 6580, 6573, and 4635 cases)

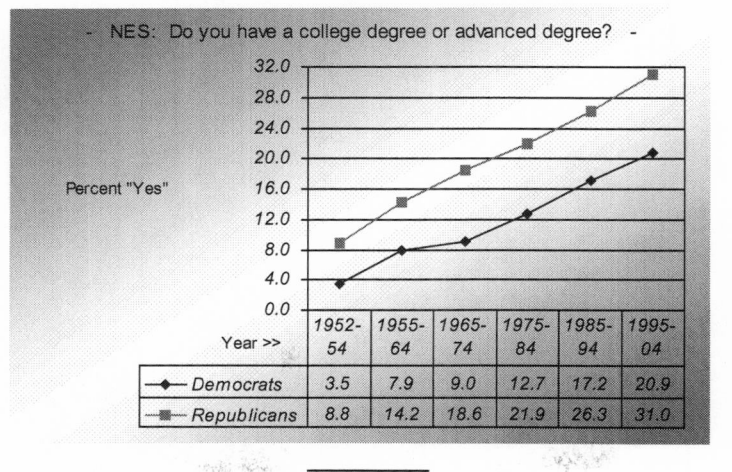

People in different family income brackets

Figure 274 shows a direct comparison of those Democrats and Republicans who reported income in the lowest 16 percent of all respondents. In this category, the percentage of Democrats has been fairly constant over the last 50 years, while there has been a steady decline in the percentage of Republicans.

Figure 274. Democrats and Republicans who place their total family income in the lower 16th percentile (combined results of several NES surveys conducted from 1952 through 2004, based on, left to right, 424, 1075, 1083, 942, 1007, and 484 cases)

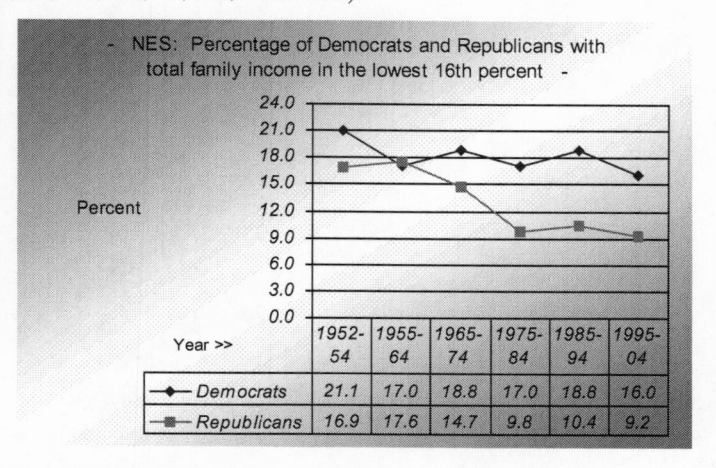

In Figure 275 we see a depiction of people who are not poor but have income that is lower than two thirds of all others. A greater percentage of Democrats are in this category, and that percentage may be increasing slightly.

Figure 275. Democrats and Republicans who place their total family income in the 17th to 33rd percentile (combined results of several NES surveys conducted from 1952 through 2004, based on, left to right, 303, 1110, 878, 1125, 985, and 652 cases)

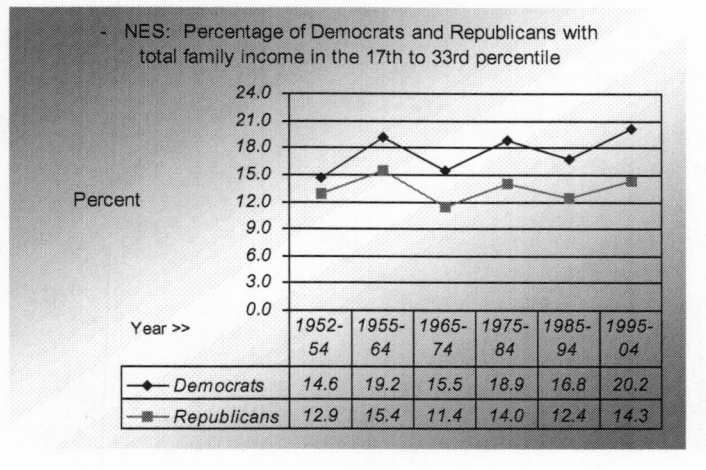

In the middle-income range (34th to 67th percentile) we used to find a higher percentage of Democrats than Republicans; however, in recent years there seems to be no significant difference.

Figure 276. Democrats and Republicans who place their total family income in the 34th to 67th percentile (combined results of several NES surveys conducted from 1952 through 2004, based on, left to right, 564, 1819, 2093, 1856, 2015, and 1060 cases)

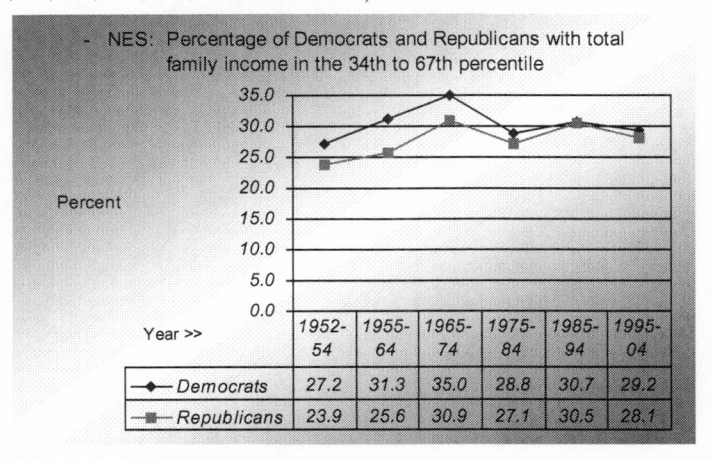

About 32 percent of Democrats used to report that they had total family income in the 68th to 95th percentile; however, this percentage seems to have dropped to just about 20 percent. About 2 percent of those Democrats may have moved up to the top 4 percent of income earners, but (by deduction) most must have moved down, relative to others. Among Republicans there has been a decline of about 8 percent reporting income in this income range. Most of those Republicans must have also moved down in income, relative to others.

Figure 277. Democrats and Republicans who place their total family income in the 68th to 95th percentile (combined results of several NES surveys conducted from 1952 through 2004, based on, left to right, 723, 1689, 1654, 1574, 1751, and 845 cases)

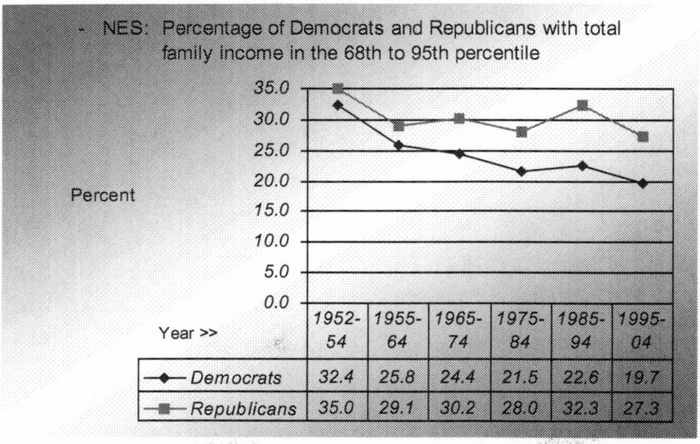

NES: Percentage of Democrats and Republicans with total family income in the 68th to 95th percentile

Percent

Year >>	1952-54	1955-64	1965-74	1975-84	1985-94	1995-04
Democrats	32.4	25.8	24.4	21.5	22.6	19.7
Republicans	35.0	29.1	30.2	28.0	32.3	27.3

Figure 278 shows the Democrats and Republicans who reported income in the highest 4 percent of all respondents. The percentage of Republicans in this range seems to consistently be at least twice the percentage of Democrats in this range.

Figure 278. Democrats and Republicans who place their total family income in the 96th to 100th percentile (combined results of several NES surveys conducted from 1952 through 2004, based on, left to right, 93, 341, 289, 366, 265, and 244 cases)

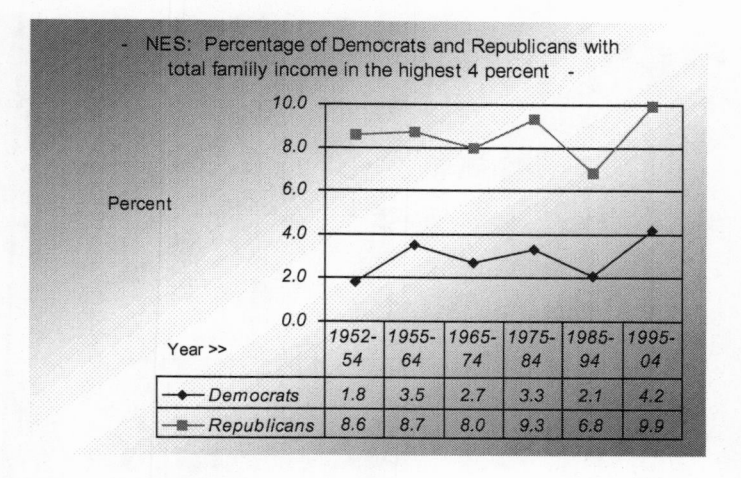

People in the "political South"

Fifty years ago, less than 10 percent of Republicans hailed from the Southern secession states. Now such people comprise about one third of all Republicans. They also constitute approximately that percentage of Democrats.

Figure 279. What is your occupational category? (Democrats) (various NES surveys conducted in 1952 through 2004, based on, left to right, 1327, 6239, 6245, 6578, 6573, and 4634 cases)

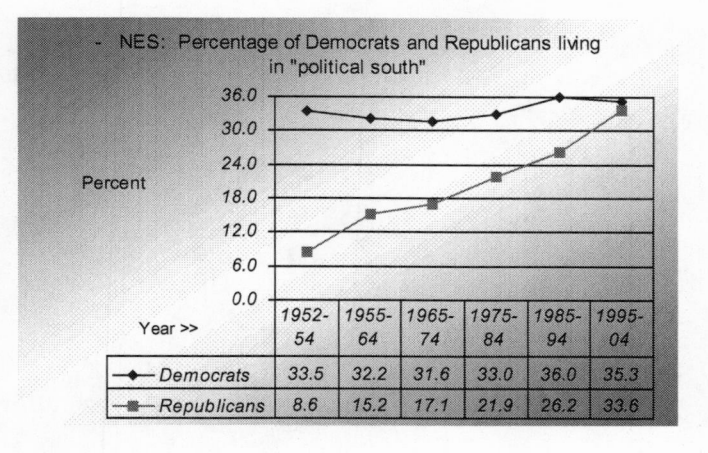

People in different communities

Most Democratic and Republican constituents used to live in rural areas and small towns. Today, the Democratic constituents are evenly divided between the central cities, the suburbs, and the rural areas.

Figure 280. In what type of community do you live? (Democrats) (combined results of several NES surveys, conducted from 1952 through 2004, based on, left to right, 1377, 3915, 3999, 4139, 3832, and 1478 cases)

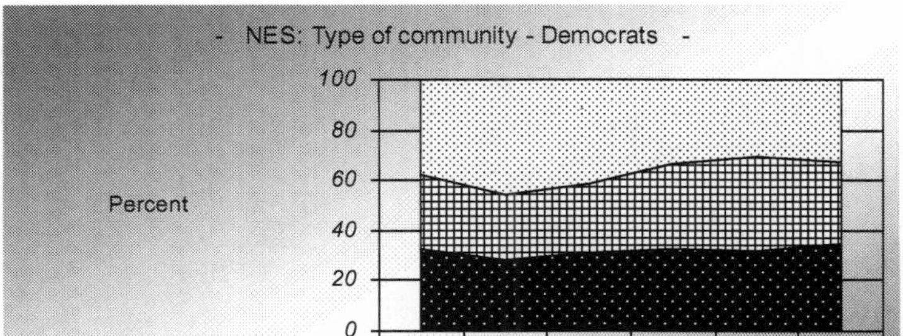

- NES: Type of community - Democrats -

Year>>	1952-1654	1955-64	1965-74	1975-84	1985-94	1995-04
Rural & small towns	37.5	45.3	41.4	33.4	30.8	32.3
Suburban areas	29.6	26.5	27.8	33.7	37.4	32.9
Central cities	32.9	28.2	30.8	32.9	31.9	34.8

On the other hand, Republicans are not divided evenly among the three major types of communities. Nearly 47 percent of Republicans live in the suburbs, while just 20 percent live in the central cities.

Figure 281. In what type of community do you live? (Republicans) (combined results of several NES surveys, conducted from 1952 through 2004, based on, left to right, 791, 2324, 2246, 2439, 2740, and 987 cases)

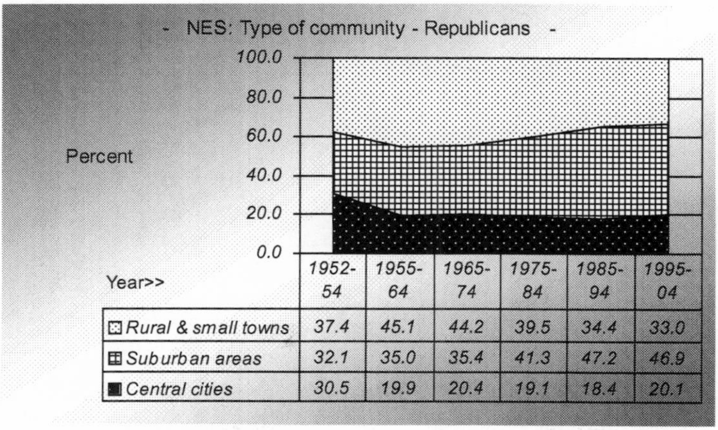

- NES: Type of community - Republicans -

Year>>	1952-54	1955-64	1965-74	1975-84	1985-94	1995-04
Rural & small towns	37.4	45.1	44.2	39.5	34.4	33.0
Suburban areas	32.1	35.0	35.4	41.3	47.2	46.9
Central cities	30.5	19.9	20.4	19.1	18.4	20.1

APPENDIX B: INFORMATION OVERFLOW AND ANALYSIS

Appendix B 1. GSS Surveys For High School Diploma Rates (relates to page 74)

Figure 282, below, depicts the percentages of Democrats and Republicans who received (at the least) high school degrees, according to GSS surveys conducted during the last 30 years. The Republican advantage has been clear; however, Democrats have mostly closed the gap.

Figure 282. Do you have (at the least) a high school diploma (men and women)? (GSS surveys conducted in 1977 through 2006, based on, left to right, 2861, 5170, 5199, 4711, 3279, and 6034 cases, with confidence level of 99+% for all differences, and with relative proportions of, left to right, .88, .81, .86, .93, .91, and .94)

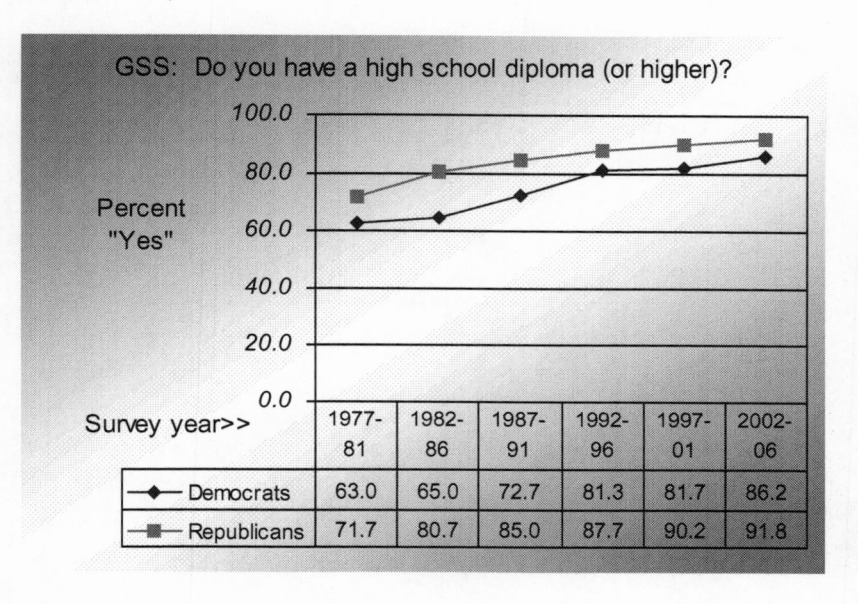

GSS: Do you have a high school diploma (or higher)?						
Survey year>>	1977-81	1982-86	1987-91	1992-96	1997-01	2002-06
Democrats	63.0	65.0	72.7	81.3	81.7	86.2
Republicans	71.7	80.7	85.0	87.7	90.2	91.8

Appendix B 2. More Surveys For College Graduation Rates (relates to page 75.

Pew Surveys

Pew surveys show that, overall, Republicans continue to have the edge with regard to college diplomas. Note that these are statistically "weighted" numbers (designed to make the results more reflective of the overall population), and are somewhat larger than the actual sample sizes (which are not shown).

Table 56. Pew surveys pertaining to 4-year college graduation rates (men and women combined)

Pew Surveys: Percentage of Democrats and Republicans with a 4-year college degree, or advanced graduate degree	Democrats		Republicans	
	With 4-yr. deg.	Total	With 4-yr. deg.	Total
Pew February 2007 Political Survey:	362	1311	308	988
Pew 2006 Biennial Media Consumption survey:	562	2202	605	1954
Pew 2005 Religion and Public Life: "	358	1392	416	1390
Pew June 2005 News Interest Index survey:	329	1206	338	1138
Pew 2005 Political Typology Callback survey:	221	905	237	797
Pew March 2005 News Interest Index survey:	181	596	141	512
Pew February 2005 News Interest Index survey:	264	973	288	920
Pew 2004 Political Typology survey:	358	1421	352	1282
Pew 2004 Biennial Media Consumption survey	462	1903	498	1575
Pew 2003 Religion and Public Life survey:	295	1228	356	1163
Pew 2002 Biennial Media Consumption survey:	518	2089	527	1888
Totals	3910	15226	4066	13607
Average percentage	25.7		29.9	
Overall proportion (Dem % divided by Rep %)	86.0%			
Confidence level	99+%			

GSS Surveys

Figure 283. Do you have a 4-year college diploma (or higher degree)? (Men) (GSS surveys conducted in 1977 through 2006, based on, left to right, 3250, 4083, and 3988 cases, with confidence level of 99+% for all differences, and with relative proportions of, left to right, .57, .62, and .71)

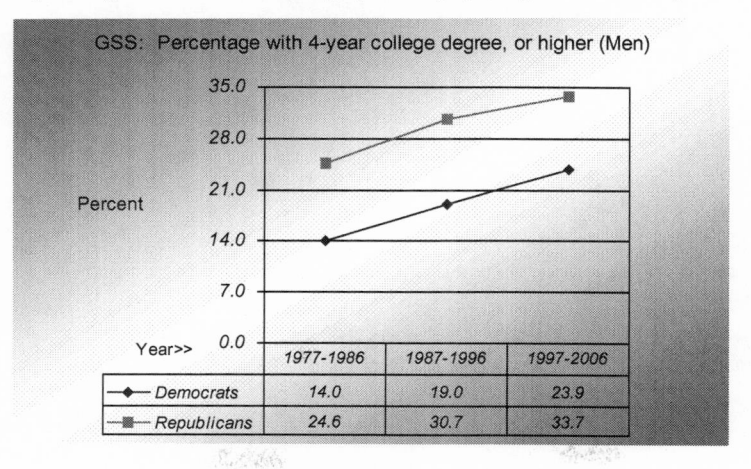

GSS: Percentage with 4-year college degree, or higher (Men)

Year>>	1977-1986	1987-1996	1997-2006
Democrats	14.0	19.0	23.9
Republicans	24.6	30.7	33.7

GSS surveys for men are similar to those of NES, and show that Republican men are more likely to have 4-year college degrees.

In the case of women, the GSS figures show less of a gap than the NES figures. These results show that Democratic women are now just as likely to have earned a 4-year college degree. See Figure 284.

Figure 284. Do you have a 4-year college diploma (or higher degree)? (Women) (GSS surveys conducted in 1977 through 2006, based on, left to right, 4776, 5820, and 5322 cases, with confidence level of 99+% for the left and middle differences, and no statistical significance for the right-side column, and with relative proportions of, left to right, .69, .80 and n/a)

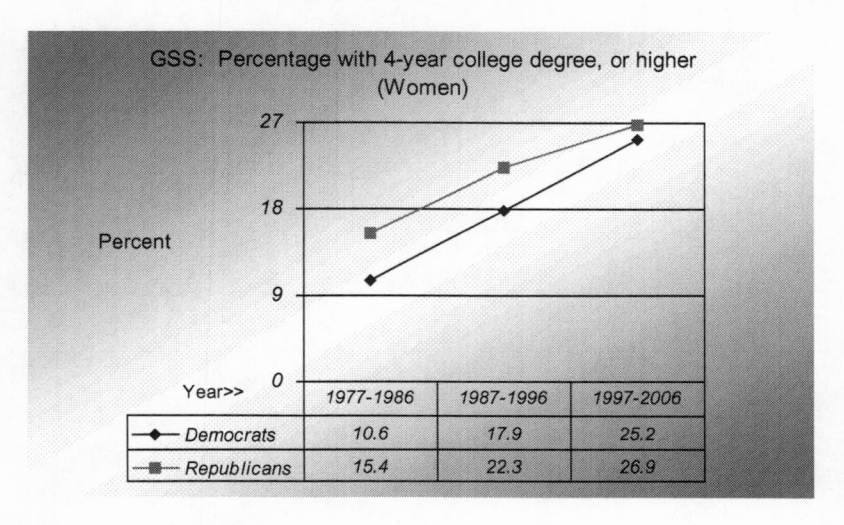

Appendix B 3. Factors That Account For The Education Gap — 30-Year Analysis (relates to page 84)

Using the multiple regression function of the SDA Web-based statistical program and GSS data for the years 1977 through 2006, I tested the relationship between several independent variables and the dependent variable, years of education (the GSS variable called "EDUC"). The independent variables tested are shown on the left side of Table 57. Each variable is expressed as a range starting at "0" and ending at "1." In the case of the first variable, party identification, being a Democrat is considered to be a "0" and being a Republican is considered to be a "1." (The assignment is arbitrary, and not meant to have hidden meanings!) As we move from the "0" end of the variable towards the "1" end, the strength of the independent variable's correlation with years of education is shown in the "Beta" column. Large, positive beta numbers indicate a strong and positive correlation, while small, negative beta numbers suggest a weak and negative correlation. In Table 57 we see a strong and positive relationship between income and years of education. (The beta number is +.300.) We also find positive relationships be-

tween education and good health (beta is .195) and between education and being Republican (beta is .062). On the other hand, being married does not correlate positively with more years of education. Rather, it is moderately associated with less years of education (beta is negative .088).

Table 57. Independent variables regressed against education — 30 years

Variable	Variable details	Beta	T-Stat	Prob.
Party identification (PARTYID)	Reps = 1 Dems = 0	.062	7.510	.000
Income (REALINC)	Over $50K in 2006 dollars = 1 Less than $50K = 0	.300	38.161	.000
Health (HEALTH)	Good or excellent health = 1 Other = 0	.195	25.858	.000
Race (RACE)	White = 1 Other race = 0	.039	4.999	.000
Marital status (MARITAL)	Married = 1 Single = 0	−.088	−11.424	.000
Political views (POLVIEWS)	Conservative = 1 Moderate or liberal = 0	.018	2.299	.022
Religious strength (RELITEN)	Strongly religious = 1 fairly or weakly religious = 0	−.010	−1.394	*
Gender (SEX)	Male = 1 Female = 0	−.006	−.851	*

*Not statistically significant

Appendix B 4. Factors Correlating With The Education Gap — 9-Year Analysis (relates to page 86)

Using the multiple regression function of the SDA Web-based statistical program, and GSS data for the years 1998 through 2006, I tested the relationship between several independent variables and the dependent variable, education (the GSS variable called "EDUC"). The independent variables tested are identical to those shown in Table 57, in Appendix B 3. The only element changed is in the number of years tested (9 years instead of 30 years). Please see Appendix B 3 for an explanation of the methodology. The results of the 9-year analysis are shown in Table 58, below. Again, high income and good health are the variables that correlate most strongly with education. Party identification is no longer an important factor. Being (racially) white correlates positively with more years of education, while being married and being male correlate negatively (although only to a minor degree).

Table 58. Independent variables regressed against education — 9 years

Variable	Variable details	Beta	T-Stat	Prob.
Party identification (PARTYID)	Reps = 1 Dems = 0	.012	.761	*
Income (REALINC)	Over $50K in 2006 dollars = 1 Less than $50K = 0	.309	21.890	.000
Health (HEALTH)	Good or excellent health = 1 Other = 0	.176	13.311	.000
Race (RACE)	White = 1 Other race = 0	.058	4.137	.000
Marital status (MARITAL)	Married = 1 Single = 0	−.052	−3.771	.000
Political views (POLVIEWS)	Conservative = 1 Moderate or liberal = 0	.016	1.064	*
Religious strength (RELITEN)	Strongly religious = 1 fairly or weakly religious = 0	.003	.192	*
Gender (SEX)	Male = 1 Female = 0	−.025	−1.906	.057 (marg)

*Not statistically significant

Appendix B 5. Calculation Of The Average Male Hourly Wage Rate (relates to page 99)

The average male hourly rate of $21.16 was calculated by putting the gender-neutral rate of $19.29 (per BLS's National Compensation Survey for June, 2006) into the following algebraic formula: .4648W + .5352M = 19.29, where .4648 represents the percentage of women in the labor force, .5352 represents the percentage of men in the labor force, W represents the average hourly rate for women, and M equals the average hourly rate for men. Since we know that the hourly rate for women is about 81 percent of the hourly rate per men (per US Dept. of Labor "Charting the U.S. Labor Market in 2006"), we can substitute .81M for the W in the formula, and solve for M.

Appendix B 6. Factors That Correlate With Hours Worked (Men) (relates to page 98)

Using the multiple regression function of the SDA Web-based statistical program, and GSS data for the years 1998 through 2004, I tested the relationship between several independent variables and the dependent variable, hours worked ("HR1"). The independent variables tested, and the results, are shown in Table 59, below. Only two of the variables correlated significantly with hours worked: having total family income over $50,000 per year, and being Republican. Note, very similar results were obtained when the income variable was changed to indicate family income over $25,000 per year. (Those results are not shown.)

Table 59. Independent variables regressed against hours worked (men) (1998-2004). There were a total of 1108 cases.

Variable	Variable details	Beta	T-Stat	Prob.
Party identifica- tion (PARTYID)	Reps = 1; Dems = 0	.079	2.242	.025
Income (INCOME98)	Over $50K = 1; Less = 0	.137	4.156	.000
Health (HEALTH)	Good or excel- lent = 1; Other = 0	.002	.062	*
Race (RACE)	White = 1; Other = 0	0	0	*
Marital status (MARITAL)	Married = 1; Other = 0	−.002	−.078	*
Political views (POLVIEWS)	Conservative = 1; Other = 0	−.012	−.356	*
Religious strength (RELITEN)	Strong = 1; fair or weak = 0	−.038	−1.238	*
Degree (DEGREE)	2yr deg. or higher = 1; other = 0	.034	1.094	*

*Not statistically significant

We see that, even after the income variable is controlled, Republicans are significantly more likely to work longer hours than are Democrats. If those re-sults are accurate, there might be some Republican traits, not yet identified, that explain the remaining differential (i.e., that explain the Beta correlation factor of .079). Of course, it could be the other way around. The practice of working longer hours could cause a person to become a Republican (for some reason un-known to the author).

Appendix B 7. The Impact Of Education On Wages (Men) (relates to page 101)

In the third column of Table 60, below, average male earnings are listed by level of educational attainment. The source is the Current Population Survey (CPS) conducted by the Bureau of Labor Statistics and the Bureau of the Cen-sus. These are year 2000 amounts, restated to 2007 values using the consumer price index. In the table's middle columns we find the percentages of Democratic and Republican males at each of the educational levels, according to GSS sur-vey results. There were no statistically significant differences between working Democrats and Republicans with respect to the high school, junior college, or post-graduate college levels (shown in rows 2, 3, and 5), so the percentages used in Table 60 for these educational levels are simply the overall averages (i.e., the same regardless of party identification). For rows 1 and 4, however, the percent-ages are different, and correspond to those in Figure 79, on page 100.

The amounts in the last two columns were derived by multiplying the aver-age earnings amounts in each row by the Democratic and Republican percent-ages shown in the two middle columns. By totaling the two right-side columns, we can estimate the expected earnings of average Democratic and Republican males, given the levels of their average educational achievement.

Table 60. Expected earnings of Democratic and Republican men aged 22 to 65 years, based on educational level

Row	Educational level	Average earnings per CPS (restated to 2007 values)	Per Figure 79*		Dem earnings amount **	Rep earnings amount **
			Dem educ.%	Rep educ. %		
1	Less than HS	$26767	10.4	5.3	$2784	$1419
2	HS diploma	39064	49.5	49.5	19337	19337
3	Jr. college	51906	9.5	9.5	4931	4931
4	Bachelor's deg.	77124	15.7	23.8	12108	18356
5	Post-grad. deg.	93135	13.2	13.2	12294	12294
6	Total expected earnings				$51454	$56337

*Only the "Less than HS" and "Bachelor's degree" rows show statistically significant differences.

**Note: The CPS average earnings have been restated to 2007 amounts.

The bottom line of Table 60 shows that, given the differing educational achievements, we would expect the average Democratic and Republican males to earn about $51,500 and $56,300, respectively.

Appendix B 8. Description Of Charity Surveys And Wording Of Questions (relates to page 131)

Table 61. Description of surveys and wording of questions asked.

Row No.	Survey/Date	Question asked in survey
1	Michigan State of the State Survey (Michigan SOSS) — 2006	Respondents were asked if they had "contributed money, property, or both to a charity or non-profit organization last year...."
2	Harris Interactive survey - 2006	Respondents were asked if they had "given money to charity ... in the past 30 days."
3	Michigan State of the State Survey (Michigan SOSS) — 2005	Respondents were asked if they had "contributed money, property, or both to a charity or non-profit organization last year...."
4	American National Election Studies (NES) — 2004	Respondents were asked if they were "able to contribute any money to church or charity in the last 12 months."
5	General Social Survey (GSS) — 2004	Respondents were asked: "During the last 12 months, how often have you ... given money to a charity?"

6	Michigan State of the State Survey (Michigan SOSS) — 2003	Respondents were asked if they had "contributed money, property, or both to a charity or non-profit organization this year...."
7	Community Fdtn Trends Survey (CFTS) — 2002/2003	Respondents were asked: "Did you or other members of your household donate money, assets, goods, or property for charitable purposes?"
8	American National Election Studies (NES) — 2002	Respondents were asked if they were able to "contribute any money to church or charity in the last 12 months."
9	General Social Survey (GSS) — 2002	Respondents were asked: "During the last 12 months, how often have you ... given money to a charity?"
10	Michigan State of the State Survey (Michigan SOSS) — 2001	Respondents were asked if they had "contributed money, property, or both to a charity or non-profit organization this year...."
11	Individual Philanthropy Patterns Survey — 2000	Respondents were asked if they had "given financially to charities."
12	American National Election Studies (NES) — 2000	Respondents were asked if they were able to "contribute any money to church or charity in the last 12 months."
13	Michigan State of the State Survey (Michigan SOSS) — 1999	In the Michigan SOSS no. 19 respondents were given a lengthy list of specific types of nonprofit organizations, and asked if, with respect to any of the organizations, they donated "money or other property for charitable purposes." In Table 28 respondents are classified as having donated if they answered affirmatively with regard to any type of organization.
14	General Social Survey (GSS) — 1996	In the GSS 1996 survey respondents were given a list of specific types of organizations, and asked if, with respect to those organizations, they had donated "money or other property for charitable purposes." In Table 28 respondents are classified as having donated if they answered affirmatively with regard to any one or more of those types of charitable entities. NOTE: "work-related organizations," such as unions are included among the listed types of entities.
15	American National Election Studies (NES) — 1996	Respondents were asked if they were able to "contribute any money to church or charity in the last 12 months."
16	Economic Values Survey — 1992	Respondents were asked: "Do you give to any charitable organizations?"

Appendix B 9. Impact of Income on Charitable Donations (relates to page 144)

Using the dataset from the Michigan State of the State survey number 42, conducted in 2006, "Total Contributions — Dollars" (variable "N9") was co-tabulated with the party identification variable called "PARTYID." The "STATE-WT" variable was selected (to provide state-wide weighting), and the results were sorted by the 8 available income brackets.

The Republican results were then re-weighted so that the Republican number of cases within each income bracket would be identical to the Democratic number of cases in the respective bracket. The Republican grand contributions mean was recalculated using the new case numbers, and the standard error of the grand mean was recalculated using the assumption that one half of the cases were a standard deviation above the mean and the other half of the cases were a standard deviation below the mean. Using the recalculated Republican grand mean, standard error of the mean, and number of cases, as well as the corresponding Democratic amounts, it was a simple matter to run a "T-test" to calculate the P value, which was .0001. This value suggests that the difference in giving is statistically very significant, even after adjusting for income.

Appendix B 10. Calculation of Federal Income Tax Amounts (relates to page 155)

Democratic and Republican federal income tax amounts were calculated using two data sources: "Historical Effective Federal Tax Rates," published by the Congressional Budget Office (CBO) in March and December, 2005, and the cumulative General Social Survey (GSS) for 2004. CBO figures are grouped into 5 "comprehensive household income" quintiles "defined by ranking all people by their comprehensive household income adjusted for household size — that is, divided by the square root of the household's size."[3] The following steps were employed to produce the Democratic vs. Republican estimates:

1. Using an Excel spreadsheet, quintile dollar-amount ranges were created for each size household, based on the 2002 "minimum adjusted income" figures in the March, 2005 release of the CBO publication (Table 1C). For example, the lowest quintile income range for a 1-person household is zero to $15,900, according to the CBO. To get the lowest quintile range for a 4-person family, the $15,900 amount was multiplied times the square root of 4 to get $31,800. This produced a low-end quintile range of zero to $31,800 for a

---

3 According to a footnote in the CBO table, "Comprehensive household income equals pretax cash income plus income from other sources. Pretax cash income is the sum of wages, salaries, self employment income, rents, taxable and nontaxable interest, dividends, realized capital gains, cash transfer payments and retirement benefits plus taxes paid by businesses (corporate income taxes and the employer's share of Social Security, Medicare, and federal unemployment insurance payroll taxes) and employees' contributions to 401(k) retirement plans. Other sources of income include all in-kind benefits (Medicare, Medicaid, employer-paid health insurance premiums, food stamps, school lunches and breakfasts, housing assistance, and energy assistance."

4-person household.[4]

2. GSS frequencies were printed by party identification and by income level for the combined years 1998 through 2004 (variable = "income98"). This was done separately by gender and separately by household population (variable = "hompop"). The GSS income levels did not exactly coincide with the CBO income ranges, so some frequencies had to be prorated between 2 CBO income ranges.

3. Another Excel work paper was created to add up the frequencies within each income quintile by party identification. Again, this was done separately by gender and separately by household population.

4. The percentages of Democrats and Republicans at each income quintile level were multiplied by the income tax rate and average income amounts for each quintile, according to the 2003 amounts released by CBO in December, 2005. This was done separately for men and women.

5. The results for men and women were then combined and averaged, to get a gender-neutral estimated amount.

Appendix B 11. Estimation Of Median Federal Income Tax Amounts (relates to page 160)

Median tax amounts were estimated by using extrapolation plus the income quintiles discussed in Appendix B 10. Democratic and Republican men and women were separately sequenced by income level using GSS frequencies for 1998 through 2004, and the medians (midpoints) of the sequences were determined. The location of each median was then identified as a percentage of the distance between the midpoints of the two nearest quintiles. Finally, that percentage was used to estimate the income tax dollar-amount paid by a person with median income.

For example, there were 2,043 Democratic women surveyed and sequenced by income. The midpoint of the sequence (person number 1,022) fell into the second income quintile, and was 21.2 percent of the way between the midpoint of that quintile and the midpoint of the next (higher) quintile. Since the average federal income tax paid by people in those two quintiles is negative $375 and $1,401, 21.2 percent of the way between those two amounts is a tax level of $2.

Appendix B 12. Calculation Of State And Local Taxes Of Various Types (relates to page 164)

This complicated calculation was performed in two parts that were then combined. First, the taxes were estimated for people under the age of 65; then they were calculated for people aged 65 or more.

For people under 65 years old, state and local taxes were estimated using information in the Tax Policy Center's publication, "Who pays? A distributional Analysis of the Tax Systems in All 50 States, 2nd Edition." That publication lists average income, excise, sales, and property tax rates, at various income levels for

---

4 The method of adjusting for household size (multiplying by the square root of family size) is prescribed in the footnotes to the CBO report.

2002, for taxpaying units under age 65. Using those results, and the distribution of Democrats and Republicans among those income levels, based upon results from the General Social Surveys (GSS) for 1998 through 2004, it was possible to roughly estimate the average state and local tax amounts paid by Democrats and Republicans — under 65 years old. This was done for men and women separately.

For men and women 65 years old and older, preparing state and local tax estimates was much more difficult. First, income tax estimates were prepared by creating 10 elderly taxpayer profiles, individualized for marital status and the varying types of income most elderly taxpayers have at different income levels. The source for these data was Income of the Population 55 and Older (2002), published by the Social Security Administration. Using 2004 TaxAct software (commercially available tax preparation software), actual income tax amounts were calculated for each of the 10 profiles, and for each of the 43 states that has an income tax — a total of 430 returns. (Yes, that was a lot of work!) A weighted average of the state tax results was created for each of the ten profiles on the basis of the number of elderly people in each state. Using those ten averages and the distribution of Democrats and Republicans subject to those averages (based upon income distributions per GSS surveys), it was possible to roughly estimate the average state income tax amounts for Democrats and Republicans 65 years old or older.

The estimation of tax paid by people aged 65 years or more required one additional step: the addition of sales, excise, and property tax. Those additional amounts were estimated on the basis of data published by TPC, coupled with GSS survey data showing the distribution of Democrats and Republicans among the TPC income and tax brackets. It was assumed that the TPC sales, excise and property tax rates, which applied to people under the age of 65, would be roughly applicable to people aged 65 years or more.

The over age 65 and under age 65 estimates were then combined in proportion to the percentages of the general population in each of those age categories.

Appendix B 13. Web-Based Social Security And Medicare Calculator (relates to page 209)

On October 4, 2004, USA Today (online) published a Web-based calculator, designed by C. Eugene Steuerle and Adam Carasso of the Urban Institute. The calculator can be used to estimate the net lifetime value of Social Security and Medicare benefits for men and women in different age cohorts, with different incomes (by $5,000 increments), with different marital status, and with different divisions of income for married couples (i.e., two-earner couples vs. one-earner couples).

The net lifetime value of benefits is the actuarial present value of all expected benefits to the retired worker and his survivors (given gender, age, income, and marital circumstances), less that present cost of all expected costs (i.e., payroll taxes paid by employee and employer).

The Medicare prescription drug program, signed into law by President George W. Bush, has been factored into the calculator; however, the calculator does not include the benefits associated with disability.

Certain simplifying assumptions were made by Steuerle and Carasso: They assumed that workers were employed from ages 22 through 65, with 5 years off from ages 30 to 34. They assumed that husbands and wives were of the same age, and that their children were fully grown (an ineligible for benefits) by the time the parents applied for benefits. For all long-term projections, Steuerle and Carasso used the April, 2004 intermediate economic and demographic assumptions made by the Social Security Trustees. A real (after inflation) interest rate of 2 percent was used for present value/cost calculations.

The calculator can be accessed on the Web site of the Urban Institute at http://www.urban.org/publications/900746.html.

Appendix B 14. Estimation Of Medicare Lifetime Net Benefits (relates to page 216)

Medicare lifetime net benefits were estimated in a two-step process. First, the expected net benefits were determined for retirees in each of 5 different beneficiary categories: two-earner couples, men with stay-at-home-wives, women with stay-at-home husbands, single men, and single women. This was done separately for Democrats and Republicans, using their respective earnings within each category, as estimated on the basis of wage information from the GSS surveys conducted from 1991 through 2004, and using the USA Today Web-based calculator (see Appendix B 13) to estimate the appropriate benefit amounts within the categories. The results of step one are shown in Table 62, and all differences are entirely attributable to differences in average income between Democrats and Republicans.

Table 62. Estimated net Medicare benefits for people with different marital status and different work-sharing arrangements. Differences between Democrats and Republicans are due to different income levels.

Average net Medicare benefits for all income brackets and for people reaching age 65 between 2005 and 2045	Dems in $s	Reps in $s
Married, with spouse who works full-time (benefit each)	209,600	205,100
Married men, with spouse who works part-time or less	463,300	444,600
Married women, with spouse who works part-time or less	476,300	471,400
Single man	196,500	193,700
Single woman	241,300	241,300

The second step was simply to multiply the figures shown in Table 62, above, times the percentages of Democrats and Republicans within each broad category. The results are shown in Table 63.

Table 63. Estimated net Medicare benefits for people turning 65 in years 2005 through 2045

Party »	Democrats			Republicans		
Status	% in the category	$—amt. per Table 62	% times dollar amt.	% in the category	$—amt. per Table 62	% times dollar amt.
Married and spouse works full-time	0.41	209,600	85,936	0.50	205,100	102,550
Married and spouse works part-time or not at all — men	0.07	463,300	32,431	0.14	444,600	62,244
Married and spouse works part-time or not at all — women	0.00	476,300	0	0.01	471,400	4,714
Single men	0.19	196,500	37,335	0.19	193,700	36,803
Single women	0.33	241,300	79,629	0.16	241,300	38,608
Total benefits	1.00		235,331	1.00		244,919

The bottom line of Table 63 shows us that, during his lifetime, the average Republican will get slightly more in net benefits than his Democratic counterpart. The amount is not statistically significant, and this is the also the case when the calculation is done on a gender-neutral basis, as is evident from Table 64, below:

Table 64. Estimated net Medicare benefits for people turning 65 in years 2005 through 2045 — gender neutral

Gender	Democrats	Republicans
Males	235,500	251,100
Females	232,500	230,500
Total	468,000	481,600
Gender neutral (average)	$234,000	$240,800

Appendix B 15. More Survey Results Related To Voting Trends (relates to page 194.)

Figure 285, below, shows the percentages of Democrats and Republicans voting in presidential elections since 1980, based upon GSS surveys. From these results, it appears that Republican voting has been somewhat steady, while the rate of Democratic voting has fluctuated. Democrats voted at a very low rate in the Dukakis-Bush election, but at a rather high rate in the Clinton elections. However, they have never been as likely as Republicans to vote in presidenti al elections.

Figure 285. Did you vote in the presidential election? (GSS surveys conducted between 1980 and 2004, based on, left to right, 4964, 4882, 3762, 5984, 4579, 3244, and 2400 cases, with confidence levels of, left to right, 99%, 99%, 99%, n/a, 94% (marginal), 99%, and 99%, and with relative proportions of, left to right, .94, .92, .91, n/a, .98, .97, and .93)

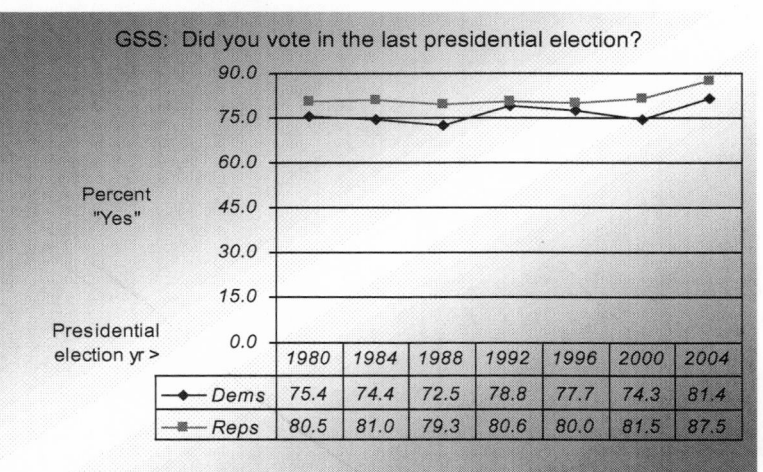

GSS: Did you vote in the last presidential election?

Presidential election yr >	1980	1984	1988	1992	1996	2000	2004
Dems	75.4	74.4	72.5	78.8	77.7	74.3	81.4
Reps	80.5	81.0	79.3	80.6	80.0	81.5	87.5

Appendix B 16. Other Surveys Addressing The Subject Of Happiness (relates to page 233.)

Table 65. Other surveys addressing the happiness issue

Survey and Question	Dems	Reps	No. of cases	Conf %	*RP
Rasmussen 2006: Is your life "good or excellent"? Percentage "Yes"	66.0	80.0	**1000	95	.83
NES 2000: Is your life completely satisfying? Percentage "Completely satisfying"	18.0	26.3	901	+99	.68
Multi Investigator Study 1998-1999: "On the whole, how satisfied with your life are you these days?" Percentage "Very satisfied"	48.8	59.4	675	99	.82
Economic Values Survey 1992: "On the whole, how happy are you?" Percentage "Very happy"	43.9	54.0	1340	+99	.81

*RP is relative proportion, which is the Democratic % divided by the Republican %.

**Case numbers include independents and others in addition to Democrats and Republicans.

APPENDIX C: INTERPRETING SURVEY DATA

The "Socially Desirable" Response

A strange survey result was noted by David Moore, Senior Gallup Poll Editor.

> In a survey on Jan. 3-5, a little over a week after the earthquake in the Indian Ocean, 45 percent of respondents in a Gallup survey indicated they had already contributed money to the relief efforts for Asian countries hit by the resulting tsunami. Only four days later, in a similar survey, the same question about contributing [to] relief efforts showed that just 33 percent said they had contributed money to tsunami relief efforts.[1]

Indeed, this was odd because, after 4 days, the number of people contributing to the relief effort should have *increased* or, at least, stayed the same. Instead, there was a large drop in the percentage who gave (larger than the margin of error).

Mr. Moore identified two possible explanations for this phenomenon: The drop in reported giving was caused by a slight change in the survey question, or it was caused by a change in social pressure. The latter scenario was described by Mr. Moore:

> Perhaps during the time of the first poll, there was such a media frenzy over the disaster that people felt they almost had to say they had done something for the victims.

> Pollsters call this phenomenon a "socially desirable" response. When social norms approve of a certain behavior, some respondents are unwilling to admit that they don't conform.[2]

This "socially desirable" phenomenon could have affected the results of this book if social pressures affect the constituents of one political party more than the constituents of the other party. For example, if Republicans have a greater need to impress survey interviewers by exaggerating their achievements, the results have probably been skewed in their favor. I simply don't know if this is the case.

The "Politically Desirable" Response

In addition to the "socially desirable" response, I believe there may be a "politically desirable" response — particularly with respect to certain "hot-button" issues, or questions asked in the heat of a political campaign. A couple of examples were noted in Chapter 2, regarding education and intelligence. In response to a Pew survey, conducted in mid-2005, Democrats were more likely than Republi-

---

1 David W. Moore, "The Elusive Truth," *The Gallup News Service* (January 18, 2005), Retrieved July 4, 2006, from Http://brain.gallup.com.
2 Ibid.

cans to overstate the Iraq War casualty count. On the other hand, Republicans were more likely to assert that Saddam Hussein had weapons of mass destruction, even after many published reports declared that none were found. Are these indications of ignorance, or do they reflect Democratic pessimism about the war, Republican optimism about the war, and/or political posturing by each side? It is hard to tell, so I avoided such controversial questions.

With respect to Chapter 4, concerning charitable donations, there was another type of question that I avoided: those concerning very specific organizations or causes. For example, one survey asked respondents if they volunteered to assist the Boy Scouts organization. I didn't use that survey question because the results would not tell us who is more likely to volunteer for charities. Rather, it would only tell us who feels more favorably towards the Boy Scouts.

APPENDIX D: A FEW NOTES ABOUT THE STATISTICS USED

There are no complicated statistics in this book. Where the underlying support for a chart or table is a two-column by two-row cross tabulation of dichotomous variables (e.g., the percentages of Democrats and Republicans who answered "yes" or "no" to a survey question) you will usually find the statistical "confidence level" (100% minus the probability value) and the Relative Proportion (RP), which I have defined as the percentage of Democrats responding in a certain way to a survey question divided by the percentage of Republicans responding in the same way to that same question. RP values that are close to one (1) indicate a small difference between Democrats and Republicans, whereas values that are substantially below or above one (1) indicate large differences.

Where the underlying support for a chart or table is a cross tabulation of two columns by three or more rows (e.g., the percentages of Democrats and Republicans that answered "yes," "no," or "maybe" to a survey question) you will usually find a Phi association value, which is a common measure of the statistical strength of a described relationship. When comparing means I give the confidence level based upon the T statistic or F statistic, as appropriate.

In a few cases, multiple regression analyses were prepared to help identify variables that, along with party identification, correlate with certain specific behaviors or achievements. These regressions, and most of the other statistical calculations in this book, were performed using SPSS software or the SDA Web-based statistical program, developed by the Computer-Assisted Survey Methods program at the University of California at Berkeley.

Unless otherwise noted, Democrats and Republicans include only respondents who self-identified as such. (independent "leaners" are not included.)[1]

---

1 Neither SPSS nor the SDA program of Berkeley are responsible for how I used their programs, or the ideas or assertions in this book.

APPENDIX E: THE SUPERIORITY OF THE DEMOCRAT–REPUBLICAN PARADIGM

> In effect, the critic is saying that there are no "entities" liberalism and conservatism. Such labeling of attitudes or constellations of attitudes is scientifically unsound.
>
> — Psychologist Fred N. Kerlinger[1]

For comparisons that are political in nature, I suspect that party identification is a more reliable measurement tool than political ideology. In the United States, ideological terms such as "liberal" and "conservative" are usually self-defined, and cannot be linked to objective and observable standards (such as a party platform), or to individuals who exemplify those standards (such as political candidates). Many people are not even sure how they fit into the ideological spectrum. Gallup notes that Americans often choose multiple ideological labels, when given the opportunity:

> What is of interest is the degree to which Americans — when given a choice — choose multiple ideological labels for themselves. Much as the census bureau has decided that many Americans need to use multiple race and ethnicity labels to describe themselves, these data suggest that Americans may view themselves as fitting into several ideological "boxes" rather than just one.[2]

On the other hand, party identification can be linked to an observable candidate, office holder, and/or political platform. Admittedly, party identity is a changeable demographic, but so are political ideology, income, marital status, family size, and education. And, while it is changeable, party identification is surprisingly stable. This was noted by Rasmussen Reports in April, 2006:

> Party allegiances tend to be quite stable over time. Despite the enormous news and political events of the past 27 months, the gap between Republicans and Democrats has never varied by more than 3.4 percentage points from the highest to the lowest.[3]

It is true that, over longer time-spans, significant numbers of Democrats and Republicans join the opposing party. (See Figure 197.) However, the relative attributes of the parties remain fairly constant — even though the people com-

---

1 Kerlinger, *Liberalism and Conservatism*, 4.

2 Joseph Carroll, "Many Americans Use Multiple Labels to Describe Their Ideology," *The Gallup News Service* (December 6, 2006), Retrieved January 2, 2007, from Http://brain.gallup.com.

3 "37% Democrats, 34% Republicans," *The Gallup News Service* (April 10, 2006), Retrieved December 27, 2006, from http://www.rasmussenreports.com/2006/April%20Dailies/Partisan%20Trends.htm.

prising them change. (If one doubts this, consult many 50-year trend graphs in Appendix A, starting on page 317.)

One might argue that partisanship is simply a collection or running tally of individual political assessments. However, there is evidence suggesting that this is not the case. In 2002, Larry Bartels (Princeton University) analyzed panel survey data in an examination of the impact of long-term partisan loyalties on perceptions of specific political individuals and events. In "Beyond the Running Tally: Partisan Bias in Political Perceptions," he reports:

> Taken as a whole, my analysis provides strong evidence of "the influence of party identification on attitudes toward the perceived elements of politics" (Campbell et al., 1960, p. 135). Far from being a mere summary of more specific political opinions, partisanship is a powerful and pervasive influence on perceptions of political events.[4]

Another political scientist, Paul Goren, examined data from NES surveys and reached a similar conclusion:

> [P]artisan identities are more stable and resistant to change than abstract beliefs about equal opportunity, limited government, traditional family values, and moral tolerance. ... [P]arty identification systematically constrains beliefs about equal opportunity, limited government, and moral tolerance. This influence, while far from overwhelming, is substantively meaningful, and therefore, can produce genuine shifts in value preferences over extended periods of time.[5]

Thus, there is evidence that party identification is strong and stable.

There is another reason I prefer the Democrat-Republican paradigm: It is less misleading. During the last 35 years, 25 to 50 percent of all self-identified "conservatives" have been Democrats, and I simply do not believe most people are aware of that fact. My studies have shown that these Democratic conservatives are quite different, education-wise, from Republican conservatives. (See Chapter 11.) Combining these two distinct types of "conservatives" is a bit misleading, and is best avoided.

For all of these reasons, I believe that comparisons based on political party identification are generally preferable to those based upon political ideology.

---

4 Larry M. Bartels, "Beyond the Running Tally: Partisan Bias in Political Perceptions," *Political Behavior* 24, no. 2 (June, 2002): 120.

5 Goren, "Party Identification and Core Political Values."

Appendix F: Survey Sources Used

For the most part, this book was produced by extracting and processing data from several large and well-respected surveys. Although I am very grateful for the access I was given to this information, the reader should understand that any opinions, findings and conclusions or recommendations expressed in this book are mine, and do not necessarily reflect the views of the surveying entities or their funding organizations. They bear no responsibility for the analyses or interpretations of the data presented herein.

In particular, I relied heavily upon the following sources:

The 1948-2004 American National Election Studies (NES) [machine readable data file] produced by Stanford University and the University of Michigan in 2005. NES is based on work supported by the National Science Foundation under Grant Numbers: SBR-9707741, SBR-9317631, SES-9209410, SES-9009379, SES-88008361, SES-8341310, SES-8207580, and SOC77-08885.

The 1972-2006 General Social Survey (GSS) [machine readable data file]. Principal Investigator, James A. Davis; Director and Co-Principal Investigator, Tom W. Smith; Co-Principal Investigator, Peter V. Marsden, NORC ed. Chicago: National Opinion Research Center, producer, 2005; Storrs, CT: The Roper Center for Public Opinion Research, University of Connecticut, distributor. 1 data file (51,020 logical records and 1 codebook (2,552 pp).

Several surveys conducted and reported on by The Pew Research Center for the People & the Press, Washington, DC, which is sponsored by The Pew Charitable Trusts. The specific Pew surveys used are cited within the text.

Several surveys conducted and reported on by the Gallup Organization, Washington, DC. The specific Gallup surveys used are cited within the text, and can be found on the Gallup Organization Web site at www.gallup.com.

Several Michigan "State of the State" (SOSS) surveys conducted by the Institute for Public Policy and Social Research (IPPSR), which is a nonprofit entity located on the campus of the Michigan State University. The specific Michigan SOSS surveys used are cited within the text.

Harris Interactive surveys found in the Public Opinion Poll Question Data Base of the Virtual Data Center network of the Odum Institute at the University of North Carolina.

Surveys conducted by Rasmussen Reports, and available from its Web site at RasmussenReports.com.

In addition, I am extremely grateful to the Computer-Assisted Survey Methods Program at the University of California at Berkeley. Its *Survey Documentation & Analysis* Web-based documentation and analysis program (SDA) was used extensively — particularly with respect to retrieval and analysis of *General Social Surveys*.

APPENDIX G: ACRONYMS AND ABBREVIATIONS

BLS – United States Bureau of Labor Statistics

CBO – Congressional Budget Office

Conf – Confidence level, which is generally considered to be statistically significant if it is 95 percent or higher, and marginally significant if it is between 90 and 95 percent. The confidence level is equal to one (1) minus the probability value (p-value).

EITC – Earned Income Tax Credit, a federal income tax credit aimed at helping low-income wage-earners. In essence, it is a form of welfare distributed via the tax system.

FICA – Federal Insurance Contributions Act (Social Security and Medicare tax)

Gallup – The Gallup Organization, a company conducting various surveys and polls, and issuing public reports on its findings

GSS – General Social Survey of the National Opinion Research Center at the University of Chicago (see NORC)

Harris – Harris Interactive, a company producing the Harris Poll, and other survey tools and reports

IPPSR – Institute for Public Policy and Social Research, an organization "extending scholarly expertise to Michigan's policymaking community" (see SOSS)

Marg – Marginal

NES – American National Election Studies, produced and distributed by Stanford University and the University of Michigan (Also known as ANES)

NORC – National Opinion Research Center at the University of Chicago, which produces the periodic General Social Surveys (GSS)

Pew – Pew Research Center for the People and the Press, which is sponsored by the Pew Charitable Trusts

Phi – Phi coefficient, which is a measure of the degree of association between two variables

RP – Relative proportion, which is (in this book) the percentage of Democrats responding in a certain way to a survey question divided by the percentage of Republicans responding in that same way to that same question

SDA – Survey Documentation & Analysis, a Web-based statistical program developed by the Computer-Assisted Survey Methods program at the University of California at Berkeley

SOSS – State of the State Surveys, which are a series of surveys prepared by the Institute for Public Policy and Social Research for policy makers in the State of Michigan (see IPPSR)

SPSS – Computer software designed to aid researchers in analyzing statistical data, originally known as Statistical Package for the Social Sciences

INDEX

Adultery, 15

Age (political implication), 260-67, 318, 332-33

American National Election Studies, 2, 364

ANES. See American National Election Studies

Apparent Intelligence, 78-9

Arrest rates, 54

Attitude at work, 105-10

Bankruptcy, 198-99

Bennett, William, 198

Bias
    against religious and ethnic groups, 182-6
    among college professors, 58
    impact on our political views, 262-3
    in the News Media, 70
    research bias at Berkeley, 285, 297-299

Bigotry, 192-85

Block, Jack, 283, 291, 296-98

Body mass, 26-9

Boortz, Neal, 163

Boredom, 7

Bottled water, 55

Brooks, Arthur C., 150

Capitalism (as a factor in happiness) 253

Carasso, A., 219, 221-23, 226, 228-31, 369-70

Cato Institute, 73, 220, 238-39

Center on Budget and Policy, 157, 164

Charity. See Donations

Childhood life, 278-80

Children, 16-21
    benefits from delaying the first child, 302
    born to teen parents, 17-8
    computer filters, 19
    development of political views, 260-64
    out of wedlock, 16-17
    preschoolers with working moms, 273
    private schools, 21
    spanking, 19

Cigarettes. See Health and fitness, smoking

Clinton, President Bill, 21, 160, 287

Clinton, Senator Hillary, 259

Cocaine. See Drug usage

Coleman, Senator Norm, 259

Colleges, political orientation of faculty, 58

Computer filters, 19

Condoms, 8

Conservatives. See Liberals and conservatives

Contributions. See Donations

Corporate welfare, 223-25

Coulter, Ann, 8, 63, 162, 178, 181, 294

Crime. See Felons

Dean, Howard, 13, 70, 97, 194

Demographics. See Appendix A

DeMuth, Phil, 255

Divorce, 13, 269, 282

Donations
  blood, 192
  impact of income level, 143-48, 306-07, 353
  impact of political ideology 150-52
  impact of religion 149-50
  to the homeless, 138-39
  volunteer services, 139-42
  Who gives more? 134-37
  Who is more likely to give?, 130-34
Drug usage, 31-2
Earned Inc. Tax Credit, 156, 169, 221, 227, 365
Education, 73-8, 327, 340, 345-7
Edwards, Senator John, 159, 254
EITC. See Earned Income Tax Credit
Elder, Larry, 156, 311
Emotional stability, 26, 111-12.
Employment
  men
    emotional stability at work, 111-12
    estimation of hourly wage rate, 349
    factors correlating with work hours 349-50
    impact of education on wages, 101, 350-51
    supervisory experience, 101-05
    Who earns more?, 95-6
    Who has the better work attitude?, 105-10
    Who is more likely to work?, 92-4
    Who works longer hours?, 96-9
  occupations
    prestige, 119-21
    types, 122-25
  union membership and miscellaneous issues, 125-6
  women
    attitudes and emotions, 116-19
    earnings and hours worked, 112-16
Entertainment, 37-44
  net surfing, 41
  reading, 41-2
  Who watches more TV?, 37-38
    sex and violence, 38-9
  X-rated movies, 39-40
Environmental efforts, 190-92
Excitement (Whose life is more exciting?), 5-6
Family friends and activities, 21-2
Federal income tax. See Taxes

Felons, 198
Fertility gap, 16-7
Feulner, Edwin, 212
Finances, 235-36, 327, 341
Fisher, Peter, 225
Football, 55
Ford, President Gerald, 79
Fried, Floyd, 152
Friedman, Milton, 158
Friedman, Thomas L., 21, 64
FSU Center for Prevention & Intervention, 17
Galbraith, John Kenneth, 151
Gallagher, Mike, 110
Gallup Organization, 364
Gambling, 49-50
Gay sex, 10-11
Gender, 320, 333
General Social Survey (GSS), 1, 2, 364
Giacneschi Center for Nonprofit Research, 148-9
Gingrich, Former Speaker Newt, 31
Giuliani, Rudy, 152
Goldberg, Jonah, 32, 195, 287
Goren, Paul, 265, 363
GSS. See General Social Survey
Gun ownership, 50-1
Happiness
  Does cynicism lead to sadness? 244-57
  versus misery, 237-40
  Who is happier?, 230-36, 358
  Why are some people happier?, 241-57
Harris Interactive, 1, 2, 364
Haskins, Ron, 223
Health and fitness, 22-34
  by income bracket, 24-5
  drugs, 31-2
  health insurance, 33
  HIV testing, 33
  mental health, 26
  overweight, 26-30
  smoking, 30-1
Health insurance, 33
Helms, Senator Jesse, 267
Heylighen, F., 242
Hillygus, D. Sunshine, 265
HIV, 33
Holidays, 42-3
Home ownership, 62
Home schooling, 22
Honesty, 199-201
Horowitz, David, 263

Housework, 115
Hunting, 52
Hussein, Saddam, 89, 359
Illegal drugs, 31
Illegitimacy, 16-7
Income. See Finances
    as related to charitable giving, 143-48
    as related to education level, 84-6
    as related to happiness, 241-42
    as related to health, 24-25
Income brackets, 327, 341
Institute for Public Policy and Social Research (IPPSR), 1, 2, 364
Intelligence, 78-9
Internet. See Entertainment and see News
Intolerance. See Bigotry
Jury duty, 193
Kennedy, Congressman Patrick, 94
Kennedy, Jr, Robert, 67
Kerlinger, Fred N., 288-90, 362
Keyes, Alan, 207
Kinder, Donald R., 260-62, 266
Kleiner, Kurt, 283
Knowledge. See Political knowledge; See Scientific knowledge
Krugman, Paul, 203
Lakoff, George, 264
Lautenberg, Senator Frank, 187, 223
Leo, John, 179, 309
Liberals and conservatives
    curious pattern, 291-94
    why terms are too vague to be useful, 286-88
Limbaugh, Rush, 69-70, 177, 183, 221, 248, 253
Lindgren, Jim, 295
Lowry, Rich, 213
Luck, 249-50
Luntz, Frank, 58
Malkin, Michelle, 178, 296
Manza, Jeff (on felony rates), 198
Marijuana. See Drug usage
Marriage, 11-16
    adultery, 15
    correlation with education, 85-89
    correlation with happiness, 242
    divorce, 13-14
    impact on work hours for women, 113
    party identification of married people, 324
    premarital sex, 15

rates, 11-12
    rates among Democrats and Republicans, 338
    reasons not married, 13-14
    Who has happier marriages?, 233-34
McCurry, Mike, 215
Medicare, 214-18
Medved, Michael, 80, 230, 260-1, 268
Mental health. See Health and fitness
Michigan "State of the State" (SOSS), 364
Military service, 186-89
Movies, 39-40
Muirhead, J. Russell, 262
Music. See Country music preference
Nader, Ralph, 226
National Opinion Research Ctr, (NORC), 2, 364
NES. See American National Election Studies
Noonan, Peggy, 35, 92
O'Reilly, Bill, 147, 305
Obesity. See Health and fitness:overweight
Occupations, 122-25, 325, 339
Optimism (lack of), 248
Overweight. See Health and fitness: overweight
Parents of Democrats and Republicans, 268-76
Party identification of different demographic groups, 317-331
Pelosi, Congresswoman Nancy, 203, 216
Percentages of the parties that are in various demographic groups 332-44
Peters, Alan, 225
Pets, 54
Pew Research Center for the People and the Press (Pew), 1, 2, 364
Political campaigns, protests, and rallys, 195-96
Political ideology. See Liberals & conservatives
Political knowledge
    based on direct testing, 59-67
    based on interviewer impressions, 67-8
    based on time reading/watching news, 68-70
Political viewpoints (development), 260- 68
Pornography, 19-20
Prager, Dennis, 137, 166
Praying, 36

Prejudice. See Bigotry

Premarital sex. See Sex, premarital

Private schools, 21

Quayle, Vice President Dan, 16-17, 75, 113

Race percentages, 321, 335

Rasmussen Reports, 364

Reading, 41-2

Reagan, President Ronald, 154, 236, 244, 266

Reasoning ability. See Intelligence

Reich, Former Secretary of Labor Robert, 91

Reid, Senator Harry, 205

Relative Proportion (RP). See Statistics: notes on statistical methods

Religion, 35-8
    as related to charitable giving, 149-50

Religious denominations, 323, 336

Retirement planning, 47-8

Rosen, Mike, 165

Sadness, 237

Schwarzenegger, Governor Arnold, 22, 267-68, 302

Scientific knowledge, 70-1

SDA (Survey Documentation & Analysis), 364

Self-esteem, 285-53

Sex, 7-11

Simpson, Carole, 58

Smoking, 30-1

Social Science Research Center, 148

Social Security
    comparing Democratic and Republican benefits, 208-12
    Texas teacher $2 billion scam, 213-14
    Who does well in the system? 204-08

Social Security tax. See Taxes, FICA taxes

Socially desirable responses in survey data, 359

Somin, Ilya (political knowledge test), 59-60

SOSS. See Michigan "State of the State Surveys"

Spanking, 19

Spending on necessities, 44-5

Statistical methods, 360

Stein, Ben, 255

Steuerle, Eugene, 205, 207-09, 212, 214-17, 356

Stocks and bonds, 47

Stossel, John, 226, 315

Tanner, Michael, 206

Tax Foundation, 153-4, 157-8

Taxes. Also see Earned Income Tax Credit
    Blue states versus red states, 153-54
    compared to income levels, 157-58
    excise, 160-61
    federal corporate tax, 161-62
    federal income
        average taxes paid, 154-58
        history, 160
        on median incomes, 159-60
    FICA taxes, 162-63, 168-69
    state and local, 164-65

Tolerance for First Amendment rights, 172-81

Trust (lack of), 244-47

Truthfullness. See Honesty

TV. See Entertainment, Who watches more TV?

Uggen, Christopher (on felony rates), 198

Union membership, 125-26

Urban Institute, 205, 355-56

Vidal, Gore, 257

Violence, 38-9, 52-4

Volunteerism, 139-42

Voting, 194-95

Wages, 95-6, 112

Weight, 26-9

Welfare
    corporate, 223-26
    social welfare, 220-23

Williams, Walter, 134

Wilson, Doug, 212